THE AVIGNON QUINTET

LAWRENCE DURRELL was born in 1912 in India, where his father was an English civil engineer. As a boy he attended the Jesuit College at Darjeeling, and he was later sent to St Edmund's School, Canterbury. His first authentic literary work was *The Black Book*, which appeared in Paris in 1938 under the aegis of Henry Miller and Anaïs Nin. 'In the writing of it I first heard the sound of my own voice . . .' he later wrote. The novel was praised by T. S. Eliot, who published his first collection of poems *A Private Country* in 1943. The first of the island books, *Prospero's Cell*, a guide to Corfu, appeared in 1945. It was followed by *Reflections on a Marine Venus*, about Rhodes. *Bitter Lemons*, his account of life in Cyprus, won the Duff Cooper Memorial Prize in 1957. Subsequently he drew on his years in Greece for *The Greek Islands*.

Durrell's wartime sojourn in Egypt led to his masterpiece *The Alexandria Quartet* (*Justine, Balthazar, Mountolive* and *Clea*) which he completed in southern France, where he settled permanently in 1957. Between the *Quartet* and the Avignon novels he wrote the two-decker *Tunc* and *Nunquam*, now united as *The Revolt of Aphrodite*. His oeuvre includes plays, a book of criticism, translations, travel writings (*Spirit of Place*), *Collected Poems*, a children's adventure, and humorous stories about the diplomatic corps. His correspondence with his lifelong friend Henry Miller has also been published. *Caesar's Vast Ghost*, his reflections on the history and culture of Provence, including a late flowering of poems, appeared a few days before his death at his home in Sommières in 1990.

Books by Lawrence Durrell

THE
AVIGNON
QUINTET

Monsieur
Livia
Constance
Sebastian
Quinx

LAWRENCE
DURRELL

faber and faber

This one-volume edition first published in 1992 by Faber and Faber
3 Queen Square London WC1N 3AU

Printed in England by Clays Ltd, St Ives plc

A CIP record for this book
is available from the British Library

ISBN 0-571-16309-2

2 4 6 8 10 9 7 5 3 1

Contents

MONSIEUR

or
The Prince of Darkness

For Ghislaine de Boysson

Contents

Contents

ONE

"Outremer"

THE SOUTHBOUND TRAIN FROM PARIS WAS THE ONE WE had always taken from time immemorial – the same long slowcoach of a train, stringing out its bluish lights across the twilight landscapes like some super-glow-worm. It reached Provence at dawn, often by a brindled moonlight which striped the countryside like a tiger's hide. How well I remembered, how well he remembered! The Bruce that I was, and the Bruce I become as I jot down these words, a few every day. A train subject to unexpected halts, unexplained delays; it could fall asleep anywhere, even in open country, and remain there, lost in thought, for hours. Like the swirls and eddies of memory itself – thoughts eddying about the word "suicide", for example, like frightened tadpoles. It has never been, will never be, on time, our train.

These were the reflections of the lone traveller in the lighted third-class compartment at the rear of the train. In the tarnished mirror this man is watching himself. It had ever been thus in early spring he told himself – even in the early student days of the old PLM. By the time the train had cleared echoing Dijon it became all but empty in this season. (He was trying to remember how long it was since he had last visited the city; but sitting there in his corner, half asleep and half awake, it seemed to him that in reality he had never been away. Or at least some part of him had always been present in its shady streets and quiet shabby squares.)

But this was a strangely different return to it; crawling out of a northern winter into a nascent spring at the summons of a blue telegram. And an awful season for such a journey! In the north a flurry of snowstorms had all but paralysed rail traffic; but down here the spring had almost decided to un-freeze the land. Once across the green mulberry-belt and into the olive-zone one becomes reassured, for even in the grey winterset of early dawn the gold tangerines hang in thriving loads as if in some Greek garden of Epicurus. His eyes rested unseeingly on the flying landscapes through which they passed.

The late traveller was myself, Bruce, and the journey was none of my choosing. The telegram which had summoned me southward from Prague was suitably laconic. It told me of the suicide of my oldest and best friend, Piers de Nogaret; more than friend indeed, for his sister Sylvie was my wife, though the telegram was signed not by her but by the family notary. It had reached me at the British Embassy to which I had been attached for the last few years as a medical adviser. "Bruce Drexel M.D. at your service" – but now how insubstantial it sounded, like an echo of far-off certainties which had taken no account of the revenges of time! The man in the mirror stared himself out of countenance. The train rushed and rumbled onwards.

He must be trying to objectify his thoughts and emotions by treating them as one would in a novel, but it didn't really work. As a matter of fact, in Rob Sutcliffe's famous novel about us all, things began in exactly this way. I was strangely echoing his protagonist, summoned to the bedside of a dying friend (this was the difference) who had important things to reveal to him. Sylvie was there, too, in the centre of the picture as she always has been. Her madness was touchingly des-cribed. Of course in a way the characters were travesties of us; but the incidents were true enough and so was Verfeuille, the old chateau in which we had lived out this adventure between our voyages. Bruce was now identifying a little with the hero very much as Sutcliffe himself was, and about whom the writer once said: "Reality is too old-fashioned nowadays for the writer's uses. We must count upon art to revive it and bring it up to date."

Yes, but what about real people as opposed to paper figments? Dying, one becomes out of date; but it brings one's friends to their senses, or should. I so often wondered about this – how to splice the real and the imagined – when I read his book. Now he too was dead and Pia, my sister, had lodged all his papers in the muniments room of Verfeuille, where the whole searing unhappiness of their married life can be studied by the literary historian. It was not that she was a rotten wife, either, for they loved each other to distraction; it was simply the sad story of inversion – it had left him high and dry, without inner resources. People like Rob become too attached, too vulnerable, and in consequence are easily broken on the block. My sister if she read these lines would put her hands over her ears and cry out "No!" But they are true.

In a few more months the three of us were to have met once again in the city of Piers' birth, to resume the thread of this bizarre friendship which had lasted half a lifetime and which had only been slightly disturbed by his last posting to Delhi. We were both due to retire this year and return to Verfeuille together, to live out the rest of our story with Sylvie behind the massive ramparts of the crumbling chateau. To wall ourselves up, in a way: to retire from the world completely: to develop and enrich this enduring friendship between the three of us which had withstood so many trials and still remained (at least for me) the central experience of my whole existence. Indeed there was nothing else in my life to which I could compare it in fruitfulness and intensity – a three-cornered love, ill-starred only because one day Sylvie lost her reason and almost dragged her brother with her. Piers hesitated and faltered on the very brink. Had I not been there I think he would have slid down the long slopes of unreason, choosing it as a refuge from his thoughts of her insanity. Now everything had changed, abruptly, brutally. Piers was apparently dead, and the man I had become could see no way forward into the future. The disappearance of my friend had overturned reality; yet the feeling of being bereft created a singular kind of tearless detachment in me, a dazed and fearless irony. The mirror recorded a grimly smiling man. Meanwhile, far away, in the green rose-gardens of Montfavet, Sylvie walked in her Chinese shawl, her lips moving in silent conversations with her dead brother. Here Bruce stands up and paces the empty carriage in a fury of resentment and pain like an animal caught in a trap.

Fatigue surely played a good part in this novel feeling of unreality which had beset me. People take time to die and the dead Piers had only just begun to make his claims on the memory of his friends. It was his body, not his memory, which was cold. Each time I was jolted awake I had to re-experience the fact of his death, an angry sting. For a moment there would be nothing, just an empty space – and then memory slid open like a flick-knife and I realised that he had gone, entered into the weird convention of the state of death, about which we know nothing which might help us domesticate the idea, tame it.

I wondered if in dying he had remembered the initiation which we had shared in Egypt long ago – at the hands of Akkad, distilled patiently from the doctrines of the desert gnostics? I know he had been deeply marked by them. In the matter of death, I mean, they were crucial and unequivocal. For after that initiation it was impossible to attach any profound importance to the notion of dying. All individual deaths had been resumed by the death of God! I remember how the idea terrified me at the time! When we said goodbye to tender smiling Akkad he told us: "Now don't give a thought to what you have learned. Simply become it as fast as you can – *for what one becomes one forgets.*"

Obviously this belonged to the other kind of death, the gnostic one which would henceforward always overshadow the death of mere time in man; the death which for Akkad and his sect was simply one form of the body's self-indulgence, a lack of fastidiousness. "Dying can be a mere caprice if one allows it to happen before discovering the big trick which enables one to die with profit," he said.

I repeated his words slowly to myself now as I stared into the flying night. I wondered where Akkad would be tonight. Perhaps he was dead? I felt separated from Piers by less than half a pulse-beat.

And yet we had been lucky, given the circumstances of our occupations and voyages, to have enjoyed an almost continuous association with each other; our initial friendship which later turned into love, had never withered on the stalk. As a youth I had come into contact with the brother and sister who lived so strange an abstract life of beauty and introspection in their lonely chateau: and from then on we had hardly quitted one another. Piers became a diplomat, I a Service M.D., yet despite all the vagaries of fate we were, at the very worst, posted simultaneously to adjacent countries. On several lucky occasions we even achieved the same posting, he to the Embassy of France, I to the British. Thus we knew Cairo together and Rome, we shared Pekin and Berne, we divided Madrid. Sylvie was our lieutenant, and when we were apart she shared us, moving from one to the other. But always we spent our summer leaves in Verfeuille together. So that despite all the changes of place and person the whole pattern of our lives (and in consequence our love) had continuity and design.

Later I had deliberately married Sylvie because she wished it. It further cemented our fierce attachment to each other. Nor was I sleepwalking, for I knew full well the psychological implications of the act. I also knew that one day the centre might fall out of Sylvie's mind; that she might have to be sent away, sequestered in the green quietness of Montfavet, the great straggling asylum which hovers among the lush streamlets and sunny bowers of the Vaucluse, exhaling something like the kinetic calm of an Epidaurus. On this score I have never had anything to regret. This three-cornered passion has held me spellbound for a lifetime and will see me beyond the grave. I knew I had found my *onlie begetters*. I was reliving the plot and counterplot of Shakespeare's Sonnets in my own life. I had found the master-mistress of my passion. Who could ask for more?

I had been walking all winter long in a country of snowbound lakes, locked in the steel grip of ice, where the wild geese hooted all night long as they straggled south. Thus walking in the grey winterscapes one comes, at every turn, upon little bundles of dispersed feathers – the snow like a rumpled dining table in the woods. The diner had left already. Sometimes the fox may have spared a bird's head, but mostly only a clutch of unswallowable feathers. A walk in the ancient world, I thought, must have been somewhat similar, with the remains of animal sacrifices at every crossroads, in green groves, on the seashore. They offered up a sacrificial death to the Gods as later on men were to offer up the first fruits of their garden plots. I felt that perhaps the suicide of Piers (if such an improbable thing were true) somehow partook of this sort of offering. But I still didn't quite believe in it. But then, if not by his own hand, then by whose? Nothing that had happened to us in the past offered an explanation for this astonishing development. And all the more so because of the gnostic ideas of Akkad which Piers claimed to have understood and to have believed in. But wait a minute!

A phrase of Akkad's comes to mind. It went something like this: "People of our persuasion gradually learn to refuse all rights to so-called God. They renounce the empty world, not like ascetics or martyrs, but like convalescents after suicide. But one must be ripe for this sort of thing." Suddenly an absurd idea has entered the sleeper's mind. Piers' self-inflicted death as being a part of a ritual murder . . . What nonsense! I had a sudden picture of my friend, quixotic to the point of innocence, repeating the words after Akkad. He had always been prepared to push things to extremes.

And Sylvie? What might she not have to tell me? The thought of her, up there in Montfavet, ached on and on in my mind, as it had done for the last two years.

And so at long last to reach home, to clatter softly and wearily into the empty station – that historic point of return and departure: but this time alone. It has always afflicted me with a profound love-dread, this shabby little station, because so often when I returned Sylvie was waiting for me on the platform, hand in hand with her nurse, distractedly gazing about her. I was always looking out for her, I suppose. The train sighs to a halt and the rasping announcements begin in the accents of the Midi. I stand paralysed among the lighted windows gazing about me.

It never changes; it looks so homely, so provisional, so grubby-provincial. You could never deduce from it the existence of the cruel and famous town to which it belongs.

Outside the mistral purred. In the slowly thawing gardens were the memorable flaccid palms set in their circles of moulting grass. There was still snow-rime in the flowerbeds.

And of course a queue of rubber-tyred *fiacres*, waiting for whatever custom the dawn train might bring in. They looked half dead with boredom and disgust, the horses and the drivers. Soon they would be sauntered away into the sleeping town, for the next train arrived after eleven. I managed to wake a driver and strike a price. I was heading for the old Royal Hotel. But as we yawed about and made some disjointed lurches towards the battlements I was siezed by a sudden counter-influence which made me direct the driver towards the river. I felt a sudden desire to see it again, its existence seemed to confirm so many things, the old river-God of our youth. So we slobbered and slid along the ancient walls, outside the bastions. It was dark as pitch, one saw nothing. Trees arched overhead. Then suddenly one heard its voice coupled with the snarl of the wind. Like cats making love. I got out and walked beside the slow cab, feeling the wind clutch my shoulders.

In the greyness the water was inky, swollen and curdled with blocks of ice which thumped and tinkled along the banks.

A faint light touched the east but dawn was not yet breaking. You might have thought yourself in central Asia – the cloudy sky in close link like chain-mail and the fading stabs of moonlight. The driver grumbled but I paid no attention. I even walked out gingerly upon the famous broken bridge, clutching the handrail as well as my hat, for here the wind whirled. A frail ghost-light lit the chapel, but there were no worshippers at that hour. A broken and renowned relic of man's belief, pointing its amputated fingers of masonry westward. I thought of Piers. In expounding Akkad once he had said something like: "What really dies is the collective image of the past – all the temporal selves which have been present in a serial form focused together now in an instant of perfect attention, of crystal-clear apprehension which could last forever if one wished." How hollow all these grave lucubrations seemed in this wind-tugged night. Nevertheless they were perhaps appropriate to the place. For a hundred years this shabby village had been Rome, had been all Christendom.

This was, after all, Avignon.

Confused messages waited for me at the hotel, but there was nothing to be done about them at this hour. I dozed on my bed until sunrise and then set out resolutely to find a coffee, traversing the old city with affection and distress, hearing my own sharp footsteps on the pavements, disembodied as a ghost. Avignon! Its shabby lights and sneaking cats were the same as ever; overturned dustbins, the glitter of fish scales, olive oil, broken glass, a dead scorpion. All the time we had been away on our travels round the world it had stayed pegged here at the confluence of its two green rivers. The past embalmed it, the present could not alter it. So many years of going away and coming back, of remembering and forgetting it. It had always waited for us, floating among its tenebrous monuments, the corpulence of its ragged bells, the putrescence of its squares.

And in a sense we had waited for it to reclaim us after every absence. It had seen the most decisive part of our lives – the fall of Rob Sutcliffe, Sylvie's collapse, and now the suicide of Piers. Here it lay summer after summer, baking away in the sun, until its closely knitted roofs of weathered tile gave it the appearance of a piecrust fresh from the oven. It haunted one although it was rotten, fly-blown with expired dignities, almost deliquescent among its autumn river damps. There was not a corner of it that we did not love.

I had not given much thought to Rob Sutcliffe until now, sitting in this grubby café, waiting for the clocks to strike eight. After my sister Pia . . . after her defection had become absolutely unequivocal and Rob knew that they would never live together again, his decline and fall began. It was slow and measured at first, the decline from clubman and adventurer and famous novelist into . . . what exactly? From a dandy with a passion for clean linen to a mountebank in a picture hat. His books passed out of public demand, and he ceased to write any new ones. He took dingy lodgings in the lower town, two rooms in the house of an "angel maker" as the ironists of the town called those old crones who took in unwanted or illegitimate children for a small fee, and with an unwritten, unspoken guarantee to turn them into "angels" in a very few months by ill-treating them and literally starving them to death. This old crone was Rob's only company in the last years. They sat and drank themselves silly at night in the den he inhabited in that ghastly house full of hungry children. His physical appearance had changed very much since he had grown a straggling black beard, and taken to a cloak and the broad-brimmed hat which gave him a striking appearance. But he had long since ceased to wash, and he was as physically as dirty as an anchorite. He was fond of the cloak because it was impregnated with dirt and spots of urine. He had deliberately taken to wetting his bed at nights now, gloating over the deliberately infantile act, rubbing his own nose in it so to speak. In micturating he always allowed a few drops to fall upon the cloak. The stale odour of the garment afforded him great pleasure. For some time he continued to see Toby, but at last he refused him the right to visit him. All this ostentatious display of infantile regression was all the more mysterious for being conscious. After all, Sutcliffe had started life as a psychologist, and only turned to writing afterwards. It was his revenge on Pia I suppose, but all the stranger for being so deliberate. Sometimes when very drunk (he also took drugs) he would beg a hack from the livery stables and ride slowly about the town, with his head bowed on his breast, asleep: the reins left on the horse's neck so that it took him wherever it wished. Even when it came to the act of defecation he chose to smear paper and fingers alike. The change in Rob was almost unbelievable. It was his friend Toby who told me all this in his low sad voice – the voice reserved for matters of gravity or distress. He had forced the old crone to disgorge all she knew after Rob's body had been recovered from the river into which horse and rider had plunged.

It was strange to sit here in the early sunlight thinking about him, and also about Piers who had also met his end not two streets away, in the Hotel des Princes. Why had he not returned to the chateau, why had he stayed on in the town? Was he waiting to greet me? Or was there some other factor involved – perhaps it was easier to see his sister? All these things remained to be discovered. It would soon be time to take up the telephone and sort myself out. Nobody as yet knew I had arrived. I wondered whether perhaps Toby was already here in response to my cable.

The reaction of the long journey had begun to tell on me; I started to doze in the café. But jumping up I went back to the hotel where I knew that a hot shower would give me the energy I needed to get through the day – the memorable day of this return to Avignon and to Sylvie.

It is much later in the year now, when I try to reassess the meaning and value of all these episodes on paper: in search of some fruitful perspective upon my own life here in the old chateau – the queer solitary life which I have at last adopted. Scribbling all this gives me something to do, I am resetting the broken bones of the past. Perhaps I should have begun it long ago, but the thought of the old muniments room with its books and memoranda and paintings, that depressed me. At every point there I am in touch with them all through their diaries and manuscripts and letters. Moreover I myself must hurry a bit also, for a personal shadow has fallen into step with me, a more prosaic medical one which I can hold at bay for a while with the needle. But I am playing my hand slowly so as not to risk deserting Sylvie if I can help it.

I knew that I would have to undertake a few of the official duties in connection with Piers' death, and later that morning I rang up Jourdain at the asylum, the doctor who had been a family friend, and into whose charge Sylvie had always been placed. He was a cheerful man for a neurologist, and made even melancholia sound like something pleasant and enviable to have. "At last!" he said with evident relief. "We have been waiting for you. She has had excellent remissions, you know, and spent a great deal of time with Piers, until this extraordinary business came about. Yes, I am as puzzled as you must be. . . . Why? They talked of nothing but your arrival and the new life you were going to start together in Verfeuille. Naturally she collapsed, but it's not a total relapse. Some twilight, some confusional states, but the picture isn't entirely hopeless. And now you are here you can help me. I am holding her under fairly heavy sedation at the moment. But why not come out to Montfavet this evening and dine? We can wake her together."

I said I would do so. Apparently Toby had given no sign of life either. I wondered if he had received my cable.

That afternoon, to fill in my time, I took a short cut across the part of the old town which lies inside the fortifications and climbed past the ugly palaces of the Popes; I climbed the green-fringed ramps which led up into the marvellous hanging gardens of the Rocher des Doms. From this vantage point one can look down on three sides to see the loops and curls of the Rhône carving out the embankments of its bed in the carious limestone, sculpting the soft flanks of the nether hills. A frail sun shone upon distant snowlines leading away towards the Alps. A little island lay below this cockpit, frozen, like a wild duck trapped in frost-glittering sedge. Mount Saint Victor stood up in the distance, erect as a martyr tied to its stake of ice. But the wind still blew steel, although the faint sunlight had coaxed out some fugitive perfumes, orange or thyme, upon the air.

Here we had so often wandered, Sylvie and I, moving from one panorama to the other. And repeating the journey now I seemed to recapture many fragments of our old conversations. Events had given them an entirely new resonance. They had become part of past history, that part of time we had shared with Piers. I saw us now as figures – rather as in Rob's novel – projected anew by the force of memory upon this vernal landscape. Sylvie's dark-lashed eyes, "borrowed from the thrush" as her brother used to say, and the black hair with its violet blackness shining like carbon paper. Yes, the past now had attained a curious nervous density, a weight which was not composed (as one might suppose) of multiple nostalgias. It was full and rich, plump as an autumn fruit. It had been so fully lived that there was nothing about it one could dare to regret. The feeling of fatality, loneliness, and so on, were constituents of the present. Up here spring was scratching at the door like a pet.

I walked absently about the garden in the cold afternoon air, retracing in my mind the slopes and contours of these ancient conversations and wondering what the future held in store for me in this bereft world.

Sylvie was now the great question mark. Would she, I wondered, ever come to herself again enough to resume some sort of life with me? Funny how confident I had been that the presence of Piers would somehow make this possible, make her return to reason, to reality. There had been neither more nor less reason for optimism than there was now, yet I had felt it. Now I was not sure – I feared the imponderables of mental illness with its imperfectly demarcated boundaries, its sudden changes of temper and altitude. It was Sylvie herself who once said: "One should always distrust the insane. They are of bad faith somehow and they know it. But they don't know how to alter it, and you doctors don't know how to cure it."

And what if the worst should happen? Why, she would elect to stay on at Montfavet in the rooms which had for so long been set aside for her, trusting only in Jourdain, her old friend and confident. I sighed to think that she might never roam the world with me again, making one member of that sad trio, husband, wife, nurse: nor even that other trio of brother, sister, lover. How close we had been before all this unhappiness supervened! I kept thinking back to those days. Piers, Sylvie, myself, Toby, Rob, Pia and Sabine with her pack of fortune-telling cards – where was she now? Did she know of Piers' death from the cards? – that would be like her. My slow footsteps crunched on the gravel. Below loomed the sinfully ugly palaces of the Popes in all their blockish magnificence, overshadowing the town which despite the resonance of its name was still hardly more than an overgrown village. The quasi-death of insanity with its small periodic remissions, its deviations into good sense, even into brilliant insight, was almost more cruel really than outright death. In my own case it seemed gradually to have worn me out emotionally – the word castration does not sound too exaggerated in the context. An affect dammed and frozen. And of course (doctors are always on the lookout) I could trace the spoor of some deep new inhibitions in my dreams, not to mention my phantasies in which I surprised myself by poisoning her. It is unbelievable when I think of it, yet is true. Standing beside the bed in grim silence with my fingers on her pulse until the shallow breathing filtered away into the silence and her extraordinary marmoreal pallor announced the advent of the rigor. And then the sweet scent rose to my nostrils, the imaginary scent of death which I always smelt: I suspect that it was the odour of morphine. Yet in this dream fantasy it was always Piers who came up and put his hand on my arm to restrain me, to exorcise me.

There was plenty of time that evening. The light was faltering away into moonlit dusk when I set out to walk across the town to the station and pick up a *fiacre*. I wanted to jog in leisurely fashion through the green fields and chestnut avenues, over the rushing bubbling streamlets, to join Sylvie. I had so often done this in the past. I was anxious to see again the little church which had always been our point of rendezvous. Did it still stand in its humble little square planted with tall shady planes? Did the old cracked bistro still have the yellow letter-box nailed to its wall? A small, a fragile point of reference in the incoherent and echoing world of her madness, of her life behind the walls of the great establishment.

I used to catch sight of her waiting for me so shyly among the trees, listening with bent head for the clip-clop of the horse's hooves. Her tremulous anxiety ignited the dark beauty of her face with its luminous eyes and white-rose pallor. And somewhere near at hand always lurked the tall, military-looking nurse clad in her stiff field-grey uniform, her white hair tugged back on her scalp and pinned into a coif. She would remain watchfully in the shadow of the trees while Sylvie advanced on tiptoe to meet me, her arms outstretched, her lips moving. It was like meeting a small child. The queer little camel-backed church was always empty too, smelling of wax and cats and dust. We entered it always with our arms about each other, the ice broken at last by the first tremulous kiss of recognition. And as always we gravitated, as if by instinct, to the little side-chapel marked with a Roman five, and sat down face to face with the large rather anodyne painting which we had come to love so much. Here she always insisted that we talk in whispers, not from respect of the place, but lest the eavesdroppers in the painting should overhear – though why these so manifestly harmless images should menace the endearments of two lovers in the silent church I do not know.

Jogging slowly along now, down these long green avenues already touched by the first spring shoots, I felt the full ambivalence of my thoughts swinging from side to side as the little *fiacre* itself swung. Queer thoughts passed through my mind, the anarchic thoughts which sprang from those unresolved childish conflicts and fears: thoughts I could identify at least. Perhaps out of Piers' death I might extract a horror and sweetness which brought me much closer to her? I, who had never been jealous of Piers while he was alive, or so I thought, managed to surprise myself with such a thought. I would have her to myself! And if she were to become sane again, then why not fecund? It was not too late . . . But here my mind balked. Once before we had taken this path, and it was a distasteful and dishonourable one. Surprised by Sylvie's pregnancy one spring some years ago, and not knowing for certain whose the child would be, I tried to solve the problem by marrying her, only to have all this uncertainty end in a provoked miscarriage. It was cowardly to pretend that her state of mind dictated it; it was our state of mind which should have been called into question. Nobody likes being a homosexual, just as nobody likes being a negro or a Jew. The marriage was only another mask for the hold I had on her brother through his affections. And yet love is a real thing – perhaps the only real thing in this bereft world. And yet how to achieve the only sort which is viable, enriching – one with no sanctions, no reservations, one without guilt?

It was no longer fashionable to ask too much of oneself; we three must have seemed a somewhat pathetic trio to the outside eye – I think of the mordant phrases of Rob about us. We were old-fashioned, we belonged to the age of piety, and perhaps Avignon was the perfect site for this kind of blind adventure which would leave no trace behind, except for a lot of mouldering papers in the old chateau which would interest nobody, and one day would be sold for scrap.

Outside, in the shade of the trees, the German nurse in field-grey waited for us, standing upright as a soldier, her arms folded, watching the door of the church from which we would eventually emerge. Once Sylvie had written on the walls of the gutted ballroom at Verfeuille the phrase: *"Quelqu'un en gris reste vainqueur."* And I knew she had been thinking of this tall dour custodian of her reason.

Yes, the church was still there, thank goodness, and the little square had hardly changed. My eyes at once sought the familiar corner under the trees, but now there were only a few aged men stooped over their *boules*. I halted the *fiacre* and went into the nave for a moment, bemused by the sleepy silence, and thinking of nothing in particular. I sat for a while absently in our little side-chapel, staring at the familiar painting which had presided over so many of our conversations. Then I set myself to think hard of her, wondering if perhaps by telepathy I might project some of this sad calm towards her. I closed my eyes and counted the breaths for a while, recreating her form mentally the while in the shape of a target, an ikon. I conjured her up – all the small-boned litheness which issued in such abrupt but sure gestures: she wore clothes of a slightly old-fashioned cut, and little jewelry. It was not hard to forge her image, her "eidolon", in the grey gloom of the little church. I tried to project towards her that part of a man which is his knowing, thinking and caring part – beyond the ego and the tricks of the mind. Yes, I saw her and another phrase of Akkad came into my mind. I repeated it softly to myself.

"Even death has its own precise texture and the big philosophers have always entered into the image of the world it exemplifies while still alive, so to become one with it while their hearts were still beating. They colonised it." But it was when Akkad said things like that, which had all the air of being quotations from some forgotten gnostic poet, that Sylvie, beside herself with admiration, would spread her hands towards him and say, "O convince me, dear Akkad, please convince me."

Unlike her brother she shared my native incapacity for belief, a lack which prevented either of us advancing very far into the tangled jungle of the gnostic world; whereas Piers took to it at once like duck to water, and only just managed to prevent himself becoming a bore, a fervent.

Time was moving on, the sunlight was slanting across the planes in a last conflagation before dusk. I broke off my reverie and rejoined the little cab. "To *Monfavet-les-Roses*," I said, and the driver looked at me curiously, wondering, I imagine, whether to feel sympathy or not; or perhaps he was just curious. The idea of the roses gave a singular tinge to the notion of madness. Indeed in the vulgar Avignon slang *"tomber dans les roses"* which had been waggishly adapted from *"tomber dans les pommes"* signified going mad enough to be incarcerated in the grey institution. We were moving through the cool evening light towards Sylvie. I wondered how I should find her.

You would say that they were simply two old dilapidated rooms with high ceilings and a predisposition to unreachable cobwebs, but they were rather glorious, belonging to an older age, part of the original foundation. But they had always been hers, set aside for her, and now it was as if they belonged to her completely. The authorities had allowed her to move in her own graceful furniture from the chateau, carpets and paintings, and even a large tapestry rescued from the old ballroom. So that it was always a pleasant shock of surprise to come upon this haven of calm and beauty after traversing the rather for-

bidding main buildings, and the succession of long white corridors with sterile-looking glass doors painted over with doctors'
names. Moreover her own high french windows gave out
directly on to the gardens so that she could virtually live in the
open all summer. Hers was the life of a privileged prisoner,
except when she happened to have a period of remission when
she resumed her place in the ordinary world. But the rooms stayed
hers, and while she was away they were kept scrupulously dusted.

She worked under the great tapestry with its glowing but
subdued tones – huntsmen with lofted horns had been running
down a female stag. After the rape, leaving the grooms to
bring the trophy home, they galloped away into the soft
brumous Italian skyline; a network of misty lakes and romantic
islets receding into the distance along the diagonal; fathered by
Poussin or Claude. The stag lay there, panting and bleeding
and in tears. None of this had changed and I found the fact
reassuring. The beautiful old Portuguese writing desk with its
ivory-handled drawers, the rare bust of Gongora, the auto-
graph of Gide enlarged and framed above the piano. Jourdain
stood by with a quiet sad smile, holding his passkey in his hand,
and giving me time to take it all in. My eye fell upon a bundle
of manuscript, and a tangle of notebooks lying about in a
muddle on the carpet – as if a packet had exploded in her hands.
"The spoils from Piers' room," said Jourdain following my
eye. "The police allowed her to carry off some of the stuff in the
hope that she might reveal something of interest. But so far
nothing. She seems to have been the last to see Piers, you see?
Come; we can talk later."

Well, but she had gone away to lie down and sleep in her
vast unmade bed with its heavy damascened baldaquin holding
back the light and neutralising it. Her eyes were closed but she
was not asleep. I could tell by the movement of her inquisitive
fingers – they were playing something like the slow movement
of the A minor; but slowly and haltingly, as if sight-reading it

23

for the first time. We made little enough noise, but I could tell from long experience that she knew we were there, sensing the fact like an animal. Nor was there anything mysterious in the fact that it was I, for she had been expecting me. It was the purest automatism for me to go down on one knee and place my finger on her white wrist. I whispered her name and she smiled and turned; without opening her eyes she kissed me warmly on the mouth, lingeringly. "Bruce, at last you, Bruce." But she said it as if I were still part of a dream she was enacting in her mind. Then she went on in a different register and in a small precise voice. "So then everything smells of burnt rubber here. I must tell Jourdain." My companion grunted softly. Then she went on at a headlong pace. "I think really that it was his way of eating that repelled me. Toby always ate in that way. Poor Toby." I took her hand, forgetting, and said, "Has Toby arrived yet?" But she only put her finger to her lips and said, "Shh. They must not overhear. He will be coming soon. He promised me." She sat up now in a masterful mood, clasping her hands, but still keeping her eyes fast shut. "Piers' diaries, they are all over the place, and I can't sort them properly. Thank goodness you have come, Bruce." Her lips trembled. "But the smell of rubber and sulphur – I can't tell which is the worse. So now I am completely in your power, Bruce. There is nobody left now who can hurt me at all except you. Do you want to kill me Bruce, to drive me to it? I must know the truth."

"Please."

"I must know the truth."

She opened her eyes at last and turned towards us smiling – a trifle tearfully to be sure but with a basic composure that was reassuring. It always amazed me that whenever I reappeared after a long absence she suddenly shed her sickness. It was like watching a diver slowly surfacing. After a moment she lay down again and turned her face to the wall saying, but this time in a confidently rational tone, "Part of the confusion is in

24

myself, you know, but mostly in all three of us at once. It is horrible to be a battleground of three selves." I knew only too well what she meant, though I said nothing, simply keeping my fingers on the precious timepiece of her pulse.

She lay sighing, and then after a while it came back, the sensation that by some enigmatic act of willpower I drew her slowly back towards reality once more. It was still a factor of control over her (which did not always work) that I would have liked to rationalise, to use like a real healer. I tried to explain it to myself by saying that with me she gradually began to forget that she was mad. In ascribing a rational value to everything she said, however confused, I provoked her into trying to provide one for herself. I pretended that it all had a meaning, and of course in another sense it did have one, if only one could have deciphered it. It was indeed literally drowned in meaning, like a flooded boat.

There is nothing stranger than to love somebody who is mad, or who is intermittently so. The weight, the strain, the anxiety is a heavy load to bear – if only because among these confusional states and hysterias loom dreadful probabilities like suicide or murder. It shakes one's hold also on one's own grasp of reality; one realises how precariously we manage to hold on to our reason. With the spectacle of madness before one's eyes one feels the odds shorten. The eclipse of reason seems such an easy affair, the grasp on sanity so provisional and insecure. While I was feeling the weight of these preoccupations she was saying: "Everything seems to have come to an end now, but has it? Three little nigger boys . . . then there were two. I am afraid of you. Bruce what shall we do?" The question was asked on such a rational note that I took the plunge and asked: "You were with him? How did it happen? Did he do it himself?" She gave a small sigh, and closed her eyes once more; she was fading back into sedation again, that marvellous defence against the importunities of the world; I felt a fool for having

25

adventured such important questions at such a time. Jourdain had the grace not to look quizzically at me. He shrugged. A tiny snore escaped her lips, and the doctor drew me softly out of that submarine bedroom into the study.

I waited there for a long while, suspended as if in a solution of silence, watching her and listening to her gradually deepening breathing as she edged her way towards the dismemberment of a drugged sleep. Jourdain was very patiently waiting too; he was an endearing man and the slight cast in one eye gave him always a sad juridical air, a tiny touch of melancholy which invaded his frequent smiles and inflected them with sadness. He sported dark suits even in summer, when they must have been stifling to wear, and white wing-collars with ties almost broad enough to be stocks. He whispered that he would come back for me at dinner-time and then quietly tiptoed away. I sat beside her for a while longer and then followed his lead. But in the outer room I started to gather up all the litter of papers and notebooks which were lying about on the carpet. It was typical of the sort of jumble of paper that Piers accumulated around him – everything unfinished, down to the last aphorism! One might have thought that a mad magpie had been at work among this heap of old concert programmes, maps of cities, rare pamphlets, notebooks and letters. I did what I could to sort and tidy, but it was not easy. Among the letters, some still in their envelopes, there were a number from me, and a number from Sylvie to me which I had sent on to him — so much did I feel that we were one person and obliged to share each other's lives, both inner and outer.

Then there were some from Piers to her, all written on the notepaper he affected which bore the legend *Outremer*. (I had noticed on her finger Piers' seal ring with the same rebus. He had always ironically referred to himself as "the last of the Templars", and the word expressed not only the family tie, for he was indeed a de Nogaret, but also the Templar pride in

26

the overseas commitment of the order. For such a romantic going to the Middle Orient was a thrilling experience – of a quasi-historical kind. He felt he was returning to the roots of the great betrayal, the roots of all anti-Christian dissent. Piers was a worshipper of the Templar God. He believed in the usurper of the throne, the Prince of Darkness.)

I pondered all these contingencies as I sat in the green arm-chair, sifting the papers and dreaming. "In the face of such evil, creative despair is the only honourable posture," he said once and was annoyed when I smiled at his serious expression. I turned the pages of a diary in which he jotted down the visits he had received during the days preceding his death. Had he given his sister the seal ring which she now wore, the *Outremer* ring? I shook a copy of *A Rebours* and more letters fell out on to the carpet. One was a note to me from Piers giving an account of one of his sister's relapses. "When these periods come on, Bruce, she hears my voice everywhere, in the woods, in the hot-water pipes, in the drone of a mosquito, crying out always 'Sylvie, where are you?' Followed by a sudden ominous wail 'I have killed my sister.' She is terrified at such times. What can I do?"

Such periods corresponded neither to the phases of the moon nor to her own physical rhythms. They seemed perfectly arbitrary and unpredictable. If we came to see her at such a time she would recognise only one of us, Piers. And here was a long rambling letter which she had written to me, but dedicated to her brother. "Dearest, you have been away so long. Soon it will be my birthday and I can scent the eachness of numbers, they mate with such reluctance. I know you cannot come as yet but I pretend. Today I waited all day for you, clothed from head to foot in a marvellous seamless euphoria. The throbbing of the almond-blossom has been almost un-bearable, I cried myself asleep, back into reality again. Now the fruit is forming and I know I love you. Bruce dear, this is Man

Friday's sole in the sand, I have it in the carpet now. Even Jourdain says he sees it, so I know that I am not romancing. Piers was a Friday child remember? My dearest, they say that now you are back from India, and yet no word. Why? You will certainly have your reasons, and everything will be explained when you come. Forgive me if I am impatient.

"I am impatient to hear about India – O how was India; how calm was India? Starving and God-drunk and tattered with dry excrement? I feel I know. Every drawn breath an infanticide, every smile an enigmatic option on inner loneliness. When I was there long ago I felt the moon of my fragile non-being was at full. The smell of the magnolia remembers me supremely. A deep sadness seemed very worth while. But locked up in the first-class waiting-room of my mind I have come to repine. Yesterday they let me pretend and I went down to our Montfavet church to say hullo to the people on the wall. Nowadays at night I seem to hear Piers walking about in the other room, but he is never there when I run to see. This place, this mockery of a place, is full of a special sadness. Jourdain feels it too. He is still here, still talking of retiring, fastidious as a leper; I taste his smoke after he has gone. The taste of iodine too."

I tested each phrase on my inner ear, my inner mind, as I thought of her sitting in the fifth side-chapel of the Montfavet church under the three oil-painted witnesses, so gauche, so awkward. On the wall at her back there was a plaque commemorating the death of a forgotten priest. If I closed my eyes even now I could read it off.

ICI REPOSE
PLACIDE BRUNO VALAYER
Evêque de Verdun
Mort en Avignon
en 1850

I was so far plunged in reverie that I forgot the sleeper next door, and when at last Jourdain came tapping on the glass for me I wondered who it might be. I was half asleep I suppose, fagged out after the long journey. However I sprang up and followed the doctor to his own bachelor suite at the other corner of the main buildings. They echoed his lifelong passion for painting, and I noticed several new additions to his collection of oils.

In order to emphasise his civil capacity, so to speak, he had put on an old and cherished English blazer — to underline I suppose that his stay as a student in Edinburgh has been a most enjoyable period in his existence. The wines were thoughtful and tenderly chambered. The food was slight but choice. And for a good while we said nothing, which is the prerogative of old friends, but sat sipping our cognac and smiling at each other. "I was about to ask you if there was any reasonable explanation," he said at last with an exasperated laugh, "and I see that you are just about to put the same question to me." He was right, I had been on the point of asking him what the devil had got into Piers. As he was fully informed of our plans of retirement and so on I could speak to him quite freely. I had always suspected him of being in love with Sylvie, but he was a man of great pudicity; when it was once a case of doing a mild psychotherapy on her he passed her over to someone else, in order, I thought, not to prejudice his doctor's control: or was it because he did not wish to feel the jealousy caused by his probings? "Let me tell you what is what for the present," he said at last as we sat down to the meal. He drew a long breath. "Piers came here on retirement nearly a year ago, and set up shop in the hotel in order to be near Sylvie as he waited for you to arrive. Everything was in order for the execution of your plan, he spoke about it twice to me with enthusiasm. Sylvie herself celebrated the whole thing by several splendid remissions – you would never have thought she had been ill at all. Piers was beside himself with joy, and she spent nearly every day with him, either walking about the town or sitting in his rooms helping him sort papers or playing cards with him – you know his passion for cards. For the last week before this . . . well, extraordinary act . . . he had been in bed with a slight cold, nothing really to worry about. You will see when you look at his diary that quite a lot of people dropped in to see him, but it does seem that the very last was Sylvie. The nurse used to collect her in the evenings around seven and bring her back here to her rooms. Mind you, it was quite appropriate that the last person to see him alive was his sister. What is odd is that she was almost in a state of collapse when the nurse arrived, so the inference is that he had already done it or had told her that he was going to do it. But at any rate she knew. From then on such facts as she produced must be held suspect, for she went right round the bend. The nurse produced one interesting point – she said that she (Sylvie) was in a fearful state because she thought herself guilty of killing Piers, for she poured out his sleeping draught for him that night and thinks that she made a mistake. The empty bottle was beside the bed, where inevitably those flat-footed police found it, and insisted on an autopsy to settle the matter. Did he poison himself, or did she accidentally do so? That is the question."

"An accident sounds more plausible. I'm reassured."

"Exactly. He gave absolutely no indication of a desire to commit suicide. I was too late to prevent the police having him carved up, but I did get on to the *préfet* who assured me that unless there is very special evidence to the contrary the thing will be treated as an accident. Which solves the question of burial. I have also contacted that strange uncle of his, the Abbé of Foulques, who has agreed to lend a moral support should the police become tedious. You know he had permission to be buried in the family vault at Verfeuille? We should get all the formalities settled by tomorrow evening. Well, that is all I can tell you for the moment." He placed his fingers on the table and reflected deeply. "It may have been Sylvie," he said, "in which case we can absolve her of any ill intent; it could only have been an accident. Yes, it must be so."

I was strangely comforted by this exposé of the situation which had at first seemed to be so full of ambiguities. At least now the whole matter was plain, and when the police came back with the obvious result things could take their normal course, the funeral could take place. As Jourdain talked, however, I saw in my mind's eye the long casual autopsy slit which stretches from below the breast bone to the *mons pubis*.

"And Toby?" asked Jourdain with a sudden testy note in his voice, "where the devil is he?" It was a question I could not answer for the moment. "We have all cabled him in Oxford. But perhaps he hasn't yet gone up, or is away on a walking tour in Germany as he so often is . . . I don't know." Jourdain nodded; and then with an exclamation he stood up, recalling something he had forgotten. "I completely forgot. I borrowed the police photos for you to see. They show the room exactly as it was when the police photographer was called in by the inspector and the *médecin-légiste*. Of course in part it is due to the fact that it took place at the Princes Hotel – what the devil induced Piers to stay there instead of somewhere like the Bristol? Funds? It's virtually a *maison de passe*. Perhaps he had special secret vices we don't know about? Anyway, whatever happens at the Princes is automatically suspect for the police. Hence these awkward questions, photographs and so on. Of course he was an amateur of *quat* – hashish – which delighted the cops. But there was precious little else of interest."

As he was speaking he was undoing a heavy black brief-case which had been lying against the sofa; from it he extracted an official envelope which held a number of photographic prints, as yet hardly dry. The glossy surface stuck to one's fingers as one peeled them. They were extremely beautiful, these still-lifes of Piers' disorderly room. Jourdain spread them out on a green card-table and drew up two chairs, at the same time producing a large magnifying glass through which one could study the detail of the room with its strange inhabitant, who lay in bed, in the very posture in which he had been found. I felt a shortening of the breath as I contemplated them. Jourdain was talking on softly, anxious to give as complete an account as he could of this strange affair. "There were several sets of prints on the empty bottle here, on the bedside table. One of them Sylvie's, which is interesting. As you know he took quite large doses of Luminash, as a sort of sedative as well as a sleeping draught. Presumably this is what they'll find in the organs."

Piers lay on his side with his knees drawn up – in almost a sketch of the foetal position; he had thrown back the sheet and the covers and appeared to be about to get up from his bed. His head was turned round towards the camera, presumably in the direction of the door, and he was smiling as if in delighted and surprised recognition, at someone who had just entered the room. It was clearly a smile of welcome. The flashlight threw into relief his pleasant patrician face and the brilliance of his bright blue eyes, which had a sapphire-like luminosity. He wore one of his old white nightshirts with the little monogram on the breast. It was like a frozen shot in a film, and it was difficult to interpret what he might have been about to do; instead of rising perhaps he was just sinking back luxuriously, and smiling goodbye as somebody left the room?

Yet one outstretched hand with its firm fencer's wrist was stretched out towards the bedside table as if to switch off a light, take up a book or a cigarette. I passed the magnifying glass across the field to examine the detail with more precision. A novel lay beside the bed. His wrist-watch and his ebony cigarette holder lay in the silver ashtray on the bed-table. In a second and larger ashtray lay a mountain of cigarette and cigar ends. I recognised the stubs of the cheroots he smoked. For the rest the room was in a state of chaos; everywhere were tea-cups, jars of jam, flowers, packets of joss, picture-magazines and mountains of books and papers. "The room looks as if it had never been cleaned," I said, and Jourdain shrugged his shoulders. "It's the Princes," he said as if that explained everything.

To tell the truth the appearance of his room was, for such an untidy man, relatively normal. Cupboards hung open revealing his wardrobe. Though he had always been a little bit of a dandy his choice of apparel was scanty, but choice, with a distinct leaning towards clothes made for him in London. A couple of medium-sized trunks were enough to house personal possessions of this kind; but the books were a different matter – Piers could not live without books, and plenty of them. This explained the sagging home-made bookshelves knocked together from pieces of crate. And there was the oil painting he liked so much, of the three of us. Sylvie in the dappled sunlight under the planes, sitting in a yellow hammock, her lap full of flowers. On either side of her we stand, Piers holding her straw hat in his hand, as if he had just retrieved it from the grass. I stand leaning against the tree, lighting a cigarette. The sky has the peculiar peeled look which is conferred by the mistral only, cloudless, hard as enamel. I went through the prints with a feeling of weakness, with a lump in my throat. Yes, there was nothing unexpected here. The only other decoration would be the famous death-map which he had been compiling of late and which had a bearing on his intention of writing a memoir on the subject of his own approaching death. But more of this later. My hand is tired tonight. I must get some order into my thoughts. Something troubled me in all this. What was it?

Jourdain dropped me at my hotel that evening after dinner, and grunted as he saw through the glass doors of the patio the shapes of two men who sat waiting for me. They sat with such an air of involuntary boredom, smoking patiently, that I almost divined who they were before he spoke. "That's old Bechet the notary, and Tholon the police inspector. They probably want to take you to see the room and ask you for any notions you might have."

I turned and bade him goodnight. "Keep in touch," he said as he let in the clutch, and I said I would. I opened the glass cage and stepped into the patio with its undusted potted palms and introduced myself to the two men – or at least to one of them; for Bechet I had already met some years before with Piers. We exchanged shocked commiseration at the news of his death, genuine enough in his case because he had dearly loved the family. He puffed and blew in his fussy way, and used his hands to say what his tongue could not.

It was unthinkable that it should have been anything but an accident, he told me, more than once. The little policeman, who looked so undistinguished in civilian clothes, did not intrude his speculations upon us. "We must see," he said quietly. "Tomorrow we should have the results of the autopsy, and the body will be returned to the morgue, to the *chapelle ardente*, where his relatives may visit him if they wish." My soul shrank back however at the thought, which was un-worthy of a medical man like myself – I know it. Bechet plunged into the details of the funeral which he had rememorised from the will. The details rendered him somewhat plaintive, for Piers was to be taken to the family *caveau* after dark, by the light of torches, there to be placed among his ancestors. But no service of any kind was to be read. "It's awkward," said Bechet, "I don't know what the Abbé will have to say. He will think that Piers was an atheist." Tholon sighed and I gathered from the volume that he harboured anticlerical sentiments. "It's vexing," said the old lawyer scattering ash over his rumpled suit, and on the end of his spotted bow tie. "In a way

34

it was worse," I said thoughtfully, "for he belonged to a sect of gnostics who live in Egypt – and they are certainly not Christians but dissenters. Hence the provision in his will, I suppose." Tholon began to look impatient now and asked me if I would care to see the room in which my friend had died. It was being held under police seal for the moment, but perhaps the contents might give me an idea to help explain the affair. I was reluctant, but felt I could hardly refuse. Despite Bechet's obvious distaste (he was like all Mediterraneans superstitious about the death of friends) he allowed his courtesy to rule him and agreed to accompany us on the short walk across the square to the hotel. I had decided to get the thing over and done with.

It was deep night now with a rising moon. The gold lantern with its legend "Hotel des Princes" swung softly in the light breeze. It was an old hotel and smelt ruinously of dust and blocked drains. We climbed to the first floor and Tholon undid some tapes stuck with sealing wax on one of the doors. The room was a pleasant size but very musty. The inspector crossed it before even turning on the light and opened a door leading out on to a small balcony; then he returned and switched on the electric light within. The bird-spattered balcony gave out on to a corner of dilapidated garden whose withered and ancient trees had long since given up bearing fruit. No doubt Piers sat out here obstinately in the icy evenings of winter to watch the light softly fading over Avignon, watching the city softly tilting into the uncaring twilight like a sailing boat turning its cheek to the wind. From here, across the network of brown clay roofs, everything slid downwards into the massive green river, which itself propelled its currents downwards to Arles with its desolate necropolis, the Alyscamps. His mind, like mine now, would have crossed the river towards the sea and then veered northward once more . . .

There was not a corner of this magnetic country that the three of us had not explored together, sometimes on foot, sometimes on horseback, or else in a dilapidated pony cart piled high with camping equipment. Often in summer as we sat down round a fire of olive-trimmings in some field near Remoulins or Aramon a moon like a blood-orange would wander into the sky and hang above the river, waiting for our return. Avignon, so small, stuffy and parochial, was in my blood. I shivered and stepped back into the room where the two men stood in sympathetic silence, waiting for me to take it into consideration and perhaps to offer some useful observations on it. But there seemed little enough to be said.

"The body has been removed, but nothing else has been touched except the glasses and the bottle of sedative from which we took our fingerprints." On the nether wall was the so-called death-map compiled by my friend. I saw Bechet studying it in a somewhat nervous way and stepped to his side to explain it as best I could. "All the names were the names of friends who had died. He seemed to attach particular importance to the fact, and used to say that each separate death had taught him something new about death, and that he was going to resume this knowledge in a philosophic essay about dying. It was connected in an obscure way with the beliefs of this sect of gnostics to which he belonged." It sounded pretty lame and stupid as an explanation but it had the merits of filling in an area of darkness. Bechet tutted with anxiety and readjusted his pince-nez. "Well. Well. Well," he said disconsolately, for death was a subject he could not stand – his whole life, constructed of a tissue of routine boredoms, had been designed to shelter him from the realisation that he was gradually approaching death. Tholon was made of different stuff, being much younger. He studied the big yellow chart with gravity. "I have noted all the names," he said, and one could sense that a formidable dossier was on the way to being assembled.

"So they are all dead?" said Bechet with distaste.

"Yes."

"But why the singular shape of the map which looks like a sort of snake?"

"It is a snake – for this little sect death in an individual assumes the shape of a constellation, the Serpent. The snake symbolises process, even time itself."

Bechet almost groaned at these obscurities. He looked quite alarmed, and I realised that it was time to spare him. So much of this must have sounded rubbish to him. "At any rate that is what he explained to me," I said hastily while the lawyer rubbed his long *ultra*'s nose and sighed.

"Perhaps," said Tholon, scenting my awkwardness, "you would care to spend a little while alone in the room? It is difficult to concentrate when one is with people. But alone and quiet you might notice something of interest. What do you say?" I hesitated. I knew that the good fellow wanted to leave me alone to say a prayer for the soul of my friend. I said I would like to stay if it did not upset anyone. To tell the truth I was anxious to see the back of them and eager to examine the bookshelf and the notebooks of my friend. There may have been a manuscript worth saving from the rapacious curiosity of the police. Tholon at once handed over the keys and the waxed tapes which I must affix. "Just lock up," he said, "and I will come round tomorrow and pick up the keys from your hotel." I thanked him. Bechet seemed eager and relieved to quit the place. But he said: "Just one thing I'd like to have an opinion about. In the will he speaks of his horror at the chance of being buried alive, and asks to have a vein severed. Would you be prepared to do that?" I said that there would hardly be any need for the safeguard in view of the autopsy, and he agreed at once, relieved.

They both went. I heard their voices and footsteps descend in diminishing echoes down the stairs; then the uneasy blurred silence of the city fell upon this tomb-like room with its disinherited objects. From time to time the susurrus of traffic might be broken by a clattering stammering outburst of a church-bell, but that was all. So this is where Piers had spent the last hours of his life! I sat down on the foot of the bed and put my hand to the turned-back sheet. It was lukewarm. The room smelt very faintly of joss as well as of drains. I pulled back the bedclothes and was not surprised to find the scarlet bedsocks he always wore to match his vivid Egyptian *babouches*. A dozen pairs of socks he had bought to accompany a dozen pairs of slippers – enough for a lifetime, as he exultantly said. "When you find your colour stick to it."

Most of the books I knew; they bore his bookplate and came from the chateau library. The notebooks were empty, so that I presumed Sylvie to be in possession of any manuscripts of vital importance. Or else the police had already swept them up. There were a few business letters in the bedside table drawers. Bills. Tradesmen's advertisements posted on to him by the Bag Room of the Quai d'Orsay.

The bathroom was in a fearful mess that was all too customary: a crumpled face towel on the floor by the *bidet* bore lipstick marks – a dark crimson-like tone which reminded me of something, a memory I could not place for the moment.

I went back into the other room and counted the cigar-butts in the big ashtray, calculating that the room had not been cleaned and set to rights for at least a week. There was also a toothmug here, presumably without fingerprints, as I could see it had been dusted over with the traditional talc. It smelt very faintly of alcohol – mouthwash, dentifrice, gin or Luminash? Impossible to say. Then I remembered something and returned to the ashtray in order to pick out two or three little cigarette ends from the darker pile of butts; they were slender and had gilt tips marked with the same dark crimson lipstick. Well, Piers did not smoke these, and his sister did not smoke at all. I pondered the matter for I knew somebody who smoked precisely this sort of theatrical gilt-tipped cigarette – loading them

38

with dried grains of hashish after puncturing them with a pin along their length: then sealing the punctures with a spittle-daubed finger. Sabine did! My heart leaped up with pleasure to think that she might have visited Piers before the end, even that she might still be in Avignon. For the colour of the lip-stick of her preference had always been, as Sylvie said, the second cousin of arterial blood. I made a mental note to ring up the old chateau where old Banquo presumably lived. Perhaps by now he was dead? But bankers never die. And yet I had a feeling that Sabine had most probably disappeared as she always did: she could never stay long in one place, a few days at most. Then she would be gone like a wind, following the gipsies into Hungary, or joining the slow caravans which traverse the wave-worn desert highways of the spice routes. I had not run across her for years, this enigmatic woman. Perhaps we should meet again here, in the context of Piers' disappearance?

I stood before the death-map, adopting something like the stance that Piers himself always took, hands behind his back, head cocked reflectively on one side. I tried to think my way into this recent mind. There were no dates on his map, just simply the bare recorded fact, the name of a human being who had, in the act of dying, turned himself into a point-event. But when one saw the whole thing spread out in this way, in a schematic fashion, one came closer to realising what had been in Piers' mind as on each occasion he quietly added another name to the fallen. Everyone must have a personal calendar of death compiled after this fashion. A war memorial, for example, never achieves this kind of coherence, for it gives too generalised a picture of death. Its universality is stressed and that is all. But in this case each separate single death had discharged itself with a throb of grief on to the heart of Piers, and the succession of falling sadnesses, like the grains of sand in an hour-glass, had gradually weighed upon his heart and his memory: until he realised that he was receiving an education for his own death. The realisation of one's own death is the point at which one becomes adult – he was never tired of repeating this proposition of Akkad's. Yes, that was the inner meaning of the map before which, for so many years and months, he had walked up and down, pondering; each name became a whole constellation of memories. From them he hoped to extract the essential philosophic meaning which would, so to speak, enlighten his own coming death and enable him to write of it with insight and truth. It was an ambitious undertaking but one upon which he had set his heart.

Over the years he has sent me small fragments of auto-biographical introduction – which was to be entitled "A Waterbiography" because he was astrologically a fish sign as was I. One little fragment I carried in my wallet, written out in his own fluent and lyrical handwriting. It went: "If I must try to describe Piers de Nogaret without benefit of mirrors I must begin by saying that his favourite word was *precarious*: whatever he wrote and thought gravitated towards or away from that word, his pole-star. In spirit and intention he was not a sensualist but an ardent Epicurean. Everything, both the best and the worst, came to him because of his sister in the first instance – for he tried to avoid loving her without avail. This was his greatest single experience, and yet he always felt that it conferred a limitation on his growth – until, that is, he visited Egypt and became a gnostic disciple of the thinker Akkad. The only other love in his life was for a man who loved him with a dispassionate singleness of intent – and who also loved his sister. The three of them could hardly tell themselves apart, became a sort of congeries of loving emotions, all mutually complementary. None of this was achieved without a tremendous struggle against their sense of rightness, logic, even appropriateness. They won, but it severed them from the world, and yet they lived a quasi-worldly life for years, which had little reality outside the company of each other. A happy trinity of lovers. Or so he makes bold to claim."

There was little else in the room to alert a detective, but I lingered on a while, luxuriating in the sense of familiarity conferred on me by these friendly possessions. I knew that I would not come back here and that sooner or later the seals would be taken off and all these items find their way back into some barn or lumber-room at Verfeuille, losing all coherence and identity. His death had invested them with a dramatic significance which they did not merit. There were some notes in the back of a copy of Swift, and I recognised the handwriting of Rob Sutcliffe. "Short story about N who to escape his sister foolishly forced himself to fall in love with a Berlin actress, very romantic, who follows him across Europe in her husband's car, dressed as a chauffeur. Shot at him in Zagreb but the weapon missed fire; he felled her with an umbrella. He had come to study the Caballa with an old Jewish sage whose name he had first heard from a psychiatrist in Zurich. She tried to pay him, pulling out a wad of notes as thick as a sandwich. He fell in love with the gesture and took her to his hotel, only to sneak off at dawn, steal the car and head north."

The tone and the matter were typical of Rob, and half the books in the chateau contained similar brief plots for stories or novels – a practice which annoyed Toby very much for Sutcliffe appeared in the end to make no use of them. They simply came to him as spontaneously as a limerick might. But afterwards he lost interest in the idea and bothered no more with it. I looked to see whether his name was on the death-map. Yes, there it was, Robert Sutcliffe. How soon would it be before some scholar applied for permission to sift through the mass of documents he had left behind in the muniments room at Verfeuille? His fame was still growing.

It was late when I got back to the hotel, but the bar was

still open and I was glad of a stiff whisky before going up to my room. I lay in bed for a while in darkness, thinking; slowly the numbness was wearing off, I was beginning to realise that I would never see my friend again.

The next morning early Bechet phoned the hotel, and with hardly disguised triumph told me his good news. We had a following wind now, for the papers had come back as well as the authorisation to proceed with the funeral. Moreover the police had waived their suspicions, thanks to the *préfet*'s intervention, and were prepared to accept the hypothesis of an accident in default of any firmer evidence. The will was in order. Only the provisions for the funeral were irksome, for the coffin was to be followed by nobody. Bechet wearisomely enumerated these stipulations in his singsong accent, and showed concern when I said that I proposed to violate them. I could not, would not, let Piers go to his grave without one friend from this life beside him, ready to see him over the threshold into the next. Duty and inclination were hand in hand, and I expressed the matter with some force. Bechet pondered and then gave in. As a matter of fact he had already had an altercation with the Abbé who was furious because he had hoped to conduct a service for Piers, and Bechet had warned him that it would be forbidden. "At any rate," he said, "the old man is determined to come, service or no service. I can't forbid him that, nor you. I will drive you over myself. If I could fix everything for tonight would you agree? I think the sooner it is over the better for all concerned. I will try for tonight and ring you back this afternoon about five. I would like to finish with the matter." I agreed, glad to feel that Piers' case was escaping from the stagnant reaches of French bureaucracy. He added: "By the way, another provision: no flowers. At least we can accept that one, can't we?" I knew the reason for this also: because they were ikons for the living soul which the gnostics did not believe in. The only appropriate and permissible flower would have been sea-lavender, then, which is a sort of fossil rather than a plant. Needless to say I did not disconcert Bechet by repeating all this strange lore.

"Sylvie can't come of course?" he asked.

"Of course not."

"All the better in a way."

"I agree."

He rang off and I prepared myself to wait for the formalities to be completed. By now the remains of Piers must be reposing at the morgue. I suppose that I should have mustered the courage to visit him there, but I could not bring myself to do it. It was a contemptible lack of courage really – and in a doctor with a wide acquaintance with surgery – to funk it. But I did. I did.

Yet the thought of getting the funeral over was itself a relief, and I spent the morning wandering round the bookshops and recalling the past. There was no longer a soul in the place who recognised me, or if there was I did not meet one. I was back for an early lunch, still perplexed by the silence of Toby who by all calculations should by now have reached the town from Oxford. But in case the night was going to be a late one I took the wise precaution of closing my shutters and taking a siesta, for the deep fatigue of the last two days had told heavily on me.

In my dreams I found my way back to the old chateau, to the Verfeuille of the distant past, that strange catalyst of a stranger love; back to the life of the past with its extra-real flavour. Verfeuille sheltered us, and within its walls happiness became an imperative. Now circumstances had scattered the pieces, an invisible hand had overturned the chess-board. But sleep is merciful. In my dream nothing had changed as yet. I turned the leaves as one turns back a vine to catch glimpses of the old house between the branches. How could we have taken it all so much for granted?

It stands high up on the westward slopes of the Alpilles and from the highest orchards you can see not only misty Avignon in the plains below, but snatches of Arles and Tarascon as well. The winding roads lead steadily upwards towards it with a graceful inevitability, passing through rich olive holdings, the grey-silver leaves ashiver at the least caress of the mistral. The plots around the old house are so rich in springs, and the soil so correspondingly rich and loamy, that the ancients planted oak and plane and chestnut to make a verdant green shade around the house and protect it from sun and wind alike. Colonies of nightingales sing there by day and night to the tune of splashing water, while the hum of the cicada, deafening in August, provided a steady drizzle, as if of strings, as a background. Of the twin lions guarding the gates of the lodge one had lost a paw and the other half of the cere-monial sword he once held so proudly, point downward; as for the massive wrought-iron gates themselves, they had been carried away and melted down as a contribution to the war effort of fourteen-eighteen. The weeds have long since turned the gravel driveway to a mossy causeway where the wheels of a car tend to skid slightly in wet weather. On this unexpected carpet of silence one turns and twines for what seems an age before the house comes into view, perched slightly at an angle in order to take the best of the sun aspects and set a stout shoulder to the northern quarter from where the butting mistral blows.

The windows, so tall and narrow, wear deep stone eye-brows, while the high donjon, a prodigiously strong square tower, dating from the twelfth century, centres the whole mass, giving a minatory touch of fortress to what is now a comfort-able dwelling merging into a farmhouse with all its clumsy dependencies – barns and stables, wine-magazines and olive-presses. The noise of cattle and poultry rules here, and the prismatic dust hangs in sunbeams. None of this will ever change. The whole of this heavy mass with its grilled windows encloses the grand central courtyard to which one gains access via a deeply vaulted passage-way – an easily defensible feature; this in turn leads to the vital heart of the place, the great well-head with its carved crucifix and its benches. At each corner of the court rises a quaint and crusty little *tourelle* from which the besieged could keep up a raking fire along the thick walls.

The main portal consists of a set of massive iron-clamped doors whose rusty teeth fold in upon each other – or once did, for nobody in living memory has ever seen them closed. Now they always stood open and the whole courtyard had the placid look of a place given over to peaceful husbandry. Chickens and ducks have taken possession of it, they wander about gossiping; a venerable goat, untethered, meditates in one corner. From the stables come the stamp of horses and the roars and sighs of cattle, or perhaps the mewing of quail in their wicker cages. An army of pigeons skirmishes impertinently about in all this with the noise of wet linen flapping in the wind. Their own headquarters is the squat bell tower, now transformed into a dove-cot, with the Roman hour-glass fixed to it.

Everything gravitates towards or away from this central court with its well – though its presiding goddess is not, as so often here, a Roman nymph, but merely an old blindfold horse which is started up each morning like a clock and then left to its own devices. Slowly and painstakingly it covers the trodden circle of its duty, and slowly through the hours the cold well-water is dispersed along a chain of stone troughs.

There were in fact several wells – one indeed in the main barn – which cater nowadays for both cattle and men by courtesy of a brisk electric motor. But the slow overflow from the ancient well, splashing into its basin, is channelled away, and conducted to the salad garden to irrigate the plants there. It is through this little garden with its kitchen herbs that one can reach the more extensive formal gardens of the chateau – for so long fallen into disrepair. They decline southward and westward and are well sheltered from the sudden inclemencies of the Provençal weather. It is difficult to imagine how they must have looked in their heyday. Ever since I knew them they have remained overgrown and unweeded, full of the romantic melancholy of desuetude. Rob used to say, "Very bad for my poetry this; it makes it all crumbly." None of us shared his feelings when we walked here, either by dawn or by moonlight. No; these gardens abounded in balustraded terraces and ornate stone benches perched at strategic points. Here and there you could happen upon a marble nymph or two in a debased and old-fashioned style, though now made really charming because overgrown by ivy or rambler roses. Here were many sheltered corners which one watched covetously for the first violets or the tender spring flowers; while along their length the beehives stood in rows.

Once all this was a profitable and lovely demesne and in the time of Piers' parents its yield represented a very great fortune. But when they died the two children did not know how to make it work and the whole enterprise became moribund from lack of effective management. It was not their fault – they had both pursued their studies in Paris and London, and for them Verfeuille represented simply a divine haven for summer holidays, nothing more. The decline was gradual but sure. Its great army of retainers began to drift slowly away to more lucrative work; war intervened, then the vine plague, phylloxera, and then a malignant drought one summer. Much of the land was sold off, and some mortgaged; the wood was sacrificed in a bad year, bringing in very little. A succession of small shortsighted follies sapped the economy of the great farm and nibbled away at its yield.

Nevertheless the estate, despite all these limitations, remained a very large one, and perhaps more beautiful because of the neglect, though no farmer would have said so. The country was marvellous, for it lay upon the flanks of the Alpilles and extended outwards from the foothills of the range pointing towards the level region where the Rhône valley widens and begins to merge into the valley of the Durance.

On the higher slopes of the land are straggling groups of self-seeded almond trees – what puffs of delicate smoke-white, smoke-pink they emit in February when they so briefly flower, turning the whole mountain-side into an oriental wash-drawing. Lower down reign the more formal olive-terraces – a silver-grey sheen the year long, for this seraphic tree sheds and renews its leaves all the time. Then as the hills dwindle away into the plain come the wide vineyards and wheat fields and vegetable holdings (once stocked for the greedy Paris market). But the plantations of fruit trees still bear, falling away in one corner to reveal the distant flats of the tedious Camargue with its lime-green ribbon of shallow sea. In my memory it will always be Christmas here, the Noel of 19—, the year that changed the direction and leaning of my life. Nothing had ever happened to me before – or that is how I felt about the events of that year. I had encountered the inhabitants of Verfeuille a year or two previously, but it was some time before, to my amazement and indeed chagrin (nobody likes to be pushed out of his depth), a classical love set in, and with it the long debate about the rights and wrongs of it. One should I suppose feel like smiling when one thinks of the painful solemnity with which we watched this marvellous ogre advance upon us, club in hand. Sutcliffe pities us, or so he says in his book, because we cut such childish figures, were taken so much by surprise. Had we never (he asks) considered the possibilities of a common passion which might sweep us far out to sea? I wonder. I recall Piers' pale serious face as he said

47

one day: "Well then, it must be love." Rob would have laughed out loud I suppose at the tone which was that of a doctor making a diagnosis – as if one might say "Well then, it must be cancer."

(I notice the shift of verb tenses in these hasty notes – they throw my memories in and out of focus, as time itself and reality melts in and out of focus when you dream.)

In those days Piers took his seigneurial obligations rather seriously and felt it very much his duty to be present for St. Barbara's day, the fourth of December – for the old Provençal Christmas begins with the planting of wheat or lentil seed in little bowls which were then set upon the broad window-sills to ripen. Their growth, and other little indications, would give one firm information about the state of the weather during the coming four seasons. At that time I think Piers nourished some ambitions about restoring the property to its old affluence; but if so, they soon declined steadily, undramatically, as did the number of servants. A bare dozen were now left – a few too old for serious labour, and a great many children who were as yet too young to be pressed into anything more exacting than the olive-picking of late November. The relationship had become a much closer one because of this depletion – poverty and lack of numbers had created the bondages of a smaller family.

But there were other factors this year, troubling ones. For Piers had as yet not announced his intention of leaving the chateau the following summer to follow a career. His nomination had only just been ratified by the Diplomatic Board in Paris, and he was as yet uncertain of his first posting. How momentous for him that it should later turn out to be Cairo! Nevertheless he was full of sadness, the thought of leaving the family home was a dire wrench. It threw into relief the stagnating fortunes of the place, the decayed husbandry of the land, the lack of financial viability. Verfeuille was bleeding to death and here he was deserting it. . . .

Paradoxically, though, a profession would enable him to keep the place going, even if it slowly fell apart. At least this way the property itself would continue to belong to him and to his sister, even though encumbered with debts. He had realised by now that he was no farmer and that in this context the condition of the place was irreversible without heavy expenditure and an increase of staff. It had gone too far. But naturally such a decision, as well as its causes, are very hard to explain or justify to family retainers whose doglike devotion and trust were completely unreasoning. He was aware of the anxiety his announcement would cause. But it had to be so, for he proposed to appoint one of the older servants as steward of the estate in the hope that he might hold his ground at home while he himself was absent on duty abroad. He had gone ahead then, while Sylvie and I had elected to stay on in Avignon, and then pick up horses at the half-way house and ride the last few miles to the chateau. Our saddle bags were full of presents, coloured sweets for the children, confetti, crystallised fruit, and little bottles of cognac and liqueurs. Also we had brought a huge family of little *santons* of painted terracotta for the crèche. No Provençal Christmas is complete without these little figures which populate and deck out the family crèche which itself does the duty of our northern Yule-tide Tree. Originally the cast, so to speak, was a small one, restricted to the Holy Family and two or three other personages who figured directly in the legend, like the kings and so forth; but under the influence of the hardy Provençal sense of poetry the whole thing had flowered rhapsodically and we had found in the shops about forty *santons*, all different. Their verisimilitude might have been suspect but they brought the story up to date with characters out of stock like the village policeman, a poacher, a Camargue cowboy, and the like. All this gear was carefully wrapped against breakages and stowed in our capacious saddle bags before we attacked the slow winding

ascent to the chateau. The horses were fresh and faced the path
in lively fashion. But a misty period had set in and the journey
needed a little caution also, for neither of us had done this ride
for several years and anyway never in winter; we had all but
forgotten the devious and winding bridle paths and fire
brakes which crossed and recrossed the main road as it rose
into the hills. From time to time all visibility was reduced to nil,
and then Sylvie, who was in a particularly mischievous mood,
pushed her horse into a canter, to be swallowed at once in the
mist. It was not a procedure to be recommended and the
second time she did it I plunged after her and punished her
with an embrace that left her breathless; feeling her cold lips
and nose against my face, seeking me out. Such was its magnetism that we became fused into this posture, unwilling to
detach ourselves from each other. I tried to at last – for I could
feel the mist condensing into droplets on the collar of my old
tweed coat; but she whispered "Stay" and it was only too easy
to obey her. We were not far off our landfall now, in a forest
of tall trees which dripped moisture all around. Among those
muttered endearments I recorded one or two phrases which
underlined her own astonishment at our situation, as well as a
doubt which was the twin of my own, and also Piers'. Ah!
Later Sutcliffe was to make cruel fun of us three in his book.
"They are so happy. They admire themselves. They have
invested a wedding cake in each other. A slice under each
pillow, O desirable treat. An unholy trinity of romantics, a love
sandwich with the perplexed and thick-thewed Bruce making
the filling." I was glad that he was later so badly punished by
my sister Pia – an ignoble emotion, but these passages were
wounding. "I have stolen you from Piers, and he has stolen me
from you? What can it mean?" I told her there was no loss to be
reckoned out. "Not with lost property – the lost-and-found
department had caught up with us three." These sounded like
inspired confidences to us: Rob would have thought us

mawkish and refused to believe in the reality of our case, our emotions. I was glad that I did not know at the time, it was only years afterwards that the book made its appearance. By that time he was himself going through a bad period and had little sympathy, it seems, to spare for someone else.

He even invented a diary for Piers to keep, describing him opening it each night to make a forlorn entry "by the grave light of two tall-stemmed candles", if you please. And this is the sort of thing he wrote to attach as a literary pendant to our situation. "It was very late in the day to realise, but at last I did. It was imperative to send them away together, my sister and Bruce: or face losing both. For the lovers had moved into such a deep phase that they had become almost alarmed for themselves as well as for me. We were held in a kind of fixity of purpose, the three of us like the rings of Saturn. One can only love like this, to utter distraction, when one is young, altogether too young. A breath of real experience would cloud the mirror. They felt unable to extricate themselves from each other, from the triune bond. In them flowed a sort of tidal sadness – the equinox of a first and last attachment; the advancing and receding waters closed over their heads. And being swept away like this they found themselves drifting towards the falls." All this was entirely imaginary; I have never been in Venice, but as he knew it well, he used a novelist's licence to transplant us there. Our intensity was of another order, less literary. Yet "Even the physical envelope, lips eyes bodies seemed to have become somehow mental contrivances only; the three inseparables seemed to themselves all mingled up, like a plate of spaghetti. But Venice did the trick, Venice exorcised the act. So the three of them were able to walk silently arm in arm among the marble griffins and the swerving canals, or sit silently playing cards on the green tables at Florian's. A strange trio, the brother and sister so lean and dark, like lizards, and their blond captive with his thickset form and rather simple peasant expression. The girl would obviously look a thorough shrew at forty with her long canny Mediterranean nose; the brother was slightly touched with romantic mountebank." So that is how he saw us when it came to give us the definitive form of print. I have never recovered from my astonishment!

And he has the effrontery to add: "Real love is silent, or so they say. But never was the green Venetian silence of the trio so energetic, never did words whispered at night burn so deeply down, guttering like candles in the sconces of memory."

None of this was as yet part of the present kiss, the present cold small nose; she had undone my shirt and placed her icy fingers over my heart. But the horses were restless now, for they had been very patient under the boredom of this long embrace and were longing for the warm stables which they knew must lie ahead, somewhere beyond the mist. Their hooves clicked, and the cold air turned their breath to pencils of spume. What could they care about the meeting of three separate solitudes? Meanwhile the imaginary romantic diarist had written, according to the novelist: "They actually dared to love, then, even though they knew that the end of all love was detachment or rancour or even horror; that it ended in despair, or even suic... But I dare not write the word." This at least was a prophetic piece of invention on his part; but it is the only thing that touches the fringes of the truth. The so-called "infernal" happiness which he attempts to describe is altogether too theatrical to belong to us. We were babes in the wood, innocents abroad.

The horses drew away, delighted by the vague outlines of everything and aching for another canter; we set off down a ride and at that moment, deep in the mist, we heard the shrill but musical voices of children, chattering and chirping. It was so uncanny that, mindful of the folktales of the country, we wondered if we were approaching a band of mist-fairies in the obscurity of the tenebrous forest. "Nonsense," I said robustly in the voice I use to reassure patients with terminal illnesses that they will live for ever. "Nonsense. It's a school excursion." But as we advanced the sound seemed to recede from us so that we quickened our pace in the hope of catching it up. And with the swaying of the horses and the meanderings of the paths the voices themselves seemed to change direction, coming now from this side, and now from that. And despite my hardened rationalist scepticism I confess that for a moment I hesitated and wondered about the provenance of those shrill voices. But on we went, picking our way and listening.

Then, rolling back like a curtain, the mist shifted aside and we came upon another path, at right angles to our own, down which poured a line of flesh-and-blood children of all ages, skipping and chattering, with their arms full of greenery. They were laden with crèche-making materials they had gathered – mosses, ferns, lichens, laurel and long polished branches of holly and mistletoe. The holly they carried like sceptres – the small-berried holly, the one they call still *li poumeto de Sant-Jan* in Provençal, or "the little apples of St. John". With a cry of pleasure Sylvie now recognised the children of the chateau, and she dismounted to kiss and hug them all and to ask if her brother had arrived safely. They cheered when they knew that we were bringing the rest of the material for the crèche. It was also a surprise to realise how close the house was: the mist had been playing tricks of visibility on us, though we were comforted to find our direction-finding so good.

But now we were engulfed in this happy throng, so that we hand-led our horses – perching the singing children on their backs. And so at last in triumph we came to the main portal of the chateau where their parents waited anxiously, peering out into the forest from time to time, watching for their return.

The familiar smiling faces were all there – old Jan, clad in his sheepskin jacket, the firelight behind him in the great hall

turning his silver hair into a halo. A little behind stood his
quiet and sturdy wife Elizo. Marius was their son and the apple
of their eye – a man of forty with broad shoulders and sweeping black moustaches. A younger man, Esprit, came out to
help us unpack our luggage. Then all the girls streamed out to
embrace us, the children and the grandchildren with names
like Magali, Janetoun, Mireille, Nanoun. Here after the ceremonial embrace we were offered the traditional posset of red
wine with its mulled spices, the old warmer-up for winter
travellers. In the ensuing babble, with all of them trying to
talk at once, we hardly noticed the absence of Piers. But he was
far from absent, for when at last we reached the great hall with
its blazing logs we saw him standing looking down from the
first landing, smiling in shadow and delightedly watching.
Then he came skipping down the broad staircase with its carved
balustrade, but a trifle shyly, as if to control his ardour, his
affection. When all the greetings were given and all the
questions answered we were free, just the three of us, to mount
the staircase arm in arm and take the long white corridors
which led to his room which lay beyond a small gallery of
pictures, for the most part ancestors, smoked black by time
and the wood fires. At the end of the gallery, in a somewhat
disconcerting fashion stood an easel on which was propped a
large cork archery target, plumped full of arrows with different-
coloured feathers. Piers spent a good deal of time practising
here with the great yew bow he had bought in London. The
whipple of the flying arrows sounded throughout the house
when he did so. His private rooms, so full of books and masks
and foils and shot-guns, had old-fashioned vaulted ceilings.
The petroleum lamps and the tall silver candlesticks threw
warm shadows everywhere. In the tall fireplace bristled furze,
olive and holm-oak which smelt divine. Everything had been
timed exactly for the Christmas feast and Piers was beside
himself with joy because there were no unexpected hitches or

delays. Moreover in two days' time Toby and Rob (the Gog and Magog of our company) were due to arrive and bring with them the light-hearted laughter and inconsequence which made them such excellent company.

We sat now, the three of us cross-legged on the floor before the fire, eating chestnuts and drinking whisky and talking about nothing and everything. Never had old Verfeuille seemed so warmly welcoming. If we had an inner pang as we remembered Piers' decisions for the future we did not mention them to each other. It would not have been fair to the time and the place to intrude our premonitions and doubts upon it. But underneath the excitement we were worried, we had a sense of impending departure, of looming critical change in our affairs – in this newly found passion as well. As if sensing this a little Piers said, during a silence "Cheer up, children. Yesterday we went out and selected the Yule Log – a real beauty this year." He described to me the little ceremony in which the oldest and the youngest member of the whole household go out hand in hand to choose the tree which will be felled for Christmas, and then return triumphantly to the house bearing it with, of course, the assistance of everyone. It was paraded thrice around the long supper table and then laid down before the great hearth, while old Jan undertook to preside over the ceremony of the libation which he did with great polish, filling first of all a tall jar of *vin cuit*. Describing it Piers acted him to the life, in half-humorous satire – his smiling dignity and serenity as he bowed his head over the wine to utter a prayer while everyone was deeply hushed around him, standing with heads bowed. Then he poured three little libations on the log, to Father, Son and Holy Ghost, before crying out with all the vigour he could muster in his crackly old voice:

Cacho-fio!
Bouto-fio!

Alègre! Alègre!
Dieu nous alègre!

Yule Log Burn
Joy Joy
God give us Joy.

And as he reached the last words of the incantation which
were "Christmas has arrived" a huge bundle of vine-trimmings
was set alight under the ceremonial log and the whole fireplace
flamed up, irradiating the merry faces of the company, as if
they too had caught fire from sympathy with the words; and
now everyone embraced anew and clapped hands, while the
old man once more filled the ceremonial bowl with wine, but
this time passed it about as a loving-cup, beginning with little
Tounin the youngest child: and so on in order of seniority
until at last it came back to his hand. Then he threw back his
head and drained it to the dregs, the firelight flashing on his
brown throat. Suddenly Piers, despite himself, was seized with
a pang of sadness and tears came into his eyes: "How the devil
am I going to leave them, do you think? And what is going to
happen to us, to It?" It was not the time for such questions and
I told him so. I finished my drink and consulted my watch. In a
little while it would be in order to tackle the second half of the
ceremony which consisted in decking out the crèche with the
candles and figurines. I was glad of the diversion, for this little
aside of his had wakened all kinds of doubts in me – about the
future which awaited us, the separations . . . Sylvie appeared
with her arms full of things, dressed now in the full peasant
dress of Avignon and looking ravishing. Everyone clapped
her. "Hurry and dress", she told us, "before we do the Holy
Family."

It did not take long. My own rooms were on the eastern
side of the house. Thoughtful hands had placed a copper
warming pan full of coals in my bed, while a small fire, care-

fully shielded by a guard, crackled in the narrow hearth. I lit my candles and quickly put on the traditional black velvet coat which Piers had given me, with its scarlet silk lining; also the narrow stove-pipe pantaloons, dark sash and pointed black shoes – *tenue de rigueur* for Christmas dinner in Verfeuille. Piers himself would wear the narrow bootlace tie and the ribbon of the *félibre*, the Provençal poet. I hastened, and when I got downstairs Sylvie was already there trying to bring some order into the candle-lighting ceremony which was almost swamped by the antics of high-spirited children flitting about like mice. She managed to control the threatened riot and before long they were all admiring the colour and form of the little figurines as they were unwrapped one by one. Soon a constellation of small flames covered the brown hillsides of Bethlehem and brought up into high prominence the Holy Family in the manger, attended by the utterly improbable kings, gipsies, queens, cowboys, soldiers, poachers and post-men – not to mention sheep, ducks, quail, cattle and brilliant birds. Then came the turn of Piers, who exercised a bit more authority, to unwrap and distribute the wrapped presents, all duly labelled, so that nobody should feel himself forgotten on this memorable eve. Great rejoicing as the paper was ripped and torn away; and so gradually the company drifted slowly away to dinner. This had been laid in the great central hall – the long table ran down the centre with more than enough room for the gathering of that year. We three were seated at a cross-table which formed the cruciform head with Jan and his wife on our right and left respectively. Candles blazed everywhere and the Yule Log by this time had begun to thresh out bouquets of bright sparks into the chimney.

It was not a place or time easy to forget, and I had re-turned to it so often in my thoughts that it was no surprise to relive all this in my dreams. I must have unconsciously memor-ised it in great detail without being fully aware of the fact at the time. I know of no other place on earth that I can call up so clearly and accurately by simply closing my eyes: to this very day.

Its floor was laid with large grey stone slabs which were strewn with bouquets of rosemary and thyme: these helped to gather up the dust when one was sweeping, as well as things like the bones which were often thrown to the hunting dogs. The high ceiling was supported by thick smoke-blackened beams from which hung down strings of sausages, chaplets of garlic, and numberless bladders filled with lard. More than a third of the rear wall was taken up by the grand central fire-place which measured some ten feet across and at least seven from the jutting mantelpiece to the floor. In its very centre, with room each side in chimney-corners and angles stood old wicker chairs with high backs, and wooden lockers for flour and salt. The mound of ash from the fires was heaped back against the back of the fireplace which itself was crossed by a pair of high andirons which flared out at the top, like flowers, into little iron baskets, so often used as plate-warmers when filled with live coals. They were furnished with hooks at different levels destined for the heavy roasting spits. From the mantelshelf hung a short red curtain designed to hold the smoke in check when the fire became too exuberant, as it did with certain woods, notably olive. Along the wide shelf above the fire were rows of objects at once utilitarian and intriguing because beautiful, like rows of covered jars in pure old faience, ranging in capacity from a gill to three pints, and each lettered with the name of its contents – saffron, pepper, cummin, tea, salt, flour, cloves. Tall bottles of luminous olive oil sparked with herbs and spices had their place here. Also a number of burnished copper vessels and a giant coffee-pot. And further along half a dozen tall brass or pewter lamps with wicks that burned olive oil – as in the time of the Greeks and Romans – but rapidly being superseded by the more modern paraffin-burning ones.

To the right of the fireplace was the wide stone sink with rows of shelves above to take a brilliant army of copper pots and pans – a real *batterie de cuisine*. To the left a covered bread-trough above which hung the large salt and flour boxes of immediate use together with the bread-holder – a sort of cage or cradle in dark wood, ornamented with locks and hinges of polished iron.

On the opposite side of the room was the tall curiously carved Provençal buffet, solid and capacious, and shining under its glossy varnish, the colour of salad oil. Then, to the left of it, the grandfather clock – a clock which was so much of a martinet that it assertively struck the hours in duplicate. Some old rush-bottomed chairs stood about awkwardly – for there was no real thought about luxury or even comfort here. The order of things was ancestral, traditional; history was the present, and one did not conceive of altering things, but simply asserting their traditional place in life, and in nature. As well try to alter the course of the planets. Beyond the bread-trough hung a long-shanked steel balance with a brass dish suspended by delicate brass chains, all brilliant with scouring by soap, flour and sand. Then among a straggle of farm implements standing against one wall was an ancient fowling piece resting in wooden crutches driven between two broken flags. The walls were heavily decorated with sentimental lithographs and oleographs, depicting scenes from the local folklore of the region; and, inevitably, with numberless old family pictures, now all faded away into a sepia anonymity – faces of unforgotten people and events, harvests, picnics and bullfights, tree-plantings, bull-brandings, weddings and first communions. A whole life of austere toil and harmless joy of which this room had been the centre, the pivot.

But the wine was going about now and the most important supper of the whole year was in full sail. By old tradition it has always been a "lean" supper, so that in comparison with other feast days it might have seemed a trifle frugal. Neverthe-less the huge dish of *raïto* exhaled a wonderful fragrance: this was a ragout of mixed fish presented in a sauce flavoured with wine and capers. Chicken flamed in Cognac. The long brown loaves cracked and crackled under the fingers of the feasters like the olive branches in the fireplace. The first dish emptied at record speed, and its place was taken by a greater bowl of Rhône pan-fish, and yet another of white cod. These in turn led slowly to the dishes of snails, the whitish large veined ones that feed on the vine-leaves. They had been tucked back into their shells and were extracted with the aid of strong curved thorns, three or four inches long, broken from the wild acacia. As the wine was replenished after the first round, toasts began to fly around.

Then followed the choice supporting dishes like white *cardes* or *cardon*, the delicious stem of a giant thistle which resembles nothing so much as an overgrown branch of celery. These stems are blanched and then cooked in white sauce – I have never tasted them anywhere else. The flavour is one of the most exquisite one can encounter in the southern regions of France; yet it is only a common field-vegetable. So it went on, our last dinner, to terminate at last with a whole anthology of sweetmeats and nuts and winter melons. The fire was restoked and the army of wine-bottles gave place to a smaller phalanx of brandies, Armagnacs and Marcs, to offset the large bowls of coffee from which rose plumes of fragrance.

Now old Jan's wife placed before the three lovers a deep silver sugar bowl full of white sugar. It lay there before them in the plenitude of its sweetness like a silver paunch. The three spoons she had placed in it stood upright, waiting for them to help themselves before the rest of the company. The toasts and the jests now began to subside, sinking towards the ground like expiring fireworks, and the time for more serious business was approaching. By tradition every year Piers made a speech

which gave an account of the year's work, bestowing praise or
censure as he thought fit. But this time his news was momentous
and would affect the fate of everyone in the room. I could see
that the idea worried him as much as it did his sister, who
glanced at him from time to time with affectionate commiseration. After many hesitations – for he changed places more than
once to have a private word with this person and that – he rose
and tapped for silence, to be greeted with loud applause and
raised glasses by the very people whom his speech would
sadden.

He stood, resigned and a little pale, while he allowed it to
subside, before beginning with the Christmas wishes. He then
went on by saying that he had been a trifle sad and preoccupied
that evening because of the news he had to give them. Not that
it was downright tragic, far from that; but all change made one
sorry and sad. "But before I speak of the journey I must make
let me speak of the new arrangements which will come into
force when I leave. First, I raise my glass to old Jan, closer to
me than my father. He will become the *régisseur* of Verfeuille
while I am absent *en mission*." The whole speech was most
skilfully executed, and touched everywhere with feeling and
thoughtfulness. He reassigned the role of each of the servants,
stressing the increase in their responsibilities and according
each one a small rise in pay. This caused great joy and satisfaction and much kissing and congratulation followed each
announcement. It was a good augury for his diplomatic role to
follow – for by the time he came to the sad part of his speech
his audience was cheerful, fortified by all this Christmas
bounty. This enabled him to come firmly and honestly to the
root of the matter and explain without equivocation that the
choice before him was to find a financial way of keeping on the
property or else to sit and watch it slowly swallowed up by
debts. He had decided to seek a post in a profession which he
knew, but, he added, there was one promise to be made. We

three would always come back to Verfeuille in the summer, to spend whatever holidays we got there. Everyone cheered and approved these robust sentiments, but for my part I foresaw that we might be forced to separate, for my medical finals were coming up that autumn, and I did not know what the future might hold in store. It would not have been possible to foresee the extraordinary fluke that landed me in the Foreign Service post within three months of passing them. At that moment I was possessed by a deep, numbing nostalgia for the land where I had spent the happiest hours of my life – in Aramon, say, among the cherry trees, on green grass, with summer round the corner; or Fons or Collias, or a dozen other spots where we had camped. A sombre sadness possessed me as I watched the preoccupied face of Sylvie.

A short and thoughtful silence fell upon the banqueters as they took in the full import of the words; as if in their minds they were trying out the absence of Piers, to see how it would feel without him. At that moment there came a light but peremptory knocking on the door of the room which made us all look at each other and wonder who could knock at this time and on this evening. The rapid knock was repeated after a pause and old Jan rose and clicked across the flags to throw open the door into the hall.

Outside it was shadowy, but framed in the winking fire-light was someone whom I took to be a gipsy for she wore the motley patchwork of one, with a brilliant headscarf and cheap but very heavy ear-rings; nor was the supposition so far-fetched for Avignon had a large gipsy colony encamped about its walls, Salon was not far away, and today would be a suitable day to beg for alms . . . But the apparition moved a step forward into the light and said huskily: "Piers, I heard you were back." The deep voice and the cultivated accent at once belied the trappings, and excited one's curiosity. Her feet were bare and dirty, and one ankle had a grubby bandage on it. Hers was a massive head with small black eyes and a long nose – at first blush one would say an ugly face. But the mobility of expression which changed continuously and the thrilling deepness of the voice were magnetic, startling. There was something authoritative and superb about the woman. Piers embraced her warmly.

This was my first glimpse of Sabine about whom I then knew little enough; indeed I only knew her name when Piers used it and Sylvie repeated it as a greeting. Later I learned to know her and to admire her – but never as much as Piers who had a regular passion for the girl. She was the daughter of Lord Banquo, the Jewish banker of international repute, and their chateau was at Meurre, a dozen kilometres away. After brilliant studies the girl had abandoned the university, and had all but taken to the roads with the gipsies on whom she professed to be basing an ethnographic work. She disappeared for long periods only to reappear at the chateau without any warning, and resume her old civilised life of a well-groomed and well-spoken only daughter. Her mother was long dead and her father lived from one mistress to the next, for the most part minor actresses. He tired of them rapidly, and replaced them frequently. He was always delighted to have his daughter back, largely for selfish reasons, for she was an excellent hostess and he entertained a great deal. From time to time, when she was in trouble, she turned up at Verfeuille and asked Piers' help and counsel. They had met out riding.

She was an unforgettable sight that first evening and I watched her curiously and rather jealously, so evident was Piers' attachment for her. On this occasion, as in the past, it was something to do with the gipsies, I do not recall what, but some sort of trouble concerning a man who was then lurking about in the grounds as far as I could gather. After listening to her low voice for a moment Piers, without a word, took up a lantern and gestured her to lead him out into the forest. They disappeared with startling abruptness through the front door. I noticed that the prudent old Jan went to the gun cupboard and produced a short carbine which he loaded before he too went to the door and stationed himself to wait there, peering out into the night, waiting perhaps for a cry for help. But none came. We could hear a sort of altercation between two male voices; then the deep voice of the girl. At last Piers reappeared swinging the lantern. He was alone. "It's all right," was all he said by way of explanation. "He won't harm her."

By now the old man had discovered that it was nearly time for the village mass. "We will have to hurry up," he said consulting the old clock, "we must set a good example on the day of the days." The company donned hats and scarves and we straggled out into the night with its washed-out late moon trying to guide us. Our feet scratched the flinty path which led away to the tiny hamlet of Verfeuille whose ancient church was now so ablaze with candles that the whole fragile structure seemed to be on fire. I walked arm in arm with the brother and sister, silent and preoccupied and wondering about the future – the future which has now become the past.

The telephone beside the bed shrilled. Bechet was as good as his word. "Everything has been arranged for this evening," he said in his fussy-complaisant manner. "And I myself will drive you over if you will be ready for me about six. Waiting in the hall, please, because of difficult parking on that narrow street." I drowsily agreed. There was a comfortable margin of time in hand which would enable me to have a bath and dress in leisurely fashion. I lay back on the pillows for a moment to recover from this welter of ancient memories – a patchwork quilt of history and sensation. And Sylvie? I rang through to Jourdain and told him what was afoot. He was surprised and also very glad that Bechet had acted promptly and that the authorities had decided to co-operate. As for Sylvie, there was for the present nothing to be done but to let her rest. Nevertheless I promised to come up and visit her on the morrow when everything to do with the funeral had been taken care of. On the one hand I felt a certain elation to think of everything formal being over that very day; but on the other hand I felt certain misgivings, for after all this . . . What? I had decided on nothing, what was I going to do with the rest of my life? I was living from moment to moment. Half my mind was plunged in the past, and half contemplated the future with a sense of disorientation and blankness. And Sylvie?

Much of this passed once more through my mind when at last that evening I sat beside Bechet in his stuffy little car, watching the twilight scenery unroll along the valley of the Rhône; the same opalescent packets of mist about which I had dreamed in the afternoon brimmed the lowland fields. Darkness seemed unduly late for the time of the year but as the time of the ceremony (or non-ceremony) had not been specified there was little cause for anxiety on this score. The old Abbé was driving up in his own car from some village further to the east. Bechet rather dreaded the meeting because of this infernal injunction of Piers about a religious service. "I have put it to him most forcibly," said the lawyer more than once, "and it is my duty as a lawyer to see that his last wishes are complied with. And I shall do it. If he so much as mutters a Hail Mary . . ." He made a vaguely threatening gesture with his chin and drove on with his features composed in a martial expression. As a driver he was a slow and jerky one, and was obviously rather concerned about mist.

It would perhaps have been more reasonable to dwell on the existence of frost on the roads which started to climb upon the steepish flanks of the Alpilles, but this did not seem to enter into his calculations at all. I think the capricious visibility played a little on his nerves, or else perhaps his eyes were weak and old. And at any rate we jogged along, carefully verifying our safety at every corner, while he engaged me in a string of commonplaces about the weather and the problems of motor-cars in winter. The tricks of the mist were certainly dramatic – as dramatic as in the dream-memory I had just dreamed – and in one of these sudden snatches we suddenly came upon a sleek black hearse which was ahead of us, and moving in the same direction. Bechet expelled his breath in a whistle and said in a superstitious sort of voice: "That must be the body of Piers being taken up to the chateau – the hearse belongs to the morgue and they gave me a rendezvous for seven." My heart did a double somersault at this ominous and dramatic vision. We now began to play hide-and-seek with the hearse in the shifting mists as we climbed. There was no frost but a deal of wet, with swatches of sodden leaves clinging to our tyres. The forest grew up round us, sombre and darkling. It was eerie to follow Piers like this, sometimes losing the hearse in the mist only to recover it again at a corner. Once or twice we were right on top of it and Bechet let out a sort of exclamation, at once exasperated and concerned. As a Frenchman from the south he would have had a superstitious nature and might have read something ominous into this long pursuit.

But darkness had already fallen now, and in the frail glow of our headlamps the country looked forlorn and all but deserted. Bechet's anxiety had increased in inverse ratio to his speed. Once or twice cars came in the opposite direction and he shied like a frightened horse and came almost to a standstill. The road had become narrower. I think, too, that he deliberately slowed down his pace in order to lose the hearse, and I was glad of the fact, for its presence afflicted me with a foreboding which was not less unpleasant for being, I knew, senseless. Half-way up the ascent he asked permission to take a rest and a cigarette, drawing the car off the road and halting it while he smoked. The darkness which descended on us when the headlights were switched off was not reassuring either; a deep thawlike night declared itself and the trees dripped moisture on the canvas roof of the car. Bechet did not speak, indeed seemed suddenly weary and distressed as he puffed his thin cigarette. The reason perhaps was that he did not quite know what to expect up at the chateau, and he wanted to give the mutes time enough to deliver the coffin and take their wretched hearse away before we arrived. At any rate the halt was not too badly calculated as matters turned out for by the time we sneaked and skidded down the last reaches of the avenue leading to the house the black car had already unloaded, and was backing to tackle the return journey to the morgue, its mission accomplished.

But the scene outside Verfeuille was an unusual one, not lacking in colourful strangeness. A tall fire of logs had been lighted – almost the height of a pyre, of a stake, on which to burn a martyr. It contested the warmth with the wet night sky. One would have thought it the eve of St. John – the only occasion in the year which is celebrated thus – but this was not the case. The logs were red hot and noisy, loosing a thick column of hot air which drove a broad trail of sparks up into the canopy of forest trees which were grouped around the main porch like silent onlookers. The front doors of the house were open and inside there were bright lights; but also wide open were the doors of the barns and stables on the left, and they too were brilliantly illuminated within. Against these complementary flamelights moved a group of rapt figures thrown into deep silhouette by the dark which stood between us, and which the feeble headlights of Bechet's car could do little to qualify. Their movements seemed slow and laboured – almost hieratic; and the object they so clumsily manipulated seemed very heavy. For example, a farm cart of the old-fashioned sort with brightly painted sideboards and a long wooden tongue which took a double yoke, was being man-hauled out of the barn. An object more fit for a fair than for a funeral, one would have said; perhaps there was nothing else which would do? One figure turning, though standing and watching the work without helping, identified itself as a thin man in priest's robes. Briefly, too, in that jumping light the painting on the side of the cart came into view – a picture of angels ascending into a blue empyrean, their dark curly heads and olive eyes conspiring with each other as they threw their appeals upward, skyward; their little white untrustworthy hands were raised in tapering fashion to form poses of prayerful propitiation. Hoof thunder followed this tableau, as a gigantic farm horse was backed out of the obscurity of a barn into the light, to be harnessed and blinkered by a hissing shadow. The fire made it nervous, it rolled its kind eyes and agitated its carefully plaited tail. It had been polished all over for the occasion like a grand piano. It moved awkwardly from one large hoof to the other as it submitted to the last ministrations of its keepers.

A group of figures, four or five, were busy about the cart now, arranging the couplings. Something black and damas-cened – a sort of scrolled blanket – was thrown over the cart and then a smaller one over the horse. The priest had taken up a pose like a golfer about to drive off a tee – he had a prayer book in hand. Bechet swore and jumped smartly into action. It was obvious that the peasants could do nothing against the venerable figure of an Abbé, even supposing them to be in the know about Piers' will and his last instructions. There was a brief but sharp little altercation in which the Abbé came off worst, for he hung his head and put away his book; but Bechet was quite out of breath and red-cheeked from the intellectual effort, and I was amazed to see that he had, after all, a backbone.

But he was not in time to prevent the manufacture of this home-made hearse by old Jan and his staff, and it would have been cruel to make them change it now. They had managed already to take possession of the coffin and push it on to the back of the cart; and now somebody ran up with a glossy black plume and fixed it to the crown of the horse's head. What a religion to be buried in, no wonder Piers had renounced it! Nor could I coax up more charitable feelings by glancing at the thin foxy face of the priest as he scornfully watched the proceedings; then he bowed his head defiantly and appeared to sink into deep prayer. I glanced at Bechet to see whether he had noticed this illegal performance or not; but he was looking the other way. I vaguely recognised old Jan, walking about in shaky fashion, but still very much in charge of things, giving orders in a low voice, and setting everything to rights. The flames rose higher, shining on the sweaty peasant faces and great paws sticking out of dark Sunday suits.

A slight powdery snow had begun to fall, but was melting instantaneously in the hot column of sparks from the fire. Cumbrously the cart was reversed now and set square upon the gravel path. The priest woke from his intercession with the forces of darkness and moved towards the cart; I caught a glimpse of a long deceitful face, narrow as a dog's. His lips were drawn back over yellowish teeth. He was very tall and skeletonic, and must have been in his seventies. The whole set of his face suggested contemptuous vexation – presumably due to the lawyer's insistence. Bechet now stepped within the pale of the firelight and introduced me. I received a glance like a swordthrust. He must have known of my existence to look at me so keenly. Then his priest's face went hard as a rock and he turned away. But by now all was in readiness. Out of the front door came shawled women *endimanchées* and Sunday men, all the retainers of the place in fact, and we formed up behind the towering farm cart in a sad procession.

We set off into the darkness, away from the crepitations of the fire, with only the music of the huge hooves to guide us.

We had one or two lanterns and by common consent they
headed the procession. Jan walked holding the horse's head,
his own lantern held aloft to light his path. So we crunched
across the gravel and then on to a wide mossy pathway which
led to the family vault which had been built in a secluded part
of the forest, thick with sycamores and planes. During this
slow descent I somehow managed to make myself known to
Jan and his son, while two of the women darted at me to take
my hand and press it to their wet cheeks. We spoke hardly at
all, but there was a note of reproach in their voices which was
not hard to interpret; it was as if this perfunctory burial were
robbing not only death of its proper dues, but also them of
their time-honoured rights as mourners. This was not a fitting
way to do things. What would become of the spirit of my poor
friend if his body was rushed to the grave without any religious
rites to smooth its sad way? Had the place and time permitted
they would have interceded with me on this score, I knew
that; and I was glad that we had delayed our journey. Now it
was too late to change things. As we approached the vault in
the deep woods we were joined by other little lantern-led
groups of neighbours and friends. Jan waved his old warped
hand to them bidding them join us, and gradually a long glow-
worm of light followed the cart.

Soon we were walking down a pathway bordered by a
broad canopy of shrubs on either side; they met overhead and
sheltered us from the powdery snowfall. I found all this a
winding and gloomy walk to the burial place. The sky above
us was silent and void of stars. We came at last to the site of the
vault with its dilapidated urns, crude *putti* and detestable
cypress trees, which had always made my heart contract with
distress – even before, I mean, there was any association involving Piers. I hated them as Horace had once hated them.
Here we halted irresolutely, the place was in darkness; but old
Jan had the key and he now addressed himself to the task of

opening the iron grille. It was a bit rusty, and I stepped out to give the old man a helping hand. After much coaxing the thing yielded. By the light of the lanterns which had been placed on the ground, we descended the flight of broad steps which led to the door of the vault. This by contrast was quite new and the lock had recently been changed. Pushed gently, it opened on blackness. We turned back for our lanterns. It seemed to me that the place had not been swept out for some long time; dead leaves littered the floor, and there were dead snails curled up in one corner. But all this was quickly remedied for one of the women had brought a straw broom with her and, while the rest of us were busy manœuvring to get a purchase on the coffin and convey it down the shallow stairway, she set to and swept out the vault at full speed.

Now there was light which enabled us to look around a bit. It was a musty enough place but larger than it had at first seemed. There were tombs of several periods and not a few cobwebbed side-chapels; but there were several blank, un-occupied emplacements, and it was towards one of these that we headed with the covered coffin. Shadows by lantern-light bobbed and danced; figures suddenly became giants or dim-inished to dwarfs. Here normally Piers should have lain at rest for a whole night and a day, while his friends and servants filed by for a last look at his quiet face before leaving the chapel to be bricked in by the masons. But now the absence of a formal ceremony created a peculiar hiatus. By the light of lanterns on the ground everyone looked at his or her neigh-bour, then crossed himself and muttered a prayer. From the Abbé's point of view this unorganised praying was little short of scandalous. He stood motionless, chin on breastbone, as if in deep meditation. In an unvoluntary and sheepish fashion we had formed up behind him in the posture of a congregation, waiting until he should return to this world and give us permission to depart. It was awkward. He stayed thus for what seemed an age; then slowly turning round he gazed at us with a vague and abstracted eye, as if his thoughts were far away. He opened his mouth as if to say something and then appeared to think better of it; he closed it again and shook his head, uttering as he did so a profound sigh. "So we must leave him," he said and turned round on his heel.

For no reason that I can fathom this ordinary remark touched off something in me, an irrational feeling of self-contempt – perhaps because I had been too cowardly to go and visit Piers in the morgue. At any rate I was seized by a kind of panic as I saw one of the farm hands advancing with a screwdriver and a fistful of brass screws. I must, I felt, look once more, for the last time, on the face of my friend before the coffin was screwed down and the embrasure irremediably bricked up. I had noticed that the coffin was of the continental kind with a hinged lid to reveal the face in the case of a lying-in-state. I stepped impulsively forward to put my feelings into practice – I had almost pushed back this section of the coffin – when they laid firm hands on my arm. Priest and notary on either side of me prevented the execution of the deed with a sudden alarm which was hard to understand. "But why?" I cried angrily as they forced me slowly back. But they were as incoherent as they were adamant. Against my will I submitted and allowed myself to be gently pushed back to the grating, and finally up the steps. It was astonishing; but of course this was no place and time for violence or an altercation. What struck me was that Bechet and the Abbé both participated in this restraining action. Their vehemence as well as their unity of purpose struck me as highly irrational. What could it be to them that I should take a last look at Piers before they closed him down? I was furious and also puzzled, but I swallowed my resentment temporarily and stood for a while on the steps gazing into the yellow pool of light and reflecting. The wind whimpered in the trees. At last there came the tapping and the screech of coffin screws being sunk into place. Then one by one the stragglers assembled once more in the dark holding their lamps and lanterns. On the way back to the house the procession slowly dissolved as we traversed the dark woods. Bechet walked beside me with the Abbé on his right. For a while he said nothing and then, feeling no doubt that silence without a platitude to ornament it would make us uneasy, gave a sigh and said: "Human life! How short and how precarious it is." But the priest said nothing as he trudged on with a kind of dogged misery. Nothing!

Inside the hall of the house a good fire had been stoked up, while the pyre outside was slowly being put out by the drizzle. It offered some warmth and cheer on such a gloomy evening. The priest and the notary (those two infamous figures of French life) settled down at a table at the far end of the room and addressed themselves to a sheaf of papers which Bechet extracted from a battered suitcase: attestations of death, burial or whatnot I supposed; or perhaps the last will and testament. At any rate they seemed much preoccupied with the business whatever it was. I betook myself to the far corner by the fire where old Jan brought me a jug of mulled red wine and sat down beside me in the chimney corner which we shared with Elfa the favourite gun-dog of the house. For a while now we sat, saying nothing. From time to time Jan gazed sideways at my face as if about to speak, and then renounced the idea – as if he could find no words to do justice to his feelings. The familiar silence of the house settled about us, except for the scratch of pens and shuffle of paper in the far corner. On a sudden impulse I said: "Jan, tell me why they did not let me look upon Piers in his coffin – or for that matter any of you? Eh?" In a sense the question was rhetorical, as I did not expect an easy answer from old Jan; I was simply airing a grievance, that was all. But he looked at me with a new incredulous expression, as if I was asking a silly question to which everyone must know the answer. I stared at him in a puzzled way and repeated "Why?" And he continued to stare at me with the same expression; then he said: "You know very well there was nothing to see. The body had no head. The men from the morgue said so. Surely you knew that – and Monsieur the lawyer? Surely he knew?"

The information was like a thunderclap. The words fell upon my ear like a deafening report. No head! "That is why they restrained you," the old man continued. "They thought you had forgotten about it." He gazed at my dumbfounded expression with sympathetic concern. It took a moment or two to get back my self-possession and accustom myself to the thought that we had been burying a headless man. But *why*? But what on earth could such a charade mean – if both Bechet and the priest were in the know why had they not told me? On the other hand perhaps it was all rubbish – perhaps old Jan had got hold of the wrong end of the stick, misunderstood a chance remark, muddled up a conversation in that old head of his?

An idea struck me; and I asked: "Did you see it with your own eyes?" He looked at me sadly and nodded. "So you are quite sure." He nodded again in a surprised way. I drank a long draught of wine and reflected. "Then how do we know for certain that the body was that of Piers?" I asked. It was his turn to look astonished; clearly the doubt had never crossed his mind. Then his face cleared, the explanation had come to him. "By the right arm," he said, "the wound."

I knew then what he meant. He made the gesture of drawing back his sleeve as he said: "They exposed the arm for all to see." Not many years ago Piers had had a very serious skating accident in Davos which resulted in a gash along the length of his right arm – it severed tendons and created a permanent disability, enfeebling his grasp with that hand. The cicatrice of this old wound was quite unmistakable. Obviously when they came to lay out the headless body they had drawn back the sleeve to expose this irrefutable mark of identity. Old Jan, in describing the fact, used a Provençal expression which is used by poulterers in describing the procedure by which rabbits are skinned in such a way as to leave their ears as a form of identification. The use of this word gave me gooseflesh.

I suppose that at this point I should have turned savagely on Bechet and demanded some sort of explanation. After all, the truth could have been quite ordinary, quite banal, and easily explicable. I should have asked but I was seized by a singular sort of constraint, almost a *pudeur*. Instead I went to the lavatory and was violently sick; while the two muttering men pursued their long conversation at the far end of the hall.

It did not last very long, for presently Bechet stood up and signalled to me his readiness to depart. I went up to them to bid the priest goodbye; he wore a haggard and sorrowful expression, and gazed at me curiously. Bechet flapped and flurried about snow on the pass and mist along the foothills. Why did I not tackle him directly there and then about the burial? I do not really know. I followed him tamely out into the darkness, having first embraced old Jan and other members of the clan, promising them that I would return soon to stay in the chateau. They made all sorts of extravagant promises about the place, but I knew it would never regain its solvency; and it was inexpressibly painful to think of coming back here all alone. We regained the car, and a moist fog swirled about the headlights, but this was a good sign for it smelt of a thaw, while here and there one felt a small push of wind from the northern sector. The merest puff of mistral along the Rhône valley and everything would become cold but clear as glass, with a blue sky to crown it.

"I'm glad it's over," said the little faded man as he manipulated the wheel of his ancient car, "in spite of the undignified rush. I must say, I loved Piers very much but I was often mystified by him. And as for the chateau I don't know how they will keep ahead of the tax people. Piers had no head when it came to figures, no head at all." The association in the metaphor emboldened me to put to him the question which had been on the tip of my tongue, but without giving me a chance he went on. "And talking of heads, my dear friend, I took one liberty without consulting you – in the interest of speed, of despatch. I have ordered a *caput mortuum* to be cast. You will have it tomorrow." So that was the explanation! "You will, I hope, pardon me for the haste. Many motives impelled me. First, I felt it was a good thing to get it over, specially for you; then, on a more selfish plane, I wanted to get the papers and certificates in order as I am going on leave tomorrow for a whole month, to Sicily. I hate unfinished business, and in my profession you know how things can drag on and on . . ." He puffed at his cigarette and gave me a friendly sideglance. "I hope tonight you will get some real sleep," he added, "because now all is in order." I suddenly felt very old, and fragile, and exhausted.

Back in Avignon the streets were wet and the rainy vistas picked out with lights trembled as if seen through gauze. I could hear the sour tang of the clock on the Hôtel de Ville as we drew to a halt under the trees in the main square. I was glad to be set down here, and to have a short walk to the hotel. I wished him a happy vacation and shook his hand. It was a relief to be alone again and I turned up my face to the sky to feel the warmish rain on it. But it was already late when at last I reached my objective and I climbed the stairs heavily, exhausted and dispirited. I had already reached the first landing when the night porter awoke and came after me with a message. A gentleman from England had asked for me; he had taken a room but at the moment he was in mine. He had ordered soda and whisky and was waiting for me. It could only be Toby, and my heart leaped up exultantly to think that at last he had managed to get here.

I hurried up the next flight and along the gloomy corridor to my room to verify this certainty and found that giant of a man spread over the foot of my bed, snoring lightly. His spectacles had been pushed up on to his forehead and were in danger of falling; his detective story bought for the journey had already slipped out of his grasp on to the floor. Ah, those spectacles! Never have glasses been so often dropped, sat upon, kicked, fractured, forgotten. They held together by a miracle, and every fracture was carefully put in splints with the help of electrician's tape. "Toby!"

He stirred, but then plunged back deeper into his sleep, his lips moving. His huge form bore all the familiar character-istics of the bachelor don – the untidy raincoat whose belt had long since vanished, the shoes like boats, their rubber soles curled up from too hasty drying in front of gas-fires after long muddy walks. Indeed his desperate trousers had traces of yellow clay at the extremities which suggested recent walks in limestone country – as well as perhaps a reason for his silence after my telegram. He had been away on a walking tour. Since he seemed to have no luggage with him save his detective story I presumed that he had first secured a room for himself, dumped his luggage, and sat down in mine to wait for me. His sleeping likeness to Rob Sutcliffe was almost uncanny; if they were not doubles, they could at least have been taken for brothers. For us they were Gog and Magog, two huge short-sighted men with sandy unruly hair and colourless eyelashes; specialists in laughter and irremediable *gaffes*. While looking down at the sleeping Toby I was also seeing Rob Sutcliffe.

Toby smelt of spirits but there was no trace of a glass in my room; but when I examined the bathroom I found a half-empty bottle of whisky, and a toothmug still half full – which went some way towards explaining his present porcine slumber.

In order to celebrate his arrival – my spirits had risen with a bound since I knew he was at my side – I drank off the measure of whisky in the glass and returned to the bedroom to wake him and claim my own bed. But his sleep was still of the deepest and I had to repeat his name twice before there was any reaction at all. "Wake up, Toby!"

He appeared to stir in coils like a python – various parts of that large anatomy changed disposition, unrolled themselves, without the sleeper himself being aware; he then scratched his thigh, groaned, half sat up, only to relax again and deflate like a punctured balloon. The eyes opened at last and examined the blurred ceiling with its scrolls and cherubs with unfocused attention, seeing everything and nothing.

It was clear that he was puzzled, that he did not know where he was. I was charitably inclined to suppose that fatigue as much as alcohol played a part in this state of utter bemusement. "Toby. It's Bruce." He now woke up with such an exaggerated energy that it seemed he might levitate and go right through the ceiling. He struggled to his feet, grasped my hand in both of his, and said in rapid telegraphese: "I suppose I am very late? Telegram was at college – been walking in Germany – was completely bowled over – and yet somehow expected something like it – didn't exactly know what – but this is it – now recognise the whole thing – the suicide – typical – damn it all."

"It's a bad dream," I said.

He nodded and went into the bathroom where he threw some cold water on his face to wake himself up. He then re-emerged vigorously towelling himself and, snorting like a carthorse, sat down on the edge of the bed and stared at me. "Suicide," he said at last, as if that were something he had never properly thought about. Then he wagged a thick finger and went on. "Bruce, you never really took all that stuff seriously, did you? I mean Akkad and all those wretched tenets he was always stuffing down our throats. You never took them at their face value – but I always did and I was always full of misgiving to see Piers go overboard for them."

I felt it necessary to apply a brake to this kind of free speculation, if only in the interests of poor dear Akkad. I said: "Toby, even if we haven't got a precise reason for this act of Piers I don't feel we have the right to jump to the conclusion that the Egyptians have anything to do with it – and I mean most particularly Akkad. They were dead against self-destruction, and Akkad never ceased to emphasise the point."

"But you didn't go as far as Piers – you were always on the fringes of the thing, Bruce. So how to know?"

"And you didn't go anywhere at all – so how dare to speculate?" I felt angry, aggrieved. It solved nothing to have idle theories spun about something so cardinal and definitive as Piers' death. "Sorry," said Toby like a sad elephant, and bit the end of his thumb as he sank into a deep reflection. "I was only trying to think of a reason, but of course there doesn't have to be a reason. Just depression or illness could account for it."

"Of course."

"He had a medical check in the autumn – I mean, suppose the sawbones found something slow but fatal like a cancer or like Hodgkin's ? It could easily . . . But I am making you impatient."

It was true. It was also a little unjust on my part. I realised that I was simply trying to work off a little of my shock and hysteria on him. I apologised and he grinned affectionately and said he quite understood. It paved the way for me to bring him up to date, to tell him all that I knew, and to describe my visits to Sylvie and to the funeral at Verfeuille. He listened to all this heavily, and with an occasional sigh. But he still shook a doubtful head. "Rob used to say something like: 'There is always a philosophy behind the misadventures of men, even if they are unaware of it.' And that's what I feel about this. Don't be angry with me. It smells purposeful."

Hence the smile on Piers' face, I thought to myself; but I was heartily glad that Toby had arrived too late to inflame the police mind with his theories. I fished out the photographic dossier I had been lent with the police enlargements. He spread them slowly over the bed and bent over them, obviously touched to the heart for he solemnly blew his nose in a grubby red handkerchief. But there was nothing more of significance to be drawn from these things now. The enigma of the welcoming gaze towards the door perhaps. I don't know. One tended to think up mysteries where none existed. I thought of the gold-tipped cigarette ends, and I thought of Sylvie and her distress on the evening of the act. Presumably these factors too would be explained when Sylvie recovered her reason again, if ever she did.

I finished my drink at last. Then I drew the curtains to watch the dawn come creeping up over the wrinkled river and over the muddled rooftops of the town where already the lacklustre pigeons were beginning to flap. Sour bells clattered the hour. "We must get some sleep," and Toby rose yawning and stretched. I felt as if I were making my first steps in a new world, a world where all the dispositions had been changed abruptly, all the proportions altered.

We agreed to meet at ten in the hall, but I slept so heavily that I did not hear the maid's knock, and when I did get there it was to find a message from Toby to the effect that he had gone out to the Café Durance for a *croissant* and a cup of coffee. It was not hard to follow in his footsteps and find him there, in the early sunlight, half asleep at a table, gazing with deep affection at his own personal corner of the city, the corner that meant the most to him – the main square. Ah! That romantic square with its horrible Monument des Morts festooned with its mangy tin lions, so typical a fancy! All squared off by the beautiful mature trees sheltering the intimate little fringe of cafés and restaurants where one could dawdle away whole days, whole holidays, whole lifetimes. I can never see it now without seeing the phantom of Piers cross it, limping to the *tabac* for cigarettes with his slight suggestion of wolf-slink; and as often I see Sylvie walking there with him, arm in arm and pressed tight to his side like a scabbard. She had that special walk with him, pressed snug to his side, proudly. In the Greek islands one has seen little seahorses walking like that, innocent sensual and upright . . . My friend was dozing; or rather he was in the benign stupor which overcame him always in his favourite city. "Ah! Avignon!" he said quietly, as much to the sky as to me. So one might have exclaimed "Ah! Child-hood!" Today was just one day added to a long tapestry of days woven by memory. At every time, and in every season, he had known the town, by summer and winter, perhaps better than any of us. For while we had so often been far away Toby had spent several months each year working on the documents in the chateau. Piers had put at his disposal an enormous cache of original material which had a bearing on the history of the Templars, the subject of Toby's *magnum opus* – "a work which will deflower the detestable Professor Babcock, and secure me the throne of medieval studies at Garbo College". It was to be understood that Babcock held diametrically opposed views about the Templars and their mysterious history. But the old man's fate was sealed, for the great three-volume work of Toby's was almost finished, and it made use of much un-published material which he had found in the muniments room at Verfeuille. Toby as a victim of the historical virus could not look at the town without seeing it historically, so to speak – layer after layer of history laid up in slices, embodied in its architecture. There was no corner of the place which did not conjure up for him delicious reveries, vivid associations.

"Will I see Sylvie?" he asked softly at last, "or would you

rather not at the moment?" On the contrary, I said, he was expected and a visit might do a great deal of good. "We can go up this evening if you wish. I only have to telephone Jourdain and let him know." But at the thought I felt weighed down again by the prehistoric depression caused by her plight – and my own. Here was time running away with us and still we were plagued by these fearful misadventures of the reason and the flesh. Moreover here I was in roughly the state of an orphan – I mean that I had severed all my ties with the outside world and had come here to settle. The few personal possessions I owned were on their way to join me. The crates of books and paintings would not be long delayed. I should soon have to make up my mind about the future – stay here, hobbled by Sylvie's plight, or go away, somewhere far away, using some medical excuse? Cowardice, I know, but when one is desperate one toys with desperate solutions. Toby suffered from no such doubts. "Of course you will have to go back to Verfeuille now," he said stoutly, "you can't leave Sylvie – unless you took her on a long sea voyage or something like that."

But I hadn't the strength to undertake a long journey in which I should have to nurse her night and day, with always the danger of a *fugue* staring me in the face, or a complete relapse into something like catatonia. Would I be forced to stay, then? (Walking alone at night, when thoughts won't sift properly, down dark roads in the rain, in the roaring northern rain which brimmed over the edges of the world I had been over and over the problem of Sylvie. Months of solitary walking.)

I ordered wine. It lay before me, glinting in the sun. It was hardly done to drink Tavel so early in the morning but I could never resist the colour or the taste; Toby, true to form, gulped at an *anisette*. His ample presence comforted me no end. Perhaps I might consider a return to the chateau if he himself were going to stay there and work for a month or two.

His company would help to make me acclimatise myself perhaps?

So we sat and watched little scenes from the life of the Midi enacted before our eyes – a delight because they confirmed the unchanging character of the place and its inhabitants. Some workmen were trying to mend the defective machinery of the old Jaquemart without success. At last the little waist-high couple of figurines gave a spasmodic jerk or two and advanced a little in order to strike midday twice – as a pure concession to the workmen it seemed, who were using extremely bad language, and didn't appear to know how the thing worked. It was a pity. The Jaquemart was one of the prettiest features of the square when they did work – the little man trotting out punctually, to hammer out the hours with his tiny mallet. But from time to time they stuck, and this was at least the third time we had witnessed an attempt to put the machinery to rights, and this time the whole project seemed to be beyond the workmen, for in a while, after a lot of desultory messing about, they started to climb down the tower. They were half way down when, as if in derision, the little figures jerked into their curving trajectory and without prompting struck midday (or midnight). The men shook goodnatured fists at them and shouted expletives.

It was reassuring in its amiable futility, this operation. Clearly the task was beyond them, and a specialist would have to be summoned to deal with the problem. We walked back to the hotel in silence, strangely reassured by this trivial scene, by this cold but benign snatch of sunlight, by the taste of good wine. I rang up Montfavet and spoke to Jourdain. He was quite delighted to hear of Toby's arrival – as I knew he would be. "She has been speaking about him quite a lot, and complaining that her rooms smell of his tobacco. Let him smoke a pipe tonight as a mark of identification. No; there is no marked change for the time being. What else have I to tell you? Yes, the morgue people have sent me round a plaster cast of Piers' face, taken by the *médecin-légiste*, or someone assigned by him. I will hand it over to you when you come."

Things were beginning to sort themselves out – or was that just an illusion born of the friendly presence of Toby and the fact that Piers' funeral had become an accomplished fact, was over? At any rate I felt much calmer as I spent the morning with Toby walking round the town, visiting the bookshops and he more immediate historical antiquities. He always felt the need to reverify his city, to make sure that it was still there, still insisting on its poetic role in the world which had by now so far outstripped it. We walked and talked regardless of the hours; then returned to our rooms for a short rest before the affairs of the evening. At dusk we jogged up to Montfavet in a *fiacre*, Toby obediently smoking his foul shag in a bull-nosed pipe and speculating on what the future might have in store for us.

Well, she was dressed in rather a haphazard fashion – in a long, old-fashioned hobble skirt and a number of brilliant scarves of different colours and materials. Eccentric, if you like. But she gave her evident disorientation a sort of tropical brilliance, like a bird of paradise.

It was depressing, it hurt, because it was such a close parody of good reason. The capricious evolutions of a child, say. Yet it was not. She seemed to be expecting us or at any rate me – perhaps Jourdain had told her something? At any rate she wore a red velvet carnival *cagoule* through the slits of which her eyes looked at us, unblinking or perhaps glittering with malice. Who can say? "There you are!" she cried, and went on: "There is no need to speculate on my identity," giving a little gesture which was somehow a forlorn caricature of an imperious one. She was like an amateur actor in a difficult play. Standing up now she said: "After all, it is all mine to do with it whatever I wish, no?" Toby lumbered up to her like a bear saying: "Of course it is," and took this velvet animal in his arms. "I recognise you," she said, "because of the smell of your tobacco. And you, too, Bruce." This was a great encouragement. But it did not change the constraint we felt, I suppose because neither of us quite believed it. Then she surprised and encouraged us by quoting a phrase of her brother's. "Here comes Toby, with shoes like boats, and a handshake as hot as a busby." This at least showed that she knew who he was. Laughter. We were both delighted, and Toby, in search of patterns of reminiscence which might, like grooves, familiarise her back into phase, went over to the piano and began to pick out tunes with one finger. This had a surprisingly calming effect: she laughed and clapped her hands, and sitting down at the card table dealt herself a hand of solitaire. The evocation of Verfeuille in winter was perfect. Toby had just returned wet through from a walk in the rain. He sits on one side of the fireplace, literally steaming. On the other side Rob Sutcliffe. Both smoke infernal pipes. Piers lies asleep on the sofa – too much wine at lunch and a late night. The rain swishes down in the park, teems on the window panes, brims the gurgling gutters. Piers sleeps; the two giants argue with acrimony about the Templars. I whittle a stick. The gun-dogs snore and tremble. It is one of those long afternoons where imprisonment by the weather becomes delightful. She deals herself a hand of solitaire. Propped in front of her is a notebook of Rob's from which she occasionally reads out aloud, though nobody pays any attention to the words. "Identity is the frail suggestion of coherence with which we have clad ourselves. It is both illusory and quite real, and most necessary for happiness, if indeed happiness is necessary." Toby, in the act of blowing his nose, cries "Bad Nietzsche!" over his shoulder. This was the scene which we were now busy re-enacting except that Piers was gone and Rob was gone. It was a frail thread to hang on to, but it held. With bowed head and concentrated air she played on, listening to the dislocated one-finger noises of Toby on the Pleyel. "Do you remember Akkad? He used to say to us: 'Hurry. Hurry. The minutes are leaking from the clocks and as yet we have only brushed the Great Cryptics.' Well, Bruce dear, I tried to hurry like he said, but I missed my footing somehow. Anyway it was always appproaching me, what Piers called 'the old fern-fingered neurasthenia' and now Jourdain thinks he understands a little but he doesn't. It's the merest presumption of medicine." I knew that only too well. In a while she got up and walked about as if she were trying to rehearse for a play. She had unmasked herself now and her eyes were full of mischief. She poured out an imaginary drink, added soda, and took it over to Toby who thanked her and drank an imaginary mouthful before setting it down on the piano. Then she lighted a real cigarette, but almost at once threw it into the grate. There was a fire laid there, and the gesture drew my attention to the fact – also I seemed to recognise some fragments of manuscript in Piers' hand. "Are you burning Piers' papers?" I said, and she suddenly stopped dead in her tracks, hand on her heart. As if recovering full possession of herself she fell on her knees before the grate and, bursting into tears, began taking out the crumpled papers and smoothing them in her lap. "Why did I do that?" she cried. "When there was nothing to hide, nothing at all to hide?"

No, there was nothing to hide. I took the crumpled papers from her and sat down to sort them while she returned seriously to her game. They were by several hands and not all by Piers as I had surmised. Sutcliffe's large florid feminine hand was very conspicuous, as was the brilliant inks he used. His loose-leaf notebooks were always exploding and letting their contents tumble about in hopeless disorder.

Meeting on the threshing floor to wrestle with death
and with love like Digenis

A railway strike produced strange things like this mountain of motionless roses laid up in a siding

Intuition has no memory, it jumps off the spool, it eludes thought memory and also causality

another tiring dream of grave allegorical figures, of sleep, cathedrals sitting in blue water on canals with wet shoes at night

a letter to Pia written in my sleep by braille

out of this tremendous chaos, Pia, I am trying to build my new and perhaps my last book. The studio floor is littered with fragments of this great puzzle

when the age gets swept out to sea and dispersed by the tides what remains will be the result of the purest accident; one-fifth of Anc Greek Drama one-tenth of Elizabethan is all we have left so why worry?

Infants are smooth and lack all swank They only have themselves to thank.

Language is all very fine and we cannot do without it but it is at the same time the worst invention of man, corrupting silence, tearing petals off the whole mind. The longer I live the more ashamed I get.

Sorrow is implicit in love as gravitation is implicit in mass.

The mechanism of causality is mighty and mathematically quite inexorable even for mental phenomena.

I sat there among these fragments of the great puzzle of Rob's unfinished novel whose dismembered fragments littered the muniments room, and heard Toby picking and picking out his one-fingered tune, merciless as a woodpecker. "Sylvie." She raised her dark head and gazed at me abstractedly, her eyes still full of playing cards and their magic. "Did Piers tell you . . ?" It was stupid of me to broach the subject at this moment, and Toby gave a grimace of displeasure. But she behaved as if she had not heard. But a moment later she said: "He had considered every possible issue before deciding that he must stick to the rules. His heart was set on it."

"On what, Sylvie?"

She produced a sad little smile and I could see that she had slipped, so to speak, off the time-track again and into the solipsism of childhood. I put the papers on the table and she read off a phrase from one of them in a low voice: "Me he will devour in the next life whose flesh I eat in this." I wondered where Piers had found that quotation for his commonplace book; also a verse by a forgotten Elizabethan:

> And so it grew and grew
> And bore and bore
> Until at length it
> Grew a gallows that did bear our son.

It must have struck his mind as a reference to her child, Sylvie's child. She shook the hair out of her eyes and said: "Remember the song the Templars sang?" I shook my head, but truthfully, for I did not know what she meant. In a small ghostly voice she sang "Oranges and Lemons, say the bells of Saint Clements." A well-enough known nursery song, though I had never heard that it was originated by the Templars. She was very earnest now, and very solemn in her dreamy way, and as the words of the song flowed out she began to enact the scene of the nursery game which we had all played when we were little. "Here comes a candle to light you to bed, here comes a chopper to chop off your head, chop, chop, chop, chop . . ." With joined fingers she executed a long line of children – guillotine fashion. Then she stopped dead, entranced, gazing at nothing or perhaps only the projection of her private thoughts on the white wall. Then she said: "Everything that happened began at Macabru, you know that. Piers knew it. Macabru changed everything."

I waited painfully for something further to emerge from this unsatisfactory meeting, but nothing more came; and soon the nurse came with her medicines and the little trolley with the frugal dinner of the patient. Jourdain, too, came and reminded us that we were his guests that evening. He was delighted to see Toby again. But Sylvie was now withdrawn, silent, in the Trappe of her private mind. "In the perspex cube of an unshakable autism." I stroked her hair and said goodbye, but she did not even look up.

In Jourdain's study, on his desk, lay the smart black velvet casket with the death-mask. It was at once like and unlike Piers – as though time had played tricks on the image like it plays on memories, distorting them. I think these thoughts might have passed through the doctor's mind as well for he said: "There always seems to be a shrinkage after death, which has puzzled me repeatedly. The image withers up. I have even tried weighing several people after death to see if this is imaginary or real. Does the personality actually weigh something? Because when it is emptied out a vast disorganisation starts, and the first sign of it is a kind of diminishing. But this is an illusion, the weight does not change." He was right, for the face of Piers looked shrunk, famished, reduced. Jourdain closed the casket with a snap and said: "Well, there it is. It's yours." I thanked him for having thought about the matter. No doubt one day, in the fulness of time, when we had got over the pangs, the first gnawing pangs of his death, it would be pleasant to have him there, in a favourite corner of the room, on a writing desk, in sunlight. I thought for a long moment about the equivocal and enigmatic quality of love and a phrase from a novel by Rob came to mind – Piers had copied it out. "In our age too much freedom has destroyed the fragile cobweb which gave the great human attachments their form and substance – their truth. Health rages in us like a toothache, but fine styles in living, as in writing, have been overtaken by loutishness."

And what of Macabru?

TWO

Macabru

THE FOUR RIDERS, ONE OF THEM A WOMAN, WHO SET off that noon from the Canopic Gate were as young as their mettlesome longlegged horses. The party was guided by a decrepit one-eyed Arab on a somewhat capricious white camel. They were heading for an oasis called Macabru which lay some way to the east of Alexandria. Yes, we were all four somewhat new to the place, and as yet very much under the spell of its skies and its vistas of many-coloured desert – here and there soothed out so like curls freshly combed: here and there so like fresh snow, bearing the perfect imprints of animals' paws and of birds' claws. As a matter of fact Sylvie had only recently arrived to stay with her brother at the French Legation, while I was putting up our friend Toby who was on his way back from Palestine to Oxford after a spell of disappointment with his Bible studies. "The more I learn about Our Saviour the less I like him. I am not going to take that sort of Holy Orders anyway." This was his most recent theme; but in fact already his addiction to drink had marked him down as rather a questionable candidate for the priesthood. When tipsy he was capable of saying anything to anyone, and if it happened to be one of his examiners? At any rate he was one of the four riders – the most amateurish I would suppose, sitting his horse gracelessly, with splayed bottom and toes turned out. He was a very large young man, his face burnt beetroot by the sun, his ears sticking out steeply – which gave him the air of trying to overhear what was being said a mile away. Thick spectacles broke up his features into reflecting planes. His sandy hair stuck out or fell down in his eyes when it needed cutting. He smelt of Lifebuoy soap and exuded a clumsy but effervescent goodwill which was contagious. Only in this case he protested a bit feeling that he had been let in for a long and exhausting ride to little purpose. It is difficult to see why, for in his disappointment with Our Saviour he had turned his sympathetic attention to the heresies of various sects which had departed from the strict canons of Christian theological dogma – so that in some ways he was much better informed about the activities of Akkad than we were.

In the case of Piers who rode a little ahead with his beautiful sister, the question was different – he had fallen under the spell of this strange man. The views of Akkad – for Piers had encountered him quite often at parties in the city during his first few months *en poste* – seemed to him something like a revelation. "I seem to understand everything he says, and I feel I am hearing something absolutely truthful for the first time – so it's all quite original for me, quite pristine. For the first time, Bruce, I can *believe* in something, a proposition about myself and the world which holds water. It satisfies me, it's like falling in love." This is the point at which Toby would groan, but Sylvie would turn her face to mine and kiss me softly. "O to hell with you ," said Piers spurring his horse.

In those days there were no real suburbs – the desert began almost at the gates of Alexandria and with it of course the damp enervating heat which soaked and bathed one, until one could feel the sweat trickling through one's clothes into one's very saddle. Our breathing was laboured. There were small villages giving (so many were the mirages) the illusion of being fictions; their reflections rose in the air or settled into the ground. Purely fictitious lakes with minarets surrounded them, turning them into violet islands. Finally one got to disbelieving one's own eyesight, and in waiting for the truth to emerge – the sordid truth, for the villages were all decayed and fly-blown, and now in the noonday sun for the most part deserted.

In one the Arab guide beckoned us to follow him, with a

sort of cheeky grin, as if to promise us an agreeable diversion. There was a naked old man chained to a block of wood set deep in the ground. He seemed dead, but the Arab turned him over with his foot as one turns a strange beatle over. No, he was alive, but mad. He mopped and mowed, smiled and salaamed and mumbled. He was as thin as an insect, but was brimming over with an insane gaiety – the blissful amnesia that all excessive suffering brings. We heard his story. He had been chained here as a punishment for some crime by the local pasha. But time passed, the nature of his crime was forgotten by the village, even the old pasha himself died, and the criminal went slowly mad with the heat and the thirst. But his madness took the form of a tremendous and exalted happiness. He submitted to everything happily. He was in a state of perfect bliss, whatever happened. Perhaps it was due to this that he survived, for the villagers brought him food and water, first out of sympathy and lastly because they felt that he was really a saint. The truth broke upon them.

Now he was cherished and fed, and people came to visit him as if he were an oracle. He had indeed become a saint, and would when he died give the village a yearly festival. Only they had no authority to free him, that would take a great deal of effort and documentation, and there was hardly anyone in the village capable of examining the legal situation or undertaking the necessary paperwork. Meanwhile he was euphoric. He kissed Piers' toe and went on muttering. The sandheap in which he lay was full of ants, and there seemed no shade for the poor man. But packets of food lay about, and having had a hearty laugh at his compatriot's plight the Arab guide suddenly turned pious, made him a deep obeisance and then went to fill a pitcher of sweet water for him. One felt helpless and thoroughly disgusted. Normally one bought out one's horror and embarrassment when face to face with such a spectacle (a beggar covered in sores, say) but in this case what good was money, what good our etiolated town-sympathy? It was hard to know how to curb one's fury, too, against the guide for having thought up this pleasing little spectacle for us. Suddenly Egypt hit us all like a hammer.

It was a sighing relief to quit the hamlet for the pure desert again. I have said there were no suburbs of the modern city and this is true – but everywhere outside it in the sand of the desert, half buried, were the extensive remains of ancient buildings, shattered archways, smashed causeways and musing lintels, and what often seemed to be partly demolished statues. So that we had some truthful inkling of the original dream-city of the boy Alexander which, according to Pliny, had had a circuit of fifteen miles and had housed three hundred thousand souls. It had gloried in palaces, baths, libraries, temples and gymnasia without number. But we were latecomers to the place, modern scavengers of history upon a scene which had, it seems, long since exhausted all its historical potentialities. It was with something of a melancholy air that Piers (who loved guide books) had read out the preamble to the article about the city in Murray. "Alexandria is situated in 31° 13′ 5″ north latitude and 27° 35′ 30″ longitude, near Lake Mareotis, on an isthmus which connects with *terra firma* the peninsula that forms the two ports."

Repeated historical earthquakes have dashed down the monuments and engulfed the place time and time again; at the time of the French invasion the population had declined to some 8,000 souls. But an infusion of new blood and a long world war restored to it much of its lost importance, and by now its central parts had become almost opulent again with villas and gardens in the French Riviera style of building, shady public squares, museums, banks and galleries. Its swollen Arab quarter was now nearly as varied and picturesque as that of Cairo; its brothel quarters were as extensive as well might be in a port which was now used to the regular visits of so many foreign warships. But the past had quite gone, and much had vanished with it. Turning slightly left towards the foaming sealine now through the tinted afternoon light it was only possible to imagine the marches of Alexander through such a haze of shimmering silence, broken only by the curses of his guides and the curious lumpy shuffling noise a camel makes in the dunes. "And yet," said Piers to whom I can attribute this sentiment, "and yet the outer furnishings of his world are still here – palms, water-wheels, dervishes, desert horses. Always!"

"Mirages," groaned Toby, "and oases."

"Some people say that it was not Siwa where he was proclaimed God, but Macabru; that is why I jumped at the invitation of Akkad."

"Romantic," said Sylvie.

"Not at all," he said, catching her wrist with a little pleading gesture. "Can't you see how marvellous history is? The presence of other people whose actions and thoughts seem to still hang about in the air? Don't tell me you can see the Nile delta without a thought for poor Euclid who obviously worked as a clerk in the Ministry of Waterways? How boring his life must have been. What a hypotenuse everything must have seemed, even love, to a poor civil servant, married with nine children, all isosceles in shape . . ."

"Enough, Piers!"

Gradually as we advanced the fatidic afternoon re- linquished much of its fearful heat, the colour began to fade into evening; objects began to take up new positions in this dying sky as watching silhouettes. This would be most pro- nounced on the Nile itself – wing of a felucca sailing south- ward into darkness! But we had to reckon with the part of the sky which hung over the blue-brown sea. "Another mouth, sicking out its alluvial muck," said Toby, and Piers said rather primly: "Once there were seven mouths, and seven cities built upon them. Now even the ashes of the ruins . . ." But they were buried completely in silt or washed out to sea. A wild sea drubbed and hummed upon these desolate beaches, beating like a fateful drum or a basoon of sadness. The sand was full of shattered shells and dead crabs, and the colour of dirty flour; our horses sank, and in order to coax them to a gallop we had to look for firm surfaces right at the sealine. Here at least we managed to let our mounts have their heads, but only for half a mile or so. The stout wind precluded all but smiles. Thick fingers of current rinsed back the bays while the undertow noisily macerated the occasional beach of pebbles. Woe to a poor swimmer on these beaches! We passed an old withered man on a mule. He seemed sunk in a trance of fatigue, but he croaked the guide good-day. This seemed to spark off a talkative vein in our own Arab. Coming alongside us with his slower animal he said: "Him very old. You don't see people very old in Skanderia. Die young, Egyptians." The observation was a true one, but he did not elaborate; I would have liked to know whether he thought this was due to the climate, the diet, or simply malefic djinns. The latter I presumed for I had been told so.

Now the shore became rocky and firm and we came upon the buried and crumbling remains of what looked like a tidy-sized necropolis, but as it was not marked on Piers' maps we had no means of telling what it really was. It tilted seaward, sloping like the floor of a theatre, and with open mouth as if it were really a stone quarry. But Toby voted it a hypogeum, I suspect because he liked the word and not because he knew what it meant; no more did I. But exposed as it was to the north it must have been filled with waves and spray whenever it blew a gale. It appeared to consist of corridors, now open to the sky, radiating out from what might have been a central courtyard. Bats flew squeaking up to the echo of the pebbles we dropped, in trying to determine its depth. But there was no time to play about as our guide was fussing about the distance still to be covered before we came to Macabru. There was a ferry to be crossed with these capricious steeds and the white camel – and even I had learned that camels are bad-tempered and inclined to bite when under stress.

When we struck the mouth of a small but violent river we turned abruptly inland and followed its course, sure now to connect with the ford which offered the only link with the further desert and the small oasis which was our destination.

But with every advance the visage of nature changed; Canopus, that desolate city, once erected about the tomb of Menelaus, lay far behind while ahead of us glinted more miles of unbreathable desert where nothing moved save little bands of swallows skimming to and fro. Clambering through the waste in which the sand drifts were in some places blown up into heaps and in others spread out into vast mattresses, where our animals sank a foot deep, and in others again, water-covered and reduced to black mud, we gradually made dogged headway under a changing sky. It had become leaden and dark with clouds in the fading daylight, a sky full of winter tones. An obstinate wind, now turned colder with the dusk, kept up its pressure on the ear-drums, and in this dull twilight the further desert looked anything but inviting. Rather it was dreary and desolate beyond all expression.

But we persevered and when the night seemed not too far off we came to a jutting little promontory with a sad little jetty barely holding its own with the boisterous snarling waters. The river was wide too at this point, and for a while we felt some real doubt as to whether we were going to achieve a crossing. From time to time, in the lulls of the wind we could hear our stirrups clink, or the dull stabbing screams of a gull, or the rasp of a heron. But night was beginning to fall. There was no sign of the ferryman on the opposite bank. We stood our ground, deliberating, while enormous crabs issuing from the holes in the river bank advanced to greet us, frightening the horses. The guide was in an ugly despair. We all shouted and yelled but our calls were swept away in the wind, and no answering voice came to offer us the promise of a passage. We felt half mad with disappointment as we saw our hopes of visiting the oasis withering away. It was in this Stygian situation and mood that I had the idea of firing off my revolver, and surprisingly enough this seemed to do the trick, for a portion of the thick dusk stirred and it was not too long before we heard a voice hailing us. And behold, the ferry boat in all its glory rounded a little spur of sand and came swaying down to us. It was quite an exciting manœuvre, the whole embarkation business, but fortunately both the horses and the camel behaved with exemplary good sense.

From then on a last village and we advanced into the desert and into the darkness; there was nothing to be seen save the desolate dunes stretching away on every side – and now visibility was foreshortened by the absolute dark. Yet the sky had cleared. We asked the Arab if he steered on a star, but this he did not seem to understand, yet he seemed quite confident of his direction and plodded mechanically on, while I took a reading from my little oil-compass just to see that we were not being guided in circles, or even back by mere accident to the river. No, he was certainly on a course, which was somewhat reassuring.

Another hour or so of this sturdy riding on uneven surfaces and we suddenly found the sky growing much lighter, as if with a false sunrise about to break through the soft horizon line to the east. Objects seemed to define themselves more clearly, and with a soft phosphorescent glow. Later we were to discover that this was due simply to the as yet unrisen moon shining against banks of soft cirrus. Everything seemed to be clearing, and it had become very much cooler. We were out of the wind now, exchanging glances with the stars which began to prickle above us on the dark carpet of heaven. Softly, with the faintest whirr of engines – indeed with far less noise than the average bus – a light aircraft rustled slowly over us with all the lights glimmering in its cabin. It made a slow turn eastwards and began to descend. The guide gave a croak of relieved triumph. The aircraft was Akkad's and it was ferrying some of his guests; there was apparently an excellent natural landing strip in the desert quite near the oasis. As a matter of fact we had been offered a trip in this fashion but being young and romantic had declined the invitation, preferring to ride. Nor had we anything to regret in the matter. But now our spirits rose in us with the confirmation that our course was a true one.

Insensibly we quickened our speed, and even the horses seemed to feel something of our urgency and began to make an effort to carry us faster. We wound laboriously up a par- ticularly large dune and were at last rewarded by a light – a soft unwinking glow in the desert some way before us. It floated, a warm rosy emanation, upon the tumultuous desert floor, promising a point of fixity in the midst of desolation: a landfall. And so we smiled at each other in darkness (there was a smile in our voices, in our banter) as we hastened over the sand.

Macabru was simply a shadow which dawn's light would break down into objects and planes; for the moment all one could say was that it was not part of the desert. It hovered on the edges of the warm light, reserving its beauties for the coming moon. But the light as we approached now broke down into many separate points, and we saw that we were approaching something like a desert encampment – the bivouac of some huge army. All was mingled and muddled by the darkness – distances, volumes, angles, objects. But as we came to it it looked not unlike another large Arab city, but this time all lit up against the darkness. It was only when we were on it that we glimpsed a slender tulip of minaret, and a patch of water rippling like a mirror – the size of a lake or the arm perhaps of the river which we had just crossed? We reined our horses on the edges of the nearest light – a fire of straw burning in a field – and here a rider came up to meet us on a great black mare.

"A seneschal," said Piers, thrilled to the core not only by the word but by the medieval formality of this meeting. I knew that he was thinking of the Crusaders – how often they must have met with this kind of Moslem reception. The tall thin man, face bearded and nose aquiline, asked us who we were in Arabic, but immediately broke into sound French when we announced ourselves, politely dragging off our light but cumbersome Arab burnouses which had been stifling us with heat throughout the ride, but which we now surrendered some-what reluctantly for the evening had turned cool. Instantly the messenger turned his dancing horse and led us down into the lighted township. Akkad had already described to us most accurately what we would see.

It was not only in the towns and bigger villages that one met with the tombs of holy men, or those who had achieved a posthumous sainthood and conferred it on a place, dignifying it with a yearly feast day. Often, and throughout the country, they stood in deserted and solitary places, and usually had a fountain or small date-grove adjoining, where a wandering dervish might pause to pray and meditate after performing his ritual ablutions: or where indeed the ordinary traveller might simply quench his thirst and enjoy cool shade on a journey. Macabru had begun modestly enough with a shrine and a fountain – but it was a real oasis with a sheet of lake water, crystal clear, where the clouds floated by day or by night. Tall reeds fringed the holy lake.

Around the tomb of the saint had grown up a small chapel consisting of one square apartment surmounted by a dome most handsomely fluted. Outside was a magnificent marble fountain of filigreed workmanship which had been donated by the local pasha, who had also endowed the place so that regular religious observances could be supervised by the three gloomy, pious resident dervishes. How well we were to get to know the curious flat dusty smell of these places, the smell of brackish water on well-washed stone; and the peculiar disorienting effect of churches with no central altar, no point of focus, save only the hanging gonfalons with their grand script invoking the blessings of the Moslem God. And always the same sparse furniture of mat, water-jug, and a coloured chest to receive the donations of the passing traveller. And thus once a year the oasis came to life in honour of the saint. A bazaar sprang up around the central palm-groves where the camels were tethered, streets mapped themselves out, a hasty but useful drainage system was dug in the sand and partially solidified by water. Even a frail system of electric lighting with myriads of coloured bulbs crossed and recrossed the streets which were now lined with multicoloured stalls selling every imaginable thing, for the fair (or *mulid*) as it had developed over the years was half secular and half religious in inspiration. Of course we saw little of all this in detail at our first entry into Macabru – just the thrilling bazaar crackling with life and roaring barter, and the lights which led back in a sweet diagonal shape towards the central chapel, which was one of some consequence. And behind the hum of human voices and the snorting of mules and horses from the dark groves beside the lake we could hear the festive beat of the little drum and the squeak of fifes. Some of the painted stalls were of wood or light wattle, but most were mere tents of soiled and tattered cloth. At the end of the pro- visional village (for that is what it became for three days every year) we came to a great striped marquee with hitching posts about its entrance where we divested ourselves of our horses and, delighted to find that Akkad had not yet arrived, plunged back into the bazaar which for us was one of the most exciting places we had ever seen.

It was indeed marvellous in its comprehensiveness, our admiration was really justified, for not only were there stalls for sweetmeats, copper ware, camel gear, calendars and so on but the provision market was as handsomely stocked as the big markets of Alexandria – from which I supposed much of this stuff came either by land or water. There was no refrigeration in those days – or at best heavy and rudimentary ice-boxes which were not easily transportable. Provisions were ferried by camel in stout sacks of gunny with blocks of ice packed round them; a herculean task. Once the destination was reached commodities like bottles were sunk down wells by the basketful, or left in the lake to keep cool. But here were exposed various kinds of meat, fresh and dried fruits, vegetables, herbs, fowls, game, fish in abundance, very fine bread, milk and fresh eggs. The country round about produced little or nothing, so that all this sophisticated fare must have come from Rosetta, Alexandria, perhaps even from other villages in lower Egypt. We wandered speechlessly about in a daze of admiration for the colours and the scents and sounds. There was a lot of rough cookery going on, and a good deal of barter for cheap jewelry. There was also a kind of sand-ring where villagers were playing at single-stick, but in mockery, amidst laughter – a version of shadow-boxing: only wielding these huge iron-shod sticks gracelessly, keeping time to music like dancing bears. This sort of sham-fight seemed to be very popular to judge by the crowd. The music however was supplied by the followers of some ladies of easy virtue who had also come no doubt to celebrate the saint's day in their own fashion. They watched the tournament, seated on horseback, heavily painted in ghoulish fashion and bedizened with feathers, grease paint and necklaces of onions and garlic. The master of ceremonies for this group was a clown who sat back to front on a mule

with his face whitewashed. He carried a monkey on his shoulders
dressed in a coloured cap and reminded one of the court
buffoons of the Middle Ages. His sallies were obviously rather
double-edged and provoked roars of laughter.

We were all so absorbed by the marvellous spectacle that
we did not know for a while that Akkad himself had joined us
and was walking smilingly amongst us; true, he had put off
his town clothes and wore an old and much darned abba and a
soft fez. But there he was, this much discussed merchant-
banker, who was equally at home in four capitals and four
languages. I did not share the deep fascination of Piers, but on
the other hand I found Akkad a most surprising and attractive
man, with quirks of behaviour and speech which always
seemed to be leading him away to the darker corners of his
own thoughts – it was as though in order to speak at all he had
to wake himself up from a trance of inner meditation. Much
that he said was scattered and disconnected, and much I frankly
did not understand – or is that true, I wonder? His physical
presence was also intriguing for he sometimes looked heavy
and fat, and sometimes thin and ascetic. I have seen him driving
across the city in those inevitable dark glasses, with a growth
of unshaven stubble on his chin and his hair parted on a different side – and I had the impression of a fattish sluggish pasha,
wallowing in riches like a Turk. At other times, at his town
house which was splendid with statues and fountains, built
round an interior courtyard which abutted on to the shady and
silent gardens of the Museum, I saw another Akkad, the cocktail version, so to speak. Beautifully dressed by London with a
buttonhole and a silk handkerchief planted in his sleeve as if it
might sprout something. He still kept the glasses of course,
but his face seemed narrower, more goat-like, his hair finer
and more sparse. Of course he sometimes abandoned these fads,
taking off his glasses to talk – and then one suddenly saw his
eyes. They were so deep, so sea-green that they filled you with

inquietude; and the faint suspicion of a squint in them increased the feeling of disorientation, for he never seemed to be
looking at you so much as looking into or around you.
Porphyrios Akkad! "I know what you feel," said Piers once,
after a long thoughtful silence. "You find Akkad too articulate,
he doesn't quite carry conviction to you, so consequently you
are on your guard. But those eyes, Bruce!"

"I know."

"And that mind!"

"You are talking like a schoolboy!"

There was no need to reply to that, for I had frankly
acknowledged that I was out of my depth for the greater part
of his strange "expositions"; even later, when I read the texts
of them at leisure I only half-saw, half-agreed . . . For his
"sermons" were recorded and Roneo-copied for the benefit of
absent members. In Piers' hotel room at Avignon there was a
ton of these fascicules, some of which I could even remember
having heard him deliver in those far-off days. As for Piers,
Sabine once said of him: "It is pitiable. He has a thirst for
belief. Almost anything might do to satisfy it." Poor Piers
was deeply wounded by this remark, as he was by mine.

Akkad was so charmed by our tremendous attraction for
the oasis-bazaar that he refused to leave us and rejoin his
guests, saying: "They will forgive a little lapse. Come, I insist.
I will show you round myself." And this he faithfully did,
explaining everything in that calm melodious voice so full of
tenderness for these colourful aspects of his native country. It
did not really take all that long, but here and there he stopped to
exchange greetings or banter with an acquaintance, or listen to
a whispered complaint and promise redress for the complainer,
so that it was about an hour before we came to the last man, the
water-seller with his special little rituals. This one was distributing free water on behalf of a rich man who had been to
Mecca and who was known for his charity. The seller, who

propped the dark slobbering skin across his shoulders, held out to us the gilded cup from which we all drank, and also held up the mirror to our faces to remind us that we were mortal and must die. An elderly sheik shared this little ceremony with us, and afterwards benignly gave the waterman a coin and made him spurt scented water on his face and beard. So we came at long last, and in leisurely fashion, to the brilliant marquee among the supply-swaying cypresses and clicking date-palms – a really enormous tent about the size of a regimental mess-tent, though the company was not so inordinately numerous.

We were about twenty or thirty people in all, I guessed, and extremely various, both as to race and colour. There were two pretty Chinese ladies, some old Turks, and then a sprinkling of more modestly dressed people who looked like minor university professors or post-office officials. Some we already knew, like Casimir Ava the tragic actor with his pale eunochoid-velvet complexion and studied poses. The stagecraft of suicide meant everything to him, and everything he read or acted seemed to hint at it; it infected his moods and physical attitudes. You could tell at once that it would end like that, just by looking at those deepset burning disabused eyes. He was Werther. He would win his own title to extinction! None of this did I know at the time; and Piers himself told me little enough about the long private sessions he had with Akkad.

There was Anne Dunbar the Ambassador's daughter, Angelo Tomasso the great surgeon, Spiro Harari the jeweller, Jean Makaro the policeman, Luther Fox of the Military Mission, Ahmed Osmanli the banker, and several others whose faces were unfamiliar. Later we were to get to know them well. The general atmosphere was that of a relaxed and pleasant cocktail party in the desert, softly lit and silently served to us by numerous servants, white-gloved and impassive Nubians.

There was no special suggestion that all the guests belonged to any particular religious or political persuasion; it was simply another social occasion. Conversation was free and unstudied. Introductions took place, people met for the first time – or so it seemed. Banter and low laughter swayed about the huge tent, swayed among the shadows thrown by the brilliant candelabra pendant on their inverted stems above the white napery of the central table. The night smelt of jasmine and hot wax. The sandy floor of the desert was hidden by a thick pile of magnificent carpets which insulated us against the slight evening damps; an elaborate series of dishes, both hot and cold, found their way on to the buffet – all in the best traditions of Egypt. The finesse and the organisation of the feast in such an out-of-the-way spot could not help but set one musing. And so the evening gradually condensed itself harmoniously and prolonged itself through the wines to the coffee and cigars without anything untoward having taken place. I myself, touched by the ardour of Piers, could not help feeling regretfully that this was perhaps all that we were going to be shown of the group's activities. I don't know why, I had not much faith in the reality represented by such breakaway sects as gnostics, and I was on my guard against the spuriously romantic. In Egypt it seemed dangerously easy to succumb to the folklore of the place – and this my friend appeared to have done. "Ah! Piers," I said, looking into his pale and impatient face. "You are in for another disappointment I fear." He clutched my wrist and shook his head; he was in a fever of excited anticipation, and his eyes followed Akkad everywhere. I loved him most when he was like this – I could read the moods of Sylvie written in his youthful eyes, which kindled almost vengefully under the spur of his emotions. "Patience," he said, pleadingly, and added: "Here comes Sabine again." Akkad was talking earnestly to a tall man in uniform.

Sabine disengaged herself from the rest of the company and came slowly towards us with that air of simple insolence which was perhaps merely a by-product of her costume – for

she was clad again like a sort of gipsy, and had travelled into
Cairo with a caravan from Tunis. Her hair and palms were
stained with henna and her eyes were dazed and stupefied-
looking from belladonna and badly applied kohl. Her feet were
bare and dirty, her toenails broken. I felt that she somehow
enjoyed disgusting people – there was no reason for wearing
fancy dress at such a gathering. She also seemed somehow
heavier, more obese, but perhaps this was due simply to the
lapping of quilted petticoats which covered her. At any rate
she looked very much the crafty gipsy of the oriental fairy-
tales, and the glass of champagne in her hand seemed almost
out of place. She stood before us, smiling from one to the other
for a moment, and then asked: "Is Toby with you? He said
he'd come." I made a vague gesture in the direction that Toby
had taken and she moved off to follow him, shaking her dark
stone-carving of a head with a little gesture of impatience and
determination. I had never really cared for Sabine and Piers
knew it; he watched me watching her with an amused irony.
"Say it," he said at last. "Why don't you say it?" I sighed at
being found out.

"Very well, I shall say it. Now that I know her her very
pretentiousness irritates me – thrusting her profligacy down
our throats all the time . . ." Piers laughed softly at my
sanctimonious choice of the words. "A desert father," he said
with his tender yet teasing eye. "Come my dear fellow." I felt
called upon to justify some of the irritation I felt with Sabine.
"I am not", I said, "the only one she irritates. Ask those Jewish
merchants who travelled with her in the caravan." Piers
nodded, with a certain indifference. "Moreover", I went on,
"she came and asked me for a consultation, and I found that she
was being treated for syphilis with herbs by a camel driver."

"Why not?"

"It's a waste of time, you know perfectly well why not."

I think really that it was her utter indifference to her

condition which most infuriated me; or was it because of Toby?
At any rate I had told her what I knew about 606, and asked
Akkad to send her to a specialist. In those days I was in the full
flush of my scientific knowledge – unaware that the dogmatic
theology of science was itself a kind of folklore, and that even
the most perfect specific sometimes failed to work. Youth
inclines towards the absolute in everything. I continued my
complaint as I watched her dark saturnine head moving among
the others, hunting for my friend. "Although she was still
highly infectious she took Toby away to the Fayum for a week."

"You are wrong about her," said Piers, "simply because
you don't know all her qualities. I asked her what she thought
of Rob Sutcliffe and why she did not marry him, and she said:
'I have never been able to envisage a love without jealousy and
exclusiveness, and have never dared to risk the business.' I
then asked her if that did not make us seem suspect to her and
she said yes it did. 'You are not real, you are figments of yourselves, love on all fours, *amour à quatre pattes*. The conventional
ménage à trois reversed.' I admit this wounded me. Then she
went on 'But then love doesn't need decoding like a cipher.'"

"She was wrong," I said. "It does. Like a cipher or a
riddle to which the answer is always ambiguous in a Delphic
way. Besides, did you think I was not jealous?"

Toby had told us that Rob Sutcliffe was planning to
sketch us into his new novel and I wondered vaguely what his
verdict on us might be – in the light of all the freshly turned
earth thrown up during his stay in Vienna. My sister had been
unsuccessfully psychoanalysed there during a long moment –
which was quite sufficient to enable Rob to acquire a bit of the
prevailing jargon which made life so distressing for everyone,
and conferred such an air of knowledgeable impertinence on
the devotees of old Freud. A little knowledge is a dangerous
thing, and these findings about the penetralia of sexual life
gave the writer a sort of justification for a native acerbity.

Afterwards, when love left him in the lurch and he became the wounded man who was such a trial to us all, he took refuge in a laughter and cynicism which were far from his real nature – a secretive one. He had at last discovered that love had no pith in it, and that the projection of one's own feelings upon the image of a beloved was in the long run an act of self-mutilation.

In the flicker of light from a dipping faltering candle I saw that slightly sardonic, slightly disdainful look, and it seemed to me full of a certain enigmatic maturity. Sabine was older than the rest of us – not in years, to be sure: but in judgement and insight. Her voyages and adventures had forged her mind already while we were still upon the threshold of our emotional maturity. The word I was looking for, I suppose, was "sphingine" – I thought of the baleful prehistoric smile of the Mycenaean women. She drew her shawl about her with a sudden gesture of dismissal, of renunciation, and shrugged her strong shoulders. Then she leaned forward to kiss the cheek of Sylvie with a humble gesture and to smile into her eyes. All at once there was something heart-appealing about this strong girl in her buoyant fancy dress – it was the warmth of a burning and candid intelligence. I saw what Sutcliffe had seen.

Much later of course I came to "recognise" her as one who, in her inner life, had thrown over the intermediaries of convention and reason which might have shielded her social self, in favour of direct vision, direct apprehension. This was the secret of her courage – of everything that made her seem so often *outré*, unconventional, out of scale. The small-minded found her simply rude and inconsiderate, whereas she was quite simply unaware of the fences they had set up about the notion of conventional behaviour. It was like being colour blind, say, or tone deaf. Once one realised this about her it was possible to make allowances, and to arrive at different conclusions about her. But it wasn't easy. For example, even now, dressed as she was . . . And then once she went outside and blew her nose in her fingers to the horror of the servants. But Akkad loved her, Akkad accepted her fully. I once saw them meet, put out their hands like antennae and touch softly, sighing both and smiling with the kind of joyous feeling normal in lovers – which they were not. Yet he loved her because there was never any need to tell her anything, to explain, to expound. At least this is what his looks sought to convey. While in his presence she seemed to become younger and shyer, less assertive, more humble. For her part her meek looks seemed to be saying: "He knows everything, he understands everything – but best of all, he knows that it is of no importance whatsoever. No need to plead, no need to convince."

Piers followed my glance as well as read my mind as I formulated these thoughts. He said mischievously: "I think that you really envy her, because she makes love *à tous les quatre vents* without ascribing an absolute value to the act: whereas we three are in the grip of an infatuation which goes on and on. How strange to have lost one's taste for other people – like losing one's sense of smell almost: why is there no word for it in English? We have deaf and blind, but nothing to describe the lost sense of smell . . . or the loss of the other thing for that matter."

Akkad was slowly making his way towards us now, and one could feel a sort of leisurely intent in his movements; nor was I wrong, for he came up to take Piers tenderly by the sleeve and place his other hand upon my own arm. "In a little while," he said, drawing us both together, "we shall invite you to come into the shrine of old Abu Menouf with the rest of us for what will be something like a religious service – or a reading of the psalms. I will be doing the commentary and the exposition. If you get bored, do not hesitate to leave and come back here. No offence will be taken. It is understood that you could be potential members of the group though as yet not set in your resolve. There will be others like you also, so do not feel that you are all alone. It should not be more painful than one of the traditional lectures on the Koran that you have heard, given by a venerable old sheik in Cairo; but of course the subject will be heretical from all points of view." He laughed soundlessly, and spread his hands out in a gesture of quaint helplessness. "What would you have us to do – sit down under the great lie and accept the rule of one we call the Prince of Darkness?" The tone in which he said this suggested more the deliberations of a stockbroker than the lucubrations of a bigot.

He went on in a lower tone: "It is not a question of making a small compromise on behalf of happiness – it cuts far deeper. Once you see the truth the way we see it you simply cannot refuse to accept. You are surrounded, cut off, severed for ever from the world as you have been living it, lost, sunk, foundered . . ." His tone remained wryly quizzical, sardonic, but his eye was very much alive, with its strange glaucous movements. As for myself, this very absence of a definitive attitude, this shying away from the mantic or the vatic, filled me with misgivings. I was young and anxious to be carried away, to be swept off my feet – just as much as my friend. But in this domain mere logical arguments, mere theological prevarications didn't seem to me to be what I was looking for. If the sort of conviction that Akkad implied was what we desired, why then rational argument was not the way to foster it. Romantic? Yes. We had every right to be. We dreamed of a perfect conviction of the truth of being which would be independent of arguable proof. Akkad stood before us in his much darned abba – the one he wore to paint his vivid water colours – and smiled his jubilant and dreamy smile. No, it would not do – at least that is how I felt. If the whole sum of human knowledge had to be put to the question then only a prophet of wrath, a poet of wrath, could do it, and could carry us with him over the rapids into the new country which was, according to our friend, waiting to claim us. Something of all this – doubts, hesitations – may have been visible on our faces for Akkad hesitated once more before resuming his more solemn manner. He looked at his slim watch and made an almost imperceptible sign to the major-domo, the tall aristo-cratic Arab who had met us on the black horse at the entrance to the oasis. The servants began slowly to bring in light silk prayer-mats and small cushions – the colour green predomin-ated. These we placed over our arms as we prepared to leave the tent for the shrine. But we were not as numerous as I had surmised – a full third of the company appeared not to belong to our group, and not therefore to be in the secret of our private congregation about the sepulchre of Abu Menouf. It was, then, an ordinary holiday cocktail party on to which Akkad had grafted the members of his little sect. It was, so to speak, a small intermission in the general celebrations of the Moslem fair, the noise of which we could still hear reverberating out-side the brilliant walls of our enclosure. So gradually, without prejudicing the pleasant atmosphere of the party, we sidled towards the entrance, following Akkad, who waited a while at the door and then turned to lead the way.

A brilliant moon poured its molten light into the lake where the tall reeds, turned ink-black or pure quicksilver according to angle, stood rooted once in their own reflections, then twice in the light clay floor of the depression. The sand of the desert could have been snow. Still as plate glass the whole world, except where here or there an insect incised the glowing surface with its struggles, and sent small wrinkles shoreward. The sky was cloudless – the moon rolled across the surface like a lamb searching for its dam. The desert air struck chill as we wound along the palm-groves towards the shrine. A dim light could be discerned from it, shining through the windows covered in painted wax paper. In and out of darkness we were moonsplashed so that one had little unaccustomed glimpses of each other's faces. I saw Akkad turned by such an accident into a grim mummy, Sabine smiled with white monkey's teeth, Casimir Ava shorn of his hair by a trick of the light looked like an old lady at prayer. I had the illusion that our numbers were swelled, not by candidates from the cocktail party, but by other unknown people who had been waiting outside in the darkness, and who now attached themselves to our procession.

The two dervishes, unkempt and forlorn though they were, held the door open for us, watchful as mastiffs. They gave the impression of knowing exactly who belonged and who did not, but this must have been an illusion for they did not know us, for example, and yet they signalled us to pass with the rest. A dark narrow stairway led us into the body of the little mosque – into a large central room very dimly lighted by tiny night-lights floating in saucers of olive oil. Because of the darkness the domed ceiling seemed as high as the sky outside, and by consequence our figures appeared diminished, and as if they were rapidly melting back into the darkness from which apparently they had been summoned.

The form of the ceremony was easy enough to discern – it was, as he had said, exactly like a Cairo sheik delivering a theological lecture in a mosque. Akkad was to be seated in the middle of the floor upon a carpet and cushion with a low table of inlaid wood some distance before him. Placed to his right and left were other tables and cushions placed for his two acolytes – one an old blind man in a white robe, the other a swarthy and bearded man of middle age in a crumpled lounge suit, but with no collar. He looked like a retired postmaster. In his hand he held a bundle of texts and a book, which he consulted, and he had the air of a stage-prompter; while the old blind man looked like one of those itinerant "singing" priests, beadles or sacristans, who can always be summoned to chant verses from the Koran in time of need. These dispositions taken up, we the auditors formed a circle at a distance round the trio, being all seated with the greatest regularity upon the

ground, and while nobody actually marshalled us in any
particular order we felt that an order had insensibly been
conformed to: the inner circle consisted of those who were
more or less the real initiates of the group and the circles
moved outward until they came to us, who were simply "onlookers with intent", as Akkad called us.

For his part he sat himself down in the sheik's place,
removed his glasses and clasped his hands before him as he
gazed dreamily up into the darkness of the mosque. We knelt
or sat in silence. The blind man waited with his chin on his
breast, breathing softly, his hearing tuned, it seemed, to concert pitch, waiting for a sign. The other scruffy individual
consulted a pile of texts and then clearing his throat coldly
announced a reading from the Pistis Sophia – but for all the
world as if he were announcing a reading from the weather
almanac. A further silence followed. Akkad appeared to pray
now, for he extended his long fingers and held up his clasped
hands. Then he leaned forward and tapped with a fingernail on
the little inlaid table. The old blind man drew a joyous slow
breath, and with a smile – looking upwards now with an
expression of great sanctity – started slowly and melodically to
recite. All three smiled at the familiar opening phrases – as
musicians might smile as they joined forces to interpret a piece
of music long known by all and loved. But the recitation was in
Greek – somewhat to my surprise; and while only the old man
uttered the words the lips of the other two men moved caress-
ingly over the polished and familiar phrases. If I say I was
surprised at the Greek it was because (knowing nothing then
of such matters) Akkad had given us to understand that the
Pistis Sophia was a Coptic text written in that language. This
was indeed so, but the Coptic of which he spoke was itself a
translation from the Greek, so that the text we were hearing
was the original from which the Coptic translators had worked.
Piers, whose scholarship was really quite profound, later

claimed to have followed nearly the whole reading with tolerable accuracy. Myself not. But the asides of Akkad were delivered in French or English and served as a quite spontaneous
commentary upon the text, uttered with too great an informality to suggest prayer, but with the deep reverence one
accords to great poetry or great music. "And it came to pass
when Jesus had risen from the dead, that he passed eleven
years discoursing with his disciples, and instructing them only
up to the regions of the First Commandment, up to the First
Mystery, that within the Veil, within the First Commandment,
which is the four and twentieth Mystery without and below –
those four and twenty which are in the second space of the
First Mystery which is above all Mysteries – the Father in the
form of a dove." (Later I came upon the translation of Mead,
and others, from the Bruce Codex and similar sources and was
so able to document myself a little bit about this weird post-
resurrectional history of Jesus.)

The odd thing about it was that it sounded not at all
oracular, but in a queer way perfectly intelligible, perfectly
sound as sense – when quite obviously if one doesn't know the
terminology, as we did not, it is the purest gibberish. I could
not judge either in what precise degree the rest of the sect
interpreted this monotonous chanting. Their heads were
bowed, except when Akkad broke into the recitation with a
dry staccato observation speaking often with a kind of restrained passion which was foreign to his ordinary comport-
ment. Such as "The more you know of man the less can you
condone the human situation under the Prince." A fearful act
of duplicity had overturned the rational order or the universe –
that is what he meant I afterwards realised. The interloper, who
had replaced the original monarch of the ages, had thrown into
confusion the workings of cosmic law. Since he came, the
Black Prince, everything had to be re-ordered, reapprehended,
reshaped; the whole of reality therefore. "The Greeks said 'All

this is untrue but it is beautiful.' But beauty is no excuse. Beauty is a trap. We say 'All this is untrue but it is real.' "

It was much later that I realised what he meant – to be of this persuasion was to remain truthful to the fundamental despair of reality, to realise finally and completely that there was no hope unless the usurping God could be dethroned, and that there seemed to be no way to do that. Had I understood more at this first encounter with the gnostics I should have been filled with the same despair as they presumably were. The implacability of process would have haunted me, as it came to haunt me later. What Akkad himself called "The very death of God", for the usurping prince had made away with the original king whose reign had been an illustration, not of nature's discord, but of nature's harmony and congruence. Under him birth and death had been fully realised, spirit and flesh, animal, insect and man were joined in a creative symbiosis of light and justice – such as we had not dared even to conceive since the date when the Prince of Darkness took his place on the throne.

I cannot say that all this did not confuse me, for it did; yet in a strange sort of way I felt that from time to time things deviated into profound sense. It is as if someone were reading to me in a language I knew but imperfectly; little patches of meaning floated out to me, sandwiched in between long passages of meaningless sound. Akkad's oracular interventions were often apt and indeed beautiful. "Who are they, then, these people? They are those who are born and reborn again unlike the Many. They recognise each other when they meet without a word being exchanged. They belong to the vertigo of nothingness, having emerged from the root of all dissent. The thrust of their souls is towards the moon of non-being, their God is he who no longer exists. How can they hope to make themselves understood? Reason is powerless – for this kind of understanding can only be soundless, wordless, breathless. Its meaning is as precarious as reality itself." Strange to read these words many years afterwards and to remember the circumstances of their delivery with such vivid accuracy. Without even closing my eyes I saw him, sitting there in his shabby old abba, looking suddenly very much older and moved almost to tears by the message he had to deliver. All the beautiful women listened, silent as fruit, some in evening dress, some in coloured shawls, all with apple-calm minds.

Part of it was litany and part ritual for once or twice the man who seemed like a prompter blew out the candles and relit them, as if to mark a distinct pause in the proceedings. He also proposed texts, uttering the first line in a solemn twang and waiting until the blind man recognised the passage and then, lifting his head like a dog, joined in on a higher register. Piers was rapt and attentive, and at the same time disappointed, I could see that; while his sister had closed her eyes and let her head fall forward, as if she were listening to music. "Thereafter there cometh a receiver of the little Sabaoth, the Good, him of the Midst: He himself bringeth a cup full of thoughts and wisdom, and soberness is in it; and he handeth it to the soul. And they cast it into a body which can neither sleep nor forget because of the cup of soberness which hath been handed unto it. But it will whip its heart persistently to question about the mysteries of the Light until at last it find them through the decision of the Virgin of Light, and so inherit the light itself forever."

I was far away as yet from "seeing" in the gnostic sense that night – of acquiring that penetrating vision which could turn us all to masks and caricatures of reality with names, mere labels; each one of us nevertheless with an "eidolon" or signature, a disposition, a proclivity visible to the naked eye of the intuition only. Within each of us struggled man, woman and child. Our passions were packed in the cool clay of our silences, ready for the oven, ready for the mystical marriage feast. . . . In this sense, and in this sense only, did I find a perfectly satisfactory rationale which subsumed my double relationship with Piers and with his sister. It was through this experience with Akkad and his sect that I at last managed to gain a foothold in that part of reality which was probably my own inner self. It may sound strange, but I now understood the nature of my love – and also the nature of human love as a whole. I saw quite unmistakably that man had set astray the natural periodicity of sexuality and so forfeited his partnership with the animal kingdom. This was his central trauma, and it also signalled the final loss of his powers over the matter – that was coming . . .

Yet despite the apparent informality of the proceedings which amounted almost to laxness one could feel underneath the structure of a method. I had the impression that something was being conveyed to me as a sense impression, and not being made rationally explicit in order not to indulge my natural faculty of ratiocination. After all you cannot ask a perfume or a sound to explain itself. By the same token I simply inhaled all this lore without trying my mind on it, trying to reduce it to some sort of canonical formula.

All this and much more was borne in my consciousness on that strange night; despite my misgivings and my distrust of hocus pocus. . . . The incident of the snake and the mummia and the wine when it came seemed absolutely natural and not a mere seductive folklore to gain adherents or convince doubters. One of the dervishes brought a large flat wicker basket which he placed at the feet of Akkad, who lifted the lid from it and disclosed a very large snake – a species of cobra which I had not seen before. It was very much bigger than the ordinary Egyptian cobra and could have perhaps been Indian. But its colour was extraordinary – a kind of nacreous pink shading into violet underneath its body. It appeared as domesticated as a household pet. It looked about with its forked tongue flicking softly in and out of its cruel white mouth; its hood was not fully inflated. A saucer of milk was placed for it with some dead flies floating in it and it leaned forward delicately to lap like a pet; indeed to facilitate the meal it slipped out of its soft basket giving us a chance to marvel at its great length. Akkad stroked it in familiar fashion, and it accepted his caress as a cat might, flattening its head and extending it for the touch of his palm. After a pause the recitation went on, though all eyes were now on the snake. When the reptile had finished its meal Akkad took it up softly and came towards us holding it in his arms, draped around him, curled, oozing, swaying. We were each of us to stroke its head, so he told us; and in spite of our fear and revulsion we made an effort to do so.

Piers and his sister passed the test easily but in my case and Toby's the snake appeared to hesitate and ruminate, and when we put out a hand it uttered a slight hiss. "Insist quietly," said Akkad, "and don't be afraid of it." It was easy to say, and we did our best to comply with his instructions, but I did not feel that the perfunctory pat on the head I gave it amounted to very much. When it came to Sabine's turn Akkad simply emptied it into her arms and snake and woman seemed to sink into a complete embrace. She murmured the sort of endearments one might reserve for a favourite kitten, stroking its head and winding it around her body. It took some time to complete this little ceremony for everyone had to touch it in turn; but when it was completed Akkad took it back to its basket and coaxed it to resume its position inside it – erect and ever-watchful however. Now some batons of incense had been lighted by the dervishes and clouds of aromatic perfume rolled about the dark corners of the mosque, obscuring outlines and transforming faces and forms. The recitation with its melodious but twanging Greek shifted key, moved in the direction of greater emphasis, as if kindled by the waves of perfume on the dark night.

Akkad sat listening, his head now bowed, like a man under a waterfall; but it seemed that he was waiting for a particular passage or a special break in the litany, for suddenly he raised his finger and the reciters paused. "Now let us partake of the holy mummia," he said in commanding tones and the dervishes advanced towards us humbly bearing large silver trays on which were a number of small bowls with pieces of mummia – or at least I presumed it was mummia. Dried mummy-flesh had been a standby in medicine for centuries, and as a doctor in bud I was curious to taste it. But dark Sylvie shuddered. The little strips of flesh were quite dry, quite dehydrated. The consistency was that of the dried fish known as Bombay duck; but the colour was a dark red, almost crimson, and the taste was faint and tenuous. I tried to place it, and found myself thinking of a faint perfume of celery. It reminded me a little of French froglegs, or the dried locusts I had once eaten in the desert outside Cairo. I despatched a wafer or two of this magic comestible without undue anxiety and watched the quantity gradually diminish as each one of us in the circle took up his portion. Akkad watched it all solemnly; but there was no specially ritual aspect to this part of the ceremony. When everyone had partaken of the mummia the dishes were taken away and Akkad, once more interrupting the recitation said: "Now let us partake of the wine."

Flagons were now brought made of some strange pottery, and in each flagon there was perhaps a teacupful of a wine mixture which tasted salt and tepid; we waited until the whole company was served and then, in response to the same gesture by Akkad, raised our receptacles in an attitude of toasting before draining them. This was the point at which I realised that some of my misgivings had been soundly based – for the wine was powerfully drugged, and one instantly felt one's senses sag and falter. Everything now began to mix and flow – what with the clouds of incense and the staccato note of the chanting, you could quite clearly feel the sudden distortion set in as the vision changed focus; yet it was not at all alarming, we were all quite at ease. Perhaps we were reassured by Akkad who said: "It will not last long," as he saw the obvious signs of our struggle against the drug.

He added, sweeping our faces with his glance: "Keep your gaze on Ophis the snake." For my part I stared at the snake with all the wild intensity of a pilot seeking a passage across a fog-bound estuary; it was partly due to visibility and partly to the drug we had taken. Everything now rose and subsided, wobbled and merged and deliquesced. The ancient serpent itself appeared to rear up to twice its height in order to present itself more clearly to us, in order as it were to preside more fully over the ceremony. But anything I say about this part of the evening is subject to caution – for we were so obviously and woefully dazed by the potion. I recall the voice of Toby saying, with a kind of triumphant indignation: "Mumbo Jumbo by Jove." But he said it unwillingly, almost sleepily, as though all but carried away by what he saw despite his native reservations. "The eyes," cried Akkad sharply, "look at the eyes."

I looked at the tiny glittering eyes of Ophis, and it gave back my glance with a queer malevolent glitter, an insinuating flicker of that forked tongue. So staring, I felt that I was rushing towards it, its head became enormous, its delicate hinged jaws open to expose long scimitar-like teeth, so white and clean. A wild revulsion rose in me, and I felt all of a sudden as if I were suffocating; I struggled to free my neck from the collar of the garment I wore, to breathe more freely. Then I shook the vision out of my eyes like someone shaking back clear-sightedness after a severe concussion brought about by a blow on the head.

It was something like a battle of will-powers. The serpent was trying to engulf me, like a python with a hare, and

I was quite determined to keep myself free. All this rose to the boil, so to speak, and then burst like a bubble, and as it did so I saw what later I was to recognise as our mentor, the usurping Prince, seated in place of the serpent, staring at me with a kind of bloodthirsty jocularity. How difficult it is to describe this sort of vision; yes, we all have the capacity during a dream to fabricate this sort of thing. But this was somehow different, though I cannot for the life of me explain just how. I saw a snake no longer but a kind of huge dung-bettle with the head of a dog; its body was armour-plated like a saurian, with black polished scales, like the body-armour of a Japanese swordsman. A single goat's hoof was visible outside the snake-basket, standing on the flags of the mosque. This whole vision kept dissolving and reappearing in the vast clouds of incense. Yet it was not quite a vision – it was certainly a Thing of particular consequence to me. I could not just dismiss it as a piece of reality distorted by a drug or a dose of alcohol. I was profoundly impressed and depressed by it, and I had a nagging feeling that nothing would ever be the same again for me. Absurd, of course, absurd.

Looking so fixedly at this strange machine-like animal-bird-insect I felt as if it were talking to me, felt it had the sort of significance which one cannot render clear by words, a deep symbolic significance of something which by-passed causality. The alchemists apparently have to deal with this sort of symbol in their work; but I was no alchemist, and I knew little enough about orders of knowledge which were not rudely scientific. I also shared a good deal of Toby's dogged scepticism. But there was much of which I was then unaware – and for example, at this very moment I was unaware that I had let out something between a shout and a shriek and tried to leap to my feet and advance on the snake. Toby heard me faintly and told me later on. Yet all movement was impossible – I was paralysed. Moreover I was all of a sudden exhausted, racked with sobs; the current turned itself off with a magical suddenness, and just as if I had depended upon it to sit upright, I found myself falling forward upon my hands. I felt my cheek touching the cold flags of the room as I came to my senses, slowly, trembling all over. When at last I raised my eyes it was to see that almost everyone in the company was in the same case, lying utterly exhausted on their carpets, tremulously breathing and gasping. It had lasted a very short time, the visionary incident. It had drained us of our attention and then left us stranded like objects on a beach at low tide. I have seldom felt so physically exhausted.

But there was one exception to the general state of exhaustion – and that was constituted by the behaviour of poor Piers which differed completely from our own. He was plainly choking, with both hands trying to tear an invisible serpent from his throat; he rose to his knees, writhing, fighting, gasping with weakness. He rolled over on his side, still struggling – and his miming of the snake, something huge like a boa, was so lifelike that for a moment one almost saw the reptile sliding round him, squeezing the breath from his body. As I say, all this was so very lifelike, and his distress so great that I started feebly to try and rouse myself to go to his aid, but Akkad smilingly bade me desist; in fact he looked highly delighted by this mimic battle and by the deep anxiety of my friend. Later he was to tell me, for what it was worth, that it confirmed the initiation of Piers, and his inclusion without further probation into the sect. He had been granted the particular sign of the snake-covenant. Myself I was reminded when he said this of the Aesculapian snake and the *incubatio* in the white colonnades of Epidaurus where the doctors interpreted the first night's sleep according to the snake-dreams of the patient. Yes, there were many connections which Akkad helped me to work out during the short time I was in Egypt with him, many resonances and affiliations.

Piers had gone so white and still that he seemed dead. But to tell the truth everyone showed the same signs of utter blank exhaustion in varying degrees, and presently at a sign from Akkad the servants appeared with soft wraps which they laid upon the recumbent forms. The great snake disappeared. Somewhere a door opened and a cold whiff of desert air entered to chase the columns of incense and bring a breathable atmosphere into the mosque. But we were all utterly dead with sleep, all of us; myself I lay in a state of dreamy half-convales-cence like a child at breast. I felt the soft material draped over me and the cushion adjusted under my head by an invisible hand, and I allowed myself to founder softly into nothingness, worn out with all I had experienced. When I awoke with a jolt it was early dawn already, and all the other sleepers had vanished with the exception of Piers who had crawled to my side and now slept quietly with his head against my shoulder. Sylvie? Toby? Gone! Moreover everything was silent save for the hum of insects in the trees outside the mosque. The sun was just touching the rim of the horizon and the whole world was saffron and lion-gold. The cold cut to the very bone of thought. I took Piers' pulse. He seemed perfectly normal now – and indeed I myself felt completely recovered from the mysterious fatigue of the night before. I was full, too, of a physical exuber-ance unusual for me, and also a tremendous mental euphoria – the kind of feeling one gets after having, without deserving it, passed a difficult exam unexpectedly. "Piers," I whispered, "I'm going to have a swim." He did not open his eyes or say anything, but a tiny pucker of a smile came to the corner of his lips so that I knew he had heard me.

I went down the stairs into the crisp dawn light; the whole village slept. It looked like an abandoned battlefield. Only an occasional horse was stirring. I walked towards the looking-glass of the lake, eager to see my own reflection in it as if in some curious way I expected to have changed, to have altered

in my physical appearance. For what reason? I do not know –
only this abstract sense of jubilation and relief dogged my
steps, and I could offer myself no reason for it. I broke into a
run along the margins of the lake, looking sideways to see my
reflection racing through the massed spear-points of the reeds.
The sun came up like a bronze medallion and its regal heat
spilled over on to the damp sand, swiftly dispelling the heavy
night dews. I looked carefully to see if there were any of the
tell-tale black shells in the shallows which might portend
water infected by the dread bilharzia but there were none and
before I could think it I was up to my waist in the icy brilliance
of the lake water, consumed again by this inexplicable joy. I
swam out of my depth and turned over to let the sun fire a
million silver drops of prismatic light on to my wet eyelashes.
It was not too long either before a second figure joined me,
and then the third – the dark girl whom I could never see like
this without a contraction of the heart. I did not say "I love
you" aloud, nor did she. Our wet fingers touched and we
formed a circle like the corolla of a flower, floating into the
silence of the desert dawn with the ancient sun on our bodies.
It lasted a long time, this swim which seemed to have some
of the qualities of an esoteric act of lustration. We were all
somehow too excited to speak or exclaim; only our triumphant
eyes met from time to time to exchange jubilant glances. It is
true that once I asked Sylvie: "Did you see . . . ?" But she
drew her breath and, nodding, cut off my sentence, as if not
only had we shared the same vision but also that it did not bear
speaking about openly.

Piers smiled to himself. He looked vaguely preoccupied,
as if he were making an inventory of his feelings, were documenting something – an experience which threw the whole
range of his past feelings into relief, so that he was forced to
re-evaluate them all in the light of this new element. *What* new
element? *What* had he seen? At this point I recall the coarse

stentorian voice of Toby (who was waiting for us on the bank
with towels and clothes) as it uttered the words "Mumbo
Jumbo" – but rather defensively, I thought. We who knew
him so well could detect something artificial in the fervour of
his exclamation. Sylvie smiled. "Akkad is waiting," he added,
feeling the water with the tips of his fingers and deciding with a
shudder that it was too cold to join us in a swim. "I must take
you to him. It's an order."

We three dressed slowly, contentedly, still making no
allusion to our thoughts and yet somehow deeply conscious
that whatever they were they had become the common property
of the three of us. It was like an extension of our loving – a sort
of new tropical flora and fauna, a private country in which we
wandered now, luxuriating in all its poetic beauty and variety.
No horses attended us here, so we set off to wander across the
sand together, led by scarlet Toby, who knew the way and who
had orders to take us to Akkad for our breakfast. It was not so
very far; we skirted some great silken mounds of dune and
came at last to a bare stone plateau, its surface worn smooth by
centuries of blowing sand so that even the coloured striations
in the rock were smooth-graven, as if by an emery board. I
had forgotten all about the little aeroplane of our host. It
looked somehow vulnerable and primitive standing out there
in the sunlight; like an insect. But bizarrely enough Akkad sat
under it in a throne-like barber's chair with inlaid arms
smothered in decorations of copper and false pearl: and with a
white cloth spread over him. His barber Fahem (we called him
the Court Figaro) bent reverently over him to lather his cheeks
while a small boy, also dressed in white, kept the already
active flies away with a whisk. It was one of the pleasing little
opulences of Alexandria for a rich man to have a portable
barber; normally businessmen in Egypt did not shave at home.
Their barbers waited in the ante-room to their offices with all
their instruments. So they were shaved ceremoniously while

sitting at their desks and sorting out the morning mail with the help of their secretaries. Akkad had simply extended the bounds of this feudal tradition; whenever he went by plane he took his own barber along. Now he peered at us shortsightedly but with an obvious pleasure – an air almost of congratulation. From the depths of a steaming towel he even said: "Come closer, I want to see your faces." And when we obliged he gazed at us keenly and then gave a sigh. "Yes," he said, "I can see that you saw him; you look so happy. And you, Piers, were accepted at once. It was a cardinal sign, your struggle with Ophis. I can read your heart, and yours too, Sylvie; for you there is going to be no looking back." Then turning to me he said: "The traditions of your education have hampered you a bit but nevertheless you saw what they did, and in the long run your native scepticism will give way to acceptance. It will be slower, that is all. But you will catch them up." Mysterious words! He submitted with a long-suffering comical grimace: to the barber's massage and the wheezing spray of toilet water spurted on his scalp. Toby said stoutly and somewhat surprisingly: "I saw nothing except a lot of smoke. I don't know what the others saw but I saw nothing."

Akkad looked at him curiously and withal in kindly fashion as if he were genuinely puzzled; for my part, it seemed to me clear from Toby's tone that he was prevaricating. But Akkad pondered the question for a long moment with closed eyes, as if he were verifying something in his memory. Then he said: "Yes, but you did see something; I will tell you what you saw. You saw something that looked like a brass rubbing from an English cathedral – the tomb of the Black Prince in somewhere like Canterbury. The vizor of the helmet was up, and you got scared when you stared into the black hole of the armoured head because you thought you saw the glitter of snake-eyes where the face should have been." Toby's jaw dropped and he turned rather pale. "How did you know that?"

he gasped, quite forgetting to deny the truth of the allegation. Akkad shrugged his shoulders and adjusted his spectacles on his nose again the better to study his man. "I was puzzled at first," he said mildly. "But now I see why you denied the whole thing; you have confused the biblical Jesus with the post-resurrectional Jesus in the gnostic context. He is simply a cipher for us. He has no connection with what you call Our Saviour (as you say quite rightly one only has to mention his name and blood starts flowing). Our Jesus comes much later in the day, and even he proved powerless to dethrone the personage you all saw last night who has had a thousand names, among them Sathanas and Lucifer. As each one brings a little of himself to what he sees you brought the trappings of your historic preoccupations, so that Monsieur flattered you by presenting himself with beaver up like Hamlet's father's ghost!" He roared with laughter and struck his knee.

Toby was as confused and discountenanced as any school-boy; but Akkad took him affectionately by the arm and said still laughing: "Come into the next room, I mean the next dune. I have ordered an absurd English breakfast for you all. After that I shall take you for a ride down to the sea and batter you with a little bit of theology – though not you yet, Toby. You are recalcitrant as yet. Your time will come later." The sun-shine was already baking and I was glad of our straw hats which Toby had brought with him; in a cloudless blue sky vultures hovered. We climbed the scarp into the next depres-sion, and really could not help bursting into laughter ourselves, the scene was so surrealist. In the middle of the sand, looking incongruously without a relevant context, stood a long table covered in spotless napery on which Akkad's munificence had caused to be laid out a superlative English breakfast of a sort that only the great country houses might have provided in the past. Leaving aside the sausages and tomatoes grilling quietly in the silver chafing-dishes, there were also several kinds of fish, including haddock and kipper, and also, laughably enough, a dish of warm kedgeree with eggs on horseback; the whole was backed up with two kinds of marmalade. We were served (on beautiful plate) by two nubian servants with gold sashes and white gloves.

Akkad was delighted with our laughter and smiled slyly as he said: "It's not what the others will be getting at all. I thought a sort of confirmation breakfast would be in order. I'm sorry to keep striking this public-school note, Piers, but my upbringing included a memorable English spell at Mournfield which I have never forgotten and which supplied me with a host of affectionate memories and many good friends." So, still smiling over this extraordinary desert scene we took our places and tucked into this breakfast with a will. "Afterwards we will ride," said Akkad. "But just you three and myself. We shall leave Toby behind to look after Sabine until we come back. You see, now that you have seen what you have seen I can fill in the picture a little with more factual things, with texts and little commentaries which relate to your presence here. You see, all this was not an accident – I mean your coming to Egypt at this time, and to me. I saw it happening several years ago during the same period of the year in the same shrine. Of course I did not know your names, but I knew you by sight and I knew your circumstances with tolerable accuracy. I was able to judge what you might do to help or hinder the group in its activities. I was also able to predict the degree to which you yourselves would benefit from the creed of the sect, the tenets of this gnosticism – which seems at first so forbidding." He was silent for a long moment now, smoking a slim cigar and drinking his coffee. "No. It was no accident," he said. "And indeed your circumstances are unlike those of most of the others – the special relationship to sex and the understanding of love in your sense . . . This was what we believe but few of us had ever experienced, at least in the singularly pure form which you seem to have realised. We will speak about that today."

No more was said; Piers hung his head and looked somewhat shy at this reference to sex, for he was always extremely *pudique* about such personal and private exchanges, and shuddered at any kind of coarse allusions to matters which he considered so agonisingly important, so very close to his heart. I think this excessive delicacy used to irritate Sabine who always tried to puncture what she regarded as an inexperienced and juvenile reserve. But then she had never made love to him –it would have surprised her. But Akkad on the contrary seemed to appreciate and respect this delicacy in him; he would not I think have agreed to Sabine's strictures (so openly and honestly expressed) when she said: "Ach, you and your little sister are overbred and over-refined. You need a streak of coarseness in your lives." She may have been right, she may have been counting upon me to supply the missing factor?

When this baroque breakfast of Akkad's had come to an end a messenger was despatched to summon the horses and bring a small picnic for each of us. "I am going to take you down to the sea, but in a different place where you have never been," said Akkad who enjoyed putting on a childish air of mystery. "A secret place," he added slyly. And then as we were mounting the horses and trying out stirrup-lengths and reins he said: "By the way, in case any one asks you, you must say that you went to a lecture at Abu Menouf, but not mention the word gnostic. You see the shrine was founded in memory of a great Wali, seer, holy man – but apparently a Mohammedan. Here in Egypt we try never to offend religious susceptibilities, and the dervishes are convinced that what we are doing here is having a quite orthodox religious service in the memory of the Saint. So we are. So we are. But Abu Menouf himself was a gnostic, and this oasis being far off the beaten track seemed a suitable place for our gatherings. We did not wish to trouble the authorities with our beliefs which have nothing to do with the social or political situation of the country. We gather twice or thrice a year here for this precise purpose. Our own patron saint is the Aescupalian snake you saw, though the dervishes are convinced that the soul (the Moslem soul) of Abu Menouf went into it when he died. It would be a nice theological point to try and establish whether Ophis is Moslem or gnostic. One day we will ask it.

"For the moment however, we claim it in the name of Abu Menouf himself who was an extraordinary old man, a wanderer over the face of the earth, a great interpreter of dreams and visions. The snake may well be his soul revisiting us – they both liked milk, which to the dervishes is proof positive. For us it is, of course, a symbol of the caduceus of Aesculapius, of the spinal column, of the kundalini-serpent of the Indians – you will be able to trace the ancestry of the idea through many continents and many religions. It is also the sacred phallus of Greece and Egypt and India, as well as the coiled intestines from which one can perform a divination by entrails as our ancestors did. All this is an exoteric scale of reference, an explanation: but the actual naked experience of Ophis cannot as you will realise be properly put into words. It will be found quite mysteriously fruitful and enriching to remember as you get older, though you will never be able to analyse it and discover exactly why. But there is much you *can* discover, there are many meanings which *are* accessible to the reason. Now come, as Byron once said: 'Enough of this antiquarian twaddle. Let's have a swim.' Only we have a ride of about two hours before I can offer you a sand beach."

Akkad led away on an easterly course and at a good pace, considering the precocious heat of the sun; and Toby was left twisting his thumbs and looking abashed, as if he had been sent to Coventry, though Akkad assured him that this was no reprisal for his lack of candour about the ceremony. We faced an hour of soft riding now, until at last we came upon a chain of blood-red hills and a large stony valley littered with blocks of stone, of schist, of crystal, it seemed; the mouth was of considerable breadth, and it was intersected with parallel lines of rock ravine where, Akkad said, the gazelles came down at night in search of dew. This was the entry to a sombre region of petrified forest which stretched away down to the edge of the sea. The whole scene was littered with petrifacts of different sizes and kinds, enormous trees, weighing tons, bared of their branches, overthrown and turned to stone. It was a weird ride through this wilderness with its dead petroliths, its solid vegetation; almost symbolic it seemed, for Akkad said nothing as he led soberly on, skirting the recumbent tree-forms. Some of the tree-trunks measured about three feet in diameter, and were from thirty to fifty feet in length! The greater number were of a species of timber no longer known to Egypt, but there were also palms here and there melted stone-solid by wind and weather. The heat was intense here and the aspect of the place, so wild and abandoned, melancholy to a degree.

With what cries of relief we greeted the appearance of a herring-gull as it hovered curiously over us bringing us the certainty that we were at last near the sea; and then with what wild pleasure we heard at last the stentorian boom of the surf on the beaches which were awaiting us, lying dazed into pearl-blue nescience by the lick of the hot sun of midday. Like phantoms we stripped naked and fell into the bursting waves, to be swiftly sucked out seawards, out of the reach of the crashing surfline. The undertow drew its hissing breaths, dragging at our ankles, but we were all experienced in maintaining a reasonable distance from the shore and so we frolicked and swam in the deafening roaring of the water. It would be impossible to describe the sense of wild elation which now possessed us — perhaps it was youth and good spirits, perhaps it was something more. Perhaps it was what Akkad claimed both then and always afterwards, that we had passed through a kind of initiation into a new area of understanding. But so much of this remained to be explained still, and I could see he was rehearsing in his own mind how he was going to approach the subject with us. He had a horror of pomposity.

At last, sea-buffeted and breathless, salt-encrusted and brown as tobacco, we allowed ourselves to be thrown up on the beach. But here another small problem arose – the sand was too hot to tread barefoot, nor was there any shade right down at the sealine. Moreover it was obvious that we would have to dispute our lunch with some large golden hornets which had smelt the fruit and the wine. However, the petrified forest came down almost to the water's edge, and one or two of the few stone trees left upright promised us a small pool of shade which we lost no time accepting. Here it was deliciously cool, for a light fresh breeze crept down from the dunes. We unpacked our victuals and suddenly realised how very hungry we were; ravenously we attacked the sandwiches of cold goose and turkey. Thirstily we drank the wine and the iced water in its thermos flasks. Then at last we settled back, replete with food and physical well-being, to hear Akkad out; it was a strange spot, this forest of dark petrifacts, this grove of ankylosed trees. From time to time there would be a small crack and a brittle piece of a stone branch would break off in the heat and fall to the ground. We leaned our backs against the dead stone and listened while Akkad, now with an air of peculiar intensity, holding the edges of his bathing wrap together and looking somewhat like a large praying mantis, began the homily which was our first detailed introduction to the gnostic canon.

How to summarise what he had to tell us I do not know; for my own part the whole long speech passed through my consciousness like a rainbow silk of different colours. It was an exposition at once allusively poetical and factual, but knitted together with persuasive coherence, and formally, intellectually, quite watertight. I think I have never listened to anything with quite the same careful intensity as I brought to this first sermon by Akkad in the petrified forest. It was I suppose because I knew that he was going to explain things which up until then had seemed to me inexplicable. Best of all, he was going to provide some explanation of the drug-vision we had all experienced. So I closed my eyes and listened to that quiet seductive voice expounding the grand outlines of the gnostic scheme.

What did he say? I can remember even after so long. He began by speaking about the sense of inner estrangement and alienation from the so-called real world which was the mark of the religious nature when once it awakes from its sleep in the world. Sometimes it awoke spontaneously, of its own accord, sometimes in response to a vision or human experience of particular intensity, or by mere accident. When it woke it quested for a metaphysical frame to contain it, to nourish it like a plant, to make it fruitful. It sought a humus in which it could flower. Of all the religions in the world, and they were as numerous as the sands of the sea, there was nothing quite like this group of gnostic systems, shattered fragments of which were all we had available today in various tongues – so well had the organised religions of the so-called perfect Good done their work of extirpation. Their adherents could not bring themselves to face the bitter central truth of the gnostics: the horrifying realisation that the world of the Good God was a dead one, and that He had been replaced by a usurper – a God of Evil. Perhaps this sounded exaggerated to us, he said, but it was the heart of the belief, and the distress and alienation of the believers was due to the deeply implanted conviction that only a miracle would ever dethrone this great Demon of Darkness, who had waited his turn so patiently and who now sat in the judgement seat over all. It was the deep realisation of this truth, and its proclamation that had caused the gnostics to be suppressed, censored, destroyed. Humanity is too frail to face the truth about things – but to anyone who confronts the reality of nature and of process with a clear mind, the answer is completely inescapable: Evil rules the day.

What sort of God, the gnostic asks himself, could have organised things the way they are – this munching world of death and dissolution which pretends to have a Saviour, and a fountain of good at its base? What sort of God could have built this malefic machine of destruction, of self-immolation? Only the very spirit of the dark negative death-trend in nature – the spirit of nothingness and auto-annihilation. A world in which we are each other's food, each other's prey.

Swiftly Akkad sketched in two or three of these despairing systems, each bearing the impress of its inventor's personality in divergences of detail: but all united in this central despair about the metaphysical *status quo*. Slowly, in his quiet voice, with its flavours of an ever mounting disenchantment he sketched in the terrible fresco of the present world, often in the form of a long quotation which attested as always to the formidable memory of this strange man. "The praying Mantis which devours its male even while it is fecundating her, the spider trapping the fly, and the *pompile* which stabs the spider to death, the *ceceris* which with a triple stroke of its sword scientifically destroys the three centres of the *bupreste*'s nervous system: and carries it off so that its larvae will be able to eat it still living, choosing their mouthfuls with skill, preserving the vital parts with a terrible science, unto the very last mouthful of the victim's flesh. Then the *leucospis*, the *anthrax*, the worm of which simply applies itself to the flank of the *chalicodome*, and sucks it dry through the skin, ingests, pumps out this living broth which is the young larvae, and then dries it cunningly, in order to keep it also fresh, living, until the last mouthful ... The *philante*, the bee-killer, before even carrying off its victim presses out the crop to make it disgorge its honey, and sucks the tongue of the wretched dying insect as it sticks out of its mouth . . .". He went on then in French, stumbling over the scientific words for which he could not find an immediate translation in English, "Quel tableau que la Création! Un massacre général! Les lois les plus féroces, les plus barbares, les plus horriblement inhumaines: luttent pour la Vie, l'élimination des faibles, l'être mangeant l'être et mangé par l'être . . . Si dieu existe il ne peut être qu'une intelligence sans cœur. . . ." He paused for a moment and then said, almost under his breath: "What implacable logic." Silence. A long silence. A very long silence.

"Then is there another kind of sense which is not just nonsense?" asked Piers, but the question seemed more addressed to himself than to Akkad, and his only answer was a look which hovered on the edge of ironic amusement. It seemed to say: "You know the answer to that question – why ask it?" I realised then that the gnostic refusal to accept the state of things constituted a particular kind of bravery without vainglory, a despair without tarnish. Sylvie lay beside me, her head on my arm, breathing slowly and evenly, as if she were sleeping; but I could see from the set of her features that she was awake, and following. And now she said in a small musing voice: "But if one believes that, what would it do to love?" Only a woman could have asked that.

The question seemed to hang there, dangling like a spider on the end of a long thread woven from its own entrails. Akkad said: "If you had seen nothing last night, or just a pretty snake, I would have been wrong in my feelings about you. But the fact that you saw something – which you cannot yet interpret, never mind – proves the contrary. In other words you are on a slope, you are sliding. There is no point in making provisos, clutching at branches on either side, asking questions, trying to pretend that you have accepted this pure experience on probation. *This is it!* It has happened to everything including this love of yours which you find strange but which for us forms a sort of disembodied illustration of the precepts of the gnostic incarnation after many many old texts. Old Hippolytus has spoken of you in his tract on the refutation of all heresies. The Myth is as follows: There were three unbegotten principles of the universe, two male and one female. One male principle is called Good, who takes forethought for the course of things; the other male is called Father of the Begotten, but he is without foreknowledge and invisible. The female is without fore-knowledge, wrathful, double-minded, double-bodied, a virgin above and a viper below. She is called Eden, she is called Israel. These are the principles of the universe, the roots and springs from which everything came. There was nothing else."

Sylvie had begun to tremble a little; she placed her small hand upon my thigh, as if to seek solace or companionship. Then she said something which had independently entered the minds of us all. "You are speaking of suicide, then?" Only a woman could have asked that.

"For the elect it was always so," said Akkad dryly, after a pause. "The poets have shown us the way. For those, in every age, who feel the deeply humiliating condition of man and nourish any hope, I won't say of ever changing it, but even ameliorating it . . . they sense the great refusal as necessary. The refusal to conform to the laws of this inferior demon leads insensibly on towards death But then death . . . What is it after all? It is nothing. It is not enough! We will all die. Yet to the pure gnostic soul the open gesture of refusal is necessary, is the only poetic act. As the Sufi poet says: 'Close thy lips so that the tongue may taste the sweetness of the mouth.' All those emblems of a hunger which engenders self-destruction, which pushes things to the very limit of the sensibility, those belong to us; and they must be strictly differentiated from the privations and prohibitions which spring from the tenets of any branch of Judaeo-Christianity. Their laws are different and based on violent repressions; ours are absolute bur personal. Refuse, refute, renounce – all religions carry in them a counter-theology. But only ours is based squarely on the sad fact that the spirit of evil has usurped the universe. Yet ordinary suicide, banal self-destruction, that is forbidden to us."

"Was it not always so?"

"No. You have seen the likenesses of pre-Adamic man and the pictures of Eden which are found in ancient texts and in ancient poets. Recorded history is too long for us to be exact about it, the mist closes in and the tracks begin to blur. But we can speak of our own age, the civilisation which is ours and in which the gnostic role has been permanently derided, attacked, even physically obliterated, whether we think of the cathars of Provence or of the gnostics of Egypt who have been forced to live under cover, in hiding. Or else to scatter and take refuge in foreign lands like the Bogomils and Bosnians. It would be wearisome to follow out this theme in detail, coming at last to the prophecies of the Tarot, but I can give you the rough outline of what we believe as true for this time. The presiding demon is the spirit of matter, and he springs fully armed from the head of classical Judaism of which all European religions are tributaries. The Prince is usury, the spirit of gain, the enigmatic power of capital value embodied in the poetry of gold, or specie, or scrip. When Christ flogged the money-changers, poor harmless men, he was not behaving in an irrational and neurotic manner. No, he had seen the Prince seated among them, smirking and rubbing his hands. He had recognised suddenly the dark glitter in the friend's eye; for the Prince knew full well what the fate of Jesus would be, just as Jesus himself knew. Our proto-gnostic had allowed himself to be trapped, deliberately. It was his masterly refusal to save himself which stamps him as one of us. But the moment of fury marks him also as very human. At least to give the demon a real thrashing in the flesh for once, in the flesh. The Bible does not say if it smarted, the beating. One hopes that it did – though of course this is childish, for it changes nothing in our blind fate, the unrolling of which is quite predictable – a dead certainty in fact. How pleasant the English phrases are, and how pregnant, when you stop to think. What could be blinder than fate, what could be deader than certainty?

"So Jesus went to his foolish personal fate, dragging humanity with him, and not even leaving behind a coherently formed system of beliefs which would distinguish him once and for all as no Jew of the Temple but a renegade Jew and a gnostic. Jesus, like so many Jews, belongs to our persuasion. We can infer this from his behaviour and his fate. His end was poetic and not theological; the cosmogony from which his spirit issued was not one of the four Ms – which characterise our own age with such a great depth of focus. I mean Monotheism, Messianism, Monogamy, and Materialism. But you can illustrate this simple thesis at every level – whether you take Marx's great analysis of our culture or the Freudian analysis of absolute value as based upon infantile attitudes to excrement. Gold and excrement, that is poetic indeed! The cornerstone of culture then is another M – *merde*. The gold bar is the apotheosis of the human turd. You will see from this how radically we poets of gnosticism part company from these Judaic thinkers. Every age has its metaphysic, and every calculus is built up upon a first term, a bedrock. Possession for Marx and possession for Freud have dictated excrement as the basic term upon which the calculus of our philosophy raises itself.

"But we have substituted another term, we have let sperm stand in place of excrement, for our world is a world not of repression and original sin but of creation and relaxation, of love and not doubt. This is what sets us apart from the others who today rule everything in the name of death. I do not need to mention other great Judaic creations of the day. They rule the hearts and minds and presumably will do so until our age comes to an end in one form or another. But one cannot wait around, one must engage one's forces, one must believe something. Self-realisation is an imperative. But how truthful dare we be? How truthful will we be allowed to be? The answer is not far to seek; we are still regarded as the enemies of the *status quo*, the vested interest which the Prince has in keeping us quiet. There is only one thing, one weapon which we hold. He is terrified by the idea of the gnostic suicide by attrition, by a steady denial of the world as it is. He is only troubled when a poet gives him the lie. Then for a moment he feels himself shrivelling in the flames. Apprehension fills his soul; but then he recalls that we are not numerous, and for the rest of the world seem to be simply a small band of wrong-headed fanatics who refuse to admit the sovereignty of darkness, who refuse to be ruled. We are not hard to crucify, and the death is an elegant one in its sad way. He can wash his hands of it before the people and the majority will accept his excuses with a bonus and a rise in pay. As far as death is concerned one must develop a certain discretion about choosing one sort from another. All questions of sorrow, fear, illness, for example must be drained away until only the pure precipitate, like calc, of the gnostic death remains. This style of mind once achieved redeems all nature for a second or two, re-establishes that self-perpetuating cycle of joy which was the bliss of yesterday –the ancient mode of yesterday.

"Yet when we say nature we really mean rhythm, and the basic rhythm is oestrus, the beating egg in its primal pouch. Naturally having lost the marvellous amnesia of sexual periodicity we live by a time-pining, time-bound, chronology. And we never forget that death sets in with conception. This alters everything, even an element like love. We are making the orgasm more and more conscious. Yet to have loved capably and methodically, to have loved with a sufficiency of attention for the fragility of the thought and the transitoriness of the act – that will teach anyone the truth of what I say about death. Ah, but once your words start to make super-sense you must either stop talking or become a poet. Choose!

"We believe also that every thoughtless or inconsequential act vibrates through the whole universe. And all the time thoughts pass through us in floods, there is no time to touch them with the wand of consciousness, to magnetise them, to redeem them, so to speak. Fish in their shoals pass not more thickly. Yet each one has ideally to be realised separately. How is this possible? Yes, there is a way, we are sure of it. There is a type of realisation which makes this possible. Ah! but the new universe has got cancer, it is evil, that is to say mediocre, to the very marrow, in the biological not the moralistic sense. It is, poor thing, twisted and luckless and out of kilter, foredoomed and star-crossed. Inferior demons have painted it in their likeness. Our hopes of stepping outside this sepulchre are very faint, but they are there. There is a way to comprehend the gnostic's giant onion of a world, the concentric circles, with the Pleroma beckoning there, the white heart of light, the source of that primal vision which for a second or two can recapture paradise. We can make amends by loving correctly.

"Thank goodness, nature's machinery is vast and intricate and completely comprehensive. There is no norm, no absolute. Every deviation is allowed for. Yet total freedom is the key we must dare to turn in order to repose her. It was not always thus, and sometimes when we are asleep we dream that it will not always be so. Our intitution gives the lie to so many of the prime notions like *omne animal post coitum triste* and *inter faesces et urinam nascimur*. These ideas belong to the impoverished world of our modern demonology."

"But how to realise?" It was Piers' sad voice now that interrogated the sea-hushed silence and Akkad sighed, though he remained smiling still. He said: "A rather cruel paradox centres about the two notions which we express by the words 'knowing' and 'realising'. You can know something and yet not realise it, not having lived it, as we say, for in our inarticulate way we are aware of the distinction. Realisation is a real sigil conferred upon an experience – like a food product which the system has passed without assimilating. And the head knowledge, the conscious product, often vitiates it by coming first, so that even if you realise it and live it, later on it has somehow lost its kinetic value as a motive force which shapes the psyche. Powerful imaginations can be dangerous; they live ideas out so powerfully that when the time comes to 'realise' them, to perform with a real woman, say, a Muse, they are either impotent or else experience the taste of ashes. Poor desperate descendant of protoman tries to still his fears by classifying them, by making an index of them. He hopes to delimit them thus, but they extend on all sides of him to infinity. So he spends his time, turning in the trap. Then he decides that there is no way out. But there is, in fact, a secret way of transcending them, of turning them to account. One must begin by pretending in order to end by realising. Pretend that you do not fear by acting fearlessly, at whatever cost. Habit is very powerful. One day you will become what you mime. The parody of goodness can make you really good."

"And what about suicide?" It was Piers' voice again, pitched on a humble and trusting note, but again as if addressed to himself.

"You are forbidden to undertake an act of conscious self-destruction. Suicide in the active sense, a bullet in the mouth, that is not what is meant. Everything lies in the act of acceptance, to join finally the spiritual trust of the mature who have tasted the world to the full and wish to be purged of the physical envelope. They join the inner circle and make an act of acceptance – that is what constitutes the gnostic suicide. They accept, then, their own execution, but it is not their own hand that is raised against them. They never know how it is carried out, the sentence, though they are told when; they receive two warnings when their time is running out, and this gives them a chance to put their affairs in order. Then, after a certain time, it can come about at any moment. An executioner and a method has been chosen, as well as a time, but not by themselves. The person who is the instrument is chosen by lot, and is always one who himself has joined the inner circle of the faithful and renounced temporal life. The procedure is one of impeccable order. In the end we imitate process and there is nothing disorderly about process, however much it may seem so. The very concept of order in nature is home-made, the product of our finite minds. In the theology of process, the queen of the sciences, coincidence and contingency rule, but never fortuitously. Never. I know it sounds nonsense, but it is so."

Suddenly Sylvie cried out: "Akkad, don't encourage Piers to take all this too seriously. He mustn't. He is far too quixotic, far too extreme. It would be very dangerous for somebody with his type of temperament." Akkad looked at her gravely and said nothing; but now it was Piers who was angry with his sister, his eyes shining. "For God's sake, Sylvie. You want me to take all this lightly? Akkad is describing my own interior mind, my own character and temperament, and you wish me to regard it as simply a sort of intellectual novelty. I feel I would go to the stake for this." Sylvie turned to embrace him apologetically but to me she said: "You see? I feared as much." In a sense this episode marked the point of divergence in all our attitudes to Akkad and his sect; Piers was determined to go on towards deeper knowledge, profounder identification with the gnostics; while I did not wish to advance further than the portals, so to speak, of their system. I felt suddenly detached and indeed a little sad as I watched the brother and sister exchange embraces to put away the memory of this little but deep disagreement. How remote it all seemed, the rest of life as we had been living it! I felt all at once like Robinson Crusoe alone on his island; below us was the drumming sea, all around us were the petrified trees and the melancholy dunes. Somewhere far away was the Alexandria of our memory, with its comfortable flats and shady villas waiting for us. We had become ghosts, uneasily haunting this strip of desert, exchanging momentous fictions about God. It was presumptuous. I lit a cigarette and smoked it thoughtfully, pondering on what Akkad had told us. There were other initiations, he had said, of various degrees of knowledge; but I felt that my own limitations of sensibility were such that I would never advance much further than this first impressive step, which had without any doubt marked my whole future outlook on life. I knew then that Piers would go on, stage by obstinate stage, towards the deepest knowledge; his whole attitude and disposition suggested it. As for Sylvie I did not know.

It was almost dusk when we packed up and set off once more across the desert for Macabru. On the return journey, not a word was spoken. It was as if Akkad had exhausted all the possibilities of language. We had been pumped dry and emptied even of coherent thought. Akkad seemed moody and withdrawn, and of course by now the fatigue of these long rides had begun to tell on us all. It was night when at last the oasis came in sight again, and we were grateful to surrender the fagged horses. Many of the guests had already gone, and the fair was in the process of packing up, of dismantling itself. By tomorrow the old silence would return to Macabru, everything would have disappeared as if by magic. That night we made plans to return to the city on the morrow, ferried by the little aircraft of our host. We ate a leisurely dinner, and took a walk in the little melting township as a gesture of farewell. Something memorable had happened here, which had tugged at our sensibilities. That much we knew.

When we finally returned to the city there was work to

be done, people to be met, so that for a week or so we were not able to join forces for more than a few moments in the evening. Then came a long autumn during which Piers launched himself into a course of detailed reading and study in the old Patriarchal Library with its warped wooden floors and leaning landings crammed with Byzantine trophies and manuscripts. Akkad had obtained permission for him to use the great library from the Patriarch himself, whose chief secretary spoke several languages and was himself a scholar capable of steering my friend among the shoals and quicksands of the desert fathers, with their hysterical condemnations of the gnostics, and the fragments of this forgotten faith as outlined by ghostly and enigmatic shapes like Carpocrates and Valentinus. Sylvie and I followed all this as well as we could, but without the candent enthusiasm of her brother who immersed himself wholly in these studies – to a degree that made his absentmindedness something of a joke among his colleagues in Chancery.

He was also capable of downright absurdities like telephoning to me in the middle of an economic press conference to say: "I think I have rediscovered the force of prayer; the thing is *prayer to what?* Remind me to go into this matter tonight." It *was* rather a problem – prayer to the God of process I presumed? It was hard to keep one's mind centred on the universe as a giant maggotry when the landscapes and humours of Egypt were so beautiful, and its passing days so enticing; moreover when one was loved. I put down the telephone and turned drowsily on my side towards Sylvie whose sleeping nakedness lay close by me, echoing the curves of my body with her own pliant limbs. Sleeping, but only in that siesta of exhausted half-sleep which is imposed by the languid Egyptian afternoons with their tepid sea-breezes and long calms broken only by the crazy hiccoughs of a tethered ass somewhere. When I closed my eyes the darkness throbbed around us and once more I returned to re-live, re-experience the soft scroll of her tongue which pressed back mine and probed steadily downwards across chest and stomach to settle at last throbbing like a humming bird, on my sex. I held that beautiful head between my palms like something disembodied, and rememorised the dark hair cropped down, and then spurred up into its chignon, the crumpled ears of a new-born lamb, the white teeth and lips upon which I would soon slowly and deliberately graft back my happy kisses. It was hard to come back mentally to the old creaking library with the fleas jumping from the cracks in the floor, the manuscripts crackling, and my friend working over those huge parchment tomes, lost in the non-world of Carpocrates – the negative of the printed world we had thought we knew well, but which now seemed a delusion, and all the more dangerous because it was so enticing. "Kiss me. Again. Once more." Commands to be obeyed when issued by a woman. There was nothing derived about these pristine acts – everything was newly minted.

Before the winter finally closed in on us Piers managed to implement a scheme he had had in mind for quite a while; he borrowed the French Embassy's felucca, and on the pretext of an official journey into Upper Egypt got it set to rights. His mission being a small one and his Ambassador an amiable man he was able to combine freedom with pleasure to a degree not usually granted to young diplomats *en poste*. I do not quite know how he justified extending an invitation to me to join the party – but the result was that the three of us found ourselves in cool weather just upriver from Bulaq, outside Cairo, preparing for a journey of two weeks and perhaps more in this handsome craft. The felucca *Nasr* was some forty feet long with two masts and a couple of cabins, and manned by a crew of seven. During a long period of relative neglect by the French it had been used to ferry fruit and wood upriver and had thus become infested with vermin. However for Nile boats no remedy could be easier than to sink it in the shallows for a while, after which it could be pumped out and scrubbed clean with sand and pumice. After a day or so it was dry and ready to load. Piers entered into all the details of the journey with the *élan* of the born romantic – you would have thought we were mounting an expedition to Polynesia to judge by the quantity of the stores which he ordered – macaroni, rice, oil, tinned foods, fruit, dried vegetables, wines. It made us feel rather ashamed later to see on what short commons the Arab crew lived – but they did not appear to grudge us our rich fare, and probably equalised things up by the amount that they pilfered from us daily and quite shamelessly. But as they were both efficient and kindly we closed an eye to their depredations, only locking up ammunition, tobacco, and such expensive frivolities as cameras and medicines. All in all, it was extremely exciting this manner of setting out on a journey by water, and despite my ironic amusement at Piers' enthusiasm I secretly envied him and shared a good deal of it. I was elected to be responsible for the medicine cabinet and the armoury – for we intended to do a bit of spot-shooting along the river banks at the end of each day; shooting for the pot so to speak.

One of the cabins was well appointed with a long divan and a heavy central work table, and was spacious enough to offer headroom and a place to put our trunks of provisions. The other had precious locker-space as well as long bunks running round the outside wall. Here we elected to sleep. There was a kind of glassed-in hatch like a conning-tower which we made mosquito proof against the long Nile evenings. All reservations made, she was an elegant and roomy vessel, and the crew were delighted by the novelty of taking aboard foreign passengers – with so many goods to be pilfered. The captain and the mate both lacked an eye, and quarrelled dreadfully; and during these quarrels they exchanged ferocious glances of a macabre kind with their single good eyes.

These cabins were to prove a godsend, for we were able

at times to work over our books, maps and papers, and barricade ourselves against the talkative importunities of the Arab crew who seemed to be dying of boredom. So it was that on a late afternoon we said goodbye to Bulaq, the port of Cairo. There was not a breath of wind stirring so that the Arabs were compelled to resort to their oars at once to fetch us into mid channel and to clear all other shipping. This they did with great cheerfulness (it is always thus at the beginning of a voyage) accompanying their energies with loud songs. We skimmed along the surface of the river, elegant as a flying fish, the spray flying under the oars. Our course lay through the narrow channel between the island of Rhoda and the mainland. On both sides of us the banks were covered in the most luxurious vegetation; while here and there as we passed we glimpsed, through narrow openings, vistas of magnificent gardens and palaces whose grounds ran down to the water. From one such palace came the strains of music and song, obviously from the harem, and our boatmen were silenced. They listened with rapture. It was, they said, the palace of the great pasha called Halim Bey, and they were most impressed when Piers said that he knew the great man, and had actually dined at his table – a statement which was not strictly accurate, though useful.

It was not long before we had passed the points of the Nilometer – and then the broad hauntingly beautiful river opened its reaches to us like arms and we found ourselves gliding across a floor of dark glass which the evening light was turning to gold. Clouds floated in this mirror with their customary languor. Our crew resumed their singing as we sped on into the darkling horizon, while we sat on the forward hatch and gazed at the intoxicating play of light and darkness over the cool bosom of the ancient river. There was no doubt that this was to be another memorable journey which would bring to an end the first year of our stay in this beautiful land. No one responsive to colour and landscape could remain the same – and when this was combined with the companionship of Akkad, and all the exciting intellectual enigmas of the place . . . Egypt as an experience had separated the old life as we were used to living it from the new which was as yet unborn, undefined, as yet only a whispering gallery of premonitions. Piers cleaned his gun thoughtfully that evening, tilting the barrels to the light and polishing them until they glittered. "How will we ever get away from this country?" he asked in despair, almost as if he had followed the direction of my own thoughts. "We'll have to I suppose, one day." But what he meant, I knew, was that we would never be able to go "back" to the old life – something new would have to be offered us in its place. After Macabru the old life in Provence seemed somehow so moribund and finished. We ached for the infant new to be born.

We drove on thus at breakneck speed towards the sunset after-glow, trying to clear the nearest waters of the river before we anchored for the first night to take stock of ourselves and the dispositions of our kit. Things looked fair enough for a light breeze on the morrow so that we might use our blunt lateen-sail as a jib. It was powerful enough both to steady us and make a little way in the veritable lakes which the Nile had carved out of the river banks in the course of its descent; for the rest we would depend on the tow-rope – from time immemorial ships on the Nile, as on the Rhône, have been man-hauled when heading upstream. But we were lucky in an unusual disposition of winds and counter currents to be able to make quite a distance upriver before the darkness threatened to close in and our crew found it necessary to seek a landfall, which they did at last after a number of violent disagreements about the choice of the place. The two one-eyed men yelled and gesticulated, and exchanged fuliginous stares. But at last they found a place to moor on the western bank.

As soon as the boat was made fast to the land by a short

pole driven into the soft earth, the boats crew kindled their dinner
fire in little portable ovens on deck and began their cooking
operations; as did also our body servant under the directions of
Piers who spoke by far the best Arabic. We noticed that the
standard fare of the Arab crew was lentil soup and bread, with
perhaps a few onions – meat was a luxury undreamt-of because
of its price. Their usual drink was usually Nile water. Yet consti-
tutionally they seemed pretty robust. On this first evening, however, as if to prepare themselves for the journey, they turned in
early with none of the usual evening songs or dances to which
we later became accustomed. A heavy damp came off the river,
and a dense ground-mist blurred all clear outlines. We ourselves ate soberly enough in the cabin, and were glad of a small
charcoal brazier over which to warm our fingers. It was the
first breath of autumn cold, and the days were to be continually
deceptive at this season – as if they kept forgetting and reverting back to the summer we had left behind. Some nights for
example were damp and cold, and some warm and fruity and
humming with mosquitoes. No two were quite alike.

But on this first evening we tasted for the first time the
feeling of spaciousness that the Nile always conveys, for its
levels are never stable, they are always falling and rising; and its
banks and boundaries shift and alter, appear and disappear
under one's very eyes. Islands emerge and fade, swallowed by
the rising tide, or else sprout up again with fully grown trees
on them by some freak of level – as if fresh from the potter's
wheel. All this was to come; but for this first evening we ate
soberly, drank a brandy with our coffee and then set our books
and maps to rights. Finally I turned in, and so did Sylvie,
leaving Piers with his diary which he was determined to fill
with news of our doings. I took one brief walk on deck before
turning in. The Arabs lay everywhere like fallen skittles,
muffled into bundles against the damp; some of them had
clenched themselves up in their rags until they looked more like

hedgehogs than anything else. A lone river wind sighed in the cordage of the ship. Then, after a long hesitation, a harvest moon came bobbing up, turning from bronze to white as it rose. It was of such a startling brightness, and penetrating all the chinks in our cabin with such a piercing glare, that Piers was roused from his book to find that the yellow oil-lamp could hardly hold its own with this moon which gave such a wild and strange colouring to the place – the books and maps, the pots and pans. Somewhere a jackal sounded, its doleful howling mingling with the distant barking of dogs. Nearer at hand on the brilliant river came the croak of some night-bird stirring. I fixed my bunk to my liking and said: "Piers don't stay up too late; tomorrow will be a heavy day." He shook his head. "I won't," he said. Later as I drowsed off I heard him close his diary, blow out the lamp, and then make his way to his own bunk. He set a pistol by his bed with a small torch, while under his pillow he placed the precious wallet which held all our passports and money and papers. I lay for a long while suspended between waking and the sweet unreason of dreams; I heard a boatman talking in his sleep, and the scatter of drops along our prow as a freshet of wind struck us. Then oblivion came and I felt my mind stretching out towards the frontiers of love and childhood, so that when I turned, and when a hand came out of the darkness to rest its fingers on my wrist I did not know whose it was.

From that point forward day merged with day and night with night to such an extent that time became fluid, distances illusory; we were moving from one dream to another, merging from one truth into another in a way that gave the lie to the banal chronology of Piers' diary which tried to segment our lives in so untruthful a fashion. When one is fully extended by day and exhausted every evening one lives differently, without the weight of yesterday or tomorrow on one's shoulders. I stored up simply a constellation of moments, a firework display of small but brilliant incidents which were like a set of coloured engravings of this great river with its moods and silences, its strange caprices and impulses. It was never still, and it compelled the imagination to follow its flight across the ancient land, as if it had been some marvellous steed running wild in the exuberance of youthful beauty. But it was sinister, too, and ruthless. Ask the huge crocodiles in the upper reaches! Here and there the hurrying water had carved up the soft banks, intruding on a nest of cobras and carrying them off, or else had invaded the shallow grave of a boatman buried, as they always were, on the tow-path they had so often trodden. A corpse whirling down the river, trailing its wrappings, as ancient as any mummy of the Pharaoh's. Or else walking in the calm evening through a forest of tall supple date palms to a village where a quaint old lady sold us milk by the tin cup and where we took the early evening flights of turtle-dove which tried desperately to rise steeply enough to avoid our guns, but were pressed down low by a river wind. These little birds would be feathered in the evening by the Arabs and then cooked by Piers. I can recall so much, but cannot give the memories order and shape, so completely had the days fused together. It did not take us long to feel the imprint of this wild life without cares and preoccupations.

We let our beards grow. We did not change our clothes despite the well-meant offers to wash them on the part of our servants who were somewhat shocked at our unkemptness. Nothing mattered but this succession of marvellous days that flew by, bearing us on their backs, as the river water bore the *Nasr*. One day in the upper reaches we came upon immense flights of pelicans which lay in – droves, shoals, what shall I say? – upon the surface of the water and showed no alarm; only when we approached quite close they did get up, or half get up, screaming harshly and beating the water with their vast wings. To Piers' utter fury and humiliation the Arab captain, without asking his permission, took up his charged gun which was lying, broken but loaded, on the hatch, and discharged it into the mass of birds, killing one outright. It upset us terribly – as if it had been an albatross; but the crew could not understand our shame and fury, and cheerfully tumbled overboard to retrieve it, the water being shallow and the day windless. It was quite an effort to get it aboard, and now the deed had been done I swallowed my anger and allowed my curiosity to get the better of me. It must have weighed about forty pounds, this opulent bird. The thick soft delicate plumage of the breast was milk white at the roots, but if you blew on it you found the top part tinged with a tinge of pink or rose colour. This shows up most beautifully when the bird rises on the wind and turns its breast slowly into the sun. It had a touching, ungainly beauty which made us regret even more the shot which had cost its life.

Before the Arabs should feather it – for they showed every sign of being prepared to eat it for dinner – Sylvie had it laid upon the hatch in the evening sunshine while she sketched it. But when dusk came it was surrendered to the cooks, and here Piers was sufficiently French to take an interest in their manner of dressing it. The meat was distressingly coarse and fibrous like old beef; but worst of all, it had an oily fishy flavour which made it most unpalatable, so we abandoned all hope of sharing in the repast. It must be said that the crew themselves showed every sign of enjoying it, greasy and fishy as the taste was. They made some attempt to burn out the fish smell by filling its stomach with live coals, but as far as I could see, without achieving anything very remarkable. But eat it they did, unto the last morsel. The Arabs, according to Piers, called this bird Gamal El Bahr which means River Camel – perhaps some vague association stirring between the hump of the camel as a place where water is stored and the pelican's enormous shutter of a beak? Who can say?

Daily the Nile seemed to increase in grandeur and magnitude, and for a whole series of days we found our path running across something like an inland sea or delta, full of lovely tufted islands, some sinking and some emerging under the vibration of the waters. They had the lonely fragility of dreams in which one could only half believe. I could see now how it must be on the other great rivers of the world, the Yangtse or the Ganges or old Amazon. A whole world passing by in a kaleidoscope of colour, yet always changing, always impermanent. All day long this feast of colour, and then at night the heavens thick with brilliant stars like the loaded boughs of an almond in blossom. Standing on deck at night, listening to far-off hyenas barking and following some spot of light from a village, one drank in an immense peace and calm, feeling the old river stealing by beneath one, licking the prow of the ship, sliding beneath the dreams of the humble Arabs like a floor of glass.

So we came to the region which throws up a few riverside mountains, so pitted and hollowed by wind and sand that they have become the home of millions of birds. Here the number of cormorants and black Damietta duck was prodigious and beggared all description; every morning at dawn, with a tremendous hurrying of wings, they arrived in huge flights from the direction of the desert. They sounded like an approaching storm; then they settled with a thunderous clamour upon the mountain scalps from which they came down from time to time to dive for fish. Pigeons, hawks and swallows also abounded here. And here too we struck relatively low flying geese with hides so thick that it seemed quite impossible to hole them or bring them down. You could hear the smack of the shot like a drum on their feathers, but they did not even deign to break formation. I tried some ball on them, but always missed owing to the height and the lack of a choked duck-gun.

And then at night, anchored under these unusual cliffs

with their sleeping bird populations, to see the white moon-light falling upon a wilderness of jewelled crags, touched in with ink-dark shadows of grottoes, chasms, caves. How small and frail was our light on the sleeping ship.

I must leave to Piers the detailed account of the journey in all its details; for somewhere among his affairs the old diary must still be knocking about with its long list of temples and towns, monuments and tombs. For my part I simply engulfed everything wolfishly, never even pausing to ask the name or the history of a site. I knew that we could look it all up later on if necessary. For me the raw experience was enough. Later of course I rather regretted my lack of documentation, for my memory was far from infallible and I tended to mix up places and times without discrimination. But Piers was indefatigable and spent a fair while every evening bringing his little book up to date while Sylvie slept with her arm thrown over her face to ward off the moonlight and I cleaned the guns or did our accounts.

When at long last we turned back for home we enjoyed a period of very favourable weather characterised by fair soft breezes and long calms, which enabled the sailors virtually to leave the *Nasr* to make her own way downstream with the current while they told stories and smoked all day. One of them, the eldest, was a sort of merry andrew and was not above dressing the part with a weird cap of jackal's skin with many hanging tails and tassels. This individual seized hold, tam-bourinewise, of an earthenware vessel covered at one end with a tightly stretched skin, and started to beat and thump on it like a drum. His fingers syncopated deftly while he launched into a monotonous air, a song at once repetitive and strangely rhythmical. At times another musician in the crew came to accompany him on a double flute, made of two long reeds, which uttered a sharp and plaintive note like a river bird. With this he improvised a lingering wavering cadenza to the original song, the audience meanwhile beating out the time with their palms and showing every mark of joy. One night, too, from a village quite near the point of our landing for the night, the peasants were drawn by the sound of our water-music and the women came down to the river's edge to dance for us – a magical, unforgettable sight under the moon.

So at last it came to an end this timeless journey into ancient Egypt; and one afternoon, listless as the calm itself, we drifted into Bulaq once more with only the current, steering our way through the various craft towards our berth where the stately Embassy kavasses waited in their regal uniforms like great ventripotent pashas for us to land. It was a tearful business saying goodbye to the Arab crew for we had become fast friends and hated to part from them. But there were papers to be filled in and signed, a manifest to initial, and various other small duties such as present-giving and tipping. All this to complete before we finally handed over the boat to the French Embassy again! But all formalities were complete by dusk and the three of us, silent and rather melancholy, climbed into Piers' duty car and told the driver to take us out on the road to Alexandria.

The night was cold, and the stars were brilliant. Winter was on the way, and my thoughts turned towards the year's end, for we had been granted a long leave for Christmas by our respective missions, and we had great hopes of spending it at Verfeuille together. I watched the glittering desert wheel past us as we sped on towards the sea; Sylvie drowsed in the crook of my arm while Piers sat beside the chauffeur in front in a somewhat Napoleonic attitude, head on his breast, dozing between military engagements, so to speak. Our headlights cut a long yellow path of light upon the dark macadam which here and there had been invaded by desert sand-drifts. We were so replete with this enriching adventure on the river! It had left us speechless with joyful fatigue.

The evening life of the summer capital was in full swing when we threaded our way into it, though by now the gay summer awnings and street-cafés had vanished at the first hint of autumn freshness. Piers had me dropped off at the Embassy where I lived in a small flat, and the chauffeur helped me carry my things up to my quarters. I had promised to join them later for dinner, though it was going to be somewhere late. I poked my head into the Chancery but everybody had gone home except Rycroft the messenger who was chaining up a bag for London. In the dispensary I found a note telling me about a patient of mine whose child was ill with measles, also a dinner plan left by the social secretary. H. E. was giving a dinner-party in honour of a visiting dignitary from London and I was bidden to hold the leg of the table as part of my social duties. The bachelors and the third secretaries in a small mission get most of these corvées. However, that was not for a couple of days, and the measles could wait. I bathed and changed, and took the lift down to the garage in search of my own car. It bore me across town to the apartment of Piers – a sumptuous enough place to suit a career diplomat who had a fair amount of entertaining to do. Needless to say it was seldom very tidy in spite of his domestics; books and paintings lay about every-where, and latterly even old missals and Byzantine parchments which he had borrowed from the Patriarchal Library with the consent of the secretary. It was into these tantalising works that my friend had plunged after his shower and a change of clothes. Dinner would be a little late, so after some hesitation I accepted a whisky and a cigarette with a grain of hashish loaded into its body by pinpoint. It was not enough to do more than soothe my weariness and bring me a quiet sedation which would stand me in good stead when at last I got to bed.

"Piers, where are you now with Akkad's little initiation? I feel I have learned all I will ever learn."

"It's hard to disentangle," he admitted softly, "but only

because the traces have been covered over by the wicked invective and propaganda of the Church Fathers, who had every interest in representing the gnostics as fostering obscene rites in their religious ceremonies. But this belief throws into relief every form of heresy, every form of chivalrous dissent from the great lie which the Church would have us live by. You will find little fragments of this basic refusal to sign the confession (to use modern Russian terms) in so many places that it is quite bewildering – sometimes in quarters not specifically devoted to gnostic beliefs. At home in Provence of course the cathars have always been self-elected and self-created gnostics. But what about the Courts of Love and their gradual extinction? The love the troubadours extolled made orthodoxy very thoughtful – in particular because it posited a new freedom for the woman, and a new role as Muse and refiner of the coarser male spirit. This was not to be relished by people who felt happier within the iron truss of the Inquisition . . . O I can't tell you how my eyes have been opened, and how grateful I am to Akkad. I've hit bedrock with this system, and I feel I shall go to the end of it, I feel it."

"Tomorrow I am going to the scent bazaar," said Sylvie in order to shut him up and change the subject which was for her both boring and somewhat frightening. She knew that her brother was capable of any quixotry, any excess.

There matters stood. The season dragged on, deepening towards the winter and our departure, which lent an air of pleasant expectation to things. The diplomatic winter season of balls and dinner parties became almost pleasurable with the knowledge that soon we should be free of them for several weeks, and back once more in France. Toby had already gone back to Oxford for a term and Sabine had characteristically disappeared again. Then there came a completely unexpected

blow for Piers in connection with our gnostic enterprise. It fell
out like this. It was our habit about twice a week to stroll down
the Hellenic end of the town to where the barber of Akkad had
his gorgeous emporium – where ladies and gentlemen alike
were barbered and scented. Here one was rather coddled and
made much of, coffee and pipes were provided, and such newspapers as had arrived from Europe by seamail. At a pinch one
could devour a cake while one was being expertly barbered.
At any rate Piers was a frequent visitor. One day he picked
up an old magazine in the shop and propped it on his knee to
read while his hair was being trimmed. He came upon an
article about hoaxes and frauds and sharp practice in general
in Egypt, and among the various types of criminals of this kind
– card sharpers, forgers, white-slavers and so on – he was surprised and chilled to find described in great detail the practice
of supposed religious initiations which had been mounted by
criminals wishing to take advantage of gullible tourists. The
various steps were carefully described, beginning with the
partnership in a secret society, of which there were many
hundreds in Egypt (all false according to the journalist); then
the attendance at a ceremony of initiation: finally . . . but Piers
read no further. His heart beat so fast that he felt almost suffocated. The astonished barber had to surrender his client half-
shaved.

Piers took up the phone to ring Akkad's office only to
find out that he was away for a few days and would not be
available until the weekend. It would not be possible to describe
the state of confusion and distress into which the article pushed
him. To make matters worse, among the illustrations was a
picture of the ceremony (identical to the one we had attended)
in the Abu Manouf mosque, over which Akkad was presiding
with an air of manifest deceit and yet imperturbably – or so it
seemed to the distracted eye of Piers. He did not know what
to do, where to turn. His whole world seemed to have turned

turtle. He took the details of the publication and placed an order for a copy with his newsagent on the way home. His brain was really spinning, and he felt on the point of collapse – so deep had been his investment in this whole business of Akkad's, so blind his belief in what he had been told. Could it all have been a fake?

I came into the flat after lunch to find him lying spread-eagled on the sofa with his face in his arms, silent and pale. He looked like a man with a high temperature, and I irritated him by trying to take his pulse. But he was wounded and distraught and accepted a whisky which he drank with a trembling hand and a vague and absent-minded stare – his whole thought was fixed upon this momentous, and to him terrible, story which threw into doubt the honesty of Akkad's actions and the *bona fides* of the sect. My alarm was so marked that at last he stirred himself to stand up and tell me the story, holding out the offending magazine in order to let me see the telltale illustrations. "I've ordered my own copy," he said sadly. "I intend to face Akkad with it. I'll have to give this one back to Fahem."

He groaned and slumped forward on the couch, cupping his chin in his hands. I read the article through thoughtfully. It went as far as suggesting that this form of cheat had originally been organised for the American tourist industry, but that the original organisers had found that not only the Americans were superstitious: from all over the Middle Orient believers came to be "initiated" as well as from Egypt itself. . . . It is difficult to describe the mixture of feelings I experienced as I read all this; in part amusement, in part relief, and in part a base desire to say "I told you so," though of course I had said nothing at all, nor cast any doubt upon the proceedings. In fact I had been as deeply disturbed and fructified by them as had been the others. And now the whole thing was called into question. . . . Piers had tears in his eyes as he said: "What do you make of it?" I shrugged my shoulders and sat down soberly.

"We have been hoaxed, that's all. At least Akkad did not charge us anything for the experience."

"I suppose he thought it was funny," said Piers angrily, striking his knee with his clenched fist. "I have a good mind to challenge him to a duel – to send him my seconds."

"You haven't any: and duelling is out of fashion. Beside what would your mission say? And if you killed him, what?"

Piers walked up and down like a caged tiger glittering with a theatrical malevolence. "One's friends!" he said bitterly as if to the paintings on the wall, "One's friends!" I caught the inexpressible contempt of his tone and said: "Piers, sit down for a moment and just think. What has this news done to our whole belief? It has simply torpedoed it, that is all. But how salutary! I wouldn't want to go on believing something false, would you?"

"But how I needed it," he said wistfully, like a child. "How it seemed to fulfil my sentiments, my ideas. O it can't be a hoax, it really can't be. Akkad couldn't do such a thing?"

He looked as if he were going to give way to tears.

There was nothing to be done about the news except to bear it bravely, like the death of a friend or the failure of some great project on which we had set high hopes. That afternoon I took Fahem back his magazine on my way to the infirmary, hoping that the whole business would gradually die down and that Piers would find some other field of study, some other philosophy to absorb his passionate beliefs. But I must confess that it did not seem likely, and I waited for the return of Akkad with some inquietude; I did not want there to be a falling out among such good friends as we had all become, for Akkad was as much Egypt to us as the country's grand landscapes – their poetry seemed resumed in him, in his gentle and poetic mind. Two days of intense despair passed on the part of Piers, who went about as if in mourning for the death of his mother; he was sufficiently upset to sleep badly and I had to prescribe a sleeping draught. Then the newsagent delivered another copy of the magazine which he propped up on the window-sill to await the moment of Akkad's arrival. It was to be somewhat unexpected. Akkad appeared instead of giving a telephone call as he usually did, and just before lunch, too, an unusual time for a visit. He stood modestly, kindly, with his green Scotch hat in his hand, on the doorstep of the flat, asking to be let in. Piers leaped up and confronted him with a kind of affectionate fury.

"Akkad," he cried, "Why did you do it to us?" Akkad blinked mildly from one to the other of us, looking puzzled. "Macabru," went on Piers. "The whole thing a bloody fake – why did you do it?" He thrust out his arms half pleadingly, half aggressively. Akkad put out his hand and said: "How did you know? When did you find out?" In answer Piers snatched up the magazine and pushed it at him, pushed it almost in his face. "This," he said. "This article Akkad!" Our friend continued to look bemused so I took a hand in the conversation and tried to find the article. Would you credit it? It was not there! I leafed grimly through the magazine page by page without finding it. This caused a somewhat dismayed halt on the part of Piers during which Akkad sat himself down by the fireplace and looked from one to the other of us with a curious expression, a sort of frail affectionate happiness as if somewhere in the heart of this situation something joyful was fermenting. I felt rather vexed with Piers, he cut such a silly figure in his childish chagrin and excitement. "Well, have you found it?" he cried impetuously, and Akkad looked on quietly with a grave face and those pursed lips. I hunted leaf by leaf through the magazine in a most exasperated way without finding the article; then I went through the table of contents most carefully. It was not there either. Piers gave a cry of rage and snatched the magazine from me to repeat the pantomime. It was no good.

The article had disappeared. He sat down with grim face in an armchair and, cupping his chin in his hands, stared malevolently at our friend who gazed back with a kind of innocent resignation, yet offered no explanation of this strange occurrence. "It was there and you know it," said Piers at last in a choked voice; and Akkad, as if to spare him further pain, nodded and said: "Yes, my dear Piers. It *was* there. I know it was there. I put it there, you see; and I put it there specially. Some time ago I asked Sutcliffe to write it for me for use on such an occasion. And I left the magazine with Fahem who produces it for clients when I tell him to. There! Now are you satisfied?"

Piers listened to this with his mouth open; his cheeks flushed with vexation and pleasure. As Akkad ended he stood up and cried out jubilantly: "I knew it. I knew it all along." Never have I heard such a ring of convincing triumph in his voice. No wonder the collapse of all his beliefs had made him suffer so acutely. But what a crazy thing to have done; I myself felt annoyed with Akkad for playing with my friend's beliefs like this. "But why, in the name of heaven, did you do it?" I asked him, and he gazed smilingly at me and replied with the utmost satisfaction: "I am so glad the little plot worked out all right. You see, it was very important, Piers, a most important test. Do you realise my dear friend that you were able to go on believing something which you *knew* to be untrue? Your belief was not shaken was it?"

"No," said Piers.

"It was not a matter of faith, but of a dead certainty, scientific certainty, we might say. I did not doubt that you were one of us, but I wanted to be reassured. So I take every opportunity to create doubt. Now, if I went further and told you that the article was not a fake but *true* . . ." But now Piers burst out laughing and turned away in mock-exasperation. "You have made a fool of me," he said, "and perhaps I deserved it.

But I hope from now on you'll take me at my face value, and not repeat this kind of hoax."

Akkad said: "I won't, but only if you promise to realise that we are treading a very narrow path between reality and illusion in this view of things. It is surprising only to those of us who have been conditioned by other patterns of thinking."

"No it is not surprising," said Piers, almost as if to himself. He picked up a letter he had started writing from the writing desk, and, switching on the lamp, read out a few lines. "Man is in a trap, according to Akkad, and goodness avails him nothing in the new dispensation. There is nobody now to care one way or the other. Good and evil, pessimism and optimism – are a question of blood group, not angelic disposition. Whoever it was that used to heed us and care for us, who had concern for our fate and the world's, has been replaced by another who glories in our servitude to matter, and to the basest part of our own natures." He broke off and looked enquiringly at Akkad, who nodded and lit a yellow cigarette. "Shall I go on?" asked Piers, and without waiting for an answer concluded with: "As for man – we are protected from the full consciousness of our own natures – and consequently from that of the real world – by a hard scaly integument, a sort of cataract, a lamination covering the actual soul. It is a coating of rubberoid hardness, difficult if not impossible to pierce. It insulates us against reality, this skin. Hence unless we make a special effort we can only see the truth indistinctly – as we see the sun, through smoked glass."

It was part of a letter to Sylvie; the two of them often wrote to each other like this. Piers put the letter in an envelope and slipped it into a green morocco-covered volume on the window seat – his sister's diary. "So far it will have to do, Akkad."

Akkad was happy now, radiant. "We cannot have it said too often, defined too often; it is such a delicate matter to slip a noose around, that every attempt is a help to us all. We need purer and purer definitions to keep us from being coarsened by the values which the world imposes on us, and which we must try our best to refuse. I think you have grasped the matter more clearly than most – perhaps your French education has helped? You see quite clearly that the stability of the gnostic universe is quite inadvertent; the conformity of matter to models or modes is very precarious and not subject to causality as they imagine. Once this dawns on you the notion of death is born and gathers force so that you start, not to live according to a prearranged plan or model, but to *improvise*. It is another sort of existence, at once extremely precarious, vertiginous, hesitant – but truthful in a way that you never thought you could be. . . ." They embraced laughingly, and all at random, as if completely carried away by the identity of their thoughts, their ideas. The good humour of Piers was now completely re-established, and he made no attempt to disguise the fact that relief played a great part in it. "What a relief," he repeated, pouring himself out a drink and signalling us to do the same. "And yet, Akkad, suppose that I had been left without a chance of learning the truth – namely that the article was a fake . . ." Akkad gazed at him beatifically and said: "This is really what I should have arranged, only I had mercy on you; ideally I should have left you to struggle with the matter, with doubt fermenting all the time and poisoning your inner certainty. But I am a soft hearted man who does not like to see his friends suffer, so I decided to tell you the truth of the matter. But if you wish, I could now go on and point to a number of senses in which the fake article is true. I mean, you could question many things about our group and we would be unable to provide convincing explanations to rebut you. Some have for example questioned the little bit of folklore with the mummia – real mummia I hasten to add. What does it do? The ceremony is buried so deep in our history that nobody could explain it – we blindly follow it; but as for its origins, they must stretch back beyond the beginnings of Anno Domini. And we procure and prepare it with great fidelity, after the ancient practices which have been handed down to the embalmers of Upper Egypt. Intriguingly enough the reference in Shakespeare's *Othello* is quite accurate – where he speaks of 'mummy which the skilful conserved of maidens' hearts'. But if you questioned that as a bit of sympathetic magic or harmless folklore I should be hard put to it to find a way of contradicting you."

Akkad sat down once more, and this time as if he were entrenching himself, which indeed he was, for what followed was a kind of marathon intellectual orgy which went on all afternoon until ten o'clock at night. It was as if for the first time the two friends had met after a separation of a hundred years. The servants kept announcing lunch and retiring again with reproachful looks. Lunch was ignored until poor Ahmed's soufflé had gasped its last. Then the meal was eaten in per-functory fashion between disquisitions, arguments, agree-ments and a certain amount of wild laughter. Sylvie had gone out for the afternoon to ride so that the three of us were alone, and I must say that this time I followed Akkad's ideas with greater ease, and I also found him both charming and beguiling as a companion even though there was a certain monotony of exposition in what he had to say about the sect and its beliefs. It is not possible to reconstruct more than a part of it – inevitably the part which most interested me. "You speak about society, Piers," he said, "but your view of it will fundamentally depend on what view you take of the human psyche which has formed it, of which it is a reflection. For us the equation matter-spoil-loot-capital value-usury-alienation . . . seems to sum up the present state of things. It runs counter to nature, that ideal nature the direction of which we believe has been usurped by an inferior demon, the Fly. Of course if you are a Marxist you will see it in the terms of economic values, labour costing and so on. If you are a Freudian in terms of an impulse-inhibition machine, excrement-oriented and for the most part hardly educated beyond the anal stage."

"And we?" said Piers. "How do we see it. The group I mean?"

"Something like the view of society that Arthur had; the Knights of the Round Table, a society of Guilds at its best. That is probably what you smell and what attracts you to us, for you are clearly of that Arthurian stock, at least by birth."

Piers burst out laughing and shook his head. "Alas!" he said, gazing at us both and shaking his head. "Alas!"

"Why?" asked Akkad.

"Because," said Piers, "de Nogaret was a traitor, the original and famous one, my ancestor. He was the King's secret agent sent to spy on the Templars. He joined them under false pretences, in order to betray them, which he successfully did. He played the role of Judas in the whole affair. Some say that his grand-parents (who had been cathars) had been condemned and burnt at the stake, and that this was his way of revenge. I would very much like an excuse of that kind to hide behind. But the fact remains that he was paid so richly in lands, manors, rivers and farms by Philippe Le Bel, that I can only think that the traditional thirty pieces of silver must have been the stake. So perhaps did he, for he went grievously and publicly out of his mind in the end. And then my family, his descendants, by poetic justice lost all he had gained by this act of betrayal – everything except the old chateau of Verfeuille which becomes more of a financial burden every year." He fell silent, and sat staring down at the table-cloth as if he were seeing in his mind's eye these scenes of his family's ancient history being enacted. I knew that these facts hurt him deeply; he could never speak of them without being upset. Even when he was helping Toby with his research into the Templars these true revelations cost him an effort to make. It was brave too, for he could easily have destroyed all the documents which were there in the muniments room at Verfeuille and so left the whole thing as the mystery it has always been. "I am a descendant of Judas," he said quietly, as he turned to Akkad, "and I don't know how that will fit into a society which . . ."

"The Round Table also had its Judas," said Akkad, and smiled at Pier's obvious sorrow. "Come, take heart. You would have a harder task if you were the son and heir of Arthur. You know, we say that the Gods are simply dogs who spell their names backwards."

It was almost dusk when Sylvie walked into the flat with her purchases and an air of subtly disquieting stillness which at once alerted the concern of her brother who rose to greet her and take her parcels from her. "Have you seen the paper?" she said, turning to Akkad. "I bought one, and look at the front page."

The face of Casimir Ava the actor was unmistakable – the professional photo showed him in the costume of Hamlet, dagger in hand. But the headline spoke of his death in a car accident on the main Cairo highway. His petrol tank exploded, no doubt from the heat, though this was rather unusual, and he had not been able to free himself and escape the sudden blaze which swept the vehicle. Piers read out the news aloud to us, his brow wrinkled with sad amazement, for he had had a particular fondness for Ava – despite the fact that his sister could not bear the sight of him. I glanced at Akkad's composed face and thought I saw a kind of resigned expression, either of foreknowledge or of already being in possession of the facts. Had he known? Of course such an item of news would excite the whole city, and the telephone could have carried it all over the place; yes, he could easily have known. And yet . . .

The singular thing was that there was a witness to the accident – no less than Jean Makaro who was chief of police in the city; he had been following behind Ava's green Lagonda and had seen the whole thing. It did also strike me as unusual that both men were part of the Abu Manouf group, and I was about to make some sort of remark about the fact when Akkad, fixing a candid and calm eye on Piers uttered a strange remark. "Now do you see that we are not joking?" he said, and rose to put out his cigarette and take up his hat.

How long ago all this was – and yet how perennially fresh it is, like everything else in the context of Egypt, with its mirages we have carried about everywhere in our memories for so many years.

It would be a charity to find one's way through this labyrinth of concealed motives, and doubtless this is what Sutcliffe's unfinished book first set out to do; but either the material proved too prolix and too contradictory for him, or the simple defection of Pia robbed him of the necessary emotional strength to create. The greater the artist the greater the emotional weakling, the greater the infantile dependence on love. Of course I am only paraphrasing in my own words what he himself has written over and over again. And now he has gone, leaving behind the Venetian notebooks and a hamper full of letters, both received and sent; for he always wrote in long-hand, and always took copies of his own letters. That is how I know so much about his relationship with Pia. He kept all her shy hesitant and accidentally brutal letters in a velvet folder of bright green colour.

"In our age it is best to work from documents," he used to say.

It has done me good to put so much down on paper, though I notice that in the very act of recording things one makes them submit to a kind of ordering which may be false, proceeding as if causality was the real culprit. Yet the element of chance, of accident, had so much to do with what became of us that it seems impossible to search out first causes – which is perhaps what led to the defeat of Rob in his fight with his last book. He was overwhelmed, he says, by realising to what degree accident had determined his life and actions. If he had never met Toby, he would never have heard of us, while it was an even stranger accident in Venice which led him to make the acquaintance of Akkad.

Meanwhile (I am quoting him) he had lost his "tone of voice" in writing, which he compared to the sudden loss of a higher register by a concert soprano. His voice had broken. This must have been after the failure of Pia's analysis, and her defection with the negress. The great Sutcliffe found himself at last on his own with only his art for company, clanking across the Lombard Plain in the direction of Venice – all the nervous sadness of the violet rotting city. It had become clear to him that the salt had gone out of everything, but in order to stop the fountain of tears which burst like a whole Rome in his heart, he had to adopt a bristling flippancy, a note of Higher Unconcern, which gave literature one of the novels still regarded in the best circles as somewhat funny-peculiar; it was self-immolating that horrible laughter. Paradoxically he could not help thinking that had Pia *died* things would have been better for him, because clearer. But simply to desert him for darling Trash, the negress . . . To be sexually betrayed is to be rendered ridiculous, and if one is famous and marvellous in one's own conceit, why it is only the sense of outrage which keeps one going. Of course these are more the sentiments of a woman than a man, and if one probed them one would reach the central chamber where the first dispositions were taken, the first complexes stored up. And how lovely Trash was with her deep rosined fiddle of a voice and her skin smelling of musk melons and her little stilted pointed accent of the deepest south; a lazy sensual toreador of the love-act, marvellously armoured against ideas like psychoanalysis or Romantic Love by the fact of falling asleep when one uttered a word of more than one syllable. "My, my," she would croon, turning over lazily on her side and falling into a coma, "you slay me, honey." To think that Sutcliffe never guessed, that it had been going on even before he had met Pia. It was infuriating. "I guess Robin's sad to death, honey."

Yes, Robin was sad to death all right, sitting bolt upright in his first-class compartment, writing another long whining letter to the pale girl – who to do her justice was suffering just as much as he was. *Pia loves Rob*, she had written it with her lipstick on the walls of the *vespasienne* in the Rue Colombe, waiting for him to finish, holding her pampered borzoi on the leash. Trash was taking an English lesson with a French whore who had the longest tongue in Christendom. What happiness he knew, in all his innocence, what pride in this girl with the slit of a mouth – so spoiled and gracile a slender body. Trash was simply a cultivated American friend from the University of I forget, who knew how to massage rheumatisms away, stiff neck, and all that. After he knew he developed a pain in the lumber region worthy of a lumberjack, but there was no Trash to help him with long coffee-coloured fingers so apt for ragtime on a piano late at night.

Thus Sutcliffe writing about himself; out of the inexplicable confusion of the Venice notebooks some sort of self-portrait does emerge; but he tried out several tones of voice and found none to fit his mood and theme. He was proposing to write about himself, to make himself the central character of his own book, but never quite found out how to situate the Sutcliffe of his invention squarely in the realm which his creator inhabited. The resulting manuscript is indeed something of a puzzle, for almost before he could get the book started his "characters", that is to say Piers, Toby, Sylvie and myself started to look over his shoulder, so to speak, and talk for themselves. He felt at once elated by the thought that he had discovered a possible impressionistic form for his book, and depressed by the incoherence in which his subjects existed. They were not articulate about anything – and specially about love, the subject which occupied him most. As for our own trinity, he was disposed to regard it as a misfortune which, with a little forethought, we might have avoided. But then, on reflection, he remembered that for years now he himself had formed (without knowing it) the third in a trinity just as ill-starred, with Pia and pretty Trash as the other partners. How should he go about the book, then? How much latitude had he to alter facts? Perhaps like this? After much hesitation . . .

"Sutcliffe – there was no limit to his greatness – became celebrated and tolerably affluent the year his wife died, and immediately set about reorganising a life which had become staled with worry and illnesses. From now on, he thought, he would set off every spring on a visit to Venice. His best friend was a raffish Oxford don called Toby Goddard, who was working on the Crusades in a chateau near Avignon. After Venice he would join his friend there for the summer. That was the plan. It was indeed not merely the plan for this year, but the master-plan for the rest of his life. Why Venice? It was rather a vulgar choice – the mud smelt so strong, the water squirmed with rats. One dares to suppose that he was merely a romantic of the trashy kind. But no, his books attest to a greatness beyond question. Hurrah! Robin and Toby were both large shapeless men, according to their friends, who were known as Gog and Magog. (Sutcliffe had genius perhaps, but was no beauty.) They both dressed rather alike, in untidy tweeds, and were both tow haired with blonde eyelashes. They also shared a fearful myopia of identical dioptry, were apt to bump into inanimate objects, sit down on invisible chairs, or bounce off each other as they shambled about talking and gesticulating. Both could walk on their hands and once had a race round St. Peter's in this way which Toby won by a short head. Venice, then, and genius . . . what more does one need? He proposed to rationalise these rather expensive journeys by telling himself that a writer needs more than a cork-lined room in which to work. Needs space, elegance and the compacted nostalgias of an ideal past expressed in stone and metal. And to hell with Ruskin. So the huge man, wrapped in his tweed overcoat which smelt like a wet animal, set forth in the year 19— to welcome a late spring on those legendary canals. Gog parted from Magog in Paris with many unsteady protestations of esteem and regret; soon this incomparable couple would be reunited in the south. In Avignon.

"He always carried about with him a black leather despatch-case full of water paints, pens, and bottles of Chinese inks and Japanese sepia blocks. So it was that the pages of his lonely letters were brilliantly got up with drawings in mauve, scarlet, yellow, green. . . . It was his way of cheating a professional neurasthenia to sit on a balcony over the loop of a canal and write these letters which were afterwards illustrated in crayon or gouache.

"Letters to whom, we may ask? Why, letters to the few friends he had in the world, like the brother of his wife who was rather a slowcoach of a doctor, distressingly sincere. He resembled his sister in nothing save the shape of his hands which were slender and delicate – but what was that to Sutcliffe? He wrote to his wife still – long chatty letters to keep her up to date with his sentiments and movements. These efforts he either destroyed by posting them down the lavatory or – if they contained fragments of marvellous writing, poignant and regrettable incidents remembered, he sent them to Toby, or to Pia's brother, with instructions that they should be spared and put somewhere safe. One day, he thought, he would fish out all this disorderly material and light a bonfire among the olives in order to say a final *Ave* to this writing life so rich in promises and so fertile in disenchantments. Yes, one day he would be an old hack, gone in the tooth, broken of nerve and talentless – dried up like a river bed. What then? Why, then, the Far East perhaps, some little monastery in the Thai hills, a bald dome, silence. Or the Trappe at Marseille where he would sit all day wearing an air of petulance like a latter-day Huysmans. Sutcliffe didn't see this part very clearly; one doesn't as a rule. Like all narcissists he was convinced that old age and death were things which happened to others – and he made inadequate provision for them, though his mirror warned him repeatedly. His teeth were getting fewer and would soon have to take on reinforcements if he was to continue eating well. His sexual needs were sharper and yet far too quick, *O ejaculatio!* He couldn't stand brothels and so was at the mercy of passing sentiments which did not often come his way. He rather saw himself as *Sutcliffe accoucheur des dames, accoucheur d'âmes.* The ideal prostitute he dreamed of merely, seeing her as a postulant discharging her obligations to a God – through fornication the human shadow drinks, the eidolon of man or woman. No use asking him what that last phrase meant. Sometimes his wife suffocated under his clumsy tenderness and felt like a conscript. If you want to know how she died read on from here. In another country, among olive trees of steel grey. In some ways for a writer whose imaginary wife has just died, death has about as much reality as a painted dog. Sutcliffe thought to himself: life is only once, old boy. All that we think and write about death is fictitious. Theology is very old ice cream, very tame sausage. Best go on hoping *pour L'amour à quatre pattes* – love on all fours.

"Affectivity, then, worn down like an old dog's molars. What you have bitten off as reality you will be forced to spit out. Here in Venice, these thoughts hardly belong to a place which so confidingly trusted in the idea of civilisation. One was forced to reconsider the idea against one's will. Sutcliffe tended to see it as some poor Penelope, trying to weave up the original couple on her loom, while she waited patiently for the return of you know who. But in this age the hero never comes, and now we know that he will never come. We must be content with *L'amour vache* and *L'amour artichaut*, he loves me, she loves me not. . . . In default of a God we must be content with that. Maybe it is all to the good. When God existed such was the terrible radiance of the thing that the ancients only dared to gaze at his behind, fearing for their eyesight and perhaps for their reason. According to Freud this led later to an irrational fear of sausages, or of being run over from behind, or impaled by father. What else to record? Yes, Sutcliffe one day fell among cannibals and was masterfully abbreviated; later at Athos he was much troubled by the indiscriminate farting from the monks' cells – love-calls of old Byzantium he supposed. . . ."

What a mysterious business.
Wound up one day like a clockwork toy
Set down upon the dusty road
I have walked ticking for so many years.
While with the same sort of gait
And fully wound up like me
At times I meet other toys
With the same sort of idea of being
Tick tock, we nod stiffly as we pass.
They do not seem as real to me as I do;
We do not believe that one day it will end
Somewhere on a mountain of rusting
Automobiles in a rusty siding far from life.
Pitted with age like a colander
Part of the iron vegetation of tomorrow.

THREE

Sutcliffe, The Venetian Documents

ARRIVED, THE GREAT MAN DUMPED HIS LUGGAGE AT THE hotel and putting on blue-tinted glasses set out to have a little walk and smell, deambulating with caution however because somewhere in this fateful town was Bloshford, the writer he hated most in the world because he was so rich, his books sold like pies; Sutcliffe's superior product sold well enough, but Bloshford carried all before him, and had managed to buy a couple of Rollses! It was vexing that he too spent most of his time in Venice – it was the site of many of his infernal novels. If ever the great Sutcliffe was in a bad temper his thoughts turned to Bloshford and the oaths mounted to his lips. Ah that bald pear-shaped conundrum of a best-seller – that apotheosis of the British artist, the animated tea-cosy! "You just wait Bloshford!" he might murmur aloud. A man who seemed to be held up by the bags under his eyes – every time he saw a bank-statement he breathed in and they inflated. A man who didn't drink and couldn't think. A man who could not plant a corkscrew straight. A heavy-arsed archimandrite of British prose. . . . When the man approached you with his bone-setter's grin you had to bite hard on the bullet.

Thus Sutcliffe taking an evening prowl among the hump-backed bridges and curvilinear statuary, a bit soothed by the breathing beauty of so much lonely water. What would Bloshford be doing now? At the flea market probably, buying a clockwork pisspot that played "Auld Lang Syne". Doubtless he had begun a new novel . . . *La merde, la merde toujours recommencée* as Valéry remarked, probably thinking of Bloshford. Enough of this.

He bought some fruit from a stall, and furtively ate it as he walked. The other half of his mind dwelt in Anghor Wat.

All that colossal winter breakdown, the nightmares, the sedatives. After nearly a decade of marriage you expect something to wear out, to blow a fuse. In this case he saw himself sitting beside the breathing slender figure of Pia like someone in an old engraving – a beastly old Rembrandt exhaling the perfervid gloom of Protestantism and a diet of turnips. He could think of nothing except her condition, and how she had got that way so suddenly. Of course, he knew it was something that had been held back, festering, and had suddenly exploded. But what? Neurology at that epoch was medieval except for its chemistry. So we were sent to a feast of psychiatry at Vienna where darling old Freud put his magnifying glass over their lives, their dreams, our hopes. It was a momentous meeting for Sutcliffe the husband, but even more so for the writer, for here was an old humble man who had given birth to an infant science. To see through his eyes was an experience like no other on earth. The writer rejoiced, for the old doctor treated all human behaviour as a symptom – the intellectual daring of this feat changed his whole life. Lucky, too, that the suicide of Pia had misfired, for thanks to this endearing old Jewish gentleman with his pocketful of dreams, the true nature of her breakdown was varnished and framed. He had not guessed that a bad attack of conscience could lead to a complete mental overthrow. This was the case, and the doctor insisted that she tell him the truth about Trash and herself. The crisis had been precipitated by Trash's threat to leave her and set up house with another girl. But this wasn't all. Standing pale before me in our hotel room, and wringing her white hands very slowly as if wringing out wet linen, she said: "This is a terrifying predicament, to realise the truth about inversion, because I really have come to love you, Rob. With all my heart and as much of my sex as I humanely can. Really love."

The great writer had to put that in his pipe and smoke it – there was nothing else to be done about the matter.

A winter of walking about in the rain down snowlit streets; overheated hotel-rooms with the smell of furry moquette; and money pouring away down the drain, down the sink, down . . . dull opiates which offered no Lethe. It was the turn of Sutcliffe to become neurotic, sleepless. But instead of losing weight he put it on, for the same reasons; he could not resist the Vienna cafés with their extraordinary range of pastry. He began to look tearfully like the fat boy in *Pickwick*, and his eyes began to give trouble. But in order to play his part he had to turn priest and listen to the whole confession of the only woman he had really wholeheartedly loved; and in her brave tearful stammering realise that really, for the first time in his life, he was truly loved. It was only this malefic predicament that had unseated them. "Robin sure is sicker than a cat, honey." Yes, Robin sure was sicker than a cat!

I only saw the old man-in-the-moon a couple of times to talk about Pia. It was enough. He was full of endearing quirks of a strongly Jewish cast – after all, who else could rename love "an investment of libido"? It was marvellous. It kicked in the rear poor little Narcissus gaping into the stream. It was intellectually the most electrifying experience that Sutcliffe the writer had ever enjoyed. Reading up a bit of this extraordinary lore he began to see some of the reasons behind his own choice of an investment in Pia – the shadow of another comparable inversion. What he had admired sexually in her was that she looked so boyish. Abrupt gestures and hair tossed out of eyes. For all her daffodil fragility she was a boy. Then he remembered once that after a fancy-dress ball when she was dressed as a soldier she came to bed still in her military tunic and the result had been more than somewhat outstanding. Never had he been so excited! But this type of predisposition could not be cured by rushing out to a brothel and ordering a friend of Baron Corvo. It wasn't sufficiently enracinated, sufficiently powerful, the strain; not as powerful as the corresponding strain in Pia. Meanwhile the great attachment had clarified itself as the genuine article . . . ahem, he coughed behind his hand, as Love.

There was plenty of time in this Venetian spring to go over all these scenes in his mind for the umpteenth time, his lips moving as he re-enacted them, as if he were reading the score of some strange symphony, as indeed he was. In the intervals he wrote a line to his ungovernable friend Toby – the accident-prone don – to cheer himself up with harmless sallies. Listen to the puttle of the vaporettos, finger that fine glass full of smoky grappa or sugary Strega with a meniscus left by the dying sunlight on the lagoon's horizon. Sutcliffe, pull yourself together, man. What do you propose to do with the rest of your life? Surely somewhere there was a dusky Annamite girl to be found, softer than promises or cobwebs?

Stirring his cold toes in his huge lace-up old-fashioned boots he admitted that he was lonely, that he really hated Venice on that first evening. He wondered whether he should not take the train south right away down to Provence which though less rhetorical and emphatic than Italy has its own lithe grace of a Mediterranean kind; as Toby used to say "something of Sicily mixed with something of Tuscany". But in the final analysis it was not landscape that irked him by its presence or absence. It was lack of company, it was lack of love. See the great man then staring into the water from a lonely table; his cigar extinguished, his book closed against the twilight. Nightfall.

But his real problem is to forget. The best way would be to let one passion cast out another. We see from this that he was rather disingenuous. He had come to Venice not only to cure his prose of words like *chrysoprase* and *amethystine* but also to cure his soul of its private hauntings. He had come here, in the last analysis, for peace of mind. There were still memories that made him moan in his sleep, or that when awake returned with such force that he dropped knife and fork and felt as if a ball of bloody rags was stuck in his throat. Such compulsive thoughts made the tweed-clad mandarin stand up abruptly and take a turn up and down the balcony, whispering curses under his breath.

To be more explicit still, it was here in Venice that she had elected to tell him everything, which explained the peculiar hold of the place. Those scenes had marked his mind as if with a branding iron. The old American duchess, for example, who entrained them into her circle. Pictorially alone the scene was extraordinary. Huge sides of oxen were delivered to the house in the Via Caravi, whole beefs split down the middle. In these bloody cradles they would lie and make love while the men in blood-stained aprons stood around and jeered. He could see the pale Pia like Venus Anadyomene in a thoroughly contemporary version of Botticelli lying pale and exhausted in a crucible of red flesh with the black glossy body of Trash looming over her. . . . Once there had been a little blood in her footprint on the wet bathroom floor, but this was her period, or so she said.

He was not to be blamed if therefore, for clinical reasons, he nursed some vague premonitory feelings about an adventure which might help him to forget a little. The image he had in mind was, as to flesh, something on the lines of Raphael – plenty of it, that is, and softer than cirrus. Vaguely he hoped for a cloud-shape but he wanted it more localised in association, more specially Venetian as to colouring. He pictured thick lustrous auburn hair, a little brush repellant, a little wayward, sweeping out at the nape into a veritable squirrel's tail which one could not resist stroking. Then also a pure intellectual beauty, work of an ancient master, which would make the saliva start to the mouth. These, then, were some of the trusting demands he made upon life in that slow Venetian spring – but they were provisional and not final. At the end one finds that one has to take what one is given or go without altogether. Sutcliffe did not give up easily, but he was prepared to bow, to face reality, to accept surprises at face value. If only to get away from the poisonous nagging of his thoughts. He reflected often on one such strange adventure which befell him one year in Stresa, with a fair girl from Périgord whose kitten-clear eyes were full of the symmetrical renown of her inner mischief. Phew! Vega burned bright for a summer, blue star of the unprepared heart. Well, he had some of these counter-memories in hand that first evening as he smiled into his shaving mirror, remembering that she had said: "You have very nice teeth and a most intelligent smile." He smiled at himself "intelligently" in order to savour the lady's approbation which in his present gloom he found comforting. It was a pity that he had to hoist his spectacles in order to see himself at all. But there! It was springtime, and soon it would be warmish, a time for fleshy desires. Ah Pia!

See him stalking, then, with his rather dispossessed air among the fountains and marble lions fancifully upon the Lido. He was wondering how long he would stand it, this inter-mittently chilly Venice, when some spring chemistry came to his assistance in the person of a young girl who passed and repassed him, walking at a much swifter pace. She was a mature enough looking person, dressed in smart black velveteen with a bright green silk shirt, plus an eye-enhancing turquoise hanky at her throat. Arresting rather than beautiful. And no wonder that her eyes had turned lime-green in a very sunburned face. It was a heavy and rather solemn prow she bore with a strongly uplifted throat – an Inca face with a heavy root to the nose and widely arched eye. She was well fleshed, well haunched in pleasant roundels, soft as a primitive landscape, promising soft rain to a parched world. Mind you, all this would be intractable bum at fifty, but she was nearer half that age. She had a clear and masterful walk – in youth one knows what one is doing, or at any rate thinks one does.

The most discouraging thing about her was that she carried a book – no, not one of his books, though he swore that if ever he wrote about her he would say it was. The second time she passed his blood chilled for a moment because the name of the author on the dust-jacket began with a B—, could she be reading a shoddy Bloshford? But then . . . relief! for by the foreskin of the Risen Lord, it was Bergson. At the end of the promenade he came upon her sitting on a marble bench in a sunny corner, covering the margins of the old boy with figures. A shopping list? He could not help wondering. He swerved about with what he hoped was an unconcerned expression and craned for another look. A tourist doing summary accounts, having overspent? He was not inquisitive by nature. Finally after wheeling about rather in the manner of a waiting vulture (he couldn't help feeling) he sat down beside her. She moved up to make room, smiling at him equably, calmly, composedly. A woman sure of herself. Later on he was to find with horror that all this maths was to do with velocity and mass, with inertia and structure, and that he had to do with a pupil of Minkowski who had grave reservations about Bergson because he knew no maths. At the time Sutcliffe didn't know that Minkowski was the trail-blazer for Einstein, but he pretended to in order to cause her delight and weaken her defences. But he didn't really want all this cultural stuff, no. On the other hand he liked women who could read and write, so why complain?

He began on a very high note with a remark about Aristotle, whereupon she loosed off about Bergson, saying something like: "It's just as if you had to have a physical model for everything before you could understand it when the thing can be stated by an algebraic equation. He has to use words which makes him as out of date as Aristotle." He was tempted to let out a shout, as if to stop a runaway horse, but he reined himself in. Classy stuff, all this; he wondered if she talked like this in bed. If so he would leave for Avignon at once. The idea came to him to ask her and she laughed a most enchanting laugh and said no, she didn't, adding: "Besides it is your fault, you started. Besides I am delighted to find someone who can talk about these things." Was she alone in Venice he asked and she said that she was with her father, but added, because he looked so crestfallen, "But I am a perfectly free girl."

This was encouraging, in view of the fact that while he could swap a good deal of jargon, his hold on mathematics was flimsy in the extreme, and when he spoke of such matters her whole mood became dangerously intense. Sutcliffe beware!

Well, even the spring decided to play a part in this adventure, for the sun came out enthusiastically in a last evening burst. From the garden of Floriani behind us came a light bogus jazz and the ticking of ping-pong balls. The air was full of melody. She really was, if not classically beautiful, at least very striking with her merry clever Jewish face, its satyrical smiling mouth, and so on. He coaxed her to a brilliant café where the dapples of yellow light played on her darkness like grains of gold – the sunlight firing at her through a screen of gold lamé. The motes dancing in her breath full of sunbeams. Intellectually she fired all her guns at him and he said to himself: yes, quite so, how clever, too true – but just wait till I get you to bed my beauty. Sitting smiling at her over the friendly Cinzano winking at the brim, he told himself optimistically that it would be like sleeping with an electrical impulse, an ohm or a kilowatt. He would wrap the whole Field Theory in his arms and canoodle her into sharing the sleep of the whole universe. To hell with Bergson. As he thought about it, his feeling for romantic Venice came back: it would be quite unlike anything that could happen in poor degenerate England where football had replaced public hangings.

For a while she wouldn't tell him her name, preferring to remain anonymous, she said, for the mild drink and the sunshine had gone to her head making her a bit blushful and youthful. When she excused herself and went to the ladies' room he instantly suspected the worst. He doubled round the corner and caught her as she was walking away from the back entrance of the café, with the clear intention of giving him the slip. She did not protest when he took her arm and shook it reprovingly. He asked her to explain this flight and she said: "Because I talk too much and I am angry with myself." The waiter came padding after them with the bill and he persuaded her, without undue difficulty, to resume her potations with him – he was prepared to hear all about electromagnetism and the speed of light if only he could go on looking at her and musing. It was the old Stendhalian crystallisation all right, and he thought back to all he had learned in Vienna about investing his bloody libido and indulging his narcissism. And all those awful silly case histories with their extraordinary language – phrases like "nocturnal pollutions", if you please. Why not "nocturnal benedictions", a natural relief from stress. "Why do you grin?" asked the girl and he found some sort of excuse for the rictus.

They talked on, weaving up a skein of bright thoughts, but all the time he realised that his conquest of her had become more and more improbable. Specially as it was now his turn to want to go to the lavatory, and he knew that as soon as his back was turned she would vanish, nameless, into the evening. Heavens, but she looked choice in her war-paint. So like a hero, like a philosopher, he decided to renounce her. He rose and excused himself, paying the bill as he did so; then he retired, gazing lingeringly at her the while and permitting himself a certain dark majesty as he withdrew, as befitted genius. She smiled at him, all warmth and affection, and he held that brown hand for a wee moment during which he recited the whole of *Paradise Lost* to himself. Then he was gone – and of course so was she.

He came back at last, but it was to face an empty chair. There was nothing between him and his bloody novel now, for when real life had nothing to offer him he fell back on the dull brooding which one fine day would squeeze out into a novel. They seemed for a moment stale, the distractions of this quaint haunt-box of a town. Old Venice glittering and lique-fying among her multiple reflections, wing of a thousand peacocks fired up into a sun-cloudy evening sky. Round and round the bloody novel like a blind horse circling a well. His hero would be called something like Oakshot, and he would be far from heroic. He is seen standing all night in the Paris – Avignon express, speeding southwards, summoned by the telegram which told him of the death, suicide, disappearance, or whatever of Pia. It had come from the brother who was in the possession of private information which might throw light on the matter. What sort ? Well, let that go for now. It would come to him later. A portrait of Trash with her lovely terracotta colouring, her expansive gestures. Throwing wide her arms and crying: "Thank you, God," when she was pleased. Did Trash perhaps fire a shot into her back while she slept? No, Trash would be cruelly satyrical – graduate of Horrid College, Nebraska, who had taken a doctorate in Human Warmth and a diploma in manual manipulation and morbid massage. O damn everything. The man standing in the lighted train . . .

"The southbound train from Paris was the one he had always taken from time immemorial – the same long slowcoach of a train stringing out its bluish lights across the twilight landscapes like some super-glow-worm. It reached Provence at dawn, often by a brindled moonlight which striped the countryside like a tiger's hide."

What sort of chap was this Oakshot? Sutcliffe yawned. Why not change his name to Rodney Persimmon and make him a homosexual publisher?

He was working off his petulance lingeringly, rather enjoying his suffering if one must be honest. He told himself that he would go to a brothel and hire some bloodless turnip of an octoroon clad in a straw mat and with a paper poppy behind each ear. That was it; but the mood did not last. Venice plucked at his sleeve – the fervent tension of flowers on stalls in the light wind, the flakes of apt sunlight, this huge museum of snowy architecture, the gallant spring, the amber women . . . in the little while he persuaded himself that he was cured, his heart was as light as a feather. He was prepared to spend the evening alone. Hurrah, yes, alone. To loiter and dine late under a striped awning over the water-wobbled, gondola-scratched canals. What would Oakshot like for dinner? Solid grumpy fare like whitebait. Not like Persimmon who was all the time on the lookout for a dauntless boy. As for Sutcliffe, he was for seafood. He made some notes on his craft on the back of the menu and asked the waiter where he should dine that night. "Item. You must not yawn up your reader. Oakshot, if he resembles Bruce, will become a bore. A serious Toby, then? It is hard to chew." He smoked slowly and decided that he missed the young lady, yes he did; there was much that she had to say about determinism in science and the new attitude to causality which was apposite to his own intentions. . . . Be careful, for these notions sound cumbrous, and a novel must speak not lecture. And Oakshot? Fuck Oakshot. If he closed his eyes he saw a gloomy tweed-clad figure eating a sandwich and swaying in a swaying train. What sort of man was he? He supposed that she had found him a trifle insincere and so disappointing. But had he enacted a really mammoth insincerity she might have loved him for ever. In science the notion of scale . . . Never mind. His attention shifted to a young English girl who was eating scampi with her fingers and saying: "What rotters the Italians are – how perfectly septic." She had had her bottom pinched in a vaporetto. Good. Good.

It was largely to drown this banal recitative that he fell to scheming up a chapter or two of his book once more. He was going to call it: *Tu Quoque* – O God, he could hear the wails of his publisher already. Why can't you give it a nice rational *terre à terre* title like "Cruise of the Beagle"? Bloshford would have christened it *Oakshot Rides Again* and left it at that. It was reckless, but with all the sumptuousness of the city around him he felt feather-headed and irresponsible. He would indulge in modish prose musings and if Persimmon didn't like it he could put the manuscript where it would do most good. By the bleeding piles of Luther, the *molimina excretoria*, he would stand his ground!

That reminded him – he had forgotten to take, as always, a few sheets of lavatory paper in his inside pockets, against accidents or paperless café lavatories. Never mind, the hotel was not far away.

There was a barrel-organ with a nice monkey atop dressed in a coloured cap with tassels, which beat time perfectly to a plaintive little version of "Solo Per Te". He sang a bit himself, huskily, nostalgically, thinking of the unknown mathematician, beating time with his fork. The long kaleidoscope of fish on the stalls were full of frenzied glittering life, winking at him: shellfish, molluscs, winkles and whales – all of them throbbing and winking away for dear life among the spattered reflections of the smelly lagoons. An old man stood there, leaning negligently on a stall and looking criminally like a Michelangelo cartoon. But if you shut your eyes you could turn him into a little coloured mandarin, block-printed by a slavish Jap. Her dark throat with the sequins floating across it like a shoal of tropical fish. Damn, why had she dumped him?

Forking up mouthfuls of fish he said: Now about this *Tu Quoque* book, and about Oakshot; let us suppose a man world-weary and world-travelled, who has spent a lifetime hunting for a philosophy and a woman to match. . . . Hum. The woman is dead. But he, who has walked the Middle East, has been marked by an encounter with a tribe of Druse-Benawhis. They feed him on lotos or whatever and induct him into the beliefs of the tribe – a kind of pessimism of an extreme cast. Actually the word is a misnomer for truth cannot be either pessimist or optimist when you reach bedrock. These ideas had come to him after an encounter with a young Alexandrian in Paris, who spoke a beguiling and negligent French, and who appeared to be in possession of a number of far-fetched and recondite beliefs of a gnostic cast. He was a member of the saddest profession on earth – a banker and man of affairs. Between ulcers, which he came to Paris to have darned, he lived in opulence in Alexandria where Oakshot had been invited to visit him. Akkad, the name. "I am not really a banker so much as a student of cosmic malevolence." The propositions of this languid fellow with the enormous soft doe-like eyes much beguiled Oakshot. Sutcliffe. "What happens after that? I don't know."

He clung obstinately to the image of the man in the train eating a sandwich as it raced through the night. At the station his wife's brother, the doctor, would be waiting, with some privileged information about the death. Or perhaps Trash would be waiting in a white sports car. "Robin, honey, I jest had to do it to her." He shied away from Bruce a bit because he judged him to be a dull fellow and incapable of anything really dramatic as a role. He was a good chap and all that, but pretty humdrum. Nevertheless Pia had loved him and some of her pollen had come off on him, so that he himself felt a certain affection of kinship for him. But he was a dull dog on the whole, and inspired no fiction.

Akkad insisted that the whole of man's universe of sorrow was the result of a cosmic lapsus – something small in scale but absolutely critical in effect. Something as small as a slip of the tongue, or a moment's inattention – on the part of God, that is – which reverberated throughout the whole cobweb. A slip of memory, the bicycle-chain of recollection, which threw all the gears out of true, altered the notions of time and place. Thus human reality was a limbo now peopled with ghosts, and the world was embarked on a collision course with the spirit of default, of evil, at the helm, guided to destruction by inferior demons. That is how cosmic justice works – one little slip and the Pit yawns open. Man becomes an *être-appareil*, an *être-gnome*. He dare not face this reality. But the gnostic boys say that if you do face it you start to live a counterlife. (Oakshot grunted in a philistine manner and decided that people who talked like this deserved to have their hands cut off above the ankles.) Alternatively, Oakshot was profoundly marked by this little discourse and felt that he had tumbled upon something which related quite distinctly to his own life, the sad marriage that he carried about inside him like a dead foetus. Another kind of life beckoned to him; these beliefs did not promise happiness, there was nothing cosy about them. But they promised truth. Oakshot sighed and lit a pipe.

Leaving Oakshot to smoke his coarse shag Sutcliffe abandoned ship, so to speak, and pushed off for a stroll. All these ideas rattled around in his noodle like nutmegs in a tin, and he made no attempt to sort them out. He promised himself instead several days of gallery-going, to bathe his wits in colour, wash out his soul in rainbows. Memory dawdled him along diverse canals in a delighted trance of architectural circumlocution to where at last, in his little shop, Gabrielli hovered like a most ancient moth, among his exquisite vellums

and moroccos. He was finishing the little Tasso which had
taken him so many years – and had been destined as an anniversary of marriage present for Pia. It was at last done, and he
had been about to send it to Sutcliffe, who made no mention of
Pia, simply saying how very pleased she would be. All of a
sudden he had the impulse to lift that withered old craftsman's
hand to his lips, to kiss it with reverence. Looking into the
glaucous old eyes he thought: we are the vestiges of a civilisation gone dead as dead mastoid. No doubt those desert boys
were right – evil was at the helm and the pace was increasing.
One could hear the distant thunder of the falls towards which
we were sliding – the distant cannonade of doom. Meanwhile
here was this little old man who had lived to see so much, frail
as a leaf, still quietly working among his colour blocks and
gold-leaf. The little book glowed in his hand like a fire opal.
Her name in gold upon the spine. Gabrielli was at peace because he was the master of his method. This was the key of all
happiness. Why couldn't he feel that way about writing books?
Oakshot hated books in which everything was carefully
described and all conversations woodenly recorded. So did
Sutcliffe as a matter of fact.

Back on the canals he suddenly found that he no longer
cared whether God existed or not – so fantastic was the sunset
that it all but sponged away his consciousness. You could have
proved anything from such a display – about God he meant. So
incredibly and painstakingly worked out and executed. Imagine
the Venetians subjected to this on every evening of their
lives. . . . It was too much. Only a blessed colour-blindness
could save them from becoming madmen or at least ecstatics.
"Look!" he cried to the gondolier who was slithering him back
to his hotel along the darkening canals, dipping like a bat.
"*Che Bello!*" Pointing like a demented Ruskin to the western
quarter where already the dying sun . . . (space for ten lines of
description full of sound and fury) "*Che Bello,* you bloody

mole." The man stared dazedly along the parabola described by Sutcliffe's cane, shrugged and grunted, finally admitting "*È bello signore.*" The great man registered impatience at this lack of spirit. "I knew it," he said. "Colour-blind."

He went up to his room at the Torquato Tasso to brush his teeth. There was a letter from his agent with a press cutting about his last book, faintly damning it in a supercilious way. He stalked to the bathroom again and with gravity dabbed out the bags under his eyes with Vanishing Cream. He was afraid of getting to look like Bloshford. As a matter of fact Oakshot had a steely bluish gaze, and hardly ever blinked, which made people uncomfortable at what they felt might be an implied reproach. People who blink too much are inevitably stupid, and Oakshot was not stupid. A little emotionally retarded perhaps from lack of sexual experience. Ever since he had climbed Everest with Tufton . . . At night one found sherpas in one's sleeping-bag and could do nothing. They suffered so from cold. Oakshot lost his trigger finger to frost bite and had to give up lion safaris. To hell with him.

But it was still going on, the day; up at this level there was still a last splash of sunlight. He thrust open his shutters and stepped out on to his balcony. At the same moment the occupant of the room directly facing his over the narrow street, did the same. They came face to face, nose to nose, so close that they could have shaken hands with each other. The little street was gay with hanging washing of all shapes and colours. He stared at the girl and she stared back at him. They laughed and sketched out gestures of helplessness. His posture said: "What is to be done? Fate is stronger than either of us. Clearly we were doomed to meet, perhaps doomed never to part."

"So it would seem," said the young lady. And emboldened by this hopeful departure of fate he permitted himself to look reproachful and ask her why she had abandoned him to his fate in that paltry fashion, condemning him to a solitary and far too early dinner?

She looked somewhat constrained and after a long hesitation said: "I knew your wife," and was suddenly silent. Sutcliffe felt out of breath with surprise. The girl added: "Not very well, but I knew her, and consequently I knew who you were, and thought that sooner or later the subject might come up and be distasteful to you. So I ran."

"You knew my wife," he said, almost as much to himself as to her. It had cast a strange kind of shadow over this incipient flirtation of minds. "I never met you, but I saw her in Avignon one summer, with her brother. I live quite near the place at Verfeuille."

Sutcliffe sat down on a chair and lit a cigarette. The girl said: "I saw your picture in the paper once." Instantly it was like a bruise which suddenly decided to ache again for no known reason. The girl facing him turned to hang up some small clothes she had washed, on the window-sill adjacent. "You need not have been unduly afraid," he said gravely. "I would have welcomed a talk about her – from anybody who knew her."

Actually this balcony meeting would be quite a good thing to happen to Oakshot; the girl would be different, a ragamuffin he had found in the stews. They spent all night in a gondola heading for the sea. Wrapped in a cloak, listening to the heart-breaking serenades of a Goldoni gondolier.

He would have to change Akkad's name of course, perhaps he might call him Barnabas or Porphyrius? You could have him saying to Oakshot in despair what he once said to me – I mean to Sutcliffe: "You are the worst kind of man to whom to express these ideas because your interest in religion is purely aesthetic – that is the real sin against the Holy Ghost." Oakshot puzzling over the grand strategy of the gnostic, the fateful grammar of dissent which . . . and of course Oakshot would consider all logical development of such ideas in the direction of suicide or refusal to propagate in cathar fashion as damnably unhealthy.

The girl had turned back towards him and her attitude had changed; she seemed confused now and sad, as if she felt guilty of an indiscretion or a gaffe. "When you knew Pia where was I?" he asked and she replied that he was in Paris and expected daily to appear in Avignon. That more or less situated the date – it was while the great nervous breakdown of Pia was cooking. His own behaviour at that epoch hadn't helped either – drink and gipsy brothels and a dose of clap. He felt guilty not to have been more responsible at a time when she needed his help. The girl stared at him wistfully, almost commiseratingly, as though repenting for having broached the subject. Sutcliffe pondered. Then she said: "Would you care to come and have coffee with me? My father has gone to the opera and I am alone." His heart leaped up when he beheld . . . He stood up and decreased his trousers with his fingers, saying: "I would of course love to, but only on condition that you don't feel sorry for me, or vexed at yourself. Otherwise you will bore me and you haven't done so yet."

She nodded and gave him the number of her room. So lightly and albeit sadly (Pia's frail shadow) he crossed the little square and found her hotel, the Lutece; curiosity prompting him to consult the register in order to discover her name. It was Banquo, and he wondered for a moment if she was not a member of the famous banking family of that name. Yes, her father must be the famous man he had heard of. "He describes himself as a famous ghost," she said later when he asked her.

She was sitting in an old-fashioned cretonne-covered armchair, clad in a green silk kimono with dashing chrysanthemums stitched all over it. In the rosy light shining from the standard lamp in its scarlet velvet hood her throat and hands were gipsy brown. Her toes with their lacquered nails were now shod lightly in Athenian thonged sandals. Well, there she was, calmly composed and amused, and very much mistress of the situation and of herself. Her confidence had come back, together with a new sympathy and she appraised him with a serious and sweet arrogance which seemed to say: "Sir, for me man is a mere epiphenomenon." It was clear to Sutcliffe that she was a darling, a heart-gripping creature, at once brilliant and disdainful and a little sad. And she was so brown, so musky. They would make brown love, musky love, full of the sapience and wisdom of disenchantment, full of the sadness of fortuitousness, wishing it might last for ever. Yes, safe in each other's arms they would watch the rest of the contemptible world as if from a high observatory. Her warm and capable hands touched his. Somewhere in the romantic and water-wobbled city bells rang out, the tongues of memory, and the faint engraving of human voices scribbled the night with song. They both sat quite quiet, just breathing and look-ing at each other quietly, with the innocent eyes of the mind. It was the right moment to speak about Pia for what she knew was of the first importance both to the husband and the novelist Sutcliffe. There was one conversation in which Pia described how she suddenly woke up and realised that she loved this loutish tousled man. And by one of those extraordinary paradoxes in which life delights, the blow of realisation came just when he was at his most odious and had been behaving abominably. (In the morning he wrote down the whole scene just as the girl told it, on the back of a menu.)

With the inevitable distortion caused by too much art it would read something like this: "She had been planning to leave him for several weeks because of his scandalous behaviour, his insulting thoughtlessness, his vulgarity: when all of a sudden it was as if a bandage had been ripped from her eyes. Suddenly in this gross overfed disagreeable man she saw the artist, divined the fragility and dignity of the enterprise which

had driven him to destroy himself as a husband, lover, bank
clerk, priest. Even as a man. She was impelled to walk out into
the street in a state of pitiful bemusement, scuppers awash with
a host of new and singular impressions. So this at last was love,
she told herself; and just at the wrong time, and with the
wrong man. She could have howled out loud like a dog with
the vexation of it. She had done nothing to deserve this. She
must never tell him. She walked up and down the dark pavements of Avignon until the number of men accosting her drove
her back to the café where he had just been slapped by a waiter.
A mass of spilled change jingled on the floor. His cane had been
impounded and was raised against him by the barman. They
were phoning the police while he sat there, white as a sheet,
like some frightened stupid animal, like a wart-hog, refusing to
leave the place without an apology. This could only go from
bad to worse. "Come with me, quick." And she jerked his
sleeve, hoisted him ungainly up. He shambled into the street
with her and was at once sick against a wall. A hoarse sob
doubled him. He said: "I finish the book tomorrow." She wept
now as she hoisted him along, the silent tears of horror flowed
down her pale cheeks. All was over with her. So this is what
they meant by the phrase "till death us do part".

Somewhere, thousands of miles away, Akkad was writing:
"They refuse to accept the findings of direct intuition. They
want what they call proof. What is that but a slavish belief in
causality and determinism, which in our new age we regard as
provisional and subject to scale." And in another corner of
Europe Freud was formulating the disposition of the artist as a
hopeless narcissist, incapable of love, of investment. The old
bastard, who saw so clearly the pathology of the artistic
situation. "People who have violent emotions but no feelings
are a danger to us all," he said to Sutcliffe once. Ah but in that
ideal world where everyone would be forced to do what they
most wanted to – an intolerable situation would be created!

At some point in time, much later on, with a new sympathy and kindness this girl closed her eyes and put her hands on his shoulders, smiling a little rueful smile of complicity. It was marvellous to feel liked, desirable. The great man felt quite tearful with gratitude when he thought of the beauty of this youthful person. He felt he ought in all honesty to inform her that he was heartwhole, and well armoured against her after all that he had learned in Vienna, first from Stekel (shaped like a pipette) and then those findings of the momentous old gent called Joy. What a fool he was to ask himself if it was quite fair to make love to her on these terms. He succumbed like a sleep-walker. How marvellous to love her and yet . . . once below the photic zone where the great fishes gawped, their eyes on stalks, like untrained neuroses: somewhere in that domain comes the clickety-click, the classical *déclic*, of the cash-register consciousness, of the obdurate thinking soul. He knew it only too well, but closing his eyes he bored into her with his mind, trying to lose himself. He had forgotten everything now, even Oakshot. He was flirting with the truth of things now; he knew that all meetings are predetermined even though (perhaps because) one hunts for the person one is anyway doomed to meet. Someone with whom one could make models of one's anxieties and set them free to float, then catch and exorcise them.

Predators, within each other's eyes lay a hundred mirror-marriages. She watched him out of the corner of her eye like an investment – the *mot juste* of Uncle Joy. What a marvellous prison, then, these self-declaring kisses, spent at random as soon as ripe, self-seeding like cypresses. He had done the mental trick that he had learned from his yoga teacher long ago. To elicit a sexual sympathy strong enough to seduce you start by copying the breath, breathing in chime with the girl, feeling your way into her rhythm. Closed eyes. Concentrate devoutly, piously. Then mentally polarise your sexual organs and enter her very softly going up and down rhythmically until she feels your sensual drive and accepts it. Touch her breasts softly, her flanks, her nipples until the gravy starts and she starts to breathe quickly, turns pale and opens her eyes. Talk to her softly, lovingly . . . In this whole transaction there was no vulgar forcing. The girl was paramount, her yes or no decided everything. But plead one could and with the power of thought and words one could excite and rough her up. O yes!

Sutcliffe was in luck; for this is precisely what the girl was doing to him. The result was that they met in a head-on collision of passions which rather scared them both. Ah this knowledgeable genius of a man, what didn't he know?

> Come, tax that pretty strength
> And try the thing again
> From pain to gather pleasure
> From pleasure gather pain.

She was lovely beyond all others, this Jewish dervish, with her sense of space and history, her echo-box of racial memories, her gallant hypomania. How deeply the night seemed perfumed by her and the silences after her deep soft voice had fallen still. That voice, O barracuda-music to the Gentile heart. A pensive cocoon of a sleeping girl with a pleasant tilt to the East. Sabine was surely her name, Sabine Banquo. Ah love with such a girl was like eating a cannibal's ear. She perfectly understood that man and woman were a single animal tragically divided by Plato; that it was a notion of the Muses. A deep friendship flared up between them between two and three-thirty in the morning – something irreplaceable and unrepeatable. And he was not even drunk. It was absolutely essential to behave as if nothing out of the ordinary had taken place. Anyway this was not love; for that is irrational. This had all the pith of an equation. "You don't want to ruin your lives?" said Sutcliffe, admonishing them both from the depths of his profound experience.

Then sleep came – we were entering the countries of sadness, deep below the photic zone with its huge gogglefish, where in the darkness the real task outlines itself like a sort of flare-path, namely how to make sense of oneself. You do not have to be an artist to recognise the imperative which is every man's. Yes but how? In this domain right sex is capital, it flenses the feelings of all the poisonous artifices brought in by the think-box in the guise of clever ideas. It is a conversion of the revoking mind into irresponsible cloud-soft laughter and smiling passion. With what a sag of misery did the genius reflect on the matter of capturing this experience in words. . . . Writers, those prune-shaped hacks in hairpieces sitting down to make a few lame pages hobble out of their typewriters – what would they see in all this? Custom-built Jewesses with desultory undercarriages made over by the diving heart into the dark hovering bird presences of history?

He had no idea what time it was when her father came in, softly opening the door with a small asthmatic wheeze. It woke her and she pulled a cover over his head. The old man said: "Asleep?" in a discreet whisper. She replied: "Almost," on a pleasant loving note.

There was late moonlight thrown back from the mirror. The old man was in full fig, with his opera cloak on, decorations blinking on his breast, and a flap-gibus in hand. He crossed the room softly, almost precariously, to place himself in front of the mirror which was full of white moonlight and the reflection from the watery streets of the city. It was not as if he were drunk, no, but rather as if he were afraid of stepping on a loose board and so making a noise. He stood there, happily but sheepishly, gazing at his own reflection and saying nothing. He stared and stared at himself as if hunting for the least defect in his appearance. Alone, he nevertheless seemed deeply and serenely aware of her sleepy presence. "How was the music?" she asked at last in French and he replied, with a deep sigh:

"Mortelle, ma fille." He leaned forward to touch the reflection of his right ear and then drew himself sharply upright, giving a reproving shake of his head. "I am staying on a few days," he said. "I have to raise a loan for the City of London."

Sutcliffe suddenly wanted to sneeze. He tried very hard to remember which musical comedy he had decided to be influenced by on the spur of the moment – or a Sacha Guitry play – and then pressed his nose between her warm breasts until the impulse left him. The man in the mirror said· "It is not enough just to keep softly breathing in and out as the years pass. One should try to achieve something."

"Yes, father," she said obediently and yawned.

'I wasn't thinking of you," said the old man.

He turned, as quietly as ever, and passed through the open door into the lighted corridor with a soft velvet goodnight. He closed it softly and she lay back with a contented sigh. Sutcliffe, replete with her caresses and disarmed by the old man's extraordinary air – for he looked like Disraeli – snuggled back into his niche and sought the deeper reaches of sleep, while she lay awake, but happily so, at his side. What was she thinking of? He could not guess.

It was almost dawn when, because she could not sleep, she switched on the subdued light at her bedside and from the drawer of the night-table took a pack of cards. She spread them out, fanned them out in a prearranged pattern on the counterpane and began to ask them questions. Suddenly she stiffened and the timbre of her curiosity had the effect of awakening him. "Do you see what they say?" she asked, smiling. "That you killed someone very close to you, I think your wife." Naturally he was by now wide-awake. What a marvellous thing to happen to Oakshot, and all the more beguiling as this lady gave herself out to be a rationalist, and then started to behave just like Newton on Sunday! "Deliberately or just by accident?" he asked, curious to judge the effect of this information on his hero.

"Deliberately."

"Tell me more," he said, aware that all this kind of fortune-telling was bogus. But to his surprise he found that she was outlining, with tolerable accuracy, the plot of the book in which he had actually managed to do away with Pia, albeit in a semi-accidental fashion. She was in fact "reading" a version of a book which had enabled him to exculpate himself from his feelings of deep aggression against Pia – his desire to murder her. He asked her if she had read the novel in question but she had not. Yet in her slow and thoughtful description it was all there: the whole Indian Ocean around the couple, the calm night sea, the tropical moon like some ghastly mango sailing in clouds. The lady in her evening gown; tippet sleeves and sequins, every other inch a memsahib. Which of the many versions, all disastrous?

Sabine laughed suddenly and said: "I cannot guarantee any of this. I have only recently started playing with it as a system. The Tarot."

System! In the book they went onto the boat deck after dinner to take the air – the still ambient sterile air. Their quarrel had been a momentous one – they had each said wounding, unforgettable things, things which could never be sponged away, excused, taken back. They were buried deep in the ruins of this collapsed edifice of their marriage, their love. How pale she was! They went slowly aft and stared down at the throbbing white wake which stretched away under the moon to a dark horizon. He tried desperately to think of something clever and healing to say but nothing came to his lips except curses. "I see it all now," she said in a low voice, and with an inexpressible bitterness. Then with a kind of effortless gesture, gravely as a dancer leaning into her opening steps in time to music, she vaulted the rail, fell, and disappeared. He had made no effort to stop her.

An alarm bell sounded and for hours now the ship turned,

the waters were sprayed by searchlights. Boats were lowered clumsily, accidental manœuvres of the oars, heads nearly banged, etc. Floats and lifebelts spattered the calm sea, voices crackled and boomed from radio and loudhailer. Nothing came of it all. Yet she had been an excellent swimmer and had won many cups and medals. In the first-class bar where he at last shambled to drink an exhausted cognac the gramophone, albeit tactfully lowered, played "Bye-Bye Blackbird". To his surprise the whole thing only irritated him; he was ashamed not to feel Pia's sudden death more acutely. In the book he had called himself Hardbane, an Anglican clergyman.

Sutcliffe dozed off at last in a mild amazement, to awake much later and find that dawn's left hand was in the sky. No; he had not pushed Pia, though in the novel someone distressed him by hinting at it. Their quarrels had been overheard. Sabine had thrown the cards down now and was talking in a low voice about travelling through central Europe with the gipsies in order to learn their language. Despite her warmth and cherish he dragged himself awake and betook himself to the bathroom to dress. He embraced her tenderly and extracted a promise to meet him in the afternoon at their first café by the water. And so with confident tread back to his own hotel, tipping the sleeping night-porter royally.

Once back in his den he pushed open the balcony doors in order to feel nearer to her and crawled sweetly into bed as if into the arms of his mother. What could be more divine than to sleep one's way forward into a sunlit day on a Venetian canal? He would wake for a stroll and a late breakfast among these stone galleries now made doubly beautiful by the experience she had offered him. But his own sense of prediction was not as acute as hers for that afternoon in the sunny café the waiter handed him a message. A premonition of the envelope's contents flashed into his mind. Yes, it was so. She was leaving Venice with her father (had she forgotten what he had said to the mirror?) Vaguely she expressed the hope that they might meet again one day, but added, on a minatory note: "I try never to let anyone become indispensable."

If anyone had asked him why he laughed so ruefully and struck his knee with his hat he would have replied by quoting Flaubert: "*Je ris tout seul comme une compagnie de vagins altérés devant un régiment de phallus.*"

He determined there and then that the whole city lay in ruins about him, and that it would be as well to depart for Avignon at once. To reinforce the decision he sent Toby a telegram and set out to locate a little car to rent for the journey.

In his little red notebook the following random thoughts formed and were jotted down, like the slow interior overflow of a stanchless music. Often they made no sense at all when he looked them over, but he believed firmly that one should have the courage to write down even what one did not fully understand. Somewhere it was "understood".

As follows:

An excellent lesson in generosity. It was clear that there was no future in an affair for her – I am too old. Steatopygous novelist.

Trash's voice echoing all the gluttony of fiddles, so deeply rosined. Coughed on her cigarette smoke like a tuba. The moon glow of her warmth, an emphysema of cordiality. Said: "Robin has enough sympathy to float a ship, honey child." Alas.

Sitting at Quartila's on the canal with Sabine watching the stars flowing by – our loving minds simultaneously ignited by a falling star. "Look!"

As in death, so in dreams, people age at different speeds, and their mathematical position *vis-à-vis* death at any given moment is not easy to calculate. One swings towards and away from, if one is an artist. Only race I know.

Her laughter was always hurt in the sound, and the subject had to be choice (Pia).

Skin smelling of musk melon and small sightless eyes with cataracts (gipsy whore) like a chapel with windows of mother of pearl or (Cairo) coloured and oiled paper.

Underprivileged hearts lodged in bodies borrowed from nymphs fashioned in gold dust.

Was told of a blind woman who was set upon by a gang of children and beaten to death in a game of blind man's buff. My informant was a doctor and when I asked eagerly for details (he had been called) he said: "She was of massive stature and she had the *cor bovinum* which one always associates with sudden heart failure."

Epistolary alpha beta theta . . . the sweet compaction of biting foreign lips.

> *Trash for President!*
> *Robin for Wingless Victory!*
> *Pia for Pope Joan*

The stifling love of the two women drove him mad with envy. He was starved, nay, mutilated in his powers of projection. He was terrified that he would be forced to fall back on the great weapon of illness.

Bad gash in a waiter's hand from a tin-opener – dark arterial blood dries violet like the ink of emperors and popes.

Two days later the little car went droning and banging and humming and snoring across the Lombard Plain in the direction of Provence with the amazing man at the wheel. Amazing because still alive and smiling. Amazing because so limitlessly great!

AN ASTONISHING LETTER

What a divine journey in the little bull-nosed Morris. We left
a plume of white fragrant dust brushing the olives right from
Lombardy to Provence, with many fertile breakdowns, many
desultory conversations with grease-beclobbered mechanics,
the new masters of our civilisation. That is the way Sutcliffe
went . . .

> Cloven by dimples . . .
> Carried off by an effulgence . . .
> Disseminated by rumour . . .
> Embalmed by inadvertence . . .
> Hung drawn and quartered by Common Consent . . .
> That was the way poor Sutcliffe went.

Yes, it is the conversation of spiritually mature mechanics
which invests the petrol engine with awesome mystery. And
the fragrance of petrol along the dusty roads leading me to
Verfeuille where I hoped, by meeting the young brother, to
renew some of the sentiments which attached me to the elder
sister he so much worshipped. (Honey, Robin is sad as a cat.)
What greater joy than to lie under a car with a man who can
explain the motions and functions of flywheels?

> The happy filth of garages
> Where men who love their mothers toil
> Like babies who their napkins soil
> The fruit of mirthless marriages.
> What odours rise from grease and oil
> The child being father to the man
> That nobody disparages
> Toiling on horseless carriages.

In my new book I must put in something in praise of the
engine. "Huddled in dirt the reasoning engine lies," exclaims

Rochester. "As this machine is to him Hamlet," cries Hamlet to Ophelia in the mysterious First Quarto. . . . No literary allusions, please.

I have been here several days now, a little sad and disappointed to find a certain constraint between myself and young Bruce; nothing lacks in courtesy and warmth, but there is a lean shadow of constraint which makes me feel how much older I am than these three young people. Nobody has mentioned Pia. Young Tobias is however in full form and gives me life and hope. But the three others – I don't know what it is – seem awkward and preoccupied by their situation which sounds so superficially romantic and is in fact extremely complicated in the jumbling of their feelings. I would not propose to write about them for fear of not being able easily to rationalise a situation which even to themselves seems weird, equivocal, anomalous. In the heart of the matter, too, I seem to detect a romantic fraud – for can love exist in any dimension without jealousy? I don't believe it. Yet in the long explanations that Toby has extracted from them, and retailed to me, that seems to be their case. But the brother and sister . . . what beauty and vehemence! Bruce is a solid boy in his blond way but nothing like as striking as the other two. They have come from the pages of old Laforgue.

For the rest I spend all morning on this high balcony overlooking a sweep of olive grove, the young man Piers I can see sitting in the lotus pose in front of the little wooden pavilion smothered in roses. He does a stint of Indian meditation every morning, and speaks of it with endearing solemnity. So does the girl.

At times the Midi, when first one knows it, seems slightly spurious in terms of its folklore, but a very brief acquaintance with its inhabitants cures this impression. One realises how old and withdrawn and intact Provence really is, and how little it is part of France. It is, rather, a separate Mediterranean nation – perhaps the impression is conveyed by the fact that it is unashamedly pagan in attitude, and a product of an olive culture. It is leaner and thirstier than the north; indeed after Valence where the olives begin the cuisine replaces cream and butter with olive oil, which gives the characteristic tonality of the Mediterranean. And as if to confirm these sudden impressions the inhabitants smile, offer one old-fashioned courtesies and appear never to hurry. They have all the time in the world because Provençal time is not clock-time as we live it in the north.

Avignon itself is somewhat dirty and dilapidated with its cracked pavements, scavenging cats and chewed walls – in some places the bastions have been worn down by time to stumps like ancient molars. Here and there a higgledy-piggledy mass of twigs on a rooftop marks the site of a raven's nest, which increases the impression of dishevelled carelesssness. Moreover for a place with such a tolling name it is a mere village, and under some aspects of weather and moonlight reminds one of some lost village on the Steppes. I am quoting Toby a little here, after he described to me a winter spent here with the tinkling river full of ice. Yes, it is a long time since the Popes had everything in hand. Their riches and their profligacy created a factitious life which fattened the reputation of this queer town. Vice and crime flourished with the counter trade in silk and bells. Day after day the long silk processions threaded their way through the monuments. Church bells and saluting guns predominated – the boom and the wingbeats went throbbing over the waters with their famous bridge. It has all vanished, and the innate vulgarity and pretentiousness of the architecture can be seen, for it is no longer decorated by silk gonfalons and mountains of blazing candles.

How long since Petrarch sighed and sobbed his way into old age, verse after dry verse like the beat of a metronome in the shrinking skull. And yet I believe in great attachments, in

the stabbing recognition that assailed him as it assailed Dante.
Freud can keep his mouth shut firmly on his cigar. The good
poet needs an unripe girl as a Muse. And yet, from one point
of view to suffer because of a hollow passion for a middle-class
allumeuse – what a tragic fate! Suppose he had won her in
marriage only to find that it was like sitting about in wet shoes?
A real novelist would find the theme worthy of him.

No, walking about here in the woods with young Tobias
I have been charmed, as indeed everywhere in this country,
by the way that the vegetation has invaded everything, colonised it. Summer-houses completely brambled-in by roses and
honeysuckle, statues covered in green ivy with only one free
ankle left to view, walls where every cranny was a nest and the
coming and going of the birds made one feel one was in the
heart of virgin jungle. Nightingales – but dozens at a time –
chanting in moist woods whose green mosses were bisected by
splashing rivulets from the overflow of pure springs. The calm
happiness and bounty conferred by tutelary water nymphs or
river Gods – and indeed the Rhône was once such a God.
Then the silky air, the ambient cool air. The quiet folded-away
quality of the chalk and limestone valleys with their sectors of
violet dust and red – the signs of a soil rich in bauxite some
wiseacre tells me. All prospects lightly powdered with the
flowing dust of clay which the hot sun had rendered friable.
And the tall bowed skies, so reminiscent of Attic scenes, fill and
empty like great sails with the breath of the rogue wind known
as mistral which scatters the olives into screens of silver-grey,
supples out cypresses like fur, and rushes to explode the spring
blossom of almond and plum like a discharge of artillery. The
walls of the crooked studio where I have been lodged (in case I
need to be alone and write) have prompted me with their
yellow photographs to indulge myself with this brief discourse on landscape – it is more or less what I can see from
my high window as I glance sideways down across the park

towards the Alphilles in one direction: and towards the cross-hatched red-tiled roofs of Avignon in another. These broken planes of red and brown terracotta fan slowly down towards a white scar of river. It is brilliantly sunny, and not in the least cold. Work? We sit for the most part before the great fireplace and eat chestnuts, Toby and I and Bruce. The constraint which I noted yesterday has begun to thaw out; the temper of my relief has shown me that I really came here because I was lonely. These are the penalties of a paper life; my best friends are all correspondents, people I deeply cherish because I seldom or never see them. The old divine Duchess of Tu, for example, writes me voluminous letters almost every week in which she has distilled the essence of her kindly and amoral philosophy of disenchantment. She smokes long green cigars, and once played the banjo in a diplomatic jazz-band. What is intriguing about these letters is the absent-minded tone – for the old darling is trying to write her memoirs in halting and hesitant fashion; sometimes when the flow gets dammed up she turns the next few pages into a letter to me. In this way I can see the gradual shape of a book emerging, and also be amused by her stories of a long life of travel and misadventure. She is the only old lady I know who relentlessly summers at the little town of Cz and this in memory of a love-affair which endured for a decade, only to be cut short by death. Cz! The nightingales in the woods and that weird inflected language.

I wrote to her a great deal while I was in Vienna, and impressed her very much by retailing many of the more comical elements in psychoanalysis; for example that all bodily openings in the dream are equal to one another. In German the vagina has been called the ear between the legs, and in some circles girls are encouraged to listen with the clitoris! The old dear has never forgotten.

This to explain myself a bit to myself – for who else is listening? Perhaps that other self who should figure somewhere in the list of viable selves; the self I had somehow hoped to "invest" in my pale and pretty Pia. What a folly to invest in anything! Old Joy invested me with a characteristic Jewish pessimism and monomania. We are dealing with a falling market, our poor little investments become year by year less valuable; I am tempted to launch myself into the rhetoric of the stock market which describes stock as being "mature" or "bearing", just like fruit trees. But the problem of a private diary whose only function is (like the scales of a violinist) to keep a writer's hand in, is to determine who is going to be amused by it? In another life poor Sutcliffe will no doubt chortle over these lonely sallies. For the moment they fill in the space before lunch: the days before death.

Of the inhabitants of Verfeuille the most striking are the two who own it, the brother and sister. They have a frail nobility of aspect and address – there is always something futile, defenceless and endearing about aristocrats. Nothing can be done for them, one feels, except to feel happy about their existence; and this is difficult, for they are often such hell on earth.

Toby has told me about them, and of course in this rather strait-laced epoch their situation is unusual. There is something unfinished and undefined about them. The word "lovers" always alarms me and fills me with distrust. In my last book a couple not unlike them both began to form and I was forced to remove them because they began to sound implausible. Why, I wonder? Piers and Sylvie have a little the air of people who have played safe from selfishness, remaining deliberately childless. They are a little like babes in the wood, somewhat lost in this rambling house and straggling grounds of a property which they neglect owing to an ignorance of country strategies. The third babe is Bruce, and this adds singularity to the scene, though the whole matter is treated with a completely natural unselfconsciousness which makes it seem as simple as a prism. I reflect on Bruce and Pia alternately: the image of their inversion dwells in my mind and provokes the slow burning fuse of jealousy, for they have achieved happiness thereby. And yet . . . I cannot doubt the pain of Pia's fragmented love for yours truly. I watch the young medical student smoking his slow pipe as he plays chess with Piers, who by rights should have been his rival. The girl wanders and reads, swims in the river, or plays the grand piano. The old chateau is full of the shadows of another kind of discontent, however; I gather that grave money troubles lie ahead and that there is a prospect of sudden separation to be faced. Piers may have to work, and the thought makes him sad and preoccupied. He is a small-boned and finely built boy, very French in temper. He is "nervous" in the sense of a thoroughbred horse. Ardent in all things, including friendship. I have wanted for nothing since I arrived. I am at ease with them both for they do not know Pia except by name. Describing their attachment to Toby, Bruce produced rather an interesting simile – likening it to the sexless *camaraderie* of explorers or mountain climbers, travellers bound by a common voyage.

Well but . . .

We sit down to a patriarchal dinner in the great central hall every evening, about thirty strong. The long central tables are joined together in refectory style, giving the room a monkish touch. Our end made a cruciform shape; but while we started off thus with workers below the salt and dons or bosses at high table the conversations and the good wines prompted a good deal of movement in both directions. Bruce went and sat by an old lady who seemed to play the role of chief housekeeper, while the shaggy old gamekeeper slipped into the vacant seat beside Sylvie and talked to her in an animated register about pheasants. Children swarmed about as if in a Neapolitan cathedral, while on the rush-strewn floor the hounds scratched and the odd flea jumped.

Uninhibited were the voices flying about like doves. They speak with a fine twang and brio down here and my own rather precise version of a French accent sounds affected. I practise their way every morning while I shave – repeating the phrase *"une sauce blanche"* as if every word in it had two syllables. This latinised twang goes trailing off through the nymph-begotten groves which echo Italy and Spain. Of course the Midi has its own proud lore and a lot of elementary nature poetry of the ding-dong-bell-pussy's-in-the-well sort, which appears to contain no abstract words, which makes Valéry's existence such a mystery to ponder over. For the rest the place engulfs one and its habits and superstitions make one feel the pagan roots of the marvellous inland sea which colours our lives.

One feels (unlike Italy) far from a catholic priest here, and to do them justice those one runs into in Avignon have a somewhat hangdog air, as if they felt vaguely apologetic for existing among the olives. So many things, however, are a genuine heartbalm like the prickles of the Pleiades rising on the night. Piers tells me that the local patois image for stars in their first state (like an etching) is "flour sprinklings". In the long evenings we play a stately game of bowls on the green sward before the front portals of the chateau in which the old gamekeeper and the steward take a thoughtful part. In the middle of the night, but late, perhaps near dawn, the unearthly shrieking of peahens in the woods. At dawn the dark girl with the gun goes stepping softly through the misty brakes, while in the nether mist moves an invisible swarm of clonking lambs. Why is it that all country ways are reassuring, touch the roots of feeling – for I myself was brought up in a town? Toby has his hair ceremoniously washed in the yard, seated on a milking stool, and draped in a white sheet. The strapping milkmaid hisses as she washes his head as if she were currying a horse. She uses *savon de Sauveterre*, the same honey-coloured cakes that are used to wash clothes. Then comes a vinegar drench which makes his hair so light and fluffy that he is aureoled like an angel and has to hold everything down with a beret borrowed from Piers.

For insomnia, for stomach pains, even for red noses, there are herbal teas of the most astonishing virtue, though it is not these which young Toby has been sampling, for after a night in Avignon he looks rather as if autumn had o'er brimmed his clammy cells. He has found a gipsy brothel, however, of the utmost charm, with music and raven-black ladies. And this is where he proposes to lead me to lighten the pains of long continence.

The old costume of Arles is going out very rapidly but the elderly folk are still proud to wear it – the high piled coif of snowy linen, with its high crown like Cretan queens, the hair twisted into a million rats-tails and spangled with coins. Dark skirts and snowy aprons. The bright lace – the *fichu* – are still there. (I am making a portrait of the housekeeper from the life.)

To love, then, to conjugate the great slow verb . . . Some people have all the luck. It would have been a pleasant thing to enjoy the artistic privileges of a troubadour, who was fully entitled to love the queen, and probably spent the days in disreputable ways while her lord was absent. *Droit du jongleur* – it is roughly what Bruce must enjoy in his quiet relationship with Piers and Sylvie. But this is not how he sees it himself. In further meditations upon the unholy trinity they form, I had a sudden small gleam of light. I suddenly saw the underlying unity of the three children as a total *self*, or the symbol of such an abstraction. Against the traditional duality-figure of our cosmology I placed a triune self, composed of two male and one female partner – a gnostic notion, if I remembered correctly. "To romantic people only the romantic can happen." This led me back to the dissatisfaction with my own rather carefully landscaped novels with their love-motivated actors. I supposed that I was not really ripe to write about the Other Thing, which I had vaguely situated in or around the region demarcated off by the word "God". That is perhaps why I caught an echo here and there of Akkad's notion of a still-born God, an abortion. I have always ferried about with me a weight in that part of me which I always symbolise as a sort of marsupial's pouch – my womb, in fact. There is something dead in there, or unrealised, soggy as a Christmas dinner. It won't get born. I have tried every kind of ergotic mixture to provoke the necessary contractions of the pouch – for even a still birth would be better than no birth at all. But no, it swings in me as I walk, all this undigested Christmas pudding, with its six-pences and holly and little British flags. Our Lutheran gut-culture, so to speak, our inner piggy bank with our paltry savings.

It is late and the strong Marc we drank after dinner has set me thinking furiously. The sharp differentiation of the sexes in our culture was shaped most probably by monogamy and monosexuality and their tabus. It was an abuse of nature. Thus the typological couple which has come to dominate our style of psyche was the baby-founding duo, husband and wife, city founders. But now comes the great revolution – praise be to Marie Stopes who has freed the woman from sexual bondage by the discovery of contraception and restored both her self-respect and her freedom. That is why the sharp distinction between the sexes has begun to blur, with man becoming more feminine and vice versa. In this context my trio of lovers must present the prototype of a new biological relationship, foreshadowing a different sort of society based on a free woman. A matriarchy, then?

I wonder.

I wonder.

The fact of the matter is that they are irritating me profoundly by posing questions of capital interest to a novelist:

namely how to render them plausible, real, for the purposes of a fiction. It wouldn't work, One would be defeated by the romantic content, if only because they are what they are – young and handsome. In order to seem plausible to a reader they would have to seem real to me – and they baffle me. If I changed their characters, however, it is possible that I could render the whole thing more convincing. Supposing Piers was a pursy fat little peasant with perpetually moist lips and the drunkard's unfocused eyes. Supposing Sylvie was beautiful but totally deaf, trailing a withered leg? As for Bruce, the village doctor – he might have a lupus stain spread like a purple caul over his face and neck. . . . Yes, that might work. Nearer to Zola, alas.

This evening Sylive played two-handed piano with Piers while Bruce stared into the fire, a little saddened by a reference made at dinner by Piers about an impending crisis which might spell a new order, a possible separation. I could not help envying them Verfeuille – there was nothing else in life they seemed to need or want. The Philisopher's Stone was theirs. Or was it simply their youth that I envied?

All day we had been pelted by a freak rainstorm which sent the temperature down and justified a deep fire of furze in the hall fireplace. It was here that I read them what Piers always referred to as "the astonishing letter from Alexandria". It came, as may be imagined, from my friend Akkad and was full of what I regarded as special pleading for his gnostic cause – though why he should have urged these things on me I cannot say. He knew me for an ironist and a sceptic, unlikely at any rate to fall into the toils of some grubby little Middle Eastern schisms. I think Piers was a little shocked when I said as much. For the letter ignited him into a frenzy of appreciation; it seemed to him that Akkad's insight matched his own. Well, the letter described a sort of nougat-land before the Fall, so to speak, before the Flood: before the fatal death-drift started which was to become the reality of our time. Akkad wrote: "Yes there was a definite time, a definite moment, which one can visualise in a manner which makes it as actual as tomorrow will be. There came a radical shift of emphasis, as marked as any historic moment like Copernicus or the Fall of Constantinople, which pushed the balance over from the domain of spirit into matter. Hints of this can be traced in the old mythologies. The whole axis of the human sensibility was altered – as if somewhere out of sight an Ice Cap had melted. The ancient vegetation gave place to our new steel vegetation, flowering in bronze, then iron, then steel – a progressive hardening of the arteries. The table of the essences gave place to the table of the elements. The Philosopher's Stone, the Holy Grail of the ancient consciousness gave place to the usurping values of the gold bar; it was the new ruler of the soul, and now the slave, deeming himself free, measured his potency against coin, against capital value, the wholly saturnian element in his nature. The dark sweet radiance of usury was born. And freedom, which is simply the power of spending – its prototype the orgasm – was shackled in the mind and later in the body. The faculty of accumulation, the usury, embedded itself in the very sperm sac of man, who began to found cultures based on key repressions – the faculty of storing, holding back, accumulating. Then came periodic bloodlettings in the shape of wars with their symbolic cutlery of steel weapons – the penis and the vagina are plain to the view as well as the lathe-turned egg of death. This death-desiring culture could only be consummated and realised by suicide. The new sacrament was to spill blood, not to spill sperm and impregnate the universe. To hoard gold and to spill blood were now the imperative, and this is the order against which our small communion of gnostics are opposed; we are quietly opting out, and in some places and times, pushing the issues as far as death. Sperm against specie.

"This basic shift of emphasis has many other, and sometimes dire, repercussions. For example duality became the key not only to philosophic thought but also to language itself whose basic brick, the word, features this central dichotomy. With everything changing scale and relationship like this, death became obligatory, mandatory, instead of being a choice, arbitrary, and under the psyche's control. Before this time you could have your cake and eat it, so to speak. You were not obliged to die if you knew how to go on living without wearing out – you could cross the time barrier into the deep hibernation of selflessness, such as the wise men of the East still know in fragmentary form, for it falls just short of immortality. But what I speak of was not the fruit of effort or meditation or the fruit of exceptional minds. It was as ubiquitous as it was optional. The sense of freedom conveyed by this state of affairs can hardly be imagined by spirits like ours, so bent and bowed are they under our perverted system of values. I can hear Monsieur Le Prince chuckle in Machiavellian fashion as he reads this over my shoulder. You will say that we only imagine him this depressing locum tenens: that he is a sort of carnival head, a totem head like the ones the Templars are supposed to have set up to replace the cross. Nevertheless what is imagined with enough intensity has a claim to be real enough. It is always useful to have a point of focus for the wandering and promiscuous mind – hence ikons and altars and shrines and herms. So, my dear Rob, if you meet an angel on the street be polite and raise your hat like Swedenborg; and if it descends like a dove on your unbeliever's head then remember that it is a Blakeian or Rilkean angel and must be fed on poetry, which is the manna of the old initiates. Yes, that other world, Rob! One sometimes sees it so clearly. Those who surrendered their lives while living in it did so with the quiet relief of a helmsman surrendering his great wheel in a heavy swell, happy to go off watch, to go below into the underworld. In other words the key to the whole stance was the redeeming of death, which is always present in the psyche and can be realised and used up like an electric charge, like a philosophic power. Failure to do this thing withers one. Today death is a limbo peopled by living.

"So it is that we believe that this world, so much misused in its powers which are wholly beneficent, and although worn to a shadow of its former seraphic self, is still accessible on the old terms to a happy few, a minority whose duty is to hold the pass, to fight a Thermopylae of the psyche until perhaps by some lucky switch the emphasis changes again and we can hope that man will no longer be turned to a pillar of salt for turning aside to gaze upon the truth. Is truth redeemable by the direct vision? Yes; we believe it is. Across the abyss of our present despair and darkness the frail light is still there, though it seems always to be flickering out. Of the two forces in play in the world the black is winning, and may win completely. When I am depressed it seems most likely. What can be done to reverse the situation? Nothing, you will say. But there is a kind of nothing which we can do creatively, which will add oxygen instead of diminishing it, which is more fruitful than fruitless. But we can't do this without facing the basic truth courageously – namely the death of banishment of God and the ascendancy of a usurping power of evil. There we stand."

The enthusiasm of Piers for this pie-in-the-sky idealism was endearing, but he read into it more than I myself could see. Perhaps I am blinkered by my mental sloth and my curiosity? At any rate these formulations make me quite impatient. I remember Pia saying once: "If one really deeply believes something one shuts up and never dares to speak of it."

Yesterday, today, tomorrow – the chrysalis of time resolving itself into the butterfly of process and death. In dreams the links seem much more clear than in waking. This week I wrote a long letter to Pia and posted it to the notice-board for messages at the Café Dôme in Montparnasse. You never know. I dreamed of her in two or three old situations and tried laboriously to analyse them when I awoke. As a matter of fact like many women she remained extremely childlike in her feeling-range. A sort of child-wife in many respects. Sometimes there is an organic foundation which stamps such girls as half-developed, and which their psyches echo. The uterus is small, narrow and elastic like that of a child. The breasts are beautifully formed but small also – mere sketches for mother-hood. The hips are transversally narrow, the limbs most gracile, the face and often the posture decidedly infantile. Many perverse trends are hidden in all this innocence – one detects a hidden criminality because of the great interest in crime stories and so on. . . .

Among other things I sketched out the story of the great theatrical hamper we carried about with us for so many years. I was always forbidden a glimpse of the contents, and was indeed implored not even to mention its existence. Pia blushed and paled in turns if ever, in a fit of exasperation, I inveighed against its cumbrousness and weight – as when we travelled by sea. It had to go with us. The label said "linen". I followed my instructions and never asked about it, never spied on her. The soul of honour was I. Then during the period before the crack when she had become progressively more anaesthetic to me sexually (I did not know that she had met Trash already) the singular old wicker hamper came into its own. What do you think it contained?

Mind you, whenever I had to go away for a while, I had a feeling that she opened it, for she moved it into the centre of the bedroom floor wherever we might happen to be. Well, I said to myself, if it keeps her happy to gloat over a lot of linen what business was it of mine? After one flaming row I left the

house, however, saying that I was going away for the weekend.
Inevitably at the station I repented and took a taxi back to the
house intending to make peace with this dear torment of mine.
Guess what I found?

She was seated on the floor before a blazing fire. The
hamper stood beside her. It was wide open now, the lid thrown
back. All around her, sitting on velvet cushions of different
brilliant colours, were dolls of all sizes and nationalities in
bright costumes. A beautiful miniature tea-set on the floor
before the fire contained real Chinese tea. My dramatic entry –
I was moist with regret and a heartfelt adoration – caught her
in a fearful state of disarray – speechless and pale. But when I
saw the dolls I seemed at once to recognise my real rivals and
an overwhelming rage seized hold of me. "So that is how it is,"
I said, and all the bile of old sterile disputes rose in my throat. I
did not clearly know precisely what I had divined in this
infantile display, but I knew with certainty that these little
homunculi must be put out of the way. They constituted an
obstacle to our relationship. I seized one, and then another,
and tossed them into the flames. I caught a glimpse of myself
in the mirror, grim-faced as a German professor. Pia let out a
shriek and fainted, while I continued the pillage of her dolls,
which I now realise must have represented a whole lifetime of
memory, of childhood. It was worse than murder. But I acted
like a maniac in a trance, unaware of the meaning of my acts,
aware only of a blasting jealousy. It was like the sack of a town.
The poor woman looked with horror-widened eyes at the ogre
who was tearing her memories limb from limb and hurling
them into the fire: then broke. I had profaned the inner reality
of her far childhood.

She lay in this sort of catatonia all night long, and when
she did awake in the morning it was with an extravagant fever
which set the local doctor talking of typhoid and meningitis.
I sat beside her bed, pale, soaping my hands and pleading for

forgiveness. But she ignored me, closing her eyes, to sink ever deeper into the sheltering fever which cradled her and which might, if her heart went on beating as it did now, manage to carry her away into the super-silence. So it was that I played my part in provoking her illness – perhaps the greatest part. Clumsy, lumbering Sutcliffe, myself, he, I.

The change in her when she did come round was marked. She had become languid, slow-witted, and protested that she was old and finished. Indeed she looked ten years older. The new crop of worry lines around her eyes I attributed to the calming drugs they gave her. But the tone of her whole spirit had changed. Partly it was revenge, and partly it was that she was in mourning for the destroyed selves, her toys. This mood endured for a good long time, and her skin became greasy and her fine blonde hair lank and toneless. Then the attacks of kleptomania began which precipitated more medical intervention and set us on the road to Vienna where (God be praised!) we learned a very great deal, though not enough to save the wreck of a marriage which had been perhaps imperilled from the beginning by the genetic distribution of the good fairy who divides things into male and female. . . . I was suddenly alone, and now I knew it. And then the return of the native – which was no return at all. It was obvious that things could never again be resumed on the old basis. And in the intervening time I had become aware of so many little tics of character which I had never noticed before. My new scale of judgement, thanks to Joy, was of some help. For example Pia could never spend the whole night in bed with a man; she must get up and go away to another bed after making love. These small and indeed insignificant things only began to become significant for me after the whole Vienna period which was at the same time inspiriting and depressing. I think because I realised that the whole system of Dr. Joy was limited and narrow in operation, though absolutely marvellous within very small limits. But it could or would never arrive at formulating something like a philosophy by which one could live. It was a lever, and as brilliant an invention of our epoch as is the petrol-engine. Anyway.

The lady in the painting, do you recognise her, under so many layers of childhood, coat after coat of whitewash? It takes a lifetime to learn to die with all you have learned, or else to live with it.

Yes, there we were with our sackload of misfortunes, and there was old Doc Joy with his grave and beautiful formulations – he refused himself every ignoble consolation when thinking about man. We learned, hand over fist, but the more we learned the less hope we had, the deeper the division seemed to go. It exasperated me when Pia told me that she only loved me because I smelt like her father. I suddenly remembered how she used to take up a sweat-shirt (I was a rowing man and still like to take a boat out for a skim): pressing it to her nose, closing her eyes in an absurd rapture. It was no compliment. Her old father, the retired Ambassador, lived on forever in Tangier, stone deaf; going for a drive in his car sometimes, or else passing away a long retirement full of bordeom by playing gin rummy or bridge. A sort of benign cyst of diplomacy who had risen by gravitation and sleek kindnesses. Poor Pia! Other smaller and more touching things. When I had reproached her for something which hung heavy on her conscience she would stand against the wall and cry into the wallpaper, throwing her arm over those poor eyes. And I suddenly saw stretching behind her a long chain of infant misdemeanours expiated by this standing against a wall. In the other life, in the old days, our nurses and our parents punished us in this fashion; and feeling reproved by my cruel words she instantly accepted the blame and expiated the rebuke in this way. It gave me a lump in the throat when she did it.

It was in a way to placate the Gods and assuage a guilty

conscience that I recounted all this to the old Duchess last week. Afterwards I was annoyed, at so obviously trying to claim sympathy. She was wise to write back about other things, about how the Duke made her take banjo lessons; also about his terrible fear of being bored. He had come to the conclusion that idle conversation was a sin. Whenever people called he retreated to the end of the garden and sent word that he was praying. As he was supposed to be a devout Catholic . . .

Another form of expiation was to take up Toby's invitation to visit the gipsies whose ragged and sordid encampments ring the walls of Avignon – they have been forbidden the interior. Here lying on some filthy straw pallet in the arms of a gipsy girl I can formulate more clearly my explanations of past events – reminded by a gipsy doll pinned to a pillow, as if for an act of sorcery. The doll sent me back to Pia, and then to odd thoughts of association which had been stirred up by the patient mage, Joy. In the layer beneath the dollies (as in a box of chocolates) were stored all sorts of necrophiliac thoughts and tendencies which lead to an exaggerated dread of graves, corpses, etc. These fears are sublimated into love for statues, waxworks, effigies, all dead objects. The reason for the fascination is the appeal of defencelessness. The corpse cannot defend itself. "Listen to that," I cry to the sleeping gipsy. "The corpse cannot defend itself, nor can the sleeper."

All round they are cooking over wood fires. The encampments hug the walls, and have been here so long they seem to have grown right into the ramparts. Here they live a sort of raffish troglodytic cave life, these birds of prey who dress like birds of Paradise, and scorn to learn a word of French – or just enough to tell fortunes under the bridge, though their real relish is quick and pleasant whoring.

Well, then, here I am in Avignon; the falling of the grey municipal night over the dusty recreation grounds trampled by the ghosts of public children . . . I walk among the empty benches and the loops of twisted wire which try in vain to encourage roses. These gardens are unlike the opulent ones on the headland with their marvellous views and splendidly tended greenery. They are more in my mood however, more contemporary.

The centurion walls girdle the sable roofs whose sliding planes take the light at different angles, turning terracotta, tobacco, violet: at times the city looks very much like a brown piecrust cooking away in its stone dish. But now twilight has its own degrees of brown dark, sprinkled in patches of shade on grass or freckling the lemon-tinted bark of the tranquil planes. And everything held superbly in frame by the headlong river which cuts its sinuous path towards the necropolis of Arles. Once, says my historian, Toby, corpses were confined and tipped into the swift river together with the burial fee; they were fished out at the Alyscamps and decently interred. Along the banks of the Rhône where I have been walking stretch the tents and booths of itinerant vendors of toys, coloured ribbons, sugar plums, straw hats and shawls; as well as wares which address themselves to the taste and judgement of agriculturalists – rope, sheep bells, sieves, harness, pitch-forks, chemical sprays and fertilisers, ploughs. The garment stalls carried the traditional blue vine-dressers' outfits, sunhats, and the great willow pitchforks grown in *espalier* at villages like Sauve. Inevitably the gipsies blend into all this, flickering here and there in their bright rags and jingling jewelry to catch unwary clients superstitious enough to cross their dirty palms: or thieving: or whoring openly in the shadow of the bushes which fringe the river. Though here we are relatively far from the sea the advent of the car and the train has brought fish to our doors and in Avignon one can eat the best fresh fish of the Mediterranean. Of course the primitive and dusty old coach roads discourage modern traffic so that in contrast to the tamer country round Nice and Monte we must seem more backward and dusty here. No matter. Things feel more authentic; everything has bone-structure and style. And the land is all the more delightful for being a little unbarbered, unshaven.

Under the famous broken bridge which the inhabitants of Verfeuille have always regarded as a highly symbolic structure, there are sometimes real dancers, during the frequent fêtes and holidays. There is also the famous cockade-snatching fight such as someone has just rediscovered on the vases of Crete. It is kinder than the Spanish fight for it does not slay the bull: it is the white-clad man who is in danger. The bullring is easily and hastily improvised by placing the carts in a ring to form an arena. The audience is mounted on the carts. Here we have snuffed enough red dust to see the summer out, and drunk enough red wine to float a gunboat. And from time to time, in a trick of slanting light, one is reminded that the Middle Ages are not so very far behind us – as a reality rather than as an abstraction. Machicolated walls grin with the gap-toothed, helot-dwarf expression of the louts in Breughel. Up against the night sky the massive and ugly factories of God loom like broken fret-saws. In the green waters of the great fountain of V., which throbs on with the heartbeat of Petrarch's verse, the polished trout swim and swarm and render themselves in all placidity to the gaff of idle boys. Darkness is falling. I am hunting among all these booths for young Toby, whose potations never cease to amaze me, and whom I will doubtless find at one of the wine stalls which offer free drinks as a kind of advertisement for country wines on direct sale at the fair. Sure enough. He stands in a clumsy and dogged way with a glass in his paw. Under his arm the latest Pursewarden much battered and full of river-sand (we bathed this morning). Vainglorious though I am I do not hold this against him for P. is the only endurable writer in England at the moment, and I gladly cede the palm to him as the saying goes. Toby has hiccups and is trying to cure them in the only way he knows. By drinking from the wrong end of a glass.

It only takes one match to ignite a haystack, or one remark to fire a mind. Piers is determined to meet Akkad on his next visit and to plumb all the mysteries of the sect; and by the same token Toby has suddenly seen the way into the centre of his own work. The little that I was able to tell him of the gnostic predispositions suggested a possible solution to the nagging old problem of the Templars – wherein had they sinned, why did they collapse? The suggestion that the central heresy might have been gnosticism suddenly blazed up in his mind and gave substance and form to all the dispersed material he had been wrestling with in the muniments room of the chateau. The mere possibility that he had a theory which might be fitted into a thesis to be offered for a Ph.D produced such a wild fit of exhilaration that it led to a three-day drunk of notable proportions. We kept meeting him and losing him in the town. At each encounter he seemed drunker, slower, more elaborate. And when Toby drank too much one was never sure what he might say or do. For example take the only taxi and cry: "Follow that neurosis!" Or recite nonsense verse: "The apple of my gender aches, I seek an Eve for all our sakes." And then of course Byron – for he sees himself as Byron and is continually addressing an imaginary Fletcher – but this happens mostly in bed.

> "*Fletcher!*"
> "*Yes, my Lord?*"
> "*Abnegate.*"
> "*Very good, my Lord.*"
> "*Fletcher!*"
> "*Yes, my Lord?*"
> "*Convey my finest instincts to the Duchess.*"
> "*Very well, sir.*"

In the incoherent maze of his rocking mind all sorts of diverging ideas and thoughts bounced off one another. "I see little point in being myself O sage," he might intone. Adding: "Sutcliffe, that huge platform of British flesh and gristle ought to be in a dog-collar. He is criminally drunk and has joined the engineers of sin. A murrain on his buttocky walk and chapped hands. Free will is an illusion honey, so is the discrete ego, say the Templars. Who impregnated them with this folly? The wrath of the nymphs was hidden from them until the last moment."

Or simply fall down on a bench and go to sleep like any tramp using Pursewarden's *Essays* as a scant pillow. Only the cold and dewy dawn would awake the unshaven sinner and drive him down to the Princes hotel, or back to the chateau.

"My advice to Robin Sutcliffe is as follows," he might add, and recite aloud while his finger marked the bars:

> Always shoot the sitting duck
> Pass up the poem for the fuck
> At worst the penalty may be
> A charge on poor posterity.

"Fletcher!"
"Yes, sir."
"By the naval string of the risen Lord
bring me some bicarbonate of soda tablets."
"Immediately, my Lord."

Somewhere, under a bamboo ceiling, hidden in a coloured transfer of tropical birds, there where the great philogists keep holiday, she may still be waiting for me. "Darling," the letter said, "Burma was such a trap. I feel I am going mad."

Wandering in the older part of the town, near the market, I found a few barrowloads of books for sale; among them a

very old life of Petrarch (MDCC LXXXII) which I riffled and
browsed through in the public gardens of Doms. It would make
the ideal going-away present for Sylvie. I was not so hard-
hearted as not to feel a quickening of sympathy at the words of
the old anonymous biographer of the poet.

> *J'ai cru d'ailleurs que dans un temps où les femmes ont l'air
> de ne plus se croire dignes d'être aimées; où elles avertissent
> les hommes de ne pas les respecter; où se forment tant de
> liaisons d'un jour et si peu d'attachements durables; où l'on
> court après le plaisir pour ne trouver que la honte et les regrets,
> on pourrait peut-être rendre quelque service aux Mœurs, et
> rapeller un Sexe aimable a l'estime qu'il se doit si l'on
> offrait à ses yeux, d'après l'histoire, le modèle d'un amour
> délicat, qui se suffit à lui-même et qui se nourrit pendant
> vingt ans de sentiment, de vertus et de gloire.*

Alas poor Pia! My mind went instantly back to the lakeside of Geneva where I had the first glimpse of the slender pale
girl buttoned into white gloves. Parasol, pointed shoes, light
straw hat. They had sent her to a finishing school and on
Sundays the girls strolled by couples along the lakeside. She
was on the pale side, and a little too slender, too much waist to
her severely tailored suit. I had a rendezvous with someone
else, and was waiting in a little café among the gardens when she
passed by, smiling at something her friend said, and left that
little ripple of complicity in her kindly glance which provoked
my interest – an interest which deepened as I watched her
eating an ice, dainty as a cat. Nothing I learned about her afterwards surprised me – it was as if I had always known about that
sad and solitary life among the great embassies, always taught
by governesses and tutors, always forbidden the company of
other children of the same age. The little brother was too young
to be a companion for her. So that even the strict Geneva
finishing school seemed a marvellous escape from her former
life. The degree of freedom permitted the girls seemed to her

to border on the dangerous. I followed her, and from a chance remark learned which church they worshipped at on Sundays. The next Sunday I made a point of joining them in these obligatory pieties. On the second Sunday I passed her a note asking her to dine with me and telling her the name of my hotel. I added that I was taking Holy Orders very soon. I did not believe for an instant that Pia would accept. But even staid and gloomy Geneva seemed to her, after what she had lived through, a carnival of freedom. For once in her life she showed a wild courage, an almost desperate courage – I mean, to use a back door and scale a low fence . . . I couldn't believe my eyes. I was completely knocked off my plate in a similar manner to old Petrarch.

> *Le Lundi de la Semaine Sainte, à six heures du matin, Pétrarque vit à Avignon, dans l'église des Réligieuses de Saint-Claire une jeune femme dont la robe verte était parsemée de violettes. Sa beauté le frappa. C'était Laure.*

How simple, how ineluctable these experiences seem when they come one's way. How calamitously they turn out. Perhaps not for the lucky, though. Nor for them.

The old doctor in Cz once told the Duchess: "I have always felt that I was a spare child, a spare part, a spare tyre. People only turn to me in distress. Nobody wants to share their happiness with a doctor."

> *"Fletcher?"*
> *"Yes, my lord."*
> *"Hand me my lyre."*
> *"Very good, my lord."*
> *"And also some purple therapy. I am a bit cast down by my hypogloomia or common hangover. Some methylated spirits, please."*
> *"At once, my lord."*

❖❖❖

> Smoking living salmon
> Stuffing living geese.
> I'm a little Christian,
> Jesus brings me peace.

(A spontaneous lyric outburst by Toby as he stood face to face with the Palace of the Popes.)

To feast on loneliness – it is too rich a diet for a man like me. Yet I have had to put up with it. Piers said: "People who can no longer fall in love can simply pine away, go into a decline, and select unconsciously a disease which will do the work of a pistol." He is not wrong. Despite the new found freedoms the area of misunderstandings about love remains about the same. The act is a psychic one; the flesh simply obeys with its convulsion-therapy and amnesia. Yes, but now that the young have at last, thanks to Marie Stopes, found the key to the larder, it will be apple tart and cream for breakfast every day, and cakes and ale all night. Why should I make such extraordinary claims upon life when I have all the gipsies of Avignon to choose from? Because I am a fool. I remember that I wanted to bleat out: "I love you," but she put her hand over my mouth and all I felt was her breath in my fingers.

In the evenings I take a long slow bath by firelight in my room; a large hip-bath does service for something more modern. A big sponge with dilatory squeezings warms my body. Then to wander the lamplit maze of the old house, taking always the direction pointed out by the distant piano. Lights blaze upon the wine glasses. How much longer will this life go on for them – living in the quiet parenthesis of Verfeuille's pulse-beat? After dinner to play a round of cards or drowse over a book. I feel all the magnet's deep slumbering passivity, the bare weight of inertia. Toby accuses me of being selfish because I pay no heed to social problems, but there is no social answer to private pain, to loneliness, alienation, the need for love. Once a French girl, grubby and unwashed, lips hewn apart with yawns, smelling like the Metro in summer, completely absorbed my affections for two months. Her reactions had been slowed down by a youthful meningitis – it had slurred up her speech, and the stiffening of the muscles on one side of her mouth gave her great beauty and stealth. A committee cannot love, a society still less. She brought me an unusual happiness, which is only the sense of wonder suddenly revived. I told Pia all about her and she listened with her patience coiled up in her like a cat saying nothing at all. I snatched off her fresh straw hat and kissed all those sunpilfered freckles with gratitude. In those days I was lighthearted and used to sign all my letters: "Well cheerio, best agonies, Rob." I little knew!

"My whole philosophy is this: that people who give one too much trouble should be arrested and turned into soap." (Toby. The last words roared out and punctuated by a bang on the table with fatuous fist.)

As for Trash, her terracotta beauty was proof of the pudding; the plum-tones softly dusted by her powder – a Greek vase dusted with bonemeal. In the morning, naked, she did what she called her personal Intonement. The text went as follows, rising on toes, hands and arms spread out to heaven:

> *Who's the Bestest?*
> *Who's the Mostest?*
> *Who's the particularly particular?*
> *Who's the specially special?*
> *All together: "Why, Trash of course!"*

The little lap-dog with its coat of scarlet velvet was named after Pia. It walked on its hindlegs with enthusiasm. When she showed it the whip it immediately got an erection. Afterwards when it died they buried it by moonlight, in tears, with loosened sphincters. Ah, the sweet mooncraft of the dark lady of the soblets!

Trying to explain to Piers that the stream of consciousness is composed of all too painfully conscious bits with the links suppressed; free association does the hop skip and jump along these points, behaving like quanta. He will not believe that the art form of the age is not the diary any more but the case-history. Anyway stream of consciousness is a misnomer, suggesting something flowing between banks. Milky Way would be more accurate. Consciousness is a smear. Come Trash my love, throw them coal black haunches over the moon! Pia's love will do you good, it will cure both your pretty dimples.

> *At night poor Robin's slanguage fails;*
> *He feels his mind go off the rails.*

Out there on the plateaus of his loneliness he feels the freezing pelagic spray drying on his cheeks. He stares and stares into the eye of the blizzard but all is wiped away by the softly falling snow. "Toby the minute you start to have opinions about day-to-day matters you cease to be an artist and start to be a citizen. Choose." But I was angry with myself for getting lost in the shallow meshes of such an argument. One should never explain, merely hint. Bruce said: "When we were younger we were actually and physically moved by books. *Seraphita* so disturbed Piers that he threw it aside and rushed into the open air; feeling suffocated at being found out. He writhed on the grass like a dog to drive away the vision it raised of a perfected love between himself and his sister." Yes, when one was young – poetry with requisite built-in shiver. Then later one finds oneself facing love affairs as full of bones as any fish – beauty bold and sweet or full of peace and weariness like Pia,

> *en pente douce*
> *au bout portant*
> *glisse glisse chérie pourtant*

vers bonheur bechamel
love, the surprise parcel
will never treat you well.

A kiss like an interval between points in mathematics, like a cigarette-end burning in the dark. I asked her once when we had been drinking a very human wine to tell me what it felt like with Trash. She coloured deeply and was silent for a long while, her eyes all the time fixed truthfully on my own, a little wrinkle of thought on her brow. Then: "Trash's body smells of wedding-cake."

FOUR

Life with Toby

WITHOUT THE COMPANY OF TOBY I SHOULD NEVER HAVE had the courage to return to the chateau; and the fact that he began so earnestly to work gave a high seriousness to our new life there. While he laboured in the old muniments room on the medieval deposits of several generations of Nogarets, I sifted softly through the archives of a more recent time – Sutcliffe's papers, his letters from Pia; from the Duchess, and from other people in his life. I occupied Piers' old studio and Toby the three guest rooms – this purely for company. So, like a couple of retired bachelors we put up a common front against the gnawings of solitude. Once or twice the lawyer came up to Verfeuille on some business connected with Piers' affairs, and once I glimpsed the Abbé in the grounds though he did not greet me, and did not actually enter the chateau. He had a long talk with one of the older servants and then sent to demand permission to visit the vaults where the family had for generations buried its dead. This was at once granted. He disappeared into the wood for an hour or two and then returned, once more to the servants' quarters, to give back the keys. Summer came and we went for long walks in the heat, in the perfumed dust of the Provençal countryside. Toby's great study, entitled *The Secret of the Templars*, was well on the way to being finished; it had taken him a number of years as far as the execution was concerned, but of course many more if one counted the length of time he had actually spent reflecting upon the subject and reading round it. It was a lifework, and his reputation as a historian would stand or fall by it. It was a strange period for me. We spoke little about the tragedy of Piers, and once a week we rode down to Montfavet to spend a few quiet hours with Sylvie. But for the most part it was long walks and early rising. I felt less of an orphan.

It was during this period that Toby decided to read me a few of the opening passages from his book in a suitable décor for it – a deserted Templar fortress which stood on the dry flanks of the steep ravines beyond the Pont du Gard – that bronze masterpiece of Roman plumbing, constructed apparently of a stone like honey-cake and set in its steep context of rock over the slow Gardon. We slept in the fort, and that night a bronze moon rose over it like an echo. The situation was suitably romantic for the reading of a work which was designed to surpass Gibbon in style and mellifluousness. . . . At least these were the pretensions of the author expressed for the most part when he was slightly flown with wine. Appropriate too was the great fire of thorns and furze which he had stacked against the walls of the inner bastion. This huge fire bristled and roared up into the calm sky making the gloomy precincts as bright as noon – and enticing the lizards and snakes out of the rock to bask in the glare. Our blankets we had spread in a sheltered corner. Toby, placing his gold-rimmed spectacles on his nose, set our dinner to simmer and uncorked a demijohn of the old Verfeuille red which glowed in our glasses with the embers of old recollections of half-forgotten journeys and excursions of our youth by the light of the moon. Then he seated himself on a stone and took up the thick manuscript, a whole life.

"Even after six centuries of silence the name echoes on, troubling and mysterious, vibrating in our memories with a kind of tragic uncertainty, tragic doubt. The Templars! What was their sin, what caused their sudden, almost inexplicable destruction? The dust lies thick upon the manuscripts which should provide an answer to such a query, but which in fact only seem to accentuate the mystery by their extraordinary ambiguities, their improbabilities. The more one studies the evidence the less convinced one becomes that the truth has not been tampered with: that the secret has been deliberately hidden, that the so-called facts lie, that the existing evidence darkens judgement. Is there, then, no answer to the secret of their strange fate – or must we rest our case for ever upon surmises and evidence as baffling as it is circumstantial?

"Across the whole of Europe and the Mediterranean Sea, from the fogs and rains of the north to the sunshine and orange-lands of Syria, Portugal, Morocco, are spread the sad relics of this order – abandoned castles and keeps which still insist, by their malefic silence and desuetude, that something momentous and tragic came to pass on that faraway Friday the thirteenth in 1307. On that date one of the most powerful religious orders the world has ever known was struck down overnight, to founder and disintegrate without defence in the fires of the Inquisition at the instigation of a weak Pope and a criminal French king. Fantastic accusations were formulated which stupefied the finest minds and hearts of this order, so long renowned for its piety, self-abnegation, and devotion to duty. The Templars were the foremost fighting arm of the day, in terms of military strength quite capable, one might have thought, of conquering the whole of Europe; moreover, from a political point of view, the knights were the bankers who handled the gold of the Kings. . . . .

"Yet at dawn on Friday the thirteenth in 1307, in conformity with the *lettres de cachet* sent out by King Philippe Le Bel to all the seneschals of France – (orders they were forbidden to open and read before the twelfth of October) – the 5,000 field officers of the Templar order, from the least important up to the Grand Master, Jacques de Molay, together with his personal bodyguard of sixty armed knights, were arrested at the instigation of the Chancellor of France, Guillaume de Nogaret. They were taken up in one night like rabbits. There is no record of a protest of any kind nor of any resistance. The main attack was launched at the world headquarters of the order, the Paris Temple. Why?

"The accusations formulated against them seem, even in retrospect, astonishing in their extravagance; one has the impression that the knights themselves were dumbfounded by them, rendered incapable of reacting out of sheer astonishment. A religious order world-renowned for its frugality and chastity was suddenly accused of heresy, sodomy, secret practices, and religious beliefs hostile to the Christianity of the day. The suddenness of the blow, the perfect timing of the attack, and the devastating nature of the charges left no time for thought, no time to prepare a defence against such outrageous suppositions. It would not be an exaggeration to say that the whole of Europe was struck dumb also with surprise; and then became scared and uneasy about the gravity of the charges and the increasing flimsiness of the evidence brought against the knights. The long sad trials began which were to drag on and on into what must have seemed an infinity of cruelty. The less the Inquisitors found, the more summary their judgements, the higher burned the pyres on which the bodies of the Templars smoked. Nobody was convinced: yet everybody was silent.

"But the silence of bewilderment or outright disdain could do nothing to help the knights in their fearful religious dilemma. They wondered, they hesitated, they compromised. Could the King be serious? Or was this a vulgar attempt by a spendthrift always in need of cash to wrest the Templar riches from them? If so, what a dangerous way of achieving his ends – for the order had a fully armed fighting force of 15,000 knights in the field: perhaps the only fully equipped and mature military order then in Europe. They did nothing. The long dreary Inquisitions into their heresies, which today cover a mountain of parchment in Toulouse, Avignon and elsewhere are extraordinarily disappointing in their lack of coherence, their ambiguities. Yet the basic fact remains that in one night, over an area of roughly 150,000 square miles a total of 15,000 persons were taken up by the authorities. There was no struggle recorded anywhere. What could have caused every single preceptory to surrender so completely? A consciousness of the innocence of the knights? A belief that an inquiry would vindicate the Order. Surprise? Yet the Templars would seem to have held every trick in their hand had they wished to resist. Their chain of fortresses, like mastodons, was impregnable, their armies were crack fighting ones. Afterwards the King, Philippe, tried to shift the responsibility to the Inquisition, saying that he had acted on their advice. But this was not true, for they were informed after the event, though they were invited to join forces with him and handle the trials in the best religious style. Nogaret had sent twelve spies into the various chapters to collect evidence against the knights. It is worth remembering that his parents had been burned at the stake as cathars by the very Templars whom he helped destroy. At any rate he ignited the pyre, so to speak, at the instigation of the King. But though the flames burned high and long there remains something mysterious and unrealised about the whole business. The truth eludes one. For example, of all the thousands of Templar knights tortured and interrogated over a seven-year span, only three confessed to homosexual acts. . . .

"But the traditional view of the matter should be set out clearly since it is the view which holds the academic field today, and there is no inherent improbability about it. It runs as follows, and the chief proponent of it is Professor Basil Babcock of Oxford:

" 'The real sin of the Templars is far from mysterious – though it is never mentioned in the long list of 127 questions addressed to each of the knights by the Inquisition. The sin was the sin of usury, and the only rational explanation of their sudden and catastrophic fall turns upon it and upon nothing else. They were, we must remember, the most powerful and widely extended money-lenders and bankers of the Middle Ages, and their enormous wealth first grew from the fact that they financed the crusades as well as taking an active part in the fighting in order to safeguard and watch over their investments. The Temple in Paris was the focus and centre of the world gold market. The Popes and the Kings were encouraged to deposit their wealth with the Temples for safety – wealth which was not locked away in the vaults but reinvested under guarantees and at a lively percentage. In sixty years of studious banking backed up by the might of the sword and the chain of fortresses stretching across the civilised world the wealth of the Templars cast a shade over the riches of Kings and Popes alike. It exercised a strange hold on the economic pattern of Europe's life. With riches comes cupidity, and with power insolence. So the stage was set for the downfall of the Order.'

"It is the purpose of this detailed study to suggest that there was in fact a Templar heresy, contracted perhaps in the Orient which, on religious grounds, and from the narrowest Christian viewpoint, justified their total destruction. While they were *outremer* in the service of the Cross they became contaminated with the secret gnostic beliefs which coloured their notions of good and evil and which qualified their allegiance to the Pope and Christendom. They became secret dissenters, and in the technical sense, or purely theological sense, supporters of the Anti-Christ of the day. At first sight this explanation of the mystery might seem somewhat bold and perhaps even rash. But there is enough evidence to support it, and we hope to show by a painstaking examination of available records that this is, in fact, what happened, though of course not all the knights were necessarily in the know. The Order transformed itself from within and disseminated knowledge at different levels – a sort of freemasonry in structure grew up; and naturally enough, because just to think such things, which threw the whole of Christianity into question, was extremely dangerous. They lost their gamble, and were rooted out, extirpated to the last man. Issues may have become confused, evidence tangled and muddled. But reason there was, and the present writer hopes to show it."

Toby threw down his manuscript and tossed some more wood on to the fire. I was silent. Despite the rather heavy rhetorical flourishes it was not bad as an introduction to his book. It was at least a direct challenge to the prevailing author-ities. I watched him pacing up and down, organising the dinner, with the light glinting on the gold rims of his spectacles. Memory seized me as I lay, sunk in a composed drowse, before the vast fire. Our shadows danced upon the walls and I thought of Plato, and then of Akkad. I thought of our lives, our travels, which now had diminished and faded into a kind of limbo where we had nothing much more to expect of the world. The fire burned, the whole of Provence (our own land) slumbered around us in the light of the dying moon. Toby was going grey at the temples, so was I. And the dead? They slumbered peacefully, waiting for us to join them. We ate in silence and happiness – the silence of deep thought: for the threads of every-thing Toby had written led us directly back to our own youth, and to Akkad and the adventures of the deserts which ringed Alexandria. I saw how the theme went now, and I could see that if Toby handled his materials with circumspection he would have a book which would not be easily superseded in its domain. He sat and riffled through it by the fire, and began to talk and expound, no longer content to read the prose in his somewhat stentorian voice.

I lay and drowsed. Some of these things I knew, and some not. I had entered, thanks to the wine, into a state of warm bemusement hovering on the borders of sleep. Yes, Avignon became Rome in 1309, just at the time of the Templar trials; Toby said: "Of course all of this I owe to that chance remark of

Rob's, and the letter from Akkad. Do you recall?" Drifting through my mind came sadder fragments from the Sutcliffe papers which I had been trying to arrange in chronological order. "Honey, Robin is all heaped up with sadness. His roses don't sing no more. He's all cased up in sorrow, poor Robin. He's gone silent, he needs subtitles, honey." Trash, with her "pretty hobbling French". . . .

"To get to the bottom of the matter," Toby was saying as he scanned his huge typescript, "one must try to see what was behind the questions posed by the Inquisition. For example, those concerned with sodomy. For while sodomy was not more rare in the Middle Ages than it is today, no stigma of effeminacy attached to it. Many Crusaders must have been of that persuasion, and of course the popular revulsion to unnatural practices went deep. Indeed the penalties were hard, though almost never invoked. The charge was punishable by being burned alive or buried alive at this time. But this was only what appeared on the statute books. Yet the Jews, for example, were never charged with sexual aberrations by their medieval persecutors. One wonders why. Even the charge of ritual murder seemed to lack any specifically sexual tinge. In the case of the godless Moslems they were merely criticised for a superlative incontinence. But – and here is a fact of great significance – homosexuality was thoroughly identified with *religious dissent* of the gravest kind – so much so that Bulgar, that is to say Bogomil, remained always by connotation a religio-sexual charge – whence later *bougre* and *bugger* evolved from it. . . . You see?"

The firelight splashed upon his grave features as he expounded; but now his exposition was punctuated by yawns. We lay watching the climbing sparks spray the night sky. The whole of this rich elucidation of the gnostic sin – some of which I had heard or read before – went drifting through my senses like a drug, illustrated as it were by a great gallery of coloured scenes from our own history, our own encounter with the last survivors of this ancient heresy. I saw the large opaque eyes of Akkad gazing at us across the whorls of incense. The great snake, the Ophis of their beliefs, rose hissing once more to the height of a man. Toby was talking with regret of the shattered remnants of Gnosticism, of how the central faith had been shattered and dispersed by the persecution of the orthodox; riddled by schisms, weighed down under the sarcasm and hatred of the early Christians, they took to the deserts, wandered into Syria where the mountains sheltered them, or followed the gipsy trails into Europe, gaining precarious footholds in places like Bulgaria which lent them such an unsavoury name. Meanwhile the Church Fathers saw to it that all accurate documentation on their lives and beliefs was destroyed or garbled. Can they have been as vile as the orthodox believed them to be? They were, after all, the real Christians. . . . I could hear the voice of Sutcliffe cry *"Libido scienti! The very albatross of unreason!"* The pitiful fragments remaining can only offer us a hint of those early systems which were grouped around the basic contention, the basic grammar of spiritual dissent. Early communists like the Adamites, for example, who proscribed marriage as sinful and declared all women common property. Sex played a leading role, if we are to believe their enemies. The first conventicles were in caves, and the religious services led to mass sexual congress. Carpocrates . . . ; Epiphanius speaks of a sect which during secret rites sacrificed a child, doing it to death with bronze pins, making an offering of its blood. They were accused of eating human flesh – and their fire-baptism is one of human flesh turned to ashes by fire. A child gotten upon a mortal woman by a demon – our old friend Monsieur in fact. The ashes were a religious viaticum, a sacrament at birth and death alike. . . .

Unsavoury?

"You know very well," says Toby, "that I have always

been in love with Sabine. She has always exemplified this horrible faith to me. Rob was right to call it a grubby little suicide academy. It isn't even a pessimism of a philosophic kind for that would be the opposite of something. It's worse, a sort of ungraduated colourless hopelessness about the very fabric and structure of our thought, our universe. A silent anguish which rises from the depths of non-being. A flayed mind still attached to the tree, but which won't give in, stays upright under the lash. How could an ordinary healthy man like me go in for it? It revolted everything in me, and yet without it, Sabine would not be half as perfect as she is. Yet it is thanks to her that I know what I do about the provisions made by the central members to do away with each other, since individual suicide is forbidden to them. You and Sylvie never belonged to the inner club, neither did I. But Piers did and Sabine did."

"Is she dead then?" I was startled.

"No. I had a letter last week from her."

"Toby are you making this up?"

"Upon my honour, no."

"Then where do the Templars come into the picture? Surely the chief charge against them was the setting up of a false God, an idol as focus for their black masses. Where does that fit in?"

He sat watching me with curiosity for a long moment and then said: "I have been thinking a great deal about what you told me. You know the mysterious idols they were supposed to set up to worship in their chapters – were they really human heads treated with natron after the Ancient Egyptian pattern – idols of Persian or Syrian provenance? I am waiting for an answer, and it must come either from Akkad himself or from Sabine. I simply dare not go any further than that for the moment. Because of Piers."

Of course I could see that in his mind he was thinking

back to our conversation about the macabre funeral – it had shaken him as much as it had shaken me. "When they decide to join the fraternity in the full sense they agree that when their time comes, and lots are cast to determine it, they agree to be murdered by someone belonging to the chapter who will be designated for the task – but they will never know exactly who and exactly how the order will be executed. You understand, I took all this for an elaborate joke for a good while, until the facts convinced me. Those names on the so-called death-map of Piers – remember? But what he was actually trying to do with that map was to assess the probabilities, to try to guess who might have been told off to do the deed. Piers had received the little package with the straws which showed that the chapter had considered his destiny. He must have been warned that only a few months lay ahead of him – it was customary. But I suppose he was curious, excited, perhaps very much afraid. It is not agreeable to be informed that one's time is up – whether it is a doctor or a gnostic who brings the information."

"And the Templars?"

"Well you know, the setting up of idols and the gnostic baptism by fire – there were hints of all that; my thought is that they were of a degenerated valentinian order. The idols represented the eons, divine emanations, and their origin was probably ophite – about which we know a thing or two at first hand."

"I see. And what about the great aerolith at Paphos which they are supposed to have worshipped under the name of Bahomet? Have you any explanation?"

"The name could be either a corruption of the word Mahomet or come from *bàphe metéos*, the baptism of wisdom. Why not?"

"A gnostic hint?"

"Yes. You know, Bruce, the Templars' primitive role seems to have enjoined them to seek out and redeem excommunicated knights and admit them to the Order after absolution by a bishop. Naturally at first they gathered up a rabble of rogues and masterless men, perjurers, robbers, committers of sacrilege, who streamed into the Holy Land in the wake of the armies in search of plunder and perhaps salvation. Unlike the Hospitallers it was a military order from its very inception. The pretentions towards chastity and spartan living were very clearly defined. Plain white was their colour, plain white wool, linen undershirts and drawers of sheepskin. Their standard was a piebald one. They offered hardship, poverty and danger as the only rewards for joining them. You see, they were not joking! They were inflexible moral puritans – just the kind that suddenly breaks under certain exotic influences. Now while they were on active service in the Middle Orient they came to grips with the Assassins, a sect based in Persia which performed ritual killings under the influence of *quat*, hashish. The leader of this sect was the Old Man of the Mountains – Hassan ibn as Sabbah, whom the Templars knew well. His assassins were free-floating mercenaries who made common cause with Saracen or Druse, or any other group that took their fancy in Lebanon or Syria. But their transcendent aim was not so much the destruction of the infidel invader as that of the Orthodox Caliphate at Baghdad. But in their way they formed a sort of Moslem military order not unlike that of their Christian adversaries.

"There is an odd similarity in the hierarchy of the groups – it extends even to the costume: the fighting uniform with the red hood for example. The whole thing was really a momentous meeting of a grass culture (blue grass, hashish, *quat*) and a wine culture – the Christian wine doing service for the redeemer's blood. Wine as a blood substitute held the Christian guilt partially in check, but not always. When it broke out, as in the siege of Jerusalem, one sees what a hecatomb these creatures could build of their fellow men. They wanted to drink blood, they could not disguise it. The assassins killed frugally, imagining they were killing minds, dry as flies."

He was silent, thinking, with his sleepy head on his breast. Then he went on. "Grape and grass cultures suddenly meet and for a while do battle. Then one side wins with the sword and loses morally. One kills like an automaton, the other must drink the blood of the victim. The Templars started going astray right here."

He chuckled and placed the sacred typescript under his head to form a pillow. "Can you not *now* see the right true end of poor Babcock? His hair will fall out around the time of the menopause, he will wilt, he will lose all his mayonnaise, Bruce."

But my mind was far away from these common-room squabbles. "Tell me what Sabine had to say," I asked and a preoccupied silence overcame him. He said suddenly: "How difficult is it to remove a human head?" "Not very difficult," I said, "and it can be done quite neatly. Just clamp off the big arteries, section the cartilage with a butcher's saw and lift."

"I do not know what to think about Piers, and the letter Sabine wrote was full of ambiguities. One thing is sure, Piers had received his *laissez-passer* and was waiting for the blow to fall. He must have confided in Sylvie, hence her relapse, her conflict, for she would have wanted to go with him and at the same time stay with you. Her relapse was a compromise which absolved her of refusing to choose."

"And the head – are you suggesting that there is some disgusting secret society trying to resurrect Templar practices with the head of the last Nogaret?"

"We won't know the truth until Sabine comes and tells us. I can think of a number of different explanations of these facts, but none which covers all the possible contingencies. In every explanation there is an odd fact or two which won't.

But usually the truth is quite simple. Suppose it was Sabine herself who had been elected to complete the task? Piers could hardly be suspicious of her. We know that she was among the last of his visitors, perhaps the very last."

"Yes, but how did he *die*?"

"Of course they found no trace of poison, but there are quite a lot of poisons which leave no trace. Fresh prussic acid for example among others . . . But of course none of these considerations would explain the removal of his head. Who took it off and why?"

"The death mask was made on the orders of Jourdain, but nothing so drastic as the removal of the head would be needed for that sort of operation."

"Of course. You know, Sabine once told me of a very clever murder which took place in Alexandria – it was on the pattern of Judith and Holofernes. To drive a nail without a head swiftly into the skull of a sleeping man . . . the hair would hide its existence. But of course in an X-ray one would see the shadow of a spike that stuck into the brain. . . ."

Far away, on the stony *garrigues* by the fading light of the harvest moon one could hear the musical calling of wolves. Provence slumbered in the moist plenitude of harvest weather, the deep contented mists and damps of fruition. The dusty roads were furrowed by the wobbling wains and carts and tractors bearing their mountains of grapes to the vats. Blue grapes dusted with the pollen of ages. In the fields lines of harvesters moved with their pruning hooks and sickles; followed by clouds of birds.

"Toby!" I said, and he gave a grunt, hovering on the very borders of sleep. "Do you really believe that something like that happened?"

"I can't tell," he said at last, "but if anyone knows the truth it will be Sabine. I have a feeling she will turn up one of these days and then we shall get the whole truth from her. I have written to her everywhere." When she was wandering the world like this she had no address, not even a Poste Restante. The faint chance of reaching her was some celebrated café with a notice-board on which one posted letters, the Hawelka in Vienna, Molard in Geneva, Baudrot in Alexandria, Groppi in Cairo, the Dôme in Paris. . . . There was an outside chance of catching her on the wing in one of these places.

If one were lucky she would reply at once. But some sort of obstinate premonition seemed to tell me that we would not see Sabine again – she had hinted in a recent letter that she too had received her quittance, her message – and that all these brain-wrenching problems would remain unanswered, lie buried in the dusty future or the rotting palimpsests of the past. Provence is particularly rich in myths and symbols, and does not like to be interrogated by the idle forebrains of modern hominids. It was like the key – the great key which the Nogarets had handed down to Piers. The legend ran that it was the key to a Templar vault where a vast treasure had been buried out of reach of the King. But where to find the lock which would fit such a great pistol-key? Piers spent years travelling about all over the country in a vain attempt to find this perhaps mythical treasure. In vain! In vain. Now the key lay in the muniments room and was used by Toby as a paperweight. There too I felt that no issue to the mystery would ever be found. It was all part of the Provençal image, the story of a land which from ancient times had given itself up to dreaming, to fabulating, to tale-telling, with the firm belief that stories should have no ending.

Dawn was breaking and a heavy dew had settled on our blankets; we would be slightly stiff and perhaps a little rheumatic as we retraced our steps to the little inn by the Pont du Gard where we had left our horses.

❖❖❖

THE GREEN NOTEBOOK
(Sutcliffe Papers)

Comedy or tragedy? Which side up, old boy. The truth is that one could make either out of our troubles. When, for example, I decided to take my "homosexual component" (O! felicity of phrasing) for a romp I instantly got a clap. After all, Dr. Joy had assured me that my choice of a boyish sexual partner like Pia argued a heavy homosexual layer in myself. Curiosity got the better of me. But it was like sleeping with a graphic mule. It was ludicrous, it was tragic, it was funny. Pia was upset when I wrote her but Trash, in telling me so, added: "Honey Rob, I'm gonna tell you I jest laughed myself yellow when she read me your letter. You crazy great man you. I'd jest love to've been with you for the kicks." Things are what you make them and a salutary clap is where one might imagine it to be. Clowns weep where angels fear to tread. For quite a while I was out of action. Sat alone of an evening mulcting a piano of tunes: Poor Rob.

A few words passed between us that evening in the sunken rose garden where they had planted Chinese tea-roses the colour of champagne. Perfumed, and yellow for Tao. I can still feel the weight of those words, like an oracle which brushes schizophrenia. Pia sat so still, hardly breathing.

At the beginning, afraid of losing her, he hit upon an idea of genius. "I must get really ill to make her love me." He did, it worked, now they are married – or were. I can show them to you if you wish.

Ah Pia, aim always for the lowest uncommon denominator. Trash, you big out-of-date Thing, come here and put your shoes in my mouth and your puss on my hat. I'll fit you, my black giraffe, and teach you to solder those rubber lips to Pia's.

In the chateau at Verfeuille when an old chambermaid died in her bed, from "natural causes" as they say, they covered all the mirrors in the house with black crêpe until her funeral.

What does it matter? Every wish contains some grain of death. The mind has an idler switch, an automatic pilot. That is where the pretty inventions come from.

Talking of collective nouns with Toby, pride of lions, flock of sheep, etc., he suggested an "amazement" of women.

In the midst of life we are encircled by the great sea of death about which we know nothing. For the sage silence is a fuel; it whistles through the rigging of the nerves like a Force 8 gale. Time has it in for us, and we for time. I was aware of this all the time, with every single kiss. At Innsbruck the *föhn* was blowing enough to drive one mad. The old novelist confided his manuscript to a traveller in Malta who on arrival in Marseille was found to be suffering from the plague. They burnt all his belongings, and that is how the work disappeared. (Coleridge.)

Sylvie says that the word "love" is a blank domino. She is right. I am swallowing my pride. *Âme sœur, âne sûr.*

When loneliness goes gaunt, Pia, nourished on long absences, honey . . .

Régine had the air of a rather vulgar duchess playing a part. Had she been a real duchess like old Tu she would perhaps have been even more vulgar but much more natural.

Cloudy white wine of Aramon with a bluish meniscus hinting of ethyl.

Swollen tongue, cloudy urine, enuresis, spatula . . . Ugh! Dying of an obscure kidney condition. The old defeated priest. I felt sorry to be so anti Christian when I saw him so nobly suffering.

Je souffre chérie, donc je suis bien portant, c'est à dire presque humain.

> *Je suis ni un refoulé*
> *Ni un cérébral*
> *Mais un vieu Epicurean*
> *Un peu ogival.*

Printer's ink from a proof gave him Scotland Yard hands. Ink lingering malingering.

The blood chirps and twitters, it is dateless;
Our ancestors send their dead tap-roots through us.

250

Her toes printed in baby powder
On a bathroom floor in Orta. Clean and pink as pigeons' toes.

Outside the window a catspaw of wind on the dark sifted lake.
One sail throbbing, trying to break loose.
On the balcony beauty takes you by the throat. Yield!

Munch the black flesh, Rob,
Thou gnostic stained with camel juice
As a woman she seemed to me

> une cherchesolitude
> une souffredouleur
> une fauchepistolet
> une polycombinable.

Ah God, for some simple mentholised concubine whose
primitive telephone is all ears.

As dolls live on in children's sleep;
So she in mine where angels come to weep.

Love tamed by a tolling life
Reason acclimatised by love
As below, so above. A wife, a wife!
My kingdom for a knife.

> Wanted: a tripod not a pulpit
> a poet not a parson

prophecy not homily
lux not lucubration.

Mon cher, parler c'est de manquer de tact.

Toby's Old Man of the Mountains
His assassins' balls were blue as fountains,
Their scrotums were deep umber
And their penises sweet lumber.

I often amuse myself by imagining a privileged communication about my case, if case it be, between Doctor Joy and Doctor Young. "This fellow Sutcliffe who is clinically suffering from an aggravated spleen due to the pangs of disprised love, much resembles the celebrated gentleman we find in Janet. Beset by a massive depression which induces listlessness, apathy, inactivity, he himself describes his state as a 'crisis of lifelessness'. He has tried everything to wrench himself free of this fearful *cafard* – for six months he kept himself drunk on alcohol or smoke. In vain. Nothing amused him, nothing beckoned. He decided at last to commit suicide, and strangely enough the moment he came to this decision he felt very much better, quite toned up in fact. The excitement engendered by the decision to die perked him right up; he had not felt so gay for ages. He smiled as he wrote all his friends touching letters of goodbye. It put him in a very good humour and he began to really enjoy life. He amused himself by firing at his reflection in a mirror, and then actually turned the weapon on himself. But he only caused himself a scratch. With disgust he noted that suicide was really too painful, and he set the thought

252

aside for a while. Then like a blue fruit the melancholia started to grow again."

For a while he could see her very clearly when he closed his eyes. Tall lace-up boots of cream-coloured kid. A long closely buttoned coat like a guardsman's trench coat with copper buttons. White kid gloves. A scarf of blue at her throat and a kind of Scotch bonnet on her brilliantly blonde head. The eyes could go sea-grey to bright periwinkle-blue, gentian-blue or soft plumbago. She walks by the lake this tall pale girl with bowed head; she is reading Amiel, and the tears of sympathy come into her eyes. Hidden away on her shoulder is the tiny vaccination mark, prettier than any beauty spot, which he had so often kissed.

The hair very fine and softly wavy, a kind of Circassian ash-blonde. For a while they navigated by the eyes, those plant-bulbs of the head, which convey everything without a sound. Two intuitives find language an obstacle, a clumsy hurdle. The eyes understand wordlessly – for words conceal more than they reveal. How hard it must be to be blind and desperately in love!

In her sleep she grinds her teeth; waking at dawn a glance of pale fire, like a sodium lamp. Naked and uncocooned I took the nymph in my arms, drawing a blank slip in the lottery of love. A doctor of literature with concrete eyes. The suave machinery of psychotalk. I walk the public gardens like a scalded hare. Fat quibbling bottoms of mothers and prams. In the shop windows I gaze eagerly at my own beauty – but all I see is a big baggy man obviously suffering from piles, sunk into his overcoat like a canvas-backed duck. I heard of an old artist who mounted the skull of his mistress on a velvet cushion with jewels for eyes.

It is night now, deep night, and my skull is full of grey mutter.

How I have come to hate this town! Full of negroes and fretful lepers with squints. Cold as a wife-swapper's embrace, and full of unverified girls. It is dead; lunatics never take holidays. "Smoked out by smoke like old beehives, the stinging vestiges of other lives."

One basic question whimpers and sobs on below all the others: where have we come from? Where are we going?

I feel terrible today, like a parenthesis between two cultures both of which I loathe. The reviews of the new book were all bad or grudging. A critic is a lug-worm in the liver of literature.

It was full winter I recall. My first in Geneva. I had stayed on because of her. I went one evening to collect her for the concert. Deep snow was falling and the wind was as keen as a razor; the frost hurt, and it was almost impossible to stand upright. They had filled the tramlines with sand as a brake to prevent the trams from skidding off in all directions like pebbles on ice. She was waiting for me in the hall of the gloomy aquarium-like apartment house where she had a flat. She was framed in all the splendour of her evening dress and the magnificent fur, against the lighted mirrors of the lift. And she was on *crutches*. In *furs*. She had broken an ankle while skiing. I stared speechlessly at so much beauty and surprise. I almost sobbed with lust.

Where would you imagine all this would end? Three guesses would not be enough. Pia had been impelled to take

Trash to every one of the places we had visited together after our marriage. I suppose I had some foolish notion about educating her sensibility, a notion which perhaps she also shared *vis-à-vis* Trash. But what could one do with darling Trash? She screamed with laughter at Venice, the Acropolis seemed to her insanitary and all broken up, Cairo made her laugh even more because of the donkeys. . . . Painstakingly Pia waded through the sum of the world's culture, following in the footsteps of the Master. And so at last they came to Angkor Wat, but by this time Trash was beginning to fall ill; the slow fever was tenacious: was it malaria perhaps? Her teeth rattled in her black face. She had sudden fits of febrile weeping, from pure fatigue. But relentlessly Pia pressed on with her lover. I think that she knew that Lokesvara held the secret to our lives – it was there, curiously enough, that we had really loved each other. You know the Chinese fancy that one has two birthplaces – one the real physical one, and one which is a place of predilection, the place in which one was psychically born. Our love was born in the upper terraces of the Bayon. Those huge mastodon faces carved out of the bare rock, the colour of putty, cigar-ash, graphite, exuding that tremendous calm – the boom of the celestial surf on the shores of the mind. Here she took my hand and held on to it like a terrified child. Slanting stone eyes, thick stone lips, in which the vision turned inwards upon the life of the mind bathing itself in the glow of reality. One realised the sheer fatigue of living in this temporal relativity, and also that it wasn't necessary. There was a way, expressed by these stone clouds, of sidestepping the time-chain. She said: "I'm terrified with joy, Rob." And now poor darling she had for company the oblivious lover. The screams of laughter uttered by Trash rang out among the statues. "It's just the damnedest thing since Cecil B. de Mille," she must have shouted. And Pia? Did she recapture the old silence and think of me? I see her walking about, pale and withdrawn, perhaps just whistling under her breath as she often did.

The entrance to the Prah Khan stays the mind with its calm surprises. A broad avenue peopled with a line of life-sized genii. On the left the daevas with their calm smiles, slant eyes, and long sweet ears pricked up to catch the music of inner silence. To the right the cold and serious asuras, round eyes, saddle noses and their mouths turned down sardonically. Both lines hold in their negligent hands a gigantic serpent, its seven-headed hood spread, its teeth and elaborate feathered crest alerted, to spread out in fan fashion before the leading figure. It is writhing, trying to escape, but they are calmly holding it to form a balustrade along which one walks, pacing up large grey flagstones. I remember the rustle of dried leaves under our shoes. Lizards like jewels rubbed their eyes and tapped the stone, curious to see strangers.

We did not look at each other because we felt shy. Immediately beyond this kind of snake balustrade the forest opens in all its prolixity; in ancient times there was a lake here-abouts but it has largely dried out, and its marshwater is so thickly covered with waterweed and lilies that it looks like an Irish meadow. You walk stiffly, indeed a trifle ceremoniously, up the long avenue of genii and through the last portal; and then you find yourself unexpectedly in a sort of labyrinth of courtyards, chambers, corridors and vestibules. An occasional shattered statue smiles out of its mutilation like a war-hero. There is a troubling stench of rotting bat manure, rancid and heavy, and in the darker chambers comes the twitter and scutter of these twilight colonies hanging in the darkness making a mewing noise like newborn babies in a clinic devoted to twilight sleep.

Then of course comes Angkor Wat itself, like a quiet but breath-snatching verification of what had gone before. The wide stone causeway stretching over a moat was empty of pilgrims. A feast of water flowers studded the water. Water upon water, trisected by these passages, and on either side green meadows alive with egrets and snowy pelicans. The five-coned towers form a quincunx, and their flanks are scooped into niches in each of which has been placed a smiling buddha shaded by a nine-headed naga like a big palm fan. As you advance the bas-reliefs start contending for your attention with their writhing motifs. Elephants with their trunks locked in deadly combat and their riders hurling arrows: chariots full of gesticulating bowmen: an inextricable swarm of dead and dying, victorious and defeated in the last frenzy of war: bridled tigers: ships with dragon prows advancing methodically over mythological rivers thick with crocodiles and great fishes. This is the world, the real world, munching itself to death. Your world and mine.

But turn away from it and you will find an immediate reassurance in the other one. The tranquillity seeps into you as you watch the sun slanting down out of heaven to turn every-thing soft as ash, violet, mushroom. Yellow-robed monks come out of the monastery of an evening to spend a quiet breath of time sitting by the naga heads; their little ivory faces quite calm and expressionless. Fit descendants of those people on the war frescoes who carry spears or trays or jars, quietly launching themselves into battle with their thick lips and long ears, marching through avenues of trees loaded down by parrots and monkeys. The little calves of the dense grey water buffaloes gambol in the dusk. Pia sits with her hand in mine, but no longer afraid. "I have understood it," she said, as we rose and began the long walk back to the waiting car.

Yes, I too had understood it; and in a certain sense it helped me rather to understand the rest – that long sad journey of the lovers and the calamity which followed on their heels. But the whole thing exists for me like a series of pell-mell cinematic images thrown down one upon the other. How the rains caught them unawares, how their car broke down in the jungle and how they found no help for a day and a night. And Trash's fever mounted until she was racked like a black silk golliwog and bathed in sweat. Some Belgians from a Catholic Mission took them into their little cantonment and put them in a grass hut where the insects engendered by the new rain swarmed and pullulated. By the feeble rushlight the little Belgian priest kept vigil with Pia, nodding off to sleep. The rain thrust downwards. There could be no doctor until it stopped and the road was mended. But in two days the noble black heart of Trash gave out while she slept, her crucifix fell from her hand to the rush matting – that is how they knew she had gone. Her body was hurried into the damp black earth to become one with it. And Pia, after sorting out her effects and writing to her brother, wrote me a full account of everything in a tremulous but meticulous hand. It was not for my sake she did this, nor because she wished to plant darts in me, no. It was as if to make herself realise fully the fact of Trash's death, to let it impact on her, pierce the numbness. She described how Trash's little wrist-watch went on twitching all night until she could not bear it any longer and tore it off from her wrist. She ran out barefoot into the jungle with some vague idea of attracting a venemous snake to bite her. But all she collected in the streaming rain were the big white leeches the size of a human finger. When she staggered back to the mission she was covered in them. They would not let her tear them away with her fingers because that left a hole and often caused blood-poisoning or infection. But the little fathers came running with rock salt and poured small quantities of it directly onto the nauseating animals. The result was extraordinary. They explode, releasing all the blood they have drunk, and wither away like a toy balloon. Soon she was freed by this method, though covered in gouts of blood – her own. "I drank a great deal of whisky to try and gag the nerves," she said. It didn't work, it never does.

I realised when I read the letter that for me the paint was still fresh, her memory green. They say that when you love someone, absence and presence partake of one another; and that you cannot really lose each other until the mainspring, Memory, snaps. Lies! Sophistries! Inventions! When I read this long letter which ended: "You will never hear from me again. Your Pia." I felt like an old blind dog which had lost its bearings – the dog in the memoirs of Ulysses perhaps.

First I tore the letter across in a fury; then realising that it was certainly the last I would ever receive from Pia I tried laboriously to stick it together again, thinking that it should be placed with the others in the little leather writing case which had once been hers. I read it over slowly again. She had taken over so many of my tics! For example when she got deeply nervous, as I did when I was working on a book, a sea of prohibitions overwhelmed her and she could no longer write cursive; she was forced to print. But this new reading only reignited my fury. I took it to the lavatory with some vague intention of flushing it away for ever, but a sudden ridiculous and involuntary impulse took hold of me so that I tore it up and ate it.

Well, it is deep night once again, and here I am in this rotting city on the snatching curving medieval river. I walk about it sometimes with distaste and boredom. A man sitting at an open front door playing a violin. The Grey Penitents awash from the overflowing canal. An old sexton digging to bury the screams of the dead. And very old people, frail dry-points, in grooved clothes. It makes one think of old civilisations where puberty was treated with tact and custom sheltered sex, aware of its preciousness. Sitting in the leafy square by the Monument des Morts and finding the women grow more desirable with every *pastis*. Perhaps I will turn pederast and go for some slender woolly negro boy from softest Africa *gekommen*.

Woman the most perishable of the vertebrates but so much more hard-wearing than man; somewhere in the kingdom of the fossils there will be an inventory of all this, printed in mud and then rayed upon a stone, to bite slowly into it over countless ages. The big defeats cut so deep that one sees nothing on the surface except the smile. And the big definite experiences come only once, alas!

Yes, you only have one bite at the cherry. The long night is coming and the darkness is explicit. It drinks as tigers drink, in stealth.

If I am still alive tomorrow I shall write to the Duchess.

The thought brought with it no consolation but I set it down here for what it is worth. The act of sexual congress as the spirit-developer, the idea-hatcher is the source of all science, all art, all information which the spirit needs as its aliment. Psychic growth is nurtured by it. Purifier of mind, sharpener of intuition, procurer of the future. But to fulfil itself and do its job it must be part of a double act, a chiming act. It is strongest when practised by the beast with the two backs. I am not being waggish – look around you at the army of the sexually defeated. Look at Rob. We impotents are great collectors of *objets de vertu*, snuffboxes, musical boxes, knick-knacks. "There's the rub!" as Hamlet says.

Then along comes Uncle Joy and tells me about the great separation from the teat and the mother which echoes on and on like sobbing in a darkened room. Poor Rob has become the champion of waiting on empty sidings, deserted railway-stations, bus-shelters in the rain, desolate cafés, midnight airports. . . . Waiting on in an agony of apathy and thinking that Trash with her skinny legs had the walk of a senior microbe.

The art of prose governed by syncopated thinking; for thoughts curdle in the heart if not expressed. An idea is like a rare bird which cannot be seen. What one sees is the trembling of the branch it has just left.

They say that if you can get bored enough with calamity you can learn to laugh. Comedians are the nearest to suicide.

> Grief clothed in days, in hours
> In places things and situations
> Grief thrown out of the trains
> Or emptied from sturdy dustbins
> Overboard from ships in sea-cremations
> From eyes or lips or refuse-tips
> Sliding like coals in chutes
> Grief thrown into disuse by miner's time
> A dustbin full of memories' old disputes
> And then to see sorrow come with its
> Stealthy foreclosing, final demands, the grave
> While super-silence hovers like a nave.

On the dark lake a boat by moonlight with its load of shadows – mounds of black grapes a-glister. Somewhere from an alp, white with spring snow, the sound of a bugle. I thought of Pia's piano teacher Mr. Valdegour, a Russian prince down on his luck. He made her play with him. He played the piano the while to allay suspicion. Later he said that it was like sinking into yielding masses of music heaped up like snow or water or cloud. Cancer of the prostate and so on. . . . Suppose, Suppose, *Suppositoire*, eh doc?

"Life", said the little tedious priest, "is always pointing in the right direction, it is always bliss-side up if only we know how to take it." Perhaps. Perhaps. But to take it you must begin by giving, and this is hard to learn.

Ah the specialised kindness of taut Christian pharisees, les *pince-fesses* who fart like tent-pegs.

Pia, that last Christmas, the tree with its withered finery. Trash in her fur cape looked like the back legs of a pantomime bear, and Pia like a small lioness in spurs. That night a necrospasm – a unique depression follows, based on reproof, rebuke, self-reproach. Yet when I was ill she looked after me like an investment. Tenderness of a gun-dog.

There is mystery in the fact that if you repeat something meaningless long enough it begins slowly to gather significance and meaning as a needle on the disc gathers fluff. It becomes a *mantram*.

I tell everyone that Bloshford was operated on for hernia by a French doctor who left a pair of gardening-gloves inside him – or at least that is how he looks. Alternatively in certain lights he looks like a stage policeman who has swallowed the pea in his whistle.

The long suit of literature? Think of the impact of Melville's years of massive silence.

Bloshford does something quite hard to do – he trivialises reality. He does not feel the need for the monotony so essential to the creative spirit. I must be very jealous of him to go on like this. Bloshford! Gr . . . Gr . . . Woof! Woof!

In the Merchant Navy an expression signifying "to go mad" is wonderfully expressive. "Riding a corkscrew" it is called.

Tall and willowy, she was one of those pretty Swedish tubes into which one empties oneself in the desperate hope of getting a good night's sleep. (Régine.)

On gazing at my reflection in a mirror: "Even a God can be the victim of binocular vision."

Flesh-hating zealots avaunt! I am for all the soft collisions I can get. I have been decocted. Soft as a boxing-glove by moonlight. Houris! Hear my call to prayer!

Roheim tells us that the Central Australian Mother eats every second child, sharing it with the older baby. He adds that they are "all heroes" and "as happy as wolves" and goes on to attribute their idyllic characters to the fact that they have suffered no weaning period and no sex-repression (latency period). A link with gnostics? Hum. "We are born mad," writes Dr. Eder. "We acquire morality and become stupid and unhappy. Then we die."

The deliberate practice of helplessness in saints and women elicits sympathy and wonder.

Toby, in a flash of sincerity, said: "I have never spoken a truthful word in my life and I have always given several conflicting accounts of the same incident – so aware am I of the relativity of knowledge and the distortion of human vision. I am a born historian, so to speak."

Trapped between conflicting notions of rest and motion, man panics his way into the tomb, rest never bringing him the peace and reassurance he needs, motion only sterile change and ideal sorrow. O! Time the great Howler!

Mille baisers, Trash, *gelatineuses et patibulaires*. *Va caresser un chameau, Garce*. I am an old elephant and my back legs need polishing.

They were actually connected by the empty space between them, the interstices between feelings so to speak, which set up this electrical impulse called desire.

SUPPOSED POEM FOR PIA

Sweet valves, in breath you will correct
The soft ellipses of my husband's sleep,
And the dull *Quand? Quand?* Repeat the
Chink-Chink of the French town's little clocks
In bogus belfries on a sour note of final
Twang. Clang! Was that someone at the door?

Today he drank pints of decorated wine,
Rods of gold wine all prizewinners.
Could one presuppose that the death
Of an ageing writer somewhere alters
Reality, diminishing a space the size of him?

It is not possible to contrast man's view
Of himself with the reality he presents

And not to feel sick unto death at such
Pretensions of a complacent little ape.

And we who say we love – how much the worse
For us and for those who possess us. Think.
Rain on my fingers, the smoke of Ithaca,
An old blind dog waiting at a garden gate.

Last night he dreamed a negress for me, another Trash,
Took her in a thicket of whispers with a smile
That smelt of freshly turned earth, the open grave.

Pia writes: "The old Asian doctor had the face of a wistful cobra, but the mind was worn like the coping-stone of an ancient well; the ropes had grooved the stone. The well of knowledge is deep and the thirst of men is endless. But they know that the wells are drying out, the levels falling."

"Mirrors were originally invented to capture the reflection of flying swallows." Sylvie. She had read it somewhere no doubt.

As Thoreau nearly said: "Most wives live lives of quiet disapprobation." A well-furnished mind in an ill-starred codpiece. (Toby.)

The wind whistles in my crows-nest of bones
In the conning tower of the skull
The sharpshooters ambush of the eyeball
Death will be only a change of code, of zones.
The python sadness shuffles in to claim. . . . etc., etc.

A kid I fell into milk. I married and was a *coq en pute*. A writer big with book I hurried to Orta like a harvest in peril. To salvage a general principle from a mass of conflicting evidence can be both science and poetry.

Toby gorged on corybantic Cambridge Sausages. Marsupial dons bellying out like sails. Galleons of furry gowns.

Les grands sensuels agrés comme moi, Robin
Les sensuelles es Amour comme elle
Dans des jardins d'agrément jouant
Comme des poules dans les basses cours
Sont plutôt agronomiquement acariatres
Selon les pédérastes, les putains et les pâtres.

Mais ce soir si ce joli temps permet
Si l'equinoxe persiste
Nous allons entendre chanter tous les deux
La petite doxologie des toiles d'arraignés.
Éplucher le gros oignon de l'univers
Nous deux cachés par l'éventail de la nuit.
Écoute, c'est le temps qui coule
C'est la nuit qui fuit. A moi Bouboul!

I have shifted this huge weight
By only a hair in half a lifetime
Of dead breath and sinew, to somewhere else,
Merely a shift of weight, you'd say,
Though it might be heavier than air
But slow to grow as mammoth's teeth or hate,
A lifetime of nails growing on after death;

Yes, I have moved this huge weight,
By less than a weightless breath
And with it the weight of my afterlife
And massive, the weight of your death.

Something has collected around this long silence, Pia, the pearl
of silence formed round a grain of sand; the golden embryo of
the inner mind promised to the gnostics. They say there is
nothing like love to develop the spirit except grief, sweet
grief. *Ah! Ce beau temps où j'étais malheureuse*, sighed Madame
de Staël.
What would we not give for Byron's ruthless charm?
Calm and fearlessness at birth should be the natural attributes
of man, but entering the gear-box of process he has been
twisted out of true, out of camber.
A wooden leg, a dimple filled with pus, a wart with an eye.
Ah! The milky bagpipes of the latent wish! Tonight Sylvie
dragging and sucking at Chopin on the piano, while I read a
book about India – the smoked dung of merchant enterprise.

Prose should have a gleam in it like mica. The glint of nervous
insight. That moonlit night in the trenches the dead were
hanging on the barbed wire like sperm in a girl's bush.
Today I have been working under high pressure weaving my
necklace of suppositories. I have come to some conclusions,
like sex is not an act but a thought: a Tip Toe Thought. (Toby
in a high state of suppressed sincerity.)

Bruce told me that when the nurse walked on Sylvie's right
side she became invisible. Cranial hemiplegia? Apparently not
however.

Pia said: "When Trash leaves me I run a temperature."
And I? And I?

I am forever writing her a letter in my head which I know will end in the Dead-Letter Office, will fall *au rebut, en souffrance*, that is why I suffer from a profuse loss of calcium. I am learning to see dreams as the expiatory device which voids the anti-social content of wishes and allows them to act themselves out harmlessly – not from civic conscience but from fear of punishment.

Later comes an embryology of boredom, we topple into the law of inertia. The sluggish foetus which won't contract out of the cosy womb life. So process gets slowed down by cowardice and slowly ankyloses. Gangrene sets in. People are born with frozen affects, and stalk the planet like dead men. In cold blood. These are the faceless hominids who cause us so much trouble by acting out what we are repressing with such heroism.

Tobor the poet for example. His young wife fell into a volcano. He never married again, and the girl became dearer and dearer to him as she receded in time. He trailed his sorrow in poems which became as heavy as lead. Finally, having become world famous, he realised one day that what he owed to her was precisely this deliberate consciousness of her death. She could not have done this for his work by simply living on. It was her death which gave his poems pith. He felt so ashamed he stopped writing.

Trash's body was a breathing bas-relief which might have appealed to a corkscrew on shore-leave. Her red mouth was a sabre-cut of laughter, like a duelling scar. Discussing me with Pia she said: "He's the sort of guy always trying to make a silk purse out of a horse's ass."

If ever I said sex was funny it was only to emphasise the enormous fragility of the enterprise. Spare us this day our classical pruritus.

Have I no right to talk about it? Why, uxorious Raphael, how he loved the act which he did not find lonely – bathed in the candy-floss of women's bodies. Nowadays all that is needed is the leaden sperm of some deteriorated schizophrenic in order to make people feel at home.

Accused by Toby of deplorable political cynicism, I asked: "What sort of social conscience and political awareness would you expect of Robinson Crusoe?" No answer. He just sat there working his finger in his ear and his foot in his shoe like a sexually aroused tomcat works its tail paddle-fashion. He told me about a friend who left everything and went to Peking where he lived with a girl called Persistent Mosquito Net, a lightly toasted concubine. He beat her till she sang like a lark.

The last word pronounced by Buddha was "diligence". An uffish thought.

A Cinematograph Company has been pestering me for ideas and I have accordingly worked out an excellent subject: a film about the filming of the Crucifixion. The actual nail-up takes place away in the distance, like in an Italian painting. The three famous actresses who play the chief female parts are sitting under an olive tree playing poker on a collapsible green card-table. Like a scene transplanted from a *maison close* and dumped down here on the Mount of Olives. Their poor straw-rotted hair is tied up tight against dust in garish bandeaux. They have wrinkled skin like old elephants – years of make-up and whisky have made them patchy as a whitewashed wall in summer. They sit and grimly play, waiting for a cue. The world's girl friends – for this is a super production. They grin yellow, their teeth have been planted in their gums by surgery, but the gums are giving out, and increasing softness has given them precarious grins (pun). Like unreformed whores, *New Testament* whores so to speak, they wearily play on waiting for a client to ring. In the far distance the whole sordid little Thing is taking place. A tiresome Jewish agitator is paying for his conceit. Judas sits under a tree nearby eating an apple. They have given him enormous canines and talons like Fu Manchu. The producer is a cripple, wheeled everywhere in a bathchair. He is epileptic and has frequent fits during the shooting. I promise to supply the subtitles later on.

Women who like furs like Pia show their hidden bent for rapine. A passion for tiger-skins reveals the father-eater. Women who train their hair back into their eyes in order to toss it back every now and then see themselves as ponies – they will ride their men. Pia painted her nails the colour of coagulated blood, Trash hers white.

A dry run for a love affair, a mock-up for a kiss, someone dying of post-operative shock. Love, the old corpse-reviver . . . Thoughts closely linked like chain-mail that arguments cannot pierce.

Once upon a time he had been much intrigued by the theories which have grown up around the idea of a "double". Once it seemed proved when she entered his room while he was in bed with a fever and said: "Yesterday you had no fever when I came to you – now your forehead is burning." But yesterday he had been away in another town. Someone had entered his skin during his absence. Who?

If man did not have his illnesses he would have nothing to shield him from reality – and who could stand that?

Dinner with Banquo in that run-down shadowy chateau in the hills. He appeared to live there alone on his holidays with one negro retainer. Sabine was due to attend but did not turn up which caused the old man some annoyance. "She has become less and less fun as she has grown older and more serious, and I can't really count on her any more." He recalled with nostalgia her silly period just after university: walking into Maxim's with a young lion on the leash. Sitting beside the chauffeur of a Prime Minister dressed as a pantomime dog. Their love-affair created an international scandal. Perhaps it was as well that this period did not prolong itself unduly. "A little celebrity and one subsides into being a character."

Said that Piers' uncle has inherited the key to a large Templar treasure, and will not surrender it to Piers who does not know where to lay his hands upon it. He sighed when he spoke of the goodness and beauty of Sylvie, adding: "Though she has very distinct marks of madness in her look one always feels that to call her insane would be to put all ontology to the question." Smiling in the firelight I saw his brave old face which seemed to have foundered on the reefs of success, the disappointment which money-power brings. He was courteous, he was weary, but he manfully entertained his daughter's guest, rather pleased to have read one of my books. He offered me horses to ride. But he was very English, very London. I thought of the smoky old hotels where he lodged as a penniless boy from Manchester – they line the Cromwell Road today. Lighted all night. The same night-porters walk the dusty corridors distractedly waving enemas. Even today he slept with the same rueful smile on his face. "Come back," he said. "I spend a lot of time alone here. Company is good for me." I said I would. I meant to, but summer passed and the fireflies died and the harvest came and the rains started. I only had one wish by then:

> to melt back into the faceless ground
> without a sorrow sight or sound
> or watch the rosy corpses play
> in cinemas by night or day.

FIVE

Dinner at Quartila's

BLANFORD THE NOVELIST SIGHED AS HE SEPARATED THE master copy of the typescript from the other two, and taking up a blank white sheet rapidly wrote down several provisional titles for this new and rather undisciplined departure from the ordinary product. After several faltering attempts he decided to give the devil his due, so to speak, and to call it *Le Monsieur*. Sunset had passed him by and now evening was falling in all its brilliant phosphorescence over the loops of the Grand Canal. He was filled with a vague sense of insufficiency at having at last decided to say goodbye to his creations – they had been together for a couple of years now and he had, inevitably, become fond of them and reluctant to part from them. Besides, had he said all that there was to say about them? There were so many corners he had left unexplored, so many potentialities undeveloped simply because he had firmly decided not to write "the ordinary sort of novel".

That blasted Sutcliffe – he had grown fond of him; he had enjoyed even being pilloried by him under the disgusting name of Bloshford. Perhaps he should sue himself for libel?

Tonight he would have the first opinion on the book from the old duchess to whom he had sent the third carbon as well as many of the scenes from his notebooks which had not found their way into the definitive text. Never had he been more uncertain of a piece of writing, never had he needed advice and guidance more. Yet he implored her to say nothing until she received his telegram and the invitation to dinner at Quartila's silk-lined cellar where he would listen to her in all humility, in order to discover what he had, in fact, done. Several beginnings and several endings buzzed around him like mosquitoes as he sat on his high balcony above the water and turned the pages of his notebooks. The suicide – was that right? And he felt that he should perhaps offer a final summing up from the diary of Bruce, let us say; something like this: "The year is on the wane, the month is already November. I have let a number of weeks slip by without making any entries in my diary. I have only a few pages left, just enough to summarise briefly the final history of Verfeuille and its owners. I have decided to cease keeping a diary altogether, to lapse into silence; too much paper has accumulated around us during this long history. 'It is presumptuous to wish to record,' writes Sutcliffe somewhere and goes on, 'Anyway it is too late to alter anything; one has started to appear as a name on the death-map as if it were among the credit titles of some shoddy film.' He is thinking of the map of Piers where death assumes the shape of a constellation hanging in the sky – the great Serpent Ophis we had once seen in old Macabru. How far away it seems now, watching the rain falling among the silver olives."

Blanford re-read these words with a pang which translated itself into an actual touch of angina as he sat in his bath chair, high over the lagoons, and let his melancholy eyes wander along the delectable contours of dying Venice – the orchestra of divine buildings hallowed by the opalescent water-dusk. Soon he would have done with the book, done with the masks under which he had so successfully disguised his weaknesses and disappointments and misadventures. His cat slept with one paw still on the white ping-pong ball, eloquent and slim as the devil himself. He had chosen for his epigraph the well-known quotation from Shagbag: "The Prince of Darkness is a Gentleman". He felt ill and yet elated by the nostalgia of this farewell. Bruce's Journal was to continue thus:

"The last few weeks at the chateau were long and burdensome to live through, so impregnated were they with the sense of our impending departure; mind you, we worked hard, and

even sang while we worked at the olives, but it was a pretence
for we were all of us heavy hearted. It was cold, and some days
we were greeted by heavy cloud and skirls of young snow falling straight out of heaven, only to melt as it touched the grass.
In the short brush there was often rime. Soon the colder
December weather and the snowfalls on the high *garrigues*
would drive the hungry wild boars down towards the low-
lands where they could be hunted. With the first frosts thirst
would set in, and game birds could be lured by simple tricks
like leaving a mirror in an open field to suggest a pool of water.
The short-sighted woodcock always came down to inspect it,
whirring into the shooter's range. Hares left their snug 'forms'
in the cold grass. Ah, Verfeuille! It was hard to imagine any
other sort of life, so fully had we lived this one among the
green hills and soft limestone river-valleys. We did not know
who the inheritors would be; but we knew that the long
promised financial calamities had fallen upon the place in the
wake of Piers' death and partly because of it. Only a huge
fortune could save the place. Mortgages had come home to
roost, contracts now had to be met. It was obvious that by
Christmas the whole place would be boarded up, given over
to the field-mice, its life extinguished. Moreover those of us
who were left would also be dispersed. Toby, for example, had
decided to take his now finished and indexed masterpiece to
Oxford to touch up the delegates of the press and arrange for
its publication. With all the privileged matter he had found
among the Verfeuille papers his book planned to overturn
many accepted theories about the sin of the Templars. It was
now clear that the original de Nogaret had become a Templar
himself in order to penetrate the order and destroy it more completely from within. The role of Judas suited him admirably,
and like Judas he went mad and at last hung himself. All this
new evidence caused quite a throb in scholastic circles – for
in order to drive Babcock mad with apprehension Toby had

leaked some of his material to learned journals. Now his triumph over pedantry was to be complete. But he himself had decided to leave.

"On his last day we walked over to the Pont du Gard and sat in an icy wind on the honey-coloured stone which we thought that we might never see again, so definitive did this ending of the Verfeuille story seem to us. It was almost a relief to be done with the lame affectionate conversations and to climb at last on to the windy platform of Avignon to await the train. But inevitably we had one last drink at the café by the hideous and funny Monument des Morts with its cheap tin lions we had come to love so much. Winter had unstitched the planes and the leaves rained down in drifts scattering and skirling around our ankles. Yet it was warm for the season, autumn had been delayed. Toby blew his nose a good deal to hide his emotion. We promised each other that we would meet again very soon, and our warmth was effusive and genuine – but how heavy our hearts were! Then the long slowcoach of a train wound out across the darkness and I thought with a sudden jealous pang of Paris, and all the rich anonymity of a big city in contrast to this little town which lost all reality in winter; where the inhabitants stayed lost in their summer memories, listening to the iron mistral as it climbed the battlements, shivering their shutters as it passed.

"As for me, Bruce, I know that I cannot leave Avignon as yet – indeed if ever. I have taken a couple of rooms in the Princes Hotel, directly above those in which Piers . . . They are cheap. Here I propose to 'tread water' this winter – to use the rather disapproving phrase of Rob Sutcliffe. Already, when Toby's train had borne him away I felt a strange sort of disorientation setting in. I walked back to the hotel on foot deliberately, precariously almost, listening to my own footfalls with deep attention. In my nameless furnished room with its ghastly wallpaper I sat listening to the silence and drinking small whiskies out of my toothmug. A vast paralysis had seized everything; I was caught like a fly in a chunk of amber. To shake off this feeling of unreality I turned to sorting my clothes and papers, and to entertaining these last details in the little diary.

"The rest is soon told. Before the chateau was closed and boarded up I had the contents of the muniments room transferred lock, stock and barrel to the local museum – including the heavy and copious files and notebooks left by Sutcliffe. Among them are several unpublished books and stories and essays, as well as all the letters of Pia. One day they will presumably be sorted out and see the light of day. Meanwhile his publishers have commissioned a biography of him from Aubrey Blanford, a novelist for whom he had scant respect, but who will be coming down after Christmas to examine all this material at first hand. Of course Rob Sutcliffe would have been horrified – but I do not see what I, ignorant as I am could do to avert this fate. I suppose publishers know what they are doing. I do not feel this is any part of my business. Rob knew that one day he would have to face the undertakers of the literary trade. Anyway there is no such thing as absolute truth, and inevitably he will become a half-creation of the novelist. Who will ever know him as we did? Nobody.

"The sleepers in the Nogaret vault are to remain there; but the place is to be bricked in definitively, and a high wall constructed around it before the chateau is handed over to the new owners – whoever they will be.

"Finally there is Sylvie – my one remaining link with this ancient town and indeed with reality itself, or the small part of it which we can share. I have lived a whole privileged life of concern for her beauty and of that I cannot complain. I cannot imagine how things could have fallen out differently, or made more sense. We have come full circle, she and I." If I close my eyes I can see the dark Sylvie that Bruce must continue to visit every day till death us do bloody part etc. She sits at her green baize card table wearing tinted glasses to disguise the lines of fatigue under her eyes. Even though a woman be mad, some traces of concern for her own looks remain. Here she plays hand after hand of solitaire, her forehead smooth and unruffled. She whispers to herself and smiles very often. She is aware of his presence though she does not always recognise him – she calls him Piers sometimes. "But my silent presence seems to be comforting and sometimes dropping her cards she will sit and hold my hand for an hour or more, quiet and happy as a plant. When I leave her I usually go to the station on my way home and wait for the last train to come in from Paris. There is never anyone on it I know – how should there be. Often it is empty. Then I walk about the town at night with a sort of strenuous numbness, looking keenly about me, as if for a friend."

Blanford went to the bathroom on a sudden impulse and took off his glasses to examine his face in the mirror. A trifle sardonically – or perhaps the impression was caused by the fact of a small strabismus, a half-squint – the sort of thing which would force one to become a sort of self-deprecating type of humorist. He regarded himself and then winked sadly at his reflection.

"Strenuous numbness," he said aloud, finding the phrase a trifle mannered. He went back to the balcony moving with his swayback hesitation caused by the paralysis which always afflicted him after a day of sitting and writing with the light drawing board across his knees; soon Cade would come and massage him before he set off with the two linkboys to the cave where the Duchess awaited or would be awaiting him. She had already sent him a telegram signed by Sutcliffe which showed that she had read the manuscript to the very end, for the text read: "Refuse to be rushed off the planet in this clumsy and

278

ignominous fashion. Kindly arrange to have me die by less theatrical means. Rob." Perhaps the Duchess had not grasped the little twist about the *saut mystique*? He would see.

It is still a moot point whether Socrates, in fact, existed as something more than a character in a novel by Plato. And what of me, he thought? Am I possibly an invention of someone like old D – the devil at large? He hummed an air he had made up to accompany the riders who left the Canopic Gate etc. It had not found its way into the text. It was a plaintive little home-made air they sang in the desert.

ALL
> Long long ago in time
> Far faraway in space
> When health and wealth
> And slimth and stealth
> Were *données* of the case

PIERS
> There dwelt a man de Nogaret

TOBY
> So overbred
> So overfed

PIERS
> Who threw his life away.

It might have been fun perhaps to print it with the music. He would reflect on the matter. He played abstractedly with the little cat Satan, as he waited for the valet. He supposed he was simply another vainglorious fool of a writer with insufficient courage to tell the whole truth about life. Always gilding the nipple, sugaring the pill. But after all what was the truth about these importunate, nagging people of his, trying so hard to get born and achieve the fugitive identity of a penurious art; he thought long and sadly of his dark wife Livia. Crumbs of her had been used for Sabine (the looks and the slashing style) and for Pia, and even a certain disposition of the eyebrows (when she was lying) which was one of the features he "saw" every time he put down the name of Sylvie. "How real is reality?" Blanford asked his cat which gazed back at him unwinkingly, unseeingly – like Livia saying: "Of course I love you, silly." By a singular paradox (perhaps inherent in all writing?) the passages that he knew would be regarded as over-theatrical or unreal ("people don't behave like that") would be the truth, and the rest which rang somehow true, the purest fabrication. He wondered if in the next book about these people he could not cut down a layer or two to reveal the invisible larval forms, the root forms which had given him these projections? Like an archaeologist cutting down through successive cultures until he reached the neolithic stage of his people, their embryonic selves? He had half decided to let Sutcliffe finish and print his *Tu Quoque* if it could be found among his papers. "Poor Bruce," he said aloud picturing the boy wandering the windy streets of Avignon in the rain, waiting for him to arrive on the night train one day.

˙ In a passage in one of the unpublished notebooks of Sutcliffe he had written: "How can Bruce, a so-called doctor, not be aware that he and Piers between them brought about Sylvie's collapse, the downfall of her reason? The division of objectives in loving is something woman finds impossible to face; it threatens the fragile sense of her identity, the unity of her vision of things seen through the unique lens of human love. Once this sense of uniqueness is put in doubt or dispersed the self breaks up (itself the most fragile of illusions) and all the subsidiary larval selves, demons and angels, come to the surface to splinter and confuse the central ego."

Perhaps he should have included that? He felt so close to these people, he saw them everywhere; yesterday he had lunched at Sardou's right behind Sutcliffe – at any rate it was the back of his head. At the end of the meal a hunchback woman came in to speak to him; she was very striking and resembled Sabine – except for the disability. This version of Sutcliffe picked his teeth with a silver toothpick of great beauty and wore a green baize apron with metal buttons – was he a hall-porter from the Majestic Hotel? He looked such a *savant* from behind.

Where was Cade? Night was falling and the plaintive rivercraft crossed and recrossed among new shadows. The real Sutcliffe, so to speak, who had loaned a physical wardrobe and a few light touches to the book Sutcliffe, had indeed committed suicide but only after a great nervous upheaval. For some reason he had not wanted to deprive Rob of his reason before despatching him. "I wonder why?" he asked the cat. "Perhaps I didn't want to steal thunder from Sylvie?" He riffled among his notebooks and recovered the passage on the Bridge of Sighs, and the nervous breakdown which prefaced the final act – so theatrical, so Byronic: yet this is precisely what Sam (the original of Sutcliffe) had achieved in reality – that word again, it has a dying fall . . .

"He was filled now with a delicious vertigo, the winged consciousness of freedom which heralds general paralysis – liberty without precariousness or guilt. The kiss of euphoria. Death was no longer even an event. He existed adjacently to it, could reach out and practically touch it, it was so real. Hurrah. He heard his mind turning smoothly like a motor; it gave him powerful traction. Yes, he would go to India for a year. Learn Sanscrit, write out a cheque for a million, apologise to God. To laugh aloud suddenly and for no reason in a crowded restaurant was delectable. He found he was being naughty, mischievously eating matches or tearing up paper napkins; but he was soon coaxed to behave more correctly. When reproved he would stand up and offer a very stiff arm for a handshake. Sometimes he was forced to hide his smiles in his sleeve. His eyes seemed to have pupils of different sizes. At the café he calls for a paper and proposes to read it aloud but all that results is a deep humming noise. Nothing really outstanding; a little compulsive talk and laughter. And in the evenings in his shabby *pension* some silence, moodiness, followed by catatonic stupor."

Poor Sam, poor Sutcliffe, which version . . . ? So many of these states were interchangeable, particularly if you took drugs. (Sometimes under the influence of the drug he found the taste of mineral water altered so much that he had the illusion that he was drinking warm flannel. Next morning, however, a burnt mouth . . . But he was an honourable morphinomane as Brutus was an honourable man; his back was still a mass of shrapnel from a low burst. They had not dared remove most of it. So he was the man with the iron spine, dwelling in the shadow of multiple sclerosis which was held at bay by the stubby fingers of Cade.)

Where the devil was Cade?

Blanford rolled his way to the balcony and stuck his head over it, calling out as he did so: "Rob! I say, Rob Sutcliffe!" A few faces in the street below turned up a vague white expanse whose curiosity soon evaporated. "You see?" he said to the cat, "Rob doesn't really exist." In every rainbow there is a gap which one must leap in order to slide down to the pot of gold on the other side.

He heard the whirr of the lift rising to his floor. This would be Cade coming to set him to rights – his Fletcher. The door of the flat was open, it only needed a push. Cade had been his batman during the war and had stayed on afterwards – from sheer lack of imagination. What a cross he was to bear with his insane hatred of foreigners and their ways. The pale soapy face with its skull almost shaven, though with a water-waved spit-curl over his forehead. He was sanctimonious, superior, disapproving. He had no sex, never frequented bars or brothels;

did not drink, did not smoke. And spoke so very carefully in his low Cockney whine that you feared he would sprain something by making the mental effort. When he was abroad, among "them foreigners" he always wore a peculiar expression – a slyly superior look; and his nostrils were narrowed as if he could smell the carrion. Blanford always wondered in an amazed way why he went on keeping Cade in all his loutish ungraciousness.

The valet came into the room and without a word started to clear up with a wooden methodical air. He made the bed, tidied the bathroom, and gathered up the notebooks and placed them in a cupboard. If Blanford addressed a remark to him he did not reply but simply went on with his work with the air of someone fulfilling his destiny, an insect of utter rectitude. He had been extremely cowardly in action, and hardly less objectionable in civil life. But he was a good masseur and grudgingly did what was asked of him in the ordinary affairs of everyday life. Yet . . .

"Cade, I am dining with the Duchess of Tu tonight," said Blanford rippling the irresistible ping-pong ball along the terrace. Cade without a word laid out a clean suit and went on with his mysterious operations inside the flat. The flowers were dead and would have to be replaced. The whisky decanter replenished. When he had finally completed his work he sidled out on to the terrace with his cunning ingratiating face set in a half-smile. His finger-nails were bitten down to the quick. But he put a hand upon Blanford's forehead and reflected gravely. No word was said.

They breathed quietly and evenly – Cade like some heavy mastiff. "No fever," he said at last, and Blanford added, "And no cramps last night, thank God." For a long time they stayed like this, master and bondsman, unspeaking. Then Cade said, on a note of command, "Go limp, then." And Blanford allowed himself to flop. Cade picked him up by the armpits and with surprisingly agile movements like a lizard, wangled him into the bedroom and laid him down on the bed. He was to be massaged, bathed and then dressed – Blanford always thought: "Just like a lovely big dollie, with a D.S.O. and Bar, and a spine full of shrapnel fragments, and a male nurse for a mama."

Cade dressed him with method, moving him back and forth like some ungainly lobster; Blanford stayed with his eyes closed inhaling the grubby smell of tobacco and boot polish which his batman gave off when he worked. He chewed quids of tobacco, did Cade, and spat black and viscid. "Got the crutches back, shod with rubber," he said, but Blanford replied: "I won't need them tonight at any rate. I'll take the roll chair and the sedan."

"Very good, sir," said Cade.

Within the hour he was suitably washed and dressed for his dinner engagement; Cade helped him into his light wheel chair and thence into the lift which deposited him two floors down almost into the arms of Guido and Franzo the linkboys. It was a pleasant fancy of his to travel by this old sedan chair with its brass polished lamps, swung on the shoulders of the two linkboys. The distances were short, and it saved his energy for better things. He abandoned his wheel chair and limped the few yards to the chair, greeting the boys as he did so. Quartila's was not far off, but he directed them by a slightly circuitous route in order to enjoy the movement and noise of the canals, now settling fast into their night routine.

The old Duchess of Tu still went on sitting in the once fashionable inner room of the place whose walls were lined with opalescent satin and where the lights, tamed by oval mirrors, were kind to her wrinkles and her fine white hair. A famous beauty in her day, she still had young hands, the cele-

brated swan-neck and eyes of sapphire blue which quizzed a
world grown stale and old with an unrelenting candour, and
without vainglory. Once they had been famous, those extraordinary arched brows, the expression at once pious and mischievous, devout and impudent. She was waiting for Blanford
now as she smoked her slender gilt-tipped cigarettes in a little
jade holder and sipped absently at the typescript and notes
which lay before her. She smiled as she did so – perhaps a little
sadly. She had been his friend and reader for a lifetime, remaining always astonished by the quality of his work and disappointed by its shortcomings. "I finished this morning, Aubrey,"
she called to him as he came limping over the floor towards
her – having abandoned his sedan outside in the street. And as
he kissed her hand and sank into his place she added, "I have
ordered a well-earned champagne." He thanked her and fell
silent, holding her hand. He had decided not to talk about the
manuscript unless she did. He had not come to dine with an
old friend in order to cross-examine her. But she said: "Did you
get my telegram about Rob – he was awfully like Sam, I had to
laugh. But to go so near the truth . . . ?"

Relieved, the writer said: "In the case of Rob, it was
literally him or me. We couldn't both commit suicide. Composite he may be but a large part is not Sam, it's me."

She paused and thought about her husband for a long
moment with narrowed eyes. Then she quoted:

> Huddled in dirt the reasoning engine lies.
> These are the pearls that were my father's eyes.

And without giving him a chance to catch up with her
train of thought she added: "What laughter must have echoed
in heaven when Sutcliffe went to the altar. It still rings in my
ears."

"It did in his, as it still does in mine. In the *Tu Quoque* he
re-enacts all the great roles of the race with himself in the part,

starting with the role of Jesus – the famous film script he wrote
which caused so many suicides that they had to stop turning it.
You remember – how could you? I haven't written it yet.
When the door of the tomb was rolled back they found that the
body was gone, but on the stone floor were patches of bloody
hair and chewed bones which suggested that the disciples had
had a midnight feast in the dorm. Or dogs perhaps?

> Men or dogs.
> Gods or Men,
> Take your choice

A girl comes through the wood singing:

> 'Of which wood of woods was the True Cross made?
> Tell me, tell me, my pretty maid.'
> 'I'm going a milking, Sir,' she said.
> 'Be he alive or be he dead
> I'll grind his bones to make my bread.' "

They sipped quietly at their champagne and watched the
coming and going of other guests; soft and decorous was the
place, while from the invisible canals came the soft discreet
lapping of water and the distant chaffering of the market place.
"It's strange," he said, thinking of her husband – his friend
Sam – that we hardly ever spoke much about him until I told
you my plans for this book." She had never quite managed to
disguise the transitory expression of hurt which crossed her
face at the mention of his name. "You were going to try and
bring him back to life – that's why." She made some purely
mechanical gesture to recover her poise. "The kiss of life so to
speak." All of a sudden he felt that he had failed her – for his
Rob Sutcliffe was not Sam to the very life. "My writer inhabited
a different, a humbler world. He could never have played the
kind of trick which Sam was famous for; I mean, like putting
on a Guard's tie and a bowler in order to make the sentries at

Buckingham Palace present arms when he passed. Rob would not have thought of that."

"No. Nor Sam thought about Jesus."

"It was essential for Rob the writer to measure his stature, or the lack of it, against the big models."

"But Jesus," she mused, smiling at him.

"The first version of Hamlet," said Blanford with some small asperity. "Nailed to the mother cross he was a good symbol for the inversion which ruined his life and Pia's, as well as Livia's and my own. Don't look hurt."

"Livia was my sister, I rather loved her," said the old Duchess softly. "Whatever she did to you: and it wasn't right or good, I know that."

"I am sorry," said Blanford warmly, and meant it, as he thought of his wife (Livia), that "lay figure" as it might be laughingly called. He lit his pipe and said: "In my panic I got all my symbolism mixed up – everything to do with our personal *consummatum est* as you might say; the pretty little *non lieu*."

"You were hard on her rather," she said with a faraway hint of tears in her voice. "Not really," said Blanford, thinking of the sufferings of Sutcliffe. ("The smokeless cartridge of the nun's kiss.")

"It was better when you got on to Hamlet," she said. "Really it was, Aubrey. I don't know why Livia played you that dirty trick."

"In Hamlet," he said soberly, "it was not only an Oedipus situation, but something more complicated; he discovered that his Ophelia and Laertes were lovers. To be or not to be really meant 'Should this marriage go on or not?' Ophelia had already told him that Laertes must be the master-mistress of his passion. It was the pressure of this guilty knowledge ('I'll fit you') that bore down on him, and then, through him, on her and made them see that there was no way out of the problem except madness. Which is never any solution."

287

"Never."

"Never."

Their waiters came now and provided the bill of fare; they chose with care and discrimination from it, arguing and bantering as old friends will. Then the wine steward brought forward his wines but they elected to stay where they were with a fine French champagne, and the compliment touched him coming from her. It was a little gesture which proved that she thought that, in spite of deficiencies, his book had come off. A sudden elation filled his sails. "It was not only Livia, poor Livia," he said, "it was also my mother's death which came right with it, alongside it."

"But Livvy got all the blame."

"Yes," he said, "It's true. She had discovered that to be adored by men she only had to simulate sharing in the man's whole-hearted adoration of himself. Tick, Tock, to cut a long Tory short she laughed in her lillywhite sleeve and said to herself in the mirror: 'People with weak bladders should not climb up high ladders.'"

The Duchess smiled sadly and shook her head as he went on, quoting from his own book. "The sponge-rubber heart, the pre-stressed concrete soul, the glass-fibre emotion. . . . No, my dear, books are finished."

To his surprise she shook her head vehemently and denied it, saying, "No, the book will not lose its place or its preciousness for it is a privileged communication between two spirits and the link it forges is vital to the culture of the heart and mind, and hence to man. The contact is between two lonely and desperate souls united by an embrace. No mob-throb here! My complaint was only on behalf of Livia; I thought she could have been comprehended more."

Blanford quoted, mimicking the very accents of Stekel: "'The homosexual neurosis is a flight back to one's own sex induced by a sadistic predisposition towards the opposite sex.'

After Vienna I really comprehended the lot, but none of my new knowledge served any purpose," he told himself, and then went on aloud, "I studied Livia with all the anxiety of a man in love, and I finally managed to arrive at an interpretation of her which met the facts. That marble beauty and silence, that reserve. I had been puzzled by the role of the wedding ring in all this – for Livia was honest and truthful as girls go. It was old Uncle Fred who set up the skittles differently for me by his animadversions upon the male lesbian type who, like the male counterpart will often welcome the wedding ring which disguises her private proclivities, and at the same time gives access of approach to unsuspecting wives and adolescents of undetermined sex. That was Livia's line. And by it of course the man is overthrown. It is precisely this sort of girl who becomes a man-eater for pure window-dressing. But even in sex her aim is to overthrow the hated male." He broke off with a short and bitter laugh. "In the powder rooms of the world's great hotels when male lesbians meet they show each other their wedding rings and burst out laughing."

"O come, my dear," said the Duchess compassionately, and put a hand on his sleeve to calm him down. "Poor Livia. I am glad you cut out the blue pages from the book, about the caresses of the mantid. After all she is dead now." He took the blue pages from her and read them again slowly: "The dry marsupial's pocket of that unused vagina might have made him awake to the enormous and beautiful clitoris. Painful to penetrate, but expert in many ways, yet shamming her orgasms very often, perhaps thinking of someone else whose memory had worn thin? He didn't know. (Sutcliffe.) But then the ring – was that finance or status or what. . . . They told him in Vienna. Male lesbians like to conquer married women and the ring excites them for they are at the same time cheating the man and aping him, replacing him."

He gathered the whole mass of papers together and drank

the last of his champagne. "*Une belle descente de lit* was Livia to me." One day he had woken up to the fact that she was servicing a whole county of unsatisfied wives. No, he had not been hard on her. It had not been fair to entrain him in this adventure which led nowhere except to mutual despair. Because love did come at last, and as always rather too late to change the course of events. "The green ink, the lucky charms . . ."

The Duchess nodded a little with fatigue.

"I realise that you are right," he said at last, "and that is why I cut those passages out of the text; my arraignment of Livia drew its force from the unconscious springs of inversion in myself – my mother fixation, my woman-what-have-I-to-do-with-thee? complex; in all these bitter animadversions I was really standing on the high cliffs of my mother's death, on the plinth of the monument of words which I have set up to her memory. I understood this when Livia died – but thanks to Uncle Freddy (Freud) who taught me about this great landslide in the affairs of men. A huge chunk bitten out of the heart, a cliff subsiding into the sea after an earthquake. I knew it all, of course, without recognising it. Its impact was retroactive. I saw myself once more (forever) standing on the cold grey asphalt of the crematorium. In the nearby airfield the wind socks hovered in the western wind which doth the small rain down shall rain etc. I am standing there stiffly, head on one side. listening to my cardiac murmur; the faint gurgle of mitral stenosis – I am inventing this, hoping to punish myself with an illness. The pulse which was set going in the belly of the whale is not as yet at rest; death had simply detached it from the mother pulse, the mentor, the tutor. Now all it could feel was the swishing of the primordial waters as they closed over my silent mother. The real self starter in this homely old country bus of the body is the shared orgasm – hence the importance of the love artefact. I saw myself walking about in ever diminishing perspective like some consecrated pig with a tiny mistress like a pinch of snuff. The amazing thing was that (as Pia said in her letters) love had come, real love, that passeth all understanding. She had experienced a successful passion before Rob – it was marvellous for the complexion. It gave her whole skin a gloss like new paint. The skin itself was derived from the marble pallor of Livia who always wore the shy silenced look of a wasted childhood – of someone who had never had a birthday party, nor any shadow to cast before her parents. Yes, you are right, when she died it became necessary to invent her just as if she had never existed. That was when the big ennui set it."

"Ennui?" said the Duchess on a sighing fall.

"It's when you find yourself saying: 'If I can get through the next ten minutes I won't do it.' Feverishly you concentrate on a book of political cartoons."

The smoke of their cigarettes curled lazily skyward; they stared into each other's eyes, devoured by private memories.

"Once Livia and I spoke about suicide in low voices so as not to wake the sleeper in the curtained bed," said the Duchess slowly, as if trying to settle something in her own mind. "About the mysterious veil of amnesia (about seven years old?) which rubs out memories, making them hard to recover in full focus. Well, I compared it to a comparable veil which seems to supervene before death arrives; perhaps to cradle one by its insulating power against the foreknowledge of departure. Everyone dies blissfully, calmly, humbly and hopefully. At the end a sweet amnesia dulls the effects of pain or drugs. There comes a secret lapsing, a not-caring to go on living. Now we often get a simulacrum of this state while we are fully in life, living it fully. One becomes death-prone, accident prone, swollen with the luxury of the idea, careless, exposed. The primordial attachment to breathing is compromised. Nor do you need any special excuse to go out though of course people blame love or money just as duellers choose their weapons. No, simply catch 'flu and make no effort to fight it; founder with all hands in a smiling silence. *Sérénité . . . Pérennité . . . Mortalité . . .*"

"That is the moment Akkad watched for," he said. She opened her handbag and took out a letter with an Egyptian stamp on it; it was not difficult to recognise the beautiful precise handwriting on it as Akkad's. It was addressed to her at the country estate. The envelope had been slit with a paper-knife. He knew what was written on the single page of note-paper inside. One day he would presumably receive such a letter himself, delivered by a flesh-and-blood postman. He suddenly remembered a remark of Akkad quoted by Sutcliffe – was it in the book or not? He had forgotten.

Akkad had said: "You can't explain symbols beyond a certain depth; after that you have to live by them in order to understand them. They sidetrack the conceptual field and become part of the blood beat. In this domain one can really say 'I know' without the onus of proof, and in default of reason."

Back in the flat Cade lit a candle, put his spectacles on his nose, and opened the Bible which he read each night, his lips slowly moving over the words and forming them as he read. He would if necessary wait up like this all night for his master. When he heard the feet of the linkboys he would take the lift down and open the front door. Apart from the Bible there lay a half-darned sock of Blanford's and a few pages of heavily corrected typescript which he had saved from the wastepaper basket, and would tomorrow take round and sell to a collector for a good sum. It was an excised part of the new book. It read: "As for Toby, who thought that alchemy and astrology were the remains of an ancient, vanished neurology, the problem of the Templars seemed no problem at all. They had gone too far, clear beyond the Orphics, beyond the double sex, the gnostic two, Tiresias and all that bedlam. They lost their balance and plunged into this new and terrifying darkness where they could realise all flesh as excrement only, decay as the only truth, death as the great Motive of the usurping godhead. Cannibalism and cabeiric orgies overcame their reason. So they came to the eatable foetus of the gnostic cults – the horror of sows gobbling their own litters for which the wine sacrament was so imperfect a surrogate. Eating and defecating at once they remained blind and earthbound –were carried into the chthonic darkness of unreason. And with them the destiny of man in Europe."

Cade folded the paper and stowed it in his pocket; then he turned back to the story of Job in the silence of the Venetian night.

It was late when Blanford paid the bill and said goodnight to the Duchess; wearily the waiters hovered round him. They had come to respect this distinguished elderly Englishman who came so often to spend the whole evening talking in whispers to an empty alcove – for it was some time since the name Duchess had appeared on the death-map of the stars. The yawning linkboys would be sitting about in the dark street waiting for a signal to bring the bathchair in and roll him out to the sedan. In it perhaps he might find a letter with an Egyptian postmark. Or it might be at this moment lying on the table with all the other correspondence, in front of Cade who read on and on into the momentous night.

ENVOI

So D.
    begat Blanford
            (who begat Tu and Sam and Livia)
            who begat Sutcliffe
            who begat Bloshford

    Piers and Sylvie and Bruce
        who begat
        Akkad
        and
        Sabine
        and
        Banquo
            who begat Pia
            who begat Trash
            who begat . . .

LIVIA

or
Buried Alive

Contents

"In the name of the Dog the Father, Dog the Son, and Dog the Wholly Ghost, Amen. Here beginneth the second lesson."

"Between the completely arbitrary and the completely determined perhaps there is a way?"

"Five colours mixed make people blind."

Chinese Proverb

ONE

A Certain Silence

WHEN THE NEWS OF TU'S DEATH REACHED BLANFORD he was actually living in her house in Sussex, watching the first winter snow fall out of a dark sky, amidst darker woods, which had long since engulfed an ochre sunset. "Actually", because his own version of the event will be slightly different, both for the sake of posterity and also on stylistic grounds. A deep armchair sheltered his back from the draughts which, despite the rippling oak fire burning in the grate, played about the old-fashioned, high-ceilinged room with its tapering musicians' gallery. His crutches lay beside him on the carpet. As he put down the swan-necked telephone he felt the knowledge boom inside him, as if in some great tropical conch – the bang of surf upon white beaches on the other side of the world. She would miss reading (the selfishness of writers!) all the new material he had added to his book – a novel about another novelist called Sutcliffe, who had become almost as real to him and to Tu as he, Blanford, was to himself. He took the handkerchief from his sleeve and dabbed his dry lips – dry from the eternal cigar he needed to bite on when he worked. Then he went swaying to the looking-glass over the bookcase and stared at himself for a good moment. The telephone-bell gave a smart trill and a click – long-distance calls always did this: like the last spurt of blood from an artery. The writer stared on, imagining that he was Tu looking back at him. So this is what she saw, what she had always seen! Eye to eye and mind to mind – this is how it had been with them. He suddenly realised that he was surrounded by the dead woman's books. Underlinings, annotations. She was still here!

He felt his image suddenly refreshed and recreated by her death – the new information was so terrifying, so hard to assimilate. Goodness, there was still so much they had to tell each other – and now all that remained was a mass of severed threads, the loose ends of unfinished conversation. From now on there would be nobody to whom he could really talk. He made a grimace and sighed. Well then, he must lock up all this passionate and enriching conversation in his skull. All morning he had played on the old pipe-organ, glad to find that his memory and his fingers still worked. There is nothing like music in an empty house. Then the telephone-bell. Now the thought of Tu. It is no use really – for once you die you slide into the ground and simply melt. For a while a few personal scraps hang around – like shoes and clothes and unused notepaper with abandoned phone numbers. As if suddenly one had had a hunger for greater simplicity.

Outside children chirped as they skated on the frozen lake. Stones skidded and twanged on the ice. How would his hero Sutcliffe take the news, he wondered? Should he make him whimper in the novel like some ghastly dog? Last night in bed he had read some pages of the Latin poet Tu most loved; it was like sleeping beside her. The phrase came to him: "The steady thudding of the Latin line echoes the thud of her heart. I hear her calm voice uttering the words." There were flies in the room, hatched by the heating. They seemed to be reading Braille. The treble voices outside were marginal. What good were books except to hive off regrets? His back ached all of a sudden – his spine seemed as stiff as a flagpole. He was an ageing war-hero with a spine full of lead.

He wished his own turn would come soon. From now on they could label him "Not Wanted On Voyage" or just "Unaccompanied Luggage" – and sling him into the hold, into the grave. In his mind he gave a great cry of loneliness, but no sound came. It was a shrill galactic cry of a solitary planet whirling through space. Tu had loved walking naked about the house in Italy, she had no sense of misdemeanour, reciting aloud the 16th Psalm. She said once, "It is terrible, but life is on nobody's side."

So the Sutcliffe he invented for his novel *Monsieur* shot himself through the mirror in the early version? "I had to," he explained, pointing to Blanford. "It was him or me." The writer Blanford suddenly felt like an enormously condensed version of a minor epic. Buried alive! The crutches hurt him under the arms. He groaned and swore as he dragged himself about the room.

The consolations of art are precious few. He always had a sneaking fear that what he wrote was too private to reach a reader. Stilted and stunted, the modern product – meagre as spittle or sperm, the result of too rigorous pot-training by his mother who had a thirst for purity. The result was retention of faecal matter – a private prose and verse typical of the modern sphincterine artist. In ordinary life this basic refusal to co-operate with the universe, to surrender, to give, would in its final stage amount to catatonia! In the "acute" wards at Leatherhead they had one twilight catatonic who could be suspended by his coat-collar – suspended by a meat-hook and hung on a bar where he stayed, softly swinging in the foetal position. Like a bat, dreaming his amniotic dreams, lulled in the imaginary mother-fluid. It was all that was left of a once good poet. The whole of his life had been spent in creative constipation, a refusal to give, so now he went on living like this – a life in inverted comas, to coin a pun. Blanford reached out and touched the earlier manuscript of his book *Monsieur*. He had given it to Tu and she had had it bound. He wondered where in his imagination, which was his real life, Sutcliffe might be – he would have liked to talk to him. Last heard of in Oxford, famous for his work on his friend's study of the Templar heresy. Blanford's last communication from him had been a cryptic postcard which said: "An Oxford don can be distinguished among all others by the retractable foreskin."

He risked another thought of Tu again and suddenly felt as if he were running a temperature. Breathless, he rose and succeeded in unfastening the French window, to let in a cloud of snowflakes and a rush of cold air. Then, bending his head, he lurched out on to the lawn, watching his breath plume out before him. He rubbed a little snow on his temples with a theatrical gesture. Then he laboriously returned to his fireside seat and his thoughts.

Cade now sidled into the room with the tea things and set them down beside him without a word, his yellow puritanical face set in expressions of fervent concentration such as one only sees on the faces of very stupid but cunning people. He bore in his arms with a kind of meek pride the new orthopaedic waistcoat-brace which had at last arrived from the makers, tailored to size. There was a good hope that this contrivance might allow Blanford one day to throw away his crutches. He gave an exclamation of pleasure while Cade, expressionless as a mandarin, helped him off with the ancient tweed coat he so loved (with its leather-patched elbows) and locked him into the new garment of soft grey rubber and invisible steel. "Stand up, sir," he said at last, and the writer obeyed in smiling wonder; yes, he was free to walk slowly about, to navigate on his own two legs. It was miraculous. But at first he was only allowed to wear it for an hour a day to get his muscles used to its stresses. "A miracle," he said aloud. Cade watched him attentively for a few moments and then, with a nod, turned away to his domestic duties while Blanford, feeling newly born, leaned against the chimney-piece, staring down at his fallen crutches. Cade would never know how much this new invention meant. The valet looked like the lower-class ferret he was. Blanford watched him curiously as he went over the room, emptying the ashtrays and refilling the saucer of water on the radiator, refilling the vase with its hothouse blooms. "Cade," he said, "Constance is dead." Cade nodded expressionlessly. "I know, sir. I was listening on the extension in the hall." That was all. That was Cade all over. His work done, he took himself off with his customary silence and stealth.

> Carbon into diamond
> Sand into pearl.

All process causes pain, and we are part of process. How chimerical the consolations of art against the central horror of death; being sucked down the great sink like an insect, into the *cloaca maxima* of death, the *anus mundi*! Sutcliffe, in writing about him, or rather, he writing about himself in the character of Sutcliffe, under the satirical name of Bloshford in the novel *Monsieur* had said somewhere: "Women to him were simply a commodity. He was not a fool about them; O no! He knew them inside out, or so he thought. That is to say he was worse than a fool."

Was this true of Constance or of Livia her sister, the writer wondered. The blonde girl and the dark. The girl with the velvet conundrum and the girl with beak of the swan?

> Grind grain, press wine,
> Break bread, yours mine,
> Take breath, face death.

Where had he seen these lines underlined by Constance in a book? At that moment the telephone seemed to thrill again, and he knew at once who it was – it could only be his invention Sutcliffe. He must have heard by telepathy the news about Constance (Tu). He realised now that he had been expecting this call all day.

He did not bother to utter the usual Hullo but immediately said to his *confrère*, his *semblable* and *frère:* "You have heard about Tu," and the voice of Sutcliffe, speaking through a heavy cold, and nervous with regret, replied: "My God, Blanford, what is to become of us?"

"We shall go on sitting about regretting our lack of talent; we shall go on trying to convince people. I am as grieved as you are, Robin, and I never thought I would be. I had so often thought of dying that I thought I had the hippogriff under control; yes, but of course like everyone I cheated in my mind by being the first to die. I suppose Constance did the same."

"You made my own life come to a halt when Pia died," said Sutcliffe both reproachfully and gravely, and then blew his nose loudly. "So I set up shop here for a while to completely rewrite Toby's book about the Templars – to apply a bit of gold leaf here and there, to give it such orotundity as befits a fuddled don. But now he is famous and I feel the need for a change, for a new landscape. Tobias has the Chair in History which he coveted. Why not the Sofa? He will live on in a conical dismay, lecturing loudly on the plasticity of pork to the new generation of druggie-thuggies." He chuckled, but mirthlessly. "What about me?" he said. "Have you nothing I could do short of entering the Trappe?" "You are dead, Robin," said Blanford. "Remember the end of *Monsieur?*" "Bring me back then," said Sutcliffe on a heroic note, "and we shall see."

"What happened to the great poem and the *Tu Quoque*

book?" asked Blanford sharply, and Sutcliffe answered: "I was waiting to get over Pia a bit before finishing it. It was cunning of you to make Pia a composite of Constance and Livia, but I never felt I could really achieve the portrait of her simply because I was blinded by love. I wasn't cruel enough. And I wondered about Trash, her black lover. I think your story is better than mine, probably sadder. I don't know. But the death of Tu, of poor Constance, should be celebrated in verse by an Elizabethan."

For some reason this irritated Blanford and he said with asperity, "Well, why not a poem called 'Sutcliffe's Salte Teares upon the tombe of Tu'?"

"Why not?" said his fellow writer, his bondsman, "or perhaps in seventeenth-century style, 'Sutcliffe's Big Boo-Hoo'."

"Poetry," said Blanford on a lower key, talking almost to himself, "which always comes with sadness; poetry, in the jumbo version of the supermarket, enough for a whole family. The economy size. Robby, you can't go on being cheerful in Oxford. Shall I send you to Italy?"

"Another book? Why not?" But Sutcliffe did not sound too sure. "I really think it's your turn to write one – and this time the true story of your love, our love, for Constance and indeed for Livia despite what she did to you, to us, to me. Would it hurt too much if you tried?" Of course it would. Good grief!

Blanford did not answer for a long moment. Then Sutcliffe said, in his old flippant vein: "Last spring I went to Paris with a girl somewhat like Pia-Constance-Livia. The word *archi* had come into vogue as a prefix to almost everything. Our own translation would be *super*, I suppose. Well, everything was *archi* this and *archi* that. I realised that one might describe me as *archicocu*, what? Indeed I went so far as to think of myself as absolutely *archicocuphosphorescent*."

"In a way I did tell the truth about us," said Blanford haltingly. "Livia carried me out of my depth. I had always needed a feather-simple girl; but Livia was only fit to have her tail spliced by a female octoroon. Damn!"

"Aha! but you loved her. We both did. But where you lied was to graft onto her some of the femininity of her sister. You made her a female quaire not a male." After a pause, during which both writers thought furiously about the book which Blanford had called *Monsieur* and Sutcliffe *The Prince of Darkness*, their faltering conversation was resumed. If lonely people have a right to talk to themselves couldn't a lonely author argue with one of his own creations – a fellow-writer, Blanford asked himself.

"A hunt for the larval forms of personality! Livia was, as far as I am concerned – " Sutcliffe gave a groan.

"A powder-monkey in Hell," said Blanford almost shouting with pain, because her beauty had really wounded him, driven him indeed mad with vexation.

"A dry water-hole," agreed Sutcliffe. "Who is Livia, what is she?"

> All our swains commend her.
> Perfection's ape, clad in a toga
> And beefed up by the shorter yoga
> A Cuvier of the sexual ploy
> You forged a girl out of a boy.
> You wielded flesh and bones and mind,
> She was attentive, tough but kind,
> Yet unbeknown, behind your back
> She sought the member that you lack.

"Enough, Robin," cried Blanford in a wave of regret and mind-sickness as he thought of the dark head of Livia on the pillow beside him. Sutcliffe laughed sardonically and tormented him with yet another improvisation.

I am loving beyond my means
I am living behind my moans!
O!
Tra la la! Tra la la!
Toi et moi et le chef de gare
Quel bazar, mais quel bazar!

Blanford supposed him to be right; for the story for him could have begun in Geneva – on a sad Sunday in Geneva. It was cold; and ill-assorted, straggly and over-gummy were the bifurcated Swiss under a snow-moon. He closed his eyes the better to hear the tumultuous chatter of stars, or dining later at the Bavaria with her face occupying the centre of his mind, he engulfed the victorious jujubes of mandatory oysters. Ouf! What prose! *Nabokov, à moi!* In hotels their lives were wallpapered with sighs. Then tomorrow on the lake, the white stairways to heaven splashed with a wrinkled sunshine. "My sister Livia arrives tomorrow from Venice. She is anxious to meet you."

That was Constance, made for deep attachments as a cello is made for music – the viol's deepness on certain notes, in certain moods. It was ages before they had both realised that the words which passed between them had a certain specific density; they were registered and understood at a level somewhere below that of just ordinary speech. The sisters had just inherited the tumbledown chateau of Tu Duc (hence the nickname for Constance). It was near the village of Tubain in the Vaucluse. Not too far from the one city which, above all others, held for him the greatest number of historic memories.

Here, Sutcliffe interposed his clumsy presence on Blanford's train of thought; sniffing and adjusting those much repaired spectacles of his. "But Livia had what excited you most – the sexual trigger in the blood; she deserved to be commemorated in a style which we might call metarealism –

in her aspect of Osiris whose scattered limbs were distributed all over the Mediterranean. Enough of the pornocratic-whimsical, Blanford. For my part I was hunting for a prose line with more body – not paunch, mark you, but body, my boy."

"Remember, Rob," Blanford retorted, "that everything you write about me is deeply suspect – at the best highly arguable. I invented you, after all."

"Or I you, which? The chicken or the egg?"

"The truth of the matter is that we did not really know much about ourselves in those old days; how happy it made one just to squander our youth, lying about in the deep grass eating cherries. The velvet English summers of youth, deep grass, and the clock of cricket balls marking the slow hours of leisure between classes. The distant clapping when some-one struck a ball to the boundary merged with but did not drown the steady drizzle of crickets. We slept in the bosom of an eternal summer.

"Tu once said that nature cured her own fertility imbalances by forcing sterile loves up on – illicit in the biological sense. Of what avail our belief in freewill? For her we were sleepwalkers caught in the current of an irresistible sexuality." He said aloud: "Poor enough consolation for the cowardly Robin Sutcliffe, sitting in that sordid house, drinking his way towards his goal – the leap from the bridge. His Charon was the twisted black woman with the crow's beak, who could procure something for every taste."

"I suppose so," said Rob with a sigh. "The bandages, the whip, the handcuffs – I should have put more of that into the book, instead of leaving it for you. She let her dirty rooms out by the hour. I came there hunting for Pia, just as you came in your turn hunting for Livia and found her in bed with that little hunchback with the pistachio eyes."

Blanford winced; he remembered the cracked bronchial

laugh, gushing out amidst cigarette smoke and coughing. She had said of Livia: "*Une fille qui drague les hommes et saut les gouines.*" He had struck her across the face with his string gloves. He said to Sutcliffe sternly: "It is your duty to demonstrate how Livia was tailored down to the sad size of Pia."

"Pia dolorosa," said Sutcliffe. "It would be more than one book, then?"

"Well, squinting round the curves of futurity I saw something like a quincunx of novels set out in a good classical order. Five Q novels written in a highly elliptical quincunxial style invented for the occasion. Though only dependent on one another as echoes might be, they would not be laid end to end in serial order, like dominoes – but simply belong to the same blood group, five panels for which your creaky old *Monsieur* would provide simply a cluster of themes to be reworked in the others. Get busy, Robin!"

"And the relation of form to content?"

"The books would be roped together like climbers on a rockface, but they would all be independent. The relation of the caterpillar to the butterfly, the tadpole to the frog. An organic relation."

Sutcliffe groaned and said: "The old danger is there – a work weighed down with theoretical considerations."

"No. Never. Not on your life. Just a *roman-gigogne*."

"The more desperate the writer the more truthful the music – or so I believed then. Now I don't know. I wonder a great deal about wrongdoing in art, in a way I never did before."

"My dear old Rob, crime gives a wonderful sheen to the skin. The sap rises, the sex blooms in secrecy like some tropical plant. Take an example from me."

All that snowy day Blanford went on talking to his creation, trying to explain himself, to justify his feelings and his thoughts. He was trying to sum it all up – from the point of view of death.

"From the ambush of my disability I watched and noted, hungry for disbelief. I watched my Livia coming and going in the mirror. I watched her walking about Venice from my high balcony, and I saw the woman who was spying on her at my request – for rather a stiff price. Livia was always looking back over her shoulder to see if she was being followed – clever, slender, nervous, and very caryatid, she had won my heart by her effortless sensuality. What a marvellous death-mask that dark face would make – ascetic, heart-shaped and pale. The way the lips and hands trembled when she became passionate.

"My God, what a muddle – it was Constance I really loved. She could have been my second skin. What a strange phrase, 'The rest of my life'. What does it mean? Surely that little rest – the steady diminishing of time – begins at birth? When you discovered you had married a homosexual what did you do, Robin?"

"The foolish fellow put a pistol to his brow."

"Even a writer must be truthful to decay. You burst out laughing first – the predicament was so foolish."

"But worse still, I really loved her, Pia," said Sutcliffe. "It was an unlucky dishonour forced upon me. But have you lived with one? They burn up your oxygen, being maladapted and out of true. They remove the classical pity which love engenders. The sadness which amends. And their beauty is like a spear, Blanford."

"Like a spear, my boy, like a spear."

"In Regent Street, in a sordid pub, a woman I had never regarded as being in any way intuitive listened attentively to my moans and said, 'Someone has wounded you very deeply and for utterly frivolous reasons. You should try to laugh and tell yourself that one is always punished for insincerity.' Damn her eyes!"

"She was right. But she had never seen Livia at bay, with flashing eyes, lying for dear life – you see, she could not bear it really, her inversion. She wouldn't admit it to anyone. With her back to the wall she fenced desperately. Tied to the wheel in the sinking vessel of her self-esteem – as who is not? – she foundered in my arms. I had had her closely watched for a little while when one day . . . my servant Cade had to return to England for his mother's funeral and during his absence I moved into the Lutèce on a narrow street; there I sat at evening watching the dusk fall, and the lights spring up over the canals. The street was so narrow that the balconies opposite were almost touching ours, or so it seemed. Three floors up, Lord Galen sat reading the *Financial Times*, full of the sense of his oneliness. I joined him for a cocktail and there, standing on his balcony, I looked across the street and saw the light snap on in a dark room opposite. Two women were just waking from their siesta – yawning and stretching. One rose and came to the balcony to thrust the shutters wide. As she did so the mouse raised her face and her eyes met mine. It was my spy, naked, and behind her in the rumpled bed Livia was drowsing, her fingers on her sex, dreaming – as if fingering a violin one is about to play. Her eyes half-closed, she was presumably riffling through the portfolio of her phantasy life. She had evidently seduced my spy! It was all over in a second. The girl retired, and so did I. Furious and thunderstruck, I said nothing to the old banker, who was particularly worried about the state of copper that day – he had once looked after some of my mother's modest investments for her and was never free from the delicious anal gnawing of money."

Sutcliffe: "So you were crushed with fury, and went

down to the bar; the porter gave you a fat envelope full of marvellous press cuttings, fulsome ones, interviews and pictures. I have always wanted to question you a little about them. For example, you are reported as saying 'I have never sought fame and fortune in my work. I sought happiness.'"

"Yes, I did say that. I thought that."

"And happiness, have you found it?" Sutcliffe put on the adenoidal voice of an interviewer.

"You find it only when you stop looking, Rob."

"And have you?"

"No."

"Why not?"

"Now that would be worth answering but I don't for the life of me know how to."

"I thought not. When you got back to the flat later you played on the little harmonium a whole grisly toccata."

"Yes, the background music for a nervous breakdown. And I reflected on all the psychoanalytic twaddle about our oceanic sexual drives. And in my manly agony I cried out, 'O God, my God, why didst Thou let me marry a Principal Boy?' When Livia slept with me who was she really loving in her imagination, in her phantasy? Who was my rival, the dark lady of the sonnets? And how could I find out? She had carefully masked her batteries. Once set off by the hair-trigger of a simple kiss she turned her face to this veiled form and used me as the *machine à plaisir*."

"And yet she was full of ideals, Livia."

"All ideals are unattainable – that is what makes them worth having. You have to reach for the apple. If you wait until it falls you will be disappointed – you will realise that it is imaginary."

"The apple of gravity, Newton's wish?"

"Exactly. And besides, never forget how much in the dark we all were about our selves, our predilections, our ruling passions. It took a trip to Vienna with Constance to teach us just a very little."

"It resolved nothing, it only unsettled you to know the truth about your sexual predispositions."

"Perhaps; yet knowledge is a sort of exorcism. I am very grateful to Constance, who was the only one among us to read German and thus have direct access to what was being written in Vienna and Zurich; moreover despite the abandoned studies she was already a fine doctor. She explained Livia to me satisfactorily."

"To what avail?"

"To no avail; of course it wasn't enough, it never is, but it enabled me to sympathise with her, to understand many things, like, for example, her deliberate grubbiness at times – the revolt against her femininity, the desire to insult the male. Then always restless, always wanting to be on the move. Several times a day she had to walk down to the village because she had forgotten to buy this or that. It used to puzzle me, it seemed almost deliberate, and of course it was. As Constance said, she was simply a man-at-arms on the look-out for a pick-up! Surely this was valuable, all this information? Eh?"

Sutcliffe deliberated for a moment, and Blanford lit a cigar, saying: "Soon there will be nobody to talk to except you. It is extremely sad – what shall I do for company? You bore me so! It will probably lead to madness."

"We will write a book."

"Of what will it treat?"

"Of the perennity of despair, intractability of language, impenetrability of art, insipidity of human love."

"Livia and Constance, the two faces? Transposed heads!"

"The two faces. You see, Aubrey, the male invert loves his mother, the female hates hers implacably. That is why

313

she won't bear children, or if she does, makes changelings or witches. What we thought we found was that Livia really loved her sister Constance – that is why she set out to marry you, to cut Constance out. She could not bear to think of you coming together."

"But Livia slept with many men."

"Of course, but it was with brave contempt, to prove her own maleness, her masculine superiority. A talented Chartreuse. She would run with her bleeding male scalps and show them to her girl friends. This was a way of advertising her wares. 'Look, this is all men are worth, so easily scalped!' "

"Alas, it was only too true." Sutcliffe fingered the little tonsured part of his own huge cranium where recently the baldness had begun to show through. "After Pia I had to buy a hairpiece," he admitted. "And specially after all this psychoanalytic gibberish. All I learned was that male lesbians are notoriously kind to dogs – but I am not a dog and don't qualify. Another question – was Jesus a lesbian?"

"Cut it out," said Blanford, "I can't bear idle blasphemy."

At this point Sutcliffe sang the little psychoanalytic song he had once made up to celebrate the great men of the science; it went

> Joy, Young and Frenzy,
> Frenzy, Groddeck and Joy.

He broke off and said suddenly: "*Et le bonheur?*"

"Exactly."

"It cannot be impossible to find. It must be knocking about somewhere, just out of sight. Why don't we write a big autobiography? Come on, punish everyone!"

"The last defence! All aboard for the last alibi!"

"What does a man say when his wife leaves him? He cries out in an agony of fury: 'Thrice-tritrurated gasometers!

Who will burn sugar to this tonsil-snipping tart?' "

"Or seek the consolations of art: the little choking yelp of Desdemona is pleasant to dwell upon."

"Or he will become a widow and in desperation take up with some furry housemaid who will in due course be delivered of some rhubarb-coloured mite."

"The Kismet for novelists with cook-housekeepers. But I have only Cade, and he can't cook. . . ."

The snow went on falling out in the park with its resigned elms full of rooks' nests. Blanford pondered heavily upon human nature and its uncapturable variety while Sutcliffe in his Oxford rooms turned and put a log on the fire. Toby was coming to lunch with a young girl undergraduate. Then he took up the phone once more and said, "The relationship between our books will be incestuous, then, I take it? They will be encysted in each other, not complementary. There would be room for everything, poem, autobiography, short story and so on."

"Yes," said his creator softly. "I suppose you have heard of that peculiar medical phenomenon called the teratoma? It is literally a bag full of unfinished spare parts – nails and hair and half-grown teeth – which is lodged like a benign growth somewhere in a human body. It is removed by surgery. It appears to be part of a twin which at some stage decided to stop growing. . . ."

"A short story lodged in a book?"

"Yes. Do you know at what point Pia began to love you? I bet you don't. It was when you behaved so outrageously at Unesco and fell into the big drum."

"You mean Shakespeare's birthday? They should never have asked me."

"You should never have gone. And then to arrive dead drunk and take your place on the rostrum among the greatest modern poets, all prepared to render homage to the Bard.

And with Toby in the audience cheering and waving a British flag. It was obscene."

"Not entirely," said Sutcliffe, slightly huffed, "it had its moment of truth. Besides, nobody could contravert my twelve commandments – the indispensable prerequisites for those who wish to make works of art. They were particularly impressive when shouted through a megaphone in a hoarse tormented tone. Why didn't you use them?"

"I will one day when I write the ridiculous scene. You made Ungaretti faint. And then having recited the whole iniquitous catalogue of drivel you fell into the Elizabethan madrigal society's big bassoon, festooned with wires and microphones."

"Rather like Ophelia," said Sutcliffe. "But I stand by my commandments whatever the French say. Let me repeat them to you lest you have forgotten or mislaid them." He cleared his throat energetically and recited them for the benefit of Blanford, who wrote them down in shorthand on the pad at his elbow.

He left a long pause for admiration or applause and then said: "Alas, it ended badly, but it was none of my fault."

There was another longish silence during which Sutcliffe blew his nose in a plaintive sort of way, feeling that he was disapproved of by his mate and pawn. Then he said: "Where will Tu be buried and when?"

"Tonight," said Blanford coolly, with a reserve he was far from feeling. "In the chateau vault, by dispensation, and no ceremony, no flowers. Some lanterns, I suppose, perhaps some torches."

"Will you go down to Tu Duc?"

"Later, when everything is settled and the château boarded up for the winter. I love the rain falling over Avignon with all its memories. There is a certain melancholy luxury in

* See Appendix for full text of 12 Commandments.

316

feeling that everyone has gone, one is completely alone. The place to experience this best of all is on deserted railway stations at night, empty airport lounges, all-night cafés in the town."

Sutcliffe said: "And Livia, who in my own personal life and book turned into Sylvie and went mad? What about her in this context?"

"Livia disappeared, was last heard of on the road to Spain with the old negro pianist. My last news of her was some years ago now, from a girl who had known her; it was in one of those houses which cater to special inclinations – indeed the identical house where you lodged with the old crone. From time to time I passed by just in order to check, because once I had found Livia there, shaking with fatigue or drugs, trembling from head to foot. She said, in a bleary tearful way: "Unless someone takes care of me I am finished." I realised then that I loved her and would never desert her; and all the while a voice inside me was raging and shouting 'Fool!' "

"That was where I hunted for Pia."

"We took her to the kitchen, tottering, and set her down on a stool, imploring her to eat something. The hag buttered some bread. Livia suddenly burst into tears and said, '*J'ai failli t'aimer*,' and the tears ran down her long sweet nose into the plate. Still crying, she began to eat, looking so like a small child in her tearful hunger that I was overwhelmed. I sat there biting my lips and remembering so much that she had told me.

"One day in a dark cinema a woman placed her hand lightly upon her thigh and she felt her whole nature tilt like a galleon in a wind, to run seething through fresh seas. She did not move. She did not speak. She offered no response. Then she got up and walked out of the cinema without looking round. In the vestibule she felt so ill she had to lean her head against the cold tiled wall. A hand touched her sleeve and a voice said, 'Come, let me help you.' And so it began. And as she diminished in my life I started to reinvent her on paper as accurately as I could. Once when she had gone and I was lonely I took another girl from the same establishment to a hotel – purely for the comfort of sleeping with someone who knew her and could talk about her, even though what she had to tell me was wounding. Cynically and with a strong twang to her French this poor creature told me about Livia's exploits in great detail, adding as she did so: 'She gives good value, that one. Among the girls who like it she is known as Moustache.' My dear Rob, my beloved was known as Moustache to her ingles!"

"Perhaps you were wise to make Pia passive rather than active – it gave her a dimension Livia lacked, a pathos."

"But Livia was magnetic, and much harder to paint. I was forever trying to push a bit of femininity back into the lady, like trying to fill a dolly with sawdust, trying to fill an eye with a drip, trying to fill a mind with a prayer. Then she would disappear for a few days, to be brought back by the police dead drunk or else be run to earth in a bar, guttering down, guttering out. You, know, her health was a worry, she was never very strong, and she persistently brutalised it. But her charm! She was irresistible, she smelt of perils and disenchantments. Men could not resist her, and she longed to be able to respond. Yes, she gave herself, but it was only a smear of a woman who responded to the kiss. Affectively she was anaesthetic, her soul was rubberised."

"How funny," said Sutcliffe. "I suppose you discovered the real truth once the wedding-ring was on her finger. It was just like that with Pia, I had all sorts of vague notions that even though she was wild and unstable she was redeemable – a little bit of settled ways and stylised married life . . . I should have known by then how to detect the quaire (feminine version of queer). After all she could neither swim nor dance, and in love she went all anaesthetic but kindly – her kisses were one-dimensional and softer than moths."

"That was not Livia. Her favourite nail varnish was called Sadist Red, and she operated with a violence and zeal of a piglet at dug. A real predator, she liked to wear the fur of wild animals. Lean tomboy of the sexthrust, it was she who impregnated me with her despairing, anodyne, phantasy sensuality."

"Why were you so annoyed about the ring? In my case I felt that Pia had taken an unfair advantage, and wanted to continue in her old style under cover of the status and the stability I offered her. I felt swizzed."

"In my case it was the ring itself – it had belonged to my mother. I had all the tortured and confused impulses of only children, sickly in youth and consequently spoiled. School was torture, other people were torture. She was my only girl, mama, and I remained a *vieux garcon*, a bachelor, until she died when I thought that my loneliness might be less unendurable with a woman about the house. Of course I had had this long love-affair with Constance in between; but she never wished to remarry. Anyway Livia had disappeared somewhere in Asia and in those days it took years before a presumption of death permitted one to dream of divorce. You deformed her a bit in Pia."

"But you are to blame, for making her passive instead of active. Pia, looking so lovely in her white night-dress, obligingly put herself into a state of abstraction to pump out her husband (tenderly, dutifully) but like a collector 'blows' a bird's egg. For the rest, lying warm in bed she played with a masturbatory little curl, and I suppose dreamed about her *fouetteuse*, or her *frotteuse*. Why not? What is cheaper than dreaming? But infantile dreams which recover an early sex life are as feverish as the dreams of an anchorite. Great

Amputator of Egg Bags, save us! The lady was a *station de pompage* merely."

"Childhood, with its gross sexual and psychological damage to the psyche – what a terrible thing to be forced to undergo. No really, Rob, one does not stand a chance!"

"They believed in God. Jesus on pedals! How could they?"

Blanford threw his cigar into the fire and thought with a sudden wave of nostalgic passion of Tu. She rose before his inner eye walking by the lake where they had once and for all staked a claim in each other's minds and bodies; he heard her low voice reading from the book about Nietzsche, whom they had come there to seek.

"What happens," said Sutcliffe thoughtfully, "according to the wiseacres you consulted with so little profit – what happens to the penis is coronation followed by decapitation – the king bowing so low before the ladies that the crown falls off on to the red carpet. Isn't that right?"

Blanford agreed and amplified the statement with a voice full of distaste. "The head lends itself particularly well to the expression of bisexual conflicts, and can cunningly represent both male and female genitalia. Both girls were highly specialised in migraines of great intensity. There are vaginal haemorrhages which can be stopped by the cocaine pad to the inside of the nose. The guillotine, remember, was called *La Vierge*."

"A fig for all this folklore," cried Sutcliffe. "All will end in munch and you know it. The black flag of pure cannibalism will be unfurled. If narcissists (artists) cannot love, what right have they to kick up such a row?"

"You're right."

"*Si on est Dieu pourquoi cochonner?*"

"You're dead right, as they say. What a useful phrase."

Blanford could hear his creation tearing open a bag of potato chips and starting to champ them as he reflected furiously upon these all too alembicated ideas. Blanford thought of his childhood. "An only child is doomed to nostalgia and uncertainty. Nobody will ever guess what it cost me against all my fears and despairs, to teach myself the profession of letters. Solo, solitude, solace ... everything beginning with Sol the father, Sol the Son and Sol the Holy Ghost. She lingered for many years, did my mother, bedridden, suffering from an ill-identified malady which purported to be a heart condition. I think now that it was some grave glandular disturbance – the thymus perhaps. It gave her languor, it gave her a skin like a magnolia; her breasts remained firm and her teeth good to the very end. We lived, she and I, without a father in number twenty-seven Ruskin Road, South Norwood – a gloomy house called The Larches, with arch statuary on the lawn and a fountain which had rusted and would not play. We shared everything, even sleeping – as one might share careers of common silence. Yet I hear her sighs in my dreams now. What a torture it was to pack up my little tuck-box, count my money and set off to school, having assembled my books and kissed mama goodbye. Sterling, the old butler, drove me shakily down to the country – my school was near Arundel – in the ancient Morris. He was a randy old Cockney and he used to say: 'Next week, d'you know what, Master Aubrey? Why, I'm going on a right bender – don't tell your mother because she thinks I'm respectable. In a way she's right, I am. But not on my holidays. I've got a couple of birds right over the pocket in Brixton, and I'm simply thirsting for a bit of knuckle, Master Aubrey, really thirsting.'

"My father had been a scientific don in a minor university; the photographs depicted a large, discordant-looking man with black lace-up boots. I stared and stared at the vague memory-bank of his face but it radiated nothing. 'Come, hand me my pins, my net and my killing bottle, and leave me in peace.' He said that to my mother once who found it inconsiderate. It upset her. The house was full of badly stuffed geese and wildfowl, and in his study was a cabinet containing shelves and shelves of brilliant butterflies all mounted expertly on slabs of cork. I would have to do without all this until the end of term when Christmas came round. Again! The smart toy of the crib, and sex awoken in some little old mistletoe-man with a red peak, at night, in the snow, driving his tinkling harim of reindeer across the snowy roofs.

"Sometimes at night, walking across London, to see scores of silent frozen girls offering their bodies for sale under the blobs of yellow gaslight. Hurrying home to mother with castdown eyes, dying of smothered desires and the all too real fear of syphilis. So my whole life took its direction from there – my mother had rendered me a lamb, ripe for the slaughter; Livia supplied the shears. Cause and effect, my lad, that is why I had to encourage you to have a richer and more robust childhood. Your people were millers, say, from the north country, with a firm fortune and coming of authentic peasant stock. I saw your prototype once, dining beside me in Avignon and I jotted down in my notebook. 'She is rather frail, but he huge with an egg-shaped cranium and a face which had funny and rather unworldly expressions on it. They smelt of industrious love-making and yawned all through dinner.' "

"Thank you. Was I at school with you?"

"We were both at different schools together."

Sutcliffe answered a ring at the doorbell and then came back to the phone to say briefly: "Toby has arrived. For my part I told everybody that I lived in Ireland in a fairy's armpit. They gave the impression of believing me, I never had trouble like you. Your laughter was a private strategy, mine was whole-hearted."

"I am not so sure," said Blanford thoughtfully, "though it is true that I was loved by a mummy without margins. Result: I wrote tonsured poems in the style of Morris. But I soon came to my senses. The result was not vastly different – we both ran into Livia, but in my case I presented a very simple target, and the motive of course was my unrecognised love for Tu. By the time your turn came you were less vulnerable because of your tough youth and were able to surmount the catastrophe with commendable humour. You at least were able to stand on the Bridge of Sighs and, waving your stick, exclaim aloud: 'Help me, Pia, help me! I am going down by the stern like Laurel and Hardy!' I could never have done that. I was after something else – a cumulus of thought subsumed in one bold metaphor. I had realised something concrete, namely that small art creates a throb, big art a wholesome vertigo. I tried to teach you this in your dealings with the people around you, so that your writing might have pith and irony. But since human consciousness distorts in the act of observing, you and I, seen by a third person, are perverted images of one another. We exchange highly diversified memoranda about the state of our attachment, just like real lovers entering that state which probably never existed. Poets exchanging cowrie shells, not real coin. Unless the images sting you awake. Robin, before you obediently killed yourself, you scribbled in the margins of your unfinished manuscript poem – the *Tu Quoque* – the words, 'Of course like Tiresias I have breasts which see all, and a forked tail in the shape of a lightning conductor. And yes, hooves.'"

Sutcliffe roared with laughter and crunched away at his chips, while in the background Blanford could hear the bearish sounds of Toby clearing his throat and the voice of a girl. He could not imagine her face as he had not yet invented her. That would come, he supposed. O God! Writers! Sutcliffe said: "Toby has been making up an imaginary obituary for you for *The Times* – you know he makes a little cash from working in the graveyard bringing obits up to date. Here's a passage which will please you: 'It is said that when rich he twice refused the thistle.' "

"But the money gave me books and travel and secrecy. And anyway one can't do better than one's best. What more would you like to hear from me if I bring you back to life?"

"About Tu; about Livia; about Hilary the brother and Sam. About the lake, and about Tu Duc and the Avignon of those early days. About us, the real ones."

"Then let me ask you one question," said Blanford sternly. "Just how real do you feel to yourself, Robin Sutcliffe?"

"I have never stopped to think," said his only friend after a pause. "Have you?"

"And you want to know about your own youth? Of course I endowed you with mine, for we are about the same age."

"But different milieux nourished us."

"Yes, but the age was the same, and an age is a state of mind. The twenties – that was purely a state of mind."

"Tell me the details, it will help me to act."

"Very well."

Blanford closed his eyes and let his memory draw him back to the very beginning of the story.

"It was to be their last term at Oxford and Hilary had invited them both to journey with him to Provence for the long vac. Neither he nor Sam had then met his two sisters, Constance and Livia. Indeed, they knew nothing of them at all. But recently, with the death of an old aunt, young

324

Constance had inherited the little chateau of Tu Duc in the southern Vaucluse, not far from Avignon. The Duchess of Tu, then, was the obvious nickname for her. The children had spent many holidays there once upon a time in their extreme youth; but in her old age the aunt became first eccentric, and then mentally unstable; she turned recluse, locked herself up, and allowed the whole place to fall into ruins around her. The rain and the wind settled down to finish what negligence had begun; the weight of winter snow cracked the black tiles of the roofs and entered the rooms, with their strange scrolled bull's-eye windows. In the rambling, disorderly park, old trees had fallen everywhere, blocking the paths, crushing the summer-house under their weight. The once-tended green plots were now a mass of molehills, while everywhere hares skirmished. They were to live largely on jugged hare that summer!

"Hilary, to do him justice, did not minimise the hardships they might have to face; but the prospect of southern sunlight and good wine was enough to offset any qualms they might have had. And then there was another capital factor – they had both youth and good health. Constance would meet them in Lyon, while Livia would come on later to join them, in her own time. Hilary mentioned Livia's name and frowned affectionately as he did so – as if he found the fact of her existence somehow troubling. His deep family affection for her had a sort of qualified, formalised air, as if he did not wholeheartedly understand her as did Constance. His way of talking gave one the notion that Livia was the wild and unpredictable one, while Constance was the stable and utterly dependable one. This proved to be more or less the case later when they got to know the truth about them – whatever that might mean. But Livia now spent all her time in Germany.

"It was this promise of a wild and somewhat primitive holiday which explained all the heavy camping impedimenta they found stacked up against their arrival in Lyon – they had sent it on in advance. Massive camp-beds and sun-helmets, sleeping-bags, mosquito nets – perfectly ridiculous items which had been invented for safaris in lion-country or for scaling the Indian Himalayas. But none of them knew old Provence at first hand, so perhaps these precautions were excusable.

"Today the world which fathered them is a remote and forgotten one; it was a world wallowing in the wake of one war, trying to gather itself together before plunging irrevocably into a second. Their youth had enabled them to escape the trenches – in 1918 they were still just under military age, though Sam nearly managed to join up by a subterfuge; but he was found out and sent back to school; whence, to Oxford where the three, though so different, became inseparable. Hilary was the ringmaster of the little group, for he had more experience than either of the others, and he always led the dance. As a boy he was blond and tall and had ice-blue eyes like a Teuton. Sam was tow-haired and rather massive in his awkward gentle way. I was ... how was I, Aubrey Blanford? Let me see.

"A bit of a slowcoach, I suppose. Sam boxed and Hilary rowed, while all three of us hacked a bit and when possible rode to hounds in a post-Surtees manner.

"I was the least mercuric, the most sedentary of the three, and my poor eyesight made me an indifferent athlete, though I fenced well and even got my blue for it. The post-Wildean twilight of Oxford was no longer a place to cool the mind – the stresses and strains of the war years still weighed on us by proxy, for many of the men who had seen blood and action in 1918 had come back to university to finish studies interrupted by the war. A disturbed and wild crew they were, like foreign barbarians.

"Yes, it is difficult to describe that world, now so

forgotten; its values and habits seem to have retreated into the remotest recesses of time. Do you remember it – a world in awkward transition? The new thing was violent and brash, the old had ankylosed. All that the war had not killed outright lived on in a kind of limbo. Intellectually, let us say, Anatole France and Shaw were at the height of their fame; Proust despite his prizes had not yet won the general public. Henry James versus Wells.

"Was I born old? I never seem to have had a proper youth – mine began at Oxford when I met Hilary. If he was by far the most sophisticated of the three of us it was due to chance. His father had been a diplomat and the children had always travelled with him to his various posts. This stiff old gentleman was something of a stickler for ancient forms, and wherever they went they had tutors and learned the language of the place. Thus Hilary and his sisters became good linguists and thoroughly at home in places which were, to me, semi-mythical – Middle Europe, for example, or the Balkans: Rumania, Russia, Greece, Arabia. . . . It is true that Sam and I spoke laborious French and Italian, with a smidgen of German. But in the case of Hilary he 'possessed' three languages in the French sense of the word, and smattered in four others. All this he turned to good account and took excellent degrees at Oxford. His objective then was archaeology, his hero Evans, and his heart he had set upon exploring the labyrinth at Gortymna which remains unmapped to this day because of its great extent.

"And Sam? I have a picture of him in the back of my mind, lying in the deep grass at the edge of a green cricket-field crunching an apple and chuckling over Wodehouse or Dornford Yates. You must remember that we were overgrown schoolboys then to whom even dull, but raucous London was an excitement, a dream. While Paris was Babylon. Sam's ambitions were simple – all he wanted to do was to climb

Everest single-handed, and on his return rescue a beautiful blonde maiden from a tower where she had been imprisoned by an enchanter, and marry her. Later on he would like to set off on his travels with her disguised as his page and join the Knights of the Round Table. You will see the disastrous effects of Malory on a guileless mind. In my case, I wanted to be a historian – at that time I had really no inclination towards this hollow servitude to ink and paper. I pictured myself doing a definitive book on some aspect of medieval history and winning an Exhibition to Wadham, or something of that nature. As you see the bright one was Hilary, with what he called his 'Minoan tilt' – for his plans and projects opened windows on the world of Europe. Am I right?"

"I suppose so, but it's a bit pedestrian your exposé – it proves that the dull historian is not quite dead in my poor Aubrey. I would have gone about it differently myself."

"Tell me how."

"I should have enumerated other things like school ties, huge woollen scarves, Oxford bags, college blazers, Brough Superiors à la T. E. Lawrence, racing cars with strapped-down bonnets, Lagonda, Bentley, Amilcar. . . . The flappers had come and gone but the vamp was present in force with her cloche hat and cigarette holder."

"I had forgotten all that."

"It is the small things which build the picture."

"London."

"Yes, and the places we frequented in London most of which have disappeared – wiped out one supposes by the bombings?"

"Like the Café de Paris?"

"Yes, and Ciro's and The Blue Peter, The Criterion Bar, Quaglino's, Stone's Chop House, Mannering's Grill, Paton's, The Swan. . . ."

"Good, Robin, and then the night-clubs like The Old

Bag O' Nails, The Blue Lantern, The Black Hole, and Kiki's Place. . . . We simply never slept."

"The music of shows like Funny Face ('Who stole my Heart away?') Charlot, and the divine Hutch smoothing down the big grand piano and singing in his stern unemphatic way 'Life is just a bowl of cherries'."

"Just before dawn Lyons' Corner House, everyone with yellow exhausted faces, whores, undergraduates, all-night watchmen and workers setting off on early jobs. The first newspapers appearing on the icy street. Walking back in the pale nervous rinsed-out dawn, the whole way back across London – over Westminster Bridge and into the baleful suburbs of the capital; perhaps with the memory of some whore in mind, and the ever present worry of a dose. Marry or burn, my boy, marry or burn."

"I did both."

"So did I. So did I."

"And so we come to the misty slip at Lyon where we waited impatiently for Constance and filled in the time by loading all our ludicrous equipment aboard the *Mistral*, a huge flat motor-barge with a capacious hold and enough deck space to take a few passengers. The hold was already battened down and covered with a tarpaulin which gave us a large flat area for lounging and eating; it was not envisaged that we should spend the night on her, but ashore. And then, amidst all these foolish deliberations, the stacking of our gear – you would have thought we were setting off for the Pole – the girl arrived; and with her, suddenly the whole summer too took place – I mean the consciousness of it, the density of its weight. As yet we were only in the mulberry-tree belt of dishevelled Lyon and its sprawling green surroundings. Far from the dustry garrigues as yet, the olive oil, and the anisette. But with Tu one saw what it was: it was sunlight filtered through a summer hat of fine straw onto bronzed shoulders and neck, creating a shadow that was of the darkness of ripe plums. It was ash-blonde hair made rough but silky by too much sun and salt water. It was a neck set perfectly on slender but strong shoulders, it was an eye of periwinkle-blue, which could turn green with the light, an eye full of curiosity and humour. She had cut her foot bathing, and her limp was explained by a bandage. She looked at us without much ardour or interest, I think, but with friendliness because we were her brother's friends. I felt at once that she shared some of his superiority over us – some of what I would call nowadays sophistication. 'Sorry I'm late; it was the train as usual.'

"Our skipper was a grave rotund man, who had the air of a great character actor out of work. His old sea-wolf yachting cap was cocked at a jaunty angle, and his liberality was not in question, for he produced frequent glasses of strong wine and urged them on us as a protection against the inclemency of the weather. What inclemency? The weather was perfectly fine, the old man obviously raving. Nevertheless the full beakers of Côtes du Rhône put us all into a great good humour; Constance sipped from her brother's glass and asked permission to put on shorts which he gravely granted. We winked at one another. The skipper's wife allowed her to make this transformation in the little cabin below which contained a cage bird and some old prints of the days of water haulage on the Rhône – really not so far away in time.

"We were fully loaded for Arles but were waiting for two more passengers who had been delayed. But they were not to detain us for long, and they were profuse in their apologies. One was a lanky, raffish-looking individual with a yellowish complexion and hair all in tufts about his greatcoat collar. He had a kind of shabby air of majesty, but it was only much later, when he advanced to the prow and let fly with an aria from Verdi, of tremendous volume, that we realised we were in the presence of a star from the opera of Marseille. The other was a humble, elderly man with a crown of white hair and the venerable appearance of a beadle. He had a brown old face which was full of character, and he regarded the world around him with an air of slightly impudent amusement. He seemed, however, a man of some real cultivation, not only from his manner but also because he carried under his arm a volume of poems, and actually sported (it is only now in retrospect that I recognise the fact) in his lapel the golden cicada which betokens a member of that famous poetic society the Félibre. Everything about our skipper – his rotundity, his accent, his gestures seemed to fill this old gentleman with delight. I realise now why, they were both from Avignon, which was also our landfall and from where we hoped to find a carriage to take us to Tubain, if Felix was not at the rendezvous with his spluttering little consular car.

"The hooter gave a hiss and a boom, while drops of steam dribbled down the funnel; we had cast off and were away almost before we knew or felt it. Lying at ease on the spacious deck we saw the sunlit world turn slowly about us, spin faster and faster, and begin to slide away to stern. We swept under a great bridge where the silhouettes of a few onlookers were set against the arc of a sky of utter blue. Constance settled herself among the cushions thoughtfully provided by the gallant old skipper and apparently fell asleep, which gave me a chance to observe her and be struck once again by her beauty, and her resemblance to her brother. The fine blonde hair at her temples was, I thought, finer than the work of silkworms; her sleep was light, she smiled at some happy dream or thought. I would never have dreamed that she was as shy as Hilary, so formidable did her self-possession seem to us poor Englanders, bursting with conventions and the need to worship. Many years later when in a letter I made a reference to this first meeting she wrote on a postcard the one word: 'Shyness'.

"There was no sign of all this in the pose of the calm sleeping girl on the deck. Hilary, if my memory serves, rapidly got on good terms with the old poet and fired questions at him about the places through which we glode so smoothly, over a river suddenly widened by the green junction with the Saône. What I did remember was the droning voice of my geography teacher as he told us its history, softly touching the big wall-map with the black malacca cane which also, in certain contexts, served him to give us the brutal thrashings which were then the order of the day in most schools. They did no harm, I might add, and indeed were really useful as a rough and ready absolution – for one expiated one's sins this way and forgot about them once the blue weals had gone. While those hundred lines or hundred Hail Marys never really did the trick.

"But this first enticing venture towards the south, towards the Mediterranean, has got itself mixed up and superposed upon the many other times when I returned to Tu Duc to spend the summers there. 'The Rhône rises in Lac Léman,' said the droning voice of my geography teacher."

At this point in Blanford's recital Robin Sutcliffe cleared his throat and chuckled and made a noise like someone snuffing. "I bet I can tell what you think of now in that context."

"Carry on. Tell me," said Blanford.

Sutcliffe said: "The Chambre Froide of the central abattoir at Geneva. Of all the extraordinary places to sit and watch the Rhône rise. It was there that Pia took me to tell me that she had met poor Trash. It was a singular place to choose, perhaps more apt than it appears at first sight. The great factory that is the abattoir is built over the lake, remember, and at the back of it there is a little glassed-in restaurant built right over the water, where the personnel of the place take their meals. They call it the birdcage, if I recall right, and it is certainly small. Naturally the prime food is the meat. Trash had found it one day on her wanderings – she had been sent to order a carcase for the old American lady's birthday-party – one which would unite all the queers and queens and quaires of the town. Here among the swinging carcases on their big hooks the butchers in their bloody aprons had a festive air. They found Trash very much to their taste, and after several of the younger ones had refreshed themselves with her they invited her to the canteen for a glass of wine.

"Without this invitation it would have been impossible to find, for the entrance was actually through a huge meat-safe which was usually kept closed. Naturally the place was not open to the general public, it was reserved for the butchers and their friends. But a few people had discovered it and the supervision was lax. Well, I remember sitting over the water listening to this sad recital of Pia's fears and regrets; and all about her love for me which made me blow my nose rather loudly because I was touched, and I felt awfully as if my heart had been broken with a sledge hammer. To be hugged by a boy in a blood-stained apron – Ugh! Of course it was Trash who had been hugged, but now Pia was going to try the same thing under the tuition of the negress. It upset me so much this recital (the foolish girl was asking for my encouragement, for my absolution, repeating that she could not live without me and that I must understand). . . . I got so damned livid with her stupidity in succumbing to the lures of that male succubus with a slit that I rushed out of the place and took a taxi to Trash's hotel with the intention of thrashing her. Luckily she was out and I cooled down as I walked by the lake."

"Lucky is the word," said Blanford, "when I took a dogwhip to Livia for one of her misdemeanours I put her into a transport of sexual delight. Bathed in tears of pain and gratitude she fell to her knees and started licking my shoes. She was my slave now, she told me, utterly my slave. And she kept repeating, 'O why didn't you do it before?' I was disgusted."

"And the abattoir restaurant?"

"If I must disinter Livia's thoughts – it was she, the original of Pia, who took me there – I must record that she adored the smell of blood and fresh water. Indeed everything about new blood delighted her. It reminded her of her first period – she had been so poorly instructed, and was so innocent, that she thought she was bleeding to death like Petronius. And then, of course, the sorrow because it was the first physical proof of the lack of manhood she so coveted inside herself. The tremendous sadness of realising, as she said in her own picturesque phraseology, that she was a boy scout with a vagina. My dear Robin, she did not actually suffer the embrace of bloodstained boys, but she dreamed about it; only in her case the butcher was an elderly man who looked like her father. While we sat over the water and I saw her face suddenly go dead and transform itself into the resolute face of a tough little sailor, something guttered out like a spent candle. My love, like a sick fish, rose to the surface belly upwards. Under the floor of our birdcage the lake-water, narrowed and sluiced by the two banks, gathers speed, as if it could smell Arles already.

"The driving channel was a dark shade of amethyst verging on ultramarine; but right in the middle there was a portion raised like a muscle in a forearm, a green muscle of water which seemed to have more thrust than the great body in which it was embedded. Following the direction of my gaze Livia said: 'You see the green ribbon there? It's the

Rhône setting off on its race for the sea.' I hear her voice, I see the water, and a thousand thoughts throng in my mind. The great rivers of the human sensibility threading the jungles and swamps and forests of lost continents. The big rivers like Nile or Mississippi ferrying their human freight from one world to another. Though short in length our Rhône was one with them as was its cousin the Rhine. . . .

"Livia told me that one night she had been taken by her lover to La Villette where an old kind butcher with the face of her father had, on request, hobbled a cow which was about to be destroyed, and made a swift incision in its throat, like slitting an envelope. He held it by the horns, though the animal felt nothing. But the jet of blood spurted out into the tall wineglasses they proffered. They drank copiously while the old man watched in kindly fashion. Later they had trouble with a policeman for they were both splashed with blood, and it was difficult to explain how they had acquired these smears. But you, Robin, above all will have easily explained Livia's aberrations satisfactorily to yourself by now – didn't you take a degree in Philosophy and Psychology?

"What always bothered me was the question of a stable ego – did such a thing exist? The old notion of such an animal was rather primitive, particularly for novelists with an itch to explain this action or that. Myself, I could hardly write down the name of a character without suddenly being swamped by an ocean of possible attributes, each as valid and as truthful as any other. The human psyche is almost infinitely various – so various that it can afford to be contradictory even as regards itself. How poor is the pathetic little typology of our modern psychology – why, even astrology, however suspect as a science, makes some attempt to encompass the vast multiplicity of purely human attributes. That is why our novels, yours and mine, Robin, are also poor. There were many Livias, some whom I love and will love until my dying day; others fell off me and dried up like dead leeches. Others were just larval forms in the sense of Paracelsus, umbratiles, vampires, ghosts. When she had definitely gone she sent me the taunting telegram which seemed to amuse you.

> A little bit of addled Freud
> Won't take you far towards the void.

"But the letter to which the thought belonged was written from Gantok and she had headed it, 'On the road to Tibet'. It was long, rambling and inconsequential, and it upset me so much that I destroyed it. But I remember one part in which she wrote: 'You cannot imagine what it is like to find myself in a land where beautiful six-armed Tsungtorma raises her lotus-soft palms.' It was a fair enough criticism of my literary method – why not six-armed psyches? Would it be possible, I wondered, to deal fairly with a multiplicity of attributes and still preserve a semblance of figurative unity in the personage described? I was dreaming of a book which, though multiple, embodied an organic unity. The limbs of Osiris, scattered as they were round the whole known world, were one day united. Out of the egg of futurity stepped that dark and serious girl who was to say one day, with a confident contempt, 'Anyone can see which one of us he loves.' One discovers these things years afterwards, in another context, perhaps even in another country, lying on the beach, pressing warm pebbles against one's cheek. 'What did you do?' I asked Constance. She replied, 'I suddenly realised that I must get free of her, she would always block my light, my growth. I embraced her so hard it drove all the breath from her body.'

"The Livia of that epoch was dark and on the thin side – a contrast to the fairness of her sister. She had beautifully cut cheekbones and eyes of green, while her black soft hair seemed to fly out of the crown of her head and flow down the sides in ringlets reminiscent of Medusa – the snake is quite an appropriate metaphor. Her beauty was not obvious, it came in a sudden kind of revelation. But of course, she slouched, and always had her hands in her pockets, and a cigarette between her lips. We were conventional enough to be shocked by this. But I was dazzled by her brains and her abrasive and articulate way of speech. The voice was deep, and from time to time an expression came into her eyes, a tense fierce expression, and one suddenly saw a man-at-arms peering at one out of a helm. I was too inexperienced to recognise the carapace of her defensive masculinity. But whenever she looked in the direction of Constance, whenever she found us laughing or talking with animation, another more calculating look came into those clever eyes. She could not stand the complicity of our obvious friendship whose warmth at that time was innocent of all ulterior purpose.

"Livia set herself quite deliberately to work upon my obvious inexperience. An easy target. Later when I came to wonder about the shape which events took in the lives of us all I thought that perhaps Livia's role had been less conscious than I had thought; she also was just an instrument registering the electrical impulses set up by a suppressed childhood jealousy. Being wise after the event is one of the specialities of elderly novelists. Quack! Quack! Of course she had no choice, none of us did. It was the peerless beauty and brilliance of the elder sister which magnetised the younger; and I must go on to add, the brother as well. For Hilary, too, formed part of this constellation, and I think that he also found the easy rapport between Tu and myself disquieting, to say the least. But whenever a brother and sister are very close together they naturally fear that marriage, on either side, will wantonly separate them. But Livia was a born conspirator, and once she had decided to prevent anything maturing between Constance and myself she set to work to undermine us – with what success you know only too well; I was captivated by this lizard-swift girl who flattered me in ways which now I would find grossly obvious. But, inhibited as I was then, her praise was manna.

"At that time Tu was taking the first distasteful steps in general medicine, and already had decided not to continue it to the end. The coarse jokes of the students as they handled the fragments of human bodies disgusted her. They betrayed their fear of death thus, the internal shrinking from having to carve up the bodies of drowned, unidentified people, tramps, suicides and the like. Flesh bloated, disfigured, or smashed beyond recognition. And then the smell of formaldehyde following one about the draughty schools! It got into one's clothes, aprons, skirts, white skirts. The loathing was impossible to overcome wholly, though for the present she persevered. Her only inspiration was her anatomy tutor; he was so mad on his subject that his enthusiasm fired her. Once after a particularly bad street accident in Gower Street she saw him pick up a severed arm, wrap it furtively in an evening paper and hurry off to the laboratory which was hard by. Perhaps there was a hope that some less taxing science like chemistry might answer where general medicine and surgery had failed her? She was waiting to see.

"With Livia, alone, swimming in one of the numerous rock pools of the Pont du Gard while the others climbed to the top of the great aqueduct, I discovered another person – not less touching and appealing than her sister, but made of harder and more consistent material. It was very attractive, this down-to-earthness, and even later when I kissed her the lips that met mine seemed deliberately cool and questing and self-possessed. But her fingers were always cold – now I would tend to associate the fact with guilt over treachery; not then. Livia was a dream, impossible to regret, even today."

Sutcliffe cleared his throat and said: "Pia had little of Livia's forthrightness, nor her deep voice. Her own voice was melodious contralto, a fitting instrument on which to play the passive score you wrote for her – and with which I myself don't really agree. I cannot really imagine a Livia in tears. She was always seen walking alone or sitting alone in the middle of the night in deserted cafés, just sitting, staring into her coffee. Her lips were thin when pursed – you forgot to say that; and her eyes had a bitter glimmer. I like that. You fused her uncomfortably with her sister to make Pia, or rather I did, but I was following the hints left by you in the black notebook or the green. Livia had a special little look of smiling contempt when she saw a kitchen; but Constance's face lit up with joy – as if a musician had suddenly come upon a concert-grand in perfect tune."

"I think the trouble is that you are thinking one-dimensionally all the time, like an old-fashioned novelist. You do not seem to be able to envisage a series of books through which the same characters move for all the world as if to illustrate the notion of reincarnation. After all, men and women are polyphonic beings. They know they had previous lives, but they are not sure what they were; all they feel is the weight of their karma, the poetry of previous existences registered in the penumbra of past time."

"How sick I am of the time notions."

"So am I, but the obsession is the age's. We have at any rate come to terms with it, we know that calendar time is a convenience and not a truth. Time is all one sheet – and just as the germs of an illness, say tuberculosis, are there inside one, ready and waiting to be called out by circumstance, so from a temporal point of view are the maggots already in the flesh waiting patiently for the temporal circumstance of death to set them free. Pia into Livia, Livia into Pia, what does it matter? – somewhere in that recess of time they are conscious of each other, of their origins."

"You could go further back still, then?"

"Exactly."

"What are we, then, if not simultaneous artists, 'perishing symmetrically', to borrow the phrase of Madame de Staël?"

"But Livia – even Livia could cry, though you wouldn't believe it. The first time we made love as children was among the rhododendrons at the Pont du Gard, when she was starting to wean me away from my admiration for Tu. Even then she was the expert, the ringmaster, the instigator – and I followed her suit in a sort of daze. It took me dozens of love affairs afterwards to recognise when a lover is sleeping with an imagined phantasy shape, or even with herself. Now I would not be so easily deluded. But then? Yet afterwards she went and laid her head against a tree and gave a small dry sob. It seemed quite private, and was most striking – for even in an exhibition of weakness her self-possession shone through. Before I could place a loving arm over her shoulders the spasm was over and done with. Nor would I have recognised at the time what was an obvious act of contrition – for after all she loved Tu, and hated to do her down. Indeed she loved her all too much to surrender her to me. I only saw all this years afterwards. And reflecting on it, and the possible pity of it, I wondered whether perhaps she had not done me a service in imprisoning me – in preventing me from contracting a love for Tu which could prove premature, ephemeral? If I wasn't experienced enough for Livia surely I was even less so for Tu? Perhaps it is as well to learn to drive on an old, or at least used, car before investing in an expensive new one? I don't really know. But I think it was salutary to have the experience of Livia at that time – though the displacement was at once responsible for other changes, notably in the attitude of Tu herself. I asked her once if she had been in love with me at that early time and she wrote back, 'Yes, I suppose, though I did not know what the word meant then. I was suffering from a sort of undiagnosed pain which was connected with your existence. It took time to master it. It was a case of third-degree burns. But look, I am still alive, happy and breathing.'

"Later, much later, in the flush of her new Viennese science Tu was able to pronounce upon her sister with greater self-confidence – though of course it changed nothing. 'You must treat her with great compassion, for she belongs to the great army of walking wounded in the battle of life. Our mother deserted us, and died far away in another country, never showing the slightest interest in our well-being or even safety during the war. We have a right to a grievance, and a sense of insecurity. Livia was forced to grow a masculine carapace in order to defend herself against life. It is a great nervous strain to keep on subsidising the man in herself. Perhaps she realises it. At any rate nothing can be changed now – she is fixed, like a badly set fracture. It would have to be broken and re-set, and in terms of the human personality this would not be possible. Indeed it would be dangerous to try, specially by analysis. You might overturn her reason.'

"And of course, when I reflected upon Tu herself, I wondered why she did not manifest the same characteristics of a disturbing environmental inheritance. And finally, this is the point at which her new baby science of Freudianism fell apart. If two people share the same environment and circumstances, why would one fall ill and the other not? It is one of the major puzzles and annoyances – for who can doubt the basic accuracy of the diagnosis? I reflected for a long time on the matter without reaching any real conclusion; but the facts were plain, in that Tu was a woman and had the fearlessness of a woman fully conscious of herself. In some strange way she had overcome the hatred for her mother's shade which had had such a crippling effect upon Livia.

"But all this comes long after that sunlit slide under the bridges of Lyon, gathering momentum as the river thickened out and began its headlong descent through a limestone country of such prolix variety that there was not a moment when something new did not catch and fire our attention – it was not only the rosy baked little towns with their castles and battlements which excited one. They were like punctuation marks in a noble poem – a Pindaric Ode, say. It was the consciousness that we were passing out of the north into the Mediterranean; the rich mulberries which had made the silk of Lyon world famous were soon to give place to the more austere decoration of olives, shivering and turning silver in the mistral which followed us down river; a wind of such pure force that if one opened one's mouth it was instantly filled with wind. We were moving from a cuisine based on cream and butter to one more meagre, more austere, based on olive oil and the other fruits of the Athenian tree. We were moving towards the sea – blue bodies of swimmers in the gulf, blue waves drumming the coves and *calenques* of Cassis. We were moving from liqueurs towards the ubiquitous anisette of the south.

"One after another the Rhône bestowed upon us its historic sites and little drunken towns, snuggled among vines, bathed in the insouciance of drowsy days and drowsy silences broken only by the snip-snop of the secateurs among the vines – the holy circumcision which ends the elegaic summers of Provence. The very names were a spur to what imagination and instruction we had – between us we assembled a few shreds of knowledge based on old guide books. Yes, Vienne succeeded desolate Mornas whose very name seemed to echo the sadness of old wars and ruined husbandry; then Vienne with its funny spur – but no trace of the classical splendour recorded in the histories. It must have been the Bournemouth of the ancient world – diplomats retired there from service; the most celebrated among them was Pontius Pilate who spent his quiet retirement there after leaving the Middle East with all its tedious and vexatious problems and stupid agitators. We saluted him in a glass of rosy wine. The river ran through a number of locks and barrages, each with its watchful guardian in his glassed-in perch who took our details before expelling us out of the lock-gates at an altered level, to speed on once more southward.

"As Vienne disappeared round one of the broad curves of the river Hilary looked back at it thoughtfully and said, 'It was there that the Templars were officially abolished.' He spoke as if the event were of momentous significance, but at that time I did not know very much about the Templars – just the broad details of the ancient scandal perpetrated by a King of France and executed by the hooded monsters of the Inquisition. Hilary stood there, gazing back along the water, lost in thought. But now Constance was awake and had succeeded in charming the old Félibre – the Avignon poet; fired by her beauty, and delighted that she knew some French, he proceeded to recite to us, his face creased up like a fine soft handkerchief. It was the first time I had heard Provençal spoken – there seemed to be moss packed between every syllable. Its soft lilt made one think of Gaelic; it echoed the meanderings of the great river with its sudden little tributaries and the occasional mysterious islands of sedge and weeping willow which came up at us out of the distant hazy blue and vine-green. From time to time the lean wolf-like man at the prow practised a trill or a series of sky-shattering head notes, looking round him after each paroxysm, as if for admiration. It was some little time before we were suddenly aware that we were in the presence of a master-alcoholic, an amateur of *pastis*. What matter? He was in tremendous form.

"At one our hampers were unstrapped on the deck and the two French passengers were happy to join us; Hilary had made the purchases in the town before our departure, and with the skill that comes of experience. Never had the delicacies of the French table tasted like this, before or since, washed down as they were with the simple sunlight of a great wine. Never had fresh bread tasted like this. So this was Provence! Cloudless sky, tall planes with their freckled outer skin glimmering like trout in a stream – reflected in the flowing green current. Then weeping willows, like great character actors entangled in their own foliage, and later as we climbed down, lock by lock, towards Valence, the smell of dust, honeysuckle, convolvulus. Objects occupied a place all to themselves; one little donkey – the only donkey in the whole universe, the essence of all donkeys – trotted along a path with its panniers full, raising a plume of dense dust. At Tournon our poet launched into a history of wine – while on the opposite bank glowed like jewels the vines from which came the senior wines like Côte Rôti, St Joseph and so on. We tasted some, we trinked, we came back aboard in fighting form, ready almost to take part in the opera, snatches from which our fellow-passenger continued to sing. The sun burned like a brazier. The skipper's wife opened an umbrella – the mistral had offered us a respite – and settled to her knitting. Round the massive curves of the Rhône we soared, doing almost twenty knots I judged with the current at our backs. At Condrieu an old bent man in a sea captain's hat waved a paper flag at us, evidently recognising one of our number. We all waved back.

"That evening we came up with Valence as dusk fell – our skipper appeared to hate hurrying and we had lost a great deal of time at Tournon. We tramped dazedly ashore, full of the fatigue of sunlight and wine, and found ourselves a grubby billet in a small hotel – Valence was disappointing in spite of its Napoleonic associations, and we turned in very early as the skipper had warned us that the voyage would be resumed very early the next morning.

"But in the cool pearly light of dawn, when we made our way back to the ship we found that the skipper, amidst violent expletives, was trying to counter a mysterious form of engine-trouble which prevented the motors from firing. And here to everyone's astonishment Sam came into his own and after a short and intense examination of their intestines, proffered a diagnosis and a remedy which, being acted upon, set the whole matter to rights in a twinkling. So once more we were sailing down the Rhône spattering the sky with snatches of Verdi, half bemused by the rich verses of Mistral. But we had lost time, we had lost quite a bit of time, and it was late evening before we suddenly rounded a curve of the great river and were treated to a spectacle made more remarkable by a suddenly visible full moon rising in rhetorical splendour over the ramparts of Avignon. High above the city perched the Rocher de Doms – the hanging gardens of this deserted Babylon. It was as if fate had chosen to delay us in order to repay us with its inspiring entry into the city which was later to come to mean so much to us – we did not know any of this then. Now, as I think back, I try to disinter that first impression – the marvellous silhouette of the town magnetically lit by moonlight pouring over it from the direction of the Alpilles. It is still the best way to see it – by water and from afar; and with the historic broken bridge pointing its finger across the river. And the little shrine to St. Nicholas with its bright lamps of benediction for seafaring folk. We had been gliding for nearly an hour among silent islands and deserted channels, watching the bare spars of the Cevennes rise on the night sky. And now suddenly this severe magic. It took much more experience of the town to come to the astonishing conclusion that it was only beautiful in profile – the actual Palaces of the Popes are hideous packing-cases of an uncouth ugliness. Nothing here was built for charm or beauty – everything was sacrificed to the safety of the treasures which these buildings housed. But you must walk about the town to find this out. It is a cathedral to Mammon. It was here our Judeo-Christian culture finally wiped out the rich paganism of the Mediterranean! Here the great god Pan was sent to the gas-chambers of the Popes. Yet seen from a long way off the profile and the promise of the town – they are heartbreaking in their sweetness of line; and by the light of the moon marmoreal in their splendour.

"We had arrived. With a roar we started reversing engines now in order to brake our descent and enable us to moor firm to the shore in that racing river. The boat drummed and throbbed. A small group of gentlemen, all suitably decorated, were waiting for our fellow-passenger on the quay – his name, by the way, he said, was Brunel. They seemed if anything somewhat subdued – they had an air of affectionate sadness as they waited for their friend. Then, as the distance shortened, one of them, a tall and distinguished-looking man in a topcoat, and sporting a beard (much later I was to recognise the poet Peyre from photographs), stepped forward to the gang plank and in a low voice uttered the words: 'He is dead.'

"A mysterious scene to me then – yet I scented that there was something momentous about it, though I could not tell what. Much later I read a modern history of the Félibre, the poets who have been the lifeblood of the region's literature, and discovered the names of that little sad group waiting under the ramparts of the city for Brunel. Their welcoming embraces were long and loving – one felt in them a sort of valedictory quality, perhaps for their dead fellow.

"But behind them in the shadows lurked Felix Chatto with the clumsy old car which would ferry us over the river to the tumbledown mansion which Constance had inherited. Felix, too, had just come down from Oxford and despite his passionate desire to become a banker had succumbed to family pressure and entered the consular service. His uncle, the great Lord Galen, owned a vast property quite near Tubain, while Felix himself was the recently appointed acting consul in Avignon. The two of them were to prove extremely valuable to us in many ways during the period – nearly the whole summer – it took to settle Tu Duc into some semblance of a habitation. No, I exaggerate. The old place was still very sound structurally, though showing signs of neglect which rendered it barely habitable. Water, for example: the pump on the artesian well lacked an essential spare part which (Sam again) had to be more or less re-invented. In the far depths of the grounds was a lily pool full of carp; the tall flukes of the artesian formed a most decorative shape on the evening sky – but though there was plenty of wind, and though the sails turned loyally, no water flowed into the tower, and thence into the kitchen of the old house. We were forced for a few days to resort to buckets drawn from the lily pond, which incidentally afforded us delicious icy swims when these activities made us too hot. The keys fitted the doors, yes, but very approximately: Felix had brought them with him. And it took a while to discover that there was not a lock on the house which had not been put on upside down, and which consequently had to be opened anti-clockwise. Later on we got so used to this factor that one always tried the anti-clockwise turn first in dealing with locks in Provence.

"The first few nights we slept on the terrace by the light of the moon – and began by setting the kitchen to rights in order to cook our meals. A little pony-trap secured our lines of communication with Tubain where we found enough shops to satisfy our modest needs. Here again the resourceful

347

Sam shamed us all by actually doing some respectable cooking with Constance. The tall shadowy rooms were full of heavy, spiritless furniture, dust-impregnated, and we had to move all this old stuff into the patio to beat the dust out of it and polish it up. The wood floors creaked agreeably but were full of fleas, and called for paraffin-rag treatment. The wallpaper was shredding. On the steep terraces large green lizards, insatiably curious, came out to watch us at work; they were obviously used to being fed and seemed perfectly tame. The cupboards in the bedrooms were full of linen, white with dust, while the big central dining table with its scarlet cloth still had plates and glasses on it – as if a formal party had been suddenly interrupted and the whole company carried off by the devil. In effect the old lady had been taken ill very suddenly, and fortunately for her, during the visit of a friend who was able to find a doctor. She had been taken to a clinic in Avignon, never to return.

" 'How atavistic the sense of possession is,' said Constance. 'I am mad about this house merely because it is mine. Yet it's hideous. I would never have dreamed of buying it. And anyway, I don't believe in possessions. I am ashamed of loving it so much already.'

"We lay in the pond with the cool water up to our necks, chatting among the lilies. She wore her straw hat tilted back. Her hair was wet. Every evening it was like this as long as the moonlight held. Hilary and Sam played chess on the terrace with a little pocket set – Hilary was watching the dinner. We had discovered the local anisette – the *pastis* of the region; surely the most singular of drinks for it coats the palate and utterly alters the taste of a good wine and good food.

"There were owls in the tower, there were swerving, twittering bats in the trees, but as long as the heat of the long grass sent up insects into the evening sky the swallows and martins worked close overhead, swerving in and out like darts, to take the spiring insects in open beaks with a startling judgment and accuracy. One could hear their little beaks click from time to time as they snapped at an insect. And then of course the steady drench, the steady drizzle of cicadas in the great planes and chestnuts of the park. All succumbing and sliding into the silence of the full moon which only the dogs celebrated, together with an occasional nightjar and the plaintive little Athenian owl called the Skops. Coming from the cold north we were continually amazed by the beauty and richness of this land. There was only one old man who worked on the property and he lived far away in the valley; but after the first week he brought up a venerable blind horse and set it to turning about a water wheel, fixed to one of the shallower wells. Mathieu, he was called, and he was very deaf."

Poor Blanford! His reveries had carried him so far afield in the past that he did not notice that the telephone had gone dead. He curtly replaced the receiver, having rung for Cade to clear up the tea things. Then he moved with the stiff precariousness of a doll to the library which they had shared over the years; he had housed his own books here during his travels – Tu had set aside two large bookcases for him to which only he had the key. It was a very long time since he had taken to binding up her letters, unwilling to part with such a testimony of friendship and love so central to his inner life, his development. By now there were a number of slim volumes with brilliant Venetian leather bindings, stamped and tooled with emblems suitable to such an intimate correspondence; the little books were housed in pretty slipcases of expensive leather. He unlocked the bookcase and took out one or two to ruffle in that silent room. She would be, he felt, almost his only reading now that she had "gone". He could grimly follow the vicissitudes of his career through her letters from the first success to the time of the Q novels. Tu had been his oldest and most ardent friend; reading some kindly, ironic passages, he recovered the very timbre of that ever-living voice.

And his own replies? They too were there in her part of the library – an extensive collection of books and manu-scripts for he had not been her only friend among the artists. One way and another Constance had known some of the great men of the day. A small pang of jealousy stirred in him with the thought. But it had never occurred to her to bind up his letters, they were in ordinary office folders, as if awaiting a final sorting. Nor were her own somewhat disorderly book-cases locked. He reached down a folder and, opening it, came upon a recent letter addressed to her from the city – sometime last year, it must have been. He had the bad habit of seldom dating his letters. He poked up the fire and sat down with the folder on his knee, trying to read the letter freshly, as if he were Tu, and as if it had just arrived.

"Once again I am here alone in Avignon, walking the deserted streets, full of reminiscences of our many visits, full of thoughts of Tu Duc and yourself. Yes, here I am again in the place where, according to cards set out by my horrible valet Cade, I am due to die by my own hand, sometime during my fifty-ninth year. That still gives me a year or two of clock time; but what Cade speaks of has surely been going on for a long time?

"How shall I explain it to you? For the writer at any rate everything that one might call creatively wrought, brought off, completed aesthetically, comes to you, his reader and his Muse, from the other side of a curtain. From the other side of a hypothetical suicide – ask Sutcliffe! Indeed this is the work of art's point of departure. It need not happen in the flesh to the performer. But it is indispensable to art, if there be any art in the commodity he fathers. Bang!

"Constance, the poet does not choose. The poet does not think of renown, for even the voices which carry the furthest are only the echoes of an anterior, half-forgotten past. The poetic reality of which I speak, and which Sutcliffe might have deployed in his unwritten books, is rather like the schoolchild's definition of a fishing-net as 'a lot of holes tied together with string'. Just as impalpable, yet just as true of our work. Art is only to remind.

"I think, if Cade is right, I shall have enough time to send this project down the slips; afterwards Sutcliffe can flesh it out and fill in the details. Come, let us buy some time for our clocks – a nice juicy slice of time. I must add in all honesty that Sutcliffe is somewhat scared of the idea. When I outlined it he said: 'But Aubrey, this could lead anywhere.' I said: 'Of course. I have freed us both.' The notion of an absolute freedom in the non-deterministic sense alarmed him. As usual he became flippant, to give himself time to reflect. Then he said, 'What would you give me if I wrote a book to prove that the great Blanford is simply the fiction of one of his fictions? Eh?' You know the answer as well as I do, but I could not resist saying it out loud. 'The top prize, Robin Sutcliffe, immortality in the here and now. How would that suit you?' This left him very thoughtful in a somewhat rueful way. He is lazy, he doesn't want to co-operate one little bit. He lacks my driving ambition.

"No, Constance my dear, ours shall be a classical quincunx – a Q; perhaps a *Tu Quoque* will echo throughout it. We will try to refresh poetry and move it more towards the centre of ordinary life.

"Then later, when the blow falls, and I disappear from the scene, it will have to do duty, such as it is, for my *star y-pointed pyramid*. Ever your devoted A."

TWO

Humble Beginnings

LANFORD NAVIGATED FRETFULLY ABOUT THE HOUSE, talking to himself a little with Constance in mind – there seemed so much still to say to her. His fingers crept along the shelf of her Latin and Greek poets towards the volumes which contained their correspondence. "I know that poets make more boom and slither, but novelists can create personae you loathe or adore." He riffled the coloured pages and then read aloud: "Your notion of Sutcliffe intrigues me. Some detail please. I hope he won't become a provincial Heathcliff."

He had replied, "You ask about Sutcliffe? I cannot tell you for how many years he lay silent, living a larval life in the cocoon of my old black notebook. I did not know what to do with him – though I kept jotting away as directed. It was essential that he should differ greatly from me – so that I could stand off and look at him with a friendly objectivity. He represented my quiddity I suppose – the part which, thanks to you, has converted a black pessimism about life into a belief in cosmic absurdity. He was the me who is sane to the point of outrage. Often I kissed you with his mouth just to see how it felt. He never thanked me."

He sat down with the volume on his knee and stared into the fire once more – into its coiling shapes he read snakes and ladders of fire, a crusader burning on a pyre, a scorpion, a crucifixion.

Yes, a different background. Sutcliffe might get born somewhere north of Loughborough, say, to decent Quaker parents. Millers of grain? He was a scholarship boy who had won an Exhibition to Oxford, and then, like so many others, had found himself thrown upon the slave market of pedagogy. He had edited a few cribs which were badly reviewed by a tiresome clanging professor – and thus lost the chance of a post as a translator. Poverty intervened, and since he had nothing special for which to starve, he accepted the first opening which presented itself. He found himself teaching French and music to schoolgirls at Hymendale, a clergy orphans' establishment, where half the staff was ecclesiastical and half lay. Whence his downfall. For nuns called to dons, dons to nuns, deep to deep, dope to dope. . . . It was really not his fault.

Hymendale was a suburb of Bournemouth, that salubrious south coast resort, which even then was geared to the retirement requirements of professional men and colonial civil servants. Privet hedges, eyes peering from behind curtains, a draughty gentility; silent streets awoken only to the clip clop of the milkman's little van. It was a fine place to develop inner resources – so he told himself grimly as he grimly did his daily walks, twice round the sewage plant and once there and back along the cliffs in the rain. Ah! the eternal rain! Eight hours a week spent with his sallow, skewer-shaped girls with lank hair and torpid intelligences. *Que cosa fare?* He saw himself even then as a rather tragic figure, trapped by fate in this religious treadmill. He played the role to himself for all it was worth, sometimes being overheard laughing aloud – a harsh sardonic bark directed at the greasy teeming sky. The pubs in the place shut early and were full of tobacco smoke, at once acrid and throat-drying. There was one reasonable bookshop, Commin's, as well as a lending library, and of course two cinemas. He buried himself in books, thanking God that he could read enough French to amuse himself. We must imagine a rather large, short-sighted man clad in shapeless tweeds perforated with many a nameless cigarette and pipe hole. He had a stalking walk whose buoyancy suggested an inner exuberance which he was far from feeling. No; he was guilty of over-compensating.

Loneliness led to this passionate self-communing, which in turn led to somewhat eccentric behaviour – at least by the standards of such an establishment. For instance, on Sunday morning, when the class formed up in the quad to draggle to chapel in its desultory Indian file, Sutcliffe (who led the procession in gown and tippet) liked to imagine that he was engaged in other, more romantic activities. Thus one Sunday he would be leading his cricketers out into the field to win the Ashes back from Australia; he snuffled the wind, gazed at the light, sucked his finger boy scout fashion and held it up to determine the direction (before sending in his bowlers). He cleared his throat and made a number of finger signs to invisible umpires, directing the position of the screens ... and so on. On other days he was the leader of an African tribe, clad in nothing but a tiger-skin, and waving a knobkerrie as he walked, chanting under his breath to the rhythm of inaudible drums. He was head of the young hunters and they were going out for lion – nothing less! On other occasions he enacted a priest leading victims of the Terror towards the guillotine. The clatter of the tumbril on the paving stones of Paris were practically audible to the listener. It goes without saying that this intense miming and the strange postures were looked upon by his superiors with misgivings. But they were simply the outward and visible signs of an intense inner life.

There was nobody he could talk to, so he had developed the habit of talking to himself – interminable low monologue of the inner mind. People saw only the outward expression suited to these thoughts which passed in him like shoals of fish. A popping eye, lips pursing, eyebrows going up and down. His nose twitched. Often (he blamed this on the diet of spotted dog and treacle tart) he had piles which divided into three categories, namely Itchers, Bleeders and plain Shouting piles. For his walks he used a shabby old golfing umbrella and vast boots with hooks and eyes. "I was formed by Doctor Arnold," he was wont to tell himself, "whose wife much enjoyed his melancholy long-withdrawing roar." When he was overcome by depression he sometimes went down into the town and for ten shillings and a Devonshire Tea gave Effie a furtive caress, which only increased his sense of despondency and alienation. Effie was a barmaid at The Feathers and a good enough little soul, very modest in her demands upon life. She was indeed sweet but O the cold apple tart between her pale, frog-like legs. He bought her presents because he felt guilty at leading her astray — she was really a good girl and not a whore. She had a marked tendency towards cystitis. But the town, the monotony, the rain and the people can drive you to do anything. One thing about her intrigued him – the way she cocked her little finger over a teacup with such an affectation of gentility. . . . She did the same in bed as if to confer some of the same sort of gentility upon the love act. He adored this. For some reason not known to science Sutcliffe had the habit of carrying two french letters in the turnups of his broadly cut trousers. They were very expensive these things, and he kept them only for Effie; after use, he washed them out and pegged them up to dry on the mantelpiece of his little room for an hour. They had the word EVERSAFE printed on them. Effie insisted on protection and was affectionately responsive to such little attentions. She liked this man who suffered so often from chilblains and who walked about on his toes with rather a mystified air. She would have dreamed of marrying him perhaps, but he was a gentleman and it would not have done.

His duties entitled him to a little room with a fireplace, with a separate entrance onto the quadrangle – and he always dreamed of enticing some secret woman to visit him. But who? He had a small harmonium of the wheezy sort and a copy of the Forty-eight of Bach, which he played for his own amusement, but not too loud. For the rest he read opera-scores at night, eating an apple the while; occasionally he moved his eyebrows and let out a roar to correspond to a full orchestra unleashing top sound. Vaguely in the back of his mind a project was forming itself; to write a new life of Wagner.

Why not? Sometimes on his walks he saw a point of darkness move indistinctly upon the horizon repeatedly expunged and dimmed and recreated. A ship, forsooth! He waved his umbrella and cheered. All this monotony might be a good aliment for a poet but what if one had no gifts? Sometimes he got so lonely that he could have set his bed on fire.

Sister Rosa must have also suffered from it, perhaps more acutely, for she had come to England from some dusky clime. She was pretty, with a mischievous face, and an octoroon as to complexion. He caught her examining him in chapel, and she gave a dark rosy blush. He smiled at her and she smiled back in a way that suddenly made him feel that for her spring was not far behind. There had been some trouble that day with the Sixth; he had been summoned to the head and asked if he was really "doing" Mallarmé? "Just giving an account of the period," he had replied. The Mother Superior raised a white finger and said, "Mr. Sutcliffe, I know I can count on you not to let anything too French or too suggestive pass. It is a great trust we have put in you in giving you the Sixth. Please guide them in the paths of blamelessness, even if it means *stealing through* the classics rather than doing them in detail."

"Do you mean censoring them?"

"Well, yes, I suppose I do."

"Very well," said Sutcliffe grimly and withdrew. He had already planned a bowdlerised Mallarmé to meet the case. "*Le chien est triste. Hélàs! Il a lu tous les livres,*" he wrote on the blackboard in the classroom. It would have to do for today. Surely the English with their love of animals could not complain of *that?* But as he sniffed the air he felt that trouble lay ahead. The pieties of the place argued ill for free thinkers. He was thinking this over when. . . . But this needs a new paragraph.

Poor Sister Rosa, too, was bored to death. Her English was very bad, and it was in the hope of finding someone to speak to her in Congo Pidgin that she had appraised Sutcliffe whom she knew to be teaching French; almost inhaling him with her mind as she raised her neat little muzzle and tip-tilted nose. The inside of her lips were blackish purple, her teeth were small and regular, her smile delicious – or so thought the quivering Master of Arts. Boredom makes strange bedfellows, he could not help remarking, for he knew that all this frantic emotion was a little bit invented. When he closed his eyes he saw her naked on his shabby cot in the alcove, lying back with her eyes closed. Her dark skin tinted like rum, molasses, ginger . . . and so on.

For her part she found it vastly dispiriting to spend hours arranging waxed fruit on the High Altar of the chapel. Nevertheless it gave her access to Sutcliffe's pew which was convenient. At the next service he found a flower on his hassock and a highly suggestive Catholic bookmarker tucked into his hymn-book. The ingenuity of women! Sutcliffe blushed all over with pleasure. It was the work of a second to scribble on the endpapers of the hymn-book the magic words, "How? When? Where?" in French. If he did not add "How much?" it was because he did not want to hurt her feelings by being *too* French. After all, she *was* a bloody nun. Now a short pause supervened, for what reason he could not tell – the designs of nature perhaps, or the feeling that she had gone too far, or something of an administrative order? Hard to tell. Anyway he left another message inviting closer co-operation and tried to fire her by singing very loudly when interpreting hymns whose words ("Nearer My God to Thee", for example) could be taken in more than one way.

At last she yielded – though her handwriting was so inchoate that he had difficulty in making out the words "Tonight. Room 5". Sutcliffe swelled up with desire and pride. That evening he played Bach remorselessly and with keen impatience. He had never been into the nunnery side of the establishment, and while he supposed that they shuffled to bed fairly early he thought it wise to let them get to sleep before starting his own invasion of the premises, EVERSAFE in hand, so to speak. To tell the truth the prospect rather quailed him – wandering about in the gloomy corridors of a nunnery. He waited until midnight before embarking.

He crossed the quad and entered the silent building which showed not a spark of light anywhere. He made brief use of his pocket torch and mounted to the first floor. The numbers were not only battered and almost effaced, they were not in serial order – or so it seemed. But at last he hit upon a room which he took to be numbered correctly, pressed the handle of the door and felt the warm air flow out into the corridor. He stepped into the blackness and stood for a moment to let his eyes accustom themselves to the dark. A figure in a bed stirred and he heard what he took to be a welcoming sigh. "Sister Rosa," he breathed and switched on his little torch.

The Mother Superior gazed at him in terrified silence, with starting eyes; if she had had her teeth in they would have been chattering – but they lay and grinned in a tooth mug beside the bed. Sutcliffe let out an incoherent exclamation of utter panic. Her wig was on a stand by the bed and she wore a nightcap. He was about to turn and run for it when she turned on the light and exclaimed, "Mr. Sutcliffe, what are you doing here?"

It was difficult to explain. He spread his arms and pretended to be sleepwalking; then he awoke with a theatrical start and said, "Where am I?"

It carried no conviction.

As time went on the story changed shape almost as often as it changed hands or tongues; some of this was due to Sutcliffe himself who had the ingrown novelist's habit of embroidering on behalf of novels as yet to be. Thus in one version she produced a pearl-handled revolver and fired a shot through his coat-tails – in fact, he was not wearing a coat. In another equally implausible version she opened wide her arms and legs and cried, "At last you have come to claim me!" thus forcing upon him a distasteful and unholy conjunction of souls and bodies. It was the only way to keep his job.

But what really happened? She cried, "Mr. Sutcliffe will you leave this room at once!" and this he did with some alacrity. In the morning he was summoned before the board of governors and dismissed with effect from lunchtime – hardly leaving him time to pack before catching the London train. He felt bad about having betrayed Rosa too, for on his way to the station he had a glimpse of her sitting upright between two granite-faced Carthusians in the little black bus of the school which could be converted into a hearse in times of need. Her cheeks were very flushed and her eyes cast down.

Once back in London he returned to the seedy agency which had found him the job and described the circumstances of dismissal to the little Cockney manager whose catarrh and adenoids took turns at interfering with his articulation. He heard Sutcliffe out, shaking his head sadly. "Not very clever," he said more than once. "You know what I should have done? Bicycled to the doctor's and asked for a prescription against sleep-walking." He spread his hands. "Then when the board called me up I would have a watertight excuse." Sutcliffe whistled. "I never thought of that," he said.

"Next time be more wily," said the little man.

"Or less susceptible to female charms."

"Quite."

He turned once more to his sordid register and went through a list of vacancies tracing them with a broken thumbnail.

So the long cultural calvary continued for our hero until (after many humiliations) he rose to glory and affluence by his superior merits. Yet looking back on these episodes in later years he was not displeased with some of his handiwork. When the class, for example, asked him what the last words of Verlaine were he had replied: "Happiness is a little scented pig."

But leaving Sutcliffe to his picaresque early adventures, the thoughts of Aubrey Blanford once more returned to those earliest memories of France, and of Provence. They were wonderfully pristine always – as if only yesterday:

There they were, for example, lying in the pond among the open lilies with the cool lapping water up to their throats, breathing in the silences of the abandoned garden, which, like the house itself, was full of presences which would have been real ghosts if only they had been visible. Doors which opened and shut of their own accord, footsteps on the main staircase at midnight. Voices which whispered names so softly that it was always possible to attribute the noise to the rustle of ivy in the changing wind. With shifts of temperature –

when the heat from the kitchen rose to the first floor – all the cupboards creaked and burst open as if to embrace one. In the dense foliage of the garden there was always a flickering of things just seen out of the corner of the eye. When one turned and looked directly there was nothing. And there was one loose tile on the footpath by the *potager* where every night at dusk one heard a footfall: someone passed and made it click.

Sometimes if you opened the cellar door a black cat flowed out which answered to no name, no blandishment, no caress. It made its way softly through the hall, to disappear by a side door. An animal? Or the ghost of one? It was like a portfolio of sketches of suave postures – something to grace a fashion plate.

A long time later Hilary said that he had once seen a girl in a white evening dress walking by the lily pond reading a letter; what struck him was that the blackbirds gave no sign of seeing a human being and were actually flying through her – or so it appeared. She passed into the trees and took the path to the house; he waited uneasily for her on the balcony but she never appeared. In the afternoons by the little coach-house someone beat the dust out of an invisible carpet. All the silences of the place seemed dense with things just waiting to materialise. A sense of immanence. Constance loved this; at night she was always blowing out the light and sitting in the dark trying to "see". But Livia could not stand it, and after a few days would find an excuse to set off on a camping-trip or spend a few days in neighbouring Avignon where Felix gave her his tiny spare room.

And then the portrait gallery, the three heads! This long gallery was an extension to the house with broad windows running the whole length of it and lit with white panes of toplight; the trees sheltered it from the direct rays of the sun. Now it was empty, for the old lady had sold all her portraits long since – an unremarkable collection by all accounts – and kept only three smoky heads printed in the typical ancestor-style of safe academicians of the last century. And now almost obliterated by corruptions in the pigment. The names too were hardly readable, though one could make out the word Piers on the portrait of the pale young man with a frail and consumptive expression, and the word Sylvie below that of the dark intense girl, who might well have been his sister. The third picture had fared worse and it was literally not possible to tell whether the subject was a man or a woman – only that its colouring was blonde and not dark, its eyes as blue and lucid as Hilary's. All three portraits were draped with black velvet, which created a singular impression on the beholder, who could not help wondering why. Was someone in mourning for them? Did it betoken some special religious gesture – a consecration? Who were they? We were unable to find out. On the back of one picture, written in yellow faded ink was the phrase, "Chateau de Bravedent". To study them one had to draw back their velvet covers with a gold cord.

Felix Chatto, no less intrigued than we, had spent a lot of time and energy trying to find out the meaning of this laconic inscription and the location, if possible, of such a chateau; in vain. "I swear there is no such place in Provence," he added with a sigh, "though of course one day it might surface again as the lost medieval name for a place." We were sitting downstairs then at the oaken kitchen table, having lunch. "And perhaps it is better that way – not to know, I mean, and to go on wondering about them. It would be difficult to invent a romantic enough story to suit that strange trio. And in my view you are wrong about the third person – it is really a woman, not a man. The fingernails are not painted." But of course this proved nothing and he knew it. But then: why the dusty velvet coverings? Were they dead?

Nevertheless the existence of the three and the name of

the apparently non-existent chateau exercised a great influence over the musings of Blanford; they existed as obstinate symbols of something to which the key had been lost. He said to himself sadly, "If only I believed in the novel as a *device* I would incorporate their story in a book which had nothing to do with real life. Bravedent!"

Livia turned her face to him; she had been sucking a coloured sweet they had bought at the village shop. With a swift motion of her tongue she passed it into his mouth and sealed it with a bitter-sweet kiss on the lips. He was lost, Blanford. He found such effortless happiness almost painful.

It was only now, in this backwash of time, and from these heterogeneous documents that he could follow out the slow curve of this *amor fati* – this classic attachment to Livia. When he asked her what her mother was like, for example, it was Constance who replied to him: but at some other time, in another context, for Livia simply looked at him with those dark eyes gone like dead snails and licked her lips as if about to speak, but nothing came. Constance wrote in a letter: "I remember an old, old lady with a piercing blue eye, whose cheeks had subsided for want of teeth and whose ill-fitting false ones did not fulfil the role completely. She had been a poor actress before she married. Now she was mad with regret and forever dwelling on ancient pleasures which had fed that sick vanity. The world of diplomacy – a world of kindly lampreys – provided a delusive background for her needs. Underneath the surface excitements the demon of accidie had her by the hair. She had always been avid for the meretricious, and when her shallow beauty faded everything turned to hate – but chiefly against her children because of their own youthful beauty. Not for her the Great Inkling! Here she was, subsiding into ashes day by day, while we were flowering. Soon she felt herself swelling with pure malevolence, a loathing strong enough to carry, she hoped, even beyond the grave, to blight our lives, to maim our spirits! She complained that her breasts were flaccid because she had nursed us too long, and tried everything then available to plump them out, except surgery. Even that absurd *ventouse* which was supposed to make them firm by suction. We have had to wade though all this powerfully projected hate without quite understanding it – except now, retrospectively. Forgiving it is another thing. Look at Livia!"

He was looking at Livia, at that face which for him spelt an invincible happiness; he was not so much wounded as astonished when the youthful Sam described her eyes like dead fish-eyes and her hair as dandruffy, adding that he could never care for a girl like that. The angle of vision is everything. The poetic vision is manufactured to meet desire. This experience was forming him, and would give him his first short story, which in the long run was what really mattered. But without her and the frightful jolt she gave him he might never have entered the immortality stakes with his first study of the circle she frequented in Paris where she was at this time a professing painter, prone to cubism. His inexperience shielded him from recognising the group of charming if effete personages for what they were – and they were careful not to enlighten him. She lived thus, in happy ambiguity, within this kindly group of homosexual friends whose charm and sensibility were undeniable. As a little band of outlaws they had grouped themselves into postures of social consequence; it was a wise precaution for they were for the most part rather insipid people and they knew it. Their social commerce betrayed a certain fragile uncertainty ... they felt somehow one-dimensional; almost opaque. They telephoned each other several times a day, as if to reassure themselves of each other's existence. They issued bulletins about their health and the state of their art which were like certificates of identity.

Later, when Constance was full (a little too full) of her knowledge, she expressed the cruel paradox of Livia's case more clearly; indeed the total narcissism which is expressed in inversion derives from the sense of abandon by the mother. But crueller still, the sexual drive which alone satisfies it consists of a mock incest precisely with her abandoner. But such a proposition would only have made Livia swear – and the oaths she used turned ugly in her mouth, accompanied as they were by expressions as distasteful as those of a sick bird. A phrase came to mind from the black notebook, where he was trying to lay down a few guide-lines towards a sketch of her character. Looking at Constance with remorse, regret and hate, Livia thought, "There is nothing more enraging than the sight of someone who is unwaveringly, naturally and helplessly good." After all, Constance had her own deceptions to live through, though she was at last able to swallow their absurdity and pretentiousness and write, "Love is the banana-peel that laughter-loving reality leaves on the pavements for men and women to skid on." The thing was that she comprehended and pardoned her sister because she loved her, and for her sake she always hoped against hope that our relations would survive despite the drawbacks. Blanford could not remember just when he made a note in his diary which said, "I fear she lives on tittle-tattle and smoke; I have married a rattle and a snob." But even that was not the worst of the matter; the central feeling of loss was to get denser and richer as bit by bit Livia grew more sure of herself, more careless about hiding matters.

The mind has limits, the body limits; the equation is easily made, the limits quickly reached. It was all my fault, thought Blanford, leaning forward to poke the fire. It was a case of transposed heads. Constance and I were slow to recognise each other. In all this amateur bliss I one day overheard a telephone conversation with Thrush, the little Martinique lover, which made me prick up my ears. In a different voice, one that I had never heard before, she said: "I simply made up my mind to make him marry me." Turning, she saw me at the door, and replaced the receiver. I said nothing and after a while her obvious anxiety died down – I suppose since I offered no comment on this remark. "It was just Thrush," she said, "we are going to the Opera tonight." She knew that I could never stand opera. But just for once I had taken the number of their tickets and had bought myself one in the Gods. I went that evening and easily located the stalls she had reserved; but the seats were occupied by other people whose faces I did not know.

It is only the context which renders such things painful or pleasurable – all that was basically wrong was Blanford's gruesome lack of experience. He knew that now. It was the pliant and lovely Livia's destiny to initiate him – and of course those we initiate we mark for life. "Nature's lay Idiot, I taught thee to f**k," she could have exclaimed as Sutcliffe did on another such occasion; nor would the glancing echo of Donne have been out of keeping. No. But the period of ardour and illusion led on and on for more than a summer – could it perhaps have gone on for a lifetime? – until by an unlucky accident he came upon the letter she had forgotten to hide or destroy and in which everything was made clear. His heart sank with sorrow and disgust; it was not the reaction of a moralist – it was simply that he found the deception cruel and unnecessary. From it all he suddenly developed an exaggerated hate for the little group of neuters – *les handi-cappés* – and by extension for the Paris he had always found grotesque, but vividly alive and nourishing. How would he stand August now, swollen with the knowledge that he was being run in tandem with some black-hearted Parisienne? He started to write her letters, and to leave them everywhere in the flat. He had moved to a furnished room but still had the key of the flat and used his bookfilled study to work in. He was still raw from the pleasures of her beauty and the excellence of her love-making; there was a poem of that period in which he described her with felicity as "a constellation of fervours". It was published in the *Critic* but he did not show it to her. Thrush, then, was the ringmaster? It was suddenly like being dropped on one's head out of a tree, or diving into an empty swimming pool. With one hand he did some automatic writing in his black notebook. ("The new sexual model will incorporate death somehow as the central experience. The lovers will float to the surface belly upwards, dead from exhaustion.") He wrote an indignant description of his discovery to Constance but did not post it. And years afterwards, in discussing this period of time, he felt glad that he had not, for Constance was busy with profounder matters, and still much hampered by her sexual inexperience. It was this same summer perhaps that she decided to marry Sam – which also called for long and elaborate reflections later on. But in one sense the shock was most salutary for Blanford; he was suddenly able to see all round himself; it was as if he had been living in a dense fog and suddenly it had lifted. It was a real initiation, a real awakening. He suddenly saw, for example, what the two lovers had done to Thrush's husband. He was a pious and swarthy little man, pleasantly coon-coloured and with dense ringlets. It is doubtful that he actually was conscious of what was going on – the notion rested on the edge of his mind like an ominous premonition. He began to feel first an overwhelming lethargy – the affect had started to bleed; the two vampires knew their stuff all right!

But first of all they made him rich and fashionable, a consultant for film stars and bankers, and that sort of animal. They lobbied him decorations of one sort or another, and made sure that he went to all the first nights and cocktail parties. It was about six years since he had last slept with Thrush, though they lived in tender amity; but he began to retire earlier and earlier, gripped by fatigue and the shadow of something like diabetes; until he took to having dinner with the children in the nursery and going straight to bed with them; he yawned more and more and looked vague. Retiring thus from the fray every evening he left the *champs d'honneur* free for the lovers and their doings. Once or twice they talked of finding him a substitute woman – a pretty *repoussoir* like Livia but he had no energy left for such a project. So thoroughly had they done the work of affect castration that he had gone all anaesthetic. As for Thrush, *animatrice de petit espace* that she was, she kept him soothed and tranquil in his striped pyjamas. In her he had an impresario who had guided him to wealth and social success – should a man ask more? But Blanford could see that this same gloomy fate of Zagreus was going to be his unless he watched out. What to do? As he wrote in one of his letters to Livia, "Of course marriage is an impossible state with all its ups and downs, lapses, temptations, renewals. But the only thing the tattered old contract sets out is that you accord the primacy of your affections to someone, this side idolatry. The cheat was that yours were not free to bestow. It is all that sours me."

He was left with a mountain of scribbled exercise books – an attempted exorcism. But it did little good. It was as futile as founding a society for the abolition of bad weather. Yet the loneliness taught him discipline. There is nothing more beautiful than Method.

About Blanford; before writing the first words of a novel in his Q series he would close his eyes, breathe serenely through his nose, and think of the Pleiades. To him they symbolised the highest form of art – its quiddity of stillness and purity. Nothing could compare with them for noble rigour, for elegance. It was in order to cure this rather dangerous proclivity that he had invented that mass of conflicting and contradictory predispositions called Sutcliffe – a writer who recited the Lord's Prayer, putting a Damn between every word, before addressing *his* novel.

Blanford took an overdose of sleeping pills and had horrible dreams in which he was forever helping two nymphs on with wings they rejected. He imagined them lying together in the sand – Livia's face like an empty playground waiting for children, her large vague pale brow . . . The long middle finger which betokened bliss in secret.

Nor was it any solace to think hard thoughts about Thrush; apart from this unhappy situation he found her delightful. But he told himself that she opened her mouth so wide that she resembled a hippo, folding her food into it. As a matter of fact, even when she laughed her eyes cried "Help!" He could dimly intuit the terrible jealous insecurity that ravaged the two quaires – the negative of his own, so to speak. Once in the rue St.-Honoré when he was waiting for a massive American businessman (they had the simple authority of trolleys, comforting), the dentist came up to him in a bar and got into conversation. They only knew each other by sight then, and Blanford felt a kind of clinging, pleading quality in the encounter – as if he were hoping to find some solution to his case in a talk with Blanford. But they were ill matched for an exchange of consolations. He told himself that Thrush had a vicious, thirsty little French face; but it wasn't true and he knew it. He felt as if his brains had cooled and dripped into his socks. He could have written an ode called "A Castrate's Tears beneath the Shears" – but the tone was wrong and he delegated this to Sutcliffe who would come along in good time with his own brand of snivel. And then, on top of it all, to be unfair to poor Paris which all of a sudden became loathsome to him. He noticed now the dirty hair, cheaply dyed, and never kept up from meanness – so many brassy blondes with black partings. And in August the refusal to shave armpits. . . . The town smelt like one large smoking armpit. Acrid as the lather of dancers. And then the selection of sexual provender – perversions worthy of wood-lice. Well, he had come there for infamy in the first place, so what the hell had he got to complain about? He would die, like Sutcliffe, in the arms of some lesbian drum-major, dreaming nostalgically of hot buttered toast between normal thigh and thigh. Indeed he would go further and become a Catholic and enact the funky deathbed scene – the spider on the ceiling and the shadow of a priest and a notary. . . . It wouldn't do, said the voice of Constance, and he knew that it wouldn't. Eheu!

Under the shock of this misadventure Blanford suddenly found that he could read people's minds, and a sudden shyness assailed him; he found now that he lowered his eyes when faced with newcomers – the better to listen to the sound of their voices. It was the voice he was reading so unerringly. People thought that he had become unusually shy of a sudden. (In some lower-middle-class bedroom Sutcliffe heard his tinny wife say, "*Chéri, as tu apporté ton Cadeau Universel?*" And he replied, "*Oui chérie, le-voilà.*"

THREE

The Consul Awake

THE PRO-CONSUL WAS RULED BY THE DEMON OF INSOMNIA, the royal illness; lying with his eyes fast shut in his little cage of a villa with its creaky bed, old chest of drawers and flawed mirror – lying there suspended in his own anxiety as if in a cloudy solution of some acid – he saw the sombre thoughts passing in flights across the screens of his consciousness. The hours weighed like centuries on his heart. Memories rose up from different periods of his life, crowding the foreground of his mind, contending for attention. They had no shape, no order, but they were vivid and exhausting – at once silky and prickly as thistles. Each night provided an anthology of sensations betokening only hopelessness and helplessness; this handsome and quite cultivated young man who dreamed of nothing so much as a post in the Bank of England (the excellence of his degrees justified such a hope) had been unwittingly sold into slavery by a mother who adored him with all the passion that centres about only children. How had this all come about? He knew only too well. "For you it's *diplomacy*," said his uncle, Lord Galen, one day, conducting the full orchestra of his self-esteem. His opinion was never asked and he was too weak to resist the little corsair who had become his mother's lover after the death of Felix's father. The boy had been weak and irresolute enough, the man was even more so. So here he found himself in a minor consular post in Avignon – a pro-consul of the career, if you please, but paid a mere pittance for his services. Yes, here he was, half dead with boredom and self-disdain.

The Office had not even had the decency to declare the post an honorary one – which would perhaps have forced

Galen to make him an allowance. He was paid like a solicitor's clerk. He was only allowed a part-time consular clerk to keep his petty cash and type the few despatches he ever wrote. There was nothing to report and if there were any British subjects in Avignon they had never shown their faces. The villa was buried deep in dust-gathering oleanders and poinsettias. If only his mother could see him now – a Crown Servant! He gave a croak of sardonic laughter and turned on his side. Yet she must be proud of him. A flood of unformulated wishes and hopes, suddenly floating into view, directed his memory to a picture which made him always catch his breath in pain, as if he had run a thorn under his fingernail. He opened his eyes and saw her sitting withered up in her wheelchair. Looking at the dusty electric bulb hanging naked from the ceiling he went over his history for the thousandth time. His father had died when he was very small; years later his mother had conducted a long and decorous affair with his brother, the dashing Galen (extremely discreet, extremely ambiguous) until the increasing paralysis confined her to this steel trolley, pushed by a gloved attendant dressed in a billycock hat and a long grey dustcoat. Felix could hear the munching of its slim tyres on the gravels of gardens in Felixstowe, Harrogate, Bournemouth. When her illness grew too severe she had been too proud to continue her affair with Galen – she could not bear to see herself as a drag on him or on his career. He accepted this decision with guilty relief, though he vowed that she would want for nothing. He kept in touch through her doctors, though he did not write directly any more – he had always had a superstitious hatred of ink and paper. He had been taught that things written down can turn against one in the courts, that was the root of the feeling. But even had he written she could not have answered for she could no longer hold a pen; and as for speech, her own was slurred and indistinct. Her jaw hung down sideways, there were problems with saliva. Deeply shocked by her own condition, the dark eyes blazed with a sort of agonised astonishment. Her attendant was called Wade. In his billy-cock hat he wore the feather of a cock-pheasant. He was now far closer to her than either her son or her lover. She was impatient for only one thing now – to die and get it over with. . . . Wade read the Bible to her for two hours every night.

Felix groaned and rolled over in bed, turning his face to the ghastly wallpaper with its raucous coaching print. He breathed deeply and tried to hurl himself into sleep as if from a high cliff – but in vain, for other shallower thoughts swarmed about him as the fleas swarmed in his bed, despite the Keating's Powder. This time it was exasperating memories of the official pinpricks he had incurred in trying to obtain a new Union Jack to fly from the mast which had been so insecurely fixed to the first-floor balcony of the villa. During the usual Pentecost celebrations, which were closed by a triumphal gallop-past of the Carmargue *gardiens*, some fool had discharged a gun in the air – *un feu de joie* – and the charge had spattered the sacred flag with smallshot, so that now it looked like a relic left over from Fontenoy. Felix simply could not fly such a tattered object any longer and, having described the circumstances, invited London to replace it. But nothing doing. An immense and most acri-monious correspondence had developed around this imperial symbol; the Office insisted that the culprit should be found and sued for his sins, and lastly forced to replace the object; failing that, said the Office of Works (Embassy Furnishings Dept.), the flag might have to be paid for out of Felix's own pocket – a suggestion which drove him mad with rage. Back and forth went these acid letters on headed paper. London was adamant. The culprit must be found. Felix smiled grimly as he recalled the leather-jawed horseman whose racing steed had struck a bouquet of sparks from the cobbles as it went. The man indeed who had so narrowly missed him, for he had been standing on the balcony at the time to watch the procession. A foot to the right and there would have been a consular vacancy which the Crown Agents would have been happy to advertise in *The Times*. He had even felt the wind of the discharge, and smelt the cordite of a badly dosed home-made charge. And the flag?

And the flag! Should he, he wondered, try to get it 'invisibly mended"? There was a new shop in the town which promised such an amenity. But an absurd sense of shame held him back. Would it not seem queer for a shabby consul to sneak about the town with a tattered Union Jack, trying to get it repaired on the cheap? Yes. On the other hand if he flew it as it was just to spite the Office there was a risk that some consular nark from Marseille might see it and report adversely on him. He sighed and turned again, turning his back on these futile exchanges, so to speak. And so then Galen had quietly replaced his father, had taken command of everything, school-fees, death-duties, house-rents, etc. In fact he had actually become his father, and as such infallible. He pronounced shortly and crisply on everything now; his will was done, rather like the Almighty's. The overwhelmed and frightened child could do nothing but obey. Galen had, as a matter of fact, demanded worship, but all Felix could supply was a silent obedience to the little man with the plentiful gold teeth which winked and danced in the firelight as he outlined the splendid life which the Foreign Service held in store for the boy.

So here was Felix listening to the sullen twang of the mistral as it poured across the town, dragging at shutter fastenings and making his flagless flagpole vibrate like a jew's harp. The consular shield below it had also taken a few pellets but the damage was not extensive. It merely looked as if some hungry British subject had taken a desperate bite out of it in self-defence. "Whatever you do, Mr. Chatto," the Foreign Secretary had admonished him before handing him his letters of credence and appointment, "never let yourself become cynical while you are in Crown Service. There will be many vexations, I know; you will need all your self-control but try and rise above them. Sincerely." Well, if he had been in a laughing mood he might have managed a feeble cackle. Indeed his shoulders moved in a simulated spasm but in fact his face still wore the pale, dazed expression of a sinus case which aspirin could not relieve. He could smell the dust being blown in from the garden – dust and mimosa. In the spaces between assaults the wind died away to nothing and left a blank in the air into which seeped fragments of ordinary sound like the bells of St. Agricole. The theatre would be emptying into the square by now and despite the foul wind the cafés would awake for a spectral moment; it was too chill to do more than hug the counters and bars and drink "*le grog*". It was early yet, all too early. Like sufferers from sinus and migraine he was used to seeing the dark nights unroll before him in a ribbon of desolation.

But his real calvary began well after midnight when he rose, made himself a pot of vervain *tisane* and slowly dressed, pausing for long intervals to gaze into the bathroom mirror or stand in bemused silence before the cupboard mirror gazing at his own reflection in it, watching himself dress slowly, knot his old school tie, draw on his shabby college blazer with the blazoned pocket. Who was this familiar shadow? He felt completely disembodied as he looked, as he confronted his own anxious, unfamiliar face. He drew on his black felt hat, stuffed his wallet into his breast pocket; then he stayed in the sitting room gazing at the print hanging over the chimney – a pastoral scene of goats and cypresses. With one half of his mind he heard the throbbing of the wind and registered its diminution with something like satisfaction. Perhaps in another twenty minutes it might sink away into one of its sudden calms. He would pause awhile before setting off on one of his all-too-frequent night walks round the town which he had come to regard as the most melancholy in the whole world. Its eminence, its history, its monuments – the whole thing drove him wild with boredom; mentally he let out shriek after shriek of hysteria, though of course his lips did not move and his consular face remained impassive, as befitted a Crown Servant.

Yes, the wind was subsiding slowly; a clock chimed somewhere and there was the long slow moan of a barge from the river like some haunted cow. He licked his finger and traced the dust upon the mantelpiece. The little hunchback maid who came in for an hour of dusting every morning was fighting in vain against the ill-fitting shutters. As for food, Felix arranged his own light meals, or crossed the square to the little penurious café called Chez Jules where they made sandwiches or an occasional hot dish filled with chili and pimento. He threw open the door of the office and stood for a while gazing down at his own imagined ghost – he saw himself writing a despatch about the flag. What furniture, what entrancing ugliness! He enumerated it all as he sipped his tea and stirred a loose tile with the toe of his suede shoe. There was a mouse-hole in the wall which he had stopped with a pellet of paper manufactured from a particularly exasperating and stupid despatch from head office. It had assuaged his feelings and had apparently discouraged the mouse – though God knows what such a poor creature might expect to find here to eat. Books? He was welcome to the consular library. Felix had a small suitcase of private books under his bed, mostly poetry. But now he was looking at the shallow office bookcase with its reference books which were apparently all that a consul ever needed in order to remain efficient. The F.O. List with its supplements made quite good reading. It soothed him to discover the whereabouts of long-lost London colleagues. When he wanted to gloat he looked up some fearful bore like Pater and read (his lips moved as he did so) the small paragraph which recited all his early posts, sinking in gradual diminuendo towards the fatal posting. Consular Agent, Aden. He could hardly forbear to let out a cheer, so much had he disliked Pater while he was being "run in" in the London office. Then there was Sopwith too – another victory of good sense. He had been posted to Rangoon. On the whole then, Avignon might not seem so bad. But he had no money to get to Nice or Paris, and Galen would never have lent him the large slow Hispano which coasted everywhere with its goggled negro chauffeur – trailing long plumes of white dust across the vernal olive groves. What else was there for a decent self-respecting mouse to feed on? *Consular Duties* in six volumes? A volume of consular stamps and some faded ink-rollers which thumped out a splayed crown if properly inked. *Wagner's Basic International Law* – a huge and incomprehensible compilation. *The British Subject Abroad*, a guide for Residents. Skeat's *English Usage*. *The Consular Register*. *The Shorter Oxford*. All this to keep his despatches in good trim. There were also a few grammars and detective stories. The whole thing was pretty shabby and anyone having a look around would realise (he told himself) that Chatto was very poor, and that Lord Galen was either quite oblivious of the fact or wanted to keep him so. As for pro-consuls in posts as remote as these, they were hardly paid at all, and certainly never got accorded consular *frais*, expense accounts, which they might disburse in the pursuit of pleasure. Moreover Felix had no private income, so that his mind was always pinched by the thought of overspending. Even when people found him agreeable and invited him out to functions he was apt to decline for fear that he would never be able to invite them back. Nothing gives one that hunted look like poverty; and there is no poverty like having to swallow the backwash of extravagantly rich relations, who cannot help patronising you, however much they may try not to. And on such an exiguous budget, in a remote place, everything became a terror – the necessary doctor's visit, an operation, a false tooth, broken spectacles, a winter overcoat. All these possibilities gnawed at his mind, depleting his self-confidence, poisoning the springs of his happiness.

Well then, night after night, as he lay in the coarse sheets, he went over these factors in a trance of sleepless misery; his history seemed to stretch like an unbroken ribbon of distress and anxiety right back to the father's death and his sad schooldays. (His reports always said something like "Could do better if day-dreamed less".) His only refuge had been books; and now he was beginning to take a faked interest in Catholicism because it made one friends and took up time. He felt that unless he could find himself fully occupied the weight of his present boredom and anguish might unseat his reason and lead him towards what was then known as "a brain fever". He whispered, "Oh God, not that," under his breath when the thought came into his mind. Someone to talk to, for the love of God! When he received a note from Blanford telling him of the summer to be spent near Avignon, tears came into his eyes and he gave an involuntary dry sob of pure relief.

In these long night-silences he felt rather like the town itself – all past and no recognisable present. Did Galen know about them coming down – he did not know if Blanford was an acquaintance of the old man. How could one tell? Galen never even bothered to signal his frequent absences and returns – he spent several months a year in the tumbledown chateau which he was too mean, Felix supposed, to restore.

He moved about all over Europe following the threads of the cobweb he had spun with his fortune, playing the game of banking and politics. Everywhere he was accompanied by Max, his negro valet-chauffeur, who in certain lights looked dark violet; and the dumb (literally) male secretary whom Galen had deliberately chosen for himself, saying with a laugh that he knew how to give orders and get them obeyed. A secretary did not need a voice, a nod would suffice.

It should be noted also that where Galen went Wombat went too, seated on a mouldering green velvet cushion with a monogrammed crown printed on it as befitted the animal's pedigree, for Wombat was the imperial cat of this strange, rather sad, motherless household. Max, who loved the thing, carried it everywhere most ceremoniously, as if he were a chamberlain carrying the royal chamberpot of a King. Wombat was half blind and dying of asthma, and if offered the slightest attention or civility like an outstretched hand or a friendly sound, would react unamiably by opening its throat to hiss, and rearing up in anger. When Galen had had a drink or two in the evening he used often to wax sentimental and inform Max that the cat was his only friend; everyone else loved him for his money. With Wombat it was real love. But when he reached out his hand the animal spread its throat and reared like a cobra opening its hood as it hissed – thus avoiding the old man's caress.

No, he had little enough thought for Felix, though every Christmas he received a penny Christmas card of the Woolworth type featuring holly and a robin. It was always signed by Galen but the envelope was made out in the secretary's awkward hand. In summer, then, it was dust and wind and noise, and Keating's Powder and ceremonial processions of scruffy nuns and priests; in winter it was frost and ice and the river swollen to three times its mean summer levels. *Le cafard*, in fact, in its most exaggerated form.

Perambulatory paranoia, they would one day christen his case, of that he was sure.

He had set Blanford's postcard up on his desk as a talisman; he leaned over to read it anew now curbing his impatience by breathing slowly several times. Then he locked up his petty-cash box with its sheets of stamps and the six blank passports in the little wall-safe. He stepped out into the garden of the house, drawing the door to behind him with a soft click. How he hated that door with its ill-fitting lock. It was a glass door with a feverish design executed in squares of cathedral glass; when the sunlight fell upon it it produced extraordinary colour effects on the face of anyone crossing the hall to open it. The features became suddenly the colour of a blood-orange; then, in sharp succession, blue, green and livid yellow. Such theatrical changes often gave the unwary caller a start.

He turned up his coat-collar and, placing his cane under his arm, drew on gloves as he began the slow martyrdom of his night march across the town.

The westering moon drooped towards the battlements and as he turned the dark corner by the abattoir which rang all night to the sound of flushing waters like a public urinal he saw the familiar little lamplighter trotting along ahead of him with his shepherd's crook with which he turned off the street-lights – for only a few corners of the town had been able to afford the new clean electric lighting. He reflected with a selfish pang that he would be sorry when the whole town went electric because the little lamplighters not only marked the hour for him (the lights were turned off at two) but also afforded him a kind of welcome night-company on his walks. He skirted the smoky grey battlements with their crenellations. By now perhaps even the gipsies would have retired to their tents and caravans – they kept up the latest in the town, as far as he could judge; he followed the little lamplighter who padded along ahead of him making almost no sound, and only pausing to put out a lamp with his little crook. It was like someone beheading flowers one after the other; the violet night rushed in at once with its graphic shadows. At the rue St.-Charles he mentally said goodnight to his familiar and turned sharp right towards the Porte St.-Charles which here pierced the massive walls of the town. One emerged upon the apron, so to speak, of the bastion – a dusty *terrain vague* punctuated with tall planes whose leaves had begun to turn green. Here were great areas of shadow and few lights – a fitting place for the enactment of mischief, a corner made for throat-slitting, settling of accounts and active whoring. The gipsies had not been slow to find it and to settle on it – in defiance of the law which from time to time ordered them to leave. In vain. But now their fires had burned low and they had taken to their caravans where frail night-lights burned behind curtains. A point or two of lights could also be seen in the tents and the makeshift shelters where they lay, piled together for warmth like a litter of cats. Felix half envied and half feared them, and as he heard his own dry footfalls change in tone as they passed between the ramps of the tall gate his hand always strayed involuntarily to the electric torch in his pocket, though as yet he had never had occasion to use it in an emergency.

Yes, their fires had burned down to the embers and even their few donkeys and dogs appeared to slumber. But from one of the smaller tents a girl, awakened by his echoing footfalls, arose, seeming to materialise from the very ground, and sidled towards him whining for alms. Yes, she sidled yawning towards him like a pretty kitten, stretching out her slender arms. She could not have been much over sixteen and she was dressed as vividly as a pierrot in her patchwork quilt of bright rags. He felt a whirl of desire overcome him as he saw her beautiful face, so full of the sexual conceit

of her people. He felt almost like fainting. Hereabouts
the stout ravelins made whole barrows of dark blue shadow –
an impenetrable darkness safe from prying eyes. Why did he
not simply beckon her into one of these pools of black and
sink his consular talons into that lithe and swarthy flesh?
She would surely follow him at the mere promise of gold?

Ah! There was the rub – gold! How much would she
want for her caresses? He did not know. Anyway he knew
that he had not the courage to do such a thing; he would have
had to undo the constraints of his whole upbringing. A giant
despondency seized him as he waved away the tempting
creature. He hurried past her, feeling her predatory fingers
brush his sleeve. She was barefoot, and moved soundlessly.
Why didn't she hit him with something and then rape him
sublimely while he lay insensible – then at least he would
not feel guilty about so natural an act? But what about the
dose which would almost inevitably follow such an act? It
would be very expensive to cure a dose here, as well as
unbearably painful. It was a subject on which he could speak
with feeling as he had once accompanied a panicky undergraduate friend to the Lock Hospital in Greek Street. The
poor boy was expiating a twenty-first birthday party spent
at The Old Bag O'Nails in the usual way. Felix out of
sympathy accompanied his friend to his first few drastic
"treatments": he watched these agonising sessions with fear
and repugnance. The background, too, was daunting – the
long marble-walled latrines hushing with water, the rows of
high white enemas and their long slim tubes. . . . Could this
really be the only cure for this foul disease? First the bowel
filled and refilled with permanganate (Condy's Fluid) which
the patient was encouraged to piss away with whatever force
he could command. Then he must submit to the cleaning and
scraping of the sensitive mucus surfaces inside the urethra
where the infection lay. The surgeon inserted a small catheter

shaped like a steel umbrella in the organ and gradually opened it in umbrella fashion, to distend the member. This was supposed to break down and detach the infected parts so that they could be ejected and discharged. It was agony for the patient. Once seen, never forgotten.

And the mere thought of these sessions lent wings to him now, strengthening his resolve to repulse the girl. He quickened his pace and turned away down towards the pretty little railway station with its dark palms. The girl showed some disposition to insist but was soon overtaken by yawns and contented herself by spitting in his wake as she turned aside to regain the tents. The last train had gone out, the first of the new day was still far off. From somewhere among the dark quays came the sharp clanging of milk churns being man-hauled and stacked in the dark sheds against the arrival of the morning milk carts. The refreshment room was also closed at this hour but one naked bulb burned on in it and through the frosted glass he could see the old peasant and his wife washing glasses and teapots and sweeping the flags with tattered straw brooms. He would have liked to drink a grog but they would not open to him until the first train of the day shook the silent station with its clatter and squeals. The *fiacres* still stood outside the main entrance under the clock whose hands had pointed to two-twenty for the last three months. Would it never be mended? The drivers were wrapped in old blankets like effigies, the horses appeared to be asleep standing.

Porte St.-Roche, Porte St.-Charles, Porte de la République – the last led directly to the heart of the town, the throbbing little square around which everything of social consequence was grouped – the Mairie, the handsome old Theatre, the Monument des Morts with its disgraceful but delightful tin cartoon of symbolic lions and the flag-waving Marianne. . . . How well he had come to know it all; he was no longer a hesitant tourist, inspirited by the romance of its history, but one of the forty thousand residents now, his spirit almost embalmed in the boredom of its silences, its frowning churches, its shuttered shops and cafés. The horrifying thing was that this sort of life corresponded most favourably to the best posting available to a young consul, apart from working in a great capital or a town as big as Marseille or Lyon or Rome. After years of expiating his sins like this in places like this he might aspire to the rank of Consul General, though still resting debarred from the mainstream of career diplomacy – for the "real" diplomats were a chosen race, a trade union, a closed circle.

Turning his back to the station he addressed himself to the second massive Porte de la République and entered the inside of the bastions. In the summer he often took the opposite direction and walked over the suspension bridge to the island; but this was rather a sinister place and pitch dark, and he had no stomach to be set upon by footpads. Besides, with the present wind and temperature he could, by taking this anti-clockwise walk, shelter within the walls from the worst inclemencies of the weather. He moved towards the little chapel of the Grey Penitents set incongruously upon its dark canal with the stout wooden waterwheels forever turning with their slopping and swishing sound. From St. Magnagnen one ducked into the terrifying little rue Bon Martinet (the name struck a chord always, though the exact association escaped him for the moment: later Blanford supplied the missing fragment of the puzzle). It was so narrow and dark that one's shoulders brushed the wall on either side and when one passed a dark doorway one prayed that there might be nobody waiting for one in it with a knife or a rope. This emerged – you could see the light at the end of the tunnel – directly upon the canals; this part of the town was the domain of the tanners and dyers, and the paddlewheels which would have driven a decent-sized steamboat, turned night and day though the actual trade had fallen largely into desuetude.

Here the darkness was like wet velvet; he paused, as always, at the entrance of the chapel and recited the inscription over the entrance to himself in a whisper. Mostly he took out his torch hereabouts to read such things. This was the Grey Penitents – the Black ones were situated in a further corner of the town. He pushed the door and it squeaked open upon blackness. Sometimes he sat for a moment in one of the pews. There was an electric bell in the wall with the name of a priest – a duty-priest, so to speak, always ready to take confession if summoned. One night he had "disgraced himself", as he would have put it if he had been describing it to someone else. In an access of misery he had entered the church with some intention of praying; but when he found himself in the pew facing the cold repugnant statue which was to act as a focus for this novel set of emotions his spirit strangled within him, he became choked. He felt as if the centre was sliding out of his mind. He understood what the phrase "wrestling with the dark angel" meant. But in his case it felt more like the slimy tentacles of Laocoön which closed around him and from which he could not disengage himself. There was nobody in the place, the silence echoed to his deep panting. At last, overwhelmed by these stresses, he crossed the aisle and pressed the bell. Underneath it there was a card with the name of the duty priest typed on it – *Menard*. Then he stood aghast at what he had done. The sepulchral sound of the bell died slowly away in the further entrails of the building, awakening nobody, arousing no answering sound. He stood there feeling now as foolish and as irresponsible as before he had felt anguished. Ringing for a priest at two o'clock in the morning – it was a scandal! And yet, surely if the religious crisis were a truthful one, a serious one, no priest could complain of the hour – any more than a doctor complain of a night call by a patient *in extremis*? But no, he felt a guilty fool for importuning the church at this time of day. Yet silence was all that his frantic ring had elicited. He stood there with head cocked on one side. In the dark street outside two cats started their macabre love-wails. Where could he be, the priest? He felt stupid, blameworthy, undeserving of consideration since he himself had shown so little. Turning, he ran to the door and opened it onto the dark causeway with its swishing canal and impassive paddle-wheels turning. Then he closed the door of the chapel silently and leaned his head against its oaken panels, as if to cool his feverish forehead with the cold touch of the wood. As he did so he heard the shuffle of footsteps entering the chapel and the clicking of the confessional wicket. A priest had, after all, answered his summons. The thought panicked him anew and turning, he hurried away into the darkness leaving priest and chapel to their darkness and silence. What a bad show this was! It took him an effort to confess it, not to the priest, but to Blanford who later joined him on these night marches, when they were hunting for traces of Livia. It was here too that Blanford untangled the associative strands which made rue Bon Martinet so evocative. The Marquis de Sade!

"It has one thing, this town, for me. The huge span of human aspiration and human weakness are symbolised by two figures from its bestiary, so to speak. I mean Petrarch's Laura who invented the perfect romantic love and the Marquis de Sade who carried it right back into its despairing infancy with the whip. What a couple of guardian angels!"

Felix pushed on doggedly now towards the next bastion, the frowning Porte Thiers where he started to cut diagonally across the sleeping town. Once or twice he passed signs of life, like an old man on a bicycle who passed him riding so

slowly that it seemed as if his journey had begun a long time
ago – back in the Pleistocene era perhaps. His bicycle bobbed
and bounced upon the uneven cobbles and flags of the street,
but quite soundlessly. The old man himself looked neither
to right nor left – was he perhaps asleep? Then he coughed
sharply and Felix nearly jumped out of his skin. The little
wooded Place Bon Pasteur slumbered among its dense
planes under which the nearby inhabitants had parked their
prams and bicycles and carts which would soon be pressed
into service when the market opened. From the end of the
street he caught a glimpse of a frail light shining in the
cavernous tin shed which housed the three trams. At five their
squeals would awaken the toughest sleepers in the town – for
they traversed the whole length of it. It was all the towns-
people had in the way of public transport – the two large and
shaky motor buses were a recent innovation and given over
to tourism; they slumbered outside the Hotel Crillon and at
ten would carry their fares off to inspect Aigues Mortes and
the Camargue. There was a shadowy figure with a storm-
lantern moving among the slumbering trams with an oil-can,
servicing them for their daily work. Dawn was as yet a
premonition in a clear mistral sky prickling with stars – a
mere lightening of the sky at the furthest edges of futurity;
but it was like a faint chord struck somewhere far away that
echoed here, for the bird colonies in the dense foliage of the
trees which sheltered the beautiful old market had started to
stir and stretch and converse. In the Clinique Bosque he saw a
faint bud of flame under a coffee-urn – an alcohol lamp. In
the Banque Foix a night watchman stirred and clanked open
massive bolts to let in the two shapeless old ladies – the office
cleaners. Somewhere in a nearby street an invisible whistler
executed a phrase from a popular tango, and then broke off,
as if in embarrassment.

This was the hour when Quatrefages at last fell asleep

in the Princes Hotel, with the lights still burning on – he could not bear the dark. What would Felix have done without the *thought* of poor Quatrefages, the knowledge that poor Quatrefages was alone among the forty thousand souls, awake all night as he himself was? The warmth of this thought made his wanderings somehow possible; the lean youth was a sort of symbolic companion for the consul, a poor scholar who was also, like himself, a serf to Lord Galen. Quatrefages looked like some sleepy raven in his rusty black *tablier* which he wore over his clothes when he worked; on this work-apron he wiped his pen with its steel nib during his pauses; his hand was a copyist's Italian cursive, as beautiful as Arabic script or a Chinese ideogram. Though why Galen should retain the services of this poor scholar to decipher and copy medieval documents, was for a time something of a puzzle. . . .

The dark, famished-looking youth had had quite a chequered history before he found himself here, immured in an ill-lit bedroom of the Princes Hotel, working with the savage concentration of a slave on the projects which Lord Galen had proposed for him. His story began with the Church – he had once been a sexton and then a curate of the Church, but a scandal accompanied by the poisonous gossip of a small village had unseated him – he had been defrocked unjustly, or so he felt. His ardent religious faith died in him there and then and was replaced by an overwhelming sensation of loss – as if the whole outer darkness which lay outside the narrow field of the doctrine had rushed in and taken possession of his soul. "Possession" is not inapt as a thought – for he now became convinced that God could not exist and that atheism was the only honourable philosophy for a logical person like himself. He had wasted his whole youth in mumbo-jumbo. In the grip of this despairing belief – for it did not render him happy, this train of thought – he turned his attention to evil with the same single-mindedness as he had once devoted to an orthodox goodness. The path led downwards by obscure stages towards symbolic mathematics, enigmas, emblems and the shadowy reaches of alchemy and astrology. On the way he discovered orthodox mathematics and became, to his own surprise, a very able performer. It was an accident, but a fruitful one, that had resulted in him being co-opted into the department of Lord Galen's business which was called "Trendings"; here a group of four young mathematicians analysed graphs of prediction as to their future movements up and down the scale. It was over these large and pretty graphs that Galen pored at night, wondering whether to sell or to buy. His little band of statisticians provided him with a rough guide to the disposition of his markets, and while they were not infallible there was quite a large element of correctness, in what they found. Here Quatrefages found himself in congenial surroundings; he was well treated, relatively speaking. As he was afraid of the dark and could not sleep until dawn, for the most part he elected to do his work at night. He would sit over the old teak drawing-boards in the uninspiring offices of the firm, his long pointed nose slanted towards his papers. He looked like some sleepy raven; his nails were bitten down to the quick, his fingers always a bit inky, his trousers frayed where the bicycle clips went. His small black mouse eyes were full of a sullen brilliance and impatience. His dry cough and eternal light fever spoke of tuberculosis; indeed his whole physiognomy was that of the old traditional *poitrinaire*, and he had once been placed in a sanatorium where they had collapsed a lung to let it mend. In vain.

But the tell-tale coughing, which sometimes doubled him up and brought tears to his eyes, did not affect the determined steadiness of his work, despite the aching boredom of the matter he had been set to analyse. Always at the end of his night prowl the young consul made a short detour in order to stand for a moment below the lighted window; to breathe in, so to speak, some of the spectral courage and anxiety of his uncle's bondsman. At such a moment his divided feelings about his uncle – hatred and affection and amusement – rose and subsided within him like a sea. Yes, he hated him; no, for how could one? Like everyone with a silly side Galen was endearing. Every afternoon he boxed with the violet negro for a couple of rounds, puffing and blowing and wiping his nose in his glove like a professional. His partner had once been a real professional and he moved round the ring (which had been set up in the garden) as lazily as a moth, fully aware that he must not hit his boss – for Galen would have died on the spot. So they moved in a strange ballet, the dark boxer grazing the ropes with his back. He wore lace-up kid shoes and a much decorated belt whose medals gleamed richly. From time to time he sent out an exhibition punch – a shadow-punch so to speak – which stopped just short of his rival's small chin. Galen's answering blows might have been aimed at the moon, they were so inaccurate. The negro moved aside, but just once in a while, took a flick upon his violet forehead and gave a deep grunt of admiration.

How beautiful Max was to watch! The negro can do nothing which does not aspire towards dancing. Even his exaggerated shuffle round the ring with the hint of gorilla-like menace – the whole thing was light as air, volatile, buoyant and undeliberate; one felt it was almost as arbitrary as the flutterings of a cabbage-white among the flowers. Yet there was science in it even though the arms hung limp as empty sleeves. Suddenly this classical punch would evolve itself like a bee-sting. Max whistled to himself, little mauve tunes, blues. From time to time he breathed a word of advice to his partner, "You gotta breathe with yo bones, sah," he might say, and shaking his head add, "sure damn thing." And

Galen would obediently try to breathe with his bones. After two rounds, speechless and puffing, the old man turned to whoever was watching (most often it was poor Felix) and said: "You see? It's the secret of my iron constitution."

Galen would rise very early in the morning and have himself driven to the main station to see the first train go out towards Paris; he had done this all his life, wherever he might be. Trains were an obsession. The intoxication of the platforms smelling of coal and oil, the bustle and clamour of passengers and porters loading baggage and freight – the whole indescribable chaos and order of the operation never failed to thrill him to the bone. And the farewells! A whole life, a whole human situation is illustrated in the farewells of lovers, friends, married couples, children, dogs. The clang of closing doors, the kisses, the shrill whistles, the red flag, and the steady champ of the engines belching white plumes into the blue sky – it brought him to tears still. It was perhaps by one of those cruel paradoxes in which fate delights that the railway had become connected to the sole tragedy of Galen's life – the inexplicable disappearance of his adolescent daughter. He had spent a fortune trying to trace her or at least to solve the mystery of her disappearance. One supposes that this sort of thing happens every day – to judge by the press, which comments on it for a while and then forgets it. Fifteen schoolgirls accompanied by two nuns from the Sacred Heart Convent, took a Sunday excursion train to London from Sidcote. When they arrived at Waterloo one girl was missing – Galen's daughter. It may be imagined what measures were taken to explain this extraordinary fact. Had she fallen from the train? No; had she absconded? The train was a through train. Her fellow pupils said that about half-way to London she absented herself to go to the lavatory. She never reappeared. Galen was beside himself with horror and

incredulity. Every field of enquiry was pursued with all the
ferocious relentlessness of a father almost beside himself.
It was years ago now, but the memory was still fresh, his
room was full of her photographs and hand-painted Christmas cards. He wept unaffectedly when speaking of her. One
day in London he unburdened himself to his clerk Quatrefages, who was then buried deep in his alchemical studies.
In some vague way Galen hoped, by revealing the degree of
his own emotional weakness and commitment towards the
memory of his child, to move the boy and win a little sympathy from him – he was such a taciturn creature with his
bitten nails. To his surprise Quatrefages produced a ring on a
pendulum and asked for a scale map of London and Surrey –
so that his divining machine would plot the course of that
fatal journey and perhaps offer a solution.

Galen watched with fascination as it swung to and fro
in the lean hand of the clerk. Finally Quatrefages said, with
a note of finality, "She was not on that train, the children
were told to say she was. The nuns were lying to excuse their
inattention; at the station she was taken by a gipsy." Galen
reeled with hope and delight. So she might still be alive, then?
After all, through the whole course of Victorian fiction the
gipsies were always responsible for the disappearance of
children, and often of grown-ups also. "Is she still alive?" he
asked in a paroxym of anxiety, "if so where should I look?"
But Quatrefages did not know – or so he said. The truth
was he did not want to go too far, as he was making all this
up in order to secure a bit of a hold on this funny, aggressive
little man. He had found a way. Soon Galen was dropping
in for chats, and ineluctably the subject would drift towards
his great obsession – the whereabouts of Sabine. He initiated
an elaborate study of all the gipsy tribes, a sort of star map
of their movements across Europe, and sent his agents
hunting equipped with photos. At the yearly world gathering

of gipsy legions his agents were waiting for their caravans to arrive from all over Europe at the Saintes Maries de la Mer. He began to find superior qualities in the French clerk – the boy became precious simply because one day he might find the missing clue to the child's whereabouts. As their intimacy grew he offered him a new sort of secret job – one he would not have confided to just anyone. Quatrefages, stupid as it may sound, was now hunting for buried treasure, nothing less, in the tangled mass of documentation which surrounds the Templars and their heresy.

Sometimes Felix stood for a while in the little square beneath the inspiring square of yellow light where once a gallows had stood, and mentally hanged himself; in the pale moonlight his body swung to and fro in the wind, softly creaking and clanking in its chains. A felon of laziness and cowardice if ever there was one. Ineffectual, too. As for Quatrefages, for all his apparent youthful inexperience and all his pretensions to esoteric knowledge, he had kept a fine French sense of proportion where self-interest was concerned. Happily. It was largely through him that Felix had obtained the part-time use of the little Morris automobile, a blessing they shared in amiable enough fashion. The clerk had asked Galen for some form of transport to enable him to travel about Provence, examining ancient sites and ruins and consulting scholars. He used the machine a fair amount, but for the rest of the time it belonged to the Consulate and undertook other duties. Felix drove himself vaguely about the delectable countryside, swollen with his sense of loneliness, and trying to render it endurable by investigating the grand dishes and finer wines of the area; for though Avignon was not Lyon in richness and variety where cuisine was concerned, nevertheless much remained to marvel at in the realm of country cooking. Even in its poorest corners France seemed quite inexhaustible to one raised on ordinary English fare.

Yet the sense of vacuum persisted, and the healthy sleep to which a youth of his age might claim a right, resisted; hence the night patrols in a city where after dark so little life seemed to exist. The few bedraggled and furtive ladies of the night were amiable but hardly appetising; they packed up at two, with the latest *café dansant*. Only the gipsies had colour and movement, and the courage which he himself lacked. Seekers of a late night out were perforce obliged to "go to the gipsies" and risk a police sweep and an ignominious appearance in court. And then the other question ... Felix shook his head. Wandering among the stray cats feasting on fishheads and vegetable garbage from the over-turned dustbins outside the "Mireille" he pondered on the fate of consuls, and saw with hungry misgiving the manic moon in her slow dejected fall towards the lightening skyline. He yawned. Somewhere he had read that dogs denied sleep for more than four days automatically died. And consuls? He yawned again, this time from the soles of his feet.

Consummatum est. It was nearly over now. In the darkness ahead he heard the sweet whisper of the great underground ovens of the bakery with its cracked sign "*Pain du Jour*" at street level. The shop was open though still in darkness. The sleeping woman sat wrapped in her black shawl like a rook. The clink of the bell woke her and she sat up to serve him. The little cubicle smelt heavenly – with the rack beginning to fill up with loaves and croissants, with *fougasses* and doughnuts and *brioches*. Felix walked slowly home inhaling the two croissants in their slip of tissue paper. The wind had dropped as it always did at dawn. He pushed open the rusty garden gate and let himself into the musty little house, greeting its familiar smell with a renewed spasm of depression. God, even the palm tree in the garden was dusty – while as for a hideous aspidistra on the balcony the maid would have to wipe it leaf by leaf with a damp cloth, as usual.

He went to the kitchen and made some coffee. On the floor in the corner lay a wooden crate he had cracked open; it bore the insignia of the Crown Agents, Gabbitas and Speed. He had ordered it to be sent on to him when leaving London. No sooner said than done, for the Crown Agents had been constituted to offer solace and comfort to diplomatic exiles with their combination tuckbox and gift-parcel deliveries. His was the smallest and most modest order of this kind – two whisky, two gin, two white sparkling Spanish wine and two Bass. That was all for the liquid solace; but there was quite a range of kitchen commodities which might be more welcome in Africa, say, than in Europe; but Abroad was simply Abroad for the Crown Agents: with a capital letter, too, as in Hell. You could also give these damned parcels to your fellow diplomats at Christmas if you wished – it saved time and thought. In the Service they were known as "consolation prizes" – consoling one against the horrors of foreign residence, among the lesser breeds of the Kipling kind, or simply among backward European states like France with its froglegs and polluted water.

Some of the tins like Plum Jam he had already extracted. On the kitchen table stood a tin of Bumpsted's Bloater Paste beside a bottle of Gentleman's Relish and Mainwearing's Pickle Mix. The consul sat down and stared hard at these sterling products. Imperial Anchovies, Angostura Bitters. Pork and Beans, Imperial size. Lea and Perrin's Sauce . . . A profound homesickness overcame him. He had seized in passing the postcard from Blanford with all its exciting promises for the coming summer; but their arrival was some way off as yet. He poured himself a large cup of coffee and hunted for milk in his little ice box which was by now iceless and dank. The milk smelt suspect. However . . . the sun was coming up; he had defeated another night. Today was his day with the Morris. He started to unpack the crate and put the pots in the cupboard, arranging them like a fussy old maid so that their names were facing forward. Then a sudden impulse overcame him and he did something he should never have done; he smeared bloater paste on his croissant and ate it with a groan. It was delicious.

There would be plenty of time for a couple of hours of sleep before the maid knocked, but lest he should oversleep by any chance he retrieved the little alarm clock by his bed and, rewinding it, set it for eleven. Then he undressed and climbed yawning into his virgin bed, turning off all the lights save the small bedside lamp, for he proposed to "read himself to sleep" as usual; and the book most suitable for this exercise was *The Foreign Service Guide to Residence Abroad*. It had a blue cover with the royal arms, rather like an outsize passport, and the text had not been revised for forty years owing to a mistakenly large first printing. Together with a Bible and a Book of Common Prayer, it was the statutory going-away present accorded to young officers on their first posting abroad. The hints and instructions contained in it had a wonderfully soothing effect on insomniac consuls. Take the chapter called "Hints to Travellers":

> Officers should take soft caps for sleeping, in a travelling bag; soft shoes to replace boots, a "housewife", a couple of good mauds, a bottle of bovril, a small spirit lamp, a bottle of spirits with cups and saucers, spoons and biscuits. Also a stout sponge bag with two wet sponges in it, a soft towel, a face flannel, a brush and comb. The pillows should be made to roll up tightly and are best made of thistledown and dandelion-down. A travelling ulster with loose fronts is very useful as one can undo the clothes beneath; it should have deep pockets. Always carry an extra pair of gloves. Always take a small book of soap leaves with a small handbag; thus hands can be comfortably washed with one leaf. With a wet sponge and a soap leaf the dusty and tired traveller can always

freshen up his face and hands. It is a good wrinkle to carry an Etna spirit lamp, also a tin of mustard leaves, a medicine glass, sticking plaster, a water bottle, and a flask of good brandy in case of sudden or obstinate illness en route.

On and on went this soothing and comforting rigmarole; across the sleepy vision of the consul passed a long, an endless, line of kindly, colourless yet courageous men in pith helmets followed by their baggage, bulging with brandy flasks and Etna spirit lamps. Now he had joined the long senseless safari – forever deprived of watching the ebb and flow of copper shares on the pretty coloured charts of Quatrefages. And what the devil was "a couple of good mauds?" He would give anything to know. But now sleep had definitely come to claim him: the book dropped from his hand to the carpet and with an involuntary gesture which had become mechanical one hand went out to switch off the little bedside lamp. Felix slept a surprisingly deep and healthy sleep which would be broken by the alarm just ten minutes before the maid arrived to set his little house to rights.

The trams had started squealing and with them came the battering of bells that had once irritated Rabelais so; but he heard nothing.

FOUR

Summer Sunlight

B UT AT LONG LAST THE SUMMER, HIGH SUMMER, WAS upon them, with the promised arrival of the four firstcomers to the old manor house. Felix was in such a fever of excitement that on the expected day he hardly dared to quit the landing stage over the green swift water for fear of missing them when they stepped ashore. He walked distractedly about in the wind, talking to himself and ordering numerous coffees in the little Bistro de la Navigation hard by the river, with its one-eyed sailor host.

There was quite a group of people waiting there, on the *qui vive* for the premonitory whiff of sound from the ship's hooter as it rounded the last bend – as much an accolade to the view of Avignon from the water as a triumphal signal of arrival. In the meantime he had been busy on their behalf; he had visited the house a number of times already, sometimes by car or bicycle, and indeed once on foot; and while he could not get into it until he obtained the keys from Bechet the notary, he had a picnic or two in the dilapidated garden and the herb *potager*, now run hopelessly to seed and weed. Sitting under one of the tall pines, inhaling their sharp odour, he ate his six sandwiches and drank his red wine, dreaming of the excellent company he would enjoy once they arrived. Nor was he wrong – their arrival and their gaiety exceeded all expectation; he was to find himself adopted at once, and the manor of Tu Duc was to become a second home. They were to spend many an evening together sitting round the old kitchen table playing twentyone; and he even once succeeded in inveigling Quatrefages to accompany him for a dinner, which rendered the boy less morose: the little clerk even expanded enough to show them a series of bewildering card tricks. But the chief factor in his happiness was without doubt the absence of Lord Galen, for the old man had decided to take his liver to Baden-Baden for a cure and had disappeared leaving no word as to when he would return. It was marvellous. The consulate remained closed almost permanently, while Quatrefages downed tools, left his Crusader maps pinned to the walls of his room, and embarked on a series of probably unsavoury adventures in the gipsy section of the town – the quarter known as Les Balances.

Livia appeared, fresh from Munich.

And with her a new element entered the camp, for the icy serenity of the girl, and the hard cutting edge of her character, made an immediate impression on them all – but of course mostly upon the too susceptible Blanford. Yet Felix too in his own fashion was enslaved, for she teased him into a sort of sisterly relationship which tightened his heart-strings with a youthful passion. He could refuse her nothing; even when she asked for the use of the spare room, a sort of glorified alcove, at the consulate (for she was too independent not to find Tu Duc oppressive) he could only limply agree while his spirit performed cartwheels at the thought, and Blanford turned pale. Blanford turned pale.

But despite all the dazzling variety and pleasure of that first summer encounter, more important elements were to form themselves which hinted at future developments and subtly transforming predispositions to come. Sam and Hilary, the inseparables, were the chief inciters to adventure and travel; only when Livia appeared did Hilary seem to take on a new constraint, his ice-blue eyes became evasive and thoughtful as he watched both Felix and Blanford foundering like ships in a gale. Constance and Sam somehow remained in a friendly comradely relationship – something not difficult for a knight-errant born to endure. Sam was not made of flesh and blood, but of flesh and books. And in the blonde, smiling Constance he had found a worshipful lady who only lacked a tower to get locked into. . . . . All this, of course, has to be interpreted backwards – for while events are being lived they travel too fast for easy evaluation. Blanford noticed many things which his inexperience could not interpret. In part he reproduced all these errors in Sutcliffe to record some of the surprise they gave him when at last the truth (what truth?) dawned. One day Livia burned Hilary's wrist with her cigarette and he smacked her – and in a trice they were tearing at each other's hair like savages. Well, brothers and sisters. . . .

They had found a hunchback maid who came from the village every day; she had worked long as a *serveuse* in a brothel, so they learned afterwards. The experience had given her insight into the ways of men – she read a bedroom when she entered it, as one reads a book. She interpreted the whole scene like a sleuth, the disordered pillows and blankets, all had something to tell her. She often smiled to herself. One day Blanford, passing the door, saw her pick up a pillow and inhale it deeply. Then she shook her head and smiled. Turning she saw him and said in her hoarse way, "Mademoiselle Livia!" Yes, but it was the bed of Hilary that she was making. Things do not strike you at the time; ages later Livia bit his hand with her white teeth and he suddenly remembered the incident. And with it the kind of strained attention with which Hilary heard him say at the end of that summer: "Hilary, what would you say if I asked Livia to marry me one day?" The hard blue eyes narrowed, and then flared into rather factitious congratulatory warmth; he squeezed his friend's shoulder, however, until it hurt, but he actually said nothing. Later when they were having lunch he said, out of the blue, "I think you should make sure, Aubrey." And Blanford knew at once that he was thinking of Livia. It takes

years to evaluate such tiny glimpses into the multiple meanings of any single human action. As Sutcliffe one day said to
him in one of his notebooks: "Right girl, old boy, but wrong
sex. Hard luck!" At another moment in another notebook the
poor old novelist had jotted down the remark; "My mother's
sterile affect was cocked like a trigger to fire me into the arms
of Livia, or of one of her tribe." Then another thing, another
glimpse – for Livia had now spent several days, or groups of
days, lodging in the box-room of the consulate – with its
clumsy cupboard in which Felix had found a place for a small
wardrobe. When Blanford, at the end of the summer, said
to Felix, "I am going to propose to Livia when we leave here,"
he received a strange wondering look from the youth –
which he rather condescendingly interpreted as jealousy.
Several thousand light years afterwards when Blanford was
recording the strange manoeuvres of his double Sutcliffe,
he met Felix by accident on a rainy platform in Paris, as he
was just setting off for the south; and now Felix told him
what that lost and forlorn glance portended. He did not
repeat the scathing estimate of her character by Quatrefages,
who at that time spent one afternoon a week devilling at the
Consulate, keeping the petty-cash box in order. This report
on her was quite gratuitous and spontaneous on the part of
the little clerk and somewhat shook Felix by its terseness.
Yet ... he himself had strayed into his guest's room while
the maid was cleaning it and had seen, hanging up in the
shabby cupboard, some articles of male wear which aroused
his curiosity. And there was no doubt that late in the evening
she often disappeared in the direction of the gipsy encampment. Why not? She was young and adventurous and may
well have felt the need of a male disguise. Indeed Felix said
as much, on a note of mild indignation, to the little clerk; but
the latter shook his head and said laconically: "I know. I
myself frequent the *gitanes*." And this too was true. Mind you

(as Blanford told himself) it did not matter – he would not, for anything in the world, have renounced an experience which had literally scorched him awake, precipitated him from raw youth into adulthood. In a sense this was the worst part of it; somewhere, in some dim corner of himself, he must have perversely enjoyed the kind of suffering she was to inflict on him. When he said as much to Felix, the latter warmly praised his loyalty and generosity, which naturally disgusted our hero. "O God, Felix," he said in anguish, "it's not that. I'm trapped. I can do no other. I am fuming with impotent rage."

But he was not the only one to be grateful to the girl; Felix was hardly less so, for Livia, by joining him more than once on his night walk, had performed a miracle – she had made him fall in love with this small and dismal city. *Venite adoremus* said the chipped gold sign above the chapel of the Grey Penitents, almost as if the church had divined his mood, his abandonment to his love for this mysterious and eccentric girl. She sat so docilely hand in hand with him in the silent pews, listening to the thresh and swash of the paddles revolving. She said, whispering, "Go on and pray, if you wish. I have never been able to." But his shyness constrained him and he felt himself blush in the darkness. Nor would he have changed his position for anything, for the feel of her rough little hand in his was bliss. How marvellous, how romantic it all seemed, and how beautiful she was, this Livia who talked about painting and seemed to know everything about the history of the place which had for him been up to now an echoing prison. As for the gipsy side of her character – why, she had been the most brilliant student of the Slade School in the years when the influence of Augustus John was at its height; all students worth anything ached to become Carmen. One night when she disappeared he ran into her by chance in the eastern sector of the town, and she was walking arm in arm with a gipsy girl; behind the couple, as if offering protection or surveillance, came a couple of lean gipsies leading a mule. They were shabby as pariahs, and had a brilliant scavenging gleam in the eye – as if they had just done a successful robbery. Livia dressed in tattered pants and was bare of foot – another passion of hers was to walk about barefoot. That summer she cut her foot on a piece of tin and the wound turned septic; this immobilised her for a while and she accepted the ministrations of Felix with brusque good grace. In the evenings the gipsy girl hung about the consulate quarter, but she always made off when Felix appeared.

Only with Quatrefages nothing worked; Livia and he simply hated each other, and hardly bothered to hide the fact. Later they came to an interesting compromise, for the little clerk blackmailed her into co-operating with him in one of the numerous enterprises of Lord Galen – one which also concerned the gipsies.

What had happened was this: the gipsies had taken up a second headquarters in the corner of the town known as Les Balances, where a number of disreputable and tumble-down houses offered them precarious shelter. Prompted by a hint from Quatrefages, they had removed the heavy stone flags of the floors and started to dig down beneath these shacks, to arrive at a layer of civilisation much anterior to the Papal period of the town. Amphoras, grave headstones, armour, domestic remains, tessellated pavements, they had made one of the richer archaeological finds of the period; and all this material was surreptitiously placed in sacks and sent up to Galen's chateau by mule. Livia, details of whose doings among the gipsies had come to the ears of Quatrefages, was content to lend her good offices to these ventures rather than have him tell anyone about her own tenebrous adventures; and indeed was responsible for securing one or two of the larger pieces which might have been salted away by the band who were vaguely aware that someone was making a larger profit than they were from these finds.

But for Felix the real felicity of that first summer was not merely the marvellous evenings spent at Tu Duc, it was to walk half the night with this dark girl with her haughty face and bare feet; her thin body was erect as a wand, and she seemed to feel absolutely no fear in the darkest corners of the town – some of which made the flesh of poor Felix creep; like the terrifying rue Londe for example with its one gas lamp set askew in a wall so mossy and so dribbling with damp that it exuded a death-chill. Here the shadowy doorways were set in such a way as to afford perfect cover for a footpad. Obviously she felt nothing of all this, for she did not cease her quiet conversation as they travelled down it – perforce in Indian file to avoid the contact of their shoulders with the rotting walls. One thing she had determined to find – a famous Avignon shawl such as her mother had had as a young girl. Alas, these fine kashmirs were no longer made in the old town.

But it was Livia who made him sit and listen to the wakening birds in little squares like that of Le Bon Pasteur, or the Square des Corps Saints with its ragged plashing fountain; or Saint Didier, set slightly at an angle to the rest of the universe, but not the less evocative. And with these night rambles the whole harmony of the Mediterranean south swept over him, filling his consciousness with gorgeous impressions of star-sprinkled nights in the old town – the six of them seated under a tree in front of some old bistro like The Bird, drinking the milky anisette called *pastis* and waiting for the moon to rise over the munched-looking battlements of the city. Once Livia managed to procure them horses from the gipsies and they rode across to the Pont du Gard, to picnic and camp the night on the steep hillsides, overlooking the jade-green Gardon as it swirled its way to the sea. Sometimes, too, Blanford invited himself into town for a consular walk with them both, much to the chagrin of Felix, who looked quite crestfallen when his friend appeared on the scene. But Blanford was as much subject to the magnetism of Livia as Felix was – he simply could not resist forcing himself upon them, though he inwardly cursed his lack of tact. Yet it was Livia who seemed glad, and who indeed seemed to favour him quite unequivocally over Felix. The crestfallen consul was forced to witness, with exquisite pangs of jealousy, the two of them walking tenderly arm in arm, while he followed wistfully after them in his college blazer, uttering fearful imprecations under his breath. Nobody took any of this with high seriousness – it was simply youth, it was simply the spirit of an intoxicating summer felicity among the olives and cherries of Aramon, of Foulkes, of Montfavet or Sorgues. Often, looking back on this halcyon period, Blanford had the sudden vision of them all, standing upon the iron bridge at the Fountain of Vaucluse, gazing down into the trout-curdled water and listening to the roar of the spring as it burst from the mountain's throat and swept down past them, thick with loitering fish.

But if ever in the years to come Blanford might feel the need to account for the enigma of this fierce attachment to Livia there was one scene which quite certainly he knew would rise in his memory to explain everything. Once when Felix was away for a few days Livia gave him a rendezvous at the little Museum in the centre of the town – at four-thirty in the morning; punctually a sleepy Blanford turned up to find the barefooted girl waiting for him at the dark portals of the place with a swarthy gipsy. Dawn was just breaking. The gipsy had a massive pistol-key in his hand which fitted the lock; the tall doors swung back with a hushing noise and ushered them into the red cobbled courtyard; and as they did so they heard the inhuman shrieks which came from the interior garden with its tall dewy plane trees. It was the crying of peacocks on the lawn. They passed through tall glass doors to reach this interior courtyard which exhaled a strange sort of peace in that early light of day. The taciturn gipsy took his leave, having confided his key to the girl. Together they loitered through the galleries with their massive water paintings of the Italian school – lakes and viaducts and avenues depicting imaginary landscapes during the four seasons of the year. Portraits of great ladies and forgotten dignitaries stared urgently at them in the gloom. Then they came to the Graeco-Roman section and after it to a small glass-roofed room with manuscripts and documents galore.

Livia, who seemed to know the place by heart, opened the cases one by one and showed the bemused Blanford medieval documents which mentioned the marriage of Petrarch's sweetheart, and hard by, some pages of hand-writing torn from the letters of the Marquis de Sade. It was strange in that silent dawn to hold the white paper in his fingers and read some lines etched in a now rusted ink. He had forgotten that both the libertine and the Muse were called Sade, and were from the same family. . . . Now Livia was at his side, then in his arms; she closed the precious cases and led him back to the cool lawn where they sat side by side on a bench trying to feed the peacocks with scraps of stale sandwich which he had had the forethought to bring with him. "Soon I shall be going back to Germany," the girl said, "and you won't see me until the next long vac – unless you come with me; but I know you can't as yet. Such wonderful things are going to happen there, Aubrey; it's bursting with hope, the whole country. A new philosophy is being built which will give the new Germany the creative leadership of Europe once more." It sounded rather puzzling, but Blanford was politically quite ignorant. He had heard vague rumours of unrest and revisionism in Germany – a reaction against the Versailles treaty. But the whole subject was a bore, and he presumed that some new government would bury all these extravagances once and for all. Besides, a new war was unthinkable and specially for such trivial reasons. . . . This is why Livia intrigued him with her romantic talk. So, more to humour her – for he adored the flushed cheeks and the joined hands which showed her enthusiasm – than from real interest he said: "What was the old world, then?" Livia shook a lock of hair impatiently out of her eyes and said: "It died in 1832, with the death of Goethe; the old world of humanism and liberalism and faith. He exemplified it; and its epitaph was pronounced by Napoleon after he met Goethe; it was an unwilling tribute to the world which the French Revolution was then destroying. '*Voilà un homme*,' said Boney, himself a child of the Directory, and the harbinger of the Leninised Jewish coolie-culture of today. With the death of Goethe the new world was born, and under the aegis of Judeo-Christian materialism it transformed itself into the great labour camp that it is. In every field – art, politics, economics – the Jew came to the forefront and dominated the scene. Only Germany wants to replace this ethos with a new one, an Aryan one, which will offer renewed scope for the old values as exemplified by Goethe's world; for he was the last universal man of the Renaissance. Why should we not go back to that?" Blanford did not see quite how; but her sweet enthusiasm was so warming, and the tang of her kiss so unmanning that he found himself nodding agreement. Livia's new world sounded like the Hesperides – as a matter of fact any new world which had a Livia in it elicited his instant support. He said: "I love you, Livia dear. Tell me more about it, it sounds just what we need to escape from all this fervent dullness." And Livia went on outlining this marvellous intellectual adventure with heart-breaking idealism and naivety. When he mentioned Constance she cried: "I can't bear her devotion to all the Jewish brokers of psychoanalysis, to the Rabbinate of Vienna. It's dead, that whole thing. Its barren mechanism betrays its origins in logical positivism." Blanford was far out of his depth here – he knew very little about these factors and personalities. Livia went on in torrential fashion: "Long before these barren Jewish evaluations of the human psyche, the Ancient Greeks evolved their own, more fruitful, more poetical and just as reasonable. For instance, before that bunch of thugs who ruled Olympus there were others like Uranus who ruled the earth and was castrated by Chronos. Those severed genitals were thrown still frothing and writhing into the sea, and the foam they generated gave birth to Aphrodite. Which world do you prefer? Which seems the more fruitful?" Blanford could only repeat, whispering in that small stag's ear the stupid words, "I love you and I agree."

She touched his face – the haptic sense – and the poor fellow was mesmerised; he was in love, and so full of glory and distress that he could have accepted anything without query provided Livia was part of it.

Here on this moist fresh grass they lay, with their arms under each other's heads, staring up into the clear warm sky with its rising sunlight and light musical clouds – herald of another perfect day. It would soon be time to slip quietly away, locking the doors behind them, and make their sleepy way back to Tu Duc through the olive groves turning to silver in the breeze. The kisses of her hard little mouth with its thin lips, sometimes cut in expressions of smiling contempt or reserve, held a world of promises for him. She had promised to spend her last few nights in his room. "I shall be back in Paris again in three months if you want me," she added, and Blanford began actively, resolutely, planning ways and means to accept this marvellous invitation. Gazing into the *camera lucida* of the eye's screen he saw a vastly enlarged version of Livia, one which filled the whole sky, hovering over them both like some ancient Greek goddess. It seemed a fearful thing to have to share this marvellous creature with the others – but there was nothing to be done for the terms of reference dictated that they should do almost everything together. As their departure began to shape itself into a fact – at first the summer seemed endless and their return to the north a figment – it became imperative to go on as many excursions as possible, to see as much of the country as possible before the fatal day dawned. Constance was staying on in Provence to try and fix up Tu Duc a little against future habitation; Sam and Hilary and Blanford were to affront their final examinations before selecting a profession. The centre of gravity was slowly shifting. At dawn, unable to sleep, and heading for the lily pond for a dip Blanford came upon the two sisters naked upon the flagged path, walking with sleepy silence towards the same objective in the dusky bloom of daybreak. Slim and tall, with their upright carriage and hieratic style they looked like a couple of young Graces who had slipped out of the pantheon and into the workaday world of men, seeking an adventure. Blanford turned aside and waited until he heard the ripple of water; then he too joined them, sliding soundlessly into the pool like a trout. So the three sat quietly breathing among the lotus flowers, waiting for the sun to rise among the trees.

It was like a dream – the wet stone heads of the sisters, like statues come to life; the dense packages of silence moving about the garden suddenly drilled by a short burst of birdsong. "Perils and absences sharpen desire," says the ancient Greek poet. In all the richness of this perfect summer Blanford felt the pang of the partings to come – vertigo of a desire which must for the time being rest unrequited. Her wet hair made her look shaven; her pretty ears stood out pointed from her head, like gnomes at prayer. From the sunny balcony where breakfast waited they could see the swifts stooping and darting; how beautifully the birds combined with gravity to give life to this wilderness of garden which Constance had sworn never to have tidied and formalised. It was full of treasures like old fruit trees still bearing, strawberry patches, and a bare dry section of holm-oak – a stand of elderly trees – which had a truffle bed beneath.

Days had begun to melt and fuse together in the heat of Provence, their impressions of heat and water and light absolutely forbade them to keep a mental chronology of their journeys, jogging about the gorges of the Gardon in the old pony-cart, or taking the little toy train down to the sea to spend a night on the beach and attend a cockade-snatching bullfight at dusty Lunel. Ah! the little pocket train, which plodded down to the flat Carmargue, to take them to the Grau du Roi. It had such a merry holiday air; the carriages were so bright – red for the first class, yellow for the second, and green for the third. All with the legend PLM modestly painted on them. The long waits in tiny silent stations where the guard sometimes braked to a walking pace so that he could loiter in a field beside the track and gather a few leeks. When you were dying of thirst how good the fresh water from the pump at Aimargues tasted; it was really intended for the engine, but once the machine had drunk its fill it was the turn of the passengers. Once Hilary even used it as a shower while they were waiting for the connection which was to carry them down to the Saintes. In the dry heats of summer the odours of the sand and the sea came up to them from the beaches – and from the inland maquis that of thyme and rosemary bruised by the flocks of sheep. Sometimes they sat in a siding and let a train pass through from Nîmes which was full of the little black Carmargue bulls used in the cockade fights. Small stations on the roads to paradise, signal boxes at the end of the world; they would return after these excursions dazed with the sun and sea. And then in the evening Blanford would hear the sweet voice of Livia intoning the AUM of yoga as she sat in the green thicket behind the tower, re-charging her body, re-oxygenating her brain. Remembering a phrase from another life, "The heart of flesh in the breast is not the *vagra* heart; like an inverted lotus the valves of the flesh heart open by day and close by night during sleep."

The sleep of the south had invaded also their love-making, giving it a tonality, a resonance of its own; with Livia it was simple and rather brutal. He would never forget how she cried out "Ha" as she felt the premonition of the orgasm approaching; it was the cry of the Japanese swords-man before the shock of his stroke. And then, so extreme was the proof that she lay in his arms as if her back were broken.

Eating their picnic lunch among the brown rocks above the Pont du Gard, watching the eagles wheel and stoop, they all – as if by sudden consent – felt their minds drawn towards the thought of the impending future with the inevitable imperatives which choice would force upon them. Blanford was perhaps the luckiest for he would inherit a modest income which he would have no difficulty in supplementing by academic work – or so he thought. The brown-skinned Sam was less self-assured as he mused. "I shan't have a private income, and with the little intelligence I have in-herited I don't suppose I could get anything sensational in the way of a job. To tell the truth the Army seems the likeliest *pis aller* – though I am not very militant." He had been an active member of the Oxford Officers Training Corps and could with luck get a commission in a line regi-ment. Constance rested her arm lightly in the crook of his brown arm and smiled up at him, confident and at ease. There was no stress in their loving, while between Livia and

Blanford there was a kind of premonitory hopelessness; they were in that limbo where destiny, like an undischarged bankrupt, waited for them. They had gone too far to retreat now even if they had wished.

Hilary said: "I am going to surprise and perhaps pain you. I have been seriously tempted by the Catholic faith. I have the notion of really taking it up – if that is the word. I thought after next term to go into a retreat and receive instruction in it. I can easily do a little tutoring for a living. Then we'll see if the thing is lasting or wears out." He smiled round at the others, feeling suddenly abashed and unsure of himself; once these sentiments had been uttered aloud they seemed far less substantial and enriching than they had been before. He climbed down to his favourite diving plinth, above the river, poised, and suddenly fell like a swift to furrow the jade water far below. Sam sighed and rose to follow, followed by Blanford. Suddenly, by this brief conversation, the future had materialised before their eyes.

Blanford had brought a pretty little ring which he hoped to give to Livia, but the act seemed somehow embarrassing and confusing; he had not sufficient courage to indulge in definitive declarations – the only kind which would approximate to what he felt. And Livia needed none; she stared at him, smiling her hard little smile, holding her hand in his. They would meet again in Paris! Ah! in the cafés of that great epoch one arrived, distraught with love, and called for ink and paper, envelopes and stamps, while a concerned waiter, having supplied them, rushed for a *cassis*. Thus were great love-letters born – they would be sent by *pneumatique* and a helmeted motor cyclist would deliver them, like Mercury himself, within the hour.

Blanford decided to send her the ring by post when she had returned to Paris. On the last evening but one they went for a short walk together among the olive groves and Livia surprised him by saying: "I always think of you as a writer, Aubrey; people who keep copious diaries like you always have – they are really writers." She had noted his habit of scribbling in a school exercise book nearly every night before he got into bed. It was a self-indulgence he had, like most lonely people, permitted himself from early adolescence. And it was here, unwittingly, that Sutcliffe got born. Once at school one of his diaries had been pilfered from his locker and a teasing youth read out some passages aloud to a circle of laughing and taunting schoolmates. It was fearfully humiliating; and to guard against a repetition of such a torture Blanford had attributed his thought and ideas to an imaginary author called S. He also firmly lettered in the title "Commonplace Book", and put a few genuine quotations into it, to suggest that he was simply copying out things which struck him from the books he read. But slowly and insidiously S began to take shape as a person, a flippant and desperate person, a splintered man, destined for authorship with all its woes and splendours. To him he attached the name of the greatest cricketer of the day – also rather defensively; Sutcliffe was, in the cricket world, a household name. Yet over the years he was fleshed out by quotations which suggested the soliloquies of a lonely and hunted intellectual, a marginal man; Blanford took refuge in him, so to speak, from a world which seemed to him quite insensitive to intellectual matters, in fact calamitously philistine. Later when the great man actually emerged on paper and started his adventurous life of sins and puns Blanford was to adapt a hymn for his use, the first line of which was "Nearer My Goad to Thee." But this was much later. Now he simply looked into the eyes of Livia and replied steadily: "I don't think I could be imaginative enough, I'm too donnish I think."

But she was right.

And looking at her, watching her smiling at him, a

simple thought came into his mind, namely how marvellous not to be blind! Livia said: "Who is this S you are always quoting?" So she had been reading his exercise books behind his back! He answered "Schopenhauer" without a flicker of expression. But in the back of his mind was already looming a large fleshy man with pink knees pressed together, penis *en trompe-l'oeil* as he might say, whirling dumb-bells before an open window. The original Sutcliffe who was to keep his emotions in a high state of chaos; one of those novelists all out of shape from too frequent childbearing. Perhaps he was a poet? Yes, he wrote verses. Some had been published in *Isis*. He would send some to Livia in order to bolster her faith in him as a creative person. She had taught him several yoga *asanas* and now every morning he obediently performed them while he thought of her sitting somewhere out among the olives beyond the tower in the lotus pose which seemed to cost her no effort at all, intoning the Aum; or lying in the corpse posture, snuffing out her whole will and body, and by her meditation "swallowing the sky". He was rather afraid that all this was very much a fad, though he admitted to feeling better after it.

It was by these strange byways and unfrequented paths that years later he was able to track down that corpulent soak, that ignoble ape, Sutcliffe, whose vulpine quivering nose reddened at the approach of whisky, and whose shaggy body rejoiced to feel the warm thrust of alcohol in the nerves. Where did this extraordinary *alter ego* come from? He was never to discover.

Livia was looking at him curiously – a snake with a trigger in its tongue, a cat with afterthoughts. . . .

And now Felix Chatto came up the drive on a derelict bicycle and brought them an invitation from Lord Galen; it was for a farewell dinner before he took his own departure for Berlin. It would be agony to squeeze their swollen feet into socks and shoes, to unearth shirts and ties. . . . But they could not refuse the old man. Anyway it would be a good training for their return to the city after this bemusing Provençal holiday.

FIVE

Lord Galen Dines

WHEN I WAS A BOY", SAID LORD GALEN WITH A
massive simplicity, "I read a book called *The
Romance of Steam* and I have never forgotten it. It
had a red and gold cover with an engine on it and it began,
"The steam-engine is a mighty power for Good." Nobody
could tell if he were joking or not. He fell into a muse and
pulled his upper lip. Max the chauffeur, now transformed into
something between a major-domo and an Italian admiral by a
costume specially created for him, diligently carved the roast
chickens in their chafing dishes before serving them. His
black dress-trousers had a broad gold piping, and in the
lapels of his dress coat he carried the insignia of a *sommelier* –
a master of Cellars. It was he who had trundled up to fetch
five young people in the Hispano, and they had been very
grateful for the lift, for the walk was a long and dusty one
from Tu Duc.

The house Galen owned and occupied sporadically
throughout the year was as characteristic as the old man
himself – it had been built quite recently by a Greek arma-
ments king with whom he had business dealings; one old
tower was all that was left of the original chateau which had
stood on the site. All the rest had been rased to clear the
ground for the modern villa – architecture of calamitous
joviality – which, however, stood in handsome shady
gardens. "Nothing old-fashioned does for me," said the old
man forcibly; adding, "I have never drunk life through a
straw, you know." Jutting out his chin.

The original name of the house had been "The Acropolis", but Lord Galen, with characteristic Jewish modesty,

had renamed it "Balmoral"; the large painted board which announced the fact always gave Felix Chatto a twinge of horror as he turned into the drive – his taste had been educated to a very high pitch of refinement. The inside of the house also caused him pain by its exuberance; it was the kind of house that a successful but ignorant actress might order in Cairo. Masses of marquetry and leather and cretonne; the salon was raised on pillars so convoluted and painted that they resembled barbers' poles of the old style. It was wonderfully modern and slightly profligate in atmosphere. And on this particular evening they found a new visitor present who seemed to belong to it, to be most appropriate to the satin and damascene and scarlet leather. They had none of them met the Prince before, nor even heard of him; but it soon transpired that though he was an Egyptian prince of the blood he was also a business associate of old Galen. His presence lent a singular and appropriate touch to all this oriental décor for he wore dove-grey clothes, and dove-grey London spats over tiny boots polished like mirrors. His grey waistcoat sported pearl buttons, and he wore a stock which set off to admiration a lean and aquiline face which was almost as grey as the rest of him. In his lapel he wore a gold squirrel, on his finger a scarab ring.

Lord Galen performed the presentation with just the slightest trace of unction, adding afterwards, "Prince Hassad is an old business associate of mine." The Prince seemed extraordinarily meek, he ducked shyly as he shook hands; his hands were small, bird-like, twiggy, and he seemed glad to reclaim them after every action. Beside him on a chair lay a richly chased fly-whisk and a gorgeous fez with gold tassels of great lustre; the green band indicated not only his royal antecedents but also the fact that he had made the traditional pilgrimage to Mecca. At first blush it seemed that what was striking about him rested on the fact that his dress was exotic, his person foreign. But within a few moments the impression changed; they felt they were in the presence of some sort of oriental saint who sat so modestly but vividly before them, his face bowed, looking shyly up under his brows as he gazed from face to young face. His English was almost perfect, his French without a trace of a foreign accent or intonation. If ever the fact was commented upon the Prince was apt to say, smiling: "I learned both languages young. There is nothing else to do in the Royal harem but study."

"Champagne," said Galen with a lordly wave and there was a suggestive popping among the rock plants in the winter garden where the dumb secretary presided over a cocktail cabinet; and what a treat it was in all that summer thirst! The Prince sipped a glass and placed it beside him on the table; he was much reassured by the fact that they all talked French as well as English.

Constance, of course, won his immediate attention and admiration by her smiling good sense and swift French; it was to her that he chiefly addressed himself in order to explain himself and expound his habits to all of them – aware perhaps that he must seem a story-tale figure in the French country-side. "I am travelling north into Germany in my carriage, and Lord Galen is coming with me to transact some business on behalf of Egypt." Galen looked rather doubtful about this; he had offered to drive north in his elegant car, but the Prince had quietly insisted on the huge state landau with its four horses – a desperately slow method of getting about. He had also expressed a somewhat alarming wish, namely to visit a cathedral or two on the way north – a sentiment that Lord Galen found slightly morbid. But the little Prince was proposing to enjoy himself as a deeply civilised oriental should do when abroad, and there was nothing for it but to fall in with his wishes. But at night, in bed, Lord Galen gave a groan when he thought of their slow progress across

Europe in this royal contraption. At the moment it reposed in his garage where the two uniformed black Saidhis were currying the horses and watering them.

Needless to say, the Prince made an instant hit with the inhabitants of Tu Duc, though hardly less markedly with Chatto and the taciturn Quatrefages who had put on a tie for the occasion and whose flushed face suggested that he had perhaps had a drink or two to stimulate his courage for such a frightening occasion. Perhaps the Prince sensed this, for he at once paid the boy some special attentions, questioning him softly in his patrician French, and soon the clerk was quite at ease and sufficiently self-confident to venture on talking in an English which was not bad despite his marked accent. So the exchange of politenesses proceeded until Max with a grunt announced that they could come to table if they wished. The Prince put down his gold-tipped cigarette and asked permission to wash his hands; his body-servant, a tall Nubian clad in the scarlet sash of the royal *kavass*, helped him, holding the towels for him to wipe his hands on, and then sprinkling the royal fingers with scent at the end of the operation. The Prince dabbled some scent on his face also. Then he came modestly to table, where they all stood and waited for him; Lord Galen placed him between the two sisters which seemed to please him very much as he instantly engaged Constance once more in small talk.

From the kitchen came the clatter and chatter of the three young farm women who had been conscripted for this fête by the secretary; he himself took his meals apart in the study. "Every year", said Lord Galen happily, "I have this little beano as a farewell treat before leaving France. But it's the first time I have welcomed the Prince to my table." He beamed round him while Prince Hassad with his shy smile made a little self-deprecating *moue* of the lips, as if the allusion embarrassed him. "I am glad to be here," he said, and added:

"particularly because of the work you are doing on your romantic project, in which I find it very hard to believe. We Egyptians are very suspicious people."

"Quite right. Quite right," said Galen with approval, "but our little project is not all fancy, you know. We have certain definite lines of enquiry laid down. This treasure is not a will o' the wisp, eh Quatrefages?"

The Prince shook his head doubtfully. "As an investment?" he murmured, almost under his breath. He motioned to his servant, who had taken up his traditional food-taster's position behind his chair, to leave. It was as if he did not wish for an eavesdropper in the room in case the conversation became confidential. He looked prudently round the table and said: "Perhaps after dinner I could be given some facts about your search. Then I will be able to judge." Then, turning aside with a more definite air, he asked Livia to tell him what monuments he should see in the vicinity, and in her usual forceful way she offered to be his guide if he should so wish, at which he looked hesitant but grateful. "There is so much to see," said Lord Galen with a regretful sigh, "but I never seem to have the chance." The grotesque cat of the household which lay on its velvet cushion in the corner of the room gave a croak. It had smelt the chicken. Lord Galen regally cut a piece from his own portion and had it despatched to her by Max who got a serpentine hiss for his efforts. For such a frail-looking man the Prince was surprisingly adroit with knife and fork, and was soon deeply involved with second helpings and vegetables which he forked on to his side-plate, preferring to eat in the French fashion – to enjoy meat and vegetables separately. Nor did he neglect his glass of Tavel, which he held up to the light with a professional expression of appreciation, to admire its topaz glow. "Though a Moslem," he confided in his host, "I am anything but a fanatic. But I never overdo things in case my wife catches me." He gave a small sweet chuckle and lowered his eyes again.

"Of course," said Lord Galen soothingly, "to drink a little – it's all harmless jollity." Quatrefages had been taciturn and talkative by turns, had been flushed and pale also; Felix knew him well enough to decipher these indications. They betrayed that he had been drinking absinthe again; it made him fiery and apathetic by turns. Now he produced his little pendulum from his vest pocket and allowed it to swing over his glass of wine for a moment. Everyone watched him with interest, as if he were about to do a conjuring trick. But no. After a moment of intense study he put away his divining instrument and drained his glass, giving an involuntary belch as he did so. They all smiled indulgently but he gazed about him with a bloodshot eye and made a sign for Max to refill his glass, which the butler did, but not without an anxious glance in the direction of his boss.

Lord Galen was talking, however, and had not noticed this small diversion. He was talking about the pleasures of Germany, of the pleasant journey they were soon to enjoy together. "Pleasant and I hope profitable," he added. "The brothers Krupp will come in their special train into Austria and we shall become good friends, yes, very good friends." An emotional man, he felt the tears of friendship rising to his eyes. It was to be a most meaningful meeting, he assured the Prince. The Nubians would get what they wanted cheap because of his other interests. Felix whispered an aside to Blanford: "He doesn't seem to know what is going on over there." If Quatrefages divined by the pendulum, Felix divined by the stock pages of the *Financial Times*. The sinister drift of events in Germany had been an object of his concerned study for some time; why, even the Foreign Office Intels had been showing diplomatic unease about the situation – and here was Galen blithely chatting about financial speculations and business interests for all the world as if the country was stable and productive, and in a fit state to welcome foreign investment.

Normally Felix would have said nothing but now his curiosity got the better of him and he said: "I personally don't at all like what appears to be going on there. I am surprised that the situation has not alarmed you." Lord Galen bridled and said: "Situation?" And this gave Felix the chance to give a brief and rather succinct outline of the state of affairs in Germany and the possible issues. To all this Lord Galen listened with a condescending smile, but attentively; he rolled bits of bread in his side-plate and popped them into his mouth. But he politely heard his nephew out, and seemed no whit abashed by the nods and murmured agreement of the old Prince who seemed at least as well informed as Felix if not quite as anxious as the consul. In fact he was delighted at this diversion which he had been too polite to initiate, but which might clear up a lot of points which were still obscure to him. He glanced from one face to the other, trying to divine whether Lord Galen, under his somewhat ineffable air of serenity, was not playing a game with him – a game of investor's poker, so to speak.

But Livia, too, seemed to be on the side of Felix, for she too nodded agreement to the propositions which he put forward. When at last the question of Jewry came up Lord Galen had had enough of his nephew's presumptuous exposition and he held up his hand in a kind but firm way. "Everything you say sounds true, but I can assure you, Felix, that I know the contrary – I know because I have been there, and I have seen with my own eyes. You will imagine when first the press started these rumours about anti-Semitism that I took note, and indeed I felt a vague alarm. As a Manchester man I could not ignore it." For some reason he disliked and avoided the word "Jew" – perhaps because of old schoolboy associations? He preferred to use the circumlocution "Manchester man"; it sounded almost as if one were a member of an Oxford college. He repeated on a lower note, and more impressively: "As a Manchester man I could not ignore it. I was both personally and financially concerned, as you might say. So what did I do? Why, I went into the whole thing, I went over myself and investigated the state of the country and nature of the opposition to the government. Now, if I had had the slightest doubt, would I have invited you to come from Egypt? All the way from Egypt, eh? An old friend, eh?" There was a long pause in the conversation during which he and the Prince beamed at one another. But Felix shook his head and Livia stared at Galen with profound curiosity – was he just ill-informed, or just pretending in order to deceive the Prince?

Lord Galen was deceiving nobody but himself. "I went so far as to see the leader of the National Socialists himself. I spent a whole weekend with him in face-to-face discussion about his plans and sentiments." He looked round triumphantly and paused.

Then he lowered his voice and went on: "It was not possible to distrust the assurances of such a man; his sincerity was absolutely convincing. Mark you, he was no hotheaded youth but a mature man who had been through the whole war as an ordinary sergeant. He had seen the whole thing from the inside. He spoke most movingly and simply of the sufferings of his country, and of the political indignities the Allies had forced upon it. His only desire was to redress these wrongs and live at peace with the world. He gave me the most explicit outline of his policies and convictions – it was really heart-warming, I was touched almost to tears. We had been really very hard on the Germans. He was right to feel a certain mild resentment about the fact. But his whole attitude was grave and measured and his views long deliberated. And this is where I was first able to question him closely about the

423

alleged anti-Semitism of his party. There was no doubt that
the man was sincere – his whole face and manner betrayed it.
He knew, he said, that nobody could pull the wool over my
eyes, and that I was free to judge as best I may, but for his
part he could guarantee that the whole press campaign was
false, and had been stage-managed by political opponents.
His party were even thinking of creating a second Jewish
state, more stable than mandated Palestine, somewhere in the
East. He spoke with passion and conviction – and if ever I
trusted a man I trusted him. He showed me a long memorandum prepared by the party department of demography
about a Jewish state of ten million souls and asked me what I
thought of it. You can imagine my excitement. It was the
dream of the race to have a place of their own. It was most
reassuring to feel that a modern political leader could think
along these lines. He said with a smile: 'You see, Lord Galen,
in some ways we are more Zionist than the Zionists.' I found
him very splendid indeed."

Galen gazed round at the company whose expressions
varied from polite incomprehension to incredulity. Felix
listened to his uncle with startled astonishment, Livia with a
sort of tremulous doubt – was he roasting the Prince? The
rest of them neither knew very much nor cared whether these
views were true or false; only the Prince seemed delighted by
this brief exposition, and not unfamiliar with its details. His
clever grey face was like a silk handkerchief, folding itself
into smiles. He said with an air of elation: "And the contracts,
P.G. eh?" Lord Galen nodded.

"I was coming to that," he said; "it was right at the end
of our talks that we discussed the financial situation of his
Party. It was, to say the least, precarious, for he was facing
powerful vested interests who wished to see other leaders
take the helm of state. If he did not get into power what
would become of his dreams of founding a small Jewish

state? This is what made me think. I sounded him out on the whole question of foreign investment and he told me that he would offer substantial concessions in the future against present aid. In the light of all that had gone before I felt that the situation held out great promise for myself and my associates. Nevertheless, I never act hastily, and I once more went over the whole ground. It was clear to me that this was the chance of a lifetime – to offer a massive contribution to party funds which would be paid for later by wholesale business concessions. I consulted everyone – naturally some were highly doubtful of my good sense, or of his good faith. But my arguments prevailed, and pretty soon we hope he will get in, largely thanks to us; meanwhile, the document which we spent half the night discussing was signed solemnly by us both in the presence of witnesses. I brought it down tonight to show everyone."

He inserted his fingers in a cardboard tube and eased out a scroll which he unrolled and held up before them. It was typewritten and the seal looked expensive with its wax eagle. But it was too far for anyone to read the text, and after a brief exposure of it to the company, he prudently replaced it, smiling the while at the memory of his astuteness. The Prince made as if to clap his hands in appreciation of his host's business acumen.

Livia said she was feeling unwell, and rose with her napkin to her lips; it was nothing, she said, she wanted a breath of fresh air, that was all. They all rose from their chairs to register concern, but were ordered to remain seated, while Constance said: "It's nothing, but I'll go with her," and the two girls made their way out of the house on to the warm green lawns where Livia sank on her knees and then lay fully down and began to turn slowly from side to side. At first it seemed like some sort of paroxysm but in fact it was only an attack of laughter so strong that she was forced to cram her fist between her teeth as she laughed, rolling back and forth. Her sister squatted beside her and watched her with smiling curiosity, waiting patiently until the laughter died away into exhaustion. Livia produced a small pocket handkerchief and mopped up her eyes. "The old fool is giving them money," she said, still a trifle tremulously. "How they must be laughing." She rose now, sighing, and allowed Constance to dust her down. "I thought I would explode at table," said Livia, "and be forced to explain my laughter. Sorry for the diversion. But it's the joke of the year."

Constance knew little and cared nothing about all these problems, so she held her peace; but she linked arms with her sister and together the two women re-entered the dining-room once more where the Prince was just saying: "I also have a car to carry my luggage – but it is a lorry really because I travel with so much luggage." He sighed. In fact, as they later found, the auxiliary vehicle was a very large removers' van – the kind known as a pantechnicon. It carried, apart from the Prince's personal belongings, a crew of three servants. At the moment it was drawn up outside his hotel in Avignon, watched over by a kindly policeman; the Egyptian Embassy had signalled the authorities that the Prince was travelling in France.

The French customs had already been dazzled by the extraordinary contents of the van; all the Prince's boxes were made of rare wood and covered outside with coloured silk and inlaid with metal filigree. There was a royal coffin worthy of Tutankhamun. Expensive bridge tables. Enough plate and cutlery to give a banquet for thirty people. When later he showed them these wonders, which included four of his favourite hawks in case he might be in the mood for hawking, he was good enough to explain that what might seem rather superfluous to them was really very necessary for an Egyptian prince, because one never knew. One never really knew. But all this transpired a little while later when their acquaintance with the Prince had ripened. For the moment they sat at table still, but now over brandy and cigars, while Galen cracked walnuts vividly and chatted knowledge-ably on the subject of investments. The Prince drank off quite healthy swigs of cognac for a man who looked so slender. "Of the other matter – your buried treasure – we will speak later!" His tone was bantering, amused, which somewhat nettled Quatrefages, who glared at him.

The clerk was rather suffused now with drink and his mood was, from the point of view of an outside observer, fretful and precarious. Felix eyed him with curiosity and affection and wondered whether he was going to break out into an impassioned speech about the treasure. As a matter of fact the French boy, always a bit touchy, resented the Prince's smiling scepticism about the seriousness of the work they were doing; why, he wondered, did not Lord Galen insist upon it and say something in defence of it? But he sat mildly rolling bread balls and thinking while the weight of the Prince's scepticism grew and grew.

At last Galen said: "The tradition is a long one and it's been hunted for by many people; a lot of money has gone down the drain hunting for it, so far in vain. More than one consortium of interests has tried its hand. But it is only recently that some documents have come to light which might pin-point the *place*. There is no doubt that there was a treasure and that it disappeared during the trials of the Templars for heresy. After all, the Templars were the bankers of kings with enormous fortunes in their care. In the docu-ments of the trials which are being deciphered and printed in Toulouse it is clear that the burning question for the investigators who tortured them was financial rather than ecclesiastical. Where had the treasure gone? The questions of heresy were all very well – the Inquisition looked into that very thoroughly; but what the Chancellor of Philippe le Bel wanted to know was where the hell they had put the boodle. This is why the trials were so long drawn out; they could have popped off the whole lot of the Templars in a few months. Why did they hang about? They were hoping for a lead which would guide them to the treasure. That was the only thing that obsessed the King – for the state was bankrupt."

He paused and turned to his clerk for confirmation and support. But Quatrefages glared at his plate in a brown study. The Prince was unsmiling now; he had suddenly remembered the stories of buried treasure which figured so largely in Egyptian folklore and the idea appealed to him. His doubts began to be qualified by the reflection that if there were nothing to the story but hot air surely it would not have attracted the attention of a renowned business baron with a reputation for flair and strong dealing? But he realised that he had offended Quatrefages by his bantering tone and he made amends now, reaching out to touch him on the wrist in an apologetic way which quite won the boy's heart and put him once more into a very good humour. *"C'est vrai,"* he said to the smiling old man, "it is true; we have some very precious indications. It is probably a crypt now covered in grass. Part of a chateau or a chapel or a monastery. The sign was an orchard of olives planted like this...." He drew an envelope from his pocket and with his fountain pen sketched a quincunx of trees.

"I think", said Galen, "the thing would be for you to visit Quatrefages' little office at the hotel and see how he is tackling the matter. It's great detective work. The scent has led us as far as Avignon or its immediate surroundings. We are going through the records of the chateaux and chapels in the immediate vicinity of the town; there are plenty of them, as you may imagine, because of its importance as a religious centre during the period when the Popes made it their headquarters. But there's hope; o yes, we have hope. That little affair with King John gave me confidence in my own private intuition. You remember? That also looked foolish, but we won through, didn't we?"

It was perfectly true. Chatting one day to a young Oxford historian at a reception, Galen had been intrigued by a remark dropped at random; the subject of treasure had come up – heaven knows in what context – and the young don enumerated several examples of buried treasure from his history studies. Among them, and one which he found perhaps the most curious, was the loss of King John's treasure in the Wash. One would have thought that that at least was traceable; the depth of the channel was negligible and clearly marked. The local movement of tides and sand bars at the ford was extremely limited. Yet despite the efforts of several generations of treasure-seekers nothing had ever come to light. The treasure itself was the most important ever to be lost in England – almost priceless indeed. This stray remark was enough to fire the admiration of Lord Galen who had always fancied himself as a sort of poet of the commercial instinct. He made a note in his little red morocco notebook and called a meeting.

He knew, of course, that in law all treasure trove belongs to the Crown which has the right, but not the obligation, to reward the finder with a bounty. Lord Galen felt that if he could secure a government promise to reward him to the tune of fifteen per cent for anything he might find, the project might prove to be worth his while. The Prime Minister was a personal friend and was coming to dinner with him the following week. He took the opportunity to explore the situation. He was given a fair wind. Dealing at such a high level with such matters one does not ask for guarantees or formal contracts. He would, he said, be content with an exchange of letters serving as a declaration of intent. Of course it was a risk. The project was a costly one and might end in failure. The Government had nothing to lose. The upshot of the matter was that he was able to attract finance for the project and indulge his sense of romance by having the Wash surveyed from the air and inviting engineers to devise the sort of machinery necessary first to locate, then to raise, the buried treasure. It had taken over two years, but had at last been successful. Lord Galen became as famous in Fleet Street as he was in the City. The profits were extremely handsome.

"I agree," said the Prince on a note of contriteness. "It was fully justified by the outcome, and a lesson to sceptics." Galen accepted the accolade gracefully, nodding his personal agreement with the remark. "That is why I thought of you, my dear Prince, when we embarked upon this little venture – which is perhaps a trifle more risky even than old King John. Many more people have tried to locate what we are hunting for – and there is always a chance that someone might have found it and kept the matter secret in order not to surrender it to the French Government. But I have made exactly identical arrangements with the Government here, and have reserved a fine meaningful percentage for my shareholders. The rest is a matter of science, of luck, and the flair of Quatrefages who will bring you up to date on what we have so far found."

Quatrefages looked steadily at the Prince and nodded gravely. "We will speak," he said on a note of confirmation. And the Prince stroked his hand once more with a warmly oriental gesture, saying: "Of course; we understand each other, no?"

At which the conversation once more became general and the contingent of guests from Tu Duc began to feel a faint disposition to yawn despite the earliness of the hour. The candles had burnt down and begun to drip. Max docked them and changed some for new. "I think", said Felix, "we should consult the clock and perhaps start moving off in good order." But a sudden loneliness assailed Lord Galen at the thought of spending the night alone with his asthmatic cat. His voice became quite quavery and pleading as he said: "O do not go so early. Let us have a last stirrup-cup on the terrace. After all who knows when we shall meet again?" Blanford felt the words entangle the muscles of his throat as he looked at Livia across the table. She smiled at him with a slow affectionate expression, but he was so deeply sunk in his own conjectures that he did not respond. How brown she had become – almost the colour of a gipsy! All of a sudden he too was assailed by a fearful sense of anguish and disenchantment – later he would recognise this as premonitory; but an irrational and boundless fear of what might come to pass for them all, and in particular for himself and Livia who inhabited so temporarily this little enclave of passionate feeling in the immensity of a hostile world. The darkness inside was now (for they were on the terrace) matched by the darkness without.

They sat over new whiskies and coffees to accustom themselves to the faint glimmer of stars. Occasional fireflies snatched in the deep grass of the lawns which that year had not been mowed. The faint wind had turned a point or two northwards and brought with it a welcome and refreshing chill which towards dawn would cause (Felix noted this) a heavy dew upon the leaves and window-panes. "It's beautiful," said Lord Galen with an unwonted warmth of feeling as he gestured towards the star-scattered darkness where the dense mists turned and shifted, now hiding, now revealing the vibrating depths of the Provençal night sky. They heard Max yawning his violet yawns within as he disencumbered the table; each time he passed the stricken Wombat it snapped blindly at his ankles.

Lord Galen contemplated the long empty reaches of insomnia which awaited him as a condemned man might think of an age of servitude ahead. He had started taking sleeping pills which guaranteed him some rest but was depressed to notice that he needed increased doses to maintain the equilibrium. It was the time of night when the thought of his daughter echoed and ached within him with a dull neuralgic insistence, poisoning his peace of mind. Sometimes after midnight he rang for his secretary and bade him produce the chessmen. They would sit silently hunched over a game until the first pale streaks of dawn woke the birds in the park. Sometimes he took a stroll in the icy dew, his footfalls silenced by the deep grass. It was rare that he could return to his bed on such occasions. He hung around until five-thirty when he heard the alarm go off in Max's room. Pretty soon the yawning black man would come and give him breakfast in the kitchen – waffles and maple syrup. Galen ate hungrily. By then he had already despatched his yawning secretary to his room. Soon it would be time to dip down the dusty hill into the town and watch the first passenger train set off for Paris. . . .

Rehearsing all this in his mind he felt the weariness and spleen assail him anew. "I suppose you all want to go to bed," he said at last, rather bitterly. "I can see you yawning and stretching, Felix – not very polite." Felix sprang to attention, metaphorically speaking, and blushed his apologies. He too was quailing at the thought of the night which confronted him; this temporary sleepiness would serve to get him to bed all right, but after an hour or two he would find himself switched on like a light and unable to prevent himself rising to make coffee, and at last, to walk the silent town. They smiled now at each other but the weariness engendered by their thoughts suffused the air, and at last the Prince, fearing that people could not leave before a prince of the blood took

his leave, called in soft Arabic for his landau. The tall major-
domo was standing just inside the drawing-room, and relayed
the message in a low voice. There was a long period of confused noise and at last the travel-apparatus of the Prince
rumbled round the house and came to rest before the flight
of marble stairs where the restless horses struck sparks from
the cobbles with their hooves and whinnied softly. *Noblesse
oblige*.

The Prince accepted his fez and fly-whisk from the
hands of his servant and then turned smiling to take his leave.
"Well, if you young people will forgive me. . . ." he said,
pressing their hands for a second in his. "I will expect you all
to a drink tomorrow in my hotel at seven." He did not wait
for a formal acceptance, but turned to embrace his host in the
French fashion, giving him a dab on the cheek with his lips.
He smelt aromatic, he smelt of camphor like a mummy – so
thought Lord Galen as he returned the accolade. Now the
Prince climbed into his coach and turning back said: "Can I
give anyone a lift? Surely Mr. Chatto? Quatrefages, no?"
They accepted his offer in order to spare Max an extra detour.
As they stepped into the landau and sat down beside the
Prince he remarked rather unexpectedly: "I feel like a bit of
fun tonight, to be sure."

They rumbled off into the darkness and the Prince
began a long and animated conversation with his staff in
guttural Arabic. He seemed to be asking them for information
about something. Then, aware perhaps that it was somewhat
impolite to talk in a language the others did not understand,
he ventured on an explanation directed largely at Quatrefages. "I am asking them to take us to a good house – surely
there must be a nice *pouf* in Avignon?" Felix choked with
astonishment but Quatrefages acted as if he had foreseen such
a departure and chuckled as he slapped the Prince on the knee
in a manner as familiar as it seemed to the dismayed consul

downright vulgar. "Of course, of course," said the clerk with a gesture towards the night sky, as if invoking all its starlit bounty upon the head of the grinning Prince.

Felix found that something distasteful had entered the expression of the Prince; those grave, sweet expressions, those silent modesties, had given place to a new set of facial looks – a trifle perky and monkey-like. He looked elated and full of zest; it seemed as if his intentions and desires had become a trifle debased, a trifle vulgar. "You aren't taking him to a brothel?" he said *sotto voce* to Quatrefages, who himself had changed but in a milder degree. He looked slightly tipsy and insolent. "Indeed I am," he said in an airy way, "the old darling is a Gypp and needs a cleanser. He will absolutely love Riquiqui. I will hand him over to old Riquiqui and see what she can provide." Felix looked miserable and alarmed. The Prince was talking Arabic again, heedless of them. "If he catches something," said Felix, "my uncle will never forgive you. Anyway I shan't go; it's too risky. If my uncle thought . . ." Quatrefages said simply but trenchantly "F**k your uncle."

The advice, Felix felt, was apposite and chimed with his own feelings. But it was all too easily said. Moreover he was not at all sure how the sentiment could be implemented. It was partly his cursed uncle and partly the dignity of the Foreign Office which nagged him. He sighed under the importunity of these ideas and set his mind firmly against this frivolous excursion, stifling all his regrets. Actually he would have given anything for an evening of good fellowship and a touch of profligacy. Ah well! The coach went stumbling and swaying through the dark olive glades to where at the outer edges of the darkness the lights of the city gleamed; from the quarter of the gipsies there came a thin plume of wood-smoke. It was still early. Owls whistled in the secret trees. The faint rumour of the city gradually evolved itself from their own noise of creaking coachwork, jingling harness and clattering horseflesh. The Prince was in a great good humour as he sat with an arm thrown round the shoulders of Quatrefages. He was occasionally slipping into his elegant French now as a concession to his companion. "I have a few small oddities of conduct", he said thoughtfully, "which are not unusual for a man of my age. Do you think they will understand?" Quatrefages gave a reassuring grin as he answered. "At Riquiqui they are used to everything, they cater for everything. And as they are frequented by the chief of police they are very much *à l'abri*." Reassured, the Prince beamed and squeezed his knee.

Felix had never been to Riquiqui's sordid establishment except with Blanford – and that for no questionable purpose. Once they had hunted for Livia during a night walk and the gipsies had directed them to try Riquiqui. The sordid surroundings and the darkness did not commend themselves to the two young men; and the personage of Riquiqui herself inspired the worst misgivings. She had opened a cautious inch in response to their tapping upon the rotten oak door. The little side street in which the house stood was pitch dark, and smelt of blocked drains and dead rats. The houses immediately to right and left of Riquiqui's had fallen down or been knocked down; their foundations gaped. Weeds sprouted everywhere. Blanford professed to find the place sinister but romantic – but of course he was lying. Felix was plainly nervous.

Riquiqui had enormous breasts bulging out of the top of a sort of sack dress, divided at the waist by a primeval drawstring. She had a wall-eye which gave her the air of looking over your shoulder while she spoke to you – which they found disconcerting. Moreover, lupus had ravaged her impure face – a burst of purple efflorescence covered one side of it. She tried to present her clear side rather too obviously, but from time to time she was forced to turn and present the diseased profile with its great splash of suffused blood vessels turning to crimson-lake and purple. A faint candle illumined the scene – the gaunt stairs behind her. She could give them no indication of Livia's whereabouts though she seemed to know, from their explanations, the person they were speaking about, for she nodded a great deal and said, "Not today" repeatedly, which suggested, at any rate, Livia was in the habit of calling in at this disreputable establishment. Curiously enough the information, far from depressing Blanford, elated him; he admired the insouciant and courageous way Livia went her own way, busied herself with her own affairs, without expecting their protective company. But Felix found this attitude inconsequent, even compromising.

But tonight, he told himself, there was to be no such excursion for the consul. Pleading a slight headache he had himself dropped off at the station; there was still time to sit and relax at the buffet over a coffee – after the bustle and conversation of a party he loved to spend a few moments alone, thinking his own modest thoughts. A train had pulled out for the north; the engine gave a whiff or two, as if it were calling back over its shoulder. The little *fiacres* stood anchored in the monotony of their function as train-waiters. Later when he set out on his walk he might feed the horses a sugar-lump or two if he felt lonely; this would lead to a conversation with the sleepy drivers.

But for the moment he had had his fill of conversation. The Prince had rumbled off into the darkness with his coach. From the neighbouring livery-stables came the noise of horses coughing and stamping. A bell trilled and wires hummed. Avignon was beginning to settle down for the night – that long painful stretch of time which must somehow be affronted. Felix yawned – yes, it was all very well, but would it last? He paid for his coffee and sauntered across under the frowning darkness of the Porte St.-Charles. It would not take him long to return. Then he would undress and go to bed doggedly; yes, doggedly. But as he neared the villa his nerves gave a jump for there was the figure of a man sitting on his front door-step smoking and waiting for him. It was a mere silhouette; he could not at first make out his identity.

For a moment he hesitated timorously, and then, cursing himself for a coward, advanced with a deliberate *sang-froid* to reach the garden gate. "There you are!" cried Blanford cheerfully. "I wondered if the Prince had taken you off on a binge." Felix recounted his journey home in the coach and Blanford chuckled. He said, "I suddenly decided not to go to bed; we got Max to drop us off and walked the quarter of a mile home – it's not far, after all." Felix opened the front door and entered the musty little villa. "I wondered if you would be walking tonight," said Blanford; and suddenly Felix seemed to sense the loneliness and misgiving behind the words. "Is there anything wrong?" he asked unexpectedly and Blanford shook his head. "No, it's just the end of this perfect holiday and one doesn't want to waste the time on sleep. I went home dutifully with the others but couldn't get to sleep, so I headed for town."

Yes, there was something lame about this long explanation. Felix put a kettle to boil and prepared to make some coffee. Then the explanation of Blanford's tone struck him forcibly and made everything clear. Livia had disappeared, and he had suddenly missed her and decided jealously to come and see if she were with Felix! It was true. Blanford could not help it – though he cursed himself roundly for butting in. He was propelled, as indeed Felix was, by a quite uncontrollable jealousy, which came and went in spasms, and which both struggled to surmount by reminding themselves that they should really be above such feelings. It was no good.

Thinking of all this, Felix poured out the dreadful Camp coffee which was made of liquid chicory and smiled acidly upon his friend as he said (unable to disguise the tone of quiet malice in his voice): "I suppose it's Livia again?"

"Yes," said Blanford surrendering reluctantly to the truth, "it's Livia."

Felix was suddenly furiously contemptuous of this spoilsport friend of his. His pent-up feelings broke loose. "And just suppose that she wanted to be alone with me, to walk with me?" Blanford nodded humbly and said: "I know. I thought of that, Felix. I am most awfully sorry. I just couldn't resist coming here. I felt I had to find her. I am so sorry, I know you care for her too. But I have asked her to marry me later on. . . ." His voice trailed away into silence while his friend sat opposite trying to convey his disapproval and annoyance by small reproving gestures. As a matter of fact, at a deeper level than all this superficial annoyance, he felt a certain misgiving about Livia as a suitable person to marry. To love and if possible lie with – yes. "Marriage", he said sharply, "is quite another affair." Blanford detested the curate's tone in which Felix uttered this sentiment. "Yes," he said, becoming rather acid in his turn, "it happens to be my affair at the moment. That's why I took the liberty of coming. But if my presence upsets you I can take myself off. You only have to say." Felix was on the horns of a dilemma here; for if he were alone and sleepless later on he would welcome company; but if Livia was driven off by the presence of Aubrey . . . it would be far better if he went home now. Which solution was the better? He went into the bedroom to consult his little clock. The hour was pretty advanced now, and the likelihood of Livia coming rather remote. He returned to the disconsolate Blanford and said: "Were you thinking of a walk, then?"

Blanford shook his head and said: "Only as far as

Riquiqui's to see if I can pick up her trail. It's a lovely night."

It was a lovely night! The words echoed in the skull of Felix as he apportioned the last of the coffee and decided that he would not go to bed, he would after all walk. Moreover he now sensed that behind Blanford's tone of voice lurked an anxiety, a fear almost of the gloomy and ramshackle quarter of the town which he proposed to visit in search of the girl. He couldn't resist a slight touch of malice in his own voice as he said: "I suppose you'd want to go to Riquiqui's alone?" Blanford looked up at him and said, somewhat humbly, "On the contrary. I'd welcome company. You know that that whole section of the town scares me a bit – it's so disreputable with its bordels and gipsies."

This went some way towards mollifying Felix who betook himself to the bedroom where he changed out of his formal suit into something lighter, and topped it by his college blazer and a silk scarf. Through the half-open door he caught a glimpse of the glorified alcove which served as the so-called spare room where Livia sometimes lodged. The little cupboard stood there with its door ajar; he had already shown Blanford the male kit hanging up in there. He himself had never seen her in full disguise, though once or twice she had worn trousers to wander about the town. Blanford had made no comment – no comment whatsoever. What did he think? Felix could not say. For his part he found the whole question of marriage unreal – despite the magnetism of her beauty to which he was as much bound as Blanford. But there was something else which had qualified his passion. It was something he remembered with a certain shame – it was not in his nature to spy on people; yet, one evening, in a sudden fit of curiosity and without any conscious premeditation, he had walked into her room, opened the wardrobe and felt in the pockets of her brown cheap suit for all the world as if he knew that he would find something there – which indeed he

439

did. It was a slip of paper torn from an exercise book – a love letter no less, but written in arch, lisping style, as if by an adolescent girl.

"*Ma p'tite Livvie je t'aime,*" and so on in this vein, but riddled with misspellings and turns of phrase which suggested an uneducated and very youthful author. Felix examined the hand with the magnifying glass which was always on his desk, and decided that it was not the writing of a gipsy but of a schoolgirl. But his investigations went no further and after a moment of hesitation he replaced the note where he had found it and went whistling light-heartedly back to his office, glad in spite of himself that his rival was being betrayed. From time to time he frowned, however, and tried to banish the uncharitable and unfriendly feeling – for he was a good-hearted boy who believed in friendship like the rest of us. Yet it kept coming back. Sometimes, walking beside Blanford he repeated the words in his mind, "*Ma p'tite Livvie je t'aime*", almost letting them come to the surface and find utterance. It was very vicious, this sort of behaviour, and he did not approve of it; but he could not help it.

They finished their coffee and Felix put the cups and saucers into the sink in his usual somewhat fussy way. Blanford waited for him, smoking thoughtfully with an air of profound preoccupation touched with sadness. A curious polarity of feelings had beset him – somewhere in the deepest part of himself he was actually glad that Livia was going, that they were to be separated for a time. It would take a weight off his mind, as the saying goes; he had indeed become a little impatient with himself, with the extent of his complete immersion in this unexpected infatuation for a girl who, more often than not, seemed hardly to know he was there, so remotely distant did she seem from all thought of him. The force of this attachment had somewhat exhausted him, and he knew for certain that it had prevented him from enjoying

Provence as deeply as he might have done. Loving – was there some sort of limitation inherent in it? This was the first time he had ever asked himself the question plainly. But the answer eluded him.

"*Avanti*," said Felix, who out of boredom had started to study Italian; and together the two young men crossed the withered garden and advanced among the criss-cross of tenebrous streets and alleys which led them towards Les Balances, that desolate and ruined quarter sloping down towards the rustling Rhône. "I don't suppose she really gives a damn about me," said Blanford unexpectedly, throwing his cigarette onto the pavement and stamping it out with petulance. He was dying for Felix to contradict him, to come out with some reassuring remark, but Felix was not going to pander to his mood. "I suppose not," he said composedly, looking into the deep velvety sky, smiling to himself. Blanford could have strangled him for his composure there and then. He made up his mind to find Livia if they had to walk all night; and when he found her to pick a quarrel with her, to try and make that dry little lizard of a girl cry. Then they would make it up and . . . here he lost himself in pleasant reveries. But what if she had returned home and was snug in his bed while they were wandering about like a couple of fools? It was amazing how his spirits soared optimistically at one thought and then sagged earthwards at its successor. Somewhere at the bottom end of this keyboard – among the bass notes – there lurked migraine and the ancient neurasthenia. They waited for him. He always carried a couple of loose aspirins in his pocket. He took one now, swallowing it easily. *Absit omen.* "It is not easy, I have never been in love before. And whores scare me a bit."

Felix took on a man-of-the-world tone as he said: "O pouf! I regard them simply as a disagreeable necessity in a puritan age."

"I once got clap after a bump supper," said Blanford gloomily, "and it wasn't at all gay. It took ages to get itself cured."

Felix felt an unexpected wave of admiration for his friend; so he had suffered in some subterranean lavatory decorated by horrific posters depicting all the possible ravages of sexual intercourse indulged in without a rubber sheath? The man was a hero after all! "It must have been dreadful," he said with a suddenly alerted wave of sympathy and Blanford nodded, not without pride. "It was, Felix."

They had started downhill, sloping along a set of streets which straggled from the height of the Hotel de Ville to the actual medieval walls which alone prevented them from seeing the scurrying sweeps of the Rhône. A glimpse of Villeneuve on its great promontory – that was all; and a coffin-like darkness in whose soft shifting exhalations of mist prickled a star or two. Felix had brought a torch, but used it sparingly in the deserted streets. The noise of their footsteps sounded lonely and disembodied in the night. The municipal lighting hereabouts was haphazard and sporadic. The last two streets they crossed to reach Riquiqui were in dense darkness; the pavements had melted away, and occasional cobble-stones lay about ready to trip them up. The quarter was an undrained one and smelt accordingly. Riquiqui's establishment stood at an angle in a *cul de sac* and its doors opened into the street. Bundles of old rubbish lay about – broken chairs, bits of marble, sheets of tin, lead pipes and refuse. It stood, the house, like the last remaining molar in a diseased jaw; on either side there was a weed-infested waste land with the remains of low walls. A window gave out into this gloom with a yellow and baleful light. But the hallway of the house seemed to be in darkness, to judge by the blind fanlight over the door.

There was no sign of the coach either – which Blanford

had christened "The Prince's Pumpkin" – but this could have been dismissed and sent away to the livery stables where its horses were lodged. Or perhaps they had gone to some other establishment of the same category – though there were not many in the town which enjoyed the reputation and indeed the official protection of Riquiqui, for she also lodged people and operated (if such a thing can be believed) as a foster mother to waifs and strays. But she nevertheless remained in a somewhat ambiguous position as one who kept a house of ill-fame and was a friend to the gipsies; they called her "angel maker" for the children confided to her care were unwanted ones and would soon – so the popular gossip went – be on their way to heaven to join the angels. The very fact of her existence was explained by her payment of bribes, in cash and in kind, which was at least plausible; for she was fairly openly frequented by minor officials and the lower echelons of the police force. The two young men trod the streets of this raffish quarter with a certain native circumspection, though Felix once or twice whistled under his breath as if to register confidence.

At least they stopped before the door of Riquiqui and Blanford advanced to tap upon it with timorous knuckles. It was not much in the way of a summons and it evoked neither light nor voices in response. They waited for a while in a downcast manner. Then Felix picked up a brick from the gutter and made a more reasonable attempt at a knock – he didn't like making a noise in the street at this time of night. Supposing that nearby windows were thrown up and exasperated voices urged them to go to hell? They would scamper away like rabbits. But no windows were raised, no voices admonished them; worst of all there was no sound from behind the unyielding front door of the brothel. An exasperated Blanford tried a couple of kicks, but this was not much use either as he was wearing tennis-shoes. They waited and then knocked again, without the slightest result. The silence drained back into the darkness. The only movement was the stirring of large birds in the ragged storks' nests on the battlements. Somewhere – not really so far, but sounding as if it were situated at the other end of the known world – the Jacquemart struck an hour, though they were not quite certain which hour. "Not a sound," breathed poor Blanford with a sigh of despair. "There must be someone there."

Reluctantly they started to move away when Felix had a brainwave; his torch played among the rubbish heaps which filled the abandoned ruin at one side of the brothel. There were some oil drums in the corner and they gave him an idea. He rolled one over the mossy surface and placed it against the wall under the lighted window, mounting it very slowly, with a thousand precautions; for he did not wish to fall among the foundations and break his back. At last he levelled off, and, holding onto the wall, craned his neck towards the light. "It's a lavatory," he said in a low voice. "They've left the light on and the door open." Then he drew a deep breath and said: "Jesus! There they are! Just look at our old Prince!"

Blanford, consumed with curiosity, hurried to take possession of his own olive oil drum and was soon standing up against the wall beside Felix, gazing into the lavatory and, through it, into the relatively well-lighted hallway leading to an inner courtyard full of divans and potted plants of somewhat decayed aspect. And sure enough there was the Prince, spread out on a sofa, and perfectly at ease; while Quatrefages, clad only in a shirt and red socks, sat by his side sipping whisky and talking with the greatest animation. It took a moment or two to register the more piquant details of this scene which had all the air of taking place in some small theatre – it looked a bit unreal.

The Prince had divested himself of everything that covered the top half of his grey little body; he sat, so to speak,

clad only in his heavy paps, and had a sort of chinless grandeur. His nether half was clad in lightweight Jaeger combinations which stretched to the ankle and through the fly-slit of
which depended the royal member with its innocent pink tip.
Quatrefages also presented a somewhat equivocal appearance,
being clad only in a shirt and socks. He was clearly engaged
in a long explanation or exhortation addressed to Riquiqui
who stood almost out of range and half in shadow – so that
it seemed that the clerk was talking with animation to two
outsize breasts bulging out of a dirty shift. Beside them stood
a puzzled female dwarf with a hideously rouged face as if
ready for the circus; she was clad in white organdie with a
marriage veil. Moreover, she was jingling with trinkets and
had obviously been dressed against a very special occasion.
As a matter of fact she had been specially dressed for the
Prince, but now his companion was expressing the Prince's
discontent with her, and indeed his general discomforture,
presumably because of her age. Yes, it was not hard to follow
the train of the argument. The dwarf was too old and too big
to appeal to the Prince. But they were being polite about it
and the horrible little creature bobbed her agreement and
dipped lovingly into a big box of Turkish Delight which the
Prince had pushed towards her. She had huge, discoloured
teeth like rotting dice.

As for Riquiqui she appeared to be at her wits' end to
meet the unusual demand. Languidly the little man extended
a hand and indicated that what he desired was much smaller,
very much smaller. He lent weight to his argument with
flowery little gestures which indicated clearly that there was
no question of ill-feeling or bad humour involved. He was
asking, not commanding. His tone was civilised and equable.
He proffered the box of loucoumi and Riquiqui in her turn
dug out a cube of Turkish Delight and wolfed it, licking the
powder off her talons, before dusting her shift to remove the

last traces of it. Then she held up her finger as one who sees daylight at last and bustled off, leaving them to their whisky. The misshapen little phantom of pleasure followed her, ripping off her bridal veil with an abrupt gesture like an actor quitting a wig as he left the stage.

Left alone, the two occupants of the centre of the stage – the suggestion of intimate theatre was irresistible because of the severely framed scene and the brilliantly stagey lighting – reloaded their glasses and conversed in low tones. The clerk was flushed and jovial-looking in his somewhat unclean shirt. The Prince in his long combinations looked quite regal still in an attenuated sort of way. He scratched his small decoration and exuded amiability. They had not long to wait, for at last Riquiqui burst in, flushed with success, hand in hand with two little girls dressed in a manner appropriate to a First Communion. Their faces were heavily rouged, which gave them the appearance of wearing painted masks through which they peered with unafraid but puzzled wonder. She paused, the huge woman, for dramatic effect as she entered, presenting her charges boldly but hesitantly. *Eureka*! She had remembered the existence of a couple of "angels", no doubt.

The result was a foregone conclusion. The Prince's radiant features expressed his delight and relief; he looked like a small boy who was turning cartwheels from sheer elation. Quatrefages folded his arms after setting down his glass and beamed upon the lady while the Prince extended his hands to take hers and move them half-way to his lips in a simulated kiss of congratulation. The two little children stood mumchance, but with a kindly air. They were sucking sweets. The Prince stood up and embraced them warmly; then he waved his arms and muttered something in Arabic and his major-domo (who must have been waiting in the shadows, the wings, so to speak) entered the lighted stage leading two large and beautifully groomed Afghan hounds on a gold leash.

The Prince clapped his hands in ecstasy and gave a little crow of laughter; he beamed round on the assembled company. Clearly everything was in order now. The next stage. . . .

Riquiqui threw open a side door which gave on to a bedroom of the house which had been decorated in the most extravagant fashion; a vast damascened bed lay under a lozenge-shaped pier-glass. It was covered in a gold cloth, and the shelf above it was full of children's dolls clad in folklore costumes. The walls themselves were draped with scarlet shawls and the whole context suggested a scene from *The Phantom of the Opera*. The little manikins looked as if they were the shrunken bodies of real children which had been patiently and fastidiously pickled before being dressed as harlequins, Arlésiennes, Catalans and Basques. Into this décor she ushered the Prince, now amiably holding the hands of the two children. The dogs, now off the leash, followed at his heels like well-drilled servants who knew their duty. The stage-set was so piquant and the actors so unaware that they were being observed that the two eavesdroppers almost forgot to feel the anxious disgust which had started to seize them.

But it was at this moment that Quatrefages entered the lavatory right under their noses and closed the door on this equivocal spectacle. He sat himself down on the throne and proceeded to more primitive business. They soon could hear his grunts and sighs right under their chins. It was quite a dilemma – they did not wish to be discovered in this spying posture. And they were suddenly aware of the precariousness of their station, for they could not simply jump down and run away. In the darkness one could have broken an ankle. So they stayed on, mentally swearing at the wretched clerk, and hoping that he would soon finish and restore them the lighted stage and the grotesque Egyptian. On the other hand, they could hardly pass the rest of the night standing up there

447

on the oil drum watching the sexual evolutions of this
Mecca-blessed libertine. A wild indecision reigned which
matched their general situation; neither spoke because
neither could think.

No doubt their frustration and gradually mounting
discomfort would have sooner or later forced them to take a
decision, but fate determined otherwise, for Quatrefages
completed his business to his own satisfaction and pulled the
chain; and as if by the same token the door was thrown open
and the brightly lit stage once more revealed to them. There
was a slight change of disposition – the door of the inner
room was almost closed and even by craning the neck it
would not have been possible to see with any clarity exactly
what the Prince and his livestock were up to. Riquiqui was
sitting down in a manner so relaxed as to suggest the puncture
of an inner tube; and she was profiting by the absence of the
Prince to renew her attack on the box of gummy sweets.

The little hunchback crossed the stage – now nude –
and seated herself at what appeared to be a small upright
piano covered in coloured shawls. She began to pick out
monotonous little tunes on it with one finger. Quatrefages
firmly retrieved his drink and spread himself over a divan
with a relaxed and gluttonous air. The conversation flagged.
There were a few indistinct sounds from the direction of the
Prince's room but nothing very concrete that might be interpreted. The whole atmosphere had become now slack and
humdrum, lacking in great interest, and Blanford began to
find his toes going to sleep. It was clearly time to get down
and go home. He was about to express this thought to his
friend when there was a sudden irruption onto the little stage
which all at once reinjected vitality into the drama, brought
everything alive again.

The major-domo burst clucking and chattering into
the room once more (apparently through the front door, for

they heard the bolts shriek) and demanded the presence of his master at once. When he was advised to be patient his voice jumped a whole octave and his hysteria mounted to the ceiling. Greatly daring (so they thought) he threw open the door of the bedroom and revealed a scene of almost domestic tranquillity – the Prince on the bed surrounded by children and dogs and himself wearing a communion veil at which the children were both laughing heartily. He shot up indignantly, forgetting to remove the veil, and let fly a stream of Arabic oaths at the head of his servant, who, however, continued to babble and gesticulate. Apparently the gravity of what he had to relate alone justified this intrusion. After a moment of wild rage the truth dawned on the Prince and he sat up to listen to what the excited man was actually saying. Whatever he at last began to comprehend had an altogether electrifying effect upon him for he leaped out of bed with commendable agility and dashed into the next room, heading for the direction of the front door and crying in a high bird-like tone and in the English of Cairo, "They have pinched the bloody coach."

Such was the excitement of the two men, such was the velocity of their movements, that everyone took fire, everyone was sucked into the procession in spite of themselves, whirled into the drama by the sheer momentum of the Prince's dramatic dash. The two young men balanced on the oil drums outside also gave way to a wave of panic as they realised that the whole of this sudden surge led towards the open street, where they might be discovered in this ignominious posture. They jumped down and by the beam of the torch picked their way through the shattered detritus of the old foundations walls.

But the Prince and his servant, with the trajectory of comets, had rushed into the street, and as if quite mesmerised, so had the rest of them – Riquiqui, Quatrefages, the little naked dwarf, the dogs and the communicating children. They all stood gazing about them in a daze of wonder and confusion and anger, for the coach which had apparently been standing before the front door, had disappeared. The Prince stamped his naked foot on the pavement with a gesture of febrile vexation, while his servant, as if to make quite sure, ran to the corner of the street and quested about generally like a gun-dog trying for a scent. Then he came back shaking his head and muttering. The Prince gazed around him, his regard travelling from face to face as if for sympathy. "Who could have done it—" he said, and Riquiqui, who had shown less surprise and consternation than the others, replied, "It's the gipsies. Leave it to me. Tomorrow I will find them."

The company was so absorbed in this little drama that they greeted the appearance of Felix and Blanford in an almost absent-minded way, hardly greeting them; but when they brought evidence to suggest that the coach had been stolen some good time ago (for it had not been there when they arrived) they managed to kindle a little interest. They were, after all, potential clients – so thought the little dwarf, who tried to link her arm in that of Felix, to his pained horror. "I will call the police," said the Prince in a sudden burst of childish petulance. "I will telephone to Farouk." It carried little conviction, for there he was with his little member protruding from his long woollen combinations.

Quatrefages, after a moment of reflection, led him muttering back into the house of pleasure and this time Blanford and Felix followed them in order to have a drink and to reassure themselves about the absence of Livia. Quatrefages, overcome by a sudden pudicity, became aware of his naked condition and hunted for his trousers before pouring out more whisky; the Prince retired haughtily to the inner room with his dogs and children and banged the door, leaving instructions that he was not to be disturbed for at least an hour. Blanford sipped his drink and heard the tinny piano tinkle. He felt suddenly terribly sleepy. Quatrefages said with a malicious grin: "Livia has gone to the gipsies."

So she had been there that evening, and had given them the slip as usual! Felix could not repress a slightly malicious side-glance at his fellow sufferer; but Blanford looked more angry than sad. He was telling himself that this would have to stop – this infatuation would have to be brought to an end. "It leads nowhere," he said aloud, talking to himself. At last the real truth of the matter had dawned on him – but like every glimpse of truth it was only fleeting and provisional. With the other half of his mind, so to speak, he was still lamed by his inner vision of her, of her sullen magnetism, of those expiring kisses which had ignited their minds. He did not care for the sardonic remarks of the clerk nor the cynical looks of Felix – the matter was too important, went too far into the gulfs of hopeless sentiment, of bewitchment, for the others to appreciate it.

He hugged his mood to himself, ignoring the rest of them, treasuring every little stab of pleasure or pain which it brought. What did it matter what Livia was or what she did? A strange metaphor came into his mind which expressed the exact nature of this attachment – a metaphor which centuries later Sutcliffe would use when he tried to define his gross attachment to the pale wraith Pia, who was a diluted version of the girl Constance, Livia's sister. But in his present mind it was Livia who provoked this thought which one would have had to be an alchemist to understand. What he loved in her was her "water" – as of a precious stone. It is after all what is really loved in a woman – not the sheath of matter which covers her – but her "signature". In the middle of all the chatter and movement of the brothel he found himself brooding upon this fact in all its singularity and wishing for a scrap of paper on which to jot it down. He

would have liked to incorporate it into his diary but he knew
that by the morrow he would have forgotten it.

Suddenly an enormous lassitude had taken hold of him.
"I want to go home," he said yawning, and to his surprise
Felix pronounced himself of the same disposition. Blanford
felt so lonely he could have gone out into the dark street
and waved vigorously to imaginary people. Quatrefages said
he would come too – "*J'ai tiré mon petit coup*," he said modestly.
And the Prince? Why, he was to be left; the major-domo
would see him safely home to the Imperial where he had
taken up his headquarters. Already a substitute pumpkin-
coach in the shape of a town *fiacre* had been summoned and
stood at the door. But the night was no longer young, and
the three young men felt sallow and spent. So they set off
across the town on foot, finding some refreshment in the
dark coolness which was full of the scent of lemons and
mandarines and honeysuckle. Felix would be the first home,
then the clerk; Blanford wanted to sit somewhere and watch
the dawn come up, to let his thought of Livia ripen like some
huge gourd. The pain was in the pleasure – a novelty for
him, he realised.

The night had waited for them – a great paunch of
silence upon which the ordinary sounds of the city hardly
impinged. Somewhere an ambulance raced with its tingling
alarm; there was something vengeful in the peals of its bell,
he thought, as it hurried back triumphantly to the hospital
with its trophy of maimed flesh. They heard its signals
diminishing as it dived through the outer ramparts towards
the suburbs. Felix yawned. Blanford, sunk himself, felt the
whole weight of his unexpressed narcissism heavy inside him,
like dough or wax, waiting to be kneaded into some sort of
significant shape – by what? – but he did not as yet dare to
think of himself as an artist. It was like a blind boil which
could not discharge itself except in insomnia or in those

sudden dispositions towards tears when some great music stirred him, or the glance of light on some ripe landscape pierced him. For others these vague intimations of beatitude, these realisations of beauty were enough in themselves simply to enjoy. But he came of that obstinate and unbalanced tribe which longed to do something about them – to realise and recreate them in a form less poignantly transitory than that vouchsafed by reality. What was to be *done*? That was always his thought, and he fretted inside himself at the notion that there was nothing, that he could do nothing, there was nothing to be done.

A brief wind ran the whole length of the street and turned a corner, disappearing in a gusty whirl of dead leaves, pouring itself into the throat of the invisible river whose slitherings and strivings they could hear as they approached it. When the sun came a thousand leafing planes would mirror themselves in its greenish waters. Here at last was the Consulate. The pavements were still warm and, because they had been washed with water and Javel, gave off the smell of incense. Felix too felt the gnawings of a nostalgic sadness. "I am sorry you will soon be gone," he said, but comforted himself with the thought that after such a summer he had happy enough memories stored against the winter with the rains and snows it would bring to the city. "I must ask for some leave," he went on, enlivening his thought with the prospect of meeting the others somewhere, perhaps in London. But Blanford's thoughts were of a graver cast – for there was to be no more Oxford after this term. Life was spreading its wings. What was to become of him? He would have enough money to live on – but what would that serve if he had no passionate aptitudes which he might fulfil? Tinker, Tailor, Soldier, Sailor ... what was he to do with his life? He had shown Livia the two little lyrics in the University magazine and he thought that she had looked at him with a new respect; but this was probably imagined. As for the poems they were quite nice pastiche, without an ounce of real feelings in them. Could she not see that? He sighed aloud as he walked. Quatrefages also seemed to be touched, through his fatigue, by the prevailing nostalgia. He gazed at the dark sky and shook himself like a wet mastiff. "Life is only once," he said unexpectedly. Felix now turned yawning into the gateway of the Consulate. "Remember the car is mine tomorrow," he told the clerk who shrugged his shoulders with indifference. Felix paused inside the front door for a moment to listen to their receding footfalls on the dark pavements. Soon the lamplighter would emerge to gather his blossoms of light, shy as a squirrel. Soon he would be alone again in this oppressive city which could only be enjoyed if seen through the eyes of Livia. In spite of his yawns he made the effort to clean his teeth before subsiding into his bed – for he was rather proud of their evenness. He told his sleepy reflection sternly: "I shall not cry myself to sleep because there are no golf courses on the moon." It was a declaration of faith, in a manner of speaking.

The two others walked silently side by side, each absorbed in his thoughts: but as they began to near the little square where Quatrefages' garish window shone out of the dark mass of the darker hotel, their steps began to lag. Despite the fatigue the clerk was reluctant to part with his companion. Truth to tell he was of a timorous nature and was always afraid to return late and alone to his room for fear of finding someone or something waiting for him. He imagined perhaps a very old tramp, sitting in the armchair waiting patiently for his return; or a blind man with a white stick and a great white dog. They would have come to propose some sort of compact with the Devil. He frowned and shook his head at his own stupidity; yet he wondered at the same time what excuse he could give which might persuade Blanford to mount the stairs with him and enter his room – just to reassure him so that he could now turn off the light and get some sleep.

It seemed absurd to propose yet another drink but that is what he heard himself doing, and to his great delight Blanford, who seemed in some obscure way to have divined his feelings, accepted the invitation. The clerk could not believe his luck. His dejected walk became all at once buoyant and nervous, his lassitude slipped from him. As a matter of fact Blanford was always intrigued by a glimpse of this extraordinary office whose walls were covered with death charts of the Templars, each with his date of execution. In the corner lay an unmade bed and a side-table covered with the impedimenta of the insomniac in the shape of bottles of pills and tinctures of opium, packs of cigarettes, and a cluster of books on alchemy and related topics, all bearing the marker of the Calvet Museum.

A pile of children's exercise books were propped up on the mantelshelf. A white chamberpot stood under the bed decorated by a cluster of roses in bloom. The whole centre of the room was taken up with the sort of trestle tables with angle lamps such as an architect might set up to draw a project in detail – or else perhaps the kind of tables upon which a paperhanger might set out his wallpapers before brushing the glue on to them. There was a small alcove in which stood a crucifix together with a bottle of whisky and several small mineral water bottles. The room smelt damply musty. It was situated on the blind side of the street and never got any light. It was heavy with dust and the little lavatory-douche was in a dreadful mess – towels covered in hair cream and, strangely, lipstick. The drains stank. Everywhere cigarettes had burnt out and left a dark burn – even on the wash basin. One wondered how there had never been a fire there. Quatrefages poured out a warmish drink and dragged out an uncomfortable chair for his guest to sit upon.

But Blanford preferred to stand and examine the charts on the wall with their suggestive datings, and the now lively Quatrefages followed his gaze with an air of pride. "We are down to the last of them," he said, "and we know for certain that they had managed to hide the treasure where neither Philippe nor his Chancellor Nogaret, who conducted the persecution, could lay their hands on it. This is why things dragged on so. The Templars would confess to anything but they would not divulge the hiding place. From other documents, some pretty enigmatic, we know that five of the knights were in the secret. But we don't as yet know which. But we have some clues to go on which seem pretty definite." He paused to drain his glass and cough loudly. Blanford, whose curiosity had got the better of him, asked a few questions and then, suddenly and perhaps rather rudely said: "Livia told me that she thought you had discovered the place, the vault, the chapel or whatever, and that there was nothing in it. That the treasure had been pinched ages ago. . . ."

The change in Quatrefages was as sudden as it was marked; his sallow complexion had become strained and laboured. He sat down on the bed and croaked out an oath: "Livia knows nothing," he said, "nothing. The gipsies tell one all sorts of things, but it is false. I have not found the place as yet. But of course Provence is full of ruined chapels and empty vaults destroyed during the various religious upheavals. But nothing that so far corresponds with the evidence of an orchard – the 'Verger de Saint Louis' – where the plane trees were set in a quincunx like an ancient Greek temple grove. No, as yet we have not found the place."

Blanford felt all of a sudden apologetic for having made this intrusion – the more so because he suddenly felt that Quatrefages was probably lying to him. Or was it Livia? At any rate none of this was his business, and he had no intention of making the little clerk feel that he was not to be counted upon, or that his word was not believed. "I am sorry," he said, "it was not my business and I should not have repeated gossip."

Nevertheless, whatever the truth of the matter was, the agitation of Quatrefages seemed somehow excessive, and Blanford could not help speculating upon this fragment of gossip which had slipped from Livia's lips quite casually, seemingly without malice or premeditation. "When we do discover it," said the clerk, his eyes glittering malevolently in his nervous paleness of feature, "that will be the day to rejoice." Blanford turned away to the great wall charts of the dead Templars and as he did so the dawn broke softly in the open street below. Its faint tinges of yellow and rose coloured the walls of that sordid room, almost like some signal from a past full of mystery and significance.

The dead names glowed like jewels, like embers still breathing in the pale ashes of the past. The names slowly recited themselves in his mind, each with its hush of death and silence cradling it. Dead cavaliers of the piebald standard! Raynier de Larchant, Reynaud de Tremblay, Pierre de Tortville, Jacques de Molay, Hugues de Pairaud, Jean du Tour, Geoffroy de Gonneville, Jean Taillefer, Jean L'Anglais, Baudoin de Saint-Just. Inhabitants now of history, destroyed by blind circumstance, by the zeal and cupidity of the lawless ages. "One wonders what they were guilty of," he said aloud, more to himself than to anyone. His eyes traversed the great names again, lingering over them, savouring the mystery and sadness of their premature deaths by starvation, torture, or the burning pyres of the Inquisition. It was a riddle which would never be read, an enigma which still intrigued and baffled new generations of historians.

Quatrefages sat on the edge of the bed leaning forward and concentrating – as if he were trying to follow Blanford's train of thought, to read his mind. His face was flushed now, the fever had come back; and he was full of drink and beginning to feel it. "What were they guilty of?" he repeated aloud in a sharp cracked voice, so curiously at variance with his natural tone that Blanford turned curiously upon him and said: "Well, what?" But it was now clear that Quatrefages was very drunk indeed; he stood up and swayed and began to snivel. "The greatest heresy the world has ever known," he said in an exalted way; he clenched his fists and raised them on high, for all the world as if he himself were standing on a high pyre, feeling the flames rising around his feet, and testifying to the truth of a belief which ran counter to the whole structure of an age's thoughts.

Blanford watched him burning and crying there for a moment, and then reached out a tentative hand, as if to soothe or console him against so much excessive feeling. He felt also a little guilty – as if his idle remark had somehow provoked this orgiastic recital. Quatrefages was now a-tremble with emotion. He was like a wire through which passed a current of a voltage almost too powerful to bear. "You don't know the truth," he said incoherently and his lips began to wobble as he spoke, his tears to choke him.

Blanford was able to glimpse now the zealot who lived underneath the external guise of the young man – the carapace of industry and probity and politeness which made up the outer man. But now it was as if a switch had been thrown, first by the drink and then by Livia's remark – the image of a dam came into his mind, or one of those *écluses* on the Rhône through which their barge had slid. The current had pushed down all the debris of Quatrefages' solitary and secret life – sitting there agonising over long-dead knights, and trying by guile and science to pick their pockets. "We are like grave-robbers in the pay of Galen," he cried with a bitter vehemence, still standing in his theatrical attitude of human sacrifice. "They have reduced the whole thing to a vulgar matter of *fric*, of booty. They have missed the whole point of this tremendous apostasy. Blanford, *écoutez*!" He took his companion by the shoulders and shook him so violently that his drink was nearly upset and he was just able to set it down and free his elbow in time.

Quatrefages sank back on to his bed and plunged his chin moodily into his fists. "That is what is killing me," he said in a lower key, suppressing the drama in his voice a little; "the ignominiousness of what we are doing, and my own part in it." Blanford's reactions to this sort of outburst were typically Christian public-schoolboy; he felt shy, alarmed and overwhelmed. He cursed himself for having unwittingly provoked this storm. He did not want to witness Quatrefages' self-recriminations and breast-beatings. If he so much disapproved of what he was doing why did he not re-sign? It was easy to simplify matters thus – he knew that. But he suppressed a sigh as he sat down, prepared to let the clerk talk himself out. "I began in good economic faith, and then I began to get more and more curious about the Templars – not about their fortune but about the nature of their heresy. To defy the reign of matter as they did, to outface the ruling devil – that was what intrigued me. Yes, they quietly built up an almost unassailable temporal power – they were the bankers of the age. And these great constructions were their banks, their prisons."

He waved an arm vaguely in the direction of the Papal Palaces on their elevation above the river, now doubtless turning rose also, petal by petal, spire by spire. "The knights were systematically destroyed by the hooded anonymous butchers of the Inquisition in order to secure the succession of what they now knew was evil – the pre-eminence of matter and will in the world. They were the instruments of Old Nick himself who was not going to have his throne shaken by this superb refusal of the knights; he was not going to submit without a struggle. The death wish against the life wish – God, you know, is only an alibi in all this, only a cover-story. The real battle between the negative and positive forces was joined here – and all Europe in the coming ages was at stake." He paused and licked his dry lips. Then, draining his glass in a wobbly way, he said, almost in a whisper, "They lost, and we lost with them."

The two of them stared at one another for a moment and then Quatrefages gave a hopeless little chuckle and put his head on one side and, half closing his eyes – like a bird putting its head under its wing – said: "I know why you look at me like that. You are saying to yourself that it is preposterous to feel so strongly about a mere historical event. You are right. But we are living out the fateful destiny of European man which was decided then – right here in Avignon. We are taking part in this materialist funeral of living man. Yes, they were suppressed and deafening clouds of propaganda were pumped out over them to obscure the real issues and blacken their names. They were accused of every kind of sorcery, whereas the only conjuring they indulged in was the flat refusal to continue living the great lie of civilisation as it was then ordered. Of course it had to be kept secret, for it was heresy, in the strict terms of the epoch."

He fell silent at last. Blanford stared at the great wall maps: among them was a series of architectural studies of the various Temples and their disposition. He was, he concluded, in the presence of a harmless young maniac who had allowed his head to be turned by the bogus speculations of the popular mysticism which was at the moment all too fashionable. The Rosy Cross, the dimensions of the Great Pyramid, Madame Bavatsky.... He knew the line of country fairly well and indeed had read quite a few books about these matters – but without being swept off his feet by what he regarded as enjoyable fantasies. "What does it *matter* if there is a treasure or not?" cried Quatrefages passionately, waking up temporarily to resume his theme. Bang! "To add a little more *fric* to Galen's fortune? But I think there is no treasure; I think Philippe Le Bel got it all. I have not mentioned this to anyone because I am not absolutely sure – but our search for the quincunx of trees concerns another sort of treasure. That is what I really believe. But who can I talk to about it? Nobody! Nobody!"

Again he banged his fist upon the bed until the springs twanged. The whole confused details of his own apostasy, his own refusal of the body of Christ, the cannibal totem, rose up to choke him with a sense of his unworthiness, his insufficiency. He let out a groan. Blanford said rather primly, "I do understand a little bit. You mean the Philosopher's Stone, don't you?" But the clerk was plunged in his reveries and only nodded abstractedly, as if he were listening to some distant music too absorbing to allow him to shift his attention to what Blanford was saying. "But that is not the sort of treasure one finds in the ground, like a crock of gold containing a liquid rainbow . . . is it?" The question was useless and deserved for answer the silence it got. Quatrefages now whispered something to himself, quietly and confidently, nodding his head sagely and with resignation. Then he sank sideways on to the pillows cradling his heavy head in his hands as if it were a Roman bust, and fell asleep. Blanford watched him for a while with curiosity and sympathy; his mind seemed to burn with such pathetic intensity in his lean body. Now, sleeping there, with his long nose aimed at the pillow, he looked touchingly defenceless. His wrists were so very thin. As the light had already been turned off there was nothing left but to tiptoe from the room and down the creaking staircase.

He paused to whisper a word to the sleepy night-porter who was putting his improvised bed to rights. Then down to the icy river and the bridge which steered away from the wakening city to the wide green hills beyond. He set out in a new burst of energy to walk back to Tu Duc. Everything on that joyful morning seemed to gleam like a new coin – a newly minted currency of vivid impressions. He felt words stirring inside his mind, like some long-hibernating species which a tardy spring had wakened only now, struck by the romance of the green swirling river and the cypress-punctuated hills he was approaching. To really appreciate a place or time – to extract the poignant essence of it – one should see it in the light of a departure, a leavetaking. It was the sense of farewell in things which impregnated them with this phantom of nostalgia so important for the young artist.

He felt the lure of language stirring in him, like a muscle stretching itself, cramped from long disuse. He did not know how to contain nor what to do with all this happiness. He approached the sleeping house across the unkempt lawns, cutting the dew with every step and feeling the moisture soak into his tennis shoes. A black cat sat on the mat by the kitchen garden – just like in his first nursery-book. But more wonderful still; from the rumple of bedclothes which hid the secret form of the naked Livia he could only pick out one slender hand with its long fingers relaxed and extended – one finger yellow with tobacco stains. He stripped and crawled in beside the sleep-sodden half-drugged nymph and, glad that she slept on, set himself to studying every feature of that slender expressive face with its striking alignment of bones and planes.

He tried to pierce with his eyes the very real bewitchment which transformed it; he realised that what he saw was not Livia but his own transfigured version of her – the reflection of his love. Beside the bed was the little box with the cheap wedding ring he had bought in Lunel from an old Jewish lady in a booth which sold lottery tickets and betting slips. He slipped it softly onto her unresisting finger and, like the unwise mooncalf he was, kissed it. He made love to her at her whispered request, though she neither opened her eyes nor in any way altered the disposition of her body; he moved her about as she lay there, quite limp, rather like one of those articulated "lay figures" that artists and dressmakers use.

Their united spirits seemed to wash down the long river together, entangled in one another, and then far away out to sea – the deep sea of a new sleep. But in order to leave her undisturbed he took a blanket to the balcony and curled up on the stones in the vanishing dew, his sleepy head pillowed upon a damp towel. In the half-sleep of fatigue the whole gorgeous gallery of Provençal images unwound inside his mind as if on a giant spool. There were so many memories he did not know what to do with them. He heard Livia stir and, turning on his elbow, gazed through the open balcony door. Yes, she was sleepily awake and sitting up in bed; but he was not prepared for what he saw now. She was gazing at her ring-finger with a curious expression of horror he had never seen on her face before. It was the expression of someone who suddenly finds a scorpion on the lapel of a jacket they are wearing. Her lips all but cried out: "Who would have done this?" and with a gesture which combined anger with repulsion she snatched off the ring and flung it with all her might into the corner of the room.

He heard its sour tinkle as it bounced about on the floor. It was quite a shock – something went dead and cold inside him as he took in this involuntary gesture of rejection. He too sat up now, to watch her sink back with a sigh into her bed and draw the covers over her head as she foundered into a deeper sleep. The ring! Blanford reflected on these mysteries and on the independence of Livia as he crossed the wakening garden and plunged into the icy waters of the lily pond; what did it mean? It was Livia who had entertained his callow addresses and his suggestions about marriage. She had shown no distaste for such a thought before. But here she was standing beside the pond, poised for a dive. "What has changed?" he asked her quietly, rather painfully, though he did not know what he might have to fear in her answer. "I was not ready for it," she said, "Not yet. Perhaps I shall never be. We'll see."

But then to make up for this disturbing hesitation she launched herself into the water and came swirling into his arms to kiss and embrace him anew, her body glittering like a fish in a net. So their peace was restored and their solidarity of feeling – yet in the heart of the matter Blanford felt the prick of sadness, of some unachieved intimacy which lay between them like a shadow. "I missed you everywhere, gipsies, Riquiqui's, Felix, Quatrefages. . ." He smiled at her but he all of a sudden seemed to wake up with a jolt and tell himself: "She lies as simply as she breathes – about everything." Later he hunted for the ring but it had gone. She had reclaimed it, then? He did not ask her.

SIX

Talking Back

THE LONG SERPENTINE THOUGHT, AFTER SO MANY parentheses, came at last to rest in his silent mind. A very long silence fell, which seemed to both of them as if it might prolong itself unto eternity. "Hullo!" cried Sutcliffe twice, on a note of almost childish anxiety. (Ghosts always get alarmed when they are not in full manifestation – when they are off duty, so to speak – for it seems to them that they are in danger of ceasing to exist.) Yes. Suppose, I mean, that Blanford forgot to think of *him*! What then? It would be the end! And Blanford himself was, at that moment, bowed under the same thought, for he knew that once the ghosts, which together go to make up the collective memory, cease to care . . . why, one goes out like a light. Ask any artist! For a moment he was quite tongue-tied, he could not answer; in his imagination he had let the old-fashioned receiver fall upon the arm of his chair as he gazed into the fire with frigid intensity, for he had seen the face of Constance there, and it was curling up with the flames, it was disappearing. Sutcliffe could hear his uneven, heavy breathing. "For God's sake," he cried, "why don't you say something, Aubrey?"

But a sudden sense of helpless inadequacy had overwhelmed the writer as he wondered how to compress and condense into a few pages all the events and impressions of that short period which had come so abruptly to an end with the outbreak of the war. This brief glimpse of Constance had suddenly revived it all. It had been so extraordinarily rich, so bursting with promise; then abruptly the whole period had sunk out of sight, into the dark night of Nazi Europe. But what was he saying? For almost a whole year the war had actually been declared, though nobody had moved. The French lurked among their block-houses, wondering at the extraordinary paralysis which had gripped the whole of Europe. Meanwhile the life of Paris and London appeared to continue unchanged – the postal services were normal, for example, the telephone worked, the skies were as yet empty of planes. Yes, a few greasy-looking barrage balloons had appeared above the Thames. Somewhere, in some dim and amorphous region of the group-mind, feverish preparations were being made to forge a weapon which might contain the launching thrust of the German forces. But somehow nobody could believe in it. In all the soft paralysis there was a luxurious hopelessness, a valedictory sensation of the doom which must overtake the great capitals, one by one. Bye-bye to Paris and Rome, to Athens and Madrid. . . . One had a wild desire to revisit them quickly for a moment, to feel their living pulse before it was stilled forever. But even this was late in the day, after the formal declarations had been made. Yet for months, even years, before one could see some sort of war coming, see the horizon darkening. They had lived with this thing and knew that there was nothing to be done.

Tiny incidents, mere crumbs, remained still in Blanford's memories of that epoch, as if they had been simply markers to point the direction of the prevailing wind, the death-wind. How he had lent Sam the money to buy himself a uniform, while down in Provence Constance waited for him, for Sam, with a calm and smiling solicitude which so expertly masked the depth of her feelings. It was no time to decide to marry, but that is what they had done, and walking into his room at Tu Duc she came upon him awkwardly examining his fancy dress in the mirror with an air of rapturous astonishment. She did not actually weep but he put her head on his shoulders and began to laugh at his foolish expression. Meanwhile he said to himself, aloud, in the mirror:

"If she doesn't love me in this get-up she never bloody will."
The trousers had to be altered, the waistcoat set more snugly.
And here Felix came to the rescue and found a tailor in
Avignon. Sam had only a few days' leave before returning
to Oxford and the war. It was not entirely in bantering terms
that he said: "I was really worried about being unemployable,
and now look at this excellent job, so well paid. And bags of
promotion, too, if one is energetic." This was on the platform waiting for the train to Paris. Blanford saw Constance
turn away to hide her emotion and he engaged his friend in
banter to hide his own. The whole world was breaking up
under them like some old raft. It was deplorable to be so
callow, so undemonstrative.

Yet there were certain modifying certainties, among
them the general belief that the Germans would never
penetrate the Maginot Line whatever their bombers might
do to the cities. If there was war, even a long war, France
would remain geographically intact, so that some sort of
civilian life would go on until it ended. The famous Line
was to France what the Channel had always been for the
British. In the back of everyone's consciousness there must
have been obstinate archaic memories left over from 1914,
stalemates on the Somme, and so on. Nobody thought
about mobility, even later when it was clear that things had
gone well beyond compromise. What then? Felix had received
orders to stand by and aid the evacuation of British subjects
should the storm break – and then to hand over his Consulate
to the Swiss. And here came a remarkable and most welcome
discovery. The three of them – Hilary and his two sisters –
were of dual nationality and would claim Swiss citizenship.
Their clever old fox of a father had had them all born in
Geneva. Neither Sam nor Blanford, however, could claim
such an immunity from action, while for his part the latter
wondered whether he should not declare for conscientious

objection. Felix offered him all the necessary documentation but he was gripped by conflicting uncertainties. The fate of the Jews had become clear, and while one could be against war in general one could not really turn one's back on this one, when such terrible issues were at stake. Yet for the time he did nothing.

And then somewhere in the middle of all this period comes a spell in Paris with Livia, a spell which ended in that fatuous marriage anchored by a wedding ring which was never to be worn. A disorderly, roughcast sort of student existence in the fourteenth arrondissement. A Livia who was always busy and preoccupied though he never found out what she was doing. But she was out at all hours in all weathers, and she talked in her sleep and drank absinthe with disquieting application. The little rented flat was a shabby enough place, but there was a table at which he could write so that one basic need was satisfied, though at this time he wrote mostly long letters. Yet stirring deep in the jungle he could hear the rustle of those animal doubts which came creeping upon him. He began to wonder what he had indeed done. At times when she was drunk her laughter was so extravagant as to be insulting. At times he caught glimpses of unusual expressions on that pale face – hate, malevolence, disdain. It made him feel fearful and sad, as if some vital piece of information was missing – the presence of a shadow which stood forever between them. There was. She had become so much thinner that her looks had changed. The head of the cicada had become narrower, the face an adder's.

Then his mother's health began to falter and flicker and he was called back to her bedside where he gazed long and earnestly into that once familiar face, now pained to see that the long illness had altered all its stresses, composed it in new planes and lines, as if to copy on the outer skin the fearful loneliness and despair of the inner mind. She had things to tell him about her small fortune, and she had discovered that she could not trust Cade, the valet. He opened her letters and in general kept a spying eye out over her affairs. She had longed to give him notice but in all his other duties he was so perfect and so dependable that she had not dared. In this, as in all other things, she was lucidity itself, and even when she sank back into a last deep coma he did not think that she would die – indeed the doctor warned him that she might linger on a long time yet, so strong was her heart. Nevertheless he spent that day at her bedside, holding that frail hand in which the pulse continued to beat like that of a captive sparrow. In these long silences his mind went about its business slowly and densely. He wondered much about Livia and about his own future. His mother was leaving him a small marginal income, as well as the London house which could be let. There was also a small cottage on a farm outside Cairo where his father had spent many summers pursuing his entomological passion with silent assiduity. This was a mere shack, though, and there was hardly any land around it. Nevertheless, it was like a window open upon another country.

Another problem: if she should by any chance wake, ought he to tell her that he was married to Livia, or was it better to keep the whole matter a secret? Already there was a sneaking premonition that he had embarked upon something which might become a capital misadventure. Sitting in that grey light of a suburban nightfall, trying mentally to align her ticking wrist with the ticking of the grandfather-clock in the hall, he wondered a little bleakly what would come of it all. In a sense it was good to have the war to think about – for it dwarfed purely human schemes, and one could shelve them temporarily. And yet he did not think there would be a war, despite all the signs; history was like some lump of viscid porridge sliding slowly down a sink, but with such an infinite slowness! Their gestures, their hopes and schemes, seemed to be somehow insubstantial, chimerical. Meanwhile the frenzy of Paris was still teaching, and he realised how pregnant were the lessons he had learned in this all too brief residence there – the capital of the European nervous system. So many valuable acquisitions: how total freedom did not spell licence, nor gastronomy gluttony, nor passion brutality.

The old streets down at the fag-end of the rue St.-Jacques which smelt of piss and stale cooking were the mere folklore of life lived in a relatively waterless capital where the women did not shave under their arms, and preferred stale scent to soapy bath water. In summer the smell of armpits in the cafés was enough to drive one mad. Yet everywhere the river winds cradled the velvet city and one could walk all night under a canopy of stars worthy of grand opera – the brilliant glitter of outer space impacting upon the shimmering brilliance of a world of hot light.

Appropriately enough she had given him a rendezvous (for the marriage) at the old Sphinx, opposite the Gare Montparnasse, where the respectable exterior – a family café, where families up from the country came to eat an ice and wait for their train – masked a charming bordel with a high gallery and several spotless cubicles. A simple bead curtain separated the two establishments, but such was the pleasant naturalness of things in the Paris of that day, that often the girls, dressed only in coloured sarongs and with the traditional napkin over the arm like waiters ("no spots upon the counterpane, please") came out to meet friends and even play a game of chequers with elderly clients whom time had ferried lightly into *impuissance*. "How marvellous," she said when she came, "if you could take all this with you to smoky

470

Euston." He had told her about his mother, that she was dying; he would leave immediately after the ceremony, which was performed by a very deaf consul and duly entered in the Consular Registers. The Minister then offered them the traditional glass of champagne under the tactless portrait of an idealised Wellington. He was a kind old man but he could not keep his horrified gaze off the dirty feet of Livia in her sandals. Later, much later, when Blanford asked Livia why she had done it at all she replied with a contemptuous laugh: "It seemed so unimportant; so I made you a present of something you wanted."

All this and much more passed through his mind as he sat holding the wrist of his dying mother – a flight of impressions like a brilliant surge of tropical fish across the dim aquarium of his student life. On the other side of the curtain of adolescence was a Paris full of bountiful surprises – a Paris where all the whores had started to take German lessons. The teachers of the German Institute were overwhelmed with requests for classes! A Paris where nobody shaved under the arms. At the Sphinx where he went rather sedately to play *belotte* and drink (with a timid air) an absinthe, which he hated, he had met a charming friend of his new wife, a negress of great beauty with a smile from here to there, and hands which roved into any pocket that presented itself. Livia found her "killing", and derived such amusement from her Martinique French that he was forced to enjoy her as well. Curiously enough she did shave under the arms, though she said the girls in general did not because a swatch of hair excited the customer and was good for business. He was extremely frightened of these unexpected revelations of turpitude, but it was after all romantic and he was in the rapt middle of Proust, and France was after all ... what exactly? He had never been in such an extraordinary ambiance before, a sort of ferment of freedom and treachery, of love and obscenity, of febrility and distress. A life which was so rich in possibilities reduced one to silence.

Nor for that matter had he ever been really in love before, whatever that might mean. The brilliant little taxis which flashed about the town like shooting stars were their favourite transport. Whenever they rushed off the macadam on to a cobbled thoroughfare the kisses of lovers in the back began to hobble and shake as if with an extra passionate emphasis conferred by the *pavé*. And quite apart from the greater beauties of this most beautiful of cities they were made freemasons of the company of its lovers, holding hands dutifully on the Pont des Arts, sitting heart joined to heart at the Closerie des Lilas or the rumbling Dôme. Floods of new books and ideas swamped them. He read relentlessly to keep abreast in quiet cafés and parks. It was the epoch of puzzling Gertrude Stein, Picasso, and the earlier convulsions of the American giants like Fitzgerald and Miller. He was sufficiently mature, however, to reflect that Europe was fast reaching the end of the genito-urinary phase in its literature – and he recognised the approaching impotence it signalled. Soon sex as a subject would be ventilated completely. "Even the act is dying", he allowed Sutcliffe to note, "and will soon become as charmless as badminton. For a little while the cinema may conserve it as a token act – as involuntary as a sneeze or a hiccough: a token rape, while the indifferent victim gnaws an apple." He added: "The future is more visible from France than anywhere because the French push everything to extremes. An audio-judeo-visual age is being born – the Mouton Rothschild epoch where the pre-eminence of Jewish thought is everywhere apparent, which explains the jealousy of the Germans."

Standing at night on a quiet bridge with the whole of reflected heaven flowing beneath them, silent, rapt. "One day you will despise me," she said, talking as if to herself.

One star was ticking over the lemon water. He said to himself: "Pity and she don't match and never will." And here he was – most inappropriate of men, a writer, watching from the abolished tower of his male self-esteem refunding his youth into these silences with this dangerous girl. "In two months' time I am going away, perhaps for good," he said, but he didn't take it seriously, just as he didn't really take the war seriously. Sutcliffe chided him from Geneva where he had landed a temporary job tutoring. "It's all very well to sit up there in your private Pisgah," he said, "but kindly note that Pisgah is the Hebrew word for an outdoor shithouse. It was here that old Moses quietly, while shifting the load of guilt, in the posture of Rodin's *Thinker*, *thunk*. My last words on leaving the school were as follows: 'The school will get no more half holidays unless secret practices cease and a new detachment is born, say a detachment of dragoons, firing off maroons.'" He went on after a pause, "But when I left, after my scandal, such is a frailty of the female organism that there was an outbreak of mumps, chiefly among the nuns."

But in spite of the confusion of this period Blanford was thinking, he was looking around him and taking stock as well as taking notes in his little student's *calepin*. Like: "The old seem to be praying for a war to carry off the young; the young are soliciting a plague to carry off the old. Fortune's maggot, I nestle in the plenitude of my watchful indifference."

She was his, and yet she was not really completely present. Reality, fine as a skin on milk, was called into question the whole time by this disturbance of focus aided by alcohol or tobacco or other unspecified drugs. Shaving himself in the bathroom mirror he realised that he had been pretending to be sane all his life. Now, even while kissing her he did not know which state of mind to assume. To overhear a thought thinking itself, to eavesdrop on a whisper of a truth formulating itself – this was his new state of mind. He began a book – the whole thing seemed to write itself. It was the purest automatic writing. It was a vignette of life in the country somewhere – a country which he himself had never seen. It was overwritten and shapeless so he destroyed it. Yet something important had happened to him – on the mystical plane, though that seems a rather pompous way of speaking about the intervention of "reality prime" into his scheme of things. (He tried saying "I love you" in several ways, in several keys, at several speeds, just to try and imagine what it was she heard when he did.) But what he realised was that from that moment onwards nothing he did was frivolous. It could be bad or good or even just inadequate or indifferent but it would be fraught with his own personal meaning, it would have his finger-prints on it. When he dared to say as much to Sutcliffe, his bondsman groaned aloud: "I see it all," he declared, "another novel written by the automatic pilot," and when Blanford looked at himself in the mirror he could see that in fact his expression was a trifle portentous – swollen, as if he had a gumboil. His self-esteem had boiled over.

Anyway, would there be time? They were pushed by the anxieties of the age to try and drink in everything before the war swallowed it up – that meant Edith Piaf looking like a cracked plate and singing like a cracked dove. "*Mon coeur y bat!*" That meant the new cinema – which had by now forfeited its chances of becoming more than a minor art by the invention of sound-track. It meant piles of saucers growing up under one's drinks at the Dôme while voices spoke of Spengler and the thirteenth law of thermo-dynamics. . . . God! it was good to be alive, but it was an agony also, and he felt it all the more when the slow measured rhythm of England replaced the throbbing Paris rush. He

managed a brief visit to Oxford to see friends and collect
belongings, and found it strange and secretive and tongue-
tied – "theological dons in their Common Rooms dancing
round the *filoque*," as Sutcliffe was to put it. For his part
the great man had started to do yoga by the lake. "Come,"
he said in magisterial fashion, "sharpen your intuitions in
the cobra pose."

Blanford did nothing of the kind. His thought-glands were
too soaked in alcohol, his mouth tasted itself through a coat
of fur. He was happy in a distressing sort of way, dwelling
in the great shadow of happy fornication with this buccaneer,
this bird of paradise. "I am young and handsome," he told
Sutcliffe, "and self-possessed as a cervical smear. I want to
enjoy myself before age sets in and I suddenly go blue as
cheese with a heart condition. . . ."

Publishers, he pretended to himself, were bursting their
braces with desire to receive a new masterpiece, and here he
was destroying everything he wrote as fast as he wrote it.
In a friend's studio here was a grand piano on which from
time to time he would practise. He played Schubert for her
until she wept, and then innocently fell asleep, chin on paws
like a Persian cat, a catspaw. Self-pity engenders oxygen and
she was very sad to be sad. He started to write the memoirs
of The Superfluous Man, but found he lacked the art. A
pelican, he was trying to drink a little blood from his own
breast.

> The tirra lirra of the public purse,
> The piggy bank whose use we learned from Nurse;
> The affect cannot hoard its wild regrets
> Except as dark repressions in cold sweats.

"I see you have a poetic turn?" said the patronising
Sutcliffe. "I too dabble, and before leaving England I tried
my hand at everything, even Sapphics which have never
been done well since Campion. Listen!

475

"Deliciously sapped by the swish of thy swansdown chemise
I perch on a porch in Belgravia pansexually pooped."

It was full of false quantities and not at all a real Sapphic,
but what was the point of arguing with Sutcliffe? It was clear
that he was pained and lonely, and probably had toothache
as well. He struck a chord, a sad diminished seventh, to wake
the sleeper but she slept on.

> If pianos could polish themselves
> They would be turned to cats;
> In mirrors of self-esteem efface their lust
> Licking their likenesses to dust.

Suddenly Constance appeared in Paris and strangely
enough with her the war became suddenly real – as if she
herself had declared it. She was very much thinner and yet
calmer, and she had had what she declared was a momentous
series of meetings with Freud in Vienna. She had attended a
conference of psychs at which he had presided and they
had taken a fancy to each other. Other meetings followed
and the result was that now she was a wholly submitted pupil
of the old man whom she now vehemently declared to be the
foremost thinker in Europe.

"Here! Wait a moment!" said Blanford, shocked by so
uncompromising a hero-worship, and of course she laughed.
It was obvious to her that he, in common with nearly all
so-called intellectuals of that epoch, understood next to
nothing of the modest provisional theses of the old professor.
How to make it clear? She took him by the shoulders with an
affectionately admonishing air and said: "From now on it
has become impossible for anyone to write *Hamlet* again,
do you see?" He did not see, did not wish to see much beyond
the dancing points of her bright eyes and the grand flush
of colour with which she announced that she was meeting
Sam secretly that evening, and they were going to get

married before the war broke out. "It will be a long sad stalemate of years perhaps," she said. "They will never get through the Line and we will never have the force to go after them. Meanwhile, lots of bombing and short rations and stalemate." It was of course the general view, hence the strange kind of stagnation in which they lived. But she had other fish to fry as well for she suddenly changed her expression from gladness to bitter gloom. "Where is Livia?" she asked with a kind of waspish sharpness. How should he know? Nobody could keep track of Livia's movements; sometimes in desperation he left her little notes on the notice-board of the Café Dôme for she turned up there from time to time.

Constance paused for a long moment with her chin on her breast, thinking; then, as if coming to a decision, she said: "All right, well, I shall tell you then. In Vienna I saw a German newsreel of some great Nazi rally in Bavaria – there she was, plumb in the centre of things, dressed in a German uniform."

The news was electrifying and numbing at the same time. What could it mean? "Are you sure?" he said weakly. Constance nodded and said: "Never surer. She was full in the camera for about ten seconds, singing and giving the salute. She looked out of her mind. I am terrified for her."

Blanford did not know what to say, so acute was his shame. "She has never confided in me," was all he could think of in the way of self-defence. But even at this late stage the full extent of the tragedy which was slowly being enacted in Germany failed to register – its impact skilfully dulled by false propaganda and censorship to which they were as yet unaccustomed. They walked a little together in the Luxembourg, mostly in silence, trying to shape some sort of true perspective for their future lives – but only vague prospects and qualified hopes stretched away from them

into ... what? But at least Constance was sure of her basic
direction. She had joined the Red Cross on the medical side,
and with her Swiss passport proposed to be of some use in
the crisis to come. Sam had a fortnight before rejoining his
unit in Britain. Tonight, after getting married, they would
take the old train from the Gare de Lyon, and spend a brief
honeymoon in Tu Duc. She asked: "Why don't you two
come for a few days? Hilary can't, he is still in his Scottish
seminary." But he sensed that it would not have done. They
parted with warmth, and on his side with a pang of vague
and imprecise regret, as if he feared that their friendship
might be qualified by his marriage. It was silly of course.
The old certain stability of things had melted into something
new – a sort of state of limbo. And in the midst of all this,
glowing like a precious stone, was the memory of Provence
and all it had held for them on this first rich encounter with it.
The richness was overwhelming, and in his own dreams he
returned again and again to the old house lying so secretively
among the tall trees, in a silence orchestrated only by the
wind and the ripple of river which passed through the garden.

As they parted she said in a sudden little flurry of
agonised feeling: "Do you think I am doing the wrong
thing? I wouldn't like to hurt Sam." He shook his head but
he felt the shock of her words. The question meant that, in
fact, she *was* doing the wrong thing, and that somewhere in
her inner consciousness she knew it. But what made him
feel ashamed was his own sudden feeling of elation as he
recognised the fact. He felt it was horrible and quite unpardonable. He would seek absolution in thinking up some
extravagant present for her in London.

Cremation is a clean and unemphatic way of disposing,
not only of your dead, but also of your thoughts about death
and any fears and misgivings they might engender. The rain
melted down over everything, a soft blue rain which pearled

down the windows of the old respectable Daimler they had hired for himself and Cade, the only two mourners. The coffin looked small and very light. It lobbed slightly as the hearse gathered way. He had been extravagant about the flowers because he knew she had loved flowers, yet an obstinate parallel thought crossed his mind as he wrote out the cheque, namely: "I never received a moment's affection from either side of the blanket." He felt aware of some sort of emotional attrition, of a withering away inside himself – a kind of poverty of affect which art and literature might only pretend to redress. Perhaps later, in middle life . . . yes, but would there be a middle life, with all this war business going on? To his surprise he bought a new car on an impulse and paid for driving-lessons. He retained Cade's services for a year, but offered him an extended leave to revisit his family in the north. When all this was over he would drive down to Provence and wait there for history to declare itself.

The crematorium was a gaunt-looking place, of an architecture so frivolous that it resembled an abandoned Casino in Southern Italy. The plume of smoke which rose from behind the main building flapped upwards into the rain and then flattened out across the fields of concrete which surrounded the place. The whole area was tastefully laid out with gardens full of daffodils and other Wordsworthian aids to memory. But there was quite a waiting list of bodies for cremation and they were a few moments early. They were set down to wait, and optionally pray if they wished, in a small ante-chapel which did duty as a waiting-room. The suburban church architecture of the chapel was of glacial coldness and infernal ugliness. The altar with its cheap cathedral-glass saints wallowing in the crepuscular gloom shed a dreadful Sunday School light upon them. On the wall in the corner there was what the cricketer in Blanford recognised as a score board such as every school buys for its

cricket field. Instead of a score however there was the programme of the day neatly indicated in detachable lettering.
Theirs was to be preceded by three other cremations – those
of Mrs. Humble, Mrs. Godbone and Mrs. Lamb; then came
Evelyn Blanford. They must wait their turn? Cade ostenta-
tiously prayed and the chief mute sycophantically followed
suit. He was a Dickensian caricature of fruitless respectability
in his old and scruffy top hat and withered tail-coat. His
cuffs were dirty and had been arranged rather impres-
sionistically with the help of nail scissors. He was wheezy
with asthma and false devoutness. Blanford closed his eyes
and breathed deeply through his gills, praying that this might
soon be over. It was astonishing how deeply upset he found
himself to be – he would not have suspected this wave of
intense sorrow and loneliness.

The officiating clergyman was a robust and pink young
man with a touch of bustle about him, as if he were anxious
to get through the work of the day as soon as possible. But
he was very detached and otherworldly as well, and one
might have supposed him to be cremating some headhunters
from darkest Borneo rather than respectable suburban
matrons from fondest Folkestone. Blanford felt rather put
out by his offhand manner and the hint of cockney in his
speech which made Holy Writ read like an advertisement for
Glaxo. But at last the session wound to its end and Blanford
was suddenly aware that throughout the length of the
service his mother had been slowly sinking into the ground
before their eyes: the coffin slowly sinking down the trap
into the operational part of the concern. The young man
achieved perfect timing, for the last word of his peroration
coincided with the muffled clap of the doors closing, after
having launched the coffin onto the rails of a subterranean
railway. They heard it whirring off down the chute. The
machinery was a trifle squeaky. Then followed a long

silence during which the mute turned to them and said, "Of course you'll be wanting an urn, sir?" "Of course," said Cade sternly. "*Two* urns!"

The man tiptoed off after saying: "I will meet you outside at the car." The parson shook a pale pork-like hand and took his leave. They were free. Blanford was wild with relief and regret. And yet speechless as an anchorite.

They had not long to wait outside the chapel before the beadle-like mute stalked round the corner of the building, holding in his arms two grotesque *bonbonnières* a little larger than the traditional Easter egg, which he distributed with an air of conscientious commiseration. Cade almost snatched at his, and to Blanford's surprise, actually beamed with pleasure, as if he were receiving a gift which brought the greatest joy. Then he caught the curious eye of his master upon him and scowled his way back into his normal taciturnity. Blanford felt a fool sitting in the back of the Daimler with an urn in his lap, and as soon as he could he placed it gingerly on the nearest mantelpiece. Ashes to ashes, dust to dust. . . .

But he was aware that a deep fault had opened in the ground under his feet – the past was now separated from the future by it. The taste of this new freedom was unnerving, as was the knowledge that if he chose to live modestly on what he had inherited he need not seek employment. A life of quiet travel and introspection seemed to sketch itself upon the horizons – yes, but with Livia? Yes, but with a war? History with the slow fuses of calamity smouldering away . . . He had selected a modest hotel from which he started to take long afternoon walks in the rain, passing more often than not the gates of the school where Sutcliffe taught and read music so many moons later. Once he even went into the close and sneaked a glance into the chapel which would so often echo with the great man's voice. On the white cliffs mewed up by seagulls with the voices of sick kittens he felt the (valedictory?) rain pouring off the peak of his hat, the shoulders of his coat. Is there only one sort of death for us all, or does each death partake of the ... valency, so to speak, of the life it replaces? It would be marvellous to know. Suddenly there came into his memory the dark intense face of Quatrefages saying: "I believe Eliphas Levi when he says that the devil is God's ruins. If you embark on the path to sainthood and fail to achieve your goal you are condemned to become a demon."

Suddenly Tu Duc rose up in his mind's eye and vibrated with an almost unbearable longing; it had all been too brief. What he must try and do, he suddenly thought, is to drive down there and await the war in the seclusion of that little village of Tubain. If he was called up, well and good. (He was still envisaging a 1914-type war.) Yes, he would leave this week and see what Livia thought of the notion – would she come too? If they had to start a married life together surely that would be the most propitious way and the right place to do so? From the window of his bed-room, which gave out onto the recreation ground of the local school, he could stand and watch the boys during "break" and marvel at the unchanging habits of schoolboys through the years. Their habit of buying a tin of condensed milk and punching a hole in it – the sweetened version. This they would suck like monkeys all day long. The older Victorian versions of sweets were still on the market – like the Sherbet Dab, which made you dream you were in bed with the Queen of Sheba. It was rather expensive. Other boys bought an orange and screwed a sugar lump into its skin. This wound could be also sucked with pleasure. Most magical of all was the Gob Stopper, almost the size of a golf ball, which shed successive coats of colour as one sucked. ... His own schooldays seemed half a century away. He often stood there in a muse until dusk fell, and then darkness, while once in a while the moon, "in her exaltation" as the astrologers say, rose to remind him that such worldly musings meant nothing to the hostile universe without. Even war meant nothing? Yes. He would write poems in invisible ink, then, and post them to himself. Was he then *doomed* to be a writer? All circumstance seemed to be at his elbow to prompt him.

> Mirrors will drink your image with intensity
> and bleed your spirit of its density,
> for they are thirsty for the inner man
> and pasture on his substance when they can.
> The double image upside-down
> They drink their fill – you never drown.
> They echo fate which is not kind
> O sweet blood-poisoning of the mind!

It was not too bad a description of the acute narcissism necessary to become a poet. He was anxious to be away south but the Probate people kept him an extra week. It was a strange new sensation to have money in the bank, to be able to write out quite decent-sized cheques. His allowance had been a very modest one, and he had tailored his needs to meet it. Now he bought some clothes which he much needed. But the result of all this was a bad attack of panic-meanness, and for a few days he lunched in a pub on short commons, almost choking himself with Scotch eggs and other such heavy fare. Back in London things were rather different. There was some sense of urgency. He met fellow undergraduates already in uniform and talking of foreign postings. Air raid sirens were in full rehearsal. The newspapers were full of hypothetical battle fronts bristling with arrows. A national daily asked "Where are the War poets?", and the Ministry of Propaganda set about creating some, though this was difficult, as to be really efficacious they would first have to die, and at the moment there was so little chance. Or so it seemed.

But Austria! The bombs, the parades, the curfews self-imposed from panic, the bands of uniformed thugs roaming the streets all night, surely all this was moving in the right direction? In London the left-wing poets announced that Plato was a Fascist and his mature thought was exemplified by Hitler. It was Syracuse all over again. Blanford had no literary contacts, only a few donnish ones. He aspired mildly to be a historian and apart from a few sporadic attacks of verse had little interest in the world of so called literary values. The scene was not wildly exciting. It was still fashionable to fustigate Lawrence, while at home the "serious critic" devoted energy to wondering if Walpole had genius. But Austria was another matter!

All this was preoccupying Sutcliffe no end, for he was stuck in Vienna, waiting for the treatment of Pia to yield some "concrete results" – what a cliché! He was waiting for her to "come to herself" – what a cliché. And this new science was a sort of hedgehog of cross-reference in which one could only have an approximate faith. He spent most of his time in a pastry-shop round the corner, on the square by the Somethingstrasse, 'twixt the so-called Rathouse and the office for the registration of foreign Labour. His German did not exist, so he lived in a sort of fearful fog. He waited for his darling, engulfing the while, at breakneck speed, those ponderous sweetmeats, puffs and flans for which the capital was famous, and feeling himself covered with spots at each new intake of sugar. They lived in a small hotel-room where they returned each night in trembling silence to eat a sandwich while he brewed a coffee in the lavatory. Then slept. She turned her back to the horrible folksy wallpaper and sighed and trembled and talked in her sleep all night. There was no more communication between them; there was nothing they could say to one another that would not wound, would not spoil the chances of this fragile "treatment". It was a real war situation, and moreover it was a costly one. Blanford was touched by his plight and sent him quite a large cheque which was no sooner cashed than swallowed up by the treatment. But Rob had discovered that all the barbers in the capital were females – there were no male figaros. In black dresses with white frilled collars and cuffs they attended to the male scalp at all hours of the day and night. It was his only solace, to be soothed by the fingers of one of these amiable maidens and have his scalp tingled by some alcoholic concoction which made him feel as if he had gathered a halo.

In that small world of neurological patients and terrified Jewish intellectuals who could see the world coming to an end, they made a number of good friends, but the best among them was a dramatic and beautiful Slav whose extravagant and fleshy *ampleur* was somehow wonderfully sexy and composed. She was a writer and a new disciple of Freud, and she spoke of poets then unknown like Rilke and even of Nietzsche whom she claimed to have known – which made them laugh in secret. But they liked her, and she developed a deep fondness for poor Pia.

He stood in the late spring wind – cutting despite the time of the year – and watched his newly acquired motor-car hoisted up into the air at Dover and then plonked down with a shudder on the deck of the ship in which he proposed to travel. He was fearful lest the bump damage its interior – which he visualised vaguely as something very fragile: an engine made of china and supported by hairpins. But it worked well enough when it was discharged again and he set off in a gathering twilight for Paris, driving with immense devoutness on the wrong side of the road. He had been assured that he would soon get used to it and indeed by the time he reached the capital he felt quite at home in the new vehicle. He had avoided thinking too explicitly of Livia partly because he was still in a state of concern and distress about the news Constance had brought, and feared to force a breach between them by demanding an explanation: and partly because with one side of his mind he was troubled by the vague intimation of a side to her life which might in the long run prove fatal to this painful attachment to her.

To his surprise, he was reassured to find the flat empty – or apparently empty, for after a long moment of questing about for evidence of her possible presence in the form of cigarette-butts or journals, he became aware that there was indeed someone in the bathroom at the end of the corridor. He heard the flush clank, and then the sound of running water in the basin. There was light also shining through the fanlight over the door. In this new mood of hovering irritation mixed with sadness, he tapped lightly with his finger and turned the handle, to find that the door was unlocked. As he did so the girl standing naked in front of the long mirror turned also and confronted him with a bold and impervious stare. No, both adjectives were quite incorrect – it was simply the calm animal quality which made him qualify her gaze thus. It was as if he had interrupted some self-assured pussy-cat at her ablutions. In fact she had just finished shaving under the arms with a small safety razor which he recognised as his own. She had swabbed the pits with a sponge and patted them with a rolled towel. Now she was simply there, and her great bronze face with its marvellous Easter Island eyebrows gazed equably at him full of a keen friendship. A vivacious light shone in those sumptuous eyeballs, the light of tropical islands, where all thinking is muffled by sunlight. "She went this morning," said the Martiniquaise hoarsely, setting her fine head back to clear her helmet of dark hair off her shoulders. "But only a moment ago."

This was the girl whose French was so "killing"; and in her satiny nakedness she was of great beauty but also of great strength. The figure was athletic – that of a discus thrower or an Amazon of the javelin. But she was friendly, and had no thought but to please.

It was indeed her professional cue to be so and an endearing paganism shone warmly out of her eyes and mind. Those little tip-tilted breasts she leaned towards him now in a soft gesture of shy friendship. "Take me," they said, "I am all antelope. I am all musk-melon. I am spice-islander." He raised his hand perhaps to slap her but she did not flinch, she almost appeared to welcome the blow – perhaps as a sort of expiation; his hand fell to his side again. He stood there quite still and listened to the ticking of his own mind – no, it was his wrist-watch. The woman said, "All finish with her – *fini*. *Elle a dit à moi!*" She tapped herself on the breastbone, stretching her long throat-line the while, with the dignified mien of some Polynesian queen. Yes, it was finished. He suddenly realised that, and, wondering at the irrationality of the human mind, he asked himself which of two reasons was the stronger. Was it because of the sexual betrayal as much as because he had discovered her opening his letters? Curiously enough the second reason seemed every bit as wounding as the first. He had old-fashioned notions about marriage and privacy, the fruit of his English education. "You say nothing?" said the woman, and he agreed, shaking his head and staring steadily at her until he felt the small prickle of incipient tears starting up. He felt ashamed of them.

She moved towards him in sympathy and then his hand, groping for a handkerchief, encountered the black rubber dildo which was still attached to her pubis, buckled on to her body by a section of dark webbing with a fastening at the back, over her rump. He took it awkwardly in his hand. There were little metal buckles round the crown of the penis, presumably to add pleasure. But what an extravagant invention, and how coarse compared to the tender and sensitive organ for which it was so pathetic a substitute. She poked it against him and laughed. Then with hands behind her back she undid it, with the gesture of one who unbuckles a sword, and let it flop to the floor where it lay, a grotesque trophy of their coupling minds. He turned on his heel and went back into the small salon, where a tremendous confusion reigned. In his haste he had overlooked this tangle of lipstick-marked towels and torn paper wrappings – marks of a hasty packing-up and departure. Through the open door he could see the unmade bed, with the pile of old newspapers lying beside it. Standing there, breathing softly and considering, he felt the weight of his grief mixed with both anger and relief. But where was the letter of farewell which she must undoubtedly have written and left somewhere? The dark girl must have scented his confusion and divined the reasons; she went to the cupboard and opened the door. It was there with a few of his clean shirts. It was terse and to the point. She was going into Germany and not coming back if she could help it. They must divorce.

About the sense of failure there was no doubt, but it was perplexingly supplemented by a feeling of freshness – the fresh wind of freedom which quickened all the staleness of the last few weeks, all the doubts which he now realised that he had been stifling. It was with a pang of remorse for this feeling that he watched the dark girl change into a clean frock and express herself as ready to accompany him towards the inevitable consolation of a drink which would topple sadness and free him once more to see the world for what it was ... an absurd way of putting it. The new world that was

beginning to emerge from the slime of history – would it be
so very different from the old?

> Boys and girls come out to play,
> Children of the *godmichet*
> Now let each seraphic mouse
> Between the thighs keep open house
> Let their uncanny kisses rain
> Upon the upturned face of pain
> In grief at having lived in vain.

In the Sphinx all was light and the pleasant frenzy of
welcome by all the acquaintances he had made when he was
last there. The Martiniquaise disappeared about her tasks of
pure ablution round earth's shores – his Keats was rusting
visibly – and left him to the silence and introspection of his
notebooks which even by then had started to gather their
aphoristic fungus, their snatches of verse and prose. He
plunged his hearing into the swathes of coarse talk and
laughter, his sense of smell with delection into the smoke of
cigars and Celtique cigarettes. Friends came up to salute
him, students from the Midi with warm accents so different
from the curt Parisian parrot-accent. *Didonk mon gar comment
sava* – his ears transliterated sound and conveyed it to his
limping understanding. No, his French was not bad, just
rather slow. It would have been appropriate to reply: *Cava
très mâle* – with the circumflex. But really he was too
despondent about his circumstances to appreciate his own
feeble witticism. He set himself to drink ardently in the
traditional manner of the jilted Anglo-Saxon. Later he would
break up the bar, get himself knocked out and put in custody
for the night. This would obviate sleeplessness and idle
thoughts about suicide which would be simply anachronistic –
since the whole of Europe was bent upon that course. It
would be pretentious, an individual act of the kind. Even
if the hemlock, love's castration-mixture, worked. Who did

he think he was, Socrates? Passing to and fro, leading her clients up the stairs or dismissing them at the foot, the dark girl took the time to stroke his shoulder or hair. Was she trying to fire him? He bent more closely to his book.

The fatal absinthe did not so much fire the blood as alter the heartbeat, anaesthetise one; one became steadily gloomier and more wretched until, just before the cataleptic trance of oblivion, one was seized with a positive epilepsy of joy, a frenzied ecstasy in the mode of St. Vitus. One pulled beards, danced with chairs, imitated famous ventriloquists. The police came. He had never as yet gone beyond a second glass of the mysterious and milky liquid. Yet already the first stage – that of an unsteady torpor – had seized him. His desires had become unwieldy, infused by a sort of sulky passion. He gazed around at the long bar with its patient and attentive clients sipping their drinks and allowing themselves to be fondled into heat by the all-but naked girls. Trade was brisk. In the outer café beyond the bead curtain a harsh music burned like straw – *la vie* forever *en rose*. The next time she passed and placed her hand on his head he was sufficiently emboldened by hemlock to run his fingers up into her fork and touch the moist fountain of youth under her sarong. "*Viens, chéri,*" she breathed, and buttoning up his *serviette* to secure his precious notebooks he lurched to his feet and obeyed. Quick as a swallow now she ducked back to where the Madam of the house sat, enthroned in wigged splendour like a very very old ice cream of a deposed empress, watching keenly over the form of her female stable. The girl took a *jeton* and was given a fresh towel which she draped over her arm like a waiter. They then mounted the stairs, negotiating them very successfully, and at last entered the little cubicle which was white and clinical and decorated only by a hideous eiderdown on the bed and a crucifix over the bidet.

The divine spasm assuaged nothing, nor did it modify the hunger it was intended to cure. He saw it now – with a phantom of disgust – as an act of barren retaliation. But skin was as glossy as ivy, breath as sweet as newly minted cocoons, so who was he to challenge fate, especially after his second hemlock? It was later that he discovered that she had managed stealthily to empty his wallet; happily his rentier's low cunning had foreseen something of the kind and he had placed two-thirds of his *fric* in the hind pocket of his trousers which he kept firmly in view at the end of the bed. It remained only to catch a homely clap now and he would be all artist. The serpent lay beside him breathing softly, waiting for him to recover his strength, fondling him the while to see if there wasn't another kick in the old *manivelle*. As a sort of testimonial to his masculinity she sowed a few love bites, little *suçons*, upon his throat and shoulders. Heigho! So this was the creative life as lived in this seamy capital? He had begun to feel somewhat of an initiate by now, though his mind still flirted with anger and sadness.

But here was a new problem – his walk had gained a strange swaying amplitude which was unwonted; coming down the stairs he had sudden flashes of vision which made him feel that he was falling backwards into a prism of yellow light. Dismayed, and a trifle alarmed – he was perfectly sober, only his legs flirted with gravitational fields beyond his knowledge – he hung himself on the bar again, in order to gain time. Though he asked for nothing he found another bloody hemlock standing before him and in his shy confusion drank it. Faces were pivoting in the mirrors, other girls seemed eager to share their favours with him. He clutched the wad of notes at his bum and allowed an attack of meanness to overwhelm him. By breathing deeply and evenly he steadied the optic nerves and then steered his way majestically into the night, tenderly unhooking the ivy-soft arms and fingers which sought to stay him, and keeping tight hold of his diary-notebooks.

At the Dôme there was a crowd gathered in the inner dining-room around a radio from which poured stream upon stream of terrifying rhetoric in a voice which by now the whole world had come to know only too well. The barmaid – a rather handsome little second-hand widow in a good state of repair – had provided this curiosity for them, though she knew that almost none of her customers understood German. It was simply the spectacle that riveted them, the phenomenon of that grating snarling voice; the sense they might well guess. And then the roaring applause. He thought of Livia. But what was he doing here? What had prompted him to enter another bar? The answer was a thirst, a raging thirst. He realised the folly of drinking so much Pernod, and called now for a pint of champagne. It hardly mended the situation, except that the coolness was invigorating. But now he was really drunk and his subsequent wanderings gathered impreciseness as time wore on. He lost his briefcase and his umbrella. Thank goodness he had had the sense to leave his passport back in the flat with other and more valuable papers. . . . He nearly fell over the Pont Neuf, enjoyed the conversation and esteem of several hairy clochards, and was finally knocked down by a taxi in the Place Vendôme, whose driver, appalled by what he had done, had the humanity and despatch of his profession, and loading him into the back raced hotfoot to the American Hospital in Neuilly where his confusions were worse confounded by drugs intended to secure him some sleep while they investigated his bones.

He informed the doctor seriously: "The whole of humanity seems simultaneously present in every breath I draw. The weight of my responsibility is crushing. A merciful ignorance defends me from becoming too despondent." He was told to shut up and sleep, and was reassured that while no bones were broken he had been much "concussed", which accounted for some of the bells ringing in his head.

Deus absconditus, the shaggy God of all drunkards' slumbers, now invaded him, and in his mind's mind he found himself wandering the ever green lanes of a southern landscape, hand in hand with the sort of Livia he had dared to imagine – one he was never to see in reality; or else seated at the stained old table in the garden covering page after page of his notebooks in a hand which he vaguely recognised as that of Sutcliffe. Time stretched away on either side of the point-event of each drawn breath, back into the subfusc suburban past, forwards into a veiled future, but somehow as yet void of significance. The writer, *l'homme en marge*, writing the Memoirs of a Marginal Man. On the title-page he had written, in this large flamboyant and rather hysterical hand: "All serial reality is by this writing called into question." The radio went on and on in his head, roaring and foaming. An ape fingering a safety catch – Europe was holding its breath. He bent his aching head lower and wrote on, "I have no biography; a true artist, I go through life like a character in one of my own books." To this S added, "My first experience of an audience was when, as a fattish youth, I played Adipose Rex in the school play. Since then I have often dreamed of living in a deserted school (life?) full of empty rooms, open doors and clean blackboards; yes, life waiting for the scholars of breathing. Comrade, continue that poem in invisible ink, ask yourself why the Dalai Lama has no Oedipus Complex." "Silly, because he has no parents. . . ."

The sirens wailed once or twice briefly like supercats *en chasse*. These were practice calls only but they wrung the heart. Marriage to her would be like drinking wine from a paper cup. What he had really needed was the smell of warm sirloin, smell of cooking in fair hair which had bent over the stove, the scent of celery in the armpits. Already he seemed to have lived a dozen lifetimes with her, all in the same cottage. For years afterwards they would remain, the claw-marks on the door where every night the dog scratched to be let in, the scratches she had made with her key around the lock. Suddenly the voice of Sutcliffe admonished him: "Aubrey, you have a mind like a fatty chop. Be silent or be completely fascinating. Never bore." The poor fellow could not have felt in any better humour than his bondsman yet he persisted in being flippant – though at times his voice was quite squeaky from fatigue. He quoted:

> Our old telluric artichoke,
> We sucked her leaves but nothing woke;
> The cactus of the primal scene
> Had mogrified her sweet demean.

Blanford, always slow to retort yet determined to get some of his own back, sat up and said: "Rob, you haven't the talent to rub a bit of polish off the primal apple; you are simply an old football full of pus."

Somewhere in the course of his military training at Oxford he had come across the expression "omega grey", and had been told that it was the scientific designation of the deepest grey before complete blackness; now as his troubled sleep swirled about him, changing form and colour and resonance, it seemed to him that the whole of the outer world beyond the window of the white ward was painted in this colour – the almost black of death. Omega grey – the phrase echoed on in his mind, though whether he was asleep or awake he could not guess. This drug-bemused reality was filtered through a mesh of discrete sensations, containing fragments of the recent past juxtaposed or telescoped upon fearful contexts. He saw the body of his mother transformed by a neo-Cubist painter into a series of porpoise-faced nudes. Her teeth were all but opaque, her gums fashioned in gelatine.

Swollen to enormous size she floated over the Thames to defend it against enemy aircraft; moreover she was all grey, camouflage grey, *omega* grey, the last colour before the dark night of the soul settled over them like a new ice age. There would hardly be time enough to achieve that state of beatitude and equilibrium which for him was already associated (wrongly) with the creative act. What was he doing here in this molten bed, fuddling while Rome burned? He should have been telling his beads and praying aloud.

He pressed his palms on his eyelids and sent showers of sparks flying across his eyeballs. Yes, it was there, the state he vaguely hankered to achieve! It already lay somewhere inside him in a completely unrealised form – or rather he knew it was there without being able to locate it. It was like hunting through the house for one's spectacles when they were on the top of one's head, perched on one's crown. A vomit of words, linked by pure association, floated below his visions like the subtitles to an incomprehensible film written by a lunatic. (The drunkard's word list is sometimes the sage's also.) A vision of Livia with her finger to her lips.

> The weather is breaking up, my puss,
> The cards are down in autumn stars

In his dream he told her: "The maddening thing is that what is to find cannot be looked for. You are trying desperately to acquire what you already possess but do not recognise. Meditation brings on a state of perilous heed – it is not mere daydreaming. All this would be risible if it were not so serious a matter." To which she replied sweetly, shaking that fine cervine head: "At any moment tell yourself that things are much better than they have any right to be." What sophistry! In the streets he saw the faces passing, omega-grey glances upon pavements of omega grey. Yes, there was nothing that did not lead somewhere – yet everything also had a built-in trap that at any moment could become an obstacle.

Suddenly the scene changed to a basement in Vienna – he knew it to be Vienna without knowing how he could know; for he had never been there.

A swarm of violins started up somewhere and through half-closed eyes he saw the fiddlers performing their hieratic arabesque – girls combing out their long hair. Bearded candles in the darkness gave them not rose or carmine, but the uniform pork tint of omega grey. A slowly folding line of music from some fugue wrapped them all in a melancholy tenebrousness. There were a dozen or so people there, but he only recognised the faces of Sutcliffe and Pia. There was something startling about their attention and he suddenly realised that they were listening, not to the music which welled from the radio, but to the distant crepitations of musketry and machine-gun fire, punctuated from time to time in the furthest corner of space by the soft thud of a mortar. There was trouble almost every night, they told him, and they were forced to live by a self-imposed curfew, more or less. It had, however, not been going on long, but the persecution of the Jews was beginning.

Then, abruptly, as if the scene had been "cut" like a film sequence, they found themselves walking timorously among deserted squares and startled public statuary, with a light spring snowfall blurring everything and obliterating skylines. They were heading for a quarter of the town which was predominantly inhabited by the intellectual élite of medicine and the arts. Here were the practice rooms where right round the clock one heard pianos playing scales and snatches of classical music, heard sopranos giving tongue, heard the gruff commentary of tubas practising. The nationalists had been busy wrecking this quarter during the earlier part of the evening and had been driven off by police, or else had had their attention diverted by other prey in other quarters where the inhabitants were easier to bait or intimidate. They had, however, left a legacy in the form of two large bonfires burning away – mounds of medical books doused with petrol. All the windows were open and the flats from which these articles had been seized and hurled into the street appeared now to be empty. All the lights burned on, furiously on, as if outraged, but there was no human form to be seen. Then Pia saw the old-fashioned sofa half in and half out of the window on the third floor, and she gave a wild sad cry. These were the old consulting-rooms which the penurious medical crew could hire specially cheaply, for they were subsidised by the university. The sofa! She had recognised one of the old consulting-rooms which an impecunious Freud had shared with Bleuler when they were making their first halting steps towards a theory of the unconscious. It was the same old leather-covered monster of a committee-room sofa upon which the master had (it seemed a century ago now) invited her to recline. On it, writhing to and fro like someone in a high fever, she had embarked on that strange adventure which as yet seemed to be never ending; one promise succeeded another, one remission followed another relapse. Now this fond critical instrument of torture hung there like a maimed crocodile.

In the wild cry of recognition with which Pia greeted this spectacle was mixed all the anguish and reverence she felt for this shabby symbol posed so outrageously upon the window-sill – like a woman too fat to get out or in now, irretrievably stuck, waiting for the fire brigade to rescue her. As a matter of fact they could be heard approaching some streets away, though their customary moaning signals were mixed with the sinister mesh-like sound of caterpillar-tracks upon concrete. A light tank prowled across their line of vision a couple of street corners away. They had been joined by a small group of medical students who were in a high pitch of excitement – they all looked as if they had been drinking.

Now a man had appeared at the window from which the sofa protruded – a sort of janitor it would seem, from his green apron. He had been going round turning off lights and closing open doors. He paused irresolutely for a moment before the sofa, obviously wondering what to do about it. It protruded so far that it was impractical to drag it back, though he seemed at first tempted to try. It was hanging by its back legs above the burning street. The students began to gesticulate and shout in a desultory fashion, though without any clear idea of what might be done to ameliorate the present situation, the smashed lamp standards, the burning books. Suddenly the concierge at the window came to decision. With a heave he disengaged the back legs of the ugly old crocodile and catapulted the whole thing into the street, where it fell upon one of the burning piles of books. The sirens had come much closer. "Quick!" cried Pia, quite beside herself with anxiety, for the sofa had begun to smoulder at the edges. "Quick!" People gazed at each other wondering what she could mean, but she herself had darted forward and caught the old crock by the shoulders, pulling it with a frantic, almost superhuman force, until it was clear of the flames. "We must save it," she said. "Rob, for Christ's sake . . ." Bemused and puzzled as he was he broke into a clumsy run and, without for an instant understanding what their objective might be, helped her tug it clear. Other students now, equally in the dark, came to their aid, and acting like lunatics they picked it up and set off at a trot for the nearest shelter. The whole performance was totally spontaneous and unplanned. It had been sparked by the intensity of her cry and the concentrated passion of her actions – she looked like someone in a trance. Obviously this tattered object was of the utmost value and importance to her. Obligingly the crowd helped her save it and drag it to the relative safety of an air-shelter with a wall where they placed it under a tree. They were all panting and yet somehow exultant. From the other end of the square now burst the police and the fire-engines, dramatic and noise-bearing as a whole opera. It was time to shrink back into the shadows and disappear. They left the old sofa sitting there in the light snowfall.

Events had moved so fast and so dramatically that they themselves were quite out of breath with astonishment at what they had done. "What will you do with it?" cried Sutcliffe now, aware that they could hardly house it in their little hotel, and she thought fiercely for a moment, her pale face bowed. They were already walking fast, almost running, towards their hotel, trying to select untroubled streets where they would not meet patrols. Friends were waiting for them at the hotel – among them the Slav girl – and they ordered coffee in the tiny shabby lounge where they would, as was customary, hear an account of the day's happenings both in the capital and in the world – the outer world which loomed over their daily minds like a storm cloud. "Whatever happens we must keep it," said Pia decisively, in the middle of a conversation about something else; and he knew she meant this stupid old sofa for which he himself felt nothing. Had she gone mad? He asked her, but she was already explaining what they had done to her friend whose face lit up with a triumphant and generous approval. The two women, he thought, were as superstitious as savages. What would they plan next?

The outcome was even more unexpected than he had any reason to suppose. Medical students, friends of the Slav, now arrived upon the scene, and they warmly approved of this absolutely medieval gesture. (They would be selling indulgences next!) They were young and impetuous and determined to rescue the totem. The only problem was to decide what should be done with it. There were several lines of thought. One wished to give it houseroom in his flat, another thought it should be carted to the Faculty and placed in the hall – but of course the medical authorities, who had hardly heard of Freud, would have had a fit at the very suggestion. Suddenly Pia pronounced upon the matter with so much vehemence that everyone knew that she would not be gainsaid. "It is mine," she said, "and I intend to keep it. I shall send it to my brother in Avignon. I have quite decided." There was no more to say; all that was left was to decide upon the details of transport – how the devil could one send a sofa? Obviously by rail. Yes, but what about transport to the station? Here one of the students, who worked part-time with an undertaker, suggested that he borrow the hearse to transport the holy relic. "Yes! Yes!" she cried and clapped her hands exultantly. "That is what we must do. I shall telephone to him tonight."

So it was that, at five in the morning, Mr. Sutcliffe found himself seated with an air of ludicrous amazement in a large black hearse, in front of what to the average passer-by must have seemed something like a very large corpse wrapped up in a brown-paper parcel. They had indeed enveloped the charred old article in several layers of brown paper, the better to label it, and to their surprise there seemed to be no problem about sending it. It would await arrival in Avignon.

Blanford had followed all this hazily, through the heavy meshes of his dream, and he conveyed his approval of the whole initiative through the usual channels – the pulse-beat of the blood. But he had decided that Constance must have the relic, not Pia; and as he carried more weight in everything to do with real reality, he knew that he could override the present decision, and persuade a carter to take charge of the sofa and ferry it up, not to Verfeuille but to Tu Duc. He said as much and to his surprise Sutcliffe did not demur – it was a measure of his indifference to the relic. He had come to hate the whole science of psychowhatsit, which promised the moon and came unstuck at every corner.

"Very well, *maître*," he said ironically, "if you say so. How is Paris treating you?"

"A pleasing priapism rules the waves," said his incoherent and maundering *alter ego* or *summum bonum*. "The croissants are brown as mahogany. I saw her at dusk, reading in a public garden, and I longed to approach her and ask where she had been. She had disappeared for nearly a week. But I dared not. I sat on an adjacent bench and told myself that it was not her, it was just someone who resembled her. She was reading one of my unwritten novels – with pious intensity. Beside her lay a bag with a half-eaten croissant in it. She was sunk in profound thought, I could see that, and would certainly be sulky if approached. I closed my eyes and waited. When at last she got up to go I saw that indeed it was not her but someone who resembled her. The discarded paper bag lay where she had abandoned it. I scattered the croissant for the birds and went home by the lake in order not to give her the illusion of spying on her. But of course when I got back there was, as usual, nobody at the flat."

> Little grains of splendour,
> Little knobs of lust,
> Make a writer tremble,
> Loving is a must
> Nor can he dissemble
> When his heart is bust.
> Let all young women bring me their emulsion,
> Gods are born thus with every fond convulsion!
>   THUS SPOKE ZARATHUSTRA!

He went on foundering more and more deeply in these patches of dream-nightmares which stretched away on all sides of him to the horizon, feeling his mind being feverishly ransacked by the combined fevers of medicine and alcohol. The dark streets of Vienna had been replaced by Paris. Night-watchmen everywhere, a tribe of scowling lurkers, loveless as poets whose minds had become viscous with fatigue, waiting for dawn. Broken glasses, club feet, *arthritis deformans*, huge clubbed thumbs. He kept waving his arms and protesting, trying to obliterate these images of menace, but they persisted, they gained on him.

His eventual release from hospital, albeit rather reluctant, was something that he simply had to accept – it would have been malingering to stay comfortably between the sheets with nothing worse than post-alcoholic depression and a touch of shock. The kindly taximan who had knocked him down came to see him and offered him a free ride back into his *quartier*. The young doctor, who was called Bruce, saw no objection. The hospital cashed his cheque without a tremor, leaving him enough change to resume civilian life once more, so to speak. Back then to the empty flat, deposited at the Dôme by his kindly overturner. But once home he became suddenly aware of his weakness, and sat down on the unmade bed with a thump; his desolation continued to manufacture discordant images of loss, but they were more inconsequential now and less forceful. Where could he find some rest – the loneliness in this little box-like flat was intolerable. If he went back to the Coupole or the Sphinx he would be undone. He hid therefore in a local cinema, feeling the fleas jumping about his thighs while he watched the amours of that most congenial of all funny men, W. C. Fields. "Dharling banana, where's your sense of humour? Fragrant yam, you are my dish." Wondering vaguely – the subtitles were hairy with age – how all this would translate. Provide your own version. *"Clafoutis imberbe*! *Potiron du jour*!"

When at last he struggled to his feet and sought the exit, night had already fallen, the mauve-magenta night which was part street-lamp and part aerial radiation of white light against the blue-black sky of cheap fur. He was hungry; he scuttled to the Dôme and ate bacon and eggs with energy, gazing round with distaste at all the other representatives of the arts and crafts who surrounded him. Pride of lions, skirl of loafers, extravagance of poets. No, he would go far away, he would eat liquid mud on toast in far-away Turkish khans. Far far from the dungy altars of the Nonconformist mind. He would order a clyster for all parish Prousts of the Charing Cross Road. He would ... On the cusp of a mere nod the waiter replenished his glass. He realised that he was still calamitously drunk in a reactivated sort of way. His blood coursed. He was surrounded by Africans with beautiful fuzzy heads and booming tones. They had all come to Paris to gather culture. Here they were, screaming for worm-powders. What was to be done? Great sweet turbines of black flesh innocently cutting slices of Keats or Rimbaud for their evening meal. A wholesome cannibalism when you thought of it. *O Grand Sphincterie des Romains*! O spice routes of the poetic mind which lead to the infernal regions below the subliminal threshold. Metaphors too big for their boots, literature of the S-bend. Wind in an old chimney – fatherly flatus? He should be more modern, go into business.

> To shit, to codify a business lunch
> A pint of lager and a brunch.

He had ordered various things for which the tally of saucers did not work, so the waiter had issued him with little price slips. It was on one of these that he jotted down a few figures, trying during a coherent patch in his thoughts to mobilise his reason and estimate what his expenses might be when he left Paris on the morrow, as he now intended to do. When it came to pay the waiter tore up these slips as he cleared the table. Then he noticed that they were scribbled over and he turned pale. "*O Monsieur!*" he exclaimed, beside himself with vexation, "*j'ai déchiré vos brouillons!*" He was under the impression that he had inadvertently destroyed the rough notes of some foreign poet of genius. His confusion was touching, his relief when he was reassured on the point, hardly less genuine. Blanford realised that he was madly in love with Paris. He had much to learn from these extraordinary people, for whom the word artist meant so much.

He felt steadier now in wind and limb, and visited the garage where he had left his car, to reassure himself about the servicing, and as to whether he might find it available for him at six in the morning, for he planned to make an early start and perhaps lie for the night at Lyon. All was in order, happily.

He went for one last drink to the Sphinx with the intention of bidding the Martiniquaise goodbye – with the present ambiguous and ill-regulated state of affairs he felt that he should really tell her of his movements, in case Livia reappeared and wished to know where he might be found. But the girl was not there that evening, she had gone to the cinema, though nobody knew which. He wrote her a message and left it with the presiding Mama who regally accepted to see it delivered. Then he drank his drink and departed, making his way back to the sad little flat, so empty now of resonance and tone – as if even its memories of the events which had taken place within its walls had gone dead and stale.

Nor could he sleep – images floated him beyond reach of it. He was hunting down the great rat of the emotions with a heavy stick in a dark house, creeping from staircase to staircase, pausing to listen from time to time. The night was full of the noise of cats feasting on garbage and each other – stale cats, the fitting symbol for temple women, all faceless claws and minds and civet. He threw up the window and stuck his face against the sky – the whole of space, sick as an actress, living in a state of permanent and thoughtless manifestation. He would be glad to get away from the Sphinx where trusting little Benzedrine Papadopoulos opened her twiggy legs to show a black bushy slit with a red silk lining. Farewell to Livia and the dry copyists' succinct word for craving – four letters beginning with L. Avignon radiated the memory of peace and contentment, and tomorrow he would be on the road once more.

In contrast to the affairs of the world, his own were more or less in order; the little flat would revert to its owner automatically for the rent had not been paid. He had wound up all household bills, debts to the newsagent, and the like. He was vacating Paris – it was a hollow enough feeling. He passed by the Dôme and scanned the letter board which contained as always a wealth of messages which waited patiently to be reclaimed. There was nothing from her, and he was a fool to have expected anything. On an impulse he copied out a poem from his notebook and placed it in an envelope with her name on it. It was valedictory enough to suit the occasion; he felt inexpressibly sad about the whole business, about the whole failure to connect, to unite. He was also alarmed for her safety – for he was, unaccountably, still deeply attached to her.

BURIED ALIVE

for Livia

A poem filling with water,
A woman swimming across it
Believing it a lake,
The words avail so little,

The water has carried them away
Frail as a drypoint the one kiss,
Renovation of a swimmer's loving.

Attach a penny calendar to the moon
And cycle down the highways of the need,
The doll will have nothing under her dress;
With an indolence close to godhead
You remain watching, he remains watching.

When she smiles the wrinkles round her eyes
Are fitting, the royal marks of the tiger,
The royal lines of noble conduct.

Virtuous and cryptic lady, whom
The sorrows of time forever revisit,
Year after year in the same icy nook
With candles brooding or asphodels erect,
Stay close to us within your mind.
These winter loves will not deceive,
Unplanned by seasons or by kin
They feast the eye beneath the skin.

SEVEN

Prince Hassad Returns

NOR WAS HE THE ONLY ONE RETURNING TO AVIGNON, he discovered, for he later found it bruited that Lord Galen and the Prince had already come rumbling and roaring and careening out of Germany together in a high state of emotional and intellectual disarray. It had not taken long for the gimlet eye of the Prince to pierce to the heart of Galen's romantic folly; he could hardly credit what it revealed of the whole catastrophic investment. Among so many miscalculations of the same order, this one stood out as a monument of the purest insanity – and so fearfully expensive to boot. Never in Galen's long career as a "gentleman-adventurer" (he was fond of the phrase) had he committed such a fearful "bloomer" (another he favoured). Indeed the blow appeared to have all but demolished him – at all events temporarily. His sang-froid had turned its back on him. He walked with a stoop, giving the impression that the disaster had actually aged him. You felt he was worn out with the long and humiliating journey back to sweet reason. At all events they drew up at Les Balances in Geneva for an orgy of accounting and numerous vital meetings with paler and paler executives. To tell the truth Prince Hassad was less bruised, less cast down, for he had invested nothing in the scheme. In fact he hovered on the edge of smiles, although his cumbersome coach caused endless annoyance in the parking spaces of the city and his staff much excitement. It was Galen who bore the brunt of it all; try as he might there was no disguising his asininity.

The Prince had, heaven knows, been the soul of tact, but from time to time a mortal chuckle escaped him. He struck his knee and wrinkled into lizard-like smiles of a private nature; but Galen could quite well guess why. Though the little man in his royal green-striped flower-pot actually *said* nothing his chuckles lodged like barbs in the tender cuckold flesh of his associate's consciousness. Things had gone so far that they had actually been threatened with arrest unless they decamped – and this by the Nazis! Galen rather wished now they had been arrested – his sadness would have been sub-limated by an expiation of sorts. "Well," said the Prince, "it is no use just going on brooding. We have made a ghastly incoherence. You must save what you can." He was kind enough to pretend that he had shared the misfortune. "Look on the brighter side," he said, turning Stoic. "In two or three months we shall all be dead – you have read about the nerve gas in the *Tribune?*" Galen obediently thought about his approaching death and felt quite cheerful of a sudden. Yes, there was no use brooding. The Prince picked his teeth and reflected; he had spent all day at the Egyptian Embassy, telephoning and sending telegrams in cipher. "My dear friend," he said, "you will go on to Provence and arrange your affairs. I have things I must attend to. I will follow in ten days' time and we can decide everything else."

"You aren't leaving me?" said Galen, pulling his under-lip and pouting. "Only for a while," said Prince Hassad, "and I think the best thing for you, my friend, is to wind up things here and then go back south. I will send off the coach ahead. In ten days we meet again and then there will be big decisions to make. I fear I must leave all my new friends in Avignon and return to Egypt for a while, until we see what form this war takes. There is a big Italian Army on the frontiers of Egypt, for example, and we don't know . . . well, *anything* as yet.* As for you, it is impossible to disguise your

* See Appendix.

incoherences." (His perfect English had nevertheless small and unexpected flaws of usage.) "So why not make the best of them and just be frank. Eh?"

Lord Galen considered being frank, with his head on one side, like a fox-terrier. "Just admit I've been a fool?"

"Exactly."

"I never thought of that," said Galen and looked suddenly relieved. Nevertheless his sorrow and humiliation were not unduly lightened by this decision of the Prince to desert him in Geneva for a few days and take the express for London and just when he needed company and sympathy too! But Hassad insisted that he had a number of things to attend to before returning home, and that these must be despatched before, in the popular phrase of the hour, "the balloon went up". The image of a bright Montgolfière – Europe itself no less – floating up and out into the unknown empyrean of the future was suitably frivolous.

After the comparative calm of Geneva, the cud-chewing capital *par excellence*, it was strange to sit in a first-class carriage of the Golden Arrow as it drew away from frenetic and gossipy Paris where one could secure a laugh at cocktail parties by giving the Nazi salute. (The Prince was terrified when he thought of it.) He sat bolt upright in his corner seat mechanically doing the *Times* crossword puzzle and waiting for the lunch gong to summon him swaying down the corridor towards a hearty but insipid meal.

Yet the quicksand of an international lethargy was still the factor which so mysteriously dominated everything. Time, from being a solution, had become a jelly. On the outer fringe of things everything seemed in a state of violent agitation. There were trumpet-calls, denunciations, sabre-rattlings, government pronouncements ... but the whole in a sort of void. People scurried about like rats, hoarding food or making testamentary dispositions or booking tickets for

America. But these gestures were somehow shapeless and without pith because, in fact, nobody could believe that human beings in this present stage of civilisation could conceive of a war – after the lessons of 1914. The little man said to himself: "It is because it is quite unthinkable that it must happen. People want death really, life poses too many problems." Things proceeded, he had observed, by cruel paradox. He sighed heavily, for not the least of his concerns was with the vulnerable and defenceless England towards which his train was racing, shrieking aloud in tunnels, and leaving behind it a thick black plume of smuts which always managed to settle themselves on his grey spats and on the astrakhan collar of his finely cut overcoat. Everything would have to be cleaned the instant he got back to: London! The word made his heart race, for surely there would be a letter from his little Princess in the diplomatic bag? It was cruel to have left her for so long alone in the dusty old palace on the Nile with nothing much to do save to paint and read and dream about his return. "My partridge!" – the endearment escaped him involuntarily as he thought of her.

The ceremony of the passport control, followed by the abrupt change in the scale of things – the new toy landscape after Dover – set his thoughts wandering in the direction of his youth as a young secretary of Embassy in an England which he had loved and hated with all the emotional polarity of his race. How would she withstand this cataclysm? Would she just founder? He trembled for her – she seemed so exhausted and done for, with her governments of little yellowing men, faded to the sepia of socialism, the beige of bureaucracy. And Egypt, so corrupt, so vulnerable, was at their mercy, in their hands. . . . Long ago he had made a painstaking analysis of the national character in order to help in the education of his Ambassador, dear old Abdel Sami Pasha. But it had been altogether too literary, and indeed altogether too wise. He had distinguished three strains in the English character which came, he was sure, from Saxons, Jutes or Normans – each Englishman had a predominance of one or other strain in his make-up. That is why one had to be so careful in one's dealings with them. The Saxon strain made them bullies and pirates, the Jutish toadies and sanctimonious hypocrites, while the Norman strain bred a welcome quixotry which was capable of rising like a north wind and predominating over the other two. Poor Sami had read the whole memorandum with attention, but without understanding a word. Then he said, "But you have not said that they are rich. Without that . . ."

The long struggle against his English infatuation had coloured his whole life; it had even imperilled his precious national sentiment. How would they ever drive them out of Egypt, how would they ever become free? But then, would it make sense to replace them with Germans or Italians? His glance softened as he saw the diminutive dolls' houses flashing by outside the window, saw the dove-grey land unrolling its peaceful surges of arable and crop, like the swaying of an autumn sea. Yes, this country had marked him, and his little Princess used often to tease him by saying that he even dreamed in English. Damn them, the English! He compressed his lips and wagged his head reproachfully. He lit a slender gold tipped cigarette and blew a puny cloud of smoke high into the air, as if it would dispel these womanish failings of sentiment! Womanish! The very word reminded him that the whole of his love-life and his miraculously happy marriage had been tinged by London. He hoped that Selim had not forgotten to book the suite at Brown's Hotel – the Princess loved Brown's and always sent the porter a Christmas card from Cairo.

But then Egypt was one thing and the Court quite another; their education had modified fanaticism and turned

them willy-nilly into cosmopolitans who could *almost* laugh
at themselves. It came from languages, from foreign nannies
and those long winterings at Siltz or Baden-Baden or Pau. It
had etiolated their sense of race, their nationalism. The French
distinguish between knowing a language and possessing it;
but they had gone even further, they had become possessed
by English. The other chief European tongues they knew
accurately of course, but for purely social purposes. There
was none of the salt in them that he found in English. . . .
Nor was everyone at the Court like him, for some were more
charmed by French, some surrendered to Italian. But it was
his first firm link with Fawzia, the passion for England. Even
when he was at Oxford, and writing anti-British articles in
Doustour under his own signature! And paradoxically enough
she loved him for it, she was proud of his intellectual stance.

The thought made him stamp his spatted foot on the
floor of the compartment, stamp with delight like a little
Arab horse. He had first met her at the Tate; poor darling, she
was piously copying a Cézanne, pausing for long drowsy
moments to dream – so she afterwards averred – of a Prince
who would suddenly appear from nowhere and ask for her
hand in marriage. This made her copying somewhat haphazard. She was chaperoned by the widow of a Bey whose
son had been at Oxford with him, and this gave him the
excuse to exchange a few words with her, and then to be
presented to the Princess. She curtseyed in an old-fashioned
manner, and he bent over those slender fingers, feeling quite
breathless. Indeed they both paled at the encounter. "It was a
moment of silk," in the Arabic phrase. Her dark eyes were
full of ardour, idealism and intelligence. He put on his gold-
rimmed spectacles in a vain attempt to seem older than he
was. The three human beings – everything had become
dream-like and insubstantial – took a slow turn up and down
the gallery, emitting noises about the paintings displayed. He

could feel the words coming out of his mouth but they were like "damp straw". Inside him a voice was saying, over and over again, "Fawzia, I adore you!" He was terrified lest his thoughts be overheard, but she preserved her demure dispositions, though her heartbeat had reached suffocation point. The kind duenna absented herself for a moment and they talked on. He was electrified. *She appreciated Turner!* "We must place him beside Rembrandt," she said firmly, indeed a little school-marmishly. But how right she was! He felt he would start vapouring with devotion if this went on, so he abruptly took his leave with a cold expression on his face which dismayed her for she thought that it was due to disdain for her artistic opinions. She stammered upon the word "Goodbye" in a way that made his heart exult, though he continued to look grim as he stalked out of the gallery. Outside he smacked the back of his hand with his grey gloves, then smelt it to see if any trace of her perfume remained before continuing this reproachful simulacrum of self-punishment. Towards the next religious festival he permitted himself to send her a large and handsome folio of colour reproductions from Turner, expressing the hope that she did not own it already. She did, but she pretended the contrary, and expressed a rapture not the less sincere for being feigned. They met briefly at a number of functions and exchanged quaint fictions of conversation in public, almost suffocating with desire as they spoke. He did not quite know how to advance from this point. He was now a graduate, yes, and though heir to a large fortune in cotton and land, had no precise job. Moreover, their attachment having been launched upon such a high romantic keynote, could not be allowed to sink down the scale and revert to the humdrum. I suppose it was very Shakespearean, but they both believed – privately, secretly, separately, passionately – that nobody had ever loved with such intensity. He was anxious to keep their love free from every taint of Parisian frivolity for he considered French notions about love to be so much straw, vanity and *trompe-l'oeil*. In this period of indecision they made several important discoveries. She found, for example, that his eyes turned violet-green under the stress of aesthetic emotion, as when he spoke of the Turners in the Tate. On his side, he became more and more enraptured by her small vivid hands, so swift in action, and yet folding into her lap like rock-doves. His doctor told him that he was suffering from heightened arterial tension, and gave him a sleeping draught, but he preferred to lie awake and think about her.

Then the way opened before them. His father, after a second heart attack, wrote and told him that he must really consider getting a job and also open negotiations for a wife. He proposed to use (he said) some *piston* in the first instance, (he preferred French culture to English and thought his son's passion unhealthy and indeed unpatriotic): the second contingency he left open, being a wise man. So it was that the Prince found himself a young diplomat *en poste* in his favourite capital; and the young lady received a formal letter which had first been submitted to her aged mother, asking whether he might declare his intentions towards Fawzia. The Arabic he chose was pure though somewhat florid. Afterwards he found that she had been much amused at being referred to as "the person in question" and for a while she signed her love letters with this sweet superscription. Yes, permission was given for them to meet, to speak. The die, as they say in bad novels, was cast.

His good genius, too, must have overheard his prayers, for his choice of a meeting place for the critical encounters with his beloved could not have been more happily chosen. He would call for her, he said, towards the late afternoon and take her for a short drive along the river. She must bring a shawl as the evenings were sometimes chilly and he proposed to show her a sunset before delivering her safely back to her mother's house in Kensington. Call he did, but in one of those smart horse-carriages, with a cockaded and billycocked driver in the Victorian style. There was a whole rank of these smart vehicles, drawn by beautifully groomed horses, which occupied a station near Buckingham Palace – a perfect draw for the sentimental tourists who loved to be photographed in them when visiting London. He was not too formally dressed – just enough for a London sunset. She had put on some finery and had obediently borrowed a shawl from her mother – shawls were old-fashioned articles of a past decade, so this was rather distasteful to her, but it was too early to be disobedient.

She was charmed by his originality and rendered slightly tremulous by his presence. She had practised accepting his offer of marriage in a variety of voices but could not quite decide which to choose. She was going to leave it to fate to decide. For his part he was equally mixed-up but deep down he felt that, in some obscure way, the issue would be decided not by him, but paradoxically enough, by the painter Turner. He began to talk diffusively, discursively, about him, his secret life, the magnitude and simplicity of his vision which ran counter to that of his whole epoch. He quoted, with flashing indignation, the judgement of Constable. ("Paintings only fit to be spit upon.") And she trembled with sympathetic pain and sadness. What pitiable blindness! But his eyes had turned colour again and she felt the deep stirring of her emotions, so deep in fact that she squeezed her thighs hard together in order to allay them. They jaunted out of the Park and took the river at Battersea Bridge from which they could already see the preliminary conflagration of a late spring sunset with all its sultry brutal saffron and carmine. "We shall be just in time," he said. "Do you always do this?" she asked and he nodded with fervour. "Ever since my first

Turner," he said, "years ago now. It is different in each season." He took her hand and pressed it. "It is so very personal," he went on, "and nobody seems to know it. It is his store cupboard, so to speak." Then he broke off to inveigh against the Tate for keeping the vast quantity of the artist's paintings in a cellar and refusing to expose them. And then against Ruskin for exercising censorship. "Shame!" she cried.

How broad it was, and how placidly it flowed, the Thames, under the massive and thickset old bridge. There was little traffic on it at this hour so that they were able to hear the rustle of river traffic, distant hootings, even voices. Spars moved upon the evening sky. All London lay around them in the expiring light. The note of the horse's hooves deepened as they reached land once more, and quite shortly the driver turned sharply to the right, to follow the long sad walls of a factory upon whose river frontage they would later notice the florid legend Silver Belle Flour. On weekdays one could peer through the gates and see flour-whitened figures like snowmen going about their tasks with the air of participating in some medieval rite. But on Sunday all was quiet. Only the children of the poor played their eternal cricket and football upon grass trodden bald by their boots. It was a depressing corner, slummy and down at heel, and she wondered idly where they were going. But it was not far, their destination, for the little church of St. Mary the Virgin still flourished like Martha's Vineyard in the midst of these gaunt deformities of factory and tenement. When they drew to a halt at the slender iron gates which opened upon a green lawn, she saw that there was a great sweep of skyline open to the west with no cumbersome buildings to break it down and arrest the mind. She looked keenly about her with her bird-like grace. "You will see with His eyes!" he cried suddenly, exultantly – and indeed on an almost theological note, so that she wondered for a moment whether there was not to be a touch of religious fanaticism underneath this exuberance. "Whose?" she asked, turning quite white, her pulse a-flutter. "His!" he said sternly and would vouchsafe no more.

So the year 1777 came to meet them across the river water in the form of St. Mary the Virgin, with its four eloquent pillars holding up, caryatid-like, the deep-roofed porch. The spire, the clock, the green belfry – so spare yet so vivacious in execution – set off the whole with unemphatic charm. The whole thing seemed to them a paradisiacal model of what village church architecture should be, should stand for. The growling circumambient toils of London around them faded before the calm of these innocent precincts. The grass was crisp and bright before the church, and was studded with a few tall trees. But it was small in extent and ended in the stout sea-wall against which lay a couple of ships, marooned by the tide and lying on their sides with their spars almost in the garden. She did not dare to exclaim, "How beautiful!" for that might have seemed banal. Instead she murmured the Arabic word "Madness!"

The angle of inclination to the place, too, was inspired and set it at a slight cant towards the curving western corners of the further river, where the dense forest lands gave it a shapely horizon full of screens through which the late sun filtered. The view, so light and airy, could have hardly been any different when the church was first opened to the parish of Battersea five years before Blake elected to marry his Kate there.

Mr. Craggs, the verger, was waiting for them faithfully with the keys, as he always did, for the Prince took the precaution of phoning ahead when the weather promised a fine sunset. Despite the rules, Mr. Craggs had been suborned by the munificence of the Prince's tip. "Never less than an 'ole suffering," he informed the awestruck clients of the The Raven, or those equally awestruck in The Jug and Bottle or

The Old Swan, which practically abutted upon the little church. The Prince had once read in a novel by Thackeray that a sovereign was an "adequate recompense" for a special service rendered, and though the coin was no longer in ordinary use he had his bank send him a dozen every month. It worked wonders, he found. But apart from this he and Craggs had become fast friends, and now the verger was enslaved by the Princess; he helped her down ardently if somewhat creakily, for he was a martyr to lumbago. "Well I never, Master Ahmed," he said, "what a nice young lass." The Prince blushed proudly. But today Craggs happily could not stay, for he had a meeting of the Legion – or so he said. "I shall 'ave to 'op it I'm afraid." But he had placed the old oak chair at the strategic place. "I know I can trust you to replace it, sir, and put the key in the 'ole in the wall." It was ancient ritual all this, and the Prince nodded. "Have a nice sunset, then," said Craggs agreeably, winding his woollen scarf round his neck and placing a battered bowler hat on his head. The operation gave him a moment of polite and very tactful hesitation – time to enable the Prince to extract a whole suffering from his waistcoat and press it upon his friend? Craggs gave a false start of surprise as he always did, and then promised to drink Egypt's health and the lady's, before stumping off into the evening. It was so calm. They were alone. The cab withdrew to the pub to wait.

"How kind he is," she said. She had already climbed the two stairs to the deep balcony of the church front. "He has even put a chair out for you. I understand everything now. What a view!" She sat down in the clumsy oaken chair and gazed past the balconies of The Swan to where, on a level horizon and fretted by forest, an unframed Turner sunset burned itself slowly, ruinously away into a fuliginous dusk, touched here and there with life as if from a breath passing over a bed of embers.

"No!" he said, with the same extreme bliss written on his face. "As yet you do not understand. Fawzia you are sitting in His chair, in Turner's *own* chair which he bequeathed to the church! He sat just here to study the light effects, just where you are sitting, for God knows how many years. . . ." He all but choked with his ardour. To see her there, seated in the Master's own chair – the cockpit, the vantage-point from which he had embarked upon the great intellectual adventure of becoming himself! His fingers touched the expensive engagement-ring in his pocket – he had had it specially made for her in Nubia. He placed it on her finger now and she submitted with bowed head, only giving a small sniff, perhaps a suppressed sob. And suddenly he felt triumphant. "Of course you will, won't you?" he said, sure of his response; and like a rock-dove she replied. "Of course I will. Of course I will."

He sat himself down on the steps at her side, and thus they waited for darkness to fall, hand touching hand, speechless with joy. Even when it came time to replace the holy chair by the pulpit in the dark church and replace the keys in the 'ole, they did not utter a sound for fear of shattering the gorgeous complicity of the moment. She felt as if the ring weighed a ton.

So they clip-clopped home in lazy and loitering fashion, and she was glad of the shawl as they drew near Kensington and her mother. The entire contents of the casket labelled Human Happiness appeared to have been emptied upon their heads from a spring sky. He saw her to her house porch without a word and then, dismissing the cab, set out to walk across London to regain his flat. He felt like a comet, trailing the fire of the painter's inspiration which chance had bestowed on them.

From thenceforward, he reflected now, as the train ground its way towards the capital, everything had borne fruit, and their marriage had become the envy of less lucky friends. She had asked the young Farouk to give her away – her father was dead, she had no male relations, and she had the right to do so, for soon the stripling would be King. This the young man did with grace and style, surprising everyone by his gazelle-like adolescent beauty and his courtier's address. How he had changed now, thought Prince Hassad, stubbing out his cigarette. The caterpillar-like sloth, the sudden rages and fits of weeping . . . What a fate! Yet when he began his reign it was like the début of a Nero, an auspicious entry upon the world of power, full of authority and idealism. He sighed as the new image replaced the old in his memory.

Then followed the good years in London as a young attaché. The wind had set fair for them, London liked them. Their children were beautiful and clever, without problems.

The magnetism held, and here his little wife showed brilliant insight for she adopted more than one role with him. When she was pregnant with their second child they ran away to France and played at being artists in a secluded *mas* near Avignon – two months of bliss. She let herself go, was dishevelled and out of breath as she bent over the cooking pots, while he reverently prepared her vegetables. Her breasts were full of milk from which he drew frequent swigs. They were both of them none too clean, too, like joyous peasants. Her hair smelt divinely of cooking, her body of spices and sweat. He adored her *boeuf en daube;* she admired his wood-cutting and fire-lighting, as well as his fashion of polishing glasses. He snuffled into her wild eatable housewife's hair like a truffle hound on the scent. All this was very good for the gestation of their little son. In the years to come his love-making would profit from all their happy abandonment, their sensuality. "From your way of making love," he said, "one can see that he will print up quite beautifully as a man, little Fouad." They avoided all that was fashionable but they did visit Saint Tropez, a tiny hamlet of scarce a dozen cottages, where already the famous and inebriated Quin-Quin had opened her shop and offered to sell Fawzia a scent which was really vulgar, something from the bazaar. A scent which threw open its arms to you and said "*Me-voici!*" But the Prince was doubtful about its propriety if she wore it in London. "You would excite the whole Embassy unbearably," he said.

Of course there were mishaps as well and shoals to face, as in every marriage, but nothing can withstand devotion. During her third confinement he contracted a vexatious though slight venereal infection from a young lady-in-waiting fresh from Cairo and was very much cast down by the misadventure. But Fawzia took the whole thing in her stride and nursed him with a passionate devotion. She was glad to have an excuse to show the depth of her attachment to him; she almost thanked him for giving her the chance to show how irreplaceable she really was and how magnanimous. He was overwhelmed with wonder and joy. He suddenly realised what a real woman is capable of facing. It was a little frightening. He swallowed his humiliation and submitted to her tender care like a child, glorying in the feeling of security and forgiveness. (The lady-in-waiting was banished back to Cairo, however, in very short order.)

Far from separating them, this little contretemps brought them closer together. He could afford to be weak with her for she scorned to take advantage of his weakness. "Goodness!" he said. "You are extraordinary!" He meant it.

She smiled grimly, almost scientifically.

"I love you," she explained in her somewhat inconsequential fashion, "not because you are my husband but because you are such a man!" He echoed the word feebly though he did not contradict her. Long may she cherish the illusion, he told himself. She kissed his brow and he fell asleep filled with the density of this loving memory. The other children were told he had gout.

So life led them on in tranquil fashion until it became obvious that he would soon, by pure gravitation, rise to a rank which entailed responsibility as well as hard work – neither were really to his taste. And in the more recent years they had both rediscovered Egypt and found that Cairo had begun to occupy a much larger place in their thoughts than hitherto. It was not to the detriment of London, far from it, it was simply that they both felt the need of a change of scene. They wintered as often as possible in Upper Egypt, and always left it with a pang. Perhaps a new posting? He tried to lobby himself something in Alexandria, but failed. There remained a distasteful choice between the Embassy in Moscow or the one in Pekin – neither tempted him. Then the brilliant notion dawned – why not become a private man again and really take in hand his large property holdings, together with the three or four old palaces which his father had left him, for the most part tumbledown edifices in handsome gardens lying along the Nile? The single one they had done up for themselves largely satisfied their ambitions and their needs. With the others, she had started to play – for her architecture was a game, an eternal improvisation, and he loved to see her haphazard fairy-tale palaces being realised on a more modest scale in mud brick and cement. Business, too, diverted him in such a slippery capital as Cairo. He had a marked aptitude, he discovered, for bluffing and performing confidence-tricks – all business in the Middle East is a variety of poker. It was a relief, too, to finish with protocol and precedence, the ramifications of which he had found so silly. For example, the courtesy rule which forced one to keep a person of superior rank always on one's right, even walking down a street, even in a taxi. One had always to be scuttling

round people or cabs to see that this silly custom was observed – or else your visitor treated you with marked coldness,
or went downright into a diplomat's huff. Phew! All that was
over. He could play cards all night, even cheat if he wanted.
One of his first civil acts was to win a large sum (by cheating)
off Lord Galen who fancied himself as a brilliant courtier and
card-player but who was as innocent of guile as a newly
born child.

The last kilometre or so before they entered Victoria
was taken at a walking pace – why, nobody could tell him,
but it was so. This enabled Selim to walk along the platform
beside his carriage, however, and make agreeable miming
faces. The Embassy had sent a car for old time's sake, and
Selim who was acting as chargé came with it to bring him
his correspondence. He held up three magenta envelopes
which contained letters from the Princess and smiled broadly.
Selim of the quiet studious foxy expression was a Copt and
had all the reserve and resilience of that enigmatic race or
sect. He smiled rarely, and always grimly, for preference at
the discomforture or defeat of others less wily than he. But
he was an admirable diplomat. They chatted like old friends
in the car on the way to Brown's, and the Prince delivered
his news which Selim was burning to hear. "As I told you in
my telegram from Geneva – not the one *en clair* – Lord Galen
committed an incoherence in Germany, but it was useful to
me. I have it from the highest authority that they will not
move for a while yet. These peace parleys and last-minute
attempts to find a solution will be allowed to fizzle away for a
while. Then . . ." He cut the air with his palm. "As for the
Italians they have orders to do nothing for fear of upsetting
Arab opinion. The build-up is purely a defensive act; even
the British are not unduly alarmed. They know the Italian
capacity for making mud-pies." So the talk went on, and the
gloating Selim was delighted by Hassad's lucidity and the

compactness of his mind. There were at least two long telegrams in the matter.

Meanwhile Abdel Sami Pasha, now long retired, had asked him to lunch at his club, and all that remained was to ask for official permission to send a private telegram *en clair* to his wife. There was nothing to fear about this either, in spite of the dramatic overloading of the wires due to the war situation. "The only thing," said Selim, "is, I did not ring the verger of St. Mary's – it looks like rain today." The Prince said that he would do that himself after lunch with Sami; Selim bowed his head, and after consulting a pocket memorandum said that that was all the business he had for the Prince. "How long will you stay?" he asked. "Just a couple of sunsets! After that I must get back to Provence and get the P. and O. to cart all my affairs back to Egypt. It's all arranged. And Farouk is sending the royal yacht to Marseille. No problems at all, as you see, my dear Selim."

They embraced warmly, with genuine warmth, for had they not been brothers in arms "in the Diplomatic"?

It did not take Hassad long to arrange his possessions in the Hotel and then to take a taxi to the gloomy old reception rooms of Sami's club in Burlington Street. They had not met for quite a time and the older man had become very white and frail. The Prince greeted him tenderly and said: "Excellence, you have venerable-ised and so have I." It was the polite way of dealing with the matter in Arabic. They talked shop for a while and his European news was duly delivered and debated. For his part the old man announced that the British would buy the whole cotton crop for that year – one problem less. "But," he went on sadly, "poor Egypt, so divided! Everyone is on a different side. Everyone hates the English, yes, but who loves the Germans except Maher? Farouk favours the Italians, but only because they are weaker even than us. . . . What a business!" They ate their slow lunch to the tune of a good wine. "As for you, young man," said the old diplomat, "I do not wish to reproach you, but from what I hear your life has become very . . . very *vivid*!" The word was exquisitely apt. Sami prided himself upon the fine apposite Arabic of his despatches. "Vivid is the word," the Prince admitted, and hung his head. "What does Fawzia think?" said Sami – he loved them both like his own children. The Prince said: "She gave me a terrible shock and that started everything off." He sighed heavily. Sami said: "Was she untrue to you?" The Prince reflected deeply and laid down his knife and fork before he answered. Then in a low choked voice he said: "She became a journalist."

Sami was silent – a silence of sympathy and commisera-tion. "Goodness!" he said at last. "Under her own *name?*" But here the Prince shook his head; at least it had been under a pseudonym. But the basic fact was there. "We drifted apart after that, I don`t know why. In Geneva they tell me it is the menopause, that it will last three years, and then go away."

"That is quite different," said Sami with relief. "If it is an illness. Now my prostate . . ."

The conversation prolonged itself over coffee and cigars until it came time to say goodbye which they did with a tender sadness – who knew when they might see each other again in this uncertain world? Rain had begun to fall, a light spring rain, and the whole prospect became blurred like a window-pane. The porter's taxi drew up and the Prince got into it ordering the cabby to drive to Battersea. It was a very unpromising weather for tea-time and he hesitated a moment, wondering if he should not rather go to Simpson's for a crumpet and an Indian Tea. But he wanted to read his beloved's letters at St. Mary's, so that he could tell her so in the long cable Selim would send to her tonight. The place would most likely be locked, but if by luck the key was in the 'ole . . . It was! The creaky lock turned and admitted him to the empty church which smelt of varnish and industrial floor-polish. He tip-toed in, why he did not rightly know; perhaps so that he should not disturb old ghosts? The rain rustled on the roofs and on the water of the river. A wind shook the foliage of the trees. There was only just enough light to see. He sat in the Master's chair to read his precious correspondence which was full, not only of the unwavering affection of this model wife, but also with the delicious small-talk of family life – essential information about children's teeth and examinations and local scandals. The Nile had behaved very capriciously and had risen by fifteen feet in a night, washing away the little turret and hexagonal tower which she had been building for him – somewhere where he could "get away from everything and just sit and think". "Drat!" said the Prince. It was an old-fashioned expression he had picked up from his nanny. "Drat!"

Ruefully he thought of the period when he himself had been just as zealously faithful to her, just as single-minded. For years. Then suddenly in middle life shadows had fallen upon him; irrational fears of impotence, of glandular dis-orders, had been among them – and others less tangible. But he felt that he could not discuss such matters with anyone in any detail – unless it be a psychoanalyst of equal social rank to himself. And where to find such a person? It was a real dilemma! He had even consulted witches: to no purpose. Ordinary doctors gave him ordinary advice, prescribed tonics with unnerving names. But he hoped that they at least would be proved right, and that this period of delightful frenzy would come to an end and leave him in peace once more.

He read on slowly, voluptuously, and as he did so the evening outside suddenly lightened with some rays of un-expected sunlight. Tucking the letters back in their envelopes, which smelt of frangipani, he crossed the church with his light step and threw open the door. The whole sky was a sheet of flame! It was as if Turner himself had come back to welcome him, to give him a last sunset before the end. It might be years yet before he saw another. He did not take the heavy chair but sat upon the steps to inhale the dying light of the sun as it bobbed down to the rim of the horizon. It was like watching a stained-glass window being slowly shattered. And it was for him he felt, – for them both. He took the letters out and kissed them for the sake of old memories. A line came into his head, "An Empire upon which the sun never sets." It was setting now over England! And by the same token, towards the north a balloon was going up – lurching heavily, greasily, awkwardly, up above the river. But what nonsense! The real Empire was in the primacy of the human imagination and that must always outlast the other kinds, or so he had believed. The sun was setting, the balloon was going up. He must return to his hotel and make his plans for the end of the week. He replaced the key reverently in the 'ole and walked back to the bridge.

At the hotel he found that Sami had sent his manservant with a bottle of medicine for him – for his "condition", so the visiting card said. It had a terrifying Arabic label and was clearly full of sherbert, the standard Cairo cure for impotence. It was called SFOUM, and that was roughly the noise it made when water was poured on it. One dose was enough. The rest he emptied down the sink. That night he walked a while in the park and then took a cab for half an hour to see the sights, Piccadilly, Oxford Street, the Palace. Who knew how long before he might see them again? But his long cable to his wife went off punctually, as Selim had promised.

EIGHT

Lord Galen's Farewell

DIRECTLY UPON HIS ARRIVAL IN PROVENCE LORD Galen, with a characteristic gesture, invited everyone to dinner – as one might call a committee-meeting to announce a bankruptcy. It was rather fine of him; one saw his essential kindness and innocence. He did not wish to disguise his shame; he stood in front of his own fireplace, empty in the summer save for a basket of blue sea-lavender which gathered dust but withered not, and he allowed a tear to course down his tired cheek as they came into the room, Felix, Constance, Blanford, and Sam resplendent in his "heroics", as he called his service-dress. The old man held out his two hands, asking only that they should be pressed in sympathy after his tragic blunder. Blanford found it moving so to demand the silent commiseration of friendship from them, and his heart went out to Galen. Max blew his violet nose in noisy sympathy and prepared them drinks – whisky mostly, from the ancient cut-glass decanter which had been the gift of a business friend with good taste. The Prince had not yet arrived. Galen hoped he wouldn't suddenly give his eldritch chuckle during dinner.

"I do not need to tell you about my mistake," he said meekly, without theatre, "for you know already! The Prince and I escaped just in time. I have lost a fortune and betrayed my own folk. Nobody will ever speak to me again in Manchester." He hung his head.

He had actually prepared them for this dénouement in the document he had sent Constance by way of a dinner invitation. There was nothing to say; he was most lovable at that moment.

He turned, sighing, to place his glass upon the mantel-shelf; the remains of his old cat Wombat gave a low gasp. It reminded him for a moment of the Prince's chuckle, and he frowned upon the memory. "It has been a calamity," he admitted, "and the whole thing my fault. Crest-fallen is the word. Yes, I am quite crest-fallen!" He bowed his head briefly and in some mysterious way managed to give the impression of an old rooster with bowed crest.

Shyly, from the depths of their youth, they raised their friendly glasses to toast him and to register their concern and affection; and at that moment there came the characteristic rumble of the Prince's coach as it drew up before the house, all its damascened paintwork glittering with high polish, and even its horses burnished and cockaded in the best pantomime tradition. Blanford had last seen this sort of thing at the Old Vic, when Cinderella was carted off to the ball in her transmogrified pumpkin. Quatrefages rode with the little man. He had become very friendly with the Prince, who for his part treated him with affectionate familiarity, often throwing an arm round his shoulder as he talked. ("*Il est redoutable, le Prince,*" explained the lean youth to Blanford during the evening; "*il connaît tous les bordels de la région.*") It was not surprising, for the Prince like a good Egyptian had taken the precaution of calling on the Chief of Police during his first week in the city, and of inviting him for a ride in his coach. His knowledge now (compared to the limited knowledge of Quatrefages) was all but encyclopaedic. Lord Galen, however, while full of respect for the blue blood of the Prince, steadfastly refused to share the pursuits of the royal amorist. "He must have his little spree," he might say, cocking his head roguishly, "but I need my eight hours!" Nor did the Prince insist, for he had all the tact of a gentleman of the old school. He went about on his lawful occasions, secure in the knowledge that apart from the factor of diplomatic privilege accorded him, he also enjoyed the esteem and respect of the Chief of the Police des Moeurs, who was not above giving him a ring at the hotel to pass the time of day. But he had, in a relatively brief delay, accumulated a lot of new acquaintances whose appearance was not somehow altogether reassuring to Lord Galen. There is an indefinable something which makes a gentleman who belongs to the *milieu*. It exudes from his person – some of the heavy slothful quality that emanates from the person of a great banker, or a promoter of national schemes which collapse in dust, or of an international criminal, a diplomat, a Pope. The Prince's hotel was now full of sinister silent oracular personages, who spent hours locked up with him, discussing business or (who knows?) pleasures as yet to be experienced. There was a heavy air of mystery which hung about the velvet-lined double suite of the Prince. The telephone was always going. They smiled, these dark hirsute people, but the smile was not full of loving kindness; the smile was like the crêpe on a coffin.

"I wonder who all these new people *are*," said old Galen in perplexity. "I ask him but he just says they are associates." He was a little bit put out by the Prince's discretion, and also a tiny bit anxious lest promising business mergers might be taking place just behind his back. At any event it was past worrying about, as he had decided that, in the light of the general war situation, his best move was to return home and brave the critics. After all, not everyone might be abreast of his activities; and this fearful mistake might as yet be hushed up. But he was very sad, he lay awake at nights and brooded; and in the deepening twilight of peace, dissolving now all round them, he felt the renewed ache of his missing daughter. So far all his expensive researches had yielded nothing concrete, though at times Quatrefages hinted that fruitful discoveries were just around the corner, not only on this topic but on the more challenging one of the

Templar treasure – that mouth-watering project which, though he could not foresee it now, was to cause him the unwelcome attentions of the Nazis who were to prove hardly less romantic in their intellectual investments than Lord Galen himself.

But all this lay in the fastnesses of the futurity; tonight was a quiet and sedate affair, imbued with a valedictory atmosphere. He bade them welcome to one of the finest dinners one could command in the region and the amateur gourmets of Tu Duc did ample justice to it. But they were sorry when the old man said: "I have just decided to return to London the day after tomorrow. Things are slowly going from bad to worse and I feel that I must be at my post in the old country if the die is cast and England finds herself at war." It was true, he was moved by a patriotic impulse, but it was mixed with the feeling that it would be more prudent to be nearer his investments. (As a matter of fact, as the Prince explained to Quatrefages, he was not going to London at all, but to Geneva.) He was just naturally secretive, he did not want gossip. And yet, with half his mind, he felt the welling up of warm sentiments for the Old Country. Tonight he talked in a warmly human way of what might be expected to happen after the hypothetical war – for even now the whole thing seemed such madness that one half expected a last-minute compromise or perhaps an assassination to change the trend of things. "We must move steadily towards greater justice and great equality of opportunity," said the old man, appearing to be unaware that such sentiments had been expressed before. He filled them with his own pure and innocent conviction. At such times he would actually inflate his breast, almost levitate, with idealism and emotion. He wished the whole world to have a second helping. Usually this was after dinner over a *fine à l'eau* and with his Juliet drawing smooth as silk.

The Prince also seemed a little sad and withdrawn into himself; he did not like partings and there were partings in the air now – just when he had stumbled upon several very promising lines of activity with his new associates. When Galen first probed him he did not reply directly in order not to shock the old man unduly. It was also a bit from a desire to keep his new friends as far as possible to himself. He had been carefully and conscientiously studying their portraits in the police files which had been placed at his disposal by the head of the Gendarmerie, who had himself been offered a marvellous job in Cairo at an excellent salary, in order to train the Egyptian police. The whole situation was full of promise – only this wretched war threatened to compromise his initiative; if only one could be sure that France would remain free. . . . He thought of the great gallery of photographs of his new friends: Pontia, Merlib, Zogheb, Akkad. . . . Such prognathous jaws, such cuttlefish regards, such jutting forelocks, such rhinoceroid probosces! It was wonderful! Yet they all looked just like great religious figures, like Popes in mufti. He stroked their images mentally like so many imaginary cats. Perhaps he should tease Galen? He gave his dry little clicky chuckle, and saw his host stiffen with pain. "You ask about my new associates?" he said. "I wonder if you would be surprised if I told you they were all bishops and abbots and chaplains and parish priests – all *religious* men?" Galen looked really startled and the Prince released another dry click of a chuckle, though this time he softly struck his knee and followed it up with a laugh, a small laugh, aimed at the ceiling. He looked like a chicken drinking. Quatrefages, who was in the secret, gave a hardly less wounding guffaw. But Galen could now see that his leg was being pulled. "Indeed so?" he said, slightly huffed, slightly pipped.

"My dear," said the Prince, "I was choking. You must allow me my little choke from time to time. *They are all great criminals.*"

"*Criminals?*" echoed Galen with a swishing indrawn breath. "You are associating with criminals?"

"Alas," said the Prince, "I wish it *were* so, for they would be so useful. But the situation does not permit me to risk any Egyptian money on their schemes. This wretched war . . ." It was as if every thought ended in the same *cul de sac*, the brick wall of the war situation. The Prince now explained that in France, when the great criminals became too hot to hold, they were submitted to a sort of exile in one of three great provincial towns, Toulouse, Nîmes, Avignon. They were forbidden to return to Paris. But in these towns they could reside at liberty and cool their ideas. How lucky, he added, that Avignon turned out to be one of these towns. It had provided him with a host of new contacts of the right sort, and had things been different he would by now have initiated several new schemes on behalf of the Egyptian companies he represented. Galen listened with popping eye.

Delighted by his theatrical effect the Prince permitted himself to embroider a little in his almost lapidary English. "Though they are all well bred," he continued surprisingly, "yet there may be one or two who would think nothing of sentencing a rival to *death!*" He paused for a moment and then continued, "They simply have them clubbed insensible and then thrust through the medieval *oubliettes* into the Rhône!" He talked as if the river were choked with corpses. "Goodness me!" said Lord Galen, startled by his obvious relish. "What an idea!" It gave a whole new dimension to business methods.

A few more such sallies followed, but to tell the truth Blanford felt that the evening had begun to lag on in a rather spiritless fashion, as if its back had been broken by the approaching war and the impending separations. Outside the moon was high, and the vines seemed very still, with no breath of wind to stir their loaded fronds. Quatrefages became very thoughtful and sad when Galen told him that he must, in the coming week, close his office and transfer it back to London. "So soon?" he said and Galen nodded decisively. "I know it's hard," he said, "but something tells me it is time to move."

It was, and for once his intuition was correct. But how ironic it seemed that the weather was maturing towards a record harvest – never had the prognostications for the wine been so full of tremulous optimism! "I could, of course, stay until after the *vendanges*, if I wished," said the Prince. "*Après tout* Egypt is to be neutral so I could do as I please. Nevertheless I fear I must go too. The yacht can't wait for ever." He was thinking lustfully of all the up and coming young wines which were raising their proud crests upon the gentle slopes and terraces around them: and not less of all those shaggy old champions once again distilling and renewing their golden weight among the hundreds of square kilometres of vine stretching away on both sides of the swift green Rhône. The very thought made him thirsty. He suddenly became as merry as a cricket. "Must you really go home?" he asked again, and again Galen said he must. "Well, so be it," said the Prince, raising his paws to heaven; and he closed the subject with an invocation to Allah, the Decider of all things.

"But I must not overlook anything," said Lord Galen extracting from his breast pocket a tiny scarlet memorandum book which contained all his engagements written down in a minute spider-scrawl. "I must not forget to go down and play with Imhof once before I leave. It's over two months since I went, and he must get awfully lonely down there in Montfavet surrounded by lunatics and alienists. He loves a game of trains!" Trains – it was the magical draw of the model railway which the authorities had permitted Imhof to construct in the hither end of the asylum garden! Blanford had been invited once to accompany Lord Galen to see his unfortunate ex-associate in his confinement. "Because," he said, "you have a very soothing presence I find. You say little but when you talk it is with a public school accent. Imhof will like that."

It was somehow typical of the essential inconsequentiality of Galen's nature that these arresting things should be said, one after another, as if they were all of the same order of thought; for him, Blanford reflected, nothing was really unusual – it all flowed together with a phenomenological impartiality which carried the colour and tone to Galen's innocent mind. "It must be dreadful," the old man continued while they were bustling down the green lanes leading to Montfavet, nestling in its bowers of roses, "to be condemned to excrete always through a slit in the stomach wall directly into a rubber envelope. Yet he doesn't seem to mind, he is positively *cheery*. He has had a very bad time has Imhof." He went on to describe the slow downfall of his partner's reason in equally colourful terms – terms which startled Blanford out of his ordinary equability and made him glance suspiciously at Galen, wondering if perhaps all this rigmarole did not stem from some secret sense of humour. But no, he was quite serious. It was no leg-pull. He described the first symptom which betokened the overthrow of Imhof's reason. "He went into shops and asked the price of things. Then he would just give a high cracked laugh and leave. It startled people."

Imhof, it turned out, was a massively built, red-headed man who looked like a market-gardener or a station-master with his crumpled black suit and heavy cheap watch-chain. He was rather unshaven as well and smelt strongly of shag. But he gave no sign whatsoever of recognising Lord Galen, and stared at him uncomprehendingly. His model railway was, however, rather an ambitious affair, with several large stations and plenty of engines and rolling stock. But it was obviously too big for one man to enjoy and he grunted with pleasure when Lord Galen started to behave masterfully with switches and points, and make coal and passenger trains perform their various functions. They did not speak but exchanged little grunts of pleasure now as they played like a couple of absorbed children, a perfectly mated couple. They got down on their knees and directed expresses to race in various directions. No words were needed, the railway was in the hands of two experts. Blanford felt deserted. He sat for a while on a bench, and then went for a little walk among the magnificent rose gardens from which the establishment took its name. It was from one of these corners, hedged in by vivid flowers, that he saw emerge a tall frail girl with long and shapely hands. She came towards him, slowly drawing a shawl about her narrow shoulders. Her dark wavy hair framed a face which was beautiful but too thin; her shoes had very high heels. She advanced slowly with a smile and said: "So you are back? O! how was India? I am dying to ask. How calm was India? Nowadays at night I seem to hear Piers walking about in the other room, but he is never there when I run to see. Did you meet him in India? Does the smell of the magnolia still remember me supremely?" Blanford did not know how to react. Though obviously an inmate, her speech was superficially so coherent and her pale beauty so striking.

They stared at each other for a moment in silence while he hunted for a word or a phrase which might suit so strange an occasion. She smiled at him with a tender familiarity and reached out her hand to place it on his elbow, saying: "Of course you did. It is obviously there you met him." Blanford nodded, it seemed to be the right thing to do. They took a few steps and on the other side of the flower-bed he saw an open French window giving on to a room furnished with a certain old-fashioned luxuriousness. There was a tapestry on the wall, and a concert-grand in the corner. Scissors and a bowl of flowers on the terrace explained what she had been doing when the sound of his step on the gravel had disturbed her. "I knew it all the time," she said again, "I knew you would come from him, from Piers." At that moment a flight of birds passed close overhead, and at the whirr of their wings a panic fear seized her. Her face clouded, her eyes became wide and glittered with apprehension. "It is only the birds," he said, hoping to soothe her, but she gazed at him wildly and repeated hoarsely, "*Only* the birds? What are you saying?" Huddling the shawl round her thin shoulders she hurried away towards the terrace and the open window. He stood quite still until he heard the latch click home. Then he made his way thoughtfully to where the two grunting men moved about on the ground like apes, releasing their marvellous models with a high skill and a perfect enjoyment.

It was a full couple of hours before Galen came to himself; it was as if he at last awoke from a deep trance of perfect, transcendent happiness, and sighing, took his leave of Imhof who gazed unfeelingly at him, watched him move away, and then bent down resolutely once more to his trains. Nothing was said about the public school accent. There had been little chance to use it, so mute had been the harmony of the two train-lovers, so deep their concentration. As they drove away Galen said, sighing with repleteness, "Poor old Imhof. I so often think of him. He made just one big miscalculation and pouf! it played on his reason. A fearful bloomer! Shall I tell you? It was during a water shortage in England, a scandal. All the newspapers went on about it, and the Government asked people to save water as much as possible. Then the press said that the Englishman's bath was the reason and gave statistics about the millions of tons of water we waste. It was here that Imhof got the idea of buying all those bidets – hundreds of thousands of them. He said that if England could be got to accept the bidet we could all make do with one bath a week. The saving in water would be immense. I forget the details but he spent millions on advertising his idea, and at the same time, not to be caught short, in buying up all the bidets he could find. A massive investment all lined up in warehouses on the coast waiting to invade across the channel." He gave a sad chuckle. "They are still there. He seemed not to realise that one of the hardest things to do is to get a national habit modified. Bidets!"

Remembering this occasion, Blanford reflected compassionately upon Imhof and his bidets while the old man thoughtfully circumcised a cigar and struck a match to light it. He leaned back now in his chair and smiled round at them; he had expiated his guilt by his sincerity and now felt calmly himself again, though of course still saddened by the whole affair. Constance and Sam said little, and it was assumed that they were preoccupied with each other and deaf to the appeals of mere sociability. But she was filled also with a weight of apathy and weariness which astonished even herself. They were like people living upon the slopes of a volcano, Vesuvius or Etna, resigned to the knowledge that one day, nobody knew when, the whole of the world they knew would be blown apart by forces beyond their imagining. And yet they continued to respect social forms like automata, like the Romans of the silver age, when the Goths were already gnawing at the walls of the civilised world. As if he had intuited this feeling of remorseful apathy in her, Lord Galen patted her hand and sighed deeply. "If this goes on," he said, and everyone knew what he meant by that, "why, money will become quite worthless." He looked round the table. "And it's a great pity. It has given us so much pleasure. Indeed there is something very inspiring about money." The word was strangely chosen, but one could feel what he meant. Money, thought poor Felix, working his toes in his dinner

shoes. He had contracted a hammer-toe from his solitary
walking about the town. Money – if only he could get his
hands on some. Blanford himself had a twinge of panic. "I
suppose all investments will collapse?" he said with some
alarm. The Prince nodded. "It depends," he said, "some will.
But if you have armament shares. . . ." Lord Galen now called
to Max to wind up the old horn gramophone and set off the
traditional *Merry Widow* waltz which closed all his dinner
parties. They took themselves to the quiet terrace where
they were supplied with drinks hard and soft and tobacco for
Sam's pipe. It was curious that no mention had been made of
Livia, and Blanford wondered suddenly if they knew anything about her – was it perhaps a tactful silence? But then
on the other hand nobody had mentioned Hilary either. The
moon shone upon their glasses. There was no wind, but
away over the hills there came a tremor of summer lightning
like a distant bombardment going on, which must herald
one of the thunderstorms which traditionally ushered in the
harvest and the autumn. The Prince asked Blanford whether
he would not like to visit Egypt. "I would be happy to engage
you as a personal private secretary if that were the case. You
would live in the Palace and meet the best people, the *top-
notch*. It is a very picturesque land."

The proposal was startling and novel and tickled the
youth's fancy. He asked for time to consider. As yet his own
personal affairs were not sufficiently in order, or so he felt, to
embark on what promised to be so exciting and enriching a
career as that of social secretary to a prince.

Now, turning aside, the Prince addressed himself to
Felix Chatto. They took a turn up and down the balcony and
on the lawn, linked arm in arm. Felix was very flattered to be
treated with the deference due to a senior diplomat, as if he
was in possession of state secrets of the highest importance.
The Prince gave a résumé of the political and military state

of things and asked him to comment upon it with a becoming modesty and a keen attention. Rising to the occasion Felix did his best to present the balanced analysis so dear to the hearts of diplomats and leader writers. As usual it all depended on If, When and But. The Prince thanked him warmly. "In a few days," he said, "I am going to have a little *spree*. After Lord Galen goes. Do not be offended if I do not send you an invitation, my dear. It will be rather an advanced sort of spree and you have a professional reputation to look after in this beautiful but somewhat sinister little town. But don't take offence. You will understand everything when you talk to your friend Quatrefages." But Felix needed no briefing, he could imagine very well what the little spree would entail. "I must pay back some social debts to my new friends," explained the little man, and the young consul saw in his mind's eye all those faces like crocodiles and ant-eaters and baboons, all dressed in dark suits with improbable ties and fingers with black hair sprouting through their rings. "I shall quite understand," he said seriously, "and I take it as a compliment, sir, that you should bother to explain to me." The Prince squeezed his arm and gave a ghost chuckle.

They broke up relatively early that evening, pervaded by a sense of weariness and loss. Perhaps because he felt that this was probably the last occasion they would meet round his table, old Lord Galen tried to infuse the occasion with a touch of valedictory ceremony. He called for a toast to the Prince and to Egypt which was willingly drunk, and which, by its unexpectedness, pleased the Prince very much indeed. He for his part replied by calling for a toast to His Majesty the King of England. He sprang up as he uttered the words with alacrity and a genuine enthusiasm. He had been received at Court with great kindness, which had seemed to him quite natural and unaffected. Besides, one of the younger members of the Royal Household had elected herself his mentor and

Muse. What he admired so much, he told Chatto, was that in England you could do almost anything without getting into the newspapers. You felt so safe, while in Egypt those dreadful socialist and communist papers were always on the lookout for scandal. "They don't like the upper class to have a little spree. Why are Marxists such spoilsports? I have never been able to understand it, especially when you think of the morals of Engels."

The car came, with a tearful Max at the wheel, and they all said goodbye to the Prince with a genuine pang. When would they all meet again? Nobody could tell, nobody could say.

The inhabitants of Tu Duc took their leave with Max in the old rumble-dusty vehicle of Lord Galen; Quatrefages and Felix, since they were going into the town like the Prince, were offered the trip in his coach. The journey passed in friendly silence; the Prince spent most of it exploring the cavities between his teeth with a silver toothpick of great elegance. He said no more about his spree until the changing tone of the horses' hooves upon the cobbled avenues of the town told them that they were almost home. "The little spree I spoke of," he told Quatrefages, "will be at the end of the week, perhaps when Lord Galen has left the country." Quatrefages asked if he could be of service in the matter and received the reply that everything was going to be arranged at an official level. "It is much safer that way. But I hope you will honour us with your presence. I think the occasion will be a memorable one – in all this fearful war-indecision which prevents us all from thinking or planning. They ring me up all the time from Abdin Palace with rumours and scares, telling me I must return. The palace yacht is already at Marseille waiting with steam up. But I think all this is quite premature."

The others elected to be dropped at Tubain, and to walk

the rest of the way in the deep moonlit dust, under the long avenues of planes and limes. And in silence for a change. Not necessarily the silence of despondency, but a silence which held the whole world of futurity in solution, as it were; the silence in which one waits for an orchestra to strike out its opening statement. Constance linked her little finger to theirs and walked with her face turned upward towards the moon. On the way, flickering among the trees like a firefly, came a bicycle-lamp which fluttered towards them and stopped. It was the son of the post-master of Tubain who had been up to the house to deliver a late telegram, and found nobody in. It was for Sam and they all knew what must be in it. It was only the date of his recall which was in question. He tipped the boy and said goodnight to him before opening the slip of blue paper. Blanford struck a match which gave a yellow hovering splash of light sufficient for him to read the contents. He gave a sigh. "I leave on Sunday," he said, in a tone of elation; it was understandable. It was far better to know for certain – at least one could prepare the event. Yes, they all felt better armed against the future this way. They would have a few more days together before the parting. Constance was going back to Geneva for her work – she would quit Sam in Paris. Blanford would stay on for a while with his little car (which was at present in a garage, being repaired and serviced), and wait upon events. Never had he felt more useless, more undecided about his direction. The Egyptian project was most tempting; but would a war not qualify it? He presumed he would be called up, and as he could not conscientiously object, he would soon find himself in uniform like Sam.

They crossed the garden in single file, under the cork-oaks with their snowy crests, and turned the creaking key in the tall front door. The familiar smell of the house greeted them in darkness; it smelt of long forgotten meals, of herbs and of garden flowers, it smelt of cobwebs and expired fume of candles. All at once it seemed a pity to go to bed without a nightcap. In the kitchen they lit a paraffin lamp and by its mild unhovering yellow light sat down around the scrubbed and sanded table to brew tea and to play a hand of gin rummy. Blanford opted for a glass of red wine instead, however, despite the lateness of the hour and his general abstemiousness. It was late when they at last bade one another goodnight, and even now with such a fine moonlight outside it seemed a shame to go to bed; so he walked down to the water and took a silent, icy swim, letting the rushing wings of the water pass over him like rain. Closing his eyes he seemed to see in memory all the black magnetism of the dark light which shone out of the earth, whether among these trees and vines or out of the bald stone garrigues and pebbled hills with their crumbling shale valleys. Among these rambling dormitories of shards Van Gogh had hunted the demon of his black noonday sun – and found it in madness. Only when one was here did one realise how truthful to the place was his account of it. He was beginning to realise the difference between the two arts, painting and writing.

Painting persuades by thrilling the mind and the optic nerve simultaneously, whereas words connote, mean something however approximate and are influenced by their associative value. The spell they cast intends to master things – it lacks innocence. They are the instruments of Merlin or Faust. Painting is devoid of this kind of treachery – it is an innocent celebration of things, only seeking to inspirit and not coerce. Pleased with these somewhat rambling evaluations he scampered back to the house and to bed, shivery with cold all of a sudden, so that he was forced to climb between the sheets with his socks on. He would have liked to read for a moment or two, so delicious was the moonlit air outside, but sleep at last insisted. He sank to the pillow as if beheaded.

Down below, in the sleeping town, the pro-consul

paced out his long penitential walk from bastion to dark bastion; the moonlight only emphasised the shadows, creating great caves of pure darkness out of which he dreamed that some brilliant gipsy might emerge and pounce on him; but more likely it would be a footpad. His fingers tightened upon the little scout penknife he carried on his person, not so much for security as for tedious pro-consular uses, such as cutting up string to make parcels. The prospect of the war filled him, strangely enough, with elation which was somewhat shame-making. Naturally he would never have confessed to such a thing publicly, for he wished nobody harm and was personally too much of a coward to hanker for firearms – he was in fact rather gun-shy. But the reality of war if it came. . . .

If he had been guilty of imitating the rather pretentious formulations of Blanford he might have told himself that the reality of war (death) if it came would render back once more all the precious precariousness of life which had become stale with too much safe living. It was not a question of swimmers into cleanness leaping à la Brooke, but simply a breath of fresh air in a twice-breathed suffocating age. If it came he would join up at once. He would welcome all the restrictions which went with the uniform. He would glory in the savage discipline, for too much freedom gives you vertigo – you are looking out into nothingness all of a sudden. Nothingness – your own portrait! Much later he would realise that this feeling was echoed by the whole of the Nazi Youth!

Apart from that, he had started a course of physical culture with some vague notion of fitting himself for the fray. He read a cheap pamphlet on yoga and realised that he was walking in the wrong way, his breathing rhythms were at odds with his steps. This made him walk in a self-conscious, rather stilted fashion as he remembered the instructions of his pamphlet. "Ordinary people breathe eighteen times a minute but in the best yoga practice you can get down to less than ten and that will do. But three a minute is really good!" Three a minute? He found himself counting the paving stones and holding in his breath, only to express it in a swish when the strain became too much. Surely this was not right.

But at dawn even he found relief in his weariness, hurrying home along the empty streets now drained even of the moonlight. Time was still there, a slowly discharging wound which the daylight would stanch. But first a little rest. He too climbed into bed and slept, but not before passing in review the sleep of the others which he could picture so clearly. Blanford all tousled, with his head under the pillow, Sam snoring, Constance invisible. Somewhere quite nearby the Prince lay, with a small piece of muslin over his face to defend him against moths – he dwelt in mortal terror of being eaten up by a moth, like an old tapestry. He had wrapped his one false tooth in silver paper, to avoid swallowing it in his sleep. It lay beside him with his beautiful ivory-covered Holy Book. Up there in Balmoral Max snoozed in a sort of cupboard which smelt of dead mice. The poor little secretary preferred a hammock in the garden. Lord Galen lay in his great bed all serene. He wore a night-shirt with frilled white cuffs which he got from Mannering's. It had his monogram on the breast. He slept with his mouth open and from time to time squirmed out a great snore which might be phonetically transcribed as "Gronk-phew"; Felix remembered the Prince saying, "He is such a good man that he is prone to be *spoofed*." And now war was coming.

> Once it was Bread and Circuses,
> Now it is all Dread and Carcases.

Where had he read that?

Yes, Blanford slept, but in his excitement he woke early while the others were still asleep, and tiptoed to the kitchen to make himself coffee. This he took back to bed where, lying luxuriously half asleep, he sent his roving mind as Felix had done, to visit his friends in their several sleeps and to try, by projection, to realise them more fully. Did he know what they felt or was he simply privileged to imagine – the writer's illness? He hardly knew. Yet it was so clear to him that the girl who slept in the afterglow of Sam's embraces was already ahead of them all in a certain domain whose real existence they hardly as yet realised. As for Sam, still drunk on the huge honeycomb of these first kisses, there seemed little beyond death and separation to consider, to evaluate. He had suddenly started to realise that he was now dying, quite softly dying. Mind you it would take time, but it was quite irrevocable. Most people hid their faces and refused to look this moment of realisation in the eyes. He slept on triumphantly in a cone of silence. The realisation itself was a victory, and it had nothing to do with the war. It would have come anyway, simply because of the contact with Constance, she had grown him up, though he would have been hard put to it to describe just how and why.

Even the notion of death offered a sort of hidden glee, it had been mastered! This whole absurd and mysterious business had been sparked off by a simple conversation in which the girl had said, "It will seem to you quite mad but from early on in my adolescence I seemed to have set myself a sort of task. I was trying to want only what happened, and to part with things without regret. It made me sort of on equal terms with death – I realised that it did not exist. I felt I had begun to participate in the inevitable. I knew then what bliss was. I started to live in a marvellous parenthesis. I also knew that it wasn't right to know so much so young. . . ." The effect of these words on Sam was indescribable. He was struck dumb. It was as if he understood exactly what she meant, but that the words had by-passed his reason. Later, much later, she would be able to add to this in a letter to Blanford by saying: "An overwhelming thirst for goodness is a dangerous thing and should be discouraged. I hunted not an ethos but the curve of a perfect licence charged with truth – however disconcerting pure truth might be! I was an alchemist without knowing it. Idiot!"

There they were, sleeping all, quite unaware that their dreams were models and outlets for their future acts. He had fallen asleep again, Blanford, and this time it took Sam an effort to wake him. "No time to lose," said Sam, "these last few days are precious. To horse!"

In some old book of aphorisms he had been surprised by the observation: "A superlative death costs nothing. The lesser ones are the more expensive." Was it Montaigne? He could not remember.

NINE

The Spree

THE PRINCE'S LITTLE SPREE PROMISED TO BE OF SUCH royal magnitude that the excited Quatrefages, when he got wind of the details from the inhabitants of their brothel – their common brothel, so to speak – at once borrowed a bicycle and scorched (the metaphor is an exact one, for it was at noon) out to Tu Duc with news of it. It must somehow be seen, he said, despite protocol considerations; even if only from afar. He himself was, of course, actually invited, but out of considerations of delicacy the Prince had decided to omit their names from his list of matchless crooks – perhaps just as well. But ... he had rented the whole Pont du Gard, and with it the whole of the ancient Auberge des Aubergines which abutted thereon. He was already busy transforming the place to suit his notions of how a spree should work.

The Auberge was a strange, rambling old place, admirably suited to this kind of initiative, with its collection of Swiss chalets hugging the cliffs of the Gardon, buried in plane-shade, leaning practically over the green water. Though it was not a residential hotel it had a series of large inter-connecting upper rooms which in summer managed to accommodate tourist groups or clubs devoted to archaeology or Roman history who selected the monument as a point of rendezvous, and sometimes camped out in the neighbouring green glades along the river. The cuisine was what had made it famous, and this was, of course, an important part of the spree. But it was not all, for the Prince, who was a man of the world, knew his France well. He knew that in this spirited Republic any citizen may call upon the *préfet* of any region to floodlight a notable monument at a purely nominal cost, simply to grace his dinner. When he himself had been young and madly in love with his Princess Fawzia he had offered her dinner here, served on the bridge itself by his liveried waiters; just the two of them, quite alone. He always remembered this early part of his married life with emotion. And now the great golden span of the Roman aqueduct was going to hover above their revels, its honey-gold arches fading into the velvet sky of Provence. His heart leaped in his breast when he thought of it. He became absolutely concave with joy. No detail must be left to chance.

Quatrefages had participated in some of the discussions as a friend and helper, and was able to attest to the Prince's thoroughness. He retailed these scenes with amusing irony, even imitating the Prince's accent to perfection. When he had asked, "*Et le gibier?*" the Prince had given him a reply straight from the heart of Cairo. "*Ne t'en fais pas, Bouboule,*" which came from some old musical comedy which time had encrusted in the Cairo soul. His henchmen were already out on their errands. Even the *gibier*, the game, was coming to the party from several different corners of the land, mostly Marseille and Toulouse. The Prince had announced that he liked the girls to be *plantureuses, bien en chair*, which explained the huge collection of cartoons after Rubens which finally arrived at the Pont du Gard. Whenever had one seen so fine a collection of sleepy sugar-dolls in all their finery, and their war-paint, a-jingle with doubtful jewelry and glinting with *toc* – the very perfection of the Arabian imagination? It was clear that the old Prince had been stirred by inherited memories of the Khedival entertainments of Cairo a century ago.

Quatrefages was so engrossed in his exposition that he did not hear the sound of the approaching car in which Felix sat bold upright in a straw hat looking like a rabbit, and tremulous with indecision. He was still not fully confident of this steel animal. Now everything had to be repeated for his benefit, and he listened with a slight pang of envy, simply because it sounded such a picturesque notion to give a party there, in the heart of the country. Preparations were already advanced; period furniture from all over Avignon, rented at ruinous prices, was being bundled into lorries and trundled out to the Auberge. In actual fact, they would only be about a hundred strong. "But the fifty girls are all *en or massif*," said Quatrefages, involuntarily licking his lips. "Marseille has outdone itself to provide sumptuous dollies."

"But where do we come in?" said Constance, who was also beginning to feel that they ran the risk of missing a treat, purely by being regarded as too virtuous to participate in it. "Indeed?" said Blanford. Quatrefages chuckled and said, "The roads after eight o'clock will be closed to motor-traffic by the gendarmerie at the request of His Highness. Obviously you won't be able to get in. But I have an idea. You can watch it all from the top of the Pont du Gard – the ballroom windows open on that side and you can see in. I know because once when I was spying on a girl who I thought was doing me down I came there and sat on the top with glasses. She was dining with a man I suspected. I saw them both quite clearly. If you take those little opera glasses you have, you will also see everything from the top."

"Yes, but to get to the top . . .?"

He gave an impatient shrug of the head and took out a fountain pen. On the local newspaper he swiftly outlined a sketch map of the country immediately surrounding the aqueduct – a drawing which stirred their memories at once for they had walked here. "Do I need to go on?" he asked. "Here is the sunken road near Vers. You climb that slope following the broken arches and the masonry. Then suddenly you turn a corner and . . ."

Yes, you walked out into the sky, and the great crown of the aqueduct with its deep water trench lay beneath you. You walked out, in fact, upon the top of it as if upon a bridge.

"I see," said Blanford thoughtfully. "Yes, it would be possible."

"Of course it would be possible," said the impatient clerk, irritated by these slow English lucubrations, this slow chewing of the cud. "You would have a ringside seat."

"When is it to be?"

"Tomorrow. You will *never* regret it!" His solemnity was amusing.

He went on with his exposé of the details and they could see that indeed this was to be no mean entertainment, but one worthy of such a splendid setting and . . . so, well, gallant a company. Yes, they really must go! If nothing else it would take their minds off the perpetual nibbling of thoughts and doubts about the war and about the impending separations. How well such an event would have rounded off a normal summer holiday, how well it would have suited the time too, situated on the cusp of the harvest, with the closing festivals of wine and bullfighting to look forward to! Never mind. Go they must.

So they set off from the house after dinner the next day, by a low and rather famished moon – late in her exaltation and fast in her setting; a deep autumnal haze lay over the land which hereabouts looked so Tuscan in its rounded forms and paint-brush cypresses, its hamlets and villages all to human scale, its rivers small but sturdy and full of trout. Soon the greenery would give place to the more dusty uplands of the garrigue, all stone and shale, and for much of the time regions both parched and waterless. They followed the instruction of Quatrefages carefully so as to avoid the traffic restrictions of the gendarmerie. When they reached Remoulins, for example, they did not cross the bridge – they saw lights and gendarmes on the further side. They turned right, as if for Uzès, and rolled along deserted roads which fringed the river bank, swerving from side to side to follow broad sweeps of the Gardon. The Pont du Gard was already lit up for the feast, its great bronze form lying in the sky like a stranded whale. Underneath it, on a flat mossy glade among the rocks, the Prince had caused a brilliant marquee to be run up, where he sat on one of his pantomime chairs to receive his guests. They were disgorged by their cars among the groves of willow and walked the thrilling fifty yards or so freckled by the light of reflectors, advancing dramatically towards the theatrical hovering aqueduct above.

The Auberge was warmly lighted also, and the whole upper storey had been converted into a sort of harem, with its walls covered with priceless rugs on hire or loan, and cupboards and coffee-tables and filigreed mirrors fitting enough for the Grand Seraglio itself. All the antiquaries of Avignon had contributed their mite to this impressive display. Pinned to a curtain was a beautifully lettered panel which read LADY BOUDOIR POUDRERIE WATER CLOSET. It was comprehensive, it left nothing to chance. On the morrow Quatrefages was to steal it and give it to Blanford who attached it to the outdoor earth closet at Tu Duc, being always glad to point out the felicity of the Cairo French, for "poudrerie" means not "powder-room" so much as "powder-magazine". The great open hearth of the Auberge was ablaze with dry vine-tendrils, crackling and snapping away like the horns of enormous snails. Somewhere in the inner heart of the establishment an orchestra was tuning up softly, suggesting the presence of a dance floor or a ballroom. Everything was in hand.

In order not to over-complicate matters they had elected to travel in one car, despite the crush; this had the further advantage that Felix was able to loan the consular

car to his invited friend for the trip. Quatrefages in *tenue de
ville* looked splendid, though somewhat nervous. He had
actually seen a few of the arrivals from Marseille who were
to be accommodated on the morrow at a hotel. He was
enthusiastic. "They all look as if their periods were overdue –
it gives women a wonderful neurotic magnetism. I saw at
least two superb dollies like great caterpillars, covered in
pollen." Felix was a bit shocked by the relish of his friend.
Quatrefages had drunk a whisky or two with the Prince's
major-domo and was in a fine state of exaltation. "Remember
the message of the caryatids?" he asked, shaking his finger
at the abashed consul into whose car he had now inserted
himself. "A girl should always try to look ever so slightly
pregnant." It was an old chestnut, invented in the past by
Blanford and which had tickled him enough to stay in his
memory. "Whatever happens, dear Felix," he said, "don't
miss it."

So here they were bowling through the sweet glades
of cherries and mulberries; from time to time the brilliant
aqueduct emerged upon the blackness to their left, and was
then swallowed up by the greenery. They could hear the
river grinding its teeth down below to their right. Then
came the left turning which normally would carry them
right up on to the bridge itself, and here stood a policeman
with a pious air and a white barrier which he had placed
across the road. But they now pretended they were heading
for Uzès and passed him by with a wave, to curl down the
long avenue of cool planes until the sunken road by Vers
came up and here they drove most carefully on an appalling
surface until they came to an olive grove which crowned
the slopes. Here it was not possible to continue by car and
they started to walk on the shaly slopes among the snatching
bristles of holm-oak and thorn. It was harder to navigate
in the darkness than by daylight.

The hill was a wilderness of dividing paths and fire breaks; but ahead of them was the furry white light of the reflectors and they navigated upon that until, with the sudden surprise of actors who walk unwittingly out upon a lighted stage, they reached the culvert which marked the first arch. And here began the circumspect descent upon the crown of the aqueduct with its metre-deep gulley – the channel through which the spring water of Vers was conveyed to Nîmes in Roman times. Here they could perch like birds in a high tree and rest their elbows on the side of the trench, to gaze down upon the princely revels below. The idea of the opera glasses was also a brainwave. They had originally been bought for the performances of the Opéra de Marseille, but lately had been much out of use, lying about the house. Now they trained them like sharpshooters upon the Auberge below, and found that, as Quatrefages had said, they had an excellent view of half the great dining-room, one side of which opened into a sort of sun verandah.

The proceedings had already begun with a certain regal formality; the male guests, who were all unaccompanied, had been received in the pavilion and had been offered an aperitif of the Prince's devising – possibly laced with cantharides? Quatrefages indeed wondered about the matter as he gulped down his portion of the fiery colourless brew. The company looked even stranger at night than by daylight. They were all dressed in dark suits which were uncomfortably warm for the time of the year, and they gave the impression of being weighed down by their cravats and heavy rings, and greased hair. At this stage there was no sign of the women. But at last, when the assembly was complete, the Prince beckoned to his guests to follow him, and led them, as if they had been a cricket team, through the glades towards the Auberge, which had stayed all this time in almost complete darkness – just a candle-glimmer here or there which betokened movement. The Prince held in his hand his little gilt fly-swash with its length of white mare's tail hanging from it. It was rather like a conductor's baton. With it he tapped on the closed doors of the Auberge and they sprang open at his behest. At the same moment the whole dining-room was flooded with light and the advancing cohort of guests gave a collective gasp of pleasure. To the right of each male guest there was to be a *naked lady of pleasure*! Those already in place clapped and shouted and vociferated in ladylike fashion as the dark-suited men advanced with a thirsty air, each to find his place card with his name upon it.

No phantasy had been spared, it was clear. Constance chuckled almost continuously at the scene as her glasses picked up now one corner and now another of the ballroom. The men, as befitted their superior sex, sat on chairs with high gilded backs, like thrones; the girls upon velvet piano-stools. The Prince dominated the table as a good host should. Behind his chair stood the three dignitaries of high office clad in the most wonderful service robes of scarlet and gold, with green facings. One was the official food-taster, who would not be pressed into service tonight; the other two, one on each side of his chair, were bearing on their right wrist a tall hooded falcon. The Prince's rank entitled him to this dignity, just as a Scottish aristocrat is entitled to his bagpiper. The dinner began with a swirl of conversation and popping and waiting . . . a little sticky as yet, despite the fiery aperitif.

The men looked like shy honey-bears at Sunday school. "But not for long, I don't suppose," said Constance, who had voiced this thought to the others. The scene was full of variety and charm. In the bloom of the candles the women looked as sumptuous and grandiose as the require-ments had stipulated. "*J'aime les grands balcons arrondis*," the Prince had said, perhaps with his guests in mind. And here were the great rounded balconies in all their splendour, covered in fresh violets and jewels and scented in a thousand extravagant ways. The merriment was slow to emerge but it was just as well, for this sort of dinner-party, in which so large a part of the thrill is the marvellous food, should begin on a note of attentive reverence. This fête was no exception. They were, after all, Frenchmen, which meant that they had an innate culture of the table, and also of the human heart and person. Even the most curmudgeonly and bearish of the guests was a born appreciator of *la bonne chère* and turned his eyes to heaven from time to time with ecstasy; some kissed away bunched fingers in the direction of the *cuisine* and the cook. With the tucking of napkins into collars a new ease asserted itself and the conversation flowed in harmony with the excellent wine. Quatrefages, who was not particularly attracted to balconies, found himself with a big shy round dolly with a vulgar laugh, but with all the right instincts for she pressed his knee throbbingly and gave him infinite seafruit to sup. Slightly fuddled as he was, he nevertheless realised that he had never in his experience eaten food so exquisite, yet so simple. The shade of Brillat-Savarin must have turned mumbling in his grave to bless the table of the Prince. So exceptional was it, that he thought for a moment of saving the menu to bestow on Constance, and then he realised that it was useless – it would be like confiding the programme-notes of some superlative performance to a friend. What could they imagine from such a bare recital of the elements of this divine repast?* Where the devil had the old boy found the champagne? Lost in wonder and ecstasy, he allowed himself to be tweaked and tickled and fed like a Strasbourg goose. The watchers on the top of the aqueduct were vastly amused by his beguiling air of helpless content.

It was long, the banquet, but so full of fascinating detail that they were completely absorbed in the watching; towards

* Nevertheless see Appendix.

the end some scattered little sorties took place, to enable couples to dance a stately measure or two on the dark balconies outside. These took place with a slightly absurd formalism, which suggested that the dancers were none too sure of their feet. The orchestra remained invisible, but waltz and tango and "slows" figured on a repertoire which was calculated not to prove too tiring for people after such a mammoth dinner. But to the regret of the watchers the lights progressively became more and more discreet – one last cavernous flare as from the mouth of hell took place with the *crêpes flambées*, that was all, which conferred on each hairy face the kind of dark light which Rembrandt has marked as his own. It was a tremendous success, the snapping of paper favours and even – a stroke of genius – the wearing of paper hats which pushed the scene from the plain picturesque to the absolutely side-splitting. Elderly rats in strange paper hats, waving their cigars at the universe! What a marvellous touch of lunacy was conferred by this simple touch. And the dancing became a trifle more treacly – the ladies swathing themselves more amply, more amorously about their partners, or spreading their arms wide like galleons in full sail – or combine harvesters, to select a metaphor by Felix who found it more appropriate to the approaching *vendanges*.

So things went on in a slightly more sentimental key – even the Prince trod a bird-like measure, but his affections seemed to vary a good deal; several large unplucked-looking girls were competing for his attentions. All that money! All that food! "He has found another lovely word," said Felix. "He says 'spiffing' when he means 'top-whole'."

Their spirits began to droop a little – perhaps because of the notion that the visible part of the revels was finished. Constance thought lovingly of the Thermos of hot wine and the sandwiches which awaited them in the car. Then suddenly the universe was blown out and the whole darkness of the sky came down on them as forcibly, as palpably almost, as a lid. They could not even see each other and the distance between them and the revels seemed suddenly to have lengthened, so that they felt miles high in the sky, seated as if in an aeroplane. Caution also was indicated, for a frolic up here in the darkness could cost a life or a limb. They waited to let their eyes accustom themselves to the dark, but before this happened another kind of light assailed them.

From below there was a succession of bangs and strings of coloured snakes hissed up into the air around them, only to spit out their hot coloured stars and plumes and subside groundward again. They scored their beautiful trails on that dark lambent sky, and their stuttering, pattering trajectory carried them right over the bridge on which they lay. It was relatively short as firework displays go, but the colours and forms were choice, while down below, at water level, fizzed some grand yellow Catherine wheels, and a set piece which looked somewhat like a *santon* of Provence eating olives at the pace of St. Vitus. From afar off they heard the distant clapping and cheering, and now, since the new darkness seemed to be permanent, they crawled back along the stone tunnel and up onto the hill. It was a bit of a scramble, but once on the other side they made better time with the aid of a torch. It had been worth it!

A dense dew had been falling, ripe with the premonitions of the harvest; it dripped from the quiet olive under which they had parked the car. How welcome the wine was. Yet a heavy mist hemmed in the further visibility. As they drank their drink there appeared a sort of secondary cloud, moving up the hill towards them, and they recognised the character-istic clatter of hooves and tonking of bells which betokened a shepherd, who came across to get a light for his cigarette, and was glad of a sip of wine. He spoke in a sing-song southern French. As he puffed and warmed his palms with the cup, his dogs crouched beside him attentively, and the frieze of sheep strung out on the hill behind. Their hooves bruised the sage and set up a dense perfume in the windless orchard. The old man said: "The War has begun," but his tone was one of such incomprehension and unconcern that they could hardly take it seriously. How did he know? He had heard it at the Mairie at midnight. But in a land so poorly equipped with wirelesses rumour makes do for fact to a great extent – and this particular rumour had been often encountered already. And yet . . . It was disturbing. They said goodbye to him, shaking his rough hand, and piled back into their car which took some moments to start.

The heavy ground mist cleared after they had negotiated Remoulins and were safely launched upon the road to Avignon; for about ten minutes there was some disposition to doze, but as they fronted the last hillside before the famous bridge, they all came full awake again and began to debate whether to go home, or whether to go into the town in search of coffee and croissants and some truthful account of what was happening in the outer world. "It's too late to go to bed, and too early to get up," said Blanford, "and Felix is the only one who feels normal at this hour." As a matter of fact Felix was elated – almost the whole night had passed in delightful fashion for once, and here he was, happy and wide awake – only a little disquieted by the peasant's remark about the war having begun.

To town then, but Avignon itself was as dead as a door-nail – even the bakers had not started to warm their ovens, while no cafés were open, not even at the Gare. They tried a last chance and crossed Les Balances on foot, skirting its sordid and gipsy-ridden tenements, worthy more of Cairo than of a European city. They dumped the car at the Papal square. But here too, alas, the little Bar de la Navigation was shut fast. They began to feel dispirited.

But in one of the side-streets near the ancient tanneries with their foul network of canals, they heard the throbbing and pulsing note of a powerful engine or turbine. It sounded like the engine of a ship. "It's an old friend," explained Felix, "come and have a look at it! It follows me in my wandering at night, in the first week of the month every six months it 'does' this quartier during the hours of darkness. Then it moves on round the clock." It looked to them like a variety of fire-engine, and it bore the arms of the town painted in gold on its muddy flanks. "What is it?" asked Constance and Felix replied with a knowledgeable air, "It's the *pompe à merde*. You see, there has never been any main drainage, here all the houses have pits, dry pits for their only sanitation. Well, these are sucked out during the night by this old mastodon of a thing. They are all proud of it. They call it 'Marius'."

Mastodon was the word, though it had a long rubber proboscis like that of an elephant which had entered a front door and descended into the cellar where the privies were. The sucking and slobbering were fearful to hear, and the shuddering and drubbing of the pumps fearful to behold – it was like a clumsy animal, sweating and straining at its task, Blanford thought. "It is sucking out the intellectual excrement of the twentieth century in a town which was once Rome. The dry pit of the human imagination perpetually filling up again with the detritus of half-digested hopes and fears, of desires and resolutions." It was a bad sign he thought, frowning, to see metaphors everywhere; though he was not the only one. Constance said softly, "An anal-oral machine most appropriate to our time. Like the Freudian nursery rhyme."

But here afflicted by a sudden modesty she decided not to repeat it aloud; she would whisper it to herself instead.

When the bowel was loaded
The birds began to sing;
Wasn't that a dainty dish
To set before the King?

There was a light in a nearby bistro where the driver of "Marius" was already ordering his coffee and a small marc to drive off the excrementitious odours with which he was forced to live. Well, it was a profession, just like any other. . . . The others joined him at the *zinc* but Blanford stayed behind, fascinated by the old machine sucking and slobbering its way through the centuries. On one side, the old wrinkled dawn was coming up in coral and nacre, and down here at the same time the stench of excrement was spreading over the whole quartier. Soon it would be time to wind up the rubber hose and drive "Marius" away to its stable, for this kind of sump-cleansing was only done during the night – for the sake of decency, he supposed.

But now he was really tired. A quotation came into his mind. *Inter faesces et urinam nascimur.* Yes, it was appropriate enough. It had been, after all, Augustine's "City of God", transplanted once upon a time to this green and innocent country.

Appendix

* page 18
Full text of the 12 *Commandments*

1. *Faut pomper la momie allégoriquement.*
2. *Faut situer le cataplasme de l'art chauve.*
3. *Faut analyser le carburant dans les baisers blondes.*
4. *Faut faire faire, faute de mieux et au fur et à mesure faire forger.*
5. *Faut oindre le gorgonzola du Grand Maître.*
6. *Faut respecter le poireau avec son regard déficitaire.*
7. *Faut scander les débiles sentimentales avec leurs décalcomanies.*
8. *Faut sauter le Pont Neuf pour serrer la main d'une asperge qu'on trouve belle.*
9. *Faut caresser inéluctablement la Grande Aubergine de notre jour.*
10. *Faut pondre des lettres gardées en instance, tombées en rebut, Poste Restante, l'Amour O crème renversée.*
11. *Faut dévisager la réalité à force de supposer.*
12. *Faut cracher les tièdes et décendre les incohérents.*

* page 210
Readers who remark a slight divergence between so-called "real" history and the order of events adopted in this novel will, it is hoped, accord the author a novelist's indulgence.

*page 258
*MENU POUR LE BANQUET DE PRINCE HASSAD AU
PONT DU GARD*

Consommé glacé à la tortue
Gratin de crevettes roses en bouquet fait
Darne de saumon sauce Léda
Cailles aux pêches du Pont Romain
Médaillons de veau Sarah Bernhardt
Gigot d'agneau Grand Pétrarque
Aubergines en bohémienne
Champignons truffés Sautebrau
Salade Olympio
Plateau de fromages des douze Césars
Fruits rafraîchis des premières cueilles
Crêpes flambées à la façon de Madame Viala du Pont Romain
de Sommières
Café et Marc du Grand Daudet

❖

Blanc Aligoté 1927
Rosé de Pierre-feu
Morgon 1937
Champagne Mouton Rothschild
Quinze liqueurs

❖

CONSTANCE
or
Solitary Practices

for Anaïs, Henry, Joey

AUTHOR'S NOTE

This book is a fiction and not a history, but it is based on in-
numerable conversations and a residence of fifteen years in
Provence; though here and there I may have taken a liberty
with the chronology of an ignoble period, the sum of the
matter has a high degree of impressionistic accuracy as a portrait of the French Midi during the late war. I have also studied
serious historians like Kenward but owe more to French
sources like the books of M. Aimé Vielzeuf of Nîmes.

I originally intended to carry two texts in the appendix –
that of the Protocols of Zion, and that of Peter the Great's
Testament. The former, however, is so prolix and cumbersome, as well as being available elsewhere in critical editions,
that I abandoned the idea; but the Testament of Peter is such a
singular document and so apposite to the times as well as to this
book that I decided to leave it in.

In conclusion I would like to acknowledge with gratitude
the lynx-eyed surveillance of my text by Mrs Helen Dore which
saved me from many errors.

LAWRENCE DURRELL

Contents

*Pour Faire Face au Prince des Ténèbres
qui a un royaume formé de cinq éléments
le Père de la Grandeur évoque la Mère de
la Vie qui, à son tour, évoque l'Homme
Primordial qui a cinq fils : l'Air, le Vent,
la Lumière, l'Eau et le Feu.*

Cahiers d'Etudes Cathares,
Narbonne

ONE

In Avignon

IN THE BEGINNING THE TWO TALL GATE-TOWERS OF MEDIEVAL
Avignon, the Gog and Magog of its civic life, were called
Quiquenparle and *Quiquengrogne*. Through them the citizens
of this minor Rome passed by day and night, just as memories
or questions or sensations might pass through the brain of
some sleeping Pope. The clappers of the great belfries defied
the foul fiend with their rumbling clamour. The shivering
vibrations fanned out below them, thinning the blood to deafness for those in the street. It was quite a different matter when
the tocsin sounded – it made a gradually increasing roar such
as a forest fire might do, or else sounded like the vicious hum
of warlike bees in a heating bottle. He had lived so long with
them as history that now, half-starved as he was, the very war
sirens seemed to resemble them. After the tremendous beating
he had endured – to the point of unconsciousness – he had been
thrown into a damp cell in the fortress and attached to the wall
with such science that he could not completely lie down, for
they had hobbled his neck to a ring in the wall, as well as
pinioning his elbows. Quatrefages had now reached a stage of
blessed amnesia when all his various aches and pains had
merged into one great overwhelming distress which elicited
its own anaesthesia. He had subsided in ruins on the floor, and
leaned his head against the wall; but the rope was just short,
by intention. The pressure on his carotid, in a paradoxical sort
of way, kept him from going out altogether. He heard the soft
rumbling of military vehicles as they mounted the cobbled
slope and rolled down into the garrison square; the rubber
wheels slithered and the engines roared in and out of gear.
For him it was as if a long line of knights were riding away by

torchlight upon some heroic Templar adventure; the garble of horses' hooves upon the cobbled drawbridge bade them goodbye. A sort of vision, born of his fatigue and pain, allowed him to delve into the real subject-matter of his life – for it was he who was documenting the Templar heresy and hoping to run down clues as to the whereabouts of the possibly mythical treasure. Now he had fallen into the hands of the new Inquisition, though the priests of the day wore field-grey and bore swastikas as badges and amulets. With them death had come of age. So this was to be the outcome of his long search – to be tortured to reveal secrets he did not possess! When he laughed in a desperate hysteria they had smacked him across the mouth, knocking his teeth into his throat. But all this came much later. . . .

As for Constance and Sam, they were not alone, for the whole world seemed to be saying goodbye; yet the present was still a small limbo of absolute content, of peace, among the vines. The high tide of a Provençal summer would soon be narrowing down towards a champion harvest which must certainly rot, for by now the harvesters had almost all been called to arms, leaving only the women and children and the old to confront these other armies of peaceful vines. There they stood, the plants, in all their sturdiness, staring up into a sky of blue glass, with all their plumage of dense leaf and dusty fruit spread out as if in an embrace.

The lovers were very inexperienced as yet, neither knew what a war was, nor how to behave towards it. This created an uncertainty which was made more agonising by the fact that their love-making had only just begun; they had wasted more than a month of adolescent skirmishing before coming to terms with each other. Their vertiginous embraces could not disguise the stark gaps in their physical knowledge of the love-act. And now, on top of it all, to be overtaken by the unwanted war which might be forced upon them by a mad German house-painter: no, it was impossible to believe in this war!

But Sam's uniform had arrived – it was as if the war had advanced another stealthy pace towards them. It needed altering, the uniform, and the cap was a trifle too large. Sam felt both glory and foolishness as he tried it on before the mirror on the balcony floor of the old house. She said nothing as she lay humbly naked on the gold and blue coverlet, cupping her chin in her hands. He looked so sad and abashed and so very handsome – a naked man in a military tunic and cap without badge as yet! Sam gazed and gazed at himself, feeling that he had undergone a personality change. "What a pantomime!" he said at last, and turning, embraced her impulsively with a wave of desperate sadness. She felt the buttons cold upon her breast as he pressed himself upon her with the ardour of his uncertainty. In the prevailing world-madness they had decided to do something quite mad themselves – to get married! What folly! Both said it, truly both felt it. But they were anxious to get closer to each other before parting, perhaps forever. Meanwhile the damned uniform had been the cause of the first quarrel among the four boys during that marvellous summer.

It was soon over; it occurred while they were playing pontoon by moonlight on the rose-trellised verandah where day-long the lizards dozed or skirmished on the crumbling walls. It had been largely Blanford's fault; he had started it by being pompous and high-minded on the subject of conscientious objection and had added fuel to the irritation this had caused by sneering at men in uniform who had surrendered their identity to the "herd-mind". It was the fashionable talk of the day in literary circles. The moon was so bright that they did not really need the old and shaky paraffin lantern which stood by them on the table. "Cut it now, Aubrey," cried Hilary, and his sister Constance sharply echoed him, "Yes, Aubrey, please." But she could not forbear (for Sam had looked really wonderful in his new uniform) to add her own barb to the conversation: "Just because Livia has been making you suffer so much, keeping you on a string all summer!" Blanford paled to the ears as the shaft went home. He had really had a miserable time with Constance's sister who had provoked in him a self-destructive calf-love which she only half-assuaged while at the same time manifesting an almost equal partiality for his young friend the consul, Felix Chatto, who now sat furiously staring at his hand and saying, "Your bank, I think!"

Livia had made fools of them both. No, it was not by mere caprice, that is what made her so fascinating – it was simply that there seemed to be no continuity between successive impulses, she jumped the points and did not bother to reflect upon any hurt she might be causing. She was either heartless, or else her heart had never been touched. It was vexatious to think of her in these terms, but there were no others. Both Aubrey and Felix were hovering about the point of making definitive declarations when she suddenly took herself off as she had always done in the past, leaving as an address a Paris café and a second one in Munich. Poor Blanford had even gone so far as to get her a ring – she had allowed it to get to this point. No wonder he was behaving in such an acid way, conscious of his own miscalculation but also of the huge weight of the love Livia had provoked in him. And then on top of this the cursed war!

It gave Constance a sudden pang as she watched them from the upper window of her room, their rosy, youthful features full of trust and inexperience, so unfledged and so uncertain. Her brother Hilary sat in his usual way, one leg over the other with his cards held lightly in his brown fingers. How handsome he was, with his blond hair and his fine sharp features and blue eyes! His bearing expressed a sort of aristocratic dis-

dain which contrasted with the simplicity and warmth of Sam's
address. Blanford and Felix were less striking – one might have
divined that they were just down from Oxford and were bookish young men. But Hilary looked like a musician, sure of himself and fully completed as to his opinions and attitudes. At
times he even gave the impression of being a somewhat supercilious young man, almost over-sophisticated and over-bred.
He lacked his sister's gorgeousness and her warmth. His coldness masked him, where she remained always vulnerable. She
felt sorry now for having stung Blanford and tried to make
amends as best she could, while Sam, from the depths of his
intoxication (after all, he was *loved*), allowed his magnanimity
to overflow in expressions of friendship which were, for all
that, quite sincere and full of concern for his friend. Earlier that
evening they had all been down to the weir for a cold swim and
Sam had said, "Constance is always asking me how you can let
yourself be made miserable by Livia whose behaviour never
varies, and is quite predictable." Blanford groaned, for he knew
what was coming: another dose of the intoxicating Viennese
lore which Constance was stuffing down their throats from
breakfast to bedtime – all the Freud she was acquiring in the
course of her studies in Geneva. "Livia is a woman at war with
the man in herself, consequently a castratrice," said Sam; it was
extremely funny, his expression as he uttered the words. He
himself understood nothing of these sentiments, he had learned
them by heart from his beloved, who had a tendency to be
rather bossy in intellectual matters. "Constance can go to hell
with her theory of infantile sexuality and all that stuff," said
Aubrey manfully.

Actually the whole theory fascinated and repelled him,
and he had eyed with distaste the clutch of pamphlets in German which she carried about all through the summer. "Freud!"
He knew that one falls in love, oh yes, for quite other reasons.
Livia had discovered one of his notebooks and, without asking

permission, had riffled through it. She was lying on the bed and as he came in she looked up, like a lizard, like a snake, as if she were really seeing him for the first time. "I *see*," she said at last, drawing a surprised breath. "You are a *poet*." It was an unforgettable moment: she went on staring at him, staring right through him as if by some optical trick, right into his future. It was as if she had suddenly invented him anew, invented his career and the whole future shape of his inner life by the magic of such a phrase. One cannot help loving someone who divines one so clearly, throws one's whole obscure destiny into clear focus. What could she have been reading among his sporadic scribbles? Just squirts of thought which one day might become poetry or prose or both. "My death goes back a long way to a time when women were coy or arch, or both, or neither, or simply MUD – the outstretched legs of mud into which I dribble my profuse and living blood, my promise of need, while my harp, whose sinews echoed all time, rebounded on the silence where it found it." She did not have to add that it was beautiful, her eye said it for her. He felt found out, both elated and terrified.

Hilary dealt them another hand and became snappy and priggish about Blanford's decision to retire to Egypt with the Prince. "It will look like running away," he said, and Blanford snapped back, "But I am, that is precisely what I *am* doing. I feel no moral obligation to take sides in this ridiculous Wagnerian holocaust." Constance reproached her brother at once, saying, "O, let's not spoil this marvellous summer we've had. . . ." and instantly the images of Provence, of Avignon, and the sweet limestones of the surrounding hills rose in their memory with a sort of lustful repletion. What an experience it had been – the whole Mediterranean world opened before them as if on a scroll.

"I'm sorry," said Hilary and Blanford echoed, "So am I." They had been living in the vast, echoing, ugly old house for weeks now, in close friendship and affection. These small bickerings left a bad taste. Tu Duc – that was the name of the place. Constance had inherited it. The name rang in their minds like a drumbeat, signifying everything they had encountered and enjoyed during this long, unhurried stay above a village which was only a stone's throw from Avignon of romantic renown. City of the Popes!

Later that night some of these regrets surged up among the dreams of Constance, but not too powerfully to spoil the moonlight on the window-sill, the smell of honeysuckle and the deep gloating warmth of the male body beside her. It was marvellous to spend the whole night with a man, to feel the drum of his chest rising and falling under her fingers while he slept. Their love-making was becoming increasingly expert with practice. At times it seemed that they were on a toboggan travelling at ever-increasing speed down a dizzily whorled snowrun. A toboggan often out of control. "Sam, for goodness sake: I am terrified you will make me pregnant." She had not foreseen this love affair and, though an emancipated young woman with the whole of science at her fingertips, she had left what she called, rather irreverently, her "tool kit" back in Geneva. Nor could Sam help himself. "I can't help it," he gasped, and steered her more and more forcefully towards the slow dense crisis which at last overwhelmed them. They were panting, exhausted, as after a race. Sam, who specialised in quotations from limericks to which he could never put a beginning or an end, quoted from one now: "So he filled her with spunk, and then did a bunk, that stealthy old man of Bulgaria."

That was awake, but it was when he lay asleep that she could spend ages watching him, head on elbow, full of the mystery of his lazy gladiator's body which seemed to store heat like a vacuum flask. She loved to feel the soft tulip of his sex lying against her side, in repose now in his deep sleep, but so quick to wake at her summons – at a wave of a wand almost, and it woke the sleeping cobra of their youthful desires. Her blood ran cold when she recalled that for more than a month he had not spoken to her, had stayed cold and distant as a star when she was simply dying to become the target for his affections. She had pretended, like a fool, to be having a love affair with an older man, a psychiatrist, and the result of this foolish piece of boasting had been to chill Sam to the backbone; how long it had taken to rectify this silly error! As a matter of fact she had last year slept with a doctor, but that was curiosity, and she had no mind to repeat it, so insipid had it turned out to be. But now Sam! In him she had succumbed to the least intelligent, the most simple-minded man you could imagine. But she was ferociously in love now, she felt like a wild cat; she had decided that she would endow him with all he needed of marvellous brain and sensibility and insight – all these treasures she had reserved for him. He would realise through her all that she divined in him now, hidden under his callowness and shyness, under his fitful reserves; she would pierce through his crust of flippancy, the friendly footlings of his idols, like old Wodehouse, and strike sparks off his inmost soul! How he would have trembled, poor boy, if she had put all these sentiments into words. It was bad enough as it was, his feeling of total inadequacy! But such a programme would have put him into a real panic.

In the middle of the night he woke her, and turning her face to him asked in a husky whisper, "Tell me, darling, do you think me a coward for offering my services?" It was obvious that Blanford's thoughtless talk had wounded him. Nor was he satisfied with the passionate, simple complicity of her embrace, though an agony of sympathy was echoed by it. "Answer," he said doggedly, as one might demand something in writing. "Of course you are not! In spite of that stupid vote in the Union – typically Oxonian! Of course you are not!" she said hotly again, hugging him to her until she was all but out of breath.

"It's quite right that England doesn't mean anything to Aubrey – why should it? But I should be hard put to explain why it means anything to me."

He closed his eyes upon the word and saw a sort of jumbled composite picture of grey buildings, low hills, and wrinkled rivers, and backing them all the romantic image of the golden Kentish Weald in harvest-time, raised like a golden buckler to heaven. He was reminded, too, of a brief and awkward love affair with a girl who was picking hops. He had been lent one of those funny little oast-houses by the parents of a friend, ostensibly to study. The affair was awkward and pitiful, though the hop-picker was brave and beautiful and as blonde as Constance. But what a trial their ignorance turned out to be, for she feared pregnancy, and he feared some venereal affliction about which he knew hardly anything! In the lavatory of a nearby pub there stood what looked at first sight to be an automatic fruit-drop or cigarette machine; but it was full of French letters. The legend said, "Place two shillings in slot and tug handle of the Dispenser sharply!" What a wonderful word – "Dispenser"; what a miserable wreck of an affair; what a beautiful girl worthy of someone more experienced and more at ease; what a fool he had been not to show more skill and kindness! But in spite of everything the shining Weald was there, in his inner consciousness, raising its blazing corn to heaven under a deafening sunshine! In a sense, too, weald for weald, Constance had become part of this picture, had merged with it. (All these matters would sort themselves out once the war was over – if ever it decided to break!) At lunch he had said, "How I wish the damn war would break!" which Blanford had echoed with, "How I wish I could wish!"

Now they lay in each other's arms, burnished dark gold by the sun, and asleep, oblivious to scurrying of mice in the old house, or the remote snore of one of their friends from an upper attic. It is strange, too, that they did not feel more helpless – but then they were full of the delusive elation which love brings. Thoughts scurrying in the attics of the brain, the feet of mice among the dying apples, the presence of ghostly women whose voices were brought by the wind, conversing, complaining, keening. The house was like an old schooner, creaking and groaning with every shift of wind. And yet in their dreams sadness came, sadness overtook them as they thought of separations and bereavements and death – yes, even death was there sometimes; and the tears of distress at their goodbyes trickled down the sirens of booming liners, saying farewell. What a confusing business! In dreams they felt the pains which waking they cared not to show.

Lord Galen's bizarre mansion up the hill was also being snugged down for the winter, and his last dinner parties became more improvised and more perfunctory; his trip to Germany and his financial gaffe with the Nazis had thrown him into a deep depression. But he was glad to see the youthful band from Tu Duc – he had taken a great fancy to Constance and regarded Sam as a highly eligible young man despite his lack of fortune. The Prince was also often there at the hospitable table of Lord Galen, and it was indeed during one of these dinners that he had proposed outright to take Blanford on the strength as Private Secretary, and to sail with him for Egypt within a week or so. Originally it was in this context that the word "conscience" had cropped up; it represented a key consideration, after all, but it somehow stung the Prince like a gadfly. "Conscience?" he exclaimed sharply. "No one comes to Egypt to struggle with his conscience!" He gazed keenly round the table under frowning eyebrows. "Egypt is a *happy* country," he went on, "and when you think that, in terms of gross inequality of wealth, criminal misgovernment and civic profligacy it takes the highest place of any nation in the world, one wonders how this can be. The poor are so poor that they have already starved and died and come out the other side, roaring with laughter. The rich are negligent and callous to an unimaginable degree. Yet what is the result? A *happy* people! Indeed the people, wherever you go, throw up their clothes and show you their private parts, roaring with laughter as they do so. It puts everyone in a very good humour." Lord Galen looked somewhat unnerved. "Good heavens!" he exclaimed feebly, "What effrontery!" It sounded enchanting to Blanford. "What does one do in reply?" he asked amid the laughter, but the Prince was not saying. "One responds with good humour," he said evasively.

Max, the violet negro, who was Galen's chauffeur and general factotum, spent a part of every morning now draping white dust-covers over the furniture; he had started on the upper floors and had worked downwards, to leave the inhabited rooms free for living in. But it was like a swimming-pool slowly emptying itself, and at the last occasion there remained only the grand salon and the dining-room free. A piled mass of waiting dust-covers was stacked in the hall. Galen sighed. It was very sad to have the summer cut short like this, and not even to be *sure* that the whole spectre of war might not melt away into some last-minute treaty of peace. What would they do then? Could they just resume the old life as if nothing had taken place? No, something profound in the heart of things seemed to have suffered a sea-change. The beating of the German drum had presaged something – some new orientation. But the future was still so dark and ambiguous and full of portent. ("Making love to her," thought Sam, "is like doing a double jack-knife with a sword swallower.") Blanford rolled breadcrumbs and reflected. There was another, a more private reason why he loved Livia – but it would have sounded fatuous to relate it. She had left him the new Huxley, his favourite writer, with the first essay on the nature of Zen Buddhism in it, the very first mention of Suzuki, which had opened like a shaft of light in the depths of his skull. It had set him dreaming once more of faraway peoples educated in harmlessness, in places like Lhasa, by the reading of golden sutras engrossed in golden ink. . . . This, like the discovery of his avocation as a poet, was also her gift to him, a gift no other woman would ever match. Who could understand such a thing?

Yet the failure of communication between them as sexual and affective animals had been nothing less than calamitous; at times it so enraged him that he could have picked her up and shaken her like a rat, shaken some sense into her – or out of her! And where was she now? He could only guess, though it very much depended on whether she had the money to stay in such a place, even though it was only middling-expensive: the Fanechon. Up in the bustling raffish and dirty Boulevard Montmartre with its *couscous* joints and tinny Arabic cinemas. She loved this small, select hotel because the side-door of the lounge opened directly into the Musée Grevin, and, slipping out of it, she would spend quite a large part of her time wandering among the waxworks, and tracing the path of French history (or the bloodier part) through its tableaux, her face taking on a new beauty from the soft abstraction into which these shadowy scenes threw her. The agony of Marie Antoinette, the death of Marat (the authentic bath was the one on view!) and the sweet limpidity of expression with which Jeanne d'Arc walked to the stake – hours passed and she was still there, sunk in thought before these waxen reinactions of a vanished yet still living past. The fête on the Grand Canal, too, with its thrilling blue night sky and shining waterscapes, or the evening, the momentous soirée at Malmaison with the entire cast of a Stendhal novel as guests! The modern exhibits hardly stirred her interest at all. But in the suffocating little hall of the distorting mirrors she lingered a good while, trying out different postures and studying the distortions with attention, never with amusement. Then she might buy some chewing gum and slip into a cinema to dream about the length of

Descartes' waxen nose or the sly expression on the face of Fouquier. Blanford thought of her with a dull ache now and said to himself, "Poor girl, she has a past like a paw full of thorns."

It would have to be Egypt, then. "In Egypt," he assured Felix Chatto, "the girls have independent suspension, it is the latest thing." It was the latest fad on the new cars like the Morris which Chatto shared with Lord Galen's clerk, Quatrefages, and in which he promised to take Constance back to Geneva and her studies – for come what may these at least must be terminated in due and correct fashion. Sam insisted on it. Later, when he returned from the wars with the appropriate bullet-hole in the breast-pocket bible he would be carrying, she would be there waiting for him, with the whole weight of science heavy upon her shoulders! "Then you will realise how stupid I am and decide to leave," she cried out in protest. Actually these studies were helping her to understand the nature of her love for Sam. An only child, his mother had overwhelmed him with her love but, wisely, never encumbered his own powers, his need to fly. She had detached herself from him at the correct moment. She had, in the new lingo Constance was learning, broken the transfer at the fruitful moment to set him free. No *Sons and Lovers* would ever be written about *him*, she reflected. He had bathed in the mother flow, his flesh was sated and at peace – hence the sexual magnetism which those lazy brown limbs held for her. He had a skin of velvet because he had once been correctly, sensually loved as she, in some miraculous fashion, had also been. They were made for each other, their sensibilities mixed like dyes! "O! Stop *gloating*!" she told her reflection in the old pier-glass – she had become solicitous for her beauty and now made up carefully each morning and evening, lest he look elsewhere! When, however, she asked Aubrey whether her beloved did not look like Donatello's David, he had irritated her by replying in that negligent, weary, Oxonian manner, "Everyone sees himself or herself as somebody quite different. Hence the confusion because everyone is acting a part. He sees you as Iseult, whereas you are really Catherine of Russia. You see him as David, but I see only the eternal British schoolboy in love, elated because he is undressing his mother." She was furious. "Damn you!" she said and went on doggedly making up while he tried to shave in one corner of the great mirror with equal doggedness.

The royal steam-yacht sent by Farouk signalled its arrival at Marseille, prepared to carry the Prince to Alexandria. Blanford called on him at his hotel in Avignon in order to find out what plans he had made for the journey and found the little man hastily wrapping up his treasures and distributing them about the numerous cabin trunks with their brilliant filigree-worked Turkish designs in leafy gold – he must have inherited them from some Khedival ancestor. At the door stood the outsize remover's van which housed the larger effects of the Prince – his chairs and folding tables (he gave numerous bridge parties); a couple of palm trees in tubs; opulent vases and gold plate and the two peregrine falcons. He showed Blanford round all these items with evident pleasure. But he did not propose to get on the move for a day or two. Asked if there were any special clothes which might be *de rigueur* for the new post he said in an offhand way, "The Princess will kit you out. Just come with one *tenue de ville* and a tie so I can introduce you respectably. Later on you'll need some shark-skin dinner jackets, I suppose. But I know where to get them cheap for you in Alex. Here, look at this." He produced a large scarlet velvet-covered hat-box, the kind a conjuror might carry about, or an actor. It was a sort of oriental wig-box, in fact, but inside it there was a shrunken human head, a male head, coated heavily in resin but with the eyes open. Blanford was startled. "Good Lord!" he said, and the Prince chuckled appreciatively at his reaction. "It's the head of a Templar; it comes from the Commanderie in Cyprus—I had it traced when I bought it in the Cairo Souk. The Museum wanted it, but I thought it would make such a nice present for Lord Galen that I brought it to offer and please him. . . ." He paused on a note of dismay. "But, you know, he is so superstitious that he refused it; he is afraid to have the Eye put on him. Specially as he is hunting for the treasure of this Order—or rather Quatrefages is hunting for it, for him. So I'll take it back. If I tell the Egyptians that it is a Prophesying Head my enemies will go pale. Egyptians are just as superstitious as you English, more so."

He popped the cover of the silk-lined hat-box with its grisly remnant and ordered his servant Hassan to wrap it up softly in tissue paper and convey it to the wagon with all the other effects. "Phew! It is hot," he said, fanning himself with a reed fan of brilliant hue. "Egypt will be a furnace still. Never mind. Sit down, my dear boy, and let me tell you a funny joke. Laughter makes one cooler, and Hassan will bring us some jasmine tea and some crystallised fruit. You laughed, remember, when I told you about the Egyptians throwing up their clothes and showing their private parts as a greeting, *n'est-ce pas?*" Blanford said, "Indeed. It sounds delightful." The Prince, whose mind slipped from perch to perch, from branch to branch, like a bird, suddenly was diverted by a twinge of rheumatism in one of his fingers. "This damned arthritis deformans," he cried, and started to tug at the joints until they cracked aloud. When he had done he resumed his theme. "About the greeting I can tell you a funny tale which makes Egyptians laugh—it shows that we are not devoid of humour. It concerns Sir Charles Polk, the last British Ambassador. This fashion of greeting so worked upon his mind and upon his imagination that he became an insomniac. I have it from the Embassy doctor, Hassim Nahd. Poor man, if he slept he always dreamed that the peasants were greeting him in this way, and he had an irresistible impulse to throw down his trousers and return their greeting! It put him in a fever of anxiety, Hassim was all the time prescribing sedatives, but to no avail. Then one day the blow fell. London told him that the King had decided on a state visit to Egypt and that he even proposed to travel the whole length of the Nile. Sir Charles had to start making all the necessary arrangements. Naturally the Palace offered him the classic old steamer *Memphis* which had always served for this kind of state journey. The problems were not insoluble. Or rather there was only one that stuck out—if I may use the phrase without indelicacy. It was the traditional greeting. It is a long way up the river, and there are thousands upon thousands of peasant *felaheen*—in fact for such an event they would probably line both banks solid. Poor Sir Charles went pale as he thought of what might happen. He tried to reason Whitehall out of the visit, but no, it was deemed both advisable and apt on political grounds." The Prince gave a tiny snort or chuckle and, banging his knee softly, went on, "One imagines the dilemma of poor Sir Charles. What should he do? Well, you can say what you like about the British public servant, but there is nobody like him for probity and unflinching devotion to duty. He explained his position and offered his resignation. The thought of exposing his Sovereign to such an outrage had been too much. The F.O. was so impressed by his dignity and firmness that he was transferred at once with promotion to Moscow, while the Egyptian trip duly took place under the aegis of a Chargé d'Affaires, who was afterwards put on the shelf and held *en disponibilité* for nearly ten years until all was forgotten. I sometimes see old Charles in London and we talk over old times; but I never ask him what the unusual peasant greeting is in Russia!"

With such pleasant exchanges the morning wore on until the mayor called for the usual pre-prandial glass of *pastis* which enabled him to resume the state of the world for the benefit of the Prince. He, the mayor, was in constant touch with

Paris and with every bulletin of news or rumour things seem to be deteriorating further. It must end in war and yet . . . "*Drôle de guerre*," said the mayor, quoting the current slogan of the day. "They will never attack us, for they know that the French army is the best in the world. It would be madness. And then the line, the Maginot line!" On such ephemeral delusions they based their hopes for peace. "They have given us some air-raid sirens," went on the mayor with pride, "and today the *pompiers* are going to have a rehearsal at three o'clock. Do not be afraid when you hear them. It will only be for a few minutes. But we must be prepared for anything with the modern aeroplane." There was so much sunlight on the terrace and so much laziness in the air that they had the greatest difficulty in treating this sort of conversation with the seriousness it deserved. Blanford lunched at the hotel with the Prince and afterwards they sauntered across the glowing town and climbed the Rocher de Doms, the sharp spur from the platform of which it was possible to see the even sharper snout of Mont St. Victoire raising its dogged crest, bare and mistral-tormented. There was no snow now, of course, but the cold afternoon mistral had furrowed the green Rhône and bent the bushes and cypresses on the dry garrigues around them. They spent a while looking down on the town with its brown pie-crust roofs and its crooked dark streets. Suddenly the sirens started to wail, and in spite of themselves they were both startled – the more so because a real plane passed over the town in slow gyres. "One of ours, I hope!"

Had things been different, Blanford thought, what a pleasure it would have been to saunter away an evening thus in the sunny city, watching the pigeons turning and hovering among the soaring belfries, gossiping about nothing very consequential, just unpacking their idle minds of their dreams and thoughts. . . . But one felt guilty of enjoying such a luxury with the world coming apart at the seams.

Hilary unexpectedly joined them in the main square for a companionable *tisane* of *vervaine*, urged upon them by the Prince. He had not been seen all day at Tu Duc because he had come in to attend early Mass at the Grey Penitents. Now he was deeply despondent, though he tried to hide it – a mood brought on by a long talk to the curé who had assured him that France would not lift a finger to fight and would be over-run whenever the Germans wished. It was all the fault of the Jews, he had added, with all their infernal radicalism. Hitler was right. France was *pourrie jusqu'à la moelle* – rotten to the marrow with it. Hilary sighed and lit another cigarette. "A young Jewish couple committed suicide in the Princes Hotel last night, so the tobacconist told me. They were refugees from Berlin. Very young, too. He heard the shots."

They took leave of the Prince, who promised to get in touch with Blanford the moment he had made up his mind when, if ever, he was going to move. Walking past the tall doors of the Museum, Blanford peeped into the courtyard and instantly felt an almost physical blow upon his heart, so vivid was the memory of Livia standing there. In the half light of dawn she had recited a line of Goethe in her "smiling voice". He walked on now to overtake Hilary, thinking to himself, "What beautiful wind-washed days we lived this summer. I feel like an old king whose favourite cup-bearer is dead." For he knew that it was definitive, her departure, and that though they might meet again they would never again live together. The thought was not unmixed with gratitude, for hers had been the kind of magnetism which matures men. He closed his eyes for a second and saw her turn the corner ahead of him. She had learned to walk like a Roman slave – that is how he put it to himself – and turning a corner she would keel and hesitate, like a hawk about to stoop. Hilary started to hum a tune from *Bitter Sweet*, and because the melody moved him Blanford hummed in unison, to disguise his emotion. So they strode over the famous bridge towards the hillocks and the winding road which led to the domain of Constance, who at that moment was aiding Sam in the business of stuffing pimientos with forcemeat and garlic against the evening meal.

After they had walked in friendly silence almost to the gates of the old house Hilary said, putting his hand on Aubrey's wrist, "I don't want to pry, Aubrey, but what the devil were you tearing up last night? It lasted ages, like in Chekov."

"Aptly said," replied his friend with a sardonic downturn of the mouth. "In fact old notebooks, bits and pieces. I wanted to clear the decks before leaving." He paused, and then went on a trifle defensively, "Even a bit of a novel. I invented a man I called Sutcliffe – for lack of anything better – and he became altogether too real. He started following me about like gravity, as well as riding on my back like the Old Man of the Sea. I had to stop!" Hilary laughed. "I see," he said. "You should have left them to the Museum. The papers, I mean."

They turned the last corner to find Blaise the carter standing proudly outside the house, on the balcony steps, chatting to Constance and Sam, for he had come up from the station to deliver the old leather sofa which had been sent them for safe-keeping by Pia. *It had arrived!* It was covered in a clumsy skin of thick brown paper. Constance gazed at Aubrey with narrowed eyes and said accusingly, "I thought you told me Sutcliffe was invented." She held the end of the invoice which contained the name of the sender. "We will see about that later," said Blanford evasively. Together they picked up the shabby object and placed it in the conservatory among the palms, where it looked not inappropriate. Blaise did not take part in this, but stood and coughed on the balcony until the girl came back with a tray full of brimming *pastis* glasses. This cough of his was no stage effect – he had been gassed in the 1914 war. Constance had managed to secure the services of his wife as a cleaner as well as laundress, which was a great help to them.

So they all chatted awhile in the course of which, inevitably, the subject of the war rose again to the surface. "The President spoke last week – *quel con!*" said Blaise without undue animosity. "He has never seen what war is. He spoke of freedom!" It was the usual mental rigmarole without any form of pith – how could there be any in a country where the leaders themselves were so confused and so pusillanimous? As for freedom . . . The Prince had indeed remarked at Lord Galen's dinner table, "Freedom is an evanescent thing – you only remark it by its absence, but you can't define it. That is why the British refuse to understand us Egyptians with our desire for freedom. We will make a mess of things, no doubt, but it will be an Egyptian mess, our own personal mess – and what a mess it will be! But an Egyptian mess!" He had raised his head proudly and gazed fondly around him.

Sam set about undoing the string and tearing off the wrappings in which the old couch was swathed. "It's Emily Brontë's sofa," he said. "No," said Hilary, "guess again." Constance said, "No more impiety, please. It's the chair of prophecy, the sofa of divination. I shall spend the afternoon reading my psycho-whatsit pamphlets upon it and praying for guidance."

Blanford had collected a Poste Restante letter from a school-friend, bookish like himself, who furnished a bewildering description of a Paris not so much frivolous about the war as totally unbelieving in its reality. "Sitting at the Dôme you feel that it simply *cannot* take place, not in this century, after all we've seen. Yet the danger gives a strange unreality to everything – the quality of amnesia. Actions become automatic. Look, sitting here on the *terrasse* I am watching the evolutions of some hirsute porters in uniforms trying to hoist an appalling statue of Balzac by Rodin on to a pedestal; finally they have waddled it up, like a penguin on to an ice-floe, where it will soon be almost invisible because of foliage; this week it is the

turn of Georges Sand whose bust will appear in the Luxembourg accompanied by speeches which give one gooseflesh.
Such rhetoric! Yet so highly appropriate for a people which can
solemnly put a notice *Défense d'uriner* on the railings outside
the Chambre des Députés! They are the true inheritors of the
Anc. Gk. sense of civic anarchy. . . . And yet, like a douche of
icy water, reality suddenly steps in with a *fait divers* like 'René
Crével commits suicide'. (He is a poet friend of mine you don't
know.) I was bemoaning this tragic fact to a painter at the
Dôme, but he cut me short, saying: '*Ce que je lui reproche . . .*
What I reproach in him is that he had good *reasons* for so
doing. *C'est pas ça la suicide! C'est pas sérieux!* He has brought
suicide into *disrepute*!'"

Blaise the carter, rosy as the setting sun, took his leave
now, and his cart crunched its way back towards the town. Sam
cleaned the paraffin lamps against nightfall and cracked open
some packets of candles which they would set up in old
saucers on the terrace table. This week Constance and Sam had
been elected to perform all those tasks which come under the
heading of "fatigue" – and some of the fatigues like the blocked
lavatory had been distinctly onerous ones. Sam groaned and
swore, but it was rapture to be alone with her. "They lived
forever after," he said as they worked, "in a faultless domestic
harmony which gave people quite a turn to see."

They dined early that eve – *entre chien et loup* as the
French say, to indicate a "gloaming" – and afterwards the boys
grew restless and elected to go for a swim in the cool waters of
the weir, leaving Constance the washing up. Nor did she mind
this – she wanted to be alone for a while, and the mechanical
actions soothed her and enabled her to think of other things
like, for example, those enticing pamphlets, so many of them
with their pages uncut, which lay beside her bed. Love had
rather got in the way of her studies and she had a bad conscience
about the matter. So once she had put everything to rights in

the kitchen she went upstairs and secured a couple which she proposed to read there and then, and in the most appropriate of places: the verandah with the conservatory. This involved some juggling with candles to obtain adequate light, but once all was in order, she lay down with a sigh and plunged into the labyrinth of suggestions and speculations which had completely altered her way of looking at things – given her an extraordinary new angle of vision upon people, upon individuals and cultures, upon philosophies and religions. It was as if her mind had been released from its cocoon of accepted verities, released to take wings on this extraordinary adventure into the world of infantile relationships, of demons and gods of the human nursery, and bestiary. God, it made her rage to find how lukewarm everyone was about these matters – the insufferable conceit of the male mind! Sticky old Aubrey blowing hot and cold down his long supercilious Oxford nose; bigoted Hilary; silly Felix . . .

She read for an hour, listening abstractedly with half an ear to the noise of their laughter, and the splashes as they dived. Then on a sudden impulse she got up, took her pamphlets and a branch of candles, and mounted the stairs to her room, which was now filled with rosy shadows reflected back from the giant old-fashioned cupboard with its full-length mirror. She sat down upon the edge of the bed and arranged her candles upon the floor so that they threw their light forwards and upwards towards her. Then she slipped out of her clothes and sat upon the edge of the bed, stretching her legs to their greatest extent and keenly gazing at the slit between her legs as reflected in the tall mirror. With her hands she spread wide the two scarlet wings of the vulva and stayed thus, staring at this terrible scarlet gash between her white thighs – a horrible gash, as if hacked out by the clumsy strokes of a sabre. Her vagina, her vulva – what a horror to contemplate such a primitive and horrific member! If a man saw this, why, he would go mad with disgust! She gave a small sob such as a bird gives when the shot strikes its breast in mid-flight. "My cunt," she said in a low voice, still staring at it, "O my God, who could have thought of such a thing?" She was filled with a barbaric terror as she stared at the red gash. He would never stay with her if he should once glimpse this terrible bloody sinus between her two beautiful and shapely legs. She craned back, spreading the scarlet cretinous mouth wider so that it assumed an oval shape with part of the hymeneal net still across – it gaped like a whale in a Breughel painting. Poor Sam! Poor Jonah! She felt quite weak with despair and horror. In her imagination she seized him by the shoulders and clutched him to her while her heart cried out to him: "Hold me, suffocate me, impale me! I am dying of despair. What good can come of poor women with this frightful handicap?" She rose with such impulsiveness – gestures winged with despair – that she overturned the candles and had to plunge after them and set them upright again. She could have wept with vexation, but she thought it would be better not to let herself go so far until he was there to comfort her. Nevertheless she did weep a little so that should he come very late he would see the tears upon her cheek and realise that she had suffered from his absence. He would be very contrite. She would forgive. . . . She drew a veil over the scene of reconciliation.

At that moment Sam himself was experiencing a wave of despair of roughly the same calibre; a chance remark of Blanford had set it off like a firework. Aubrey had said, in his gloomiest tone: "The power that women have to inflict punishment on men is quite unmanning, quite terrible; they can reduce us to mentally deficient infants with a single glance, make us aware of how shallow our masculine pretensions are. With their intuition they can look right into us and see how feeble and infantile and vain we are. My God, they are really terrifying." Listening to this wiseacre of twenty Sam felt a sympathetic wave of horror pass through him as he thought how superior Constance was in every way to himself. Yes, what good were men? The role of Caliban was the best they could aspire to! He hated himself when he thought of all her perfections – a whole Petrarchian galaxy of qualities which made her, like Laura, supreme in love. And now they would soon be parted. He jumped to his feet. Here he was wasting valuable seconds talking to these fools when he could have been with her. How like a man! What idiots they were! He took one last plunge and rose panting like a swordfish, with arms extended. How delicious the water was, despite the desperate fate which lay in store for men! How he longed to feel her in his arms once more! *He must try to be worthy of her!* He was so intoxicated by the thought that he fell over a tree stump and ricked his ankle quite severely.

And when he did arrive at the bedroom door it was to find her asleep with the marks of tears upon her cheek. How callous, how thoughtless men were! They were just ogres with a sexual appetite, and apart from that quite unfeeling, brutal, philistine! He crawled into bed with wet hair and snuggled up close to her warm body, stirring now in sleep.

Despite these emotional polarities he was at once soothed by the physical warmth of her, and like a diver immediately plunged back into those refreshing innocent dreams of his early puberty, which always figured, like some mystical *mandala*-shape, in the form of a brilliant green cricket-field upon which the white-clad players, like druids, performed their slow reflective evolutions until the evening bell sounded four from the clock on the pavilion. The deep grass which bordered the field was where the schoolboys lay with their books and cherries. A population of rabbits almost as numerous had stolen to the edge of the field to watch as well. (The same rabbits now on many a secret airfield had tiptoed to the edge of the mown runways to watch the Spitfires as they rehearsed, landing and taking off.)

He groaned a small groan from time to time in his sleep, and automatically she folded him in her arms without waking up herself.

Two floors below, a long-visaged and weary Blanford was completing the destruction of his loose-leaf notebook which seemed to him now insufferably priggish and threadbare with all its wide-ranging sonorities. "A throw of the dice must decide whether the mates magnetise or not, whether they click and whether their product is a clear-eyed love or a mess – a mess transferable to their children." He sighed and watched it burn among the other slips, for he was using the fireplace for his *auto-da-fé*. Later they would scold him and force him to clean up his room. He had said as little as he could about Livia, it was too painful to discuss; as for news of her, speculations about her, and so on, he left all that disdainfully to Felix Chatto.

"Europe's behaviour was appropriate for those who drank symbolic Sunday blood and munched the anatomy of their Saviour." So thought Blanford's Old Man of the Sea – about the C. of E. It was pungent stuff – was he himself as pessimistic as all that? He thought and smoked and thought again; and decided that he was, and that he had done well to cleanse his bosom of such perilous stuff.

> Unhealthy couple full of sin
> Witness the mess that we are in!

Then, further on, another note which was destined to have a longer life among his speculations. "If real people could cohabit with the creatures of their imagination – say, in a novel – then what sort of children would be the fruit of their union: changelings?" He laughed helplessly in Sutcliffe's voice and took a turn upon the terrace. The night was fine, like blue silk, and the stars were on parade in force, twinkling away like mad upon the operatic blue dark.

He got into bed and sought his restless slumber, head buried under his pillow, which smelt of newly ironed linen which had been hung out in the rain. The rain! He was not awake at four o'clock – the dawn was just hinting – to hear the swish of a light shower on the trees and on the stones of the verandah outside his room. The summer heats, rising from the brown parched drumskin of the earth, had given rise to a customary instability of temperature – little summer fevers which suddenly produced large ragged sections of free-flying cloud, so low that you could almost touch them. They were quite isolated, surrounded by summer blue, and they bore small showers or sometimes even hail which slashed at the vines and drummed on the grassy ground.

Bang! The report was so loud that the lovers started up; so did Hilary and Felix Chatto who was on a camp-bed in the kitchen. "What the devil!" exclaimed Sam. Could they be shelling the city? And who? Bang! This time they were awake enough to orient themselves towards the sound; it appeared to come from the densely wooded knoll above Tu Duc where they had once been to hunt for truffles in a holm-oak glade. But who could have got a gun up that steep hill, and for what reason? *Certes*, the whole town of Avignon lay down below it, across the river, with Villeneuve at one side turning the sulky cheeks of her castle towards the left. It had sounded like a light mortar, but there were no answering shots fired and no sound of aircraft, so, puzzled and disturbed, they started to make coffee and question. "We must go up and have a look," said Hilary in an alarmed voice. The wet grey dawn was breaking through the forest. "Of course," said Sam: so they gulped their coffee, and during this time two more shots were fired by the invisible artillery. They hastened, bolted their drink and food, and started the short but steep climb towards the summit of the overhanging hill. It took a quarter of an hour, but when at last they emerged upon the green platform it was to find that the weapon was only an old *paragrèle*, or cloud-cannon, which was firing shells full of salt crystals into the black stationary clouds above them. There were two old men alone to charge and fire this small mortar with its cartridges – the charges hissed upwards into the clouds which were swollen like purses with rain; yet after half an hour the trick worked and a light rain fell like smoke upon the slopes. One of the old peasants uncorked a bottle of *eau de vie* and passed round a sip after the success of their last shot. A watery sun struggled out and turned their faces to grey and then to yellow. They toasted each other with an Eviva, and then one of the old men remarked in an offhand manner, "They have gone into Poland! *L'après-midi, c'est la guerre.*"

The cloud had burst at long last.

TWO

The Nazi

THE LANDS OWNED BY THE VON ESSLINS MARCHED WITH the sealine in a desolate corner of Friesland, but without ever actually opening out upon it. Thus they shared the high winds and foul weather without in any way sharing in its picturesqueness, its refreshing breathlessness of spray and grey cloudscape. It was brackish land, poor land, encircled by shallow ranges of low hill which gave a deceptive profile to them, hinting at their penuriousness and the pains which they must inflict upon those who tilled them. Hills bent like pensive brows; thick yellowish loam, poor in limestone, which clogged under the plough, being too clayborne for rich crops. Winter came almost as a relief here, the land sinking back into its secret silence among the frozen dykes and ponds where the ice-cocked speargrass suggested armies of swordsmen. The trees dripped noisily in the night thaws, letting fall their icicles.

It had been theirs since the early seventeenth century when the first Von Esslin – also an Egon – had entered the profession of arms and won himself some dignities and a small fortune from a lucky marriage. The large, ugly feudal manse had in some way inherited two incongruous towers and a small moat, now in use as a duckpond. It was uncomfortable and impossible to heat. Moreover, as for most military families hovering on the margins of being considered nobility of the sword, finance was a perpetual trouble. The land offered them an income from two gravel pits and a seam of very fine white clay which they sold to potters in Czechoslovakia. The old General's pension was quite substantial, while Egon himself found his staff pay just about adequate for the life he led, which did not allow him to indulge himself in gambling debts, horseflesh or actresses like many of his brother officers of the same caste but with greater means. He did not regret the fact, for he was of a serious, almost pious bent, as befits a Catholic whose origins on his mother's side had been Bavarian. But as a family they were stylised now as being of the Junker breed, and they had acquired some of the massive obduracy and obscurantism of that class – retaining, however, a special weakness, a seasonal weakness, one might say, for the music that took them each year in the direction of Vienna, a capital they had always loved and where they had always kept an apartment with lovely views out upon the famous woods. But Gartner, the family house in the hamlet of that name, was a grim place, a difficult place to love, and now that his mother spent nearly the whole year there Von Esslin himself had begun to feel the strain: he was rather ashamed of the fact that he felt almost glad when the army called him away to his duties and gave him an excuse to live elsewhere.

These were some of the half-formulated thoughts and sensations that passed through the soldier's mind as the squat staff car lunged north and east along the dunes where the sea sighed among its summer calms and the sand lilies showed their pretty summer flowers; he had, by making some specious excuses, achieved an unheard-of luxury – twenty-four hours of leave – at a time when everything, every stitch of armour, every man, was grouped upon the borders of Poland. With so much impending he wanted to bid his mother goodbye – for who knew where the decisions of the Führer might send them? The telephone had been under blackout for some days now, except for army messages, but he had managed to signal her by asking a colleague in a northern unit to detach a motor cycle despatch rider to warn her. So she would be there, waiting for him as always at the end of the long green salon, her fingers upon a book, smiling. It was her invariable pose when it came to one of his visits – it tried to suggest that all was well, life was calm, and everything to do with the property taken care of. The Polish maid who never spoke would open the door to him and curtsy silently with that shy, downcast smile on her swarthy face. Well, but . . . they had much to discuss. Things were moving so fast that everyone felt out of his depth; they had been outstripped by the speed of events. Peace was not yet mortally stricken – but it was like a patient unconscious on a table, bleeding to death.

The summer had been exceptionally hot; warm rain in August, if you please! Everything was steaming; and now the real harvest weather had come, stilly blue with appropriate sunlight. (Ideal for a campaign in the Polish marches.) Von Esslin frowned and touched the edges of his short moustache as he watched the house come into view at the end of a long winding road lined with gracious lindens. This was his home – he repeated the phrase in his mind, but it evoked no pang of pleasure, simply the dutiful anxiety and affection which he had kept for his mother. They were very close in a way, and yet a mortal shyness ruled over their behaviour; to hear the tone in which they talked you might imagine them to be mere acquaintances, so without animation and lustre was it. It had grown, the shyness, since they were left more together, following upon the death of his twin sister Constanza, and of his father, the General. The old man had worshipped Constanza, and he never really recovered from her death; he had pined away like an old mastiff, filling the salons with photographs of her as a young woman before the slow wasting M.S. – sclerosis – had declared itself. How beautiful she had been; Egon himself had been stricken down with despair at so cruel a fate. They never discussed it, or seldom, and then gruffly.

It was different when they were separated, for then he permitted his warmth of feeling to evoke his childish attachment for her; in letters she became Katzen-Mutter, and as he wrote the words he felt the picture of her rise in his heart as a benign cat-mother, always with a great Siamese rippling at her side. They were still there, the cats; they were a passion with her.

The staff car drew up at last before the culvert covering the moat, and then gingerly crossed the plank bridge to arrive at the tall oak door behind which the Polish maid stood already waiting for his ring. She heard the driver open the door and heel-click, and then the voice of the Major General telling him to take his dressing-case inside and to be prepared to move off on the morrow at first light. This brief, barking exchange was succeeded by the jangle of the bellrope. The Polish maid opened and muttered something guttural as always; she bowed her head and sank into a half-curtsy. Von Esslin grunted something which bore a vague resemblance to a greeting and walked past her to place his cap upon the marble table and turn aside to where already the girl had opened the door into the green salon where his mother rose to greet him with a little cry of pleasure. "I did not quite believe it," she said, with her brief scentless embrace. "But how wonderful." He stepped back a pace to take her hands and kiss them with a suggestion of affectionate homage. "I haven't very long," he said, and then cleared his throat harshly as he added, "We are on the edge of war." She nodded swiftly, a bird-like nod. "But how brown you have got," she said. "It makes your scar look whiter than ever." He smiled, the joke was an old one. Once a horse had run away with him into a wood and he had cut his cheeks open by riding into a coil of barbed wire which for some unknown reason had been tied upon a tree. The wounds were clean and he did not think to have them dressed or stitched – the result being the neatest simulacrum of duelling scars you might imagine. Despite his explanations his mess refused to believe that he had not in secret indulged in the old samurai-style duelling match which had been for many a year banned in the army, but which from time to time tempted young officers to practise it in secret. The more he denied this, the less he was believed. Was he not a

Prussian? Such cases were rare but they did occur, just as from time to time someone had to be court-martialled for fighting a duel. The scars remained, grew whiter as his skin browned in summer. He was rather proud of the implication in a childish way; and at the same time ashamed. They were like stigmata to which one was not entitled but which could not at the same time be expunged. They laughed together at the absurdity.

"Come and sit beside me," she said, "and tell me what is happening. Here we know nothing, the wireless is broken."

He obeyed her and sat himself down on the sofa, sighing as he did so. "Things move so fast," he said, "that I risk being out of date. That is why I must be at my post tomorrow. The Führer is making lightning decisions."

The Polish maid came in with a tray of drinks and a silence of lead fell between them as the girl crossed the room. Usually when she was present they spoke in a wooden and stilted French for the sake of privacy. So his mother said now, "The Czech contracts for the clay have lapsed, but I think we have found another buyer closer at home. I am waiting now for a response." He nodded and replied, frowning, "It was bound to happen, events being what they are." As the door closed silently behind the servant his mother said, "She asked for leave to visit her parents. I thought she would not come back. I was surprised that she did." He expostulated, "*Ach* why, she has always been with us, even if she has never learned a word of German. She must feel more at home than in some Polish hovel – her parents are farm labourers, no?"

The fate of Poland cast a momentary shadow over their conversation; both hastened to inter the subject along with the sentiment of regret – it would have been too much to call it shame. He became hearty and sentimental. "It's good to feel the country flexing its muscles, facing up to its detractors. Germany has been patient for too long, the Führer is right about that. Too long."

In sympathy with the mood she altered her expression to one of suitable sternness; she bowed her beautiful heart-shaped head a little and allowed her mouth to settle into its cat-form. It was straight and hard – the expression of a soldier's wife used to confronting bereavement and sudden loss with courage, if not with a resigned equanimity. He liked this in her, this expression of indomitability. There was much left unsaid behind this façade of normality, much that as Germans they could not say. There were paradoxes – for example the German expansion into Austria had put the music festival so dear to her temporarily out of reach. The festivals went on, yes, but she felt inhibited about visiting her beloved Salzburg and Vienna as a member of a master race. . . . It was awkward; happily the Führer had shared no such feeling of inhibition. He had consecrated a whole day to the convulsions of Wagner's music, and solemnly had himself photographed with the Wagner children for the benefit of the press. He apparently wished it to be clear that the intellectual and emotional foundations of the present German postures and actions were to be traced to the artist. The spiritual justifications of the new faith were there.

And then of course there were other matters upon which they could not smear self-justificatory conversation like a salve; matters too dark, too floating in ambiguities, to form a substance upon which they might base talk not hedged with reservations. "You realise, mother, we must be *positive* now." He had a special plosive way of expressing the word, accompanying it with a short gesture, as of a man driving a nail into a door. Positive. His thoughts turned with schoolboyish pleasure to those dark tanks of his, now so peacefully browsing in the fields and pastures, the rolling lands which led towards the border. Some might have seen them as obscene steel beetles manned by men dressed in helmets shaped like ugly turnips of the same steel. But no, for him the thought of them and of their crews was one of joy unredeemed by any reservation. The 10th Brigade, the 7th Panzers – this vast grouping of steel was breathtaking in its battle-power, its beetle-power. The slither of mesh as the caterpillars cackled across the asphalt of major highways, the roar and slither of the engines – all this was a Wagnerian paeon of malevolent power which would soon be unlocked. His heart rose at the thought and yet he felt somehow tearful inside. He repeated the word "positive" again, giving it a touch of grim relish. So they sat staring unhappily into their drinks.

When he got to his room to change for dinner he found that the girl had already set out his dress uniform on the bed and had passed an iron over the braided trousers. A little touch of formality was suitable to his first evening at home with his mother. It had always been so. The silver-backed brushes and the phials of cologne had been taken from their leather slipcases and disposed in the bathroom against the shave which he always gave himself on such occasions. How well this spindly Polish girl knew the routines of his life. It was curious to think of her as soon to be formally declared a slave. . . . He thought about it, frowning, as he lay in the hot water. Then he dressed and went downstairs again to the picture gallery where he would wait for his mother to join him. The tall windows, the little bow window at the far end with just room for a sofa and a grand piano, gave it intimacy. There were a few indifferent portraits of the various members of the family, one fine Klimt, and a few glass-covered cases which held various family relics deemed worthy of exhibition. There was some vague relation by marriage on his father's side to the Kleists, and in some mysterious manner they had inherited a couple of his love letters and a manuscript copy of a play. This was perhaps the most important exhibit, apart from a couple of letters from Hindenberg to his father about military affairs. The Kleist archive was rather an ambiguous trophy, despite the poet's admitted genius. But . . . he had, after all, insulted Goethe in the most rabid fashion; and then his suicide (after all he *was* of a military family) . . . that was also somewhat awkward, in a way. Von Esslin had quite a vivid picture of the handsome couple setting off for the fatal picnic with their hamper full of cakes and fruit. Underneath nestled the loaded pistol, waiting like Cleopatra's asp. He closed his eyes the better to visualise the lake scene with its sunshine and drifting swans; he heard the sharp crack of the discharge upon the sunny silence, he saw her fall sideways upon the bench, folding down into the poet's encircling arms . . . No, one could not help but feel distaste.

When dressing he had extracted the coveted order called *Pour le mérite* and pinned it beside his own Iron Cross and the other service marks which his brother officers always referred to as "confetti". The *Pour le mérite* (which was the German Victoria Cross) had been won by his father at the end of the First World War. Naturally he treasured the medal, and since he could not wear it in public he always pinned it on the inside of his breast pocket, reserving the outside for his own more modest prizes. It gave him pleasure and a certain confidence – as a sort of talisman. He knew she would notice with pleasure though she would make no allusion to it. He poured himself a drink and, sitting down at the piano, forced his fingers to play a few airs from Strauss. How stiff they had become! He always longed to be somewhere within reach of a piano; but it was ages now since he had had the chance to play. When his mother arrived he took her arm and led her in to dine without preamble. He did not wish to make a late night of it for the morrow promised him exceptional fatigues. They dined by candlelight and spoke in low tones so that there was no chance that their conversation would be listened to – despite the firm conviction of the Pole's total illiteracy. His mother told him of the visit of a young security officer from a local unit who had asked if he might wire a microphone into the kitchen. Von Esslin was at first incredulous, and then overtaken by laughter at such block-headed service behaviour. They were so far away from the Polish border. . . .

"That is what I told him, and after a time he went away. He had not been told who you were, either."

"So!"

They talked on until the clocks chimed ten, and then she bade him rise and prepared herself for bed. It was goodbye, for she would not be up on the morrow when he left. They embraced. "Please take care," she said, and he promised that he would as he saw her to the door before turning out the lights and following her up the old-fashioned staircase. He looked round him slowly, a little mournfully. In his room the bedside light was on and the covers were turned back.

He undressed and got into bed, thinking that he might read a few pages of the detective story he had brought with him, but he found his mind wandering back to his men and machines and all the excitement associated with this entirely new form of warfare: the use of aircraft as artillery, the concentrated masses of armour. Such force could not help but burst apart any enemy by its sheer concentrated impact. How had the democracies not seen it – for apparently they had not produced a shadow of tactical reorganisation to meet the threat? It was rugby against tennis, a powerful toboggan against a *fiacre*. . . . He sighed and laid down his book to stare at the wallpaper. And then the total secrecy of command offered by the astonishing scrambler coding machine they called Enigma. No, nothing could miscarry, despite the cautious saying of his old father, namely that on the battlefield chance always ruled. Chance!

He lay quietly breathing, allowing these vagrant thoughts to pass through his mind until they slackened speed, dimmed. He fell asleep lightly now. He had just enough self-possession to turn off the light.

When he awoke it was around one o'clock; it was as if a hand had been placed upon his shoulder in a gesture at once soft and confiding. The hand of a woman. At once he rose, one might say obediently, for it was in response to a wordless call like that of some animal or some bird. The gesture was quite unformulated; he walked down the corridor like a sleepwalker and then climbed an inner staircase which led to the maid's room. It had been like this for years now, since around his fortieth birthday. No word was exchanged. She lay with her face to the wall, but with her eyes open – she did not even pretend she was asleep. He stripped naked and climbed softly into bed beside her, lightly touching her flanks with his fingers, giving the signal which repetition had made customary. And she turned slowly round, quietly but ravenously arching her skinny body to accommodate his own sturdier, taller one. They were locked in silent combat now, like two experienced wrestlers, and he felt in the spider-like grip of her thin thighs and arms a kind of helplessness, an agony of submission and sexual abasement. She bowed before him as if she desired only one thing: to be trampled, to be spurned. Yet it was only a ruse, for she felt his mounting excitement as he trod her with ever-increasing violence, with a powerful, determined passion which mounted towards a climax which would sweep them both breathlessly away into the marvellous amnesia of their double lust. With no word said, no gesture of complicity offered on either side. They were like insects answering a rhythm, a wave-length of light or a sound. Her eyes were closed in the death-mask of her little dark face with its helmet of hair – so dark as almost to suggest the hair of a Japanese doll. The sort of tresses which grow on Eastern corpses after death. Her face was pretty but terribly emaciated, terribly thin. It was the head of an adder, though the details which made it human were quite fine, good eyes and teeth. When younger she might have made the impression of being a *petit rat de l'Opéra*.

She was his, she submitted, and the thought excited his cupidity; he overwhelmed her as his army would soon overwhelm her country and people, raping it, wading in its blood. At last the climax came and in his muddled exhaustion he fell asleep on her breast to dream of his big, playful tanks nosing about like sheepdogs in the dust and clutter of the farms they had knocked down, pushing their squat steel noses through walls and hedges as they fanned out into the attack. She lay as if dead, though her lips moved as always at this moment. But he could never catch what she whispered so very tenderly while she cradled his head. It was not in German that she spoke.

Two storeys above them his mother lay with open eyes, staring into the darkness and thinking as she listened with furious concentration to the silence which from time to time blurred into the small sounds of congress which they made. A chimney-flue conveyed whatever sound there was up to her room; but that was little enough, so she must supplement it with guesswork to imagine clearly what she had already imagined so often in the last years of his father. Then silence came.

It must have been just before light when the girl woke him with a touch, herself sliding out from the circle of his sleeping embrace and into a wrap. He took no formal leave of her, simply rose in heavy silence and made his way back to his room. He took a hot shower and dressed with circumspection. Then, taking up the locked briefcase, he walked downstairs once more to where, on a sidetable in the dining-room, a coffee-pot steamed over a bud of alcohol flame and some buns of brown oatmeal lay warming in a chafing dish. He helped himself and sat down, knowing that while he ate the servant would be packing his affairs at lightning speed into the two suitcases, and then bringing them down to await the chauffeur in the hall. After that she would no longer manifest herself unless there was any precise need – she would wait behind the green baize door until the front door closed behind him. It was a time-honoured routine.

As he drank his coffee he unlocked his briefcase and flicked through the documents it held, to refresh his memory of things outstanding, things to be done when he returned to his unit. They were for the most part unclassified field-orders and annotated map references: with things moving so fast there was hardly time for signals to linger about on the secret list. Operation White, *der Fall Weiss*, had already been formulated and allowed to mature in the mind of the General Staff for some time – the Nazis were nothing if not thorough.

Then came the plastic folder which imitated a superior pig-skin, but in a flashy and debased fashion which gave the show away. This contained the two pamphlets which Dr. Goebbels had issued to them after the latest staff briefing by the Führer. They lay side by side in the pouch, one red and one blue. What was it the little crippled doctor had called them? "A cultural and intellectual justification apparatus": *Ein Kultur- und Intelligenz-Rechtfertigungsapparat*! *There* was a phrase to gobble on, and gobble he had had to with his slight impediment of speech. But what a momentous experience it had been to sit there among some two hundred or more of his fellows, his colleagues, in the new study which the Führer had built for himself in the newborn Chancellery.

They had cooled their heels for a good hour before he came, *der Kleinmann*, sidling almost shyly through the great doors with an air of preoccupation, almost of vagueness. With a fine synchronisation they rose together, stamped once and heel-clicked – echo-smack of boot-leather was like a giant licking its lips. In unison they greeted him with a hoarse, carlish roar of "*Heil!*" and an outflung right arm. To this he responded with a vague gesture of reply and an even vaguer glance, an almost embarrassed glance. Then he released the spring with the words, "Be seated, gentlemen."

They settled once more like a flock of pigeons and leaned attentively forward to catch, in its most intimate and exact sense, the purport of the words which flowed now from his lips. They began slowly at first, and then gradually gathered speed as his ideas fired them, the obsessional ideas so long harboured and polished in silence and exile. But he looked tired, as well he might, with so much upon his shoulders, so many wrongs to right, so many scores to settle with the world. He was pale also and there were times of near aphasia, as if he were still coming out of an epileptic "aura". They listened with a kind of fearful emotion to the long trailing diatribe.

And while they listened they looked around them at the immense room, memorising as well as they could the details of this pregnant encounter with the man-god of the future who was delineating for them the spiritual frontiers of the new estate. The prospects of the freedom these ideas offered made them feel buoyant and shriven; for all that they were going to do now the Führer offered them an absolution in advance. Belief – that was all that was necessary for them; the rest followed automatically. One could become drunk on such rhetoric. Many of them felt moved, their faces flushed, their breathing quickened. So it went on until suddenly, abruptly, like a motor running out of fuel, it ended and the silence flowed in upon them all.

It had taken only nine months to bring to birth this huge edifice of a Chancellery with its nine hundred rooms, plus the great operations-room and study – the cavern in which the Führer was going to live and work; to guide this huge battle-ship towards the new millennium. He had worked long and lovingly on the plans with the architect Speer. It was massive, subdued, theatrical, but of a classical theatre suitable to the age. As for the lion's den, it had all the middle-class allure of a classicism such as would satisfy the criteria of an architect used to building cafeterias. But it was impressive, because its owner, the slight man with the moustache-tuft and the side-saddle hair, was impressive. One asked oneself how he had arrived at this point. Then one noticed his eyes. . . .

Von Esslin, normally no sycophant, leaned forward and pretended to take notes; the eyes distressed him, and he disguised his anxiety in this fashion. From time to time he looked about him, taking stock of the place. The acoustics were really excellent.

The monumental room was twenty-seven metres in length, fifteen in breadth, and ten metres high. The air moved tepidly and sluggishly about it despite the well-studied ventilation of the place. The windows were six metres in height and framed in heavy curtains of grey velvet. And then everywhere there was Greek marble, specially ordered; the workmen had been generously rewarded for working overtime at Pentelikos to cut the slabs for their future monarch. Marble grey, rose and coral. Then, to offset the delicacy of these tones, there were tapestries – admirable Gobelins. The ceiling was carved into two hundred and twelve equal caissons, each one offset by mouldings of a rigid geometric style. A sculptured frieze repeated unto infinity, as it were, while upon every column flowered six double torch-holders of unctuous bronze above the initials A.H. cut in a style which hinted at a Doric order. On the cool floors glowed oriental carpets of impeccable pedigree. Three tall standard lamps of bronze presided over the massive, gleaming, walnut-wood desk and four high-backed chairs before the work-desk. It was more than convincing, it was overwhelming.

There was a sense of anti-climax when all of a sudden the discourse stopped and the Leader rose to leave them. Once more they repeated the ritual heel-clicking and the hoarse cry. Then he was gone, and the cripple came into the room and took his place, while uniformed orderlies distributed the little plastic pouch with its two pamphlets. Goebbels waited until the distribution was complete, and until the tall doors had closed behind the orderlies. Then he cleared his throat and in a quiet, unemphatic voice began his exposition; it was pitched in a low key as if to form a contrast to the harangue which had preceded it. Here they were on more familiar ground, for most of what he had to say was orthodox and free of surprises; it was what one read every day in the newspapers: the wrongs of Germany which would soon be righted, the intolerable provocations they had suffered from inferior breeds. The tone, however, was reasonable and expository. Germany had now found her true path and was going to go forward with the building of a new world, a new order of things which would be more in keeping with the order of nature. *Ordnung* – he almost sang the word; it clamped together the whole edifice of his thought. It was a rivet in the flanks of this huge steel battleship which would soon be rolling across the land and the sea, promoting the new Golden Age. But here the speaker reined and with uplifted finger warned them to keep always in mind the two basic foes of all they stood for – the two forces of darkness which they must overthrow in order to achieve their objectives. They would find the documents of the case in the little plastic pouch. They must be studied with care for they contained the whole truth of the German mission; every field commander should study them. These and only these two forces stood between them and the new Aryan order. That was the germ of the matter.

One might perhaps have expected an anthology of Nietzsche quotations, expressing all his vehement anti-semitism (sentiments which, forty years later, would prove to have been forged and inserted by the philosopher's sister and her husband); but no, the two documents which nestled in the little plastic pouch were, respectively, the text of the celebrated Protocols of Zion, which outlined the Jewish plot to conquer the world, and the extraordinary Will of Peter the

Great,* equally a plot to redeem it through Pan-Slavism.

The terrible thing was that there was nobody with whom one could discuss such matters, except hypocritically, for to express reservations about such apparent trash would at this stage have been taken as a treasonable act. Each was locked in the private cell of his doubts and fears – with no hope of an exit this side of the war. The position was an intolerable one for men who could still regard themselves as men of honour. Von Esslin sat in the corner of the staff office with these documents on his knee, staring at the sunshine upon the trees and pondering. Army folk were so innocent of all political instinct. It was best to think nothing, to say nothing – to throw oneself into the marvellous liberation of blind action; to become part of this vast steel juggernaut aimed at Poland, and leave the thinking to others who knew more than he did. These were the thoughts which filled him with elation – the promise of glory and the fulfilment of his professional curiosity in the matter of tanks. Could they be directed from division, or would the general staff have to ride on their backs, so to speak, in order to control the pulse-beat of the battle as it unrolled? He would soon find all this out, unless by some last-minute chance the wind turned and the French and English changed their orientation. Yes, but even then . . .

He was impatient to get back to his command post, to his staff unit, to his professional friends who were all as keyed up as he was; he was keen to sanction the last signal before battle, the "Last Letters Home" which would tell the troops, if they did not already know, that the die was cast, the attack ordered. When these thoughts passed through his mind he was seized by a sort of vertigo – a desire on the rampage. It was at such moments that he longed for a piano with which to assuage all the confusion of his thoughts and impulses.

How slowly history evolves! Each drop from the icicle

* See Appendix.

takes an age to form and to fall – or so it seemed to those who, like himself, waited for the definitive signal. He motored up by night, through a country of forests and marches where now the chief vegetation seemed to be of steel. At a turn in the main road, by a bridge, he came upon some sort of accident, to judge by the flare of headlights and the silhouettes of figures busily occupied around a couple of lorries which had turned turtle and lay in the ditch with their wheels in the air, like insects turned over on their backs. "An accident," said the driver. With so much traffic, in so many complicated formations moving about by night, it was hardly to be wondered at. But there seemed to be nobody of rank about to direct whatever operation might be necessary to free the road and Von Esslin jumped out and made his way to the scene. Then he saw that the lorries had contained crosses, thousands of wooden crosses which filled the ditch and the field beyond, gleaming white in the sterile lights of the halted cars. Crosses! For some reason the sight threw him into a towering rage; he began to give orders with a hysterical violence which surprised even himself. The soldiers on the scene, aghast alike at his eminence and the febrile fury of his rage, began to buzz like an overturned hornets' nest themselves. Von Esslin all but screamed. He ordered the drivers to present themselves and berated them. All three were put upon a charge at his behest. Then, still fuming and feeling almost faint with the force of his emotion, he returned to his car and resumed his journey.

He soon forgot, for the mighty rhythm engendered by the Grand Army in movement is irresistible, is all-engulfing. They were all diminished as individuals, shorn of their personal responsibility by the power of its motion. Its coils and meshes held them fast while its gathering momentum rolled them irrevocably down, as if on the breast of some great river, towards the fulfilling ocean. But a river of chain-mail, a river of meshed steel. Von Esslin, once he had regained his place in all the warmth and tension of friendship with his fellow adventurers, found himself as if upon the bridge of some great raft, rolling with ever-gathering speed down towards the deeps which beckoned them; towards the new human order which they had been set to build and to inspire with their presence. He looked around the map caravan at the brown, intense, beefy faces and the big red hands; his heart swelled with emotion, with affection for them all. From the depths of the night they were setting out towards a new dawn – by the time the sun was up the whole face of history would have been changed!

The edges of the darkness trembled and here and there the horizon flickered with light, as if from a distant storm's sheet lightning. But they knew it was the first rumour of engagement, the armoured units in their delving had already locked horns with the enemy scouts. The whole symphony had been set in motion within two hours of dawn; the great animal was uncoiling itself, at first gingerly and then with increasing confidence and speed, unfurling the darkness with its few points of necessary light as it got into gear, with only the suffused roaring of an ocean grinding upon shingle to herald its advance across the plains.

At first light the air bombardment was to begin – an innovation in tactics which blasted vast ragged holes in the front. They might have been forgiven for imagining themselves to be taking part in some great historic saga, were it not for the distasteful bearing of the special units which were attached to them. The prisons had been scoured to brim their ranks. They would follow the fighting men and start the task of pillage, rape and extermination which was so carefully embodied in their official directives, issued on the field-grey signal paper which the para-military Schutzaffeln affected. "Fear of the Reich must be instilled at whatever cost. No effort must be spared." They were a special breed, these men, furtive and monosyllabic and withdrawn. The officers smiled without unclenching their teeth; they exuded guilt and unease as do all people who enjoy inflicting pain – jailors, inquisitors, shop stewards, executioners. The concentration camps had allowed their choicest disciplinarians to gain prestige in the hated and feared death's-head uniform of these modern centurions. The regular knew them to be lackeys on whom the authority to murder had been conferred; their shame ignited his own, for he knew that their task was to turn the whole of Europe into one smoking knacker's yard.

They moved forward now from darkness into light and soon came to the edge of those endless plains of yellow harvest wheat, still under a cerulean sky which would soon be full of small black specks swerving and chattering like distant magpies. Then sound came, volumes of it, varieties of it all mingled into one earth-trembling concave weight upon the flinching ear-drums; they could not hear themselves speak. Their mouths worked. And slowly, from two ends of the horizon, the world began to burn, the wheat began to burn, racing as if to meet them.

Seventh and Tenth Panzers had been unkennelled like hounds and directed deliberately across this flaming prairie, racing to make contact with the invisible foe. They had supposed that their speed would carry them through, but a sudden ambush supervened, the fires elongated, unrolling before them as they raced, and they found themselves encircled by the flames. Von Esslin saw his cherished tanks going off like chestnuts, their petrol tanks exploding in the heat. The command car turned back, hesitated. He swore at his driver and urged him to continue, to follow the armour, but by now they were at the edge of the flame area and more vulnerable than the exploding tanks. It was only a minor incident in an uninterrupted chain of successful actions – they were almost bored with the reiterated signals which told of objectives attained, objectives over-run, enemy units bypassed or completely encircled. A small setback, yet it played upon his *amour-propre* and he felt culpable as well as cheated of something – what he did not know. He was relieved to discover that he was sitting in a puddle of blood; a nasty cut in his forearm had soaked him. In his excitement he had experienced no pain; now the wound began to smart. He called for an orderly and stripped off his coat, the better to present his wound for bandaging. Dense smoke had succeeded the panorama of flame. Units were poking about in the black charred stubble for his exploded chestnuts of tanks. There was a bit of shrapnel in his sleeve; the orderly picked it out and handed it to him saying, "A souvenir, sir." Von Esslin's humour was restored by this trifling expiation. At this rate they would soon be in Warsaw.

THREE

Into Egypt

THE EMBARKATION WENT OFF WITHOUT A HITCH AT DEAD of night and by morning the royal yacht was well out to sea en route for Egypt.

In his notebook Blanford wrote:

Immortality must feel something like this for a poet. Suppose I were to tell you that here, in perfect peace, we sail eastward under cloudless skies upon a windless cerulean sea with not one Homeric curl in it. . . . The *Khedive* is the royal yacht which is carrying us into Egypt and safety. No, it is totally unreal to find myself here under an awning of brightly striped duck, lounging beside the calm Prince, drinking a whisky and soda with grave reflective delight. Contemplating the abyss which has opened at our feet – the war. The Prince himself has been transformed into an imposing maritime figure, for he has put on yachting *tenue* complete with white trousers of some magnolia-soft tissue, set off by a blazer and an old heraldic yachting cap bearing the insignia of both the royal house and the Alexandria Yacht Club. The blazer is all Balliol, Oxford.

From time to time, so pure and so encouraging is the air, we doze off for a few moments; then we awake and continue the Arabic lesson which is going to transform me into a linguist If there is world enough and time.

(My darling, these lines, somewhat to my surprise, are written to you and not to Livia. I write them because I feel freed by the probability, nay certainty, of never seeing you and Sam again in this lifetime! I write them from the part of myself which has slowly and secretly turned to you. Typically enough

I did not recognise the situation at first. But Livvie did. I noticed her jealousy but not its cause. I did not realise the truth until I was on the very brink of kissing you goodbye. But Livvie did and hated you accordingly – as much as one permits hate for a sister. I simply did not know or did not realise until the train bore you away.)

And so here I am, like a younger version of Tibullus without the sea-sickness. My poetry is crowding on sail. My mother is dead, my friends dispersed, my future uncertain, my solitude a delicious weight. One feels in all this a sort of affirmation for some early promise made by the good fairy. She must have said: "This one will be introspective, cut off from ordinary life, proficient in solitude but subject to enchantments because of his insight."

The old yacht has been provisioned in the most imaginative way – caviar, champagne, whisky, nothing lacks. We sit down to meals of fervent Frenchness served by great bronze servants with the tones of gongs, clad in booming white and gloved spotlessly to the forearm. Unruffled in their dignity and truth, like great aristocrats, they disburse kindness without servility. It is my first taste of Egypt, the marvellous hieratic servants of the Prince, serving our food on matchless plate. It worries the Prince sometimes. "I suppose that if we were to receive a plebeian torpedo I would be asked to regret the loss of all this stuff – even though it isn't mine. Farouk would be furious of course. I suppose he is insured." I had never thought upon the matter. Kings get given everything – do they need to insure? I yawn and stretch like Cleopatra's pet cat.

The ship's library is full of Victorian fiction amassed by Farouk's English nannies. But among a small yet choice Arabic section there is a play which the Prince considers to be an excellent introduction to his country. "It is by a friend of mine," he says, "and it is entitled *The Death of Cleopatra – Masra Kaliûpâtrâ* – it is very suitable for you, yes."

It is pleasant to know that Cleo was known as "Kaliû-pâtrâ" by her subjects. The collapsing world she knew could not have been vastly different from this one – a question of scale merely. Catastrophe is catastrophe, whatever the magnitude.

All around us, according to that scratchy oracle, Ship's Radio, a war rages. The fleets of France and England threaten to cross swords. Somewhere lurks an Italian fleet, showing great discretion, thank goodness. Meanwhile (as if at the fabled heart of some great hurricane, the core around which it has moulded itself), we float onwards, serenely, in untroubled silence save for the quiet purring of the motor and the languid plume of smoke from our great funnel. Onwards towards the white cliffs of Crete and then Evnostos, the harbour-home of the Alexandria basin. It is too good to be true.

"Mr. Blanford, I would like to ask you a favour on behalf of myself and the Princess."

"Certainly, Your Highness."

"May we call you Aubrey? It simplifies things."

"But of course."

"Thank you, Aubrey."

"Not at all, Your Highness."

So the Arabic lesson winds slowly on its way, interspersed with a hundred and one interruptions and interpolations by the Prince. Among them he urges upon me a book about Egypt written by his own nanny, a Mrs. Macleod, and entitled *An Englishwoman on the Nile*. He says that it is full of striking observations; it lists many of the queerer things about Egyptian life. I open it as he talks and see that it begins admirably indeed, with the words: "In Egypt one acts upon impulse as there is no rain to make one reflect."

In the cocoon of this fine warm air it seems a sin to go below, so we order our dinner to be served us upon a tray, and eat it while we are still idling on deck. From time to time a

typed news bulletin comes our way with the compliments of
the radio operator, but its contents sound mad, inconsequential, out of all proportion to this grave sinking sun and
still sea. We had, however, contacted Alexandria and were to
expect an escort to join us before midnight in order to see us
safely to port. The great harbour with its immobile battleships
and cruisers, both French and British, would have been an
impressive sight, I suppose, but we were to be spared it; for
after dinner the Prince was summoned to the bridge where he
was able to make use of the land telephone to call someone who
would relay his message directly to the authorities and obtain
permission for him to land, rather unorthodoxly, at the Palace
of Montaza rather than in the Grand Harbour. He explained
that this would lighten the journey a great deal and enable us to
get ashore without fussy *douaniers* and security officials. "The
English will be obstructive as usual, and won't like it; but they
will have to lump it if Farouk says so, and now he knows he
will jolly well say so!"

We retired early to get some rest, leaving everything to
these grave brown beadles of servants, who spoke so thrilling
deep and smiled like pianos among themselves. And sleep I
did, to be woken by a brown hand on my shoulder, shaking me
with extreme reverence while a brown voice said, "Master he
say you to go uppy stairs now. He waiting." I dressed and made
my sleepy way on deck, where I found the Prince in high good
humour presiding over all our baggage. "I was right," he said
joyfully, "the English are most furious with me."

We went ashore in darkness in a large motor launch
belonging to the Egyptian navy and landed at the water-gate
of a palace plunged in utter darkness; then, after much chaffering, somewhere a switch was thrown and a sort of combination
of Taj Mahal and Eiffel Tower blared out upon the night.

It was my first exposure to Egyptian Baroque, so the
simile is surprisingly apt. To blare, to bray – so much light in so

many mirrors of so many colours – the effect was poly-morphous perverse, so to speak. . . . I realised that I was going to fall in love with the place – I saw that it was a huge temple of inconsequences. Silently pacing these matchless Shiraz carpets which paved the vast saloons my spirit was intoxicated by scarlet leather, golden studs, lapis lazuli, cat's eye, and every-where mirrors spouting light like deserted fountains. For the reception rooms were empty, not a soul was about. The state lavatories were the size of Euston, but the chains clanked on empty cisterns. We hesitated, irresolute.

Then the Princess manifested, coming down the great staircase half-asleep, wrapped in a white kimono of soft feathers like a small, yawning swan. They stood gazing at each other, expressing such a wealth of desire and delight that it was exquisitely moving to the onlooker. Etiquette prevented them from embracing in public after the plebeian style made common by the cinema. They behaved birdfully, like birds, which have no arms to grab hold with; they spread their wings, so to speak, and whispered each other's names with humble rapture. The Prince kissed the tips of her fingers; then, with a little sob, like an excited child, she rushed away to dress for the journey. While we waited, a sleepy palace servant encouraged us into the vast dining-room where the chandeliers now shone upon tables laid for breakfast with coffee and chocolate and fresh croissants and cream. I felt extraordinarily heartened to see people who could love each other so devoutly; it was so unlike Europe where serious thinking about passion has really come to a standstill.

We embarked in two dark limousines, leaving the staff to disengage the Prince's affairs from the yacht; there was some concern, for a fresh wind was springing up and the anchorage was not a sound one. However we got our bags, and I travelled in the second car piled high with them. A vague impression of the Grand Corniche with the sea slapping and the wind knuckling the palms. Then dark ribbons of road across the desert. I fell into a troubled slumber, lulled by the smooth engine and the feeling that time had no joints.

I write these words some days later, seated upon a shady balcony overlooking the Nile which runs as smooth as a razor across the garden's end; it is sulphurous hot, I trickle as I write. My wrist sticks to the paper, so clammy is it, and I am forced to press it upon a blotter in order not to smudge. But I am happy. A whole new world opens before me. I have fallen on my feet. I was rather dreading the Princess – I felt sure she would instantly divine all my deficiencies. But she took my hand and held it for a long moment while she gazed earnestly, thought-fully into my eyes, with a deep preoccupation as if she were listening to sacred music. Then she sighed with relief, dropped my hand, and said, "He is all *right*!" Whereupon the Prince gave a small chuckle and said, "She *never* trusts me."

I am all right! What more does one need to hear about oneself? A wave of confidence swept over me, and I realised that I would certainly make a success of this rather vague assignment as English secretary to the Prince. It is also pleasant to begin to feel part of a family – my upbringing had not accustomed me to such warmth. Nor are my statutory duties very onerous; the correspondence is fairly heavy but will be easy to despatch in a longish morning of work. Remains the social side – I feared this; but here I am treated with great consideration. I am not forced to hand round drop-scones for the English tea parties of the Princess. But I do it. A complete wardrobe was being supplied to me by the centenarian tailor of the house, in beautifully cut mint summer silk.

The town house of the Prince (for they also appear to own an abandoned palace at Rosetta and a summer villa at Helwan) is not exactly a castle. It is the size of a medieval prince's hunting lodge with extensive dependencies, indeed a sort of nabob's country seat. Parts have been shored up against ruin, parts have been allowed to subside gracefully and melt back into the primeval mud of Egypt – the black viscous element from which everything seems to be fashioned. One wing is full of corridors boarded up as a safety precaution against floors which have been ravaged by termites. The furnishings are modest compared to those of the palace of our arrival, and all is a bit dusty, decorations, furniture, mirrors, everything; but very faintly, like powder in a wig. Time and neglect and the river-damps have hazed the clear outline of things. On the other hand there is distinction in the quality of the paintings and bibelots, the plaster mouldings. They had not just accumulated, one felt, but had been individually chosen and desired and cherished for their aesthetic feel. Though they were various, not matching in a uniform way, they lived on in harmonious and coherent discord. The whole place felt nice, smelt nice. Extraordinary cats abounded. The dissonant shriek of peacocks made one jump. The Nile smelt old and sad and disabused, turning green like oxidising copper, but imperishably itself, unlike any other river in the world. At dawn I saw a fisherman standing in quiet expectancy by the river bank, as if waiting for the sun to rise; presently it did, and the whole insect world began to buzz and bubble in the warm ray which burned the last mists from the water's surface. The fisherman took up a mouthful of water and blew it out in a screen of spray against the sunlight, revelling in the prismatic hues of the water-drops.

In the morning I heard moans from an outhouse and the sound of strokes and swearing; I enquired of the Princess what this might be, and she informed me demurely that it was Said, their young major-domo, receiving what she described as a "smart slippering" for some domestic fault. "Ah," added her husband, "you no doubt recall that the royal sceptre of Egypt was always the rod. And with our servants there is no way to combat the progressive amnesia which comes over them, gradually accumulating until they seem quite mental, quite unable to hold anything in mind. Then they begin to forget things and break things and it is time for a kindly reminder. About every six months I reckon. You will see the difference in Said tomorrow. Today he will sulk because of the insult to his honour, but tomorrow . . ."

"And your secretaries – do you have them slippered?"

The Princess clapped her hands and chirped as she replied, "I told you he was all right." But the Prince cocked an eyebrow and said, "We have much worse reserved for the secretaries!"

I am not the only secretary – there are several others, each with his own domain of activity; but they all vanish at the end of the day while I stay on to dine *en famille* or else alone in the magnificent suite of rooms I have been allotted. Everything is new and curious, so that for the moment I do not find this padded life of an honorary attaché becoming wearisome. But I have always enjoyed being on my own and I indulge the bent several evenings a week in order to write letters or scribble notes such as these sporadic annotations on the margins of history. For the moment I feel cut off from the world, almost from the human race. Egypt is like some brilliantly coloured frieze against which we move in perfect ease and normality. The country has declared itself neutral, and its cities are "open cities" – shimmering pools of crystal light at nights, of choked bazaars and traffic-laden thoroughfares by day, of lighted shops and brilliant mosques – a parody of the true Moslem paradise. We read of blackouts elsewhere; in the City of the Dead you can practically read a newspaper at the full moon. I feel at once exhilarated and lost, exultant and despairing. The world has been cut off, abbreviated to the confines of this lighted city between deserts where all is comfort and plenty. But for how long? Nobody dares to think about it.

The disturbance of the mails has called forth new conventions like the air-letter; I have armed myself with a package of them, but to what end? Will England still exist by the time my letters arrive? A profound despondency rules over this underworld of forebodings and hidden fears – I speak as much for my hosts as myself. They are beginning to realise the depths of their affection for the misty island where they had spent so many happy summers hating the English. And France, too. "France, *halas!*" It sounds somehow sadder and more absolute in Arabic, like an overturned statue. It has in it a hint of the wailing Aman-Aman (Alas-Alas) songs of the radio which scribbles over the silences of every café with the voice of Oum Kalsoum, the nightingale from Tanta. . . . I suppose *kaput* would be the translation of *halas?*

I was formally presented to my fellow scribes by the Prince himself. Professor Baladi was tall and slim and spoke fluent English. He had blue eyes and a fresh colouring and wore his red fez at a jaunty angle. He had an endearing desire to represent himself as a man about town and hinted that he would be available to assist me in exploring the city – a most useful offer. He carried an ebony-headed walking stick with great care, like a sceptre of an inconceivable preciousness. We clicked. So it was with a slower and muddier gentleman, Khanna, a Copt, who seemed at first a little shy and taciturn. Confluent smallpox had given him a skin like a colander. He had a preference for speaking French, and to express an opinion cost him a great effort. He was a brilliant soul in strict hiding; he trusted nobody. There was reserve here, but none of the animosity I had feared.

Yet the power behind the throne, so to speak, was a young and quite disarming Syrian, by name Affad. He was, I gathered, a millionaire in his own right, and only appeared upon a number of boards to support the Prince, out of pure affection. He was a remarkably attractive character with rather misty, glaucous eyes and a helpless appearance; slim and tall, he gave a curious sort of androgynous feel upon first meeting. I thought he must be some brilliant homosexual of the ancient ilk, for like Alcibiades he had a faint lisp. His line of talk was most amusing, self-deprecating, satirical; it was clear that nobody could long stay immune to his deadly charm. In dress he was of a negligent elegance which almost suggested a fashion-plate. His English was faultless, he possessed the language fully and his apparent incoherence and almost ineffectual mildness was really a ruse in order to call forth affection. When he wanted to make it so, his talk was brilliantly incisive. "Well, but I have been expecting you for some time," he said, to my surprise. "It has taken him an age to find the right sort of secretary for his work, and once he met you he cabled me that you would be ideal and that he would try and make you an offer." I wondered what I could have said to create an impression upon my first meeting with the Prince back there in Provence. As if he read my thoughts, Affad smiled and answered the question for me; the solution could not have been more surprising. "The Prince heard you say something most interesting about Apollonius of Tyana, and it made him realise that you would find yourself at home in Egypt." What could I have said? I racked my brains to remember. Yes, perhaps I had mentioned something about gnosticism in Egypt in relation to the Templar heresy – to Quatrefages or perhaps to Felix. It was nonetheless astonishing. The Prince himself was far from being an erudite, an intellectual, so why should such a remark. . . ? I thought idly of the dried and resined head in his red hat-box. I wondered what had happened to it.

Meanwhile Affad poured me a drink and assured me that I should find my post a deeply satisfying one from several points of view. This I was beginning to believe. Never had I fallen among such agreeable and gentle folk. To work for them, with them, promised to be easy and pleasurable.

There remained my compatriots; we spent a morning and an afternoon upon them, since form decided that I must at least

register at the Consulate and fill in an availability form in case
I should ever be called up. My passport was examined by a
disagreeably lordly little grocer's assistant (it would seem)
called Telford – *Mister* Telford, sir, if you please! He was thus
addressed by his sycophantic pro-consul. "You will have to
stay on call for the present. I can guarantee nothing."

The Prince was nettled by his tone. "Well, I think I can,"
he said icily, "we are seeing H.E. this afternoon and he is aware
that Mr. Blanford is engaged as my secretary." Telford shrugged and handed back my passport with disdain. "So be it," he
said and waved us away into the noisy street where the Prince's
car waited.

In the afternoon we went up to the Consulate to sign the
book and to make our obeisances to the Minister. He was
sitting in a deck-chair far out upon the dusty lawn, a thin, tall,
rather attractive man in his shy way. He had chosen a strategic
spot midway between a couple of large water sprinklers which
were hard at work in the heat keeping the paper-dry lawn alive.
The water pushed large blocks of tepid air about around his
chair, giving the faint illusion of freshness and coolth. We
stepped between the columns with care so as not to get our
trousers sprinkled, and were received kindly enough by the
Minister, whose servants came running with further deck-
chairs which were placed with equal strategy round about us;
also a table upon which appeared in due course a large English
tea complete with rock cakes, ginger biscuits and drop-scones.
How strange it seemed to find this in Egypt! I commented on
the fact and our host smiled and said, "You should find it
reassuring, should you not? With the present situation on our
hands we shall need all the morale-building tea we can get."
Then he added as he stirred his cup, "I have had you officially
'frozen' for a year, as the saying goes. This means that H.M.
regards your job as a privileged one and essential to the war
effort." I did not quite follow how and was about to ask, when

the Prince turned to me and did the explaining himself. "It's because I am a Colonel on the Military Mission, and also head of the Red Cross in Egypt. That is why H.E. wants you to keep an eye on me and see that I don't get into mischief by inviting Mehar Pacha to lunch one day, eh?"

The Minister did not rise to the jest but on the contrary looked rather pained. "You will soon know," he said, turning to me, "just how lucky we are to have someone like the Prince to consult on policy. Egypt is terribly tricky politically, and doubly so at the moment with the present options."

The talk then generalised itself into gossip about the war situation which, despite some lucky strokes on our side, was still appallingly full of hazards; it gave a highly provisional air to these orders and dispositions and it was obvious that the Minister was weighed down by these fearful contingencies which hedged us in between the deserts, still with inadequate forces and armour to confront the worst that the enemy might think up. He did not say any of this, but his tone implied it – and of course the facts of the general situation were so widely reported that there was nothing secret in the matter that any newspaper reader might not know. Our tea-party ended on an amiable but subdued note. "I know that you will be in and out of the Chancery on business matters," said the Minister as we rose to shake hands, "I will tell my social sec to see that you receive all standing invitations. But if you ever need to see me personally, don't hesitate to ring up and come round." We thanked him for his warmth. A swerve of the water sprinklers sent a gust of cool air towards us; it dislodged a leaf from the bundle of despatch-paper on the little wicker table. I picked it up as it fell to the ground and handed it back. It looked at first to be a cipher. Then I saw that it was a game of chess described in cablese. He thanked me as he took the paper back and said, "I see you caught a glimpse of the positions. Do you play chess?" But there I had to disappoint him. "Canasta, bridge or pontoon – nothing else." We took our leave.

So the long days of my secretarial engagements outlined themselves, full of variety and novelty. The interests of the Prince were multifarious; as president of the Red Cross he had a fine set of offices in the centre of the capital, where I was accorded a small room by the teleprinter from which I had to harvest a huge correspondence; then there was the dusty, agreeable Consulate which he so frequently visited – though here he had no foothold. We wandered about the Chancery at will. My palace office was the central one, the key to everything else. But the Prince, as an honorary Colonel of Regiment to the Egyptian Field Artillery, was also entitled to an imposing office at headquarters which he adored visiting in his uniform – a British colonel's outfit topped with a traditional fez. He wore a spray of service decorations on his breast and it was obvious that they gave him immense pleasure, for he stroked them unendurably during formal conversations with the obsequious young officers of his regiment.

Yes, this new world is full of colour and sensation; nor would it be possible to overpraise the beauty of this gorgeous, dusty city with its bubble-domes topped with new moons, its blazing souks, its brilliantly lit riverside suburbs, its bursting shops. The whole of Europe is in darkness and we are here in a night-long incandescence permitted only to the cities which have been declared "open". No bombers snarl out of this velvet-blue night sky. There are no signs of the war save the soldiers on leave. Occasionally, just before dawn, a stealth of tanks and carriers might emerge from the barracks and rustle across the deserted roads, making for the desert on tiptoe, as it were; but so circumspectly that they make less noise than the thudding of camel pads on the asphalt – for just before dawn long columns of camels bring in the vegetables to the town markets together with other loads like cotton, reeds, *bercim* – clover for animal fodder.

"The Princess rather mocks my uniform," said the Prince, "but I keep it for it enables us to picnic in the Western Desert when we want; without it I would be a civilian and the desert is out of bounds to ordinary civilians. That reminds me, I must have you gazetted to the Egyptian army as a volunteer second lieutenant. Then you can come as my aide." An alluring prospect – to wear British service kit with a scarlet flower-pot on my head. Strangely enough, both Prince and Princess were deeply moved when I walked in on them, dressed in full fig complete with tarboosh. "Now you are really one of us," she cried, and tears came into her eyes. I looked an awful fool in the flower-pot.

England was an occasional pang, an occasional twinge of conscience away; the new life was all-engulfing in its variety, while the information which it proffered so liberally was persuading me to see this ancient country not as something exhausted by history, existing through its ruins, but as something still thrillingly contemporary, still full of an infernal mystery and magic. Of course I owed most of this to Affad, though at first, while I was settling in, I had little to do with him; my fellow scribes occupied the centre of the stage. Professor Baladi, for example, with his quaint Victorian-novel English, could have earned music-hall renown had he so wished. "Mr. Blanford, I esteem that there is nothing more sublime in nature than a glimpse of an English lady's bubs." He watched me curiously for my reaction, head on one side. "Really, Professor, you are making the blush start to my cheek." He laughed airily and said with a certain archness, "I only said it to make you chortle." And so I obliged him with a chortle – or what I took to be such a thing, something between a chirp and a giggle.

"I have been told that the Egyptians are mad about pink flesh, hence the pimp at Port Said who offered his little daughter, crying 'all pink inside like English lady'." It was a very old joke, but he had not heard it, and it threw him into a silent convulsion of decorous laughter; tears poured out of him. He mopped them with the sleeve of his coat. But we had put our foot in it. We realised this when we caught a glimpse of our fellow-scribe's face – the face of poor Khanna the Copt. He was crimson with anguish and evidently deeply shocked. Baladi did a wonderful toad-swallowing act as he saw this, and his laughter abated somewhat, subsiding away into sighs touched with contrition, though from time to time a small seismic convulsion seized him midriff, and at the thought of the jest he hid his face for the space of a second in his sleeve. I thought the best way to atone was to go all silent, speechless and industrious for a full quarter of an hour, in order to let the dust settle. Outside on the green lawns the sun shone, the sprinklers played, turning and turning their slim necks like sunflowers. Somewhere in the palace the telephones rustled – their bells had been gagged, for their sound was judged indecorous. I pondered the war news in the *Egyptian Gazette* and allowed England a slight ache of nostalgia; but secretly my heart turned to the Pole Star of Provence – a Provence now forever peopled by Felix, Constance, Hilary, the vanished friends of that last summer of peace. Where might they all be now? Dead for all I knew. And the most painful evocation of all, that of Livia. Last heard of in Germany – the girl I had insisted on marrying, like a fool.

When Khanna withdrew to soothe his ruffled feelings and relieve himself in the ornate lavatory by the reception hall, Baladi jerked a thumb at his retreating back and whispered, "I think we pipped him rather." I agreed solemnly.

"If you are free on Saturday night," said Baladi, with the air of wanting to compensate me for my sparkling conversation, "I will ask you to accompany me to a house of joy for a little spree." I accepted, but faint-heartedly, for I had just drifted into an affair with a young officer of the Field Transport Corps, a volunteer unit of rather over-bred girls which supplied the army with drivers, secretaries and field-messengers. One of these had taken a fancy to me and invited me to dinner at their mess. Anne Farnol, a Slade student, was a girl of about twenty-eight with brilliant blue eyes which kindled with bright intelligence and sympathy at the slightest excuse. She was unusual among the rather frigid dollies of her unit, for she exuded warmth and femininity which sorted ill with her martial attire. Yet when she sprang to attention and saluted before my desk the gesture had great charm. She brought the Embassy despatch-case which contained Red Cross minutes of which I took possession on behalf of my liege lord the Prince. For a moment, while I sorted the papers out, she accepted my invitation to sit down and smoke half a cigarette, which I cut for her with the office scissors. This pleasant little ritual and the idle, friendly conversation which accompanied it had become a feature of my existence on Mondays and Fridays. I had warmed under the smiling gaze of this military young woman who wore her small lifeboat hat (these were, I afterwards discovered, known as cunt-caps among the girls themselves) and smoked her ration of tobacco, though she always refused coffee.

So the invitation to dinner fell naturally into place; and one evening I found myself in front of a smart apartment block of buildings in the Sharia El Nil, negotiating a lift which took me to the fourth floor where her small apartment was. The door was ajar and there was a note on it to say that she had just slipped out for a moment, but that I was to make myself at home and await her, which is what I did. I spied upon her in her absence, examining the poor meagre treasures around which she had woven her new nomadic life – postcards of Hastings, a family group, father and mother and then a handsome young man with hurt eyes clad in a sculptor's smock. He held a mallet. The husband, I supposed, for she wore a ring on her marriage finger. A sudden sadness, inexplicable really, came over me. I riffled her sketchbooks. The room was deep in the scent of flowers – where else do flowers smell like they do in Egypt, as if they had just passed through the Underworld and across the breath of an open oven?

I sat for a while so, smoking and reflecting, upon her balcony above the buzzing thoroughfare beneath. She was beautiful and self-possessed and I desired her, yes; but my infernal English upbringing stood in the way of any enterprise which might bring about a fitting conclusion to this chance meeting of exiles so far away from the beleaguered island. She came at last, looking somewhat pale I thought; she had been back to the mess to draw her ration of whisky in my honour. I was ashamed, for with what the Prince was paying me I could have brought her a case of the stuff. I made a mental note to have one sent. She was as sensible as she was beautiful, and thanks to her my stupid diffidence which so often gives the impression of sulkiness, was thawed out, and I began to tell her a little about my life and ask her questions about hers. As a married officer she was entitled to a flat of her own, while the other girls of the unit, or those not in her position, had to be content to live in a sort of Y.M.C.A. with strict hours and visiting rules. It was quite late when I rose in awkward desperation and made a gesture to simulate departure. I walked out on to the cool balcony; the night all round was deep, furry and dark, while directly below us the street blazed with light. We stood there in the darkness looking down, like gargoyles on the leads of some medieval church – just two heads sculpted in darkness. I had at last the courage to say, "I would like to stay with you," and she put her hand on my arm, saying, "I hoped you would – I am so homesick, I sleep badly and this town makes me restless."

With the lights turned off, the flat became a dark burrow lit at one end by the theatrical flaring light of the street. We made love suddenly, precipitately, with a sort of involuntary desperation. She was still in uniform, I felt the cold buttons of her tunic on my flesh. It was terribly exciting – so much so that she began to weep a little bit, which increased my lust for her. Afterwards we lay side by side on the bed in the darkness and I could feel the steady drumming of her heart and the little shudders of pleasure slowly diminishing. I lit a match to look deeply into those steady blue eyes, which stared at me through their unnecessary tears. "It is the first time I have made love to an officer on active service; it's wildly exciting to do it in your uniform. Let's repeat it." But she was already slid from her clothes and lay naked in my arms, smelling gorgeously of some Cairo perfume and our own delightful rankness. Our kisses grew steady, we composed and aimed them with more love, more direction, less haphazardly. All night we lay in each other's arms, too excited to sleep more than fitfully, in short snatches. And we talked in whispers, sometimes falling back into sleep in mid-phrase.

The next day I watched the dawn come up over the desert from her balcony while she lay buried in the heaped bedclothes in an abandon of quiet sleep. The night had brought us both a wonderful animal happiness and a new calm. I felt a disposition to sing as I put the kettle on in the tiny kitchen and prepared the table for an early breakfast, for we both had offices to attend before the heat of the day declared itself. In her tousled, sleepy awakening she looked divinely beautiful and vulnerable. Yawning, she joined me and let me help her to coffee. "Strange what contentment," she said, shaking her head, "and yet nothing we do has any future, any meaning. Everything has become sort of provisional and fragile. I mean, next week I may be dead or posted. So may you – no, I forgot, you are not really in the war as yet, so you can't feel the strange posthumous feeling about things. Does it matter what one does? It has no future, no substance."

"If you go on philosophising at me like this, so early in

the morning, I shall quote Valéry to you."

"What did he say?"

"*Elle pense, donc je fuis.*"

"Unfair to my sex."

"Sorry."

A wonderful feeling of physical well-being possessed me; I had not realised that, despite my present colourful and delightful activities, I could be a little lonely – simply for lack of the sort of company which I would, for preference, keep. I hoped that this bond would continue and strengthen, despite the threat to it posed by the chance of postings to other war theatres, like, for example, Syria. I had, in my optimism, even ventured to sketch in a few possibilities as to our spare time. I knew that my hosts (I could not bring myself to think of them as employers, so kind and familiar were they) would be delighted if I were to discover a personable English girl to visit museums with, or make desert excursions with. . . . It seemed that fate had put a lucky experience in my way, perhaps to make me forget the harvest of bitter memories I nursed of Livia and the Provençal summer she had virtually ruined by her behaviour – that of an *allumeuse*, to put the matter plainly. Now she had diminished in size, so to speak, though not in poignance; but this new experience might help me to qualify the pain of the old. Perhaps I was too forthcoming, for my companion did not respond to my suggestion with anything like my own exuberance; indeed, there was something rather lame about her responses, though she agreed in principle, and even allowed me to suggest taking tickets for a recital of native music.

Two mornings later at my desk I awaited her arrival. I had already halved the statutory cigarette which she accepted. But no Anne manifested herself. After quite a longish interval another girl appeared – indeed, Anne's commanding officer – and it was she who bore the despatch-case. Placing it on the desk before me she said, "I suppose you have heard about Anne?" I looked blank, as who might not, and shook my head. The girl drew up a chair and sat facing me across the desk as she said, "It's been a bit of a shock to us all. She's dead. She was discovered on Thursday morning."

"But I went to dinner with her."

"I know you did; she told me where she could be reached if need be."

"Was it an accident?"

"No. Suicide."

She had taken the big estate car which formed part of the unit's car-pool, tanked it up fully, and then parked it in front of the garage, as if to await a duty call. There was nothing suspect in such a gesture; their work often fell at irregular times, irregular hours – they were, after all, on active service. But after dinner, when the mechanics went home and the Arab watchmen locked up, she borrowed the keys of the night watchman and sent him home. Then she drove the car into the garage, and into the hangar where cars were washed – it was practically hermetic when the sliding doors were shut. Indeed, when they were you could not tell there was a car inside at all. She locked the garage from the inside, turned out all the lights, and started the engine of the big duty car. In the morning of course she was found dead in the driver's seat, a death by carbon monoxide poisoning. "She left no messages for anyone. I have the unpleasant task of writing to her mother, who lives in Hampshire."

"But why on earth?" I exclaimed in an outburst of chagrin. It is absurd, but I have noticed that one often does this – it seems such a personal affront! "She seemed so well and so happy." The commanding officer eyed me for a moment and then said, "She said nothing to you, then? When she came to the mess to fetch that bottle there was a service signal for her saying that her husband had been lost at sea. He was in minesweepers apparently. She just put it in her bag and went off to join you for the evening. Nobody but I saw the signal. I think it's the reason why for the suicide at such short notice. What do you think?"

I could think nothing. I was speechless, in a daze.

To have appeared and disappeared with such startling suddenness . . . I felt absolutely bereft, not only deprived of her warm physical presence but also of the future of meetings which might have been in store for us. It was as if she had over-turned the desk at which I was working. If my business associates found me distracted and thoughtful that day they did not remark on the fact. I felt completely dumbfounded. And it was with an effort that I picked up the threads of my daily life in the city. Fortunately there was plenty of work to do; indeed my sleeve was being plucked at almost half-minute intervals, so that I could at least use the excuse of my duties to occupy my attention. I thought the image of the girl would fade quite soon, for I knew so little about her; but on the contrary she continued to exist in memory with a remarkable clarity of outline and focus. She was like a statue in a niche, corresponding to nothing else, cut off from space and time, yet quite complete and separate. Anne Farnol! The modest name vibrated on in my memory for whole months which succeeded her disappearance from the scene, from the war, from time.

The war! The Prince was much preoccupied during this period with the economic affairs of his own country as well as those which menaced the structure of European affairs. The Red Cross, which at first seemed to me to be a time-wasting repre-sentational job, proved on the contrary a most valuable source of information, a veritable port-hole open upon the new Nazi Europe; moreover, it was based in Geneva, and the traditional neutrality of the Swiss had not been violated. Nominally at least the Germans were still signatories to the Red Cross convention, and the servants of the organisation still enjoyed a quasi-diplomatic status which was everywhere accepted. I was surprised to hear the Prince announce one day that he proposed to visit France one day soon, when "things had settled down a bit". And suddenly my own world, the lost world of friendships and youthful happiness which I had interred in the fastness of my memory, returned vividly to me in the form of a letter addressed to me which tumbled out of the scarlet despatch-box one day. It was from Constance. From *Constance*! I could hardly believe my eyes as I gazed upon that familiar handwriting, which I had never truthfully expected to see again. In a flash the whole vanished reality of things reasserted itself; I was deluged by memories. It was only a short note, a "trial" note as she put it, in order to see if she could locate me through the Prince. She knew of his Red Cross connection, and the postal link through Turkey was still holding. But there was something more important she had to tell me, and that was that Sam had been posted to the Middle East and would soon be here, if indeed he had not yet arrived on the scene. I sprang up from my chair, almost as if he stood already at my elbow. Sam! It was fantastic news; for he must certainly know how to go about finding me. The very telephone directory would have the Prince's number listed.

"Tell him from me what a sod I think him, for you know he has never written at length; he hates writing like you all do. The last thing was a picture postcard of a fat woman from Worthing on the back of which he had scribbled:

> The weather here is mild and balmy.
> I'm awfully glad I joined the army.

"Just wait till I get my hands on him. I will prove Hilary's contention that marriage is a martial art. O Sam, you low-down swine, hiding your laziness behind the pretence of security regulations!"

I carried the letter about like a talisman, excited beyond measure by this sudden rekindling of the past; my loneliness had burst into a blaze, so to speak, and I was moved as well, for she had also mentioned me with affection. "You down there, alone in silence like a rising moon, building up your poems out of selected reticences, please, *please* write!" I did better, I sent the Red Cross a deft telex to be transmitted to her with a few scriptural passages signalled by references, all of which ran to a decent-sized letter; the superficial impression created was of a confidential letter on Red Cross matters coded out thus in quotations from the Bible. But the important thing was to spark the contact, and indeed within a week or two a bundle of letters for Sam arrived on my desk through these semi-diplomatic channels. It remained for Sam himself to manifest, and when he did I was surprised to learn that he had been in this theatre for some little time. Indeed, the bronzed young officer who one day sprang to attention and saluted as he stood in the doorway of the Red Cross office was clad in full fig as a Desert Rat, bush-shirt, suede ankle boots and all. He announced himself as "Captain Standish of the Bluebell Girls". We hugged each other like Turkish delight, with tears in our eyes, so deeply did we feel the fatefulness of the meeting. "How marvellous to find you sitting here quite unaltered, old gloom-bag Aubrey, with your eternal notebook and slyboots expression; it restores my faith in nature, if not in the army, which got me out here so safely. And all to meet you again. O, let's start a quarrel about something trivial shall we? Just to celebrate? You and your old Zen Cohens" – this was his version of *koan*. "The only *koan* I've learned is the British army one – shit or bust. It's terse and to the point."

"What!" I cried. "I must not forget!" And opening my safe I took out the treasure trove of her letters and placed them

before him on the desk in a triumphant fashion. "Good God,"
he said fervently, and it seemed to me that his face fell a trifle.
He looked sort of abashed – perhaps with guilt for not having
written to her. He stood and looked at them, but did not fall
upon them as I would have done had I been in his place.

He took them up awkwardly and instead tapped the
package softly on the knuckles of his left hand as he talked.
Perhaps he wanted to be alone to read them? Of course, that
was it! I dismissed the matter from my mind. "I didn't come
before," he said, "I wanted to wait for some *real* leave – like
this, a whole week. Besides, I was posted off to Greece briefly
with some odds and sods of units and guess where I have just
come back from – you'll never. *Thermopylae!* The Hot Gates
themselves. I was visiting fireman to the New Zealanders. Then
back here. And at your service. Now can you put me up, or
shall I go to Dirty Dick's?"

The palatial dispositions set this doubt at ease for I
occupied a veritable apartment with several separate but inter-
connecting bedrooms, and one of these was made ready for my
guest, who sang and whistled joyfully in the shower, picked
fleas out of his vest which were, so he said, ancient Greek fleas,
and borrowing some civvies from me sent all his own clothes
to the cleaners of the palace. They would all be back at dusk,
spotlessly cleaned and ironed. Such was the luxury in which I
lived. It created, he said, misgiving about my writings – the
worst thing for a writer, he had been told, was soft living. "This
way you'll never succumb to absinthe or syphilis or something,
which I gather is absolutely necessary to meet the case." I
shook my head. "On the contrary, every vice is open to me, and
every drug from hashish to scarlet cummerbunds – which, by
the way, I have been talked into wearing with my white dinner
jacket. Promise not to laugh if we dine with the Prince – he will
be delighted to see you again, and the Princess equally to meet
you."

He agreed somewhat sombrely, anticipating perhaps a social evening, but was relieved when we dined alone with the couple in the vast echoing dining-room. He had supposed that we should have to be tactful about the Prince's rather questionable behaviour when he was in Provence, but to our surprise we found that the Princess seemed to be fully informed of his various "sprees", and completely understanding about them. One realised her great strength in this, and also the reason for their marvellous attachment. It was really a marriage, not an artifact. We drank, in our excitement, rather too much champagne and elected to go to bed at a decently early hour, to lie in adjacent bedrooms with the doors open, talking sleepily far into the night about everything under the sun. I noticed that Constance's letters lay unopened upon the mantelpiece and speculated vaguely as to why they had stayed that way so long. Perhaps he was shy about being unable to answer them as they deserved? He had always accused himself of being tongue-tied and paralysed by shyness. But now they were married. . . . I found the matter something of a puzzle, but I was not disposed to probe for mysteries which might not be there. In due course we would speak of her.

In due course we did; I woke well after midnight to see my friend standing naked on the moonlit terrace on which the full moon blazed, staring down into the garden, completely still. He must have heard me turn, or known in some way that I was awake, for he turned at last and crossed the brilliant terrace to stand at my window and talk to me as I lay there in the dark room. "The thing is this," he said, and I instantly divined that he was about to explain his reluctance to open his wife's letters. "I feel a complete traitor to Constance, to all she believes in, to all we both believed in. That is why I hesitate to open her letters. You see, Aubrey, I don't hate the war at all, I like it; and it's marvellous to have a good moral excuse to wage it. Our war against the Hun is just, and we must win it. Of course some wars can be bad, but some have been of the greatest use to the human race, like the Persian War fought by the old Greeks. You simply do not know what an engagement is like, going into battle. Your blood freezes, your heart trembles to its roots. I have had no experience comparable to it. Beside it, love-making is a charming adventure, nothing more. I know, what I am saying is horrible, but it's the truth. Adventure, I was born and trained for it; I know it now. And if I survive this lot of thunder I shall join the army for life!" He stood quite still now, with hanging head, as if abashed and waiting for the reproof which these sentiments must certainly evoke. I did not know what to say. I was disgusted beyond measure at such glib propositions. "I know what you will say and think; but I am only describing what I see. The lack of individual responsibility is so wonderful – it enables the whole race to act from its functional roots, in complete obedience. Hardship and danger are splendid medicines for softness. And the girls are available now in a way they never were. They smell the fox, smell the blood like packhounds. They are so happy that you should be torn from their arms and flung into the pit – still alive, so to speak. It's like being a baby torn from its mother's arms. What kisses we are reaping! How can I explain all that to Constance? I shall come back to her changed in quite unforeseen ways, but without the power to describe it all, and feeling a traitorous shit – which of course I am now from your point of view." I groped my bedside table and found my cigarettes. We both lit up and started smoking furiously, deep in thought, like two mathematicians beating their brains out upon a problem in physics. "How can I tell her that?" he went on. "All that I have seen would seem to justify what she feels about war, what you feel about it. I have seen some horrid things, things which freeze your mind. But this desert war is marvellous – you engage, and if you lose the toss you fall back forty miles and re-form. Glorious! I have seen some fearful accidents on all sides, some suicides. I saw a bayonet charge by the Essex which was of such scrupulous malevolence that I couldn't believe I belonged to the same race as them. I have seen chunks, whole arms and ankles literally flying off a column being machine-gunned at low level by a fighter. They fire slugs the thickness of a child's wrist in sharp bursts like a spray. They use up the oxygen by their speed and leave you gasping in the middle of a litter of human spare parts. It's horrible, it's wrong . . . what can I say? I wouldn't have missed it for anything. O Aubrey, say something!"

But I was dumbfounded, thunderstruck. I was also rather shamefaced at having been caught out in a moral dilemma which I had never resolved; perhaps the slick moral judgment was mine, and mine the condemnation? Inevitably, and without quite meaning to, I found myself becoming sententious. "My experience has been limited so far as a non-combatant," I said. "And surely humanity's mishaps suffice – do we have to add to them by wars? Last week I was asked to go down to Port Said and read for a weekend to some remnants of the Australian Div. There were about two hundred young men, all cases of blindness. They were waiting in transit to be repatriated. It was terrible to see their white, shocked faces and fluttering eyelids, and their panic, for they were new to this world of blindness. I felt sort of ashamed, as if I had no clothes on. I read to them from *The Bible Designed to be Read as Literature*, etc., etc., the gospel according to Gollancz. It was a strange experience to hear the 16th psalm in the atmosphere of the first-class saloon of a cruise-liner. Instead of looking down as one does when poetry is read or music played, they raised their faces like chickens, as if the words were pouring down on them from a cloud. I was glad to beat a retreat after an hour. Despite the profuseness of the education officer's thanks I gathered that my 'pommy accent' offended some and spoiled the experience for most."

While I talked he had put the light on in his room and unearthed a decanter of whisky; we had a drink there in the theatrical moonlight of the Egyptian night.

"There's one thing I want to ask – a favour," he said at last. "I took the liberty of putting your name on my blood-sheet, you know, the next-of-kin sheet we all have to fill in."

"But why?" I said.

"Well, just in case I get stopped in my tracks by some-thing, I would like to feel that it was you who would break it to Constance; you would be able to explain it better than anyone and offer what consolation one can in such circumstances. I felt it sort of kept the good tension of the last summer in Provence – as was appropriate. Is it all right with you? Unless you don't want the responsibility of announcing the dismal fact of my departure for the land of shades . . ."

"Of course not," I said, getting back into bed and switching off the light. "Let's catch a glimpse of sleep before the sun comes up."

"Done," he said with an enormous healthy yawn. "Done!"

Turning and tossing restlessly, eager to achieve sleep before the dawn with its first mosquito rendered it almost impossible, I heard him muttering on, pursuing the same line of thought which had caused us such an amazing exchange of confidences.

"It's awful how we all want in one way or another a certificate for glory," he said sadly, and groaning, fell asleep.

He was up well before me, and was sitting on the terrace reading his correspondence with affectionate attention – our talk had dispersed his doubts and fears. Somewhere a soft breakfast gong sounded and I groaned my way to the shower.

"Awake at last," he cried, with a revival of his usual high spirits. "I saw you lying there, dauntless as a sausage, snoring your head off, and I could not help but appreciate your

645

contribution to the war effort. It sounded like distant gun-fire."

The Prince was up and in a somewhat testy mood, unlike his usual lark-like good humour. He was reading the war news in the columns of *Al Ahram* and shaking his head over the non-committal communiqués issued by the staff. It was one of those rare periods of stalemate where nothing particular was happening. But it was not of this that he wished to speak. "I sometimes wonder," he told us, "if the British really want to win or not; they behave in such an extraordinary way. You know about our agent? Well, we have a Nazi agent living in the summer-house at the bottom of the garden; the gardeners found him and he offered them money to leave him alone. Can you imagine – a German archaeologist who speaks perfect Arabic? As you may well imagine, I rushed to the Consulate and told them, expecting they would send someone to sweep him up and shoot him. Not a bit of it. That detestable and supercilious Brigadier Maskelyne said, 'We make a point of never disturbing a nesting agent.' And now they are even proposing to supply him with equipment. Is *this* war, I ask myself? If all the agents are going to be left alone and even kept supplied . . ." He did not appear to imagine that it would be very much worth our while to try and infiltrate German or Italian Intelligence, and as he was almost hopping with irritation it was wiser to leave him in ignorance of the facts of life.

The conversation turned upon the few days of relaxation he had immediately accorded me with the appearance of my friend; no effort must be spared to make Sam's leave as agreeable as possible. A marvellous series of alternatives was proposed – excursions to the four corners of Egypt, visits to countless ancient sites. Only time was the enemy, circumscribing this little holiday. "Nevertheless," cried the Prince with energy and determination, "between the lot of us we shall certainly see that he has a good time." His vague gesture took in not only his wife and palace staff but also the various secretaries and his friend Affad.

Indeed, the banker Affad was the most charming, diffident and resourceful of the Prince's associates, presenting himself as an eager host, and his invitation was made the more tempting by the fact that he was about to set off on a journey by water – a Nile journey: moreover, in a well-appointed little ship belonging to the French Embassy. We hardly realised the magnitude of our luck until we had been two whole days aboard this pretty pirogue travelling up-Nile, a water world which is like no other. It was all too brief, for halfway up to the nearest big town we were to be dropped in order to return to Cairo by car, since my friend must not overstay his leave, or even risk such an eventuality, while this return would enable him to enjoy a little of the company of the Prince and Princess to whom he had taken a great fancy. But this little journey proved delightful as a sort of extension of our untroubled Provençal summer – the links formed there still held. Indeed they seemed almost forged anew, so ever-present seemed Constance and Hilary her brother, seemed Felix Chatto the consul . . . seemed even in ghostly form the dark shade of Livia. Where would she be, I wondered? And Avignon with its looming skyline against the blue sky – the cathedrals which Hilary had always referred to as "disused prayer factories, with no noise of bumble like turbines coming from them". The thrilling swish of mistral in the pines. It was all these, it was all here.

More piquant still was the fact that Affad's other two guests proved to be a French couple, of meridional persuasion; "*les ogres*" they were christened, for their family name was LeNogre. They were brother and sister, twins to the hour, inseparable – Bruno and Sylvaine by name. The boy was a young attaché in the Free French Embassy; his sister kept house and entertained for him. They owned, or so he said in his calm, studied English, an old derelict chateau in the village of

Villefoin, not very far from Tubain where "our" chateau, the house of Constance, was situated. Why, they had been there that summer – we could all have met! There was a gleam of sorrow in the dark eye of Sylvaine as she stated the fact. The expression on her face, the shape of her features, her way of holding her head, reminded me most acutely of someone, though I could not for the life of me think whom. The thought was troubling, like the attentions of a fly one could not brush away; but my obstinate memory refused to yield up the key to those dark features. Her brother was deeply preoccupied and ashamed of the way France had fallen, and of these base chicaneries of the French Mediterranean fleet which refused to join the Allies. However, the Free French movement was now a fact, and within the year De Gaulle would have twenty thousand Frenchmen in the field under his leadership . . . so that all was not lost. Yet it was touching to see so young a man wounded in his national honour by the collapse of his country and its wholehearted espousal of a Nazi peace. But, he added ruefully, "I am surprised at the strength of my own feelings – I did not know I had any. I am just the average French intellectual, and you know how cynical they are!" Sam reassured him in his tactful way by saying that something very similar had come about in England. "I was very much criticised for joining up," he added, with a side-glance at me, "as Aubrey will tell you." All of this was true; we had all been living in a fool's paradise. It has taken Hitler to blow off the tent top and show us what a circus the political world really was.

These young people were hospitality itself, and soon the large centre cabin with its enormous table and hanging petrol lantern was well and truly taken over – our belongings were disposed upon and around the bunks which lined the walls. The big central table with its sanded benches was where we sat and ate or played cards, or spread out our maps and writing materials. We were staying with them too briefly to have accumulated much luggage, for they were planning a trip of some two weeks and were very well equipped with everything in the way of tinned food and ammunition for their sporting guns. But the mood was so tranquil, the coilings of the great river so suave and dense with beautiful islands and groves, that we quite forgot that the pastures which bordered it were thick with quail and turtle-dove. While we were with them there was no shooting by common consent. That would begin, said Affad, when they arrived in the true north, the crocodile reaches. One ached to be going with them. Not the less because their visit to upper Egypt was to end with a ride out to a distant oasis where a famous country fair was to be held, and where a clairvoyant of renown was to be encountered who would tell their fortunes. "I don't mind about the fortune-teller," said Sam, "but the oasis sounds everything one has read about. What a damned shame." But the two "ogres" professed not to be unduly superstitious and would, they said, be delighted to offer themselves to the fortune-teller as subjects.

We dined that night by lantern light, while high overhead the night sky spread its carpet of brilliant stars and a frail new moon shone. It was quite chilly on the water and the freshets of evening wind rapped upon our prow as we drew into shore to anchor for the evening meal. Our consciousness had already been lulled and subdued by the thump of bare feet upon the wooden deck and the quavering, trailing songs of the watermen as they guided us southwards. The river opened and closed like a fan – suddenly enlarging its confines into whole estuaries or small lakes, only to fold back into its own narrow bed for a space. Kites hung in the higher airs, keeping up their steady relentless patrol, but all along the banks we met brilliant rollers and kingfishers, and the little rock-doves of the desert fringe with their plaintive small cry: "Too few," they seemed to say, "too few."

The ever-changing light all round expanded and contracted solid outlines and distances so that the eyes, travelling in pursuit, were mesmerised by the apparent make-believe. "Lord bless you," exclaimed Sam, inappropriately crossing himself and repeating the Latin grace in use at his Oxford college. "You couldn't describe it to anyone because you can hardly believe it yourself."

Palms and tombs, tombs and waterwheels and palms. Islands rising and subsiding in the mist. A river which flowed like smoke between the two deserts in a luxuriant green bed full of paradisiacal plants and trees. "No wonder dervishes dance," Sam went on, and Affad smiled his approval. "Who wouldn't?" But with the rising light came also the glare and the parching heat, so that at midday the sky weighed a ton. "Tell me what surprised you most about Egypt," said Affad curiously; he was genuinely curious and not merely in search of compliments. To have replied, "O everything" would have been at once too easy and not sufficiently exact; for my part what had assailed me was an extraordinary sense of familiarity. To throw open one's shutters at Mena House and find oneself with, so to speak, a personal Sphinx squatting outside one's window, patient as a camel . . . They seemed great playful toys, the Sphinxes, and despite the complete mystery which surrounded their history and meaning, curiously warm and familiar – domesticated animals, like the water-buffalo or the camel. And then of course the desert itself had been a complete surprise. One came upon it, came to the edge of the carpet of human plantation and there it was like a great theatrical personage, waiting serenely. It was at once a solitude and also homely as a back-garden. But as much an entity as the Atlantic; one could not just walk into it for a stroll, for its shapes were always changing; at the least wind all contours changed, and one's tracks were expunged at a breath. No more could one decide to go for a row in the Atlantic without misgivings. The desert was a metaphor for everything huge and dangerous, yet without so seeming. Parts were slick as a powdered wig, parts shallow with pretty coloured rocks and clays, striated with the marks of vanished caravans; parts were like a burnt-out old colander full of dead cinders. Rosy winds sighed about it at dawn, or when the desert wind called *khamseen* set upon it, pillars of rusty blood-coloured wind raced as spume races ahead of the waves in an Atlantic storm. But riding across it one found certain animals quite at home, oriented and self-possessed; the rat, the *jerboa*, a kind of jack rabbit – how did they manage it when there was no cover at all save scrub? Packs of wild dogs wandered about with the air of living off the land – but what could they find to eat? Heavy dews at dawn and at midnight provided moisture of a kind for insects like mantises and locusts. But dogs? The desert offered a different sort of providence; its terrible frugality engendered introspection and compassion. God!

Some of this I managed to say and Affad listened keenly, with interest. The desert fringed our present skyline, but here we were gliding upon the glazed reaches of the Nile which offered the contrasts of cool surface wind and sparkling water, not to mention the gorgeous panorama of river-craft with its thousand eye-coaxing sails of different hues. Here the felucca came into her own, dominating, like some great queen of antiquity, the river upon which she had been built to travel. The beauty of function, the elegance of purity and stress. No one could see a felucca and not feel it to be a symbol expressing the unconscious essence of womanhood. But feluccas have no need to be fashion-conscious. The way they press their cheeks to the river wind is as invariable as the wind itself, which imposes on them a formal geometrical precision of trajectory. They run down river upon a few sweet angles of inclination – and they surprise one with the feeling that they are among man's choicest and rarest creations, which indeed they are. Their field of action is limited and more exacting than ocean navigation. The Nile flows directly down out of the heart of

Africa into ancient Greek history – like the spine of a cobra. Its feluccas are controlled by the river winds which arrive and depart like soft-footed servants whose work is dedicated to these swallow-cut, pouting lateen rigs. A shivering goes through them like an electric current all day long, and they slide down river as if on a cord, then abruptly come to a halt and everything is becalmed, frozen in the middle of a tactic; the feluccas bow their heads as if the wind when it comes will behead them. Instead the glass floor starts rolling again, and quietly they turn to left or right to resume their journey. Here and there you might encounter one ferrying sugar-cane and wearing an eye like some apt Aegean echo; but the eye will be an Egyptian eye – the eye of the camel, in fact, with its double set of eyelashes. One will recognise the ship as a Greek vessel manned from the Greek colony at Edfu. The whole of Herodotus gazes out of that kohl-traced eye!

The people of the river too are special and apart, different from the mundane and banausic town Egyptians. On the banks they superintend the criss-crossing water-channels and tend their dates and their vegetables, but always with time for a salute and a hoarse cry of welcome which invites the wayfarer to sit and sup with them. The women strike one more than the men – their magnificent carriage upon the treacherous river banks. They are black-avised as warlocks and wear their black cowls with formality and disdain. But their smile, fuller of ivory than a male elephant in rut, flashes out of toil-worn faces packed with all the majesty of hunger. They glide along like the unconscious patricians which they are, and their bear-like, gloating walk seems to draw its rhythm from the pace of the Nile's green blood, flowing steadily from some distant wound in the heart of Africa.

"For me," said Bruno, "it was chiefly the tombs, dug so deep into the ground, and yet so snug. I have never seen anything comparable to the tiny kings lying there in their painted cocoons surrounded by their toys, as if the world of childhood also passed with them through the barrier of death. But what am I saying – 'barrier'? I was struck by the facts of that marvellous workmanship, all those frescoes so brilliant in their colouring, were to lie there unobserved by human eyes through the centuries. The little kings and queens with their toys, slowly drying out in their awkward sarcophagoi (the word means flesh-devourer in Greek, no?); their attitude to death was quite different from ours, or indeed from their contemporaries the Greeks' with their asphodel-splashed underworld expressing all the sincere and open regret which the thought of death brought. They had no impassivity about death – it was terrible and sad and uprooting, and the end of every happiness. They refused to allow themselves any factitious consolation. And yet they were also naive, they felt if they wailed enough, made enough noise they might make death relent. But the Egyptian? This massive, slumbering, vegetal life of silence and vacancy, strapped into one's swaddling clothes, the mummy wrappings . . . Then I realised that the word eternity really meant something to them – an eternal waiting – but for what they did not know. Time existed forever in massive extension – to the very confines of the human consciousness. It was frozen, their thoughts as well as their tears were frozen by the sepulchre, but there was no repining for death was real, and it existed like the next room exists while we are talking in this one. I got a shock off these strange little mummies, planted like vegetables in the shaly valleys. Even to sit beside them in the tombs and hear one's own heart beating was a strange experience. And the toys? Reaching out one could actually touch their touch upon them, the touch of children's fingers! But the quality of immobility, of waiting without thought, without hope, without desire, is something you can see in the peasants today as they wait for the sun to rise or set, or for the station to open, for the first train to come. They wait like inanimate objects, like sacks of grain, like chunks of marble. There is no buoyancy in them – just the enormous load of their waiting. One can read into their posture some of the immobility of the little kings in their brightly painted tombs. The word 'eternity' comes into the mind, the whole field of consciousness becomes one eternal waiting-room. Even the dust does not gain upon one in these bright tombs, for they are sealed and the little kings exist now in a tepid vacuum of eternity. They can get no older now, nor will they ever get any younger; but at least they have achieved a perpetual immobility, a perfection of non-being beyond moon or sun."

"How beautiful the women are!" cried Sylvaine. "They don't seem to fuss very much about the veil either."

"It's hard to work as they do and wear it."

"I hope they abolish it one day. What eyes!"

"What eyes!" echoed Sam and added, in garbled quotation, "She walks in beauty like the Nile." But it was an apt enough paraphrase for what one felt watching the women upon the banks, their tall frames moulded from the darkness of water and clay, brown as terracotta. In them you felt the great river with its sudden eddies and slow oozings, its lapses and languors. Yes, the river was her clock-time, she walked in time to river's green blood, the Nile-pulse which throbbed in that velvet smooth element. The warmth of these villagers was inspiriting, smiles of charcoal, ivory or magenta, sudden flashes from the turret of a veil; and then the hoarse, bronze laughter of the man, brazen heads laughing, bronze arms raised. All suddenly cut off by a bend in the river, decapitated: their voices drowned by the shrieking of waterwheels whose wooden squeak is the most characteristic sound of the Egyptian night.

The pilot smiles as he answers the wave of a whole village – but the smile passes like a breath over embers and then is gone, lost in his dark abstraction, his nilotic amnesia. Slowly the villages pass out of sight; night is falling, soft as a great moth. These big lumbering men and women have all the humbling dignity of dispossessed monarchs. They are paupers, ravaged by want and illness. The old stand about in attitudes of deafness, like so many King Lears. And yet their land is a paradise – nature's exuberance has gone wild. You see cork oaks ravaged by ants, honeysuckle climbing into palm trees, water-laved rock carved into the heads of elephants. But everything enjoying a seeming aloneness under that burning sky. Dusk to darkness to starlight. A fish jumps. Then another. Then a sudden shower of silver arrows. It is to be our last night aboard.

A faint river wind favours us, keeping the night insects at bay, so we are able to have our dinner by candleshine on deck – a smoky flapping light which we would soon extinguish in favour of a young rising moon. We grew sentimental and spoke of *après la guerre*. The French couple unhesitatingly expressed their intention of returning to Provence to spend the rest of their lives in the old tumbledown chateau of their ancestors. Bruno wanted to write a book about the Templars – apparently there was a mass of unpublished matter in the muniments room of the chateau.

"You will come too," he cried warmly. "I feel you will. I know you will. We will be happy living there with just each other for company!" I hardly dared to extend my wishes so far, though Sam seemed ready enough to promise so far ahead. I could not envisage any end to this war, and a deep sadness took possession of me. I thought of Anne Farnol and wondered how many like her would be forced to abdicate in the face of fate. Then, with a jolt, I "recognised" the face of Sylvaine; it is strange how small things stick. I had seen her for a while in the lunatic asylum of Montfavet near Avignon. I had been taken there by Lord Galen to visit a friend of his and I had glimpsed a dark girl, a patient, walking in the rose garden. So very like Sylvaine, the dark, bird-headed girl – they could have been twins as well. I told her this and she smiled and shook her head. "Not me," she said, "or me in another life – who can say?"

We had become such close friends now that it was quite a wrench to envisage this parting; just round the corner was the little town where tomorrow our car would wait to ferry us back to the capital where we were expected to dine with my Prince. Another small sadness too was that soon Sam would be going back to the front – and everyone knew that there was a big battle impending in the Western Desert. My heart turned over as I thought of Constance and watched her handsome, insouciant mate packing his kit bag.

On the morrow it was all goodbyes and regrets, unfeigned enough, for the whole voyage had been a miracle of comfort and delight. Yes, we would all meet again, we swore it. Then with a melancholy thoroughness we packed our affairs into the big camouflaged staff car which bore the Egyptian army crescent. The return journey was a whirlwind of dusk and clamour as we swept through the villages on the river bank, scattering livestock and villagers alike by the noise of our triple horns. There was some point in this speeding, for the capital was a good distance away – and indeed we only arrived at the palace with half an hour to spare before dinner. As my servant wound me into my cummerbund I heard Sam in the shower talking, half to himself and half to me: "So Constance doth make cowards of us all, eh? As a matter of fact I wrote her a long letter from Greece; but God knows if it will ever reach her through the army post office. Anyway, I feel the better for having talked to you. Will you write her about my visit? You have so many more nouns and verbs than I." I agreed to do this.

The servant brought in a parcel of clothes and started laying out a desert uniform with Egyptian army tabs. Sam watched this curiously, wondering what it could mean. "I have been created an honorary lieutenant in the Egyptian army for tomorrow. Apparently the picnic place is technically out of bounds except to troops." It was some time later over whiskies in the scarlet leather salon that the Prince himself added the details to this explanation, smoking a hashish-loaded cigarette in a long yellow holder.

"It has always been our favourite picnic place, an old Coptic monastery in ruins, Aby Fahym. Now since that corner of the desert has been cleared of the Italians I have asked H.Q. for permission to revisit it. You will see how pretty it is, though mostly knocked down. First the Italians took it, then the British kicked them out; then they came back, then were kicked out again. Each time they knocked a piece off it. There was one old monk who refused to move; he lived in the ruins, crawling about like a lizard. Both sides fed him, he became a sort of mascot. Finally he disappeared in the last British attack which took the place, and since then has never been seen. He will obviously become a legend in the Coptic Church; but meanwhile you will see how pretty it is."

Next morning we set off by car and motored to the desert fringe where we were met by horses and a string of camels: slower moving traffic, so to speak, but more adept when it came to carrying heavy baggage, tents and suchlike. Everyone was in high good spirits. The party had been joined by two young staff officers from the Military Mission, an Egyptian liaison officer and an R.A.M.C. doctor who seemed to be on good terms with the Prince and Princess and answered to the name of Major Drexel. He professed himself to be "swanning", very much as Sam himself was. The Princess with some hauteur refused the horses and camels which she described as "Bedouin folklore" and elected to lead us in her comfortable estate car with its special tyres. So we set off in a somewhat straggling party to complete the first part of the journey which was undertaken with circumspection, for the route led us first through a network of minefields until we hit the final wire with its command cars and straggling tanks on duty. Here we provided our permits and documents and were ushered into the desert as if into a drawing-room by a ceremonious staff officer who took the trouble, however, to compare map references with the liaison officer and insist that we went no further than the feature mentioned on our permit. "At least, we take no responsibility for you beyond that point."

The Prince puffed out his cheeks with a proud and disdainful expression. "There is no danger at all now," he said, "I have it on the best authority."

"Very well, sir," said the ruddy staff officer. "On you go, and a happy picnic to you."

A light wind sprang up, not enough to create sand, yet enough to cool the middle hours of the day. The light with its dancing violet heart outlined this strange primeval world of dunes and *wadis* through which we wound our way; quite soon, like a ship which clears the horizon, we would be moving by the studied navigation of the compass, or the stars. It gave one a strange feeling of freedom. Once a small arrowhead of planes passed overhead – so high as to look like a formation of wild geese, and far too high to let us read their markings. Sam rode with the Princess, and I on another horse with the Prince. The whole journey only took about an hour and a half. We came at last to a small oasis and a series of grey escarpments, forms of striated rock, which shouldered up into the sky. "Look!" someone cried as we rounded a shoulder of dune. We saw a small oasis and within a few hundred yards the Coptic monastery came into view. Aby Fahym must once have been very beautiful, though now it was rather knocked about; one had to decipher its turrets and crocketed belfries anew to rediscover its original shape and style. But almost any building in that strange, romantic site would have seemed compelling to the imagination. The two main granaries were joined by a high ramp in the form of a bridge. The Prince was highly delighted and gazed at the old place through his glasses, exclaiming, "Well, it's still there, the old Bridge of Sighs. They haven't knocked it down after all." He superintended the setting up of a shady marquee with childish pleasure, even going so far as to knock in a tent peg or two himself with a wooden mallet, until a shocked servant snatched it from his royal hand and reproached him in guttural Arabic.

Carpets were spread, divans appeared, as also the latest creation from Italy, a portable frigidaire which held countless bowls of sorbet and iced lemon tea. We were all thirsty and did justice to this initiative, seated in a wide semi-circle around the Prince. The conversation had turned to politics so that, excusing ourselves in a whisper, Sam and I set out to trudge up to the monastery. "We might put up the missing monk, eh?" said my friend with boyish elation. "There may be cisterns or cellars below ground – there's little enough cover above," I replied. We had both had a good look at the place with the Prince's binoculars. On a ridge quite close to the monastery I had seen some red markers planted in the sand and wondered if somebody was surveying the place – I thought them to be for theodolites, perhaps. Somewhere to the right, upon a profile of sand dune and sky, moved a line of light tanks and command cars engaged on some obscure military manoeuvre. We turned back once or twice to wave to the colourful party in the oasis below. The camels were groaning and being bad-tempered. Then we addressed the last part of the slope and entered the baking gates of the little place. It had been built with a mixture of straw, brick and plaster which gave the walls, or what was left of them, a strange appearance of wattle-moulding in brown hide. But there was no sign of the monk, and no sign of any subterranean cellars where he might be hiding. Disappointed, we lingered a moment to smoke a cigarette, and then retraced our steps – or at least began to do so.

Then it happened – as suddenly and surprisingly as the

capsizing of a canoe. The suddenness was quite numbing, as well as the immediate lack of sound which gave the illusion of a whole minefield going up silently around us. A series of giant sniffs and a crackle of splinters followed a good way after the first seismic manifestation – the desert blown up around us in picturesque billows and plumes – a whole running chain of puffs, followed after a long and thoughtful pause by the bark of the mortars, for that is what they turned out to be. "Christ," shouted Sam, "they must be ranging." Another series of dry crackles followed by puffs seemed almost deliberate, as if to illustrate his remark. We began to run awkwardly, stooped, hands spread out like startled chickens. The red poles I had seen must have been ranging markers. We tried to set a course away from them, running sideways downhill now in the thick sand. Out of the corner of my eye I saw that the party in the oasis had also been alerted. There was a stir of alarmed recognition. They pointed at us as we ran stumbling downhill towards them, and the servants in a sudden access of solicitude started running towards us, as if to avert the danger from us. There was a tremendous burst now – it went off between my teeth, my whole skull echoed, my mind was blown inside out.

With scattered wits and panic fear we raced, Sam and I, along the side of the dune, in the hope of cover. But before we reached our objective we were overtaken by the whole solid weight of the desert. It was flung over us like a mattress. We collapsed like surfers overtaken by the rollers of the ocean, like ants overwhelmed by a landslide.

It seemed as if huge fragments of this shattered desert composure were blown about on all sides of me; my brain swelled and became full of darkness and sand. I felt my tongue swell up and turn black with heat, I felt it protrude. All this while falling sideways into space and vaguely hearing groans and whispers magnified on my right. Then thump – someone or something buried an axe in the middle of my back and the pain spread out from this centre of crisis until it reached the confines of my body, tingling in the fingertips like an electric current. I tried with all my might to rise to my feet but there was no traction to be had. My companion had fallen too, propelled skidding by the same sandspout as my own. And now in a lull came the crackle of shell splinters among the hot rocks, the sizzling spittle of the invisible guns.

From this point on everything becomes quite fragmentary, broken up descriptively like strips of cinema film, with just a frame here or there showing an image, indistinct and alarming. And even more alarming were the shattered fragments of conversation, or of voices calling. Guttural Arabic shouts and sobs – the servants in their devotion had shown great bravery. They reached us as we fell half rolling down the sandhills, in a welter of bloody smears which had begun to print themselves on the new khaki drill of our uniforms. I suppose we were picked up, joints all loose like rag dolls, and transferred bodily to the canvas tarpaulin which allowed Drexel to examine us, but only perfunctorily for the firing had become nearer at hand, and the whole party was retiring in the utmost confusion, leaving half their possessions behind in the oasis. In a moment of lucidity I heard the Princess say, "God! my veil is covered in blood." Sad and reproachful she sounded. And then Drexel saying, "Give me a chance; I want to examine them." And the Prince suddenly petulant says, "He is a doctor, after all." I was moved about moaning and thumped down on canvas; I heard the clean clicking of scissors and felt air where my clothes were being cut away from me. Then in a lower register a voice I could not identify said, "I think the other one's gone." There were groans of vexation and the curious whimpering noise of the servants – to echo the anxiety of their employers was a formality of good manners. They did not fear death as much as blood, black blood which oozed like the Nile, or spouted darkly from a severed artery, or inundated a whole section of the skin with wine-red smears. "There's a field dressing station by the wire," said Drexel. "We can clean them up a bit there; but for the rest . . . what can one do?"

"I shall never forgive myself," said the Prince in a low, hissing voice. "The whole thing is my fault."

A smatter of Arabic voices now took up the tale, cajoling, excusing, explaining, or so it seemed. The sun seemed to be playing upon my very eyeballs. The pain was one continuous even throb now, with its own anaesthesia – when it reached a certain degree of intensity one fainted away for a moment.

Now the shuffle of car wheels and the grinding of gears; we were heading back for the wire. Somebody suggested whisky and water but Drexel said, "Not with such bleeding please."

"I shall never forgive myself," said the Prince.

A sympathetic group of voices hovered like an overturned beehive at the wire. We were treated with kindness and despatch. The officer was disposed to crow over our mishaps, but the Prince bit his head off with a crisp, "That's enough. Can't you see we have two casualties? Where is the dressing station?"

Dust and whirring sand, and flies settling on blood in swarms. A needle, a drink of cold water, sleep.

I was not to know till later that Sam was dead.

Nor that the guns responsible for the accidental assault on us had been our own – Cypriot mule-borne mortars at target drill.

In the month-long agony of lying half insensible from shock – both the shock of my friend's death, and the post-operational shock from all the spinal excavations I had had to undergo in the "cleaning-up" process – much else had happened. Cade had appeared from nowhere, to my dismay and consternation. Thanks to the Prince he had succeeded in getting himself transferred to the Egyptian mission and appointed to me as a batman. It was intended as a kindly gesture on the part of my hosts. How could they have divined the depression and horror I felt to wake and find, sitting at the end of the bed, the yellow weasel of my mother's last days – her manservant and reader of the Bible, Cade? He sat there in expressionless silence, with an air of profound disapproval of everything – Egypt, the war, the Prince, my disposition – everything. It took less than nothing to start him off whining about the army, the Germans, the war, the peace, the weather. He wore his puritan life like a dead crow round his neck. Every day I was tempted to sack him, and yet ... He was useful to me. He had once been a male nurse in an asylum and he knew how to wash and change me, and how to massage my splintered limbs. Also my eyes seemed to have been affected by my other tribulations, and I allowed him to read to me – the new correspondence which flowed out of Geneva: the letters of Constance, who by now was fully abreast of events, in possession of the truth. "So Constance doth make cowards of us all," I heard Sam's voice in my ear as Cade read her brave letters, so full of a contained hysteria, so free from bravura. "I am puzzled, for it has keeled me over: yet in a way it was to be expected. Aubrey, send me every scrap of detail, however horrible. I want to experience as deeply as possible this terrible yet perhaps most valuable experience. Did he speak of me, did he miss me? Why should he? He loved me, and was as free as a butterfly, his wings turned sunward. Here in the sleet and snow it all seems unreal – down there by the Nile. By the way, I thought for a long time your Sutcliffe was imaginary, but I find he is all too real. What could you have meant by that? I am treating his wife – standing in for a colleague on leave of absence. What a *ménage*! He asked to see me, I complied. He brought up the question of Freud's sofa without my prompting him and I knew he was 'your' Sutcliffe. I told him it had arrived safely.

We are friends now, close friends. He is a weird man. Strangely enough, the sort of man a woman could love. An old wart-hog with dandruff – so he says of himself. It has meant a lot just now, with Sam, having someone like this to talk to. Aubrey, please recover, please tell me all."

Cade folded the letter with distaste and looked at the wall-paper with a mulish expression devoid of emotion. I was tempted to sigh. "If foreigners did not exist the English would not know who to patronise," I said angrily, and I asked him to take a letter back to Constance. He seated himself at the desk with the portable typewriter before him, waiting, his pharisaical hatred of everything flowing out from him into the room in waves, in concentric circles. Horizontal, I drew a long breath and hesitated peevishly, for Constance had now made a coward of me: I simply could not tell her the truth. I would certainly report that he had died instantaneously with a bullet through the head. After all, what did she really want to hear? "His spine was shivered, his organs splattered with thorns of shrapnel, the works of his watch shot into his wrist? Nothing could stop the flow of blood, our blood. The car cushions were daubed, the canvas sheets on which we lay were smoking with flies. Rib-cage stove, thorax broken and bruised, ankles snapped like celery..." It was disgusting. Moreover, what was the point? Worst, it was selfish. It was not part of her loving, it was a medical therapy to test her professional composure. No, I could not tell her the truth.

Every day now the contrite Prince came to sit by my bed, for the most part with the Princess; but usually they separated these visitations. She came in the afternoon to have tea with me, he just before lunch to discuss any work problems which might have arisen in the morning, for we kept up the pretence that I was still in his employ, neither side wishing to let the relationship lapse.

For the rest, it was Cade who waited upon me now, who

664

dressed and fed me; why did I tolerate this man whom I found so detestable? His insolence – examining the fillings in his back teeth with the aid of my shaving mirror, doing his hair end- lessly in the bathroom with my combs and brushes! Sometimes he did not answer when I spoke but just looked at me, his head on one side, with a benign contempt. But when I raised my voice his assurance wilted and he became a slave again, cringing though still loitering. Was it because he had witnessed the death of my mother? Or because it was to her that he had read the Bible every night? Nowadays he kept up the same practice, spectacles on the end of his nose. His lips moved as he read. . . . He sat now before the machine, his head bowed, waiting. I simply could not bring myself to write to Constance through such an emissary. "That will be all, Cade," I said, much to his surprise. "I am beginning to ache. I'll record a letter later." He looked at me keenly for a moment and then got up, shrugged, and removed the typewriter. They had loaned me a little magnetic recorder, and this meant I could have my recording typed out in the Red Cross offices and so keep it from the prying eyes of Cade. "You can go now," I told him. "I am going to sleep for an hour."

The unhappy conventions of grave sickness – I had not known them before; you become a burden to those who nurse you. The dressings and the drugs and the tiptoe people only emphasise what you would be only too glad to forget – your utter helplessness. The world closes in, one affronts it from a lowly horizontal position; those who help you you come to hate. For me at this stage the future had vanished as inexorably as the past – even if the war lasted a century it would not modify my condition. And how ignominious to be put out of action by one's own side! Drexel came in sometimes in the afternoon to talk to me, and showed me the pictures he had taken on that fatal afternoon. The Bridge of Sighs, so-called, in the far distance, with Sam and me in the foreground turning to wave –

within a minute of being blown up! I was glad of his presence, for he could examine and talk about my wound; Cade had simply held up a doubled fist and said, "You got an 'ole this size in your spine, sir." Drexel for the first ten days assisted at night with the dressings and bindings. "You will have to be re-strung like an old piano, I am afraid; thank goodness we have a first-class orthopaedic unit with the Indian Div. But you will need at least two more ops which I don't think can be performed here – so delicate; unless the Prince has some foreign talent up his sleeve. Ask him." But the Prince had nobody except competent local doctors – Egyptians of his class were used to being treated in Zurich or Berlin for any malady graver than a common cold. I entered the dark tunnel of this illness with a tremendous depression, for my whole life seemed to have been compromised by it. Sometimes in the shuttered afternoons with the white ripples of the Nile reflected on the ceiling of the tower-room into which I had been moved for convenience, I awoke in the blaze of fever to see my valet's face bend over me to take thermometer readings to log my progress. Then there came as well exhausted days of remission and coherence where I found I could speak and craved company. The Prince's children came and played in my room sometimes: I tried to get them to pass me the holster on the mantelpiece which contained a service revolver – part of my Egyptian army kit. But they refused, and must perhaps have told someone, for when next Drexel came I noticed that he broke it and tilted out the cartridges. Neither of us said anything. "Different sorts of fever," he said once, quietly. "My own is a girl with dark hair and black eyes." I did not know it then, but the reference was to Sylvaine, the dark sister-*ogre* with whom we had travelled up the Nile. The information came from Affad, who also dropped in regularly with papers and presents of chocolates. "It's a strange love trio," he said, "quite worthy of Ancient Egypt. They have great plans of retiring from the world after the war and locking themselves up in their Provençal chateau."

After the war! "Have you seen the news?" I asked him, and he replied, "Yes, I know." How could anyone dream of an afterwar state? He lit a cigarette and quoted some Chinese sage: "In this life they are only dreaming they are awake." Yes, it was true – we lived like parvenus, like vulgar provincials in the city of God. And now to be helpless in a foreign land, far from love and its familiarities, strapped down to an ironing-board with a pound of lead on each foot and the plaster sticking to the hairs of the skin in an agony of heat . . . I had been assured that it would not be for long though. I closed my eyes and saw Constance walking by the grey lake, a whole landscape of iron-black trees quivering under snow. I would have given anything to be walking beside her. "I took them to the oasis of Macabru – you should have come. There is a little sect of gnostics who meet there at this time of the year; they carry on ancient rites and beliefs. They admitted us, and we took a good deal of hashish and had visions." He laughed softly. I asked him, "How would you define gnosticism?" but he only shook his head doubtfully and did not answer.

The coming of Theodora changed everything. She was the new nurse from the Greek Hospital in Alexandria who had been drafted to Cairo. The Prince without telling a soul had engaged her to live in and look after me. One morning she was simply there. She stood in the doorway divesting herself of her shawl and eyeing me a little sideways with her yellow goat's eyes, as if she were listening to some invisible pulse-beat. She said good morning with complete assurance in French and Greek – her accent sounded very plebeian in both languages. Then she rolled up her sleeves and came towards me slowly, stealthily, as one boxer approaches another to deliver a blow. At this moment Cade came in, and turning to him she gave him a long yellow look and then pointed at the door, saying,

"*Moi massage le Monsieur. Sortez.*" The manservant slunk out of the room without a backward glance.

"*Ego eimai Theodora,*" she said in Greek, tapping upon her own breastbone with long capable fingers. "*Je suis votre infirmière Theodora.*" And with that she started to massage my ankles and toes which felt as if they had been buried in the ground for a century. She turned me deftly this way and that with the voluptuous air of a small girl playing with her doll; and finally when she made her way towards my midriff it was dolls indeed; I felt a whole surge of new life awake in my loins, new oxygen enter my lungs. The massive vascularity of the big blood vessels was invoked by her strong fingers in their apt progress. "*Et comment ça va là?*" she asked at last, taking up my faltering tulip in strong fingers and kneading it as if for the oven. "Did they not check if it worked?" She was both out-raged, and at the same time delighted by what she had accom-plished, for brave tulip was the size of a Montgolfière and still growing. "*Assez,*" I cried, but my voice must have given me away; the truth was it was delicious. And bending down over me she brought me to a climax so thunderous that I thought I had burst all my stitches. Never had I experienced such an immense slow orgasm – its ripples ran like the tributaries of the Nile throughout the whole nervous system. With this bold stroke she restored me to life and I knew that I could only get well. It was so intense that I started to cry, and bending down tenderly she licked my tears away, dabbing my eyes with a handkerchief. "*Enfin!*" she cried triumphantly, "*C'est ça. Tout va bien.*" And then added in Greek, "*Sikoni monos tou,*" which later I learned meant "It stands up without prompting." Indeed so it was to be, for every day she took tulip for an outing, and every day I waxed in vigour with all this delightful target-practice.

Later, as I grew stronger, she straddled me with her long lean legs and repeated the miracle even more slowly, sharing in the pleasure herself this time. It was rape, the infantile dream of being tied down and raped forcibly by someone who smelt like your mother and had the eyes of a goat. Tall, lanky Theodora was, like her great namesake, a gem. With her I rose from the dead.

FOUR

Paris Twilight

THE GERMAN OFFENSIVES FOLLOWED SO FAST, ONE UPON another, that they left the German General Staff almost breathless with exultation. It was as if all they touched turned to gold – they had difficulty in catching up with themselves. They lived with the unexpected, each victory seeming so easy and so inexpensive that life had the signature of a great adventure. Their own casualty lists were so ridiculously low that it seemed almost beyond belief that within a few months they had shattered and dismantled all the powerful armies surrounding them. They were left sole possessors of the field – a field which now seemed to be expanding itself limitlessly, effortlessly, with only the distant Caucasus mountains as a boundary to German ambitions. All reservations were gone. They were madly in love with the Leader who seemed to them now to have righted every wrong, to have subjugated the traditional enemies of the Reich. The feeling of invincibility made them drunk. The future of Germany was opening before their bemused eyes as if on a huge screen. History had turned turtle and a new German Empire had come into being overnight.

Von Esslin had never been so certain of the appropriateness of his emotions. It was almost with tears, which he uncharacteristically allowed to grip his heart, that he stood to the salute on the sunny Champs Elysées and watched the Leader gliding down through the silent crowds, standing upright in his triumphal car, pale of face, distraught of mien. No wonder he looked pale after the strain of plotting all these vast manoeuvres, directing whole armies like clouds to do his bidding. The giant brain of that little figure had launched Von

Esslin like an avenging catapult first into Warsaw, and now sheer through the Ardennes into a France taken so much by surprise that resistance was nil. The French General Staff had been knocked off their perch. Chaos now reigned. Von Esslin's tanks had behaved with exemplary skill and force – but with such unexpected speed that they had run out of petrol and lost touch with command; had been forced to hold up ordinary commercial petrol pumps like gangsters. It had been great fun. At every halt he could hear the laughter of his "young lions" as they stepped from their machines. Sometimes in sheer exuberance they would burst out laughing and pummel each other playfully. Resistance? There had been a little light skirmishing, that was all. A few *franc-tireurs* had been summarily shot against the walls of village *mairies*. All's fair in love and war! Instructions to the German troops were to administer swift and fatal justice to any who might stand in their way or hesitate to acclaim their triumphant passage. The terrified inhabitants of the towns and villages they entered were in no state to withstand the murderous élan of the Nazi advance. They sank speechless before this grey tide of men and machines. God, but it was beautiful to watch the panzer divisions fan away at speed down the country roads – not unlike the start of some speed trials, say the opening of Le Mans! The dust and whirl of their passage shook the earth and reverberated throatily in the sky. They passed strings, groups, columns of dispirited and disoriented prisoners aimlessly walking in every direction of the compass. They had no point of reference in a world where both morale and communications had failed them. The encircling German forces might appear from anywhere. Of course the heavy fighting was taking place far away to the West, but even here the catastrophe had already declared itself; the defeat was unequivocal. The sunny weather made the run-in on Paris almost a holiday event and Von Esslin felt himself to be getting quite brown from the sunshine; he sat in the back of the staff car with the hood down. Yes, it was not perhaps very wise, but there it was, victory is like strong drink. There had been some light machine-gunning from the air, but it seemed to the Germans in their present euphoria as light as spring rain merely; it rippled the corn and knocked branches off the trees. Von Esslin found himself humming an air from *Don Giovanni* as he read the coded messages which ordered him to group his armour around Belmoth. There was some resistance in that area and once or twice they crossed the tracks of some heavy artillery moving up that way. But no trace of a real road block, no ambushes, no gross air movement. It was wonderful to be alive. They ate ravenously under an oak tree and monitored the crackle of messages coming in; all the real hard work was being done away on the right flank.

While they were eating there came a slow drift of motorised infantry moving up to clear the sticky villages and a great friend of Von Esslin hailed him: "Klaus!" They were enchanted to meet, and overcome with laughter at this piquant encounter so near to Paris. The young officer elected to spend a few moments sharing a sandwich with Von Esslin and exchanging such news as he could mobilise after a night and a day of speedy advancing upon a non-existent enemy. "I can't believe it!" he kept exclaiming. "I hope there is no catch in it!" The elder man patted him on the back and assured him that there could not be. "In one week, when we are billeted and organised, I shall meet you in Paris, at Feydal on the Champs Elysées, and we will drink a vintage champagne in honour of the Führer."

The young officer took the challenge as seriously as it was meant to be taken. He stood up and clicked out his salute, and then took the General's hand in his, saying, "Seriously?"

"*Ein Mann, ein Wort*," said Von Esslin with an explosive

good humour. "My word of honour!" And indeed the somewhat rash promise was redeemed exactly on time, for the two
of them met on the appointed day and hour and found a table
in the sun at which to drink the promised toast. Moreover the
Leader himself was there to look in upon the drinking. It was
unforeseen, but it gave the toast significance.

But there was still some resistance ahead; Von Esslin felt
the tanks and infantry gradually building up behind them like a
wave. A staff officer reproached him for travelling thus in so
very vulnerable a car, and though nettled he accepted the
greater safety of a command car with a turret. All that night
they were bogged down with this invisible resistance ahead,
and then towards dawn it eased; it was as if someone had
pulled a plug out of a bath. Everything started to flow again
and a new momentum was achieved.

What surprised him – yet war is like that – was that he
seemed to have missed all the major engagements of this
period. They felt almost like holidaymakers. He had a confused memory of his young bronzed giants stripped to the
waist, wading about in the ripe corn. It was beautiful to see – in
his heart bourgeoned a renewed love for Germany. But what
the devil was actually happening? He called for operational
signals and a field orientation, and in doing so made contact
with another of his cronies and contemporaries, a General
Paulus who telephoned him to sketch in the background, the
backcloth against which, like a blind man, Von Esslin was
advancing. It was from Paulus that he learned of the tremendous exodus of the civilian populations of Belgium and the
northern sectors of France – the thousands upon thousands
who sought an imaginary safety in the southern parts of France
which they believed would be behind the lines.

"What lines?" The German advance had been so hectic
that frequently these marching hordes arrived in towns and
villages only to find that they were already in German hands!

Confusion was total—their victory was more than just physical, it was quite as much psychological. All the little towns in the southern sector were already swollen with itinerant refugees for whom no sort of preparations had been envisaged. In Toulouse and Nîmes people slept on the pavements like gypsies. And during all this period of turmoil and upset Von Esslin's forces advanced without undue stress or strain until they lay not far from the open road to Paris. It was unbelievable. Nightingales were singing in the woods. They had captured the contents of a wine cellar and the General sipped some wine and ate a biscuit for his lunch, though he spoke long and earnestly to his troop leaders. They must spare no effort to contain any disposition towards drink in the ranks of the tank-troopers. But how marvellous, how warming victory was! Terrified peasants here and there gave the Nazi salute in a cringing sort of way; then, delighted that they had not been shot at, they smirked. "The French will welcome us," he thought, "for their heart was never in this war, and we have much to offer them in the New Order." He nodded with a frown, as if he had need to insist on this point, to convince himself.

The world unrolled itself around him with a grand polyphonic flamboyance; he was dazed with the march of affairs. Moreover one of his tactical ploys had come to the notice of the Chief of Staff and earned him commendation! It was a lucky accident. Yet it had seemed to him self-evident, obvious—just the sort of thing that improvises itself in the heat of battle. In the general surge forward they had here and there met with road blocks and some spasmodic disposition to delay them. He had passed his panzer on to the adjacent railway line and let it crackle down the permanent way, to turn the flank of these obstacles. The use of railways . . . it would go into army manuals on tactics. It had been vastly amusing to watch the tanks hopping on and off the main line in order to let trains go through – the French Railways system simply could not admit to the existence of a war, much less to German tanks flopping in and out of their railway stations like so many rabbits. Here and there they fired a few bursts at a train, but it was largely for the fun of the thing. Once they even emptied an express – the people came scuttling out deathly pale with their hands above their heads. "What to do with them?" asked a bronzed patrol leader as he nudged them amiably towards the waiting-room of the station. "There was a French officer – that one over there – who fired at us with a pistol." Von Esslin turned curtly away with a bark: "You know your orders." As he got into his car again he heard the ripple of a machine-gun inside the station.

The rest of the tank brigade turned right across fields and joined the general advance upon a main road now littered with abandoned farm wagons and personal belongings. It was a great temptation to stop and examine all those burst suitcases from which protruded every sort of gear. Thank goodness, they were on wheels and moving fast – he would not have to read them a lesson about looting. That was to follow, of course, but in systematic fashion, in a punitive manner. Indeed the whole philosophy of their campaigns had already been laid down for them. They were to be just like Napoleon's: campaigning *à la maraude*, as the French would soon find out. For a moment Von Esslin swelled with pride, and then the sentiment was swallowed up in a sort of guilty fury. France was finished! He struck his boot twice, hard, with a cane and immersed himself in deeply gratifying memories of the noise his steel-meshed caterpillars had made upon the railway lines. A flight of planes ahead of them swooped down and started chattering like magpies. Their advance slowed. Thick smoke and a series of thuds spoke of an engagement ahead; a burst oil drum had flooded the road and the hollow tanks swished about, as if in heavy rain. He pulled them off the main road and into the green fields on either side of it. It was late afternoon, soon dusk would come; they must gain as much ground as they could before bivouacking for the night. He called back for a few bus-loads of infantry to support the tanks as they combed the forest, firing odd bursts into the greenery in order to flush out troops which might be hiding there.

Once it had become fact it seemed so obvious, so inevitable, the total victory which had already altered the fate and disposition of so many nations – the British rout, the French collapse, the Low Countries ... So many and so diverse were the successes that it was impossible to sketch in the boundaries of a future – for it spread out in every direction. He was not simply being Junker when, in response to the question: "In your view what should we next consider doing?" he had replied acidly: "I am a soldier of the Reich, I have no views. I simply do what the Leader says." His interlocutor, a staff officer in the map caravan section, looked disgusted. Nevertheless he saluted and bowed in agreement, trying to keep his look free from irony. But the truth of the matter was that Von Esslin was rattled – events had outdistanced him and he had genuine difficulty in marshalling them into coherence. He hoped that he might soon find himself back on the Eastern Front – a vague sense of *malaise* haunted him, something at the heart of the French collapse. Nor did the cringing, hysterical reception afforded his men by the citizens of Paris do anything to allay his sense of disorientation. They kicked some police units out of their billets in Avalon and took possession of this sensitive entry to the capital. But pretty soon the general efficiency of their forces had carved out a reasonable way of living – which afforded Von Esslin frequent short leaves to Paris where he found that the girls eyed his uniform with great respect. Once a young *fille de joie* asked him if he would care to come with her and give her a good beating with his cane. She would consider paying him, she said, which was at least original. He was shocked, and contemptuous of the French race for taking their defeat so contentedly. He muttered some opprobrious epithet and hurried on over the bridge to the *quais*, where he found many German books which he bought and sent home to his mother. The mails were now getting through and he heard from her every month or so; in exchange he wrote to her to retail his adventures and to describe Paris, which he had always found so fascinating, and which was now, in defeat, almost more so.

When he had drunk a cointreau or two he became flushed, heavily sentimental, and in these moods he would sometimes escort a street walker to her grubby lodgings. But the period in question was brief, like the withdrawal from the southern sector of France, and within a few months he found himself posted with his armour to Tulle – on the edge of the occupied zone which he himself had always been convinced could not co-exist peacefully with the occupied north. France was like a Christmas stocking – everything had been pushed down into it, refugees, Jews, criminals, and members of a hypothetical Resistance; not to mention the fact that the Allies were sending in agents the whole time in an attempt to gather information and to promote insurrection. It was rumoured that Von Esslin was to have a new command, and he pondered deeply whether it might not be something to do with the push into Russia, for nobody he knew had believed in the factitious pact that had been signed – it had been a manoeuvre to free a flank against Russian perfidy while France was dealt with. Nor could one be very much in doubt about future possibilities, for the armoured build-up in the north hinted of such preoccupations. Meanwhile, the absurd *drôle de guerre* had given place to an equally *drôle de paix*! The French really believed that it was only a matter of time before the two million French prisoners were released to them, to be accompanied perhaps by a general German withdrawal from the country after the signing of some sort of peace pact and the payment of an indemnity. It lingered on for months, this fatal misapprehension, in spite of the desert battles, the battles for Greece, Yugoslavia, and so on. People clustered round the symbol of a France which would retrieve her freedom and greatness, though the old Marshal Pétain, with his avuncular speeches and ineffectual acts, was hardly the man to inspire such hopes. Anti-British feeling was at its height, for the English by their ill-considered bombings and hostile activities risked upsetting the Germans who would then obviously punish the French civilians. In the midst of all this confused and incoherent sermonising they managed to establish for a few months a life as quiet as any seminarist's, with frequent Paris leave for troops, Avalon being so near, and plenty of time to refit and rekit against the next round – whenever that might be.

In the meantime, as Von Esslin wrote to his mother, some new units had come in to anchor alongside them and he had found four or five bosom cronies whom she knew well – old Keller and Le Fals and Kranz; they made up a four for bridge in the mess of an evening. They also made their descents on Paris together in jovial Bavarian style, and all being of a Catholic persuasion they attended many services in some of the great churches and cathedrals of Paris. "The music is marvellous," he wrote, with real feeling, "and I am often reminded of Vienna where we so often heard an unfamiliar mass, only to discover that it had been written by a Mozart or Haydn for that particular church!" But though this period was rich in its enthusiasm and carefreeness there was an invisible preoccupation growing up in the back of his mind; it seemed like an ever-lengthening shadow over the future. At first Russia had opened up before their eyes like forest fire, like a volcano erupting – the scale of the assault was dumbfounding. But now new elements had begun to intrude – resistance in Africa, in Russia, in the Balkans, in Norway . . . It was slowly thickening, like a dish of lentils from too fast a cooking! He brushed the feeling aside as somewhat of an illusion, but it persisted.

Nevertheless . . . a thousand bombers over Cologne! And the B.B.C. radio programmes from over the water gathering self-confidence and density – always with that ominous drum-beat taken from Beethoven! He was impatient now for some action, in order to avoid such reflections.

The new Government of Vichy was all smarm and affability, but it was obvious that without the weight of German forces watching over it its life would have been a precarious one, so evenly were the French divided between those who genuinely favoured Nazism, and those who found the occupation intolerable. For the moment the public had not felt the full weight of the German yoke. But it would not be long before the shortages and the ration-cards brought home the sombre reality. But such general considerations hardly touched the fringe of Von Esslin's preoccupations at that moment; his speculations about the future were crystallised by the visit of three Vichy functionaries who arrived in an old car one morning and demanded audience. They were, so they said, attached to the French Second Bureau and they announced that within a matter of weeks the German army would move into the unoccupied zone as a sort of unofficial police force for the Vichy Government. Von Esslin was to be part of this operation.

It threw him into a frightful rage to hear these shabby Frenchmen deliberating upon his future, and he was almost tempted from spite to put them under arrest. His face flushed dark as he told them, between clenched teeth, that he took his orders from the German High Command only – from nobody else; they were abashed by his vehemence and apologetic for the gaffe they had perpetrated. Nevertheless one of them showed him a letter of appointment signed by the *Reichs-führer S.S. und Chef der deutschen Polizei* – no less a personage than Himmler himself – and Von Esslin's heart sank. As a soldier he resented being a tool of the politicals and a weapon used by them in their secret wars. Nor would it have been any use to ask the rank of the new appointee – he might simply be a modest colonel-general and yet still have the power to report directly to Berlin behind his back and manipulate the armed forces by remote control. Besides, Von Esslin did not want a quasi-civilian posting in a backwater, with no possibilities of promotion. He applied instantly for a posting to the Russian theatre, but the message remained without answer. Silence fell. Perplexity grew. He heard no more of the dark-suited Vichy functionaries. Then one day his orderly told him that someone was waiting for him in his office and he found Fischer there, installed in a swivel chair, cap tilted back, paring his nails with a paperknife. "Good morning, General," he said with his lazy and insolent smile, but he made no move to rise. Von Esslin remained standing and gazed at him silently. He wore the S.S. uniform, but with a shiny black greatcoat that hid insignia. He had very light blue eyes of great brilliance and weakness. It was as if you could see pieces of the sky through his skull, for the eyes did not join in the smile. "Pray be seated, my General," he said, smiling, showing perfect white teeth. An incandescent smile but without any heat. "You are in my chair," growled Von Esslin. He did not want to take the suppliant's seat in his own office. The younger man shrugged and rose. He was tall and thin. He had rings on his fingers. At first blush this might have hinted at an innate effeminacy, but the impression was rapidly dispelled by the empty eyes. They might as well have been the empty sockets of a Roman statue, so little did they convey of sensibility or intelligence. He turned slowly towards the window and briefly traced a pattern on it with his forefinger. Then he turned round once more and again flashed Von Esslin that brilliant smile, empty as a neon sign. "You will get marching orders on Monday. I will go on directly and be waiting for you when you arrive."

Von Esslin sat down massively and treated the young man to a grimly bad-tempered smile intended to express his disdain and resentment of such cavalier manners. "But of where do you speak?" he asked, and the young man answered, "Avignon has been selected as the headquarters of the force, you will group there. The S.S. will quarter quite near at hand. All this is to help the Vichy régime – they fear the situation is sliding out of control; too many communists, Resistance groups, Intelligence groups. We shall have to begin with an impact. You will receive a list of villages where hostages are to be taken and liquidated." He looked suddenly sick and sad, like a sort of blond Mephisto wounded by a memory. Ruminating, his tongue travelled round his teeth, as if to gather fragments of something he had eaten. Then he said abruptly, "I look forward to working with you. General, do you play chess?" Von Esslin said that he did not, though in fact he did. "Pity," said Fischer, and once more gave that dazzling, disconnected smile. His skin was very pale, his cheeks bloodless and anaemic-looking, his eyelashes of a lightness that was practically albino. "Pity!"

"What is your rank?" asked Von Esslin in a heavy, boorish tone; of course it would make no difference to the day-to-day issues. From his accent he thought he detected a sort of clever Munich garage mechanic in uniform. Fischer pulled down the collar of his greatcoat sufficiently for Von Esslin to see the characteristic insignia of the Waffen S.S. "I thought so," he said. Fischer nodded with satisfaction. "We will work together very well," he said, and added, but in a much politer tone, "May I see your hand, General?" Caught by surprise Von Esslin laid his hands out before him on the desk and the young man leaned attentively over them for a second, though he did not touch them. Then he straightened up, smacked his lips and said, "I thank you." He went to the door, and standing by it, with the doorknob in his hand, he allowed his right hand to sketch a formal salute of great punctilio, at the same time bringing his heels softly together. Was it mockery? It was hard to decide, with that dead, smiling face gazing at him. Technically he should have risen and responded, but he was still full of anger, so he contented himself with a curt nod. The door closed behind Fischer, and Von Esslin turned with despatch to his telephone. He must find out from Paris what was brewing, what the future held for him.

When he managed to contact operations he was told that movement orders had already been despatched, that he would have them within a few hours, together with details of the units engaged. So! He felt a touch of perplexity and unease grow up inside him as he listened. It was to be a take-over, no resistance was to be anticipated; he would consolidate around key towns and pave the way for the French Milice – the recruited Nazis of French origin. One of his oldest cronies was high up in postings, and Von Esslin broke the rules of military etiquette in telephoning him to say testily: "Forgive me, but do you know any reason why my transfer is being passed over? This is almost a civilian command they offer me! Why?" His friend's suppositions were not very elaborate. "Passed over?" he said diplomatically. "That is hardly the word *surely* – you have been *mentioned* quite recently and that means despatches. It's just an administrative bungle which will sort itself out in good time. Be patient."

As a matter of fact Von Esslin found these blandishments anything but reassuring; his mind once more began its hovering around a private thought which had for some time been troubling him. Was his Catholicism going to tell against him professionally? The idea had already presented itself to him more than once, though so far there had been nothing to confirm it. Well . . . once or twice he had heard ironic phrases fall from the lips of S.S. officers which hinted that one could not compromise between God and Hitler. Once he heard a young man say: "When a Nazi goes to confession . . ." but the rest of the phrase had been lost in ironic laughter. Then again, on another occasion, there had been a reference to a Nazi storm-trooper on church parade which had also led to strenuous guffaws. Was this new posting a tacit indication that his religion had come to the notice of his superiors? Shaving in the mirror, he went guiltily over the last few times he had been to church with his friends – *they* would hardly have informed on him? Why "inform"? "You are being stupid and suspicious," he told himself aloud, and stepped into his bath with a sigh and a shrug of the shoulders.

That night the detailed orders came and he read them through with cynicism and distaste; those Waffen units, why so many? They were going to break civilian morale, he supposed, in the traditional way; the Waffen units were Himmler's personal toy, and consequently almost a law unto themselves. On the other hand Von Esslin's own command had shed a lot of tanks – they were wanted for Russia perhaps? But there was no doubt that as a command this was going to be a backwater of little importance where nobody could expect to earn glory and advancement. It was not exactly a slight, yet he almost felt it to be one. There was nobody to protect him up there at the General Command, nobody to whom he could appeal privately.

He felt suddenly very much alone.

FIVE

In Geneva

THE STREET IN GENEVA AT THE END OF WHICH THE OLD
Bar de la Navigation stands runs back from the lakeside
with its bulky Corniche and scrambles up a steepish
slope. It is an undecided sort of street, it seems at cross-purposes
with itself, for it begins as a modest side-street, becomes for a
block or so a wider boulevard, then breaks off abruptly to
become a narrow dog-leg passage giving on to an evil-smelling
court full of lidless dustbins. It was precisely this air of
lugubrious secrecy that endeared itself to our hero (heroes,
rather, for Toby had appeared in Geneva to join forces with
Sutcliffe). It seemed to them the ideal place for those confidential mid-morning potations and games of pool for which
the Foreign Office had invented the phrase "elevenses", after
the hour of the morning when one feels one most needs a short
swift drink, or a long "unwinder", to use slang.

They were both engaged on what was then known as
"war work". In the damp basements of the Consulate (below
lake level) a flock of new temporary offices had been created,
each separated from the next by a wooden partition. Services
of the most heterogeneous sort rubbed elbows. Oxford had
sacrificed Toby to the needs of M.E.3 (counter-espionage),
while a disgruntled Sutcliffe, pushed out of Vienna by the
troubles, translated confidential German documents for the
Military Attaché's department and waited angrily for his wife
to be restored to him by the psychiatrists. It cost the earth. She
was housed at the Prangens clinic across the lake. (Every
morning he used to go out on the balcony of the small flat
which he shared with his friend, and shout aloud, "I want my

wife" in German; but it appeared to have no effect on the
unimaginative Swiss.)

The two huge men, so like ninepins, shared as best they
could this ugly flat which was impossible to keep in decent
order. Chaos reigned; neither was tidy, neither could cook.
They heated up tinned food in a saucepan of hot water and ate
it with sadness and disrelish, under the belief that they were
economising. On Mondays a desultory charwoman did what
she could to restore some order in their lives. In the evenings
they often sat down to play poker, wearing pyjamas with broad
stripes and eyeshades of yellow celluloid like the croupiers at
Las Vegas. Their raptness might have persuaded one that they
were playing for higher stakes than matches. Ah, the nights
of the early war, fading down into the blue lantern-lit dusk with
their dense fogs smearing visibility on the lake! The Swiss
army was on "alert", the country mobilised, the towns blacked
out, though not entirely. It was almost a curfew, with most bars
and bordels closing early. The world lived in a tension without
remedy. The authorities had tried the air raid sirens and found
they worked. The noise was deeply depressing and reinforced
an innate tendency to stay at home and drink tea laced with
applejack or plum brandy. Toby called these confections
"spine-twisters" from the shuddering caused by the first
mouthful. Aptly.

The potations of mid-morning, however, were different,
consisting of hot grogs with brown sugar (despite the muggy
climate) in a vain attempt to defeat the chronic bronchitis they
shared, the result of smoking too many Celtiques – the *tabac
gris* of over-run France. This affliction rendered the morning
cacophonous, due to a joint symphony of coughing so violent
that it brought the Swiss couples who lived below out on to the
landing, wondering if they should call for help. Sutcliffe
imitated a young cat being tried for size, Goddard a surly
Turkish porter being mauled by a bear. Sometimes they united

to imitate the national anthems of various nations, or else to repeat in musical coughs the phrase "*Le docteur Schwarz est un pot de chambre*". Schwarz was the analyst who had fled from Vienna carrying with him his choicer and richer patients – for not all could find the money to move with him. (Sutcliffe's overdraft did not bear thinking upon.) It was Schwarz who had been bitten by a paranoid patient and granted a month's leave to recover and attend to his infected ear-lobe. "Such are the love-bites analysts receive," commented Sutcliffe bitterly to Constance when she answered the phone. "I wish my wife would react as positively." But Constance was not there to be made fun of; she turned the jest coldly aside, saying, "I will certainly see you if you wish for any information. I am abreast of the dossier, but I am only standing in for Dr. Schwarz, holding the fort. I am not treating her, though I have established contact with her and had several talks. You may come at ten tomorrow." She was disposed to be rather priggish, and received a rather unfavourable impression of him due to his dirty fingernails and lack of physical spruceness. Sutcliffe was intimidated by her beauty, but had only the faintest idea of who she was. Then came an accidental reference to Blanford in the conversation and she saw his eyes widen. "Goodness!" he cried and sat staring at her. "You must be Constance, the other sister."

"Then who are you?" asked Constance with hesitation, for a sort of feeling of familiarity had begun to grow up inside her, vague as a cloud. His name fell with a thud upon her ear. "It's not true!" she exclaimed. But it was, it was he. They sat silent for a long moment, staring at one another, and then she began to talk rapidly, erratically, still not quite sure of her man. But the sofa of Freud clinched the matter – for she had seen his name on the invoice. "So after all you are real!" Sutcliffe laughed and said, "Everybody is real."

It was a crazy thing to say, if you were someone who did

not believe in fairies, but then he was given to immoderate optimism when in the presence of beauty, to which he remained forever susceptible. But he smarted under her coolness, he found her a right bitch and he told Toby so. "*Une garce,*" he said, preferring the French word with the broad vowel sound spread like legs: like those satisfactory words and phrases he treasured – "*gâtisme ou le relâchement des sphincters*".

His friend looked at him with interest and asked, "Why are you so much up on end?"

Sutcliffe replied soberly, gravely, "I am sure that Aubrey will end up in love with her and I understand why. It's those sea-green eyes and the snow tan. But she's a real Swiss prig."

"But she's English."

"She's both: a double priggery."

She had initially refused to meet him on social terms, outside the consulting-room, and he supposed this to be a question of medical etiquette, mixed with the evident distaste she seemed to feel for his company. So he was surprised when she telephoned to his office and said in her rapid, rather strained way, "I feel I was rather uncivil to you, and probably hurt your feelings; I am sorry if it is so. I would like to repent and also accept your kind invitation to a drink. This evening, if you wish." He was both elated and nonplussed by the sudden change of wind. "Good," said Toby when informed, "if she's medical she might give us some tips about geriatric aid. I am putting up feebler and feebler performances with the typists' pool. Little Miss Farthingale is languishing, and I am heartily ashamed of the poor motility of my product. The damn stuff can hardly swim, it turns over on its back and floats. The girls are right to protest." Sutcliffe clicked his tongue disapprovingly. "We can't ask her that. You will just have to live with your humiliation, Toby. But come to think of it, why don't you try a Diplomat's Aid?"

"What's that, may I ask?"

"Get a nice thick office rubber band and make a tourniquet for your closest friend; place it rather high up and fairly tight. It will work wonders. I learned it from the little Indian typist. She says that in the Foreign Office . . ."

Toby was elated by this information and unearthing a series of rubber bands from his briefcase he retired to the lavatory in order to find something suitable for his troubled circumstances. Sutcliffe walked down to the lake to meet the ferry, for he despaired of anyone finding the little bar, just on a set of telephoned instructions. It was tea-time and the day was fine. Constance waved to him from the deck and he replied.

She was not at her best, she looked tired and strained. Indeed her general appearance, for a girl who liked to be well turned out, bordered on the unkempt; her white mackintosh was not too clean and a missing top button had been replaced by a safety pin. Her hair had been badly cut and was all puppy dog's tails. The truth was that she was still in a state of semi-shock, almost collapse, due to the news of Sam's death. It was simply amazing – for they had both imagined that they were strong enough to face up to such an eventuality, that the life-giving power of their magnetic love would resist even this sort of separation. Love makes you naive, she realised it now; they had been acting a part, the part of two golden immortals from some romantic opera. Now here they were, under the wheels of the Juggernaut – or rather, she was; in a sense he had escaped and left her to gather up the remains of the thought "death". No, that was not all, for some days after the news she had received to her surprise one brief letter duly transmitted by the Army Post Office to the Consulate. It had made an elaborate journey, the voice of her dead "husband". Yes, all of a sudden the word had resonance, an old-fashioned gravity and pith. The whole of her small apartment by the lake seemed impregnated with it. That is why she had taken to sleeping at her office in the clinic, on a camp bed against the further wall.

Everything, even her work, seemed suddenly insipid; the chance collision with Sutcliffe now filled her with conflicting emotions. She wanted to avoid talking about Sam with half of her: with the other half she realised that it might help her to find her way out of this temporary numbness, the way back into life. So here he came, patient as an old dog, to ask for news of the pale slender girl, who was now sliding away down the long slopes of melancholia which would lead only to mania.

"I should not visit her at the moment. She will only start wringing her hands and weeping again – all day long."

"But you know as well as I do, she holds me responsible for everything, and it is not fair."

She shook her head. "Nothing is fair with the insane." Sutcliffe placed his hands on the top of his head like King Lear and said, "I destroyed her dolls. How could I have been such a fool?" But the trouble went deeper than that, much deeper.

"The negress calls every day, and with her she seems a little better. They play noughts and crosses."

"It's appropriate to the day and age," he said bitterly. "Indeed when one sees the state of the world one wonders why one should call her back to it – supposing we could."

Before going to join Toby in the bar they walked a while in the gardens which border the lakeside and she told him of Blanford's wound, which made him, rather unaccountably, chuckle.

"I must get in touch with him again," he said, nothing more. But when she mentioned Sam's death – as a therapeutic measure in order to take its pulse, so to speak – he looked at her with sympathy and a certain rough affection. "It's just the beginning," he said. "Have you seen what they have reserved for the Jews?" Who had not? "Anyway," she said, "Freud is safely away even though all the books are lost; but copies exist here, thank goodness." He looked at her with interest and said, "Did you know him?" She nodded and smiled, as if at the memory of a pleasant and rich meeting. Indeed it had been the great turning-point in her life and she was prepared to defend the old philosopher to the death. Sensing this, Sutcliffe was prepared to tease her a little; under his breath he sang a stave of "Dear old Pals" in an amended version.

> "Dear old Fraud, jolly old Fraud,
> We'll be together whatever the weather."

"O cut it out," she said, "I am sure you don't believe it." He grinned, for he did not. "I got to know him quite well," he said, "and he was no humbug. He gave me several interviews and outlined his system with great elegance and modesty. He emphasised its limits. He gave me half a dozen consultations on the couch to show me how the thing worked, which was jolly decent. The thing is it doesn't – not for anything really serious, anything like psychosis."

"He never pretended it did."

"But Schwarz did, and it is his messing about that aggravated the condition of my wife; but that's not your affair, I suppose, since you are only a locum."

"Well, I can't pronounce on his cases," she said with the light of battle in her eye. "But I am glad you met Freud himself."

"He was very amusing with his Jewish moneylender touch. I teased him a bit about love being an investment – invested libido. But the old darling was serious. Jews can never see themselves from the outside. They are astonished when you say that they are this or that. They are naive, and so was he, very much so. The way his hand came out for the money at the end of the hour, when the clock struck, was a scream. I asked him if he would take a cheque but he said, 'What? And declare it to the Income Tax?' He insisted on cash and when he put it in his pocket he shuffled it until it tinkled, which put him in a great good humour. He looked just like Jules Verne at such moments; indeed there was a sort of similarity of imagination between the two fantasists. Anyway the idea amused him for he had read and admired Jules Verne. But when I told him that the whole of his system was a money-making plant, to be paid for just listening, and by the hour, he chuckled. 'People want to suffer,' he said, 'and we must help them. It's the decent thing to do. It's not only Jews who like money, you know. Besides, the hand-to-hand payment is an essential part of the treatment. You feel the pinch or the pain in your infantility.' "

Constance mistrusted the depth of his knowledge in the clinical sense. It was one thing to talk all round a subject in terms of philosophy; it was quite another to adapt it to a therapy. "I am boring you," he said, and she shook her head. "No, I was thinking of other things, of that whole period when I started medicine. Tell me more."

Sutcliffe, when they had retired to the bar once more, called for drinks and said, "There is little more to tell. I was with him for such a short time – sufficient however to foster a great respect. The biggest pessimist since Spinoza. For the last session I brought him the fee in coin of the smallest possible denomination. I had a little leather bag with a drawstring round the mouth, which I filled with farthings or their equivalent. He was quite surprised when I presented it and told him that it was his fee. 'Good Lord,' he said with a laugh, 'you've got diarrhoea!' "

Toby drew on his pipe and listened with half an ear; he was not really abreast of the subject and knew little of the personalities under discussion, but Sutcliffe seemed well enough informed. "And then we left Vienna, and old Fraud moved back to his flat to a new consulting room, abandoning his gloomy rooms and the old couch where she had set out all the elements of our married life like someone sets up toy soldiers for a battle, or dolls for a picnic. But when I spoke to the old boy about us he simply shook his head and said, 'The story of narcissism is always the same story.' I felt an absurd temptation to weep for myself and wring my hands, but to what end? He told me that I must sublimate the distress in a book, which God knows I have been trying to do from the very beginning – even before I felt the distress, so to speak. I have from early adolescence suffered from *Schmerz, Angst,* and for good measure piles. My first publisher gave me an advance to write a cookery book about Egyptian food. I was wild with joy and took ship for Egypt at once. But the very first meal I had – there was a French letter in the salad. And things have gone on like that ever since." Under the rather lame banter she felt the massive depression and the stress. In his rough lumbering manner she found something comforting and helpless; he was like an old blind bear tied to a post. For her own part she had her own share of distress to cope with; she realised that she did not want to go back to her cold sterile little flat with its over-flowing bookshelves and undone washing-up. Since she had received the letter from Sam she had suddenly taken it into her head to flee across the lake; at least at the clinic she had the company of other consultants and nurses, while even the presence of the insane all round her seemed to afford a paradoxical sort of comfort. But now the evening was drawing on and Toby had a dinner engagement. He bowed himself away with solemnity, hoping to have the pleasure once more . . . The seventeenth-century sentiments became his vast form very well, he was made for awkward bows and gawkish scrapings. That left Sutcliffe. She thought: "It must be strange to exist only in somebody's diary, like Socrates – we only have Plato's word for his existence."

He was thinking: "And this book which I have always had in deep soak, when will it be finished? When I stop breathing? But the idea behind this furtive activity has always been that ideal book – the titanic do-it-yourself kit, *le roman appareil.*

After all, why not a book full of spare parts of other books, of characters left over from other lives, all circulating in each other's bloodstreams – yet all fresh, nothing second-hand, twice chewed, twice breathed. Such a book might ask you if life is worth breathing, if death is worth looming. . . . Be ye members of one another. I hear a voice say, 'What disease did the poor fellow get?' 'Death!' 'Death? Why didn't he say so? Death is nothing if one takes it in time.'"

She was thinking: "To be instructively wounded is the most one can ask of love. What innocents we were! Now I see it all so clearly. Some marriages just smoulder along, others chime by couples, but in ours we were blissed out. What luck! But how hard to pick oneself up after such a knockdown blow. What now? I shall live alone like Aubrey, sleep alone, on my right side, pointing north-south; yes, quite alone."

He thought: "To commingle and intersperse contingent realities – that's the game! After all, how few are the options open to us – few varieties of human shape, mental dispositions, scales of behaviour: hardly more numerous than the available Christian names used by the race. How many coats of reality does it take to get a nice clean surface to the apprehension? We are all fragments of one another; everyone has a little bit of everything in his make-up. From the absolute point of view – Aristotle's Fifth Substance, say – all persons are the same person and all situations are identical or vastly similar. The universe must be dying of boredom. Yet obstinately I dream of such a book, full of not completely discrete characters, of ancestors and descendants all mixed up – could such people walk in and out of each other's lives without damaging the quiddity of each other? Hum. And the whole book arranged in diminished fifths from the point of view of orchestration. A big switchy book, all points and sidings. A Golgotha of a book. I must talk to Aubrey about it." He bowed his head while an imaginary audience applauded lengthily.

She thought: "To wake up one day with a vision of Absolute Good! What would it be like?"

Sutcliffe, who sucked a pipe in order to supply a substitute against smoking cigarettes, threw it down and lit yet another Celtique, snapping his fingers defiantly at his own reflection in the gloomy café mirror.

The drink was beginning to tell on them; she felt quite unsteady and all-overish. "We must eat something," he said and bade the taciturn waiter produce his dismal menu. He read it through, groaning: "*Plat du jour*, baked beans on toast. Let's have that."

She was too weak to resist for they must eat something or be completely dismasted by the alcohol. Besides, it prolonged the evening, for she had not yet decided whether her courage would permit her to resume residence in her flat which was hard by, or whether she would need to go back to the clinic across the lake. This at least set a time limit upon the decision, for the last ferry left at eleven at night. Her heart was beating much faster and from time to time she felt flushed and a trifle incoherent. The food was produced and they fell upon it with zeal. "What a swiz life is," said the big man between mouthfuls, "I saw an advertisement for a smart secretary for my office, and I answered it only to find that the girl in question – O dear! Masses of dirty hair attached to a broomstick. So I sent her to Toby's department where they are all colour blind." She was not listening. She was thinking: "How intensely one dreams of the past." She said aloud, "I keep dreaming of the last summer we had in Provence – it is so vivid. Small things come out so clearly. Sometimes very trivial things about Hilary my brother and Aubrey. Do you know, when Aubrey became absolutely insufferable with his preaching about how superior to us the French were we set up an ambush for him. The one subject which he always brought up at the end of one of those futile arguments about Art or Sex was the richness of the French language. It had many more pejorative epithets than English, he would assert loftily. It got on our nerves so much that we rehearsed a little act and whenever he brought this up we used to chant in unison, with terrible facial grimaces, the half dozen or so which he always cited. It doesn't sound funny but if you saw the grimaces and his own crestfallen blush . . ."

"What were they?"

"*Cuistre*! *Mufle*! *Goinfre*! *Rustre*! *Jobard*! *Goujat*! *Fourbe*! *Gniaf*!"

"Good. I didn't think his French was up to much."

"At any rate we cured him that summer."

"Good."

But she sighed and said, "I wonder what he is doing now, all alone in that palace with the Nile flowing on his ceiling."

"I can tell you," said Sutcliffe, "but it's only a novelist's guess. He is listening with ever-increasing irritation to the nasal whine of Cade, his servant, who is massaging him reproachfully. Cade has found out about the goings-on with the Greek nurse and he is saying, in his lugubrious Cockney accent, 'For my part, sir, I never go with a girl without wearing a conundrum.'"

"I must try and get home," she said, "but I need help after all these drinks." They negotiated the gloom of the place with its vast dusty clumps of furniture and arrived in the street only to find that it was raining—an autumn drizzle for which neither was prepared. "The quickest is my flat," she said, glad that the issue had been decided for her by an extraneous factor. "It's just around the corner." They scurried with as much despatch as their condition permitted and reached the house in somewhat unsteady shape. Here she had a struggle to find her key, but find it she did and they took the lift up to the second floor. The place was very dusty and had clearly not been inhabited for a while; there was washing-up about and through an open door one saw an unmade bed. But the little studio room over the lake was pleasant and the sofas were comfortable, which invited Sutcliffe to relax while she went in search of further drink. There was only vodka left in the drink cupboard and this, she realised, was going to be fatal to him; but it was obvious that he had already decided to fall where he stood – he had shaken off his clumsy shoes and was examining the big toe of his left foot which protruded from a torn sock. "I like these Swiss suburban flats," he said, "they are homey. There is always a *membre fantôme* on the hallstand and a Valéry open in the loo. They are inhabited by psychoanalysts and abortionists."

"Thank you."

"Not at all."

"I see you don't believe in science."

"I do, though; but in the poetry of science."

"And happiness?"

"Has nothing to do with the matter. You cannot create this obscure and marvellous field of energy – *le bonheur* – by advocacy or the whip, by force or by guile, but only by pleading. Poetry begins there, and prayer also; they lead you to a thought, and science comes out of that thought. But the pedigree is long." He broke off and erupted in a string of hiccoughs which rather alarmed him. Then he went on: "The sixpence in the plum pudding must be taken on trust. We must believe. It is really there. It is the holy Inkling."

"You are babbling," she said reproachfully, and he shook his head sadly over her, saying, "You have received a tremendous shock with Sam's death." And at this, quite involuntarily, they both burst out crying simultaneously, joining hands. It was such a relief to discover that she could produce so human a reaction at last; he cried like an old horse, she cried like a humble adolescent, awkwardly and noisily. And while she cried she thought: "The arrival of death on the scene brings an enormous sense of the sweetness of things – the richness of impermanence which one has always avoided, feared. 'The dying fall' is true for all of us: clowns, heroes, lovers, cads, fools, freaks, kings, commoners, the sane, the mad, or the silent."

She laid her distraught drunken head on his shoulder while he, unmanned by emotion and exhausted by his potations, stroked it with his coarse palms and repeated helplessly, "There, my dear, there." And all the while she was thinking: "The long studied suppuration of confessional analysis! The fatigue and intricacy! The weeping wall of the Jewish spybrain hovering around schemes of investment; picking the scabs off wounds and wondering why they bleed. Scar-tissue of un-assuaged desires!" Then she burst out: "He wrote me such a foolish letter with nothing in it but schoolboy jokes and just one good sincere passage. Wait, I'll get it. I left it in the loo."

She had wanted to tear it up and flush it away but instead had put it beside the bath where the steam had gummed half its leaves together. Now she picked up the flimsy mass and peeling it like an onion found a sheet. She read out: " 'Connie, death is nothing and that is the truth. Pain of course one fears a bit, but amnesia comes with it. Our great weakness, the place where we all cave in, and can't take it, is love.' "

"But the letter," said Sutcliffe, "it's all glued together." She replied: "I know it by heart. But it came too late. That is why I am so terribly upset. In it he told me that whatever happened I must keep the child, for we both practically knew for certain that I was pregnant; at that time I told him that I would certainly not hold him up by having one, in case when he came back he no longer felt keen on me."

She knocked on her forehead with her knuckles. "I was being noble. I did not wish to risk that he might stay with me against his will because of a child begotten in haste and by accident during the war. After all, I thought, when our love re-establishes itself there will be time enough to have another one.

So I made away with it. I made away with it. And hardly had I done so than the news of his death came, and of course the child became infinitely precious – if only I had kept it!"

He realised now the full extent of her distress and guilt. She stood in the centre of the room with hanging head and relived that cold afternoon in the little apartment of the old doctor – lying spreadeagled in a dentist's chair hoisted against a white pane of glass where the clouds from the lake surface reflected themselves. Lying with her legs apart while the old man talked rapidly, confidentially. Pain and anaesthesia melted and blended. Then the mountains of wadding to stay the bleeding. The old man came with a slop-pail in which the foetus lay, the fruit of their love, like a little greenish tree-frog, with perfectly formed fingernails and toes. It was still alive but tremendously exhausted. It lay like a half-dead swimmer washed up on a forlorn coast.

Realising his role as confidant, his therapy, Sutcliffe plied her with questions, made her spit the whole poisoned lot of it out into his lap. They talked on and on in the darkness and in the intervals between the sound of their voices they heard the whewing of gulls or the bray of a ferry-siren mixed into the simmering noise of rain on the windows. The topic of their conversation, their common distress, united them in a harmonious web of shared emotions; but the slow spirals of alcohol in the blood led them further and further towards incoherence, and at last into the fastnesses of sleep. His snores replaced his sobs, and gained in splendour as he slept, his head on her companionable shoulder. It was dawn when she woke with a start – the night had folded itself away like a screen. On tiptoe so as not to wake her confidant she betook herself to the kitchen and set going a copious breakfast which she knew she would need as much as he; though it was early she made haste, for she had work to do across the lake. Sutcliffe slept on, quaking into a snore from time to time, his frame wobbling jelly-like and then settling again into its mould. He too had work that morning and would be glad of the hot shower and the plate of bacon and eggs when he awoke. Nor were the promptings of reality unhelpful, for the telephone rang and cut through his sleep like scissors. Constance answered it briefly and turned to her guest who was beginning to stretch and yawn his way back to life. "It is Schwarz," she said with relief, "he is back on duty again and I can return to my own cases at last. Is there anything that you would like me to tell him when we consult later on this morning? Or to tell her for that matter?"

Sutcliffe pondered heavily. "I was once promised that she could go for walks round the lake in the afternoons; what has happened to that idea?" Constance shook her head. "I did not hear of it. Perhaps she showed a disinclination to meet you? I will find out." He lumbered to the lavatory, having selected an old copy of *The Times* to read there, leaving her to clear the place and lay their breakfast table which she did with despatch and care, for the extent of their alcoholic abuses had rather alarmed her in a medical sense. The murdered bottle of vodka lay there, showing its teeth, so to speak. Had they really put away so much? Noises from the lavatory answered her question. She tapped on the door to ask if he was all right. "Yes, thank you," he said. "I was just lost in the liana of my lucubrations as I unwound the *Times* leader. Rigorous, cleansing prose. After this I shall totter to my office, as pretty as a virgin with horns. Ah, my head!"

But the weather had cleared and a fragile sunlight enhanced the lake mist with its gleams. They embraced warmly as they separated. "O thank you, my dear," she cried impulsively and he spread wide his arms in a gesture of resignation. "Fifty-fifty," he replied.

It was no more than the truth. "And do remember that if you wish to send Aubrey a message I can have it sent over the

Red Cross teleprinter." Sutcliffe chuckled again and nodded his head vigorously. "I certainly shall," he said with a smile. "But above all, Connie, please keep in touch with me now and help me if you see any way."

"Of course."

The little office smelt of Turkish cigarettes rather than French, and he knew at once that his partner Ryder had been in that morning; it was equally obvious from the litter of press cuttings and half-typed pages which adorned the desk next to his own. That week there had been an awful lot of technical articles to translate from Swiss and German periodicals. Laboriously, in a frenzy of tedium so to speak, they were wading about in search of the scrambler device which rendered the codes of the German "enigma machine" so impenetrable to their own Intelligence. Thousands and thousands of articles had been combed, and thousands awaited them. Ryder and he were building up a "scrambler file" which would contain almost all that was known on this abstruse topic. Ryder – astonishing for a regular officer – was a brilliant German scholar and had been delegated to this pedestrian task, which he performed with discipline and good humour. A small peppery young man with a toothbrush moustache, he was always on time; he drank and smoked most moderately and lost his temper infrequently. Sutcliffe hated him, because he always felt that Ryder's professionalism showed his own behaviour up for the lackadaisical sort of article it was. Sometimes when Ryder criticised a passage in a translation he would feel that he was steadily turning blue with rage. He gritted his teeth and felt the muscles at his temples squirm with irritation.

But he had to accept these strictures for what they were – observations from someone with superior knowledge; and bow to circumstance, for Ryder was head of the section, and their translations went in under his name and signature. Sutcliffe was only a clerk. How hateful it was to be a subordinate!

He slumped down at his desk and felt his gorge rise as he turned over with one finger a clump of cuttings from the German press. He was about to address himself to his file when Ryder himself walked into the office, beaming and holding two champagne glasses in his right hand and a bottle wrapped in a wet cloth in his left. His springy bantam's walk was made more pronounced today by his obvious good humour. "Today," he said, "is a day for a celebration. So I brought the necessary. A drink is in order. H.E. yesterday sent us a strong commendation, and is putting me in for a gong." Sutcliffe groaned with disgust. He was about to say, "Is that all?" when his companion went on: "But that is not the reason. Last night I got through to London and I gather that at last they have started to get the hang of the damned scramble device on the model – the only one – we've squeezed out of Jerry so far." That was indeed great news and worth celebrating, for it implied being delivered from any more articles of scientific purport in the near future, and the thought made Sutcliffe happy. But . . . much as he would have liked to toast Ryder's "gong" his overwhelming hangover with its waves of deafness and nausea made the prospect something of a dilemma. Nevertheless, he did not wish to seem churlish. "Just a little," he cried feebly, but his companion, full of goodwill, filled him a brimming glass and pressed it upon him saying, "Come along my lad. Here's to us!" Ironically, too, the wine was a yeared Bollinger of almost carnal subtlety and while Sutcliffe's stomach quailed his palate hungered for the treat. He closed his eyes and with a sort of lustful despair, like a man diving off a cliff, he thrust his nose into the beaker and took aboard a vast draught of the precious stuff. How good it tasted, yes, but as it whorled its way down into his stomach it set up all the foreseen reactions, at first slowly, then in more explicit spasms. Retire to the lavatory he must, and in haste; to his intense fury he was disgracefully sick. It seemed somehow symbolic of the whole mess they were in – the mess the world was in: the mess in the heart of reality itself. "First free drink I get on Hitler and look what happens!" And with the news so bad, the future so dark, it was not possible to hope that there might be another. Ryder said, not without admiration, "Some hangover, I must say!"

Sutcliffe groaned and resumed his place at his desk, pale as rice. "It's the Grand Climacteric," he said, "I knew I would reach it one day." And in answer to Ryder's question as to what that might be he replied with dignity, "The Grand Climacteric is the moment at which the problem of when to die takes precedence over that of how to live." The lavatory mirror had deeply reproached and dispirited him – his eyes appeared to be poached in liver extract. Nor was the burden much lightened when Dr. Schwarz telephoned and told him with unction that the afternoon walks for his wife had been sanctioned on condition that they took place when he was not about; he must not see her lest she feel that she was followed or in any way persecuted. "Persecuted!" he lunged out the word contemptuously at the good doctor, who for his part added, "She will be accompanied by her friend – the negro one – who has agreed to come and fetch her between three and four in the afternoon." He hoped that this would meet with Sutcliffe's approval.

So began the afternoon ritual which from now on would dominate his life in the afternoons; the pale blonde girl and the slender vivid negress (so often clad in violet, magenta, orange) walking slowly arm in arm along the shores of the grey lake. Behind them at a great distance came Sutcliffe in dark glasses and hat, coat-collar turned up in a furtive manner. He did it in order to see her; he could not resist the urge to do so, for she still ached him and dominated his restless imagination. The illness, uncoiling as slowly as a python, poisoned his self-possession by its remissions and labyrinthine metamorphoses. He followed the two of them as one might follow a funeral, muttering to himself, sometimes suddenly striking out to left or right with his cane, as if to strike off the heads of imaginary flowers, for none grew on the bitter grey concrete reaches of the Grand Corniche.

From time to time the dark girl might pause, point at something, and speak, often with laughter and buoyant gestures; she had a ringing sane laugh and a big mouth like an open umbrella. Her pale companion never smiled, however, for she had been shocked into silence. Yet sometimes she echoed a word here or there in a small and precise tone, puzzled by its unfamiliarity. Her whole manner suggested that she had regressed in panic to the age of ten.

Far, far behind them walked the solitary bondsman of this unholy trinity, nursing in his mind murderous thoughts about destiny and the treatment of Dr. Schwarz. "You know damned well," he might tell the absent doctor in his mind, "you know damned well, Schwarz, that the subconscious is fished out — there's hardly a sprat left. So you are driven back to base, my lad, with the old fashioned mind-fuck machine of an electro-convulsion-therapy jag. Any poet will tell you that the basic illness is the ego which, when it swells, engenders stress, dislocating reality. Then the unbeknownst steps in with its gnomes and *Doppelgängers*; but once you realise this simple fact your positivism falls from you like a cloak. The penny drops, the *jeton* engages, and you have the Dalai Lama himself on the wire; what comes out now is poetry — that highly aberrant act of nature! It lies the other side of a crisis of identity, stresspoint, flashpoint, turnstile. Once in these calm waters one reads new meaning into things." So, lumbering along in his operatic disguise, he might stop to stare hard at the back of his wife as he resumed his monologue. "Thus and only thus does one become a great lover, shedding the scar-tissue of old dried up love-poems; despite my chain-smoked eyes and lamprey's smirk I have become at last the One I really was all along. A lover made for the intensive care ward of some great asylum on the lake, where Connie in her white smock with her bunch of keys moves gravely among the toys they give to lunatics in a vain attempt to curry favour with them. Schwarz, when you step outside Christianity and look back at it through the bars your blood runs cold!"

The girls ahead of him paused at a stall which was selling fresh *beignets de pommes*, apple-fritters, and bought one each; suddenly Sutcliffe felt violently hungry from all this pious cerebration. He could not wait for them to continue their walk so that he might himself approach the stall in sneaking fashion. He watched them wolfishly as they bit into their hot fritters, happily licking the icing sugar from lips and fingers. The simple gesture had transformed them into schoolgirls enjoying an afternoon off. The pale one almost smiled, as if the sweetness of the sugar dust brought back vague and long-vanished memories. Once more they resumed their quiet stroll while Sutcliffe's stomach contracted with desire and the saliva rose in his mouth. It was an agony to wait for them to take themselves off to a reasonable distance, leaving him free to hurry to the stall and snap out an order for a couple of these delectable comestibles. He watched their retreating backs against the grey mountains, himself standing still, holding a fritter in each hand, his eyes full of tears. Guilt overwhelmed him. He ate ravenously, astonished at his own febrile lust. Vanished scenes came to mind – of when she lay in his arms with her eyes closed, sleeping like Ophelia among the lilies; even then her mind was fraying and he had an obstinate notion that if he managed to make her pregnant it might condense her wits. But she behaved as if she did not understand what his desire might mean. She obeyed him like an animal but without emotion, according him every sexual liberty but without a hint of participation. Their kisses expired in air, and no child came of them. He wrapped his coat more closely around him now and resumed his prowling monologue with the absent Schwarz – the eminent Black, which symbolises death to the psyche of the Christians. Death, the old specialist in unhappiness, always there, unhurriedly waiting for the phone to ring. The while over grey Geneva the soft pornic clocks choked out their chimes: at night old teeth ached in the fragile mouthscape of the indented coast. "What precautions *can* one take against the suicide of a patient?" Schwarz had asked humbly; he spread his hands to suggest the vastness of utter impossibility. "None." The Christian mind is a wonderland of smut, so thought the unhappy writer as he lumbered along. Why was it so hard to imagine a reality without qualities, and an illusory soul? The whole of Europe was dying of blood-poisoning because of this inability. As indeed they both had been, long before she abdicated and renounced the safety-nets of logic and reason. It was all very well to be clever – how bitterly he regretted all those self-consciously ironic propositions he had advanced in his conversations with her, stupidly imagining that she might through them admire the brilliance of his intellect. As when he remarked that the whole paradox of love for him lay in the fact that one wanted something permanent but which did not last too long. He had been well repaid for his lack of sincerity in his loving! The white-coated doctors had gathered around them in clusters, their voices softer than moths.

Thus had opened the Vienna period with Freud and Jung – the sweet-and-sour pork of psychoanalysis, so to speak. Taking apart the clumsy old folkweave Unconscious with all its terrors and aborted ardours. He got the hang of it fairly quickly and was dazed by the suggestions it opened up; in those enthusiastic early times nobody knew that these marvellous vistas ended in a *cul de sac*. If there was a dropped stitch in the folkweave there was nothing that could be done – unless of course by suicide which unravelled the whole cloth. Nevertheless he had learned much from this stay. It had been a test,

and a stern one. Drink and cream cakes had done for him.
Someone, perhaps Freud himself, had assured him that strong
characters are nearly always constructed around some grave
central weakness, a central flaw. We live in a state of over-
compensation for this flaw; our tears of pain solidify into jewels
of insight. "The sickness of the oyster is the pearl." But after a
drink or two had cooled him he realised always that if happiness
had not come his way it must have been because he had never
really prepared himself to receive it. Now, after such a long
period of misadventure, he realised in what sense Western Man
had got his priorities wrong; the target was not between the
thighs, but between the eyes – the pineal gland of the white
vision.

Other memories surged in upon him as he watched the
two receding figures of the women ahead of him. Soon they
would reach the end of the Corniche and it would be the signal
for him to turn aside and scuttle into the side streets, safe from
recognition. Trash the negress was very animated today, but
he was not near enough to hear that robust laughter; happily,
for it would have put him in a rage, by reminding him of how
she had provoked a scene of violence in a Sapphic club in underground Vienna, and all because he had followed them, wistfully
hoping to detatch her companion, to reclaim her, so to speak.
In his rage he had shaken his fist at Trash and promised to beat
her up; he had received a box on the ear which made his head
sing. The door was slammed in his face, and the Judas clicked
shut, leaving him alone in the draughty street, now smelling of
night and approaching snow. He turned aside into a café and
drank his wits into a curdle of incoherent shames and loathings.
Trash was not a woman, she worked on batteries, so he told
himself. On the coat-hanger in the café entrance he had noticed
a walking stick hanging on a peg. It gave him an idea. He
would burst in upon them and administer the necessary punishment to the negress who had thrust herself between his sick

wife and himself. When he went wandering back with the stolen weapon he found to his surprise that the door was ajar. He entered somewhat unsteadily but with the gleam of battle in his eye and slowly negotiated a corridor lined with heavy damascened curtains which smelt suffocatingly of dust and the piss of cats. He had hardly got inside this high-ceilinged saloon when the lights went out with a snap and he realised he had fallen into an ambush; for from all sides naked figures leapt through the curtains and started to belabour him with sticks and umbrellas. His hat was pulped, his tie torn off at a single wrench; he was beaten to his knees and forced to defend himself wildly with his stick, and though he got in a smart cut or two he was soon disarmed and overwhelmed by the invisible girls – for he smelt they were women, for all that he could not see them. It was lucky that they did not break anything apart from his spectacles which were expensive ones. He drew himself together as best he could from this rain of blows and thumps. He retreated slowly, ignominiously, on all fours in the direction of the passage which led to the front door, and once outside they were content to let him go in peace. He scrambled out into the street covered in bruises and sweating with humiliation. He stood for a while swearing at the sky but refreshing himself with the prickle of light snow on his face . . .

Ah! But now the women had turned to begin the return journey; it was his cue to make himself scarce, and this he did with alacrity, hopping across the main road and into the anonymity of the side street, making his way slowly back to his office, where he might stay until six before joining his donnish friend at the flat, or heading directly for the homely old Bar, so ill-lit and gloomy and full of sombre furniture. It was the appropriate cocoon for the two bachelors. Here he ordered a drink and sat down with the Geneva newspaper which was so clumsily compiled and written that it seemed to him to be the work of an analphabetic moron from the nearby snows. Even the war news which was enough to strike a chill of despair into any citizen's heart somehow emerged from its smudgy paragraphs as without significance; it was partly due to the French written by Swiss – like porridge poured into a guitar.

Finally Toby appeared, stalking gravely into the establishment; he so much enjoyed being a spy, albeit a desk-bound spy. He wore dark glasses and a hat with a huge brim; he looked over his shoulder all the time, sure that he was being "shadowed". He looked under the table for gunmen and under the bed for kidnappers. He was the fully fashioned operational secret service man. Sutcliffe was bored with all this absurd behaviour and had started to play tricks with him, to give him something substantial to fear instead of these fantasies of power.

He told him lies about odd phone calls, and spoke of the mysterious presence of a black saloon car, a German Horch with bullet-proof windows which patrolled their street sometimes after dark. It was full of armed men; he strongly advised his friend to ask the service for a bullet-proof waistcoat, lest he be attacked on his walk back from the office. At this however Toby demurred – the waistcoats were heavy, he said, and might give him a hernia. However he was impressed by this propaganda and wore an air of nervous precaution when he walked the open street.

Now he entered the old bar in high good humour, hanging up his coat and hat as he boomed a welcome full of gratitude. "My dear fellow, how to thank you .. ? Your rubber bands ... a wonderful contrivance worthy of the best civil service in the world . . . secret service too . . . saved my honour this very lunch hour . . . Miss Farthingale was able to say with Galileo, *eppur si muove* . . . it obviated the need for her to wear spurs, thank goodness, and carry the good news from Ghent to Aix . . ."

He placed his briefcase in a strategic place where he could keep an eye on it, and motioned Sutcliffe away to the pool table for a game of French billiards, switching on the lights and checking over the balls which clustered in their wooden triangle, a formation suggesting the symbolic properties of the Grand Pyramid's square root of five: symbol which faraway Blanford was even then thoughtfully contemplating in a big book of engravings concerned with such abstruse matters. From time to time they talked a small bit of shop, but for the most part they pursued this wholly absorbing occupation in silence, enjoying the long meditations between strokes, between remarks. Then once they were relaxed they replaced their cues in the rack and resumed their places at their customary table where Toby looked at his watch and said that there was just time for a stirrup-cup before they must face the awkward problem of a dinner neither knew how to cook. "I see your Ryder is in for a gong," he said. "It won't do him any good; the damned military don't like civilian gongs being dished out to their people by poor old ambassadors." Sutcliffe said, "He could hardly refuse." Toby wagged his head and added: "The man has a poorly aspected Saturn I suspect." The door opened with a clink and Toby exclaimed: "There you are! I was wondering what had happened to you." It was Constance! Sutcliffe looked reproachfully at his friend, since he had obviously expected this visit – doubtless she had telephoned him. "You could have told me," he growled.

Toby looked haughty and said, "It was all top secret – so she told me – and I respected her confidence, didn't I, my dear?"

Constance looked more rested and better groomed than upon a previous occasion, or perhaps it was simply that with the familiarity of their friendship she had flowered. On the other hand it may have been that expurgating her conscience with Sutcliffe through alcohol and conversation had acclimatised her feelings of reticence. But whatever it might have been the warmth and simplicity with which she took her place between them spoke of an affectionate complicity. Moreover she now had a topic of interest, of burning interest, to discuss. To Toby she said, "I am sure you have heard my news independently, because for some reason not clear to me everybody seems to suspect the Prince of being a double agent." Toby nodded gravely. "It is absolutely false," she said. "He criticises us very harshly at times but he is completely pro-Allied in sentiment. Anyway, he is the topic of my chatter – because I have just had a long communication on the teleprinter saying that he wants permission to land here for discussions." All this Toby knew, as the old Prince had been the subject of some highly confidential exchanges with Cairo, from which it had become clear that his movements were causing concern and alarm since he threatened to return to the unoccupied zone in France for reasons unspecific enough to be described as "business consultations". Toby had no fast views on the matter himself but he was in honour bound to echo the sentiments of his office, which in turn relayed the sardonic suspicions of Cairo, whose saturnine Brigadier Maskelyne could see no virtue in the old man, nor any sense in letting him gallivant about Europe conveying, no doubt, military appreciations and perhaps even coded messages to the Germans. Maskelyne wanted his journey blocked if possible, and proposed that once in Geneva he might be snowed under with prevarications and visa problems. But this was easy to say, harder to execute, for the Ambassador in Egypt was very much on the side of the Prince and, if appealed to, would certainly try and facilitate his request in the teeth of Army Intelligence. The only thing to do to achieve the desired end was to cause muddle and as much bureaucratic confusion as possible around the matter in the hope that the discouraged old Prince might get bored and renounce the journey. This Toby expounded to Constance

with care, watching her ever-growing impatience as he outlined the business. "You don't know the old man," she said,
"he is not only an absolute darling but also very pig-headed;
and he has plenty of people who would be on his side and
against your detestable short-sighted Intelligence Branch.
Mark my words."

Toby sighed and called for drinks, in order as he put it to
himself to give her time to cool off; but she returned almost at
once to the attack with: "Anyway, the die is cast, for the Swiss
have given him a visa and the Red Cross have cabled the
Ambassador." Toby nodded and sighed. "But the army controls transport on a priority basis. If they pretended that there
is no room for two months . . . that is what Maskelyne is
wondering . . . How much power does the Red Cross carry, I
wonder, in Cairo?"

She chuckled. "You will soon see. The old boy will be in
the air tomorrow and through Turkey by the weekend. He has
already asked me to call a meeting, and I have alerted Felix
Chatto to convoke it."

"Another name I seem to know," said Sutcliffe, feeling
rather out of his depth. "Isn't that the consul? I thought so."

"Of course, you know perfectly well. I have no further
doubts about your identity. You were with Aubrey in Vienna
when Livia, my sister . . . She who disappeared just when war
broke out."

"Did Aubrey really love her?" To her surprise the girl
found herself blushing as she replied hotly, "Of course he did.
Who else?"

"And Felix also?"

"You can ask him that yourself. He is here in the Consulate, open to the public all morning."

"And Livia?"

"Vanished. I saw her in a newsreel film of a great Nazi
rally. She was in uniform. After that no news. I don't dare to

speculate, Robbie." He was delighted by this mark of intimacy. "Yes, do call me Robbie, that is what Aubrey calls me; it brings me closer to him. After all we owe you a great debt, your Freud sent us to Vienna. Poor stricken Pia! Not that it did any good, alas!" She put her hand on his arm and squeezed. "I am sorry," she said. And now Toby called them to order. "We are wandering from the point, which is this: is the old bugger going to get through and start up all sorts of conspiracies and projects? I have no one to shadow him." She laughed and replied confidently, "He won't need it. I can guarantee his *bona fides* if you wish. He is staying at the Orion where he has always had accommodation set aside for him since he left Egypt years ago."

"And he will have the latest news of Aubrey," said Sutcliffe, and then stopped short, confused, for the remark seemed to raise up between them the ghost of the vanished Sam. The girl nodded. She looked a trifle pale. She added that the Red Cross was anxious that whatever proposals the Prince might have should receive the attention of the security authorities, "Therefore I ask your department to send a representative to the first general meeting where he will give an account of our work in Egypt and then raise whatever else he has in mind. I only come into it as a medical adviser to the organisation for the Swiss area. I have no sort of jurisdiction outside it. But I have been invited to form the meeting in this way so as not to waste time."

"I can't blame Cairo for being thoughtful about the old boy," said Toby. "If I had Farouk on my card index, working day and night to help the Germans, I would be very thoughtful too. Yes, of course we'll send someone, probably me, since I know something about how you spent your summer before the war, and we are having quite a business getting agents into the unoccupied zone before the door shuts, as it soon must."

"Why must it?" asked Sutcliffe and his friend replied,

"There is too much going on. Finally they will get fed up and occupy the whole place. Meanwhile we are making hay despite the French who are making things hell for us and collaborating very nicely with the Boche."

Sutcliffe was secretly piqued that Toby should have kept the arrival of Constance secret from him, and in revenge felt bound to make them laboriously explain everything to him – to expiate their sin of collusion. His friend, feeling the reasons behind his testiness, resolved to take them all out to dinner at the Lucrèce where, despite rocketing prices, good food was still to be had. The question of the Prince was for the moment shelved, and the evening passed in friendly persiflage and banter.

SIX

A New Arrival

BUT CONSTANCE'S PROPHECIES CONCERNING THE PRINCE and his powers proved well founded, for within the week they found themselves standing on the windy airfield in a darkness punctured only by the runway flare path, waiting for the aircraft which was bringing him to Geneva. He had evaded every obstacle with ridiculous ease. "My boss is in anguish," said Toby. "He has forbidden me to mention the Prince's name in the office as it gives him toothache. Cairo is furious."

"Everyone is always furious with him," said Constance, "but it does no good." The reception committee consisted of Constance and a ventripotent Swiss banker, representing the Red Cross, Felix Chatto from the Consulate, Toby with his elaborate air of spycraft, and the Egyptian Chargé d'Affaires, smooth as an egg. They could hear the noise of a plane droning about among the mountain peaks, its note altering with altitude and position – presumably it was the old English Ensign crammed with passengers. So they hoped at any rate. The airport buildings were in darkness except for a few dimmish lights in the lounge. It was cold, the smell of autumn was in the air. It was not hard to imagine the dark freezing cities of Europe which must already, due to curfews and food shortages, have huddled themselves down to sleep or watch through the silent friendless hours of the Nazi night. The bar was not open in the lounge or they would have drunk a defensive coffee or whisky against this notion of vicarious misery. At last out of the darkness of the sky a plane materialised and they realised that it must be theirs. It rolled quietly to a halt at the end of the runway to disgorge its passengers, for the most part military or diplomatic figures, but among whom, very sprucely clad, and

714

with a fresh buttonhole in his lapel, walked the Prince with an unhurried gracefulness. The little group formed a semi-circle into which he came smiling from face to apparently familiar face; but he stopped when he saw Constance and gave a sudden little leap of recognition. In a moment he had his arms round her, squeezing her shoulders until it hurt her. At last when they disengaged and he had freed her she saw with emotion that his eyes were full of tears. "There is no doubt that it was our fault," he said under his breath, "the Princess said to be sure to hide nothing from you. It was my fault and hers, that dreadful picnic. His death, *aïe*!" He raised his finger and tapped it softly upon his forehead.

She squeezed his hands, as if to comfort and exonerate him from so much feeling, so that he at last felt free to turn his attention to the others, to greet each and every one of them with the punctilio due to his condition. He had a special word of acknowledgement for Felix Chatto, whom he remembered from Provence. The young man was delighted to meet with acclaim for his political percipience. "I remember your political judgements," said the Prince, "and I took good note of them while your foolish uncle made one bloomer after another." It was music to the ears of Felix. Having done his duty thus the Prince then made his excuses for the lateness of the hour and for the fact that he was too tired to prolong the evening. If he was to be fresh for the meeting on the morrow he must really get a little sleep – and who could begrudge him this?

The flock of official cars followed the dark Red Cross limousine bearing the Prince and the banker to the former's hotel, and then as they approached the town, dispersed in their various directions. Felix dropped Constance off at her flat and kissed her cheek as he said goodnight. The Prince had given her a large envelope from Aubrey Blanford containing messages and manuscripts for her to read and she was anxious to examine them before going to bed.

On the morrow they met in the Consulate ballroom which was so often used as a boardroom of a temporary kind, and here the Prince, freshly laundered, so to speak, presided with aplomb. He had recovered his twinkle and the suavity and crispness of his professional manner. He began by giving them a brief account of the state of the war from the point of view of Egypt. "I am irritating the British very much," he admitted, "because my Intelligence is so much better than theirs; you see, being neutral we still have diplomatic representation behind the German lines and normal confidential bag facilities. So it's not to be wondered at that I know a good deal. Naturally we pass on all we can as Allies, but often we are not believed, they think we are double agents and passing planted information to them. . . . Goodness, how suspicious and mistrustful they are as a race!" The central heating was on full blast and, finding it a trifle too much for him, he pulled out a small Japanese fan from an inner pocket and fanned himself as he continued his exposé. He was lucidity itself, and beginning with the rape of Poland he went through all the succeeding events in order; it aged them to hear him. Each great battle or disaster sank into their consciousness like a nail driven home. Dunkirk, Sudan where France fell, the Battle of Britain, the fall of Paris. "What is to be expected now?" he went on. "I can tell you, though I don't know the date. And don't tell the British, they won't believe it. But all my contacts agree and all my sources insist that an attack on Russia is imminent. This will relieve pressure a good deal, but not in the desert where Axis forces are building up again."

He now turned aside to purely Red Cross matters concerned with budgets and balance sheets and appointments. "My journey has somewhat intrigued everyone but in fact there is nothing specially confidential about it. I am bearing messages to various people, and I must briefly visit Sweden and if possible Paris. I hope to get the necessary exequatur this week for both; but while I am busy talking to the Germans, I

want to propose that we have some representation in the unoccupied zone of France. Aix? Marseille? Avignon? I don't
know. You may think it not very urgent but in fact my own
guess is that the zone will not remain unoccupied very long; it
is too easy for the British to filter agents into it, and whatever
there is of dissidence and resistance to the Germans can form
down there more easily than in the industrial north. And you
know what the French are like. They won't obey orders and
they are completely selfish; sooner or later there will be a gaffe
and the Germans will come in with a heavy hand and take over
the zone. We need someone there to make sure that Red Cross
supplies get through and are properly distributed to the medical people. I cannot see that the Germans will refuse such a
request since they are still signatories and we have not been
repudiated." The Committee heard him out with quiet respect;
nobody had specially clear-cut views about their field of operation, nor were there any very thorny budget problems. In
Egypt all appeared to be going well and even the new Axis
build-up was being faced with confident determination.
"What would you?" said the Prince. "The war will last another four or five years, then peace will come; though what
sort of peace and on what *sort* of terms I cannot tell you! Even
though I appear to be a know-all . . . there are limits. You will
have to consult Nostradamus!"

That evening there was a reception given for the Prince
at the Consulate to which only Felix was invited. Constance
had work of her own to do, while Toby's department never
figured on the social secretary's invitation list because of its
confidential nature. The Prince was in great form. "Felix!" he
cried, "if I may call you so, for we are old Provençaux, no?
Felix, I want to speak to you frankly about your uncle, Lord
Galen. I fear he has been misplaced by the British and will
commit incoherences." Felix Chatto groaned and threw up his
hands. "I share your views alas," he said. "The appointment is

disastrous. The P.M. must be out of his mind!" Lord Galen was the new Minister of Culture and Information, and had taken up his new post with great style and an elaborate incoherence special to himself.

From every point of view the appointment had been regarded as extraordinary. It was not that Lord Galen lacked all culture – except such as might be acquired by someone who had spent a lifetime on the stock exchange: there were other objections as well. The fact that he was an eminent and widely known member of the Jewish community would give Nazi propaganda an easy topic of comment about the culture of the Allies; moreover the appointment had irritated all the intelligent Jews already involved in the struggle. "And then, your uncle made an inaugural speech at his first press conference which was of fantastic inappositeness." Here the Prince got up on tiptoe, spread his arms in an imitation of Lord Galen's public manner and said, in broken tones, overcome by emotion, "Culture . . . our heritage . . . we must . . . do everything to preserve it . . . it's so precious . . . we can't ever do without it . . . precious heritage . . . I mean to say, what?" The Prince shed his imitation like a cloak and pursed his lips, shaking his head reproachfully the while. "It is not possible. He is drawing ironic applause everywhere, like Ramsay MacDonald in his heyday. And you know he gave Aubrey the fright of his life; poor Aubrey woke from a siesta to find Lord Galen standing at the end of his bed with outspread arms like an eagle, intoning: 'O my dear Aubrey, the first victim of our culture . . . the first young writer to be wounded by enemy fire . . . I will get you an O.B.E.'" They both laughed at the thought, imagining the face of Blanford waking to find this dark cultural apparition at the foot of his bed. The Prince went on: "I pointed out that Aubrey had been shot by his own side, and he was extremely irritated. No, I don't think the appointment can last long. There is not enough culture to go round with him in charge.

And you know, Felix, I am an old friend and love him dearly, so I am not just being malicious about the matter. He is a *disaster*!"

Felix was delighted by the sincerity and familiarity of the old Prince's conversation; it somehow set the seal upon his own new maturity, for he himself had changed very much since the outbreak of war. First of all he had secured a vastly superior posting to Geneva – ironically enough he had moved heaven and earth to get himself called up for the Air Force, but with no result. The Foreign Office had "frozen" him in his new duties which were not too arduous and only mildly confidential. Best of all, Lord Galen had been so impressed by the eminence of his new rank that he had offered him a rather handsome allowance upon which he could not only live in good style but also run a small car, which greatly aided the image carried by his rank. The change in him was rapid and very much for the better; he became quite at home in the more famous *auberges* of the town, and indeed in the more respectable night clubs. He even managed to conquer his innate timidity enough to invite the occasional dance-hostess back to his flat for the night. He had grown taller and very much more handsome and assured the Prince that he would be happy one day to accept a Cairo posting if it could be arranged. "Of course it could. The Minister is my friend," cried the little man with vehemence. "He would do anything for me. It's thanks to the Mount of Olives, as we call him, that I am here really, in the teeth of those old Arab Bureau slyboots. I will start work on it as soon as I wind up here and in Paris and go back to Egypt. We will speak more of this matter – this is not the place."

Everything, for the Prince, had a place and an appropriate time; it was amazing how he kept things so sorted out in the filing cabinet of his memory. Most people in his position would by now have succumbed to the role of "delegating" to an assistant. It was this quality which made Constance sure that he would devote some of his private time entirely to herself –

there was a whole sea of conversational matter between them which had not yet been taken into account. She quietly stood back and waited for him to complete the first social evolutions on his agenda. Sure enough after a week during which he had sent a bunch of red roses to her flat every morning, he proposed lunch and a drive round the lake in the afternoon.

It was a brilliantly sunny day despite a fresh wind off the distant snows – for already the traditional autumn decor of Switzerland was beginning to assert itself; the Prince, compensating for his short legs by a prop in the form of a cushion, was at the wheel of the office limousine. They set off in a sort of bemused silence due to a sudden attack of shyness which took them both by surprise. "How strange," he said at last in a puzzled voice, "I feel that I don't know where to begin. . . . Isn't it strange? Help me, Constance, will you?" She smiled, and shaking her hair out of her eyes said, "I know. What a strange sense of inhibition! Dear Prince Hassad, forgive me. Let us begin with him, with Sam." He recognised at once that she was correct in her assessment of their mutual reluctance to talk of the death which nagged them. He began to talk now, quietly but with emphasis, about the fatal picnic party and the Bridge of Sighs, and he could feel her physical tension, the timbre of her anxiety, as yet hardly even translated into physical form, though her fingers trembled slightly as she lit a cigarette, and she turned away from him rather abruptly to gaze out of the car window at the fleeting lake scenes they were passing. Once launched, however, he spared no detail, for all the world as if he were anxious himself to unload the full burden of his guilt, to expurgate the whole incident for which he knew himself to be responsible. Indeed he was paradoxically a little hurt when she said sharply, "There is no real question of guilt. I think we should drop that notion, it leads nowhere. The same thing could have happened in Piccadilly with a runaway taxi, you know that as well as I do. Only . . ."

"Only?" he echoed, gazing at her.

"The thing has filled me with impatience and anger and the sensation of uselessness. I have been seriously thinking of going back to the U.K., shelving all my commitments here and finding something useful to do there. After all, there something real is happening, they are being starved and bombed. They are in the thick of it, while here we are skulking on the outskirts of reality. The Swiss get on my nerves, they are so dull and gluttonous."

"I know what you feel," he said thoughtfully, "but I think you should not act in too great haste. You are doing valuable work here; and if you did move I can think of more useful places for you to occupy. No, I don't agree." He shook his head somewhat sternly. It made her smile affectionately and putting her hand fleetingly on his arm she said, "You sound reproachful."

"No, but for someone so clever not to recognise that you are only acting out of a sense of guilt. You want to be punished, that is what, so you seek action, fear, discomfort."

He was right, of course, and she knew it. "I am just run down," she said. "I'm tired of the insane, I need a change. But a radical one." They drove on in silence for a while. Then she went on: "I've got so jumpy, and that is a bad sign in my line of business. Yesterday a dying patient threw his slops at the nursing sisters – they are nuns in my ward – and screamed, 'You don't love me at all. You love Jesus, you hypocrites! I want to be loved for myself! Take your hands off me, you bloody masks!' To my surprise I burst into tears – a poor advertisement for a doctor."

"Well, you will need a change; how would you feel about a visit to Tu Duc? I have to visit Avignon quite soon; I saw the German Mission yesterday and they have agreed to get Berlin's authority to have Red Cross representation in the unoccupied zone – though I don't think it is going to remain unoccupied long. What do you say – a trip into enemy country, so to speak? It's a rather *unSwiss* remark, I am afraid."

"Back to Avignon?" she mused, for the idea seemed quite chimerical, unrealisable; the rail system was dislocated and the frontier closed, this much she knew from the steady flow of visitors which passed through Geneva, as often as not to call upon friends and relations taking treatment in various clinics. The city has been from time immemorial a vast sanatorium as well as a political cross-roads. Its present neutrality was nothing new; a spycraft and international banking were still flourishing, and the buzz of loans and mergers was always in the air. The Prince found all this delightful, suggestive, invigorating.

"In fact," he said, "when the post is approved I will offer you first refusal of it. It might suit you for a year to work there for us, and come back to Geneva every other week. To keep on your flat and continue your present job in a less exacting sense. What would you say?"

What could she say? The prospect was such an unexpected one that she could hardly visualise it to herself, much less take a decision involving it. When they had left Provence they had envisaged saying goodbye to it for years, perhaps forever. In the case of Sam it had become indeed a case of forever; she closed her eyes and conjured up the battered old balcony upon which they had spent so much of their summer, the woods dripping now with the first winter mists and heavy dawn-frosts. The melancholy road winding down past Tubain towards the silent town with its assemblage of belfries and towers, its cruising walls still hairy with stork's nests, its gypsy-infiltrated bastions.

"I don't know. I must think."

"Of course you must," he said, "and the post has not yet begun to exist, so you have time ahead of you to consider it."

"I shall do so," she said, and with that the car which had

stolen back into the grey town, took an abrupt turn and entered the drive of the Egyptian Legation. On the steps under the portico a young man was alerted and came towards them. He was a tall and extremely handsome personage. The Prince tooted softly at him and said, "Ah there he is at last! This is Mr. Affad, my conscience, my guide, my banker, my confessor – anything you wish. I know you will like him." He was indeed an extraordinarily attractive man with his quiet and well-bred air, his attentive serviability. He opened the door of the car and offered her his capable brown hand, saying as he did so, "I am by now a friend of Aubrey, a firm friend, so I have no hesitation in asking you to please accept me too as a friend. I have heard a great deal about you, and have been hoping to meet you. There! I have said my piece." She asked if he was with the Prince and he replied that he was. "I am supposed to be his business adviser and to keep him out of mischief, and I try to. But it's not always possible."

It was nearly tea-time and the Prince led the way to the garden where in a glassed-in verandah full of hot-house blooms there stood an elaborate tea-table prepared for such as wished with cakes of every sort. A servant also appeared with water for the tea-pot and they seated themselves comfortably around the metal garden table to have a cup of China tea. Affad seemed about to embark on a remark involving some of the Prince's business when he caught himself up and lapsed into silence; noticing this the Prince said, "It's all right, Affad, you can talk in front of *her*; she is a close friend." Affad looked pleasingly confused and replied, "You read my mind wrong. I was about to start talking shop, but it was not for security reasons I braked: it seemed to be impolite to talk shop before a third party – that's all." The Prince wagged his head impatiently and said, "Hoighty-toighty, what a pother! She won't mind if we speak freely, eh my dear? I thought not."

He turned to Affad and said, "Well."

The banker produced a small red notebook from his pocket and turned the pages. "Very well," he said, "first the journey to Sweden and to Paris is fixed. Communications are so haphazard that it may take longer than you think. I have had a long talk with the astrologer Moricand. It is true that he was invited to visit Hitler but he could not get through the lines with all the fighting, so he returned here to wait."

The Prince was absentmindedly feeling in his own pockets for a memorandum book with the manifest intention of jotting down some notes, but he came upon some snaps of his children and began to study them carefully, with a pleasure that was almost unction. He listened to his adviser with only half an ear, so to speak. "Astrologer!" he said vaguely. "What next?" The children stood staring into the camera with their doe-like regard. "How beautiful they are, little children," mused the Prince. "Each carries its destiny in its little soul – a destiny which slowly unrolls like a prayer-mat." He was suddenly overcome by guilt and came to himself with a start. He put the photos away with despatch and turned back to Affad who was saying, "You know, he lives by predictions, like a sort of Tiberius; there is great competition among soothsayers to capture his ear. We may turn this weakness to our own profit later on. I am glad you brought your Templar head on the off-chance. It's the kind of thing . . . we shall see. But what seems imminent is Russia; the whole machine has wheeled round in that direction. I suppose with Greece defeated and the English pinned back in Egypt by Rommel the little man feels free to move: no flank problems."

"I have so many irons in the fires," sighed the Prince to Constance. "I must also arrange a trip to Vichy. The Jewish community of Egypt is offering vast sums to ransom their own kith and kin in France and I must find someone who has the ear of Laval. That is why Avignon, you see; then also the British have unearthed some new intelligence which informs us that the Nazis believe that the Templar treasure still exists somewhere in the Provençal area of France, indeed that Lord Galen's team had actually pinpointed the place but were forced to decamp before they could dig it up. Two members of the staff who stayed on have been arrested already, and one has died under torture. Ironically enough a secretary who was dumb, and could not speak to them! They thought he was just being obstinate and tortured the poor chap until he died. What a world, what vermin!" He stood up and said, "Well, I have things to settle before I leave." Tenderly, reluctantly, he took his leave of her, promising that he would contact her directly he got back, perhaps in ten days or so. "Affad will drive you home. He is going to stay on a while here, and has messages for Aubrey's friends."

"I can tell you where to find them," she said, "with a fair degree of certainty; they foregather almost every evening about this time at a rather disreputable old pub. I can show you where it is if you are going to run me back to my flat, which is quite near."

"With pleasure," he said, and the three of them crossed the rotunda and descended the marble stairs into the drive where the old limousine waited for them. The Prince did not make heavy weather of his goodbyes, for he did not think he would be long away. Time proved him to be mistaken but this was not to be foreseen now, as they parted company among the green lawns and gravel stretches of the Egyptian Legation. Affad drove very slowly and carefully, talking to Constance in a low voice about ephemeral, indeed frivolous, matters until they reached her flat, after they had passed the bar and he had duly taken note of its address. He was really an extraordinarily attractive man, or at least she found him to be so; but as she did not approve of this feeling she frowned upon it and upon him and informed herself sententiously, "Charm is no real substitute for character. There!" Nevertheless she stayed chatting to him in the car for a moment, telling herself that she must be nice to the friends of the Prince. But she found herself admiring his brown hands as they rested on the wheel of the car, and the easy negligence of his dress; for his part he found her very beautiful but slightly mannish – he mentally tried divesting her of all that beautiful hair and crediting her with a moustache. It was a trick he often used when he wanted to "see" into the character of someone, to change their sex mentally. Often it was quite a revelation. But in this case the moustache didn't really fit, and even as a boy she made a very pretty Narcissus. He gave up at last and said, smiling, "The Prince says you are now an analyst. I suppose you treat our dreams as bottled wishes." She laughed and replied, "More or less."

And on that note, with a laugh and a warm handshake, they agreed to part, though he asked if he might ring up and keep her informed of the Prince's movements. "Of course," she said and wrote down her number. The car drew away, and turning the corner, came to a stop outside the old Bar de la Navigation, where Sutcliffe who had just missed an easy shot was using very bad language. Seeing the car he cried to his friend, "There's the black car, Toby. Look out. There's an armed man just crossed the road. He's coming in here." That performance was so lifelike that Toby almost bolted to the lavatory to hide. It took a moment to reassure him, though Affad did not look at all like a gunman; but when he said that he had just come with messages from Blanford everyone raised their heads and expressed great interest. Affad obtained a drink from the gloomy bar-tender and joined them round the billiard table, to talk while they played on. It was his first introduction to the little group of which he was soon to become an inseparable part.

SEVEN

Orientations

THE HARSH WHITE LIGHT OVER THE GREEN BILLIARD table outlined the massive forms of the two stout men, making a contrast with the more slender silhouette of Constance, who had agreed to form a trio with them. It was a restful way of spending the twilight – nobody had spoken for a full ten minutes. Seated in an armchair by the cue-rack sat the negligent and elegant form of Affad, who was watching intently and drawing from time to time upon a cigar. The balls clicked contentedly as they rumbled about the green cloth. Sutcliffe paused to take a swig of his beer and said, for the fourth time that evening, "I'm blowed if I know what has been eating you; why, I mean, you have come to this decision, which seems futile, romantic, dramatic . . . I mean to say?" He chalked his cue petulantly, as if to alleviate his perplexity and annoyance.

Constance showed signs now of creating a "break", so that she did not answer directly; she pursued her advantage until a missed stroke halted her progress. "I have told you why, but you won't grasp it. I want to do something more active. What good is a poor psychiatrist when the whole world has gone out of its mind?"

Toby failed to exploit a lucky shot now and whispered a very abrasive epithet to himself. "It's just maidenly vapours," he said disagreeably. "Believe what you please," she snapped, "but at any rate I am going into France to see for myself if such a posting wouldn't be just what I need at the moment. I know what you are thinking – that all this is a backlash from Sam's death; but that only catalysed things! My dissatisfaction with medicine has been going on a long time, and it's not connected

CONSTANCE

only with that, it has also to do with being a woman. Yes, damn it, being a woman."

"How is that?" said Affad curiously, for she had sounded quite specially intense. "What has being a woman got to do with the matter – and specially this journey?" Constance chalked her cue with robust determination and said, "A woman doctor is no good. The masculine shaman is too strong for her, she will never be taken really seriously even though she is twice as good as any man. When the door opens and the doctor is announced the appearance of a woman doctor creates anti-climax. The patient's heart sinks when he sees he has to deal with a woman when he needed to see her husband. Woman can cure, all right, but only the man, her husband, can *heal*. It is all rubbish of course but the patient's soul *feels* this, his infantile soul feels it; for when illness comes one becomes a child again, helpless, passive. What can a woman do? O yes, she has learned a trick or two from her husband about chemicals; but she can't convey the massive authority and warmth and paternalism of the man-doctor." Toby shook his head firmly and said, "I think you are exaggerating, Constance." The girl pursed her lips as she played on, letting her theme elaborate itself in her mind.

With compressed lips and concentrated eye she bent to her strokes, while her sigh of exasperation filled in the moment or so of respite. "I know what I am talking about," she went on sadly. "After all I've been in this business for years, some of them in general practice before I specialised. I can only say that, however good you may be, and I reckon I'm good, being a woman spoils everything." Pausing, she transferred her cue to her other hand in order to give a thumbs down sign in the Roman manner! "Even if you perform miracles of healing! We are working against a shaman of great antiquity and great tenacity. It will take several hundred years for us to come to terms with it – if we ever do. It isn't possible, is it, to imagine

Hippocrates as being a woman—though God knows, why not?"

Toby seemed about to launch indignantly into a tirade in response to this pessimistic formulation, but Sutcliffe motioned him to be silent so that she could continue; he was genuinely puzzled, while the silent Affad was deeply touched and looked away, as if what she had said had had the effect of wounding him. How beautiful she looked at this moment of doubt and contrition! "Tell us more," said Sutcliffe quietly, "It seems so strange."

"Very well," she said, "let me give you a simple example. It is not possible to examine a male patient without making him undress and actually palping him all over. Just the classical routine examination, I mean. Well, I don't know any man who can respond to this elementary routine without getting excited sexually, and in some cases even getting an erection! This should not be so, but it is. I have had to evolve a technique in order to get over this situation—which is as embarrassing for the patient as for myself, for neither of us wish to let sex intrude upon such a transaction. I talk to him all the time, telling him what I am doing, localising his interest so that he forgets his risk of excitement, often by pure shame or funk. I say, 'Now I will examine your liver, so! If it hurts just say.' So I talk on and he takes an interest in his liver. As for touching him with my hands, which can be powerfully exciting, I have adopted another ploy. I bought the short drumstick that bassoon players use in orchestras. It's stubby and has a rubber head. I plant this cold instrument on the organ in question before following up with my hand! But in God's name what a bore this whole thing is! Now in psychiatry the sexual game is only verbal and one can counter male or female susceptibility more easily, or so I imagine. Also one does not have to *see* one's patient, which helps."

"Is beauty no help, then, in healing?"

"It's a great hindrance; it's only in loving that Beauty is a help, in my opinion. And when you are dealing with science there is no place for it."

All three men echoed the word "Science!"

"Yes," she said defiantly, "Science!" Affad lit another cheroot and murmured, "In an ideal world science should be love!" He stared curiously at the girl; she had a way of concentrating her eyes as she stooped to a shot which fairly made them shine with blueness. "But you will still be connected with medicine," he said, "even if you take the Red Cross posting, no?" She nodded and said, "In a sense. But it's purely administrative – distributing medicines and food. What a relief that will be! But first I must go and see for myself."

"A descent into the pit," said Toby dramatically. "I hope nothing goes wrong."

"What could go wrong?" But Toby shook his head and did not answer. In truth he hardly knew. Constance, when she thought of this journey with the Prince, felt a sudden little wave of exultant excitement. It must have been, she reflected, much the same for Sam when he put on his uniform and let a train carry him away towards a war. It was stupid, of course, but one could not help it.

She was meeting the Prince for dinner that evening in the old Hôtel Orion where he was always pleased to lodge because of the mirrors. "Wherever you turn, wherever you look, *there you are!*" he said exultantly. "Sometimes you are taken by surprise because you didn't know you were there, but you *were*; and then sometimes people can watch you without you knowing, or you can watch them. When one is alone there is nothing like a lot of mirrors to make you happy!" He busily counted the number of his reflections as he attacked the smoked salmon. Constance followed suit, wondering how long the Swiss would manage to live in such luxury, ringed about as they were with battlefields. "When do we set off?" she said and the Prince replied, "Tomorrow afternoon. Remember, no very heavy baggage as we have to change trains at the frontier and walk with our valises. And wear the grey uniform with the markings. I thought of abolishing my tarboosh for fear of being shot at or taken for a spy, but I think on the whole it's better to stay natural even though distinctive! And after all we are to be met. And then, finally, we are *only* staying for ten days or so initially, eh?"

"Very well," she said, and returned home to pack her exiguous possessions which included stout walking shoes and tweeds and a heavy overcoat, for the season was late, and despite the marvellous summer the winter was upon them. Then, as she tested her two little valises for weight, she felt some of the excitement wear off, to be replaced with a mixture of curiosity tinged with dread. It was not necessarily going to be specially tough – just different, that was all: or so she told herself. Her taxi brought her to the station at the prescribed time, just as the Red Cross car drew to a halt with the Prince sitting upright in the back. He waved gaily.

After many a delay they were shown to an unheated train which promised them ample discomfort. It went slowly, too, and the Prince, a true Egyptian, groaned as they mounted into the snowy alpine passes on the way to the frontier. He worked his toes in his polished boots. Their breath turned to spume, whitening the air; they shrank into their coats and buried their hands in their pockets. "Well, we mustn't complain," he said with an attempt at cheerfulness. "Nobody invited us." This was somewhat obvious, for apart from their own presence aboard there were no other civilians – everybody else had an apparent function. There were a few railway officials, some police and soldiers, and a *douanier* in bright uniform. Moreover their speed was funereal – it was as if they feared an ambush or explosives planted on the line. Soldiers swarmed in the country-side, and the signals seemed heavily guarded. And so at last, somewhere at the level of Culoz, with its double helix of line, the train came to a halt and all the lights went out. This was apparently the temporary frontier. The uniforms changed with the language and everything became much louder and more imperative. "*Schnell*!" cried voices, and feet trampled the dark confines of the railway sheds. Their hearts sank, it was so dark.

They had to navigate by the light of lanterns and torches and to carry their baggage for several hundred yards of dark permanent way; then at last round a bend they came upon the new French side, a brightly lit station full of soldiers and officials. There were long wooden forms in a customs shed, presided over by officials and soldiers, aided by a group of French Fascist Milice, looking sinister and depraved in their dirty mackintoshes with distinguishing brassards ornamented by swastikas. Eyeing them with distaste the Prince said, under his breath, "When the sewers are flooded up come the rats!" It was most apposite, for the swarthy line of faces, insolent and rapacious, were indeed rat-like. Their papers were scrutinised with an insulting thoroughness; as if these riff-raff were trying to memorise their very passport photographs. After this they entrained once more and this time they had a carriage to themselves, albeit once more unheated. After another delay they moved off into the night, but with an elaborate stealth, and with no lights on, sometimes drawing to a halt, sometimes accelerating: the whole impression created was one of indecision, as if they were now travelling through unmapped country in which anything might happen. Around them spread the white snowscapes of this winter land – they dared not hope for more clement conditions much before Valence where the olives of the French Midi began. It was eerie. Aloft there was a dazed-looking moon. It looked as if it had been bled white. Constance dozed, or tried to do so, while the Prince produced a pocket torch and a thriller and proceeded to read for a bit, nibbling at a ginger biscuit the while. "I am trying to put myself into a good mood," he said. "One *must*!"

It was the right attitude, at any rate, and she tried to compose her mind to influence the quality of her sleep. She was in a bad humour, though, and obscurely enough this passing irritation had been provoked by the fact that at the frontier she had heard a group of French soldiers, but regular ones for all their grubby disarray, discussing with great earnestness whether snails were tastier if simply roasted, or whether a sauce improved them. It was so very French that it made her want to laugh and swear at one and the same time! The French attitude!

"Tell me more about Affad," she said.

"He's a strange fellow, a queer fellow," said the Prince, thinking with great rapidity like a bird, his ideas beating in his breast – but at the same time remaining absolutely motionless on his branch, so to speak. He was seeing his friend "in his mind's eye", as the saying goes. "You see, his wife's mother was a friend of ours, still is, in fact, an old school-friend of my wife. It is she who lives here in Geneva and looks after the little boy. She has a vast house on the lake and is still very beautiful, tall and dark like a statue, and never speaking, just huge dark eyes. Affad was between the two Lilies, as we used to say, to tease him. Both mother and daughter were called Lily: there was no father, it was something of a scandal at the time. But they were absolutely alike, both dark and statuesque and un-speaking, with the power of looking at you as if they looked down a well. Uncomfortable, their silence and their regard. First he was friends with Lily the mother; he says she often used to ring the bell of his flat and when the servant let her in would come into the sitting-room and stand by the fireplace looking at him, never saying a word. Sometimes she lit a cigarette and smoked thoughtfully for a moment, but silently. Then, as if a new impulse stirred in her, she turned and left the room, just as unsmiling, just as vague. He got used to these visits, but they hardly exchanged greetings even. It was un-canny, he said. Then he met the daughter Lily and to everyone's surprise he married her. She was a striking beauty like her mother, severe as an Egyptian goddess, selfish as madness but of great purity and justness. Many men were after her, but she was unaware. One day in her hearing Affad said something like: 'There is a certain kind of independence in piety,' and the remark – I'm not sure it's right, but something of the kind – had an extraordinary effect on her. She fell hopelessly in love with him. I repeat what he told me. It was at a crowded cocktail party. She said to him, as if to confirm her bursting heart, 'Would you say those words again, please?' and he did. So she stayed with him, true as a magnet until the break. That is how our Egyptian women are – tuned to the mind like feathers."

"And the child?" she asked with curious sympathy. "Where is he?"

"Here. That is why Affad comes so regularly to the place. The boy has the same eyes as his mother, indeed also as his grandmother. Lily's eyes, violent deep eyes, wounded eyes, they burn in his little head like suns, Constance, like suns."

He paused for a moment, deep in thought, caught in an abstraction of memory as he re-enacted these scenes in his mind and tried to evaluate them.

He went on: "In English poetry they say 'orbs' for eyes – yes, that is what he has, two black *orbs*!" The word took on an extraordinary colour as he rolled it out. "I think they all hoped that some medical treatment might cure him, something new like your analysis, whatever that is. . . . But so far nothing has. *Orbs*!" he repeated, thrilling to the sound.

"Analysis!" she quoted hopelessly, overcome by the realisation of her professional helplessness. It worked in such a limited field, this cherished analysis of theirs. You could only reach a certain depth; after that your penetration was compromised and involuntarily you began to invent, you began to start reading in Braille; distortion set in. The vision grew turbid. Limits were reached, the ship grounded on hidden reefs. Intellectual insolvency set in – the so-called cure was really only a promissory note. "It would not work," she said, "that is not the sort of thing to do any good."

"It is like a culmination of the two women's speechlessness, his . . . what d'you call it? Yes, autism. O dear, such sorrow we have all had for poor Affad, such sadness when you thought about his reality. At first they seemed to have found a unique relationship, they drifted about like clouds together. They gave the impression that they thought the same thoughts, even that their breathing synchronised. It is a long time now and he has recovered his calm, I suppose. But he still comes here to see about the boy. He told me that before going to the house he goes down to the Corniche – he knows the hour – to watch the great black car pass along the lake. Lily takes the boy for a short drive every afternoon, still looking sincere and beautiful, without a crumb of discontent, staring ahead of her just as the child does. He sits beside her in his sailor suit from Harrods with H.M.S. *Milton* lettered on the hat. You see what I mean? Once he took me to watch them pass. Afterwards he asked me what I thought and I did not know what to answer. What was the sense of his question, I wondered? The boy's eyes were full of energy, he seemed to see everything, he turned from side to side. Why would he never speak? Affad told me that only once did he hear Lily – the mother – take the initiative and speak before a crowd of people. That was at the theatre during a performance of *Phèdre*. She all at once stood up very gravely and raised her hand, crying out in a deep hoarse voice, yet calmly: 'No! It must stop. It is too much.' Then, turning round just as calmly, she left the theatre with her hands over her ears. People are so strange, don't you think? Her beauty was phenomenal and her gravity was like a charm, it silenced people." Constance found herself dozing at last.

The train jogged on across the snowlit fields with the sleeping girl and the reading Prince. They trailed through Grenoble which was in darkness, and thus down into the plains which led them onward towards Valence. It was late when they finally drew into the silent and empty station. The city around them was asleep, though here and there shone sporadic lamp-bulbs in tenement rooms. By now, too, they were tired, and hardly realised that the train was no longer moving. Indeed the dawn was breaking when once more things started to warm up again. A covey of grey soldiers clanked down the platform at the double with their equipment and embarked, but in absolute silence, which seemed to them very singular. But now, as if stimulated by the new arrivals, the train gathered speed and in the icy dawn they found themselves running through a countryside as yet untouched by the snow, along the Rhône of "hallowed memory": the catch-phrase came into her mind as she watched it gliding beside them, and recalled their own youthful descent of the river – now it seemed a century ago. The willows, the fortresses, the vines – they were all still there, then? It seemed inconceivable. The consciousness of distance and separation suddenly afflicted her with a pang of sorrow for that last memorable summer. Superficially, then, nothing had changed, Provence was just as it had always been.

As if to celebrate the cold sunrise in an appropriate way the Prince produced a thermos flask of hot coffee and poured her a cup. It was delicious, as were the ginger biscuits which he always carried with him against emergencies. "How clever of you to think of it," she said. "Like a fool I imagined there would be drinks and sandwiches available." She had somehow not associated war with shortages, she realised; yet it was obvious. "I shall have a good deal to learn, I can see," she told herself, settling more deeply into her overcoat. Thank goodness for the sunlight on the plains, glinting among the mulberries and the olives. But her education in war was not complete – there was more to come.

Some way before their destination they came upon an old-fashioned railway viaduct which spanned the line, and gazing absently up at it she saw, turning in slow evolution at the gusty tugs of mistral, six faraway swinging forms which some part of herself instantly recognised as human. They had been suspended from the iron balustrades which spanned the viaduct arch, and then allowed to tumble into the void beneath. Brought up short with a jolt, they must have endured a brief moment of agonising discomfort before paying the price for whatever offence it was that they had committed. They lay there against the sky, hanging from the reddish spars of the old viaduct like dolls, turned by the wind as if on a slow spit. Their heads were set crookedly enough on their shoulders so that they looked like quizzical members of a Greek chorus, or else perhaps like strange birds. Their presence there, so high in the air, served as an elaborate warning – but for whom and against what? Once she had seen dead magpies nailed to a barn door with a similar intention. She felt cold. "Look!" she cried sharply on an imperative note and the Prince looked, studying them for a long moment before saying, "Signs and portents of the master race! Six human beings!" To himself he thought, "Their long quibble with reality, circumstance, contingency is over, and so quickly and direly! A small, small click, a tiny bone displaced." Suddenly he felt very old and very vulnerable. He went to the window and watched the swaying figures intently, following them until they went out of sight, as if to steep himself in the notion of war, the reality of war. "I see the Germans have made themselves quite at home," he said bitterly and took up her hand to kiss it before sitting down once more. They fell into a gloomy silence which was only broken when the engine shrieked and slowed down – they had reached the station of Avignon, their destination.

The station was almost empty except for the troops who had travelled with them, and it was not difficult to pick out the little group of civilians who had come to meet them. They stood in a dispirited circle, eyeing the train and chatting to each other; then they caught sight of the visitors and broke into smiles. There was Bohr, the Swiss consul, who was representing quite a number of belligerent nations apart from his own country – for example the interests of Britain and Holland as well as Belgium. Beside him, looking resigned and sardonic, was the doctor who acted as liaison between the medical corps and the Red Cross. He seethed with provincial gallantry when he saw that he had to do with a pretty woman – the wearisome French skirt-fever was her own diagnosis. He would obviously have to be put firmly in his place! The third member of the group was a small and extraordinarily pretty women in her thirties, with hair almost as blonde and lustrous as Constance's own. Her style, her smile, were gallant and spontaneous, and immediately one felt in her presence that one had made a warm-hearted friend. At least this is what Constance recognised at once.

The reception offered them by the little party was cordial if a trifle restrained – as though invisible witnesses somewhere out of sight might have been observing, taking notes. Bohr had already been introduced to Constance by Felix Chatto in Geneva; he was a large heavy man with an unimaginative expression and a thick dark suit. He was heavily polite but monosyllabic. The doctor was called Bechet, the girl in the fur coat Nancy Quiminal. Constance knew from her files that she was a married woman with two small children; her husband was a musician in the city orchestra who was bedridden at present with some unspecified disease. For some years Madame Quiminal had busied herself in representing the Red Cross in a southern province of which Avignon was the principal town –

the *chef lieu*. Her manner was so cordial and persuasive that Constance immediately fell under her charm, as did the Prince. It was almost arm-in-arm that the two women turned to leave the station. Military guards sniffed at their papers like mastiffs but said nothing and waved them through the barrier. Superficially nothing had changed: but then yes, for all the little horse-drawn *fiacres* had disappeared to be replaced by a couple of ancient taxis and two or three buses. The palms looked sick and mildewed. "How sad," said Constance remarking upon the change, and the doctor said sardonically that he thought the horses must have been . . . he made a large and comprehensive gesture . . . eaten to compensate for the defective meat supply. Yes, meat was in great demand and fetched astonishing prices; but recently it had been impossible to find any at all, even on ration cards. Constance was all contrition. "O please forgive my lack of tact." But Nancy Quiminal only squeezed her arm and chuckled as she said, "We are starving slowly; you will see for yourself. Yet everyone thinks that Marshal Pétain is a god and trusts the Nazis." There was bite in her way of expressing herself, and perhaps the doctor found it too sharply pointed as a remark for he added, "You must look on the bright side, my dear. The doctors are worried because with this shortage of food nobody will be ill any more, and they will be out of business. Starvation if it is not pushed too far has its uses for the public."

"You have no children, doctor," said Nancy, with a grimace. "As for Pétain and Laval . . ." but she did not finish her phrase. They managed to secure places in the largest taxi for the brief run along the outer circuit of the ancient walls. The river looked turbid and uneasy. The Prince rubbed his hands with anticipation – he was looking forward to a hot bath and a drink. But the old Europa looked hopelessly unkempt. Its pleasant inner patio was adrift with unswept autumn leaves. Its dim and makeshift lighting arrangements argued a power shortage. Moreover it was unheated; the main lounge was cold and damp. The manager came to greet them – he knew them of old, but it was with sadness that he advanced to take the hands of the Prince. "Excellency," he said sadly, and made a vague gesture which somehow expressed all the unhappy circumstances with which they would have to come to terms in this new world. "O dear," said the Prince, "all those nice wood fires!" The manager nodded and said, "All the wood has been sent away, trainloads; not only firewood, Excellency, but all kinds of woods used in carpentry. *Kaput!* And one wonders why. So many trainloads. Meanwhile we are here . . ." The bar was lighted with candles and looked rather like its old self. They were given drinks and sat down for a moment of briefing before surrendering their new friends. The Swiss informed them that they were expected for dinner at the Military Governor's villa. He turned to Nancy Quiminal and the doctor and said, "Unfortunately you are not included in the invitation, I don't know why." Their alarmed faces at once cleared and their upthrown hands registered an immense satisfaction. "Thank God," said the doctor, and set about taking his leave of them. It was clear that Nancy Quiminal felt a certain relief when he went; there was a sort of constraint in her manner which now vanished. It was as if she had been unwilling to talk freely in front of him. This, Constance recognised, may have had nothing to do with the situation – it was probably just a meridional convention – for in the Mediterranean countries nobody trusts his neighbour; he suspects that he is plotting against him, or talking ill of him behind his back. Quiminal was a Protestant from the rugged country around La Salle, whereas Bechet was from Arles and probably Catholic. Now the two women felt free to speak, and under the quick sympathetic questioning of Constance Nancy picked up her courage and told them just what it meant to be living under very stringent rationing of food, fuel, clothes; and under curfew also which made the nights seem interminable. In full summer they would be stifled alive in the airless habitations of the lower town. And then, of course, there was the ever present danger of being denounced to the Milice; its members would invoke the Gestapo, and anything might result from such a thing – deportation, imprisonments, or even ill-treatment at the hands of these thugs. After half an hour of these exchanges the Swiss looked at his watch and said that it would not be long before the staff car came for them – they might perhaps like to wash their hands and prepare for the ordeal. "Well, I shall be on my way," said Madame Quiminal briskly. "You can give them all my love, I don't think." With a bitter little grimace she shook hands all round and walked briskly off into the dusk, saying that she had to prepare dinner for her two children. Apparently she had somehow managed to come to terms with the Germans and find ration cards which enabled her to feed them. One hardly dared to imagine how . . .

The staff car with an escorting adjutant was duly waiting for them in the little square with its half-stripped winter trees. The three of them entered it with rather the feeling of being diplomats about to present their credentials – which was roughly the case, despite the ambiguities of the German position. It was gratifying that as yet the Red Cross had been overlooked, had not been repudiated by the Nazis. They might still have some sort of tenuous influence over them, then – or so they imagined. This grimly social event hinted as much.

Constance's heart beat faster as she saw that the car, after crossing the bridge, took the curving narrow country roads which led through the foothills towards the villa where once Lord Galen had held court with his absent-minded pronouncements on life and art: where the violet chauffeur Max saw to everything, protected his Lord against every encroaching reality. It had been taken over for the nonce as the General's residence, as well as the senior officers' mess – an arrangement which suited Von Esslin not at all, and made him feel more than ever slighted by the Party. He felt as if he were a sort of local concierge, for he alone lodged there, but he was forced to eat and drink and fraternise with a crew of senior Waffen S.S. officers, including the one who was in overall control of the Gestapo, Fischer. This dire situation in which he found himself made him gloomy, monosyllabic. To assuage his mutinous thoughts he had resurrected an ancient monocle with a golden rim which he hardly needed any more, and which he usually reserved for special occasions of military weight. He planted this object grimly in his right eye, aware that it made him seem aristocratic and forbidding. At the mess table he sat upright, as if deaf, rolling breadcrumbs; he was cold as an iceberg. It was into this somewhat frosty situation that the Command signal had fallen, ordering them to "permit and assist" the implantation of a Red Cross official who would be coming in from Geneva to make contact. It was rather vague – whose responsibility was it, the civil arm's or the military's? While they debated the matter there came another signal, this time from the Consulate in Geneva, telling them to stand by to receive a Prince of the Egyptian ruling house who was representing the Red Cross! Egypt! The business began to take on a vaguely political hue, for the Eighth Army was locking horns with the Africa Corps in the desert and something useful might be gleaned from such a visitor. Von Esslin decided to shoulder the responsibility, though he could not have guessed how apposite it was for them to receive their guests in Lord Galen's old villa with all its memories.

Constance pressed the Prince's hand and his own gave an answering pressure of sympathy, divining her excitement as the car turned into the familiar ravines clothed in *maquis* which tended towards the secluded glades where the iron fences began to mark Lord Galen's old boundaries. "There's the house!" she cried and the Prince took her hand once more, though this time he did not let it go until they stepped out upon the gravel which fronted the villa; indeed he went further, for he held it as they mounted the steps of the portico with its hollow Greek columns and together entered the spacious drawing-room, like actors entering on stage. Behind them lumbered the Swiss consul, a trifle out of breath, and slightly intimidated by the circle of silent officers who rose to greet them. They were for their part astonished, for nobody had told them to expect a pretty woman to dinner, and the Prince suggested an intriguing exoticism with his tarboosh. The Swiss grunted some fairly approximate explanations concerning them, and the officers approached formally, one by one, for the ritual handshake of welcome. But the stark astonishment of the General was the most marked of all; he let his monocle fall with surprise, it tinkled against the buttons of his dress uniform. He turned red, and seemed half disposed to bow rather than touch her hand. Nor was his confusion dissipated when her name was pronounced, for he saw in her the near-double of his vanished sister, Constanza – the same reserved beauty, the same tilt of mind, independent and serene. He withdrew his hand from its contact with hers with a sudden impulse, as if he had been stung by an insect. She had the impression of someone large, shapeless and somewhat guile-less; he was rosy and touching – as so many of the brutes were! He mastered himself, but inside he felt quite overcome, for they had started to speak now and he heard her crisp Hanover accent with its stylish intonation. She was of good family!

The Prince spoke somewhat halting German, though it was serviceable enough for his present needs. Fischer now came forward, full of assurance, but strangely tongue-tied. Von Esslin quite understood why – the lackey had been brow-beaten by the girl's accent and her masterful social insouciance. She saw with disdain a sort of gigolo with heavily greased hair brushed back from a high forehead. He had the flash good looks of a tailor's dummy. Somewhere no doubt he must harbour some deep social resentment against life – she tried to sketch in his disposition as women always do with men, so terrifying and so unpredictable do the creatures seem. It was the self-defensive gesture of her tribe. She felt more at ease with Mahl who was a blockhead and silent, and with short-sighted Smirgel who wore dense pebble spectacles over eyes which seemed made of bluish tweed, with no reflection in them. But he had a certain donnish distinction, and she was not surprised later to hear him referred to as a "Professor" – for that is what he proved to be. Drinks were brought on the scene to accompany the politenesses now exchanged. The officers drank heavy sweet wine or else whisky. Constance chose the latter to allay her fatigue and to stay her hunger, for the journey had made her quite ravenous – hunger could not be stayed with sandwiches and biscuits and such scraps. She hoped that they had had the sense to procure a good dinner.

While waiting upon the event she politely answered questions and blithely accepted compliments on her German – they had never heard an apparently Swiss girl talk such an aristocratic version of the language; it was hard to believe that she was not German, with her blonde colouring; it was harder to believe that she was designated to become the representative of the Red Cross in Avignon where very few people spoke the language. At dinner, which now followed and which proved to be quite eatable, Constance and the Prince flanked Von Esslin who acted as host. Fischer sat at the far end with the consul. On his left there sat a tall saturnine officer of rank called Landsdorf. He was very deaf and conscious of the fact. In the middle of the dinner the Prince let it be known that he was familiar with the house, that he had often been here to dinner during the years of peace. This roused the interest of both Professor Smirgel and Fischer, though it was the latter who said, "You mean Lord Galen?" The Prince admitted as much. "A rich Jew who was trying to locate the famous Templar treasure?" He was all attention now, tense as a cat, as he waited for the Prince's response. "Yes, though with no luck I believe. Or so he told me, for he is in Egypt now. I saw him last month." Smirgel put his head on one side and stared with his tweed eyes for a long moment before he put in, "But he located something – a possible place, no? Luckily for us, his clerk and his secretary stayed behind to help us in our own researches. You know the Führer is actively interested in the project in which he deeply believes. It has been prophesied more than once that he will find it." He depressed his cheeks and bent his head down until he was staring at the white table-cloth, in order to hide the faint smile which played about his lips. It was not sardonic, the smile, but shy and uneasy. The Prince said boldly, "I personally think it is all rubbish, it is just local folklore." They looked at him curiously but said nothing; they went on eating in silence, waiting as if to hear him continue; but he too fell silent now. Mahl coughed once, a sharp bark, and Landsdorf, believing himself to be addressed, looked up and cupped his ear to receive the message. "Nothing," Mahl told him. "Nothing."

Constance was frankly puzzled by the obvious disarray of the General who seemed hardly to dare look at her directly – except once when the Prince announced that she might become the Red Cross nominee and he stared fixedly at her for a brief second before timidly replacing his monocle.

"In my case," said the Prince airily, "I am from a neutral country and have several propositions to put before the responsible people here – if I can find who they are. For example . . ." he drew a deep breath before embarking upon a subject to which he could not foresee very clearly the German reaction. "The Jews!" There, the word was out! "With whom do I discuss the Jews? I have proposals of the most far-reaching kind from the Jews of Egypt to present to someone. Who is it?"

They looked at each other, the five German officers, with an awkward complicity disguised in a stylised hauteur; it was as if the introduction of such a subject had been a gross breach of good manners. Von Esslin stared at the far horizon and cocked his ear in the direction of Fischer who, after a moment of thought during which one could look into his features as if into a well and see right back into his childhood, smiled and moistened his lips. Constance was amazed for none of them looked really hangdog, really guilty. They all believed in what they were doing! The most troubled was the General, and he had the air of ruminating over matters far removed from the present exchange. "You must see Vichy," said Fischer, "Laval – the bureau for Jewish affairs. Remark, it won't do any good. It won't stop this – he calls it *prophylaxis*!" He gave a smile, a snake-like grimace in which the eyes did not join as he resettled the cutlery beside his plate. Mahl chuckled lazily and added, "Now the French Milice has arrived with its new uniform all will be well." This released a spring and everyone felt disposed to smile in agreement. "What new uniform?" asked the Prince curiously, and was given a description of it by the contemptuous Fischer. Khaki trousers, blue shirt and beret. "No doubt they will wish us to salute them in the street!" he said, his voice full of merriment, and his audience of uniformed men guffawed in polite fashion. "Very well, I shall call upon Laval," said the Prince, "since you have no powers, since you are simply the instruments of the old Marshal." They did not quite like this; as a diversion Constance who smelt the hostility in them said, by way of a palliative, "*Aber*, my own problem is one you can solve, General, I am sure. I own a house just outside the village of Tubain. If I accept this Red Cross post will I be allowed to live in it while I work in Avignon? I used to spend the whole summer there once, and it would be easy to open it up. Would you permit me?"

All at once everyone felt relieved, for here was something they could comply with easily enough. They felt suffused with archaic gallantry. "I see no reason why not," said the General amiably. "Indeed we have the very man with us – hey there, Landsdorf!" The deaf officer cupped his ear and had the situation explained to him by Professor Smirgel who had not ceased to cast hungry and admiring eyes upon Constance ever since he had heard her patrician accent. Landsdorf looked surprised for a moment and then nodded quite vigorously to indicate that the eventuality was well within their scope. Constance's heart rose with pleasure. "It will however be very cold, and perhaps not really safe," said the General as an afterthought. "But I am sure you can arrange things to suit you; perhaps to share it? And the Red Cross will have transport, no?"

They surmised as much and Mahl became very knowledgeable on the subject of black market petrol as compared to the rationed variety. They were still canvassing the subject when the signal was given for them to retire into the comfortable cretonne-covered armchairs which adorned the diningroom. Smirgel managed to sneak himself into a seat beside Constance with an eagerness which at first she took for sexual attraction – it caused her misgivings that she was admired by this goat-like creature. But it became rapidly clear that he had other interests in mind. "Did you also know Lord Galen?" he said at the first opportunity, and when she replied in the affirmative went on, "Did you know what he was doing?" It was rather a thorny point and she hesitated for a moment before saying, "Very vaguely. He was a businessman. Perhaps the Prince here would tell you more." But the Prince was disposed to be modest. "I was his sleeping partner; he was trying to find the Templar treasure – we found almost everything but that . . . Greek and Roman statuary, medieval ware, ancient weapons . . ."

They looked at him with respectful attention. "But treasure there was *none*!" he said emphatically. "*None*!" There was a long silence. Everyone had half-inclined towards Smirgel, as if he perhaps was the oracle who alone had the right to pronounce upon the subject – as indeed he had, for his sole task was to do just that. He looked quizzical now, as he lit a cigarette; then, watching Constance closely as if for a reaction, he said, "That is not what we hear from the chief clerk Quatrefages, who is our prisoner and whom I have interrogated myself. I must add that the question is an important one for us as the Führer has a particular interest in the matter. I am here on his special instructions to try and solve the mystery."

The Prince looked rather peeved at this, for his suspicious mind toyed with the idea that perhaps after all Galen had unearthed the treasure but kept the secret to himself; perhaps he knew, Quatrefages knew, the whereabouts of the orchard with its fabled quincunx of trees? But no, it could not be! Lord Galen was too much of a fool to be able to manage a double-cross like that without giving the show away. He shook his head in a decisive manner and said, "No, it is impossible! At any rate, *we* did not get it. Nor did we ascertain whether it really existed. Quatrefages had been dismissed already when . . . you gentlemen crossed the border into France."

Smirgel was lying, in order to find out how much they knew – that was how the Prince summed matters up. It was obvious that the Nazis knew nothing either. But they had the task of convincing Hitler of the fact, and that could not be easy. He sighed. He would take up the matter again with Lord Galen when he was next in Egypt; could something be done for the poor clerk? "Where are you keeping the boy?" he asked, but no answer was forthcoming and the Prince let the matter slide, busying himself with preparations for a visit to Vichy with its notorious bureau for Jewish affairs. Meanwhile Constance agreed to show Landsdorf where the house was – he would call for her on the morrow and motor her out to Tubain, simply to familiarise himself with the spot and decide whether such a scheme was feasible so far from the town and the protection of the armed forces. This sounded somewhat disingenuous. "I am not likely to be shot by the *French*, after all!" she said, and Landsdorf turned a trifle red. "Nevertheless!" he said, and they shook hands on the deal.

The duty car duly motored them back into Avignon later in the night; they were stopped on the bridge by an armed patrol whose task was to enforce the curfew which had been declared for eleven o'clock, but their shepherding adjutant made himself known and assumed responsibility for them. The hotel was in darkness, but as they tapped upon the front door the manager rose from the depths of an armchair where he had been dozing against their return. He had prepared a tray of something hot, and also hot water bottles for them to take to bed. They were glad to turn in, both being preoccupied and tired by the journey – a fatigue and depression that lingered on in irritating fashion. It was reinforced by a vague impression of unreality as if everything were swathed in cotton wool. The depression and sadness of the whole community seemed to be leaking out into the atmosphere, infecting it; even with the brief glimpse they had had of the town they had the impression everywhere of faces crashed down into depression. They had smelt the stench of war now; it was more than the smell of folly, of disaster. It was the smell of intellectual disgrace, of human deceit. Constance sat on the side of her bed, warming her hands round her coffee cup, and thought back over the evening she had just spent. A lighted candle puckered the darkness about her. She found herself recalling the conversations, she went over them meticulously, as if to come upon some clue as to what made these soldiers perform their acts. Suddenly the thought came to her: "*They are not ashamed of what they are doing!*" And of a sudden a chill of pure terror entered her heart.

She got into bed and turned out the light, blew it softly out, to settle back in the cold sheets which smelt of damp. In her restless sleep she dreamed of the blue gaze of Fischer, its fixity and its mineral-like quality as of some worn-out gem. It was a gaze full of unconscious sexual information. He could deprave, this man, simply by smiling. In him she felt some buried puzzle which had never been deciphered yet. And yet there was magnetism, compared to the others who were easily understood, easily classified. The General was a harmless fool as apt for good as for evil – provided it came in command orders. He had looked quite confused by her beauty, he would be easy to handle if need be . . .

The subject of this somewhat unflattering judgement had, for his part, also retired to bed – or, more accurately, retired in search of sleep which was to prove extremely elusive on that particular evening, coloured as it had been by the strange new visitor – in the guise of an apparition, almost. Constanza! He bathed in the memory of her blondness, of her warm blue regard, and the sentiment permeated his sensibility with tenderness made the more rich because its object was someone long since dead. But there were confusing cross-currents, rapids and shallows, which perturbed him, prevented him from sinking into his usual heavy slumber. There had been the letter from Katzen-Mutter, for example, which had stung him to the quick with remorse. It was a brief sad letter about the family house but which, halfway through, recounted the suicide of the Polish maid; she had stabbed herself through the heart with the old dress dirk belonging to some forgotten regimental outfit, and which had always been on the wall in his room, over the writing desk. On the desk itself she had left a message in clumsy German which read: "I do not wish to be a slave." His mother did not expressly reproach him, nor in any way suggest that she might have known what the relationship between them had been . . . yet! It was as if she had known, and he felt a profound shame for something of which he could not be accused of being guilty.

It came, too, hard upon a field episode which his rank obliged him to witness – the "judicial execution" of twenty citizens in a small village near which a *franc-tireur* had fired upon his panzers, killing two troopers. It made him feel old, indeed mad with fatigue, but he behaved with a dutiful stern-ness, walking up and down the line of dead with determined step. There was hardly any blood. They had fallen in all kinds of positions. They looked, with their shabby black winter clothes, like a clutch of dusty fowls lying beside the tiny war memorial. He returned to his office in the fortress with a splitting headache, feeling the two separate emotions of the two distinct events blend inside him and trouble his composure. He wondered if he was perhaps getting influenza. But that night and the next he dreamed of the Polish maid, and on waking he realised that he must find some way of attending confession. He must find a priest. And here once more the cursed ambiguity of his position as a Catholic came upon him like a huge weight. Why not the Cathedral? Indeed why not – but he could not, as force commander, move without escort for fear that someone might take a pot shot at him. Kidnap a priest, then? He laughed gruffly. Simply join a congregation for mass, then? He spoke very bad French!

The situation worked upon him. He became a prey to constipation and colitis – childhood illnesses which no longer responded to senna or castor oil. And now, miraculously, after meeting Constance all was well. He knew he would have the courage to insist on being shriven somehow – he would go to the Grey Penitents' chapel, he would go out to Montfavet with Smirgel; what did an escort matter? Nobody would notice, after all. He felt elated, as if this strange meeting had been an omen of a favourable sort. Constance! He had nothing to read and he felt the need of a calm half hour before sleep claimed him. He turned with renewed perplexity and respect to the little official booklet – the intellectual absolution offered by Dr. Goebbels. It was hard going, the Protocols of Zion, and he was not too sure about the historic role of gold in the matter; he felt an exaggeration somewhere but, after all, the document was an official one: who was he to question facts endorsed by Rosenberg? Rosenberg, himself a Jew – so he had learned! It was even more perplexing. Yet he was in a sudden mood of relaxation, almost of euphoria. Proof: his blocked entrails performed their duty now with rapture, with profusion, as if to make up for days of costiveness. Overwhelmed by the feeling of relief he slept, having made a mental note to visit the chapel of the Penitents on the morrow.

But to Constance sleep did not come so easily, troubled as she was by the memories of the dinner and the empty stare of admiration from the blue eyes of Fischer. It made her impatient, she tried to analyse the dynamism of the glance and came at last to the conclusion that it was his capacity for cruelty and mischief which gave him an almost sexual radiance. She was angry with herself for feeling such a thing and reflected ruefully that at any moment the woman keeps in mind, like undeveloped negatives, several sexual possibilities, several choices which circumstances might put in her way. She turned with impatience to a more troubling topic – Affad; when she had called at the hotel the Prince had asked her to see him, for Affad was indisposed and in need of a prescription from a doctor. "The simplest is to ask you," he said, "though he is dead against it, doesn't want you troubled." She took the lift up to the elegant suite which Affad occupied and found him lying quiet, staring at the ceiling; he blushed with vexation when he saw that it was Constance, and expressed his displeasure with the Prince. "Nonsense," she said briskly, "it's much quicker for me to make out the prescription." "Very well," he said unhappily, "I have run out of Paludonin, that is all." She sat down by the

ORIENTATIONS

bed and said, "I shall get you some." But she took his wrist in order to feel his racing pulse, and at once remembered her conversation about medicine in the bar with the two friends Sutcliffe and Toby. Perhaps he did too, for he turned scarlet and turned his face away to the wall, with a womanish gesture of shyness. She was, so to speak, left alone there with his pulse and her science – and bereft of words. It was as if he had slipped off a glove. But what came into her mind was a thought which confused her in her turn. She did not quite believe it, but she felt certain that he had fallen deeply in love with her, and the thought was both chastening and elevating. It forced her really to consider him, to evaluate him as a possible person she might love in her turn. A woman is a creature who keeps all her options open. "You have a blazing fever," she said, because saying something filled an awkward space, and he nodded at the wall, keeping his eyes closed. "If you could just give me the prescription," he said, and it was clear from his tone that he was anxious to see the back of her. But she had not brought her printed prescription block, so she elected to slip down to the pharmacy at the corner in order to fulfil his request. "I will send the bottle up with the *chasseur*," she said. "It should pull down the temperature dramatically – but you know that." He nodded once more, and lay as if asleep. "Thank you," he said. "By tomorrow I shall be up once more."

She thought this episode over very carefully as the lift swung her down to the main hall; trivial in itself, it nevertheless vibrated inside her like the echo to something long wished for, ardently desired. At dinner she asked the Prince to tell her about Affad, and followed with great concentration an account of his business life and his education in three countries. "He is really a sort of strange mixture of businessman and mystic. Perhaps he is a homosexual without being aware of it – I don't know." The Prince made a face to express his amusement at this hypothesis. "I certainly

753

don't think so myself," he added more vehemently.

All this and the emotional indecisions provoked by the encounter with Affad she recalled with great vividness bordering indeed on a sort of anxiety because of its ambiguousness. She was not ready to love anybody. Turning and tossing in bed she squashed the tepid water bottle against her toes to try and warm them. But even though sleep came, it was late and unrefreshing. At dawn she was up and dressed, anxious to take a walk across the town. Her feet on the stairs woke the night porter who had overslept and he let her out of the front door on request but without approval. "What will you do?" he said in a wondering tone. "Just look," she replied, and set off for a brisk walk to fill in the time before the planned arrival of Madame Quiminal who was coming at ten to take her to the offices which had been proposed as a centre for Red Cross operations. The town had always been somewhat dirty and dilapidated, so that at first blush little seemed remarkably different about it. Then the smell of rotting garbage became pronounced and she observed mountains of it, overflowing from dustbins and packages everywhere – the stray dogs had enjoyed a field-day in dragging all this stuff about the main square where it mingled with the drifts of fallen leaves. No café was open so early, and the only public phone booth opposite the post office had been used during the hours of darkness as a sort of urinal by persons unknown. There were wall-portraits of the Marshal in a number of places but they were mostly defaced or covered with impotent graffiti. More imposing, for they reflected a history more recent, indeed of burning actuality, were the large command posters attached to walls and trees around the main square; they recorded the death sentences pronounced upon captured *franc-tireurs* by the German High Command. In some curious way the letterpress, crowded together as it was, gave a faint hint of Gothic script most appropriate to the subject, while the red ground upon which the whole was printed was precisely the dull red of arterial blood which had been, from time immemorial, used on the bullfighting posters. The dark red of bull's blood, upon which the crooked cross had been overstamped. Sighing, she read through these condemnations, heavy in spirit, wondering how human beings with so short a span of life at their disposal should seek in this way to qualify and abbreviate it with their neurotic antics. It was a mystery. A deep-seated self-destructiveness was the most one could diagnose about such a state of affairs. But it involved everyone. You could not opt out. Even those comfortable neutrals up in Geneva, though they thought themselves out of reach, were involved in this calamitous historic process – it would reach them in time. Her absorbed steps led her in and out of the medieval cobweb of streets, past the Princes Hotel, where once (so Felix Chatto had averred) Blanford had spent an afternoon with a girl in a room belonging to Quatrefages the clerk. She had completely forgotten this incident until now. She followed the curving walls of the outer bastions, past the little bread shop which had always been the first to open in the mornings because it supplied the buffet of the railway station. But now there was no light in the interior and on the door there was a notice which read *Plus de pain*, which must have struck a heavy blow of dismay at the French soul: such an idea was unthinkable. Maybe it would bring home to the citizens of the town the reality of the New Order. On she walked and the north wind rose and sparkled through the bright sky.

Back at the hotel the Prince sat in the breakfast-room with a bad-tempered expression on his face, spooning up the meagre fare provided for him while opposite him, with an ingratiating expression on his goat-like face, sat the Professor of last night, Smirgel, who seemed to have taken a great fancy to this new friend. "We could not speak freely last night in Von Esslin's mess," he said, "and I wanted to ask your help with the question of the Templar treasure." The Prince in a somewhat irritated tone said, "I've told you all I know." Smirgel made a soothing gesture with his hands and said hastily, "I know, sir, I know. But I have only recently arrived, sent by the Führer specially to deal with this problem and this has put me in rather a delicate position. For example your clerk, Quatrefages, has been very difficult; first he lied and then he pretended that he was tortured, while now he is pretending that he has lost his reason. I say 'pretending', but I am not sure."

"Why should he be pretending? He will probably die under interrogation like the secretary of Lord Galen – he was 'pretending' he was a deaf-mute, I suppose?" Smirgel hung his head and allowed the Prince's high indignation to sweep over him in a wave. He even nodded, as if he accepted full weight of the incriminating charge. Then he said, "All that was before I arrived; now things are different; we are proceeding in another manner now, with caution and sincerity."

The Prince looked as if he were about to throw a plate at him. He swelled up for a moment, filling his lungs with air, and then said, on an expiration, "The last information we had from Quatrefages was that we now knew the names of the five knights who were in the secret. It was a question of trying to trace through them the famous orchard with its quincunx of trees – I ask you! A hopeless quest, I should say."

"You do not believe it exists?"

"I did not say that. Lord Galen seemed quite convinced that it did; but he is a strange whimsical man and could, I should think, be capable of believing anything. But Quatrefages offered us hope, and that is as far as it went. Clearly your inquisitors have driven him out of his mind, thus ruining any chance of getting hold of such information as he might hold. How typical! Where is he now? Is he to be seen?"

The Professor deliberated for a long moment before answering; then he said, "In the asylum at Montfavet – where he can receive treatment and follow a sleeping cure to try and straighten out his mind. He was in the fortress but there was an attempt to help him escape by the gypsies – he was always their friend, no?"

"Of course he was; they were doing a lot of the digging in the part of the town known as Les Balances – they found most of our statuary. We bought it for very high prices."

The Professor gave an elf chuckle. "Our people thought it was Foreign Intelligence which wanted to free him because of the secrets he knew. Hence the interrogation. But you have confirmed my own surmise – it was just a friendly act by the gypsies who were his friends. Thank you, Your Highness." He stood up, for in the mirror among the clustering palms in tubs he had caught a glimpse of Constance returning. "I don't wish to disturb you any longer. But if there are any other after-thoughts please let me know – here is my number. I could arrange for you to visit him, if you so wished – either of you." For Constance had seated herself and after nodding good morning, was looking from one face to the other to try and seize the thread of their conversation. The Prince explained, "It's about Quatrefages. He is in the local asylum. This wretched treasure – now it's Hitler who is after it, one can't imagine why. He can't need the money I shouldn't suppose!"

The Professor permitted himself to say, with a becoming unction, "The Führer's motives are not pecuniary, I can assure you; his interest is a mystical one, to trace the roots of the Templar beliefs, the secret of their downfall. German free-masonry was also involved in their history – I suppose you would know that?"

He seemed anxious to justify himself and indeed re-open the conversation, but he received no encouragement from the Prince, who nodded curtly and with a dismissive air said, "Ah, I see Madame Quiminal coming into the hotel. Let us order some more breakfast for her, shall we?" The Professor accepted his cue and made his departure but not before giving Constance a card with his phone number on it. "In case you might ever have news for me, or information for me," he explained hastily and saluting turned away to make room for the newcomer who came smiling to their table. She was grateful to spend a moment with them before the office opened. "I will be frank," she said. "I have been told that the hotel can afford real coffee because its patrons are army people." But though the coffee was good the hotel seemed completely empty. Although Nancy Quiminal was handsome in her unusual fair-skinned way she was clad in rather a perfunctory fashion, and her shoes were very worn. She caught Constance's eye as it roved over her attire and she said, "*Eh bien*, I know. You are looking at my shoes with surprise." "On the contrary," said Constance, "I took a walk this morning to look at the shops – there is nothing in them! And when I think how *chic* the town was as a shopping centre." Quiminal made a grimace. She did not comment further. But when they rose to go she asked if they might take the bread and croissants with them because one never knew . . . She wrapped them swiftly in a paper napkin and placed them in her much used shopping bag. Then she led them to where their new office was to be created in the back block of apartments which adjoined the handsome central Mairie which looked out over the famous square with its formal Monument des Morts wreathed in metal tracery of breath-taking flamboyance, and contrasting so definitively with the sobriety and ampleness of the theatre. The great central court of the Mairie with its fat classical columns was swept with icy draughts, for a traditional mistral had begun to blow. "We will call on the mayor," said their mentor, "but don't say much to him; he is one of them." She jerked her head with contempt and looked as if she were about to spit. They climbed the beautiful staircase in silence, digesting this information. But it was only to be expected that the Germans would appoint people they could trust, and Constance said as much, *sotto voce*. But Nancy Quiminal said, "No. He was here before. Anyway it is for you to judge." And she threw open a door on the first landing and ushered them into a handsome high-ceilinged apartment where M. le Maire sat at a vast desk, his shoulders bowed under a quilt whose function was to keep him warm enough to sign the documents which issued from his department. He looked both pleasant and quite intelligent, and offered them chairs with courtesy and a certain dignity. "I have heard nothing official, but I gather from common gossip that you are going to come and install yourselves here for the Red Cross. I would say welcome, if things were not so difficult. My poor country!" He saw them eyeing a portrait of Pétain on the wall behind his desk, and made a grimace of distaste and sadness. "Ah, the Marshal," he said tenderly, "without him it would have been worse – a *total* defeat! He is saving as much as he can, but even he is not superhuman." There was an awkward pause; Madame Quiminal rose and excused herself, saying that she would precede them to the offices which had been set aside for them. "I think M. le Maire will want to talk to you for a moment by himself," she added tactfully.

For the mayor it seemed an unexpected idea. He asked them a few questions about the sort of organisation they were minded to father upon the town, and seemed quite pleased at the idea that through the Red Cross they might have access to medical supplies and food parcels for the new prisoners. "All is chaos," he said, "for the moment. There are new camps being used as transit camps for prisoners. . . . Supplies are always short." Then, somewhat to their surprise, he said that while all knew that Madame Quiminal was indispensable to the Red Cross she was not . . . here he paused to seek the right phraseology: she was "not a woman to whom one could say everything". Constance showed her surprise so plainly that the mayor went on to explain that he had nothing against her personally, she was very good at her job. "But there are ambiguities. They say, for example, that she accepts the favours of a German officer, indeed the head of the Gestapo here!" This really took the wind out of Constance's sails; she felt her nascent indignation subside in astonishment and sadness at the thought. "She must have her reasons," she said with asperity and the mayor agreed with his gestures that there was no doubt about the matter. "Nevertheless," he said, "it makes one hesitate. You see, there are many people who are frankly on the side of the ... enemy. One has to be rather careful. But there, I don't want to depress you with such matters. Come, I will take you to your offices myself."

Together they negotiated several corridors until at last tall doors opened upon a pleasant suite of rooms in one of which sat Nancy Quiminal at a desk devoid of paper as yet, knitting and reading. The mayor made his adieus with a formal correctness full of reserve.

Outside in the square there came the tramping of boots as a contingent of infantry crossed it on the way to the fortress where they were quartered. It was a strange sight. Constance stood at the window watching the soldiers, lost in thought; the town was all but deserted. Where, one might wonder, were all the inhabitants of the famous city, normally so eager for diversion that the faintest hint of marching feet, or of drum and trumpet, impelled them immediately into the open streets and squares, keen to mingle into a procession or join a dance-measure? A few shabby housewives skulked here and there like mangy cats, holding empty shopping-bags. Members of the new Milice – *les barbouzes* as they came to be called – strutted awkwardly about in their newly minted apparel. Latins are always conspicuously dangerous when they are serving an unpopular cause for money. It would have been folly to smile at their get-up for they were armed with out-of-date but still quite serviceable weaponry.

They had taken an oath to save the French nation from a besetting Jewry and on them was beginning to fall the onus for the rounding-up of the victims; it had become almost as familiar a processional feature of the town's life as the dustbin round had once been, and would again be when they got it going. The air of solemn legality was absolutely breathtaking when one understood the issues at stake. Constance could hardly believe her eyes as she watched them pass down the boulevard upon their appointed errand, flanked and headed by motor-cycle combines.

The most important thing, she reflected, as she stood on the balcony of the Mairie which formed a most useful belvedere over the town, was to make her appearance as commonplace and down at heel as possible, so as not to appear conspicuous in so much shabbiness. The Prince, who stood beside her, stirred uneasily in his cold shoes and said, but without much conviction, "I suppose it will all settle down one day." He had spent an active and not unsuccessful morning in taking up old contacts dating from his Provençal sojourn, and he was relieved to find that many had gone to ground in strategic positions – some in the *police des moeurs,* some in the Milice, some in road-haulage and land speculation. With their help he had even made a brief visit to the brothel where he was accustomed in the old days to pass an occasional evening, but he found the girls somewhat dispirited and depressed. Their clients were now a superior officer class, but mean with the money. All the girls had been issued with ivory swastikas which they wore over their tin crosses and birthday medallions. They were pleased to see the Prince, though they at once concluded that he was pro-Nazi and this somewhat dampened their elation. Nothing he could say would convince them of the contrary. Nor was there time to do much more than distribute some sweets to the pallid rachitic children. It was with something of a pang that he said goodbye.

There were days when one felt like this – that all was lost, or that the war could not be finally won in under a decade. How could one blame people for not believing in the Allies, for picking up the shattered pieces of their lives and trying to reassemble them again, even in the shadow of the black swastika? He sighed and she looked at him affectionately, saying, "You are in a mood today, aren't you?" He nodded. It was true, and there were a number of reasons. He was not happy about leaving her here in order to go north for discussions over the Jews which he now felt would be fruitless. He had thought at first that the French were simply hostages to fortune, forced to do the bidding of the invaders; he had been disillusioned and disgusted to discover that, on the contrary, quite a number were active anti-semites at heart and only too glad to assist in the persecution of this gifted and ill-fated tribe. He had heard stories of the French concentration camps which froze his blood with indignation and horror – places with such poetical names as Rivesaltes and Argelès, as Noé and Récébédou in the Haute Garonne; but nearest of all was the camp of Gurs in the Pyrénées, which had become a byword for its open brutalities. He became quite pale as he retailed these stories to Constance. "I have been wondering what we could do, if anything; could we ask to visit them? I know, it's premature. I'm jumping the gun. Let us get established first. O my dear, things are much worse than I imagined. These Germans, they are not only foul, but they revel in foulness for its own sake. What have we done to deserve such things in this century?"

She did not know what to say to console him. Almost every day now the buses went the rounds of the old town, openly, industriously, like bees from flower to flower, combing out their human prey with all the appearance of solemn legality. A uniformed officer presided, holding a typed list of names of the wanted Jews. Nor did the victims ever seem to fly, they waited in a kind of paralysed apathy for the green buses to draw up at their door. There was never a struggle, a protest. The Gestapo was using the familiar green buses known to Parisians, with the broad balcony astern, secured by an iron chain and bolt. This made a characteristic click as it slipped into place. Years afterwards Constance was to remember that little click in the post-war Paris, for the same type of bus was still in use.

She was thinking of other things. She said, "Tomorrow I am to visit the house once more!" She squeezed his arm as she said the words in order to make her voice sound even and natural. It was hard, for emotion and excitement welled up in her when she thought of that bleak little manor-house in the woods, with its high windows and dormer roofs set at ungainly angles. It stayed in her memory like a human face – the face of some meek old housekeeper worn down by a life of household cares. She recalled the last look back at it, as the gate clicked shut – clicked shut upon what had now become the last summer in Eden before the Fall. She had some vaguely stirring premonition that much would be decided by this visit, though in telling herself this she could not exactly explain in what sense, nor fully account for the heightened sense of expectancy. It was as if she might meet her lover there once more, by accident – or something of that order. What rubbish!

The chilly airs at last drove them back into the bright high-windowed rooms of M. le Maire, but not before they had become aware that down there in the almost deserted square a new sort of movement had begun to come into being; by slow seepage a crowd was forming and advancing gradually down the side streets towards the Monument des Morts. It increased in density as it slowly pushed its way through the narrow arteries which all led in the direction of the Mairie with its wide central square. Yet the pace was slow, almost leisurely, like that of a flock of sheep being coaxed along; in this case, though, the shepherds were uniformed men armed with automatic rifles, a sight which stirred their every anxiety. Their thoughts turned to reprisals, punishments, massacres – the last months had conditioned them to expect the unexpected. But no, apparently, for the mayor took his place beside them inside the sheltering windows, and said, "Ah! It's the bicycles." She echoed the word at him in surprise and he smiled reassuringly and said, "It is for today, together with the handing-in of shotguns."

They saw now that the crowd indeed consisted only of cyclists wheeling their machines; they were ushered, urged, guided into the main square where under the tutelage of the soldiers and the Milice the bikes were abandoned on the ground while the owners were motioned back to the perimeters of the square to become no longer actors but spectators of the scene which was about to take place. It took a little time but gradually the thick carpet of bicycles spread over the ground; many of the owners, now watching from under the trees, were schoolgirls. They were in tears. They felt that something dire was to befall their machines and they were not wrong. Quiminal caught sight of her own daughters in the crowd and asked to be excused so that she could descend and offer them her comfort against the loss they were to suffer. She slipped across the square towards the pretty young adolescents, herself as graceful as a doe. She put her arms comfortingly round their shoulders and spoke to them smilingly. A silence fell for a moment.

Presently there came a stir and some senior German officers made an appearance, obviously to preside over the proceedings and to emphasise their significance. They climbed up on to a dais, whereupon a signal was given at which, with a rustle of steel meshes, two light tanks wallowed into the square, like bulls into a ring, and commenced to devour the bicycles with great zest. Like minotaurs they addressed themselves to the fallen bicycles and reduced them to shivers with their jaws. The officers watched with approval, the crowd with disdain and sadness. The operation proceeded with speed and method.

The carpet of bicycles was gradually rolled back, and as gradually the Milice started to dust the residue of steel towards the centre of the square, forming it into heaps for disposal. Here and there a bicycle which had arrived late on to the scene was fed to the tanks like a Christian being fed to the lions. "It's unbelievable," cried Constance, watching. "What unbelievable spitefulness!"

"*Au contraire*," said the mayor, who had come back to her side after taking a telephone call, "it's a calculated military move to prevent messages being carried to the Resistance in the hills – supposing that there is such a thing!"

"In what way?" she said, and he smiled as he replied, "A bike does some ten miles an hour. They already control petrol and the cars. It would be hard for me to send a message to the hills, and harder now without bicycles. They are very thorough, our friends."

Together they watched the systematic destruction for a long moment, the conversion of the bicycles into mounds of dusty steel fragments. By now, too, brooms had been produced and the watching crowd was invited to sweep the débris into the middle of the square where a lorry might gather it all up. "*Ainsi soit-il*," said the mayor sadly. "For those who live in the villages and shop in town it will be very cruel indeed. Horses would come back into favour – but I fear the majority have already been eaten! What more can I say?"

There was nothing to be said. The performance was over and now the shepherds began to manifest impatience with the sloppy, tearful crowd which still surrounded the square, as if unable to disperse, to tear itself away from the sad spectacle. Those who had come from the villages were indeed wondering how they would get home. Now they were ordered to disperse, with gruffness; they obeyed slowly and reluctantly – too reluctantly for the Milice in their new get-up. There was a menacing clicking to accompany the orders as the firearms were primed for action. Those with brooms started to sweep literally, at the feet of the crowd, driving it back into the side streets from which it had emerged to form this assembly – now riders sans steeds. Nancy Quiminal had rejoined them now, still smiling but albeit somewhat tearfully – on behalf of her daughters, so to speak. "It's too much really," she said. "Every day something new. The poor *lycéens* are stricken to the heart, for their bikes were gifts for first communion or good work or whatnot. Thank God we live in the town."

When it came to taking their leave she elected to walk Constance back to her hotel, and together they crossed the icy marble halls of the Mairie and descended the broad stairway outside which a lorry was busy sweeping up the litter left by the bicycle episode. A chill wind stirred the trees and Constance thought with distaste of the unheated hotel and her cold bed which awaited her. As they fell into step Quiminal said, "I would have liked to have you home for some tea – I managed to get some fuel for the old wood central heating today: but I am expecting a visit, alas! I suppose the mayor has told you about me?"

"Yes," said Constance, surprised and relieved in a way that there should be no secrets between them. "He warned me against you!" Quiminal smiled. "Good," she said. "It's his duty and his right. He is for Pétain – what can you expect?"

"But I was surprised."

"Were you?"

"Yes. I wondered why; and moreover I wondered why Fischer of all people. But it's not my affair, after all."

They walked in silence for a while and then the French girl said, "It isn't much of a mystery really; I have a husband I love who is dying of a rare spinal complaint. He is bedridden. A musician, an artist! At all costs my two children must eat and drink – no sacrifice would be too great. My job as documentalist with the municipal library vanished with the war. My work for the Red Cross earns me a pittance as you know . . ."

"I see. Therefore!"

"Therefore!"

On an impulse the two girls embraced and said no more. In the window of the bookshop which angled the narrow street they saw a cluster of slogans and pamphlets and portraits of the Marshal which suggested that the bookseller had responded to one of the "warning visits" of the Milice. Yet on the outside of the window, written perhaps with a moist piece of soap, were the words "*le temps du monde fini commence*". It was like a douche of cold water, life-giving and sane and truly French in its cynicism and truthfulness. Quiminal laughed out loud, her composure completely restored as she said, "*C'est trop beau.*" It was as if a ray of light, a glimpse of the true France, had peeped out at them through the contemporary murk of history. They walked on awhile before the girl said, but almost as if talking to herself, "It is he who controls the lists of the taken." Constance guessed that she was speaking of Fischer. An expression of weariness and sadness settled on her features. "Sometimes he 'sells me lives' as he calls it. I buy as many as I can!" For the moment Constance was silent, though she did not quite understand the purport of the last words. But she felt great warmth and sympathy for the girl and admired the world-weary resignation which was so very French, and so very far from everything that she herself might be, or might wish to be. The basic Puritanism and idealism of the north held back from such an open acceptance of life with all its hazards. But there was no knowing how she might have reacted under similar strains, similar circumstances. Much later Nancy Quiminal was to describe her strange harlot-like relation with Fischer. The names of the Jews and other undesirables gathered up in the weekly list of *battus*, as they were candidly called by the Gestapo "beaters", were transcribed on long spills of paper and in this form were delivered to the Mairie where the

Etat Civil of the victim could be checked and his or her name transcribed in the register. There was nothing underhand about all this, it was legal and above board – it satisfied the Nazi sense of self-justification for what they were doing. But then Fischer would arrive with these lists, unbuckling his belt and throwing it upon the hall table like a wrestling champion making his claim, issuing a challenge. She had to wait for him there in a kimono of silk which he had sent her – ready for business. But sometimes they sat and talked and drank some stolen liquor, a bottle lifted from the house of one of his victims. For the most part, however, the Gestapo did not loot; they gave a note of hand for everything they took, for they revelled in the intense legality of their actions. Naked on the bed with her, he would become heavily playful, touching her body and her lips with the long spills of parchment-like paper, and asking her whom she would buy from his list. It was the sexuality of the satrap – he allowed her one or two, sometimes three, slaves of fortune. Their names were crossed out and were not transferred to the great official register. Such victims were surprised to be released the next day. But it did not always work, sometimes he was captious and capricious; after promising her he withdrew his promise and reinstated the names. It was a curious way to redeem these unfortunate hostages – by her very embraces. It was queer, too, sometimes to come upon them alive still and walking the streets, unaware that they owed their good fortune to her. But even this sacrifice did not always work, for Fischer went through variations of mood; sometimes he was full of vengeful thoughts and desires and she found him hard to handle. Once he asked abstractedly why her daughters were never present when he visited the house, and she did not answer, though a cold thrill ran down her back. She had to beg for every sou, to plead, to wheedle, and he would gaze at her with that bright dead smile, anxious that she should grovel; sometimes half-playfully she did, sinking to clasp his ankles,

768

and he stood there with his hands on her shoulders, suddenly switched off, his attention elsewhere; he gazed into some remote distance and went on smiling from the depths of this complete abstraction. She described him as "*un drôle d'animal*", and mixed with the distaste and disgust for this relationship there was a certain pity—an inbuilt French regret at the spectacle of someone who deliberately chooses the road to unhappiness, who revels in self-immolation and the misfortunes of others. Sometimes he fell asleep and had nightmares during which he cried out and wept, and once after such an occasion he discovered the adolescent sources of much of his instability based on shame—for he wet his bed. It was a shock, and he did not reappear for some time—it was she who, needing money, set about finding him. But all this information came later; on that first evening the two women merely shared a coffee at the bar of the hotel before saying goodbye and promising to meet on the morrow for the visit to Tu Duc.

The Prince was in a poor humour that night, and not at all disposed to travel north as he must; he felt he had a cold coming on. His room was cold, his feet were cold. "And yet I must," he said gloomily, "the General's movement permit specifies times and days, and I mustn't miss the connection since we have to cross into the northerly departments. Damn! I saw the old boy coming out of the church at Montfavet; he looked very sad and weary, perhaps the Creator gave him a talking to . . ."

"What were you doing there?" said Constance.

"I went to try and get a glimpse of Quatrefages; they gave me permission—Smirgel, the slimy one, took me. My dear, Quatrefages is really floating, really *dingue*. Walking about like Hamlet. He was sure I had come from India with special private information for him! I ask you! No, he's not all there. Perhaps it's the drugs, though Smirgel says not. They are keeping him most preciously in the hope of discovering . . . what rubbish it all is, I must say!"

EIGHT

A Confession

IN THE CASE OF VON ESSLIN MATTERS HAD FALLEN OUT somewhat differently, for he had not been slow to act upon the wave of optimism occasioned by Constance's visit. It was almost with euphoria that he motored down into Avignon bound for the Grey Penitents, for he had been visited by a new idea concerned with the problem of mass and confession. His boots clicked firmly upon the pavements of the little causeway which crosses the bubbling waters of the canal, with its old-fashioned wooden paddle wheels. He went with only a modest escort, so as not to draw too much attention to his exalted rank, and also because he did not like to fill the street with armed men unless it were on a professional basis, so to speak. The great portals of sodden wood sighed open and he stepped from stone on to wood, and from daylight to the fragile light of candles burning everywhere. The little chapel was deserted though ablaze with light, as though the time of a service was approaching. The three wooden confessionals, so like telephone booths, were open. Beside them was an electric bell and a card with the name of a duty priest who, apparently, could be summoned in case of need. Von Esslin sat down in a pew for a moment, then knelt in prayer, as if to prime his gesture, to purify it, before it was executed. Then he pressed the bell and listened with bent head until the echoes died away in the depths of the church. Outside one could still hear the hushing of the waterwheels as they spooned away at the dank canal of the ancient and now vanished tanners. At last from behind the altar, moving very slowly, very sluggishly, there came a burly priest with a massive square head on which the shock of greying hair was cut *en brosse*. Von Esslin sprang into a salute as the figure advanced and then, relaxing, said in his halting French, "Father, I would like some information. On behalf of many of my officers, where can they hear mass and attend confession?" The insolent dark eyes stared at him with a toad-like composure; the priest's face stayed expressionless as he reflected. He looked the General up and down with no trace of servility. "There is only one priest who knows German," he said at last, "at Montfavet. I will telephone to him and you can go there when you wish and arrange with him. When would you like?"

"In an hour," said Von Esslin, elated to find that he might shed his burden so summarily. "Is that possible?" The square-head bent his chin to his breast and said, "Very well. In an hour. I will telephone to Montfavet now." It seemed almost too good to be true. The priest turned abruptly on his heel and went slowly back towards the altar. Von Esslin watched for a moment, a trifle put out of countenance by his cursory attitude. Then he too turned and made his way out of the candle-gloom into the sunlit street where his escort awaited him. He had one or two official calls to make and he undertook them now in order not to present himself too early at the little church of Montfavet – he wanted the priest to have ample time to contact his German-speaking *confrère*. So that it was a good hour and a half before he broached the winding tree-lined roads which lead towards the ancient village. Everywhere the streams were in flood, they ran hissing and gushing among the green meadows. Larks flinched in the blue sky above. His spirits rose again and he heard himself humming a tune from an opera under his breath. How long ago, how far away, the world of music seemed!

The car with its escort rolled across the green sward in front of the old church and came to rest. Von Esslin got out smartly and with springy step made his way into the gloomy interior. He no longer felt timid about the matter – he had convinced himself that he really was acting on behalf of his brother officers. But the church was empty and there were no lights on – only such light as filtered through the tall windows on to the big, undistinguished holy paintings. After a moment of irresolution he entered the side chapel marked IV and sat himself down in patience for a while; then, thinking to improve his hour, he took to kneeling at a *prie-dieu* and ventured upon some propitiatory prayers to the Virgin which might serve as a sort of scaffolding to the more important confession which was to follow. The sound of footsteps – a strange shuffling footfall – brought him back to himself. The priest had entered from behind the altar and was halfway across the church to where the confessional stood, its oaken doors invitingly ajar. He was a tiny figure, stunted and swart as a black olive, and his eyes glimmered with intelligence. But from the waist downward he was grievously twisted, his whole haunches thrown out of symmetry so that he walked half-sideways with a laborious swaying rhythm. All this happened so fast, however, that there was hardly time to form a clear impression, for the little priest with open arms beckoned him into the confessional with an air of kindly complicity. Von Esslin obeyed and found himself in semi-darkness now, facing an empty slot in the wood, for the priest was not tall enough to reach it. He heard the little man's rapid exhausted breathing as he began with the opening flourish of his *peccavi*, "Father, I have sinned."

The responses and interventions of the little priest came back in German all right – but with so rich a Yiddish accent that for a moment the General nearly burst out into an imprecation. It was as if the gods were making a jest of him! Had they set a Jew to shrive him knowingly? No, it could not be, yet was there anything to stop a Jew from becoming Catholic? Was there? Was there? No, nothing. He was nonetheless briefly possessed by a confused sense of outrage and involuntarily his hand sought the butt of his revolver, his fingers fiddled with the safety catch in a futile, aberrant manner.

The accents of a Viennese psychoanalyst, forsooth! It turned his conscience sour to hear that unmistakable slurring upon certain words. Yet how silly all this was! It cost him something to proceed with his confession, but he managed to stumble through it and receive the expected admonition and mock-punishment which would, according to the strategy of the faith, absolve and pardon him. Yet the contretemps almost made him feel that the performance lacked real conviction. It set him arguing with himself. It was in something of a state of perplexity that he had himself driven back to his headquarters in the fortress. His staff had taken over a regular warren of interconnecting chambers, all giving through one central door on to the main corridor – a security officer's dream. And here on the wall, leaf by leaf, they were laying out the maps which delineated not only his somewhat ambiguous command but also its relation to general troop dispositions further north. He supervised all this with undiminished élan and good humour. The news from Russia, though not disquieting, nevertheless hinted at diminished momentum, of halting to regroup, of stiffened resistance. Well, with such extended lines of communication an occasional pause for consolidation was only to be expected.

That evening Fischer was alone in the mess, reading and re-reading his one and only intellectual possession, Kropotnik's *Chess Problems*. The younger man seemed moody and disinclined to converse, which was quite in keeping with the General's own mood. He ate his dinner with a haughty silence. In his memory he still lingered over that singing, swaying Yiddish intonation, as in words or phrases like "*Welch einen Traum entsetzensvoll* . . ." He wondered if the little priest might figure one day upon a Gestapo list? There was disrelish in the thought.

The next day dawned chill and misty with skirls of fine rain; the German officer appeared on time, sitting rather stiffly upright in his duty wagon – the posture somehow seemed to illustrate his deafness. He was full of a shy punctilio, but was not unhappy to be escorting two pretty women – for Quiminal had elected to join Constance for the visit to Tu Duc. There was mist on the swollen river as they traversed the famous bridge, leaving behind them the flock of churches and belfries and taking the road to the hills. Constance sat in front beside the driver, eagerly reading off the landmarks which memory rendered precious.

NINE

Tu Duc Revisited

A S FOR AVIGNON, SHE HAD NOT AS YET REALLY MADE UP her mind whether to stay or leave – her resolution had been somewhat sapped by the obvious disgust and distress of the Prince who was dismayed by the thought of leaving her behind when he took his own leave. All the sadness and barbarity of the place with its medieval sanitation – how would she face all this alone? He asked her this, and Constance herself did not quite know how to answer these questions. It was as if she were waiting for a sign or portent which would decide the matter for her. But meanwhile the rich tapestry of her memory spread itself all round her, illustrated by these fine forests and sweet limestone hills full of pure water. The German officer drove stiffly but carefully, walled up as he was in his deafness; Nancy Quiminal had fallen silent, though from time to time she shot a thoughtful glance at her companion. How silent the roads were! The countryside looked, in such wintry light, ominous and beleaguered – as indeed it was. It was not far to go, but Tubain was tucked away in a secret hollow of its own, so that when they arrived the seclusion of the place gave them the impression of having travelled many leagues.

The German switched off the motor and the sound ebbed away from them into the forest. There stood the little manor, damp-stained and unpainted, its gutters swollen with fallen leaves, overflowing upon the front steps and the broad stone verandah with its climbing rose trees. They sat, the three of them, and said nothing.

"Is this the house?" said Quiminal and when Constance nodded, went on, "I came here once, very many years ago, as a small child; an old mad lady lived here? Yes. We brought her eggs!" Constance climbed down and said, "I must just see if everything is the same." The familiar click of the gate greeted her. Everywhere gutters oozed and dribbled for it had rained that night, though now the sky was clear. The garden lay, as always, in its own atmosphere of ruinous isolation, waiting for the burden of summer bees, for the song of blackbirds or cuckoos. The kitchen window was still broken; she peeped in upon the table at which they had so often sat to eat or play cards. But the hearth was piled high with vine snippings and paper – a suggestion of habitation which made her heart leap. Was someone living here? She turned abruptly aside and cried, "We must go down to the village and get the key; I must see the inside." The French girl shrugged and said, "*Bien sûr*." But as Constance turned, her eye caught a ghost of movement amid the forest trees and following it discerned a man hovering about in the distance, obviously hesitatingly, haltingly wondering if he dared approach. It was Blaise the carter who, together with his wife, had played the role of caretaker for them during that last summer. She beckoned him urgently and at last, with misgiving, he approached, though he only recognised her when he was quite close. Then with a bound he came to her side and took her hands. "They have arrested you, then?" he said in a low anguished tone. But she smiled and disclaimed the fact, and they were far enough away from the car for her to whisper a brief account of her fortunes, and an explanation of what she was in fact doing there. He followed her explanation with narrowed eyes, urgently and with a sort of fearful concern. But when she hinted that she was all but thinking of returning to live at Tu Duc he threw his head back and gave a harsh laugh of pure rapture. "Wait till I tell my wife," he cried, "she will be mad with joy."

"But first I must see what state the inside of the place is in," she cried, for she was still hesitating, and taking the key from his pocket he said, "Come. Enter. All is as you left it. It is perfectly habitable."

It was strange to step into the dark kitchen with its ceiling-high cupboards and scoured white table marked by the cutting knives of past cooks, among whom she could now number herself. She ran a finger along the white mantelpiece and saw that it gathered no dust; who continued to clean and tidy here now? His conversation supplied the answer – it was his wife. But leaping over all these considerations he asked impulsively, "And the boys? How are the boys?" She was caught unawares, and felt all of a sudden assailed by shyness. "Well," she said. "Very well." He insisted, "And Sam?" She realised with a sudden shock that Sam was still, for him, alive on this earth – it gave a strangely relative colour to the fact of his death. She went on to volunteer the fact that he was in Egypt with his friend Aubrey, on active service. She was suddenly swept away by the luxury of having him, her husband, restored to her in this factitious way. She positively drank up his impulsive "Bravo" and squeeze of her hand. The echo of Sam went on repeating itself in the empty room, the empty house; she could talk freely about him because he was still alive! The psychologist in her reproved this weakness, but the lover rejoiced; just to talk about him as if he lived helped her surmount the agony of deprivation which she had been forced to bottle up by her false professional pride. Moreover this was the signal for which she had been waiting. She would stay on in Tu Duc with the shadowy mythical Sam, sole possessor of the truth of his death, so to speak, until her sorrow and hunger were worn out; she would work through the rich vein of his death and Blanford's incapacitation – the horrible accident which had encapsulated itself inside the greater and more wounding accident of the world at war.

"I am coming back here to stay," she said, and when they were back at the car she repeated this in a more excited tone to

Nancy Quiminal who nodded brightly and said she saw no reason why not. There was just enough of the old furniture to make it livable; the rain droned and drizzled on the glass roof of the verandah with its coloured panes. The old analytic sofa stood there, silent, passive, patient as an ideal analyst. She sat down upon it for a moment in passing and heard the twang of a spring. "In dreams begin responsibilities," she quoted to herself; it was a dream with which she would have to deal – a past Sam and a future Sam, transformed and assimilated, and all bound up with the memory of a dead child. It was terribly rich and painful still, this material; but also fecund as only sorrow can be. She would live it all out here on this hillside with its good memories and bad. The wife of Blaise now appeared and added her cries of surprise and welcome – and incredulity at the thought that Constance might come back once more to live at Tu Duc. They promised to have it all ship-shape within days; Quiminal said that her sister's vacated house was full of linen and cutlery and furniture. "I must get permission first," said Constance, "and see the Prince off. He will be angry with me when I tell him." After lingering goodbyes the car bore them back towards the town, Constance craning to catch diminishing glimpses of her "chateau" amid the green screen of woods. They were silent on the way back, completely silent. It remained for the Prince to be voluble, to argue with her; but arguments only strengthened her resolve. "The loneliness *alone*," he said. "What on earth will you do there alone? No telephone, no radio, winter, snow, curfew . . . My goodness, Constance, *soyons raisonnables*!"

"I am staying," she said, taking his hands in her own strong ones. "When you go I'll move up there; I feel the need, don't you see?"

"Just like a woman!" he said, for he was in a real huff. "Come," she said, "you knew it was a possibility when we set out. You yourself suggested it indeed. That is why I packed my

affairs in the two suitcases which you are going to send me with
the first courier." He made a growling noise and cleared his
throat. She pressed his small hands and went on, "I will arrange
the whole matter, residence, transport, and so on. The farmer
and his wife will look after me. I'm two minutes from town with
a duty car."

They parted sadly to go to bed, and next morning when
she came down he had disappeared. A car had called for him
before first light, and he had taken his affairs with him, leaving
her a brief and angry note. "I'm taking my things as I may
decide to return to Geneva direct. If you wish to stay I can do
nothing. I will send on your things. *Please* arrange to come
back *frequently* for consultations at least with Affad."

She felt suddenly bereft, abandoned, and consequently
sad; she had counted upon him coming back to give her his
support until she was settled in. Now . . . But from other
quarters the news was better. The mayor had won the right to
have a Red Cross duty car at his disposal with a uniformed
driver, though it would have to fly a swastika. And the deaf
officer came one day to announce that a villa further up the
road from Tu Duc had been earmarked as a strongpoint. This
meant that there would be frequent patrols in the vicinity and
that Constance could use the duty car to be fetched each day
and lifted home each night. This was a great convenience, and
they marvelled at their luck. Everything was turning out well –
save for the disapproval of the Prince. Nor did she know
whether he would come back this way – or had her insub-
ordination driven him away for good?

"I don't care," she said. "I think we have the General to
thank for all this. I hope there won't be any strings attached to
it." There did not seem to be, for the General himself did not
manifest; he was making his own personal arrangements to
move, for at last a suitable villa had been found as a residence
for him; at last he could vacate the mess which so weighed on

his nerves. He did not so much as deign to mark the event by a dinner or an announcement – he simply disappeared one day with his batman and the half dozen or so valises which housed his affairs. He had inherited Lord Banquo's old residence, where he would have the ministrations of batman, cook, A.D.C., and a signals officer who functioned as a shorthand-typist. His responsibilities had grown, his command had become more "critical" in the professional phrase. All this coincided with the first battle definitely lost in Russia and several small but sharp reverses in the Middle East. The plot was thickening, the wind of victory was blowing less strongly. He was glad now that he had left the old mess, for these factors would certainly have caused constraint. Something was changing, had changed; the old cocksureness was no longer there. But the anonymity of his swift departure from the mess had angered the susceptible Fischer who celebrated the occasion in his own way by giving a beer party at which he himself became hopelessly drunk. They felt a sense of release, like schoolboys when the master has left. They sang songs and ended the evening by shooting at candles, having set up a branch upon the mantelpiece, before the tall mirror which gave back their reflections as they stood to aim; the heavy slugs made a satisfactory crunch as they buried themselves in the glass or in the wall. Hardly anyone hit a candle-flame – the object of the game. They were so drunk. But they laughed immoderately, and in the intervals shouted out songs and war-cries. When his pistol was empty Fischer sat exhaustedly in a chair, leaning against the wall, and said to his nearest companion, "You know what I like? Hostages! When you stop a bus or workmen's train. You see their faces and you say: 'I want you, and you, and you'." He set his face to imitate himself in ruthless mood. A pause. "I say: 'Get down.'" He allowed the command to sink in and then continued. "They say, 'Who, me? I've done nothing. I've done nothing, why me?' And I say, 'I know what you've done. You get down and quick.'" He swept up his pistol to support the commanding tone. Then his face crashed, disintegrated into a smile which became a guffaw, expanding into a paroxysm of loud laughter as he slapped his knee and repeated, for his own private delectation, the phrase: "Who, me? I've done nothing." He would never forget the look on their faces when they said the words. And he went on laughing in a maudlin delight. The party wound its way to a slow ending, past midnight. A young Waffen officer decided to imitate the Russians by breaking empty glasses in the fireplace. They were invited to imitate him but few did; the gesture left them very thoughtful. The thought that it might be ill-timed, however, did not affect Fischer who loyally disposed of two beer tankards in this fashion before somebody took his arm and cajoled him back to his normal sober sense. He looked haggard and ghastly when at last the party broke up to go to bed. It was their farewell to Von Esslin with his excruciating aristocratic ways, with the reserve that froze. Naturally his name was not mentioned, though the fact was tacitly accepted by them. Only Smirgel the intellectual had remained quiet, had taken no very active share in the proceedings, contenting himself with a quiet smile from time to time to show that he did not disapprove.

But to be alone suddenly is another matter, alone in a town which in its new guise was no longer the sun-golden, leisurely town she had known. The winter wind, the whirling leaves, the seething river below the ramparts all went to make up a revised image against which she now had only the fact of her loneliness to place. It was true it was desired and willed and self-induced – nor would she ever have repudiated it for she felt it to be necessary. Yet with the departure of Prince Hassad a twilight fell, a winter twilight populated by Germans, and the bitter world of shortage and curfew which they had brought with them; a world of ration-card and movement-order which slowed down the course of everyday affairs and made all of them apathetic and ill-tempered, cold and underfed as they were. And supplies were short, or had to be hoarded if they were not simply appropriated by the Germans. Here she knew how to use both force and tact – and her knowledge of German helped her in her numerous altercations with supplies officers or small functionaries trying to curry favour with the German authorities. For a while she even managed to invoke Pétain and plead for a shallow margin of independence, but the image of the old Marshal had tarnished so rapidly in the light of the forced deportation of Jews and the drive for manual workers for the German war-industry that it conveyed little force; already public disgust with his antics and malpractices had become marked, and the present discontent was soon to be followed by despair as it finally dawned upon people that their boasted independence was completely hollow. Yet in a sense the resulting shame only made them hate the English more for having refused to do as they had done. Above all, *they* should not be encouraged to create incidents here in the "free zone" for which they might all suffer – for the German reprisals were swift and not too selective. Nor did it take much to annoy them. In one random machine-gunning they could, and often did, account for a whole village. The posters with their rusty blood-coloured texts proclaimed the fact quite clearly: "The German High Command will extend no clemency to *franc-tireurs*. They will be punished ruthlessly."

The day she chose to move was a Sunday, and she had invited Nancy Quiminal to come and help her make the change-over. If she had any fears or imaginings about a life in Tu Duc which might be one of loneliness and privation they were rapidly dispelled by the warmth of her welcome, by the evident relief of Blaise the carter and his family, not forgetting the three children he had fathered. The whole house had been scoured from top to bottom; a fire of vine snippings blazed warmly in the narrow hearth, its flames twinkling among the copperware hanging on the wall – they had left behind a serviceable *batterie de cuisine* for some future visits unspecified. Cutlery, table linen, sheets and blankets – all had been reverently locked away by the good man's wife, only to be revived now for Constance who was astonished by the transformation. There was even a drum of paraffin in the outhouse with which to fill the small lamps with their warm gleam. She felt quite tremulous as she sat at the scoured kitchen table and watched the fire blaze up and felt the heat turn her pale cheeks to rose. Stray thoughts of Sam did not help her composure and though Quiminal felt the temper of her emotion – she pressed her fingers – she could not guess the reason behind the mood. It was the secret poignance of Sam's invisible presence – he had once polished the little lamps with pieces of newspaper and carefully stacked them in the cupboard against a future summer – they all had believed obstinately in *that*. Blaise had found a hidden bottle of wine at a good degree of alcohol and they were each given a small beakerful to toast the "success of the house". It was so marvellous – the leaping fire, the smell of food already cooking (a *ragoût*) on the old-fashioned range with its coal bullets, the chatter of the children . . . all this was a good augury for her stay, Constance felt. She would live and work in the kitchen, would use the big barn-like pantry as a dressing-room while at the same time keeping on her own bedroom – the one shared with Sam, because it turned its back to the north wind. In fine weather she could emerge on to a kind of verandah conservatory which, though water-tight, was so smothered in rose creepers that it filtered the light and one felt almost as if at the bottom of a pool. Here the old sofa lay at anchor, waiting for happier days.

They had brought modest rations with them – some rice and vegetables, some coffee and cheese. She had persuaded Nancy Quiminal to stay the night after much cajoling, and now the wife of Blaise delightedly made up the bed in Blanford's old room. "It's almost like being on holiday!" cried the girl. "One simply doesn't feel the Boche up here – and yet we are only a few kilometres from the town."

It was true, the Germans had hardly shown their faces in this small hamlet; the fact had enabled Blaise to make his dispositions for winter as he had always done, behaving as if there was no war, no Germans, no shortages. In Tubain he had done what he had always done at the end of the year; he had bought two geese, a couple of piglets, and half a dozen chicks. His backyard gave out upon pure forest. It was easy to dissimulate and disperse these modest purchases in such a way as not to excite the cupidity of any passing patrols. In an old Provençal chest he had hoarded up some flour, rice, tea, and a collection of dried herbs for medicinal teas – *tisanes*, so beloved by the French as a defence and counterbalance to a too rich cuisine. He made his own wine every year in a modest enough quantity but at the expense of the neighbouring vineyards where, after the harvest, a free-for-all is permitted to make a clean sweep of inferior grapes which the harvesters have rejected or missed. This is called *grapiller*, and everyone of modest means goes a-graping after harvest and with what he gathers makes his own home-made brew. So Blaise. His wine was of good colour – like a good Frenchman he held his glass up to the light before drinking it off: and it had "nose", just the very faintest wraith of a trace of earth-coolth, cellar-warmth, odourlessness of human hands which have plucked the fruit, redolence of the magma of decades from the great vine-presses . . . *presence*. All this romance and folklore seemed immortally true and real in the warmth of the leaping fire and the rosy light of the lamps, lit well before their time to lighten the dark kitchen. The wife of Blaise was called Colette, and she was a proud and robust woman from the Protestant sector of the Cevennes, slow to kindle "like holm-oak" as the saying went, "but once alight, burning forever". She had long since adopted Constance, and was genuinely thrilled to think that she might spend the dreaded winter ahead with them in Tu Duc. This vivacity and sympathy was not withdrawn from Nancy Quiminal either, for it was almost impossible to resist her good looks, sincerity and forth-rightness. They found themselves bringing the "latest news" from Avignon to this couple for all the world as if they lived a hundred miles away; but it was sombre news of punishments and arrests – and in some cases gratuitous brutalities for which, illogically enough, they had been ill-prepared. Sights they had not been prepared for: like civilians hanging on the branches of a plane tree opposite the Papal city. Or in another part of the town a dog and a youth hanging from a first floor balcony. There were stories attached to all these bloody incidents and Nancy Quiminal told them in her low melodious voice. A pained silence followed, while the gaze of Colette, with all its dark intensity, passed from face to face, as if questioning them as to the meaning of such events. "You will not be afraid here?" she said at last to Constance, and seemed reassured when she shook her head. "Much less than in town I can assure you." There was, indeed, no curfew here and no patrols, which some-times took a pot-shot in the direction of a forbidden light during the obligatory blackout. Nevertheless like true peasants the family turned in early, but not before Blaise had crept down to the cellar and tuned in his ancient radio to listen to London for news of the war. This was very dangerous and might one day have dire consequences, but he could not resist this one link with the outer world; it made their Crusoe-like existence up here, perched over the village of Tubain, tolerable. "One thing," said Colette. "There is a good deal of movement on the road after dark. If someone knocks don't open. It's safer. Many people are escaping to the hills, to avoid forced labour, you see. From the end of this road, they turn aside into the forest and gain the hills like that. This is the last point. They pass at night, sometimes one hears them talking. Once I saw cigarettes in the dark. But I always lock fast and so far nobody has tapped at our door."

However they dined very early, for the winter dusk fell betimes at this season, and then the children were sent up as warming pans to warm the beds made with fresh, rain-smelling sheets. The little boy insisted on performing this service for Constance's bed, for he had been hopelessly in love with her since the beginning of the last summer. He lay still and thoughtful, gazing open-eyed at the ceiling, remembering how she looked when almost naked, in her old-style bathing costume. He groaned. He had been so jealous of Sam. He put his hand upon himself and imagined how it would be if he could get Constance to make free with him as his sister so obligingly did when they played in the barn. He groaned again and turned from side to side in a small paroxysm of desire. (And to think, thought Constance to herself, nobody noticed such things before Freud discovered infantile sexuality. It is quite unbelievable.)

Then she admonished herself by saying, "Dear me, being schoolmarmish again. Every mother must have known it, seen it; but social convention gagged her, she couldn't speak about it." Yet she was not so sure. As for the famous infantile sexuality there had been an incident during that memorable last summer which had been anything but equivocal. It had happened one morning when Sam had forsaken their nest-warm bed, to brave the cool of the weir and gambol among the water-lilies, leaving her half-stunned between love and sleep. The sun would soon be up. So, lying there, dozing dazedly, she felt the sheet drawn back enough to admit the smaller body of Blaise's son who slid down beside her, into the circle of her arms, to shower kisses upon her sleeping face. She awoke surprised and lay there nonplussed for one long moment, unable to formulate a form of conduct to suit this forbidden intrusion which at the same time seemed almost innocent because of the youth of the young

Tarquin, who did not seem able to help himself. He was in an agony of love. Emerging through the barrage of tiny bird-like kisses she found herself saying, "*Non. Non. Arrête!*" but even as she uttered them she felt his small throbbing penis tremble and discharge like silk against her warm sex. What should she do? It was a quandary! The speed of the assault had taken her by surprise.

She managed to utter the saving words without undue priggishness but it was already too late, the deed was done, and the boy's transfigured face spelt out the innocence of his emotion. His weapon had now started to shrink and wilt, he uttered brief smothered cries of pleasure and buried his face between her breasts. This would not do, and she was about to take a more forceful and definitive line when providentially they heard the latch of the kitchen door down below click open, and a step fall upon the kitchen flags. In the most miraculous way the boy disappeared – as if into thin air; it was an act of the purest de-manifestation! He slipped out of sight and sound so swiftly that she could not even formulate her aroused reproach, and even began to wonder whether she had not dreamed the whole episode. But no, the little pool of semen was there, proof positive, with droplets caught hanging in her bush. She dozed again, or tried to, until the reappearance of Sam and the renewal of his caresses, his cool flesh turning warm under her responses. They made love once more and slowly, a little wearily; and because the incident and her own arousal made her feel a little guilty she felt overburdened with the truth and the desire to confess – or nearly as possible! She needed to feel a vicarious absolution in this richer, deeper coupling with her mate. "I've been raped," she said, but in such a way as to make it sound a jest. Obligingly he took it as such and said, "By what – by a dream, or a wish, or a clergyman's thought?"

"Yes," she said, but not specifying.

"Well, you are pretty warmed up," he said, with a mock

sigh of sadness. "One always has to thank the other, *l'Autre*, the Lodger, the sod . . ."

"Homosexual ploy, that," she said, proud of her new analytic skill. "Ah, the public school."

"If there were world enough and time," he said, most unexpectedly, and bit into her bottom lip until it hurt intolerably. "Constance, you as my *ideal* girl will always keep a gilded dildo for doldrums – as when I go to the wars, like." She felt him deeply, deeply sad.

"You authorise me, my Lord?"

"Anything you do is fine," he said. "Only because it's you, that's how I feel it."

"Only because it's me?"

"That's it, that's how I feel it."

They lay staring into each other's eyes as if mesmerised for a long moment before he turned on his elbow and groped for a life-saving cigarette. "My dear," she whispered, and put her arms upon his shoulders which were still cool from the waters of the weir. He did not mean a word of it!

As absolution that was all there was and it would have to do. . . . And now, remembering these past events, so sharp in memory's focus, she told herself the real reason for her decision to stay – it had not even been clear to herself until a moment ago. The truth was that for all these people Sam was not dead, he was still in an unspecified somewhere which would one day divulge him again and restore him, blithe and unharmed, to this landscape, to these people. It made her a little shamefaced to realise this, for she had rather strong views about sincerity; but she needed time to herself, time to stare Sam's death out of countenance. Here she could live without having to give an account of herself or of him. For how long she could not tell, but evidently one fine day, when she could resume life to the full, there would no longer be the need to cheat. She would assume his death before the world.

The fire in the range blazed up now, and their dinner which consisted of a large *ragoût* of various palatable scraps, conjured from God knows where, and eaten with that rarity, a home-made loaf, smelt marvellous. The children came down and announced that the beds were blazing. Their mother despatched them to bed betimes to save fuel, but they refused to go unless their father gave them a glimpse of the family of ferrets which he had just managed to acquire. They were kept in a large wooden mousetrap of the old-fashioned kind, one with several compartments, almost like a small apartment. Blaise said, "To call in the farm-guns as the Germans did could have spelt starvation for many – perhaps it still does, who can say? But I thank God for the warrens of rabbits in the forest, and for these little fellows. I had ten conies yesterday. Aren't they pretty?"

The ferrets were sleek as very tiny greyhounds; they slid about their cage with an evil composure, their eyes gleaming as they made a queer little clicking sound. The children were given their glimpse but not encouraged to caress the little animals. "To bed," cried their mother. "Kiss the ladies goodnight and off you go!"

Constance did not fear that the son of Blaise would risk renewing his addresses as she had successfully quelled him by hinting that if there were any renewal of such behaviour she would inform his father of it. The boy turned pale and from then on avoided her stern eye whenever chance brought them together. The threat weighed heavily upon him, as well it might. Nevertheless now, after such a lapse of time, the event itself did not weigh so heavily, and she kissed him lightly, giving his shoulder a squeeze. They locked up the little duty car in the great barn of the Bastide where Blaise lived as caretaker to absentee tenants; it would not do to let the motor freeze in the whirling mistral which had risen upon the night, like an outrider of the coming snow. They said goodnight and locked themselves in the kitchen, having blacked out the room with scrupulous care. Nancy Quiminal played a hand of solitaire on the kitchen table in order, as she said, to calm her spirits before sleeping. Constance brewed a *tisane* of sage – she had picked some in the field outside the house.

When they crawled into their tepid beds and bade one another goodnight Constance felt that for her the war had really begun; this was her first night of it and Sam was still alive, had been unobtrusively salvaged from the wreck of the world.

Both girls slept badly, unaccustomed to the sense of emptiness engendered by the country noises which came to their ears from the garden with its sombre greenery and tall pines and chestnuts, and from the strip of forest which lay beyond the high road. It was not fear, but strangeness which bade them rise before first light and set the old oven going to brew morning tea. They had begun to move imperceptibly into winter – the dawn showed it with its sullen crimson gashes, its clouds wind-scarred from the fitful mistral of the night before, its ringing frost upon the highroad leading to town. Quiminal remarked upon it when the little duty car rumbled and skidded downhill to the town, and added, "Now our troubles begin; the cold will soon strike." But they were in good heart after all, the trip had refreshed them, and they supported the insolence of the soldiers at the checkpoint on the bridge with a vexed resignation. Now they could see the point of having a uniformed driver to conduct them, for he would bear the brunt of such encounters with the soldiery. It was as good as having an armed guard. "Paradoxically enough, our dangers will come from the *maquisards* when once they form – if ever they do." The loathing and despair engendered by Vichy was apparent from her tone.

But good news awaited them in the form of permission to travel about the area replenishing medical stocks in hospitals and clinics, and this task was delegated to Constance, as the newcomer, a fact which rejoiced her. Here was a chance to move about, to restore her contact with the Provence they had once known as a playground; it was as yet not quite a cemetery, despite the depredations of the Germans. Even in chains, like this, denied all the brilliant trappings of its bullfights, Corsoes, village fêtes, religious or secular foregatherings – its life-giving ethos of pious joy and unbridled paganism: even now as it was occupied and defeated, it emanated life and hope. So long as there was one point of light in the bleak world there was hope. And Constance was irrationally proud that it was England which had fed this flame. Though the defeat and the betrayal hung heavy, people had begun to feel that it was redeemable. It was sufficient to hope for the moment. And in the final analysis hearts rose to realise that already France Libre under its youngest General had twenty thousand French volunteers under arms . . . None of this could be said; but in every look cast at a German soldier or at a member of the Milice there was a buoyancy which conveyed the thought. The insult was there to be read, which is why both the Huns and their instruments took special pride in their routine cruelties. It was their reply to the silent reproach of the public's charged silence. A new kind of hate had been born, and it was with anger that they filled the trains to bursting point with poor half-demented souls from the camps, bound for the better equipped camps in the north. It was with deliberate pride that they ordered them to go slowly, at a walking pace, through the town and over the famous bridge, so that everyone could see their captives. In olden times they would have impaled them and stuck their heads on pikes to be exhibited along the walls, over the gates of Avignon. Yes, but the enormous numbers of such quarry precluded such a medieval gesture, or else certainly the Nazis would have revived it, as they had revived ritual beheading.

Sentiments and emotions such as these are difficult to express to oneself unless they are illustrated by some concrete instance which stands forever as a marker, a history which clinches the matter. So it fell out for them.

One such train, full of children and adolescents – some girls – slowed to a halt upon the main line at dusk, in a light skirling snow. The doors of the wagons were open or ajar and from them flowered these pale, exhausted faces in abstract expressions of estrangement or grief. It was a bereavement just to see them and to know oneself helpless to aid them. The Red Cross truck was crossing the sidings below the main road when the lights held it up for the train to pass; the whole expressive object with its penitential cargo of suffering passed directly across the vision of Constance as she crouched beside the driver. Their own cargo consisted of medical supplies bound for Nîmes and its clinics, but it also contained a treat of one hundred whitemeal loaves for the children. The flour had been hoarded and saved with great difficulty, and every week this little offering was given to the young, either in Arles, Nîmes or Aix. It was not much, but it cost thought and time – and a certain sharp practice. As chance would have it, Nancy Quiminal was at Constance's side, for she had asked if she might be given a lift as far as the Lycée, and she shared the sombre vision with her friend. But she was quicker-witted than Constance, for as the train lingered at the level crossing she gave a sudden gasp as an idea came into her mind; and before anyone could ask what she was at she had leapt out of the car and thrown back the tarpaulin which sealed the back. "Come quick," she gasped, and before she even fully realised the intention behind the gesture Constance followed suit, bounding into the road under the dully amazed regard of the uniformed driver. They seized the two laundry baskets filled to the brim with fresh loaves of bread, and dragged them up the concrete slip to the waiting train, uttering little breathless cries to attract attention. It was like feeding seagulls; the hands floated in their anxiety above and around their upturned white faces – the wagon stood too high off the permanent way for them to hand the loaves, they must pitch them. But not one fell down, not one was missed, while here and there on the frozen faces glimmered something which approached a smile of gratitude, or perhaps something more inscrutable, like an expression of desireless fatigue and pain.

The baskets were almost empty when the expected re-action came; a whistle blew once, twice – a piercingly urgent note. In the distance, way down the long platform, a slim figure in the uniform of a Nazi lieutenant gesticulated and shook his fist to mark time with the string of imprecations he was uttering – too far away to be audible. But the action was sufficient to bring down retribution on their heads, for nearer at hand some burly civilian figures who looked like stevedores or lorry-drivers broke into a jog trot towards them, growling like mastiffs, their boots striking sparks from the concrete of the platform. One undid his belt as he ran, the other brandished as a weapon a pair of long wool-lined leather gloves, elbow length – murderously heavy. The two girls saw them ad-vancing out of the corner of their eyes, but they kept their minds resolutely upon the task they had set themselves, and by the time the first two men reached them in a scuffle of boots and a welter of guttural oaths and snarls, their baskets were empty, down to the last loaf. Then the sky flew apart as the men – they appeared to be either Czech or Russian muleteers – waded in with their blunt weapons and crashed them down upon their poorly defended heads. They cried out in protest of course, but this only enraged their assailants and the blows redoubled in violence. They shrank down, shielding themselves as best they could with their arms, but to little avail. They were beaten to their knees, and then even lower until they were almost on the ground, gasping under this punishment.

By now the youthful officer was also upon them, his pale face contorted with a rage which hardly allowed him to speak, uttering imprecations and orders in a voice which sounded almost like that of an adolescent. Here a moment of inattention came to the rescue of the two girls crouching on the platform. The German's language was obviously foreign to the two peasants and they turned heavily round upon him in order to try and understand what he wanted of them. It was only a moment, but it sufficed for the quick-witted Nancy to cry, "Quick! Run for it!" And suiting the action to the word both girls raced along the platform, their feet barely touching it, or so it seemed: like duck upon the surface of a lake. The men turned growling and started to pursue them, but in a half-hearted surge which ended at the gate of the level crossing. Their quarry had darted sideways into the narrow streets of the town, while the driver of their car had had the wit to reverse into a nearby side street to await their return. Meanwhile they still ran frantically, in tears with rage and excitement at the humiliating beating they had received, but also aware that their escape had been providential – further down the platform they had seen soldiers running up, their rifle butts at the ready. One blow could crack a skull.

They burst at last into a small *estaminet* known to Quiminal and under the stolid and unimaginative stare of the landlord behind the bar – a man known for his Vichy sympathies – asked if they might dress their wounds in his toilet. Nancy had a lump on the back of her head, fortunately masked by her hair, and a mass of smaller contusions; Constance a black eye and a cut temple which would necessitate the wearing of dark glasses for a good week. It was mercifully limited, though both had aches and pains, bruises and sprains almost everywhere. And shock: they were still pale and trembling at their own audacity. By the time they went back to the bar the expressionless peasant behind it had set up two glasses and plenished them with yellow rum and sugar upon which he now poured hot water before pushing them forward and motioning to them with his head to drink. It was a generous gesture considering his sympathies and in view of possible consequences for himself – for already a platoon of soldiers wandered down the street checking identities, perhaps (one never knew) searching for them?

They took their drinks to the darkest corner of the establishment and drank gratefully, in this way calming themselves down before any further action. They decided to separate, Quiminal being quite near her objective; so Constance set out alone and managed to find her car and driver in a side street. Snow had begun to fall; the train had vanished into the slate-grey skies of the northern hills. Their journey was not a long one – Nîmes lay about an hour away, tucked into its dry scaly heaths called garrigues. But checkpoints were many and quite systematic, and even their quasi-official status availed them nothing. But it was at one such checkpoint near Bezouce that a familiar figure from the past floated into her presence with his arms spread to embrace. It was like some archaeological survival from a forgotten epoch – Ludovic the Honey Man, whom they had encountered in the Cevennes, and along the dusty roads of Provence so often, so very often. He was one of those unforgettable figures of the local genius who bear the full Mediterranean stamp: generous, copious, inexhaustibly rich in humour and earthy vivacity.

He walked like a bear emerging from its grotto, arms spread wide, radiating a massive benevolence. He recognised her at once – he had a peasant's eye sharpened by a lifetime of fairground practice. No country fair had been complete without the presence of this great expert, who blazed and roared and crackled like a forest fire, cajoling, teasing, provoking, inspiring his customers to invest in one of his choice honeys – "honeys from the bosom of Nature, perfumed by the Virgin herself" as he was accustomed to declare – though in prevailingly Protestant country he used other terms. "My God," said Constance, "It can't be true. . . . Ludovic!" Moreover he had with him his honeycoach as he called the great furniture removal van which he had had adapted to the needs of his exacting craft, his hives.

His horse, disshafted, cropped the grass in a nearby ditch; his capacious honeycoach with the back let down stood in a field beside the checkpoint. He had been busy selling his produce – his young son was still at it – to the German troops who manned the post in a good-natured way. Also to the passing traveller who, while his papers were being checked, strolled across to buy a pot of this "veritable nectar of the gods". It was more than an apt word spoken in jest – it was true: there was no honey on earth as delicately perfumed as the honey manufactured by Ludovic, for the simple reason that he followed the blossoms with the rotation of the seasons and took his cleverly constructed hives with him. It was work of great refinement and delicacy, like the blending of a fine wine. His great coach had been decorated by a local artist with scenes from the Fête of the Tarasque – the mythical dragon-monster of Tarascon which enjoyed a whole festival procession on its own; this gave it some of the sharp brilliance of a Sicilian country cart with painted sideboards. In this contrivance he jogged his way about, following an exacting itinerary which began in High Provence with the first chestnut blooms and linden, and gradually descended the slopes of the Cevennes towards the plains; in his mind he had a complete map of his choicest blooms and their location. And with each flavour he had recourse to one of his four "widows" as he called them, who busied herself with the bottling and labelling of his produce. He also carried in his head a clear and detailed chronological chart of the various country fairs of which he was such an ornament. But just in case of doubt he always carried with him a copy of that extraordinary great compendium of learning, *Le Lahure: les foires de France*. From these pages he could tell you the time of day, year, hour of every festival and fête, not merely in Provence but in the whole of France. It was his only reading matter, and when he had nothing to do, while "the bees were working" as he put it, he would lie under a tree reading it with massive attention; and when he tired of it he spread a red handkerchief over his face and slept massively and often convulsively. After every seventh snore his whole face contorted and he appeared to swallow a large mouse. Then, recovering, the sound would be renewed. They sat together now under a bush by the cart, to discuss matters again, after so long a time apart.

He was full of complaints; his pots of honey sold well to his new clients but the roads were getting very difficult, movement was difficult, fodder for the horse was difficult. He had become quite a scavenger for scraps in what was once a land of plenty. With his large clasp-knife he cut off a hunk of cheese for her which tasted delicious, "situated" as it was by a glass of wine. He was full of quaint expression: "*Il faut le situer avec un coup de vin.*" The meaning presumably was to wash it down with the wine. Whatever it meant the act was appropriate and the wine delicious.

"Well, what do you say now?" he asked with flamboyant gloominess. "What a pretty mess we are in – what did I tell you long ago, eh? The youth of France has gone work-shy and gun-shy – and here's the result. The country ruined and the Hun in charge." He glared malevolently at the young soldiers who were circling round his quaint coach, eyeing it with curiosity. "I shall soon be out of business. Life in the hills has become hard and dangerous."

"The Resistance?" she said, kindling, but he shook his head disdainfully and replied, "There's no such thing. Simply slave-labour on the run, dodging the draft in order not to go to Germany. The hills are full of them. But they are hungry and dangerous. The Germans must be mad."

There was nothing vastly original in the complaints of Ludovic; but it was amazing to see that he was still in business, plying his anachronistic trade despite the upsets caused by the Occupation. He had grimmer tales to tell, of course, as who had not, for he came from the poor devastated villages which had suffered reprisals for sporadic impulsive action by the odd *franc-tireur* or peasant driven mad by Nazi exactions. The smoke of burning barns and houses was still fresh in his nostrils. "And I can tell you that before the last shot is fired, I will fire one, I will take one of the swine with me, that I promise."

They talked in this strain for a while and then he said that he must get going as he hoped to reach Remoulins before curfew time to avoid trouble. "When will we meet again?" he added sadly, "now there are no more fairs, and I have to sell in towns where I am tolerated, like Carpentras and St. Gilles. Let me at least take your address." It so happened that he knew Tubain, and this cheered him up. He reharnessed his horse with a prodigious amount of purely theatrical roaring and shoving, while the little boy giggled himself witless. Then side by side they both waved to her as they clopped off down the road, while she rejoined her taciturn chauffeur and set off once more for Nîmes to despatch her business. She had been wondering what to say about the missing loaves of white bread, but when Ludovic had heard her story he at once offered to make good the loss with a dozen large pots of a choice honey, and nothing she could say would change his mind. He loaded them himself into the back of the car, expatiating on the virtues of honey for young people with big appetites and growing limbs. "Pure honey nourishes the intestinal flora," he added inconsequentially but with an air of disinterested medical gravity. Where on earth could he have picked up such a phrase, she wondered?

But after the warmth of this encounter – a voice emerging

from prehistory it seemed – she found the journey turn cold and forbidding again. The grave heathlands through which they were starting to mount looked austere and forbidding, like cruel drypoints which soon the snow would mantle and hide. Her head ached partly from the belabouring she had received at the station and partly from the strain of conversation with Ludovic who conversed in a wild and whirling manner and in a high register complete with a whole repertoire of extravagant gestures. A conversation with him was like a whole season of opera. But how well she could recall the smell of the croissants they ate at breakfast daubed with his lavender honey. Blanford made the sacrifice of cycling down to Tubain for the bread and croissants almost before first light each morning. The honey of Provence – how romantic it had seemed to them then as they sat round the breakfast table smearing it on their bread while Blanford read them the head-lines in the newspaper and commented thereon with gravity and a touch of pomposity.

So a new rhythm began and as the nights grew longer and the country a prey to the frost and the tearing mistral the journey home each night, or at the end of each professional visitation, grew more precious, more than ever desirable. Sometimes she kept the duty car for the night, sometimes she was dropped at Tu Duc at dusk. It was bliss to know that there would be a small fire in the grate, a lamp lit, an oven heating. It made her almost guilty to enjoy the mothering of the peasant girl and the warm solicitude of her husband, who had always brought off some *coup* in the matter of food for them, and sometimes even wine or a *marc* of smoky intensity.

At other times, but the occasions were rare, she managed to bring with her Nancy Quiminal for a night. Nor were there any special alarms, though once or twice at the end of the year, at the full moon, she heard steps in the road at night. But nobody stopped; as for the patrols, they made so much noise with their service cars and motor-bike combinations that it was possible to plot their journey from afar; she got used to the particular swarming noise of the Volkswagen and Mercedes engines. These coveys of armed men passed regularly, at stipulated times, and they did not seem to be seeking for any trouble in this lonely corner of the countryside. After a few weeks she could tell the time by them almost, though she was careful to avoid them if she could where her own movements were concerned. She sought no contact with the patrol station up the hill.

One day some small indisposition had made her ask for the afternoon off, and she spent the after-lunch period in turning out the upstairs rooms where, here and there, in corners and cupboards she found odd relics of their last summer stay; a bundle of newspapers, some old letters, a torn sweater belonging to Blanford. There was a little frail sunshine and she opened the window upon the garden to capture some of it. As she did so she heard, or thought she heard, the faint pure sound of a voice down by the weir – a voice pitched slightly above the steady drumming tone of the water. In fact it sounded exactly like the voice of Livia, her vanished sister, and, like her, it was intoning the *Aum* just as she used once to do at the beginning of her yoga sessions. Quite dazed with surprise Constance leaned out of the window, craning to see if there was anything which might substantiate this, for she told herself that it was a figment, a trick of memory – this low pure sound upon the cold air. Twice the voice intoned the word and then fell silent. Constance closed the window with a bang and made her way downstairs at breakneck speed. She slipped out of the verandah door and ran lightly down the avenue of planes into the dense patch of forest which bordered the weir. As she ran she parted the bushes with her hands, half afraid that at one such gesture she might reveal something so strange and frightening that she would be struck dumb with astonishment. She really did not know what to expect, so that it was a relief to discover nothing to correspond to the sound. By the old weir the frosty grass was trampled, yes, but by rabbits. There was no sign of anyone. Nonplussed, she turned and retraced her steps towards the house. And in the final alley she came nose to nose with Blaise. "You heard it?" he said, and she nodded.

"Does it sound like your sister to you?" he went on. And when she nodded he said that he had heard the sound twice before but there had never been anyone when he went to investigate. "But once my wife said she saw far away a girl on a bicycle heading down the hill for Tubain. It was too far for her to see clearly."

"My sister Livia?"

The thought echoed on in her mind, striking it with a deep amazement because of the improbability of such an eventuality. What would Livia be doing here? Strangely enough this question was soon to be answered, though for the moment she put it aside in order to apply herself completely to the work which had now become more exacting because of the season of frost and wind. For journeys now one had to count upon occasional sunny days when roads were not too frostbound. The close friendship with Nancy Quiminal ripened day by day until they were as close as sisters – closer indeed than she had ever been with Livvie. They undertook alternate journeys, dividing up the responsibility.

Once Nancy came back from a visit to Aix and told her that she had seen all the Paris intellectuals playing at *boules*, rigged up in *berets basques* and complaining bitterly about the food shortage. "I felt such a disgust and shame that I almost wept – but then what else could the poor things have done?" Indeed. Constance was reminded of this one evening when she arrived to overhear the children of Blaise playing in the barn among the haystacks. They were exchanging caresses, making free with each other, and at the same time repeating memorable recipes of long-vanished dishes. It was one way to allaying their hunger in the prevailing dearth – she was both touched and amused. If only Sam had been there to share such things with – yet in a special sense he still was. And then from the conversations with Blaise suddenly some ancient French would rear up its head in the middle of a phrase; she was on the lookout for these cherished exceptions. As, for example: "*Quand l'arbre est vertueux taillez le en bol.*" Or else: "*Madame, je vous signale que le zinc est une matière noble!*"

Then one evening something unusual happened; the duty car dropped her at the corner of the forest path – it would return on the morrow – and she made her way on foot for the last few hundred metres, glad to breathe in the forest for a moment before closing her door upon it. It was dusk, with a fading light. Outside the garden gate stood a duty car with a soldier at the wheel. She peered in at him and with a movement of perplexity invoked an explanation of his presence there at such a time. But the chauffeur did not wind down the window. He simply pointed to the house and then turned away his gaze with an air of brutish insolence. Seeing that there was nothing to be got from him she opened the gate and entered the little garden. And peering through the lattice of the old-fashioned windows into the kitchen, now warm and rosy with firelight, she saw a German officer seated before the blaze, but with his chin sunk upon his chest, apparently asleep. For a moment she thought it might be the General – an irrational enough surmise – and then, peering more closely, she made out the profile of Smirgel. He slept on under her gaze, he seemed hardly to be breathing, with his grey eyes doubly hooded, once by the heavy vulture's eyelids which covered them, twice by the thick-lensed glass with which he covered them. He heard the snap of the latch as she entered the room and drew himself upright in the chair, sighing and rubbing his eyes apologetically, shamefacedly. His greeting sounded ingratiating in its warmth and she was too startled to return it. Instead she said curtly, "What brings you here?" He looked at her for a long moment during which she discerned that his attitude towards her had changed – it was stern now and earnest. "My duty," he said sharply. "We have never really had a talk, have we? Not a really warm confidential talk, have we?"

He stood now and watched her as she went about her conventional duties, taking off her coat to hang on the hook behind the door, smoothing her hair and unpacking her shopping bag, arranging her few spare articles of kitchenware on the tall dresser. Over her shoulder she said, "I trust you know my status, if this is intended to be an official interrogation?"

"Of course I do," he said and as if to punctuate the thought gave the shadow of a heel-click. "I came to put before you some of my own problems in the hope that you may supply some answers. Your sister has been very helpful – of course you know she is here?" Her consternation both puzzled and elated him. He said, "You did not *know*? She has not made contact, then? How strange, for she spoke of you all with great affection, great affection." Constance sat down with some abruptness upon a chair before the fire. "So Livia is here after all?" she cried, almost in a fury, and the officer nodded. She is a nurse now in the Army," he said. "She is working on shock cases at Montfavet – and Quatrefages is in her ward, in her care. Why have you never asked to see him?"

"Why should I? I have only seen him once or twice; I know nothing about his activities except that he worked for Lord Galen. Livia on the contrary knew him much better. But what intrigues you about all this business? Lord Galen and the Prince were partners, hunting for the Templar treasure – mythical as it is I suppose. They thought they were on its traces. Or so I understood."

Smirgel said almost sadly, "So am I, so are we, and so far with little result. I will be frank with you. We have been able to do little with Quatrefages because of his health which has

CONSTANCE

broken down under the strain of our rather harsh questioning. This is all over, now; we have placed him out of reach of the Gestapo – you know that my department belongs to the Foreign Ministry, I report direct to Ribbentrop while Fischer and his colleagues depend upon Himmler. You can imagine there is some rivalry, as in any organisation. So that much that I know is not known to Them." A very fine contempt had now entered his tone of voice upon the word "Them". But she also felt the implication that whatever she told him would be held in confidence. It was puzzling. Later, in discussing this very perturbing visit with her friend Nancy Quiminal, the latter said, "Of course you were puzzled – you were for the first time hearing the voice of the born double agent – he was taking a sounding." Constance's kettle was making a slurring noise. Without more ado she poured out two cups of sage tea and sat down opposite Smirgel, examining his face with attention as she said, "You will please now tell me what is on your mind, or ask me what you have to ask. I cannot stay up all night. I am tired after a long day."

"Of course. Of course." For a moment he was sunk in thought, coiling (so it seemed) and uncoiling his long spatulate fingers. He placed his hands about the cup as if to warm them, and spoke now in the most friendly, kindly manner, as if the act of participating in this little refreshment had brought them much closer together. "I'll tell you everything," he said, clearing his throat. "I will admit that I am under a little pressure, simply because my master is, because the Führer is himself deeply interested in this matter; not, you realise, because of the fortune involved (suppose there were) but just because other astrological predictions which have been made in the past would be confirmed by such a find. You see?"

"What a farce," she said, and he nodded as he said, "From one point of view, certainly it so seems. And yet who can say? The world is such a strange place, and we are busy refashioning it anew . . . we must have all the facts if we can. Now, let me carry on the story. When you were all here on holiday you were very friendly all together, Galen, Prince Hassad, your brother, the consul, and Quatrefages. At that time the last-named had made advances to Livia and been refused by her, so that he nourished a violent hatred against her. So *she* says. There is no reason why not. You were all young and on holiday. But during this period Quatrefages gave her to understand quite clearly that he had managed to pinpoint an orchard with a family vault or crypt in it which showed every sign of being the site they were all looking for. To us he denied this. Anything he might have said, he adds, would have been to seduce her. All they did discover were Greco-Roman remains dug up by the gypsies. We have accounted for most of these pieces, some were sold to the Louvre, some to New York. Can you add anything to this?"

"Nothing," she said. "Livia is the only one who might have had such information. But had it been true either Galen or the Prince would have blurted it out, I'm sure. There was no secrecy about this purely financial adventure, nothing esoteric."

"*Au contraire*," he said sharply, with a warning finger raised. "Quatrefages is deeply steeped in the lore of the gnostics and the Templars. All this apparent rubbish had great symbolic importance for him – he felt himself to be on the track of the Grail, the Arthurian Grail, nothing less. The treasure might have been a simple wooden cup or a priceless chalice or a loving cup buried by the knights; it could have been the cup out of which Jesus drank at the Last Supper. It was not money or specie he thought himself hunting!" His look of triumph matched her own look of surprise. She did not know what to say, the whole matter was so surprisingly novel. He now leaned forward – he had a long neck like a lizard with a pronounced Adam's apple – and said, "This is what interests our Führer, a lost tradition of chivalry which he wishes to re-endow and make a base for a new European model of knight-hood. But of a black order, not white."

"Chivalry!" she said contemptuously, standing up before the fire, her cheeks rosy with warmth and a vivid anger. "I suppose you have not seen the trains pulling out of the station day after day?"

He looked at her in amazement. "You surprise me," he said, "for I thought you would have grasped by now the scope of the New Order, the terrifying new order which now through German arms is trying to establish itself in the western world. You do not see beyond the fate of a few Jews and gypsies, and such riff-raff which will soon be swept away together with the whole Judeo-Christian corpus of ideas based upon gold – for in alchemical terms the Jew is the slave of gold. Spiritually we are on the gold standard of Jewish values. At last this has been recognised, at last someone has dared to break away, to break through into the historic future. You cannot belittle the enormity of the evil we have unleashed in order to outface it; we Germans are a metaphysical race *par excellence* – beyond good and evil stands the new type of man the Führer has beckoned up. But so that he perfects himself we must first go back and start from the wolf, so to speak. We must become specialists in evil until the very distinctions are effaced. Then he will come, the new man whom Nietzsche and Wagner divined. You underestimate the vast scope of the new vision. Our world will be based no more on gold, but on blood – the document of the race-might."

Constance felt the weight of this discourse fall phrase by phrase on her mind, creating an ever-growing shadow of apprehension and horror. Her flesh crept – she realised for the first time that she had, in fact, been in danger of underestimating the vast hysteria of the German belief in all this hocus pocus and Wagnerian black magic, because it did not seem that people could act upon such propositions. Here was a whole nation welded together and orientating its activities in precisely this grim sense.

"But it's a pathology," she exclaimed with a violent disgust, and to her surprise he smiled and nodded his head, as if he took it in a complimentary sense. She said to him with ever-growing dismay, "How innocent we were, how trusting! We were raised not to believe in politics but in man and his innate capacity for justice and a search for equity and happiness, and now this thing." She stared intently at him, seeing him for the first time as a new kind of species, a new kind of insect. He looked like a praying mantis, with all the cold mechanical fury of such a thing in love. After a long pause he continued in a low voice, talking as if to himself, "Nature can be both purposeful and frivolous. One must watch out. Also wasteful, a spend-thrift. We are not imitating her in everything. But the minute you understand the far-reaching conception behind the New Order you cannot withstand its black violence and poetry. We are not washed in the blood of the Christian lamb, but in the blood of inferior races out of which we shall fashion the slaves which are necessary to fulfil our designs. It is not cupidity or rapacity which drives the Führer but the desire for once to let the dark side of man have his full sway, stand to his full height. Seen in this way Evil is Good, don't you see?" He raised his hand and sketched a blow upon the table. But he did not deliver it. He, too, had now a high colour, a flush as if he had been drinking. He found it difficult to support the look of the two contemptuous blue eyes which fixed themselves upon him, it was so obvious and so extreme, her feeling.

There was a long moment of silence, during which she stared fixedly at him – fixedly yet absently for she was intent upon the purport of what he had said, and indeed still shocked and surprised at so trenchant a revelation of unholy faith in this black cause. As if he followed her inner thought he said, "If I have reservations in anything it is perhaps because of our timing which has placed a great burden upon our men and materials. In my view we should have dealt with Communism first – how everyone would have welcomed that! Later the turn of the Jews would have come, more gradually. But what's done is done, and must be followed out to the end. And of course war is a game of chance as well." He suddenly took up his briefcase and hunted in it for a document which he extracted from among a number of photostated materials. "*Tiens,*" he said, and the French word sounded strange on his tongue, "I thought that this might interest you – our service intercepted it. It's addressed to all heads of diplomatic missions abroad and signed by Churchill himself, as you see. At this moment to harbour illusions is rather dangerous, don't you think?"

She was curious enough to take the document and hold it to the light. It was a circular of a standard Foreign Office kind, and had been sent not in cipher but *en clair*, showing that it was not of any great secrecy. But the text had a characteristic ebullience, for it said, "By this end of this year our fortunes will seem to be at their lowest ebb, with bad news coming in from every theatre of war. Nevertheless I can with reason authorise you to feel a distinct measure of moderated optimism. A radical factor has at last emerged from the picture. The enemy has begun to think defensively for the first time; he is stockpiling in rear areas on a scale which proves that he envisages coming retreats. Maybe later historians will describe this as being the real turning-point of the war."

"Why do you show this to me?" she asked, genuinely curious, and he shook his head as he took back the document and replaced it in his briefcase. "Do you think it is a fake?" This made her angry and she said, "Please go now! You have no right to question me." He nodded sadly and said, "Very well. Then, my message is that your sister wants to see you if you can tomorrow at four at Montfavet. May I say you will come?"

"Of course I will."

His heels snapped, he saluted, and went through the door into the garden without another word. Constance sank down in her chair and tried to master her surprise at this extraordinary visit.

She heard the car doors close and the motor start as it slid away down the slope towards the town. At the same moment there came a scuffle of footsteps upon the garden path and Blaise burst into the house with a shotgun under his arm, white with apprehension. "I thought they had come to arrest you," he gasped, mixing anxiety with relief, "and I was ready to *les descendre tous les deux*". This was stupid behaviour and she cried, "For God's sake put the gun away!"

"Have they gone, then?" he said, looking wildly round as if to despatch a couple of hidden Germans lurking in the shadows of the kitchen. "Yes. Gone!" He expelled his breath in a swish of relief. Then in a typical peasant gesture he took a handful of salt from the bowl on the table and scattered it in the fire where it sparked off in blue points. "*Malédiction!*" he exclaimed – it served as an anathema on the departed Boche. "Sit down, Blaise," she said, and made him a sage tea while she told him the news – namely that Livia was indeed there and that on the morrow they would meet. It gave her a strange feeling of tremulousness as she did so. After so long, and in such a weird context. She went to bed early that night but slept badly, and was glad when day broke with its wide, wind-washed skies which presaged a day of sunny calm without wind, welcome respite after a heavy spell of mistral.

She despatched her routine duties on the next day with a perfunctory impatience, feeling that time was gnawing at her, and at last after lunch took the duty car and aimed it in the direction of Montfavet, circling the ancient walls of the town, and slowing down only for the two military checkpoints where, however, she was waved through because of the pennants on her car. The deep woods, the narrow roads came into play at once, so that within a few minutes she found herself lost in the snowy country; there was ice on some of the small saddleback bridges, and while some streams were frozen others foamed and gurgled and overleapt their narrow banks. It was like a landscape around Oxford which she remembered with a special affection because of a youthful love affair which a special kind of tenderness on the part of an undergraduate had rendered memorable. It was something one could not go back on. Now the deep woods sprang up on every side, and presently the car turned sharply and sidled into the little square planted with planes outside the little grey church, the place of rendezvous. She had switched off the engine to idle across the grass verges and come to rest at the main door of the church, which stood open. She saw nobody for the moment so that she entered the church formally dipping her fingers in the holy water stoup and signing herself. Then she saw Smirgel; he was sitting in the small side chapel on the left-hand side underneath a large, bland painting, and he was making notes in a loose-leaf folder. He looked up with a start, as if surprised to see her there. Constance looked equally at a loss. "She is outside, in the square, she is waiting for you," he added. Constance turned back and passed from the gloom of the church to the square lit by the bleak afternoon sunglow. Sure enough, standing upright in a somewhat military attitude at the far end under the planes, stood a figure in a field-grey uniform with a nurse's badge. She did not really recognise her but she advanced with a certain tremulous care, as if she were a bird, so as not to frighten her away, saying, "Livvie, dear! Is it really you?" The nurse appeared to regard her for she nodded, yet she kept her face in half-profile, turned away towards the ivy-covered wall which lined the church precincts. In a hoarse voice she answered, "Yes," and then, motioning Constance towards her, like Hamlet's ghost, as if she had something to impart, she said, "Constance, come here." And with that she sat down upon a stone seat and still keeping her face averted went on, "I could not get in touch before, partly not to compromise you – I did not know what you were doing: partly because . . ." Here a sort of hard misery took possession of her and abolished the end of the phrase. In anyone less harsh of tone it would have seemed the equivalent of a sob – an uprush of anguish. In her it just sounded unqualifiably hard, like the cinders of old emotions.

"I came here to help get the truth out of Quatrefages," she said. "But I have failed, and he has turned the tables on me."

"Livvie," said her sister, "why are you turned away like this, why don't you look at me?"

"I've lost an eye," said Livia laconically. And then continued to speak in a hollow resonant voice and with apparent indifference, asking for news of Blanford and Hilary. When she heard of Blanford's grievous wound she bowed her head briefly, but said nothing. "And Sam?" she said with a sharpened note of interrogation. Constance drew a breath and answered, "Sam is dead, killed in action." And as she said so it became for the first time a fact. Sam died now as a reality, as the figment she had been carrying around inside her like an unaborted child. "Sam dead?" said Livia in the same harsh tone. "Ha!" as if she could not quite believe it. Constance said clearly, "Sam is dead, Livvie. Sam is dead."

It was astonishing to feel a sort of relief in the depths of the statement, yet it was truly a relief suddenly to feel the ghost of Sam recede, diminish, and then all but disappear – at least to reduce itself to something of quite manageable proportions. It made her ashamed, this unexpected trick of the emotions. What a trickster life was, and how merciless to our self-respect. It was almost as if the open statement had all at once revealed a hollowness in the very calibre of her pain, had shown it up as,

CONSTANCE

if not a sham, at least as something exaggerated.

"Well, that's that," cried Livia in her harsh corncrake's tone. "You will have to lump it, that's all."

But with the new sense of liberation brought by this confession Constance was also suddenly feeling the weight of her experiences here in the city. As if she had been unaware of her own fatigue. But Livia was talking now, still with the averted face, still out of the side of her mouth. "I have been up to the house once or twice, but I did not wish to embarrass you – I can imagine your job must need tact. Meanwhile I felt I must talk to you quite urgently if only to say goodbye and to tell you that Quatrefages has turned the tables on me, he has denounced us all as Jews. Smirgel is trying to keep this from the Gestapo but it can only be a matter of time before I am recalled. Perhaps suddenly in a few days."

"What rubbish," said Constance. "Surely you can tell them the truth?"

"I became a German subject, unlike you."

"But it's preposterous. I shall go and tell them that we are English, if you won't."

"I should wait until something happens before doing such a thing. Besides, you are technically Swiss, remember? They would not believe you more than me!"

"I shall ask to see the General," said Constance with an angry self righteousness. "I shall talk to him."

Livia shook her head and sighed as she said, "Things are in such a tangle that one could expect anything. I just tell you to warn you, but I ask you not to do anything rash that might compromise me further. Are you going to see Quatrefages?"

"Should I?"

"I don't know. Why, after all? He is pretending to be mad in order to avoid further interrogation, that is all."

"I won't see him," said Constance on a sudden note of resolve, "specially if he is playing us off against the Nazis."

Livia gave a world-weary shrug and sighed again, a pain-laden little sound. "Well, I'll say goodbye, Constance."

She stood up, still at the awkward half-angle to her sister, face turned away. Constance upon an impulse cried out, "Livvie, dear, do you still believe in . . ." she did not know quite how to phrase the question that was on her mind ". . . all this?" she finished rather lamely, though the comprehensive gesture of the hand was intended to encompass everything, the whole world crisis provoked by Nazism. Livia started to move off towards the trees, though she took the time to answer, "Yes. More than ever!" and there was nothing in her tone to belie her response. But she moved away towards the trees with ever-sharpening stride. Constance stopped with vexation which was at once swallowed by compassion for her sister, and she hurried after her saying, "Livia, wait! When shall we meet again?" To this however Livia had no response, and as the distance between them increased it was clear that there was not going to be one. Constance stood and watched the tall figure losing itself among the trees.

She turned back into the dark church to where Smirgel sat, absorbed in the notes he was making. He made room for her in the pew but she preferred to remain standing as she said, "Can't you do *anything* to help Livia? You know the real truth about us all, after all." He smiled his slow, obsequious smile. "The unlucky thing is that the information was confided to the Gestapo, not to my department, hence the concern. However it is too early to worry. If anything happens I will come and seek your advice, if I may."

"I thought of seeing the General," she said, for the idea still worked upon her despite all she knew about divided commands and internal rivalries among the occupying forces. Smirgel threw up his hands. "The General!" he said on a note of mocking commiseration. "He is so weighed down by his new command that he can think of nothing else. Since now the possibilities of a second front are beginning to take shape, Avignon becomes a very important strategic point to group both material and reserves. Wait and see in a few weeks." Vaguely she had followed some of the gossip about a second front, and a possible attack upon the French Riviera coast, which would cut off the German armies in both Italy and Africa. But she thought this was simply part of the propaganda war, not something serious. It was disconcerting, yet heartening, to find that the Nazis were giving credence to such ideas. "Von Esslin is in heaven," went on Smirgel. "He was pining for Russia and feeling he had been overlooked; now his command is of supreme importance and he has a whole new staff on his back. I don't believe that he would have time for you, even if he wanted to see you."

"We'll see. I must reflect."

Nor was his somewhat cynical judgement (his frankness astonished Constance) so far off the mark, for Von Esslin, after a long period of apparent neglect, during which the whole region appeared to have been earmarked simply as a back area for convalescents from the Russian fronts, suddenly found himself centre stage with a vastly increased responsibility carrying all the possibilities of professional advancement with it. The change in accent was electrifyingly sudden – fruit of some new propaganda suggestions about a Second Front – and all of a sudden he was having support troops and tank companies wished upon him in quantities too large to camouflage, too numerous to house easily in this rather barren, backward land of austere towns and empty heaths. Not only that – a whole riff-raff of pioneer regiments composed of renegade Russians and Czechs and Poles had been drafted south, designated for new, unspecified labours which had as yet not been defined. All was flux and uncertainty; and meanwhile the Allies had begun to pay some attention to the bridges over the rivers. The disposition of the rivers – it was the real nightmare of Von

Esslin. Often in his dreams the great operations board in the Castle Intelligence room floated into his vision: the Rhône, Durance and so on with their great speed and vexatious lateral cuts along the limestone outer skin of Provence. From the beginning of time they had been military hazards – preventing the Romans from reaching Britain, preventing Hannibal from reaching Rome, preventing . . . He was not sure on which side of the Rhône to keep his tanks, his precious unwieldy panzer forces, now doubled. So he kept them always in uncertain movement, crossing and withdrawing, forming and dispersing. It was wasteful in fuel. But with the new bombing patterns . . . The British had replaced the slovenly high-level bombardiers of the U.S. Air Force. They came low and were thorough, methodical; very little civilian damage seemed to follow in their path, but meanwhile the goods yards of the railways had begun to suffer, while bits began to fly off the precious bridges, the panzers' lifeline. Theories of a south European landing on the Riviera were doubtless exaggerated, yet nevertheless this new phase marked everything with a new accent of uncertainty and concern. (He had received two new decorations, which was highly pleasing. His mother was delighted of course.)

But the war had slowed, was beginning to drag a little, while this heavy stockpiling in his area was rather a perplexity. He sent out to hunt for underground caves capable of being enlarged into vast ammunition depots. Of course one thing that was quite easy in such a country of calcareous limestones was to pierce the topcrust with roadmender's tools, and seek out caverns which might suit such a purpose. But it was tedious and long, and there appeared to be no geodetic surveys of the lonely garrigues which might provide clues. Then all too easily one stumbled into underground workings of abandoned Roman mines only to find that they were full of water, possessed by some secret river, which only gave a sign of life during heavy rain, but then burst its banks, overshot its levels.

Not to speak of the Rhône itself, guzzling mud as it swept down from Geneva, increasing velocity steadily until before Avignon it developed almost twelve knots of speed. The slightest level-change in this context meant all the islands and the estuary in the centre flooded, while the water snaked its way into the cellars and granaries of the medieval central quarters of the town.

The town began to suffer sleepless nights as the bombing sharpened; from Lord Galen's best bedroom Von Esslin could hear the sirens, and hear the ambulances plying their trade after each attack. Holes in the pavements became a common-place. But he had grouped his armour round the castle at Villeneuve, regretting its prominence as a target but insisting to himself that if the bridge was put out of action he could at least disengage in a westerly fashion; but . . . this was no con-solation if one thought of an enemy coming up from, say, Nice. He was teased by all this problematic strategy. Yes, things had changed, there was a new kind of urgency in the air. One day he received a personal order from the Leader telling him to turn out and witness the execution of three "conspirators" in his sector. No explanations were offered. In a cold blue dawn he watched as three young Austrian aristocrats, brown and slender as sheepdogs, entered the prison yard where they were attended by an executioner wearing a top hat and morning dress; their heads were clumsily hacked off with an axe. The General went back to his office in a quiet rage. He had not even been told their names nor why they were being executed. He did not deign to ask either the Gestapo or Smirgel – an icy formality characterised their relations. But he took pleasure in crossing them whenever he could, for he was after all, the military power while they were the civil.

The ill-omened Fischer was back once more after a refresher course in his macabre trade. He had done fatigues and courses in several of the more notable camps, and the experience had been hardly inspiriting (yes, he had been expecting something inspiring and uplifting, something also a little reassuring). He was tired like everyone else, but lately the way people looked at him without saying anything had begun to play upon his nerves. And then the camps – things were being slowed down steadily for they simply could not cope with the influx of men and women destined for the incinerators. He read a carefully reasoned Gestapo report on the matter which told him that it was no easy task to dispose of bodies – their fats and acids were hard of disposal, made poor and over-acid manures, were not suitable for soaps. It cost a fortune to gas and burn them. In spite of technical advances the rate of obliteration would have to slow down to keep pace with the machines and work task of the present system – some four hundred murder camps. He had walked dispiritedly around Buchenwald in the feathery light snow which creaked under his boots, brooding on the problem. How charming was the forest which surrounded the camp. Snow had made the slopes brindled with dark points of charcoal, stubble-like. Here in this peaceful decor had walked Goethe and Eckermann of whom he had never heard. The tall chimneys of the crematoria fumed softly on the blue icy air. Burning bodies stank like old motor tyres, he reflected, and blood hissed like rain on dead leaves. The situation was a wretched one – they had miscalculated – a humiliating state of affairs for a country with such great technical resources, such long experience, so many fine brains; but there was nothing for it, the whole process must slow down to keep pace with the available means. The latest lists of detainees would be pended and they would be allowed to return to their homes on a temporary basis. Pity. Among them was the little priest of Montfavet – it had not been difficult to convict him of having Jewish origins. It was his own fault, drawing attention to himself by absolving some of the senior officers, friends of Von Esslin. The names of the officers in question had been noted and filed for reference. But the arrest of the little priest had been a pleasant way of checkmating the General, with his superior airs!

Things at Tu Duc had changed somewhat also with the advent of heavy rainstorms followed by frosts and ice-bound forest roads. In the park another tall pine had been torn down by the mistral. It made a tremendous tearing din in the night, the owls flew whewing in all directions. The old conservatory sprang a leak and rain dripped into it, falling upon the old Freudian sofa, so that it was necessary to rescue it and drag it into the kitchen where at least Constance could lie at ease on it before the fire.

To her intense annoyance she fell ill, with high temperatures, raging migraine, toothache: indeed a whole congeries of petty troubles which all added up to an overwhelming fatigue, slowly accumulated over months. Strangely all this had tumbled in upon her like a sandcastle by the simple act of announcing Sam's death to Livia as a historic fact. With that announcement and the realisations of the stark truth she had begun to feel bereft, dispossessed. What was she doing in this bitter and beautiful country?

She must ask for leave, there was no other way of dealing with it.

Her bedroom being so cold, she spent much of her time spread out upon the old sofa in front of the fire, devouring the pamphlets and books which she had brought with her. While the wind rattled the casements she reflected that it might have been upon this very sofa that Dora or the egregious Wolf Man . . . But who the devil in this country would be interested in such things? It gave her a great sense of loneliness to be locked up here with all this information, like a bank vault, while all round her the icy country was in the grip of the monotonies that war engenders. What she needed now was a spell of calm by the lake, and to this end she contacted the

Swiss consul who came up to call on her in his old car. Yes, he was planning on a leave, and would be glad to offer her a seat in his car, but first she must really manage to shake off her ills, and scramble to her feet. The journey, though not fearfully long, was an arduous one, for as soon as the roads approached the mountains the ordinary amenities of travel – hotels, electricity, garages – failed them. But he would certainly go, and take her with him, when the time was ripe. It would anyway take a little time to get the necessary *laissez-passer* for the two of them, for Geneva must be contacted via Berlin.

Buoyed up by the thought of escape from the town and its problems she actually persuaded herself back into a state of tolerable health once more, and used her sick leave to walk in the surrounding forest which was, more often than not, snow-bound, though the paths were free of access. She would come back to the kitchen grate before dusk, glad of its warmth and the secrecy with which it invested her impoverished intellectual life: a few trivial pamphlets – she gnawed on them like a dog upon a bone. But the death of Livia was completely unexpected.

As with everything concerning Livia, it seemed motiveless – or simply to belong to that category of events which history might later sum up as a sort of entropy. The sorrow, the abandon, the refusal – it was all there in the gesture: and at the same time a cry for help from the nursery of the human consciousness, for like a hunted animal she had crept back to the one burrow which had once been hers, for however short a time, in that forgotten summer. It made Constance groan in sympathy with what she imagined that profound pain must have been like to her inconstant sister; to carry the weight of it inside her like a stone. She hung there so still, some graphic illustration for a study of conceit – intellectual *hubris*, which had been her darkest driving force. Yet how had she got in and when? Later Blaise found the abandoned bicycle in the shrubbery by the pool, and one of the big Venetian shutters with weak hinges had been forced. But there were no other marks of her entry, and she had taken the stairs up to "her" room without turning aside into the habitable rooms where Constance dwelt.

That actual intimation of the fact too was curious in the manner of its advent. They had had an afternoon of blusterous tramontana, continually changing direction and force, and exploding the light snowfalls with mischievous gusts. But towards dusk it ceased abruptly and gave way to a watery sunlight and open sky, preludes to nightfall. She could not say with any accuracy that she "heard" anything, no, but at a certain moment she raised her head from her book like a gun dog who scents the presence of game. She had a feeling that something somewhere was beckoning to her, called for her attention. She stood up and stayed stock-still for a long moment before setting off to follow this enigmatic signal through the labyrinths of the intuition. Once in the hall the stairs beckoned as they always do. It was like following a note of music – perhaps only to find at the end that there was somewhere a musical tap dripping in a dry tin basin. No, but this was soundless. Up she went, and on the first floor there might have been an excuse to hover a bit, though all the rooms were shut. She threw open the doors with a definitive air, but nothing was revealed apart from traces of mice in the dust, and the obstinate tapping of fronds at the window. It was a long time since she had come up here. Next came the semi-landing with the lunette window, and here the door opened under the pressure of a single finger, and with a sigh and creak. She entered very slowly, gradually revealing to herself the hanging figure with its contrite downcast head, chapfallen now and pale from lack of blood. But all very orderly and condensed – there was no sprawling. The lost eye looked like the withered belly button of some medieval saint. With its light extinguished, the whole face, with its spectral planes, looked penitential, daunted by adversity. The pinions were quite explicitly Gestapo in their expert fit – you could pinion your own arms easily with them. The hair was sad and tired and the partings full of dandruff.

She took the pulse, though it was merely formality; the stillness told all. Then for a moment she hugged the ankles of the form, crying "Livvie! Livvie!" Then came the problem of releasing the body from its ropes – how could this be done without Blaise? Suddenly she took wing, racing down the stairs and out across the garden to the house of the couple, calling him now in urgent tones, telling him to bring his axe and follow her. Together they retraced their steps until once more they stood before Livia's body. A dull thwack of Blaise's axe and it swirled and thumped at their feet upon the floor of the little loft. Blaise crossed himself over and over again and muttered prayers of a sort. Constance sank down upon a chair.

The pain she felt now, accompanied as it was by a frustrated vexation which cast her back into the deepest depths of her childhood, was as physical as it was banal, though she could not give it a true location – what a crazy mixture of migraine, ulcer, cystitis, all coming so suddenly upon so much fever and fatigue that it seemed to lay rough hands upon her shoulders, pushing her down to the hard kitchen chair. She had put her hands over her ears and pressed them tight but this was not to hear the hoarse question of Blaise, addressed partly to her and partly to the world at large: "*Mais pourquoi?*" Indeed it was the capital question, but it had been asked of Livia since her birth, for nothing that she did or was entered into the sphere of rational explanations. That echoing "Why" had resounded already in the mind of Constance as she stood, holding the hanging body round the thighs to ease the weight on the rope and facilitate the task of the axe, weeping all the while with the tears coming from some remote and secret stronghold of infancy. The "why" extended in every direction, on all sides. Why, for example, had they not been more alike since they were brought up together by the same inadequate child-hater, deprived of the cuddling and caressing which form the self-esteem of the body so that its image can project faith and acceptance, sure of itself? This was how Constance "read" Livia when she thought of her as a case. The bitter narcissism, the jealousy, the withdrawn and melancholy character had evolved out of this background which Constance had shared with her; Hilary much less, for he had been sent away. Exasperation raged within her as she gazed down upon the face, fast setting into its mould of final secrecy. She had seen much of death professionally, but that is not the same thing.

Livia had fallen awkwardly with one leg doubled half under her, and she looked now like a dummy, a lay figure such as dressmakers use for their models. Blaise corrected the posture and then, after a moment's thought, took off his scarf and lashed the ankles together. Meanwhile her sister sat there and stared at her, though she was really staring at her own thoughts and memories. What lasted was the stinging exasperation – never to have been confided in. And now this maladroit and graceless act to round everything off; she hoped, Constance hoped, that it would not compromise her own departure to Geneva. It was a troubling thought, and as if to echo it, Blaise said: "What shall we do with her?" His own mind told him that it would be best to bury her in the garden in some secret corner and say nothing to a soul. . . . But this did not appeal to Constance who could foresee searches and questionings following upon a disappearance of that kind. "Happily Madame Nancy is coming this evening with the duty car, so we can take her down to the morgue and I can approach a doctor to certify her death. At least I hope so." The decision somehow released her frozen energy, and she went into action to prepare the body for easy transportation, pinioning the arms and covering the features. Then they rolled Livia in a coverlet and tied the form once round with a piece of cord. Thus she might be easily carried out of the house. Blaise also was concerned that his wife should not see the body – he said that he would tell her about the matter later on, when all was in order. "Let us have a drink," he said, "a good drink. What an unhappy thing!" And for once Constance did not refuse the drink in favour of tea or coffee. Between them they placed the silent form upon the sofa, there to wait until they could get it into the back seat of the duty car. Constance hoped that there would be no hitch, or that Quiminal had not forgotten her promise.

"No, no," said Blaise; "If she said she will come, she will come. She is a Protestant, after all."

He had hardly uttered the prophetic phrase when they heard the peculiar and characteristic seething noise of the Volkswagen engine and the whine of its tyres on the gravel before the gate. They stood up somewhat irresolutely and waited for the girl, who walked down the garden path and clicked open the latch of the kitchen door, to find herself face to face with them. It surprised her to see Constance looking positively ill with distress and Blaise whose sorrow for his friend gave him a hangdog expression which would have been hard to interpret had not the blue eyes also taken in the wrapped and silent dummy on the sofa. She turned and put her arms about Constance, saying simply, "Tell me! *Raconte!*" and haltingly Constance told her the little they knew about the motives of Livia, and also about their recent meeting at Montfavet. Quiminal sat down on a chair and tapped the finger of her gloved hand upon her lips. "We must avoid any trouble if possible," she said with decision, and her firm tone re-invigorated the resolve of her friend, who went to the sink in the corner and washed her face and hands slowly and methodi-cally, while they both thought of ways and means to deal with the situation; somehow it would have to be declared – at least to the local authorities – and indeed explained. Slowly a plan began to dawn on them.

Quiminal said, "Are you fit to come with me? Good! Then you will take her directly to the morgue, dropping me off at the office. I will join you as swiftly as I can with a doctor and with Smirgel – it would be wise to implicate him as he is likely to help rather than hinder. Do you agree? You know the morgue people already." Constance had been down once or twice to identify or advise them on civilian corpses picked up by the police. Yes, it was feasible, and this way she might avoid taking Blaise with her into town to help – it would spare him unwelcome publicity as a contact of hers. "We'll have a try," she said and jumped up with a new resolution.

Blaise was disappointed but said nothing; he went off to rejoin his wife. Together the two girls managed to carry and arrange the figure in the back of the car, somewhat awkwardly to be sure. Then they set off upon the icy road to Tubain, knowing that they must reach the town before nightfall. This bleak winter dusk with its hint of frost and snow was ideal for such an expedition. The sentries on the checkposts were half-asleep with the cold and could not bother with them – they waved them on almost with impatience. And so across the bridge and into the enceinte of the massive walls, threading their way towards the quarter where the morgue lay. Quiminal was duly dropped off by the square and scampered off like a hare to perform her part of the bargain. Constance went on alone now until she came to the ugly little building which had once been an abbatoir and now did service as a morgue. She ran up the steps and, pressing the bell, lifted the flap of the letter-box to shout through it the name of the warden: "François! *C'est Madame Constance.* Open up please. *Oui, c'est le docteur.*" With the customary sloth and groans the old man turned the key and the high doors swung open. "What do you bring?" he said, seeing nothing but an apparently empty car. "A client," she replied according to the time-honoured pleasantry among those who dealt in corpses with as much emotion as a butcher does with meat. Grumbling, he turned back and she followed him to take one end of the old and stained stretcher into whose stout frame the slender wrapped form was placed, to be carried into the building where Constance herself elected to undress it before placing it in one of the long oak drawers which covered one whole wall of the establishment. François groaned and grumbled as he assisted her, but it was largely about the difficulty of running things in the present conditions. "Don't blame me for the smell," he said with bitterness. "How do they expect me to operate on half-power? No refrigeration plant could take it. The place is beginning to smell to high heaven." He rambled on between groans as they conducted the body to the theatre where it would be placed upon a marble slab – an old-fashioned one which recalled those upon which fishmongers displayed their catch half a century before. "Careful with her – she's a friend," cried Constance in the face of his clumsy and negligent gestures, his attempts to undo the figure which was so professionally tied up by Blaise. "Let me do it."

"How old is it?" he said, and then, "A woman did you say?" But he recoiled when he saw who it was. "It's the nurse of Montfavet," he said, "I know her all right." This was an unexpected departure. He went on, "But she is in uniform, part of the army. We can't take her in here." This was one of the distinctions which Constance had foreseen and feared. She was examining those dreadful bruises upon the throat when a voice from behind her answered the objection. It was the voice of Smirgel and it said, "I will be responsible. Please do go ahead. A doctor is on his way here." He seated himself upon the only chair and seemed about to make notes or fill in forms or perform some clerical work. Meanwhile they turned on the arc lamp above the high operating table, and which at once threw up the surroundings with its light. They were in a large crypt with white tiled walls, somewhat greasy; a number of hoses depended from the ceiling, with one of which they were now able to wash the quiet body – water so hot that it contributed a distinct tint of warmth to the marble flesh. They cut off the body's dark hair which Constance put in her handbag – she would afterwards make keepsakes from it for the three survivors of the shared summer. Strangely enough while she was doing this Smirgel came to her side and stared down upon the recumbent figure for a moment before he gave a very small, a hardly audible sob, but whether of affection or contrition, or both, it was impossible to judge. Constance eyed him keenly and most curiously. "Was she anything to you?" she asked, on the spur of an impulse, but the German did not answer. He went back to his seat where he crossed his legs and closed his eyes. They went on with the preparations, drying her and cutting her nails short. Then came the cheap cotton shroud through which her shorn head peered with an expression of nervous vagueness. And now came Quiminal with a man who was apparently a doctor for he carried the forms which attested to the death of someone "from natural causes". But first he went through the parody of verifying the death by placing a stethoscope upon the pulse. (The strangulation marks were hidden by the shroud.) Then he went into the outer office and wrote industriously for a moment upon several forms which he thrust upon Quiminal before taking his leave in perfunctory fashion.

Now she was ready; but before tilting her off the table Constance asked for the traditional scalpel which the old man kept handy for such a purpose, and made a deep incision in the artery of the thigh, binding it up with a strip of tape against leakage. So she was propelled on a spider-like trolley towards the huge filing cabinet of oak which, like a gigantic chest-of-drawers, held the dead. "And the funeral?" said the keeper, who was about to start once more upon his theme concerning the current, and the difficulties of refrigeration. "She will be buried," said Smirgel unexpectedly, "with full military honours. I have seen to everything." Constance looked at him curiously. It seemed so strange that he should seem to be so moved. "Do I come?" she said, and was relieved when he shook his head. "I can't ask you, it will be in the Citadel."

Poor Livia! What an apotheosis!

They would, she supposed, fire a salute over the grave. "Natural causes" is after all the best description of such events, so refactory do they seem to human logic. A siren sounded somewhere: they had forgotten the war for a moment. The car stood in the dark street waiting for them. All of a sudden Constance felt passionately hungry, for she had eaten little or nothing all day. In the pocket of her greatcoat she found a slip of chewing gum which would have to sustain her until she got home. And Quiminal: "Do you want me to come?" she asked Constance. "Or would you prefer to be alone?" Constance nodded on the word alone, but then another thought struck her: "If I don't reappear at the office tomorrow it's because the Swiss consul has come and we've left for Geneva; you will not forget to come up and fetch the car?" It was agreed, and after a warm embrace the little car set off to carry her home across the bridge. The Rhône was ominously high; Constance's dimmed headlights did not meet with approval from a passing patrol which hooted at her. She slowed to shout "Emergency" at them, and then took the desolate and dark side-roads leading away into the hills.

The whole episode throbbed inside her, matching her fatigue which came and went in waves, stirred, it would almost seem, by the swaying and bucking of the little car. So that was the end of Livia, an end with no beginning, with no explanation. Had she been Smirgel's mistress? An idle enough thought: Livia belonged to nobody. She thought of her now, lying wrapped in her cotton *burnous* in the great sideboard –

what else could one call it? – of the morgue, a companion now
for tramps picked up in the frozen ditches, or elderly and half-
starved citizens of the town laid low by frost on their shopping
expeditions. She would lie there all night in her abstracted,
withdrawn death mood, the silence only broken by the little
withered noise of the machinery working at half-current. She
would never see her again; she repeated the words "Never
again" in order to come to grips with the idea. It was as though
someone had thrown a stone to make a sudden hole in the décor
of their lives, just as Sam's death had done; smashed reality like
a pane of glass. She realised then to what extent the dead
exercise the profession of alibi-makers for the living; she lived
in part because she was reflected in these people – they gave her
substance and being. And then another, heavier thought
visited her: what would Aubrey feel about it? Should she tell
him or wait for someone else to do so? She had a sudden picture
of his expressive face conveying sadness, and with a shock of
surprise felt a sudden wave of love for him. The beloved old
slowcoach of the almost forgotten summer. In one of the cupboards upstairs she had found a discarded and forgotten exercise book of his which still contained notes and jottings,
though now half illegible from damp. Moreover the book had
been torn across and obviously flung carelessly into the cupboard. She made no attempt to decipher any of the annotations,
feeling that in some way it would be a violation of Aubrey's
privacy – he was, like her, touchy about such things. But she
put it carefully in a folder with the intention of returning it to
him when next they met. She could not have possibly guessed
how soon this would be: the surprise must wait upon her
return to Geneva and the Head Office.

At the house, however, there was another surprise. A man
sat in front of the fireplace warming his hands, or trying to for
the fire was almost out. It was the Swiss consul. She greeted him
wonderingly. "I didn't see your car," she said, and he explained

that he had hidden it in the trees. "As I warned you, it is very sudden; we must start for Geneva tonight, as soon as you can get ready. I have had the *laissez-passer*, everything is in order. But we must hurry. I will tell you more when we get on the road." It would not take her long, for her affairs were in tolerable order, her packing almost done. "Very well," she said, between exhaustion and elation. "Very well."

She went upstairs to where the cupboard stood which housed her few clothes and rapidly completed the packing of her small suitcase; with this and a briefcase of papers and toilet gear she rejoined her companion who was now betraying every sign of anxiety, looking at his watch, and standing now upon one leg, now upon the other. Blaise appeared to lock up after her and take the keys. She explained rapidly and in low tones the chain of events which concerned the fate of Livia, reassuring him that there would be no repercussions to worry about. Then the three of them walked into the forest clearing among the tall planes to where the diplomat's car stood with its double pennants in their leather sleeves and emphatic diplomatic insignia. The consul slipped off the leather cases and released the flags – one Swiss and one with a swastika. He climbed in and started the motor. "I am ready," he said, and Constance made her goodbyes, promising to return before the end of the month. They moved off slowly down the hill and turning away from the city engaged the complicated loops and gradients of the northern road, which soon brought them down to river level. It was possible to increase speed, though in places the Rhône was exceptionally high and ran in the counter sense within a few metres of their wheels.

But the run was not all to be so calm for already at Valence they ran into a cloud of command cars buzzing about like insects to clear the main highway; they were deflected to side roads and were not sorry, for they ran through remote and beautiful villages which seemed deserted. Obviously there was a push southwards being organised, forming like a cloud upon the invisible horizon. The car was cold but the steady murmur of the powerful engine was reassuring, comforting. Apart from the grand turmoil in Valence they ran into no other traffic of consequence, but it was well after midnight when they reached the border and were halted by a military barrier. Lanterns and hurricane lamps flared everywhere inside a disused railway shed, a desolate rotting edifice full of wooden sleepers. Some human ones also.

Here they were roughly told to get out and shift their baggage on to trestles for inspection, which they did, yawning. After a methodical search through their affairs they were permitted through, though she had to walk the hundred or so yards of dark permanent way while the Swiss, being a diplomat, was allowed the privilege of driving his car along a dirt track, to emerge behind the barbed wire which marked the Swiss frontier. A man was waiting for her arrival, lurking in the shadows.

"How ill, how pale she looks," he thought as he watched her from his point of vantage in the shadow of the building. "And her hair all in rat's tails and dirty." He had half a mind to turn away and vanish, for he had not been expected and would not be missed. But his heart held him there, like a compass pointed upon Stella Polaris, yet without the courage as yet to go forward, to announce himself. She must at most have expected a duty car with a driver. He thought of that abundant blonde hair with a pang of memory. Now her head was casually done up in a coloured scarf tied under her chin. She looked like a French peasant from the occupied zone, dirty, listless and tired. He had not expected to find her in such a state of fatigue and disarray, and he did not know whether his presence might make her feel humiliated. But retire he could not, nor advance, nor decide anything whatsoever for himself.

He was revealed to her sleepy eyes by a bar of gold light

thrown from a doorway suddenly opened by a militia man. "Mr. Affad!" There was no ambiguity in her relief and enthusiasm; she went up to him in a somewhat irresolute fashion, as if about to put out her hand; but they embraced instead, and stood for a moment yoked thus, absurdly relieved and delighted by the other's presence. It was wonderful to feel his body breathing in her arms. Caresses! That is what she had been missing all this time, she realised, that is what her own body hungered for. Yet she had thought little of him, and had never as far as she could remember, dreamed of him. Now all of a sudden she was set alight by the touch of him and the firm resolution of his arms around her. She relinquished him with regret for she was obliged to introduce him to her travelling companion. To her delight she distinctly saw a frown of jealousy appear on his charming face. It was wonderful to see him feign a coldness he did not feel now, imagining heaven knows what about this portly and unimaginative figure who was all too anxious to relinquish her and head for home. She thanked him suitably, promised to keep in touch about their joint return to duty, and turned to follow Affad who already had her affairs in hand. His private car, an old American sedan, stood at the side of the road, and they piled into its warmth with gratitude. As he started the motor he said, "Look at me, Constance," and she obeyed, though it at once made her conscious of her appearance. She put her hand up to her hair and slipped off her scarf. "Why?" He smiled. "I wanted to see how you look when you are away, working."

"Grubby and crow's-footed, as you see."

He said, "Not for long. How tired are you? I have told the hotel hairdresser to stand by for breakfast-time."

"Bless you. That would be marvellous."

"But first I must tell you my real news – before you go off to sleep. Constance, we have managed to get Aubrey on to an exchange list of badly wounded prisoners of war – fifty

German against fifty English. They will come here in a week's time. Once here he can detach himself and we must see that he gets medical treatment – whatever is needed for his condition. This is where you come in. I have his whole dossier now; you will be able to study it in detail and judge. Are you listening?"

"Of course I'm listening," she said indignantly. "I am bowled over, that is all. What a miracle!"

She had planned to call back at her flat but it was not to be thus; the hour was against them. Heavy fog and a dirty white light did nothing to enhance the beauty of the lakeside town they were approaching with suitable caution. There was no traffic, fortunately, but they were obliged to hoot a warning on the curves of the hills – a sound which echoed dolefully on their ears. They were moving towards the outer suburbs now among green foothills still partly encumbered with fresh snow. She had an attack of yawns which made him smile. "Poor Constance!" he commiserated. "You could sleep for a month – and so you shall. But for today . . ." He pointed a long forefinger at the clock on the dashboard which said four o'clock. "We have fallen askew; nothing will start before six-thirty now. The best would be to come back to my suite – you know how big it is. I can give you a whole small flat to yourself, bathroom and all. Have you a change of clothes with you? Very well, then wash and have a nap. This afternoon you can go down to the hairdresser and – well, anything you feel up to. I have some mail for you, too, which is also in my room. What do you say?"

"And Aubrey? When will he get here?" The very words filled her with amazement, as if she had not fully realised the meaning they conveyed as yet. The image of Sam and Aubrey walking arm-in-arm over the bridge at Avignon came back to her like some ancient yellowed snapshot found at the bottom of a trunk. "I can't take it in," she said again and again, and then yawning fell into a deep slumber which only the sudden switching off of the motor eased into dazed wakefulness. They were at the hotel already and her companion was ringing the night bell. A sleepy hall porter opened to them and took their possessions; in the lift she leaned against Affad, almost asleep again, which gave him an excuse to put an arm about her shoulders and guide her towards his suite. Once there they explored the adjacent rooms which he had never bothered to investigate. They were sumptuous double rooms each with a bathroom which was still packed with toilet articles, soaps and scents and oils which were part of the hotel propaganda of the day. "I'll take this one," she said, relieving him of her case. "And I shall have a long bath and clean-up; then I'll come *chez vous* if you promise to be kind to me and not too violent. I need cherishing." It touched him to the heart – her disorder and grubbiness. "I understand you," he said gravely while she looked at him carefully, keenly with her fine eyes. She was actually asking herself, "What *is* it about short-sighted men that I find so attractive? And these long cervine heads . . ." But she went on sternly, as if to warn him against her inadequacy. "You see, I can't love any more; like someone with prolapse or hernia, I'm forbidden to handle heavy objects – all the mysterious symbols of attachment, heavy metaphysical baggage. I am a simple junior psychiatrist, a sorcerer's apprentice. A devil's advocate . . ." she tailed away into yet another yawn.

"I am demanding nothing of you," he said, though he knew this to be untrue. He was irritated by her attitude.

"I know," she said. "Sorry to be prosy. It's a poor return for your thoughtfulness. It's fatigue and the feeling of un-reality – all that hot water and soap after my usual hip bath and a boiling kettle."

"I am going to doze a little," he said, though he knew himself to be far too excited to sleep. Constance nodded her approval. "Maybe I will too, in my bath," she said.

It was marvellous to hear the swish of the hot water into

her bath, and to finger all the toilet delicacies on the shelves. She would have liked to use everything, all at once in one terrific and wasteful splurge, but of course it would have been to no purpose; the oils and soaps cancelled each other out. Nevertheless she sank sighing down in a nest of violet bubbles, submerged completely until all she could hear was the thick drumming of the water as it rushed into the bath. She washed her hair, so badly in need of the shears, and wrapped it in a towel before falling magistrally asleep in the warmth, her head against the back of the bath. Such sleep – of the very bones it would seem – no opiate could have procured for her, and diminishing the hot flow to a steady trickle she relaxed as if for eternity.

Affad, too, was weary, for he had had no sleep while waiting at the frontier post – simply a fugitive doze in the back of the car. Now he changed into a thick winter dressing-gown and turned in, reading for a few moments by the light of his bedside lamp. For how long he did not know, but he woke with a jolt to find his bedside clock showing six, and the yellow dawn light over the lake gradually increasing in strength. There was no sign of Constance and he thought it probable that she had also taken to her bed in one of the two spare rooms of the suite. He would not have disturbed her for worlds. Then he heard the annoying and persistent sound of the over-flow running in her bathroom. He listened to it for a long moment, trying to decide what it might signify. Had she left the tap on and gone to bed? Had she gone to sleep in the bath, oblivious to the running water? Perhaps he should investigate and turn it off? He allowed curiosity and anxiety to master his disinclination and gently opened the bathroom door to see what was the matter. But unexpectedly she had crawled out of the bath and on to the wide table – the masseur's settee so to speak – after wrapping herself in the heavy white burnous of towelling provided by the hotel. White in a white decor, she slept quietly, her head still rolled up into a seashell shape. Her lips were parted on the faintest suggestion of a half-smile and she heard nothing of his stealthy approach. In all that whiteness and steam he tiptoed to close the tap, and was turning away to leave when he noticed the blood flowing down from the couch, from the half-opened gown, the half-opened legs – a red pool into which he had inadvertently trodden with his bare foot and printed the tiles. What awakened her was the sudden cessation of the noise from the bath, and dimly through half-opened eyes, and with a half-awakened mind, she saw that he was there and held out a hand to him in a gesture of sympathy which was a pure fatality, for he approached her now and pressed her, all warm and snuggly, in his arms. "O God!" she groaned. "I'm bleeding. It's too soon." But the gradual strengthening of his embrace was accompanied not only by kisses, warm and shocking in their precision, but the excited whisper: "Bleed! Thank you, Constance. Bleed!" He was overwhelmed with gratitude for he realised that it was for him, this dark menstrual flow; and turning her slightly to depress her legs and pull her downwards towards him he entered her softly, circumspectly, disregarding her faint mewing protests, which soon subsided as she quietly opened herself to him, profoundly and completely, made herself the slave of his lust in a way that had never before happened to her. Where, she wondered, had she acquired the experience to react so absolutely? It was not enough to tell herself that it was simply that she realised herself to be deeply in love with him. He stood there bending over her for a long moment, doing no more than kiss her, embrace her. He was inside her but he did not move. He waited in deliberate cunning for her to stir the first; he waited for the suspense to become intolerable. "You will get covered in blood!" she said at last to disguise the movement which took possession of her loins with a mock-attempt to rise and disengage. But now he had begun the fateful rhythm which joined their breaths to the universal pattern of breath. She tried to protest to herself, telling herself that this must not be; but he only drove his slender horn ever deeper into her.

Even now she felt called upon to assert some of her feminine independence, to assert a loving domination over him by her sheer physical strength. She decided that she would force him to a climax first by the sheer strength of her young animal control, the strength of her sphincters; and he felt the challenge as she seized him for it summoned up all his own strength and litheness, his defences against a premature dispersal of force. "I see you are smiling," he said between shortened breaths, while she replied "Yes," punctured with little gasps, adding, "You will give in first." He shook his head: "No." Still she smiled, and he closed his eyes in agony and put his head on one side. "Please!" Constance said boastfully, "My sphinxes are strong and in good repair. I *order* you to come." He fell forward under the discharge of her kisses, proud now at her victory and keen to share it. It was only some time later that she knew that he had given her the victory which he would have been quite capable of forcing upon her. But now she felt wildly exultant. They lay exhausted in all that blood and steam like stricken martyrs to human bliss. She had known it all along, she had known that it would be like this, that he would be like this; why had she closed her mind to it and stayed deliberately in Avignon, away from temptation? Paradoxically, to remain faithful to Sam! The thought filled her with astonishment – how old-fashioned the gesture seemed!

"I can see nothing," he said, blinded by the steam, "even your face is dim, like a wet water-colour. And I have printed the tiles all over with my bare feet – your blood, Constance." He refilled the bath once more, carefully hanging up his own wrap, and stepped into it to lie at ease, deeply thoughtful, watching the filaments of dark blood wash off his skin and hang in the warm water before dissolving. "I feel like Petronius."

But she was appalled by the mess, and had started taking measures to clean it up with damp towels, unwilling that the room service people should see it. "Come," he said. "It's their job, Constance. Come in here with me, it's not too hot for you." It was something of a jam but somehow she managed amidst much laughter to squeeze herself beside him and to shrink down sufficiently far to have the water level up to her neck. They were like eels in a jar. An enormous depression suddenly seized hold of him, and she noticed with a passionate concern which she was rather ashamed of showing and said, "O, what is it? What has happened, have I displeased you?"

He shook his head and said, "No. I have an overwhelming desire to make you pregnant – it's crazy. I have not slept with anyone for several years and I wasn't really prepared for you. I thought I was, I lived on hopes as you must feel all too clearly. But I am in disarray. You have scattered everything to the winds. I feel numb, dead, like a mummy. Can you bring me back? I doubt it."

"What happened the last time?" He smiled sadly, but did not answer. Then: "In Alexandria someone who is quite continent, apparently uninterested in sex, causes alarm and disquiet. In Arabic they say, 'He has a penis with three heads', and nobody can use it – that is the sense."

"Am I too young for you?"

"Even if you were, what difference? This thing!" He pressed his fingers upon his body in the vague region of his heart. She took them and placed them upon her own hot cheeks. "So you wished to anchor me to my loom and spoil a promising medical career?" Still troubled he was able to reply, "I could, yes."

She lay there for a long time, saying nothing, stretched beside him like a young lioness, one hand lying possessively upon his article, cupping the sinister-seeming scrotum like a nest-tumbled bird gathered up. Soft as a cloud her spirit started pouring into his and she felt, like a ship answering a shift of wind, the mast rise into the sky of his unrealised desire. But he had not finished quite for he said, "But sperm can be a poison if it is not fresh, or poorly documented, or sick like the sperm of deteriorated schizophrenics and others; undue retention can cause illness, brain fever, mind-squeeze, one can witness this in hypocritical cultures based on puritanism like yours. Sperm needs to be cultivated, it is really riches, money in its physical aspect, the girl should all the time be making more and more, manipulating the scrotum, caressing it, counting her change. She must feel it psychically coming down the urethra drop by drop, she must welcome and husband it, and let the parched womb rush at it, unleashing the ova like a pack of hungry wolves. They must both act towards each other with the highest degree of conscious effort; the more they render the orgasm conscious the deeper in phase they will be, thus the purer the child and the more harmonious the race. This takes so long to express but there is no mystery about it – real women have always known it. When a culture starts going downhill the first victim is the quality of the fucking and the defective documentation of the sperm – by documentation I mean oxygen, just lack of oxygen, which is race-knowledge, genetic nous."

Half-sleeping now in each other's arms, their desires prospering with every breath, he whispered on, telling her about the history of sex, why it had always elicited fear and an exemplary piety. It was an engine fuelled by the mind and the coarse manifold of sperm which was needed by the thirsty soil of the womb. Alone the man could do nothing, alone the woman could not resolve the dilemma of her earthly needs. And this was the base of thought and feeling – in every order of perception. The primal vision of man and woman, the primal fig leaf, the primal asterisk – they dwelt in this domain of high-tension wires whose fearful fragility was manifest every time a kiss went astray or a desiring look missed its target. "It's terrible; we can do nothing without each other. Each is the other's fatality – you with your little handbag full of Easter eggs and farthings, but attached to another, and over which you have only temporary and fleeting control: instead of having it always near, on you like a real handbag, full of powder and lipstick and French letters; and then me, a sleep-walker from the beginning of history, mesmerised by your two galactic bubs, the spring of eternal youth, which gave me my first drink on earth and comforted me from the assault of light and sound, and the agony of trying out a new stomach and lungs. Mama!"

So the sleepy commerce between them entered upon the domains of an attachment where the physical and the mental made common cause; but she realised that he had opened up something inside her mind by this conversation, had primed her, and that if they were not careful she would become im-pregnated. It was as if he had hypnotised her into this delicious satyriasis; she was dying to feel, to prosper and harvest his orgasm, but he hung back, as if reluctant – in fact to sharpen her desire for him. They lay in an agony of impatience with thoughts of loving obedience pouring out between them like some vast waterfall. "Now!" she said. "Wait!" he replied, en-grossed mentally in trying to accord their breathing, their very pulse-beat. Already he could sense the rich void of repletion they would enjoy afterwards, lying like drunks in each other's arms, driven to sleep like sheep, into a pen. He turned her lightly towards him and loosed the sails, feeling them draw breath, feeling their craft heel and strain and then gather weight with a shared ecstasy guiding it. She realised that she had never known what love was, what it could be. She was terrified to feel so much at his mercy, and at her own. To sur-render, to yield, to abdicate and receive – it made her feel dangerously vulnerable. She said sadly, "Ah, but you are joking and I am serious; you are going to be disappointed in me. I am only a scientist at heart. I believe in causality."

He raised himself on an elbow and looked closely at her, as if seeing her for the first time, as if she were some strange insect which had alighted before him on the counterpane. "Alchemically speaking, nothing can be achieved without the woman, without you; your thighs are the tuning-fork of the male intuition. You strike the spark, we light the fire in the hearth and stick you with child."

"O yes, Herr Professor," she said meekly.

They both laughed. "O no, you don't," she said in her new relaxed and confident mood. "This is a male plot to make our relationship neurotic. I'm not playing. Let us begin with ourselves, only ourselves. I'm only an old Freudian, and can't see further than my nose."

"You live in the spare parts of other people's dreams, neologisms among the nightmares which project themselves into your own daymares of violence and panic. Which *somnifère* do you take? Constance, we are full of ideas which remain obstinately homeless. I want to share, to share." There was a tap at the door and a breakfast tray appeared as it opened. With an unpremeditated gesture they both drew the sheets over their heads and lay motionless, as if in deep slumber, until the tray was placed by the bed and the maid withdrew. Then they burst out laughing, throwing off all the covers and engaging with a sudden new-found fierceness in a love bout which was deliberately pain-giving. The violence was delicious, she felt with horror and pleasure his vampire's *suçon* on her throat under her ear. It would leave a tell-tale blue mark which would need careful powdering out. Damn! But this time it was he who called the tune and she was surprised by the controlled strength of that tall, somewhat awkward body with its bony girl-like motions. At the same time it made her exultant, the inner recognition that he was completely fashioned as a male, and capable of making her groan softly with pain, to hurt her without leaving bruises or blemishes, with the sole exception of her throat – but this was a piece of pure vulgar sexual boasting and she would tell him as much. She found herself trembling under his assault, trembling at her good luck in being after all able to plunge deep into an attachment without reserve – she who had felt herself dried-up and empty of all emotion. Suddenly the thought of Livia smote her, she saw her dead face, and between pain at the memory and pleasure in the present began to cry, which made him desist. He was apologetic now; he had been thoughtless when she was so tired. Then he added an amazing thing: "And shocked too by Livia's death."

She sat up in bed, wrapping her kimono round her and said, "How on earth . . ?" but he shook his head gently to reassure her and explained, "From Smirgel, of course. He has been in our pay for a long time." It should not have surprised her, but it did. "Whose pay exactly?" she asked, and he replied, "I didn't mean the Red Cross, silly, I meant the Egyptian army, so called. It's an independent net. The British feel happier with their own old-fashioned methods and men like Quatrefages – whose field of vision is very limited. We work independently, though of course we share our labours with them when there is anything really important. But they never believe us – they don't believe in Smirgel, for example."

"Neither would I," she said. "He is a real Nazi believer, he confessed as much to me and gave me the whole gospel. I would never trust him. Really not, not an inch."

"He is a double operator, perhaps," agreed her lover equably. "But we have had a long history together. I must tell you how we've saved his head more than once from Hitler's impatience and Ribbentrop's. Head for a head, so to speak."

They rose and as they breakfasted he told her more in his quiet, smiling voice. "You see poor Smirgel in another light, but in fact the wretched fellow is quite astute, quite clever; he must be to have kept the ear of Ribbentrop. But he did not bargain for Hitler's impatience to get to the bottom of the Templar heresy and all the mystery surrounding it. Not only that but the rumoured treasure which they buried somewhere and which crackpots like Galen try to unearth. Hitler views them as a heretical sect convicted of religious malpractice, and he wants to found an order of black chivalry – if I may coin a phrase – to take their place. Mad, of course, absolutely mad! But when he has nothing better to think about he gives Ribbentrop a shove, or his replacement, and the shove is duly communicated to Smirgel. Recently there was some talk of replacing Smirgel, but we managed to save his head by providing something on account, so to speak. Did you ever see the dried Crusader head which Hassad carries about in a scarlet hat-box container? You did? Well, we allowed Smirgel to discover this, based upon the confession of Quatrefages. Everyone was delighted. At last something tangible! Moreover we cooked a pedigree for it. It is supposed to be the prophesying head of Pompey which the Crusaders believed was imprisoned in the cannon ball which tops Pompey's Pillar in Alexandria. Once in a while the thing is alleged to utter a prophecy, but in one's sleep; one has to have it beside the bed. Do you know where it is now? Beside Hitler's bed. He half-believes, is amused and intrigued, shows it to everyone. Who can say what a shrunken head knows?"

Who indeed? Alas, there was no way of planting ready made speeches in its mouth to influence the ideas of the monster; but for the time being Smirgel was being left relatively alone with his routine duties and was concentrating on the build-up and the dumping which was going on in the new command, herald of who knew what?

"Where can we meet at the earliest sheer possibility? What are you going to do today?"

She was going to look in on her flat and tidy it if need be, visit the office, and then perhaps try and locate Sutcliffe, to make belated contact and let him know that she was back. Had he heard about Aubrey coming?

"Indeed he has. He groaned and said, 'It's a hard life for those of us who live vicariously.'"

She said, "Rob Sutcliffe will have to pull his weight now and stop bothering so much about her" – she expressed this opinion in rather an offhand way. "His devotion is so exaggerated that it will soon seem suspect to us, Schwarz and me."

"You must tell him."

"I will."

But despite these pious sentiments once more they fell asleep in each other's arms, and if from time to time her mind cleared and she awoke it was to a dazed abstraction which heralded something like a new life – a new attitude to her life. She felt so strange! Everything had irremediably changed.

Yes, with all this she had suddenly, dramatically assumed herself, her full femininity – something which had remained always a sort of figment, a symbol which gave off no current. To be a woman in this sense it was not necessary to be a mother, or a wife, or a nun or a whore – all these documentary forms of living were quite secondary to the central state. The doctor in her had made a discovery of the first order! To achieve some understanding of the role of the female – why, it chimed with her art, it was implicit in the craft of her job. The female was the principle of renewal and repair in the cosmic sense, it was she who made things happen, made things happen, made things grow. She was the principle of all fertility even though she might be disguised in the trappings of Mrs. Jones. (He had been brutal with her once – his joy had over-brimmed into a possessive lust, and the pain he inflicted was harsh and hard to bear; but she welcomed it, as a martyr welcomes the burning pyre.) He had split her down the centre as if with an axe.

"Turn again," he had cried, and she submitted and turned, quite prepared to die in his arms – but the poetic figure of speech was now the relevant one, for she "died" in the Elizabethan sense, and her own wanton cry of delight rang out on the silence, expressing many things, notably the thought: "So I can love, after all!" though up to that moment she had never once considered herself incapable of loving. It was as if she had simply not known what the animal was. His face looked so tense, so withdrawn: she recognised his male weakness, his alarming precariousness of feeling, his absolute need for the support without which no advance was possible, no creation within his own scope. This realisation made her suddenly conscious of her own strength, as if she could now use a whole set of muscles which up to now had lingered on in disuse. She glimpsed the tantric left-hand path of which he was always talking, and which so much irritated her scientific mind. He had given her much more than his love, he had given her the full maturity of her gift, her medical skill. "O thank you, thank you!" But he made a vague hopeless gesture and groaned, saying, "I don't know why the devil I am telling you all this gibberish – it will make you love me finally, and you'll find all other men insipid for about ten years after I leave you, as I have to. Damn!" But the trick was done; she possessed the secret of her own soul now, and her generous kisses and smiling eyes told him that there was nothing to regret for either of them henceforward. The imp was out of the bottle.

A bell rang somewhere and she sat up. Good God! It was late afternoon! She had slept all day, and Affad lay beside her once more. How had he come in without waking her?

He woke from his deep trance-like sleep and rubbed his eyes, saying, "That means a new drum of paper for the machine. Smirgel has become increasingly talkative, he runs on and on. It makes you think of the agony of silence spies have to endure, for keeping a secret is a real effort, like wanting to pee during a march past. He can talk to nobody. Except me. He has become like a chatterbox wife. I keep trying to shut him up but to no avail."

"I understand nothing of all this," she said, and as he rose and hunted for a wrap in the bathroom he told her to follow him and see for herself what it was all about. They tiptoed down the cool corridor to what seemed like an outside lavatory – but was a rather solid-looking room with a steel door, which bore a sign proclaiming it a power point with dangerous wires. "Do not enter," said the notice, and "do not touch".

"That is just camouflage," he said and opened the door with a small key to reveal a comfortable office-like room with a tickertape machine punctually extruding what appeared to be news items or stock reports. "It's Smirgel," said Affad with a chuckle. "He has become very alarmed and excited since the first attempt at landing. I am drowned in information." He indicated the piles of striped yellow transcription paper which littered the floor and with a grimace said, "I hardly dare to go to sleep for fear that I will find myself strangling in the coils of this infernal ticker. At any rate he works for his money, Smirgel. Look!" The machine clicked steadily on, the paper lengthened. Affad opened a hatch and replaced some paper drums with new ones, passing them into the jaws of the rotor and securing them to ensure continuity. "Where does he do this?" she asked curiously, impressed by the element of risk incurred. Affad said: "In the so-called dangerous wards at Montfavet-les-Roses, separated from the half dozen or so madmen by a bead curtain and a frail door. He is scared stiff. But it's the safest place. It was suggested by Dr. Jourdain, to whom we owe much. By the way, what sort of chap is he?"

"The doctor? Rather mannered, highly cultivated and very pro-English. He wears a college blazer – he studied at Edinburgh. Has a death-mask on his desk. I think he is secretly in love with Nancy Quiminal, though I never speak of it to her, nor has she mentioned it to me. But that is all I know!"

He sank into a chair and allowed the long paper streamer to pass through his fingers as he slowly read the progress report of the agent. "The interminable list of Jews deported – nearly forty thousand now, it's hardly to be believed," he said with sorrow. "Smirgel always sounds grimly approving – I suppose from what you say he could hardly feel otherwise."

"It is sickening."

"Yes. And doubly so, for we shall never hear the end of this calamitous blunder; the Jews will extract the last ounce of blood from our horror and repentance, they are masters of the squeeze. We will have to hang our heads in their presence for a century at least."

"You don't sound as if you like them very much."

"I am from Alexandria, I live with them and know their problem to be insoluble – so brilliant and fragile they are, so conceited and afraid and contemptuous of us. After all, Constance, the Gentiles did not invent the ghetto – it's they who wished to lock themselves up with their monomania and their pride and cosmic solipsism. The little I know about racial discrimination I learnt from them – once I had the temerity to want to marry an Orthodox Jewess in Cairo. I was offering a quite straightforward and honourable marriage. But the row it caused! Everybody, up to the Grand Rabbi, meddled in the affair, while the parents of the girl locked her away for safety in an asylum, pretending she was mentally afflicted. From which I was forced to kidnap her and force their hands, which I did. But it opened my eyes to the whole matter of race and religion – everything to do with monotheism, monolithic organisation, everything mono, which leads to this self-induced paranoia called Western Civilisation. . . . The Germans are simply following out the whole pattern in their usual gross fashion. It's heart-rending, senseless, barbaric. But even the Jews are not helping themselves! Anyway, let's hope we are in time to rescue at least half of them. Not to mention gypsies, tramps, jailbirds and 'slaves' of every persuasion. It isn't only the Jews, you know, though of course they make the most noise as a majority."

The paper was perforated at regular intervals so that one could tear off each sheet and assemble the strips in the manner of a book, giving easier readability. She helped him to do this, to assemble his dossier of information for him. It was strange to see the city from this angle of vision, to see it in depth, so to speak, and not from the blinkered viewpoint of a Red Cross employee operating in a strictly limited field. Here she could read of troop movements, of reprisals against isolated acts of sabotage, of the steady stockpiling going on under the Pont du Gard. Several thousand Czechs and Poles had been drafted in to do the work, presumably because they would be less likely to leak the information – already they had created a sizable language problem, not to mention problems of public order in the surrounding towns of Nîmes and Avignon. Their drunkenness had rendered the streets dangerous in the twilight hours before curfew – the only time when the housewife was able to shop. Happily they were only sketchily armed, the group-leaders carried pistols and pick-helves. As night fell lorries went round the town picking up the fallen and shoving them aboard in variously comatose states: and the city breathed again. But Smirgel's despatches listed two important brawls which had led to the death of two Vichy policemen and the rape of a girl of ten. There were also punitive actions against so called "terrorists" in the surrounding hills – but these were mostly work-shy youths trying to dodge the forcible deportation which had been decreed by the Germans. It was nothing to burn down a whole village, while a few exemplary hangings was argued to be a necessary deterrent to further lawlessness. But the tide had turned at last, there was no doubt: the iron jaws of the Allied war machines had begun to close on Germany slowly but inexorably. What would they do with the new world which would be born when once the guns fell silent? They did not know, for the old would be somehow buried in that fateful silence of peace. She felt consumed by restlessness at the very thought of peace, as if she could not get rid of this war-time insomnia, this persistent feeling of having her heart ravaged by the brutishness of human behaviour.

It was agony to separate, but their duty called them to do so. The next meeting was, by common consent, to be in her little flat for dinner.

So again that night the bed floated them both out to sea like some precious catafalque. Reality and dream again became coeval, time and space commingled. When sleep came it was deep as death might be.

But not entirely, for now they awoke always upon a new world both of unique privacy and of Promethean simplicity – for pain mingled with the pleasure and the reassurance of their passion. Yet in spite of this profound intimacy, this flirtation of private minds, she was still hungry to get nearer to him, to devour him woman-fashion. Almost in exasperation she cried, "O have you no other names, Affad, no Christian name? Must I invent a nickname to lay claim to you?" And to her surprise he replied, "Yes, I have, but I have never liked anyone using it after my mother died. She pronounced it in a special way."

"May I know? May I use it?"

"I am called Sebastian."

"How did she pronounce it?"

He hesitated for a long moment, staring curiously at her. Then he said, "Sebastiyanne, with the accent on the last syllable. There! I have given away my soul to the devil!"

"My love, surely not that! Surely not that, Sebast*iyanne*?"

He said nothing but lay in the stillness of his wakeful drowsing with eyes firmly shut as if he dared not open them upon the rapturous face of his lover. He was debating deeply within himself, resisting an impulse to shed tears of joy and helpless fatigue. In a whisper she repeated the name, and said, "Was it like that?"

He shook his head and replied, "No. It won't do. Call me Affad like the rest of the world. Keep the other for yourself."

The revelation and the name had brought them much closer together. But lest the claims of ordinary life be neglected she permitted herself to add after a moment, "God! I am so hungry. I think I will die." He at once shook off his sleep and said, "I will make you the breakfast you deserve. Tell me where everything is and leave it to me." Which she was weak enough to do, guiding him in whispers, once more half-asleep.

"Bacon, sausages, eggs. O certainly God exists," she whispered, to which he added piously, "God bless our happy home," as he struggled into a borrowed kimono.

It was marvellous to be waited on.

"You would make a wonderful slave," she said, still mentally smoothing herself, her psyche, down as a cat might lick its own coat clean after a love-bout. He had collapsed into a state of complete submission, resembling a case of deep shock. To feel him so passive and so enslaved had aroused her to the highest pitch. Afterwards, exhausted, bathed in sweat, she said reproachfully, "You never seem to let go, damn you; you are always *there*."

He put his arms round her, as if to comfort her for her disappointment. "There is nothing to let go," he said, "I feel I am *there* the whole time, at the centre of you. I am trying to eat you alive, to swallow you like a boa. But it is not easy: you will take ages to digest." They lay breathing into each other's mouths, full of the convalescent sweetness of this transient form of death in life while their desires roved about them in packs, as yet unsatisfied, the remnant of truthful impulses perverted by lack of zeal. "In your work," he said, as if the formulation had cost him deep thought, "you are the bonds-man of the ego, but in mine I begin with the *Vor-Ich*, the pre-self, the *pre-self*, my dearest Constance. The marvellous little pre-self like an acorn, like an unshelled penis, like a lotus bud . . ." He began to laugh at her exhaustion. She tried to get up more than once, but fell back each time into his arms, sleep-impregnated, her whole body in deep soak. At last with a groan she turned and tore away this veil of nescience, and made her yawning way to the lavatory, pausing only to draw hot water for his bath. "Lie in peace," she said, "it is well earned. And let me make you the bath you deserve!"

Later on they parted once more, but gravely, reluctantly; he watched her set off walking along the lake reaches, the long Corniche, towards the bankers' city, with her head bowed as if in profound contemplation. His eyes followed the lithe, striding figure with its impenitent head set so firmly on slender but strong shoulders, its look tilted slightly upwards, giving it a youthful urgency. It was as if she had forgotten all about him – she had swallowed him like a drink, and turned her mind back lifewards. But she was very deeply shaken, and when at last she entered her office at the clinic it was to sit blindly before the mountain of dossiers, staring at her own fingers. She remembered some words uttered by the good Schwarz during a seminar: "*Aber*, Constance, man is not a natural product of nature – he is an excrescence like the truffle, a cancer, an illness, it is only his high gamy flavour that makes him acceptable!" He was smiling, of course, though the words were seriously meant. He believed that when man had sacrificed sexual periodicity it was the fall into a freedom he could not manage. He could not face the freedom offered by choice, whence history.

During the afternoon she fell helplessly asleep and dreamed archaic dreams of haunting incoherence. Somewhere from the deepest recesses of memory there swam up upon the white screens surrounding her bed – dream of a hospital – a painting she had once loved, *The Parting* of Chirico, with its clinical rigour, its glacial detachment which freezes the optic nerve like anaesthetic; the palette cool, the tone-range Roman as befitted partings where grief bit too deep for expression. A mental foliage of rusty wire, barbed into drypoints of fingers or leaves or hair, bundles of twigs birds organise into the cradles and nests from which one flies into comfortless futures of thought. He had taken his ***** in quiet fingers and countered the web of tensions in her by his deep ***** and careful *****. He could hardly tell what ***** for it stirred the classical cocoon of all vice, opening and shutting her lips with his ***** while she for her part ***** and reaching into wealth behind her groaned as she *****. She concentrated on the screen memory to assuage her pain. (Paintings are to bring calm.) How deeply he hurt her now with his ***** and his violent *****, each awkward spasm lifting itself into the centre of her *****, the flower and branch of all sex. Still she clung to the lovers' goodbye, the turning away, the imprint of the primal crime, the original fall, thought catapulted into matter and fixed by Saturn into the hysteria of dust. O God! It was friends who parted in the painting, not lovers, for they can never be separated, the flesh having grown together. Such scar tissue would put them at risk. "Tell me again the *****; you know how it shames me."

Fragile as a nautilus afloat their sexes plumbed the innermost recesses of sinus, heartless as a forgotten creed, the numbing pain of the bruised bones conveyed their own amnesia. The meaning of lovecraft only grew out of parting. The breath hissed like seething milk, the whip rose and fell, but in the painting your ***** is completely ***** and you hear nothing while the imaginary figures were not designed to feel the blows. Sebastian, Sebastian, Constance, Constance. The stepping stones yield as one treads on them. The painting is complete. In the turret of the church the clock has struck two and the lovers are still there, unwilling to part with all their ***** so

fresh the ardour of genitals created to pierce and fill. Why go?
Why not stay? Soon it will be morning and all options will be
renewed.

But while you look at the ***** the couple is slowly dissolving, the acid has reached the armpits, the fair breasts, the
throat. "I am *****," she cries out in harsh triumph and he
increases the summary rhythm of his loving ***** to danger
point. Then drop by drop into ***** will go like seeds pouring
in to a drumhead. Tonight will be fatal to someone's hopes.
The whip rises and falls, the painting changes. We are lovers
who have buckled under history's pressures. Later the historians will come and set out the typology of contemporary
humours to measure us by.

The painting faded and in its place there shone out from
the heart of Avignon, lambent like the Grail, the old smoky
masterpiece of Clément, half-obliterated by grime; she saw
again so clearly its weird mixture of elements—a sort of
Paradise Regained painted, superimposed upon a *Last Supper*,
as if printed upon a gossamer veil. The painter had called it
Cockayne, and Smirgel had received a grant to clean its
blemished surface. The sleepers were asleep in their chairs, the
candles had melted and run all over the place. Strangely enough
it was outside in a grassy meadow, sheltered by a coloured
marquee. There were gold coins lying about in the grass,
handkerchiefs, articles of wear. Parts took place in the
seventeenth century, Christ had the head of Spinoza. Judas
looked with a conger's gaze. The wine had been doped,
perhaps? Had they all fallen asleep at the table? Maybe the
gypsies had sneaked up and cut their throats while they slept?

She woke with a start to find Schwarz smiling at her across
the desk.

Schwarz smiled as he watched her, but his smile, as always,
contained a sort of undertow of gravity while his ugly, lined
old face contained a great sweetness of emphasis. He sighed

and said: "It's a long time since we two made love. I was thinking so today because it is Lily's birthday." Lily had been his wife. They had been together since they were students at medical school. Then they broke up, and when the Nazis came he fled from Vienna, leaving her behind. The news that she had been sent to Buchenwald finally leaked through and the full realisation of his own cowardice and callousness had caused him a severe breakdown through which, and indeed out of which, Constance both nursed and guided him. She was supposedly his student and he her controller, so the situation was paradoxical in the extreme; in order to keep their relationship private and unprofessional rather than formally medical and subject to all the boredom associated with a psychological "transfer" he had been allowed to make love to her half a dozen times until he came to his wits, and returned shamefacedly to his responsibilities. "So long ago; yes, so long that now it seems never when I think back. It has all washed away. But you are still here, my friend; we are still friends. What a lesson you gave me in sagacity – you were ahead of me in your completeness. *Ach*! It sounds clumsy. I am thinking in German." He clicked his tongue reproachfully. Indeed his English and French always had a Viennese slant.

Constance said: "You had a moment of doubt – you lost your centre of gravity. It was lucky I was there to catch you. But you'd do the same for me, would you not? Indeed you may yet have to certify me! My present behaviour . . ."

"You can't regret being in love?"

"No. Of course not, who could? But this Egyptian lover of mine is employing a strategy completely at variance with your established ideas of how the couple couples."

"You mean sexual deviances, variations?"

"No! No!" she said vehemently. "Absolutely not. Not a shadow of such oriental treats. But a reversed affect technique entirely new to me, to us, and which gives brilliant results.

And which he seems to regard as being in the very nature of things. I thought for a while that it was simply that we complemented each other perfectly, that was all. But it's more than that and it deserves our attention as psychs." She lay back in her chair for a long while, quite silently reflecting. Then she dragged herself to her feet and went to the blackboard on the far wall of the consulting room. Old Schwarz gave a chuckle. "I know," she said, "I know. I am going to sound pompous; but it is very singular what this so-called gnostic man believes about us; when the couple was created out of the original man unit, clumsily divided into male and female parts, the affective distribution did not correspond at all with the biological. The sex of the man is really the woman's property, while the breasts of the woman belong to the man. Wait! I know it sounds crazy unless Affad himself expounds it, but it seems to work, it's not a hoax. The male and female commerce centres around sperm and milk – they trade these elements in their love-making. The female's breasts first gave him life and marked him with his ineradicable thirst for creating – Tiresias! The breasts are prophecy, are vision! Her milk has made him build cities and dream up empires in order to celebrate her!"

Schwarz cried, "Wait, Connie, wait. Let us record some of this; you will want to use it. Don't waste it while it's so fresh." He quickly changed the magazine of the wire recorder and switched on the small microphone which hung by the blackboard. She had drawn two rudimentary figures, a male and a female, facing each other. She joined them with a single stroke repeated three times at the level of the eyes, the breast and the sexual organs. "Now," she said thoughtfully, "this is how we envisage the affective discharge in sexual congress – mouth attacks the mouth, breast the breast, sex the sex. But in his idea of the affect link the male sex is really the woman's handbag, it hangs at her side while her breasts belong to him with their promise of nourishment. Their souls trade sperm against milk. And of course in the practical sense the quality of his product depends in her care and manipulation of the money-bag. Exchange rather than investment! Barter!"

"But when you actually *make* love?" said the old man with some bewilderment. They both burst out laughing. She said: "He simply abandons himself, lets me have what belongs to me. The woman, according to him, should be perpetually counting her small change, manipulating the scrotum manufacturing the sort of product which will biologically enrich the race and not just impoverish it – what is happening at the moment. Indeed, hers is the complete responsibility for the erection, she can build it at will when she pleases, even if the man be tired. He is quite powerless in this sense. Poor Affad, he'd be horrified to think I was scientifically interested in his marvellous gentle love-making. That is another thing, making love with a sincere belief in this kind of reversed affect relationship leads to simultaneous orgasm – almost every time. It is built into the exchange. It sounds such rubbish doesn't it?"

"Yes."

She herself looked so overcome by these strange formulations that Schwarz could not resist the desire to tease her mildly: "What do I hear?" he said with a strong Jewish twang. "Simultaneous ejaculation every time as well as almost permanent erections in the male? Surely Christmas is coming! *Aber*, Connie, it's too good to be true." Truth to tell, she looked a trifle shamefaced herself, to be so carried away by her subject. She blushed. "You know," said the old man, "it may just be a very lucky encounter with someone who really suits – such things have been heard of, and with all the apparent miracles you mention. But for the great run of people there is no joining, no chiming, no click. They just rape each other dismally or exploit each other or become prematurely impotent, lose all their hair, go into politics. It may be unique, your love, his love."

She nodded ruefully; you could not erect a universal principle with only one example to go on. It had to work in every case, to be a rule and not an exception. Schwarz thought he had wounded her with his banter, so he came to her side and patted her shoulder. "I share your concern, my dear, who could not? We deal all day with guilt and violence and insensitivity – any solution would be marvellous to hear of. Especially as we are all hungry for an antidote to violence and what you speak of is gentle love-making."

"Yes. Gentle with a respect for the other person and a full realisation that the sexual act is a psychic one, the flesh and bone enact but the psyche directs. But the reversed affect . . ." She laughed again and threw down her chalk. The telephone rang and the old man answered it, embarking on a long conversation with a fellow doctor. She listened to him abstractedly, thinking her own thoughts which still hovered about these psychological evaluations of her love-experience. She ached to be with Affad again – and to reprove the feeling she frowned and bit her lip. But the desire persisted and she recalled how for long stretches of the night she had lain at his side, quietly building up his strength as she had been told to do, "counting her change" as he had put it irreverently, preparing with care and concern an erection which she would in her own time demolish. . . . Schwarz went on talking but as he did so pushed across his desk one from a pile of monographs and offprints.

It was a recent contribution to the medical journal of Geneva on the grim topic of sexual violence inflicted on women during congress – either by homosexuals on each other, or by particularly aggressive males upon females. The Americans had christened this fist-thrust form of sex – the pushing of the clenched fist into the vagina – as force-fucking or fist-fucking, and the surgeon who had written the paper signalled a prevalence of cases suffering from physical damage to the head of the uterus. The general belief that men should show their masculinity by being as violent as possible was causing the woman partner physical damage, he asserted. As Constance riffled through the article, Schwarz made a number of enigmatic signs to her to suggest that here was the answer to her talk about gentleness in love-making, harmony in desire, unity in building the network of powerful love-sympathies which reward the lovers with the dual orgasm. She nodded grimly. Yes, this was her answer indeed. Fist-fucking!

Schwarz put down the phone and said: "Violence to be equated with inability to ejaculate, or simply badly, or praecox or what have you! But pain is *also* exciting, Connie."

"I hope I didn't give you the impression that we have started a Sunday school; pain is part of the play, but not a cruelty-substitute for incapacity. This oriental style uses everything, but modestly – the target is the double orgasm which is the base of all dialogue – even in the genetic sense."

"Which remains to be proved in my view as being general to all men!"

"Of course," she said humbly. "I am a fool to try and attribute universal laws to what might be a solitary experience. I wonder what poor Affad would think if he could overhear us."

"That you had a rather chilling, analytic mind – it augurs ill for romantic love, if that is what it is."

"Not quite that either," she said, but she felt rather a fool for having been so youthfully enthusiastic. She switched off the recorder and eased out the cartridge which she slipped into her pocket. Yet the subject itself would not rest, and she felt impelled to pursue it while the memory of her night-long dialogues with Affad was still fresh – for where else would she find a listener and critic so apt to evaluate and recognise what her lover had had to tell her? Schwarz could scent this and was himself sufficiently curious to try to encourage her to pursue her theme. In the silence they smoked, and she walked slowly up and down, deep in thought.

"Well, you are in love," he said at last, gravely, but just as gravely she shook her head and replied, "No. The word has no context. It's a commitment far beyond that in a way, because we are sharing something. Most people just follow out their immediate desires and when they dry up they are at a loss. They don't share an experience together step by step, building it. We are much closer now, at the start, than most married people. So, it's worse than being in love, as you call it, and much surer. It's oriental or Indian in origin, I suppose, but it has its own scientific rationale."

She told him of Affad's theory about oxygen, the basis of everything, the genetic food of both sperm and ovum, without which they were, according to Affad, "poorly documented", ill-equipped to help the race struggle to maintain itself; about this element or quality which was the real nous, the genetic "document" upon which almost everything depended, including the quality of the product on both sides. "When the quality of the sperm deteriorates a whole culture can be put at risk – which is what is happening now in the whole Hegelian West! And the first sign, the first signal of alarm comes from the woman who is biologically more vulnerable and more responsible than the man for the future which they literally weave like a tissue with their kisses and caresses. The spool upon which time is woven in the ancient Greek sense – not to mention the coming child which contains, like a grenade, the elements which will unfold into a full-sized skeleton with limbs, teeth, brain, hair . . . Where should we situate human love in all this vast context? Yes, you are right, I *do* love him, but not in the way you think – but because he showed me this schema of which I had a *profound* need. At last I can rest my intellect upon something which seems solid! As he says, 'When the asterisk marries the figleaf all is well.' The rest is this marvellous amnesia of love-making where all we have to do is to bring home the harvest. It seems another world altogether where people debate 'love', where couples bring their cases against each other, and marriages wallow and founder. But it's not only that, my dear, it has a direct bearing on my poor art, my little cottage-industry psychiatry. I understand Miss Quint much better than I did!"

They both laughed; Miss Quint was one of the quaint old ladies among her patients whose fantasies and Victorian timidities had given rise to such a strange psychological state, a dream-world worthy of Lewis Carroll, a garden of puns and weird spoonerisms. "When I told Affad about Miss Quint, how she had christened her vagina after her cat, and how she claimed that it not only mewed in complaint when the milk had turned, but also followed her about and jumped on the beds of her friends, he was absolutely delighted. He said, 'Nature always supplies essential information in the form of ailments. But she is right about her pussy.' When the documentation is poor or incomplete the woman knows it at once – indeed it creates a state of alarm. The quality of loving, of coupling falls off, and the man's erections become compromised, his sterility sets in. All this not seen from the selfish point of view of a couple becoming tired of each other, but as a form of cosmic calamity threatening the race and its mental balance. Love-making this way is unaggressive and deeply logical."

Schwarz began to become a trifle plaintive. "Are we going into marriage guidance or matrimonial aids?" he asked wryly, and added sadly, "Yesterday my nice old philosopher Ginsberg committed suicide, Connie, and he had promised to confide in me the secret of the universe. But he left no message – or perhaps the act was itself the message, like love is supposed to be?"

She smiled. "You are right to shoot me down – I must seem unbearably prosy about all this. But I never heard this sort of thing before or experienced passion in such an un-requitable way – as if there were no floor to it. And it doesn't come from a man, it comes from an attitude. Why shouldn't I try to catch a hold on it and rationalise it? It might serve others like me, like I *was* before Affad arrived, bleating in the wilderness of my logical positivism?"

"Indeed! Indeed!" said the old man, touched. But to himself he said: "It smells of Vedanta! Ah, these clever Orientals, what would they do in our shoes? With every damned illness our whole culture is called into question! Damn Affad!"

Indeed! She said: "Doctors with all their phobias and philias, like statues from some Graeco-Roman museum. You begin to realise that we are cannibals in fancy dress."

"It doesn't help!" he said gloomily.

"It doesn't help!" she echoed just as sadly.

A nurse brought in a tray with coffee and cakes and for a moment their attention was deflected from these abstruse matters. "Gosh!" she said with surprise, helping herself, "I am absolutely ravenous! What a surprise!"

"I wonder why," he said drily, sipping his brew.

It was marvellous to have someone to whom she could talk, with whom she could discuss these burning topics. She kissed his forehead piously and thanked him for listening. "I should charge a consultation fee," he said.

It freed her to continue this feverish disquisition upon her new experience. "Being in love with an Oriental is eerie because we are so different. He is like a piano of perfect tone but with no sustaining pedal. I mean that we do not share the same historic pedigree, intellectual connivance. My soul, my heart is of a more recent manufacture, sixteenth- or seventeenth-century – the world where sense, sensibility, sentiment were formulated as modes of enquiry and expression, where romantic love first threw up its narcissisms, its Don Juans. His backcloth is a huge hole in space, something vast, an Egypt of utter blank indifference to actuality. I live in the contingent, he in the eternal – in prose rather than poetry. It is superior in its way, though a trifle top-heavy: I can snipe at it with my humour, which is the weapon of my insight. But I would pay for a refusal to abdicate to his maleness, and he vice versa with my femininity. It's made me see that my love for Sam was only a transaction and not a full commitment – we were eaten alive by reciprocal sentiments. I also see now that the old-style couple is simply a fortuitous composition designed by lust; the new one I envisage could be triggered by desire yet be fragile as a wine or a water-colour which are both compositions and which can achieve aesthetic value, be beautiful in a geometrical way like a bird's nest or a cradle for the future. For the first time I feel optimistic about love, do you hear? Love!"

"O God!" said Schwarz with the full weight of his Jewish pessimism compounded with a Viennese upbringing. He was thinking: man is born free, free as a nightmare. We live forever encroached on by future and past, the dead and the unborn. Both live in the full horror of a perpetual present. *Aïe*! And here she was getting enthusiastic about contrapuntal fucking or about lying all night kissbound in a honeysuckle sweat as the vulgar tavern song said! Doctors were people of limited uptake, limited intellectual outspan, faulty insight. Their function was simply to reveal what was already known but unrecognised. A monotonous and limited role, like that of the coprophagous beetle forever rolling its balls of dung. What did it matter?

"What does it matter, Connie," he cried, "if you can find some well-earned happiness? You alarm me, you are far too articulate. You will *bore* him." She nodded and said, "I know. I am in danger of becoming too bossy – I could bore him, as you say. He already says that women who think should be lapidated by psychiatrists." Schwarz said, "I wish you would stop walking about as if dragged by a huge dog or propelled by a high wind. I'm dizzy."

"I am sorry," she said, all contrition at last, and sat down at the desk with a fair semblance of composure. "But I have been thinking of ways to formulate it. Look, it's like the contrast between a cathedral and a mosque. The mosque has no altar, no centre of focus. In it the truth is everywhere, though the whole is in fact oriented only gravitationally, aiming at Mecca. The cathedral is not oriented geographically, but inside it is focused upon a special spot, the High Altar, where the critical blood-sacrifice takes place. This is, so to speak, the butcher's slab of the Christian transaction. Here the wine is diluted, the bread is cut up and consecrated. This place is also the telephone booth from which one can ring up God and try to strike a bargain with him for one's individual soul – that precious figment! All right, I know I sound rather like old Sutcliffe weighing into you about Pia, but there is the whole contrast between us – mosque and church. But this thing outweighs the difference, it's common to either. Affad in discussing it spoke of it being calculated by an 'engineer of love in terms of *puissance massique* – the mass-power of weight-ratio' I must say it sounds as elegant as it is esoteric, but I know what he means."

"Damned if I do," said the old man doggedly.

"Of course you do."

She felt as if she had been separated at last from the world against which their science was fighting – a world of attachments without resonance, adventures without depth, embraces without insight! The embrace of Affad had in some singular way acted upon her as the drop of scalding olive oil had done upon the cheek of sleeping Eros. Perhaps she had even been cured of that obstinate old dream of all women, to become indispensable to someone's happiness – the running sore of self-esteem, the old dysentery of human narcissism. . . . Or was that too much to hope?

"I'm going home," she said abruptly. "I am in no mood to work, and I have so much leave accumulated that . . ."

"I know," he said with resignation. "Go on home."

She felt she could not last another moment without seeing Affad again, so she took her leave and went back to join him at breakneck speed – but only to find an empty room and an un-made bed beside which, to her surprise, disdain and concern, from a medical point of view, lay the little hashish pipe which smelt recently used! He walked in while she was sniffing at it like a suspicious cat and she put it behind her back while they embraced. Then she wagged it at him, saying, "You didn't say you smoked."

"Must I reveal everything? I am Egyptian after all, yes, I smoke." But he added that it was neither very much nor very often.

"Does it matter?" he asked.

"Only because you do."

"It's harmless," he said. "It's ritual."

She was relieved to hear it. She took herself off to the kitchen to make some tea while he searched slowly and methodically along the bookshelves for something which might interest him. "Ah, this bogus science!" he exclaimed as he caught sight of a series of blue-backed books, a psycho-analytic series. "It doesn't go far enough." She said, "How do you know?" and he sat down slowly balancing his tea-cup as he replied, "Hear my story, then. My parents were very rich, I was brought up very carefully but all over Europe to give me languages and make me quite at ease in every society and every circumstance. But I was shy, and, being sheltered, very slow to develop. I mixed badly. I preferred to lock myself up and indulge in abstruse studies like alchemy and mathematics – Egypt is the right place for that sort of thing, indeed everything occult. An only child, I became very solitary when my parents died, locked up as I was in a vast flat in Alexandria with few friends. My gnostic studies led me to a small group of seekers among whom I found Prince Hassad, and became his man, so to speak. Apart from these people – they were of every rank and circumstance – I frequented nobody. Then by an accident a charming and ardent young woman drifted into my life and took possession of me completely. Our marriage lasted seven years, but the child we had turned out to be deficient intellectually and the shock separated us for good. My wife went to live in the monastery of the Copts at Natrun as a solitary hermit. Her old mother took charge of the boy: she lived in Geneva, that is why I come here so regularly, to see how he is getting on, and to see her and give her the news of Egypt. After that calamity I went on alone, I had lost the taste for any other close relationship, so I made do, and got to like it. Once or twice I may have had a chance encounter with a woman but I made sure that it was ephemeral – some tired cabaret artist or street walker. But this was exceptional and due to loneliness – perhaps thrice in all these years. So I am hopelessly out of practice, and can be easily put to flight if you find this situation too demanding. It was in this state of fragility that I encountered you and was attracted, heaven knows by what, for I have known greater beauties and met more massive intellects. I took my courage in both hands and with great daring tried to stake a claim to an experience which – clearly I am wrong about this – seemed to me essential if I was not to die of spleen and boredom during this senseless war!" He yawned in an outrageous way.

"I have never heard a more self-centred, a more masculine declaration of love in my whole life!" she said with a certain amusement in her voice and an unwilling tinge of admiration in her heart – for this shameless egotism was accompanied by propitiatory caresses and endearments. They were lying down now, side by side, and had kicked off their shoes.

"Don't you like omniscient men, men who are too sure

of themselves? They give such confidence, they say. When
first I saw you I had a tremulous premonitory feeling which
told me that I would be excused every fatuity."

"Wrongly," she said, cobwebbed herself in the drowsiness which he seemed to project with every measured breath.
My goodness, she thought, soon they would be making love
again, it was quite deplorable that it should seem so inexorable.
Also behind the sleepy persiflage of his speech – so belied by
the gentle but perfectly assured rhythm of his caresses – she
felt the deep vibration of an anxiety in him, a lack of confidence
in himself which made him send out these wistful probes in
order to take soundings in a possibly hostile world around him.
Or was it that he found the habits of solitude hard to break and
the society of a woman, even a cherished woman, menacing
and disquieting?

"No," he said, for all the world as if he had been reading
her thoughts as they passed in her mind, "none of those things
really – perhaps a little of the last might come later! My main
concern was to preserve you in this world – I felt you might
become suicidal in Avignon like your sister – and if possible
to bring you back where I could approach you. That is why I
told Smirgel to look after you very carefully, or answer for it
with his head!" She was surprised. "So *that* is why he kept
persecuting me with his solicitude? I thought otherwise."

"Poor man! he was doing his duty. I even came down to
Avignon once myself – it was a great temptation to call on you,
I don't know how I resisted, but I did. I knew your hours and
movements. What heroism!" She felt a sudden pang of regret
that he had not done so, yet it might have served no purpose at
that time, living as she was. Affad then was hardly more than a
thought in the back of her mind, without real substance, a
faint beckoning thought without a tangible future. "What
part did Livia play in all this?" He replied drowsily, "None.
None at all. Smirgel loved her, that is all. You know he was

there in Provence when you all were, working in the town gallery restoring the medieval paintings. He met Livia then. It was he who introduced her to the Nazi philosophy of the time. When she went to Germany it was to stay with him – he was an art critic in Hamburg."

"Did they live together in the accepted sense?"

"I don't know. I never asked him. They met in Avignon where he was staying. She became a party member through him and later on naturalised. He started by using her to spy on Galen, then went and fell for her."

The thought was horrible to Constance and vastly increased her sympathy and regret for her dead sister. There was a long silence now, and she feared that they might both slide away into sleep unless some new topic were introduced, so she said the first thing that came into her head without quite meaning to: or perhaps it only *appeared* to be involuntary, one could not be quite sure. At all events what she said was: "Will you marry me?" This had the desired effect – it was sufficiently unexpected to make him open his eyes. "Did you say 'would' or 'will'?" he asked cautiously. He placed his lips to her cheek and heard her answer quite distinctly, "I said 'will you'!"

"Of course not," he said at once. "At least not in fact. Whatever gave you such an idea?"

"I thought not," she said, amused. "I just wanted to make you writhe, that is all."

"Mark you, in certain undefined and relatively unimaginable contexts I would, I could, I *might*. But of course I won't."

"That was very closely argued," she said.

"Surely you follow my reasoning?"

"Only too well; supposing I were pregnant?"

"Why should I when you are not?"

"Casuist and philanderer!"

"You are like the Catholic Church, Constance. This is nothing but a hold-up." He quoted disgustedly, "Will you, won't you, can't you, might you, must you, would you ... what a catechism for a right-minded gnostic to come up against. Of course I won't!"

"Very well, then, goodbye!"

"Goodbye," he said equably (how terrible it sounded to her ears), and shut his eyes once more, adding, "Marriage may be dead as a doornail but the real couple hasn't begun to manifest as yet. At least not in the West. It will need a new psychology – or perhaps a very old one – to inaugurate the coming dispensation. O dear! It sounds terribly schematic, like cutting along the dotted line. On the other hand we can't go on as everyone is doing. The world is coming to an end faster because of the waste, the misdirection of affect. I want to begin the new thing with you."

"Truthfully," she said, "I don't give a damn about theoretical considerations. I just want to be loved by you, stop."

But she was lying and they both knew it.

Their attachment had been born into a new age of sexual friendship which would create new responsibilities and problems in the measure of its new freedoms. But somehow not for them – what he had told her made her sure of it. Yet the whole subject-matter of his thinking was still full of mysteries – perhaps even absurdities, who could say? She was still, after all, a hostage of the logicians and consequently full of scepticism. He seemed so intellectually cocksure, a bad sign in a man, and particularly an Oriental. She lay beside him and watched him sleeping so peacefully, his head turned away in half-profile from her. What, she wondered, was the meaning of the little slip of thread round his throat? Some people wore a christening chain with a cross on it, or else their names graven upon a talisman of a saint. Perhaps, like a true Mediterranean, he wore it against the evil eye – but where was the usual blue bead? Beside the bed there was a pair of nail scissors which he had been using to clean out his pipe and settle his plug of hashish. Half in a spirit of idle mischief she took them up and placed them upon the thread as if to cut it. At this moment he opened his eyes and saw what she was doing. A look of horror and supplication came over his face, and he gasped, "For goodness sake!" Constance, delighted at the alarm she had created, withdrew her scissors and said, "I knew it! The Evil Eye!" And she put the scissors back on the side table. He said, "One can't turn one's back for a moment! You were actually going to sever my lifeline, were you? And so carelessly? If I had fallen back dead upon the pillows – where would you have been then?" She could not quite make out if this were banter or not. "Explain!" she said. "What is the thread?" And slowly fingering it, he told her dreamily that it was a signof his affiliation to the little Orphic group of which he had spoken more than once; it was the umbilical cord which united him with the buried world they were trying to bring to light with their association.

"The little thread is flax, grown on the Nile. We have imitated the Indians in that. It's the sign of the yogi, of his frugality and his mental chastity. The Templars wore it as a belt – and those idiot Inquisitors took it for some secret sexual symbol arguing a homosexual affiliation. Idiots! The double sex was quite another thing, a syzygy of the male and female affect."

"Would you have died if I had cut it?"

"Just to punish you I would have tried! But I would have regretted it, for it stands for other things. My fate, woven by Moira, the fates of Greece, my umbilical cord through which I connect with the rhythms of the earth yoga. No, not died, but been sad and regretful."

"I am sorry. It was thoughtless of me."

That night she asked her lover: "Did you know it was going to be like this?"

He looked at her and slowly nodded but said nothing; he

closed his eyes and appeared to reflect very deeply upon her question. "Did you, tell me truthfully?" She put her fingers upon the drum of his chest and felt the deep rise and fall of his breath, the archaic oxygen-pump which fed his thinking and his love-making alike.

"It isn't like a love affair at all," she said aloud, echoing a thought which had been formulated by her mind a while since. Their relationship had developed an odd kind of continuity so that it seemed to be a succession of small surprises, their endearments were like stepping stones towards . . . towards what, exactly?

"It is in fact the prototype, the original love-affair which we've tumbled into by luck: or perhaps a design we are not wise to. Today's loves are mostly debased currency, the timid investments of undischarged bankrupts with nothing to offer but undocumented sperm, trivial aggressive lusts, stuff of little richness. Sperm without oxygen, and with poor motility, will never reach the Grand Slam. All that is the domain of Unlove, Constance, it's not our concern."

"But where are we going?" she asked in a low voice full of concern. "We seem so linked now. I have changed so much in such a short time."

"It's only the beginning – that's why I hesitated so much. I did not want to go away as I must soon."

So, inchmeal, their love advanced.

And yet there was some inward check, for from time to time there would be moments of abstraction when she discerned an expression of tremendous sadness on his face; he might stand staring at the lake, or simply transfixed before the mirror in which he was knotting a tie, while this shadow of immense distress settled upon his features – it needed an effort to shake off. Then it was replaced by the look of loving wonder which he always wore when looking at her, talking to her. But she was alarmed by this sudden change and once, surprising it as she awoke (he stood by the balcony gazing down at the water) she cried out, "What *is* it that comes over you, comes between us all of a sudden? You must tell me. Is it someone else?" He laughed, and came to sit on the foot of the bed. "Yes, I must tell you because it concerns us both in the long run – it's aimed at us. Yet it's so fantastic that it is hard to realise, its novelty is so unexpected. Constance, I have been to Canada and I have seen the thing – what they call the Toy: the bomb, the new one." He fell silent for a long moment, staring at the pattern in the carpet.

He had visited the smithy of Haephaestus so to speak, the flaring forges where the huge grenades of the atomic piles roared and shivered, as if about to give birth, while the boiling steam and water rushed from the sluices and filled the air with dense acrid warmth; and outside the vast snowscapes like another inclement Russia, snow falling in the quarries with their long caterpillar-lines of linked chariots. He shivered in his soul when he remembered those shivering and sweating grenades full of a new fever.

"I had to report on this to the small group of Alexandrian searchers to which I belong and which I sometimes direct. I won't bore you with all that. But what I saw – my dear, all that is going on now, the fighting taking place, is already as out of date as the Battle of Hastings. We are fighting with bows and arrows. Compared to what has already arrived, the Toy."

"I had heard some vague talk about it from a patient who was a Viennese mathematician."

"It's not the war that's at issue. This thing is aimed at our bone marrow, and the bone marrow of the earth we live on. It confers sterility or genetic distortion – we will be born without heads and legs like illustrations to the propositions of Empedocles. Constance, nature has lost all interest in us; from now we are orphans! And how appropriate that a Jew should have triggered this murderous extract of pure matter, what a terrible revenge of the Semitic brain – a really Faustian denouement awaits us; it completely dwarfs the war, what matter who wins or loses? It is a shadow-play, for both sides are orphaned by the same stroke." He was trembling so much that she took his hands in her own strong ones and succeeded in calming him without speaking. "Not only that," he went on at last on a quieter note, "as if that were not enough – woman is compromised; in her we are destroying our nurse and muse, the earth."

They sat for a long time, as if posed for a photograph, she with her head against his shoulder, he with his arms round her shoulders. "You see what comes between our kisses?" he whispered at last, stroking her attentive and beautiful face. "When man starts to *feel* with his reason, with his intelligence, why, Monsieur is there!"

"Monsieur what? Monsieur who?" she asked.

And then, "We are being too serious," he said all of a sudden, briskly, shaking off the enormous weight of this ugly daydream, and at the same time feeling absolved because he had told her, had spoken it all aloud; at last there was someone to whom he could really talk. As she was putting on her clothes she said thoughtfully, "There must be a strategy for being happy. It's our duty to find it!" How like a woman, he thought.

"No such thing," he said.

She found some of his thinking interesting, but some downright silly. "How like a man," she said, "you are just feeling out of your depth, that is all; the new polyandry has scared you. But honey, the woman was always free, though not always allowed to say so openly. Is it a bad thing to come clean? She can now indulge her always dream of being an unpaid prostitute of pure benevolence, a public benefactor. She has become a collector – seven men to one woman seems about right – I have worked this out from what my patients have told me. Farmyard mathematics!"

"It doesn't work," he said. "Would that it did!"

"I know. But why not after all?"

"Because the poor quality of the male sperm becomes at once felt by the woman who is now the assailant. Anxiety and poor erections set in. *Ejaculatio praecox*! The poor little vagina must be likened to a little animal always eager for its nourishment. The sperm literally feeds it, it bathes the walls with their mucous membranes, it permeates the whole flesh and psyche. You can taste the odour of male sperm on the breath. The vagina starts to die of inanition, to falter from hunger; a hundred men with inferior sperm cannot feed it. In the gnostic sense a sperm which is poor in oxygen is deficient in the needed nourishment; it is poorly documented, poor in oxygen and the fruits of thought."

"Go on," she said, for it seemed a new and unusual way of looking at the sexual act, at the economy of the whole transaction. But he had turned quizzical now, as if he did not for a moment expect her to believe his theories. Smiling, however, he went on with his exposition: "The walls of the little animal – prettier often than the mouth of its owner – gives out a replete hum when the quality of the sperm is high or well-documented as we say: like a beehive or a small dynamo or a cat purring. The possibility of making a strong child with rich brain content and powerful sexuality presents itself and is eagerly welcomed by both lovers in their psyches. But with poor-quality sperm the poor little animal becomes parched and withered; sperm with no spiritual axis cannot feed the woman's ideas or her feelings. The more she performs the more diminished she feels. Genetically she is being starved, her ideas become poor and exhausted, the joy of living deserts her. And then comes the last stage." He put on a story-book voice and wagged a cautionary finger at her as he said, with great assurance. "Guess what? *Nymphomania!*" She clapped her hands at this revelation. "The girls begin to scratch themselves to

death; the men find that they cannot achieve a climax easily –
even younger men. Their hair recedes. They go into
politics . . ."

"Or come to the analyst. I have restored the hair to two
tired men, and have heard of analysis unblocking the sex drive.
But you must know that. Where did you pick up your psychological knowledge?"

"Here and there. But I went to a woman and she could not
resist my honesty – she fell in love with me."

"And?"

"And!"

He took her hand and put it to his cheek. "Your life is full
of hazards because as yet your science is inexact. She went mad
and was locked up: she writes to me, long, long letters of self-
reproach for having loved me. Yet there was nothing between
us of a personal sort – it all went on in her head!"

"Love! It's all done by mirrors!"

"Exactly. But I don't care. I invest! I love you!"

"Prove it."

He shook his head. "We are living out the death of the
couple, the basic brick of all culture."

"You are out of date and out of focus," she said.

"Out of date and out of fashion, rather," he admitted.

She said: "It's all going too fast; you understand too
much; I shall use you up too soon. I had imagined this relationship being slow, full of hesitations and nuances and unwitting
naivetés. I wanted to build it slowly, match by match, like a
ship in a publican's bottle."

He: "I thought you were too beautiful to be really
clever."

"You are not against me because I am a Freudian and a
doctor? I was scared to death that it might make a sort of
shadow between us – that I knew too much to be sufficiently
feminine to appease you, to get my hooks into you: but it's

been so easy sliding downhill, *en pente douce*. I have forgotten how to brake."

"It's a sign of our intellectual abjectness that psychology with its miserly physical categories and positivist bias should prove liberating and enriching as it does; it proves that the psyche is seriously ankylosed by the rigour of our *moeurs*. The real seed of the neurosis is the belief in the discrete ego; as fast as you cure 'em the contemporary metaphysic which is Judeo-Christianity manufactures more I's to become sick Me's. On my word as a Professor!"

"O Lord! you *are* anti-Freudian after all."

"No. I revere him, I even revere the purity of his un-shakeable belief in scientific reason. His discovery was as important as the microscope, or the petrol engine, a sudden enlarging of our field of vision. How *could* one not admire it?"

"Okay. I forgive you. But there is one thing most aggravating about you – I'd better tell you now, right at the beginning, instead of waiting until we are divorced . . ."

"Well?"

"You talk as if you had some privileged information which is not accessible to me. It's typically masculine and it makes one inclined to sympathise with the heavy brigade – as we call the clitoris club in the clinic."

"It's a serious charge."

"Have you?"

"No."

TEN

The General

THE MISADVENTURE WHICH VIRTUALLY COST VON ESSLIN his sight was also, by a paradox, instrumental in saving his life, for it supervened at about the time when the tide had turned and hostilities in and around his Provençal stronghold were sharpening to a climax. It resulted in his being incarcerated in an eye clinic near Nîmes, there to lie in sombre darkness with a pad over his eyes, drowned in self-reproaches and self-questionings. Whatever his body decreed, his soldier's mind was still on the active list, and the little radio by the bed brought him no consoling news, though the bulletins were under heavy censorship. Heaven knew how much was left unsaid. But truth to tell, his own decline had been going on for some time, for a year or more; this sudden flurry of a build-up involving so many new officers and material had only emphasised a fatigue which had slowly been gaining on him since the Avignon command had first become his. Though not unduly introspective he found himself often wondering about the cause. It was not only the calamitous withdrawal from Russia which could hardly be disguised any longer, nor the failure in Egypt and Italy, no. It was the inability to speak openly about them, and thus to devise ways and means to stem the tide until they could re-form their ranks. He did not believe the war lost, but still under debate, while there was plenty of life in the old German war dog yet to redress the failures of the past and assure future victory. But in other times the subject would have been discussed and ventilated, there would have been great conferences of strategists, self-criticism, truthful, intelligent assessments of the situation. But in this case one

could not voice a single criticism that did not touch the question
of the Leader's good faith, good judgement; what was at stake
was quite literally the divinity of the Führer – who dared to
gainsay that?

And then . . . Von Esslin had aged, he felt the gradually
lengthening shadows of a change of life start spreading before
him; his reactions were slower. The younger officers grew
impatient with the timidity of his troops' dispositions and felt
that the three lateral rivers had begun to obsess him. In the
fortress, standing in front of the great European chart with its
interlapping sections, he still held forth, terminating his discourse with the old, once dramatic gesture of placing his thumb
upon Avignon and spreading his fingers to turn them in a slow
arc to show the extent of their strategic coverage – the gateway
to Italy and the Côte d'Azur were both comprised in this
expository gesture. The thought of a landing further north was
a novelty which he did not take into account: others would
deal with such an eventuality. But the numbers needed close
supervision, things had become very crowded, not only
because of the wounded from the Russian front but also because
of the hordes of slave-workers or volunteer Fascists of all
nationalities, even Russian, who were tunnelling the vast
underground corridors of the new dumps under the Pont du
Gard. He had vague thoughts about his retirement in a few
years, of what he would do with himself; but here a thrill of
incertitude swept his mind. What sort of world would he
retire into? In order to call himself to order and replenish his
morale he commenced a close study of the Protocols of Zion
and the Imperial Testament of Peter, the documents he carried
with him always in their little plastic envelope. It calmed and
even invigorated his mind, this regular study every evening.
But he felt rather cut off and a trifle moribund as he contemplated the impatient energy of the younger officers, and
so often read on their faces expressions of a smiling con-

descension when he was talking. He was annoyed to discover
that he had been accorded the nickname of "Grandfather" by
the command. It only emphasised the gulf which was spreading
between two generations, two historic attitudes. He began to
drink rather heavily.

It was at this moment that he was informed that he could
release his servant for regular soldiering and replace him with
a slave-prisoner if he so wished; at first he was regretful, for his
batman had been with him quite a time, but his regrets were
short-lived once Krov appeared upon the scene, saluting
smartly with that captivating smile, at once so knowledgeable
and so self-deprecating. He was handsome and slender and he
turned his youthful agility in the direction of making himself
indispensable. In a world full of surly mastiffs he was something quite new, a ray of sunshine. What was there he could
not do? Sometimes Von Esslin enumerated his skills with
amazement – and he said that his family background was rich
bourgeois; his father had been a doctor. Cook, sweep, maintain, polish, set to rights . . . Banquo's old house had never
shown to better advantage; gardener, handyman, mason,
electrician . . . every new problem showed Krov's versatility
accompanied by charm and good nature. His German was
imperfect and he made delightful mistakes which sometimes
turned into puns of great felicity. Von Esslin recounted these
to his mess and earned hearty laughter for his new slave. Krov
exercised a charm over his master which was positively
Mephistophelean. He tended and brushed his clothes with
passion and frequently made some small adjustment of dress,
brushing off a crumb or cigar ash from Von Esslin's tunic
before letting him depart for the office. The old man was
bemused by his good luck – never had an establishment been
run so efficiently and with such warm good-feeling. "Ah,
Krov," he would say, "how did you never marry? You would
make a very fine husband. Or perhaps a wife, eh? Ha! Ha!"

"I did, I was. I have two children."

"Where?"

"I don't know where they are," said Krov quite seriously but without undue emotion. "Somewhere they must be." Von Esslin felt a wave of sympathy heavy as lead around his heart. "Well, I must be going, I shall be late," he said and stumped off. Poland!

Sometimes when he came back for lunch he might find Krov sitting on the front steps of the villa in the sun polishing his boots and shoes; he would spring up and salute with his warm smile of greeting, so obviously glad to see his master back that Von Esslin's heart was warmed and he became almost human, almost talkative, despite the official warning that there must be no fraternising with slave-labourers. Or else he might find him on top of a ladder arranging the grape trellis on the garden balcony. It was difficult when one received such superlative and willing service not to fall a victim to it, to become a little slack and dependent. You had only to say "Bring me a clean handkerchief, Krov," and the youth would dart away like a deer to find the article. Sometimes when he lay awake in bed the General's thoughts turned homewards and sometimes he accorded the Polish servant a sad passing thought. Krov's country villa had been in roughly the same region – bought against his father's retirement, he explained. His master grunted, but did not ask him for any more details about Poland before the war. But in a fit of elephantine playfulness intended in some profounder way to show his awkward gratitude, he learnt a few words of Polish from the little phrase book which the servant carried and both pleased and surprised him by saying "Good morning" in that language; but only when they were alone, of course. And when Von Esslin fell ill of a 'flu Krov nursed him tenderly, even feeding him with a spoon when he had a high fever, as one would a child. The old man was touched and grateful, though he refrained from thanking him openly, for after all he was only doing his duty in the official sense.

It proved a welcome change. Krov afforded him company and interest at a time when he was withdrawing from the coarse jovialities and philistine high spirits of the mess with its new faces.

He tried in unobtrusive ways to lighten the burden of the younger man's slavery, but it was difficult to go against field instructions which insisted that his slave was "expendable" and should be "used up in hard labour". He feared that Krov must present himself to the world as rather too well off, too well fed. He felt reckless, however, and even got him some cast-off clothes with boots and a tattered green mess jacket in which he served meals, which he did with professional aplomb. His cooking also was something special. Von Esslin was so charged with intellectual infatuation about the slave that he wrote and described some of his virtues to his mother who replied by saying, "It's as if you speak of your son." The observation struck him quite forcibly. One day when he cut his hand opening the car door he found a sympathetic Krov rushing to bandage it up, first dressing it with ether – he knew where everything was. His speed, tact and sympathy made the elder man say to himself, "But he really *seems* like a son to me," a sentimental idea which was so novel that he all but felt tears start to his eyes. "There!" said Krov at last, satisfied with his skilful bandage. "That will hold firm until tonight when we'll change it. Would you be in need of any anti-tetanus injection?" The General snorted with scorn. "For that little scratch? No." Krov said, "Anyway, the trigger finger is all right, so you can still shoot, sir, without any difficulty."

"Yes." Von Esslin smiled.

The weather had been so variable that one did not any longer know what to make of it; snow was followed by rain and warm winds, then frost, then sunshine again. The mean temperatures rose and fell like the waves of the sea. Now, during his convalescence, they had entered a sunny passage which was almost like summer; he could spend the afternoons out of doors, among the vines at the edge of the copse, reading or writing letters while Krov scurried about his tasks in the house, all the while humming or singing under his breath songs in his own unfamiliar tongue – songs which pleased the old man as much as the fine tenor of the singer. But of course he could say nothing to compliment him. The evenings too had become more supportable since Krov had shown him how to play solitaire. How strange life was! He often wondered nevertheless how Krov could maintain such a continuous amiability – for a man with his country over-run, his family dispersed and lost, his people sold into slavery, it was astonishing. There must be times when he felt the tug of sadness when he thought about these things? It was better not to let his thoughts take this direction, however, for it was the sort of situation which would never be redressed under the New Order.

Krov had placed an old fashioned rocking-chair which he had found in an attic at the end of the garden and it was here that the General sat in the evening to read or write; if the weather was at all chilly Krov put an old military cloak round his shoulders with great solicitude. It was from this habit that the shooting developed, for during the handing in of the guns as dictated by the Army a number of rather fine ones naturally figured among the general run of cheap farmers' twelves and sixteens. These were naturally regarded as "on loan" to the occupier, and when there was a shoot they were distributed to all senior officers. In this way Von Esslin "inherited" two fine hammerless twelves which he used once or twice for duck on the Camargue. But now, from his rocking chair, he found that on days of mistral his little hillock where the house stood was in the direct line for the evening flight of turtle doves and partridge. The turtle doves could hardly make headway against the wind and certainly not gain height; pressed down earthwards by its violence they flew in little gasps, little bursts, digging their way into the wind, and at each stroke falling back towards the earth once more with a lost momentum. They presented a very easy target even for such a moderate shot as Von Esslin, and on flight evenings he usually disposed of a dozen for dinner with rapidity and ease.

Krov went out of his way to encourage such activity, for he knew how to pluck and dress the birds which fell to his master's guns; sometimes when the flights were big and he had nothing to do he might take on the role of loader, thus increasing the speed of Von Esslin's firepower. On the evening of the accident the wind had come up but the day had proved so very exceptional that one felt one was in the month of August; only the clipped and raked vineyards belied the thought, for as yet the first green pilot leaves had not appeared on the black crucifixes. But birds there were in plenty, and the General popped away at them while his slave loaded the smoking guns for him. A certain wilful confusion hangs over the incident which now took place – some believing it an accident due to the General's thoughtlessness. What actually happened was as follows. Beside the chair of the General was an extremely damp mud parapet which was still soaked with the heavy rain of the preceding days. Inadvertently – he was to claim that the action was inadvertent, though nobody believed him – Krov in exchanging guns lightly stuck the barrels in the muddy bank, thus stopping the ends with heavy pellets of soil. He wiped the end of the gun before handing it to Von Esslin and busied himself with the second weapon. Now came the accident. The old man had got into the habit of discharging both barrels of his sparrow-shot together, aiming just in front of the dover-flights so that the birds dived into the sprayed pattern of lead. But this time when the hammers struck the gun blew back, the barrels exploded and the stock flew off; he received the blow-back of the charge full in the face. Enough to kill one outright, as they said later when dressing his complicated criss-cross wounds.

He turned in horror and perplexity, his features runnelled in trickles of blood, powder-markings and mud, as if to invoke the help of Krov; then in a flash he saw that his servant must have been expecting the accident for he had prudently stepped behind the old olive tree, and had his hands half-raised to his ears, as if anticipating an explosion. Von Esslin roared like a bull and stood up shaking all over with shock and pain; but in the roar also was another note, a note of pain and sadness and affliction at the betrayal of his affections by the Polish slave. He stood trembling, looking at him, with his smashed-looking face, and then slowly sank to his knees, grabbing the chair and overturning it as he fell face downwards in the grass.

Unfortunately there was a witness to the scene in the form of the A.D.C. to the General; this young staff officer had been looking for him in order to deliver a service message of some urgency; the house being empty he went out into the garden, and just as he located his chief he saw the whole thing take place; he also saw the incriminating move of the servant as he hid behind the tree. There was no doubt that Krov knew it was going to happen, and was therefore responsible. Consternation seized the young soldier as he saw the General fall, heard him roar with pain and anger. The sparrow shot whizzed in the bushes. The whole thing was so sudden that he stood stock-still before having the presence of mind to race to the General's aid, at the same time blowing his whistle to alert the duty picket, which now came thumping and panting out on to the balcony with a clatter of useless rifles. Krov was already beside his master, down on one knee, when the officer arrived, so that together they managed to take up the still writhing form and carry it towards the balcony; here someone with presence of mind had produced a stretcher, and the General, who was still swearing and groaning, was piled on to it. The heavy duty wagon had a capacious end with fold-down seats, and this obviated calling an ambulance. The thing was to get him to the general hospital in the Citadel as quickly as possible. They hoisted the wounded man in. Then the officer drew his Luger. To Krov he said, "You are coming with me."

Krov did not show any particular emotion, but he asked if he might go to the lavatory. The officer said he might, but with the door open and with himself posted outside, his weapon at the ready. They drove in silence to the Fortress where he turned out the guard and asked the officer of the watch to convene a provisional court martial for that afternoon. Then he announced what had happened to the duty officers and confided to the operational telex the news that the Senior Commander had had a serious accident and that a bulletin about it might be expected from the medical staff that same evening. Nor was this long delayed, for they washed the blood and powder and mud from the face of Von Esslin and pronounced with relief that all the wounds were superficial but that the explosion had only compromised his sight. He was almost completely blind and likely to remain so, if not forever, at least for the foreseeable future. A command was out of the question in such a case, and it would not be long before a replacement arrived to take over. It was of course catastrophic in one sense for the *amour-propre* of an active man to be plunged in the dark like this, with the prospect of hospitalisation and retirement to look forward to as a future. Apart from the shock and the pain, the stitches in his cheek and chin, he was beset by a fearful sense of despondency and utter helplessness. An oculist came and tried various kinds of light upon the eye, but was non-committal about the future. The eyes must be given time to settle down, he said, for they too were in a shocked state from the accident.

Accident? That evening a drum head court martial heard the evidence of the A.D.C. concerning the guilt of the Polish servant in grim silence; it was not thought necessary to ask the wounded man whether he would concur to this statement or not – the thing was so conclusive. Krov was sentenced to death by firing squad the following morning. It was not the only execution, for a couple of *franc-tireurs* were also going to be executed. The General sat in a chair by the window. His face had been repaired and dressed. He sat there patiently under the full weight of his near sightlessness – how unfamiliar it was! Yet he recognised the voice of the A.D.C., who came to tell him about the verdict on Krov, hoping no doubt to please him by this summary revenge. But the old man said nothing. Finally the A.D.C. took his leave, closing the door softly behind him. When the nurse came in to the room she found her charge still sitting by the window, but his chin had sunk on his breast and he was breathing rather more rapidly than usual, which indicated nervous stress; it was most necessary to make some bright conversation to infuse a bit of optimism into the General. She was right. He was soon chatting away in his kindly fashion, thanking her warmly for all that they were doing for him. When the question of his convalescence came up the oculist invited him to the eye clinic in Nîmes where his progress could be checked. It was only a question of clearing up – and there was no Krov to undertake such an operation. Finally a couple of clumsy orderlies assembled his few possessions and helped him into the duty car. In this way he cleared the decks for his successor.

All this, in much abbreviated form, was retailed by Smirgel in his secret bulletins to Geneva, and he was even able to supply the name of the new Commander. It was Von Ritter, a stern disciplinarian and party man, as ugly as he was unprincipled. The news of his appointment caused a ripple of interest, for he was fresh from some spectacular civilian reprisals in Russia. His arrival was celebrated by a mass hanging of twenty "partisans" in Nîmes: they were actually youths who, to dodge the labour conscription, had taken to the hills where they lived like the shepherds. They were unarmed, but what matter? It would teach everyone a good lesson.

So the news of the new dispensation filtered through the opaque medium of the gossiping Intelligence agencies, and the name of Von Esslin was gradually obliterated from the reports. In Geneva as in Avignon the cold set in again with high wind and heavy snowfalls.

ELEVEN

Confrontations

AROUND THE COMPANIONABLE GREEN BAIZE OF THE billiard table moved the two figures of Affad and Toby, each with half his mind on his ball and the other on the subject in hand, namely, did Ritter's appointment prefigure a policy change; or was it a ruse? For Toby "it smelt ratty". The accident was an excuse merely to replace an old-fashioned regular with old-fashioned notions by an active, fire-eating young general who would ginger things up. Affad shook his head: "You over-elaborate the obvious. I believe Smirgel." Toby sighed with resignation and said, "As always. But you just wait. That man is going to fail you."

"I have asked for an independent medical check on the matter, so we'll see who is right." Then, in order to rub a little salt into the open wound of British Intelligence he went on, "By the way, I did not ask you people for the dates of the Second Front landings, I got them from Cairo. I did not want to embarrass you. But here on this visiting card I have jotted down the false dates which I have passed to Smirgel. You will find quite a response to them already – a whole lot of armour has been shunted north to contain this hypothetical landing – but I am sure you know that."

Toby swore silently for as a matter of fact he did not know, though it would not have done to say so; he looked vexed, however, and Affad smiled, for he liked teasing him. The result was that Toby missed his shot and vented his spleen with an audible oath which did service for both groups of sentiment.

The Secret Service was really no fun at all. One was always being upstaged by some other agency and one was forced to accept old-fashioned histrionic methods of work, some of them elaborated at the turn of the century. It was the influence of bad fiction like the Sherlock Holmes series (which he adored); the Foreign Office believed that every spy should carry a big magnifying glass with him night and day in case of footprints. And here this blinking Gyppo Prince went about openly tapping telephones ... "Nobody tells us anything," he said plaintively, and by a lucky shot broke even.

Constance who watched them thoughtfully from the corner where she was answering letters in her swift shorthand said, "I find it galling to hear you two talk – you know more than I do about Avignon, and yet I live and work there, and my job takes me everywhere. Poor old General; how sad to lose your sight!"

But the new General had wasted no time; he had sacked subordinates right and left, signalling for new staff appointees whom he could personally trust to be "firm", and had spread terror into all departments including those which dabbled in counter-espionage. "Smirgel himself is scared and wants to shut down his transmitter for a week or so to let the simmering settle down. I must say when I see these whopping reverses and withdrawals in Russia I can't help feeling that that little embalmed head we supplied is giving Hitler pretty destructive guidance."

"Let me tell you the most important news of all – for the first time I see a faint hope that we might just win the war. Lord Galen has been *sacked*." Both men burst out clapping with delight. "O not that we don't love him," explained Sutcliffe. "But really we want to win, don't we?" They explained that Lord Galen, in order as he said "to show up the other side for the rotters they were" persuaded the War Cabinet to announce that no monuments of historic or aesthetic value in Europe would be subjected to bombardment. Moreover he had this piously announced over the radio. The result was not hard to foresee for at once the Nazis took advantage of this knowledge and turned it to account in their ammunition stockpiling. Toby said, "For example that mysterious dump they have coded as W.X. in Avignon is being burrowed out slap under the Pont du Gard – you must have noticed a vast increase of activity around the Remoulins area. Huge teams of foreign workers are being housed in makeshift huts all round about in the garrigue. It's quite an operation. But finally somebody has tumbled to Lord Galen's role as a hot potato, and he has been invited to abstract himself from the task of Information. May God be with him in his new post in the colonies."

"No colonies for him. He is too clever for them. He will suddenly emerge as an admiral."

"But tell us your news," said Toby, turning to Constance apologetically. "How have things been?"

"It sticks in my throat," she said. "It's an unheroic story of discomfort and sadness, with sporadic little outbursts of danger or outrage, shootings and disappearances. Bread from maize full of straw and other sweepings. Coffee made of mud. Hungry children. Queues for medical attention. I feel ashamed to live where I do, eat what I eat, thanks to Blaise and the office and the black market in everything."

"And Livia, is she really dead?"

"Yes." And she told them how and when.

"And no clue to why?"

"I could think of none, save that such a stark gesture was in her character, and that it may have been somehow connected with the failure of her central beliefs – though she said not. But who could see the face of Nazism from close up and not want to retch? She was not a fool. But I am aware all the time that you probably know more than I do about everything. Perhaps you have answers to all these questions."

"No," said Sutcliffe. "Perhaps Affad has, though; we don't use the same source of supply as he does."

"Smirgel?"

"Yes."

"But Quatrefages is surely just as likely to be untrustworthy; remember all his romancing about Galen's child and the Templars? He would tell you anything."

"He is not alone, there are others."

They rose to play and she returned to her correspondence, pencil in hand, making draft notes for the replies to letters which would later be typed. Toby opened the game with a magistral flourish. "It's all very well for you to jabber about the Jews, MacSutcliffe, but I find it sometimes most irritating the way they go on; why, the last bunch of intels were extraordinary. They were not only reporting each other in Paris, but some had actually joined the Milice. As if it were not enough to be more industrious and more conceited than everyone else!"

"Whatever you may think of Jews," she said, "you would not stand by and see those trains pull out and hear Smirgel's snigger."

"Speaking as a historian," said Toby, "if the whole thing weren't tragic it would be risible. Do you realise what the Germans want? They want to be the Chosen People – they have announced the fact. They want to do away with the Jews so that they can take their place. It is quite unbelievable – if you told me I would not believe you. The Chosen Race! Whose blood is thicker than whose? Washed in the blood of whose lamb if I may ask? This is where Luther's great worm bag has led them. It's like children snatching at each other's coloured balloons. But to descend to the total abolition of Jews – it would take a really serious metaphysical nation to do that!"

"According to Affad it has a metaphysical base: it is an involuntary organic reaction, like the rejection by the stomach of something disagreeable, against Judeo-Christianity as exemplified by our present world philosophy which as you know is dominated by brilliant Jewish thinkers."

"Illustrate, please," said Toby, trying an awkward shot which lost him the match. "Damn!"

"The triad of great Jews who have dominated thought – Marx, Freud, Einstein. Great adventurers in the realm of matter. Marx equated human happiness with money – matter; Freud found that the notion of value came from faeces, and for him love was called investment; Einstein, the most Luciferian, is releasing the forces sleeping in matter to make a toy which . . ."

"O God," she said in dismay, "don't tell me you are half-hearted about Nazism? I've just come from a country which can't make up its mind. So many French seem indifferent to this purge which Laval calls a 'prophylaxis', if you please."

"I don't think the Russians are any better," said Sutcliffe. "We have a number of distasteful choices – the world as a kibbutz, with obligatory psychoanalysis lasting a lifetime and replacing Catholicism . . . and then atomic robotisation I suppose. It makes me feel all old-fashioned; I don't know what to say."

"*Honi soit qui Malebranche*," said Toby.

"And it's all very well you being pious, but all this started with the French, the Republic having no need of *savants*. And Jews like that foul painter David presiding on committees to cut off the head of Chénier. Tumbrilitis has slopped over and reached the whole world now. To think that the first statue which was erected by the revolutionaries was one to the Goddess of Reason!"

"It still goes on; I used to wait for her outside the ivy-covered building in Raspail which houses part of the University, against which wall I taught her how to hold her chopsticks. Love was never the same again, in the light drizzle falling on our faces, sticking our kisses like postage stamps upon each other's lips. Above us, written on the wall, nay, engraved in it were the fatal words: '*Université. Evolution des*

Etres Organisés. Ville de Paris.' It was the equivalent of 'Abandon hope, all ye who enter here', though we did not know it at the time . . . and now Schwarz has her in dark keeping which harmeth not. Or so you say."

"I can't follow," she said.

"Wait till Aubrey comes. He will tell you all about Hitler and his ideas."

"It will be your first meeting? No?"

Sutcliffe looked at her in a curious fashion but said nothing. At that moment a familiar voice said, "They arrive next Monday by air from Cairo." Affad stood at the door cleaning his glasses with a pocket handkerchief. Her heart turned over involuntarily, which surprised her: she did not as yet know how to behave in the presence of other people. But he came lightly across the room, avoiding the two players, and after kissing her sat down, putting his arm in hers. "All this confusion and talk about Hitler and Jews comes from one factor – the refusal to see that the Jewish faith is not a confession but that the Jews are really a *nation* bereft of a homeland and forced to become the world's cuckoo. This is where we have permitted ourselves to work against the British and further the claims of Palestine. Of course the British are scared about their Arab oil, but nevertheless it is of world importance that the Jews be housed nationally. Then it does not much matter what form their Judaism takes, monotheism or whatever. But we persist in treating them as simply a confession."

"Well, as a convinced Freudian analyst I feel a bit compromised; perhaps I am Jewish from this point of view."

Sutcliffe said, "You know what Aubrey would say – he would say that you are simply running what the Americans would call a massage-parlour of the soul. You cannot analyse Psyche without coming upon Cupid."

"But that is exactly what Freud says."

"Does he?"

891

"Of course."

"But Cupid is simply an investor, not a god."

"That's another matter."

"A Luciferian remark if I know you."

"I did not mean it as such."

"How about Libido?"

She sighed a long sigh and decided not to deliver the heated exposé which seethed inside her. She rose.

"Let's go, I'm hungry."

Delighted, Affad sprang to his feet at once. "I was just about to say the same. Where shall we go?"

Sutcliffe said, "Somewhere where we can join you for coffee, before the office opens."

"The Old Barge" – everyone echoed the name of a familiar haunt, a boat converted into a restaurant and anchored against the quay, hard by the elegant and well-tended gardens. It was central to the town, not too smart or expensive, and very close to the Embassy. They took their leave of the billiardaires, as Toby called himself and Sutcliffe, and drove to the appointed place. They were suddenly, unaccountably, shy with each other. It was difficult to understand. "I know," he said at last. "It's because you seem so different all of a sudden, sort of sophisticated and well turned out, and far too beautiful for safety."

"Whose safety?"

"Mine! Everyone's!"

"I suddenly felt I needed to get away from you, to stand off from you in order to see you more clearly; I am going to desert you after lunch and visit my old clinic to see how they are getting on with my old patients."

"And tonight?"

"I must sleep in my flat, alone."

He used a lot of bad language under his breath, swearing in French, Arabic, Greek and English, but what the target of these objurgations was he could not say – it had nothing to do with her, and everything to do with this strange love-predicament. Just when he most wanted to seem a man of the world, sincere but experienced. "What are you mumbling?" she asked suspiciously, but he only shook his head and said, "I was swearing at my own lack of subtlety. I should have got tickets for a concert. It would have been one way of being together without chewing each other with our eyes."

It was hardly surprising that they lacked appetite as well, though she found an excuse in the fact that she had only just arrived from a starving country and was not used to all this abundance. But she drank a couple of stiff whiskies – a fact which he noted with disapproval. They were joined fairly soon by their two billiardaire companions who were indulging in their usual desultory wrangling. "Just because our old friend Blanford is about to manifest, Robin here has set up as a new Einstein, just to *épater* him. On the bathroom mirror he has in lipstick $E = mc^2$ with the legend ERECTION EQUALS MEDITATION PLUS CONNIVANCE SQUARED. As if that were not enough he had added on the mirror in the hall, MEDITATION OVER FORNICATION LIKE MASS OVER FORCE YIELDS REINCARNATION. I do not think either Blanford or Einstein would approve, but there it is."

"It's the fruit of my inmost supposings," said Sutcliffe, a trifle coyly. "It's such a bore just going on being a cricketer." He was referring to his famous namesake, now in honourable retirement. "Can't one change hearses in mainstream? Why not Jack the Stripper or someone more colourful? I shall ask Aubrey when he comes if it's all the same to him."

"Will you come to meet him?" she asked curiously, and he said, "Of course I will, if you will drive." But she did not believe him. Somehow she thought he would avoid the meeting. On an impulse she decided to go home to bed, but once she walked into her flat a terrible desolation seized her by the hair. She telephoned Affad and he came to her, as swift as magic.

They looked at one another for a long moment; and then, no word said, they went outside and got into the car. He felt as if he was hardly breathing, he was pale. Once they reached the hotel they rang for the lift, and still silent went up to his room where he at once drew the curtain to shut out the daylight, while she was naked in a flash and in his arms. She was so excited that she wanted to live out a sort of expiation, and through clenched teeth she whispered, "*Fais-moi mal, chéri. Déchirez-moi.*" To hurt her, to drive his nails into that firm body – yes, but he wanted to bide his time as yet for their breathing was not in synchro. They would scatter the precious orgasm, mercury all over the place like a smashed thermometer. "Ah, you are holding back!" she cried in anguish, and scratched. "I'm not, Constance." She began to laugh at their precipitation, and their disarray, and then the laughter turned to tears and she buried her face in his shoulders and planted a dejected blue bruise on the fine brown skin. Two arms, two legs, two eyes . . . an apparatus both for surfeit and for bliss. *Tristia!* What a tremendous novitiate loving was – no, she was taking it too seriously. It was just beauty and pleasure. He was saying to himself, "It is like drinking a whole honeycomb slowly. O Divine Entropy – even God dissolves and melts away. Ah, my poor dream of a committed love which is no longer possible because of the direction women have taken."

Suddenly he gave her a tremendous slap across the face, and almost before she could react with surprise and pain he was on her, had taken her by the shoulders and penetrated her; and to still her cries of rage and injured pride he sealed his mouth upon hers. There was no doubt who led, for now he mastered her and inflicted orgasm upon orgasm upon her like welcome punishments. And suddenly, after a struggle, she accepted the fact, she played the role of slave, knowing that her perfect submission would tire him sooner and bring him down to her feet once more. The charm of that inner compliance excited him beyond endurance almost; later he told her it was like being covered in honey and tied down to an ant-hill, to be devoured slowly kiss by kiss, ant-mouthful by ant-mouthful. So the time ran on until the two exhausted creatures fell asleep.

"I knew this would happen," she said much later, combing out her hair in the mirror. "I simply knew that I could be something to you." Then added, "Bloody fool that I am!" Almost every day now they dined at her flat, which enabled her to show off a culinary aptitude which was fair to good for a bachelor girl, and which he appraised as well as praised with discrimination; then he helped her stack the washing up for the servant and played a little on the sweet, small upright piano which was her solace in times of melancholy, and on which the ponderous Sutcliffe amidst sighs swathed himself in the moods of Chopin. Affad did not play as well as she did – good!

He stood up and said, "Were you happy as a child? I think I must have been because I never asked myself the question. I stood between my father and mother, each held a hand, as if between a great king and queen, two gods. It would have been unthinkable to regret or doubt. I lived in a dream, and it is still going on in the depths of things, for me. Yes, still going on." And he softly repeated the word which he did not like others to use: "Sebastiyanne."

They lay down side by side on the couch, fully dressed and thoughtful. He said, "You know, this war is coming to an end, slowly but surely. Italy has been turned inside out like the sleeve of a coat. I have been checking the reports of all posts. We have a date now for a landing in Europe in full force. It is all coming together, becoming coherent, and the Germans know it. They will turn very nasty now before they are finally convinced. How right Tacitus was about their national character. How marvellous the British have been to hold on, how can we ever thank them?"

"What do you see beyond – what sort of world?"

"A smashed Europe like an old clock; it will take about six or seven years to get it working again, unless the Russians decide to prevent it ever working. They will emerge from this thing strong, while we shall be exhausted."

"I shall stay here," she said, "and operate from here if I can. We shall see. But meanwhile, for the present, we mustn't forget that Aubrey arrives tomorrow at dawn. Sutcliffe has panicked and retired to bed with a heavy cold. He dare not look upon the face of his Maker, it would seem."

He slept quietly where he lay, and she in her turn also did so, though she first made herself more comfortable in a silk dressing-gown, and combed out her unruly hair in the bath-room; the little radio was on but turned quite low. She heard Chevalier singing "Louise" and for some reason she felt moved, tears came into her eyes and threatened her make-up which she was too lazy to remove. She restored her looks and her composure with the help of a tissue and told her reflection, "All this will end in a fine neurasthenia, you see."

She unlaced his suedes and drew them softly from his feet, while he hardly stirred; what had he been doing to get so tired? Then she arranged a rug over their feet and crawled under it, nestling beside him, trying to remain quite still, almost breathless like a bird, so as not to disturb him. In the middle of the night she woke to find him staring at her with his eyes wide open, so intently that for a moment she wondered if he were still asleep. But no. "How marvellous!" he whispered and in a flash was asleep once more. She felt proud and con-tented, as if she had suckled him. Her own sleep was troubled lightly by questions about the future – intellectual nest-building which she reproved. It seemed hardly an hour before the little alarm clock squealed and they woke reluctantly upon

896

the darkness, to envisage the distant airfield in its remote valley under the snows. The car was sluggish, too, but at last they got it going and crawled across the sleeping town towards the lakeside where there was much more light, with a distinct promise of a clear dawn coming up apace.

"Can I smoke?"

"No. Or I shall too."

"Very well."

They drove on in sleepy silence, until he asked: "Have you precise plans for Aubrey Blanford's treatment? You said you had seen a detailed dossier."

"Yes I have; there may be one fairly big operation and two minor ones to do, but the picture is not without hope. I have invoked the aid of Kessley and his clinic – he is by far the cleverest surgeon for the job. Aubrey is young still and in quite good physical shape. There is no need for a gloomy prognosis in his case, as in some of the others. I have made all the arrangements – a pleasant lakeside room, and of course the hot water spa right at his elbow. Let's see what he says."

The airport was hardly awake, and the bar provided them with deplorably weak coffee and a croissant. But they were glad of the shelter and the warmth, for outside on the field a chill wind was blowing. In a while they heard the distant droning of the three Ensigns which were bringing the chosen fifty to safety and medical aid. They circled the field once or twice before making their run in one after the other. They came to rest and taxied up to within hailing distance of the terminal before releasing their occupants – a cluster of uniformed nurses and orderlies, followed by a mass of stretchers and wheelchairs. They waited patiently, trying to sort out the throng with their eyes. "There!" Affad said at last; as a matter of fact it was not Blanford he had recognised, for he was huddled in his wheelchair, covered in a rug, and deeply asleep. It was the snake-headed valet, Cade, who wheeled him out of the plane and towards them. He wore a kind of desert uniform with a bush-jacket, and his service cap sported a cock feather. "Good morning!" he cried cheerfully as he saw Affad. "Here he is all safe and sound. But sound asleep," and as if to explain, Cade groped at the feet under the rug and produced an empty whisky bottle. He frowned and said, "Too much of this for my liking, but what can I do? I have to obey orders." He gave a brief canine smile, full of yellowish teeth. The sick man stirred.

He seemed to Constance to be very much thinner than she remembered, and indeed more youthful in a strained sort of way, but surprisingly brown, which gave the tone of fitness to the general impression he made, lying there asleep.

Presently he woke, due perhaps to a slight jolt of his wheelchair or some unaccustomed change of silence or sound or temperature – a cold wind blew across the airfield and the air was full of cries and greetings. Yet he woke smiling a trifle shyly, to give each a hand, saying, "I'm sorry to be in this disarray; it was a long twelve-hour flight and my backache drove me to gag the pain with whisky, which annoyed Cade." She told him with genuine delight that he had not changed – yes, he had allowed a small moustache to grow, that was all. Nor had she, he said, and blushed with a sort of delighted confusion, with emotion at meeting, so to speak, with a survivor of that last Provençal summer. Yet both made the same disclaimer: "Ah, but inside!" she said, and he agreed that the change was there, though invisible. They felt aged in the heart of their experience. He held on to her hand as they talked, as if to draw from it warmth and support; and Affad, feeling that a third party would increase the dilemma of constraint and shyness, said a brief fond word and took his leave, on the understanding that she would ride in the ambulance with Aubrey, and that he himself would send a duty car to the clinic for her.

Some provision had to be made for Cade and the wheel-chair, and this she arranged with the driver of the ambulance, squeezing in beside him so that she could keep Aubrey's hand in hers while they drove in companionable silence to their destination. "It's quite unbelievable!" he said once, and that was all; but she noticed that he was feverish and a little hysterical, no doubt due to fatigue and the claustrophobia of the journey in an old-fashioned plane. At any rate he berated Cade for trivial lapses or oversights with an unusual violence and outspokenness. The hireling did not reply, but simply drew his lips back to expose his teeth with an expression of pain, or as if he were a dog about to snap. His resentment he showed by breathing hard through his nose. Aubrey saw that she remarked this departure with curiosity and coloured as he said, trying to laugh the matter off, "One becomes a bit of an old maid, as you see. We quarrel like an old married couple – Cade is the wife." Disgusted, the valet pretended not to hear. He looked out of the window with his dogged expression, impatient of their arrival at Dr. Kessley's clinic. It did not take very long before they turned into a well-tended property full of green grass and firs, and dotted about with elegant chalets. At one of these they disembarked and found their way to his quarters which delighted him by their seclusion and the beauty of the view. "I was hoping for snow," he said. "I wanted to see snow again." Dr. Kessley made his appearance and created a most favourable impression on the patient by his modesty and by the fact that he was fully abreast of the case. Constance he called by her first name, which increased the sense of intimacy, of being among friends. "We want you for a few days to do nothing but take hot water massage in the spa waterfall and sleep a great deal; we want you completely at ease and relaxed before we go any further. You have received excellent attention in Cairo for the first stage – there is no work to be undone. We can continue from the present state of affairs with some confidence. I suppose you know about your condition." He said that he did; Dr. Drexel in Cairo had given him a thorough brief as to the general shape of things. "Good," said the surgeon and took his leave.

They busied themselves in getting him washed and put to rights before tucking him up in his bed. While the valet was out of the room she said, "You know you will have expert nursing here; you could get rid of Cade for good if you wished."

He shook his head. "Not yet."

There was a silence during which she was wondering whether her suggestion had upset him in any way; Cade re-entered the room and went about his tasks in silence. His presence imposed a constraint upon them, so they smiled at each other and said nothing. Then the valet left the room again on some pretext and Blanford was able to say, "I can't sack him yet. He is my only link with my mother. Every day he tells me some little thing, some little incident about her which enables me to see a bit further into why I hated her so much and so unjustly; I *must* have, to find myself in this situation – I don't believe in chance accidents. It's a situation which might keep me childless."

"But that's *Freud* on women," she said with some surprise.

"Everything he says about women is true of men," said Aubrey Blanford with a sudden return to the old curate's tone for which they used to tease him so remorselessly in the past. It was so delightful, the serious way he said it, that she clapped her hands and laughed as childishly as she would have done had they both been at Tu Duc. She could not refrain from kissing him warmly, which made him blush with pleasure. "O childless one!" she said, adopting for a moment the mock-papal tone of Sam. "Will you let Cade psychoanalyse you?" And he made an impatient gesture.

The duty nurse came in to be presented to her patient and it was time to take her leave, so Constance felt, for her car had already been signalled as waiting in the drive. She would leave him to acclimatise and return on the morrow, she said, and he acquiesced. Kissing him again almost rapturously she said, "Thank God you haven't changed – still the old sobersides Aubrey Blanford Esq. I am so happy about that." He was less so: "I have changed profoundly," he said gravely but with twinkling eyes, "but for the worse; I have become a cynic. I want you to take a message of disdain to Robin, for his cowardice in not daring to face me; I know he has retired to a flat with a lift too narrow to accommodate my wheelchair. There he is throwing a fit of influenza as an excuse. Tell him that he will be punished by the visit of a dark woman of unexpected force and glory with whom he will be forced to couple." But she decided that she would leave him to deal with Sutcliffe on his own, without her interference. She bade him goodbye without precisely saying so. "Don't be too annoyed with Robin, he really is under the weather." Yet Blanford answered darkly, "I am annoyed because my power is not absolute over him – he is after all my creation; but he can some-times break loose and show traces of free will. My domination is incomplete, damn him. I told him to come to the airport. He mutinied. He must be punished!"

Leaving him, Constance drove back to her old clinic to find Schwarz, who was delighted to see her, as always. Pia and Trash who were passing through a relatively tranquil period, were working together on an ambitious tapestry. The subject was Clément's celebrated painting from Avignon, *The Land of Plenty: Cockayne*, which had been com-mercialised by Gobelin among other masterpieces. The quiet work, the skeins of colour, absorbed them both and they sat before the white window, quiet as nuns. Constance had to wait awhile for Schwarz to finish with a young ardent American analyst who was working with him, and who was submitting to his "control discussion" concerning some patients who were giving him trouble; they were apostates from the Rudolf Steiner groups so numerous in Geneva, and their astral theology was unfamiliar to the young man. His voice carried plangently and plaintively through the door of Schwarz's office: "So I gave him the suppository you prescribed, but in his present state he can't keep anything down."

"*Down?*"

"Sorry, up."

"I see."

Apparently, though apostate, the patient still had fragments of theosophical belief clinging to his thinking. "What do you propose?" said Schwarz.

"He's the most religious of the two; he's been deep into what he calls Astral Communication – so deep he had an attack of Poetic Apprehension – that's what he calls it. After that his wife refused to sleep with him. She said his breath smelt of embalming fluid. Boy, that Apprehension was certainly a bitch. I've locked him up with a sedation mixture."

"What else can we do?" said the old man; it was a question he always uttered with a strongly flavoured Yiddish accent; and he repeated it now to Constance. "*Aber*, Constance, what can we do?" He had half a mind to try an insulin shock convulsion-therapy on Pia but Constance had pleaded so earnestly against it that he had abandoned the idea. "You'd blow out what little brain is left," said Constance. "After all there's a whole situation attached to the matter of her illness, and it concerns several people." Since the discovery of Affad and the vertiginous glories of their affair she had become much more sympathetic to people in love – had even begun to see the elephantine love of Sutcliffe as moving rather than grotesque and preposterous; while the manoeuvres of the innocent and warm-hearted negress added both charm and despair to the whole business. Pia whined and whimpered like the sick child she had become, while Trash answered her with force and energy, saying stupid things with great conviction in that sweet dark voice, heavy as a bass viol. "I wanted us to sleep in one great bed," she told Schwarz once. "There'd be room for everyone, for Robin and Pia, and even their friends could come for a fix when they felt that way. My mother always said Never Refuse; and the preacher at the church said Give It All You Got. But Robin won't and Pia won't. Would it help if I went away?"

"No. You've tried that; Pia is still too fragile for anything drastic. She would withdraw again. We want to keep her in the field of vision still."

It was an unearthly waste of time and talent and medicine. Doctors nowadays are supposed to cure everything, even soul-complaints. But what could a priest have done anyway?

TWELVE

A Visit from Trash

T HE AFFLICTION WHICH LAID ROB SUTCLIFFE LOW WAS
of his own making, compounded for the most part of
sheer alcohol and *tabac gris* in immoderate quantities,
irregular meals and unusually large doses of medicines like
aspirins and vitamins plus a geriatric invention of the Swiss
called Nix which was supposed to make you younger. Now he
lay, feverish and snorting like a billygoat in a rumpled bed,
smarting under the sallies of his co-sharer and workmate who
resented having to play nurse to a man who would not see the
Embassy doctor because he was called Bruce Hardbane. "I am
superstitious about names," he explained. Nor would he see a
Swiss because that would mean his having to pay for a consultation; the Foreign Office provided free medical supervision. Toby was already late for the office but he stayed to mix
his colleague a grog to take with his aspirin, and then swept
into his threadbare overcoat and smartly disappeared from the
flat. Sutcliffe sighed; another long day to spend supine with too
much of a headache to read, and no company to divert him
from gloomy and aggressive thoughts about Bloshford who
lay also supine with a hole in his back, but in incomparably
prettier surroundings, looking out upon the lake. He would
have rung Aubrey up to insult him but the telephone was out
of order for the nonce. There he lay like the Brothers Grimm,
like the Brothers Karamazov, like the whole tribe of guttering
Goncourts, steeped in sadness.

He was surprised to hear the lift start to mount in its cage,
and even more so to hear it stop at their landing while its
occupant vacated it and sent it down again before advancing
up to the door of the flat and giving a little tattoo of the finger-

nails upon it before pushing it open – for it was always ajar. He was delighted to think it was a surprise visit from Constance and called her name aloud triumphantly, but who should walk in with dramatic slowness but the negress Trash? "The ogre!" he cried aloud, swearing a little. "How did you find me?" She looked utterly beautiful, like a black pearl – as a matter of fact she wore large pearl earrings which looked divine on that black satin headpiece. Then the most magnificent furs in which she was sweating lightly, giving off incensuous musk of gorgeous body odour. Robin raised himself and snuffed her like an equatorial balsam wafted from the still vexed Bermoothes of his heart. He knew that she did a little mannequin work for Polak's, and that they let her borrow furs sometimes – so this sombre plumage worthy of the helm of the Black Prince must be on loan. "I jest had to see you Robin, honey," she said, advancing to sit on his bed, and at the same time laying a large hand, graceful as a coffee table, upon his forehead. "You're quite a mite feverish," she told him, and he lay back, putting on his haughty and disagreeable expression. "What brings you here?" he said, trying to "rasp" as one would if one wrote it in a novel. For a while there was no answer to his rasp. He watched rather uncharitably while she took a swig at his grog, burning her cherry-red mouth. "Is there anything wrong with Pia?" She shook that black mausoleum of hair in a negative sense. "She is being sedate until two," she said. "But we've been talking and I told her I was coming to see you and tell you what we think." She opened her red maw like some great sea-whore in search of some plankton; modelling furs had brought out the seal in her. She said confidingly, "You ain't ill, Robin, you jest ain't strivin' enough; you gotta latch on to the affirmative, man, like the song says, and eliminate the negative. You gotta *be* it Bing's way! I guess you are jest sad cause you ain't got a good girl to plough, Robin. Them Embassy dames are mighty cold turkey, isn't that it?"

He thought, "I could not love thee dear so much loved I
not killing more." But really she was right, this ebony glisten-
ing pillow consultant. What he needed was pillow music or
even a pillow fight with an untrussed nun. The terrible thing
was that she seemed half in love with him herself, even a little
jealous of his cold turkey, for she slipped her warm hand inside
his pyjama jacket as she talked and scrumped softly at his chest
hair and Tiresian tits. "Listen," he said, "I'm ill, Trash." She
shook her head playfully and said, "Not really, Robin." He
was just not striving, she repeated, but clearly her ploy was to
soften up his resolve before producing her revelation, whatever that might be. But she smelt wonderful, like a whole
coconut grove, and as her hand went slowly lower the most
delicious ripples of sensuous reaction spread in slow curdles
over the stagnant pond of his unused body. She began to hum
softly now in her deeply melodious contralto, some sort of
wanton spiritual to mine his defences – never very strong. It
was a cradle song calculated to disperse influenza and restore
health together with an unswerving and invincible erection.
Rob groaned with pleasure, and as he did so her fur fell open
and he discovered that she was naked under it save for stockings
and shoes. "You can't do this, Trash," he croaked, but already
she had guided his costive fingers towards the moist scarlet
slit, her second mouth, where they found their tender purchase
in the one place which made her lift her head with pleasure
and snuff the air like a tigress, moving slightly to feel his finger
caressing her vital trigger. When she was ready she threw off
her fur and mounted him with delight, like a child with its first
rocking-horse. He was angry with her and it put him on heat,
so that he turned in an excellent dogmatic performance which
had her groggy. They melted at last into the supreme fiction of
joining with a sable orgasm of deep lust and pith. She was made
for love, this nymph! Kiss, kiss, the taxonomy of virtuous
compliancy with nothing grim, nothing furtive, just the

cryptic vision of wholeness. It was Eros versus Agape. And here he was, condemned to spend his life shooting his brains through his fist because this nymph refused her jumps. He lay there in a tousle feeling that he must smell of babies' milk stools and antiseptic soap while she panted beside him, her breasts as fresh as dewponds. "God, Trash!" he said with a sadness the size of a cauliflower. She had begun to recite the 16th Psalm in a whisper. "*Don't*," he said in an agony and Trash replied, "She said if I did you would say yes, you would agree." He grew angry and said, "Come on now. Out with it! What do you want?" But she was rousing him again, her skilful hands were trying to rebuilding the sandcastle of his erection which the tide of their passion had demolished. "Give me that hangin' fruit, Buster," she muttered as she grabbed and manipulated his choicest possession. But now he revolted against her and refused to get an erection until she answered his question. He did this by closing his eyes and thinking of ice cream. She was dismayed by this unusual display of independence and took herself off to make water which she did with enough noise for four thoroughbreds. Then she came back and standing by the bed said, simply, pregnantly, "We have decided we want to go round the world. Will you let us?"

The question was so astonishing that for a moment he was nonplussed. "What world?" he asked at last. "The war is nearly over. Pretty soon we shall be able to get going. You see, she wants to give me all the culture you gave her, Robin." "What on *earth*?" he said, genuinely puzzled. She must have heard of the Allied landings and the latest triumphant battles which had all but driven the Germans out of Europe and back to the fatherland.

"The war is far from over," he said, and she said, obstinately, "Yes it is, soon will be, now the U.S. Marines have landed. You don't know the U.S. Marines, Robin. I know the

U.S. Marines. They got the biggest pricks in Christendom."
He did not know what to say. "Do you mean they *are* the
biggest pricks?" but she shook her head determinedly and said,
"No. GOT the biggest I said."

"The Lord be your shepherd," he said, praying to
heaven for sweet reason to supervene. "Sit down, Trash, and
let me explain about the war." He took a deep breath, and
assuming the sort of tone and accent of the B.B.C. producer of
"Tiny Tots' Hour" he explained to Trash that even if by some
miracle everything stopped tomorrow and peace was declared,
it would mean years before conditions returned to normal:
certainly all travel as private individuals would not be possible
for years as yet, unless one managed to represent some
organisation civil or military. She sat listening to this logical
exposition with bright and attentive eyes, nodding from time
to time, and moistening her lips as if about to speak. But on he
went, listing all the ugly calamities of the past and the present,
and trying to draw a portrait of a future which would be heavily
compromised for ages yet; to demobilise, to repair cities, to
revive shattered economies, to rebuild civic habits . . . it would
take an age! And here they were talking about travelling round
the world like tourists.

"Don't you see, Trash?" he said, with something like
agony, for now it looked as if she had been thinking of
something else all the time he had been exposing his case to
her.

"You could come with us, Rob. She told me to tell you.
So long as you don't get mad at us. She only wants to give me
the culture you gave her." He snorted wildly. He had inherited
a sum of money from an old aunt which carried with it a condition: that he spend it in travel. Nothing more desirable, what
with the war coming on – at least everyone seemed to feel it
was. So he took Pia on a lightning-rod tour of the basic
antiquities of the world, first Europe, then as much of the

Orient as was within the reach of railways and flying-boats. They came back dazed and confused, but with all the money gone, and a library of prospectuses and travel brochures. Pia went through it all with speechless gratitude – God only knew how much she had taken in, but the journey marked her. And it was invaluable to him, of course, as a guide to places he knew he did not want to see again. To do India, cockroach by cockroach, for example, was beyond all imagining; the original *cafard* must have dwelt there in the plains. But the Himalayas now, there one could stay forever. He found Pia lacking in all serious instruction, almost analphabetic, yet they met a Nepalese lady nun who said that she was spiritually very advanced – higher up than he was. "You do not have to be clever to be wise," said this pleasant woman who had been educated at an English school and spoke Druid fluently. He loved Pia more than ever after that, he smothered her with instruction and kisses thicker than flying fish in the Indian Ocean. But she turned up her nose at the *Kama Sutra* and said it was "unhealthy". She thought the Taj Mahal would have looked nicer in brick. Now she wished to impart all this wisdom to Trash, darling Trash, who sat with her hands in her lap – her coat lay open like her thighs. She looked a bit crestfallen, as if her mission had failed. "When would you go?" She shrugged and said, "Whenever it's possible. We only want you to say YES, because she won't do nothing without your okay; you know that, Robin. But if you jest say yes we can start collecting the guide books and planning. It will save her mentation, honey, just to be told 'Go Ahead'." His face cleared. "So *that* was all you wanted? Just my okay?" She nodded. "Of course you can," he cried robustly. "Of course you can go. You *shall* go!" Whereupon she threw off her skin and did a soft shoe routine crying, "*Wow and Superwow!*" over and over again. And then a short eloquent verse which went:

"When I wanta
I've simply gotta
When I have ter
I simply Must!
Babe, have I got a Wanderlust!"

It was clear that she was already on the journey. "What a gift-horse you turned out to be," he said, and made as if to re-open sextilities, but she had to rush off and tell Pia. In a flash she was gone, forgetting her earrings.

Sutcliffe tried them on and found that they rather suited him; he put them carefully aside. One day he would walk into the Consulate wearing them. It would create, he hoped, quite an effect. But now the telephone thrilled and he took it up to hear the central exchange assure him that the line had been re-established. His heart sank a little for there was no longer any excuse not to ring Aubrey, the Blanford-Bloshford who presided over his life. He took up at last his battered address book in which Constance had jotted down the clinic number. He asked in an agitated falsetto if he might speak to Mrs. Benzedrine Papadopoulos, but of course Aubrey recognised his voice. "Speaking," he said, and Sutcliffe groaned aloud. His mentor said, "Why are you groaning like a Heathcliff in labour when you are only a common Sutcliffe in disfavour; what have you been triturating, you common fellow, while my back has been turned?"

"I have been ill," said Sutcliffe with a deeply dramatic expression, "and now I am ringing to tell you that I have been raped by Trash – very enjoyably but against my will. Pure rape!"

"It is not possible; you are fictions."

"Have we no future, then?"

"You have contexts, but no future and no past."

He laughed and then recited:

> "Tell me, how do fictions fuck?
> All our swains commend their pluck!"

Sutcliffe improvised in return:

> "Like shucking grain, expressing pain,
> Emptying opiates to a drain."

But he was listening with close attention to the timbre of Blanford's voice. He knew that very often his emotions under stress were masked by a deliberate and perverse flippancy – he retreated into his private despair like a crab under a stone, and was not to be dislodged. Fundamentally there was a lack of passion in him, a power-cut now so markedly symbolised by the physical disability under which he laboured. He grunted, and Blanford who had been following his thoughts said, "Everything you say is true."

"I said nothing," said Sutcliffe. "I merely thought a lot. It's as if we were versions of one another set upon differing time-tracks. Reality is very fatiguing."

"Exactly," said Aubrey. "Be ye members of one another – the good book invokes you."

B. "Which book? Yours or mine?"

S. "Mine. It's a better title, I think."

Blanford sighed and said, "Mine is still unfinished, but I have an ant-hill of notes which should help me complete it. When did you finish yours?"

"When I heard you were coming."

"What is it called?"

"*The Prince of Darkness.*"

"Hum."

Sutcliffe could not forbear to quote his Shakespeare: "The Prince of Darkness is a gentleman."

"You must manifest at last," said Blanford in a changed,

sharper tone; his bondsman recognised the grim note and agreed with surprising meekness. "I knew we must meet one day in order to exchange versions – it's in the order of things. Maybe we can help each other solve a few problems – some of yours, for example, are not easy. What about the lovers?"

Blanford replied with irritation, "Since you like Shakespeare so much you'll know that journeys end in lovers' partings."

"Ah, the pity of it!" said Sutcliffe ironically. "How are you going to make a job of that? My own version corresponds to the reality. She will be hurt by his going but unbroken. In my version he offers to take her with him and she refuses."

"Dead true!" cried Blanford with pleasure and surprise. "How the devil did you know?"

"You know how I knew!"

Blanford paused and then said, "You must come now, the sooner the better. Come to tea at four, and don't forget to bring your version since it's complete. It will help me, as I am in a bit of a muddle. Yesterday she spent the afternoon with me and I started to read her bits of my book; but in the middle dozed off, and I fear with without permission she did a brief riffle of the rest, while I slept. I am vexed, she was supposed not to know until he went back to Egypt."

"Unconscious sabotage?"

"Of course. I'm jealous!"

"You are no artist, then."

"Let's leave that open. I am waiting for you this afternoon at four. I shall recognise you at once. I will cry, 'Doctor Liebfraumilch I presume', removing my topee."

He put down the phone and reflected for a long moment; a sudden world weariness afflicted him. What would he not have given to tip the whole damned bundle of manuscript into the lake. The incident of yesterday afflicted him, nagging like a toothache. Constance had come to spend an hour with him, unfortunately towards siesta time. He had read her a passage from his book, but sleep had overcome him. He turned back to it now and re-read it, recalling the scene between them. It went:

"Akkad in his stained brown *abba*, looking so fragile, so weightless, as he sat upon the sand went on: 'From the cosmic point of view, to have opinions or preferences at *all* is to be ill; for by harbouring them one dams up the flow of the ineluctable force which, like a river, bears us down to the ocean of everything's unknowing. Reality is a running noose, one is brought up short with a jerk by death. It would have been wiser to co-operate with the inevitable and learn to profit by this unhappy state of things – by realising and accommodating death! But we don't, we allow the ego to foul its own nest. Therefore we have insecurity, stress, the midnight-fruit of insomnia, with a whole culture crying itself to sleep. How to repair this state of affairs except through art, through gifts which render to us language manumitted by emotion, poetry twisted into the service of direct insight?"

"Art?" she cried, angrily. "Rubbish, Aubrey!"

"Art!" he echoed firmly.

"Out!" Constance, wearied and exasperated beyond reason by this wilfully mendacious reasoning, put out her hand thumbs down and stared sighing out upon the calm lake. Suddenly he broke out, as if to refute her thoughts, "You see? He is not joking, the fraternity is quite decided to pre-empt death by voluntary suicide – you might call it that, though actually the blow is struck invisibly, by someone or something else, an instrument of their collective fate, so to speak. O God, can't you see?" He could read the expression of angry disdain upon her face.

"Well, it's one way of saying goodbye," she said coldly. Truly, Affad might have spared her all that had grown up between them, luxuriant as some tropical jungle, since he had known from the beginning that it must all come to nothing – that sooner or later they must come up against the blank wall of his voluntary disappearance – despatched by an unknown hand selected by an invisible committee in conclave back there in the deserts of Egypt? The whole of her training, her science, her practice was dedicated to working against this cowardly principle of suicide and abdication. And they spoke about art as if it were some sort of vitamin. "Art!" she said aloud with disgust. She was dumbfounded by the pusillanimity of men! The psychologist in her recalled all she knew about aberrant states like autism or catatonia, with their stark suggestion of a narcissism overwhelmed by reality. She thought of the diffident and troubled gaze of her lover's sea-green eyes with compassion mixed with hatred. So he was a weakling really, and not a man. And this playing about with abstruse gnostic states was surely dangerous for him, for his equilibrium? She told herself, "It's when the mind strays out of touch with its own caresses – its own catlicks upon the body-image of itself – then it loses the power to cherish and restore itself through self-esteem. The actual tunic of the flesh dries up, man becomes an articulated skeleton, that is to say, a machine."

Art! Who cared about that? Inwardly she laughed sardonically; outwardly she looked cold, white, numb and a prey to a thousand indecisions. "I think I shall leave the Red Cross and get back to my job if it is still possible," she said, and he gazed at her in puzzlement. "I know," she said, staring back, "it's running away, and I don't approve of it. But I need time to think." But escape in the direction of Avignon was, she knew already, no more possible; and anyway surely her excess of feeling was itself misplaced, for surely they were all under sentence of death, the whole world? All Europe was a suicide club, was it not?

These notions increased her vexation. Why did she feel such a keen sense of reproach towards him simply because he was a card-holding member, so to speak, of this absurd suicide confraternity with its cowardly refusal to face the world as it was? It's because (she thought) Eros demands a false reassurance, a promise of immortality, in order to flourish – and "flourish" simply meant to bear a child. That was it! In the depths of herself she had planned to love by extension into the future, to share a child with him. This abrupt reminder of his possible disappearance at any moment, it was unnerving. The feeling that it compromised the continuity of love – the purest illusion – made her draw back. And now she became furious, not only with him but with herself as well. She had been cheating at cards, so to speak. The sleepy Blanford watched the play of thought and emotion on her angry face with curiosity.

They were silent for a long moment; then he took up the manuscript once more, saying, "It's only a novel, the bare bones of a draft of a story based on true findings. I was led to it by a lot of sporadic and scattered reading first of all: by the mystery of the Templars' abject surrender and their obvious guilt. It was Affad who told me they were simply gnostics dedicated to cross swords with Monsieur instead of putting up with his rule. Then I took up the threads right there in Alexandria. They are not joking you know! The cult of the human head is with us even today. In the novel the death-map of Piers was an attempt to assess his chances – he had put the names of his friends on it, under the names of the Templar knights. He suddenly realised that his number was up – but who was going to strike the blow? I haven't finished the book yet but in the final version it could be Sabine." He paused before going on in a slower tone: "Suicide was forbidden to them, so it *had* to be some sort of death-preempting ritual murder. But of course it is only the inner circle of the confraternity who take this vow; as their ranks thin others are elected. Affad had to wait years he tells me. And of course there is no way of knowing when he will get the message – the short straws gummed to a piece of rice paper with his name on it. The letter with the Egyptian stamp."

There was a pause. "Schoolboys!" she cried in accents of distress.

"Affad is leaving the day after tomorrow. He rang me and asked where you were. He thinks you are going to be bitter and reproach him for what you once called his 'pre-lapsarian twaddle'." She smiled a trifle wistfully. "Perhaps I shall, when next we meet."

She had sent the car away, and now set off to walk back around the lake shore; at their old meeting-place opposite the promontory near the town approaches she saw the car of Affad standing, its engine uncovered, apparently in difficulties. Its owner was trying to execute some inexpert repairs, or remedy some defect in a fashion that seemed almost laughably inept and despairing. He was no good with machines, as he always said, and the machines knew it. He saw her coming and for a moment did not know quite what line of action to take – it seemed so ignominious to be stranded there with an expensive car. So he did nothing, simply stood still and smiled sadly at her in all his humiliating dishevelment. When she was still a little way off he said, "Have you heard? I've been recalled at last." She said nothing but went on walking towards him, looking at him with such hungry intensity that one would imagine her to be storing up memories of this moment against his fatal departure. "You have come to reproach me," he said, and she shook her head. She had suddenly seen him as he really was, she had seen his *eidolon* in all its gentle passivity and feminine warmth. There he stood, covered in oil and with his hair standing on end, pained beyond measure and quite humiliated by his defaulting motor car. She felt a tremendous shock of sympathy, a warmth about the heart, and with her eyes full of happy tears, put her arms round him, as if to comfort him in his defeat. A new pang had shaken her, and with it a new and quite unexpected magnanimity. "Yes, I came to reproach you, damn you." But the malediction was not really meant as such – it was an endearment. He looked at her with his sad, protesting, sea-grey eyes. She said, "I really came to thank you for giving me the key to myself – teaching me to live and create without a man. I owe you that." They kissed exultantly. She added, "I know you are ready to take me back with you, but I am staying here where I belong; perhaps you will come back, perhaps not. We shall see." His look was a whole discourse of rapture and deep gratitude. "With so much death in the world surely we have a right to a little love?" she said. "Let's not spoil this, diminish it by pettiness or play-acting."

She got into the car and pressed the self-starter. By some miracle it worked. They drove off along the lake. Never had friendship and love joined forces in this way for her. It was as if henceforward she understood everything, no more turning back. It was the right way to part even if it was not forever.

"What will you do with yourself?" he said, putting his arm round her shoulders, for she had elected to drive. "We may have years ahead of us."

"I shall pursue my obstinate theology course – building the Taj Mahal on an icefloe, as you call it."

"Deciding how many psychoanalysts can dance on the point of a pin!"

"Of Jews an infinite number, I feel sure."

There was a long silence as they watched the blue lake unrolling beside them, and then he said, "What made me so suddenly and acutely aware that perhaps I wasn't being fair to you was a conversation I had with the Prince; for the first time on a somewhat acrimonious note. He said that in the present state of my engagements – about which you now know I don't doubt – I was not free to love you. In the most literal sense. I could not prejudice my commitments towards the committee –

it would be like breaking the chain of belief which binds us. Like breaking a letter chain. In fact, that I was loving you under false pretences and he, the Prince, was jolly well not going to have it!" He could not help grinning affectionately as he mimicked the tone of the Prince's voice. Constance smiled also, "Good for him," she said, "at least somebody loves me."

Affad said, "I am duty bound to go back and consult the brotherhood as to my chances of freeing myself from them. If I could achieve that I would be free to return to you – it would change everything. One could envisage another sort of life based on this experience. Would you encourage such an idea?"

"You would never do it," she said after a long pause. "It's your whole life. You would be wrong to try. I'm sure when you reflect – when it comes to the point – you will feel bound to them, to the organisation, and not to me. Outwardly I will still be there, of course, and nothing forbids us to continue to meet. But the inward landscape has changed, and that may well be for good, forever."

"For love it's the acid test," he admitted. "But I refuse to pre-empt the future. In my present mood I feel sure that I am going to free myself and join you while there is still time. Constance, look at me." She turned her bright eyes on him for a second and then bent them back upon the road. He said, "Can I leave you a hostage of a kind – a hostage of a strange sort? I have been meaning to ask you if you would study and pronounce upon the illness of my little son. I hesitated; but now I feel it is right to ask you if you will see him while I am away. Will you?"

She said nothing, but her eyes filled slowly with tears, though she did not shed them. An appalling thought had come into her mind, shocking in its baseness, namely: "He wants me to cure his child in order to recover the love of his wife." How could she think anything so foul and so untrue? In order to expurgate the fearful supposition she leaned towards him and kissed him quickly on the mouth. "Of course I will, my darling," she said, "of course." And he thanked her, saying, "Lily suggested it long ago. She will be glad. And the thought will link us while I'm away."

They drew up at the office of the Red Cross and left the car in the courtyard. It was an appropriate place to say goodbye – even a provisional goodbye. She kissed him and walked away towards the billiard bar, leaving him to look after her with his gentle and hesitant regard which somehow held finality in it. She seemed as she walked to overhear the voice of Sutcliffe say, "There are no more great loves, my lad, just Snakes and Ladders instead."

Soon there would only be reminiscence left, going backwards into time as one unwinds, undoes an old sweater, on and on towards the dropped stitch, the original sin. Most love just lapses from satiety and indifference, but he had given her a version of the old text which one could continue to follow out, like a salient dialogue which went on even in absence. The rendering conscious of the orgasm as a gradually shared experience, it was like something new to science! Later the thought of him would perhaps ache on like a poisoned arrow, but for the moment she felt only her exultation, her solidarity with him.

This love was a separate culture. The world like some great express switches points without asking anyone's permission, passing from tobacco smoke to wine, from steam to sail, satyr to faun, from one calculus to another: we live under the thrall of its symbolism. One simple default, a switch thrown too late, and the giant can be sent howling and hurtling from the rails out into the night, into the sky, among the stars. It was hard to try and see things clearly. Twixt *vérismo* and *trompe l'oeil* they were doomed to try to live and love. That night, watching dusk fall over the impassive lake which reflected a heartless city, she seemed to see death and love like a single centaur joined at the waist walking through the ice-blue waters to reach her.

THIRTEEN

Counterpoint

SUTCLIFFE, DESPITE HIS DISPOSITION TO WAGGISHNESS and frivolity, was nevertheless a most obedient slave. Obsessions usually are. He materialised on the chair beside the bed just as Blanford woke from a somewhat unrefreshing sleep, opiate-imposed. "Well," he said robustly, "at last we meet. Dr. Dyingstone, I presume." Sutcliffe nodded gravely, and said, "At your service!"

They both burst out laughing as they eyed each other. "I imagined you as much fatter," said one, and the other replied, "And I much thinner." Well, they would have to make do with reality – it was all they had to work on; it's boring, this question of there being several different versions of a self, so to speak, no? Sutcliffe had actually combed his hair and donned a respectable suit – it might have been described as *tenue de ville*, his get-up. With him he carried the battered scarlet minute-box with the monogram of the Royal Arms on the lid; it contained his novel – the "other" one. "What are you calling it?" asked Aubrey curiously, and nodded when he heard the title, to show that he found it suitable: *Monsieur*. His own version was not quite finished, and he hoped during this convalescence to complete it, taking his cue from Sutcliffe. His visitor held up the red box and said, "It's all here!"

"The whole quinx of the matter. Your quinx?"

"No. Your quinx, rather. My cunx."

Aubrey gazed admiringly at his friend and chuckled as he said, "By the five wives of Gampopa, you keep up a pretty recondite style. Quinx to Cunx, eh?"

"A dialogue twixt Gog and Magog."

"Between Mr. Quiquenparle and Mr. Quiquengrogne."

"Ban! Ban! Ban! Caliban!"

"That's the spirit!"

It was marvellous to see eye-to-eye like this. Sutcliffe had already spotted the whisky decanter in the corner with the tray full of glasses and soda syphons. "May I?" he asked politely, inclining his throat and trembling wattles in its direction. Without waiting for an answer he crossed the room and primed a glass. Then he stood and admired the lake view while Aubrey watched him with an affectionate if somewhat disembodied air. "My vision, like yours, is not absolutely panoramic yet. it's selective: so there is always the blind spot." Sutcliffe nodded, frowning, and said, "It's the point where Monsieur intrudes on the cosmic scheme. The Counterfeit Demon in the pages of Zosimos. Or in more modern terms the demon figuring among the electrical properties of Faraday."

"I was delighted to find that he was reborn to the R.A.F. Command as 'the gremlin' and is still with us. His uncles – the joker in the pack of cards and the Hanged Man of the old Tarot – are proud of him."

"And no wonder. He lives a very full life."

"And now that the war is ending, Robin, what is going to become of us? With our sad bifocal vision and the awful sense of *déjà vu*?"

"We will go slowly out of date like real life."

"I doubt that; much remains to be done."

"Where?"

"In the city! We return there!"

"All of us? To the dead city?"

"As many as remain. The survivors of love."

They reflected on the probability with doubt, almost with distaste. Aubrey said, "In the Templar legends there is one crediting the Last Supper with having taken place in Avignon. *If five sat down to dine which was Judas?* So runs a riddle without an answer."

"Will Constance come?"

"Of course! Constance is a key."

That seemed a slightly less bleak vision of the future. At any rate to Aubrey it seemed still a way ahead – the other side of his convalescence. Here he must lie for months as yet, woozy from drugs, with reality dissolving like a tablet in spittle.

"In my version," he said, "I return to Provence with the *ogres* after a war something like this, having retired from the world to a chateau called Verfeuille. It's unsatisfactory; something about their ill-starred love wasn't right – you will help me there, I hope. The reality we had lived was more engrossing than the fiction, which was unpardonable. Now we are going back at a different angle, and with a different crew, so to speak."

"Can't I opt out, go away, right away?" cried Sutcliffe in exasperation. "To India, say, or China?"

"You want to go back into life and you can't," said Blanford with his bitter smile. "Nor can I – it's back on to the drawing-board, back to the blueprint stage. Back to Avignon! There are only two ways out of Avignon, the way up and the way down, and they are both the same. The two roses belong to the same family and grow on the same stalk – Sade and Laura, the point where extremes meet. Passion sobered by pain, an *amor fati* frozen by the flesh. The old love-triangle on which Plato based the Nuptial Number taken from Pythagoras, a triangle the value of whose hypotenuse is 5."

"Quack! Quack!" said Sutcliffe irreverently. "You will not distract me in my search for the perfect she, the mistress of the sexual tangent, *les éléments limitrophes*. I demand as my right love-in-idleness, a Laura unconscious of her fate, *femme fatale, féotale, féodale*."

"Instead you will find only the 'five-stranded' Tibetan breath, the 'mount' or 'steed' of white light, and a titanic silence with no geography. A tall tree with the sap arrested in its veins."

"But where?"

"In Avignon, rose of all the world."

FOURTEEN

By the Lake

T
HE DAY DAWNED SO UNUSUALLY WARM OVER THE LAKE
that Blanford grew impatient to be lying thus, gazing
across the green lawns to the still blue water. Why not
a sortie? His first operation was in two days' time. "Cade," he
said, "today is my birthday. I want to get a breath of air. I want
to go for a push along the lake. I want to celebrate the birth of
my mother's death. Get a chair and a rug, and bring your
Bible. You will read to me as you used to do to her." To his
surprise the valet looked almost elated as he bobbed his assent
to the idea. "Very good, sir." Tucked down in rugs, elongated
in the rubber cradle, Blanford hardly felt the rubber tyres on
the paved Corniche. But he was still drowsy and also light-
headed from calming drugs, and his thoughts evolved in
pericopes without a sequential pattern.

"Cade, we shall never see Greek drama as the Greeks
themselves saw it."

"No, sir."

"For them it was an expiation."

"Yes, sir. Shall I read? And where from? D'you want
'In the beginning was the Word'?"

"No. 'The Lord is My Shepherd', rather."

"Very good, sir."

The words reached deep inside him and he felt his bowels
moved, his entrails plucked by their ravenous splendour of
language – an English which was no more. And paradoxically
while he listened he thought of other things, of Nietzsche's
missing essay on Empedocles, of madness, of evolution, of the
emergence of man from the belly of the time-bound woman,
and with him all nature. Slime and warmth and water-lulling

plants and infusoria and larval fish. The Creator thrusts his hand into the glove, up to his arm, as into a sausage skin, and then withdraws it while a collection of wet organs rushes in to develop into man. A weird assemblage of arms, legs, eyes, teeth, gradually sorting themselves into completeness: a ditto of mental attributes flowed out like electricity playing – sensation, ideation, perception, cognition: the whole held together by the centrifugal forces of the spinning turntable of a world. *Whee*! Then each in its category rose – plant into tree into fish into man, whose mind's eye would lead him into the mischief of paint, words, music and above all buildings to exteriorise, celebrate, and even house his body – living, as a temple, dead, as a tomb. Hubris came somewhere after this and with it dread. The antlers of the god grew on his temples, he went mad, dared to *see*!

He discovered fire, wine, weapons and tools, but also the stone-fulcrum for building, the enigmatic formula of Pythagoras, the arm of gold. (Every man his own true pyramid.) He could not detach himself enough from the maternal shadow to understand Death and come to terms with it, even to harness it as he harnessed rivers. (The Druids had a way perhaps?)

The voice of Cade ran on like gravel in the stream of the language; his coarse diction gave the words a robust music of their own. The vowels swelled like sails. Meanwhile Blanford's mind played hopscotch among the pericopes of fond ideas which might one day inform his prose. "The crisis came when early man first lost sexual periodicity, for then he risked running out of desire. The race was imperilled by his indifference. So the anxious divinity, Nature, invented the specious beautiful crutch of Beauty to spur him on. What could be more unnatural, more delightfully perverse? Looking through each other's eyes the lovers saw more than the memory of each other, they saw 'it', and were at once humbled and captivated.

The body knelt to enter the mother-image like a cathedral and to die, so that the fruitful larval worm could hatch its butterfly, the nextborn soul, a child."

"In the midst of life we are in death," said Cade.

But, Blanford thought on obstinately, the Greek ideal of Beauty was a wonderful invention, for its value was transferable to other things, projected like a ray from man's own precious body. Artisan and his artifact improved into art pure. Beauty can reside, like the smell of musk, even in functional machines: substitute-bodies enjoying proportion and bias (callipygous women with haunches rich in *galbe*). Mental orgasm can be approached, abstract as paper-money or music or rain. The poet droops, suffers and invites his Muse – a one-man intensive care unit for the romantic invalid! You cannot look upon Eve future with impunity, for she carries within her the seeds of the idea of Death!

Yet within hours of death bodies begin to unravel like old sweaters, dissipating into random chaos again, mulch, mud, *merde* mind. Hail-hungry ghosts! Shades of the Luteran wormloaf of the world-view drawn from big intestines with their slimy code. The great dams of consciousness admit only trickles of reality through them – thirst is rife, the waters of life everlasting. On the great treadmill of consciousness what outlook can he have, the poor neuro-Christian twisted out of his original innocence? Cade was silent now, walking with lowered head staring at the ground below his feet. "What are you thinking, Cade? You never say." But the servant only shook his head in a determined way and showed yellow teeth in a nervous smile.

Sweet as geometry to the troubled heart, Method was born and the magician's footrule. Mental faculties separated into kinds. Ah, maniacs, so rubicond and exophthalmic! Ah, melancholics, so dark and shaggy and pale from excess of black bile! Love became mania. "Then I saw her ther, my lyttel quene." Hebephrenia set in like a tide, the helpless laughter of schizoid niggers. Fordolked, my masters, fordolked! *Morfondu*! Knocked for six!

Cade said, "At times she was not herself, sir. She said to me: 'Cade, I have gone beyond love, now I hate everyone, even my own son.' I was afraid for her reason."

Blanford listens, head on one side, and hears his own heart quietly beating under the rug. It was these small unexpected insights which were valuable. One thinks one knows better always; then comes the truth like a thunderbolt. He told himself that love overcomes magic by its very powerlessness. Both Merlin and Prospero gave in, surrendered their weapons at last, repletion was all.

> The meaning of meaninglessness is the code of
> the Grail
> As Merlin divined it, it never can fail.

Once replete with this knowledge he could retire to Esplumior, his island home, to play cards forever with his friend Prospero by the hushing sea. The old game of Fortune, played with a Tarot pack without a Hanged Man! Esplumior!

He heard the voice of Sutcliffe admonishing him: "More work for the Institute of Hallucination and Coitus! You want to combine ratiocinations in a Pelagsian fuck and it won't work. Even Trash knows that. She told me yesterday: 'Sperm washes off, honey, but love don't wash out. It's with you to the end. You have to wear it out like an old shoe.'" When they met now they would greet each other simultaneously with the words: "*Salut! Bon Viveur et Mort Future! Salut!*"

He had carried with him the clinic cat which purred quietly on his lap under the rug, like a small motor. What a peculiar kind of concentration it is that leads to the artistic product, he thought. One exudes a kind of emblaming fluid, an agonising ectoplasmic exudation, memory. The way a cat coats a mouse with its saliva before swallowing it – anointing it with a slimy coat to make the passage of the gullet easier. Was this the way to invoke shy Psyche, the love-child asleep on his mother's wedding cake or his father's coffin?

> The bazaars of silence where she dwells
> In double childhood, eyes in all the wells.

The end of death is the beginning of sex and vice versa. Children are abstract toys, representations of love, models of time, a resource against nothingness.

Suppose one wrote a book in which all the characters were omniscient, were God? What then? One would have to compose it in a death-mood, as if dawn would bring with it the firing-squad. But this is what the artist *does*! Does poor Constance really grasp what Affad is saying – namely that in trying to render the orgasm conscious he is trying to extend the human understanding of what, up to now, has been regarded as apparently involuntary and unpremeditated? This is real love!

> The couple was dead
> Ere we were wed
> All under the greenwood tree!

Maybe, however, she thinks him simply disinterestedly interested in human virtue but unable to regard it, as so many do, as a guarantee against The Thing – cruel fate which is indifferent to theological distinctions. Stupidity and hypocrisy, the indispensable elements for illness and consequently for religion! O thieve me some happiness, Constance, I am tired of steeplechasing with this tired out old cab horse! My soul camps in the ruins of India while my mind is gathering dolphins' eggs! *Le double je de Rimbaud*! The double game!

The whole strength of the woman comes from a studied self-abasement, an Archimedean fulcrum; and young girls taken warm from under their mothers' wings, stolen from a warm nest still need mothering awhile. In this pleasant morning drowse he saw them come, hip-swinging, callipygous nautch-dancers, *sécheresses, vengeresses, castratrices de choix,* and he knew that the guillotine was invented by a homosexual French-woman. "Cade!" he said sharply, "Amend thy trousers, for the flies have fled!" She was beautiful with her swarthy rose-black skin and the apricot-fashioned mouth sticky as a fresh hymen – the silkworm's tacky passage across a mulberry leaf. Kisses that clung and cloyed. What was the name of her father, the old banker who made love to his dog and wintered in Portugal – a caninophile, gone in the tooth, gone in the wind? As Sut-cliffe remembered her she wore the white nightdress like a uniform, a carnival disguise, archly, coyly. More appropriate would have been a butcher's smock with fresh bloodstains from the abattoir! There they sit, while we lie alone and suffer, sticking ripe plums up their arses, as happy as a sackful of rats! Memory is like having a dog on your back gnawing at your eyeballs. Venereal fevers shake the heart's dark tree. The Happy Few – *ceux qui ont le foutre loyal*!

Realising that all truths are equally false he becomes a posthumous person, makes his shadow melt away. All shadow-less men are perfected in their *ghost*! The cinema in the head has fallen silent.

In science the exact is by consent the beautiful and seems new, pristine. In language beauty lies in the explicitness, in the nakedness of thought clothed in a sound. He saw Constance coming towards them across the gardens, waving. Her strange lithe walk was full of an endearing eagerness, an unspoiled freshness of approach as if some new discovery awaited her when she reached you. It was like someone walking a rainbow. She took his hands softly in hers and he said, "You are the only one who realises how frightened I am. Thank you." She was in love, she was glowing with the experience – one can never disguise it. It seemed so strange, for here they were alive and in their own skins, while round them for miles stretched the dead, the countless dead. Yet, he thought, Constance and I are really equidistant from the darkness on the circle of probability. Tomorrow perhaps an absence, a hole in the darkness which rapidly heals up, closes over. "I know you are," she said, "and in a way it's good as a reaction." The walk with all its fevered ratiocination had tired him and he felt a little tearful. He dabbed his eyes with a tissue while Cade with a sudden surprising tenderness patted his shoulder. "I say to myself all the time, 'Why die? Why go? It's so nice here!'" There was no short way to counter this mood of depression, so she said nothing, but helped the valet set him up once more in his mountain of pillows. All of a sudden he felt much better; he was used to such mercuric swings of mood. "The torn notebook you brought back," he said, "did you look in it?" She had not. "It's got some of Sam's jottings in it, among them poems like

> Because he was a decent chap
> He wore the fairies gave him clap
> But Mrs. Gilchrist took the rap
> Because he was a decent chap."

There were other trifles which amused them for a while but then she had to leave to keep an appointment and he took his sleeping draughts and composed his mind to sleep, sipping the while a green tea which she had left him and which Cade prepared. He fell once more to dreaming in slogans and pictograms, trying to visualise the words as he thought them. "Secret Practices – lovers sharpened by slavery. A committee of dolls ruling everything. *Terrain giboyeux à vendre pour roman à clef.* He who once vaccinates the novel with heraldic doubt, must poke to let the sawdust out!"

On this note he fell asleep at last and was only woken by

the silver chiming of his little travelling clock. He was surprised to find Constance sitting at his bedside, watching him sleep, deeply thinking. It was reassuring in a way to renew his hold on life again through her – for the effect of pain and drugs and fatigue had begun to make him live in a sort of twilight state, between realities, as it were. Constance was real, she rang out like a note in music. But profoundly sad. "He's gone!" she said in a half-whisper. "O Aubrey, what a dilemma!"

There was a tap at the door and Cade entered the room with a silver salver upon which there lay a letter. He smiled in his sly conniving way as he said, "There's a letter for Mr. Affad, sir." They looked at each other in total indecision. "But he's gone," she said at last, and Blanford put out his hand to take up the envelope and examine it. The postmark of origin, the Egyptian stamp . . . He said sharply, "Very well, Cade. I'll take charge of it. You may leave." As the door closed behind the manservant he said to her, "I am going to confide it to your care and discretion. Wait until you can give it to him personally. Let the present issue resolve itself first. Don't hurry, don't tempt providence. Wait!"

"Alternatively to open it myself, to see what it contains, to be sure . . . what a temptation!"

"That is for you to decide of course. The temptation of Eve in a new form. Darling, do what you feel you must."

The girl rose and took the letter. "Or else just to tear it up and throw it on the fire! Why not?"

"Why not?" he echoed. She stood for a while looking down at the letter in her hand. Then she said, "I must think about the matter. I must really think, Aubrey."

He watched her slow and perplexed retreat across the green lawns of the clinic towards the car park where her car awaited her. What would she do? It was a pregnant decision to take. He could not for the life of him predict.

FIFTEEN

The City's Fall

FOR THE HISTORIAN EVERYTHING BECOMES HISTORY, there are no surprises, for it repeats itself eternally, of that he is sure. In the history books it will always be a Friday the thirteenth. It is not surprising, for human folly is persistently repetitive and the issues always similar. The moralist can say what he pleases. History triumphantly describes the victory of divine entropy over the aspirations of the majority – the hope for a quiet life this side of the grave. For Avignon, as for Rome, it would not be the first time; before the city of the Popes existed its inhabitants had seen the swarthy troops of Hannibal swimming over their thirty elephants, animals whose odour and fearful trumpeting struck terror into the Roman legionaries as well as their cavalry. Today it was a depleted 11th Panzer division, that was the only difference; much armour had been drawn off for the impending collisions of the war in the north. But the preoccupations were the same: the transverse lines of the swift precarious rivers and their vulnerable bridges.

The pressure had increased, just as the tension in the news bulletins had sharpened; all of a sudden the sky filled up with giant bombers which flowed steadily down the railway lines at dawn and dusk dropping high explosive upon the culverts and rails, or spending a whole night at work on the marshalling yards of Nîmes from which in spouting red plumes of flame one might see whole wagons thrown into the air like toys, and human figures like ants shaken from them. Of course some went astray. In some market garden or down some country road full of flowering Judas one might come upon houses which had become very tired, been forced to kneel down, even to fall: some old medieval *bergerie* turned inside out with live-stock and the farmer's clothes blown into nearby trees. The weight of the silence when the bombardment ended – that was insupportable, for the shattered fragments of reality re-assembled themselves and then one could estimate the result. Say that one had fallen in the middle of a Sunday School picnic among olive groves. You only heard the screaming then. The children blown down among the crockery, some without heads, and one leaning sideways against a tree with a straw boater dangling from her neck. The old black priest held on to his stomach as if it were a runaway horse. He was of an exceptional pallor, he was leaning on a wall, which itself was leaning on an empty space upheld by pure gravity. It was no use calling for stretchers and doctors, for yet another roar was approaching them, more bombers moving against the sunset and picking at the bridge this time; but they passed so low that one could see the expressionless eye of the rear gunners as they sprayed their surroundings with lead. The guns on the fortress responded, but the small calibre made them sound as if they were yapping like bandogs while the bombers bayed and gave tongue like hounds in cry.

Away over the green meadows at Montfavet the noise was simply a distant blur, but the flight-path of the aircraft brought them over the village at roof level so that the trees were pollarded by the rippling machine guns and showers of green plane leaves fell everywhere like a benediction from on high. The lunatics in the central courtyard gathered up all the branches they could and waved their thanks to the planes. They did not notice if here or there one of their number sat on a park bench completely immobile, or lay in a flowerbed dozing. They were used to variations in behaviour. In the case of Quatre-fages it was neither one thing nor the other, for he had managed to achieve a kind of heightened consciousness which allowed him to see everything as a purely historical manifestation.

He slept in a monkish cell in the most ancient part of the building, and the light of passing cars flared briefly upon the whitewashed wall, bringing him pictures from his past, the projections of troubled memory, once full of armoured knights riding down infidels in a gorgeous array of plumes and helms – like great fowls on horseback; now the same space peopled with the dark-robed exemplars of the new Inquisition, thirsty for booty, not for knowledge. He laughed aloud, for with all the cars and tanks passing the wall went on and off in cinematic fashion, and each time it was a new picture. A feeling of continuity resided only in the fact that the one that repeated was the old Crucifixion of Clément – the land of Cockayne. It was amazing that – it had not been carried off like so much else in the town, for it was quite a celebrated work of art; so much so that Smirgel had managed to get a half-size colour print of it which he pinned to the wall of the nearby cell in the Danger Ward where he composed his despatches. Quatrefages could hear the tapping of his little cipher machine, insistent as a woodpecker. Smirgel had changed into civilian clothes of dull, pewter-coloured stuff which suggested an out-of-work clergyman; he walked now, no longer strutted. He seemed, unlike the rest of the German garrison, to have become weighed down with the gravity of things, whereas for the others a new anxiety was mirrored in their sharp squeaky commands and the restless running to and fro at speeds which suggested the movements of an undercranked ciné film. The armour had moved off, and they felt bereft, uncovered; reports now spoke of landings on the Côte d'Azur in the area of Nice. The three squadrons of spotter aircraft upon whom they relied for firm intelligence had been bombed into immobility and silence. Nor was it possible to interest the high command in their plight, for all eyes were turned on Normandy where the battles were absolutely critical not only for their own future but also for armies further south – not to mention the Italians!

From the personal point of view, however, what Quatre-fages most deplored was that the noise had silenced the amours of the frogs in the lily ponds, for he loved their deep thrilling bassoons, loved watching them in the love act, their throats swollen out with lyrics, like human tenors at the music festivals of Marseilles. He had been taught that their love clamour could be scripted, after Aristophanes, with the phrase *"Brek ek kek kek Koax-Koax"* a pretty enough transcription of the sound. But after a few days of this he thought that the sound became *"Bouc Bouc Bouc-Emissaire"*. Yes, that was it! And how much more appropriate it was. He used to lie for hours by the pond, flat on his face, with his chin on the side, to watch them as they struggled amorously, sometimes in chains, tacked on to each other by simple imitation – three frogs, let us say, with a dead female at the end of the line, still penetrated by her mate who could neither disengage himself nor rid himself of the younger ones which had clambered on his back. Quatrefages was at heart a kindly youth and he spent some time with a long metal spatula which he had stolen from the kitchens trying to disengage the dead from the living. The little animals were so much on heat that they made no further distinction. The younger and less experienced, driven mad with the delicious copula of their lust, clambered anything that presented itself, alive or dead, male or female. This complete abandonment to ruthless passion was wholly admirable. Sometimes to send himself to sleep he drowsily imitated their plaint, laughing and hugging himself with waggish delight. With the disappearance of his reason, in the formal sense, he had been filled with a wonderful notion of freedom. And now great changes were in the air. The hated Milice had suddenly disbanded and thrown away their uniforms, though some had kept their small arms before heading for the hills where ambushes organised by the Resistance awaited them.

He heard Dr. Jourdain call out this choice information to

Smirgel as he locked or unlocked one of the doors in the ward; the information had come from a casual visitor on a bicycle. How empty the town must feel! He began to wonder if he might not return there for a while and make a mental inventory of everything which had changed. He had never seen a siege but he had read of many and could predict much of the present reality, like the bands of famished dogs which roamed about, driven mad by the noise and the lack of food; they set upon the heaps of uncollected garbage and the piled dustbins with a will. Meanwhile odd bands of leaderless men, not very numerous but distraught – Poles? Russians? It was not quite clear – roamed about armed with sticks. They manned the ferries which buzzed back and forth but lacked passengers.

But it was far from the end, you would have thought, to see Ritter and his staff, pale but determined as they went about their tasks in the fortress and ensured their control of the roads and bridges by frequent patrols, lightly emphasised by the appearance of an occasional heavy tank which fired a few rounds across the river, or into the surrounding hills from which came from time to time sporadic ripples of gunfire, one presumed from partisans or infiltrators, or even runagates from among the forced labour groups hidden in the forests. Only the pile of cigarettes beside him – the butts thereof – suggested that Smirgel himself was under strain, for the rate of his bird-like pecking remained slow and calm. He worked from shorthand notes on the back of service messages or grey envelopes, building these into the messages that Affad received by the lake of Geneva and, as like as not, transmitted to Toby in his cellar. He gave a succinct and sharply focussed picture of the new command at work, recounting their high morale under this determined party general whose perpetual toothache made him seem to be grinning always. A rictus of pain served as a permanent facial expression. Small, slightly round-shouldered, he had the long ape-like arms most suitable for declamatory gestures before a map; he took over from Von Esslin's old-fashioned rhetoric and produced a new version, with up-to-date oaths and outlandish jokes which made him strike his thigh with imaginary amusement, though the grin of pain did not change. To him they owed a new idea of some consequence. The plum target for the bombers had always been, would always be, the railway bridge over the Rhône. Since he had been told that when the time came he would have to retreat upon Toulouse it came to him that an ammunition train halted on the bridge might, if hit by the Allies, blow up and inflict a marvellous, undreamt-of wound to the town which he had come to hate so profoundly. Alternatively, if the Allies knew about the train they might spare the bridge. With this in view he had commanded an empty train to be backed into a siding at Remoulins and quietly loaded with the more powerful and effective explosives from the great underground ammunition dump in the hills near Vers. This would be his parting gesture to Avignon! The train arrived in the darkness of a moonless night and was shunted up on to the bridge before being deprived of its engine and abandoned. Meanwhile the town was also abandoned in all but seeming, for it was most effectively covered from the new base in Villeneuve across the river, and within a protective shoulder of medieval wall which, in the event of the train being blown up, would protect the Germans adequately from blast. They were within days of leaving now and they knew it, but it was necessary to keep up a show of force to make a withdrawal across country more safe. They had "leaked" the train as well so that after some days, bombing switched to other targets and other bridges, thus avoiding catastrophe for the town. It was only when withdrawal became a fact that Ritter elaborated his ideas, and decided that it would be pleasant to make sure of the explosion after all; why should the train not blow up within moments of their retreat?

He would, he thought, give orders for time fuses to be set along the whole length of the train, and these they could light as they departed. He imagined himself, some miles off in the hills towards Nîmes, suddenly hearing the dull, ground-rocking boom of the explosive and seeing the sky behind him grow white suddenly, as if drained of blood, and then red, deep red! How he hated this town – and more so now when everything was shut and bolted with not so much as a cat on the streets. Half the population lived in the cellars underneath the cathedral, secure from bombs but with no sanitary facilities. Moreover they seemed unable to organise themselves in any fashion whatsoever. What filth, what misery!

But the fuses would entail special knowledge, and the only sappers left in the command were a small Austrian unit whose job would be to sink the ferries and dynamite the eastern approaches to the town. He decided that he would call upon them to prime the train. But when they were driven down to the bridge and learned what was expected of them they suddenly mutinied and flatly refused to be a party to such an act which might inflict incalculable damage on the town. This severe blow illustrated how low morale had fallen in the occupying force and it could only be met in one way, according to Ritter's military code. The sappers were pinioned and set against a wall in the inner fortress which had already – to judge by the traces of bullet marks along it – served as a point of execution. So as the long column tapered away into the night, crossing the river and taking the road to Nîmes, it left behind fifteen more dead and the silent train. The grateful townsfolk later buried them in consecrated ground and covered their graves in roses.

In the town nothing stirred; most people had either gone underground or taken to their heels with whatever provisions they could lay hands on. All the doors and gates of the fortress hung open. The departing troops had expressed themselves in

939

a manner which had become for them conventional in war. Everywhere there was excrement, on tables, on chairs, in doorways, on stairs. And of course notices warning of booby traps, another speciality of the German army. Smirgel had spent his last few uniformed days in an unconspicuous manner, though it was clear that he, like all the other agencies around him, was winding up his affairs and preparing to move off with the regrouping. He had allowed his cipher clerk to pack up the impedimenta of his modest office, burn all standing instructions and late messages, and load whatever remained into the army lorry which was at his disposal. He himself would come on later in the little staff Volkswagen which was his. Instead, however, he found his way to Montfavet, and burying the car in the deepest recesses of a convenient grange changed into the anonymity of civilian clothes and resumed his despatches with all the calm of a provincial recorder reporting upon his home town. Avignon had practically become that for him after so many adventures. He had been up to the mess to pick up his small kit, plus the precious volume of *Faust* which he always anchored beside his bed – a verse or two at night secured a good sleep, he was wont to say with a chuckle. Everyone had gone. The last orderly was putting the finishing touches to the baggage. He was a bullet-headed Swabian corporal with a sense of humour. He saluted and said, "Shall I show you something funny, sir officer?" and when Smirgel agreed led him into the garden and opened the door of the earth closet. Surprisingly there was someone sitting on the roost and it was Landsdorf. At first you did not realise that he stayed upright because he was leaning back against the wall. His chin was raised like a chicken drinking. He was dead. He had shot himself through the soft palate with his service Luger. The corporal burst out laughing, and Smirgel nervously followed suit though his laughter ended in a croak and a sigh. He had liked old Landsdorf.

But the German was not the only one. Up in Tu Duc there had been little enough movement, except at night by small groups; the main troop movements had been along the great highways, the bombing mostly across the river. Blaise could, if he wished, watch everything without taking part, simply by climbing the hillock in the wood and overlooking the town from the open glades at the summit. At night he went to ground like a fox, locking everything up very carefully and extinguishing every gleam of light. How then could he have not heard the fusillade which cut short the life of the honey man Ludo? The ambush into which he had strayed with his one-horse caravan was barely three hundred yards away up the forest road. Blaise heard nothing, and would have known nothing had not a passing woodcutter whom he knew come stealing out of the wood to borrow a light for his cigarette butt and told him that he had just passed, higher up the road, a mutual friend of theirs, done to death by the Resistance – a presumption based on the fact that the overturned caravan which lay half in the ditch was liberally daubed with red paint proclaiming the victim to have been an informer. The woodcutter told his tale with angry emotion. Such an error seemed almost inconceivable. It always does. Yet in war as in peace it is like that – one is hurt by one's own side.

Like good Provençaux they knew they must bury their friend, and with a heavy heart Blaise called his wife and marshalled spades for the three of them. "Take some sacks," said the woodcutter, "for he is all in pieces." They walked in grim silence up the road until they came to the site of the calamity: the caravan half on its side in the ditch, the dead horse and the pool of honey mixed with blood. The man was just ahead – he had fallen with outspread arms, as if he had tried to protect his horse, to explain, to plead. His body appeared to smoke, but it was just the carpet of sleepy bees which covered his bloodstained frame in its tattered shirt and scarf which stirred from time to time, giving a fictitious life to the still form. The machine-gun had traversed the whole interior, quite riddling the hives. It had cut its target into several separate pieces. The woodcutter was right, the old olive-crop sacks were useful. In them they assembled the fragments of their friend and the head of his horse and carried them a little way into the forest until they found a suitable place for the long slow dig. The caravan they dragged off the road and hid in the bushes, also the body of the horse. The bees did not sting, they drowsed on in the bloody honey, as if shocked. Nor was there any trace of the little boy, the son of Ludovic of whom he had been so inordinately proud. Happily? Yes, perhaps he had escaped. In affairs of this sort there is always a missing child. In this way history manages to perpetuate itself.

It was going to be a long dig. The earth in this forest glade was not too soft. But the wife of Blaise had had the forethought to bring a supply of bread and cheese, two cigarettes, and a small bottle of fiery *marc*. They rolled up their sleeves, and marked out the grave of Ludo. But before beginning to dig the wife of Blaise put her arms round her husband and kissed him on the mouth with all her determination – something she had never done before.

With method, slowly, they worked late into the night, while always to the left came the shock of distant explosions and stabs of white light waxing and waning as the bombers came swishing in like great winnowing fans to release their loads.

The crisis was ripening like some ugly fistula. At the asylum Jourdain woke one morning to find that the kitchen staff had vanished, leaving no stocks of food for his lunatics. It was critical, something would have to be done, but what? The telephone had gone dead. There was nobody to appeal to. In order to calm himself he sat for a moment cross-legged before the full length mirror in his flat and performed a couple of yoga postures with the appropriate breathing. Then, in order not to waste the last of the hot water, he took a long and leisurely shower and shampoo. He donned his college blazer and dressed in formal fashion with a dark shirt and a college tie. Beside his bed lay the proofs of his new book on schizophrenia, at which he gazed lovingly. It had taken ages to formulate these scattered observations drawn from his flock and to translate them into theory. He read a passage to himself in a whisper, frowning with critical pleasure: "My proposition is, then, that the state of schizophrenia is not one of mental disorder, but one in which a different sort of order rules. When you shout 'Go away' to a fly, are you presuming upon its knowledge of French? And if it goes away dare one suppose that it in fact has understood? For the schizophrene . . ."

He sat down on the bed and reflected on his plight with bitterness; here he was, with a hundred and fifty mental patients to feed and wash, and with no staff to help him perform this miracle, and no food in the kitchen. "*Merde!*" he cried aloud after a moment, solacing himself with an echo from the exasperated soul of Cambronne. "*Triple merde!*" But he realised that this would not get him very far. Then he heard steps in the corridor and the insect-like pecking of the spy's machine. The main generator still held for a while, but for how long? Its charge would soon expend itself – three hours was the most! Then even the spy's little apparatus would be silenced. He listened grimly for a moment. Then he took his last whisky bottle from its hiding place and selected the two glasses from the bathroom before making his way to join Smirgel.

At this moment the stick of bombs fell on the house and the gardens with a mind-swamping roaring that abused all consciousness. A vast pall of dust rose now – he saw himself standing there with a bottle, and with his clothes apparently smoking, as if he were on fire. An invisible hand pinned him for ten full seconds to the nearby wall and then released him so that he fell like an unjointed doll first to his knees, and then flat, with a scream that he himself hardly recognised. It took an age for the dust to settle and for him to verify that he was physically unhurt, and that the precious bottle remained unbroken. As for the howling and drumming of his charges, the screams and laughter, he was used to these sudden waves of feeling, often provoked by nothing tangible. Here at least there was a good excuse; half the building was peppered with holes, holes which seemed like new magical doors through which one could get "outside" – the symbol of prime reality to a prisoner of any category. He joined Smirgel and without another word they drank down a life-giving draught of alcohol, listening gloomily the while to the noise of falling rafters and crumbling masonry. The distant cannonade of the town had diminished now; it was they who were in the centre of the stage. Yet apart from that one fortuitous stick of bombs nothing more fell upon the asylum. Nor was there any need, for the one salvo was destined to change their whole lives, the pattern of their behaviour. It had blown holes in every ward wall, and it had shaken every door off its hinges. How open the world seemed to Quatre-fages, who had also been blown to the wall of his cell and had cracked his skull on the iron bedrail. But from the window now he saw them all emerge, walking with circumspection, on tiptoe, gazing about with wonder at "outside" from their "inside", being born again. The square was slowly filling up with them, each with his personal vocabulary, the triumph of his destiny over reason! The Crusaders of the new reality!

The main gates still stood, but only just, for the hinges had been blown to pieces. How slowly the inhabitants emerged into the quiet square under the trees, some of which had fallen! The silence was brand-new after the thunderclap. The two men, Smirgel and Jourdain, watched from an upper window, glass in hand but forgetting to drink, so preoccupying was the scene. The whole staircase leading to the Dangerous Ward had gone, leaving a theatrical looking arch through which the hungry inmates were now making a surprised entry upon the life which they had abused and rejected. Smirgel's flesh crept, he was terrified of lunatics like all deceitful people; it was as if these criminal ones with their pious and deceptive air were poisonous snakes set suddenly free in a bathroom. "My God!" he said. "Your Dangerous Ward!" But the doctor's professional interest had been awakened and he leaned forward eagerly to watch, as a supporter watches the home team, full of sympathy. "It will be most interesting to see what they do," he said, and the German stared at him as if he were mad. Now everything suddenly fell into place, reality reasserted itself for them thanks to the bombing.

The asylum, set in green land, abutted upon two farms, and often the inmates were encouraged to help the farmers with the agricultural work, while the series of vast cellars and stables were rented out to the farms. The doors of these caves had been stoved in, and they revealed the four animals, two horses and two cows which shared their labours. They shyly ducked and snuffled in the gloom, dimly aware that something unusual was afoot for it was late for ordinary work, and the clients seemed unduly numerous. A vague indecision hovered in the crowd, their purpose in seeking the light had not been yet revealed. It was Quatrefages who condensed everything, who now endowed them with a purpose and a coherence. Raising his arms he gave a few imploring cries and beckoned them to follow him into the stables whence they dragged the four long carts, old-fashioned hay-wains which so often had brought in the harvest with their sincere aid. "*Allons, mes enfants!*" he cried with such fervour that everyone was galvanised, everyone rushed to join him with chirps and moans of happiness. They felt the beauty of function, the beauty of belonging to method. The doctor at the window watched them carefully, jealously;

the dangerous and the harmless together, what did it matter? But the dangerous were his special possession, he treasured them. "Baudoin!" he shouted suddenly. It was Baudoin de St.-Just, the notorious murderer who looked so quietly pious – all those years he went to confession and never once mentioned the fact! The man looked up and waved merrily like a schoolboy. "The harness is on the wall inside!" the doctor told him, and the man turned away obediently into the darkness to find it. Out came the cattle in a sort of foam of agitation. They smoothed and patted them, some curried them with leaves; and under the leadership of Quatrefages they harnessed them to the wains with shouts of indifference. Then there was a scramble to get aboard, though no fighting as with normal people, just a few in tears and one with stomach-ache. "Are they all there?" said Jourdain with keen interest. "I don't see Tortville the butcher nor Jean Taillefer. O yes! There he is. Where did he get that knife I wonder? What people! He will be troublesome tonight." Smirgel: "But not to us I hope." Raynier de Larchant was preaching a sermon – he was never dangerous when allowed to play on a piano. Moreover you knew where he was. His mother confided as much before he ... Molay, Pairaud were looking dazed and sullen which was not so good. The wains were harnessed. With one single push the great courtyard gates tumbled over and quivered in the dust. A shout went up from every throat. The wains were chock-a-block. Vaguely the crowd sensed the similarity of the situation to half-forgotten harvests and fairings, to village fêtes and dancings on the famous old bridge. Quatrefages mounted a horse and started to lead them. He looked around him, joyfully, childishly, and brandished a pick-helve like a broadsword. "We will find food and water in the town," he informed his forces, and they set up a ragged cheer. He caught sight of Jourdain on the balcony and swept him a mock bow as he cried again, "To the town!" But to the doctor he shouted, "I will lead them to Rome!" and curiously enough the occupants of the wains and those who tagged along overheard and took up the cry. "To Rome!" they shouted, growled and piped. "Onwards to Rome!"

Jourdain sighed. "Science is wonderful!" he remarked apropos of nothing in particular. They watched the motley throng form up behind the wains as if for a harvest or a funeral or a fairing. "This is the way revolutions start, by accident," he went on, for he could hear that somewhere in the crowd someone had given tongue with the *Marseillaise*, and as the distance lengthened they heard the marvellous verses begin to take shape. "If anything can make one march on an empty stomach, that song can," said Smirgel, shaking his head. But now they noticed that the bombing seemed to have stopped. The doctor held out his hand as if to feel whether it was raining or not. Indeed a light shower had started. But the silence which flowed in was absolute, and one could hear the rain purring like a cat. Smirgel asked if he might have another drink. "Well, the Swiss Army has closed the border. The Allies are moving up on us from Nice. I have enough petrol in my little car to take us somewhere where we might find some scraps to eat, north or east, I leave it to you."

"Did you notice how once they united in a purpose music was necessary to mark time, to mark step?" In fact two of the "dangerous ones" had found tambourines and a trumpet, relics of some village band, and beat out an admirable rhythm with them, while the trumpet choked and squeaked. The doctor sighed again as he heard the diminishing chant and thought of *Cock Lorel's Boate* and the *Bateau Ivre*. "Have you ever heard of The Ship of Fools?" he asked his companion but Smirgel shook his head. It would take too long to explain the medieval notion of treatment for lunatics, specially to a German, so the doctor dropped the subject. "There is one person I didn't see," he said, "and that was our great stationmaster Imhof, by the way he is English. I wonder where he has got to." But Imhof had slept through it all, comforted by the model train which he kept under his pillow; he hardly stirred when his pulse was taken.

The two men made their way down to the old cowshed where the German's car lay hidden; they were still undecided about which direction to take. Only one thing seemed certain: there would be no point in following the procession of lunatics towards the town. That way lay trouble – or that is what they surmised. They would sneak across country to the Fontaine de Vaucluse and then turn north. Who knows?

Now that the bombers had gone away the little procession was filled with renewed confidence, and made good time on the road to Avignon, the tambourines keeping them in a good humour when they were exhausted with singing the anthem. Quatrefages was transfigured, like an actor now, turned into a medieval knight bearing high his standard. From time to time he thought of the great wall in the hotel with "his" Templars and their dates recorded on it – the solemn procession of forgotten knights. No, not forgotten, so long as one person could remember them! History was like that – a negative of which one was the print, the positive. He thought: "People are not separate individuals as they think, they are variations on themes outside themselves. Think: Galen's daughter progressed could be Sylvie who was only imagined, who could be Sabine child of Banquo. The lost remain the lost, the found the found. Oranges and Lemons!"

The trumpet blared.

On they went boldly, extravagant in their fine optimism, the mad leading the blind, the blind leading the sane. "Variations on themes," he repeated aloud, "Just as a diamond is a variation on carbon, or a caterpillar on a butterfly."

They approached the mother city with confident tread, sure of their welcome, sure of food and drink. For its own part

Avignon had begun to stir from its forced sleep. The silence
and the emptiness had at last evoked some response; a few
faint news bulletins had managed to penetrate the overwhelming sense of desolation and hopelessness in which they had
existed for so long, tortured both by the enemy and by their
own fascist kind, the Milice. As soon as the mayor of the town
found the incredible thought of an empty city begin to dawn
in his mind, he opened his front door cautiously and surveyed
the deserted streets with suspicion mingled with mounting
elation. No noise but the rain, the soft thistle-sifting rain of the
Vaucluse. "*Ils sont partis*," someone said above his head,
someone behind a shuttered window. It was as if they were
trying out the phrase, so long rehearsed in the mind: though as
yet it had no real substance and they did not dare to fling back
the shutters. The mayor gave a small sob and groped for his old
bicycle. Very slowly and circumspectly he set out on a tour of
the walls, bastion by bastion, feeling the rain on his neck like a
benediction. Yes, they had gone; once more they were master
of their fate as he was master of his town. He returned to the
Mairie and unlocked the doors, throwing them wide. Now
people were emerging from holes and corners, from cellars and
stables and garrets, saluting each other in hushed voices and
gazing about them. The mayor, filled with a sudden vertiginous
ecstasy, raced up the stairs to his office and went out on to the
balcony. He was going to do something he had not done for
years, namely call his friend Hippolyte, the *pompier de service*,
who lived opposite the Mairie on the square. Cupping his
mouth he roared, "*Hippolyte-e-e-e!*" After the third bellow
he saw his friend trotting towards him across the square
waving his arms. "*Ils sont partis, partis, partis, partis!*" the
words were taken up and repeated, rattled like peas on a drum.
The first act was to announce the fact to the town in time-
honoured fashion through the town-crier, and Hippolyte,
already in uniform, had already started to assume his official

responsibilities. He had belted on the sour kettle-drum and fixed the rubber hooter to his bicycle handle. At the four quarters of the town he would now announce after a preliminary klaxoning, followed by a long ripple on the kettle-drum, "*Oyez! Oyez! Oyez! Official announcement by the Mairie. The Germans have gone. The curfew is lifted until further notice.*" At each repetition he was mobbed. More and more people came forth from the ruins, many in tears, some with great difficulty because of age or wounds or for other reasons. Hippolyte was kissed and embraced almost senseless. And slowly the crowd began to wend its away towards the cathedral and the main square over the river. To celebrate, to give thanks, to express their overwhelming relief – that was the first instinctive reaction to the news. Perhaps M. le Maire would speak? But when they got to the square they found him at the head of a dense crowd ready to lead them to the cathedral for a service of thanksgiving.

Within the echoing precincts (there was only candle-light, the electricity had cut out) the atmosphere echoed with an extraordinary fervour, with tears and groans, with sobs and cries – for everybody had something or someone to mourn and few had recovered enough to manage to rejoice with any wholeheartedness. And so many were hungry!

The service was long and though improvised upon the occasion elaborate and memorable. Who would wish to relive those years again? Down in the town, however, new crowds had begun to form of a dissimilar caste and colour. They were composed of a heterogeneous collection of men and women of the lower layers of society, workmen, sempstresses, night watchmen, farm-hands, mechanics and railway-workers – a laic image in sharp contrast to the bourgeois image produced in the cathedral. A dozen such groups milled about with conflicting or parallel intentions centred vaguely about a civic celebration. Their activity was only co-ordinated by mood, for they had not decided whether to give the proceedings a political colour (there were many Communists, as usual well organised) or simply a national and patriotic flavour. Gypsies had come forward now, crawling like snakes out of nowhere, also Arabs in their indolent and lustreless fashion, waiting to start picking pockets; then an amorphous band of "slaves" composed of Czechs, Russians and heaven alone knows what other breeds swept down south by the tides of war. Worst of all, though perhaps most suitable to the scene, was the appearance of some great casks of red wine which were at once made available in the square by the Monument des Morts with its frieze of debased lions and flying heroines, vaguely evoking both Marianne and Mistral's dearer Mireille. All the cafés now opened and did what they could to promote festivities. Some had bricked up their cellars at the beginning of the war and now were content to release stocks of drink which had ripened in the darkness for those who drank harder stuff – *marc, calva, fine.* . . .

The procession from Montfavet finally joined forces with the forming surging crowd at the Magnagnon Gate where they were wildly applauded as being – so people vaguely imagined – a body of country people who had done something gallant to resist the Germans, perhaps even killed a few, to judge by the histrionic attitudes of Quatrefages. He was on the one hand acting out his role, shouting the word "Citizens!" over and over again as if he were about to make a speech; and at the same time inside himself he was quite serious and was talking to himself in his mother's voice, encouraging himself, soothing himself. He had bad stage fright. Moreover he feared that someone, perhaps a member of the Milice, might take a pot at him from a balcony. But they advanced with a will, driving their carts into the centre of the melée and letting the crowd surge approvingly round them. By now, to compensate for the lack of light, fires had been lit everywhere, as if it were the

Eve of St. John; at almost every street corner there was a blaze throwing sparks up into the drizzle which was soon to part dramatically upon a gaunt moon. With the leaping light and the capering shadows, the cries and the crack of wood, the whole scene resembled some wild *kermesse* taking place in the appropriate decor of the medieval walls of the second Rome.

But if Quatrefages was shouting the word "Citizens", his echo, the mad preacher from Anduze, Raynier de Larchant, was producing a headier slogan, which had the power to ignite souls. With his shock of white hair and his deep-set eyes he was an impressive figure – a generation of Protestant worshippers had been swayed by his delivery. He threw back his head and roared like a lion the words "Vengeance!" and "Justice!" This roar punctuated their progress like a ripple of kettle-drum music. Though mad, he knew how to carry the crowd, for everyone has something to expatiate and everyone seeks retribution. In this wild, colourful way they advanced towards the central square of the town. Some bread had appeared from somewhere, but there was precious little food, so that the floods of coarse wine and spirits kindled and warmed the hearts of the demonstrators with speed. Here and there people reeled. Incidents exploded on the screen of light – a man fell into a fire and was rescued by children. There were no police to interfere with the folly of so many fires. They were all hiding in civilian clothes from the vengeance of the Milice. *Their* central propaganda office with its pictures of Pétain had been stormed and set on fire.

Here and there in a completely arbitrary and unorganised fashion dancers had appeared: each music had its little circle, like eddies in the vast crowd. In one corner the celebrated wooden-legged Jaco set up shop with his wheezy accordion. Where *had* he been? everyone asked. All through the occupation there had not been a sign of him, and suddenly here he was again, quaffing the *pinard* and playing *Sous les toits de Paris* and *Madelon* as if the whole world had become a *guingette* and all the people revellers. In another corner fragments of the town band tried hard to assemble a *farandole*, for this type of folklore seemed appropriate to a nationalist and patriotic celebration. A tribune had been erected, at one end and suitably covered by flags and decorative emblems. One vaguely thought that here the mayor, backed by the town band, would make an excessively long peroration and end by burning the Nazi flag before the approving eyes of the people.

It did indeed start like this, in a confused sort of way. The band was reduced to three instruments, it was true, and lacked drive, for the soloist played a violin. But they played the national anthem creditably as an introduction and then the mayor in his sash started to orate, though he could hardly make himself heard above the buzz and roar of the crowd. Moreover the crowd was restive, they were after other game; vaguely they would have liked to execute some Nazi criminals on the spot to express their feelings of frustration and pain – for of course many had lost friends and relatives in the carnage of the years of war. The long tally of savageries, deportations, tortures and murders still lingered in the consciousness, their memory hung like a miasma over the music and the dancing, the relief and the joy.

The mad preacher's roars, calling for justice and retribution, could not have come at a more apposite moment, for just as they burst into the square with the firelight dappling their cows and horses, there emerged from the old quarter of the Balances another procession, of women this time, marching in a bedraggled column with lowered heads, and guided by a guard of youths and prostitutes and old women, some with lighted torches. At first one thought them penitents, perhaps come to offer thanks or some signal sacrifice to the forces of liberation. But no, they were those who had collaborated in whatever degree with the occupying forces. Some had been the concubines of soldiers, some had fraternised, unaware that they were being noted down by that group of festering moralists who plague the decency of every town by their puritanical fervours. Many had done nothing at all, they had simply been pretty enough to earn the jealousy of old maids who had "reported" them to the Vichy police, or sent in their names anonymously as "fraternisers". They must pay for it now. A roar went up from the crowd – they were not after all going to be deprived of a summary vengeance on someone or something. "The scissors!" they cried. "Where are the scissors?"

A corridor of fires the whole length of the square was cleared and organised by the crowd, while the victims were mobilised at one end in a group, looking pathetically like a group of schoolgirls about to participate in a race. They were in fact about to be forced to run the gauntlet, launched by a committee of old hags who brandished several large pairs of scissors such as dressmakers use to cut up lengths of cloth for their creations. Each was first shorn of her hair, had her face smacked soundly and her dress torn or pulled down over her shoulder; then with a sound push she was launched upon her course down the gauntlet where the public waited to take a smack at her with a belt or a switch. Conspicuous were the old women who in this way compensated for loveless lives, calamitous disappointments, or simple childlessness. They whipped away as if they were invoking fertility on the young bodies of virgins – they say that in Roman Italy statues were whipped to provoke fertility. The victims, for their part, though they cried tears of shame and indignation at the cries of "Prostitute!" were glad enough to escape with their lives, for the mood was ugly and the crowd under the influence of the drink had become temperamental and capricious. Already a fight or two had broken out among the spectators, and there were several disputes among armed onlookers somewhat the worse for red wine. But the best was yet to come.

It was rather like a Roman triumph, in which the best and most lucrative hostages, or those whose rank carried prestige beyond the common crew, were displayed at the end of the procession. So it now proved, for with a crackle of drum beats a smaller group emerged from the shadows guarding a single prisoner, *pièce de résistance*, it would seem of the evening's pieties. She, for it was a woman, walked with a deathly pale composure inside a square of guards who looked vaguely like beadles, though they carried the short trident of the Camargue cowboys as part of their fancy dress. They guarded her preciously though she did not seem to need guarding. She walked quietly with apparent composure and lowered head but her pallor betrayed her mortal fear – her skin glowed almost nacrous in the warm rose of the *flambeaux*. Her hands were tied behind her back. "*There! There!*" cried the crones as the little group advanced. "There she is at last!" It was clear that they spoke of the Evil One herself. The woman as she advanced overheard the tumult and slowly raised her head. Her wonderful head of blonde hair rippled upon her shoulders, her blue eyes were wide and cold. Her nervousness gave her the air of almost smiling. It was as if she had stage fright, she hung back in the wings, so to speak, for she had never acted this part before. "*Up! Up! Up with you!*" cried the crowd, indicating the rostrum upon which at last they mounted her, attaching her wrists to a column of wood. A pandemonium of rage broke out. The women with the scissors scuttled up on to the dais and waving to the crowd histrionically made as if to chop off her tresses, pulling them to full length so that they gleamed like the fruit of the silkworm's agony. "Justice!" shouted the madman down below and the crowd echoed him. "Vengeance! Justice! Prostitute! Traitor!" The scissors began their work and the blonde tresses were shorn and thrown into the crowd as one throws meat to a pack of dogs. They were torn to bits. Meanwhile the phalanx of kettle-drums – for new musical reinforcements had arrived – kept up a heart-shaking tattoo, such as might accompany the last and most dangerous act of a trapezist. They tore down her dress until she stood there clad only in her shift; the more they tried to debase her the greater her beauty was. Her little ears were pointed, like those of a tiny deer. And now they poured water on her head and shaved her with a cut-throat razor until she was as bald as an egg. "Shame on you!" they cried hoarsely, for she did not seem to be repentant at all, she did not weep. The truth was that she was too afraid. Everything had become a blur. She felt her wrists tugging at the post. They held her upright, for she felt on the point of fainting.

Then came something which, though quite unpremeditated, might easily have been expected, given the context of such an evening. She was pelted with refuse from the dustbins. God knows, there were enough of these. A pile of refuse built up around her feet. Eggs were not plentiful. Then a young man, extremely drunk, mounted the stage and rather unsteadily produced a heavy revolver. The crowd roared. He took up several menacing postures as he flourished the weapon and pointed it at her, so as to show the crowd what her deserts should really have been had they not been true patriots and civilised people. That is, at any rate, what the majority of the crowd thought.

As for the young man, so far-gone in wine, he was bursting with civic pride and a deep-seated sense of misgivings about his own inconspicuous role in the war and the Resistance. He longed to affirm by some dramatic act that he was an adult and a warrior of principle. Lurching about on the rostrum in front of the victim he took the roars of the crowd for approval. At first he had had in mind to fire a few shots as an alarm, or a *feu de joie* or ... to tell the truth the devil only knew what. But this was the hated concubine of the Gestapo chief, after all. The cries which exhorted justice and vengeance had gradually worked on his fuddled adolescence until, almost without thinking, he placed the cold barrel of the pistol against the brows of the tethered woman, right between the eyes, and pulled the trigger.

As always in such instances there are people who say they did not mean it, that it was all a mistake, that they were misinformed; and it is true that a moan of surprise and shock was heard from the crowd but it was rapidly drowned in the roars of approval and the music of the kettle-drum. Nevertheless a silence fell, or a lessening of noise, and the crowd wept, for people felt that they had gone too far. And then pushing into the crowd came a small group of nuns who quietly but firmly forced their way up on to the stage to take possession of the mortal remains of Nancy Quiminal.

Then as if to finally wash away and quite expunge every trace of these ignoble proceedings a thunder broke loose and it began to rain as it can only rain in the City of the Popes. Gutters brimmed and overflowed, leaves were broomed from the trees, the fires hissed and spat but went out. And the crowd began to slink away, at first hiding under eaves and in doorways, and then disappearing for good. The curfew habit was still deeply engrained. By midnight the rain had veered off and a candid moon shone in the sky. There was no sign of either enemy or friend. Even the lunatics had disbanded. Each had gone about his former task as if he had returned from a holiday. De Larchant had found his way to the cathedral where a terrified sacristan who recognised him surrendered the key of the organ loft. The grave strains of Bach suddenly swelled like a dark sail in that lightless cavern. Taillefer had gone back to the railway station to resume his job. Baudoin de St.-Just sat at a table in the rain outside the café playing a hand of solitaire with a pack of cards he had appropriated.

It was towards morning when the night watchman of the morgue heard horses' hooves followed by the sour buzz of the night bell. He had only just turned in after a full evening of work without light and his temper was ruffled. "What now?" he growled aloud as he opened, expecting some emergency delivery from the town. But it was only a pale tall man with two girls, his daughters. He had a letter from the mayor authorising him to see his wife's mortal remains. It was the husband of Nancy Quiminal, a man never as yet seen for he was bed-bound by illness. Once he had been a musician and had played in the town orchestra. He was pale and thin and ravaged by illness, and so weak that his two daughters held him by the elbows. The night watchman touched his forelock to him awkwardly in a gesture of sympathy. The nuns had dressed and composed the body and tucked it into its white winding cloth. They awaited only a *pasteur* now to arrange for the funeral. And then the medical certificate, what of that? Was it murder or judicial murder or what? Finally it would prove to figure as an unlucky accident. The family was in no position to contest the official view.

He hoisted a white blind and wound up a long handle so that the long chest-of-drawers swung towards them. Then he drew out a drawer to reveal the quiet form of the murdered woman. She looked like a little wakeful gnome in her snood, she was bald as a baby but with alert little ears like crocuses. Yet what affected them most was the sweet panoramic regard of the wide open eyes, the blue French eyes which held just a gleam of satirical humour in them. There were no powder-markings, just the blue hole neatly drilled between the eyes. The children were on the verge of tears and it was time to go. Her husband put out his hand to touch her pale cheek, left it for a moment and then withdrew it. He said he would come back in the morning and attend to the details with the authorities. But he never did. It remained for her two daughters to accompany their mother to a pauper's grave – the *fosse communale*.

A day or so later French troops relieved the town and at long last the bells of Avignon recovered their fearful tintinabulation which once, long ago, had driven Rabelais wild with annoyance. For the city the war had ended.

Appendix

LAST WILL AND TESTAMENT OF
PETER THE GREAT

IN THE NAME OF THE MOST HOLY AND INDIVISIBLE TRINITY, We, Peter the First, address all our successors to the throne and to the governors of the Russian Nation!

Almighty God, to whom we owe our life and our crown, has endowed us with his light and supported us with his might, and He has made us come to see the Russians as a people called to dominate all Europe in the future.

I base my thoughts upon the observation that most of the European nations are in a state of old age bordering on decrepitude towards which they are hastening with big strides. In consequence it is easy and certain that they will be conquered by a new and young people when it has reached the apogee of its growth, its maximum expansion. I consider therefore that the invasion of the Occident and the Orient by the northern peoples is a periodic mission decreed by providence – which by analogy in the past regenerated the Romans by barbarian invasions.

The emigration of the peoples of the Polar regions are like the overflowings of the Nile which, at certain fixed times, enrich with their rich silt the impoverished lands of southern Egypt. I found Russia like a small rivulet and I leave to my successors a great river; they in turn will make it into a vast sea destined to fertilise an impoverished Europe; its waves will overflow everything in spite of the dykes which faltering hands may dig to restrain them; waves which my successors will know how to direct. With this objective in view I leave them the following instruction which I commend to their unwavering attention and constant observation.

(1) To keep the Russian nation in a constant state of warlike readiness, keeping the Russian soldier forever at war, and only letting him have a respite if there be need to ameliorate the State's finances; reform the army and choose the most opportune moments for launching it into the attack. Turn things in such a way that peace can serve the needs of war, and war those of peace, all in the interests of the greatness and growing prosperity of Russia.

(2) Address ourselves to the people of cultivation in Europe, reaching them by any possible means – the officers in wartime and the scholars in peace, in order to let the Russian nation profit from the advantages of other nations without losing her own.

(3) Take part whenever we have the chance in popular affairs and legal disputes in Europe – above all in those which touch Germany, which interest us more deeply as being nearer to us than the rest.

(4) Divide Poland by fomenting internal dissensions and jealousies on a permanent basis; seduce the powers that be with gold, influence the Diets and corrupt them so that they favour the election of a king; seek out dissenters and protect them; send in Russian troops to foreign nations and keep them there until there is a suitable occasion to leave them there for good. If neighbouring states make difficulties, appease them temporarily by splitting up the place until such time as one can secure what one needs to hold permanently.

(5) Provoke Sweden as much as possible until she is forced to attack us, giving us a pretext for conquering her. With this objective in view it is essential that Sweden be separated from Denmark and Denmark from Sweden – by carefully encouraging their rivalries.

(6) Always to give German princesses in marriage to Russian princes in order to increase the number of family

alliances; thus to bring the interests of both countries closer together and win Germany to our cause, asserting thus our influence.

(7) For our trade orient ourselves in preference towards England, a power which has great need of us for its fleet and could be useful to the development of our own naval power; offering in exchange for gold our wood and other products, establishing firm links between their sailors and traders and our own, so that we can increase the scope of our own trade and a naval power.

(8) Advance our power without a halt northwards along the Baltic coast and southward around the Black Sea.

(9) To get as close as possible to Constantinople and India, for whoever rules over these regions will be the real ruler of the world. In consequence we must provoke unceasingly troubles between Turks and Persians. We must establish shipyards along the Black Sea, gradually extending our domination over it and over the Baltic — two land masses necessary to us if we envisage the success of the plan. Accelerate the decadence of Persia; penetrate as far as the Persian Gulf; re-establish if possible through Syria the ancient trade routes to advance to India, the entrepôts of the whole world. Once arrived there we will no longer need the gold of England.

(10) Seek out and maintain with care the Austrian alliance; appear to support its growing ideas of domination over Germany, but at the same time secretly fomenting the jealousy of princes against Austria. Operate so that both states ask for Russian aid and allow us to exercise over them a protective role which will prepare our future domination.

(11) Interest the Royal House of Austria in the plan for clearing the Turks out of Europe and neutralise its jealousies over the conquest of Constantinople either by

provoking a war with the older European states, or by sharing a part of the conquered territory with her; this we could take back later.

(12) Unite all the Orthodox Greeks who are divided or who support schisms throughout Hungary and Poland; gather them together and support them so that they constitute in a group a sort of predominant and sacerdotally important body; thus we will have many friends amongst many of our enemies.

(13) Sweden partitioned. Persia conquered. Poland subjugated. Turkey defeated. Our armies reunited. The Black Sea and the Baltic guarded by our sailing ships. For the moment we should propose, separately and in absolute secrecy, first to the Court of Versailles, then to that of Vienna, to share with them our world empire. Should one of them accept – inevitable if we know how to flatter their self esteem – we must turn one against the other and wage against them a battle whose issue is in no doubt, seeing that Russia will already hold all the Orient and a great part of Europe.

(14) If by chance both refuse the Russian offer – a highly improbable issue – we must set alight conflicts which will ruin them both; then can Russia at a decisive moment launch an attack on Germany with her forces concentrated.

(15) At the same time two vast fleets will set sail, one from the sea of Azov and the other from Archangel, full of Asiatic troops to join forces with the Black Sea and the Baltic fleets. Our army and navy will advance and cross the Mediterranean and Indian Oceans, on the one hand invading France, on the other Germany. Once these two regions are conquered the rest of Europe will pass easily and without much effort under our control.

That is how Europe could and must be subdued.

SEBASTIAN
or
Ruling Passions

to Simone Périer
of Montaury by Nîmes

ACKNOWLEDGEMENTS

Thanks are hereby extended to Dr Torhild Leira who gave permission for the author to use hints from her beautiful article in the *International Review of Psychoanalysis*, vol. 7, pt 3, 1980, entitled 'The Release of Tears'.

Contents

ONE

The Recall

THE PRINCE WAS IN A VEXATION. HE HAD DECIDED ON the spur of the moment to return to Egypt with Affad whom he took to task very severely for having succumbed, as he put it, to the "whim" of falling in love with Constance. He pursued the theme doggedly as they rode in the official limousine towards the airport of Geneva. "It was completely *uncalled* for," he said, "in view of your superior experience and the *engagements* you had entered into with the seekers." He was referring to the small brotherhood of gnostics in Alexandria to which they both belonged and in the tenets of whose creed they both deeply believed. Yes, on this score Affad felt deeply guilty, deeply betrayed by his own desire. The face of Constance rose up in his memory as if to reproach him for what he could not help. "You had no *right* to fall in love," the Prince went on testily. "I will *not* have her hurt." Affad made an impatient noise in his throat. "There is no such thing, as you have said. We must find another word. I will not have *engouement*. It is something of another order. Not infatuation at all." (They were speaking French, their tone was high.) Then after a long silence Affad said, "The experience was new to me; I ran aground – *j'ai calé*. Prince, it was not myself acting. Besides, you talk as if you were in love with her yourself." This put the Prince into a fearful rage because it was true. He made a cryptic gobbling noise like an offended turkey and blew his nose in a cambric handkerchief.

The problem was insoluble. Surely the insidious goblins of love had ceased to exist on the thin moral fare offered by the modern world? Affad was thinking with deep desire mingled with remorse of that secret field or realm which constitutes the

971

moral geography of the mystic. His friend Balthazar had once said ruefully, "I thought I was living my own life but all the time it was really living me without any extraneous aid. It had taken half a century for me to realise this! What a blow to my self-esteem!"

"Your behaviour is out of date," said the Prince again. "Since contraception things have changed. Women were once unique events in the life of a man; now woman is a mere commodity like *hay*. Availability has bred contempt."

"Not Constance!" he said.

"Of course Constance!" said the old man.

Affad thought back in silence. When he had first seen her he had been unable to believe his eyes, so original had her style of beauty seemed. ("I hate people acting out of epoch," said the Prince vehemently, and he intended the remark to wound.) "In fact so do I. But in any given moment of time some part of us is out of date, stays chronologically prehistoric in the most obstinate way. The kisses of ancestors take firm possession of our senses; we are mere distributors of love, not inventors. Even less investors."

"Fiddlesticks!" said the Prince.

"I was alarmed to find that for once this demonic sentiment was not moribund. I tried to escape it in vain, I really tried!"

"Fiddlesticks!" cried the Prince and gave a tiny stamp on the floor of the limousine. He was beside himself with . . . not only moral vexation but also jealousy. Affad said, "You are behaving as if I were a curate who had been untrue to his vows of chastity. I won't have it." But this was unfair, the business was much graver. It was in the most literal sense a matter of life and death and sacrifice. He had fallen short of his own intentions. In ancient times human sacrifice was invented to placate this particular demon. Think of the hundreds of imberb boys and impubert girls it had needed to placate the Cretan minotaur! "On my last birthday my old aunt Fatima sent me a telegram saying, 'Death is of no importance to It: why then to you?' Was she wrong?"

"Yes, she was wrong," said Affad, out of sheer contrariness, for the Prince was very annoying and there was no point in continuing to give in to him. On theological matters it was another affair – he would have to face the Star Chamber, so to speak, and answer for his fidelity; but this was an inner committee which had every right to probe his sincerity. They had never heard of Constance, like the Prince. "As a matter of fact Constance herself took a rather robust medical attitude to the sentiment you so much disapprove of," he said, and he felt the Prince's mind pucker up around his affection for the girl. She had once referred scornfully to love's *angoisse vésperale*, evening distress, but then had softened of a sudden, tears had come into her eyes, she had put her hand over her mouth as if to discourage a disposition to cry. Under her breath she had added. "Mon Dieu! Quel sentiment de déréliction!"

"Well, I suppose it is all fiddlesticks, as you say, but it is an expensive form of folly. She will take to her bed with a high fever and transfer her *angustia* to her medical duties. How to face those huge heaps of dead leaves, the neurotic patients who besiege her?"

They rode on for a while in silence, the Prince cracking his finger joints with an ill-tempered scowl. That brave girl, he was thinking, having to defend herself from the charm and folly of this suave python of a man. It was quite maddening for he loved Affad also as he would have loved his closest friend.

"I hardly dare to confide my distress in you because you react so violently. What would you say, I wonder, if you knew that I had been trying to make her pregnant – to face total and irrevocable disaster, so to speak, which would have united us definitively. Eh?" The elder man jumped at the confidence but did not comment upon it; he just sat looking straight ahead for a long moment before asking, "Does she know yet? For certain?" and Affad took his arm affectionately as he replied, "Unfortunately yes!" Rather surprisingly the Prince turned his birdbright glance upon him and said with unexpected sympathy, "Bad luck! Poor girl! But it would have rendered your decision to leave her even harder, even more cruel. You have behaved like a great coward in all this business, I feel; you have failed on both sides, Eros and Thanatos. Yes, you may well hang your head, my boy. And I suppose you blame love for all this lack of moral fibre?"

"Fiddlesticks!" said Affad in his turn with a blush which showed that he had felt the force of the reproof. His thoughts had come full circle and settled into the deep gloom engendered by his self-reproach and by the knowledge that in the last analysis it was the secret brotherhood which had the ultimate claims upon his life, and that at any moment they could foreclose upon his future. What a curse it was, after all, this love which set friend against friend, lover against loved. The whole circle of his friendships had shifted, been displaced by Constance's choice of him.

He had spent a no less gloomy moment at the bedside of the recumbent Blanford whose friendship he now treasured almost as much as that of the Prince. "It was my fault for letting her see passages from the bloody novel; it made her understand how crucial your beliefs were to your life . . . you hadn't told her, had you? O God, I am so sorry. But from her point of view you are simply ill, so to speak; you are suffering from a dangerous form of religious mania which she must be dying to cure in order to keep you!" Affad wrung his hands as he listened. He implored his friend to spare him any further analysis. The "bloody" novel lay before Blanford on the bed. He touched it wistfully from time to time with an air of deep regret. "Sebastian, please forgive me!" he said.

Affad rose. He stood for a while looking down upon the

troubled face of his recumbent friend with affection and sympathy. "Aubrey!" he said aloud and fell silent. Just the word, like a note in music. He did not add a goodbye for it would have seemed out of place – for he was not going anywhere in the profoundest sense. But he did add: "Please write to me when you feel like it; I am not sure when I shall come back, but my intention of the moment is to return in three or four months."

"I know you will come back. I have begun to see a little way into the pattern, the apparent confusion is beginning to make sense. I realise now that I came to Egypt because I was ill, I was afraid of the man on my back. I did a Sinbad in the hope of ridding myself of Sutcliffe – you will have noticed my various attempts to dispense with him, to make him commit suicide for example, using the bridge as a symbol. I had to have my spine shot into holes before I realised that the only way to deal with the Socratic Voice is to concretise it, let it live, manifest itself. Then it becomes a harmless ghost, it passes off in a fever, it writes the classic phrase for you. It can do everything but love. That you must do for yourself."

"O God!" said Affad dismally. "*Again!*"

"I had formed him just as one forms a renal calculus – or a teratoma, or the shadowy figure of one's twin which must be thrown by the ever-present witness of birth, the placenta. To hell with all this verbiage! The creature is alive, he is coming to lunch, he will even get an O.B.E. in a while for his services to the Crown. O God, Sebastian, I wish you were staying; I have learned so much from you!"

Still his friend said nothing but simply stood looking down at him affectionately. Blanford had become very thin and pale and drawn-looking; the spinal operations had taken their toll of his health, but so far they had been successful, and the surgeons believed that the next and most critical would be the last. After that it was up to the musculature to recover its tone once more, and for the patient to begin to dream of sitting up, and then walking once more. It seemed such a dream from this vantage point in time. He himself hardly dared contemplate the thought for fear of an ultimate disappointment. He poured out some mineral water from the bottle at his bedside and drank down a draught, but not without pledging his companion ironically in the harmless brew. Alcohol for the nonce was forbidden or he would have proposed a drink in token of farewell. But it was better thus.

So Affad had taken his leave in a thoughtful and sorrowful silence. And the same afternoon while the nurse was bathing and dressing Blanford, Constance looked in for a brief, unexpected visit – the new Constance, so to speak. For she was pale with sleeplessness and professional stress and her talk was languid and of an unusual vagueness. She did not mention her lover, nor did he, for his own distress and confusion were further deepened by the obstinate knowledge that he himself loved her and regretted the harm caused by his selfishness and self-importance. They sat for a while in silence, her hand lying upon his arm, full of an unstressed affection, and perhaps a tiny bit pleading, as if for sympathy. They were not at the end of their surprises, it would seem. It was the death of Livia, now.

To her immense surprise the information had come as a profound shock to Felix Chatto, of all people – he had been almost physically knocked over by it. All his new social assurance and devil-may-care airs had deserted him. The easy splendour of the man of the world – it had vanished, to leave in its place a frightened undergraduate. It was indeed a profound puzzle to the boy himself – yes, while Livia was alive he had lavished an adolescent attachment upon her; but he had never had any faith in his own feelings, he just enjoyed making his friend Aubrey suffer – as apparently had she. Now with the knowledge that Constance brought him he had made the discovery that, after all, he must have loved her – for he loved her still, retroactively, retrospectively – he was sick with the thought of her disappearance, even though he had hardly spared her a thought in all these long mysterious months during which she had vanished and her continuing existence could only be supposed! (I am sick, thought Constance, of sitting at bedsides and prescribing sedatives!) But this paradoxical behaviour touched and interested her, as much as it seemed to surprise the boy himself. He was, for example, avid for every scrap of information concerning the death of Livia; he wanted to know in great detail how she had been found, how the body had been cut down and disposed of, even such minor points as the slit vein in the thigh – Constance had humoured the old superstition about being buried alive by accident in which her sister had believed, and made sure with a femoral incision! She remembered her own insistence upon every scrap of detail in the case of Sam's death – how she had implored Blanford to tell her everything down to the smallest fact, pain her though it might. It was a way of mastering pain to absorb it like this – she now recognised that Felix Chatto was doing the same thing.

It was curious also that the references to Smirgel, the German informer who had enjoyed a somewhat enigmatic if not mysterious relationship with Livia, touched a chord in the memory of Felix – for he recalled that when they were all together in Provence before the war Livia's disappearances often seemed attributable to the existence of a German scholar who had been entrusted with the task of restoring some of the more famous paintings in the town collection. He was rather older than Livia and seemed a harmless, scholarly personage. Was it Smirgel? And did their attachment date from then? She must ask Affad to find out; then all of a sudden she felt the wild pang of her lover's absence like a knifethrust in the loins.

"It *must* have been him, Smirgel!" she cried with undue emphasis, to stifle the pain of the memory. "He told me he was restoring two famous ones. One was Clement's *Cockayne*."

Where had this memory surfaced from? She did not know. Felix said: "Someone was filling her head with stuff about Goethe and Kleist and Novalis with which she would bore the devil out of poor Aubrey who was reciting Keats in his sleep. Somehow I must get over this soon, I can't let her spoil my life by accident like this." So love had its ignominious side also?

Constance walked back to the clinic in a quiet despair at ever restoring the world around her to some sort of coherence. She told herself: "There's a barrier that goes down between you—the process starts at *first sight*, Shakespeare was perfectly right, like Petrarch, like Marlowe. Click! Of a sudden you are thinking each other's thoughts. Every other mental predisposition seems meaningless, trivial, vulgar. . . . There is nothing more to understand, it would seem!" Clouds had formed and swung low over the lake preparing for one of those electrical thunderstorms which punctuate life in mountain scenery. She was still living out the supreme collision of that first embrace, now so far back in time that it seemed prehistoric. Yet it was there, ever-present on the surface of her thought. She had changed very much. In the margin of a book she had borrowed from Sutcliffe she had found the scribbled words: "The same people are also others without realising it." The wind had risen and the waters of the lake were marked with dark prints of paws. The sky had swelled, as ominous as the nervous breakdown she could feel approaching her across the water. She tried once or twice to weep but it did not work; her mind was as dry as a bone. Then it started raining and she ran the last hundred yards to the ferry with her handbag held above her head.

Schwarz her doctor associate sat like a graven image at his desk reading the *News of the World* raptly. After long days spent with the insane he found these excursions into reality, as he called them, most refreshing; in this long catalogue of crime and folly, of mishaps and maladies, he felt that the real world was asserting itself, marking out its boundaries. It saw precarious, full of penalties – for one slip of the tongue or the mind and one became food for the doctor or the psychiatrist, a tenant of this quiet hotel set among lawns and orchards beside the lake. Here among the worm-casts of old theologies they knew for certain that science had abdicated, that the law of entropy ruled. Reality which was once so very "real" now only manifested a "tendency to exist"! All truth had become provisional and subject to scale. Truth was only true "on the whole". Someone, perhaps Schwarz himself, had scribbled upon the blackboard above her desk the verse:

> Though dice thrown twice
> May remain the same dice
> Yet chancy their fall
> For hazard is all!

But when he looked up from his paper and caught sight of his colleague's distraught expression he felt a thrill of sympathetic alarm, for he knew his Constance well and knew the limits of her strength. It was a moment of great stress, of great danger, he could feel it. He folded his paper and drew a deep breath, deciding as he did so to make a lightning decision. He would not indulge the advancing illness by suggestions of rest and careful sedation – he would risk exhausting her further but pushing her onward into a case which might occupy her mind and temper her distress. He said, hardly giving himself time to think the matter out, "Look, Constance, I have come to a decision about Mnemidis, but I want to talk it over with you before acting. I have decided that we should surrender him to the authorities and freely admit that we can do nothing with him. He is too sane or too mad. It's idle to talk of treatment. Besides, I am afraid of him, which is bad in a therapist! I was listening to the transcriptions again last night. It's no good. He is acting all the time, even to himself!"

Constance was already on her feet with her cheeks flushed. "You *can't!*" she cried with a vehemence that did his heart good to hear. "He is the most *interesting* case we have ever had. What a waste to let him rot away in the high security prison for twenty years, without trying to at least document the paranoia. It would be a shame – what on earth are you thinking about?"

"My skin, frankly. He is dangerously sane and altogether too articulate for our safety. I'm lost, Constance. Listen for yourself – everything he says is true and yet it's all false. It all comes to the boil, slowly and then . . . bang! – a crime. From another point of view it's a waste of time, of our time, for there are cases we *can* help. Don't you see?"

"No, I don't! And if you won't continue with him I shall take your place. I'm not afraid of him. Besides, you have the old 'Malabar' at hand if anything goes wrong, gets out of hand. I implore you to reconsider the matter; let me take a hand for a bit with him. He has not discussed the actual murders yet, has he?"

'Not in detail; he is busy trying to justify himself at the moment – and with what ability, it's hair-raising! I am supposed to see him today. I was going to tell him about my decision and pack him off back to prison to complete his sentence."

"Shame!" she said, and taking his hand in her own firm grip went on, "Let me take over the session from you. Besides, I need something to get my teeth into, something to keep my time fully engaged! Mnemidis the impersonator would be just it. Please let me!"

Schwarz made a show of hesitation and indecision. But as a matter of fact he was seriously wondering whether the decision was in fact a wise one; various factors in the case made him wonder whether the arrival of a woman doctor on the scene would not aggravate matters. He hovered between all these contingencies with an exquisite sense of vertigo. By doing this in order to restore the balance he felt was at risk in

Constance he might . . . "O Jesus!" he said, and he was not a pious man, although a Jew, "O Jesus, help!"

In hospital parlance the "Malabar" was just a strong-arm man who was always on hand to deal with dangerous or refractory patients. There were several in the employ of the clinic, but Pierre was their favourite – a giant negro from Martinique who combined overwhelming physical force with a warm gentleness, a ruthlessness of affection that had even the most difficult patients at his mercy in no time. "Pierre is bringing him – indeed, there they are! If you feel you *can*, then perhaps you should, Constance! But I have misgivings. Look at them."

The guard and the patient advanced through the forest side by side at an easy pace. Mnemidis was of a slight build but with very long arms and a strange domed head which gave him a somewhat professorial look – belied by his curious and sordid record. He glanced furtively sideways and upwards at the negro face of his keeper; they could not hear what he was saying but his expression was ingratiating. The negro did not walk, he sailed serenely onwards with eyes half closed – almost, you might have said, a sleep-walker. But he had one hand twisted lightly into the cuff of Mnemidis' coat and with this invisible leverage he was actually propelling him gently in the direction of the psychiatrists' lodge with its array of confessionals. They watched for a moment; then Constance was at the door. "I shall take him today," she said with a new decision, "and give you a rest." But Schwarz called after her: "Maximum security, don't forget, please!" He had not forgotten the episode with the metal paper knife which could have cost him at the least a wound, at the most his life.

But Constance was an experienced practitioner of the black arts, and as she slid into her seat at the bare desk she tested the soft bell which might summon a waiting "Malabar" to her aid, and also checked the hidden Judas through which

Schwarz, if he so wished, might cast an occasional glance into the theatre of operations. A recording apparatus existed though its functioning was often doubtful because of the fixed microphone. A patient lying on the couch was fairly recorded, but if he became agitated and moved about as so often they did, or even simply sat up – as Mnemidis was just about to do – why, the recording was scrambled.

She composed her hands upon the desk before her and waited for the door to open and for Pierre to usher in his charge, which he now did with a kind of dusky dignity which showed kindness and insight – for there is nothing more humiliating than to be shoved around when one is ill and knows it. But then Mnemidis might have phrased it otherwise for he spoke of it as "feeling real", and contrasted it with less heightened states which he called "feeling normally unreal". Quite a card, this man who sidled into the room looking about him as if recognising invisible onlookers who would certainly be amused by his predicament. "And where is Dr Schwarz?" he demanded at once on an insolent note and waited for Constance to explain the substitution. But it would have been an error to do this from a sitting position while he stood over her, and to redress the situation in her favour she said with quiet authority, "You can lie down, please. And put your handbag on the table where we can see it." He did not like this at all and flashed alarmed glances everywhere, but she waited there impassive, staring at him, until slowly he started to consider obeying her. It was important that the female handbag (in cheap crocodile skin) should be deposited between them, for it contained his power, his malefic genius. It was probably quite empty, but for him it was a kind of bomb, at once defensive and aggressive. So long as he put it down somewhere he was disarmed. Well, he put it down, and she sighed with relief.

He lay there for a while, smiling and pouting at old memories, while she watched him thoughtfully and reproached herself for the fact that underneath everything – if sincerity counted for anything – she was disposed towards this audience because she half hoped to hear the name of another Alexandrian: her lover, Affad! Even though she knew that they could never have met or had anything to do with each other! Mnemidis had hardly seen the place since his acting gift took him all round the world. "Where to begin?" he repeated wistfully, under his breath. Then after a long pause he drew a deep breath and began: "The thing is this: how could things have been otherwise? What could I do? Have you ever thought about the predicament of being God for example – suppose one were? You couldn't act otherwise. In my case – ah! listen carefully. In my case I was born without aptitudes or inclinations, and with little enough brains or beauty. I was just *there*, my mind as smooth as an egg, but with no direction, apparently good for nothing, and so society must suffer me. . . . O God, the emptiness, it leads directly to a state of alienation, one feels the fact of being a sort of cosmic mishap! The intense *boredom* is crushing. In my case it led however to a state of grace. By an accident I discovered a *sortie*. An opening. I found that without being actually great you can slip past the sentries into greatness, without waking the sacred geese . . ."

A spasm of violent nausea seized him and he turned up his eyes into his head in a frightening grimace which seemed almost epileptoid. It died down slowly, leaving him pale and weary-looking.

"Well?" she said, in order to keep contact.

"Well!" he echoed. "One night at a party, suddenly and quite involuntarily I uttered a false laugh, in a vague desire to amuse. The cracked hysterical laugh of a servant girl. It had such an instant success that I was as if stamped for life as an impersonator. I became in demand at parties where I would laugh until I had everyone shrieking with mirth, or trembling with anxiety for sometimes it went on too long, I could not break it off." He put his hands to his throat as if exploring old bruises.

"Then gradually the voices came, I developed a whole repertoire, it was like becoming a hotel with someone different in each room. Yes, but you could mix up the keys if you weren't careful. Laughing professionally before a public – that is something different. I began to voyage among the living and the dead – at the suggestion of my lover, an old man weighed down with his culture. Werther, Kleist, Manfred, Byron, Hamlet, he could not divest himself so he voided them all on me. I did not read anything, you understand, but he directed me and coached me and instructed me so they were more real to me than if I had read them myself. Gradually as I improved in richness I added other touches, sudden frightening grimaces, choking and falling, enacting a shooting star or a flash of lightning. A pistol shot, a groan, a sigh – Casimir developed these thoughts and planted them in me so that I enacted them. But now I had entered a new domain of total joylessness. I felt the strain. You see, right from the beginning this man had enslaved me against my own will. It's common enough in Egypt, this sort of magic. When I refused his first advances he used magic. His wife Fatima told me long afterwards how it worked – she too was forced by his threats. He forced her to perform fellatio on him, holding her by the chignon, clamped. With his free hand he dialled my number and engaged in a long amorous pleading conversation – leaving me in no doubt as to what was being done to him and by whom. At the moment when he felt his sperm pass into the mouth of Fatima I felt it also for he had visualised my 'eidolon' as we say. I cried out and dropped the phone, but it was done. Next day I woke with a headache and a fever and a sore throat. I dreamed of him. I was on fire. Finally I was so exhausted by the mental waves he was sending me – the sheer weight – that I capitulated and asked him to come. I could not wait, I was in a frenzy of capitulation.

THE RECALL

"So it came about. He was active and vicious but very clever and a magician with money. But his look was so sad and disabused, his eyes so ignorant of smiling, that it gave one a thrill: one was talking to a dead man, one felt. He used to say, 'Time is rusting away inside me, my heart is full of barbed wire.' I no longer hated him, the hate had dulled. I was his slave and I hated only myself. Yet he must *pay* one day, I felt it. I was not surprised when the stranger came from the city with a message. A new era had already begun. The veins in my head had started to swell with water, throbbing: echoing: booming! It was this stranger who asked me if it wasn't right that Casimir should *pay*, should die. There was no other real solution, it would seem; the little group of his friends had turned against him. They were looking for a passive instrument – that is how he put it. Passive. Instrument. I watched him curiously when he was asleep, he seemed so near to death already. Once he felt my gaze on him and he opened one eye and said: 'You know this is with my *full* consent? Don't be afraid to act if they ask!' Could it be possible that he knew?

"I had started my tricks already – I was imitating his voice on the telephone and ordering things from shops, all in his name. A mountain of jewellery was what I felt I needed to counter my ugliness. He knew but said nothing. As for Fatima, I left her for another occasion, another country, another method. The symptoms were much the same but the powder left no trace in the organs though she had already denounced me by letter, for she had been warned."

Constance listened with intense concentration to this professional monologue, to this desolate man, empty of all feeling. He went on: "I discovered that even when I was *acting*, I myself was only acting. Where had I gone? My I? My eye?"

The desolation of the liar! He was nodding slowly with the mandarin-like nodding of the morphinomane – though he was not one in real fact. He was only illustrating time running on, running out. "Tick-tock," he said. "So it goes on. Tick-tock. Do you carry a watch, like all doctors do? May I see it, please?" As a matter of fact she did, in the fob-pocket of her white smock. It was a pretty little timepiece, slightly ovoid, almost egg-shaped. She placed it on the table before him and he took it up with a sort of shy rapture, examining it with close attention, holding it to his ear. Then he swallowed it right before her very eyes and they gazed at each other with silent amazement, for he himself seemed astonished by his own action. It was important not to over-react, as with a child who swallows a peach-stone. She stared. "Why," she said at last, "did you do that?" and he shook his head with a childish expression of wonder on his face: "I don't know. I suddenly needed to stop the world. It was stronger than me. I stopped *his*, didn't I? In spite of our romance I stopped it thoroughly, once and for all. But this wasn't very clever of me, I admit."

The hour was up according to the electric clock on the wall and she rose. "I will tell Pierre," she said. "He will know what to do."

"I don't feel like apologising," he said and his underlip trembled as if he was about to start crying. She pressed the bell and the vast form of the negro appeared in the doorway, smiling. She explained what had happened in the most matter of fact way and seemed by her tone to reassure the sick man for he smiled and nodded. Pierre took his sleeve with a tactful nonchalance and they set off back to the dangerous ward together, walking away circumspectly through the trees. She watched them disappear and then slipped back to her own room, only to find that Schwarz had also gone. A passage from his new book was on the typewriter and she bent down to read it. "But Freud like Darwin was truthful to the point of holiness. Their devout scientific atheism had the necessary rigour to produce results. When you look through a telescope of high magnification you must hold your breath so the image does not waver. Now, how poor the dialogue has become. Not science but semantics rules! Paris, instead of playing a seminal role to replace the murdered Vienna has reaffirmed its lesser role as the capital of fashion in ideas, of superficiality. Spindrift of politics fabricated by educated poltroons with taste. *Barbe à papa*, a candy-floss culture."

Schwarz had grown increasingly critical of the French rôle during the war. "As Darwin himself noted: 'To reason while observing is fatal – but how useful afterwards!'" While she read, her colleague himself appeared, with his mildly sardonic air of curiosity and amusement. "Well?" he said, and she gave an account of her session with Mnemidis and his gesture with her watch. He laughed with delight and said: "Poor Pierre will have to spend his days stool-watching until it reappears, if it ever does. How do you know – he may digest it! Thank God, however, for the session seems to have done *you* some good!" As they talked he had placed his fingers upon her pulse. "And your colour is good once more!" Perhaps the demon of this fatigue would pass and her composure be restored by itself? "I have had another insulting letter from Sutcliffe, probably written when he was drunk." He took up a sheet of official notepaper and read out slowly, "'Schwarz, you bloody man, supporter of lost causes among which Love looms largest, why not try another method? Instead of fretting about *changing* the world, why not realise and accept it as it is, admitting that its order is divine, that reality, of which we are part, realises itself *thus*. Swallow the whole thing whole! If you did, if you do, the great paradox will supervene; the world will automatically and irremediably change itself and of its own accord. Or so they say! Farewell!'"

"He has been drinking again I don't doubt. I think you must really join him one day for a game of billiards."

Schwarz looked startled. "Blood sports! Me?" He made defensive gestures with his hands. They were finished for the day and uncertain of how to fill up the evening. He thought he would probably go to the cinema, while she thought with dread of her empty flat. It seemed more than ever desirable to unearth some company which might help her to pass the remaining daylight hours without too much room for introspection! Schwarz seemed equally solicitous about her balance. He said, "Constance, when are you going to see the small boy of Affad – the autistic one?" She sat down and reflected. "I don't know. I am in such a disturbed state at the moment that I thought to let things settle down a bit."

Schwarz shook his head. "I should start at once," he said, "at least to make the opening moves. After all, there may be nothing to be done. The children of the rich and purseproud are always in the greatest danger."

Children!

She remembered Affad declaiming in a mocking voice something like: "Children! you were born to disappoint your parents as we have all been, for our parents built us gilded and padded cages to live happily-ever-after-in – and look what came about: exile, bereavement, folly, voyages, despair, ecstasy, illness, love, death: all life in a single stab like a harlot's kiss."

She was thinking sadly of the absent Affad and suddenly coming to herself she saw that Schwarz was contemplating her with solicitude and concern, trying to estimate just where she stood in the face of this crisis in her affairs. "My God! what a shabby profession it is – or perhaps it is us, worn out by the sheer magnitude of the task and the limitations imposed by inadequate knowledge. I have started dishing out pills, the first sign of morbid frustration. And our job is to teach our clients how to rediscover a state of joyful nonchalance in the face of things, something as calm as death but just *not* death . . . And here we are falling sick ourselves. I'm worried about you. You have become a bore." Thus Schwarz.

"You mean in love! I know it!"

"But that is not why he left?"

"No. It's more complicated."

It was both more complicated and yet quite simple, quite transparent. "You know what I think? I think I will try to patch up my wounded self-esteem by buying that fur coat which I need for the winter. I have been putting it off all the year. It seems just the moment. Do you think it will save the day?"

"Yes. The instinct is sound!" he said, not without a tinge of irony. He was about to add that it was one of Lily's habits when she felt depressed, but was suddenly assailed by a pang of depression at the thought of her, at the thought of having betrayed her, as he put it to himself. When going to the cinema he tried to avoid the newsreels which preceded the big film, lest they show scenes of the advances into Germany. "And those pictures," she said, "that's another reason – I found them on Affad's desk, the whole exhibition folio spread out on the floor. They are mind-blenching in their horror. It's quite beyond weeping. One wanted to bang one's head on the wall from sheer incomprehension. How *could* they? How *could* we?"

Schwarz sighed and drew obscure diagrams on the writing pad at his elbow.

The confusions caused by the onset of war had been great, but had given place to a certain artificial order during the prosecution of it over a period of years. Some sort of haphazard system had emerged based on the prevailing military and political options. Now with the return of a hesitant and fragmentary quasi-peace this factitious order was once more disturbed and on an even wider scale, for the whole world by now had reeled out of orbit under the hammer blows of the sick Germany. The confusions engendered by this peace were almost worse; Switzerland was an oasis of calm, an island, compared to the surrounding hinterland which was so fully occupied with the disbanding of armies, resettlement of disturbed populations, onerous shortages, dislocated communications, broken civic threads everywhere which must be retied, respooled. The terrifying photographs of which she spoke had been taken by the armies as they advanced, and they were of concentration camps and their inmates. Everyone had known about the extermination camps, it is true, but people find things hard to realise, to accept what they might intellectually know. The Red Cross had received all this frightful documentary material with instructions from the military and political arm to give it the widest possible publicity; and to this end the pictures had been enlarged and an exhibition formed which showed the work of the camps in all their dreary horror. The idea was to mount a travelling public exhibition together with an illustrative text in several languages. Blanford had been approached for that and the whole project had been the subject of a number of committee meetings.

"I was intrigued to see from the minutes," said Constance, "that you came out rather strongly *against* the display idea for the pictures. We thought that as a Jew the subject . . ."

Schwarz made a noise like a snort and said, "*Aber*, Constance, I am first of all a doctor, and my decision was according. The subject is horrible, the injustice and horror palpable, but on such a scale should we turn it into a peepshow? Of course the thing must stay on the record and we will somehow have to try and forgive what it will be impossible to forget. But finally this whole-scale outbreak of German *lustmorder* was a national aberration on a fantastic scale. What is even more interesting though is that they managed to start the French off behaving like that at first; doubtless the British would have followed suit if the Channel expedition had come off. All this raises a medical and philosophic problem of such great importance that we must try and study it coolly, as we are trying to study Mnemidis. What a triumph it would be if we could throw that Faustian switch and get him working with rather than against us. Roughly, all that was in my mind when I voted against."

"I see."

"I wonder if you do. I know that Affad does because I was able to discuss it with him, and of course in the new book I try and deal with the whole matter in general terms. Our whole civilisation is enacting the fall of Lucifer, of Icarus!"

She felt a rush of affection for all that he had given her over the years and a quickening of love and admiration for the dignity of the man and his faithfulness to his craft. He worshipped method like the wise old god he was. "Affad was right when he said that the most tragic thing about the German decision to abolish the Jews was that their solution, for all the horrible pain and suffering it brought, was profoundly *frivolous* – cruel paradox! For the problem of the Jews is far more serious, not less, concerning as it does an alchemical *prise de position* on the vexed question of matter. Demos Demos Democritos . . . now we see that matter is not excrement but thought. If we have come to the end of this cycle and are now plunging into a hubristic *dénouement* I can't help as a Jew being deeply proud of the tremendous intellectual achievement of Jewish thought. I am thinking of our three great poets of matter. What a stupendous Luciferian leap into the darkness of determinism. Will there be time to correct the angle of vision, that's what worries and intrigues me? This Jewish passion for absolutism and matter has already started to modify itself – entropy is the new sigil! Freud arrived on the scene like a new Merlin to take up the challenge of the Delphic oracle. He resolved the riddle of Oedipus. A Hero! He paid for it with his organ of speech, just as Homer and Milton each paid for his inner vision with his sight! But the confusion of gold and matter is a philosophic problem, and you can't deal with it by abolishing the Jews' physical presence. Our racial passion must become less visceral and more disinterested. The Jewish mind cannot *play* as yet! O Christ, what does all this rigmarole matter? Who will read my book? They will say that I am anti-Jewish!"

"Yes," she said. "I am familiar with this line of thought because of . . ." – strange that she should have a kind of inhibition about pronouncing his name – "Affad!" There! but it made her feel shy. "Unhappily we still have a need for heroes. Myths cannot get incarnated and realised fully in the popular soul which seeks this nourishment with sacrifices, for reality is just not bearable in its banal daily form, and the human being, however dumb he is, is conscious of the fraud."

"Yes. It's what that bastard Jung is up to. Affad approves a little bit but not entirely of his attitude. The alchemical work is in distillation or decoction – the personal ego decants itself in thoughts which are really acts and slowly, drop by amazing drop, virtue, which is voidness, precipitates." They both laughed, he with that sardonic helpless Viennese despair which had taken so many generations to form. It was not cynicism. It was a profound creative distrust of the dispositions taken up by reality, by history. He said softly, "A sort of *pourriture de soi* . . ."

They were both wondering what Mnemidis would have made of this conversation – highly articulate as he was. How could one talk to him about such matters, which were after all vital for his health, his recovery? His response would be "acted": for him all love was the genius of misgiving, which rules the human heart.

Schwarz was sick to death of this world and its works. Even as he felt the pulse of Constance under his fingers he felt rise in his own soul the thick sediment of despair, like the lees of a bad wine, which dragged him always towards suicide – the suicide which always seemed to him so inevitable. One day it would claim him, of that he was sure. At such moments when the demon had him by the hair he wanted to bury his face between the breasts of a woman and hide from this all-pervading idea.

"I dreamed last night that we killed Mnemidis with one simple injection; you helped me. We were so happy to be delivered from him!" He sighed and cleaned his old horn-rimmed glasses and he thought to himself, "It's a question of patience. The vast weight of cosmic submission, the inertia of mass, will prevail over all."

"I'd like a dry Martini," she said.

"Done!" he said, stripping off his white tunic.

They took the ferry across the lake whose glassy surface reflected the coming night, and made their way with slow steps across the town – carefully avoiding the old Bar de la Navigation, for they did not want any more talk – and slowly arriving at the main station of the town where they sought out the first-class buffet, incomparable for the size and quality of its pre-war Martinis. The barman was an old friend, and had in his youth worked at the Ritz in Paris. Yes, they wanted to sit quite quiet in a companionable silence. And this came about as planned except that as they sat down he said, "I am profoundly worried about you." And she replied, "I know you are – I have a juicy neurasthenia coming on, like influenza. It will pass, you will see." No more. Just that and the alcohol burning in the mind like a spirit lamp. And of course, dimmed by the heavy doors, all the distant romantic stirring of trains arriving and departing.

Recently, within the last three months, she had had an accidental meeting with someone which she would soon come to regard increasingly as providential; it surprised her that she had not mentioned it to him, since it had involved her in an entirely new programme of personal health, personal endeavour: moreover in a field which she had long regarded as suspect and without much interest for a scientist. Walking one day along the old rue de la Confédération with Felix Chatto, en route for a coffee-shop where they could gossip, they came face to face with a small white-clad figure which at first neither could recognise. It at first looked like an Indian saint, a yogi of some sort. Its mane of white hair flowed down on either side of its dark negroid features. It was clad in white in the manner of an Indian *sadu* or holy man, and it was walking barefoot on the grubby pavements. This was the figure that spread its arms in a signal of surprised recognition and stood stock still, smiling at them. Who on earth could it be? They peered at the apparition, peered through the tangle of silver hair, as one might peer into the jungle, intent on the identification of some strange animal. The little sage had the advantage of them for he said, "My goodness, Mr Chatto, sir, and Miss Constance, fancy meeting you! What are you doing here?"

What were they doing there! And slowly piercing the obscurity of the Indian saint's disguise they gradually found with the help of memory another face emerge, developed like a photograph. "Max!" she cried, and with a short interval of prolonged puzzlement Felix Chatto echoed her with "Max!" Then they were all three shaking hands, embracing, talking at once. It was the old valet-chauffeur of Lord Galen, whom they had last seen during the last summer they had all spent together in Provence; the old negro boxer who used to be Lord Galen's humble sparring partner on the lawn at daybreak! How was it that he had so completely vanished from their thoughts – the violet chauffeur who often dressed like an Italian admiral? "Max!" she said, "You have changed so much – what has happened?" And in his affectionate excitement he almost reverted to his old Brooklyn-negroid tones. "Doogone it, Miss Constance, everything! Just everything! Ah been in India a while now and ah've learned a new science. Better than the old one-two!" He spread his arms and his face took on an angelic expression of bliss and devoutness. They both felt suddenly abashed by Max in this new incarnation, this new disguise – if disguise it was. Still holding their hands in his he explained breathlessly how the transformation had come about. "When Lord Galen went home I decided to go to India. I had received several invitations from an old man who made a lot of sense to me – I met him in Avignon. He came to the boxing booth where I used to drop in for a work-out. But he wasn't a boxer, he was a wrestler and a yoga-maker. I got to working with him a little, and was intrigued enough to visit him in Bombay. Thanks to him I became a yoga-maker and teacher; when I was through he asked me to run one of his groups right here in Geneva. So here I am!"

It seemed almost unbelievable; such a transformation of personality in such a short space of time, it seemed almost like witchcraft. They dragged him off to a coffee-shop where they sat him down before a dish of tea and cakes in order to ply him with questions about this new departure. The only one of them who had shown any interest in yoga as a method of health regeneration had been Livia; but perhaps this fact had not been known to Max at that far-off epoch – indeed her own initiation into the science had come about in Germany during her flirtation with National Socialism. But Constance did not mention her name – why should she? The gravity and simplicity with which Max talked about the change of mind involved in developing from a pugilist into a yogi was more than merely interesting – she was struck by the distinctions he drew and the simple vividness with which he enunciated them. How he had changed! India had even improved his English, as well as giving him at times a tiny touch of a Bengali accent. Constance was beside herself with joy, and when Felix Chatto was forced to take himself off to the office she had stayed on for a full hour, profoundly interested in the psychological change which had taken place in this old friend. "Of course our studio yoga isn't a therapy as such but since I have been here I've seen such dramatic changes in people due to its practice that I have begun to wonder jest what in hell it is. Now doctors are sending people to us that they can't handle. Our classes are full of young people suffering from stress and tension of spirit – on their way to crack-ups we help them to avoid. In India they'd be surprised, since there's no ego to get mentally stressed up with, so to speak. But why don't you come and see the studio? My, it's classy, it's downright classy. And I'm the boss locally – crazy, isn't it?"

Later that evening she actually did visit it with him and watched a hatha class under the instruction of a young girl. It created a sort of echo in her, a half-formulated desire to become part of it, to learn the ritual. After all, what was her medical practice about if it was not concerned with the problems of stress in its extreme forms? Why should she not study this ancient method for a while and see what bearing it had upon her own formulations?

Later still, sitting in his tiny office drinking more tea, it seemed to her the most natural thing in the world for him to lean forward and touch her knee as he said, "You know, I believe you could work with us and learn something you could turn to use. Maybe, if you had the patience . . ."

She smiled and replied, "I've always had the patience to learn something new; but tell me how and where to begin." And the negro smiled and went on patting her hand as he said, "If you like I'll step out with you to the ten cent store where you can buy yourself a cheap yoga mat. It's the first really important act, for you will find it very important for you; you'll get sort of stuck on it. It's like all your work and your breathing, and your whole mentality soaked into it while you work on it, or maybe just lie on it and rest. They don't cost much, they are just little eiderdowns as you saw in class. But it's good to get a colour you like and keep it always around you – you'll want to anyway. The thing becomes precious, like your own hymn book. It's a record of your strivings." He went on in this vein while conducting her downstairs and across the inner court-yard to the front entrance on the street. They ambled across to a store and she duly bought herself the small eiderdown as required. Then she accompanied him back for her first lesson. The studio was indeed rather a grandiose modern establish-ment forming part of a flourishing Turkish bath. When they re-entered the main courtyard she was struck by the singular vision of two yoga students diligently burning up their eider-downs on a lighted brazier. Astonished by this aberrant conduct she stopped and pointed it out to Max. "What on earth . . . ?" she cried, nonplussed. He burst out laughing: "They've *realised!*" he said cryptically.

She was completely nonplussed. "But after what you have just been saying about yoga mats . . ." she said in bewilder-ment, but he only shook his head and laughed at greater length. "Listen," he said at last, "there is nothing mysterious about what they are doing, but I don't want to go into merely intellectual explanations. It's better left – the subject for the time being. Later on you'll get it for yourself."

They resumed their trudge up the stairs and then, as she debated, a sudden intuition flashed upon the screen of her thoughts. She stopped dead and said, "I think I have got it! Attachment!"

"Yeah," he said with a grin. "That's it!"

She surprised herself by this sudden and quite spontaneous formulation. Where had it come from? Obviously she must have read it somewhere – for after all the whole subject of Eastern metaphysics was quite foreign to her study and indeed her interest. "You know more than you realise," he said happily. "Now I'm putting you in the beginners class so you can jest learn the alphabet; later on the letters will make words and then the words will make sentences – that is if you don't get bored and jest drop the whole thing. It does happen and it

997

isn't important. The science is for those who reely want it and need it and are prepared to make an effort. Like me wanting to become a *champ* – it was an obsession, and I made sacrifices to get there. However it didn't work, I didn't have the class. Then age took a hand and I lost out."

"And now?" she asked.

"Bless you, I'm jest happy without any kind of after-thoughts. They showed me how one could meditate sweetly and gradually harmonise with the goings-on of the whole wide world!"

"It sounds great!"

"It certainly is. I'm telling *you!*"

And so had begun her insinuation into the mysteries of the craft, and now while she thought back upon it she realised why she had never mentioned it to her colleague. He had once or twice hinted that all such matters whose provenance was Indian were somewhat intellectually disreputable in a scientist of the twentieth century: and she valued his good opinion! If ever asked she had been wont to say that twice a week she took a relaxing Turkish bath in the town. So the yoga had remained a secret between herself and Max. Yet not completely – for later Affad had redeemed this whole field of knowledge by admitting something that neither Max nor Schwarz could have admitted – namely that the heart of all these dissimilar sciences was the same heart. Max knew no science and Schwarz no yogic lore; she felt herself to be intellectually living in a double life between them, each with his claims upon her time and intelligence. If driven to it Schwarz would even quote Kipling on the question of East being East, etc. But thank goodness one day Affad took up the discussion and surprised her by saying quite simply that "Einstein's non-discrete field, Groddeck's 'It', and Pursewarden's 'heraldic universe' were all one and the same concept and would easily answer to the formulations of Patanjali." Her heart leaped with joy to hear this, for the whole weight of such tiring speculations had been pressing upon her mind, causing her anxiety and muddle in her thoughts, not to mention doubts about her methods. Of course! And one more reason to love Affad – insight was so much more important than physical beauty. As they sat confronting one another in silence she had the sudden physical feeling of his presence beside her – perhaps at that moment he was thinking of her, desiring her. Trains came and went and the forest of human feet pounded the dark pavements of the quais outside the bar. She drank and listened to her own thoughts as they scurried hither and thither like mice: all thoughts of the past. It was strange how this breach in their relationship had stopped her in her tracks – she felt quite futureless, everything lay in the past and was bathed in the sunshine of reminiscence. O where was Affad now?

TWO

The Inquisition

WHERE INDEED? THEIR PLANE WAS DELAYED IN TURKEY by bad weather – the Prince behaved as if it had happened deliberately in order to annoy him further. Nothing would convince him that the Turks ("they have souls of mud like the Nubians") had not organised the whole thing from the depths of their anti-Egyptian feeling, even the weather which was so inclement. They spent a sombre weekend watching rain and cloud lying like smoke upon the echoing vistas of the capital – at its best a proud and sinister place. Even the beauties of the Bosphorus were dazzled and rubbed out by the wind and waves, and a racing darkness. The pleasant excursion to Eyoub which they always took was hardly tempting in such frowning weather. Moreover the subject of the journey and that of Constance weighed heavily between them; indeed every time these subjects were touched upon the Prince flew into a vehemence and was so acid that the long-suffering Affad began to wax irritated. They sat among palms in the hotel, where the Prince impatiently read out-of-date newspapers and cracked his finger-joints while Affad played solitaire on a green card table in a self-commiserating sort of manner, swearing from time to time, under his breath and in several languages. The coming Inquisition filled him with guilty gloom and apprehension.

After one sally by the Prince he turned on him and said, "I implore you to drop the subject – I know your views on it too well! I know that I have to face the enquiry and answer for a gross and lamentable failure of nerve – but let me prepare myself quietly for it and not be chivvied out of my mind . . ."

"Who is chivvying *who*?" growled the scowling Prince,

1000

and Affad replied just as testily, "You are. And if you don't stop I'll take another plane."

The Prince snorted with contempt. "*What* other plane I'd like to know!"

It was very much to the point. They had sent a telegram announcing their tardy arrival in Alexandria. The Prince after a moment of silence could not resist a resumption of hostilities. "I hope you'll have the grace to confess that you have exercised a baleful influence on the poor girl – among other things encouraging all this yogi-bogey stuff she has got interested in."

"It's something you would do well to get interested in yourself before you fall apart, Prince. Those awful attacks of sciatica, for example. You could dispense with all those injections. And then your belly . . ."

"What's wrong with my belly?" said the Prince haughtily, mounting his high horse.

"The Princess thinks it too protuberant."

The little man snorted. "People of my rank cannot be expected to stand about in artificial postures dressed in a loin cloth, nor live on goat's milk. Who the hell do you think I am, Gandhi? And all this physical stuff, in my walk of life and at my age . . . it's preposterous. You have influenced a serious scientist with all this Indian mumbo-jumbo. And you, with a degree in economics and humanities!"

It was Affad's turn to pass into a vehemence. He drew a breath and said, "It is quite gratuitous and you are behaving like a Philistine, which you are not. I have already explained to you exactly what yoga is about in scientific terms. There is *nothing* in it that contradicts western science at any point. It is simply spine-culture intended to restore the original suppleness of the muscle schemes of the body and to feed them on oxygen with the help of the lungs. You treat the whole body as a key-board and muscle by muscle get it back into optimum condition, as supple as a snake or a cat, ideally. The *asanas* are breathing codes. They teach the muscles their role and finally the movements become sort of mental acts. The muscles are oxygen-filled and get to become almost mental acts when they move."

"Rigmarole!" said the Prince firmly. "Mere rigmarole!"

Affad produced a characteristic grunt of indignation. After all, he had not known in any detail the extent of Constance's preoccupation with these new lessons she had started taking – nor indeed did it much concern him, except that they were valuable: for he himself had followed courses in the science long ago and had profited from them. He had in fact cured a recurrent spinal complaint in a period of two years of methodical practice. "Mental acts!" he went on heatedly. "And once informed the muscle stays in trim eternally, or until decrepitude sets in, or illness. I fully approve of her investigations, for that is what they are. And philosophically speaking the whole process is one of progressive cosmic helplessness. It relinquishes its resistance to entropy, and the basic realisation which meditation brings is really n-dimensional. *You* could do with a bit of that yourself. After all your own sexual follies foisted on you by that *idiot* house-doctor of yours! Involving children and dogs and so on, just because you began to fear impotence and were scared to talk to the Princess about it."

This was beginning to be extremely unfair, and the Prince clenched his fists for all the world as if he were about to punch Affad in the eye. He inflated his lungs fully, as if about to launch into a tirade or utter a shout, but he did neither; he remained poised, as it were, for a long moment, and then burst into a prolonged chuckle. "You brute!" he said, and aimed a make-believe blow at Affad's abdomen. "What an unfair thing to say!" Affad shook his head: "*Au contraire*, a moment of yoga would have set your doubts at rest in the matter and avoided all sorts of compromising and ridiculous situations – for a man of your rank, I mean, since you keep bringing it up!"

The Prince reflected deeply, nodding as he thought. "It was a terrible period," he admitted, thinking back no doubt to the brothel in Avignon where he had once organised what he was wont to describe as a "little spree". The thought gave him cold shudders now. Thank goodness he had confided everything in the Princess and with her help recovered his balance, as well (to his surprised relief) as his virility. Now when he thought back upon that period he had cold shudders, for it was clear that if the Princess had left him it would have been not because of his sexual misdemeanours so much as his lack of confidence in her as a confidante. She was keen on her role as wife and helpmeet. He sighed. "Thank God all that is over." And now all of a sudden his evil humour deserted him and was replaced by an affectionate concern for his friend and for the reception he must get from the small committee in Alexandria who awaited the sinner's return. The executive arm of the fellowship was limited to three members who operated with a formal anonymity on behalf of the whole group; but as they were rotated with great regularity every year it was not possible to guess in detail at their composition. Thus the Prince, who would have loved to try and intervene on his friend's behalf, or to use his influence to secure some sort of favourable view of his crime – the word is not too strong – was checked by the fact that he did not know whether he had a personal friend among the three to whom he might appeal. . . . The very idea was of course immoral and unthinkable in the gnostic context, but then it was not for nothing that the Prince was a man of the Orient and impregnated with its labyrinthine strategies!

The night drew on and the thunder rumbled. Affad relinquished his solitaire for some sleepy general conversation before suggesting that they should go to bed and not wait for a summons from the airport which would never come because of the wind and pelting rain.

They shambled up to bed like sleepy bears, and were

woken at three o'clock with the intelligence that the plane was ready to leave within the hour, and would touch down at Alexandria—an unusual concession to the Prince's eminence and also to his wire-pulling which was, as always, inspired.

They dozed for the most part in the ill-lit plane and made their way slowly across the waters, tossing and swaying into Egypt where the inadequate aerodrome had been alerted to light them in along a flare path manifestly too short for any but small wartime planes. A bumping and grinding landing rounded off this disagreeable journey; a chalky greasy dawn was coming up as the office car rounded the last headland by the dunes and entered the sleeping town with its soft whirling klaxon pleading with strings of early camels plodding to market with vegetables. "I shall say no more—except tell me as soon as you can what they say," said the Prince and his companion nodded, smiling wanly. "It's impossible to foresee their judgement," he said, "because it has never happened before, an apostasy like mine. O Lord! It will have created a precedent." He sounded close to tears of misery, which indeed he was. The Prince left him—a dozen servants had been waiting all night on the steps of the town house, wet and miserable but faithful as dogs. They whipped open the door and conjured away his baggage. Affad was driven on; his more modest house was set in a grove of palm trees, back from the boulevard. His garden ran beside that of the museum, and indeed from his cellar there was a secret entrance into its basement. Sometimes after dinner he took his guests through the secret door and into the gloomy crypt where so many treasures (which could not be shown for lack of space) stood or lay, shrouded in sheets. Indeed the museum itself was most charming by yellow candle-light, and he used to carry a branch of Venetian candles with him on such occasions. But his own house was more modestly staffed than that of the Prince; a cook and a butler, the faithful and negligent Said, made up the whole staff.

As his key clicked in the door his valet Said rose from the armchair in which he had spent the night's vigil and advanced, rubbing his eyes but smiling delightedly to see his master again. Affad greeted him affectionately and stood steadily divesting himself until the servant carried away his coats and freed him to advance and make a loving tour of the home in which he had spent so many years of his life – many of them quite alone except for the servants. A clock gave off a soft musical chime as if to welcome him back. The statue of Pallas and the stuffed raven were still on the ledge above the fanlight. His books were arrayed on either side of the Adam fireplace – a fine array of friends. He advanced, touched the covers with his fingers as if to identify and greet the author of each, and then progressed towards the group of Tanagra figures in their glass case. He licked his finger and touched the glass to verify if Said had cleaned in his absence or not. But in reality he was searching for something. The servant came back with his mail – a meagre collection of bills for water and electricity, and appeals for hospitals and homes. No, it was not that. He knew that they must have summoned him to a rendezvous. Normally such a missive would have been slipped under the door. He questioned the servant, but no, he had seen nothing like that. He sat down for a moment and drank the coffee which had been prepared for him as he reflected. Finally in some perplexity – for he had expected an instant and peremptory message – he took himself off to his sumptuous bathroom for a bath and a complete change of clothing, not without a certain feeling of relief. Perhaps the whole business might be delayed for a while? On the other hand, he longed to have it over and done with as summarily as possible.

The weather had changed, it had become suddenly sunny and clear, though the cold sea wind persisted. He dressed carefully and taking a light overcoat walked slowly down the boulevard to the Mohammed Ali Club, greeted here and there by a friend or acquaintance who was pleased to see him back, resuming his Alexandrian life once more. It was on the notice board of the club that he found the missive he had been expecting, addressed to him in a hand he did not know and on a paper without letterhead. It said succinctly, "You will attend an exceptional meeting of the central committee at midnight tonight in the burial theatre of the museum crypt." Only that.

He knew what they must mean by the phrase "burial theatre"; it was the furthest part of the museum crypt and had been at some time part of a necropolis. But successive generations had altered it according to more recent motives until it clearly had served several purposes, with its small arch and portion of nave, and its little amphitheatre. It was a mixture of chapel, Greek theatre, and lecture hall admirably suited to the meetings of their society with its need for lectures or discussions of procedure or indeed prayer-meetings and the reading of minutes. It was called "The Crusaders' Chapel" and "The Coptic Shrine". In its further depths it contained some sculptured aeroliths and some drums of stone purporting to be Babylonian sculpture – a sort of map and calendar of the world supported by the coils of a huge serpent. How well he knew the place! It was here that new members were sworn in and their first act of submission heard. And how very appropriate that it should be an amalgam of so many different things, so suitable to a city which had made a cult of syncretism! It was here that he must answer for his defection. He must attend, then, in due form and order, to hear their reproaches and accept whatever punishment or obloquy was his due. He had not a leg to stand on. He wondered what sort of punishment could be envisaged for such a case.

Preoccupied by these grave deliberations and wounded by a sense of guilt, he ate a solitary lunch at the Union Club, where he found himself agreeably alone in the gaunt dining room. But appetite he had none. Then he walked back to his house and took a siesta – fell into a profound sleep which took in at one span all the various fatigues of the journey. Indeed it was already dark when he awoke with a start, summoned by the little alarm clock by his bed. There was time in hand – too much of it. He had begun to feel impatient. Some invisible hand (for there was no trace of Said) had prepared him a light supper such as he was in the habit of ordering when theatre-going kept him out late. He hardly touched it, but he drank a glass of champagne. It was mildly stimulating, mildly encouraging. Then he hunted for the black carnival domino, supposing that it was the appropriate thing for a penitent to wear. Indeed if the society had any formal uniform it was that, though it was worn as informally and carelessly as the fur tippet and cape of a master of arts. Nevertheless carnival time was their most important yearly meeting with its significant – *carni vale* – farewell to the flesh, as suitable for their Manichean creed as for the Christian.

Punctually at five minutes before the hour he visited the lavatory through the window of which he could study the profile of the museum which at this hour was normally deserted. Yes, there were lights on the staircase, so the three Inquisitors must have made their way in to wait for him down below. For his part he preferred his own private entry. He slipped downstairs and through the kitchen into the cavernous pantry where the private door answered noiselessly to his yale key. He had a pocket torch to light his path as he stepped into the gloom of the crypt. With beating heart he traversed the first cell, a sort of antechamber, and then the second, from which he could see a distant light and hear voices. Was he too soon?

No. The door to the theatre had been blocked by a drum of carved stone and when he arrived there a voice from within called his name and asked if it was indeed he, to which he replied in the required language, "None other". He rolled aside the stone and entered the theatre where they waited for him. He was to sit in the centre, he saw, under a floodlight of great theatrical force, while the three Inquisitors occupied three adjacent stone seats in the main hall, the main theatre. The lighting allowed them or perhaps devised by them was so arranged that all he could see was their hands upon the stone dais before them. They were but vague shapes, and with even vaguer voices. He strained at first to see if by chance one of them might be an acquaintance or personal friend. In vain.

So he entered circumspectly, rolling aside the stone drum, and bowing to the three pairs of white hands sat down and bent his head forward upon his breast in a formally penitential gesture of respect: not for the rank of the Inquisitors for they had no formal rank, having been elected by lottery, but for the organisation they represented with its beehive-like grouping of cells.

A voice intoned, "Sebastian, Thoma, Ptah, Affad Effendi?" and he replied in a whisper, "None other". And he felt himself reverting to his Alexandrian self, his Egyptian self. Each name was like the unfolding of a mummy-wrapping, in a way unbandaging his youth with all its fragility. He felt rise in him, like nausea, the long years of solitude and philosophic speculation which had gone to form the person that he now was, and an involuntary sob rose in his throat. He peered into the dark shapes of his three invigilators but could not discern anything except the vague outline of their heads. Only their ghoulish white hands lay before them on the stone tables which were bare save for a small Egyptian knife with its point turned towards him. Yet the voices, whether they addressed him or spoke together, were matter of fact. He studied the spatulate hands of the one who had spoken his name and felt the vague stirrings of familiarity. Could it be Faraj? Neguid? Perhaps Capodistria? Or Banubula? Impossible to be sure. He gave up.

"Do you know why you are here?"

"Yes."

"Tell us why."

Overwhelmed by the gravity of his fault as only a philosopher could be, Affad answered with a sob in his tone, "To answer for my sudden defection. To be punished, admonished, expelled, executed – whatever you may decide is suitable for this unheard of act of treachery. Even now I find it inexplicable to myself. I fell in *love*." The word fell like a slab of stone closing upon a tomb.

One of the Inquisitors drew in his breath with a sharp hiss, but Affad could not tell which one it was, nor why. He fell on his knees and stretching out his hand like a beggar soliciting alms said, "It seemed to me then that there are spirits of love sent into the world who, if recognised, cannot be resisted, *should* not be resisted at the risk of betraying nature herself. I found myself in this impasse. Hence my apostasy, which I have now fully revoked and abandoned."

There was a long silence. Then the first pair of hands to have spoken clasped themselves and the voice belonging to them continued to speak but in an unhurried and sorrowful manner. "You do not know all," it said. "But you know full well that the strength of a chain is the strength of its weakest link. You were prepared to snap the chain of our corporate activities, to prejudice the whole spiritual effort represented by our attempts to face the *primal trauma* of man, namely death, and all for the sake of a *woman*. So much we all know. But your letter in which you asked leave to forsake the movement, thus prejudicing every single member in it, welded as we all are by sacrificial suicide . . . this was unheard of and provoked a crisis of grave indecision bordering on despair. In the meantime your election had been decided upon by ballot – you are the next, *were* the *next* sacrificial exemplar of the death-confronting fraternity. Your telegram retracting this decision came after the ritual letter had been sent to you. You can imagine the dismay and confusion you have caused the brotherhood."

"But I have not received any letter," cried out Affad from the depths of his misery. "When was it sent? Where was it sent?"

"It had already been despatched when your own communication was received; there was confusion and delay. But the letter of sacrifice containing the details of your death-confrontation and the time allowed you to prepare . . . it was sent to Geneva where you were then, and, it was thought, likely to remain."

So the blow had fallen! He had, after so many years of patience, at last been elected. Extraordinary emotions assailed him now, discharging themselves in his heart so that he felt at one and the same time proud, sorrowful, and in an intermittent way wildly elated, as if the adventure for which he had longed for so long had begun. But then doubts intervened; would it be cancelled in the light of his apostasy? Suddenly deep gloom replaced the elevation of spirit at the very thought.

"I implore you to let me go through with it. Let my retraction be accepted, let me redeem my crime by the act of sacrificial fulfilment according to the vow I took." In the silence he could hear his own heart beating loudly, anxiously. What if this bitter cup should be taken from him, just because of a momentary weakening of his resolve? How remote the painful image of his love seemed at that moment of self-abasement, of cringing self-immolation! Seeing himself with her eyes he realised just how despicable he would have seemed to her could she see him now. And also how amazing, for under the veneer of sophistication and formal culture there now appeared the initial gnostic Manichee born of those long deliberations and fasts and mental exercises. Constance would have been afraid to see him almost grovelling before his Inquisitors, pleading with them to restore his death! What appalling fantasies men harbour – that is what she would think. But he brushed her from his mind like a fly; and now truly he

really wanted to die. The whole tide of his disenchantment with
the human race and their way of living rose in him and overflowed into a measureless pessimism. And love had made him
wish to turn his back upon reality and blinker himself with
transitory passion. To wake and sleep with her. To engender
a child – *a child!* What a trap he had prepared for himself. Still
with his beggar's gesture of the outstretched hand he cried
hoarsely, "I implore! I implore!" But in a paradoxical sort of
way he was also imploring Constance to forgive him, to release
him, to understand the full extent of his religious dilemma. The
voice went on: "It is the more painful as all three of us, sent
here to make a judgement on you, were originally converted to
the gnostic posture by your homilies and your formulations!"

That was the cruellest cut of all! His own converts had
become his judges – if that was the word. At any rate from his
own point of view the matter of the first importance was to
have his retraction accepted; then he must set about finding the
fatal letter. It must have been sent in the diplomatic pouch
reserved for Red Cross affairs and be somewhere between
offices in Geneva.

A long silence had fallen – the three dark figures seemed
to have fallen into a temporary inertia. Then the second one
said, "The judgement must be debated and voted upon. Other
consultations must follow. This cannot be achieved before
tomorrow at midday. The result will be communicated to you
by Prince Hamid. You should go now and wait upon the judgement which will be neither merciful nor indulgent but just and
logical."

The posture had cramped his legs and he rose stiffly to a
standing position and unsteadily bowed his thanks to the
invisible group. Three pairs of hands briefly rose in farewell
and as briefly subsided upon the stone. He groped his way to
the door and switched on his pocket torch to light him back
through the crypt. Behind him he heard the low murmur of

their confabulation begin. What would the upshot of it all be?
Surely they must accept his sacrifice as foreseen long ago – the
year when three and then five, fellow believers went calmly
into infinity armed with the hope, indeed the belief, that their
sacrifice turned back the tide of dissolution and offered a pattern
of hope to the beleaguered world?

He climbed back into his house, mounting the stairs in
dazed exhaustion. He was violently sick. A clock struck three –
it was very late. Soon dawn would be breaking. His quiet bedroom . . . the bed had been turned down. Could he sleep, he
wondered? Could he sleep, with such great affairs impending?
To make sure of the matter he prepared a strong dose of a
sleeping draught and with its aid sunk into sleep as if into a
cavern; and here came the dreams of the forgotten Constance,
memories of their love in all its unexpected variety and tenderness. Everything that he had simply abolished when talking to
his judges returned like a tide and swallowed up his emotions.
When he awoke it was already past eleven. There were tears on
his face, on his cheeks; he indignantly washed them away in
the shower, glorying in the swishing water. Then he put on
his old rough *abba* instead of the habitual silken dressing-gown
and went downstairs to the great glassed-in central hall where
the brilliant whiteness of daylight caressed his small but choice
collection of statues and the tropical plants which framed the
further end leading into the garden. A fountain played – he
had always loved the sound of water indoors. There was even
a group of brilliant fish. Pastilles of incense burned in the wall
niches. He sat himself down at the recently laid table and
poured out some coffee. In a little while the Prince would
telephone and tell him the verdict of the three, the 'executive
cell'. Quietly, as he sat there and listened to the water running,
he went back in memory to the remote past when first these
gnostic notions had begun to germinate in his mind. Step by
step he had been led backwards in chronological time, negation

by negation, until he had come up against the hard integument of Greek thought – a strange and original manifestation of the human spirit. It had assimilated and modified and perhaps even betrayed these successive waves of esoteric knowledge which, like a tropical fruit, were the harvest of Indian thought, of Chinese thought, of Tibetan thought. He saw these dark waves of culture pouring into Persia, into Iran, and into Egypt, where they were churned and manipulated into linguistic forms which made them comprehensible to the inhabitants of the Middle Eastern lands.

Greece was the sieve, with its worship of light and its unbending propensity for logic and causation. The Greek philosophers, one by one, took over the world-pictures of different peoples and wove them up into self-consistent philosophical systems. Pythagoras took up the Chinese world-system, Heraclitus the Persian, Xenophanes and the Eliatics the Indian, Empedocles the Egyptian, Anaxagoras the Israelite. And finally, in a mind-crushing attempt at synthesis Plato tried to bring together all these foreign influences and harmonise them into a truly Hellenic world-view both spiritual and social, both scientific and vatic . . .

These ideas and memories excited him so much that he got up and walked up and down the hall with his hands behind his back, reliving the thrilling agony he had felt while he first formulated them for himself under the tutorship of old Faraj the philosopher. Yes, but before Plato even, came the wise Mani and his disciple Bardesanes – they were the hinge between the Orient and the Occident. He clasped his hands and felt anew the thrill of his first affirmation of allegiance to the 'pentad' and the 'triad'; in poetic terms these were the five senses and the three orifices. But in fact for the Buddhist psychology it spelt the five *skandas*, bundles of apprehension, reservoirs of impulse! He remembered so well the impressive way Faraj had said, "My son, the Manichean Prince of Darkness combines the forms of five elemental demons: smoke (δαιμον), lion (fire), eagle (wind), fish (water), darkness (δράκων). In Greece his prophet is Pherecyrdes. . . . Out of this mixture of studies and fasts and meditations the Thing had grown and grown until one day a man unknown to him had knocked at the door and gained entry. He was old and dressed like some Coptic tramp, but of great presence. He said simply, "My son, have you considered death, the primal trauma of man?" And Affad had nodded, for the person and the question seemed familiar, as if he had waited a century for this event to occur; and beckoned him to a seat. So the adventure had begun – death as an adventure!

They could not deprive him of his right at this stage. He had earned it by those long solitary years which had so puzzled his fellow-citizens that they had hatched the most extravagant rumours about him, just to account for the fact that he lived alone and had no attachments; the life of a seminarist or monk. They said that he must be a secret homosexual, or impotent, or bewitched, or had taken a vow with a view to entering holy orders! And all to explain why in a city of debauch and casual venery he kept himself apart, though he lived a full enough social and business life. Now he went slowly round his possessions saying goodbye to them one by one, just as a rehearsal, to see how much he was attached to them and how much it would hurt to leave them. He still gloated over them – the obsidian head of a Roman cup-bearer, two cloud puffed *putti*, the skull of a woman covered in gold leaf from a desert tomb. No, but the cord was cut in the most profound sense of the word. He was no longer owned by them. His feelings were sharper when they consulted smaller, more trivial things. On his dressing-table the latch-key Lily had given him, his first toy soldier, a grenadier with no head. One drawer was full of a jumble of small items incomprehensible to any but himself; a dance-book from carnival with his own name filling up every space, written in the hand of Lily. ("I don't want anyone to put their arms round you.") Yes, at times his celibacy had become a fearful burden, specially in springtime when the first dry desert winds struck the capital; it was agony not to have a girl in one's arms, in one's bed. Sometimes in an agony of loneliness he walked down to the dark Corniche to watch the moon rising on the sea. In the darkness they called to one another, the lovers, with names like Gaby, Yvette, Yolande, Marie and Laure. How they ached, the names!

One night he passed a girl alone, standing quite still, looking at the sea, and actually brought himself to speak to her. "Are you alone, Mademoiselle?" She gazed at him for a long moment, as if sizing him up, and then replied in soft, disenchanted tones, "Too much for my liking". They walked quite unhurriedly the length of the Corniche, talking like old friends, and when they reached the outskirts of the town again he asked her to come back to his house with him, for he did not wish to spend another night alone. She hesitated for a moment and then quietly agreed. Together they walked back. When she saw the relative luxury of his home she said, "You must be very rich, then." He replied, "Well, I am a banker by profession." But her reaction was one of relative indifference. She was a gentle, rather passive girl, pleasant-looking rather than pretty, but not vulgar. They had at first spoken Greek, but now it was French. Her name was Melissa, she said, and by now she had warmed to his gentleness and lack of brashness.

The rest seemed to follow naturally and he enjoyed the immense luxury not only of lovemaking but also of sleeping and drowsing beside this gentle and composed and somewhat melancholy woman, who was not a *fille de joie* in the professional sense but something more like a *grisette*. They warmed to each other though neither made any effort to arrange a further meeting. She did not, perhaps, think it was her place to do so. He wanted to write her a cheque, having no cash on him, but she would not take it. "I am with an old Jew who is jealous and goes through my bag. And I couldn't cash it until Monday. Give me two or three of your cigars, the Juliets, he likes cigars. I could say I stole them or bought them." But this did not seem to him adequate. "Melissa, give me your address and I will send you a money order by post." But she did not want to do so. When first they reached the house they had talked and joked, and when he asked if she had never been married she had laughed and slipped the paper ring from his Juliet on to her ring finger and held it up, turning it this way and that as if it had been a real ring with a precious stone in it! "Alas, my family is penniless, I have no dowry." But she did not sound preternaturally sad about it.

In the morning, when she departed with the three cigars for her lover, he found that she had left beside the bathroom wash-basin where she had performed her toilette the paper ring, and beside it the world's oldest contraceptive device, namely a pessary carved out of a small slip of fine sponge and impregnated with olive oil. It was washed now and dry, and as he thought of it, the history of it which stretched back into the remotest corners of Mediterranean mythic lore, he picked it up and together with the ring slipped them both into the drawer of his dressing-table among the other souvenirs of youth. This was now among the objects to which he was saying adieu, and for a brief second he wondered what had happened to the girl, for he had never seen her again after the night spent together. The objects themselves might have come from some Stone Age grave so remote did they seem: yet they had poignance.

These reveries were interrupted by the chirping of the telephone. He awoke as if from a trance and made his way across the hall to hear the voice of the Prince at the other end of the wire – full of relief and suppressed sadness. He said, "They have just rung me up with the result of the whole enquiry. Your retraction has been accepted and your rights have been restored to you . . ." He paused for a long moment, awaiting who knows what reaction from his friend. But Affad stayed stock-still with the receiver to his ear, drinking in the news and still saying not a word. He was like someone who learns that he has won a great lottery, speechless and uncomprehending. For the first time he realised the enormous attraction of death, and the secret lust for it which animates human beings. Fear and lust. In the distant recesses of memory he heard the voice of Constance saying (as she did one day when they were discussing the matter), "But it may be that you are deeply schizoid without knowing it or feeling it!" It had made him laugh at the time, for what could such formulations possibly mean in the context of a reality such as the one he was embracing?

"How marvellous," he said in a low voice, cherishing this sense of voluptuous completeness. The Prince went on, "The letter had already been sent to you when they received your abdication, hence the confusion. Now it is in order again."

"But I received no letter," said Affad.

"It must be in Geneva waiting for you. I think they sent it to the Red Cross pouch – you know all the problems we face today. First the British, that meddlesome fool Brigadier Maskelyne is always prying for British Intelligence, and then the Egyptian police are convinced that we are a subversive political movement . . . So care must be taken. But the letter has been written and the details worked out."

"They did not tell you any details? How long have I got, for example, and where must I expect the last scene to take place?"

"No, they told me nothing. I suppose in Geneva itself, though I don't know when. I have sent an urgent signal to try and trace the letter. It must be in your tray in Geneva but we might as well make sure."

"Who wrote it? Who would know? I would like to know

whether I must say goodbye here and return there or whether I have some months ahead of me."

"Only the letter can tell you that."

"Can't you ask the committee?"

"My dear, I don't know who they are. I was told the little I know by a voice, an anonymous voice. It was someone I did not know, so how could I ask someone? Who?"

"I see." It was very vexatious not to be in full possession of the details; it was like planning a long voyage and not being in possession of the tickets.

"I foresaw your puzzlement," said the Prince, "and I tried to find out myself by telephoning to Samsoun. He was not sure but thought that you would be expected to be present in Geneva for the next few months. And things are more conveniently arranged abroad, as you know. I should act on that assumption until we find the blasted letter and can be sure. Say goodbye to Alexandria leaving you!" It was grim to quote the famous poem at this moment, but the Prince was overwhelmed with sadness at the prospect of losing an irreplaceable friend, and nervous excitement makes one do tactless things. "Yes," said Affad slowly, "I think you are right. I shall do just that, and in my own time. How strange it will feel! See you later in the day." He rang off and went to dress. Then he walked down into the town at his usual leisurely pace, first to drop into the Bourse and renew old acquaintances in their offices, then to study the fluctuations of the market. Everyone was so glad to see him back that for a while he almost forgot the valedictory nature of these visits. People thought that he had come back after a long stay abroad to resume the old life of the banking community of the city. He went to the club to read the newspapers, or such of them as were still alive after the war. There was a Rotary meeting going on upstairs and he made a surprise visit to it, to join in its deliberations and greet other older associates.

That evening he changed into a habitual dinner jacket and joined the Prince's dinner party at the Auberge Bleu to keep up his reputation for pleasant affability: and as he was a good dancer, his reputation as a tolerable ladies' man. Once or twice he caught the Prince staring at him with a sort of hungry, affectionate curiosity, as if he were trying to evaluate his friend's feelings, but Affad had never been demonstrative, his expressions were not easy to decipher. But during a brief exchange he said, "Tomorrow night I am going out to Wady Natrun to see Lily for the last time; may I tell her that she can count on you in the future if she needs help?" The reproachful glance of the Prince told him that his question need not have been asked.

"Will she see you?" he asked.

"I do not know. I will try."

Lily was another preoccupation. Somebody had once asked him at a party, "Who is that girl you were talking to? *The girl with the tears in her voice?*" It expressed the sense of poignant rapture of her tone, a voice swerving like some brilliant bird from register to register. What had become of her soul, her mind, now that her body no longer counted for her – sleeping in some wattle hut in the middle of the desert with only the hideous summer sun for company? He sighed as he thought of the desert. It too was an abstraction like the idea of death – until the life of the oasis made it a brutal reality. Yet what terrible longings the desert bred in its addicts! "Yes, surely she will see me," he told himself under his breath. He said goodnight to his hosts and walked down to the seafront for a breath of air before facing the night. The sea was rough, but playfully so, resounding to a rogue wind from the islands. It dashed itself on the rocks below the Corniche. Few people were about, but here and there was a group of friends returning on foot from some party or other. Once he heard the soft strains of a guitar vibrating in the distance. The museum slumbered in darkness with all its trophies – did the statues manage to doze for a moment during the Alexandrian night? The light in the hall had been left on by the thoughtful Said; he found his way to the kitchen for a late cup of tea which he took up to bed with him; he would have liked to read, but his eyelids felt heavy and as he did not want to lose this valuable predisposition he did nothing but just lay there drinking his tea and watching the shadows on the ceiling and thinking of Constance. What would she be doing at this hour? he wondered.

Soon they would come to the end of the road and she would have to find a new path through the future. It weighed in him, the sadness, but there was also mixed with the emotion a sense of relief and fulfilment. He slid softly, as if down a sand dune, into a harmless, dreamless sleep.

The next evening he took the desert road and drove in the cool of the day along the narrow tarmac road which united the two capitals, Cairo and Alexandria. The heat haze had subsided, the sky was clear with the promise of a ghostly moon to light his return. His anxiety as to whether Lily would see him or not had sharpened today, for he had begun to have new doubts. Night was coming – he could feel the evening damps rising to his cheeks as the open car traversed the dunes towards the distant green splash which marked the site of the oasis. He would perhaps arrive before the great portals were closed upon the darkness, perhaps not. It did not matter, he could always knock, he told himself.

The monastery gradually rose up out of the sand with its curiously barbaric atmosphere – as if it stood somewhere much more remote, perhaps on the steppes of Middle Asia? The cluster of beehive buildings were glued together in a vast complex of brownish stone: pumice and plaster and whatnot, and the colour of wattle smeared with clay. This light, friable type of material offered excellent insulation against both desert heat and also the cold of the darkness during the winter.

The palm groves stood there, silently welcoming, with their weird hieratic forms, benignly awkward. But the great doors had been shut and he was forced to lift the heavy knocker and dash it upon the booming wood once or twice and to swing upon the thick bellrope which set up a remote interior jangling in the distant recesses of the place. At last a monk opened and interrogated him, and having given the name of Yanna correctly he was allowed to send him a message and to take a chair in the waiting-room with its dense smell of candlewax and incense.

The principal Coptic father of the monastery had been once a banker, but for many years now had retired to this life of silence and contemplation, though he ruled the place with an iron hand and vaunted the efficiency of its activities. He was completely bald and had a heavy, Chinese-looking countenance which contained, deeply embedded, two eyes of penetration and pertness, always twinkling on the edge of laughter. Affad greeted him with affectionate familiarity and explained that he had come on the offchance of an interview with Lily as he was planning to go on a long journey and wished to see her before he went away: also to give her up-to-date news of the child . . . Yanna debated and sighed as he did so, shaking his brown dome of a head doubtfully. He said, "Nobody has seen her for ages now; food is left and the dish is emptied and put back outside her hut, so we know she is alive, that is all. But she was in a bad way, a significant way. She once wrote me a message saying, 'I have begun to see colours with my mouth and hear sounds with my eyes, everything is confused. If I take a pencil in hand I make letters a foot high. I must retire and cure myself again.'" They gazed at one another, reflecting. "The best would be just to go and try. She can only refuse, you can only go away after all." He crossed the room to the wall upon which there was a large framed picture of the oasis with the grouping of the buildings clearly marked, thinning away into the desert where there were the cells, mere wattle shelters which housed those who had chosen to live as solitary anchorites. There were also a few lean-to shelters for sheep against the desert winds. He placed his finger on one of the star-shaped huts and said, "There! I will give you the monk Hamid who takes food, he will show you the way; but my friend, if she is unwilling don't insist, I implore you!" Affad looked reproachfully at his friend and said, "Of course not—why do you say that?"

"I'm sorry. It was out of place. I apologise."

The old monk who was the night-janitor of the monastery now appeared bearing in his hand a dark-lantern and a wattle basket with some fruit and a bowl of rice. He bowed and grunted his assent when he had received the orders and, turning, led the way across the complex of silent buildings and thence through a large lemon grove which, like an outpost, opened directly on to desert dunes with here and there a fringe of palms.

It was quite a stumble across the sands and Affad could not help noticing with admiration the curious ease of movement of his companion: his walk was a sort of glide across the difficult terrain. The lantern with its single candle seemed on the point of going out all the time; but a frail horn of moon was rising through the dense fur of the night mists. So they came at last to one of the remotest cells beyond which lay nothing—just the uncompromising sea of sand curling and flowing away into the empty sky. In such a place the sight of a stone or of a distant bird of prey would stand out from the whole of nature like a sun-spot. He shivered with a pleasurable distaste as he thought of life here, how it must be; to be alone with one's thoughts here, and *nothing else to distract you away from thinking them.* The old man grunted, put down the lantern some way from the wooden door and gave a strange hoarse cry, as if to some domestic animal: a sort of "Hah!" or "Hey!"

For a while there was no response and then they heard a

shuffling noise, as of a broom sweeping up dead leaves, or of someone rustling old parchment, old newspapers. But no voice. The janitor advanced to the door, and after placing his ear to it, drew back and said hoarsely, "Someone is here to see you." At the same moment he beckoned Affad to come and stand beside him, and by the same token, to make himself known. Affad did not know what to say, everything had flown out of his mind. He said at last, "Lily! Listen! It is I."

There was a further rustling sort of commotion and then the door opened violently and a gaunt, ragged figure appeared, shielding its face from the dim light and chattering with excitement like a sort of huge monkey. He cried out her name again and the chattering subsided a little while her voice – such as it was, for the sound was as disembodied as if it came from some kind of instrument – called to the old janitor, "Go and leave me!" And the old man, taking up his lantern with a submissive reverence, glided away into the surrounding night. Now the light was indeed dim, yet he did not dare to reach for the little electric torch he always carried in his pocket. She was like some rare bird which might be disturbed by the light, might disappear in a panic. How did she look now, after all this time? He could not guess.

It was as if she had lip-read his mind for she said slowly, "I wonder how we look now, after all this time?" They stood listening to each other's breathing, just their antennae touching, so to speak. Then he said, "I have a light, if you wish to see." Actually he wished to see her, to evaluate how she was, from her eyes. Silence again. "Shall I show you?" She said nothing but just stood, so he slowly reached back into his pocket for the little torch which always aided him plant his latchkey correctly. He held it above his head like a douche and switched it on so that the light flowed down over his countenance; at the same time raising his head. She gasped. "It does not look like you at all," she said. "Not at all."

He was dismayed and a little astonished because it seemed that she was talking about someone else, to somebody else. He had the sudden impression that he was now impersonating somebody he did not know, had not met. "What is your name?" she asked, with a touch of peremptory sternness, increasing his discomfort, his sense of being there under false pretences. "Surely you know," he said. "Surely, Lily!"

She burst into tears, but very briefly; after a single cry the current was switched off, so to speak, and she knuckled her eyes free and said humbly, "I have forgotten. Not speaking for long, my memory has gone." Her wild look of sadness was replaced by one of savage expectation. She took his wrists and shook them softly. "Shall I guess?" she said slowly. He nodded. "Yes, Lily, guess." She bowed her head on her breast in deep contemplation. Then she gave a small snort and said, "It is like a gigantic crossword puzzle, only instead of words just sounds to be filled in and colours!" She was speaking of reality, he quite understood. It made him feel helpless and morbidly sad. "O God, why can't you remember? Can't you remember when you dropped the basket and all the eggs were broken – *every last one?*" She gave a cry of amazement, youthful and lyrical, her face cast up to the sky as she pronounced the word, the elusive word: "*Sebastian!* At last I have got it. O my darling! How could I?" And now she was really crying and in his arms, her fragility made all the more striking by the tension, the electric current flowing through her body like wind through the foliage of a tree. He held her humbly and with pity and a wild desire to make amends to her for the short-comings of the world which had allotted her only half a human mind, but not (cruelly) withdrawn the capacity to love! He groaned in the inside of his own mind, groaned. It was stupid, he knew. One always feels that one should be able to cure the whole world. That one is to blame for everything, every iniquity. It was a form of false pride, he supposed.

He felt that what was needed at that moment was to give her confidence, and so with a kind of necessary innocence he sat down on the ground before the hut, pocketing his torch. And after a moment of indecision so did she. So they sat in the dust facing each other, like Arab children. Now her breathing had become less laboured, and her fingers had ceased to tremble, so he felt that he could embark upon a recital of his adventures since last they had met. Nor did he omit anything, speaking about his attachment to Constance with a kind of puzzled sincerity which seemed to her very moving, for she stifled a sob and put two fingers sympathetically upon his wrist. He told her that Constance was to try and evaluate the position of their son in medical terms and decide upon what treatment, if any, was best for the case. But even as he spoke she shook her head softly from side to side as if she had already made up her own mind about the matter, and that it did not offer much hope.

And then about himself. "I have received my own orders as well; you know that for some time I was quite expecting them – well, now the die is cast, though for the moment I haven't got the actual details. But this will be our last meeting, of that I am sure. So I must thank you for everything, and for having put up with my shortcomings as you did. It was not your fault that things turned out the way they did." O dear! It was the truth and yet it sounded terribly prosy when put into words; and why the devil did he have this sense of contrition? Had it been his fault? Lily was like a butterfly born with only one wing – otherwise perfect in every way. The fatal handicap stood in the way of fulfilment – or perhaps simply changed its prerogatives. She would sit there in darkness now, perhaps for life after life, gazing at a hole in space throughout the full length and breadth of time. He could see her whole future of darkness in his mind's eye – as if she stood on the bridge of a liner; the night was a liner, slowly travelling through absolute darkness towards an undisclosed goal somewhere in the darkness ahead. "Well," she said humbly at last, "So you must go at last. We must all go." And she gave a sigh full of world weariness and passed into a kind of compassionate silence, still touching his wrist with her fingers. After a long time he stirred and rose, and they embraced and stood latched one to the other in a final decisive gesture. Kissed also. It was like kissing the face of a rag doll. Then he left her.

He drove himself back across the desert in a state of dejection and exhaustion, glad of the car's tinny radio which accompanied his thoughts with the monotonous ululations of Arabic music unwinding its quartertone spools forever upon the moonlit night. His headlights put up startled desert creatures – were they hares? They fled so fast into the surrounding darkness that he could not say for sure. And then at last the dispiriting city of chromium lusts and avarice and boredom! How well the music illustrated its suffocating monotony, its limitations of growth, squeezed between two deserts! He would be glad to get away again. Abruptly he snapped off the radio and allowed the swishing desert silence to fill the hull of his car. It was late. He was exhausted by so much fervent thought. The house was dark except for the hall light. He felt suddenly sad and mateless. He lay down on his bed fully dressed and went to sleep at once, only to be woken by the discreet knock of Said as he came in bearing a cup of early morning tea. He drank it with relief and treated himself to a long hot shower before going downstairs to where his breakfast awaited him beside the small lilypond with its whispering water.

At ten the phone rang and a somewhat irascible Prince asked him where the devil he had been, "because I was trying to reach you last evening and there was no reply". Affad explained; but he was intrigued by the note of concern, almost of alarm, in the Prince's voice as he went on, "I spend almost the whole day on the phone to Geneva – you will imagine the difficulties, the bad lines and so on—in the hope of finding out about your famous letter. It was delivered to your office, and thence taken by Cade to the clinic, thinking you were with Aubrey, but you had gone. Now comes the funny part: Aubrey gave it to Constance, thinking that she would certainly be seeing you. But apparently she did not, or forgot it. At any rate she seems to have it, but after a series of calls to her consulting rooms I managed to get Schwarz who tells me that she has gone on leave of absence, to have a rest. Of the letter he knows nothing. It's to be presumed that she still has it?" Affad was puzzled by the tone of the Prince for it conveyed a notion of alarm, which did not seem to match the rather commonplace facts of the case. After all, a letter had gone astray, but was not lost. He said, "You sound sort of strange."

"I am a little put out," admitted the Prince, "and I will tell you why. When I managed to get through to Aubrey and he said that he had handed it to her he said that she had been angry and depressed, and said that she had half a mind to put it into the fire or tear it up unread. You see, she disapproves very strongly in ... well, in *us*, all we stand for. I wish to hell he had not been so indiscreet. But you see that if she were to do anything impulsive like that it would constitute a sort of technical miscarriage vis-à-vis the central committee. I could not foresee the reaction, but once more you would come under fire." Affad groaned and agreed. "I would have liked to tell Constance direct that any attempt to interfere with the course of ... well, justice, historical justice, in a sense, might put you in a gravely prejudicial position ... But now she has gone away somewhere and we don't know for how long. I have left a message with her colleague Schwarz, but he is a pretty vague fellow like all analysts. Anyway I can do no more."

"Thank you, anyway," said Affad. "I see no undue cause for worry. But of course once a woman disturbs a sequence of events by a rash act ..."

"Exactly," said the Prince. "It always makes me nervous when a woman intervenes. Things usually get into a tangle. At any rate, for the moment there is no undue cause for our fears. Have you made any plans yourself?"

"I haven't yet said goodbye in Cairo so I plan to spend a few days there this week. Back Saturday."

THREE

Inner Worlds

A S FOR CONSTANCE, SHE HAD AT LAST TAKEN THE ADVICE of Schwarz and left for the little lake house which they used for weekends of leave. It lay in a sunken garden and was built over a boat-house containing the precious motorboat of Schwarz, which he had christened *Freud*. There was also a tiny skiff which they used when they wished to sunbathe on the lake or to visit the local *auberge* for lunch or dinner. It was a delectable corner and there was no telephone – a fact which set off its quality of seclusion and quiet. As ideal for work as for rest, then.

But in her present disturbed mood it would have been hard to think of rest, so she had done what she had so often done before, namely taken her work with her in the form of the medical dossier which the central clinic had built up out of their investigations of Affad's son; a document which depressingly reflected the objective medical view of the child as "a case". It lay before her on the rough deal table together with her typewriter and a cluster of pencils and notebooks. She shrank from it somehow, for she could foresee its dispiriting evaluations of human misery, and the inflated vocabulary which could hardly disguise the almost total ignorance in which their science lay shrouded. Nevertheless. One must begin somewhere, one must make an effort to understand, the hunt for exact observation was their only *raison d'être*. She could hear the cautious voice of Schwarz cutting into her thoughts to warn her, "Yes, but method, while desirable, must remain an art and not dwindle into a barren theology – the sort of superstition upon which dead universities exist!"

Okay. Okay. *Symbiotic child psychosis with marked*

autistic traits. As she read the portrait of the small staring face in the sailor hat, fervent in its withdrawn impavidness, gazed out upon her from the slowly gliding limousine. It was of course the face of Affad in miniature that she watched.

> The child was referred by a hospital where he had been kept under observation for three weeks of tests at the request of his father and the child's grandmother; the mother, who had a long record of psychic upheavals punctuated by ordinary periods during which she resumed her responsibilities, exhibiting a normal but hypertense relationship to the family circle when she was at home. But during periods of collapse or stress she herself returned to her home in Egypt and had herself committed as a voluntary patient for rest and treatment. The evolution of the boy's childhood seems to have been normal and regular, but after the mother's first disappearance for long from the scene during his sixth year, he fell ill with a fever which resisted accurate diagnosis, but which kept him in bed for several months during which the present traits slowly evolved. The behaviour pattern was sufficiently striking to prompt parental anxiety and the father sought medical aid. The case was referred to my care and a fairly detailed and intensive period of observation and evaluation followed, during which I saw the child for several hours a day. His grandmother was permitted to stay in the hospital with him, though he himself exhibited neither alarm nor curiosity and stayed sunk in the apathy of his condition.

The report had been written by an old friend and fellow-student of Constance, a wise and experienced neurologist not lacking in insight and affection, with children of her own; and it was extremely detailed, though as always with such a subject, consistently tentative. She heard Schwarz again: "Despite such a river of verbiage we know damn all about the human condition either in health or in sickness. Yet we must slog along." Slog was the word! Constance made herself some tea and returned to the thoughtful and painstaking document of her friend.

The standard preliminary tests showed no trace of anything pathological. There seemed to be no history of lues or any other family illness in the background. Cerebral computer tomography registered normal states.

Up till the time of his illness which could have been touched off by the crisis of his mother's departure, his development had been somewhat retarded as to speech and the making of sounds; but not sufficiently marked to warrant real anxiety – some children are slow to learn to speak. But from the illness onwards his autistic behaviour grew so marked as to prompt a question as to whether he were not actually deaf and not responsive to sound-signals. Yet this did not seem to be the case for at some loud noises he turned the head, but very slowly, and his look was blank and incurious. Sometimes he stood quite still with eyes narrowed as if he were listening to some inner noise, though his reactions remained expressionless and stony. He submitted to caresses with equal indifference, and if a human face approached his would look away or look through it into some imaginary place, as if something or someone were waiting for him there. His great physical beauty makes it easy to be fanciful about him. But he was like a mechanism which proves defective, had stuck definitively at a certain stage in the building. With both eye-contact and physical contact lost one became somewhat hesitant about an explicit diagnosis of the case. I myself alternated between notions of cerebral damage, pure autism, shock and hyperkinetic syndrome: since whenever he did move the procedure was almost ataxic in its lack of coordination, though always violent and directed towards some inanimate object around him, into which he often sank his teeth before dropping it and then standing still, to stare at a wall or door with total expressionlessness. He did not behave destructively with his hands, tearing things apart, but simply sank his teeth into them, and then dropped them.

His grandmother with whom he lived was herself a somewhat dramatic old lady, and seemed disposed to help, but owing to her defective French and Italian did not seem able to provide much understanding which might be of medical aid to a would-be physician. The boy was named Affad after his father, a businessman who came frequently to see him but lived in semi-permanence in Egypt and did not reside in Geneva. The old lady lived in great luxury in her own lakehouse with several servants, a large private limousine as well as an expensive motorboat for outings, on which the little boy always accompanied her after being carefully dressed for the occasion in true Levantine style. The family came originally from Alexandria in Egypt.

In these circumstances the child lived a strange non-life, or a life of total non-cooperation despite the presence of kindly servants. His vast playroom was full of toys which he ignored, even the musical ones, like the toy piano and drum and xylophone which would normally tempt a child. Of course with both father and mother absent there was a lack of family atmosphere about his life, but many children suffer such conditions without becoming ill. This could be a subsidiary reason but did not seem to be central. Nor could his father offer any clues; he was a somewhat effete and withdrawn figure, fashionably and even elegantly dressed, but overcame the first impression of insipidity and proved extremely articulate, though of course completely in the dark as to the child. His own medical history offered none either, and he seemed depressed and concerned about this highly intractable condition which had, as he put it, rendered his child as silent as a mummy. I obtained his active agreement to venture upon a series of tentative visits to the child with a view to trying to penetrate this mask of impassivity, or at least come to a definite conclusion as to the causes. I spent over an hour in his presence about three times a week, just to observe his habits, however passive they might be. He was taken out on the lake sometimes in the big motorlaunch, dressed up and clean. He liked to sit and trail one hand in the water, though without any evident pleasure. The other excursion was in the limousine which went slowly along the lakeside for an hour or so. He sat looking at the passers-by and the houses, but saying nothing, impassive.

He does not refuse food but he has still to be fed, although old enough to feed himself; nor does he show any preference as to dishes. He goes through the actions of eating with indifference. He sleeps restlessly and sometimes groans in his sleep or whimpers and has been known to suck his sheet—but this is a fairly normal suckling hangover like thumb-sucking; one is tempted to think that it would be too easy to assume his condition to be the result of shock at his mother's departure. I would say rather that the shock touched off a more deeply based anxiety historically situated in the remoter past, and was concerned with his suckling problems. I suspected that the mother might have been guilty of depriving the child of its milk either from distaste for the whole business, like so many mothers; or simply had broken off the suckling period in favour of the bottle at too early a stage. Of course this is a traditional view after Klein, yet it is rather puzzling that he showed no disturbances over eating now, that his whole condition seemed to be independent of a food problem.

Here the dossier came to an end and there followed some notes in the hand of Schwarz which began:

By ill luck this unsatisfactory preliminary sketch could not be amplified as the therapist was forced to return to Canada on duty and owing to staff shortages we could not allocate another for many months, so that the situation was allowed to drift and at the time of writing has not markedly changed. All the elements described here remain constant, and the life led by the child maintains its steady rhythm. I think it desirable that we try and penetrate a little further into the obscurity of his condition. There are a number of things which have not been tried; for example a pet, say a kitten. It is hard to resist a kitten playing with wool or a rolling ping-pong ball. Harder to resist the advances of a puppy. Then, what effect if any have images? Images projected on the nursery wall could be tried, just to see whether they raise the tone of his response. What about music while he sleeps . . .? I throw out these suggestions at random. I think, however, that since you have gone as far as to promise your friend a consultation you should perhaps take the place of the therapist and continue the portrait of this (in my own view, looking in from the outside) classical autism!

The dossier was marked in her name and with the classification numeral of her post-office box. What should be done, she wondered, that had not already been done by her more experienced colleague?

Wind rose off the lake and whirled the shutters closed;
she set them to rights and after checking the moorings of the
skiff set about cooking her frugal dinner in the cosy kitchen
with its wooden walls and waterscape. The moralist in her
frowned a little at herself, at her eagerness to come to the rescue
of the child, for she felt her intention to be not quite pure, not
quite disinterested. After all, had it not been the child of Affad
... what would she have done? Most likely deserted it in favour
of more interesting cases? Perhaps. "You are still showing
your vulnerability," she told herself, and with the thought a
wave of hatred swept over her – hatred for Affad and the
appalling game of cat's cradle he was playing with her attachment. Damn him! And damn that collection of dismal death-
worshippers projecting their infantile death-wish out of a
ruined Egypt! "I thought the Germans were infantile enough,"
she said to herself, "and that the Mediterranean races were
older and wiser ... what a fool! How naive can you be?"

All this self-recrimination did not however help her to
come to a decision about her clinical role in the affair of the
child. She would sleep on it and decide in the morning whether
to go through with it or simply to pass it to some other
therapist. There were several skilful and devoted people she
could think of who were quite as capable as she was, and would
be glad to round off the portrait of the robot-child. It cost her a
pang to think this, however, and she slept badly, dreaming of
him with a fervent sadness.

In the morning she woke and at once recalled the description of Affad as a "somewhat effete and withdrawn figure".
This annoyed her, though the feeling was, she knew, utterly
irrational. But her own new appearance was pleasing, it was
part of the attempt to rehabilitate herself in her own eyes, to
rise phoenix-wise from the ashes of this destructive and barren
attachment. She had bought the fur coat and some handsome
winter gear, she had changed her perfume and she had allowed

her hairdresser to alter the style of her hair and wave it differently. It really became her very well – and here there was nobody to see it, to admire it! "Serve you right," she said vindictively to the shade of the departed "effete and withdrawn" one. But she had not been able to resist dropping into the office to seek the approval of her colleague. His reaction was most stimulating. "God! Constance, you look ten years younger and just fallen in love again – how I wish *that* were true!"

In a way, so did she. But the business of sick-leave had been settled and underneath her war-paint lurked the old nightmare of fatigue. He saw the dossier under her arm and nodded his approval of her intentions. In the meantime they were proposing to place Mnemidis under prolonged sedation to see whether a simple rest might not alter his disposition. She felt less badly about leaving the case to Schwarz, who was quite obviously not the therapist to handle it; yet she also regretted her own absence because of the intrinsic fascination of the case itself. Schwarz sensed this and said, "Don't worry about Mnemidis. He is in a pious stage at the moment and has borrowed all the books he can lay hands on. When he next appears on vaudeville it will be in scenes from the Bible I should suppose. *Aber*, what a freak!"

The silence of the little house was broken only by the lapping of the lake water at the wooden jetty. The sun came out and enabled her to move her books and papers on to the lawn which was kept neatly trimmed by a visiting gardener who was invisible except on Mondays. She slept, woke, and slept again. Ate a dazed meal, and was overtaken by a real fatigue now which could only be purged by a siesta which prolonged itself until the night was falling. It seemed that the accumulated weariness of centuries was expressing itself through this long slumber and that she would never be free of it. But on the second day the weight was sloughed, and on the succeeding morning she woke early and on an impulse plunged into the lake – a shock like diving through an icy mirror. She groaned with anguished joy as she towelled herself back into rosy warmth and padded to the cosy kitchen for her breakfast. The rest had done the trick; she had more or less shaped out her line of action over the child. Still in her dressing-gown she drank coffee and ran swiftly through his very unsatisfactory dossier. Then she took her car and motored to the nearest hamlet which boasted a post office and telephoned to the mansion on the lake. A servant answered her and in a short time she heard the deep but uncertain tones of the old lady asking her what she wanted. When Constance gave her name, however, the old lady gave an "Ouf!" of relief and said, "We have been waiting for you for days. I thought perhaps that you had forgotten ..." Constance sounded suitably shocked as she repeated the word: "*Forgotten?* How could I?"

They elected to meet at teatime on the same afternoon and by the time Constance had parked her car at the gate-house over the water she had no need to ring the bell for the old lady was already in the garden waiting for her behind the grille. She fluttered a white handkerchief in a sort of furtive signal, as if to an accomplice, and came towards the gate almost on tiptoe. "I am so *glad* you have come!" she said in her histrionic gasping way; she had a trick of rolling her eyes as she spoke which invested her speech with a sort of subdued frenzy. It conveyed urgency, and also confusion. It was very Latin.

But when they had shaken hands and looked each other up and down there came a moment of relief, of relaxation, almost as if on both sides the encounter had been somewhat dreaded. The old woman now became serious and stepping back drew herself up and settled her features anew into a severely unforgiving expression, as if calling herself to order after having shown an excess of feeling.

"What will you do?" she said hoarsely, and Constance

shaking her head, replied: "For the moment gain *your* confidence and begin to watch him quietly."

"We are just going out for a drive – *the* drive: perhaps you would care to come with us?" It was a good chance to infiltrate herself into the pattern and she at once accepted, at once followed the old lady through the herb garden with its miniature maze to the garage where already the black limousine waited with a gaitered and helmeted chauffeur at the wheel. He had already thrown the switch which rolled back the garage doors. "His nanny will bring Affad down," explained the old lady, as she allowed the old chauffeur to help her into a warm dark overcoat. "She won't be long."

Nor was she. She appeared quite soon and tried in passing to let the child attempt the marble staircase, but he was so slow that she finally swept him up into her arms and moved towards them, smiling a welcome. She was a fresh-complexioned and rather pretty Swiss girl and Constance already knew that she had her nursing degree and was fully in the counsels of the doctors; moreover she was most eager and willing to help. They exchanged smiles full of conspiratorial warmth and Constance bent briefly to kiss the impassive small face of the boy, who took no atom of interest in their movements or intentions, so familiar to him was the routine drive round the lake edge. He sat beside the old lady, stiffly upright, and with one hand upon her forearm; the two girls sat immediately in front on the fold-out seats. The chauffeur, who was separated from them by glass, checked the speaking tube to make sure that messages would reach him correctly, and switched on the radio in a very subdued manner. They moved off to the faint strains of a Strauss waltz, a strange, disembodied sound which did not disturb the nescience of the child who sat looking out upon the world without curiosity or elation. His little dark face was like that of some great bored plenipotentiary making a familiar state progress through a familiar country, a familiar ritual. Withdrawn as a Buddha he sat, watching the alien world from his perch in the absolute. There was no conversation of a general sort. Constance watched the little boy discreetly in the mirror but the observation revealed nothing, suggested nothing. She must talk to the nanny; and this she arranged sotto voce, suggesting a rendezvous in town where they might exchange views. She already felt that the old lady could contribute little to their debate except expressions of her own intense anxiety, and there was no point in this. On the other hand Constance did not wish to seem to operate behind her back, so to speak. So she broached the subject, pleading a discussion of technical matters, and to her surprise the point was taken without demur; so that the following day the nurse met her at the "*Renon*" for a coffee and a discussion.

She had read the dossier and indeed knew Schwarz already in another context. "Can I tell you what I think of it?" asked Constance, seeing that the girl looked rather doubtful about it when it was mentioned, though she seemed not to want to pronounce upon it in any definite way. "Yes, please!" she replied, and Constance said, "I am not very keen on kittens and toys which make noises; it is not just a question of motor response one is looking for, but a reaction at a deeper level, which can only come from inside himself. How can we help that?" The look of relieved delight on the girl's face changed it utterly; she clapped her hands with delight. "*Exactly* what I thought! No clever tricks for us. I am glad you think so too. There must be subtler ways of waking him. But I am *delighted*. I know we can work together now."

It was a great relief to Constance to find a willing and enthusiastic helper in a common cause; she had feared both jealousy and incompetence in the nursemaid, and neither fear was justified. She was able straight away to arrange her own times of duty and also to launch into a long and detailed list of questions as to the child's reactions to sleep, to food, to hot

baths, to massage, and so on. There was little enough to be
gleaned, for the subject showed neither special preference nor
any really significant aversions. He was simply absent from his
shell, his body was simply a package, an appendage. Yet he
was painfully like his father in physical structure, with the long
head and the same shape of eyes: only his were stone-dead
whereas those of Affad senior were both hurt and also wily and
amused. She could not help making the comparison when she
helped the nurse undress the little one and then lower him into
the warm bath in which he lay quite still like a small absorbed
frog, listening – for one could not say thinking or feeling. At
times waves of despair overcame her. Yet this change of patient,
change of objective, brought her fresh energy and enthusiasm,
and it was with pleasure that she motored the forty or so kilometres thrice a week now to assume her new role as assistant
nanny.

For the first two weeks she did nothing beyond her
routine duties of caring and surveying her charge. He looked
up when she came into the room sometimes but there was no
curiosity, no tone in his look, and for a long while she sat,
copying his breathing and attempting to influence him mentally. Sometimes, for a brief moment, he would allow an idea
to infiltrate the obscurity of his condition and might perform
a parody of rising to walk a few steps with an involuntary
clumsiness which might end in a fall. Or else he might pick up
a toy and gaze at it in an unseeing way before raising it to his
mouth to bite before he dropped it on the floor and resumed
his wall-gazing. But very gradually, and with professional
stealth, Constance advanced towards a body-contact such as
an occasional accidental embrace, or simply a pat on the
shoulder; she also developed a small array of daily habits
herself which she put on exhibition, so to speak, for his sake:
such as drinking a little milk from a plastic mug, combing out
her hair, and so on. With these she hoped gradually to draw

him towards a familiarity with the circumstantial, and to break his psychic reverie – for after all he was not asleep, he was breathing. He was just not fully alive, that was all. Somewhere there might be a switch. But all this with the greatest precaution and sans haste or impetuousness. It was important to give him the notion that nobody cared because they liked him as he was – they would not wish to influence him! All this slow acting-out seemed interminable and it was almost two months before there were the first signs of contact, but by then Constance had enlarged her own sphere of expression – she was now free to hum, to whistle, to stroke him, to move him about by hand, pick him up, even at long last to sit for long silences with her arm round him, crooning and sometimes breathing on his cheek. Her existence had dawned on him, he was aware of her for sometimes now he smiled and lifted his cheek to feel her blowing softly upon it. At times, too, he lay in her arms with a cryptic expression of enjoyment, closing his eyes, specially if there was music.

Then one day the magical weeping started, the fruitful tears began to flow; yet she was not sure of the mechanism which operated this notable and triumphant departure from the habitual nescience and withdrawal. But happen it did, and at a most awkward time, for she was all dressed up to go to a reception in the town, in order to help Schwarz who was the guest of honour of an International Psychological Association which had given him an important award, not to mention a silver medal for his work in analysis. But the Swiss girl was delayed and Constance had agreed to stay on with Affad for longer than usual.

It was not the fact that she was in a new costume that set the tone for this encounter – for he seemed to show no particular interest, though he smiled faintly to show that she was welcome, and allowed himself to be caressed and even picked up without demur. Yet sitting in her lap he lay back and

showed signs of fatigue, yawning and rubbing his eyes. One
hand seemed accidentally to touch her hair, and then suddenly
move to her face with fingers spread, and apparently with an
aggressive intent, as if to plant them in her eyes. But the
impulse waned. The threatening quality was new, though. He
whimpered as if he wanted to be released, yawned, and even
kicked a little, but she held him firmly in order to let him declare
himself more fully; evolve and fix the rather vague emotion.
But his eyes were clearer, and their focus was more profound
and direct, with a quality of alarm – no, the word is too strong –
anxiety, in them. He listened to her talk and humming with a
new attention, he seemed poised as if upon a new slope down
which he had never glided before. He gave a small moan and
opened his throat wide, though nothing came forth except a
pitiful clicking, dry and incoherent. It was like a yawn which
had got stuck. Then suddenly – it was as if the whole of reality
rushed in like a Niagara of feeling – suddenly the weeping
started, weeping of such violence and abandon that it was as if
his little psyche had exploded like a bomb and was on the point
of disintegration. She held him tight, as if to hold the shattered
fragments together against total dispersion, held him fiercely
in her sheltering arms, rocking him slightly from side to side
and almost keening his name, the name of her absent lover:
"Affad . . . Affad!" It was to congratulate him passionately for
this wonderful departure in the direction of the norm. She felt
the tears start to her own eyes, but it was important to remain
cool in the observation tower of her reason, the better to
evaluate the meaning and the possibilities inherent in this new
behaviour.

Meanwhile he wept and screamed with all his might as if to
rid himself in one cathartic expenditure of all the demons which
had held him spellbound for so long, and part of the screaming
let loose waves of aggression which made him kick and choke
and storm and grind his teeth. This savage gust of anger

alternated with waves of almost inhuman despair; he seemed about to shatter into a million fragments, to disperse, to melt. Only the warm and determined ceinture of her arms offered his psyche the chance to contain its woe and reorder the disturbed torrents of the affect flowing out of his very soul. She had never as yet heard anything like it in her professional career, though in the long and tedious confessional work associated with her trade weeping was common enough. But this inarticulate discharge had a fury and despair which was quite unique. It went on and on until it seemed he would come to the end of his voice as well as his strength.

She put him down on the floor and all of a sudden the weeping stopped, as if turned off like a tap, and the child slumped groggily back into a reminiscence of his previous role of absence and wall-gazing; but now he was beside himself with exhaustion, and when she picked him up again he at once went off into a further paroxysm of weeping, as if overcome anew with despair, the uprooting despair of the primal wound whose depth she could not as yet evaluate. Still carrying him, and he was quite heavy, she took him to the luxurious bathroom and turned on the tap to run him a warm relaxing bath. He allowed himself to be undressed while lying on the bed, still expressing a now voiceless weeping. And even when it had started to peter away into the noiselessness of utter exhaustion the face kept the hard fixity of the primal howl, so that (with closed eyes) it resembled something like a tiny Greek tragic mask. He lay so still in the water that he might have been dead; softly and sweetly she sang to herself in a small absorbed voice as she propelled him very slowly back and forth in the bath.

She wrapped him softly in the great perfumed bath-towel and then powdered him with talc before putting him to bed in the quiet bedroom with its faithful night-light burning – a tiny Christmas tree lighted by electric bulbs. Here he seemed at last to cave in, to succumb to a profound slumber, completely extenuated. For a while he turned hither and thus with a trace of his former restlessness, and then turned on his side and like a ship going down, nosedived into sleep. But he did one thing that he had never done before – he thrust his thumb into his mouth. It was an archaic gesture which suggested a fruitful and deep regression to some place of psychic hurt – like someone fingering the scar tissue, the cicatrice of an old wound. As she sat beside him and watched quietly her hopes rose for his restoration to the human world. But she frowned as she thought of the elder Affad, of his delight and perhaps gratitude: had her motives been entirely disinterested? Was it on these grounds . . .? But she shook her head sharply to banish the thought and then looked at her watch. There was half an hour before the Swiss girl came back on duty. He slept so soundly that it might have been possible to tiptoe away, but she did not wish to risk it in case there was some new and fruitful departure in behaviour to be studied. She crossed the room to the day-book and entered a few notes which she would afterwards expand into a case-history, dictating it on to her magnetophone before handing it to her typist. The time passed quickly and by the time the Swiss girl tiptoed into the room she had finished and was ready to polish herself up for the party and take her leave. As she did so she communicated the events of the afternoon and evening to the girl, who showed great delight at the news of a deviation in behaviour. "It might be the beginning of a radical shift," Constance admitted, "But we must be patient and not force."

But she herself was joyfully optimistic and so fully absorbed in her thoughts that she drove extremely badly, and when she got to the town had trouble parking. But she was not too late, and Schwarz's relief was very pleasant to experience; not less, she was forced to admit to herself, the obvious admiration of his colleagues. The new hair-style was a distinct success – that was something pleasurable to experience. But as soon as she could get Schwarz alone she told him excitedly about the events of the afternoon. He whistled with surprise and delight. "What a break-through," he said. "Maybe your original diagnosis was almost right – *histoire de biberon!* What luck if he can find his way back like an electrician going back along a wire to find and seal a break. . . . You are lucky, Constance! I never have these sharp cathartic changes, dammit! But the important thing is the whole continuity – I hope he keeps on until he discharges the whole weight of the trauma. If he does tomorrow and for a while, *please* phone me. I want to know." To her surprise, and indeed a certain mortification, she almost started to cry herself, but managed to check the impulse as she blew her nose. It was a poor advertisement for a cool and scientific therapist, she told herself bitterly.

Schwarz had done a tour of the room and had finally drifted back to her side again with his replenished whisky. "By the way," he said, "I almost forgot to tell you. I am having difficulty defending your privacy, endless telephone calls keep coming in – no, not from Affad, but from the Prince, for example asking where you were and for how long? I said you were on sick leave for at least two months, and away from the country. Is that all right?" She was a little cast down that Affad himself had sent no message, but reproved the sentiment immediately. "Of course," she said, "I owe nobody anything, I am quite free am I not?"

"They are worried about a letter addressed to Affad which came in the Red Cross pouch and which you apparently have; I can't profess to tell you what *that* is all about but he sounds very concerned, asking if you have destroyed it, or opened it or what the hell you have done with it. What do I say?"

She felt herself blushing slightly. Schwarz's glance was a trifle quizzical, although in the matter of Affad he was not fully in her confidence. "If the Prince asks again, please give him my love and tell him that the letter in question was misdirected by

Aubrey Blanford's stupid servant and I took charge of it, hoping to see Affad before he left and give it to him. However I didn't, and so I still have the letter. It is waiting for him, unless he wants me to send it on to Egypt; but he spoke vaguely of coming back soon so I put it in a safe place to await his arrival and . . ."

But suddenly at this juncture her blood ran cold, she put her hand to her cheek. Schwarz was saying, "But the old boy was in quite a bother, he seemed to think that you had either destroyed it in a fit of pique or that you had opened it yourself and knew the contents . . . what the devil is it, a love-letter?" He broke off as he saw the expression on her face. "Constance!" he cried sharply; and now she said, "Did you say Mnemidis had been at my bookshelf?" He spread wide his arms with an air of puzzled resignation. "But you gave him permission to borrow books, did you not?" She nodded, for she had in fact told him that he might have any book he wished to read, though her own shelves contained mostly text books and dictionaries and fat volumes of reference. She had really been thinking of the general clinic library which was not a bad little one, full of novels and general literature. "I *told* you he had carried off a lot of your books," said Schwarz somewhat irritably, "but he had your express permission." She nodded. She had missed the first allusion to the subject. "But the *Bible*," she said now, "the *Bible!* The letter of Affad I slipped into the Bible for safe-keeping!" She had gone quite pale and this puzzled him for he said, "Well, what about it? You can easily retrieve it. Mnemidis won't *eat* it after all, will he?" She hoped to goodness not; at the same time she was furious to think that all this fuss should be made over this petty question of a letter — though of course she knew (without really believing in them) what momentous issues hung upon its receipt. To know the hour of one's death — was it really so important? "You must ring up Pierre when he's on duty and tell him to retrieve it from the book. Mnemidis himself will be under full sedation for a while yet; he liked it so much that he asked for a second vacation from himself." He was perfectly right; Pierre would certainly secure the detested letter if he were asked. All this was quite true but so great was her anxiety and impatience that she slipped out into the lobby of the hotel and found a telephone. She rang the clinic and asked for the secretariat so that they could tell her the duty-hours of Pierre. Unfortunately he did not come on duty again until eight the following morning; the patient himself was in a sedation booth and his little room was locked up, so that it was idle to ask somebody else to hunt down the letter at such an hour. The best was to wait until Pierre came on deck again. For some reason or other she felt full of anxiety; she admitted to herself that there was really no reason to suppose that she would not recover the letter intact. Yes, but nevertheless . . . the whole matter rattled her in an obscure way.

She found the speeches stuffy and quite interminable and was glad when the evening came to an end and she was able to say goodnight to the glowing Schwarz and retrieve her car for the long drive back to the solitary lake house. She arrived late in a sort of remorseful triumph – a strange mood which shared the anxiety over the letter with the delightful sense of having advanced a pace in the direction of the child's good health. In both moods of course the thought of Affad echoed in her ears, so that she dreamed of him and woke somewhat disconsolate and disturbed.

The little alarm told her when to get her car and motor to the *auberge* to telephone to Pierre whose day watch began at eight in the morning. However, it took a moment to locate him and when she did he was at first quite startled and intrigued that she should ring so early. He listened to her with care and verified the fact of Mnemidis' borrowings; and, yes, among the books had been a Plato and a Spengler. But had been very specially glad of the little Bible, because (so he said) he had some things to confirm and verify. "C'est un drôle de coco celui-la!" confided the giant with a chuckle, but added that all the books were in the locker by his bed and would come to no harm. "Please," said Constance, "I want to ask you a favour – will you go and find the Bible? In it you should find a letter addressed to a M. Affad. It is from Egypt. If you can get hold of it I will come round and pick it up." He promised to go and have a look while she held the line. He was away for a considerable time, but this was not unusual for the high-security wing of the clinic had a bewildering number of sealed doors which one had to open first and then lock behind one.

But the letter was not in the book!

Nor was it any use repeating: "Are you sure? Are you absolutely *sure*?" Pierre felt the urgency in her tone and was correspondingly troubled. "I looked in all the books, and in the bundle of papers and folders. I also looked in his handbag to make sure it was not there. Then I went round the room, the shelves the shower cubicle, the . . . but everywhere, doctor, everywhere possible!" She closed her eyes and in her imagination photographed her consulting-room as well as the alcove with the built-in bookcase. Could it be perhaps that the letter had fallen out during the actual removal of the books? She telephoned to her secretary to ask if she had rescued any letter from the floor during her own absence, but the answer was in the negative. Where the devil had it got to? Had Mnemidis perhaps destroyed it, thrown it out into the wastepaper basket? Her heart sank at the thought of the complicated search which would have to be undertaken to verify such a hypothesis. She reproached herself for the exaggerated anxiety she felt about this trifling contretemps. Of course it would turn up, perhaps even Mnemidis when he woke might throw some light on the matter. It was best to wait calmly and let things take their course. This harangue to herself did little more than allay her native impatience for a brief spell. She looked at her watch. There would be time to verify matters for herself and still arrive (if she hurried) in time for the child's evening session which closed with dinner. She drove to her office and startled the somnolent Schwarz who was not used to late nights, and paid for them with several days of apathy and fatigue. "What's got into you?" he demanded plaintively; and she replied, "It's that bloody letter of Affad's. It has got mislaid. It has disappeared. It was in the Bible which Mnemidis took to study and which is now beside his bed covered apparently in jottings. I phoned Pierre to check. But no letter!"

With considerable exasperation she now went through her own consulting-room with a fine-tooth comb, so to speak, in the hope of tracing the article. In vain. Mnemidis had not after all taken so very many books: half a dozen in all. But of course the Bible had been among them.

She drove now up to the central clinic and the remote grey building which housed the dangerous cases, and just managed to catch Pierre as he was going off duty. Together they went upstairs, unlocking and locking a network of doors until they came to the little room where Mnemidis lived out the greater part of his strange life. The books were all there, and yielded nothing: nor did the patient's own papers, in the form of several folders containing letters and newspaper clippings. The bible was quite heavily marked up in pencil, as though he had read it with special attention. Perhaps for new impersonations? "And his handbag?" she asked. Pierre said, "It's with him. But I've been through it. Nothing!"

"Nothing!" she echoed with a sigh.

She sat down on the nearest chair and reflected deeply for an instant. The only hope left was perhaps that Mnemidis himself might provide a solution to the problem when it became possible to interrogate him—but that would not be for ten days as yet. She must possess her soul in patience until this last avenue could be explored. Perhaps he had inadvertently thrown it away or destoyed it: perhaps opened it? "Pierre," she said "I'm so sorry for the trouble I've given you. But the minute he comes round please help me interrogate him. He trusts you now, after that ridiculous episode with the egg!" The big "Malabar" smiled his slow saintly smile and nodded.

She calculated that there was just time to circle the town and visit her flat before returning to the château and her charge: she needed some clothes to wear in the little lake house by the water. While she was busy turning out a chest-of-drawers the phone rang. It was Sutcliffe, who was both surprised and delighted to catch her, though he sounded a trifle nettled that she had disappeared from circulation without leaving him a message. "Ah! There you are!" he said with a sort of testy joviality. "Perhaps you will favour me with some information as to where the devil you have gone to and why. Everybody is asking me. I have a right to know – or have I?" She explained that she had decided to deal with her fatigue by drastically reorganising her holiday-time – in fact she confessed where she was and what was afoot, though she swore him to secrecy. "That's the point," he said, "what do I tell the Prince? It's all about the fatal letter addressed to Affad. He is under the impression that you have taken destiny by the forelock and intervened."

"In what sense?"

"I mean simply carried off the letter with the intention of suppressing it or of losing it. I can just hear him saying to Affad, 'You see, the *moment* a woman interferes everything goes wrong.' So I implore you, for your own peace of mind and mine, to surrender that bloody letter to me and I will put it back in the bag and bang it off to Egypt."

"The letter has been mislaid!"

Sutcliffe whistled and fell silent. Then he said, "They won't believe you, you know."

"It's the truth," she said.

"I myself hardly believe you. Swear!"

"I swear! Cross my heart."

"They will think you have interfered with . . . well, with what they regard as Affad's destiny. I suppose you have been told about the letter, the death-signal, so to speak, and where it fits into their gnostic arrangements. O Lord!"

"Yes, I know what it means, though I take a rather poor view of all the mumbo-jumbo, and the secret society business. It's a very perverse and foolish philosophy."

"You are very pig-headed," he said angrily. "After all, the metaphysical problem is a real one. How to turn back the tide of spiritual entropy. The sacrifices are real, too. Affad is not alone, there is a man before and a man behind; he is part of a tradition which hopes to interrogate death itself. Now the old boy will certainly think you have made an unwarrantable intrusion into the affair. Probably that you have even opened the letter, or destroyed it. Do you know what is in the letter?"

"No. I swear!"

There was a long silence during which she could hear him whistling softly to himself—a sign of great perplexity and exasperation. "The whole thing is incredibly childish," she broke out, "and so Egyptian: why can't he get a copy of the message from the central committee or whatever? It is not the first time a letter has gone astray, been mislaid, is it?"

"Apparently he can't."

"Even the Prince?"

"So it would seem!"

With mounting irritation at all this portentous and childish behaviour she described the situation to him, adding that perhaps the problem would be solved when Mnemidis was woken from his artificial sleep. Sutcliffe sighed. "Well, I will do my best to put things in a favourable light, though I can foresee a good deal of scepticism about your own good intentions. They are bound to feel you are playing with them."

"If they do, then let me speak to them. I can quite easily convince them, I am sure."

But she was reluctant to push things further until this last avenue had been explored; suppose the madman had just hidden it somewhere – behind a radiator, say? Yes, but they had looked everywhere, specially in such places! "I've got to get back to my job," she said. "Schwarz is abreast of my movements and my work, if there is any untoward happening!"

It was puzzling that there was no news of Affad's return to Geneva: however, she did not wish to seem over-curious about the matter, and rang off, regained her car and set off for the château.

There was apparently nobody at home except the Swiss girl and she had to ring for a while before the door was opened; she was however radiant and smiling, though she put her finger to her lips and said, "Shh! He is having a nap. But my goodness, what a change! I hardly recognised him today. Constance, his eyes are open, he is looking, they have depth and being in them!" She clapped her hands, but noiselessly. Together they mounted the staircase and gained the elegant dressing-room which had been set aside for them, and where Constance divested herself of her coat and handbag while she listened to the report of the assistant therapist. "He did not weep for me – I'm afraid the whole transference thing is all yours! But the change was very marked, his whole face has opened up like a flower. And his smile! It's so new he hardly knows how to wear it. But don't listen to me; come and sit by him for a moment." Their silence was no longer necessary for the child was awake, gazing round him as he lay in his little bed, curling and uncurling his small hands as if he were about to employ them in doing something.

But no sooner did she lean down to kiss him and pick

him up than it started again, the weeping – but more slowly,
more consciously. He was in the middle of a yawning fit,
seized by a kind of fatigue; but he looked at her keenly, touching her hair and putting his finger almost in her mouth. And
wept. As if it were the end of the world, the end of time. She
took him up and cradled him once more, mentally encompass-
ing his whole being with her circling arms. She felt that he had
embarked upon the perilous attempt to forge for himself a
human identity, and that the principal wound in the unconscious had been found if not identified. Would that he could
weep his way back to articulate health! And today, as for some
weeks to come, this cathartic weeping was the only fruitful
dialogue which took place between them. But it also evolved,
it did not remain static. There were days of anger and days of
gloom; but very gradually, like the sun piercing clouds,
elements of relaxation, almost of joy, manifested themselves.
And these could be read upon his new face – one in which the
eyes now played their full part, expressive, curious, sometimes
almost roguish! Sometimes during his weeping he would let
her put her finger softly on his nose, chin, forehead. But always
he went the full length, crying until he was completely
exhausted, worn out, hypotonic.

Gradually, too, as she advanced tiptoe into this uncharted
territory, it seemed that she could "read" the infantile dilemma
which had stunted the psychic growth of the child. What was
also new was the feeling that now he was cooperating unconsciously with her. His muscle schemes were relaxing, he was
drawing strength from her, and from the admission of his own
weakness.

Some of the encounters sparked off other feelings, for
example aggression; he would stab at her eyes with his fingers,
or put them in her mouth with a rough intent, but which faded
into helpless tears, as though the impetus had spent itself. In
the aggression she read his reluctance to surrender to the soft

appeals of reason and health. Then at other times the weeping
ceased and he would lie in her lap for a spell, brooding as he
listened to her singing. Sometimes he carefully touched her
mouth again, and smeared his spittle round it carefully, as if
following out some inner ritual. And sometimes also he might
lie as calmly as a nursing infant making soft sounds with his
voice, "*da da va va*". Once he put his mouth to her cheek in an
involuntary gesture of affection, but was immediately seized
by contrition and reverted to his blank, sightless look, turning
his head away from her. But his eyes were at least open now,
and he could now gaze even at the world outside the window
of the playroom; or at the slowly unrolling lake scenery
opening like a Japanese fan during the afternoon drive. The
old grandmother reported that while he was still restless at
night he had long periods when he was in a good mood, and
his gestures and impulsive movements seemed less uncon-
trolled. The process would still be a long one, Constance felt,
but the orientation had now changed in a more fruitful
direction – the ship was on the right course. And with the first
successes in this field she felt the whole weariness of her profession surge up in her. What was the point of effecting a
psychic repair of this kind if one could not leave the patient to
continue the work in competent hands? Who would replace
her, who would communicate the loving care and the warmth
to the little robot when she was forced to leave? For the
moment the very evident success of the treatment was enough
to keep her happy and enthusiastic, but already queries about
the future rose in her mind; she had begun to divine what old
age was all about! It would have been so good to spend the
night with a man, instead of staying sealed off and frigid like
this, incapable of warmth, of a simple, lustful response to life.
This was the terrible weakness of setting too serious a valuation
on experience. What to do? Once she had tried to break out of
the prison of her sensibility by getting drunk at a cocktail

party and succumbing to the charms of a pleasant younger colleague. But the episode had been like trying to ignite damp straw. She was humiliated not by his ineptness so much as her own inadequacy. How right Affad had been to insist so stoutly that all sex attachments are psychic and that the body is simply a reservoir of sensation. Loving from this point of view meant that reality was not compromised, and one faded into nature as if into a colour wash!

But if there was any fatuous disposition to self-congratulation over the increasing success of her treatment it was nipped in the bud by an incident, trivial in itself, which showed how intricate and strange are the associative schemes which provoke and underlie human behaviour. Or at least so it would seem from a remark made by the grandmother one afternoon as they drove slowly round the lake. The old lady who, for all her forbidding silences, was very observant, turned her large dark operatic eye on Constance and said, "You are not wearing the scent today!"

"It's probably because I went for a swim in the lake – but in fact I am, though it's much fainter. Do I smell of it so very much?"

The old lady smiled and shook her head. She said, "No, it's just that it is my daughter's scent, Lily's."

"You mean Jamais de la Vie?"

"Jamais de la Vie!"

Constance was dumbfounded, exasperated and professionally delighted – perhaps *this* is what had given her such an immediate associative transference with the child, had enabled her to penetrate his emotions so swiftly. And the tears . . . She went back over the old diagnoses in the light of this new gleam of knowledge. How lucky she had been, for her choice of a new scent to match a new hair-style, a new character change, had been quite haphazard. Had it in fact been a key? She turned to look at the small abstracted face beside her in the

looming automobile and wondered. And if all human emotions
and action depended on such an affective pattern of association-
responses . . . It was a pure wilderness of associations, a labyrinth in which the sources of all impulse lay. Besides, it was
after all sound psychology to trace the roots of emotion and
desire to the sense of smell – its vast ramifications had never
been completely worked out, and never would be. She tried
to remember the smell of Affad – it was a sort of non-smell, like
the smell of the desert: yet somehow at the heart of its airless-
ness there was a perfume, the odour of muscat or of cloves?
(I hate literary emotions, she told herself!)

"I shall soon be leaving you," she said to the old lady, "as
I must sooner or later return to my other cases. No, don't look
alarmed! Not until I feel sure that everything is going well and
that Esther can take over. Besides, I am always there if need be
to consult. At the end of a phone!" This seemed to reassure the
old lady and no more was said about the matter.

At the end of the excursion she carried the sleepy patient
up the stairs to his playroom and set him down among toys
which now were becoming objects of interest to him.

It was in the same week that another significant departure
took place; the Swiss girl greeted her one day with a triumphant
expression and said, "Eureka! Today he lifted the glass of milk
himself and tried to feed himself. Constance, it's really
marvellous!"

And Constance knew that she would soon be leaving; the
obstinate Mnemidis had refused all knowledge of a letter in the
bible, or indeed in any of the other books. It was quite baffling.
Could he be lying, and if so why? And to make matters worse
she at last received a letter from Affad, couched in the form of
a reproach which she did not feel she merited. It made her feel
furious, and also guilty. After all, in accepting the letter from
Blanford she had had no clearly formulated plan – indeed, had
she met Affad as she expected to do, she would have handed it

over in the normal way. And here they were accusing her ... It
was really most vexatious and short-sighted.

Dear Constance: I really did not think, my dear, that
you would meddle in my affairs in such a resolute fashion;
it is all too painful, and I understand your feeling that
things can be prevented from happening by an act of
resolution ... But they can't. I regret having told you as
much as I did about the structure of gnostic belief and
the grave experiment our group is engaged in trying out.
This stupid letter would have only contained a death-
date, with no indication of how or by whom. That is the
little bit of essential information which enables us to
complete our *devoir*—without it we are just ordinary
people, dispossessed, taken unawares: the original sin!
It is the equivalent of letting me die unshriven! The
knowledge of this simple fact enables one to take up a
stance consciously towards the only basic feature of
human existence which is never studied, is always avoided,
is funked! People expire, they don't *die* in a positive
sense, "mobilised in the light of nature"! I ask you to
restore the letter to me. You have no right to it, and I
have. I cannot believe that you would betray me like this
even though you are a determinist, a behaviourist. Ah!
What a stupid charge to lay against you! I am terribly
sorry for such a sudden explosion of bad temper, but I am
both frustrated for myself, my own *salut*, to use an ironic
phrase, and also for the man or men after me. I am only a
link in a long bicycle chain. I believe you understand this,
as it is also expressed in sexual terms in our love for each
other—has it *forever* vanished? Are you cured of me?
Have you forgotten the beginning when we played cards
by candlelight with the dying Dolores?

It came back to her now with a shock; no, she had not

really forgotten, she had just put aside the memory, perhaps out of pain, for Dolores had been her best friend at school and then later in medical school. When her husband who was a musician died she cut off her beautiful hair and threw it into the coffin. But it grew again, as beautiful as ever, and so did her only child. She was a brilliant surgeon among the younger ones, but by ill luck she infected herself and contracted a fatal type of poisoning. Constance used to take Affad to the ward at night to keep her company, and the three of them would play cards on the night table. As she grew weaker the effort increased but they kept up the habit out of friendship. One night the dying woman handed over her cosmetics and said that she would like to be sure that if she died suddenly in the night her face would be made up for her before her son was allowed in to see her. They promised, and set about playing the usual game of rummy. But tonight she felt much weaker, and kept fading away, drifting into quiet dozes; until with a small contrite shudder she simply stopped breathing. They were both shaken with sadness and resignation. Constance checked pulse and breath and then drew the lids down over the sad and dignified eyes. Affad put his arms round her and she embraced him with a triumphant abandon, touching his hair and throat and ears as if she were building up his image as a sculptor might from the moist clay of the primary wish for love; to affirm, to unite, to triumphantly rescue him from time. And later on when they went hand in hand down to the deserted buttery to make a cup of coffee, Affad had said, "As you know, when one has seen someone die, someone stop breathing, one realises with a start how one breath is hooked into another, is attached to another. In between the breaths is the space where we live, between the beforebreath and the afterbreath is a field or realm where time exists and then ceases to exist. Our impression of reality is woven by the breathing like a suit of chain mail. It is in that little space, between the breaths, in that tiny instant that we have started to expand the power of the orgasm, as a united synchronised experience, making it more and more conscious, mobilising its power and fecundity with every kiss. Constance, we can't go wrong. Love can't make any other sense now for us! God, how I wish I could make you pregnant in the light of this! She had replied, "If you go on talking like this, you will!" But he had not. Nor would he now. Well, it was something real and for her something new in orientation and intensity. Better than the usual business, making love in a sort of moral pigsty of vaguely good intentions. Or not at all. Or not at all.

> My whole time here has been taken up with silly discussions about this fatal letter; and I at first thought it was all a mistake. But now I am forced to conclude with the Prince that you took it upon yourself to execute a *coup de main* in my favour. Darling, it is most misguided. Please believe me when I tell you so. The Prince is also writing you, and has telephoned so many times that I feel quite ashamed. Constance . . .

She put down the letter thoughtfully and devoted a moment of reminiscence to that faraway period – how close it was in actual clock-time, and how far away in memory! They had lived out the attachment obsessionally – was the past tense correct? She listened, stiffened to attention, to her own heartbeats as if she interrogated them. Was Affad really *over*? In a paradoxical sort of way only he could answer such a question by the act of reappearing on the scene. They had worked not just for pleasure but for ecstasy, not for the merely adequate but for the sublime, and this is what seemed to her unique about their love. It was without sanctions, without measure, and wholly double. Nor could she envisage it being over because the experience had been so complete, had marked them both so irremediably! She swore slightly under her breath and tried to pretend that the whole thing had shown a regrettable weakness on her part, but she was being insincere and she knew it. And *now* the whole damned problem of the letter had come between them. It was with a resigned sadness that she packed up, locked the little lake house, and took the road back to the city.

Her flat seemed somewhat gloomy and forbidding, so she bustled about and dusted it and generally set things to rights. An empty frigidaire gleamed frostily at her, empty as the heart of a sun. Thence to the clinic where she found a gloomy and irate Schwarz waiting for her with a nasty gleam in his eye. "Listen," he said, "I have a bone to pick with you, about this Mnemidis caper. He has been restored to us safe and just as unsound of mind, though of course rested and ready for any mischief. Constance, we cannot go on with him, whatever you say; we are simply not equipped, even the high-security wing, to look after him as he must be looked after. He belongs to the civil law, and should be returned to the authorities. If you go on poking away at his paranoia you know full well what the result will be. There is no point in incurring senseless danger or difficulty. He is quite certainly beyond our help and I think we must admit it."

She sat down at her desk and said, "What about the letter?" Schwarz sighed and said, "No trace! Did you expect any? I didn't. He could have put it down the lavatory, of course." In a sudden burst of resolution she got up and took him by the shoulders. "I feel I must go on with him until I am sure that he did not see it; grant me a month or two more and I'll surrender him as you see fit. But I must try out the matter and see – for Affad's sake."

"For Affad's sake," he echoed despondently. He swivelled his office chair round and pushed his spectacles back on his head. "Another thing! What do we do about visitors? Several people have asked to see him, including a doctor from

Alexandria who claims to have had him both as a friend and also under his wing. Now a *prison* has its security rules and all its precautions. A prison could answer these people. But we have no code of rules. Do we let *anyone* in who wishes to see him? One is a doctor, one a business associate . . ." He was in a frightful temper, she could see that. But, to be truthful, the problem was a relatively new one. "Could we not establish a visiting day like the state prison?" He said, reminding her, "what do you mean by 'close detention'? Define it."

They sat glumly staring at each other for a long moment. She knew that in this mood he would not give in unless she wheedled. It was unfair, but . . . "Please help me," she said. "I feel I am only doing my duty in making sure. It's the least I can do. And after that I promise to be good, *absolutely* good!"

So they came to a compromise about the treatment as well as the visitors, and she won her way over the misgivings of the sighing Schwarz.

But of the letter there was no sign; yet Mnemidis' way of talking about it, of answering questions about it, seemed somehow sly. He talked sideways, turning his face away, and said, "From who to who, and why? What a strange name, from Egypt certainly? Yes, from Egypt originally perhaps. Why should I have seen it? The Bible? It is full of untruths. And there are no *dates* so you cannot tell when it all happens!" In the middle of all this verbiage she imagined an occasional gleam, the barest hint which suggested that perhaps . . . But she was also aware of the desire which might lead her into a self-deception. The long sleep had done him good in a way for he was much fresher and his ideas flowed more freely. But of course what was missing was the basic connecting links between them—it was the standard paranoid configuration. And of course she was on the lookout for the first signs of persecution-delusions which pointed to danger for the therapist. Persecution was the code sign of violence, and she must be careful not to provoke this vein of feeling by too great insistence in her questions.

He had been watching the nuns from his window, for among the nurses on the wards there were a number of young nuns. He was intrigued to hear that they belonged to a silent order – he who spoke so much, in torrents, indiscriminately! "When there is nobody there I can still hear myself talking to myself, it still seems necessary – my whole intellectual formation and my expensive education all led to this state of affairs. I wish I could see some end to this situation because sometimes I am out of breath and out of voice. I get headaches even. But on goes the torture of the dialectic – the parallel straight lines which are supposed to meet at infinity, but never do. I know this because I have reached infinity, I am there, and still they haven't met." His eyes filled with tears, beautiful violent eyes which had only known one kind of rapture – death! The clock chimed, it was the end of the new session. She told him that arrangements had been made for him to see his friend the doctor on the morrow, and Mnemidis nodded, smiling enigmatically, joining his hands on his midriff like a mandarin. But the name stirred no particular echo. As for the letter, it appeared to have vanished for good. Was it worth being obstinate and keeping on?

It was at this juncture that Lord Galen, like some long-forgotten carnival figure, strayed on to the stage, so unexpected a presence that for a moment she could not fit his name into her memory. "My dear Constance," he said reproachfully, "of all people to forget *me*. Of all people!" She expressed an unfeigned contrition for she loved old Lord Galen – the mention of his name made one want to smile. And here he was, vague and wide-eyed as ever, with his rolled copy of the *Financial Times* under his arm. He carried it about as others might carry about a book of poems or a novel, to be dipped into during the day. They had lunch at a fashionable place and he signed the cheque with a flourish in the name of some international agency. In answer to her query he said, "My dear, I have come here to coordinate things. After a big war there is a lot of coordination necessary. They have made me Coordinator General of the Central Office of Coordination. I oversee almost everything and in a twinkling coordinate it! It is an immense saving of time and money for us all." She was tempted to ask him what his salary was, but refrained. He also apparently lectured, on the subject of which he obviously had a perfect command. But just what it *was* she never found out. He had learned it in America, he said. "I am very *pleased* with America!" he said, as if awarding a school prize. "After those beastly Germans it is just fine to be a Jew in America. America speaks with a Jewish voice and that goes for a lot. After all we won the war and now we will win the peace. Constance, you are smiling! Have I said something *effulgent?* I have come here to coordinate World Jewry. It may take a moment, and I may have to make sacrifices, perhaps take a cut in my *frais de représentation.* But what of it? And by the way I have managed to get Aubrey a decoration for his bravery – an O.B.E. You should have seen his face when I told him! He was pale with pride and surprise. He never expected his gallantry to be recognised but I saw to it. One word to the Prime Minister and . . ."

Aubrey's own version of these events, when she mentioned all this, was characteristically different, for the whole episode bordered on the grotesque and filled him with moroseness. "As for being pale with pride I was white to the gums with humiliation. Imagine! One day without warning the door of my room is thrown open by the obsequious Cade and a group of pin-striped notables is ushered in. It includes the consul-general and two consular clerks, Sutcliffe, Toby, Lord Galen and two other gentlemen who were described as journalists. You can imagine my alarm as they converged on me. I thought they had come to castrate me perhaps. The consul, Nevinson, held a Bible and a casket while the consular clerk held (for reasons best known to himself) a large parchment citation and a lighted candle. My hypothesis changed – they had obviously come to excommunicate me. Lord Galen then made an artless speech of fascinating inaccuracy and unconscious condescension. He praised everything except my physical beauty – my civic sense, my unflinching bravery under enemy fire, my example, my long suffering, *mon cul* – everything! I lay there between the sheets like a stale sandwich and allowed all this to pour over me. It was all the more humiliating as among them was Sutcliffe's boss Ryder whose wife had almost been buried alive in a London bombardment; she had lost a hand and an eye, while here was I . . . You can imagine. Then the consul cleared his throat and read out a long and incoherent citation written in a style which suggested that it had been swiftly run up that morning by someone on the *Daily Mirror*. Then he pinned a decoration to my pyjamas and a champagne cork popped in true ceremonial fashion. I nearly cried with rage. Then to round off everything Lord Galen imparted to us all his philosophy of life which went like this: 'The moment has come to invest in bricks and mortar. You can't go wrong if you do.' And Toby, who had just been to a Geneva bank to cash a cheque said, 'Have you noticed? The peculiarly tender way that bankers take each other by the shoulders and gaze into each other's eyes, as if they were caressing each other's fortunes which equalled their private parts?' Lord Galen hadn't, and he became somewhat huffy."

Constance cocked a professional ear to this unwonted vivacity of discourse and felt that things were very much better for Aubrey, that he was really on the mend. He could already just about stand up on his two feet and there were plans afoot for him to take a few steps during the following week. The operations had been strikingly successful. And this sudden improvement in health had encouraged him once more to think of his book, the "authorised version" of which still lingered among the disordered papers of Sutcliffe, the incorrigible and depraved shadow which hung over his life. "By the way, Affad rang up," he said a little maliciously and watched her carefully to see what the effect on her composure was. But she replied to him coolly and gave him an account of the contre-temps about the letter, and about her battle of wits with Mnemidis. He sighed and shook his head. "He will be coming back anyway," he said, "though he didn't say when. By the way, talking of scandal, I discovered something quite extra-ordinary. Lord Galen has been frequenting the *maisons de tolérance* of the city, and in one of them he ran into Cade, who has suddenly started to take an interest in the low life. It would seem that Lord Galen is having trouble with his erection and that his doctors in London despaired of securing the right stimulus for him. So after trying everything without avail they suggested the Continent as a probable place where such matters are taken more seriously. Moreover in Geneva there is a special bankers' brothel called *le Croc* which specialises in such troubles and here Cade has found a billet also."

"I wonder what he is up to? Have you asked him?"

"Yes. He scratches his head and ponders a long time before replying in that dreadful Cockney whine, 'It makes a nice change.' In his pronunciation nice is naise and change chinge. My God, Constance, with all this talk about me I completely forgot to tell you how beautiful you look – the new style is unhingeing. Kiss me, please, to show you still care – *will* you?" This gallantry was also something new, though there was no lack of warmth in her embrace; he knew how much she loved him, and that he could ask anything of her. What better therapy, he asked himself, than this? "And even a new perfume to set off the graces of the new woman! Bravo!" He knew she was trying to outface the loss of Affad, to pick herself up off the ground, so to speak. But it had to be said in all friendship, lest she suspect him of "tactful" silences.

"Did Affad say when?"

"He said soon, very soon."

"*Eh bien*," she said, trying to sound indifferent, resigned.

But in fact the resumption of her city rhythm was a welcome thing; she had decided to visit the child less regularly and hope for a transfer of trust and affection to the real nurse, the Swiss girl. She had taken the precaution of leaving her a bottle of Lily's perfume to help things along. But here in the middle morning she was able to meet and question Aubrey's surgeons about his condition and inevitably Felix Chatto dropped in for a glass, together with Toby and the hangdog *patibulaire* Sutcliffe, looking as much a gallows' bird as ever. But how happy they all seemed to see her again! And how happy she was to rejoin them once more.

That afternoon Schwarz brought the alienist from Alexandria to meet her and discuss the case of Mnemidis. He apparently wished for a brief clinical discussion before embarking on the interview with his ex-patient and one-time friend. He was a tall lean man with a rasping voice like a crow. Impeccably dressed and hatted with a dark Homburg. He carried a stick with a golden knob which gave him a slight touch of sorcerer-on-holiday. His spatulate hands ended in long filbert nails, well tended. His face was pale, long, goatlike, with sulphurous yellowish eyes, a bit bloodshot as if from alcohol. But he had a kindly if commanding presence, and he called Mnemidis "our friend" with a conspiratorial smile, and formally alluded to Constance once as "my dear colleague" which showed the quality of his manners. He had apparently brought a letter for Mnemidis, and he was hoping to spend ten minutes with him—this had already been accorded. "But I wanted first of all to tell you that I have really come to negotiate his release under guarantee. His sponsor is an ex-associate, a millionaire from Egypt who will offer you every guarantee as far as security and safety is concerned in the question of actually transporting him back to his native land. I would only like to know the actual legal matters to be adjusted: what forms must I fill in, what permissions obtain?" They talked round the subject in a desultory way at first; Constance thought that the authorities would be glad to relinquish him under caution, and be rid of him. But they would have to examine the legalities involving criminal law. "That is precisely what his associate is doing today. I expect to be word-perfect this evening and tomorrow we can start a release-plan."

"That is rather quick work."

"Well, we can be patient if necessary. Geneva is a most interesting town where we have many friends. I wonder, doctor, if you would consider dining with me tonight? I would be honoured."

She hesitated, but finally agreed; the goat-like emissary might know Affad! He might have some information. She cursed herself inwardly as she heard her own voice say, "Thank you, doctor, that would be a great pleasure." He rose to his full height and with an awkward angular gesture put out his hand to shake hers. She felt obscurely that he had been looking and talking to her as if to a person about whom he had heard a lot. But perhaps this was just another self-delusion, unworthy of such an exalted personage as a psychologist! Nevertheless she would go! Nevertheless!

He was already seated at a corner table by the time she entered the old Bavaria, with its pseudo-Austrian furnishings and sedate walls covered with framed political cartoons. He explained that he had come early to secure a corner table, having read in the paper that a great international conference was opening that day, and knowing of old how congested both hotels and restaurants became during such events. He was very much in *tenue de ville* and wore a dark stock with pearl-headed pin which made him seem like a barrister or judge. It was only after a while that she realised that he was passably tipsy which gave his discourse great smoothness; he had lost his raven's croak.

"Did you have your interview?" she asked and he said that he had had a rather unsatisfactory meeting with Mnemidis. "He is very distraught by the questions the doctors keep putting to him. He confuses them with the police. You see, he has always been in a privileged position in Egypt; you probably don't know, but he has the gift of healing among his other less pleasant attributes. He is famous and has made a fortune for his Cairo associate Ibrahim. So occasionally when he does escape and spends a few days in the *souks* of Cairo with the inevitable result, a blind eye is turned to the matter, though of course they sweep him up and imprison him again. He had the luck once to cure the chief of police of a stone, a gall-stone. After being touched by him Memlik Pascha passed the stone without difficulty, thus avoiding the operation we had all said would be necessary. As you know, Egypt is a strange, superstitious sort of place. They see the world in a different way. It is hard for us Greeks or Jews of the second capital, Alexandria, because we are for the most part brought up in Europe, and we see things with your eyes. But we also see their way. A split-vision. Of course a lot has to do with simple definitions. In Mnemidis *you* see a subject with a florid paranoia and an epileptoid inheritance resulting in bouts of acute hypomania and so on: but last night Ibrahim was telling me that he was born in the sign of the Ram; with Mars and Sun in opposition in Pluto; his moon mal-aspected in Scorpio, a magnetic dissonance between the Lion and Mercury in the eighth house ... It depends where you want to look for an explanation of the formidable double-bind which triggers him off." He turned his thirsty yellow eyes on her with a benign smiling weariness and rubbed his hands, as if he had just demonstrated something with them. She had begun to like him, for on the underside of his conversation, which was so assured, she felt a diffidence and a shyness which was most appealing. She longed to ask him if he knew Affad – after all she had accepted the evening invitation to do just that – yet her cursed pride held her bound to her reserve. What was to be done with a woman like herself?

"I suppose it is a different reality," she said, and he replied, "Very different but not less plausible once you realise how tricky words are! Our so-called scientific reality is a mere presumption suitable for certain intellectual exercises; but we dare not believe in it, completely, wholeheartedly. We cannot swear that the electron has no sex-life . . . but I am being silly! Thank you for smiling! But where the hypothesis of the individual ego with 'its' soul rules, as in a Christian state, people live in a state of unconscious hallucination. Is that too strong?"

"No. The problem has entered psychiatry."

"I don't think you are right, doctor. Or else we are talking at cross-purposes. The Freudian system at any rate works through and *with* the hypothesis of an individual ego."

"And Jung?"

"The doctrine has begun to crumble in Jung who is a Neo-Platonist in temperament. In that sense you are right. But all the discoveries are from Freud, he has all the honours. If the thing doesn't work 100 per cent, why, it is not his fault. He will become out of date just as Newton has. But for *us*, for *now*, we can't do without his genius."

"And Mnemidis, when he gets back to Egypt, will he be free to assume his old life? I mean will he be allowed his forays?"

"I expect he will be under reasonable surveillance – who knows? The police may turn him into an instrument, directing his activities: Memlik is quite capable of that. But nobody cares, any more than you care if a sportsman bags a couple of rabbits before lunch one day. In India, where everything began, this kind of human activity, obscene in itself, was undertaken on behalf of a goddess, called, I think, Kali; the murder was an act of so-called *thugee*, I was told."

"Good Lord!"

"An appropriate exclamation," he said, pouring himself out more wine. "In Cairo there is so much confusion, noise, lights, dust, fleas, people, daylight and darkness that nobody who disappears is really missed. I myself, when I was in my professional-doctor mood, tried a thing or two on our friend out of curiosity. He had a paranoid delusion that the walls of his room were closing in on him. Well, I had a detention cell specially made for him in which the walls really did close at the rate of five inches a day. You know, he reacted positively when it became obvious that it was not a delusion, it was true: the walls *were* closing in! One is at home in one's delusions and only asks to have them verified."

"Yes, I am aware of all the dialectical clevernesses, but they do little to help us find a therapy. Discussions about reality belong in the domain of the philosopher, and one pre-supposes *him* to be sane – another question mark! Are *you* happy about Mnemidis' activities?"

"No. For my part I would have him put away. I go even further: I think a healthy society would have him put away, after having tried to cure him for some years. Detention is no use."

"But?"

"But I may be wrong. The constitution of things may be juster than I am capable of supposing. Besides, look at the mess which comes about when I decided to take things into my own hands and act – Hitler! What an illustration of the misuse of the will, what misuse of human endeavour! And what is the use of getting rid of the poor Jews if you keep monotheism? It's crazy thinking."

"You should talk to Schwarz."

"I have. He agrees with me."

"Are you a Jew?"

"Of course. Everyone is a Jew!"

He had started to sound a trifle indistinct, as if the drink were beginning to tell on him; but he read her mind and said, reassuringly, "I sound drunk, don't I? I am not really. I took an overdose of a sleeping-draught yesterday by accident and the result is that I can hardly keep awake today. Excuse me."

"Should you drink?"

"Perhaps not; but after I have seen you home I am proposing to visit an old friend for a nightcap, and I must be in good form for him. Perhaps you know Sutcliffe?"

"Of course! Do you know him?"

"I have always known him. We are old hands, so to speak. I have been out of touch with him for a fairish time and am anxious to compare notes with the rogue."

"And Blanford?"

"I only know of him through Sutcliffe himself – something about collaboration on a book which wasn't going too well; according to him each one was trying to drag the sheets over to his side of the bed, and the book was suffering from it. I gather Sutcliffe has some sort of job here which he hates. As for 'our friend' Mnemidis he will be happy to get back home to Cairo. His nerves are at breaking-point under the questioning, so he says. Speaking in Arabic of course; he says you are putting a truth-drug in his food so he refuses it with the result that he is always hungry."

"O God!" she said with dismay. ". . . It's started!"

"I thought you must know, he must have said something."

"No. I was waiting for it, however! O what a dismal business it is when the persecution thing rears up. It's unfair!"

He laughed and said, "Yes: all is silent save for the noise

of swearing psychoanalysts getting the locks on their doors changed! Are you in the telephone book?"

"Yes. But I think we can ignore the graver eventualities in this case. Swiss detention is severe and exact. Still!"

"As you say, 'Still!'"

"Should I break off the interviews now before he turns nasty? Of course he himself may refuse to continue; and I was so much hoping ... However, I will tell Schwarz that the milk has turned – the expression is his."

"I should personally break it off."

It was a depressing thought to feel forced to conclude this promising line of enquiry – she could see the phantom letter slowly dissolving as a reality. Tomorrow she would recover her Bible and say goodbye to this striking madman on whom all pity and sympathy would be lost because he seemed to be completely filling a destined role, something for which he had been born. In murder he perfected himself, you might say! An existentialist formulation worthy of the Left Bank! Where the Jewish Babel was being built by Sartre and Lacan and their followers, swarming like flies on the eyeballs of a dying horse! She had had many a disagreement about this with Affad whose fatal indulgence for letters often made him excuse any sort of dog-rhetoric, or so she told him. And here they had come to the end of the evening and the fatal mental block against mentioning his name was as fast as ever. She sighed, and her companion smiled and said, "I expect you are sleepy. In Geneva one does not siesta as in my country, so that one makes a poor showing in the evening if one stays late."

"I am sorry."

"It was not a reproach."

He walked her back to her flat along the tranquil park-fringed borders of the lake, talking quietly about their patient, and about his plans for transplanting him, as he put it, back to the sumptuous apartment among the mosques which had been his before the present imbroglio had altered the balance of things. In the course of the coming week the legal side of the question would be settled, and then they would be free to devise the safe transfer of the patient. "Doubtless *you* will miss him and be full of a professional regret; but he is easily replaced, when you think of it. Almost any prime minister of any European country . . . As for him he spends hours at the little window of his new room which overlooks the kitchens. He is lost in admiration for the nuns."

"I didn't know."

"Yes. There is a silent order of nuns who are in charge of a whole wing and who do much of the catering for the whole establishment. The kitchens have big bay-windows and he can see them moving about preparing the food for the inmates, like 'feluccas' (I am quoting) for they wear those tall starched white coifs on their heads and broad white collars over their black vestments. I spent a while with him watching them, for I offered to go back with him and Pierre very kindly let me. They are very striking, they look like Easter lilies to me, the shape of the coif, and our friend wondered whether they were really silent by choice or whether they had become dumb owing to the lies disseminated in the Bible which he is reading so avidly. But he is so sane that he remains very cunning and one can't tell if he is lying or not – because he does not himself know. What a predicament to be in! Maybe it is what overturned the reason of men like Nietzsche. I have often wondered." It seemed rather a strange proposition, so she did not attempt to embroider on it. But in general how strange the preoccupations of lunatics were; what could Mnemidis find in the view of the nuns in the kitchen?

But everything has its answer. The blue unmediating infant's gaze of Mnemidis fixed itself, not upon the nuns in their picturesque uniforms, but upon the two great carving knives with which they so expertly cut up the daily bread of the establishment before distributing it deftly among the yellow baskets. He sighed when the operation was at an end and the baskets were loaded on to trays and trolleys and carried away to the refectory; he sighed as if woken from a dream of some total abstraction which had held him spellbound. This was indeed the case. His whole day orientated itself upon the appearance, as if upon a stage, of the nuns. The kitchens blazed suddenly with white light. A van drove up to the door, the back opened; the drivers lifted out a number of tall baskets with the loaves of bread in them. Into the kitchen they went and the nuns, seizing the two flashing, sabre-like products of the Upinal Steel Federation (often given away as pure advertisements) began their absorbed Christian sacrifice, cutting up the body of Christ into eatable-sized slices. In this way the Word would be made flesh at last; as for the wine, the blood, that would come later. Meanwhile the knives rose and fell, flashing in the sunlight, or poked and thrust with peristaltic suggestibility until with one hand he found himself fingering his private parts and deeply thinking. Deeply, passively thinking. Happiness lies in this sort of concentration, this surrender to one's inmost nature. What could be more innocent than a loaf of bread? It hardly felt the knife enter it, purr through its white flesh. The Upinals were terribly sharp always, they were known by the excellence of their superior steel. What better steel for a sacrificial knife, then? Mnemidis watched humbly, taking in every detail. Sometimes he broke off and made a short circle around the writing table, only to come back once more to the window and concentrate on this gripping vision of the nuns cutting up their Saviour. Give us this day . . .

Of some of this matter Constance was aware, but not of all; but the news that Mnemidis was running short of patience and simmering into revolt was depressing in the extreme. Though she had been tired at the dinner-table and was glad that her host walked her back to her flat relatively early, she found that sleep evaded her. Nor did a sleeping draught help matters, so she read a little, and then rose to make coffee for herself – a fatal decision. A profound depression seized her, and about everything – her life, her work, her profession, her future . . . It was like sliding down a bank of loose sand into a deep pit of self-reproach and, which was worse, self-pity. It would not do. She played a game of solitaire on the green card-table and after a while felt the drug beginning to work on her nerves. Sleep became once more a possible achievement, however troubled, so she risked getting back into bed with her book. On an impulse she did what she did quite often, picked up the telephone and dialled the time-clock. The announcer's recorded voice was not unlike Affad's, though the accent was different. She allowed him to recite the passing of time for about two whole minutes before shame drove her to cut him off. But her self-reproach became actualised by the dream voice of Max as he guided her through the *asanas*, forcing her to take them slowly, and at each stage to pin-point the nothingness-quotient of her mind, half narcotised now by the drug. It was clumsy, lop-sided yoga and would have merited a rebuke from the old man, but it had the desired effect for it shifted her attention from herself – sleeplessness is in the first instance simply exaggerated self-importance – and allowed her to lower herself into the warm pit of night with a mind too tired to manufacture any more dreams. No more dreams!

She slept.

The Escape Clause

IT HAD BEEN STIRRING WITHIN HIM NOW FOR DAYS, AND HE was aware of a gradually growing constraint in his feelings about the outer world – first towards his keeper Pierre and then the doctor, that handsome woman who made everything sound glib and roguish. He knew now that everything she had been telling him was false, and came from the Black Bible she had loaned him. Her smile, moreover, was false as a mouse-trap – *une souricière de sourire!* First she had thrust him down into full oblivion with her medicines: now it was this mysterious letter. He had perused it negligently, vaguely noting the date it contained, and that not precise. It said "*à partir de . . .*" which seemed to offer no very exact information. Nor had this anything to do with his own concerns – the gradually overwhelming, suffocating, feeling which would evolve slowly into the basic cold hate upon which his actions would be based. Hush! she must not become aware of his state of mind, he must pretend to be pious, for they were all Christians and had been brought up in a vengeful code, always seeking moral redress, always thinking sacrificially. For some time now when he heard Pierre's footsteps on the gravel he would hasten to kneel down and feign to be deep in prayer when the Judas clicked open. No doubt this was reported. He watched her reactions carefully when he criticised the good book; he intended at the very end suddenly to pretend that he had been converted, that after all he had come to believe in it. That would put her off her guard and make her become perhaps more negligent in her habits. He had already reflected on how much energy it would need to overpower Pierre in the course of their walk across the wood. It is true that the negro was built like a house, but that did not seem to Mnemidis an over-riding consideration. He was agile and versed in the ju-jitsu style of wrestling. And he was totally unafraid, his wholehearted self-dedication gave him the strength of a lion. He felt the current of his desire sweeping through his body like a stream of electricity. There was only one question which created a difficulty in his planning. *L'arme blanche*, in the expressive French phrase – the crucial *knife* which he needed for his self-expression. At home in Cairo he had a wall collection of them – beautiful knives of all calibres with which he practised assiduously. He could both throw and stab at will, and as suddenly as a snake striking. No real problem here. It was only the details which remained to be worked out.

The mention of Cairo now, that was a new factor in his thinking, a new promise of life and freedom. The whole matter had filled him with renewed enthusiasm for his avocation. To quit this dull grey Swiss background for the brilliant Cairo of his youth – goodness, his heart sang within him! And just as a farewell present he would, as a *pourboire*, so to speak, leave them a knife-print or two in his best vein before leaving. It would be his going-away present for the sterile world of doctors and priests and policemen. Who did they think he was? *He was, after all, Mnemidis, the one and only member of his species*. Old B., the doctor, used to tease him about this proposition, but really it was the truth. B. used to joke and say, "Now tell me to which species do you belong? Imaginary Man, Marginal Man, Fortuitous Man, Superfluous Man, Parallel Man? . . ." And he would reply, "To none, to none. I am the incarnation of Primal Man. I am perfected in my sainthood because I know not the meaning of Fear!" As he spoke he had a sudden vision of his own consciousness hanging in the air above him – brilliantly iridescent and glowing, a self-perfected globe of celestial light, throbbing and hovering in an atmosphere of pure bliss of which he was the human instrument. He was the pure spirit of the perfected Act! It had all come to him from that first day when as an adolescent he had strangled the little Bedouin child who had come to the house to beg for work. So silently, his lust glowing like a great ruby in his mind. In this way he had separated himself from the rest of humanity.

Yes, the thought of Cairo struck a new note, and the sudden arrival upon the scene of ancient associates with their promise of freedom excited him unduly. Moreover when they spoke to him in Arabic, as the doctor did, he felt quite disarmed, and incapable of keeping a secret about his feelings, about his eagerness to be done with the Swiss scene. But the doctor urged compliance upon him, and patience and watchfulness; a hasty move might spoil his chances of an escape. There were documents to be filled in, people to be consulted. Nevertheless he felt in honour bound to make it clear that since he realised that he was being systematically poisoned he found it much harder to set aside his feelings of impatience and frustration. Much, much harder.

Nor could he help noticing that his jailors had redoubled their precautions, for his person, his cell and his meagre possessions were subjected every morning to the most careful scrutiny by Pierre who dwelt lingeringly upon each object, as if he were trying to memorise it, humming softly as he did so. What charm the man had! Mnemidis ground his teeth soundlessly, feeling the muscles at his temples contract and relax. He had a secret premonition that it would not be long now, things were moving into the sort of spiral which quickened into the catharsis of action.

His intuitions seemed verified almost at once, for on presenting himself for the usual interview he was confronted by the surly figure of Schwarz who informed him that the long treatment was to be discontinued. "I understand you have expressed strong reservations about the doctor treating you,

and in deference to them I have had her transferred to another
field of enquiry. On her return from leave she will undertake
other duties. I hope this will satisfy your sense of justice." This
sounded a most elaborate and juicy climb-down, and the
patient was all smiles at his unexpected victory; he rubbed his
hands and bowed. Then his face darkened again with a
renewed wave of doubt, for it seemed to him that they were
trying to shirk their responsibilities; after all, the damage had
been done. The poison was already permeating his whole
system, and now they were talking of abandoning him. No, it
wouldn't do, it wouldn't do at all! "It's all very well," he said
at last, with a smouldering glance of contempt, "but what about
all I have been through, all the questions, the waste of time
. . . eh?" Schwarz sighed and said patiently, "I hope you will
soon forget your ordeal. Tomorrow or the next day you will
be returned to the civil authorities and they will arrange for
you to join your two friends and return to your homeland.
Surely that must please you?" Mnemidis moistened his lips
and asked if it were true. "Of course it is true," said Schwarz,
who now permitted himself the faintest tinge of joviality. And
indeed his two friends, as if to prove the correctness of the
doctor's announcement, presented themselves with good news.
The transfer was being negotiated, there was no impediment
in law, and within a week or ten days they would present themselves with all the papers and a special Red Cross ambulance
to take him to the airport where a special plane would be
waiting, bound for Cairo. It was like a dream, he wept as he
thought of it, but sadly, for it had come too late. They would
not avoid their retribution quite so easily, particularly the
woman. The whole thing had been her idea, the whole cunning
interrogatory had been devised by her with the idea of making
him doubt himself. That night he wet his bed. He was assailed
with extraordinary dreams and visions of power and omni-
potence; he became once more the child divinity whose

purpose burned within him like a lamp of grace. His tongue swelled up in his mouth like a puff adder, then his whole throat. He woke late but ready for anything. He had a feeling the hour was at hand, though for the moment the details were not clear; they would come.

When there is such a stylist in mischief as Mnemidis prepared for action, the very spirit of mischief presents itself in order to facilitate things. In this case it was the Swiss mania for insignificant detail which played the part. Before parting with their visitor it was essential that the documentation upon his case be complete; hence the long and exhausting series of blood-tests and nerve-tests, of analyses and readings, of cephalograms and cardiograms . . . the whole rigmarole of quantitative science must have a final outing before restoring him to his world of occasional involuntary murder. He had to blow into tubes, swallow liquids, stand on one leg, kneel and lift weights. He waited patiently and most obediently throughout all this, waited for the door which he knew would open. He went from laboratory to laboratory like a lamb, watched over by Pierre, whom he had come to love like a brother. But he was in a state of heightened attention, he noticed every lock, bolt and bar; yet for the time being nothing beckoned him, nothing whispered conspiratorially in his ear to say, "Now! This is it!" And apart from all this the change and the movement were refreshing for someone suffering from over-confinement.

The last of these investigations were the most elementary, and usually took place first, on entry into the hospital. There was a tank-like changing room with seats and lockers on all sides, changing-screens and douches. In here were machines which recorded your height and weight and such vital facts as general corpulence or the circumference of calves and breasts. The entry corridor to the whole complex contained noticeboards and toilets, and finally opened into the spacious dining-rooms and kitchens. It was in this tank-like precinct that the magical whisper came and communicated itself to Mnemedis.

To divest himself of the long-sleeved regulation coat of pleasant green tweed and his woollen vest he stepped behind a screen while Pierre, respecting the delicacy of one who had been "born a gentleman", did not follow him but stood and waited on the other side; the articles of clothing were thrown upon the screen and Mnemidis, stripped now to the waist, looked strangely coy and playful. Ignoring the weighing machine which stood waiting for him, he gave his jailor a sudden push with both hands, catching him off his guard, and with one and the same movement, propelled himself through the door and into the corridor where he promptly turned the key upon Pierre and went off – but slowly, thoughtfully, for he knew that if one moves slowly people suspect nothing – and entered the network of locker-rooms and privies which led to the kitchens. One cannot describe him as thinking all this out in detail; he was really sleepwalking, letting instinct guide him. Flashes of light like a summer lightning dazzled him from time to time and he blinked his eyes. He heard the voice of Pierre and the rattling of the door but was not alarmed at all. A wild certainty possessed him. The spirit of mischief was in the saddle. He went solemnly and industriously from room to room, locking each door behind him, and so at last came to the spacious kitchens which were empty. He stopped to gaze about him, noted with appreciation the warm sunlight shining through the high windows upon the spotless array of cooking utensils lining the walls. It was very Swiss in its impeccable cleanliness, the great kitchen, one felt that no germ would find a harbour there; it smelt clinical and pure, its air filtered by the clean flowing draught of fans. But he was looking for something and had no time to waste on idle appreciation of his surroundings. From his window on the opposite side of the court his gaze fell . . . just where? He made a swift calculation and changed direction. Yes, the bread-bins and the wall of tins was on the right, surely they must be there? There!

The knives, spotless as the rest, were there!

With the current of joy and affirmation flowing through his body he contemplated, giving thanks to his creator; he even joined his hands before his breast and shook them in thanksgiving, like a Christian. Then with a sneaking, smiling air of happiness, he took up first one and then the other of the knives and felt its exquisite balance in the palm of his hand; it was as pregnant with futurity as an egg. At this moment the swing-doors at the end of the kitchen opened and in swayed the monumental form of Pierre, looking puzzled, for this had never happened to him before and he found it surprising. Moreover with Mnemidis now stripped there was no sleeve to grab in order to tame and pivot him. The big man was suddenly realising that much of his mastery over things, over people, was due to familiar routines; the lack of that basic sleeve troubled and disoriented him. Nor had he seen Mnemidis ever look quite like this – blithe and exuberant, his whole bearing suffused with a glory from on high. He proposed to play cat and mouse with Pierre, but jovially, with kindliness, for he really loved and esteemed this companion of his solitary hours. He put the hand with the knife behind his back and beckoned Pierre to approach with the other, playfully, teasingly; and when the "Malabar" obeyed he dodged back and round, in and out among the sinks and cupboards. They performed a slow and somewhat elaborate ballet in this way, passing across the great kitchens in a sort of gruesome two-step for Pierre was fully aware of the knife and of the danger he was in from a sudden change of mood. It would have been wise for him to pick a weapon for himself and try to despatch the madman with a lucky blow on the head – a saucepan, perhaps: but he preferred to be patient and not provoke a flare-up of aggressiveness. He was calm and confident of the outcome and only concerned lest he might obtain a wound while trying to disarm Mnemidis. Moreover, dancing about like this they were killing time and it could not be long before somebody came into the kitchens and then Pierre could shout for help in surrounding his man. Where were the sisters? Where was the staff of the place? There was no sign of a soul. They continued on their appointed courses like two ill-omened planets in orbit — planets engaged in a gravitational flirtation which could only end one way, in a collision!

Neither was the least out of breath as yet, and watching the intense concentration with which they danced an observer might have thought their synchronised and stylised motion the result of long rehearsal. But there was method in Mnemidis' madness – to coin a phrase; he had seen a half-open door which gave on to a sort of clothes-closet which housed a quantity of aprons and gowns, of buckets and pails and sundries. He was working his slow way round until his jailor had his back to it – it was like putting a billiard ball over a pocket. This done, he attacked the "Malabar" with almost inconceivable force, giving a pious grunt which echoed throughout the kitchen. Under the impetus of this rush the "Malabar", attentive to the threat of the knife, backed away and before he knew where he was found himself pinned into the closet against the hanging clothes, against the wall, with a hand firmly clutching his throat, his own arms vaguely encircling the shorter man with force but without design. And now Mnemidis with thoughtful and considered strokes, like an experienced cook, started to lard him with the knife he held in his hand. All this seemed to the "Malabar" to pass in a kind of languorous slow motion, but in fact the blows were swift and tellingly aimed. Meanwhile Mnemidis gazed into his face with attention, almost lecherously, as if he were looking into a gauge which might tell him how successful his assault was. Negroes do not turn pale but rosy in this kind of fatal situation. Mnemidis felt his man give a crooning sound and lean forward upon him. It would be like tearing down a high curtain, he thought to himself. Both were breathing heavily now, but Pierre was blowing out his cheeks with exhaustion, and his lungs were filling and emptying very quickly all of a sudden. It was as if he had run the 100 metres in record time.

With loving penetration Mnemidis continued to hold him and gaze up into his face, now bloodless and somehow serene despite the exhaustion – a serenity which perhaps counterfeited and anticipated the inevitable death which must follow such an exchange. It was a crucial sweetness, and the pallor was highly satisfying to the author of the assault who stood, holding him upright and scrutinising him so tenderly. At last Mnemidis stepped back and gently posed the teetering giant more snugly in the mass of hanging coats. He must be losing blood rapidly, Pierre, but he remained upright in a pose at once fragile and authoritative, his arms out and his fingers crooked, but no longer on the body of his adversary. His expression suggested that he was all of a sudden deeply intro-spective, investigating his inmost feelings; to try and determine perhaps the extent of the leak, the volume of blood which was now flowing – he could feel it, soft and quite insidious – flowing down. Losing blood, yes, he was losing *blood*. He groaned, and as if upon a signal Mnemidis stepped back and shut the closet door, leaving him to stand trembling among the clothes.

By the grace of the Creator the kitchens were still empty, he had them to himself; he was very thirsty, so he gave himself a long drink from the sink and tenderly wiped the blade of his knife. Then, squaring his shoulders, he went in search of a garment which might hide his nakedness above the waist, or indeed disguise him, for as yet his journey had only begun, there was much to be done. Vaguely stirring in the back of his mind was the idea of perhaps a chef's cape or a baker's white coat, or a doctor's regalia, but what he indeed hit upon was even more impenetrable as a disguise. Some of the nuns engaged in heavy manual labour like washing clothes or swabbing floors, had the habit of hanging up their robes and coifs in one of the adjacent changing-rooms which was open. He could hardly hide his glowing self-satisfaction as he found three or four of these costumes from which to choose; and most particularly the starched and all but spotless coifs. What a disguise! This huge headpiece was shaped like a lily and he slipped one on just to see how such an affair would look. He was amazed by his own face, it looked quite terrifyingly composed with just a trace of human light in the eye, and just a trace of a smile at the corners of the mouth. But he had never noticed before that he had dimples, and the better to study them he allowed his smile to broaden, to overflow as it were; the dimples belonged to someone's early childhood, as did the face now, whose contours were demarcated by the white helm of the nun. But this one was a trifle too big; he went along the line and out of the three or four available picked one which he snugged down over his head to make a perfect fit. Then he sought out the curtain-like nun's robes and picked a suitable one. All this happened in a flash; he consciously hurried things along because he could hear, somewhere in the depths of the building, a muffled bumping as if Pierre, half-foundered by the stabbing, had started to react, to fall about among the hanging coats.

The mirror gave back an elderly nun with a face full of unhealthy confessional secrets, expressions both perverted and hypocritical, but with an uncanny brilliance of eye. A nun of great experience, yet not disabused. A nun ready for anything. He almost chuckled with delight as he crept out of the closet and into the main hall, walking with bent head, as if deep in thought, and very slowly so as not to excite curiosity. He examined the notice-boards, passed them in review, and then just as self-confidently directed himself towards the wood which he traversed every day with Pierre. At once when he was under cover his pace increased, and he arrived at the little villa which housed the psychological unit almost at a run. By great good luck the office of Schwarz was empty, as also was the consulting-room of the woman doctor – the one he was most anxious to see. He sat down suddenly to reflect. Perhaps if he waited they might come, the one or the other? But the woman was more important.

He sat down in Schwarz's swivel chair for a long moment and reflected; in his mind he went back along the chain of past events – those of the last hour – in order to evolve a line of action suitable to his case and his intentions. He had retained the addresses of his two Egyptian friends, and once he had finished his scheduled business he intended to call at their hotel and give himself up, put himself in their charge, hoping that it was not too late for them to put the escape plan into operation and waft him back home to Cairo. So he sat, taking stock of himself and fingering the heavy handles of the kitchen knives – for he could not resist taking both. It was somewhat awkward having them, but each had a stout leather sheath and a scabbard, and each was attached by a tough thong so that he could loop it into the belt which held up his trousers. The long cassock-type garment of the nun was most voluminous, and obliterated all contours; it amused and excited him for it brought him back old memories of the carnivals in Alexandria. It was like a black domino. But . . . he sprang to his feet and chided himself for wasting valuable time here instead of moving on into town to further his plans. The nun's habit had two great inner pockets, one of which contained a rosary and the other tickets to a *fête votive* in a lake village. Not to mention a cambric handkerchief, with which he might cover part of his face if necessary. But it was a pity to have missed both the doctors like this. He felt a twinge of regret to leave the consulting-room without having, so to speak, made his mark, left a message of some sort. Yet what? On Schwarz's desk he saw an apple on a plate – it constituted the modest lunch of the analyst who was dieting and trying to lose weight. With his knife Mnemidis cut it in half, giving a little chuckle of pure mischief.

Then he set off at a trot through the wood, only slowing his pace when he came to open spaces bordering the main entrance, or trim gardens rich in flowerbeds where he adopted a loitering, contemplative gait, snail-like in fact, most suitable for a nun who tells her beads as she walks, rapt in prayerful union with her Saviour. He had expected by now some sort of spirited pursuit, cries of surprise, running footsteps; it was disappointing, but nevertheless. He was usually chased and pounced upon in such circumstances. But he recognised in all this the hand of fate – for he had as yet not accomplished his mission. He frowned as he walked thoughtfully towards the car park and the main entrance. There was a risk that the alarm had been given, that they had telephoned the front gate to stop all people trying to leave. But apparently not, all was quiet. It would be more than an hour before Pierre fell out of his cupboard on to the floor – under which the pool of blood had traced a path which someone would notice. No, all was normal in the office of the gate warden. Moreover, a further stroke of luck awaited the newly canonised nun, for parked outside the gate and obviously ready to move off was the baker's van which brought the establishment its daily bread. The driver, a fresh-faced youth, was just shutting down the motor hood after checking the oil. The sight of one of the sisters walking through the gate was not calculated to arouse any particular interest in the guardians of the gate who simply gave Mnemedis a cursory glance as he passed under their window. He held his handkerchief to his mouth as if he had a cold and spoke in a hoarse whisper as he asked the young driver whether he was going into town, and whether he would give him a lift to the lakeside village to the *fête votive* for which he had now two tickets. The boy agreed most respectfully to take the sister aboard, and Mnemidis climbed in beside him and snuggled down, delighted by the ease with which he had hoodwinked the authorities and broken prison. It was in the best tradition – he had never done a cleverer, smoother break-out in his whole life. He restrained a temptation to whistle a tune, and asked the young man in a hoarse whisper whether he went to church, and if so to which. "Catholic" was the reply.

Mnemidis was emboldened by the manifest impenetrability of his disguise – he looked every inch an elderly sister with a slightly waggish disposition. He took the wise precaution, however, of talking in a hoarse whisper, as if he had lost his voice, due to a heavy cold. As the nervous youth went on in *naïf* fashion to outline his religious convictions the sister of mercy put her arm about his shoulders in sacerdotal sympathy. Then she asked if during the night he was not troubled sometimes by unworthy thoughts or dreams or . . . wishes? And her hand slid softly down to caress the young man's thigh. He could not forbear to flush up and draw in his breath – it was sexually exciting to feel this apparently innocent advance. He did not quite know what to make of it. Meanwhile Mnemidis went on talking in his hoarse whisper about the difficulty of sleeping when one was young and pursued by chimeras of experiences one had not as yet tasted. Did not the young man sometimes . . . But the young man was manifestly excited now and blushing furiously. He had never had an experience of this order, and he had lost all his composure. After all, what could one say to a nun? He too felt that he had lost his voice, while the stealthy advance of the nun's hand now made clear her intention – of making free with him sexually. But the steady flow of language did not cease as the caresses became more pointed and deliberate. Finally, in a more authoritative fashion, the sister told him to pull his vehicle off the road and into a copse which obligingly presented itself, and here the seduction was consummated. The young man mixed confusion, sexual excitement and shame in equal parts. Then he conducted his passenger to the lakeside road and set her down at the gates of the park in which the *fête votive* was being held, and for which she held tickets, it would seem. The nun said goodbye with a ghoulish demureness and the young man drove off in something of a hurry, glad to be shot of so strange a customer.

But this encounter was most valuable to Mnemidis in that it gave him confidence in his disguise. It provoked no curiosity and much respect. He even tested it by going up to the policeman on the park gate and asking the time. The man drew back and saluted respectfully as he conveyed the information. No, it was completely foolproof. With a sigh of relief Mnemidis now abandoned himself to pure pleasure. He walked about the spacious gardens, visited the flower show in the conservatories and helped judge the competition by putting his judgement on to a slip of paper and sliding it into the box at the gate. Then he walked into the other corner and saw a Punch and Judy show which he found completely absorbing. He had forgotten how marvellous the facial expressions of children can be when they are absorbed by a theatrical performance. You can see the adult lodged in the youthful body; if you gaze into the eyes and let your intelligence flow into the child's face you can divine very clearly what sort of adult it will become in due course. He was delighted by this exercise, involving a thesaurus of young faces in all their moods. And then he went into a concert where gross romantic music was the keynote, and he throbbed and almost swooned to the strains of Strauss and Delibes. Emotion is permitted in a nun. He moved his head from side to side and closed his eyes with each wave of delight. At the same time his fingers caressed the forms of the knives which lay so quietly obedient upon his thighs.

He had all the time in the world, that is what he had begun to feel. He could afford to take his time. But when he spotted a telephone booth he suddenly remembered that he did not yet know the exact address of Constance's flat. But he soon found her in the supplement devoted to trades and professions, and reading over the address a couple of times unerringly memorised it.

This is where he would go when he was good and ready, to exact retribution from the woman who had so misused him both morally and physically. He closed his eyes the better to memorise the address.

FIVE

The Return Journey

WITHIN THE SPACE OF THIS RELATIVELY SHORT absence from the town Constance found that the dispositions had somewhat changed, been reshuffled. The mid-morning "elevenses" of Toby and Sutcliffe had remained the only constant, but the company of the *billiard-aires*, as Sutcliffe had christened what threatened now to become an informal club, had been increased by new arrivals. Blanford had graduated to a wheel-chair with a movable back which he could adjust to correspond to his waves of fatigue, or desire for a cat-nap. He found the atmosphere most congenial for his work, and he found that Sutcliffe argued best when he was allowed to be slightly absent-minded, half-concentrated on a tricky shot. He had his best thoughts paradoxically when he was occupied with something else – it was as if they were completely involuntary, arriving from nowhere: but every artist has this unique experience, of receiving throbs from outer space as pure gifts. Another member of the company was Max, who in a curious way felt a little lonely in Geneva and was anxious to take up old friendships; he played an excellent game of pool, and despite his new avocation as a yogi was still very much his old self, easy to tease in an affectionate way for he was so very humble, had always been despite the gaudy uniforms provided by Lord Galen. The gloomy and deteriorate old bar took on a new life; the moribund old man who ran it so very inexpertly invoked the aid of a niece or a daughter-in-law who started to produce eatable comestibles and superior brands of whisky and gin to meet the new custom. And this general disposition towards improvement had borne fruit, for among the new members of this confraternity were two of the secretaries who worked for Toby, and even Ryder, Sutcliffe's head of section, who since his wife's accident had taken to drinking rather heavily. Moreover, he was somewhat intimidated, or so he professed, by frequenting "sort of artist chaps", because he was simply "an ordinary lowbrow service mind". His misgivings were rudely set to rest by Sutcliffe.

"The word is a misnomer, it should be *autist*. I know that the animal is short of manners and lacks true refinement, but then he is tolerably happy with his vulgar streak. There are advantages in being a *parvenu*: one is shunned by people dying of the slow blood-poisoning of over-refinement. The poor artist is a fartist, and he belongs to an endangered species and needs the protection of the reservation. His compensations are secret ones. He belongs to the Floppy Few!"

"O Christ!" said the soldier in despair. "If ever there was someone in need of subtitles . . ."

But it was not always as bad as this, and he solaced himself with the more worldly company of Felix Chatto who had smelt out this informal morning gathering and graced it with his company several times a week. Geneva was short on really good company combined with complete informality, and that is what the smoky little bar had to offer, despite its impersonality and general ugliness. And the general relaxation of the atmosphere was also a sign that the long suppurating war was drawing to an end. New sorts of agency were beginning to make their appearance in the town – agencies for peace and reconstruction, not for war, espionage, subversion. The faintest shadow of a new atmosphere had begun to flower among the ruins of the epoch. Yet how exhausted they all were. (These thoughts are those of Constance.) Yes, even those who had apparently done nothing were worn down by the invisible moral attrition of war. In her own case she felt its separate weight added to the weight of the human experiences through which she had found her way with such difficulty, with so many hesitations. And now once more changes were in the air, the structure of things was shifting, disintegrating around her. Soon, she supposed dumbly, she would be on the move again, heading for some distant country, some new project. Only the thought that Affad was coming back halted her.

"Halted her" is not true either, for at the very heart of her emotion, the seat of her loving awareness of him as a man, she was aware that something had gone wrong and that she did not know how it could be put right; it was like a break in an electrical circuit, it would need mending by both sides. But if they were not together? There was the rub. To still her sense of overwhelming boredom she had begun to spend more time with Blanford, indeed whole afternoons talking to him on his balcony or lying beside his bed. Not infrequently they were joined by the massive figure of Sutcliffe, tired of pacing the waterfront on misty afternoons. It was curious, too, to hear them discussing the interminable sequences of the "double concerto" as Blanford called their novel now. He took the concerns of form very seriously and reacted with annoyance to Sutcliffe's jocose suggestions, namely that the whole thing would be much tidier as an exchange of letters. "We could have fun, spelling God backwards! You could sign yourself OREPSORP and I could sign myself NABILAC. It's the other side of the moon for Prospero and Caliban—between us we could really control things. I mean Reality or YTILAER. With many an involuntary chuckle and lots of spicy new dialogue like: 'A stab of grog, Podsnap—I mean Pansdop? Don't mind if I do, mate. Couldn't care less if I did!' In this way *enanteiodromion*, everything would be seen to be turning into its opposite, even our book which would take on a mighty shifty strangeness, become an enticement for sterile linguists to parse in their sleep."

"But hard on the reader, surely," pleaded Constance. "And of an unhealthy schizoid cast of mind."

Aubrey said, "I am deliberately turning the novel inside out like a sleeve."

"Then back," said Sutcliffe.

"Yes, then back."

"I have treated people like you, sometimes even much worse. But with no success, alas. And I was brought up on rigorous fare like Ivanhoe and Proust which enjoyed classical exactitude as to form . . ."

"But that is Culture," said Sutcliffe in his most reproachful manner. "Or if you prefer, ERUTLUC. You see, we have never been interested in the real world – we see it through a cloud of disbelief. Ni eht gninnigeb saw eht drow!" He intoned the phrase majestically and explained that it was simply the backspelling of "In the beginning was the Word!"

"So we are back to culture, are we?" she said. "And we are not the only ones. Lord Galen is being deeply troubled by the word as well."

Blanford said, "I know. He has been to see me about it. But first let me tell you about Cade my manservant who has started to encounter him at night when he prowls about the city. Cade, when he is deeply thinking, puts on an extraordinary facial expression which reminds me of that sculpture by an artist whose name I have repressed called 'Romulus and Remus founding Rome'. That is how intense it is. Then after a time he clears his throat and says, 'Sir, may I speak?' and when I nod, goes on, 'I saw *him* again last night!' A hush. 'Him who?' I ask and he says with slyness, 'Lord Galen. He was in one of the houses. They were laughing at him. They asked me if he was really a Lord because he calls his balls his "heirlooms". Of course, I said, that's why he is worried about their performance. He 'opes for a son and heir. I trust I was right, I done right.' 'Cade, you done right.' 'Thank you, Master Aubrey.'"

"I shall ask Toby to take Galen to the Swiss perverts' restaurant where they only serve fried grapes in order to break down your reserve. Is he really worried about his heirlooms?"

"No. It's to do with culture. And it is very human and touching. He has been told to see man in the raw!"

Indeed there was a good deal of truth in this, and it had largely come about because of Galen's latest and most illustrious appointment.

He sidled into Blanford's room at the clinic looking like the Phantom of the Opera; there were dark circles under his eyes. He was slightly out of breath and very much out of composure as he cast about for a way of expressing his disturbed feelings. "Aubrey!" he said, with a suspicion of a quiver to his underlip, "I felt that I must consult you, and I hope you will have time to hear me out. Aubrey, I am at a great crossroads in my professional life." He sat down on a chair, and placing a briefcase full of books on the floor at his feet, fanned himself with his hat—as if to quell the fires of anxiety which were consuming him. "My dear Lord Galen, of course," said Blanford with a rush of affection and sympathy, and put out his hand which Galen grabbed and shook with gratitude. "What is it? What can it be?"

Galen allowed his breathing to rediscover its normal rhythm before unfolding his tale. "Today, Aubrey," he said at last, "I am at the top of the tree, I have the plum job of all—I am the Coordinator of Coordinated Cultures!" He waited for it to sink in before continuing, "And yet I can't for the life of me discover what culture *is*, what the word I am in charge of *means*. I know that I pass for a well-educated man and all that. But I am supposed to work out a report which will deal with the whole future of the European book, for example, for we control all the paper. Someone has to decide what is good of our culture, and that is me. But how can I decide if I don't know what it is? And from every side they come bringing me what they call 'cornerstones' to look at. 'You must include that in your recommendations, it's a *cornerstone*,' they keep saying.

I am surrounded with cornerstones. And some of them – well, I have never been so disgusted in my life." He groped among his affairs and produced a copy of *Ulysses* by Joyce. "Aubrey! Upon my honour what do you think of this . . . this cornerstone?"

"I can see your dilemma," said Aubrey, thinking of the scabrous parts of Joyce's masterpiece. But to his surprise what Galen said was, "It's the most anti-Semitic book I have ever read. Absolutely *virulent*." Aubrey was quite bemused for he had never read it in this way. "Just how?" he asked in genuine perplexity and Lord Galen hissed back, "If as they tell me the earliest cornerstone was Homer with his hero Ulysses, representing the all-wise and all conquering traveller, the European human spirit so to speak, why this book is a wicked take-off of Homer, a satire. According to Joyce the modern Ulysses is a Dublin Jew of the most despicable qualities, the lowest character, the foulest morals; and his wife even lower. This is what our civilisation has come to . . ." He made the noise which is represented in French novels phonetically as "*Pouagh!*"

He poured himself a very stiff whisky and made a forlorn gesture of impotence, as if invoking either the sky or perhaps the shade of Joyce himself to descend and resolve his dilemma. But Blanford was genuinely aroused by this extraordinary analysis, the first of its kind, and lost in admiration mixed with astonishment that such insight came from someone like Galen. In a flash his mind seized on the notion and fitted it into a scheme which might satisfy a philosopher of culture of the kind of Spengler. European Man as the gay artificer Ulysses who had endured until Panurge took up the tale once more and made it live. And then the Dionysiac force gradually spent itself and the Spenglerian decline and division set in. Expiring volcanoes went on smoking with names like Nietzsche, Strindberg, Tolstoy, but the ship was going down by the stern . . . Lord Galen was there, floating in the sky with his arms outspread, a look of agonised perplexity on his face, crying, "Our culture! What is it? I wish someone could tell me." In his hand another "cornerstone", another virulently anti-Semitic analysis of European culture with its bias towards materialism and the inevitable exploitation of the underprivileged by the "capitalists". Céline! The form of Lord Galen settled once more like a moth upon the end of the bed to continue his exposition. "Now at last this beastly war caused by that rotter Hitler is actually coming to an end and we can hope for peace, we can work for peace. Aubrey, my dear boy, can't you see what hope there is in the air? A real hope! But if our culture goes on being celebrated by fanatical anti-Semites we shall end in another bloodbath – O God. My goodness, what have the Jews done to merit it? After all we gave you our bomb to drop on the Japanese. Our very own bomb which we could have kept to ourselves, or else charged you an enormous royalty on its use while keeping the patent private. Don't you see? But this problem came at me head on when I got my new post. For about ten years, as far as we can see, there will have to be some sort of priority system of control for paper stocks. Not only sanitary paper, Aubrey, but also school textbooks as well as newspapers and books of art. Above all 'cornerstones'. The question to ask oneself is always 'Is it a cornerstone or not? If not, out!' The whole thing has become a nightmare and has caused the whole of my committee days of acrimonious argument, and myself anxiety and sleeplessness. But I owe it to European culture to get it right. I must pass the books which are fruitful and proscribe those which aren't. But how to decide? It's all very well to suggest, as someone did, that we might get a book like this *Ulysses* rewritten in a more acceptable and forward-looking manner by someone like Beverley Nicholls, but that would be interfering, and I don't hold with mere temporising measures. You cannot rewrite a cornerstone or even bowdlerise it; I quite agree and would never condone it. But how to be sure what is what? I received a petition from the committee which said: 'In our view our Chairman for all his experience of commerce and diplomacy has a somewhat narrow view of culture and ordinary life. In our view he should perhaps go out into the world a little and see man as he is, in the raw, in order to judge the culture of which he is only a part.' I try not to get too easily nettled and I accepted the criticism in good part. Well, I must go out more into the world. But first I rang up Schwarz and asked him if he knew why everyone was so anti-Semite, and he said, yes, he did. It was because of monotheism and monolithic radical philosophies based on the theory of values. It was Judaism, he said, that irritated everyone so. He added that I was behaving like a paranoid minority syndrome in allowing myself to get upset. Aubrey, I have been called many things in my time but never a syndrome. I rang off in despair. This is what you get when you search quite disinterestedly for the meaning of a word like culture in our time."

He halted the recital of his woes in order once more to avail himself of the whisky which, Blanford remarked, he now drank in heroic doses, hardly diluted. It was obvious that this intellectual adventure had shaken him, had even pushed him into having recourse to the bottle more frequently than was his wont. "And then what?" said Aubrey, torn between amusement and sympathy for his friend. Galen groaned. "Schwarz," he said, "has got an amazing idea that the Jews *created* racial discrimination by their Chosen Race policy and their refusal to dilute the superior blood of Israel by mixing it with inferior brands. Isn't that very strange?" Aubrey said, "Well, it's one way of looking at it. It could be true like in India; the top dog complex creates instant Untouchables – which is what the gentiles are for strict Jews. Am I wrong?" Galen knew nothing of India. "Jews are not all Untouchables, on the contrary they are very generous, though of course they bargain and like to know where their money goes. But the Jew is generous, quite an easy touch in fact!"

There seemed no point in pursuing this line of thought, based as it was on a typical misunderstanding. "You win," said Aubrey, abandoning the train of thought, and with a smile Lord Galen stretched out along the end of the bed and, meta-phorically, put his head under his wing and went to sleep, looking rather like an old rook snoozing on its nest.

But he went on talking with his eyes shut – burbling, rather, for there were patches of free association as well as gaps in the slow sequence of his rambling. It was as if he were talking not to Aubrey but to his Maker. For example, at one point he raised his head and still with closed eyes exclaimed passion-ately, "No Gentile could have invented double-entry book-keeping!" accompanying the thought with a gesture of fearful vehemence. Now, however, he subsided into sleep with a somewhat fatuous smile on his face and whispered, "It was all this that led me to the *pouf* of Mrs Gilchrist. A young diplomat in search of profound sensations agreed to accompany me. I did not know of her international celebrity at the time – apparently like so many things in our time she is a chain store, and has branches all over India, Turkey, Greece, France and Eastbourne. She literally breeds girls for the diplomatic and military markets. I seemed to impress her very favourably; she said I had majesty. She was of uncertain age and with heavily tinted hair combined joviality and hysterectomy in equal parts. For a moment I almost thought I might love such a woman – Aubrey, they were right, I was in need of wanton-ness. She was, said my young diplomat friend, thoroughly representative of the age and the culture, so I could go ahead and explore on an empirical basis. There was a lot of talk about Lective (hic) Finities – another cornerstone by Goitre. I didn't follow but pretended I did until she hopped back on the nest. Then I was lost in the night of her hair – afternoon, rather, it was bright red. But lost, lost to reason. I had heard of whirl-wind romances before but never realised fully. I tell you this, Aubrey, because I don't want to hide anything from you, I want your views on culture. And besides, you know all, for in the midst of this adventure who should I meet but your man Cade who said to me, 'Lor' bless you, Milord, what are you doing in a place like this? With Mrs Gilchrist! It's like fucking a dead mouse.' He is a coarse and narrow-minded man and doesn't know what it is to empty some dull opiate, as my young diplomatic friend puts it. But things went from bad to worse for when we returned to what Mrs Gilchrist called the winter garden there were a lot of half-dressed people dancing in a marked way, some with few if any clothes. One young man in an apron and a boater, who had a flower behind each ear, stubbed out a cigar on my forearm without asking permission. The pain was terrible. I still have the scar. Another dressed in next to nothing forced me to waltz and gave me a bite on the cheek which kept me from the office for a week. Mrs Gilchrist said it was nothing, just a love-at-first-sight-bite. I was by now in an advanced condition of intemperance and not much able to look after myself. But I was making mental notes all the time. She had covered my neck in what in such circles are known as *suçons d'amour*, blue marks. But she seemed proud of me for I heard her proclaim, 'Celui-là a des couilles super-posées.' I wondered what my committee would say if they could see me. Well, whose fault was it? There was a kind of fight, and an influx of policemen and it was then I saw your man, who kindly helped me to the door. I found myself in the street sitting on the pavement with my opera hat beside me – someone had jumped on it – and being bandaged by some of the nicer girls: but of course they were going through my pockets and wallet. However, I had taken the precaution of carrying very little money and no personal jewellery of value; my signet I left in the office safe. So that all in all, while I was shorn, it was not completely. My diplomatic friend put me in a cab and – against my will – took me to another dingier place where I got stuck in the lavatory and was kicked by a curate. I protested, whereupon my friend said, 'Are you a man of the world or no?' 'Yes!' 'Well then!' I didn't see his point."

There was a long pause, some snoring and the dazed voice once more took up the tenuous thread of what now seemed to be a jag lasting over weeks; perhaps it was just the confusion in the telling. "O my God! how she talked and talked about culture. And I kept telling myself that I must remember everything in order to report to the committee. O my God!" He groaned again and wagged his head on his shoulders.

"Thelème!" he said once more. "I don't suppose the name means anything to you. An abbey somewhere in Provence, the abode of perfected felicity! It is now called Cuculotte in the Gard, centre of the hot chestnuts trade. Mrs Gilchrist sometimes goes down at Easter with her mother. Her belly is cloven with the devil's hoofmark, but her sex is as smooth or smoother than a surgeon's glove. Sometimes she turns down the lights and does horoscopes. She can see auras, she can overhear states of mind. When I told Sutcliffe this he said, 'Let everyone make his personal noise for the braying of donkeys is sweet to the ears of the Creator!' Cuculotte, she saw it so clearly in a dream. There is a woman waiting for me there who looks like the Virgin Mary but is really called Cunégonde – another cornerstone. A hole-and-cornerstone. Ha! Ha! My diplomatic youth again, the poor cynic. I last saw him standing naked, on Mrs Gilchrist's upper balcony, arms wide as he declaimed, 'Hear me, ye sperm-coaxing divinities, for I am afflicted by scrotum fever and I bring ye my purse of Fortunatus!' The Swiss fire brigade had to get him down with a ladder and I expect he has been rusticated already. O God, Aubrey, all this because they said I had not lived enough.

"But *Ulysses*, that odious book, what is one to do? Toby

says that all energetic wanderers descend from Dionysus, they are really gods of wine which gives warmth and motion and curiosity. The wandering Jew, the Flying Dutchman, Gil Blas, Panurge – O my head spins with everything I have been hearing!"

Aubrey thought with a pang of the long nightmare of Joyce's struggle to get his work published – eighteen years – and said, "You must not blacklist him, whatever you find to say against it, you must not index Joyce. The Catholics already did, and he was a secret Catholic as much marked as old Huysmans ever was. Hence the heavy liturgical type of prose exposition with its gruesome echoes and parodies of what he could not forget. No, it's rich in church furnishings, and the function of Bloom is to desecrate the Church, to shit on the High Altar. You are lucky if he doesn't recite the Creed as he shits. No, it's a real cornerstone."

But this time Galen slept and did not hear; faint snores escaped his lips though he still smiled at some cherished memory; and it was during this period that the shadow of Sutcliffe tiptoed into the room, finger on lip, and took up an amused position in a nearby chair, whispering, "Is it okay for me to be here – or is he confessing all?"

"Nearly all. He speaks of a Mrs Gilchrist whom I seem to have heard of."

"Of course. Those songs. The first scowling clap brought back from Gallipoli by the Anzacs was claimed by one of her girls. The song was plaintive – Will she give you the cherry off the cake, Mrs Gilchrist?"

"I never heard it."

"I could bring her to have tea with you; she probably does massage as well."

"Thank you, my friend, but no."

"With me too she waxes mystical and speaks movingly of the Third Eye, Troisième Oeil as she says with a classy twitch. But what really concerns her is the Troisième Jambe of men – those who had it were marvellous. 'Quel homme fascinant, il est géomètre', she would coo. Or else, 'un homme spécial; il est chef de gare mais il a des qualités de coeur!' She is what our ancestors would call an adept of splosh-fucking. As Cade would say, 'She'd fuck the tiles off the roof if you let her.'"

"I did not know you had shared this tremendous binge of Galen's." Sutcliffe nodded and said, "The real life of Geneva, capital of Calvin, goes on there. Toby found it, and it proved so restful that he often takes his knitting down for an hour and just sits, listening to the banter of Mrs Gilchrist's girls. It is the hub of this Spenglerian capital where one sees that our civilisation is the weary little monkey which sits atop the barrel organ and proffers a tin cup for alms while the organ-grinder is a large Jewish gentleman of urbanity. Toby says that Freud is the only honest Jew, just as Socrates was the only honest Greek. Yes, I have been sharing in the quest for the Golden Fleece – if I may call it that. And a fine job he has made of it. He has discovered that when the love of lamb cutlets is universal the reign of benevolence will begin. A thermonuclear Jehovah is watching over us!"

"There's a hellish lack of continuity in what you say."

"It's good sense but somewhat diluted with whisky. It will all get clearer and clearer – now that you have admitted to yourself that I exist – or rather that you only exist in function to me! Socrates only existed in Plato's mind, Freud only in Jung's, that's how the whole thing goes. It's a chain gang. Sam once had a limerick about the matter which went:

> Who sends out his cock to the Cleaner's
> Must risk quite a shrinking of penis
> Which perhaps is restored
> By recourse to a bawd
> And a subsequent transit of Venus."

"Be more precise, please; you rave!"

"It is very simple, Aubrey: if the Superego is really God the Father, then man is the only animal who has one ball higher than the other – no other carries his ingots in this position. The women have found out and here they are jousting, tossing the caber, climbing the greasy pole, wrestling in mud, writing, painting, pissing standing up, clearing their throats just like – better than – men. I am fordolked, *morfondu*, chilled to the heart by the spectacle. This is what comes of letting them share the war."

"But at least they are free and you can get at them."

"In a manner of speaking." He recited darkly the verse:

> Marsupial Sutcliffe with distinguished balls
> Sits by the telephone and waits for calls.

For a moment, like a whale surfacing, the recumbent figure of Lord Galen condensed itself and shot upright as if on a spring. "My God, where am I?" he asked in total bewilderment, and then just as suddenly closed his eyes and sank back into profound sleep once more. Aubrey said, "If he can sleep through your disquisitions he can sleep through anything."

"I haven't told you all as yet," went on Sutcliffe in a hushed voice after having allowed Galen a moment or two to engulf himself thoroughly in slumber. "I haven't told you about the Crucifixion on the most memorable evening, the last and worst. At midnight or after there came an influx of theatre people, or perhaps a carnival party, with extravagant hats and plumes and weird noses and masks. They were all more or less drunk and the naked sirens of the house had great fun in plucking their clothes from them like fruit from trees, appropriating their hats and noses and whatnot, while the whole place resounded with music and everyone fell to the knife and fork act with celerity, except for those like little Cravache-Biche who must be corrected with nettles. Don't tell me where they found them at this time of night, perhaps by moonlight near the lake. In all this the wistful Galen wandered vaguely half-undressed and on the incoherent side of his last huge whisky. There was a sudden fight, too, which was not allowed to deteriorate into fisticuffs, thank goodness, though I heard a female voice cry raucously, 'Lâche-moi, espèce de morve,' which I translated back to myself as meaning: 'Unhand me, species of snot!' The contestants were separated by two clowns and the party rolled on over our heads like the sea. More players, more music – a kind of predynastic jazz with sweet unction of clarinets calling from forgotten minarets to the faithful who crowded the tiny dance floor yapping like Pekinese. Someone was crying 'Redemption!' and I thought he was a religious maniac, but no, he was waving a banker's draft: yes, there were bankers among us, and I even saw one undressed. He looked just like other men but he was crying, 'I am absolutely frozen, my ingots, my heirlooms, my assets are frozen, I tell you.' It was not clear whom he was trying to convince. Toby was talking moodily of bringing down a secret transmitter to the *pouf* in order to sift all the available information. 'Why not install it – I sometimes have brilliant ideas – in Mrs Gilchrist's pussy? From there you command the whole wide world.'

"But I had no chance to develop my idea for a fascinating dark girl intervened and coaxed me into indulging in some conventional knife and fork in an alcove – the facsimile of a joy I would gladly have shared with her. She was of a dark, grave, Semitic beauty, and in distress, thrilling like a wounded nerve. And I felt my age heavy upon me as I gazed into those sweet wounded eyes. Aïe! Jewish girls have fur-lined pussies and simmer with sinful single-mindedness, salacious and solitary and sexual as swallows in spring: they swerve out of the dark syllabaries of sensuality with superb submission like silken scimitars swung by a sultan . . ."

"Wow!"

"Thank you so much!"

"Tell me about love. I have been forbidden it since I have been here and I am beginning to miss it. This nun's life is bad for my book. I fear that if too long out of use one surely atrophies, no?"

"I don't think so—ask your doctor."

"I have and he says not. Actually I am less worried for myself than for my baby, my book. Ah, Rob, what a strange obsession it is, this writing game! I desire the sovereign form exposed by exact method—open-cast mining, or better, heart surgery. But in order to achieve it you must first get mental pruritus, the desire to *know*, and then quietly scratch yourself to death, the paper to death with your pen. And all to what end?"

"Well, if you can't love it's your only alibi."

The thought was displeasing to Blanford, so in order to cheer him up Sutcliffe recited:

Another lovely morning in the history of Our Saviour,
I pray you children one and all, be on your best behaviour.
Put all these problems out to grass
And watch the generations pass.
I've lived my life, I've had my say,
A lucky dog, I've had my day.
Rise early, darlings, catch the dew
And may you join the Happy Few.

"What is really ailing you is a theological nagging which has little to do with your book, since it is neither a *plaidoyer* nor does it preach anything. But if you go mucking about with the discrete ego you must be careful not to make a mistake and release a whole lot of indiscreet ids. Remember that a conjuror must be worthy of his balls!"

"Well said! Nobly said!"

"And now, Aubrey, to my main theme. It is nothing less

than the Crucifixion of Lord Galen at the hands of Mrs Gil-christ and her girls, a sight of great dramatic and symbolic significance. It is amazing with what modesty and good nature he went to his doom; indeed, he chose his own doom, but it was very late in the night, towards the third hour when different realities begin to sift into each other and the Chinese distinguish finely between the day particle and the night particle, between the definite and indefinite article. There came a young lady to the door of the apartment clad in nothing but a sort of drunken dignity who raised her voice and said, 'There is a Jewish gentleman below who wishes to be crucified and has asked me if you will all oblige.' There was an immediate rush of willing-ness to please, everyone felt warm and generously disposed, but how to proceed? There were no nails to be found any-where, lucky for Galen. Meanwhile, where was he actually? For some time past he had not been in evidence and one pre-sumed him to have left or fallen asleep in some nook. But instead he had been undressed and locked into a cupboard full of brooms and slop-pails and here, after announcing his deter-mination to expiate the sins of Jewry by getting himself crucified, he waited with smiling patience. The girl in question having prepared her audience now released him and led him unprotestingly from room to room – he smiling bashfully and somewhat roguishly the while: but he was drunk beyond dead-ness, beyond coma, beyond the seventh sphere of incompre-hension. He was hazed in, worn out and living in a world of his own. He was nude and his Old Etonian tie had been attached to his principal member, and it was with this that he was led, just as Gandhi led his goat through the market-place where he received a resounding ovation. It was as if a Turkish butcher might lead a succulent fat-tailed sheep across the market place in order to beat up his clients' saliva by the spectacle. Our own saliva flowed copiously enough, but where was the impedi-menta – the cross, for example? We did not know that it was not the first time that Mrs Gilchrist had organised a little crucifixion to please an exacting client – but that we supposed would be perverse, perhaps, catering to special inclinations. Galen looked too naively happy to be a pervert, lusting after red-hot pincers or beds of nails. He turned his head from side to side as he walked through the rooms in harmless beatitude and one could not help being charmed and wishing him well in his little adventure.

"The girl having trailed her cape, so to speak, throughout the various salons, made her way, followed by a considerable crowd of enthusiasts, to the high walled-in verandah which Mrs Gilchrist called the Quarterdeck. The only furniture was a huge double bed with massive medieval baldaquin, which stood in the middle of what seemed a sort of nuptial chamber. Perhaps it was here in this mammoth bed that a youthful Mrs Gilchrist had yielded to the charms of the now phantom Major, whom she was wont to invoke as her late husband? At all events this was to be the site of Galen's crucifixion, for the two thick bedposts served admirably as struts upon which they could string him – better, indeed, than a cross, though a trifle less symmetrical as to the feet. However the concourse of maidens with cries and songs and expressions of goodwill now started to lash his outspread arms to the posts while in a Christ-like enfeeblement but with good humour Galen's head lolled and he expatiated upon himself: 'I wanted only to be good, pious and obedient,' he confessed modestly, 'I was prepared to wait for God to make me original. My dears, it worked. It worked and here I am!' He tried to spread his arms in triumph but was impeded by his fastenings. But he was not dis-countenanced, for he continued: 'The Ambassador to Banga-lore appeared before me dressed in the robes of a *khitmagar* or majordomo. He said: "Why don't you refuse the whole blood-stained Christian package, eh? Doff the butcher's apron so to speak, refuse the self-righteous futility of it all, stop being a martyr to respectability, dissociate yourself from blood-gulpers and wafer-chewers with their smithereens complex. Zonk! Bonkers! Pliouc! Be yourself even in strip cartoons! My dear Galen, relinquish your ghastly monotheism which has led to man's separation from nature and released the primal devastator in him. Pierce to the heart of helplessness, of harm-lessness, which is Buddhism. Let meditation be the mould of feeling and breath the engine of thought!"'

"In the midst of all the horseplay and noise Galen did succeed in looking something like a Mantegna Christ Crucified – all except for the foolish good humour with which he sub-mitted to an occasional tickle in the ribs. Or else a passing girl might seize his Old Etonian tie and give a tug, crying out 'Ding-Ding!' in the accents of a passing tram. Or yet another might cry out, 'They say he has dimples in his bottom like a French novelist!' But in the intervals the noble lord went on reciting the interminable Buddhist creed – for that is what it sounded like to the onlookers. 'Guilelessly, harmlessly, heed-lessly, noiselessly, needlessly, haplessly, hopelessly, toplessly, shapelessly, soundlessly, stainlessly . . .'

"At this very moment who should come upon the scene but Mrs Gilchrist herself, wrapped in a whorl of pink silk and white fur, and winnowing her way across the floor like a wild bird dragging its claws across the surface of a lake: she skidded into view exuding majesty and a certain reproachfulness. Clapping her hands loudly she was exclaiming, 'My children! My children! What is going on? Why aren't things being hurried up? What about the *extermination* of the Jewish gentleman?' And with this she chucked Galen familiarly under the chin, causing him to giggle once more – though his expression was ever so slightly tinged with alarm – for he clearly did not know what the word might connote in the mind of Mrs Gilchrist. But for the girls it contained no secret. At once from behind their backs there appeared lipsticks of various types and hues – lipsticks like the little red sex of a thousand lapdogs lusting for love. And now the girls swarmed all over Lord Galen, decorating him with intense concentration, covering every available nook of his august person with flowers, mottoes, cobwebs, hearts, arrows, as well as other less familiar *graffiti*, like the genitalia of other members of the animal kingdom famed for their lubricity. It was a veritable fertility rite which was accomplished with almost no bickering, while the subject stayed rapturously still with arms outspread, feeling for the first time in his life thoroughly appreciated, thoroughly loved and understood. But from time to time fatigue overwhelmed him and he sagged briefly in his lashings. Then came catastrophe.

"In order to draw on his back and his bottom, not to mention his legs, the young ladies of Mrs Gilchrist climbed upon the bed in force, and it would seem that this was responsible for what followed. The heavy baldaquin, worked out of true by their wrigglings, suddenly broke away from the frame and crashed down, carrying one upright with it – fortunately Lord Galen was propelled sideways out of reach of the falling pieces and thus avoided an extremely nasty knock on the head. But he still remained tied by one arm, feebly draped across the floor. There was not an inch of his person that had escaped the artistic enthusiasm of the girls and he really looked like a tattooed Maori warrior prepared for a battle, or some obscure African chief prepared to preside at a witch cult. There was, of course, a delicious panic now, with bumps and bruises and squeaks all round, and when it was clear that for the moment the rest of the bed held firm, the girls who had drawn back now closed in once more upon Lord Galen and helped him down from the cross with strokings and mewings and consoling cries lest he had been frightened by the accident. He had, of course, but in a vague way, his whole sensibility deadened by drink. So now they carried the crucified and exterminated one to a nearby sofa and laid him out in vaguely ceremonial fashion, piling cushion upon cushion on him, and leaving only his grotesquely decorated head to stick out – it was like burying a Red Indian totem pole. But it was lovely and warm with the weight of the cushions upon him and he snuggled down in great good humour, confident that he would rise again on the third day because Mrs Gilchrist informed him that he would. 'Have a little kip, dear,' she suggested. But it was not to be.

"At that moment, with the air of avenging angels, two forms appeared as if by magic, stilling the tumult with a gesture of doom. One was the transfigured form of Felix Chatto, white with shock and resentment and outrage. In his hand he waved – an appropriate symbol of disapprobation – his London gamp meticulously rolled. He carried it high, just as Zeus might carry his trident or a saint his sceptre. And he shouted in a slightly daft voice which broke under the stress of his emotion, *This has got to stop once and for all!*' The message was meant in particular for Galen but it was propelled with sufficient force to include the whole of the company. The second figure, who looked abashed and out of place, was, of all people, Schwarz who stood about disconsolately waving a stomach pump – he had been misled about Galen's condition which continued to register a mild euphoria despite the rather terrifying nature of his decorations. Felix was almost dancing with rage, his sense of *que dira-t-on* had been increasingly exacerbated as day followed day and rumour rumour about Galen's cultural researches. 'The whole of Geneva is laughing at you!' he cried and with his gamp struck at the recumbent figure, but hitting him through the cushions which gave out a satisfactory thwack. Galen's painted face worked – writhed, one might say – within its decorative scheme. He vaguely sensed that he was in a position of inferiority and just as vaguely thought to redress the situation with a reproof. 'I never expected to see you in a place like this, Felix,' he said in hollow tones, and the exacerbated young man hissed back, 'And you? I came here to find *you*, and I have brought a doctor and an ambulance. This time you will be disintoxicated once and for all in the best clinic of Geneva!' Lord Galen shrugged and threw up his hands; his underlip wobbled, and for a moment he looked as if he were on the edge of tears. 'You are judging me very harshly,' he said, with a shake of the head, 'After all I have been through, you are judging me *very* harshly.'

"Felix, still brandishing his umbrella, said, 'Someone had to do something. This last month has been a nightmare. At every turn I ran into one of your subcommittees asking for news of you, or worse still *giving* me news of your behaviour – highly unpalatable news, if I may so.'

"Felix, it is at their prompting that I undertook this path. If you knew what I have been through – dear boy, simply the American novel, nothing else! God! what a feast of violence and vulgarity and slime. I could hardly believe my eyes. And every one a cornerstone! No, Felix, there is a Communist Index and a Catholic Index and so far so good. Now I am going to establish Galen's graduated scale of acceptability and see if the United Nations will bite. God, but I am tired!' And now he had begun to look it. It was as if for the first time he realised fully that he was completely tattooed with lipstick. He gazed down at himself and gave the ghost of a whinny – the very last shadow of an exhausted chuckle. 'Well, if I must I must!' he said and held out his arms.

"For a moment there was some hesitation as to how he should be clothed for his departure from Mrs Gilchrist's establishment; but two interns appeared bearing a stretcher and having carefully wrapped him in sheets he was lowered into it, and covered with a blanket. The girls made a good deal of petting him and Mrs G. took her farewell with a light and airy kiss. And so Galen's search for culture ended."

A pause now ensued and all eyes were once more focused

on the sleeping man who had not turned a hair throughout the hushed disquisition of Sutcliffe. It was rather the silence which woke him now, and very quietly. He raised his head and said, "You were talking about me? Yes, I felt it."

He yawned luxuriously and went on: "For the first time I feel really rested, completely cured. It's been wonderfully therapeutic just lying on your feet and resting – I hope I didn't crush? No? Good!" Indeed he looked once more his old expansive, convivial self as he rose and put his clothes to rights and combed his hair. "This afternoon and evening," he said, "I must face the Central Committee with my recommendations, and we will know all!" He took up his bag full of cultural "cornerstones" and took his leave. A tight-lipped and unforgiving Felix awaited him in the car outside the clinic, ready to drive him to his office, and to make sure that he did not escape again.

"I fear," said Sutcliffe, "that this is the end of Galen the polymath and cultural dictator. I hear from Toby that he is collecting massive votes of no-confidence inside his own party, and that that monstrous ass Gulliver is trying to betray and dethrone him. Gulliver is the type that runs a pub and says 'righty-ho!' with great jauntiness. He gives himself out to be a retired naval commander but in fact was in the R.A.F. and grounded early on for L.M.F. – the dreaded citation: 'lack of moral fibre' (fervour?). At any rate Galen is presenting a pretty soft underbelly to him, and I fear the worst."

"I read some more of your drafts last night; it's queer stuff, some of it, and has a kind of bearing on what I have done. How shall I say it? You know full well that there is always something going on in the room next door and you often find yourself wondering what it might be. But it's never what you think. Your version of our book gives the presence of events, mine the absence, if I can put it like that."

Sutcliffe nodded somewhat gloomily. "Yes," he said,

"and it's because you really exist. I'm just a figment, living by proxy, turned on and off at will like a memory. I'm only as real as is necessary. My existence is contingent. Our books are linked without being interlocked, if you see."

"Hail!"

"Hail!"

"Be ye versions of one another, says the Bible!"

"Husband thy immortality, says Job."

Blanford gazed long and thoughtfully at his fiction and said, "I have given you a bad time, I know; that awful marriage, and all the sadness. But now at last we are both moving towards our apotheosis, you as a fat, sad oracle, me as a post-war crock with designs upon the Underworld only. No more love, no more apple-pie in the sky. Life will become an extended reverie – and of course a number of us must die. Don't forget it. You at least can't do the whole thing, you are limited to a fiction's dying. But the result can be moving or instructive or both. I shall be so glad to get you out of my system at last, my Old Man of the Sea!"

"What you mean is that at last this terrible but blessed war, which has prevented us from thinking about ourselves – or even *for* ourselves – is coming to a close and we are soon to be thrown back on our own resources. Winter quarters for the 10th Legion, and Iron Rations!"

"I am in love with Constance!" he suddenly blurted out like a schoolboy attacked with the squitters.

Sutcliffe looked quizzical and just a trifle ironic. "*Enfin!*" he said. "Something that was not in the script! Something unexpected! But it could be untrue, couldn't it? You yourself are fond of pointing out the self-deceptions of others . . ."

"To hell with you!" Blanford said, fully aware of the appropriateness of the oath. The fat man said, "You mistake me for Monsieur, doubtless?"

"Doubtless!"

Sutcliffe chuckled indulgently and wagged a reproachful finger at his fellow scribe. "You know that Affad is back, don't you?" Blanford did not. At that moment Cade knocked and entered on a note of interrogation. "You rang, sir?" Blanford looked up and shook his head. "No, Cade. I didn't." The valet looked puzzled and aggrieved. "Well, someone did ring," he insisted before turning away to leave the room. Blanford said, "Where is Affad, then, why hasn't he made some sign of life?" Sutcliffe, who was sharpening a pencil, shrugged his shoulders. "How should I know?" he said. "Since all the romantic convulsions I have hardly dared to mention him for fear of upsetting Constance."

"I think," said the irritated Blanford, "that we are all behaving like a gaggle of maiden aunts and the result will simply cocker up the girl's ego—already too swollen, in my humble opinion!" Sutcliffe looked at him with an ironic smile; "Hoity-toity," he said, "such vexation now! I think we must leave it to Affad now to reappear and set things to rights."

But it was the following day that Affad suddenly appeared in their midst during a mid-morning gathering in the old Bar de la Navigation—though the presence of Constance was quite a rarity: she was usually far freer in the evenings. Yet on this fine morning she had made a detour on foot in order to catch Sutcliffe with a message about Trash—and had been persuaded to stay and have a drink.

A car drew up in the street outside and suddenly with a heartleap—a desperate sense of total heed—she saw a familiar form merge up on the glass-fronted door and heard the bell tingle as he pushed it open. There stood Affad after what seemed several centuries, though it was only a matter of months. Her first impulse was to turn away, perhaps even to flee, but she converted it in characteristic fashion. Advancing upon him with a smile of welcome she caught him almost before he had entered the room and with a kiss she stuck a flower in his gun, so to speak, saying lightly, "Are we speaking to each other or not? I have forgotten." It sounded challenging and frivolous, and she all at once repented when she saw how thin and pale he looked, and how diffident. He said in a low voice, without any trace of affectation, "Of course. I *must* thank you – I don't know *how* as yet." And they allowed themselves to be submerged in the general conversation – for his sudden appearance had gained Affad a general welcome. Every one was anxious to know how he was and where he had been; and for a moment this somewhat boisterous greeting obliterated all other thoughts. He accepted a glass of beer and sat down beside her to drink it and to exchange banter with Toby and Ryder, while Blanford from his corner watched the face of Constance with a sardonic and yet resigned expression. The distress she had suffered with the separation – and particularly the confidences she had made to him as her best friend – had touched him to the heart and had increased this age-old attachment to her image. So much so that he almost forgot to be jealous of Affad whose friendship was equally dear: as if they all lived equidistant from each other. But now there was a whole jumble of misunderstandings between the lovers and as Constance sat there at his side, smiling and saying nothing, her heart continued to sink, for she could not imagine that such a breach would ever be mended, nor could she devise ways to heal the wound caused by this misunderstanding. How impossible men were, after all!

There were other factors also which added to her anxiety and undermined her self-confidence and poise. She cursed herself for the reaction, it was so childish: but he had hardly bestowed a glance upon her new hair-style. Did he perhaps dislike it? She caught a glimpse of it in the mirror and wondered if he thought it too loud, too feminist ... But then at last when he deemed that his welcome had been well and truly lived he rose and said, "Constance, please may I talk to you for a few moments? I have things to tell and things to ask." He looked worn and pale and extremely uncertain of himself. ("Good!" she thought vindictively.)

They went out into the sunlight together and since the day promised to be so fine he suggested that they leave the car and walk along the lakeside, a suggestion to which she agreed.

Not without a certain trepidation, for she too seemed awkward and inhibited. But by dint of waiting and letting the rhythm of their walking chime he was at last able to collect his thoughts. "You know, you must know, you *must* have felt that I had decided not to speak to you again – and of course the reasons (I know they seem fatuous to you) were also plain. That is why when I came here I went to the lake house, intending to come into town as little as possible. But after I saw what you had done for the child – with your own science which I found so limited – I could not do otherwise than come and thank you for the tremendous gift." As they walked he put his arm about her shoulders. Then they turned to each other and embraced silently, clutching at each other like drowning people, and saying nothing more, it being so difficult to breathe. Near at hand was a public bench, and at last she broke away feeling half-strangled and choked with conflicting emotions. "Ouf!" she sat herself down, between tears and rueful laughter, and put her head in her hands. He came to her side and gently stroked her hair. (Perhaps after all he did not mind the new style?) As a matter of fact when they embraced he encountered the changed scent which for some reason he greeted with a sense of unease, almost of distaste. Yet he could not analyse why exactly!

"We are being punished for having done something so frivolous as to fall in love. Punished for being out of date." But all this was simply to fill in the gaps of the silence and to conceal his own overwhelming emotion – he had forgotten how much he sexually desired her. His fingers received waves of sex like electricity – he stopped short of reproaching himself! "We thought we were extremely clever and superior!"

"You are still so unsure of yourself!"

"Unsure of you, rather. I thought you realised more fully than you did how dangerous it might be to mess about with a machine you did not understand: a machine which was already launched upon a trajectory. One could lose an arm, an eye, a life. Perhaps I didn't explain very cleverly what we were up to – you thought of it as a vulgar suicide club, and of course being a spirited woman felt that it qualified my love for you – how *could* I both love you and passively subscribe to my own death from a hand unknown and at a time chosen by others? That is what you really felt, isn't it?"

"Yes." She said a little sullenly, "I suppose you could say that that is what a woman would feel. A deep disappointment in your manhood, really. I had the rather foolish notion of intervening, stealing the letter – I didn't quite make up my mind as to what I would do with it. At first I thought I would destroy it out of pure mischief and see what happened. No, I wasn't aware of any great danger because at bottom I did not take it very seriously – you had spoken of making a renouncement of the whole thing, pleading off . . . what was I to imagine? So I stole it while waiting to make up my mind and I put it in a book. Someone borrowed the book, a lunatic, and the precious document simply disappeared. My God, I'm so sorry for the thoughtlessness and the annoyance. We are trying to get it back, to find out what if anything the patient could have done with it."

"Your hands are cold." He sat down beside her on the bench and chafed them slowly as he talked. "I am as much to blame as you are, not for the letter, but for not explaining better what stood between us, and what you would have to accept in order to go on loving me. Yes, I did think of going back and attempting a renunciation, but really I knew it was hopeless. The minute I left your side I knew it was really out. I simply could not do it – it compromised the whole mechanics of the movement and what it had set out to do. I was a traitor!"

"Traitor!" she echoed ironically, and he pressed her hand, saying, "Yes. Yes. I know you think it schoolboyish, but there is a man behind me and a man before, I am part of a chain, a link. Our ambitions in a mad sort of way are scientific in the most exact sense of that misused word. We are setting up a chain-reaction which we believe could counter the laws of entropy – the irreversibility of process leading always to death, dispersal, disaggregation . . . Of course it is wildly ambitious. But, you see, it isn't just a romantic appetite for death as such . . ." He stared at her fixedly for a moment and then sighed, saying, "My God! I think you are beginning to understand. I was afraid you wouldn't – for after all it makes part and parcel of our loving: fucking is just the cement which binds together the double image we present to reality when an orgasm is shared, is reciprocally *breathed*. What does old Max tell you – surely something like that, no?"

"Yes. I was thinking of him."

"The man behind me represents the past and the man in front the future. In between those two poles I can say that I exist, only there, only in that *Now*. And in the duration I am experiencing I exist also in you, and you in me – *s'il vous plaît!*"

She was so happy that there would have been no point in being insincere and continuing to resist his warmth – though of course the brute badly needed punishing . . . "In spite of my misgivings I surrender. I am only sorry about my unpardonable intervention. But is it *all* that necessary to know the hour and the day?"

"In a sense, yes. To set one's affairs in order is only a secondary reason. But to accept the death transition profoundly is important because you pass the message on down the grapevine. What do you think societies and associations were created for? Reservoirs of energy and thought, dynamos, if you like."

"I see."

"So I feel that without that knowledge I am passing on a feeble signal. Like a dirty spark plug!" He put his arm in hers and said, "God! I am so happy I think I am going to faint!"

"Don't do that! Let me cook you some lunch. You are just faint from all your Egyptian excesses. But seriously – you have got very thin. Why?"

"I've been in the desert such a lot: one can't eat in the heat. Also I thought I had lost your respect. It was pretty bad, it made me realise that you were really a lovemate and that anyone else was out of the question – it would diminish what we had discovered in such an accidental way! I don't want to give you a swollen head so I won't go on. Anyway, it must be self-evident. What I really wanted to do was to father a child on you – by one act of perfect mutual attention: in a single yoga-breath, as you would say. Like you blow a smoke-ring, perfect and self-sustaining. Constance, why don't you shut me up?" But it was honey to her!

And there was only one way to do that and they sat and embraced so passionately that they received the curious or amused glances of the passers-by. Then at long last she proposed that they should walk back to her flat, but he had to sit still for a moment for he was in no state to stand up and walk – which amused her vastly. "Just think of ice-cream," she said, "and it will be all right!" But it was some moments before they resumed their walk. How glorious the sunlight seemed; they made a detour through the public gardens where preparations were almost complete for a local *fête votive*. Some of the stalls were already in place selling their fragile carnival wares, toys and ribbons and celluloid propellers and dolls for the children. They walked with their little fingers linked. She said to herself,

"It feels marvellous to be loved from top to toe, not an inch of you free from the honey." At a bar they ordered a bottle of cheap champagne and drank it as if it were nectar. That is the terrible thing, she thought, love is really a state of mania!

From a medical point of view it was practically certifiable. She remembered him saying once, long ago, "Constance! Let's fall in love and create a disappointment of children!" And simultaneously she recalled Max telling her that "Every girl's a one-man girl, and every man too. Hence the trouble, for just anybody won't do – it's gotta be the him and the her of the fairy tale. Humans were born to live in couples like wild doves or cobras. But then we went and lost periodicity, meat-eating came in with the taste of blood: then sugar, salt, alcohol followed and we lost our hold on the infinite!" She wondered what Max would think of Affad's gnostic beliefs and obligations. Not so much perhaps, for the true yogi knew the hour of his death, and did not need artificial reminders in order to render it a conscious act.

"What are you thinking so sadly?" he asked.

"Nothing specially sad; just that time is passing; it has become doubly valuable since all this talk about death. Which is anyway impertinent and silly – trying to pre-empt reality when destiny may well be preparing to make an end of us in the next five minutes. We could be run over by a taxi."

"You are right; we will certainly pay for all these fine sentiments! God, though, it's marvellous to see you again, feeling all signals register and echo! The strategies of nature may be boundless but *this* thing puts them under the burning-glass."

"I loathe high-minded people like ourselves. We are just the type I can't stand."

"I know. And all this self-caressing sort of talk ruins fucking. Why don't we shut up and get on with it? I feel quite anorexic – sexanorexic. If you got into my bed I would be seized by paralysis. I would just dribble and swoon. Narcissus beware!"

They reached her flat and mounted the stairs arm-in-arm, still uplifted to the point of subversion by the bad champagne they had drunk; but also now a little afraid, a little withdrawn, because of the coming shock of their first encounter for so long. He looked particularly scared. The flat was spotless, the cleaning woman had been; and in leaving she had drawn the curtains so that they wandered into a half-darkened room. And just stood, quietly breathing, and regarding each other with anxiety, and at the same time so out of their depth.

"Sebastian!" she whispered, more to herself than to him, but he caught the name and took her hands, drawing her softly through the half-opened door towards the familiar cherished bed, reflected three ways by the tall mirrors, taking the hushed light of the window upon their bright skins.

The lovers, she was thinking, belonged to an endangered species and were in need of protection; should perhaps be kept on reservations like specimens of forgotten and outmoded physical strains, wild game? But was there any happiness which was the equal of this? To be blissed-out by the kisses of the correct partner, to make love and fade? Not to squander but to husband – a perilous game, really, for it was changing even while one was in the act of experiencing it. Yet there were so many people, perhaps the most, who arrived at the end of a life of limited usefulness to find the doors of this kind of happiness bolted and barred against them through no fault of their own – just scurvy luck.

Their clothes rustled and fell in a heap like a drift, and slowly, hesitantly they enfolded each other and drifted into the warm bed, to lie for a while breathing shakily, like freshly severed twins. So conscious also that kiss by kiss they would be winding steadily down into the grave. He was remembering some words from a letter: "Nothing can be added or subtracted from what exists, yet inside this wholeness endless change and permutation is possible with the same elements." Her teeth sank into his lips, he felt the sweet galbe of her flanks and arching back.

And yet, for all the tension, at the heart of their exchanges was a calm sensuality of understanding such as only those lucky enough to feel married in the tantric fashion experience. They were squarely each to each with no fictions of lust needed to ignite them. Embraces were woven like a tissue.

But because he had lost weight she took pity on him and hunted out chocolate from the kitchen – coaxing him with it to sweeten his drowsy kisses; and since he seemed the weaker today she took the dominant role, excited to drain him of every last desire by the authority of her splendid body. She feasted on his flesh and he let her go – though he was only shamming, saving his strength. And as soon as her passion subsided a little he suddenly turned her on her back like a turtle and entered her on a wave of renewal – a conqueror in his turn, but a welcomed one. All his strength had come back in a rush, as if from nowhere. But he knew that she had summoned it, had conjured it up. At last they lay entangled in each other like wrestlers, but immobile, and still mouth to mouth in a pool of ghostly sweat: and as proud of each other as lions, though meek as toys!

The telephone rang in its muted fashion, and she raised her head in drowsy dismay: "What a fool I am! I forgot to turn it off!" She was reluctant to unwind this matchless embrace for a mere professional call from Schwarz or someone. She hung back and hesitated, hoping that the invisible caller might suppose her absent and hang up; but no. The instrument went on and on insisting, and at last she crawled from bed and groped her sleepy way to the salon – only to find that as she picked up the instrument and spoke into it, it went quietly dead on her. She had just time to say "Hullo" twice before Mnemidis (for it was he) replaced the receiver with a quiet smile, having recognised her voice as that of his doctor and tormentor. So she was, after all, at home and not absent on duty as Schwarz had suggested! It was really wonderful how things fell out without any special interference on his part: they just fell into the shape dictated by his desire! Meanwhile an irritated Constance hovered above the phone, wondering whether to switch it off or not – her professional conscience reproached her for the wish. On the phone pad was a phrase which Max had given her, a quotation from a philosopher. She read it drowsily as she debated within herself the rights and wrongs of pushing the switch of the phone. "Everything is conquered by submission, even submission itself, even as matter is conquered by entropy, and truth by its opposite. Even entropy, so apparently absolute in its operation, is capable, if left to itself, of conversion into a regenerative form. The phoenix is no myth!"

Ouf! Her bones felt full to overflowing with electricity; she was outraged to find him snugly asleep instead of awaiting her! That was men for you! Yet to tell the truth she herself was not far off the same state, and enfolding him in her arms once more she fell quietly asleep, pacing him with her heartbeats! He could not guess how long this state of felicity had lasted when at last he awoke to find her lying wide-eyed and silent beside him. "What is it?" he whispered. "Did I wake you, did I snore?" But she shook her head and whispered back, "I was woken by an idea, a marvellous idea, and quite realisable unless you have any special plans for spending your time. Why don't we go away together for a few months, to really discover each other – supposing you *have* a few months at your disposal? Why waste the precious day? I have accumulated a lot of leave. Provence is cleared of Germans. I have an old house which we could open up, very primitive but comfortable and in a beautiful corner near Avignon . . ."

"How funny," he said, "for I was going to suggest something like that; I even borrowed Galen's house for the occasion. Yes, we shouldn't sit about waiting for time to catch up with us. We should act boldly like people with forever in their pockets. Perhaps this time I might actually . . ." But she covered his mouth with her hand.

She dared not think of becoming pregnant by him, with so many outstanding issues confronting their love. No, they must advance a step at a time, like blind people tapping a way with their white sticks. Paradoxically her very elation was terrifying. With him she might even dare to utter the words "*Je t'aime!*" which had always represented to her a wholly unrealisable territory of the feelings, of the heart. But then everyone alive is waiting for this experience, with impatience and with despair. Everyone alive!

They slept again, then woke, and drowsed their way slowly towards the late afternoon when the unexpected fever awoke in him – an onslaught so sudden that the symptoms for her seemed instantly recognisable as a rogue attack of malaria. But at first she was startled at its violent onset, to see him jumping and shivering with such violence, while he could hardly speak, his teeth chattered so in his head. "I brought it back from the desert – they have been planting rice like fools, and now you get anopheles right up to the gates of Alexandria!" But if his temperature had gone through the ceiling his pulse had sunk through the floor. He hovered now on the very edges of consciousness, but without undue alarm, for he knew that it would pass. Only with fury and self-disgust, for he was dying to make love to her again. And he had broken out into a torment of sweat. She found a thick towelling dressing-gown with a hood – indeed, they had stolen it from the hotel he had last occupied when in Geneva. An ideal thing for such a state, though it took quite an effort to get him into it, for he almost could not stand because of these paroxysms of trembling. He almost dropped on all-fours under the attacks. The sudden change was quite alarming, for he was ashen-white and all curled up. Malignant malaria is well known for its sudden paroxysms of fever which arrive or depart with incredible suddenness. But here was a temporary end of their love-making: he would simply have to sweat his way through the bout until the fever left him. She heaped him with blankets while he obediently turned his face to the wall and quivered his way into a half-sleep with a temperature so high that he was all but delirious. She did not even take his temperature in order not to alarm herself! Of course there were drugs which, administered in the night, might help to bring the fever down on the morrow. But of course he would be as limp as a cat afterwards . . . Damn!

Damn also because the telephone rang at that moment, and this time it was the voice of Schwarz, sounding preter-naturally grave, as if he were trying to master a concern or an anxiety. "I have been trying to reach you everywhere to tell you that your pet patient has broken out and escaped. Yes, Mnemidis!"

She thought for a long moment and then said, "Isn't our security foolproof? What about Pierre?" Schwarz replied, "He has stabbed him quite severely with a carving knife from the kitchens. But he has clearly got away because he made a phone call to his doctor friend from Alexandria and was most excited by their news. You know they were trying to take him back home? Well, they have succeeded in getting a *laisser-passer* for him from the Swiss, and there is nothing to prevent him just meeting them and being airlifted in a private plane – which is standing by at the airport. That is why I am not proposing to get unduly alarmed by the break-out; but I have moved into a hotel and asked a carpenter to change the locks on my flat. I think you should do the same. Until we get the all clear. The Alexandrian doctor has promised to signal me when he is safely in their custody so that they can escort him back to Cairo. What a bore it is! I hope you are feeling a bit chastened for having insisted on keeping him under treatment? No? Well, you should. At any rate, Constance, don't take any chances. For the moment he is somewhere in town, and nobody knows exactly where. So . . . Be on the *qui-vive* please, will you?"

"Very well," she said, though without conviction.

SIX

The Dying Fall

MNEMIDIS WAS MAKING THE MOST OF HIS FREEDOM, HE was filled with elation at the excellence of his disguise and the anonymity it conferred, though he looked a somewhat able-bodied nun. But he revelled in the unfamiliar beauties of the old town. As for the *fête votive*, it was so very touching and innocent that he was almost compelled to brush away a tear. It was very affecting. He laughed heartily and sincerely at the vastly correct jokes, careful not to boom, however. The squeaky exchanges of Punch and Judy and the rapt enthusiasm of the children filled him with an emotion close to dread. Once in Cairo long ago a little child had come to him, perhaps ten years old, doubtless a Bedouin and lost in the city ... he had a fit of harsh coughing. It was time to be moving on. He was waiting for the evening to arrive but he had not as yet actually located the situation of the apartment he planned to visit. But there was a most convenient tourist map of the city outside the gardens at the bus stop. There was also a list of the principal avenues and a marker to help find one. He spent a long moment doing so and verifying his own position vis-à-vis the street in question. He had all the time in the world. He had already been astute enough to phone to the hotel of his two Cairo associates, and the doctor had given him the good news of his successful *démarches*, of the Swiss *laisser-passer*, and of the private plane waiting for him. Mnemidis was overjoyed, but asked for a little time before joining his associates; he had something to do in the town first, but he thought that it might be possible to meet them at the airport late in the evening, say at dinner time or just after ... All this in a fine colloquial Arabic with its reassuring gutturals. "Above all," said the doctor, "do not commit any indiscretions, for you will be locked up for good, and we will never be able to release you. Take care!" Mnemidis chuckled and said that he would take care.

But there was time enough in hand, so having fixed a rendezvous at the airport at nine with the hope of a midnight departure, he left all the details to his friend, asking only that he might be met with a parcel containing a change of clothes, male clothes. He did not expatiate upon his present disguise because at bottom he trusted nobody. But his freedom and the secrecy of his whereabouts put him in a strong position to dictate his own terms. All the rest was up to him. He decided, since the afternoon was agreeably warm, to walk slowly across Geneva, and this he did, humming happily under his breath.

His route took him across the seedier parts of the old town, the poorer quarters, full of *maisons closes* and oriental cafés and moribund hotels; not to speak of the blue cinemas playing pornographic films. The one thing the war had not changed or debased was pornography; if anything, far from reducing it, it had caused an efflorescence, an increase. So necessary is it for the scared human ego to belittle a force which it recognises as being incalculably stronger than itself – the only really uncontrollable force man knows: for even if repressed it bursts out in symbolism, violence, dreaming, madness . . . Mnemidis slackened his pace in order to take in the whole scene with a just pleasure. There were a few sleazy whores already on the street, and the cinemas were rich in promise. He lingered at the entrance looking at the stills, attracting a number of curious and amused looks for he was still in his nun's garb. What marvellous titles the films had, expressing the age-old wishes and dreams of poor man, revealing him in all his frailty. He chuckled with an ape-like sophistication!

In the rue Delabre there was *Queue de Beton* or *The Concrete Prick*; further down *Plein Le Cul* or *A Cuntfull* and further on *Les Enculées* or *The Buggered*. It was absolutely delicious! He tore himself away with difficulty. It was with deep regret, however, for he simply longed to pass away an hour or so watching the antics of a blue film – it sharpened his intelligence. In it he felt the profound succulence of abused flesh. Even to think of it gave him hot flushes. However, he could hardly enter such a place in his present garb, and of course he did not wish to draw too much close attention to himself. But how reassuring it was to think that if all went well – and why should it not? – he would be leaving the country of his unjust captivity that very night! It elated him beyond measure, and he almost made the mistake of lighting a cigarette, for he had bought a packet. But he resisted the impulse successfully. He wandered past the cinemas and along the silent avenue leading to the park. He was not far off now, and he was filled with a silent felicity for he knew that luck would be with him in this just enterprise.

The mad must be people without selves: their whole investment is in the other, the object. They are ruled by the forces of total uncertainty. At this point Mnemidis did not know, with one half of his brain, what he might do under the promptings of the other half. A delicious uncertainty!

Like the greatest of mystics he had arrived at an unconscious understanding of nature as something which exists in a state of total *disponibilité*, of indeterminacy, of *hovering*! He was the joker in the pack, he was equally ripe for black mischief or the felicity of pure godhead. It was all according to how the dice fell, the wheel spun. Moreover he recognised that nature itself was completely indifferent to the outcome – to human bliss or pain. He felt only the electrical discharge of impulse throbbing in his body, like the engine of a ship, driving him onwards to the harbour of his realisation, a mystic of crime!

There is no therapy for reason, any more than for original sin. Yet sometimes even now he almost awoke from this mood, shook himself like a dog, wondering of a sudden if some small element had not worked loose somewhere in his inner thinking ... some tiny link. But he could not bear the wave of oppression and mistrust which followed in the wake of this sentiment and he closed his mind upon it like a steel door. His mouth set in a grim line. And now here he was in the street he had been seeking, standing before the very house he proposed to visit, utterly sure that everything had been planned for him, so that he might execute an exemplary punishment in the form of a farewell to Swiss medicine. And, by goodness, the door was ajar into the hall, for Constance had slipped out to the nearest pharmacy in search of a febrifuge for her fever-bound lover. She would not be gone very long. Hence she left the flat door ajar. Mnemidis saw with deep satisfaction the black shadow of the nun like some allegorical bat mount the stairs with a kind of Luciferian deliberation – as if she had been summoned to read a service for the sick or to hear the confession of someone *in extremis*. He chuckled to find that the flat door was also open. He entered and stood for a long moment looking about him, as if to memorise the geography of the place; but in fact he was simply listening to his own heartbeats and soliciting his soul, asking himself what he should do next. He heard the faint stirring of the bed in the next room and boldly opened the door – also ajar! His heart swelled up in triumph for there was a figure in the bed, covered from head to foot in a towelling dressing-gown with a hood drawn right over the head. Its face was turned to the wall, away from him, and from the whispering and trembling he at once guessed that she must be in a high fever, practically a delirium. But it was mysterious that she should be here all alone, lying ill in this darkened room. Perhaps there was someone else in the flat? With great swiftness now he explored all the other rooms, and then subsided with relief, for there was not a soul. What a perfect situation. "I told you so!" he said to himself under his breath, and breathing deeply like a voluptuary he advanced towards his victim.

It was lucky also that he had to deal with this inert and passive form and not a target presenting more difficulties – having to struggle, use force or ruse. No, the white form lay before him as if upon a slab, waiting to be operated on; in the beautiful simplicity of the whole business he felt he could read the handwriting of higher providence. Yes, this was how it had to be! And poising himself with profound concentration he put one hand upon the shoulder of the figure and completed his work with such speed and dexterity that he quite surprised himself. There was no cry, no groan, no sudden spasm. Just a deep sigh, as if of repletion, and a small gulp – a mere whiff of sound. With knives so preternaturally sharp it was hardly necessary to thrust with force, nevertheless he took no chances and gave of his best. *Consummatum est!* A whole mass of gloom-laden preoccupation seemed at once to fall from his shoulders. It was as if his conscience had voided itself like a sack. He almost cheered in his elation. But he wiped the weapons most carefully upon the silent shoulder of the corpse and then crossed the room on tiptoe. In the salon was a writing desk with a framed photo of his tormentor looking particularly pretty and intellectual. He stared at it for a long time, smiling grimly with a satisfied air. It was here, under this picture, that he at last placed the missing letter which she had been kicking up so much fuss about during recent weeks. Once when young he had been apprenticed to a conjuror and had retained a few of the skills he learned – making things appear and disappear with professional skill. It had not been difficult to do this with the letter. But now he was going to surrender it – like a parting snub!

He withdrew as silently as he had entered, closing the flat door behind him with a slight click – indeed this is what puzzled Constance on her return a quarter of an hour later: finding the flat door shut. It was vexatious for she had no key

and she did not want to tap and awaken her patient. She returned
downstairs and rang for the concierge who had a master key
which she loaned her. She entered at last to stand in startled
surprise at the open door of the bedroom, her arms full of
medicines. But almost at once the unnatural silence and inert-
ness of the figure on the bed struck a chill of premonitory
alarm in her. And peering as she advanced she saw the bloodstains on the sheet and shoulder of the wrap. She held her
breath and let drop the package she held. She called his name
once, then twice on an even sharper note of interrogation,
alarmed by the stillness. One thin hand stuck out of the wrap,
contracted up now in death like the claw of a dead bird. She fell
upon the pulse for a long moment, ferociously concentrated
with total attention. Then with a gasp she drew back the sheet
and began to unwrap the silent parcel, letting out a wail of
anguish as the reality of the affair came rushing at her, engulfing
every feeling. How could it be real, and as she drew back the
wrappings strange jumbled thoughts and memories contended
in her head with her concentration upon the terrible reality of
the situation – the wounds! Once someone had told of unwrapping an Egyptian mummy to get at the precious eatable
flesh which is the soul-nourishment of the gnostic – and
noticing that it had been stabbed *through* the wrappings, that
is to say after its death. Now who would fall upon and stab a
a body already dead and parcelled up for the grave? The
mystery remained! Yes, it was Affad who had told her. And
now this white towelling dressing-gown was the very same
into which she had bled so copiously upon her first sexual
encounter with him. They had stolen it from his hotel as a kind
of lover's talisman. When she had uncovered his body and
made quite sure she started to faint; she had just enough
presence of mind to dial the emergency code, four-number
four-ambulance which might come to her aid. But it was someone else's voice it seemed that told the operator to summon

Schwarz to her side. Then she fainted away. And so they found her.

Half-falling, half-subsiding upon the bed beside him she was possessed of a private stupefaction which would soon (like rings widening in water from a thrown stone) become public – or at any rate more public, for this sudden abrupt disappearance from the scene of Affad seemed as unbelievable to everyone as it seemed incomprehensible to her. But by now she was on the way to recognising the handiwork of her most interesting patient. She was stunned and bemused into an incoherence of mind which alarmed Schwarz when he at last arrived, though he did not go as far as opening the black leather suitcase which housed his drugs. It seemed more appropriate that she should cry, should give public expression to her shock – not just sit bereft and stunned and tearless in a chair with blood all over her skirt. Gazing in puzzled silence at his face with its now gigantic reserve, its depth and weight. All the memoranda of past conversations swarmed over her, invaded every corner of her apprehension. She was absent-minded, tongue-tied, shocked into aphasia almost. She said to herself something like, "So the future has arrived! Life will be no longer a waste of breath!" But the dazzling fact of his death still blinded her – like stepping in front of a firing squad and refusing the bandage. Was the death of a heart impossible to accept – it had, after all, been part of the original contract? How deafening was the silence in which they must now communicate with each other!

Yet the mechanical part of reality still held together like a stage-setting defying an earthquake – once the ambulance with its duty-doctor and team arrived, followed very shortly by her colleague, a rather trembly version of Schwarz. His gestures also were part of the whole stereotype, only they were more efficacious for he knew the flat; and from the cocktail cabinet under the window he extracted the bottle of vodka. The fiery dose he poured out for her made her hesitate; but then she drained the glass and the liquid poured into her like fuel into a furnace bringing heat without joy, without surcease. Nevertheless.

The intern was making a gingerly examination of the wounds before permitting the parcelling up of the body for the stretcher. "Surprisingly little blood," he said in a whisper almost, as if talking to himself. "Considering . . ."

Considering what, she wondered? Then of course she saw that one of the crew had found a knife which seemed to correspond to the victim's wounds. It was wrapped up carefully in newspaper for the coroner. It was another of Mnemidis' little offerings. "Finish your drink," said Schwarz sternly, "and sit quiet for a moment." He felt suddenly very angry with her, irrationally angry. He could have smacked her face. This is what came of meddling with other people's destiny – he did not say it aloud, but that is what he felt. Constance said, "He told me he was leaving his body to the hospital. He said, 'I like to think that I shall end up in chunks like a pineapple; after all, I was built up that way on the assembly line!' Easy to say." Schwarz did not at all like the note of her laugh at this awkward pleasantry so he sat down and put his arm about her shoulders.

There was some documentation to be completed and here Schwarz was master; he filled in the forms with expert swiftness, talking all the while to the intern. Meanwhile the stretcher was raised and borne away to the waiting ambulance and the flat door closed. The two doctors shook hands; Schwarz had already sketched in the context of the murder. Later on, the next day, he would find a message on his telephone recorder from the Egyptian doctor which would tell him that everything had worked perfectly, and Mnemidis had duly arrived at the airport, ready to embark for Cairo. There was nothing to be done in effect. What would have been the point in trying to get the madman back? He would be judged unfit to plead and locked up once more – to what end?

SEVEN

Other Dimensions Surprised

"OF COURSE THERE MUST BE A SERVICE," SAID THE Prince with unaccustomed testiness. "Forms must be observed as he would have wished." She shook her head. "I think *he* would have been indifferent – however, we shall do what you wish."

"It's easy to talk idly," said the Prince snappily, "but quite another to deal with a reality like this." His eyes filled with tears, and seeing that, so did hers. "You can imagine how guilty I feel," she said, almost whispering, and he took her hand to press it sympathetically. He felt that her heart was still only adolescent, still burning to grow up: and now this dire calamity stood in the way of its natural evolution towards maturity. "There's another thing," he said. "You will be quite surprised by the number of people who will be touched by this sudden loss. I think the chapel on the lake will be suitable for becoming a *chapelle ardente*, and we must publish the fact in the press perhaps – don't you think?" She was too tired to think. Things were resolving themselves without her intervention. She felt that her mind had gone numb. The little chapel in question was a small architectural vestige standing among mulberry trees on the water almost. It was part of the grand-mother's property. It had not even been ordained for services – indeed had never been used except once for a christening. It would do admirably. But she was unprepared for the number of people who put in an appearance at the ceremony itself, and for the feeling which was generated by the sight of his quiet face, pale now and somewhat drawn, in the big gondola-shaped coffin in which he had been laid. There were so many humble people like office-messengers and filing-clerks and typists, some of whom shed tears of real grief at the sight! One had quite forgotten that he had played a part in the public life of the town, and of the Red Cross; then of course her immediate friends, Sutcliffe wearing a tie, Blanford in his chair, Toby, the Prince, and of course Schwarz – all with their attention oriented towards the Pole Star of his death, of his silence. But he himself seemed detached, almost as if he were listening to distant music – perhaps he was? Fragments of old conversations floated backwards through her mind, as when she once said, "Damn it, I believe that I really do love you!" And he had replied ruefully, "It comes with practice I am sure – but will we have time?" Prophetic question!

Nor had it been difficult to find a Coptic priest who, together with his youthful novice, chanted the seemingly interminable Egyptian service of the dead, their thin, gnat-like tones stirring quaint echoes among the cobwebbed arches of the upper chapel. Geneva is the capital of cults and movements. Priests of all the denominations abound. The ceremony was at once exotic and fanciful and at the same time highly conventional owing to the soberly clad group of civil servants in their bourgeois clothing.

She had spent the afternoon lying across the foot of Blanford's bed; when she arrived at the clinic he was already in the know, for Schwarz had telephoned him. Constance simply marched into the room and said, "Please, Aubrey, I don't want to talk about it, indeed about anything. Can I just lie here for a few minutes?" She placed her hand in his and gradually swam out into a deep oceanic sleep which was to last a couple of hours. Blanford said nothing – what was there to say? But he felt the stirring of his old passion for the girl and his heart drew encouragement from the soft pressure of her hand in his. He felt that one day she must come to love him. It was something that was to be forged by time and circumstance; it could not be rushed! But it was in the final analysis ineluctable.

He was terribly happy and moved by the presentiment, by the promise of a future full of happiness. How can one feel so sure, though? And was it wise to encourage such optimism? She lay at his feet sleeping like a young lioness.

But he too was a prey to new conflicts centring around guilt, for it had suddenly dawned on him that quite possibly he had hated Affad without being fully aware of the fact. It was extraordinary how the news of his friend's death had brought him a sense, if not of elation, of peace and well-being, of fulfilment almost. He was too curious about the emotion to indulge in self-reproach – moreover, the whole thing was so unexpected. But it seemed unworthy of Constance to accommodate vulgar emotions like jealousy. ("Why *vulgar?*" he asked himself.) Was his love suffering from the blood-poisoning of over-refinement? Or was it just a coarse plebian growth like everyone's? He watched her sleeping face with attention as if he might perhaps read the answer on it, to master the secret which so far he had never expressed.

"Cet homme n'avait qu'à ouvrir les bras et elle venait sans efforts, sans attendre, elle venait à lui et ils s'aimaient, ils s'embrassaient . . ." Yes, he suddenly felt the quiet suppressed fury of Flaubert's jealousy and recognised it as his own. "A lui toutes les joies, toutes ses delices à lui . . ." For *him* all the joys, all the delights for *him*! "A lui cette femme toute entière," for him this woman entire, head, throat, breasts, body, her heart, her smiles, the two arms which enfolded him, *ses paroles d'amour*. A lui tout, à moi rien! He stirred her sleeping body softly with his foot, almost apologetically for what he deemed an ignoble line of thought. Ah! This power-house of human misery and ecstasy, the cunt! What Sutcliffe called "the great tuck-box of sex". How much thought, how much science would it need to control its ravages?

She spoke now without opening her eyes so that he could hardly tell whether she was awake or not. "Did you see what the little boy did?" Yes, he had seen. "Yes, I got quite a shock, a sort of shiver ran through me. I felt the significance of his decision, the weight of it. One simple decision like that alters the whole of a life. Am I romancing?" She gave a brief sob and fell silent.

What had happened was this: in the small chapel they had formed several different groups with the family servants and the grandmother (in all the splendour of her mourning costume – superb garments, for the Egyptians are best at mourning, it has always been so): she stood away to one side with the little boy beside her clad in his eternal sailor suit with its HMS *Milton* on the hat ... while Constance stood far forward on the left so that she could watch the quiet face of her lover who seemed so inexplicably still. All of a sudden she heard the click of small heels on the stone flags and turning her head saw the boy leave the side of the old lady and walk with premeditated decisiveness across the whole width of the chapel to Constance's side. He did not look at her, but simply took her hand, and together they gazed in the looming shadows at the corpse in its gondola-like coffin. Meanwhile the service nagged onwards towards its benediction. The old lady released him with a half gesture of loving despair, spreading her hands as one who releases a cage-bird. Her eyes filled with tears but she was smiling. She realised the full significance of the act as indeed Constance did. It was hard not to tremble, but she managed an appearance of calm as she pressed the small hand which lay in hers.

It was a new role which seemed to be now presenting itself – the role of a mother, almost, which was part of the inheritance left her by Affad. It was the most unexpected of gifts, and one which she knew she must not refuse. At the end of the service she walked him back to his grandmother and handed him over without a word exchanged. But both had grasped the finality of the choice and both knew its value and its explicitness. The details could wait upon circumstance. The choice had been made and would be respected. She felt quite shaky with emotion as she joined the others in the garden outside the chapel where there was a little delay while people sought their cars. It was here that Cade came forward with a letter for Schwarz from some refugee centre.

Schwarz glanced at the printed superscription on the envelope and grumbled as he put the envelope away in his overcoat pocket, to read at leisure. "International Refugee Centre," he growled, scowling at Cade as he did so. The whole world was a refugee now that the war had at last ended. "How did you get hold of it?" he asked the servant suspiciously, and Cade replied with punctilio, in his sanctimonious whine, "It came in the Red Cross pouch, sir. As I knew I would see you here I brought it along to save time." The eternal messenger, bearer of the eternal telegram, the poisoned arrow! He was not at first to recognise the death sentence which the envelope contained.

Constance was woken from sleep by the appearance of yet another unexpected figure – a bronzed young giant of a man in uniform bearing the insignia of the Royal Medical Corps. Blanford greeted him with unusual warmth, almost as a long-lost brother. This was Drexel, the young doctor who had provided welcome medical first aid after the accident in the desert which had cost the life of Constance's first love. There was a spontaneous warmth and penetration in his regard, and a feeling of familiarity which immediately captivated her. "Bruce Drexel!" So that is who he was; and for his part the young man greeted her as if they had been childhood friends. He was eager to assess the merits of the extensive surgical repairs to Blanford's poor back and glanced through the dossier of the operations with keen interest. "You were right," said Aubrey, "to call it the restringing of an old *piano*, for that is exactly how it felt to me. But from a *piano à queue* they are gradually turning me into an upright again. There's a real promise that I may one day walk again, though I think that ballroom dancing won't ever be possible again. Never mind!"

"You are lucky to be here at all!" said Drexel reproachfully, and then stopped abruptly as he thought of the dead man, and recalled that he had been, after all, the husband of Constance. She rose to set her hair to rights in the pier glass while Drexel went on, though talking in a lower key, as if what he had to say might interest only Blanford. "You know something? Now the war is over, or almost over bar the shouting, the *ogres* are going to break free from diplomacy and return to Verfeuille once more – you remember the old dream we spoke of on the boat? The dream of *après la guerre*? Well, it is slowly coming true, I think. The old château is in pretty ruinous shape but we can fix that up slowly; and though it sounds romantic wouldn't you retire from the world if you could? Anyway I am going on down into Provence as an advance guard to take soundings for the two *ogres*. They think that by next spring we can put our plan into action for a permanent *ménage à trois* . . ." He hesitated, for Constance had turned back from the mirror and showed a disposition to re-enter the flow of the conversation once more. She sensed his reticence and hastened to say, "I know all about your plan, because Aubrey told me about it; and then I was delighted for you would be neighbours. But isn't it a little early as yet?"

"The Germans have gone, and things will slowly come back into true. The *ogres* propose to live very modestly on his pension while I have a tiny income of my own." He smiled and stretched and stood up. "Why don't you come down around Christmas and spend it with us? It's far enough off as yet to dream about."

It was curious how this casual suggestion set up an echo, a vibration in the consciousness of Constance. It was as if a door had opened somewhere in the further end of her thoughts and memories. Provence! She had been talking of going on leave ever since her return from the long gruelling spell she had spent there during the war. Why not inaugurate the peace there with a Christmas visit? "It sounds crazy," she said automatically, and the young man sighed and shrugged. "In any case," he said to Blanford, "your novel about the matter is finished: it only remains for you to see if we are going to live it according to your fiction or according to new fact, no?"

EIGHT

After the Fireworks

AND SO AT LAST THE CLOCKS RAN DOWN AND GENEVA, capital of human dissent, realised that it must formally fête the ending of the most murderous war in human history. Yet, despite everything, a war which had made her rich and confirmed her liberties as well as her boundaries. A particular day was agreed upon by the nations which would bear the brunt of the victory – celebrations seemed onerous in the prevailing exhaustion, yet it was appropriate that they should mark the event, however half-hearted, however reserved. A day of lamentation for humanity might have been nearer the mark, for to the work of Hitler and Stalin the Allies had added their own rider in the ominous word Yalta, thus completing the circle of doom which hovered over European history. Nevertheless a victory celebration had been accepted by all, and for something like a week the Swiss had been industriously transforming their lake frontage into a wilderness of medieval towers and gates and keeps which would supply a stage backcloth for the mammoth firework display which they had planned. And the new fad in town was to walk the lakeside after dinner each night to study the progress of the work, to watch the army of soldiers and civilians at work on the project, operating from a fleet of anchored pontoons over a length of several kilometres. Nothing had been seen like this since the Great Exhibition: nothing since Paris had transformed itself into fairyland for a spell just before the war broke out.

Constance walked the whole length of the lake with her colleague Schwarz several times a week now when returning from the clinic at night, or after dinner in town. It was always full of variety and interest, the slow progress of this one-dimensional project upon which the fires would burn, the lights flicker. Obscure scenes from medieval Swiss history were to be pictured here against the screen of fireworks, scenes which extolled the grandeurs of freedom and independence: perhaps, as Schwarz said ironically, also scenes which extolled banking and secret credit accounts . . . who can say? But their statutory walk was much enlivened by the occasion and they planned to dine together on Victory Night and to follow the progress of the display on the spot. "*Après la guerre!*" mused the old man as they progressed. "What can it mean? For war never really ends, like birth and death, perpetual motion . . . Before one can get to the end of one set of wishes or hopes along comes another. The options have changed! History makes a rightabout turn. I used to see much more sense in things when I was younger, consequently I was prepared to fight for them. Now it's all hollow, all empty, and I am ready to turn on the gas."

"Hark at you!" she said with indignation. "Only yesterday I heard you express a hope that Israel might emerge from the present chaos as a coherent entity. And now?" Schwarz depressed his cheeks and looked shamefaced. "It is true," he at last admitted. "I did say that I thought I saw an important role for Israel and hope she would come forth from the ruins. But Constance, the sense in which I spoke was far from political or geographical. For me the country is like a retort in which a vital experiment could and perhaps will be conducted. But this is in the domain of philosophy and religion – it has nothing to do with frontiers. I am hoping that something like the Principle Of Indeterminacy as posited by our physicists for reality will find its way into the religious values of the new state; I see you don't quite understand me so I won't labour the point. But I'm hoping for a materialism which is profoundly qualified by mysticism – a link between Epicurus and Pythagoras, so to speak. All right! All right! I think that our Hassidim have the creature by the tail and that they might help it to evolve. It would be a marvellous contribution to the future, for we can't continue with this worn-out materialism of ours, it leads us nowhere. And while we are eroding the Indian vision, drowning it in our technology, India is eroding ours, drowning Europe in all the vast meekness of pure insight!" He stopped.

"You mean the world is becoming one place?"

"Yes! It so obviously must if there is to be a future for humanity. Surely we can dream? Why should man be the only animal who knows better but always fares worse?"

This long, indeed interminable, argument of theirs wound its slow course across the weeks towards Victory Day which would mark the historic *point culminant* of things. Much of what he said was only imperfectly understood as yet by Constance and would come back to memory in the years to come – making her realise that with Schwarz she had received a sort of philosophic education invaluable for a doctor. But so often he was obscure, oracular, perhaps one could say almost 'vatic' in his vision, for he was after all Jewish in origin, with the broad stripe of mystical insight for which his race is known. The severe materialism of his apparent outlook was merely a façade to mask his other profounder preoccupations, as when he sighed, "To what extent have we the right to interfere with the principle of entropy, the cosmic submission which subsumes everything – the death-drift of the world?" It was the point at which East and West were still at loggerheads. Submission or intervention, which?

"No!" he went on. "The Nazi in the woodpile is a too strenuous orthodox Judaism which we can evolve and modify slowly into a richer complicity with nature. Absolutes spawn restrictive systems; but provisionals in their elasticity allow us to breathe."

He struck the ground defiantly with his stick and said, "I have a *right* to hope, after all!"

"That is what the Prince sometimes says!"

Schwarz snorted, for he was slightly jealous of the Prince, sensing how deeply Constance was attached to the little man. As a matter of fact the news from Egypt – which had followed the Prince, so to speak – was hardly reassuring, for all of a sudden the British authorities after years of quiet suspicion about the orientation of the gnostic groups had decided to investigate, and about twenty-five of the Prince's collaborators were at present under arrest pending an inquiry into their apparent political motives. It put him in a rage just to think of it! The shortsightedness, the imbecility, the waste of the whole thing! It really wasn't worth being pro-British when they behaved with such ill-judged stupidity! The whole storm in a tea-cup would end in nothing, for there was nothing secret and confidential to be discovered. One could already foresee the climb-down which would ensue, the apologies offered all round to the arrested club members! Goodness, what a fool that Brigadier M. was! But the realisation did little to soothe the ire of the Prince who felt that the whole operation had made a fool of him and of his pro-Ally sentiments.

Schwarz was thinking: "Larger than life or larger than death – which? The two ways, East and West!" What he wanted to do was to scale himself down to the size of his own death, which he could feel was not too far off now.

So they limped their way towards the point of victory, and the day dawned bright with church bells and religious processions – it was treated like a Holy Sunday and public holiday combined. But for the clinic this meant little difference – one cannot call a truce to the unhappiness of the insane just when one wishes, even to celebrate the end of a war. So it was evening before they found themselves at the Bavaria while outside in the grassy squares massed bands played and detachments of motorised troops marched and counter-marched to the music, waiting for the first pangs of white light from the anchored pontoons with their brilliant historic tableaux. There was ample time to dine, and under the influence of the red wine Schwarz waxed almost eloquent about firework displays he had seen in the past, in Vienna, in his student days; and once on a visit to Venice. How would this Geneva display compare in style and originality, he wondered?

But they were already walking across the park when the first maroons boomed out and the white effulgence coloured the dark air with sudden stabs of starkness, printing up the receding façades of the buildings like so many human faces and running with slippery unction from the lake surfaces tumbled by the night wind. Gradually, as they advanced, the whole axis of light slanted and the waterfront slowly took fire like a summer hillside, each section performing its duties with beauty and precision, so that the whole comprised a single jungle of impulses moving right and left, up and down, and printing out the city with every sulphurous stab, every explosion of light, every thirsty roar of rocket or meteor. And while this whole symphonic movement gathered weight the various historical tableaux began to print up, human figures began to move and bend and dance. (That afternoon the Prince had said to Constance: "Constance, you have suddenly started to walk like an old woman. It has got to stop! And you are letting your hair grow wild just like those pregnant girls who hope by doing so to conceive of a boy. Please pull yourself together. You must. Please use a little reason!") *Reason!* She repeated this to Schwarz who snorted with disdain at the word-choice. He was thinking to himself that reason made strange bed-fellows: how Socrates sought suicide like Jesus, but did not want to take the blame for the act. What a contrast to Buddha who thought that felicity and the rounded tummy were best!

They came upon a public telephone and Schwarz was impelled by a characteristic twinge of professional conscience to ring up the duty nurse at the clinic to find out if all the untoward banging and flaring had had a disturbing effect on the patients. But he refrained, he restrained the desire. He said, "The most haunting thing about human reality is that there is always something unexpected happening in the room next door about which one will only find out later on! Moreover it will prove surprising, totally unpredictable, and more often than not unpalatable!"

"Pessimist!"

"No, realist. Pragmatist!"

They advanced upon the starkly blazing water frontage, dazed by the variety of the scenes which were now being simultaneously enacted for their benefit – some from the late war, some from historic circumstances and events, some perhaps from wars to come, wars not as yet engendered in the human consciousness. The flames and scenes were striving to offer them a sort of summing-up of the years wasted in brutality and strife – in the hope that by closing the whole chapter a notion might be launched of some change of direction. Geneva was the capital of the moral reproach, the lost cause, the forlorn hope!

"When puberty came," said Schwarz grimly, "when I was around thirteen or so, a sudden terror took possession of me one day in church. I suddenly saw that everyone around me was abnormal, was ill, was mentally disturbed; I had realised that to be a Christian constituted being deranged in the purest sense of the term. The Quia Absurdam leaped at me, just like standing on the head of a rake. Moreover it was everywhere, all around me – the thirty-nine articles or the sixty-nine varieties of Heinz beans. I trembled and broke into a sweat just reciting the Creed after the parson – it seemed gibberish. Jesus was paranoid like Schmeister, driven mad by the strain of trying to break away from or assimilate the tenets of an orthodox Judaeo-Christianity. He had shared this fate with Nietzsche, the Christian syndrome. In the despair of my youth

I could see no hope of ever escaping it myself. What an experience for a sensitive youth! It marked me. Even now when I tell myself that I have escaped the worst I catch myself up abruptly and wonder ..."

A dozen blazing swans whizzed heavenward spitting out tracer; sixteen pearls hissed after them trailing parabolas of flame. Constance thought, "We look to each other for nobility of conduct, for traces of the sublime. There isn't any such thing, no such hope. How did we get such ideas and wishes in the first place? They were bound to be disappointed!"

So they walked on like fellow-bondsmen shackled by the same ideas, swollen with the despair of hopes unsatisfied, of promises unfulfilled. What price their theories of health and disease when pitted against this sort of historic reality? She could feel the greyness creeping upon the outlook of her companion, could sense the cryptic sadness welling up in his mind. How senseless this huge and wasteful celebration seemed to her! It closed no door upon the past, it opened no door upon the future. It left them disconsolate and bereft – like beached ships. Abruptly – and without even waiting to see if she followed him or not – Schwarz turned aside into a café with a bar giving on to the lake gardens and angrily ordered double whiskies, but continuing the while to gaze at the display in all its distant splendour. Under his breath he was softly swearing – a habit Constance knew full well from the past. She put a hand on his arm to soothe him, and said, "Well, look who's here!" She had caught sight of Sutcliffe and Toby sitting in a far corner, apparently deep in conversation with Lord Galen whose manner suggested the deepest elation. Schwarz showed some reluctance to join them, for it was obvious that Sutcliffe had been at the bottle, and possibly Galen also; but their appearance was greeted with such a display of welcoming affability that it would have been churlish to turn one's back upon them without exchanging a word. So they advanced towards them, determined only to stay a few moments.

After suitable greetings they took their place at the table which was admirably disposed *vis-à-vis* the continuing fire-work display, and allowed Lord Galen to monopolise the conversation, which in a curious sort of way echoed their own preoccupations and doubts. It concerned the problems which they might anticipate in a post-war state of things. "I felt quite lost and thrown aside, I must confess," said Galen, "and I did not know which way to turn my talents. I knew that one day I must return to private enterprise. Then, like a signal from On High, I learned that Imhof was dead and that he had made a will in my favour – can you imagine? I had inherited those thousands of bidets which he had stored away in Dieppe in vast warehouses, just waiting to cross the Channel and convert the English, in order to help them to save water. Think, all through the war they had been laid up there, shrouded in anonymity, waiting. Suddenly I found I had inherited them. At first I was a bit panicky at the thought but finally my old business sense came to the rescue and I drafted a careful advertisement in *Exchange and Mart*. Sure enough – there is a market for everything if you can find it – I had an answer from the Society of Jesus, who proposed to export them to the Far East as part of a religious campaign. They found a way of printing 'Jesus Saves' on them in several languages, and away they went! I was left with a nice little sum after settling up the dues involved. I was able to consider leaving the ministry with all its insoluble problems. But of course civil life was also full of grave discouragements, I don't deny it. I decided that I should diversify my investments but I did not know quite how when ... guess what ... I got an idea from Cade, of *all* people, Aubrey's factotum. I heard him say to his master, 'Lord bless you, sir, the future will be just like a past. Nothing is going to change. Everyone is going to go on in the same old way, you will see.' It carried conviction, I suddenly realised that it was true. I saw that one should still invest in the old values, the old beliefs, with perfect security. So I decided to invest seriously in Marital Aids – for soon marriage would be booming again. I founded the Agency Vulva to sell a computer of that name – the only computer with a sex-life that is really life-like – it can twitch, throb, corybant at the pressing of a button. It is most exciting and is well on the way to building itself a world market. I owe all this to the insight of Cade!"

He gazed around him with fatuous self-satisfaction, swollen with an innocent conceit at these antics. Sutcliffe banged his glass on the table approvingly and said, "I appoint myself your advertising manager. I will write you slogans of utter irresistibility like . . . 'Bring splendour to your marriage with our hand-knitted french letters.' Or for the Swiss something a bit aphoristic like 'C'est le premier pas qui coûte quand c'est le premier coup qui part!'" Galen shuddered, but with gratitude. "For the moment," he said hastily, "we need nobody. Perhaps later."

A Swiss military band with a pedantic goose-step marched across the middle distance against a blazing wall of Catherine wheels pounding out the music of Souza. Schwarz went on quietly swearing, with resignation, almost with piety, oblivious to the restraining caress of Constance's hand upon his elbow. Soundlessly, one might say, inside all this triumphant noise. His lips moved, that was all.

"I do not see," said Toby with a judicial air which could not hide a certain insobriety, "that the future can resemble the past in any way. Thanks to science the world has come to an end, for the woman is free at last, though she remains bound to the wheel of generation; she is free to spread sterility at will. The balance of the sexes is beautifully disturbed." Galen looked both perplexed and alarmed. But Sutcliffe nodded approvingly and said, "Exactly what I have been telling Aubrey, to his intense discomfiture. He also hoped that things would go on in the same old way. I was forced to disabuse him. Soon we are going to have to collaborate on a terminal book, and it's important that we should see eye to eye, so that it will be written, like all good books, by the placental shadow, me! Actually if it is to be historically true it should be entitled WOMAN IN RUT AND MAN IN ROUT. And of course the secondary result of this confused situation will be an increasing impotence in the male – *un refus de partir, mourir un peu beaucoup quoi!* My basic genetic alibi, my cockstand, will go all anaesthetic." He gave a low moan on a theatrical note. All this was calculated to increase the distress of poor Schwarz. If Sutcliffe was to be believed, what hopes could one hold out for the future of medical practice – specially something as fragile and contestable as psychoanalysis? Moreover they were *joking* about such a situation – joking about tragedy! He rose unsteadily to his feet and gazed wildly about him as if he were seeking a weapon. For the appropriateness of the subject-matter to the specific night – the victory carnival after nearly a decade of war – made the whole context ironic in the extreme. Constance rose also in warm sympathy with her colleague's fury, and prepared to set sail with him despite the protests of the others. As they walked away from the braying and banging of the spectacle towards the shadows Schwarz filled in the picture in his own mind with bitter thrusts of thought: yes, after all, Sutcliffe was right. Semantics would replace philosophy, economic judaism democracy, sterility potency . . . and so on. There was no way round the omens. But at least he, Schwarz, refused to be flippant about the matter. He *cared*, he was *concerned*!

At last they came to the last depleted taxi rank and he turned to bid her goodnight, for she had elected to stay at her flat in town for the night. "I am sorry to have been so very subversive on Victory Night," he said ruefully, "but what is there left to hope for, eh?" They embraced and he gazed long and tenderly at her before turning aside – a look which would remain with her for years, for this was the last time she was to see Schwarz alive; a look which summarised the tenderness and professional zeal which linked them in the name of their defective science.

She stood gazing after the taxi, touched by a dawning premonition of something momentous about to happen, she knew not what!

NINE

End of the Road

"ATTENTION CONSTANCE," SCHWARZ HAD WRITTEN ON
their common blackboard in violet chalk before copying the phrase again upon a sheet torn from his prescription pad; this latter leaf he propped against the dictaphone.
It bore an arrow and an exclamation mark and indicated the
pyramid of wax cones upon which he had imprinted the true
story of his death, his suicide. It would have been sad if by
some inadvertence they had been overlooked or cleaned of
their story. The cones were sorted most carefully and numbered; it was possible to hear his description and exposition of
the whole business in strict sequence. Schwarz had always had
a mania for order – it seemed to him to confer a sort of
secondary truthfulness. And in this particular case he had been
anxious to present his decision as reasonable, the act as pardonable because quite logical. Nevertheless there was some guilt
mixed up in the business, for he had felt the need to make a case
for himself.

They had both always despised suicide!

And now what?

"Constance, my dear, I foresee that perhaps you may be
a little shocked by my decision, but I did not take it lightly; it
has matured slowly over a period of time, and has only come
to a head during this week, after receiving the letter which you
saw Cade hand me – a letter which contained strange news after
so many years of silence. It told me that Lily had been found at
last and still alive! Found among the dregs of Tolbach, the
notorious camp for women, in Bavaria. At first of course my
heart leaped up, as you can imagine, and a variety of conflicting
and confused emotions filled it; but then the letter contained

news which was disquieting rather than reassuring. She had
lost her teeth and her hair, was suffering from malnutrition as
well as experiencing moments of aphasic shock . . . My first
impulse was to rush to her side, but when I phoned the units
working on the problem the doctor in charge advised me to
give them what he called "a breathing-space", for he did not
want me to be too shocked by her condition. He needed time
to feed and rest her up a little. He posted me some photographs
taken at the camp, of those who had been still alive when the
place was discovered. Lily was only one of many, but fortunately she had been sufficiently coherent to give an account of
herself, and they had found her dossier in the camp files. But
the photographs they enclosed were hair-raising in their
fierceness – this bald and toothless old spider, worn to the
skeleton with hunger – this was all that was left of Lily, the
lovely Lily!

"Connie, you know just how deeply guilty I have always
felt about her – about my cowardice in escaping from Vienna
without her, and leaving her to the mercies of the Nazis – to
almost certain death. There was no excuse, and I never *tried* to
excuse this terrible failure of nerve. But I lived, as you know,
bowed under the guilt of this act all through the war – even
sometimes perversely hoping that she might never return to
judge me – though I knew it was not in her nature to judge! But
it was there, the guilt. And then at other times I thought of her
possible return as a joyful event: it would give me a chance to
make it all up to her, to repay her for all her sufferings . . . How
skilfully we can untangle the delusions of others! Yet when it
comes to one's own one is powerless not to believe in them, not
to swallow our self-manufactured fictions!

"Of course I was impatient with myself. I tried to treat
the situation in a masterful fashion; I took up the phone and
implored the doctor to put me in touch with Lil, direct touch.
He deplored the idea but agreed and gave me a time of day

which would be suitable. But I was unprepared for the dry
clicking of her voice with its shy pauses, its lapses of memory.
It was like talking to a very old and half-mad baboon." (Here
the terse narrative was caught up with a dry sob. After a long
pause the grave measured voice of the old doctor resumed the
thread of his story.)

"I was gradually coming to a new point of realisation
about her; it was dawning on me that her return to me in this
new form was something to be dreaded rather than wished for.
For so many years the thought of her had acted upon me like a
sharp reproach; but now she threatened to become something
altogether more fierce still – a living, breathing reproach to
the man who had been responsible for her distress, her
imprisonment! I suddenly realised that I simply could not face
such a *dénouement*. I was completely unable to swallow such an
idea. Moreover this sudden violent revulsion was completely
unforeseen. It surprised me as much as it shook me. What was
to be done, then? To deny her once more? To repeat my
original act of cowardice, apparently because she was in poor
physical shape? Such a thing would be unthinkable, unpardonable! Then what alternatives were there? None. The only
choice before me was either to submit or else to vanish from the
scene. The solution printed itself on my mind with a simple
finality which was incontrovertible! I could find not a shadow
of doubt with which to counter its cold and absolute truth!"
Schwarz paused for breath and one could hear the scratch of a
match as he lit up a cigar and puffed reflectively before resuming his account.

"Naturally I envisaged something very swift and decisive,
a bullet in the brain no less. And I unpacked the old revolver,
broke it, and checked the shells. Then I put it carefully in my
mouth like the well-briefed suicide I was – God knows, when I
was a young intern I had helped clean up messes of this kind
when on duty with a police ambulance. Memories came back

to me as I sat there, feeling and looking foolish, with the icy barrel of the revolver pressing upon my soft palate. I knew of course that revolvers throw upwards as they fire and that one stood a fair chance of error if one fired it through the temple – one case I recalled had shot out his two eyes without inflicting upon himself the death he sought. The only foolproof way was to shoot upwards into the skull via the soft palate. This is what I proposed doing. What, then, was making me hesitate like this? Partly for company, and partly for encouragement I switched on the time-clock of the telephone and sat there listening to the disembodied voice repeating: 'At the fourth stroke it will be *exactly... Au quatrième toc il sera exactement...*' Don't smile! I just could not press that cold trigger. The seconds ran away like suds down a sink and there I sat, pistol in one hand and telephone in another, riveted. Another memory had surfaced – of a suicide who had actually done the trick classically, pistol in mouth. But the force of the explosion had removed the whole crown of his head like somebody's breakfast egg. An appalling mess for a young and shaky intern. I vomited violently as I worked at the cleaning up. Naturally I suddenly felt that I could not inflict this upon our own ambulance people. I rose and hunted out an old skull-cap of mine and a prayer shawl. Draped in these I resumed my vigil with the telephone and this time I stayed there obstinately, urging myself to show the necessary courage to complete the act. I had already sorted my papers, cheque books, identity kit, etc. so that Lily would have no problems when she re-entered civil life; I had even written her a cheerful note of welcome to my flat which she would soon own."

In the pauses of his discourse you could hear the puffs as he drew on his cigar and formulated what he wanted to say next. "Constance, I found I could not do it. A new cowardice had come to replace the old. I laid the pistol down – it is where you will find it. I am substituting a peaceable injection for it. It is less dramatic but just as efficacious. Goodbye, darling Constance."

His sighs expended themselves on the queer silence, and one was able to imagine what he was doing from the tinkle of the syringe against the ash-tray. He muttered a short prayer in his own language, but it was perfunctory and full of disdain for God in whom he believed only intermittently. Constance listened to all this sitting with the dead man at her side slumped at his work-desk. Then she called the Emergency Unit.

TEN

The End of an Epoch

IT WAS LATE AT NIGHT WHEN THE NEWS OF SCHWARZ'S disappearance from the scene was telephoned to Constance who had celebrated a few days of leave by staying at her town flat, thus enabling herself to see her friends and even play a game of pool with Sutcliffe or Toby. The telephone cleared its throat and set up its rusty trill. She recognised the voice of the night-operator on the switchboard and heard with sinking heart the first ominous words which spelt the end of her leave. "Dr Schwarz has been taken ill. The Emergency Unit has been asking for you, doctor."

"What has happened?" she asked, but the line had already been switched, presumably in the direction of the emergency intern, for there followed a garble of clicks and voices and finally she heard the incongruous voice of the negro stretcher-bearer Emmanuel saying hoarsely, "*Mister Schwarz he dead.*"

"What?" she cried incredulously and the deep thrumming negro voice repeated the message more slowly. The import of the words sank into her – or rather she sank into them as one sinks into a quicksand. Surely there must be some mistake? "Give me the duty doctor," she said at last, sharply, and as Emmanuel faded she heard the voice of the emergency intern, old Gregory, take up the tale. "I think you had better come up here," he said. "I am afraid that the old boy has done himself in with an injection. At any rate he is sitting at his desk and his heart has stopped, and there is a syringe in the ash-tray beside him. But Constance, there are messages for you, and your name on the blackboard. I am reluctant to call anyone in until you have had a look at the scene for yourself. I can't really evaluate it, and I don't want to invoke the police at this stage. Anyway, perhaps you know why. Was he specially depressed?"

She gave a groan and a hollow laugh and said, "When is a psychiatrist not a psychiatrist? God, Gregory, are you sure that—I mean, perhaps if you massaged the heart?"

Gregory made a sound something like a groan and an exclamation of impatience. "We arrived much too late," he said. "He is becoming marbly already—I want your okay to uncurl him and spread him on the couch straight away. Otherwise the rigor will cause problems."

"Do so if you must," she said. "I'll be there as quickly as a taxi can bring me." But when she arrived they had as yet done nothing, dismayed by the scribble on the blackboard and the dictaphone tablets. Schwarz looked so normal and so homely that all at once she conquered her fear and her distaste, and was glad to sit down at his side and bend over to study the dossier which he had open before him and which he had been studying while he waited for the slow poison to uncoil, serpent-like in his veins, until it reached his heart. Gregory watched her for a while with sympathy and said, "Yes, she was probably the last person to see him alive, you will have to ask her. I have no doubt." Constance reflected, her face wore an expression of compassionate distaste. Gregory said, "She must have come here with her latest manuscript, and perhaps he told her why— unless you already know why." Constance stood up and said, "Now please leave me alone to listen to these wax tablets—give him the chance to tell me why himself, for that is clearly what they mean. Afterwards we can decide what is what, and reflect on the role of the police in this affair." Gregory nodded and lit a cigarette. "And this girl, Sylvie, who was quite a well-known writer—what of her? Was Schwarz in love with her?" Constance shook her head and said, "No, it's more complicated than that; I started to treat her myself—she is absolutely brilliant but schizophrenic. She fell in love with me, whatever that means, and the transfer went to hell, so that he was forced to take her back on to his roster, and to pretend that I had been sent far away, to India no less, in order to release her from her obsession with me. Such are the hazards of psychology!"

"Well, the best would be to leave you to examine all the data before coming to any conclusion about the matter; he was not one to cause mysteries. Besides, this whole dossier seems to consist of love-letters – presumably addressed to Schwarz."

"No," said Constance, "that is the trouble, they are always addressed to me. Schwarz's job is to post them to me in India – for he alone knows my address and will not reveal it to her – that is the cover-story which has enabled me to stand aside and switch her treatment to him. When I last heard she was enjoying a short remission from the malady – all the more cruel because she always remembers in sane periods what she did and thought when she was mad."

"I see."

"It is the saddest of all our cases because she is a woman of the greatest brilliance, her writings are quite marvellous in their poetry. I suppose I shall have to go and see her now and pretend that I am back from India. She will find herself quite bereft without him, her beloved doctor."

Gregory stood for a brief moment smoking a cigarette with a somewhat dispossessed air; then he said, "Well, I shall go back to Emergency and see what other calls have come in. If and when you want us just phone down."

"I will."

"Constance," he said with deep sympathy, for he knew how much the old man had meant to her, "Constance, bad luck my dear!" And in his awkward way he stooped to kiss her face. And now she was alone with the stooped figure of her oldest friend, suddenly overwhelmed by the surging memories of all they had shared together – memories now abbreviated by something as momentous yet trivial as a cardiac arrest. "Ah,

my dear," she said under her breath, "why did you have to do
the one thing you most despised?" She switched on the little
recording machine and heard his voice etching itself upon the
silence of the room as if in answer to her question. As he talked
in that quiet, measured tone she examined the little phial from
which he had drawn the fatal injection as well as the empty
syringe leaning upon an ash-tray with two cigar-butts stubbed
out in it. Everything had taken place quietly and quite circumspectly; the other suicide equipment, the revolver and the cap
and prayer shawl were at the far end of the table.

The dossier was familiar, though since she had last seen
it it had swollen in size with a number of new letters, all neatly
typed carbons – presumably the originals had been sent to
"India". Sylvie must have visited Schwarz and left it behind
her. She recognised the dazzling alembicated prose which had
so much impressed Aubrey. She had told him the history of
Sylvie and shown him the early letters. She did not forget the
occasion when she came upon him as he replaced them in the
folder in which they lay. He looked up and his eyes were full
of tears of admiration as he said, "Goodness, Constance, she
has done it, she has done the trick, she has become it! Against
this all my stuff is feebly derivative and merely talented! This
is art, my dear, and not artifice." And he had begged to keep
the file so that he could read and re-read the letters. He was much
affected by the story of her life and of her unlucky illness as
well as of her poetic obsession with Constance with whom she
had fallen so deeply in love. Sitting beside her old friend and
mentor, listening to his voice recounting his last hours, she
thought over these incidents with a tremendous weariness. All
of a sudden, within the space of a few months, reality had taken
on a totally new colour; it was as if the world had suddenly
aged around her, washing her up high and dry on to this shelf
in time where she sat in a sort of trance listening to the voice of
Schwarz and resting a hand upon the immobile shoulder. But

she must have affected his centre of gravity for all of a sudden the corpse began to slide slowly towards her – she just had time to catch and steady it. Then she realised that it must after all be laid out and using all her strength she lifted and dragged it to the sofa.

It was something of an effort for her, although Schwarz was not a heavy man; but there was no evidence of the *rigor mortis* which Gregory had feared, and the corpse lay back with a supple easiness, though as she folded the arms upon the breast its eyes opened like the eyes of a doll and there was her friend gazing at her calmly and temperately from the realm of death! She drew her palm across the eyes to escape the disturbing vision. They closed and the whole face seemed to sink back into its new anonymity, a timeless contrition. She sat and listened to it expatiating upon the reasoning behind the act of departure, defending the self-annihilation which had deprived her of her oldest mentor, colleague and friend. From time to time she shook her head with reproachful resignation, or rose to change a waxen cone in the little machine. Inside herself the profound depression grew and grew, an enormous dismay which threw into meaninglessness her every activity, either intellectual or physical. The loss of Schwarz rose like a wall in her consciousness, almost as if he had been a husband, a mate, and not merely an intimate friend. Yet she was dry-eyed, composed, and kept on her features a sardonic expression suitable to such an ironic situation: but it was a pitiful boast and she knew it. The slow voice held her in thrall, the slow insidious argument unrolled itself in her mind, and she knew that reality had all but overwhelmed her, had shaken the basis of her inner composure. When at last it ended, the recording, she gave a sharp cry, as of a bird stricken by the hunter's shot, and turning back to Schwarz saw with disgust that his left eye had opened again. The other remained shut. It gave his face the faintest suggestion of slyness. It filled her with distaste. Impatiently she closed it once more with the palm of her hand, and then pressed down on both lids at once for half a minute to make them stay shut.

This time they stayed shut. She found a blanket and drew it over him. Then she set the room to rights, cleaned the blackboard, replaced the wax cones on the dictaphone and replaced some books on the shelves. The revolver and the impedimenta for the first suicide attempt she did not touch lest they might yield fingerprints or other data to interest the police whose turn it now was to evaluate the facts of the case. She took up the telephone and called Gregory to tell him about the confession of Schwarz and invite him to put things into motion. "For my part," she said, "I am going to call on Sylvie to tell her that I am back from India, and resuming her case."

But it was a distasteful prospect and she felt on the border of tears as she set forth through the pine forest in the direction of the small modern pavilion in which the girl lived – had lived for years. It was indeed her principal residence, and she had been allowed to furnish and decorate it to her own taste, so that it felt anything but clinical and austere, being decked out with brilliant hangings and old-fashioned carved furniture of heavy Second Empire beauty. It was also full of books and paintings. Her old-fashioned bed with baldaquin was set against a fine old tapestry, subdued but glowing – huntsmen with lofted horns were running down a female stag. After the rape, leaving the grooms to bring the trophy home, they galloped away into the soft brumous Italian skyline, into a network of misty lakes and romantic islets. In one corner lay the stag, panting and bleeding and in tears like a woman. Sylvie herself was not unlike the animal, but the tears had dried on her lashes and she lay in the heavy damascened bed with eyes fast shut though she was in fact awake. Moreover she knew without opening them who her visitor was. Her mind was slowly emerging from sedation to an acquaintance with sorrow and bereavement caused by

Schwarz's withdrawal from her world. "O God, my darling, so he was right; I didn't believe him when he said you would return. O my only love, my Constance! I am impatient to hear about India – O how was India, how calm was India? Constance, take my hands." She put out her own which trembled with the shock of their meeting.

Love is no respecter of persons or of contexts – it vaults every obstacle to achieve its ends. The wild spiritual attachment of Sylvie had not changed, rather it had fed on the absence of the beloved personage. Now she was trying to swallow and digest the long blank in her life for which India stood as a sort of symbol, a penitential silence on the part of Eros – for during her moments of relative sanity Schwarz had discovered that she knew as much psychoanalysis as he did: and this was a wretched enough augury for a cure and a return to ordinary life (pray, what is *that*?). It was a paradox that when she was officially mad she was often more advanced in self-understanding than at other times. So India rang out in her conversation – her only way of reforging the missing link with her adored Constance. "Has it so much changed, then? Still starving and god-drunk and spattered with dry excrement? When I was there long ago, long before you, and my love for you, I felt the moon of my non-being become full. The smell of the magnolia remembered me supremely. The deep sadness seemed very worthwhile. To be a whole person discountenanced all nature. It is different for me now that I have betrayed my brother in turning to you; I am clothed from head to foot in a marvellous seamless euphoria. In my mind your kisses clothe me close as chain-mail link by link. Only he sent you away in order to save me, but it was my ruin!"

"Now he is dead!"

"Now he is dead!"

It was as if the phrase resounding thus in echo somehow actualised the death and separation. Suddenly Constance felt weak at the knees, incoherent and shapeless, with all her joints floating with an ague. She sank down upon the bed and lay in the trusting embrace of Sylvie, aware only now of the tension of the counter-transference which she had tried to avoid by running away. The girl was kissing her with all the accurate passion of despair which was now turning to exaltation. With one part of her mind Constance was amazed at the strength of her fierce attraction for Sylvie. A whole gravitational field seemed to have grown up about this exchange, these sorrow-laden caresses. Their tears and sighs seemed to come from some vast common fund of loving sadness, and it was only when she felt her companion's hand first upon her breasts and then invading her secret parts that she came awake herself, aroused and forced to face the demons of choice. Should she allow herself to slake the love of this beautiful young stranger? And even as she asked the question she felt her own nerves respond positively, her own kisses begin to ignite under Sylvie's spell. So much for Narcissus! She was dismayed by the powerful emotions which swept her heart and only half-aware that all this was a reaction from the death of Schwarz. She had been driven out of control by it and from some depths of inner numbness had lost all power of evaluation. She was lost, washed overboard, so to speak. She clung now to the body and mind of Sylvie as if to a life-raft, happy to own this slender body, these graceful arms and slender expressive fingers. And to be loved after all she had endured was perfect heaven.

So for a brief period of time these two defeated and exhausted women would band themselves together through love and unite their strength to face an unfeeling world. In their febrile ecstasy they were become deaf to the counsels of science and reason. How intrigued Schwarz would have been to learn of this fortuitous development caused by the shock of his death and by nothing else. It was love again in one of its many disguises. Sylvie was saying, "Won't you go away now to get over it? O please take me with you! I can't bear to be left again! Take me, Constance."

And this theme too was to become an echo in the conversation of her friends – the theme of departure. After all, France was free again, although far from restored to its former glories. Sutcliffe echoed the question, and then Aubrey in his turn spelt it out. It snowballed. Lord Galen also!

The accumulated leave which Constance had coming to her spelt a whole summer and more, while Blanford was sufficiently advanced into convalescence to consider a southern holiday; Sutcliffe was waiting a posting . . . So it came about that they all met on the platform of the veteran express which served Avignon – indeed the whole eastern part of the Midi. Between them they occupied a whole section of carriage in the comfortable dining-car. "What price the *Canterbury Tales*?" said Aubrey Blanford. "The setting forth of the pilgrims, eh?" But as Sutcliffe pointed out sardonically, it was much more like an exodus of refugees. "No single complete unit like a couple, all broken up and fragmented, and in dispersion. A rebeginning of something, or an ending. This is the way that the seed leaves the sower's hand."

But Blanford's heart smote him with pain as he watched the two shy rapturous girls walking together, holding hands as they advanced along the platform, as if to give each other courage and consolation. Disgust and envy seized him, for he had been completely unprepared for this turn of events. Affad's little son – that was also a surprise, for he was delivered to the arms of Constance by the old grandmother almost without a word. Yet there were tears in her eyes as she pressed her charge forward towards Constance. The little boy went hot and cold by turns, white and red, and he clenched his fists with excitement until the knuckles were white. He had never been seized with so fierce a happiness, and the two women cherished him as if he had been their own offspring. Lord Galen was retiring to his house to mature his plans for investing in marriages of the future. Cade and Blanford were setting off side by side, living on in a state of suppressed irritation with each other and yet unable to part. Almost every day the servant remembered some new little thing about Blanford's mother – a small tesselation which enlarged the enigmatic portrait of her. Cade was sparing with these details, recognising them as part of his affectionate blackmail. Sutcliffe and Toby were supporting cast – so Toby said. They too were hoping for a restful summer in Tu Duc or Verfeuille or Meurre – they had a choice. But Sutcliffe like the others was a little plaintive. "I can't help being angry because put upon," he told Aubrey, "for, after all, what would you do if you were refused a specific and discrete identity, if you were forced to accept your role of etheric double merely, insubstantial and fantastic? Eh?"

"Better than being a product of the old button-puncher *à la* Ibsen," said Aubrey comfortably; he felt very much encouraged by this journey. "After all, Socrates was only the etheric double of Plato, he was not real so much as *true*, that is why he was so neurotic – all those fevers and fears and visions! Plato saved himself by shoving them on to Socrates' account. He was absolved from the worst by his invention. I hope you will do the same for me."

"Synaesthesia!"

"Yes."

"They will not understand."

"Nonsense! You will loom without a precise meaning like the statue in Don Giovanni, blocking the whole action, and gradually acquire symbolic weight because of your lack of personality in the human sense. Your speech is not that of a person but of an oracle."

"A semantic word – bazaar?"

"Not exactly. You will make another sort of sense in using the same sounds."

"Is semantics more antics than semen?
More suited to dons than to he-men?"

"Precisely. You win first prize, which is a battery-driven chamber-pot!"

"I shall apotheose into don."

"Cheer up, Rob. The Quinx be with you!"

"Amen!"

They sat, each following his private line of thought like a line of personal music. As for Constance, she now knew beyond a doubt, as a doctor, that man cannot do without calamity, nor can he ever circumscribe in language the inexpressible bitterness of death and separation. And love, if you wish. Love.

Cade sat somewhat apart from them all, his head bowed over his hands as he carefully pruned and buffed his large sepulchral nails. From time to time he smiled broadly and looked around him as if he dared them all to guess his thoughts.

Sutcliffe said, "And Aubrey, do you see an end to this bitter *tu quoque* – or will we go on forever?"

"They say that Socrates spent the last night on earth in silent soliloquy, alone with his Voice, so to speak."

"Inner or Outer voice?"

"Inner is Western and Outer Eastern. The Noumenon and the Phenomenon – reality turned inside out like a sleeve. It's as clear as a donkey's eyeball! Why aren't you happier?"

Lord Galen played with the stack of Order books which lay before him sheathed in rubber bands. They were full of orders for his Aids from thirsty, trusting Swiss couples. He was brooding on the marriage of the future – Adam with his great purple prick and Eve with her marsupial socket... Si vous visitez Lisbon envoyez nous un godmichet! It was prettier in English. "If you touch at Lisbon send us a dildo." It was all very well for Robin to joke ("The Swiss lover has asteroids in his underwear and spiteful hair!"), but now the war was over one must really be practical and start rebuilding the future. His couples would be anointed by computers and married by voices. In the bordel he had overheard someone say cryptically, "Elle a des sphincters d'un archimandrite Grec!" and wondered if it might have any bearing on the new devices he was fathering, the distribution of which would be controlled by the obsequious Cade as a part-time task. The whole future of marriage was an absorbing topic ("toad in the whole" – the flippant Toby with his puns got on his nerves). Lord Galen burned to serve the lovers of the future. He was hurt by the ironies of people who should have known better, like Sutcliffe: "*Mon cher*, it's going to be a case of *reculer pour mieux enculer*. We will be able to have a fuck on the NHS, with nurses specially trained by Norse fishermen for low-calibre tupping – just clickety-click and the pretty turnstile does its work. They will call it Somatotherapy."

> "Nature's fond jock-strap I taught thee to pounce
> And spiral out your orgasms ounce by ounce."

"People are so cynical," said Lord Galen to himself. "The lack of loving-kindness makes you very sad!"

Blanford was scribbling some militant verses in his commonplace book:

> Blood-gulping Christian pray take stock
> I have doffed my butcher's smock
> I have put away my cock
> Lost the key and closed the lock
> Of my passions taken stock
> Heard the ticking of time's clock
> Heard the noiseless knuckles knock
> *Toc Toc Toc   Toc Toc Toc.*

He was thinking: If we could have a summer or two of peace and quietness one might commit another novel, a votive joy, a moonshot into the future, an Indian novel. "Why not?" said his etheric double accommodatingly, "If the harvest is good and the girls beautiful enough? Why not?"

"Yesterday we devoted the whole evening to Strange Cries, Toby and I. We screamed our way into hoarseness with the macabre inventions of our fancy. We whorled and snibbed like a chapter of dervishes. Toby did the primal cry of all the nations while I toured the animal kingdom, ending up with a dog and cat fight which brought our Swiss neighbours tiptoing out on to their landings and balconies, wondering whether to call the ambulance or not. Nor did we lack invention, for after the prosaic we took to the fanciful and found sounds to illustrate abstract entities like, for example, the Magnetic Melon; some of these inventions took the skin off the Swiss mind. This morning I was in poor voice until my first drink. Last night they hammered on the door and menaced us with indignant policemen until we desisted. In the morning Toby decided to change his name to Mr Orepsorp which is only Prospero spelt backwards – though it sounds like the Welsh nickname of a man with an abbreviated foreskin. So we bade farewell to Geneva of hallowed memory, of hollow mummery."

"The *ogres* will be waiting at the station when we reach Avignon. Everything will start again when spring melts into summer. We will prune our books and re-set all the broken bones. As Dante once remarked to himself:

> See how sweet the stars are twinkling
> They have received the Greater Inkling,
> Silent, without presumptuousness
> They hang in Utter Umptiousness."

Some of these flights were to be attributed to the fine French wine served aboard the train. And while they joked the two girls sat with the little boy between them in silent rapture. Blanford thought bitterly, "L'Amour! Étrange Legume! Quel

Concerto à quatre pattes! Viens cherie, on va éplucher le concombre ensemble!"

It was grossly unfair to feel so bitter but he could not help it; ashamed, he hid in French. He was tasting the bitter fruit of sexual jealousy to the full, for he had planned to be alone with Constance. But if they were silent, the two lovers, the little boy had begun to speak as he watched the countryside spinning past them. "My father will always be watching over us from heaven. But he will not be able to come down to us except when we are asleep."

Sylvie kissed his head and squeezed his small shoulders to encourage his desire to confide in them, to relearn the freedom of speech.

"I suppose you've heard about the Prince?" said Lord Galen to Constance. "The British have arrested the entire sect on suspicion of subversive activities and the Prince just got away in the nick of time in a Red Cross plane. He is coming down to stay with me until it all blows over. I know you will be glad to see him again." It was a pleasant prospect indeed.

"If Provence is herself again we'll be able to tell, for all Spain will clamber in over the border to help with the grape-harvest. Spanish girls among the vines with names like Conception and Incarnation and Revaluation and Revelation."

"Not to mention Infibulation and Abomination and Peroration and Inflation and Deflagration and ... Phlogiston."

"How 'Phlogiston'?"

"Just Phlogiston!"

"Not to mention Adumbration, Marination and Abominable Secretion!"

"The harvest is assured. As for me, I shall be thinking about the title for my autobiography. How about *Last Will and Testicle* or *Parallel People* or *Catch as Catch Can't* or *Out First Ball* or *Options, Inklings and other Involuntary Chuckles*?"

Cade poured out the wine. The train flew on.

QUINX

or
The Ripper's Tale

inscribed to Stela
A. Ghetie

Contents

. . . must itself create the taste by which it is to be judged . . .
Wordsworth *dixit*

ONE

Provence Anew

T HE TRAIN BORE THEM ONWARDS AND DOWNWARDS
through the sluices and barrages which contained the
exuberance of the Rhône, across the drowsy plain,
towards the City of the Popes, where now in a frail spring
sunshine the pigeons fluttered like confetti and the belfries
purged their guilt in the twanging of holy bells. Skies of old
rose and madder, flowering Judas and fuchsia, mulberry and
the wise grey olives after Valence.

They were met by the long-lost children they called
"the Ogres" accompanied by the faithful Drexel. They had
come to carry out the long-promised plan of retirement to the
remote chateau which the brother and sister had inherited.
Here they were to bury themselves in the three-cornered love
which had once intrigued Blanford and caused him to try to
forge a novel round the notion of this triune love. Alas, it had
not come off. The idea, like the reality, had been too gnostic
and would, in the reality also, fail. But now they were happy
and full of faith, the beautiful ogres. Blan greeted them
tenderly.

For their own part they looked rather like the members
of a third touring company of a popular play – the two fair
women and the boy, Lord Galen, Cade, Sutcliffe, Toby and
so on. Be ye members of one another, he thought. If each had
a part in the play perhaps they could also be the various actors
which, in their sum, made up one whole single personality?
The sunshine slumbered among the roses and somewhere a
nightingale soliloquised. He had made one gesture which
adequately expressed his feeling that this was to be a new
beginning to his life. He had thrown away all his notes for

1177

the new book, shaking out his briefcase from the window of
the train and watching the leaves scatter and drift away down
the valley of the Rhône. Like a tree shedding its petals – slips
of all colours and sizes. He had decided the night before that
if ever he wrote again it would be without premeditation,
without notes and plans, but spontaneously as a cicada sings
in the summer sunlight. The fat man, his alter ego, watched
him as he did so and expressed a certain reserve by shaking
his head very doubtfully as he watched the petals floating
away in a vast whirl just like the pigeons over the town. It
would be like this after the atomic explosion, he was thinking
– just clouds of memoranda filling the air – human memoranda. The sum of all their parts whirled in the death-drift
of history – motes in a vast sunbeam.

Cade suddenly laughed and struck his thigh with his
palm, but he did not share the joke with them. Perhaps it was
not a joke?

Sutcliffe said with dismay: "But surely we aren't going
to let the ogres re-enact the terrible historic mistake which was
the theme of your great epos – the heroic threesome of
romance? Come! It didn't work in life any more than it
worked in the novel, admit it!" Aubrey did, but with bad
grace. "Three into one don't go." Pursued his alter ego:
"Though God knows why not – we should ask Constance,
for perhaps the old Freudian canon can tell us why. Anyway,
if it was good enough for Shakespeare it is good enough for
me!"

"What do you mean by that?"

"The Sonnets. The situation outlined in them would
have made perhaps his finest play, but he fought shy of it
because instinctively he felt that it wouldn't work. We must
really try to save the poor ogres from the same fate – not let
them come round again on the historic merry-go-round with

the hapless Drexel. Save them! History, memory, you promised to avoid all those traps: otherwise you will simply have another addition to the *caveau de famille* of the straight novel and Sylvie will remain forever in the asylum, lying under her tapestry and writing . . ."

"She has been trying to write my book, the one I am just about to begin by marshalling all these disorderly facts into a coherent maze of language where everyone will find his or her place without jostling or hurry. But I realise now that if you don't have the built-in intimations of immanent virtue as described by Epicurus, say, you will end up with an excessive puritan morality, and overcompensate by unscrupulousness, even by sheer bloodlust, marked by sentimentality. At the same time one must tiptoe and with care, one must advance *au pifomètre*, 'by dead reckoning'." It was obvious to both that the sort of book they sought must not repeat the misadventure of Piers and Sylvie for what they wanted to refresh and reanimate was the archaic notion of the couple, the engineers of grace through the act. Actually it had happened, and thanks to Constance, her massage and her physical pleading had suddenly awoken his spine and with it the whole net of ganglia which revived and tonified his copulatory powers. Thaumatology! the death-leaps of the divine orgasm like a salmon: the two-in-one joined by an immense but penetrable amnesia which they could render gradually more and more conscious. To hold it steady to the point of meditation where it is blinding and then slowly melt one into the other with a passion which was all stealth . . . Who abdicates in love wins all! "The Garden of the Hesperides" is within the reach of such . . . The kiss is the pure copula of the vast shared thought. "I love you!" he said with amazement, with real amazement.

"Christ!" he said. "Thanks to you I have come awake for the first time. The horrible sleeping dummy awakens!

Lady Utterly, fancy seeing you! What brings you here?" She settled more closely into the crook of his arm, but did not speak. She knew that the information she had passed on came from her dead lover, Affad. He had always said: "What is too finely explained becomes inoperative, dead, incapable of realisation. Never talk about love unless you are looking elsewhere when you do. Otherwise the self-defeating pillow-music will lead you astray." Blanford was saying: "Darling, you will be able to exhibit me in a glass case outside your consulting-room as 'The man who came back from the dead – the ape erect!' " Ah! but *she* knew that science is not interested in happy endings – that is the privilege of art!

As Sutcliffe used to hum:

> *What he believed in cannot be expressed,*
> *That's why his ideas seem partly undressed*

When insight hardens into dogma it goes dead, so they kept everything fluid yet kept on praying for more and yet more insight with which to discipline the heart. How dull the old world of "before" seemed now with its inappropriate lusts and dilapidated attachments. In the Camargue on the verandah of their little house they sat in silence watching the night falling and the fireflies twinkling like minds realising themselves briefly, abruptly before disappearing. Meanwhile she was making notes for her psychoanalytic essay on that forgotten novel *Gynacocrasy* the reading of which (it was comically pornographic in the stark naivety of its love scenes) had brought them both so much fun. It had clearly been written by a woman and Constance was setting out to prove the fact (which was nowhere stated) purely by internal evidence of a psychoanalytic-sexual kind. Blanford was amazed when he thought how much she had taught him, even physically. She had learned that the priapic conjunction is a force-harness which builds the field in which the future, as exemplified by the human child, can secure a foothold in reality. Half-joking she could say: "Now you know what you are doing when you couple with me you will never be able to leave me – it would be dangerous for your insight! For your art, the merchandise of breath, *oxygen*! We've done it, darling! The orgasm if shared in this way admits you to the realm between death and rebirth, the workshop of both past and future. To grasp this simultaneity is the key. Meanwhile in between births – the orgasm is a shadow-play of this chrysalis stage – we exist in five-skanda form, aggregates, parcels, lots, congeries. They cohere to form a human being when you come together and create the old force-field quinx, the five-sided being with two arms, two legs and the kundalini as properties!"

"Well," he said somewhat ironically, "in the new age it will be the man who is the Sleeping Beauty and who is kissed awake by the woman! Their paths join and bifurcate at the command of nature. And human truth, damn it, must become coeval with nature's basic nonchalance for the miracle to come about. As if one had to stop caring and start improvising! Of course love can be reduced to a pleasant conviviality but the wavelength or scale is low and it cannot fecundate the heart or the insight. A mere discharge cannot instruct!"

"You need to go away from me for a bit now. Not for too long. But to get your focus right for what you want to start building."

"I know," he said. "I shan't be happy until I have had a real try to make it the way I want – being serious without being grave. (The malevolence of too much goodness is to be feared!) If I could create such an edifice it would point the finger at the notion of discrete identity as being very much in question – 'Be ye members of one another' or 'spare parts', *pièces détachées*!"

"What else?" she said in loving triumph.

"Make a playdoyer for coexisting time-tracks in the human imagination. Deal seriously *at last* with human love which is a yogic thought form, the rudder of the human ship of fools: for hidden in the blissful amnesia we have just shared is the five-sided truth about human personality. Meanwhile the text should show high contrivance as well as utter a plea for bliss as being the object of art. Am I talking rubbish? It's euphoria, then!"

But in fact he was right for the idea of chronology had become disturbed – history was not past but was something which was always just about to happen. It was the part of reality that was *poised*! He would have gone out of his mind with all these intimations of another version of reality but for the indispensable beauty and loneliness of her presence. She had said: "If you want to do good without moralising write a poem", and this is what he began to feel might lie within his powers one day soon!

"You will soon be in a position to write a study of the woman as placebo – the therapy takes place even if she is not a goddess but an ordinary woman!" (Sutcliffe sounded a little jealous, perhaps he was.) She said: "But you are *right*. It's her role. And each orgasm is a dress rehearsal for something deeper, namely death, which becomes more and more explicit until it happens and revives the whole universe in us at a blow. Knowing this you know that everything is to be forgiven, none of our trespasses need be taken too seriously. Fundamentally everyone is panning for gold."

"I hate this kind of moralising," he said, "because it smells of self-righteousness. I want to be bad, just bad. It's also a way of loving – or isn't it? I know you are thinking of the philosopher Daimonax, but was he right when he said that nobody really wanted to be bad? We must ask Sabine."

And fortunately Sabine was there to ask, sitting at the table on the balcony with her eternal spread of cards before her, scrutinising the future. She was smoking a cheroot as she worked – for skrying is hard work. She said: "It's better than that, even, for the whole universe; the whole of process, to the degree that it is natural, becomes pain-free, anxiety-free, stress-free. The lion was made to lie down with the lamb – only anxiety causes fear, causes war. The same with us. Love and lust are forms of spiritual traction which a girl knows instinctively how to handle – the push and pull of sexual and bisexual feeling, the dear old Oedipus group. Unless one grasps this one goes on living with sadness – the horror at the meaninglessness of things keeps on increasing. But reality is really bliss-side-up if we want it so. Constance must purge your nursery desires, evolve your feeling for emptiness, develop the vatic sense, and persuade the heart to become festive!"

"Yes!" said Constance slowly. "And birth is no trauma but an apotheosis: here I part company with my Viennese colleagues for they were born into sin. But in reality one is born into bliss – it is we who cause the trauma with these mad doctrines based on guilt and fear. Pathology begins at home!"

"Instinct has its own logic which we must obey, we can't do otherwise. We must roll with the hunch, so to speak. It is independent of the quantitative method which just brings up samples to analyse, all parts of an incommensurable whole."

It was now that she told them the tale of Julio, the gipsy poet, and the story of his legs. He had been the only child produced by the Mother and nobody knew what his origins were for She had never been seen to "accept" a man in her caravan. It was understood that such a weakness would have in some way qualified her "sight", diminished her powers of prophesy. Julio grew up into a godly magnificence, physically of fine stature, and composed as if he had already lived on earth before. Not to mention *une sexualité à tout va* . . . He made up for his mother's shortcomings and had all the beauties of the tribe in love with him. He became the tribal bard, so to speak, though among gipsies there is no such thing. His compositions were improvised to the guitar but the words were so striking they became popular sayings. He still lives on in quotation, so to speak.

"But it was not only love-making that Julio favoured, he was also an athlete and enjoyed cattle-rustling and cockade-snatching – the variety of bull-fighting favoured by all Provence. He liked the taste of danger in the cockade fight and became a champion – unusual for a gipsy. Then came his downfall." Pain entered Sabine's quiet voice. "He was matched against the famous bull Sanglier who was also a champion, and a fierce combat ensued. Julio almost flew in this battle, and the old bull used every trick in his repertoire, for he was a seasoned defender of the little red cockade. Then came the climax. Julio slipped as he came to the barrier and lost his advantage over the bull. Sanglier bustled him to the barricades and with an experienced maliciousness savaged him. When you are passing in the Camargue and you come across the tomb of this heroic Homeric animal, say a prayer for the ghost of Julio for he had both legs so badly crushed against the barrier that they were forced to amputate them. We thought he would die of misery and physical humiliation but after a period of despair, during which he selected and rejected every form of suicide, he took on a new life. His poetry increased in vigour and gravity. He had asked for his legs back, and these he had beautifully embalmed as an *ex voto* for Saint Sara. They were placed in the grotto with the spring at the Pont-du-Gard and a cult of fertility grew up about them. But this was after his death, for he lived on for a number of years just as a stump of flesh with arms, and strangely enough his success with the women increased rather than diminished. He never wanted for women. It was said that the infertile conceived after a love-bout with Julio. All the sexual

power of his lost legs seemed to have entered his member. It
grew enormous, he was in permanent erection it seemed. I
went to him myself once or twice out of curiosity and he was
extraordinary. He seemed to bore to the very heart of the
orgasm – the psyche's point of repair, the site of its sexual
health. With the missing legs one could see that the spinal
column was really a sort of Giant's Causeway towards the
yogic self-comprehension – the kundalini, serpent-erect business. Julio had imbibed this from his mother's milk. I myself
realised for the first time that sex is not dying, it is coming of
age with the freedom of the woman. Its real secrets are as yet
only half-fathomed in the West. The mathematics of the
sexual act remain obscure. The power of five is really the
riddle of the Quinx – solve it if you dare! But the problem of
Julio is a very grave political one for us. Unless they are
rediscovered and the shrine of Sara given back to us the Tribe
can neither march nor procreate!"

> "Two down and five across, a ruling passion."
> "Tagged by the Greeks as psyche-fed?"
> "No. No. Five letters, love. I love you!"
> "But psyche-fed no less, for love's the
> Four-letter word we most recall with
> Never a crossword or dull moment. Two
> Across and one up, never a cross word!"

To codify the appetites by yoga – all kisses and sweet
stresses, sweet stretches and breathwork, guarding the deep
vascularity of muscles and veins. Then meditation, like
crossing the dark garden of consciousness shielding a lighted
candle which the least puff of wind might extinguish. You
protect this small precarious flame, treasuring it in the palm of
the hand. So very gradually your meditation affirms and
strengthens the flame and you can cross the dark garden with

it triumphantly erect – the yoga erection of the adept in Tao is this, no? Yes, in Taoist terms even love is a predicament due to the wrong angle of inclination towards the universe.

He sees no contradiction in contradiction, and to know this is the beginning of a freakish new certainty. His poetry is concerned with the transmission of an inkling, a breath of the supreme intuition which makes you laugh inside forever!

"I am grateful to Egypt – having my back shot to pieces. I might never have bothered with this yoga jape and so missed a deeply transforming experience. A religion which harbours no ifs and buts, not even the shadow of a perhaps. No sweet neurosis this, no mental chloroform pad! Formal logic dissolves and as you orchestrate the body you exchange lard against oxygen. The hunger is not to possess, to own, but to belong."

> Parts and wholes
> Wholes and parts
> Private parts and
> Public holes
> Holy Poles
> Unholy poles
> Wholly wholes.

"If you suffer from a Priapus afflicted by Saturn you will do anything to make ends meet." (Sutcliffe)

He dreamed of something as lovely and deliberate as the kisses of pretty Turkish *hanoums* in their sherbet heaven. An abundance of smiling ticklers, an alphabet of broken sighs, oriental codes of sex. And all he got was that a girl like a pterodactyl silked him off in the bus from Gatwick crying, "Bless Relaxers!" By not minding we gain a little ground.

SUT AND BLAN
SOUL AND BODY = prototypes of love and folly lie there and
play with your Vertical Banjo!

Puella lethargica dolorosa! Just kissing you was like a
telephone call from God! Why then did you go away and
ride to hounds? A non-man is worse than a con-man. He will
wither your sense and sap your succulence. "Not to know
one's own mind is for a woman the beginning of wisdom!"
(Inscription on a Persian pisspot.)

Running along the grey-green river they had seen the
famous broken bridge, still pointing its reproachful finger
across the water towards the waterless *garrigue.* Neither
Blanford nor Sutcliffe could resist the prompting to hum out:

> *Sur le pont d'Avignon*
> *on y pense, on y pense . . .*
> *sur le pont d'Avignon*
> *on y pense, tout en rond!*

"How much longer have we got together?" asked
Blanford and his alter ego replied: "One more book, one more
river. Then body and soul must end their association. I know.
It's too short. It's the only criticism one can make of life. It's
too short to learn anything."
"Constance looks ill."
"She will recover. I promise."
Rose de la poésie, O belle névrose!

But even God must be subject to entropy if he exists. Or
has he learned to enjoy and use the death-drift from perfection
to putridity? Does he live like the Taoist in a perpetual holy
irreverence?

make his bed   perhaps some passages in primal scene
take his life   verse? Maybe Sutcliffe would share a

mark his pillow
'absent wife'
darn his heel
smoke his quid
doing all
the other did
hunt the slipper
hunt the soul
Eros teach him
breath control!

Hearts-and-Flowers act with his alter ego?

Scene of the epilepsy, the pearl saliva, The tongue bitten in half, almost swallowed.

"Cybele! What's for dinner?"
"Uterus!" she said.

Carry thy balls high, Coz, *les couilles bien haut! Recuser, accoler, accusez, raccolez!*

When young my member diminished like a candle under her caresses; but age and meditation stiffen resolve and now she knows how to mature and guide the trophy of erectile tissue in order to make it act responsibly. Today I feel I could write cheques with it if necessary. (Sutcliffe)

The old valiant rises and retains its discharge politely like a clergyman at a tea-party, giving infinite service with infinite politeness. But it is entirely in the woman's gift. If she wants she can blow it out like a match! (Blan)

The elephant, if you imbibe him, teaches that art is both therapy and moral construction. Its calibre and relevance may vary. Its arithmetic is hermetic. Something goes into nothing once only. Love!

Ah! But to die of sincere haemorrhoids, or by inhaling a banana, or *d'une obésité succulente* – that would be worthwhile, artistically. And pray, why not an aberrant prose style to echo the discordance at the heart of all nature? Shackle verbs, give nouns wings, disburse the seven-pronged adjective. Divulge!

Often when they had drunk too much they would have the illusion that it might still be possible to get to the bottom of things. Dialogues like:

BLAN: What would you do if someone said you were not true to life? Eh? Reveal!

SUT: I would be vastly put out. I would sulk.

BLAN: You see, for us in the cinema age reality is recognisable and identifiable only at twenty-eight frames a second. But undercrank and the image goes out of true and becomes aberrant, that of a paranormal person, schizo or parano, whichever you wish.

SUT: Is that the complaint? Not true to life, they say? So there is such a thing to compare me with? I am undercranked and feverish? So this is what mere Relativity has done for us? Catapulted us into the Provisional, with reality as a shadow-world?

BLAN: When I asked Einstein about you, about how much reality I could accord you, he said: "You mean that pink chap who looks like a pig? Tell him from me that man only has a *tendency* towards existing. I can't go any further towards unqualified certainty about his actually being: short of a telex from God, that is!"

SUT: What a dilemma! I am simply symbolic you might say. Symbolic merely, like a teddy bear full of caviar? The people who say this seem unaware that they only camp temporally in their body as in a chrysalis. Then pouf! a moth dedicated to eating cloth. One day I shall acquire a meaning. As in the average novel, "A careful analysis of Nothing reveals that . . . Ambulances bleating for blood all night, flesh and blood. Who can sleep?"

BLAN: Wake then and write our book – a new Ulysses dying of a liturgical elephantiasis. Or dream of a girl on long thirsty legs but as shy as glue. Art has a stance but no specific creed.

SUT: It could borrow one if need be. A smother of girls would be better. You see, we only live in the instant between inhalation and ex-. This point in yoga time is the only history. But suppose we refine and purge and strengthen this small glimpse of truthful time, why, we would redeem eternity, the heraldic vision, the panoramic insight!

BLAN: Oh well, so what then?

SUT: You have me there. What then indeed?

BLAN: Philosophâtre or Psycholope
Come and join the Bank of Hope
Like royal swans in helpless rut
Or dirty ducks in hopeless goose
Wake Psyche from her trance
Lest she should die of self-abuse
And take a lesson from the dead
For history is a running noose.

SUT: So I really mean nothing? Symbol without translation?

BLAN: All symbols start like that. Happily meaning has a tendency to accrete in time around an enigma. I don't know why. As if nature could not rest without offering a gloss. In poetry the obscure becomes slowly invested with meaning as if by natural law. The big enigmas of art, simply by dint of continuing to exist, finally accumulate their own explanations by the force of critical projection. Mozart's Commendatore, for example, is regarded as so mysterious, yet because he still lives, thanks to the electric charge conferred on him by his maker, he becomes daily more significant. One day soon the "meaning" will burst upon us.

SUT: Agreed. But this information is available to the woman from the resources of her female intuition. It may remain unformulated but somewhere she knows that she is the custodian of his poetry, her role is to recognise and release the rare moth which can be housed in the most loathsome caterpillar's form. The act of sex bursts through the container of the flesh in an act of recognition. Presto! Liberation of poet-moth!

BLAN: Wow!

SUT: As you say, wow!

BLAN: *Touche-partout, couche-partout,*
Bon à rien, prêt à tout.

What about love?

A girl in grey with one dark note,
Pitched somewhere between fox and dove,
Soft as the driven television must
Like all our lovers come to dust.

Think of others who have passed this way. Lust for a comprehensive vision which death repays in dust. Nicholas De S. Better to become a best seller and spend your life fingering the moister parts of the Goddess of Pelf! E.A.P. his brain burst on the job. The perilous ascension of artistic ichor in the bloodstream, the panoramic vision – it was too much for him. It swallowed him. He was dragged by the hair into the cave of the oceanic consciousness, the Grendel's cave of art's origins; drink drank him.

(Sutcliffe pours out a drink.)

And K? As his mind ran down he grew more yellow and wasted, blooming now like a waxlight, a Jewish taper burning inside a coffin. His hands grew covered with warts which suppurated. Staring into the maw of the Jewish superego.

Tolle lege, tolle lege. Voices that St Augustine heard, of children in some forsaken garden singing for the birthday of an angel. The imperative of the poet. Hush, can you hear them?

The doomboat of our culture filling up, the ship of fools. But it only looks like that. Actually if you believe, as I do, that all people are slowly becoming the same person, and that all countries are merging into one country, one world, you will be bound to see all these so-called characters as illustrations of a trend. They may be studied through their weaknesses of which the greatest and most revealing is their disposition to love and produce copies in flesh of their psychic needs. Do you see?

B. thinks: Death seems various and quite particular because our friends die in scattered fashion, one by one, slipping out of the décor and leaving holes in it. But as a principle it is as universal as all becoming is – *semper ubique*, old boy – though the effect is slow-motion. The ship shakes itself and settles with a shiver before she dives. Experienced sailors notice the premonitory quiver and cry, "She's settling!" long before the cry goes up, "There she goes!" The spring will seem endless once back in Avignon. Constance: I love you and I want to die.

Sutcliffe had a friend who died in action but continued his erection into *rigor mortis*. This was quite a sight and caused an admiring crowd of nurses who had been on short commons for some time and were anxious for novelties. A thing like this mauve member could satisfy an army of them, they thought, and kept coming back to look and exult. But it faded with the sunset when they came to lay him out.

Blan said grumpily: "But we shall end like some old bow-wow and toddle off to Doggy Heaven in Disneyland or Forest Lawns where telegrams are delivered to Little Fido when he has crossed the Styx. Charon delivers them without a word, pocketing the dollar with a grin as he rows away.

> To each his tuffet
> And so some Miss Muffet.
> (Many are called but most are frigid.
> Some need theosophy to keep them rigid.)

> Deep in its death-muse Europe lay.
> Boys and girls come out to play.

> *Fruit de mer* beyond compare,
> Suck a sweeter if you dare.

> Ashes to ashes, lust to lust,
> Their married bliss a certain must.

> He storied urn, she animated bust.

The day when Aristotle decided (*malgré lui*) that the reign of the magician-shaman was over (Empedocles), was the soul's D-Day. The paths of the mind had become overgrown. From that moment the hunt for the measurable certainties was on. Death became a constant, the ego was born. Monsieur came down to preside over the human condition:

> To kill to eat was nature's earlier law.
> To kill to kill created a furore.
> Such abstract murder could not come amiss
> So Christians sublimated with The Kiss
> And drunk on blood they broke the body's bread
> To make a cold collation for the dead!

Listen, nothing that SUT has to say about BLAN should be taken too seriously, for he is only a creation of the latter, his Tu Quoque, existing by proxy. Is BLAN then King? Yes, in a way, but his powers are somewhat diminished, he can't see very far, whereas SUT is the third eye, so to speak. His belly-button pierces the future, the all-seeing eye of time. Is this what has poisoned the life of the solitary author as he files his nails and watches the snow falling eternally over Blandshire? Why the devil had he chosen a profession which involved him in the manufacture of these paper artefacts – characters which drained him of so much life that he often felt quite one-dimensional, himself equally a fiction of his fictions? Eh? After the publication of SUT's autobiography, in which he figured, fame was not long in coming, though both men had begun to feel wholly posthumous. But SUT became slowly so popular that he became detached like a retina, or else loosed like a soap-bubble to float about in the public consciousness like a sort of myth. He had made the English language, had the old Ripper, while Blanford had hardly made *Who's Who*.

"*O Anax* – the Big Boss, whose shrine is at Delphi, neither hides nor reveals, but simply signifies or hints!"

Similarly all writers are the same one, Blake scribbles Nietzsche's notes on the same experience . . . Trickling through the great dam of the human sensibility, charting the depths and the shallows. Sometimes imperfect texts give off the authentic radium, like the shattered lines of Heraclitus, O Skotinos, the Darkling One! It still vibrates in the mind like a drum-beat.

Rozanov whose originality lay in his truth, capturing thought just as it was about to burst like a bubble upon the surface of human consciousness, of *meaning*. Neither good nor bad, simply what is. Just inkling. A highly pathological and precarious art flowed from this practice in Western terms: in Eastern terms he was writing entirely in *koans*, not in

epigrams. To be thought of as the start of a religious quest –
doubt, anxiety, stress. The soul's traction!

SUT receives a postcard from Toby who is lecturing in
Sweden: "Come north at once! The Swedes are quite
marvellous. They have souls like soft buttocks and buttocks
like hard soles."

He has caused considerable annoyance by describing the
nouveau roman, of which they stand in superstitious awe as:
"*Les abats surgelés des écrivains qui refusent toute jouissance.*"

In the Paris *métro* he caught sight of the new woman we
have all been on edge to meet – the Rosetta Stone, fresh from
the USA. "She wore an inflatable air jacket stolen from Air
France. Trousers lined with newspaper – the *Tribune*. She
carried a traffic sign torn living from the landscape around
Fifth and Sixth, reading YIELD. She sucked her thumb when
doing nothing – nails bitten down to the quick. And twitching
with hemp smoke. A choice young cliterocrat."

The sperm does not age as man himself does. Even an
old man can make a young baby.

> Envenomed by solitude and vanity,
> Created sound and yet forbidden sanity.

SUT: (To his shaving mirror) "Ah! the dear old face,
like a bony housing for the critical motor, eyes, nose, mouth,
cruel uncial smiles, eyebrows cautious circumflex. Toughened
by weather, roughened by thought, weathered by sighs so
dearly bought. Needs repainting. The eyes shouting 'Help!'
The eyes pleading diminished responsibility."

By hoping, wishing and foreseeing we are doing something contrary to nature. *Cogito* is okay but *spero* makes man
out of the featureless animal of Aristotle: gone astray in the
forebrain.

SUT: "*La femme en soi si récherchée par l'âme. La femme en soie, brave dame.*

> *Boule Quies d'aramanthe et camfre*
> *Une veuve de Cigue*
> *Trinquer avec la mort!*
> *Cliquot Cliquot Cliquot*
> > *Trinc trinc*
> > *La Veuve Cliquot!*"

BLAN: "In the account I propose to give of your marriage I propose to heighten the colour in the interest of my fiction with additions gleaned from Constance who talked about it with sympathy and sorrow. Explaining with all the vivacity of my prose style how everything had been complicated and poisoned beyond endurance by this unlucky marriage to a captious little queen of the greatest charm and style who disguised her proclivities very cleverly, by sleeping with many men openly, and as many women secretly. It was easy, really, for you were a highly intelligent man – that is to say, a fool!"

SUT: "I was inexperienced, I suppose, and of course when one falls in love one is simply 'imprinted' by the projection of one's desire, like a duckling falling in love with its keeper's shoe. Yet I should have known. Those dry airless kisses tasting of straw were puzzling, the caresses of the mantis. Then the dry marsupial pocket of the rarely used vagina should have drawn attention to the enormous and beautiful clitoris. She was a trifle painful to penetrate but in every other respect normal and valiant. It took some time to find out that she shammed her orgasms, or else (to judge by the few involuntary expressions that escaped her lips) thought of someone else while doing. She had avoided marriage all these years, why had she turned aside for me?"

BLAN: "I don't know. Perhaps the male gender of the tribe have a weakness for young married women and the ring excites them for they are at one and the same time both cheating and aping the man. Excalibur! How joyfully they humiliate hubby and betray him! Suddenly the whole business became clear to him, the meaning of that large circle of female friends, all very feminine and unsatisfied (if one were to believe them) in their married lives. As she said, they had 'thrown themselves away' on Tom, Dick and Harry. Then of course the conventions aided things. Nobody bothers about women kissing and hugging each other, a little conventional 'mothering' is quite in order, or trotting off to the powder room together while the husbands solemnly suck their pipes and talk about holy orders!"

She was no larger than a pinch of snuff but she packed some sneeze! *Une belle descente de lit.*

S: God, what dreadful French!

B: I know. Showing off again. Go on.

Well, he found himself gradually propelled into a sort of travesty of the female role. He did the washing up and stayed behind to watch the dinner cook while she hopped off with a friend to have her horoscope cast by another friend. The telephone went all the time with a susurrus of private jokes and social plans. He opened a private letter one day in error, having mistaken the handwriting (he would never have dared nor wished to spy on her) and at once interpreted all these ambiguities correctly. Thought suddenly of the so called "masculine protest" – the tiny moustache which was so painfully removed by wax depilatory or dabbed with peroxide. The green ink, and the wearing of charms and necklaces and *one earring*!

Amo, amas, amat. Je brûle, chérie, comme une chapelle ardente! Baise-moi! Self-righteousness, hunger for propitiation, vainglory, sanctimoniousness – Sutcliffe: "At your service, old man: at your mercy."

I am adding an anecdote from someone else – Fatima,

to be precise. "Let's make love, it will be good for each other's French." It was not very satisfactory, she had all the desperation of a woman who knows she is too fat. But after all she was game and later she cried with a mixture of vexation and stark pleasure. What did I like in her? She was lush with worldliness and had a peach-vulgar face. But the smell of her thighs was rich with an instinctual sweat hinting of musk; wherever you licked her skin was dewy as a rose. I licked and licked like a *drogué en état de manque!* – her own expression.

Toby, regarding himself in his shaving mirror, exclaims: "Mean-spirited gnome! If it were not for your beauty I would leave you!" His ad is still going in the *Trib*. It runs: "Elderly vampire (references) living in kind of doomed old mansion near Avignon seeks rational diversions."

He also said: "Other men drink to forget but I drink to remember!"

The poetic substance detached from the narrative line, the sullen monorail of story and person. Rather to leave the undeveloped germs of anecdote to dissolve in the mind. Like the accident, the death in a snowdrift near Zagreb. The huge car buried in a snowy mountain. She was in full evening dress with her fur cape, and the little cat Smoke asleep in her sleeve. The headlights made a blaze of crystal so it seemed the snow was lit from within. But they forgot to turn the heaters off. A white Mercedes with buried lights. Why go on? They suffocated slowly while waiting for help which could not reach them much before dawn. Only Smoke remained. Her loud purring seemed to fill the car.

A letter from faraway London. Grey skies. Pissing in the bull's eye of a Twyford's "Adamant". BLAN was forced to write on a postcard: "Be warned that daydreaming is not meditating. Inquisitiveness is not curiosity. Beware of the brass rubbings of a demon culture. Identikit husbands and wives!"

Eclair, who wrote the review, was a generous old French pedal, tightwad like most, burning with a hard bumlike flame. He wrote about the poet as if he were a sort of stair carpet wreathed in Scotch mist. He curled his hair with hot-smelling tongs and ate much convincing garlic with his choice high-flown game. Yet he understood all, revealed all! It was uncanny. "A good artist has every reason to enjoy his approaching death – his life would have proved to be a scandal of inattention otherwise!"

B: Where do people end? Where do their imaginations begin? I have been a sleepwalker in literature. My books have happened to me *en route*. I am at a loss to account for them, to ascribe any special value to them. Perhaps they may be marvellous to other sleepwalkers, serving as maps? Who can tell? Socially I am a fig-eater. I have always believed in myself – *credo quia absurdam*! Given to baroque turns of speech, in writing I wished to substitute intricacy for podge.

> Go and catch a falling whore,
> That's what she is waiting for.
> Ah! pretty frustrate pray unlatch
> And bid poor Jenkins down the hatch.
> A rose by any other name
> Would smell as good where'er it came.
> Great Lover, that involuntary clown
> Will always having his trousers falling down.
> To scrape a furtive living from the arts
> And keep intact his shrinking private parts . . .

The lover now belongs to an endangered species for science threatens him with extinction. Maybe Stekel will have the last word on your marriage after all: "It is evident that a sadistic atmosphere was cultivated in this marriage. The fact that both parties were homosexual led to a peculiar sort of inversion. He played with the wife the role of a woman who has intercourse with a woman, and she that of a man having intercourse with a man. This bound them together. Those movements which excited him at coitus resembled the convulsive twitching of death. And surprisingly, in contrast to his fantasies of violence he was aware that potency disappeared if that woman moved. She must lie still, grow pale, resemble as much as possible a corpse. Thus he was aroused sadistically and restored to full potency."

For some reason this irritated Sutcliffe who said: "I often see us as a couple of old whores, dead drunk, who toddle off into the night towards Marble Arch, having emptied their bladders accidentally into each other's handbag."

It was obvious that in common with most of us they were hunting a spontaneity which had once been innate, given, and to which the key had been mislaid.

Though spring was here the station of Avignon was a draughty place to argue about who was going to stay where. Finally the main party decided to stay with Lord Galen whose establishment was the most comfortable until such time as the house belonging to Constance in Tubain was ready to receive them. This would give them a valuable respite of a few days to organise the plumbing and painting which was undoubtedly quite necessary after years of neglect. It was astonishing even that the edifice remained watertight and with a solid roof after so many war years. But surely all this could be put right for a summer; in a vague way the notion recaptured some of the *élan* of that earlier holiday – situated in prehistory it would seem now – when they had all been young. Before the War?

The kiss of Judas – the poisoned arrow of our history became something one could learn for kitchen consumption. Seen from the point of view of the City of the Popes it signified the truth of the matter – namely, that our whole civilisation could be seen as a tremendous psychic mishap. The baritone pigeons crooning among the tintinabulous belfries calling the faithful to prayer which had become a mere expedient, not a way of breathing.

"I am writing a defence of Inklings."

going	"Inklings of what?"	dying
going	"Of the absolute, silly."	dying
gone	"And what, pray, may that be?"	dead
	"An inkling."	

SUT said: "I have taken another and less uncommon path. Ever since I founded my group, called Mercy-Fucking for the Hard-Pressed, I have never wanted for clients. The robot did it all."

Lord Galen, who had come silently into the room in order to bid them to dinner in the grange, pricked up his ears and said: "Did I hear the word robot? Why, you take the words out of my mouth. As you know I have great post-war plans for a rational deployment of my capital in several ways. One of them is going to be in marital aids. There will be a great need for marital aids. I am trying to arrange for some to be blessed by the Pope as part of the promotional campaign. The chances seem promising at the moment."

The two men, if that is what one can call them, congratulated him with unfeigned affection and followed him down to the vast kitchens where trestle tables had been laid out for them and the vivid odours of roast pork and ginger flew about like doves of promise. Of course there was constraint – Constance with her silent companion! The little boy had found the two daughters of the caretakers and sat between them happily. The rest disposed themselves around unfinished conversations and fell to work, served by the old farm woman and her youthful niece.

How Blanford with his shyness and pain over Constance irritated the lady as he eyed her; she glared down at her hands, resenting his air of inescapable chasteness – the despair of a Prometheus chained to the bleak rock of his moral virginity. She hated him! What a self-satisfied little prig!

"My yoga teacher told me that one of the great problems of the hermetic schools was to prevent the lama turning into a robot, to prevent him falling asleep at his loom. Don't you think that is a fair comment on Lord Galen's marital aids? After all, a simple kiss describes a trajectory through the human consciousness, for it raises the blood heat and adds to secretions like sugar and insulin. You may be sure that Judas knew that."

"Pity you emptied out all those notes over the valley. You will feel the need of them."

"I have them all here, night and day." He tapped his forehead. "You will notice them coming up in my conversation because they represented my most intimate obsessions, problems I could not solve; and without a solution I could not advance in my heart. For instance, problems of form and style essential to my new book. I was much encouraged by the courage shown by Rozanov, and also by the jumpy hysterical jottings of Stendhal in his *Souvenirs Intimes* – half-intelligible as many were. They carried his authentic quirk, unmistakable turn of speech. They helped me in my search for a form. I said to myself that one does not look for great truths in a pantomime, but how refreshing if you found some in this form, no?"

"I am a modern man," said SUT, "and I think men wonderful in principle; but of all men the most wonderful seems to be me. I am sublime. Nature exhausted Herself in creating me. Other men – well, how easy to see that she ran out of ideas. They are tadpoles. Do you tell me that your yoga can cure such a conviction?"

"Yes. As it cured my back pains. Relief of stress caused by pressure of an unduly swollen ego. It could lead to trouble in the long run."

"But you are talking as if I am real. Here I have been feeling so diaphanous and now you tell me I am tangible."

"As tangible as a marker in a hymn book; but you cannot sing any of the psalms, my boy.

> The pathos of metaphor will spell
> The secrets of your wishing well,
> Brainless as odalisques must be –
> The difference twixt thee and me.
> To catch a wind, put out a sail.
> To catch a mind, put out a soul."

The wine, a wonderful Fitou, was taking its toll and enlivening the talk. They found themselves liking each other's company more than they had realised; only Constance and her companion lived in a cage of silence and ate with lowered heads. Lord Galen was joyful in his brainless way and Cade watched them all from under his drawn brows, like a mouse from its hole in the infinite.

And that beautiful profligate, the choice companion of Constance, what of her? Sometimes with a hanging head she wept silently from pure joy at her lot, at her luck. Blanford watched her superstitiously and with unwilling sympathy. She wore vast golden sashes to match torrential golden hair and blue eyes full of humour; their constant gaze made them seem like the riding lights of an anchored yacht. Lips uncials of sweet compliance. But she was never quite present, always listening to the inward monitor of a restless mind at odds with

itself. Yet watching her and remembering some of the things
she had written in the manuscripts which Constance had
shown him he realised with envy the truth of her beauty and
her genius. Softly he repeated to his own mind, "I dream of
writing of an unbearable felicity. I want to saturate my text
with my teleological distress yet guard its slapstick holiness
as something precious. To pierce the lethargy, indolence and
distress of my soul. But the boredom of knowing the truth
about things is killing me – the overturned cradle! You see,
time, which we all believe in, becomes solid if it persists long
enough. Time becomes *mass* in mathematics. For everything
is obstinately and deliberately turning into its opposite. That
is the nature of process when you get behind the law of cosmic
inertia. The universe simply does the *next thing*; it has no
programme, does not predict, knows not where it is going.
A perpetual spontaneity rules!" He was jealous of Sylvie. She
had no right to know so much.

No wonder Constance had succumbed to the appeals of
such a heart. And the epigraph she had chosen was apt for her
state – the exclamation of Laforgue: "*Je m'ennuie natale!*"
Yet he told himself: "I did not expect to be wholly original;
secretly I did not think I was really in the Grand Class. But I
decided to strive for the heights and at least make myself
wholly contemporary, absorbing all the fads and poisons and
truths of the age, fully aware of the danger of overturning my
applecart by caring too deeply. Yet simply to go on without
achieving anything of note – the idea was unbearable. And
end up in old age ravaged by the terrible priapism of the very
old – ineffectual, burning, solitary: and powerless against the
pangs of diurnal lust. Not that!"

Depth of focus is everything in passion as in prose. No
more, please God, of those big-paunched invertebrate novels
of yore, full of rose-water. An attitude to love which has taken
the tang out of tupping. Prose style known to the French

as *genre constation de gendarme.*

Reality which seems completely merciless is completely just, being neither for nor against. Sometimes he caught sight of her profile, or the head half-turned towards the source of light. How munificent her deep gloating regard, the sumptuous swarthiness. (The dead are heaped around us in a state of failure.) The single imperative of the artist (everyman) is *bricoler dans l'immédiat, c'est tout*! Reduce the work load of the heart, the tourist heart. Sutcliffe must have been following his thought for he said now: "Vulgarity in love is distressing, and for those who care about it, how vulgar Ovid is! He would work in advertising today, a laureate of Madison Avenue. Propertius, Catullus, *autre chose.*" He raised a skinful of wine to his mouth and drank. "Uncanny stuff, wine!" he said, putting down his glass. "I prefer girls of a territorial vastness whose centres of gravity are tellurian tits." Blanford disagreed as he watched the other. With her long white neck she looked like a lily in tears.

Someone commented upon the vastness of Toby's helping whereupon he said huffily: "I have signed no contract with the Holy Ghost to abstain from pork in Lent."

The mansion of Lord Galen had been built in the grounds of an ancient tumbledown *mas*, the manor house of the usual Provençal style of which little remained except several vast granges or outhouses which had been turned into impromptu lodgings against the refurbishing of the newer (and rather hideous in a suburban way) houses. During the harvest and in winter the two further ones were crammed with agricultural machinery like tractors and harrows and combine harvesters. But the one in which they sat down for meals had normally been reserved as a workshop and garage for sick machinery. Exposed on the wall of this rustic dining room was a relic of this mechanical past which had been left behind as a wall decoration. It had great charm because it was clearly an explanatory poster which postdated the invention of the petrol engine by at most ten years. A famous make of automobile offered it to their clients as something which should be on every garage wall where the mechanic could consult it. It was a detailed diagram of a petrol engine extended and exploded so that its parts could be studied separately and their functioning grasped. Each member floated in the air separately, so to speak. This poster formed the backcloth against which Blanford and Sutcliffe sat, and Constance looking over their shoulders studied it with all the medical attention it merited – in the light of her avocation, so to speak. It was an embryology of the petrol engine – the foetal body with all its crude analogies to the human – arms, legs, as wheels, the vertebral column of the human spine. Sump, clutch, cloaca maxima lungs, guts . . .

Some of this thinking was of course Blanford's when he mounted his hobby horse about the flight of the ego to the West. Indeed she could hear his voice parodying her reflections. "Suddenly the human will metastasised, the ego broke loose, took wing in a desire not to conform to nature but to dominate it! A momentous moment, as when Aristotle put the skids under the shaman Empedocles and intellectually fathered Alexander the Great, whose tutor he was! Mind you, the alchemists of old must have known where this prodigious swerve of the human consciousness would lead, this obsession to hunt for the sweetness of traction. As you know, Tibet refused even the wheel – as if to hold up the business as much as possible. Obviously an ego cult fathered upon a driven wheel promised a total drunkenness – a fly-culture over which Mephisto would preside! Yet how irresistibly poetical the quest and how beautiful this racing human diagram in stressed steel, driven by a spark, breath, the cylinder-lungs, the oxygen burning, and the exudation of the waste in calx or smoke through an almost human anus. A fire-chariot woven out of mental stress and the greed of narcissism, self-love, vainglory. It has brought us the unbearable loneliness of speed, of travel, and lastly to the orgasm of flight. As you say, by their fruits shall ye know them. It has brought no peace while a displaced alchemical thirst for gold has attracted the most insecure, the Jews, and has brought us Lord Galen and the World Bank and the Marxist theory of value . . ."

Then he would be visited by a gust of despair and add, characteristically: "O dear! I shall probably end in the condemned cell of some monastery counting the moons of Jupiter for my sins and manicuring my reputation by sonnets." But the diagram would haunt her so that sometimes she was to dream of it, confusing it with an illustration from a medical work on embryology with diagrams of the foetus at various stages of growth, its detached parts all free-floating on the page. Yet her heart applauded him when he added: "But I deplore those who want to make a funk hole or a weeping wall out of the Vedanta, however despicable our present state and however desirable it is that we change our direction before it is too late. Yet destiny is destiny, and ours must work itself out in a Western way, carrying us all with it. Perhaps we could persuade the will to stop clutching; perhaps not. Personally I see no hope, yet I draw my optimism from seeing no grounds for it. I believe in a few things still. You are one."

She had never replied to this but just walked out of the room; but she had tears in her eyes and he noticed this and his heart stirred with conflicting confusions.

But the gruff comment of Sutcliffe was also apposite to the matter. "Crude antithetical thinking", he said, "is the mark of the second-rate mind. It would be fatal to behave as if we had something special to expiate – that would be mere pretension. If you had ever seen a Kashmiri merchant or a Bengali *bunia* or a Hindu business man you would realise that the West has no monopoly in materialism and ego-worship. So there!"

It was true, of course, and Blanford knew it in his heart of minds. His version was too pat. He put aside the latter for the moment. There were more important things afoot. He managed to get the girl aside the next day while Sylvie was having her siesta, a chemical sleep, to say: "You have been up to Tu Duc, and yet you have said nothing about it. I don't even know if it's still standing. I hardly dare to ask." She flushed, overwhelmed by a sudden pudicity. She realised that the whole matter of Sylvie's presence had begun to overcloud the question of them all returning to the *status quo ante*: could he bear to live with her under the same roof? It was unpardonable, what she had forced upon him, and she knew it. Suddenly contrite, she took his arm with all the old affection and said, "Darling Aubrey, yes, it's all there and still in good repair thanks to the new couple Blaise left behind when they went north to a better job with less work. It is all as it was."

Aubrey gazed at her curiously and almost tenderly. "And is It still there – you know what I mean?" Yes, she knew; he meant the old motheaten sofa of Freud, the analytic couch which Sutcliffe had rescued from Vienna a thousand years ago. "Yes, very much so! There is one little mousehole where the stuffing threatens to come out, but I can easily darn it." There was a long silence and then came the question she had been expecting and somewhat dreading. "Are we all going to live together, and if so how?" She herself felt somewhat reluctant to answer it immediately, abruptly, without a preamble of excuse – there had been so much suppressed emotion in his voice. "I thought of giving her Livia's room for the moment. She seems to have fallen in love with it; and she has asked if she might have the couch in it, now she knows its history. She seems to have fallen in love with that too. Aubrey, these are stabilising factors, I am sure you will understand and help. Please say you will."

He gazed at her and nodded slowly. "I shall have to see if I can stand life with you – it's provisional for the moment. But, darling, I can't take up any definite position, I love you too much for that. But the whole thing has been such a shock. And I suppose Cade will have Sam's old room?" She nodded: "If you wish."

"Galen won't want to let us go; he simply has to be surrounded by people or he gets alarmed and lonely!"

"I know. But soon he will have Felix and the Prince to compensate for us. Aubrey, I hope you can face it and be patient." He said, "So do I!" but his tone carried little conviction; nor was there really any alternative, for he was not rich enough to make other arrangements. In his inner mind he swore and ranted at this turn of fate: all the more painful in that she had elected to undertake his treatment, including massage and yoga and electrotherapy. They sat in helpless frustrated silence for a while, staring at each other. She wondered whether or not to carry the story forward and tell him more about this dramatically unreal attachment which had come as much of a surprise to her as to anyone else. But she hesitated. The dilemma was even graver than superficial appearances suggested – professional considerations were inextricably mixed in with them. So it was perhaps inevitable that she should direct her steps towards the lunatic asylum at Montfavet where so much had come to pass during the war years and where her friend Jourdain the doctor still reigned. She had phoned to say she was coming, and it was with smiling deference to her (for he had always loved her but been too shy (unusual in a Frenchman) to tell her so) that he sported his ancient college blazer to remind the world that he was also an MD Edinburgh. Nor was there any insincerity in his exclamation of delight at finding her younger and more beautiful than ever. "Flatterer!" she said, but he shook his head, and then pointed to his own greying hair. Yes, he had aged quite a bit, and was much thinner than when she had last seen him. "Sit down, tell me everything that has happened since last I saw you," he said. And then, realising how impossible a task that would be, added, smiling, "Preferably in one word!" This fell most aptly; she was able to echo his smiling and relaxed mood though what she said was actually laden with sorrow. "That I can," she said, "and the word is . . . Sylvie. I have committed a fearful mistake, and a professional misdemeanour of size. I am in a fix. I want your advice, I need it!"

"Where is she?" he said. "With you?"

"Yes. But as lover, not patient." The sob in her voice startled him and he leaned forward to take her hands as he stared into her eyes with astonishment and commiseration. He whistled softly. "But after all the precautions? India? Really, I thought . . ." She shook her head and said, "I must explain it all in order – even though I can't excuse this terrible and quite astonishing aberration. Where to begin, though?"

Where indeed?

How humiliating too after so many years to come back here, not for treatment, but for moral advice – to what Schwartz always called the "dingy *baisodrome* of French psychiatry"! Talk of being made to swallow toads! She laughed ruefully. "But what went wrong?" he said, his amazement quite unabated. "After all, when first the situation developed we all behaved with impeccable professional zeal. You were alleged to have gone to India and I took your place. Then she was transferred by you to Geneva and the care of Schwarz. Then what?"

"It worked reasonably well until the day when Schwartz elected to commit suicide and I had to take over his dossier in default of anyone better. I returned from India, so to speak, and came once more face to face with her. I experienced the most dramatic and irresistible countertransfer you can think of. The base must have been some slumbering and neglected homosexual predisposition, but the motor which set it off was, inexplicably enough, the death of Schwartz, who was a dear and long-time friend and colleague though nothing more. Inexplicable! Inexplicable!"

"Love is!" said Jourdain, ruefully gazing at her down-cast blonde head and lowered eyes so full of chagrin. "It wasn't love but infatuation – though what matter our silly qualifications? It's just because I feel guilty and ashamed – I should never have succumbed, yet I did."

"And now?"

"But there is worse to come," she said, "for another strange experience awaited me. I had been locked into this experience with such a savage intensity that I think I must have been a little bit out of my mind. I could not breathe without her, could not sleep, read, work . . . Yes, but all this (I see the despairing faces of my friends) – all this melted like an icecap just when we crossed over the border into France. It was as if I had crossed into a territory policed by the part of myself which still belonged to Sam – an older self, apparently long since dead and done with. But no. I realised with a sudden jolt that I was not a homosexual at all but a woman – a man's woman. And the shock spread right through my nervous system so that I think that for a brief moment I may well have passed out. I loved just as intensely, but as a friend; the whole of the sexual component, as uncle Freud would so chastely say, flew out of the window. I was suddenly completely anaesthetic to feminine caresses. They were so light, so insubstantial, trivial as feathers. I suddenly knew I belonged to the hairy race of men. But there, Aubrey has always said that I am a bit of a slowcoach and am afraid to make love without a *garde-feu*. But do you see my dilemma now? O God!" She was pale with fury.

"But why did you come back here?" he asked.

"I had several reasons, among them some quite un-finished business with myself – I wanted to find out a little more about my sister Livia, her death and so on. Then I felt in a vague sort of way that psychologically it might be good to move her back into an old context which must certainly be familiar – though I haven't yet dared to bring her back here to see you. Yet she knows I am here, and even hesitated about sending you a message, so that she still remembers you . . . But now it's me who is in a mess, for I simply do not dare to tell her about my state of mind. I have to sham an affection which I no longer feel for fear of upsetting the precarious applecart of her mind again! It would be ridiculous if it were not both painful and humiliating. You see, she is valuable, valuable to us all, her talent, her genius even. We haven't a right to put that at risk – or at least I don't dare. On the other hand I feel like a suburban housewife who has fallen in love with the milk roundsman but does not dare to risk being divorced for it! Sutcliffe was right to laugh when I told him; instead of sympathy he said, 'I think your policemen are simply wonderful!' Like the historic American in London. I suppose he was right."

"But I don't see how your *ménage* is going to work out without stress at some point."

"I know."

"*Ménage* or *manège*! That is the question."

"Help!"

"How can I? You must live it out."

"I know." She stood up, glancing at her watch. "I must go back. But you see? Already I feel better for having ventilated the matter, even though I knew no solution would be forthcoming – how could it? It's my own mess and I must accept the fact. On the other hand I cannot see this situation prolonging itself indefinitely. I am simply marking time now."

"My poor colleague," he said drily, but with all sincerity. There was no trace of irony in his tone – for he felt the same sharp pang which touched the heart of Blanford whenever he caught sight of her downcast head and averted eyes. But he at least was not abreast of the developments which she had outlined for the benefit of Jourdain. It is difficult to know what he would have thought of them – elation, sympathy, horror? The repertoire of the human heart is a vast one, a veritable broom-cupboard. She had left the car in the little square with its silent trees and small white church which enshrined so many memories of the past. Jourdain had extracted a firm promise that she would dine with him soon in his rooms.

She stood for a while letting the atmosphere of the little square seep into her, seep through her mind.

How long life seemed when one thought of the past – especially of all those sadly wasted years of war and its distresses. Her friend Nancy Quiminal used also to visit the little church. During the *fêtes votives* she brought posies of flowers to offer on behalf of an old aunt who had been born in the village of Montfavet, and had attended catechism classes in the church, which hadn't changed a jot. Constance tried the door.

She sat there in a pew for a long moment, counting her quiet heart beats, almost without drawing breath. The immense weariness of the war years had not yet quite dissipated, while the present with its problems seemed hopelessly lacklustre. Had they come back too soon to recapture some of the *élan* and optimism of the past – had they made a fatal miscalculation? It was true perhaps that one should never try to go back to retrace one's steps to a place where one has once been happy.

A wave of depression came over her, and for a moment she was almost tempted to say a prayer of abject self-commiseration, pagan though she was. She smiled at the impulse, but compromised by crossing herself as she stood before the watchers in the painting. Who knows? It was gipsy country and the piety might work like a *grigri* . . . Then she resumed her little borrowed car and set off back to collect Sutcliffe whom she had left in town to do some shopping with Blanford.

But when she found her way back to the little tavern by the river which was their point of rendezvous she was furious to find them both drunk – not "dead" drunk but in an advanced state of over-elaboration. Blanford could be most irritating when he became slightly incoherent while Sutcliffe became simply cryptic. They had been absorbing that deleterious brew known to the peasantry as *riquiqui*, a fire-water compounded of several toxins. "O God!" she said in dismay. "You are both drunk!" At which they protested energetically though with a slight incoherence which gave the show away. "*Au contraire*, my dear," said Blanford, "this is the way my world ends, not with a bang but a Werther. First time I've tasted this stuff. It's plebeian but very consoling. *Vive, les enfants du godmichet!*" Sutcliffe at once said, "I echo that toast in all solemnity. Did you know that for several centuries the city kept its renown because twelve churches preserved the authentic foreskin of Jesus as a holy relic? Twelve different foreskins, but each one the true and authentic . . ." They had set aside the pack of cards with which they had proposed to kill the time waiting for her. "A smegma culture," said Blanford gravely, thoughtfully, and his friend said, "When I hear the word I reach for the safety catch of my hair-spray. Levels of nonentity rise with a rising population. Who is going to do our dying for us? I once knew a parson who found he could not stand the sight of a freshly opened grave; he had a serious nervous breakdown. His doctor said soothingly, 'For a congenital worrier there is nothing more worrying than having nothing to worry about.' The poor parson jumped into the river." Blanford fiddled with his purchases and said, "When I killed you in the novel I intended to leave some ambiguity about the matter. Your body and the horse were washed up in Arles. But the police were to find that the dental imprints on your washed-up body did not coincide with the records of your London dentist. A pretty mystery!"

But to do justice to Blanford it must be allowed that underneath the tugging of the alcohol with its spurious consolation there echoed on the profound sense of desolation and emptiness which followed upon the defection (if that is the word) of Constance, and her absorption in Sylvie. As for the programme for a future life *à trois* . . . it was problematical in the extreme. "It was anguish to revisit Tu Duc," he told Sutcliffe. "The great dewy orchard, its apples tight and sweet as nuns' bums. And ironically I arrived with the first cuckoo – it seemed as if the whole spring had come to Avignon to announce my cuckoldry!"

It was with difficulty that she managed to shepherd them back to the car. Sutcliffe swore that his armpits were smoking from the *riquiqui*. But they were docile enough to obey her.

TWO

The Moving Finger

D URING THESE DAYS OF SOMEWHAT FORCED CON-
viviality Constance realised that Blanford was
inwardly quite terrified of the move and all that it
might portend. He had begun to drink rather heavily, and of
course his bondsman and double followed suit – which made
them excellent company for Toby and a trial to Lord Galen
whose sense of humour was somewhat limited.

Paradoxically enough, however, the alcohol had an
enlivening effect on his talent and the commonplace book
began to fill up once more with what Sutcliffe called "thimbles"
or stray thoughts, and Blanford "threads". He wrote: "Pearls
can exist without a thread but the novel is an artefact and needs
a thread upon which to thread not so much the pearls as the
reader! It is not true that all the great themes have been used
up. Each age produces new ones. For us considerations like
this: what did they think, the women who watched the
crucifixion? They say that Buddha's wife became his first
initiate as did the daughter of Pythagoras. Those were the
days! Or, to change topics: what of the one Spartan to outlive
Thermopylae? He was left for dead on the field and came to
himself when the enemy had gone. But he could not stand the
odium of having escaped the slaughter, the suspicion of
having run away. He killed himself in despair. A Don Juan
who was terrified of women? Crusoe through the eyes of
Friday? A Life of Jesus out of Freud and vice versa?" Sutcliffe broke in with: "And love? What about love?" In his
new mood of sorrow and guilty intransigence Blanford said,
"The greatest of human illusions. It's not worth the kisses it
is printed on! Pearls before swine, what!"

"I am meditating a love story about the ideal couple. She would be called Rosealba, a girl to detonate insight if ever there was one. He – I haven't chosen a name yet, but he is the original death-yield of a love-bundle bang-plus-whimper man. Moreover it is a perfect marriage. Every morning he tells her something she does not know. Every evening he puts something so big and warm into her hand that she becomes thoughtful. They are almost dead from pure yes-ness. She has filled his heart with a glorious blindness."

Blanford protested, "It is out of date. The new discrete image of fiction is different. All the people are parts of larger people or composed of parts of smaller people, enlarged or diminished according to need. All events are the same event from a different angle. The work becomes a palimpsest with a laying out of superposed profiles. (My God! What supreme, prize-winning boredom! Nevertheless *avec cela j'ai fait mon miel!*)"

"The fourth-century Thebans were renowned for the practice of male sexual cohabitation – plus a crucial military innovation. The Sacred Legion comprising 150 homosexual couples was commanded by Pelopidas. It was the *corps d'élite* of the line regiments, and the only full-time unit. Perhaps your escaped legionary from Thermopylae committed suicide for other reasons: like the loss of his love?"

"Perhaps. I am reminded of some lines by Shakespeare: 'The fulcrum of my lover's bum / Will guarantee a nightmare come.' "

"Pelopidas."

"The first thing I do when I get up in the morning is to count my uniforms and run through my decorations, always starting with the Grand Bandage of Outer Mongolia where I was consul for a week. The artist decorated is an awesome sight. Should the poet make reassuring noises? Yum yum, yes please!"

"The sea-shell is the mystic's telephone. Only in the

sea-shell can one hear the mystical *toc sonore* and realise fully that in art a methodical licence rules, and that greatness does not stint but neither is it profligate. Finally that with every breath, every pulse-beat, every thought the whole universe invests its strength anew in reality. My friend, these bold words were dictated to me while I slept."

"In a new age of plastic caryatids we shall be permitted to change women in mid-scream. Thus to honour a secret goddess in her kilt of dead rats! Ah, you had better tear this letter up before reading it. Constance, the vatic second state you so distrust is reached without strain. I drifted into my life like an air-bubble into an old aorta. Went off bang one day and died for her. Exploded like an aneurism."

"Thank God for petrol. Arabs who are sensitive people buy women like others buy paintings. If paintings could open their legs they would buy paintings!"

But this persiflage could not disguise the deep unhappiness of the inward monitor. "I feel that I am giving off a steady glow of sex – like an abandoned dungheap!" said the incorrigible Sutcliffe. "And I have discovered a way of making Galen cry when he irritates me too profusely. Any reference to his late cat 'the wombat' puts him into a tearful state. When I twist the knife and speak of the 'old days' he whips out his hanky and says, 'Don't go on: we were so happy. I feel so lost now. Boo hoo!' He is highly susceptible, our great Co-ordinator."

"Other problems. How to defend yourself against your own self-esteem, eh? How not to look complacent when you are? There must be a gadget. The objective of the Christian is to be good, that of the Buddhist to be free. A different frequency. As death closes in more and more, illustrates itself with the loss of friends, the difference becomes more marked, one tends to take out more fire insurance. The mysterious root-force which gives enduring life to art can be felt and described in terms of architectonics, but its nature and essence remain mysterious – a dark river flowing from nowhere to nowhere. The pen touching paper marks the point of intersection merely. But when the artists of an age begin to use architectonics without humility we are in danger of losing the thread they weave. Wagner, Picasso – they are like mechanised muezzins whose prayers are recorded and broadcast on an almost political level. The intimacy has gone, the sensual exchange is not there. A microphone has intervened. As for the artist . . . poor fellow, after birth the terror of ego-consciousness strikes, the awe invades, the fear, and immediately the self laps itself in layer after layer of protective feelings to avoid foundering: like an onion, layer upon layer of defensive schemes. This is what poor old Buddha tried to counter by his policy of unwrapping the poor ego from its mummy-like swaddling clothes – the nervous aggressive reactions. He had made a capital discovery, but it is hard to convince people that the threat of nature is illusory. Yet once they twig the fact peace spreads round them in rings. But it's a whole art, to make yourself thoroughly vulnerable, even open towards death. Yes, once you are in the know nothing much matters any more, the penny has dropped. You realise that harmlessness is the highest good."

"Good art is never explicit enough."

"How should it be? It does not contain an ethic. You cannot break the code of the beauty exemplified by the rose. Ah! blessed principle of Indeterminacy which renders every eventual second of time miraculous: because all creation is arbitrary, capricious, spontaneous. Without forethought or afterthought."

"Every two seconds a mental defective is born. Nevertheless I pat the whole universe on the back and cry, 'Well done, old cock, well done!' "

"A monkey telling its nits, the priest his beads. Yet

somewhere I am sure the Great Plan exists. It is pinned out on a vast wall-map containing every imaginable reference as to our entries, exits, names, styles, natures, destiny. I'm sure!"

"You remind me of poor Quatrefages!"

"Yes. And his great map of the Templars. He has retired into the fastnesses of Montfavet – *la vie en rose*! He has not quite succeeded in convincing Galen that there is no Templar treasure to be exploited, but very nearly. The real secret treasure was the Grail, the lotus of insight. They had become infected first by the old Gnosticism so rampant in the Middle Orient (*outremer*); and then secondly and definitively by the practices of yoga – as the thread woven from millet round their waists so clearly showed. The Catholics were quite right – they *were* heretics, and their practices *did* create a danger for the Catholic world."

"Galen must be beside himself with anguish, after having invested so much money in futile research on the subject. So indeed must be the Prince who allowed himself to be talked into the scheme. We shall see next week when he arrives."

"They will find something else – a new line in widows and orphans. The war has created so many."

"A world without man – how was it before we emerged, I often wonder? Perhaps trees were the original people, anterior to humankind. Man sprang from the humus when it was mixed with water. Thus the mystics desire to regress into the unassailability of plant life – the insouciant lotus – in order to recapture the down-drive into dissolution, echoing the force we call gravity upon body and mind. What would you say to that? Excellence – the very notion of excellence comes from rarity, scarcity, paucity. Nature's robust mutations encourage species to evolve and lead the many towards the unique one. Ah! The brain's old begging-bowl! Perhaps the first fish were soluble and could not resist the rubbing water: but gradually by will-power and curiosity they learned survival. And elephants like humble space-ships floated without touching the ground . . ."

"Then came man. Woman blows man like spun glass from her womb. He is the weaker of the two, she writes his books though he executes them. Yet his sperm is her supreme document. If the quality falls off she becomes sick with malnutrition, soul-hunger, a sort of vampirism possesses her. The couple, the basic brick of understanding, is at risk. What is compromised is the sexual bonding which comes with insight."

"St Augustine was right in a way, writing letters to his punch-bag and cheeking the Holy Ghost. He was right – those who say don't know, those who know can't say . . . The corollary is that those who don't bloody know can't bloody say, yet today they make the most noise."

At this point Lord Galen erupted, clapping his hands, and said: "That is enough higher thought for today, Aubrey. Lunch is on the table, and it's mushrooms we picked ourselves."

THREE

The Prince Arrives

ALEN PLEADED WITH SUCH HEARTRENDING EMOTION for them to defer their departure that Constance took pity on him and decided to stay until the Prince arrived on the scene, which he duly did, accompanied by the newest version of Felix Chatto, now a man of the world, indeed a young ambassador in bud waiting for his Latin American republic to mature, so to speak. But the Prince was in an evil mood due to this latest contretemps with the British who had arrested twenty-five members of the secret brotherhood on the vague presumption that their activities were political and, by the same token, subversive. But for his part he was delighted to see Constance again and embraced her tenderly with tears in his eyes. He had left the princess behind in Cairo – she risked nothing from the British, he explained, as she had always been neutral; besides, she had become a bosom friend of the present ambassador, and as usual the embassy was at loggerheads with the army, as personified by the odious security brigadier who had initiated all these persecutions. "Him and an odious little man, Telford, who was a billiard marker in peace time and now enjoys currying favour with the army by supplying false information. He doesn't even speak a word of Arabic or Greek. And he's from Barnsley. I ask you, *Barnsley*!" He positively sizzled with contempt. "The real problem is, *how* can I go on loving my dear British when they let wretched people like this persecute us, eh?" He kissed her hands repeatedly, and she knew he was thinking of Affad, though he did not mention him. Instead he said: "And the boy?"

The boy had settled down very comfortably, having

found companions of his own age at the farm. He had been
instantly adopted by the farmer and his wife, and made free
of the place. What more intoxicating place than a farm with
all its livestock to fire the mind of a child? But he had also, in
some curious way, adopted Blanford; he had begun to show
a preference for his company over the others'. Often when
Aubrey was lying down – an enforced rest or siesta, say, for
his back – the boy would appear and ask to be read to. Or he
wished to play a game, or learn how to play backgammon.
Blanford found this profoundly touching, and at once complied. It was as if Constance herself had asked him for these
trifling favours. He loved the boy with this transferred love,
the rival of Sylvie, so to speak. He wondered what it would
be like to have a child of his own – he supposed that there
was no experience in life so strange and so unique as to create
another human being. Once the boy said, "You will stay with
us, won't you?" and he was surprised for he supposed that
the child had overheard some of their deliberations, their
expressed doubts and hesitations. "Would you like that?" he
said, feeling absurdly moved and flattered. The boy nodded in
solemn fashion. "You play games so nicely," he explained,
"and you always explain things to me!" An obscure shyness
prevented him from recounting any of this to Constance. But
she noticed for herself – small touches of affection and confidence marked the relation; when out walking in the courtyard, for example, the boy might take the hand of Blanford
in an absentminded way; or break step in order to let their
footsteps chime. On the other hand the embraces of Sylvie,
which were on the effusive side, made the child ever so
slightly impatient – anxious to be released. It was a strange
polarity of inner feelings, yet it must have been based on
some sort of sense of discrimination and insight, for when
Felix Chatto arrived he was immediately accepted on the
same basis by the boy, and instantly. About Felix Blanford

was not surprised – he had developed into a most charming human being. A little bit of professional success and a sortie into the social world where he might receive the favours of women and so assume himself and gain confidence – it had served him in good stead, and he had not wasted his time. His scope had broadened with his new charm; even his looks had changed, had improved. He was lean and brown now in physique and with a high sense of irony, as befitted somebody in diplomacy, where one is always in danger of being besotted by protocol and caution. And a wry sense of humour set off to perfection his shy and self-deprecating manner. Most important of all he had managed now to get upon even terms with Lord Galen and was no more oppressed and intimidated by the shadow of the great man. He was able to stand his ground and have opinions of his own. The boot was, in fact, on the other foot, for Lord Galen had become diffident and hesitant with *him*, and of late had started to defer to *his* opinions. Indeed he had even been invoked to bring some critical judgement to bear upon the Templar Treasure invest-ment – was it worth continuing the quest, or should it be given up as useless? The debate which was now going to ensue upon the matter would largely turn upon his private opinion as to the soundness of the venture. Time had enabled him to turn the tables on his seniors. All this put him into a very good humour, enabled him to support with sangfroid the Prince's own dark humour. But it was evident that on the question of their so-called investment he harboured more doubts than hopes, despite the tantalising elements which Quatrefages had revealed in the construction of his Templar wall-map, despite the reluctance of Lord Galen to relinquish all hope of finding a treasure buried in the crypt of some old castle. "I shall be sorry to play the 'killjoy'," he told Blanford, "but good sense is good sense, particularly in finance!"

"Finance again!" cried Sutcliffe later that night. "But

did Felix tell you of his mission to China, to help advise them on how to balance their budget? Galen sent him from Geneva. Did he?" Blanford shook his head. Overwhelmed by his excitement, Sutcliffe tapped his own temples with a clenched fist, but softly, and said: "I will, then. My goodness, what an adventure for Felix.

"When he arrived he found them all convulsed with enthusiasm for Zen Buddhism, of all things! Yes, I know, I know. In the Marxist Ministry of Finance they had never heard of such a thing. But they were working with an American adviser called O'Schwartz if you please and he had told them that the only future for China lay in tourism. They must provide facilities and he, O'Schwartz (he said he was from an old Irish family, Madison Avenue Irish) would guarantee the tourists. All America would rush to visit China, but it must have not only accommodation but also sports like tennis, golf, water skiing, etc., and Zen Buddhism. They looked puzzled and asked what the devil that might be. They'd never heard of it. Well, O'Schwartz told them that everyone knew what it was, it was kinda religious only needed no effort. He knew that there was money in it because the Rothschilds were on to it and it was given away free with every packet of crisps by the Club Méditerranée. Now the American tourist insisted on the best and nothing but; if he did not find Zen on the menu he would feel he was being cheated. Obediently they got to work and a professor was found who had heard of the article. He told them of the epoch-making arrival of Bodhidharma from India, where he had been the twenty-eighth patriarch, in order to become the first in China. Dazed, they heard him describe the long incubation in the cave, where the sage sat facing a blank wall for so many years until the King asked him what he had gained from the practice, only to be told, 'Nothing at all, your Majesty!' This really baffled the Chinese, but O'Schwartz stuck to his guns, and they turned to Felix for confirmation of the fact that American tourists would feel happier if they could visit, for example, the original cave or the original wall. They had sent out scouts to try and locate the original cave where the practice of Zazen was first initiated. In the meantime, while waiting for news of it, they addressed themselves to the formidable problems raised by the other requisites – the large hotels, beaches, excursions, shopping centres. Finally word came back that a cave – perhaps the original, perhaps not – had been found and was open for their inspection. But it was a long way off and would necessitate a long journey by train and jeep and finally mule. The old sage never did things by halves. It was remote, this cave. Felix was full of misgivings, but O'Schwartz was adamant. They must really take the trouble to look at it on behalf of future tourist activities. In fairness to the Ministry it must be said that they did not insist on the *original* cave – it was the relentless American adviser who did. Any bit of wall, any cave, would do, thought the Ministry. But at the prompting of O'Schwartz the Professor took charge of them and off they set on a long journey by river and pure jungle towards the keystone of the old sage's edifice. Wild country, yes, and full of rock-panthers of a beautiful ivory hue which they caught sight of from time to time, but rarely for they were shy and of a guilty conscience. This animal delights in the flesh of dogs, just as man does in the flesh of fowls. At first they divined their invisible presence as they advanced because their dogs began to disappear one by one, and noiselessly, with hardly a bark or a shriek; they melted into invisibility as if some unknown hand had sifted them away. It was unnerving – like swimmers taken by a shark. Once or twice they caught a glimpse of these favoured great creatures which seemed to have stepped out of an old engraving or a wash drawing of the middle period. At night they drew close about the fire which they were forced to light in the wilderness in order to keep the panthers at bay. They slept badly with their huddle of dogs. It was wild country with no towns and no taverns. So at last they came to the place of the cave.

The old scholar who led the party was a vague and prosy old gentleman whose exposition was blurred and whose knowledge was full of gaps. Fortunately Felix knew a little and O'Schwartz also. As for Bodhidharma the only painting extant is too late to have been done from life. The sage's eyes are crossed from his exertions. Diplopia giving the impression of the pineal eye, the Third Eye in full flower. The only painting shows the tender clown with painted tears engrossed on his face, fixed like the flared nostrils of painted rocking-horses uprearing to the winds of heaven. When the poor little king, so thirsty for instruction, asked old Bod just what forty years of speechless wall-gazing had done for him, the great one returned a somewhat dusty answer. 'Forget it, cod,' he said, or words to that effect. There was in fact nothing that *could* be predicated about the experience he had been through. Either one twigged or not; there was nothing to say about so private an inkling of truth. The King sighed. (Was memory then so tenacious? The keystone to the average human condition was, as always, stress and fret and frenzy. The squalid and chubby self was still in the centre of the picture.)

Zazen, as he christened it, was the dire and absolute procedure which enabled him to effect a breakthrough into the other register of consciousness – the open realm or field where the whole of consciousness floated, detached and sub-lime. The cave they had found was large and silent, its walls like superb natural frescos of blood-red stone – intricate interlacings almost suggesting a human hand's work. It was not here that he squatted, the sage, for these graffiti could have reminded him of things, and he was not allowed to have either associations or even memories. His purified outlook upon the

sublime was empty of every qualification! He was glimpsing
the very 'itness' of things, of all nature, if you wish. He plucked
this dense wall as one plucks a goose, or a picker picketh fruit
or moss, absently present all the time. This kind of reality
had no Therefore in it. Bodyless, Boneless, Soundless and
Meaningless – it was full of information for his parched
intuition. Reality now was sweet as a plum, romantic as
wedding cake among these neolithic veins of gorgeous stone
which he rejected in favour of a barren uncoloured strip of
cave. A far corner which was not declamatory, which was
worth its weight in . . . The tremendous plumage of nonentity
– gazing into it he realised all the riches of his inmost dowry.
All Sesame slid back – it was a simply mental knack to slide
the panel back upon the mirror of truth! The place, so
ordinary for him, would become hallowed through the bald
irreverence of the horde. Early tourists must have come. They
visited bones until they dissolved into dust. Then with
moistened finger they licked up his dust or supposed dust.
Now only the wall remained on view for a century or two –
orders of the Ministry. But 'Is this *really* all there is to see?'
they ask the guide. Perhaps one could X-ray the wall, and
catch a glimpse of the treasures inside? No, since then man
has lived on in ever-increasing embarrassment at this power-
cut in the central vision. The travel agencies can do nothing
except repeat promises of their good faith. It is not the
original wall – it proved to be too far away; so they settled
for a cave which was more easily accessible to the tourist. But
the original – Felix was aware of the importance of the
experience O'Schwartz had given him, and he was duly
grateful. In the silence of the cave he stood and counted the
golden register of his lagging heartbeats. He could not help
but think in quotation either – Plato's mystical cave with its
shadows loomed up in memory. Plato's cave was the un-
purged cave of human consciousness. The soul's bargain

basement which old B. had turned into a jumble sale! Fecit! With only his eyeballs for probes he exhausted the contents of the blank wall by a relentless attention to its focal beauty. Plucking a blank wall with primal sight – a wall dense with music like some carnal plum. This is what gave the old lad his fatal ZA – his *do-re-me-fa-so*! What he was rewarded with was something that would not melt in silence, nor pucker in wind, nor be honed by mischief-makers, nor claimed by clowns. Within it all polarities ceded. Never was it to be disavowed by the wrong love.

In this critical wall he saw a mirror reflecting the whole retrievable inward chaos of man. He harnessed the energy it gave off, fully aware that one day local fame would become world renown; yet the plight of human happiness could not be changed by simply changing the metaphors for desire. The real original sin of the affect was trying to perpetuate the transitory. Water, itself the symbol of ancient purity, stagnates without motion, without movement. This was old B.'s simple ZA! Hunting down an old spontaneousness which had once been innate, unrehearsed: pining to dwell once more, and this time for ever, in a perfected nonchalance of being! This he managed to do with the bare bodkin of his human probe – his eyeballs. The old TU QUOQUE gave place to rest and silence. As he told the king: 'Imitate plants in their defencelessness. If you are a love-child it doesn't matter if your father is only a groom. The art of fishing is never to let the fish know that you are in love with it! To heighten pleasure tighten pain. The highest sensuality lies in repressing the hunger.' What marvels of insight emerge from privation! What a marvellous topic was silence! (The king burst into tears. He had tried so *hard* and here he was: out of his depth!) All these aphorisms, the spawn of insight! It was such bad taste – altogether too literary. The soft reversal of the real provokes a wholesome vertigo in the opinionated. The hairpin bends where death attends. The secret plumage of the rock gave him the information that he needed. He marvelled at the sapience of his triumphant ZA! There was no written text, no code for this passion. A slip of the pen in the dog-days of love – he now knew how to be vigilant in silence and quite sorrowless. The sources of culture were obvious now. The origin of all drama was incest! The role of the physician was to purge our childhood of wishes.

There he sat, the old crystal-chafer, quietly rubbing his soft lampoon and daring humanity to dare."

The dry copyist's succinct word for human craving – four letters beginning with an L. Lust? Lost? Last? List? Live? Love? The choice is extensive yet intensive. The whole of this experience, the strange journey, the cave, the zany propositions of the Marxists, exercised a strange effect upon Felix; he felt changed in some profound way, but he could not have said just how. And for once he felt unwilling to discuss the experience, except to make fun of its bizarre side – the thought of Americans with cameras plodding through this field. O'Schwartz had even evolved a scheme by which they could obtain certificates of religious initiation in the Dharma – he had suborned a Californian monk to help him with his scheme. Thus the tourist would have something to show when he got home – apart from his photographs. A diploma!

Something to show! A certificate of higher indolence! Felix recounted this whole spiritual adventure to Galen who listened with an air of pained puzzlement. It was evident that the chances for speculative investment were poor and some-what chancy with those Chinks – moreover brainwashed Chinks of the left hand! Yet . . . they were right about tourism, he should suppose, if only communications opened up once more and the war-damage was set to rights. "What does the Prince think?" he asked a little plaintively, and Felix replied, "He is in a bad mood and says that he won't chance a penny on any Chinese scheme. On the other hand he is reluctant to relinquish the Templar treasure scheme. He still thinks there is hope of a breakthrough towards a real treasure. Myself, I . . ." His shrugged shoulders were quite eloquent enough. But meanwhile the Prince had come into the room silently and was in time to overhear the exchange. "It is not quite my point of view," he said rather testily, "but you must remember that I come from a land where the bazaars are absolutely crammed with lying soothsayers. I consulted one in the Grand Bazaar in Cairo in the middle of the night by the weird light of those large hissing acetylene lamps which make everyone look deathly pale, drained of blood! And what Aubrey calls 'squirms' of children jumping about like fleas. Now this old man was extremely explicit about this whole venture. He told me I was involved in a treasure-hunting scheme about which I had become somewhat doubtful, wondering whether to abandon hope. He said that I must not give up for at least another six months. He could not tell me whether the treasure really still existed, because he was too far away from the scene, but he suggested that I consult someone who was actually on the spot. That is why I hurried up and planned my arrival for May."

"Why May specially?" asked Galen and received the laconic reply: "The gipsy festival rounds off May, remember?" Galen did not but he pretended he did. Felix nodded and provided the exact date and the exact place: Les Saintes Maries de la Mer! "I will have our fortunes retold by a gipsy," said the Prince, "and we'll see whether to carry on or abandon the whole investment!"

"Fortune-telling?" said Galen somewhat unhappily. "It's not very *sound*, is it? I mean to say, having your palm read, what?" The Prince nodded his agreement to the proposition. "Nevertheless," he said with resolution, "there is so much that is questionable about the whole enterprise that one little soothsayer won't change much. I don't intend to abandon the *Financial Times*. But the one in Cairo told me I had a partner who was too cautious, believed too much in moderation. Said I must encourage him to risk more. How do you like that?"

Galen put on his wounded look. "Well, I like that!" he said reproachfully, "after all we have put up. As for lying soothsayers, we have had our share with the myth-making of young Quatrefages. And we still don't know where we are!"

But about the gipsies the Prince was not wrong, for already their slow steady infiltration into the province had begun – a leisurely penetration into Avignon and thence into the Camargue. It was probably deliberate, in order not to alarm the country people too much by a violent gipsy presence – though in smaller villages the church bells might be rung and the housewife's cry go up: "The gipsies are coming!" It was the signal to bolt and bar the granary or the barn, to get your washing off the line, and to withdraw from the window sills such items of common fare as pots of basil or of wild mint, so renowned were they for their light-fingered tactics and the brilliant insolence of their approach to the timid and the law-abiding. They invested the little towns of the Midi as cunningly as freebooters might – for that is what they were. The women would sell baskets or profess to grind your knives for you at your front door: but your eye must be sharp for while one swarthy beauty worked at the knife blades another might slip past you into the house and pilfer. But they were so good-looking and insolent and dressed like birds of paradise that one was always torn between fear and admiration, while the beauty of the women set the sap mounting in the veins of the menfolk. They were not averse to some quick sexual commerce in a barn or in the woods – fair reason for your wife's anxiety when the cry went up that they had arrived. *They did not seem to care!* That is what went home like a knife-thrust in the heart of the careworn house-wife! In their dusky skins and glowing eyes they seemed to express the perils as well as the joys of absolute freedom. Yet for all their being scattered far and wide there was only one festival a year at which they were all joined together to honour their patron saint, the dark-skinned Sara whose grottoes were in the crypt of the little Church of the Saintes Maries de la Mer, the famous village on the sea to which all their steps were now bending. But first they filled up Avignon and for a while created a kind of excited tremor in the life of the merchants and settled folk. A gipsy fiddler in the main square managed to inflame some young couples to dance to his music – he was of a northern strain and sounded Hungarian, or rather his music did. They were getting them-selves assembled in their various troupes to await the arrival of their Queen Mother who was somewhere on the road still.

Without her there could be no fête for the moon-people – for the gipsies are lunar folk. So they marked time, reading hands and tea leaves and coffee grounds until she should come.

Gradually, too, the town woke up to their exciting and distressing presence and the inevitable reaction, set in the form of increased police surveillance and minor harassments and persecutions at camping sites and in urban squares or wherever a cart and a tent appeared. In olden times – yet not so long ago – they would have been arrested, imprisoned or whipped at a cross-roads for flouting the common law, for trespassing and pilfering. Today they only had to endure a minor form of the old rabid persecution – the object being to expel them, force them to move on. There was no need for harsher measures since everyone knew that their objective was not Avignon but Les Saintes, and that they would soon ebb quietly away towards the torrid plains of the Camargue. The town was simply a staging post for the grand march southward. But it offered an extraordinary glimpse into the organisation of this mysterious ethnic group. "In one of your previous lives I learned about them from a girl called Sabine," said Sutcliffe as they sat before their glasses of wine on the broad terrace above the olive grove. Blanford nodded: "I well remember," he said, "and I have often wondered what happened to her. They said that she had gone off with a gipsy." Blanford chuckled. "It was the fashionably romantic thing to say or even to do then: before the war, I mean." Yet it had been more than that, for Sabine had been told that she was descended from the famous gipsy personage Faa, who was among the first to establish a right of entry into America. Sutcliffe refilled his glass and went on in reminiscent vein: "In my wine-jumbled brain I remember not only her favours, surprisingly tender and vulnerable, but also her conversation. I had vaguely thought of them as persecuted people simply because they would not keep still, would not integrate with settled communities. But the long saga of persecution – I had not realised to the full what that had meant to them. It had formed them and rounded them until their personalities were as solidly obdurate as an ingot. They have become incapable of change."

The Prince was listening with great attention to this somewhat drunken disquisition. "Nevertheless," he said, "in Egypt they are a sly and slippery folk – and their name is apparently derived from *gypt*, which is 'us'. If they are, as you say, unchangeable it is because they *are* change. They are like water and will take any shape, but always stay the same. And by the way, I was talking to a minor functionary of the *mairie* today and he was saying how amazing it was that so many tribes manage to get down to the Saintes for this Saint Sara festival every year. They even come from behind the Iron Curtain as you must have seen from some of the carts. Strange folk!"

But doubtless they themselves would look almost as strange *en masse* for they had hired a large red motor bus for the excursion, complete with driver. It was the Prince's idea, as he had been told of the almost intolerable congestion of traffic caused by the slow-moving carts and the horses – not to mention the vast plumes of dust which rose along the gipsies' passage, following them like a forest fire. A van such as this would free them from the responsibilities of the road and also keep them all together in a single party. Needless to say, the preparations for the trip involving hampers of elaborate food and wine put everyone into a good humour while the Prince devised ever more wonderful configurations of truffled trifles with which to tease the palates of the pilgrims – for they conceived themselves now as such. After all, they had a purpose, they were voyaging with the intention of invoking Saint Sara, asking her to take a sounding for them in the ocean of futurity. Travelling like this, in a congregation, so to speak, enabled the more loquacious (or simply drunker?) members among them to permit themselves sonorous disquisitions upon whatever subject came to hand. But the thought of the vanished Sabine touched off other reminiscences of gipsy lore and history with which the nostalgic Sutcliffe enlivened the first part of the journey through the flowering meads of high Provence which soon gave place to the sadder, flatter plains of the Camargue – country of marsh and rivulet and lake where flies and mosquitoes abounded, as well as the sturdy brown bulls of the locality which were raised as cockade fighters for the Provençal bull rings. Here too the characteristic cowboy of the land, the *gardien*, prevailed with his broad-brimmed sombrero and the trident which he sported like a sceptre of office. As the straggling columns wound dustily through his land to the sea there was need for constant watchfulness, for the gipsies were light-fingered and pilfered remorselessly while the strangers' dogs teased the bulls and snapped at the horses – the little white palaeolithic steeds which the poets of the place always saw in terms of a foam flowing over the land like waves on the blue sea which lay ahead, the crown of their journey, the church of Saint Sara.

"I feel wonderful on this wine," said the relentless double of Blanford. "I may have a tendency to boom a bit. If I do, curb me with a frown, will you?"

"I will. Anyway I see no mystery in the Gyps because I think of them as Jews gone wild. No money sense."

"Oh dear!" said Lord Galen unhappily. "Now you will start being anti-Jewish. I feel it coming. Change the subject, please!" Sutcliffe poured him out a glass which he drank off.

So they voyaged on in a pleasant state of abstraction, skimming as much as they could along the swarthy columns of "Greek" and "Egyptian" and "Romanian" and "Bulgarian" gipsies, each tribe with its characteristic music and avocation – basketwork for the "French", pots and pans for the "Greek" farriers.

Some of the horse-drawn caravans were brilliantly painted, speaking of Sicily or England. And by the wayside perched their tents in small encampments where the children lay about like litters of cats and puppies in the bluish dust. The tide, however, flowed steadily towards the sea where the little church of the Saint stuck out its abrupt butt towards the beaches, never quite allowing one to forget that it was originally a fort, a defence against the pirates who ravaged this coast. As for the beaches themselves they had become one great single encampment, as if they had been spawned by the grand Souk of Cairo. Here the various races mingled and bickered, the various musics contended against each other – and also with the noise of the waves forever bursting upon the white sand. "From Messina to the Baltic, from Russia to Spain, this people had been enslaved, tortured, often put to death: their lives were worth nothing. Long past the sixteenth century the persecutions endured. Indeed at that time anyone who frequented or succoured them was listed as a common felon and could be put to death without even the benefit of a jury." Blanford dredged up this scrap from some old conversation, from perhaps Sabine? Her name had come back to hover about him like a persistent fly: he wondered what had happened to her. And, of course, as is always the case, he was soon to meet her in the flesh again and find out!

So the little bus struggled on through the dust plumes until the broad beaches came in sight, framed by the rocking sealine. Their horses and carts had taken possession of the beaches under the watchful eye of the local cavaliers who by now had become familiars, wandering among the tents on their little white steeds. A great fair was growing up around the event which would end with a religious service and the transport of the three Maries down to the sea on a great wooden trestle banked with flowers; the whole party, bursting with ardour and joyful tears, plunging through the shallows until the sea was breast-high, and the whole cavalcade seemed to float on the water, encircled now by all the fisher boats of the little seaport, appropriately bedecked and beflagged in their honour.

Their own objective was one of the seaside cafés where they had reserved a shady corner of terrace with a vast green awning, which would serve as a headquarters from which they could sally forth into the fair at will. Here their hampers were unpacked, their plates and cutlery being disposed upon long trestle tables – all the allure of a scouts' picnic. And it was while they were taking their aperitifs that a gipsy woman approached them with a slow and curious air, as if she were looking for someone who might be found in their midst. She was awakening into an uncertain familiarity with the face of Blanford – though it was Sutcliffe who was the first to recognise her, and let out a cry of recognition. "Sabine, darling!" he cried. "There you are at last! We've been hunting for you in each other's books for ages! Where have you been?" The woman thus addressed was indeed hardly recognisable when compared to the memories they had kept of the old Sabine.

She was stout and dirty and wrinkled, and her clothes and trinkets were of the cheapest sort. Her hair was greying now, and the once magnificent eyes were a prey to myopia, which added to her difficulty in recognising those who had once been acquaintances and friends. As they peered it seemed as if they were seeing her afresh through several veils of reality, several washes of colour. Of course she had always been rather self-consciously a tramp, as so many university children of her era had been. You showed your intellectual independence by not washing in that far-off epoch. But Sabine had gone further and actually disappeared with the gipsies, which had more or less destroyed the happiness and peace of mind of her father Lord Banquo. He for his part had been an old associate of Lord Galen and had even known the Prince. So that when Sabine discovered herself to them several recognitions took place and several simultaneous conversations broke out around her past and around her father, whose chateau in Provence was now boarded up and deserted and seemed to have stayed like that throughout the war. "He's dead, yes," she said in her harsh but calm tones – it was so strange to hear that Cambridge accent coming out of her swarthy face. "They say of course I killed him by taking to the road – well, perhaps I did. But there was no other choice for me to make. I wished to please him, and there was nothing I could offer as an excuse for my choice. I even submitted to a Freudian analysis of several months in order to get myself fully explained: but it explained nothing and I was literally driven to this solution in spite of myself. It wasn't love either,

or passion, as in the novels. It was like one decides to go to
America or into a monastery. It was a sort of magnetic
solution. I was sleep-walking, and I still am. I would not
change this for worlds." And surprisingly she put her hands
on her fat hips and let off a laugh like a police siren. How
much she had changed, thought Blanford, and he had a sudden
memory of Banquo's face watching her with such admiration,
such pain, such anxiety.

She sat down and put her head on one side, as if she
were listening to herself; indeed she was. "God!" she said.
"I'm so thirsty to speak some English after so long; and yet
it sounds so strange coming out of my head. I thought I had
forgotten it after so many years of dog-Esperanto. Aubrey,
speak to me!" and she smiled this new hideous smile full of
flashing gold teeth. She tugged his sleeve affectionately,
pleadingly almost. He said, "Immediately I want to know
why! Why did you do it?"

She lit a hemp cigarillo and began to smoke in short sharp
inspirations, holding it not between her fingers but in the palm
of her hand, as if it were a pipe. "I've told you," she said,
"just as I told dear old Freud who was hunting my Oedipus
complex. Mario, the man I went to was so much older, you
see, that they thought he was a father-replacement. I ask you!"
She laughed again in her new ferociously lustful way, and
clapped her hand on his thigh. "When I came down from
Cambridge I was an economics star and I wanted to do a study
of society which would pinpoint whatever it was that was
preventing us from constructing the perfect utopian state – a
state so just and equitable that we were all using the same
toothbrush. You know how it is when one is young? Idealism.
I finally narrowed it all down to the idea of the Untouchable
in his various forms. My book was going to analyse Untouch-
ability. We were after all Jews, so it was a good starting point;
then I went to India and experienced all the horrors of

Brahminism; finally among other little ethnic puzzles I came upon the gipsy, first in the caves at Altamira and then one day in Avignon when I bought a basket from a rough-looking gipsy in the main square of Avignon. The next day when I was passing through the same square he was still there and he recognised me. He said, 'Come with me, it is important. Our mother wants to speak to you. She says she *recognises* you.' This is our tribal mother – *puri dai*, as they call her! Our tribe is a matriarchy. This old woman took my hands and predicted that by the end of the summer I would join them and that Mario would make me pregnant – which he did. She forgot to add that he would also give me syphilis! But compared to so many other trials it was nothing and I was after all sufficiently educated to get it treated. I was spellbound by the self-evident fact that I *was* a gipsy – the whole of European culture slid from my shoulders like a cloak. Mario was much older but like an oak tree. After the first night in his tent I went home and told my father I was going to leave him." Yes, but her voice held pain at this stage in the story. Blanford remembered that troubled summer when the old man locked himself up and refused all invitations. How tough women were, finally!

Indeed she looked quite indestructible in the quiet certainty of her direction. "We've done India several times. All the horrors. And Spain and Central Europe. My children died of cholera. We burned them and moved on. We speak about economic survival and I am a trained economist. But where does it come from, the ethnic puzzle? Even Freud did not know, I found. But the gipsy has resources, he has to; because often one is moving through a land which, if not hostile, does not need our pots and pans, our woven rugs or rush baskets, or our farrier work or the knife grinding. What do you do then to eat? Mario taught me the economic answer." Here she was so overcome with laughter that the tears filled her eyes. "It has been our mainstay in so many places. It is called the 'dog and duck act' in the annals of the American circus, and we even have a faded poster which we hang on the tent where it takes place." "I must see this," said Sutcliffe, and she said, "So you shall this evening. Our stars, our principals, are called Hamlet and Leda, and I sometimes think when I watch them coupling that they represent European culture – the ill-assorted couple, the basic brick of any culture; what sort of child could they make? Why, something like us!" The Prince was filled with an ardour and a compassion which showed that he recognised how remarkable a woman she was. "It is deeply affecting what you say!" he cried, brushing away a tear; and taking her hands he covered them with kisses. "It reminds me so much of Egypt!" he said. "I feel quite all-overish!" And he shuddered with intellectual admiration for this weird gipsy who was now quite at her ease – quietened by the hemp and full of joy to rediscover old friends who might well have been dead after such a long war . . . And she submitted to the Prince's admiration with great dignity of bearing, showing that she was touched and pleased to be understood. Yet how strange the English language sounded to her as it flowed out of her head.

"Hamlet is a small and apparently ageless and immortal fox-terrier, and Leda is a fat old goose, lazy and thoroughly lascivious as all geese are. But she loves being mounted by the dog, she ruffles her feathers with appreciation and honks while he, like a dog or a banker, gives of his best. I realised after the death of my own that they were really our children, our own small contribution to the way things are. How extra-ordinary the world is. Even God is dying of boredom – it's called entropy!"

"Don't say that!" exclaimed Lord Galen – a surprising interjection, coming from him – "Don't say that, please. There will be nothing left to invest in!" And now the church bells in the belfry of the fortress-church burst out in an anguish of clamour, almost as if they were answering Lord Galen's prayer! And Sabine laughed once more and said, "You must go and pay your respects to Sara now because soon the procession will begin and with such crowds you won't be able to move. Then come back here and I will try and arrange for you to be skried, or read or divined – however you like to put it – by someone reliable, perhaps even our Mother, because so many of us are cheats and rogues and bluffers. India too is thick with imposters and thieving swamis, as you well know!"

Sutcliffe murmured under his breath the folk verses they could never remember correctly.

> A slimy swami pinched his cap
> But Mrs Gilchrist gave him clap.

"No, no," said Blanford, "I swear my version is the correct one. I wish we could prove it!" And he recited the lines in another text.

> He swore the fairies gave him clap
> Though Mrs Gilchrist took the rap.

He added: "In this way the British Army made its small contribution to Indian thought. I wanted to write the biography of Mrs Gilchrist who set up the first classy tearoombordel in Benares and imported suburban butterflies from Peckham to staff it. But there was never enough material available."

As he was speaking they were all turning their heads towards the main street where there was a sudden eruption of music and a gush, literally a gush, of white steeds with flowing manes and the Camargue *gardiens* mounted on them, sombrero on head and trident in hand. They were to form the escort for the Saints in their descent to the sea, and they were clad rather formally in the dress uniform of their profession – beautiful whipcord trousers with black piping, and flower-patterned shirts topped with black velvet coats, and short jackboots. It was a uniform which melted down two different influences into a harmonious and aristocratic unity – Spain and the Far West of America. At their appearance the guitars, rather hesitant at first, burst into a fury of passion and the air throbbed with the warmth of castanets and the swing of Andalusian dances, the whirl of skirts, the snapping of coloured paper streamers. There was just time to salute Sara, though after they had done so they wondered at their own courage in facing this dense press of swarthy bodies and literally carving a passage through it.

Sutcliffe was happy to renounce the adventure when he caught a glimpse of the throng hemmed in by the aisles of the little church, whose walls were decorated with every kind of *ex voto* imaginable, depicting shipwreck, accident, fires, earthquakes, acts of violence as well as acts of God; broken heads and limbs, dying children and their parents, overturned boats and horses destroyed by accident . . . a whole hospital of woes which had been either cured or averted by the Saint who was now waiting for them below stairs, clad in her new vestal gown. But how could they get to her? She stood on a trestle table at the far end of a low crypt or cellar where the lack of oxygen made one instantly begin to suffocate, while the brilliant wave of light from hundreds of candles throbbed and pulsed – for they too were eating your oxygen. Yet light one you must, and place it in the iron chandelier as well as deposit a coin in the offertory box hard by the statue. The dull plonking of coins in the wooden box provided an accompaniment to the low haunting chanting and moaning of the crowd, forever retreating and advancing towards the gorgeous black statue of the Saint. She is black, yes, but the cast of her features is completely European, occidental. Beauty and youth and incorruptibility seem united in her lucent and happy gaze. She looks through everything into a beyond of such perfect felicity that one longs to make the journey with her. The gipsies whimpered and sweated and crossed themselves and muttered in an ecstasy of apprehension and requited love. The other two saints were rather a washout – they were just Biblical walk-on parts, but Saint Sara was bursting with superb unction at what she knew. She looked a darling who was simply burning to whisper the secret to someone – if only there were less noise and singing and general rumpus – for a thousand children added to the complications with their chirping and shoving. And the whole of this sweating humanity was pushed down into a little dark sinus of a crypt where breathing was a torment. How did she not melt, one wondered, for Sara was fashioned in black wax.

"Not for me," said Sutcliffe. "I can't face this sort of thing. One hand on your pocket book and the other on your balls ... it's too much." So he elected to go for a walk among the tents while the saints were being carried down to sea on their wooden trestle – part of the traditional service.

The beaches were swarming with families who had settled in for the usual three-day festival, around flourishing camp fires where food was roasting on the spit. Sabine walked with him, pausing from time to time to greet an acquaintance or relation, and say a word to the children at their heels.

"Coming down through the chestnut forests of High Provence we had a wonderful stroke of luck," she said, "for we ran into an absolute colony of hedgehogs: you know that for the gipsy it's the greatest delicacy of all. That's what you are smelling now. Mario is doing three or four for lunch. We dug out an old abandoned clay pit for the event. We gut them and then cover them thickly in wet clay before putting them to roast in a fire built just below ground. Have you ever eaten them?" He had not. "Slightly richer than Chinese puppy but very good in flavour. When the clay is baked and cooling it is knocked off with a hammer or a stone and all the quills and the skin go away with it, leaving the flesh exposed. I know – it must sound horrid!" For he shuddered at the description. "So I won't invite you for lunch today!"

"Sabine!" he said, suddenly stopping to look at her rather pathetically. "Darling, why did you leave me? You knew you loved me." She smiled and put a hand on his arm. "Of course I did," she said, "but you must ask Aubrey that; I could not take you with me, after all. Our lives were split down the middle, no way of joining them that I could see."

They stood for a long time thus, staring at each other while the crowds swirled round them, streaming down to the seashore in the wake of the Saints. Then they turned back against the human tide and in a quieter side street found a dark wine cellar full of barrels of local wine; and here at a dirty table they sat down and ordered a glass to drink. She was still talking with a kind of considered impetuousness, simply for the pleasure of talking English again. She seemed so real it was hard to think of her as purely imaginary. "And the big question is always 'Why?' " she said. "Starting with my sur-prised and half-incredulous father – old Banquo, as they called him in the City. I adopted it also as a form of address and it amused him. But this thing outraged him so, his sense of logic and reason. He knew a lot about gipsies and the relentless persecutions they had had to endure over the centuries. And there was one particularly savage tale which he thought might clinch the matter and dissuade me from the choice I had made. He had heard it first from an attaché of the Austrian Embassy in Sofia – you know he began as a diplomat, my father, and left the service because of the inadequate pay. In his first posting he met this little crippled Austrian – I even remember his name, Egon Von Lupian! They became friends despite the difference in age because both were mad about

orchids and collected them. Von Lupian was a leg short and
wore a wooden one with a spike in it which made – I quote –
a 'characteristic clicking sound' on the marble floors of the
old Chancery. He was a strange number – Aubrey has written
about him elsewhere. But he told my father about his childhood in Austria. He came of an ancient and aristocratic
family, and one of his uncles owned vast estates in the north.
He was a great hunter and often had the boy to stay with him.
He ran a great pack of stag-hounds in the barren marches of
his part of the country; and sometimes they would course
some poor wretch of a tramp who had strayed into their
lands. But the choice quarry was a gipsy, and if possible a
woman with a child at breast! Imagine. He remembers once
his uncle, a big red-faced man with a curling moustache
coming down to breakfast rubbing his hands and saying,
'Today we'll have the perfect hunt! It's all too rare, but it does
happen from time to time!' Gipsies had come to town in the
night and as usual had been arrested. His uncle was the chief
magistrate of the region and thus a law unto himself. On the
morrow at dawn they were to set off. It was only in after years
that he understood and appreciated the details about the hunt.
They had taken the gipsies the night before and among them
they had found what they wanted – a gipsy with a child at
breast! They were going to turn her loose and course her
like a stag!

"The pack was in training always, raised so to speak on
camphor and menstrual blood, for it was not always that there
was a quarry at hand during certain parts of the year. The
woman was taken off at dawn on a cart to a certain cross-
roads some miles from the village where the hunt would
begin. Her person and her clothes were dowsed with this
mixture of camphor dust and bran soaked in human menses.
They had an hour or more to take her out to the chosen point
and drop her for the hounds. Meanwhile in the manor house

all was excitement and anticipation. The little boy, cripple as he was, was taken up by the strong arms of his uncle and perched upon the high saddle from which he could command an excellent panoramic view of everything that took place. So when an hour had passed a signal was given and the horns began their deep braying sound soon to be matched by the bass baying of the great hounds which were almost as tall as the stags they had been raised to hunt. A medley of confused sounds and the whole hunt set off across the frozen marches in pursuit of the solitary cart and its victim, the woman with the suckling child.

"The cart with its two drivers dropped her at the agreed place, a point where three ways met, and with a last burst of malevolence whipped her away from the cart into the unknown. But she was a sturdy girl and hardly whimpered as she set off at a stumbling run into the snow-lit landscapes which surrounded her. There was no mistake now; she could hear the deep baying of the pack as it rolled across the marches towards her. There was no time to be lost. She must try and cross water somehow, somewhere. She ran vaguely in the direction of the river, but her memory was at fault for no river came in sight; and the baying of hounds and the shrill groans of the stag-horns thrilled her blood. She felt as if she were already bleeding to death as she ran – it was time foreshortened bleeding away in her! (I know something about that!) Then on a distant hill the hunt came into view. It made a brave show on that frosty morning, scarlet and black and bronze and gold. But she had seen water – it was not the river but a shallow estuary with several lakelets of brackish water. With luck she might save herself. The little boy shared the thrilling vision of it all with his big-boned uncle riding before him on the Spanish saddle. He saw the gipsy's bid for freedom fail. She managed to reach the water and walked into it almost to her waist, holding the child above her head. But the hounds had seen their quarry and they burst out of the woods and crashed through the thin ice-sheet of the lake in order to drag her down as they did the stags of the region. He heard her screams, and those of the little boy, and then everything was silent and the water of the estuary turned carnation-red as the hounds ate their fill. It was after all their reward for a highly successful hunt. The Master of Hounds and his whippers now drew rein and produced sustaining drinks for the hunters. The little boy was to be affected throughout his life by this scene, and not less by the enormous impression made by it upon the hunters. His uncle remained speechless and out of breath from the sexual orgasm he had experienced after witnessing the hounds at kill. And happy, tremendously elated! His laughter was the laughter of a maniac. As for the boy, he never forgot, and in every capital to which he was posted he commissioned a local artist to paint him an oil, always choosing this scene for subject. He had a whole collection of them at his home in Vienna – a whole gallery of *Gipsy Pursued by Hounds*."

Sutcliffe was quite pale with lust. "You have excited me terribly," he said in a whisper, and she replied, "Yes, I wanted to. We must make love after so long. We must fuck."

"Yes!" he almost shouted. "Yes, please, Sabine!"

She led him by the hand and they went first into a dark passage and then up a long flight of shaky stairs which led to a garret which she had borrowed from the servant. Here on a grubby bed they enacted the fulfilment of a crucial dream, recited the whole vocabulary of lust and disaffection. There was a sob buried in every kiss, as there always is when real couples meet. They pierce the thin membrane of time with every orgasm, they taste despair to the full. The partial joining of the love act was a torment – why could it not be for ever? "It's maddening! I love you irremediably!" she said, counting out his elderly heartbeats kiss by salt kiss.

They lay together later in tears of happiness, playing with each other and caressing each other with their minds. "I never thought it would happen again. I hardly recognised it the first time round! What luck!" And they thought with compassion of their poor creator who sat so stiffly over his wine now, watching the crowd flowing down to the sea, admiring the tears and the fervours and feeling sorry because he could not share them. He saw himself, Aubrey did, as a dead body lying in some furnished room in a foreign city, in a bleak hotel, made famous now because once a poet was allowed to starve to death in it! Paris, Vienna, Rome . . . what did it matter? Via Ignoto, Sharia Bint, Avenue Ignoble! Yes, Sutcliffe was right to reproach him with all the brain-wearying lumber he had taken aboard – all this soul-porridge, all this brain-mash of Hindu soul-fuck. He would change tack, he would reform. He would be possessed by a new gaiety, a new rapture. But where was Sabine?

Where indeed? She was lying in the rickety bed with her arms round her mate, staring over his shoulder at a corner of the ceiling and wondering whether this meeting would ever be repeated. She recited to herself a popular gipsy proverb. "In a lean season the gipsy never forgets that the cemeteries are full of gold teeth!" Why were they not free to forge their own futures? What damnable luck to be simply figments of the capricious human mind!

"Lovers," he said sadly, "are just reality-fools! There is nothing to be done about them!"

"And yet?"

"And yet! How good it is, how real it is!"

They embraced again violently and she said, "If you knew Spanish I would quote you the words Cervantes puts into the gipsy's mouth. It is less rich in English. Do you know them? Listen! 'Having learnt early to suffer, we suffer not at all. The cruellest torment does not make us tremble; and we

QUINX

shrink from no form of death, which we have learned to
scorn . . . Well can we be martyrs but confessors never. We
sing loaded with chains and in the deepest of dungeons. We
are gipsies!' " And turning her magnificent head she made to
spit twice over her right shoulder. A ritual salute. Her lover
was deeply moved. He had sunk into a profound melancholy
at the realisation that in a day or two they would separate
once more, perhaps never to meet.

But time was getting on. A flock of horsemen galloped
down the main street firing off their guns and pistols in the
air, while the deep vibration of guitars was now taken up and
underpinned by the skirling, pining note of mandolins –
Orient answering the Occident, East mingling with West.
"It's time to go!" she said, struggling back into her clothes.
"I must arrange for their fortunes to be told by our tribal
mother if possible. Hurry up and dress now. The party is
over for us, worse luck."

The evening had started to lengthen out its shadows;
they were beginning to feel footsore as they gradually found
their way back to the tavern balcony which was the rallying
point where the remains of their lunch still stood, waiting to
be packed up in the straw hampers. But there was still wine
in abundance to be disposed of, still plenty to eat . . . Therefore
Cade had hesitated to start the process of packing up, for the
party might go on all night. There was at least one person who
hoped it would, and that was Affad's child; he had by now
become quite drunk on the beauty and colour and movement.
Moreover a kindly cowboy, an elderly *gardien* on a white
steed, had adopted him for the afternoon at the behest of
Sylvie, and he had viewed the proceedings from the crupper
of a white Camargue horse, a safe enough vantage point, and
one from which one could really see everything that was
going on. The brilliantly dressed and painted saints, the
ecstasies of the crowd, the fervour and the tremendous pulse

beat of the music made him tremble with pure rapture. Never had he known anything like it. And the two women who from the depths of the crowd could see his rapture in the expression his face wore were almost as happy themselves.

By the time they had regained the balcony, however, it was to find a thoughtful Sutcliffe sitting beside Aubrey over a drink; night was slowly falling. "I have been with Sabine!" he explained. "And she has gone to try and arrange for your fortunes, though she thinks that the old girl will only accept to do three of us because it tires her so much."

As a matter of fact the witch was already drunk, though in her monumental agelessness she showed no signs of it and remained in fair coherence. She inhabited the brilliantly painted and carved caravan of the old style which was set somewhat apart from the fairground on the beach. Inside it candles and joss contended – for the wind had dropped and already the spring mosquitoes of the Camargue had started their onslaught. She was the race-mother of this small troop and everyone, even Sabine, was afraid of her; she could if she wished command the death of someone who had sinned against the ethos of the tribe – by adultery, rape or any other such trespass. Moreover she did not like or trust Sabine, whom she knew to be a woman from the world "out yonder". There was also a touch of fear, for she smelled the weight of her education, her culture. Yet Sabine was so useful that one found no excuse to gainsay her, above all when she came to propose clients who might pay well. "Shalam!" she said, twice bowing her head and pouring out another stiff portion from a bottle marked "Gin". "Shalam, Sabina! What brings you here?"

"I have clients for you. They speak English."

"Then you must stay and translate."

"I will, my mother." So they talked on for a short while; it provided an opportunity for Sabine to perform several little offices for the old lady – such as trimming the candlewicks which were burning unevenly because of the wind, and setting out the dice with which the witch literally played herself into the mood of her client, so she could "read" his preoccupations and divine their portent and shape; and also see how they would mature or fail . . . But Sabine had been right, she would not take more than three for the evening. The others might come tomorrow if they wished. And she must have half an hour alone during which time she prepared her own mind, sharpened her own faculties. A clock struck, and she said it needed winding up, an act which the younger woman performed. She agreed to transmit the message and come back with the first client within half an hour. A grunt of agreement was her only response, so she tiptoed out of the caravan and down the stairs, closing the door softly behind her.

She crossed the twilit sands towards the balcony of rendezvous bearing her message about the limitation on numbers. "Well," said Lord Galen in some dismay, "I suppose we shall have to cast lots or play at Eeni Meeni Mina Mo?" It was as logical a course as any, but they had half an hour to wrangle about it, and the final choice as a result of their deliberations fell upon Sylvie, Galen and the Prince. The others were to possess their souls in patience or submit to the ministrations of less professional seers. They did not lack for these, for as they sat at their wine the crowd threw up half a dozen cozening faces and outstretched hands of women as well as men offering a reading of hands, a guide to the future. One of the younger women was so insistent and so pretty that they adopted her and she settled like a bird of prey over the hands of Aubrey. But the language she spoke was almost unintelligible and it needed Sabine's help to decipher it. "She says you are worried about a building, a structure, something like a house which you wish to make beautiful. But it takes much writing. She is thinking of cheques and contracts – something of that order." Aubrey said, "Has she ever heard of a novel?" But there were other things also somewhat ambiguous. "Now in a little while you will have the woman of your dreams safely in your keeping, free to love you. You will know great happiness, but it will not last very long. Guard it while you have it." The advice seemed sound enough if true! But how often in the dreary routine of fortune telling must the young woman have said the same thing? As for the hand of Cade, she simply turned pale and dropped it like a hot coal. She crossed herself and spat and retreated from him with an expression of alarm. "As if she had been scalded," said Sutcliffe with amusement. "What can the poor fellow have done to frighten her?" It was not possible to find out for the girl melted away into the crowd and was replaced by a man with one eye who seemed every inch a fabricator and whom Sabine refused to encourage. She drove him off with a few sharp phrases of reproach and he left with anger and reluctance.

But with the fall of darkness new styles of celebration came into being – impromptu horse races on the sands, championships of such games as *boules*, Provençal bowling, and archery. With the Saints safely back in their niches among the *ex votos* it was time to turn to more secular amusements, so that while most of the world fell to dinner the little arenas of the village were of a sudden brilliantly floodlit and the gates thrown wide to receive their black Camargue bulls. The rest of the evening was going to be spent in bull-fighting – not the Spanish-style killing fight but the Provençal cockade-snatching ones so suitable to the temper of the place. In this mode the only danger is incurred by the white-clad fighter whose task is to snatch the cockade and skim the barrier out of reach of reprisals – for the little black bulls are fiery and carry long-horned crowns with which to defend their cockades.

Weariness was setting in, however, and it was clearly about time to start thinking of the return journey; but as yet the fortune telling was not at an end. There was nothing for it but to set the table for another repast and to replenish the glasses. This did not come amiss for some of them – notably Sutcliffe who was somewhat weary after his impromptu afternoon honeymoon. Sabine was away helping to translate the divinations of the old gipsy. The little boy had fallen asleep on a bench in a shadowy corner of the balcony, and it was clear that for him at any rate the party was over.

But when the three postulants returned with Sabine it was clear that the results had been far from satisfactory, perhaps because of the massive potations of the old lady. On the other hand both Galen and the Prince looked elated for they had been assured that the treasure they had sought so long and so ardently was a real tangible and concrete one, and not just a historic figment. But the somewhat confusional approach of the old woman had provided several enigmas, for in talking of one of them she made references to others – to Constance, for example – which were easy to decipher. But of course the usual trappings of fortune telling were present – the colourful language and imagery, for instance. Sabine's gloss went as follows: "The treasure is real and a very great one, but it is locked in a mountain and guarded by dragons who are really men. Great dangers attend the search. Nevertheless it will not be abandoned, even though the whole business could turn to tragedy. If you proceed it must be with great caution."

But despite the ambiguity Lord Galen felt a wave of optimistic elation; all the doubts and fears which had been evolving within his mind seemed set at rest. The Prince also felt elated, though of course he was less prone to believe in soothsayers. Sometimes, though . . . The reference to the mountain was tantalising, however. He shook his head doubtfully. But the person most affected by this séance was Sylvie, who returned to them step by slow step as if blasted by the weight of what she had heard. There were tears on her white face and she held her hands before her in a pleading, twisted way, as if it was their infamy which had been revealed. She had been told that her partner, companion, lover would soon leave her – indeed, that she was not any longer loved. And with this she suddenly felt the extent of her dependence upon Constance. It also clarified a lot of small incidents and occurrences – she realised that her lover was trying to find a way of breaking off their relationship, and that she was suffering with guilty feelings because of it. She was thunderstruck when she tried to imagine a world without a Constance at her side. The fearful fragility of her grasp on reality became clear – she saw herself diminishing, becoming a parody of a person, empty of all inward fruitfulness, of love. Swollen with this revelation, she felt she could hardly look her lover in the face. Drawing a shawl over her head like a gipsy in mourning she climbed back into the bus and hid herself right at the back, where soon the little boy found her and fell asleep at her side with his head in her lap. So she sat in a daze and felt the night flowing round her like the waters of a dark lake. The voices, the snarl of mandolins and the crackle of dancing heels in the main square under the portals of the church – they lacked all significance now. They referred to nothing, expressed nothing. There was no flow in things, no element of *time* to enrich the future with promises or desires. It is always at this point, when reality loses all freshness and seems unable to renew itself, that the little hobgoblin of suicide appears. Constance would have been terrified had she known of this reading entirely because of this factor. What price the psychology of the day? How untruthful it seemed, this pickpocket loving! But the one basic truth of the matter was that they must soon break up, separate from each other, rejoin the ranks of the walking dead – those who were out of love! As the others drifted back to their base, and thence slowly began to take their places in the little bus, Sylvie drew her shawl closer and tried to sleep – what a mockery! Sabine seemed somewhat anxious about her and sat for a while with a protective arm about her shoulders before returning to the café for a last chat with Sutcliffe.

For her part she was worried lest the idea of the impending breach might once more undermine Sylvie's fragile grasp upon reality. "I only hope that Constance is aware of the probabilities – but she must be because of her professional training." Indeed Constance was when she heard of the prophecy, and at once her affectionate compassion sent her to the side of the girl to try to palliate the pain of the wound. In vain, for Sylvie simply dropped her hand and said simply, "I understand so many little things which puzzled me these last days. You were trying to tell me that everything was over between us." And her lover sat beside her in a sort of choked despair, stroking the head of the sleeping boy and saying nothing because there was nothing to say. It was clear that out of this new information some momentous new dispositions would have to be taken. There was the danger, in a manner of speaking, for Sylvie had nowhere to go if she decided to leave – unless it were back to Montfavet, which in fact was what later transpired. Constance reproached herself bitterly for her own weakness, but it availed nothing: what was done was done. It remained to try and skry into the future, to the new life which so vaguely beckoned to her from beyond the screen of the present. "No," she said, "we are friends for ever, Sylvie!" And this too, in a strange sort of way was true. "Don't shake your head, darling, it is true."

From the cafe's edge, where a corner of the marquee was drawn back, Blanford watched their expressive faces with pain and helplessness. He could not hear what they said but it was obvious from their expressions that it was not happiness which preoccupied them. How he longed at moments to be alone with Constance! But what could he tell her that she did not already know?

Sutcliffe, to console him and amuse Sabine, said, "When I read somewhere that Chinese peasants stuffed up the anus of their pigs with clay in order to make them weigh more when they came to market I realised in a flash why so many American novelists write to the length they do – they have been end-stopped by relentless publishers. Subject for a doctorate: 'The novelist as many-splendoured pig'." But his bondsman who was still poring upon the distant face of his true muse hardly heeded him. He sat locked into the parsimony of his sexual insight, quoting to himself the lines: "In an inferential realisation of emptiness, an emptiness is cognised conceptually or through the medium of an image. Despite the profound nature of such inferential intuition, *direct realisation* is yet to be attained!" What was one to do? But now Cade was packing up in earnest and the bus driver flashed his lights as a sign of his impending departure. They must return northward and leave the fair to dwindle away in the darkness, under a gibbous moon.

They threaded their slow way across the sands to the main road, fully aware of how many fires still burned in the darkness and how many families lay about, sleeping where they had fallen, so to speak, on a battlefield of black wine at thirteen degrees! Here and there a child still scampered across their headlamps, bent on some midnight manoeuvre. The smoky fires damped down the moonlight into spindrift which lolled and subsided upon the surface of the inland lakes – the *étangs*. But once on the more secure purchase of the macadam-ised main road, their driver turned off his gig-lamps and let the passengers swell slowly into drowsy sleep as he set sail for distant Avignon. As Blanford slept, the whirling confetti of his abandoned notes drifted him silently into a great drowsiness. He wondered what the time was because he did not wish to miss seeing the dawn come up over the river, over the spires.

But if he drowsed his bondsman did not; the events of the day had put him in a resounding good humour, not to mention the snoutful of red wine. "Ha ha, as we used to exclaim in the tropics!" he cried, banging his knee for extra emphasis. This was mysterious – why, for example, *the tropics*? But he would not have liked to be asked to explain the outburst – for him the sheerly inconsequent and the inadvertent were close to the sublime, a kingdom of mad laughter.

"Shut up!" said Aubrey, "and let me get a speck or two of sleep." But the flying confetti with its conspiratorial messages kept teasing him with its gleams of subversive insight. "Tell me, Mr B., how would you describe yourself?" Answer: "As a mortally shy man suffering from delusions of grandeur. I have been impelled to try the path of negative capability – how to cross the river without a bridge across it. I am aware that when a culture cracks up soothsayers and false witnesses abound!" All these midnight conversations with the time-clock! (If the communication between the sexes falters the whole universe, which is imaginary, is put at risk! Of course it is pure impudence to think like this.) Ah! Catspaw of the loving mind, which takes refuge in the Higher Flippancy. To sit in a cave and argue substance away dialectically could help you to shed the skin of your mind – but how laborious a method. Is there no other? Yes, there is always The Leap! The Avignon bridge symbolises it.

The real tragedy is that the whole of the Vedanta becomes mere gossip when she smiles – and nobody is to blame because the whole Universe is indifferent to our prowess!

On they went, swaying through the darkness like a night

express, only more slowly, elbowing their way through the forests and the demesnes of divine Langue d'Oc, while Sutcliffe informed the world at large that "human beings displace a good deal of air – mostly hot air" and that "for the artist to take a vow of chastity which is quintessential for his inmost self is also to invite rape!" The lights from passing villages briefly illumined their forms, showing who slept with arm hunched up against the window of the coach – Cade: or who bowed into the immensity of sorrowing sleep – Constance. Sutcliffe was humming improvisations full of the plenitude of his genius.

> Cloud-forged and water-lulled
> From heavenly cirrus culled
> My heliocentric honey come
> Confide the treasures of thy golden bum
> To one who merits ripest sugar-plum
> Come O come!

Blanford slept and allowed the idolatrous image of his only love gradually to overwhelm his consciousness – what a honeycomb of smiles, what a pincushion of kisses! He recognised this unflinching open-endedness as a way to comprehend a poetic attitude! Its theology was resolution-proof – the religious message not penitential but exuberant. It had its laws, the right kisses always breaking a code, the right approach scoring points in the old-fashioned gymkhana of self-realisation. Like the boom of surf upon the desert lakes, his cloud of notes assailed him with both promises and accusations. "To live in a fearless approximation to nature – to cultivate the consciousness of material intangibility. To create poetically in books written from the hither side of a privileged experience – the posture of awakening. Not phrase-making but direct experience experienced, printed and disseminated. The central truth of the Dharmic brain-flash is linguistically quite incommunicable, it outstrips language, even the most conceptual forms. It is a privileged experience. But by simply exchanging a look you can tell at once whether you share this body-snatcher's love with someone else, and the laughter follows spontaneously. The glance is not such an idle combustion of acquisitive desires but a lock-step in art of the highest reticence. You cannot help hugging yourself once you realise that there is no such thing as a self to hug! And you have all the time in the world – there is no concept of impatience in all nature!"

No escape from the dozing notebook of the brain. He told himself, "You can keep lighting candles to yourself on the great Wedding Cake of the Sages, but one day you will have to cut a slice yourself!"

Sometimes the terror of the pure meaninglessness of things seized him by the hair – for there is no reason for things to be the way they are. Suppose Aristotle to be wrong, to have wallowed in pure presumption, the observer influencing his field of observation, what then? Yet he had a feeling that the notion of emptiness would save him. Yes, to savour to the full the sheer inherence of things, so pure and gentle is it; if you get still enough you can hear the grass growing. You can see landscape in terms of a divine calligraphy! Ah, the mind-numbing ineptness of the rational man with his formulations! Defeated always by the flying multiplicity of the real. "Ordinary life" – *is* there such a thing?

Yes, the observer fouls up everything by trying to impose a plan, an intention, upon nature which can only reproduce the limitations of his understanding, the boundaries of his personal vision. He disturbs the rest of the universe which has no fixed plan, but simply lolls about and goes whichever way things tilt, just as water does. What to do then? Why, play for time just as nature does! Become what you already are! *Realise*! Discontented and vigilant body so much adored, you know too well that death and life coexist.

But as he sank deeper into his loving swoon his irrepressible bondsman took up the tale, despite the gesture of reproach sketched in the air by the Prince who wanted some peace in which to work over in his mind the prophecies they had received at the fair – for as a good Egyptian he believed in the other world of alchemy and divination. "I mean," said Sutcliffe, "how would you like to be just a counter-novelist, existing on relief on charity, or in the imagination of a friend? I wake sometimes with my face bathed in tears. Ontology-prone Judeo-Christians have stolen away my heritage. On the other hand all the gibberings of Paracelsus are coming back to us under a Tibetan imprimatur!"

"Shh!" hissed Lord Galen, wrenched from a troubled sleep by these hoarse formulations which he did not understand. "For goodness sake, let us have a tiny doze!"

"The Scythian proverb says: 'Those who eat wild garlic shall prophesy by farts!' " announced Sutcliffe gravely, though he himself was gradually being overwhelmed by the weight of sleep. To himself he went on in disconnected monologue based on the scattered notes of his maker. "If I had had a harpoon I would have thrown it – how beautiful she was! Rising from bed with the early sunlight she said, 'I must wash my eyebrows or nobody will believe me.' " The universe says nothing precise, it hints. Cade slept smiling – the smile of a dwarf preserved in pickles. Galen dreamed now of symphonic ladies with proud bums and bushes like busbies, doing yoga in groups full of cosmic munificence! A little further on were clusters of Geneva bankers practising the Primal Cry in unison, also Spontaneous Laughter on all fours. In this they were joined by dumboid damsels full of stealth conducted by *prêtres caramélisés* from the *atelier* of the head pastrycook of the town. Yet throughout it all she slept on, *jolie tête de migraine*!

It was to be an evening fecund in new departures for all of them – unexpected swerves in the action. Among them, that of Felix, who was now so rich in the munificence of his new understanding of things and people. Sylvie! He sat in the speeding coach and watched her averted face with a kind of drunken vehemence, realising with an unexpected dismay that he had fallen in love with her – it is not altogether pleasant to feel powerless and bound. He felt suddenly that he had been invented for her express wishes like a bucket for a spade! Yes, but what did she feel? There was no clue to be read in her preoccupied expressions which were all ones of stress, composed around the pain for her ruined passion and its inevitable outcome – separation. What was to become of her? For some time now this realisation had haunted him and filled him with a restlessness which he translated into physical activity. He reforged his relationship with the city which had once meant so much to him, hiring a push-bike and setting off every night after dark to traverse its squares and corners with affectionate nostalgia, recalling all the bitter privations of his consular posting, wondering how he had managed to put up with such loneliness and so many petty humiliations. Sometimes he would wind up after midnight in the little square of Montfavet and press the night bell on the wall of the asylum. The little doctor was an insomniac – he knew this of old – and hardly ever sought his bed before the first gleam of dawn light. He was always delighted by the thought of late company and would hasten to stoke up the old-fashioned olive wood fire. It was he who one day told Felix that Sylvie had sent him a message informing him of her decision to return to her old quarters in Montfavet, if he would agree to welcome her back once more. He spoke with a sorrowful resignation in which there was more than a touch of asperity which signified a criticism of Constance's role in this lamentable business. A professional criticism as between two doctors, for after all she had been in possession of all the facts and in a position to foresee all the contingencies. "It's as unexpected as it is unfair," he said, "and she should be ashamed of herself."

In fact she was, deeply ashamed, but quite powerless to act otherwise, such was the gravitational pull of her lover's charm during the first months. And now?

As for Felix, it had happened very suddenly, when he happened upon a prose poem of hers which Constance had left lying about in his room; he was startled to realise that she was far from insane, she had simply been brushed with the essential and basic illumination which comes to all virgin hearts when one bothers to prepare them. The poetic life declares itself with such force that it often looks like an alienating force which dethrones simple reason. But this isn't madness – except for behaviourists! Reality has several dialects, and the most powerful are sexual ones. The sexual code, if ignited between two people who recognise how momentous an act it is, will automatically be conducted with reserve and great timidity. "Of course," said Sutcliffe approvingly, "because the seed of all meditation is in the orgasm itself!"

But after such a realisation you cannot go on in the old way, grudging away a whole life from pure lack of attention. The sublime anguish evoked by her words had moved him to the depths, and he had "crystallised" her in his heart – that wonderful gloating walk, the whole mesmerism of her beauty. Such a profane beauty as permits almost penitence after pleasure. With each new realisation of it his passion crowded on new sail, as did his anxiety also – for if she did not respond, did not "see" him, what should he do then? Sometimes she looked so distraught that he wondered if she would refuse her jumps, or bucked so that her riders fell off. A fathomless ignorance swallowed him; he realised that you cannot codify the reality of love, for it moves too fast for the eye and mind to follow it. The sweet topic of love only dealt with a parody of the great event. Ah, to become a saint for her sake, to solicit states of calm and interventions of grace on behalf of both! Sutcliffe clicked his tongue disapprovingly and quoted one of the joke *petites annonces* of Blanford: *Druide très performant cherche belle trépannée.* To improvise on the great keyboard of love! But Sutcliffe disapproved once more and cried, "Useless! Like rubbing cold cream into the belly of a dead porcupine." Until death do us nudge into the total reticence; man's function on earth is to allow it to realise itself in him. Ugh! But once you stop caring in the wrong (i.e. awkward) way, everything starts to cooperate and blitheness sets in and the lovers comprehend everything. Felix appeared in her room and wildly, impulsively, said to her as he took her hands, "Sylvie, don't let them send you mad again – let me love you! Your illness is just the growing pains of a solitary cogniser. In Japan they would give a party to celebrate the vision you have experienced! It is the first step by which the yogi gains admittance to his final omniscience! I want to marry you and look after you otherwise you will stop writing out of fear like Rimbaud! Come and live with me."

Yet as she trembled in amazement and hesitated before slowly toppling into his embrace, Constance by the same token was bitterly addressing the mirror image of herself: "You cannot be a doctor and a human being at one and the same time!"

On they travelled through darkness stained with patches of white, the noise of their springs creating around the dozing forms echoes of a secret language – voices repeating obsessive phrases over and over again, like "miniature pigeons", "miniature pigeons" or else "conscientious gypsum" over and over. Blanford listened in his sleep, reminded of older hallucinations. He reminded his other that "when Professor Dobson began to break up he started reacting with dismay to the conversation of French intellectuals, specially men with bushy beards. If any such person cleared his throat and started a sentence with '*C'est évident que la seule chose . . .*' or else '*Je suis tout à fait convaincu que . . .*' he turned pale and faint with distress and if nothing were done he fell slowly to the ground, to lie there helplessly drumming his heels."

"I don't know how you can talk after undertaking this weird prose barbecue, evolving a vexatious prose style based on Rozanov, Hegel's *Aesthetics* and Mallarmé's *Igitur*."

This for some reason irritated Blanford who felt forced into a defence of his methods. "Nonsense. I have been explicit enough to expose my thoughts most clearly. My style may be described as one of jump-cutting as with cinema film. The basic illustration is of course the admission that reincarnation is a fact. The old stable outlines of the dear old linear novel have been sidestepped in favour of soft focus palimpsest which enables the actors to turn into each other, to melt into each other's inner lifespace if they wish. Everything and everyone comes closer and closer together, moving towards the one. The great human models – the Emperors and Empresses – were related by blood ties, were brothers married to sisters. Breath by breath, stitch by stitch, they wove their winding sheet of kisses and prayers. Even before puberty she was there in my bed, the little tantric mouse. Their speech became a rainbow. After them came poets to live in a bewilderment of women. But the book, my book, proved to be a guide to the human heart, whose basic method is to loiter with intent, in the magic phrase of Scotland Yard, until the illumination dawns! The apparent disorder is only superficial and is due to the fact that part of the notes which I scattered out of the train window were notes I had borrowed with permission from Affad – the little sermons he pronounced at Macabru in the desert. Huge bundles of them were stored in the muniments room at Verfeuille. They were full of striking gnostic aphorisms and I copied many into my own notebooks. Hence the overlap.

"By the same token the people also, and even pieces of them, spare parts which are not as yet fully reincarnated. One must advance to the edge of the Provisional, to the very precipice! And when you think of it, you haven't done too badly considering that you are only a figment of my fancy; you could be considered as more than half Toby when it comes to the novel which I almost wrote and then funked because of all these considerations. Somehow you have managed to hold your separateness, your own identity . . . do I mean that? Yes, a book like any other book, but the recipe is unusual, that is all. Listen, the pretension is one of pure phenomenology. The basic tale which I have passed through all this arrangement of lighting is no more esoteric than an old detective story. The distortions and evocations are thrown in to ask a few basic questions like – how real is reality, and if so why so? Has poetry, then, no right to exist?"

Dawn was breaking with its chaste silver points of lake and forest, and their sleep entered a deeper and sweeter register; reality seemed fragile, provisional – a mere breath might blow it out like a candle, so you felt. Indeed, the snoozing Blanford who dwelt among dreams which seemed felicitous abbreviations of truth, told himself that a human being might be described as simply a link between two breaths. Oblong thoughts to drive philosophers like Quine and Frege sane, again! To siphon off love, to hive off desire, that fancy reptile by what Sutcliffe called "low grade mercy-fucking by some inadequate pixie – someone with big elementary toe-nails and salient balls!"

Memory dropping stitches; all night long in his sub-conscious played a sleek and baleful jazz – *esprit de vieux piano-bar! Le baisodrome vétuste de l'âme française!* It is not as Cioran has it *"de bricoler dans l'incurable"*, but rather "*bricoler dans l'incroyable*" once the vision makes itself felt. In the terms of the true alchemy both worldliness and vanity can be seen through and defeated by countermeasures. You need not give in to media clowns or dozing quietists. (I wish you would shut up and let me sleep.) I am six foot of pink convinced English baby and I write prose without thrust. Cade, go bring me my love-bacon, my sex-grog!

But Cade's dark nightmares were of a uniform scheme and content – picture of a huge insect as the World, using primitive factors of intelligence which worked functionally but which were devoid of affectivity, of feeling! Poor fellow, this was troubling; but nevertheless he felt himself to be the servant of this faculty. Rather like someone who finds that he can read minds unerringly. It makes him feel always a little apologetic. To see so far . . .

The World as an armour-plated saurian with an insect mind and belated feathers – the mindlessness condemned by the gnostics, but which ruled the world. The Beast! What could be done to replace such a monster by something a little more human? Apparently nothing whatsoever.

In the case of Constance the situation with Sylvie led to a breach with the little doctor who had loved her so devotedly for more than a decade. He burst out: "What a fearful aberration this has been! How could you give in to such a folly – and drag this mad girl back once more into schizophrenia and quite possibly suicide? Constance! I am angry with you because you know better. You are not Livia with her *partie à trois*! It has been an amazing folly." Constance was on the point of bursting into tears but she resisted the feeling and said, "I *fled* into this parody of passion to defend myself against the realisation of Affad's piteous death – I felt it would drive me insane. I hid like this and played for time until I could muster the courage to confront the hole in the middle of nature which he left me!" He turned his back to hide his emotion and she realised how much she meant to him. "We don't have any luck as far as love is concerned!" she went on with bitterness, "and I was rather counting on your sympathy. It hurts to be reproached."

Nevertheless he was right and she knew it. But in order not to wound her too irremediably he changed the subject of the conversation in the direction of Livia. "You tell me that you are still asking questions about Livia. But did you know that several Germans who might know something about her are still with us? No? Well, Smirgel the double spy is still in Avignon. He was able to demonstrate quite triumphantly that he was working for the British all the time with his own transmitter. But more astonishing still is the existence of Von Esslin, the German general who commanded here. He is almost blind owing to an accident and has been more or less hospitalised in the Nîmes Eye Clinic while he awaits trial on a War Crimes charge of one sort or another. There must be others around but these two are likely to be able to help, and in the case of old Smirgel they were actually associates, were they not? I mean that the two worked together up at the fortress. I have got his address in my day book since he often comes round to read to depressive patients – he enjoys doing that. So you could ring him and make a rendezvous if you wished to ask him questions about Livia . . ."

How extraordinary to realise that these relics from the war were still in existence, and still in Provence! It seemed hardly possible, so far away did the war seem with all its follies. "The General!" she thought. "Perhaps it would be worth it!"

Yes, she would visit him.

FOUR

The General Visited

FOR A SHORT WHILE NOTHING WAS TO COME OF THESE notions, but then with the first few warm days of spring they gradually took shape and turned into promptings fed by her native impatience and the impending changes in their lives – for Blanford had decided that if Sylvie betook herself off to her old quarters in Montfavet he himself might return to Tu Duc at last. Constance seemed to favour the idea at any rate. So she found her thoughts turning in the direction of old Von Esslin who spent his days cooped up in the little Eye Clinic of Nîmes in a state of ambiguous half-imprisonment, waiting upon a War Crimes Tribunal to pronounce on his dossier. He was almost blind and the prognosis for the future was so poor that he had already invested in the traditional white cane, though in fact he could just dimly see things and people, often only as outlines which he filled in from memory. He sat stiffly at a child's desk trying to learn a little elementary French in order to temper his isolation and loneliness. The authorities treated him with respectful civility proper to his exalted rank and this did not surprise him for, as he was to put it to Constance, "They understand the logic of the uniform – what is a crime after all? A soldier's duty comes first and they know it." It was one of those intellectual quibbles which left a bad taste in the mouth, like the scholar's proposition that "The Templars were the bankers of God but not of Christ"!

Things did not move with great urgency, nor were the French anxious to hasten them, for with every new move the full extent of their shameful collaboration with the Germans became more and more clear. As for Von Esslin he felt rather an orphan for he had lost touch with his family and home which was occupied by Russian troops now. What little news that leaked out was anything but reassuring. Later on he would find out that the Russian Army, responding to reports of Nazi atrocities further East, had burned the chateau. His mother and sister had perished, locked in a barn with the servants. The silence emphasised his isolation. The world had closed in and his movements were limited to a walk of a few hundred yards in the romantic public gardens of that austere fief of Protestantism, the city of Nîmes. He tapped his way across them until he found a sunny spot in which to sit, basking in sunlight whenever there was any, like an old lizard. He suffered very much from the winter cold, for the little clinic was inadequately heated.

It was of course a great surprise when Constance burst into his life as she did, without warning, and she supposed that it was the surprise of her perfect German which made him disposed to welcome her. But in fact it went deeper, very much deeper than she herself would ever guess, for through the screens of his fading vision the blonde and beautiful woman seemed to be reincarnating a screen-memory of his blonde sister Constanza – even to the name! "My name is Constance," said Constanza, and a piteous pang of joyful recognition was his first reaction. Of course confusion and disappointment followed it – he had wondered for a wild moment whether by some miraculous military dispensation the real Constanza had not been permitted by the Red Cross to cross the lines and visit him . . . It was cruel, and it took some time to accommodate himself to the truth. It was also in a way exasperating, for this life-inspiring vision had to be continuously edited and re-edited to meet the needs of the present. Moreover the sweet resemblance of voice together with her mannered stylish Prussian turns of speech went far to confirm at first blush that it actually *was*, it might be, it could be, *must* be his sister! Alas! But in their first interview while the girl introduced herself and opened up the subject of it, this thirsty delusion came down over his heart and mind like manna from heaven and it was little wonder that within an hour he was devotedly at her service and fully ready to cooperate with her in her quest for more information about Livia. His age and fragility were touching. They became friends.

What seemed strange at first was the fact that they remembered nothing of each other despite the fact of having spent so long together in the same city during the same critical period. Perhaps twice she had seen him with a column of soldiers crossing the town, face turned away, pale and remote as a cipher – which is what he was. He could not remember having seen her at all, otherwise he must have been struck by the resemblance to his sister. Of Livia he knew only a little and that by accident, for he had spent a weekend in the infirmary of the fortress being nursed for an infected tooth, and this rather taciturn field nurse was on duty that week. But the eminence of his rank had hardly encouraged them to indulge in casual conversation. Nevertheless he had heard some vague gossip about the English girl who had defaulted to join the Nazis and who was working as a staff nurse in the field force. He himself felt that such independence merited admiration and was rather shocked when the security officer who outlined her record spoke of her with pity and contempt. They were suspicious of Livia apparently, and in part it was due to her association with Smirgel who was the senior intelligence officer posted in Avignon and whose acquaintance with her dated from before the war when he had been an art student spending a period of study in the town on a scholarship. He had met Livia one day while working on the restoration of a painting and they had, with some hesitation, become lovers.

"So much I learned, I overheard, so to speak. But I gave the matter no thought as we had so much already on our hands. Nevertheless I often heard doubts about Smirgel's reliability expressed, specially because he had accepted a working brief with the English, but only in order to mislead or betray them – or at any rate this is what he said. It could have been true – why not? But in a war rumour runs wild, and nobody believes anybody else. At any rate the old field reports must exist somewhere unless the French went ahead and had them destroyed to avoid causing themselves much unnecessary soul-searching because of the past. One can understand it. They were more zealous than us all when it came to hunting down the dissenters. In my own view there would have been no real resistance at all after the first few months had we not gone ahead with our slave-labour policy. That is what set up a wave of reaction and got people evading the draft and taking to the hills. Once that started the British started parachuting in and forming an armed resistance among these runaway slaves; and of course the terrain around LaSalle and in the fastnesses of Langue d'Oc favoured such a development."

He shook his head with an expression of regret and went on: "And what complicated matters was the three overlapping intelligence agencies, often with conflicting tales to tell about the same incidents. My own role was purely military though I had access to all. I depended on the field command and had an intelligence group of my own, dealing only with that. Then came the military governor who had his own security service which he shared with the French Milice – which he loathed and distrusted, though he managed to foist most of the dirty jobs on to them. Nor did they mind. They seemed to take pleasure in roughing up their own nationals. That is why they are in such a state now, for so many animosities were created, and the Frenchman harbours grudges, he does not forgive and forget!"

He had been drawing in the gravel with his cane – a sketch of the interlapping agencies; now he tapped once or twice as he added, "You see? While nominally working together we were very much divided internally. Nobody could stand the Milice and the dislike was reciprocated for the Milice had a bad conscience. That is why they have pounced on the documents in the case. As far as I am concerned I am convinced that not a scrap of paper will emerge from it all. The dossiers are too incriminating for them. You mark my words, it will all be destroyed and a new race of war heroes will emerge from the ashes. French propaganda is very astute and they must prove they did something in order to give themselves bargaining power when it comes to the negotiations of the peace table. I think so at any rate! But then they would say I was prejudiced against them."

He sighed and shook his head in a sad, reproachful way. So the conversation ran on in somewhat haphazard fashion: it was so intoxicating to speak his own tongue again that it was almost unmanning for the soldier in him – he felt almost tearful with gratitude. Moreover to speak to this shadow-lambent version of his own beloved Constanza . . . waves of sympathy passed over his old heart like wind flowing over embers he had long thought cold. He even dared to reach out and touch her hand which did not withdraw from the contact but stayed for a calm moment unstirring in his. It fired his thoughts, this warm contact, though he had little enough to recount about Livia. No, it was obvious that she would have to try to trace Smirgel. She told him how some time late in the war – indeed, just before the general retreat – Smirgel had visited her to ask her opinion about a document which he had procured which purported to be an order of the day signed by Churchill himself. It was an optimistic evaluation of the war situation saying that the Germans had begun to stockpile in back areas and must now be considered as having gone over on to the defensive. Smirgel wanted to know whether she thought it a fake or not. Later when she thought over the episode she thought that it had been a clumsy attempt to worm his way into her confidence. But *why*?

The General provided an excited comment of corroboration to this by saying: "Good Lord! Yes! I well recall that English document with its message. It was very striking because it happened to be true. We had already started anticipating a defensive battle or two in the south of France – to consolidate the Mediterranean axis, for Italy had begun to defect and disintegrate. But even more than that I can tell you that when the Allied radio piously announced that no historical or archaeological treasures would be bombed it gave us at once a clue as to what should be done with all this precious stockpile of weaponry which was pouring into France by rail, road and water! We would mask it if possible by placing it in sites to be spared aerial attack. What better, for example, than to hollow out the quarries and caverns which abut the Pont du Gard? It was a God-given site. The kilometres of subterranean corridors and caves were ideal for the purpose. So we directed our sappers to perform and so they did. And the quantity grew and grew."

He had grown visibly rather tired and his exposition had begun to flag somewhat. But he did not wish this delicious exchange to end and he quested about in his mind to find an excuse to bring her back again. "It is time for my medicine soon," he said with regret at last. "But perhaps I will remember other matters of interest later on; would you wish us to meet again for a talk next week?" To his surprised relief she said yes. She found his obvious regret at parting from her touching. "Yes, we should meet again," she said, "just in case we have overlooked some detail or other which might help me. And next week you can pick your day because I am on leave for a few days." He was delighted and shook hands warmly as they parted.

So it was that this initial contact flowered into a series of short agreeable visits to the old man which enabled her to relive and re-experience those sad and barren war years spent in echoing Avignon. Nor were the visits valueless from the point of view of information, for many a small detail about life at that obscure epoch awoke under the stimulus of her company. Apart from this, too, she was able to secure for him certain small concessions and attentions on the part of the clinic, such as a cigarette and wine allowance – he was after all a prisoner of war and should enjoy certain entitlements due to his rank. And while the season advanced towards the more clement end of the spring she tried to assemble and collate these tiny fragments of history for her own satisfaction. At first Jourdain proved somewhat cold and hostile towards her acceptance of Sylvie's leave-taking but later when he sensed the full extent of her regrets he changed back into his former generous self, though when he heard that Blanford had decided to return to Tu Duc he could not repress a jealous pang. He knew nevertheless that Constance had decided that she would herself undertake the extensive physiotherapy which was part of the treatment for the rehabilitation of Blanford's wounded back which had vastly improved under her care. But one of the more surprising new elements which emerged from the General's recollections concerned the vast cache of arms which had been stored in the caverns and corridors of the Roman quarries of Vers and elsewhere. The regiment of sappers charged with the task of storing all this weaponry was Austrian and had ended by openly mutinying and refusing to blow up the train full of ammunition which the Nazi command had planted on the bridge over the river which commanded the town. (Had they obeyed the command they would have irremediably disfigured, indeed completely destroyed, Avignon.) The Austrian refusal saved the town, but the sappers themselves, all twenty of them, had been arrested and unceremoniously shot. The grateful townsfolk had covered their graves with roses when the army at last abandoned the town and started to retreat northward . . . So much was mere history. But the work of the sappers had given rise to strange rumours about discoveries made while they were burrowing their way under the Pont du Gard, clearing out the debris of ancient excavations to make room for their stockpile.

They claimed – at least the two officers commanding the operation – that their men had stumbled upon an oaken door set in the rock in the very heart of the labyrinth – a steel-studded door which when forced opened upon a small nest of caves of a beehive pattern. These were of fine workmanship, the walls carefully rendered to secure the place against damp. These nooks were positively crammed with treasure, all the crates carefully assembled and tidily disposed. Their astonished eyes took in not only gold bars and coin but also a small mountain of precious stones and other specie, while a Latin wall inscription gave them to understand that the hoard was of Templar provenance! Templar! At first there was some confusion and a good deal of scepticism, for the lieutenant in charge of the Austrians was a renowned liar and drunkard. Moreover he intimated that in order to safeguard their find they had carefully mined and booby-trapped the corridors which surrounded the entry to the principal cave with its door set in the rock, and that it would be perilous to attempt to visit the site without a detailed map of the booby-traps, not least because of the fear of setting off the explosive stored all round – the original stockpile which occupied the surround of caverns and corridors! If there was at first some disposition to disbelieve the contentions of the Austrian lieutenant, his story was given substance and force by the fact that he and his fellow-soldier were both able to produce some precious stones which they alleged they had abstracted from one of the great oaken chests, before shutting the place up and wiring up the surrounding caves with defensive explosives.

What irony! So thought Constance when she learned of these developments. "The Templar treasure, though at long last discovered, remains as always obstinately out of reach due to the freakish developments of a new war." She smiled ruefully for she could see in her mind's eye the expressions which would flit like bats across Lord Galen's face – hunger, elation, fear, vexation, if ever she got to tell him the astonishing story, as she supposed she one day must – foiled again! And yet . . . surely there *must* have been a map at some time, if only to enable the Austrian discoverers of the place to gain access to it once more? Somewhere, somebody must have kept a record of the booby-trappings. But all the sappers were dead, executed by the Nazis for the crime of refusing to destroy the city! And who would risk treasure-hunting in this vast stockpile of ammunition? How maddening all these contingencies were! The old soldier was all sympathy for her exasperation; yet when she told him of her excursion to the Saintes Maries and of the gipsy pronouncements upon the treasure – namely, that it was real enough but guarded by dragons – he chuckled and struck his knee with his palm, saying: "One strange thing – the Austrian sappers had been formed from a disbanded regiment of Imperial dragoons and were entitled to wear a dragon on their shoulder-flash in memory of their origins. There you have your so-called 'dragons' if you wish to interpret the prophesy like that!" It was highly plausible to a superstitious mind and she could just see the Prince lapping it up with delight. But of course the principal dilemma remained – namely, what if anything could be done about the treasure hoard? Presumably nothing in default of further information. "I see that you are vexed and disappointed," said old Von Esslin with compassion, for familiarity had done nothing to quell the ardour of his admiration for Constance, "and I quite understand. I will have a further think about the matter and see whether any solution could present itself. But of course it would be madness just to wander about in the *cache* without knowing what one was doing. This group of active mutineers were not joking. They meant business and they knew their jobs."

For a while it seemed that the whole subject had reached a stalemate and that no further advance was to be expected. Then there was a diversion which was provided by the sudden appearance of the doctor, Jourdain, at Tu Duc one middle-morning, riding a bicycle, and bringing news of the reappearance on the scene of Smirgel, the wartime double agent who had so much occupied their thoughts. "He has re-emerged from hiding to provide evidence before a war crimes tribunal about criminal activities during the last days of the occupation. He is in quite a state, as you can imagine, and is trying to save his skin and his name by betraying a number of his erstwhile colleagues! At least so it looks to me. He is an incorrigible fellow, and a liar of the first order. I have a sort of unwilling admiration for him as a specimen. From the medical point of view he astonishes me by remaining just this side of a fine full efflorescent paranoia. I wonder how he does it." Aubrey Blanford, who was listening and playing a hand of solitaire with himself, said, "Perhaps he should be writing novels?" and Jourdain smiled. He went on: "At any rate with a matching effrontery he dropped in on me for a drink and tried to sound me out as a possible witness in his favour – a role I carefully sidestepped, as I don't know what he was up to during the occupation, how should I? But I told him that you, Constance, were trying to locate him, hoping to question him in your private capacity about Livia and her mysterious activities. This seemed to make him startled and a bit distrustful. He seemed somewhat unwilling to be met again – I feared he would disappear – but after I had talked to him for a while he calmed down and listened attentively. I stressed that you would be a valuable ally for him in case of trouble with investigating tribunals and it might be worth his while to humour your request. So suddenly he gave in and said that he would meet you on condition that only you knew of the place of rendezvous. He proposes this afternoon at four – hence my appearance all of a sudden here. I bring a letter with the details."

He extracted the sealed envelope from his pocket and placed it in the hand of Constance saying, "Ouf! I am rather out of breath with all this activity, but I have done my duty. What about treating me to a glass of wine before I take myself off? It would be an act of kindness . . ." They hastened to comply with his request and the three of them sat on for a while on the terrace, in the shade of the apple trees, while Constance with a mixture of curiosity and elation opened her envelope and started to read her message, written in the spidery hand of the evasive Smirgel. It was written in German – so he had not forgotten! "Dear Madam, I understand from our mutual friend, the good doctor Jourdain, that you wish to see me. I would be glad to comply with this wish and ask you to accept a rendezvous which, owing to my present activities and preoccupations, seems suitable, as I am not entirely my own master and am very busy. Therefore I will wait for you between four and five tomorrow at the Montfavet Church which of course you know so well. I will sit in the fifth side chapel. I trust this is acceptable to you. Yours Sincerely." The signature was a squiggle. She replaced the letter in the envelope and thanked Jourdain for his good offices. They had decided in the course of these exchanges to keep him for lunch, and from the kitchen came the agreeable clatter of pans and pots.

So it was that with a westering sunlight she took her little car along the familiar roads towards the city; Jourdain sat beside her for she had persuaded him to double his bicycle into the back of her little car, folding it up as far as possible, so to speak. She dropped him first and then drove back into the shady little square with its quiet tenantry of olive trees and cypresses. She parked it against the wall in the shade and switched off the motor to sit for a moment recalling her last weird meeting with Livia in this pleasant precinct so many years ago. She recalled the precise tone in which she had said the words "I have lost an eye!"; and how she had all the time kept her face turned away from her sister, as if ashamed of the deformity. How had she lost an eye? Ruminating upon these forgotten events she slowly crossed the sunlit-dappled grove and entered the quiet church, now deserted and shadowy, to find herself at last in the side chapel under the oil-painted witnesses, so gauche and awkward. On the wall at her back was a plaque with an inscription commemorating the death of some now forgotten priest.

ICI REPOSE

PLACIDE BRUNO VALAYER

Evêque de Verdun

Mort en Avignon

en 1850

The painting was of a poor style, a poor period. And how wan, abstracted and faraway were the faces of the three presiding over this silent edifice. Yet not entirely silent, for somewhere outside among green leaves and bowers of shade a nightingale stammered out a phrase and then was suddenly silent, as if it had grown abashed. Well, she had arrived a few minutes early, so it was too soon to become anxious about the arrival of Smirgel. She closed her eyes for a moment, the better to dream of the past in this rich corner of silence with its opaque afternoon light – a place for guided loneliness across the breathing silences and the one-pointed plains of deliberate unreason towards the mystical nudge which might set the dreamer off on a new trajectory towards the light! Towards a new objective – to try and make death fully conscious of itself! In the midst of these lucubrations she found herself falling asleep in the pew she sat in, and it was with something of a start that she woke at last to find that Smirgel had succeeded in entering the little church noiselessly and sat in the pew beside her, looking smilingly at her sleeping face. She was a little bit put out of countenance as she tried to muster her questions. "Of course it must be you," she said, to which he replied, "Have I changed so very much, then?" In truth he had. He had become extremely thin and now dressed shabbily enough, while his hair had been cropped rather short – it was fairly grey. But the old deviousness and invincibility of spirit still shone in his eyes; they had narrowed with cunning and he was saying, "I have no idea what I can tell you that you don't know, but I will do my best to meet with your demands. But will you in return help me if I need help one of these days? I suppose that Jourdain told you that I am being called before a war tribunal to answer for so-called criminal activities just before the collapse, our collapse. The truth of the matter is that I was working for the British on the promise that they would take the fact into account after the war. But now on the plea that I was a double agent working for my own side they claim that they owe me nothing for such work! Can you beat it?" He sat back in his pew and shook his head self-commiseratingly. Constance felt it was wise not to allow any strings to be attached to the transaction and said, "I can't make any promises, I am afraid – otherwise we can go no further. I cannot pose conditions myself either. I was just curious to find out something more about my sister Livia and her strange and tragic ending. At that time you seemed to know a good deal about her, but I refrained from asking you anything. It might not have been felt suitable while war conditions were such as they were. But now that things are changing back to peacetime conditions I thought I might try once more. Do you see?"

"Ah! Livia!" he said, sighing deeply. "Who will ever find out the truth about Livia?" Was it an illusion or did he swallow a lump of chagrin as he spoke? It was as if the thought of Livia came suddenly upon him, without warning, to drown him in the toils of an unrequited desire and memory. She found herself watching him curiously to study the sorrowful lines which these thoughts hatched upon that deceitful countenance. He was thinking deeply, painfully – perhaps re-creating her image with its wounded eye. He said gruffly, "Of course it is useless to tell you how much one could care for such a girl – you know that only too well! But in my case memory goes back beyond the war to when I first met her. We were both much much younger, and I did not know you or your family or your home. I was a German student of archaeology, specialised in the restoration of historic objects – paintings, pottery, glass and so on. The Society had sent me to Avignon to help restore its most famous painting. I was young and ardent, a keen National Socialist as we all were then. To my surprise so was she. You cannot realise what it meant to have someone English approving of one's political direction – it filled one with relief and happiness. Moreover a girl, a beautiful one. I could not help but love such a person. I became a slave to Livia. We met every day before the great painting. She held my brushes and paints for me. Her patience was exemplary. But sometimes she disappeared from view for several days, though she would never say where she had been. For a while after we became lovers I was wildly happy and then a kind of doubt began to seep in. It was as if inside herself, deep down, she enjoyed a profound reserve which prevented her from really giving herself in love. It was as if in her heart she were listening to faraway music or voices; they gave her a kind of dreamy detachment, of abstraction which left her lover baffled and somehow unsatisfied despite the passion they exchanged. I felt cheated and sometimes proposed to break off the affair, but she pleaded with me not to – pleaded with intensity and force that convinced me to stay on as her humble servant. I realised that I loved the girl, but that she did not love me in the same way, or in the same degree. I wondered why. Then, during one of her disappearances, I had a chance to see some new sides to her character, for one of the gipsies came to me and said that I should go to her as she had fallen ill – from smoking *quat*, he said. He led me to a corner of the town near 'les Balances': and there, on the third floor of a dilapidated house which was most likely a bordello, I found Livia, deadly sick in bed, just as the gipsy had indicated. The reasons were evident also. I was alarmed and debated whether to call a doctor or not. But at last I decided to get her home first, to my lodgings which were respectable enough, before calling in a doctor."

He paused to light a cigarette and she was intrigued to see how much his fingers trembled as he did so; by contrast the tone of his recital was dry, monotonous and without emphasis. But the expression on his face remained withdrawn, almost deceitful in its deliberate expressionlessness. After a brief hesitation – as if he was not quite sure in which order he should present the facts of his story – he went on with a trifle more animation. "The gipsy had a two-wheeler, a barrow on which he exposed his wares for sale, mostly old clothes. I persuaded him to help me place the sleeping form of Livia on it and cover it with clothes and blankets. At break of day nobody noticed us wheeling her through the silent streets to my own lodgings where we managed to get her up to my rooms and into the comfortable bed, while I talked the land-lady into sanctioning the new visitor who had, as I told her,

fallen ill of a stomach ailment due to the highly spiced food:
a common enough event. I had built up a reputation for
seriousness and studious application to my books, so everything was all right. The young doctor whom the landlady
summoned was also discreet and pleasant and I was able to
confide fully in him, which was a relief. So Livia hovered for
a week or so between sleep and waking while we fed and
protected her. But for long periods during this time she lived
in a state of hallucination, she had visions; this is how I made
some new discoveries, unpleasant ones, about her past.
Because of her state of mind she was off her guard and confided in me things which perhaps in her ordinary state she
would not have wanted known. That is how I discovered
about Hilary, her brother . . ."

He jumped to his feet now in some agitation for he had
also discovered that it was somewhat inappropriate to smoke
cigarettes in the chapel and he walked to the portal in order to
throw the stub of his cigarette outside. "Hilary!" she echoed
in some confusion, standing up herself in order to let him
pass her. "What has Hilary got to do with all this?" He
looked at her keenly under depressed eyebrows as if her
surprise astonished him – as if she should have been quite
au courant with what he was about to reveal. Having despatched
his cigarette stub he turned and returned to her side, motioning her to sit down once more. It was as if he said, "Pray sit
down, because I have a lot more to reveal to you." And
obediently she sat down again under the oil-painting, but
feeling now a sort of anxiety take possession of her. And
Hilary, so long absent from her thoughts, now suddenly
became a figure of significance and colour. He had been killed
on active service with the Intelligence Corps; she had heard
vaguely that he had been parachuted into France to help the
Resistance, and captured by the Germans. That was all.

"Hilary, my brother," she said quietly, "was in the

process of taking Holy Orders when the war broke out. He felt sufficiently strongly about it to adopt a pacifist stance, and retire to his Scottish monastery, breaking off all contact with the rest of us – the order he joined was a silent order, so this was understandable. He kept this up for some years until gradually his intellectual posture changed, became modified. He joined the Intelligence Corps and offered to serve abroad with the Resistance; he was actually sent to France, but captured by the enemy and executed. *Voilà!* That is all I know. As a matter of fact I didn't ask for more details – once he was dead, what did further details matter?"

"I hope what I am about to tell you won't be unwelcome or shocking, but I wish to explain why I hated Hilary so profoundly. It was because of Liv. I don't suppose that it was the first time in history that a brother seduced his sister sexually – but unhappily it affected me. I realised from what she revealed to me that in fact Hilary was responsible for shaking her affective stability with this unlucky passion which neither could renounce. To do him justice he often lamented their fate, often tried to unshackle himself from his sister, make a desultory move or two in the direction of freedom, or of other women. But in vain. I realised now that he was really the author of my misfortune, that Liv would never come right, be cured, so long as the magnet of Hilary's presence existed somewhere in the world. All other relations were worthless to her while her brother lived and breathed. It was terrible, but the realisation of this fact poisoned my waking life. I was filled with vengeful thoughts, and indeed at long last, and quite by chance, fate made it possible to execute them."

She must have looked astonished or perhaps even dismayed, for he broke off suddenly and gazed anxiously at her as he said, "May I go on, please? I do not wish to shock or hurt you but I feel the need to explain many of my actions in the light of this overriding passion of Liv's; if possible, to excuse my own actions."

"Of course," she said, a prey now to old memories which welled up in her mind. They took on another light in view of these facts – new shafts of light struck them and forced her to re-evaluate them! "Of course," she said, "by all means let us have the truth, since we have all suffered so much from it."

He cleared his throat and resumed his painful narrative – it obviously cost him something after all to reveal these things.

"As for me, I followed much the same sort of trajectory in my own thinking – it took a few years but at long last I too grew disillusioned with the Nazis and ashamed of my own passivity in the face of Nazi doctrines and Nazi acts. I began to search for ways and means to escape the collapse I could see coming to meet us. I thought I might perhaps offer my services to the British. But how to make contact with them? One had to take a risk. I wrote a frank letter to the BBC which I entrusted – it was extremely foolhardy – to someone with a neutral passport who was going to Africa. Then I waited in a state of great anxiety in case the letter had been found, had been confiscated . . . But then one day I received a communication from a post office box in Avignon which gradually materialised, so to speak, into the person of a young French woman who ran a group of patriot agents and through whom I managed to inherit a transmitter and a code with a wavelength call-number which put me in direct touch with London, which is what I wanted. Of course it took me a little while to establish my *bona fides* but at last I did – it will seem ironic to you, but while neither side fully believed in my honesty both were exultant at having penetrated the enemy intelligence service. This was due to the selection of information titbits which I revealed, first to one side and then to the other.

Paradoxically both were soon content to accept my double agency, knowing that I could also pass false information to mislead the enemy! Indeed I was already operating a successful double option when I came to see you with that rather puzzling text which you may or may not remember. It was quite genuine, I discovered later. Secretly I was hoping that we might strike a chord of sympathy and make a sincere contact which would enable us to talk, but you proved too suspicious to offer me any encouragement and I felt unable to confide anything in you for the time, though of course the whole situation as well as the tragic dénouement weighed very heavily on me – as you may well imagine."

For a while now he fell silent and looked full of self-reproach, fingering his chin as if debating within himself whether to go on or not. He had turned quite pale as well. He shook his head doggedly and suddenly blurted out, "It isn't easy to say, but I mustn't disguise from you that fact that I am responsible for your brother Hilary's death – and in a secondary way for Livia's also." He hung his narrow head – it was as if the full weight of what he had said were now suddenly made manifest to him: as if he had difficulty in assimilating its significance. He stared at her with the face of a sick vulture and lapsed into silence, weighed down it would seem by an immense depression and sadness.

Surprise bereft her of speech, deprived her of any capacity to react appropriately to this surprising and shocking piece of information; and with the surprise came a twinge of doubt as to its veracity. With Smirgel one was always being overshadowed by the angel of doubt. One was condemned to wonder what hidden motives might lie hidden behind the words he uttered. If all this were a tissue of falsehood, for example, why tell her, Constance, about it: why reopen the subject which was obviously as painful to him as to her? Nevertheless, "Go on!" she said, as if admonishing him for his lack of courage to continue. This soon resulted in him rising to his feet and starting to pace up and down the narrow causeway between the pews of the little chapel with his hands behind his back, gathering together the threads of his slow narrative.

"As you will imagine, much of my work was concerned with the Resistance which had slowly started to become a reality, a possibility, owing to the insane slave-labour policy of the Reich which drove the young people to take refuge in the hills to escape conscription in the slave battalions. Soon almost every hideout in the Cévennes was full of shirkers. They had nothing to eat, of course, and arms drops alternated with food drops as they were slowly transformed into military formations. A few I actually betrayed to my own people in order to keep my reputation for truth, but the most not. The heavily wooded country round LaSalle and Durfort were the obvious places for such activities – the real mountains begin around there – and despite frequent military sweeps by our troops and the Vichy police it was seldom that the guerillas were surprised. But of course the whole question was eagerly debated by both London and Marseilles, and all the time people were coming through to evaluate the importance of such movements. Agents were parachuted into the Cévennes in gradually increasingly doses. Of course I kept a sharp eye on all this activity, and by now London trusted me implicitly with a good deal of secret information which sometimes I revealed to my own people for obvious reasons. Then one day I got some queries from London which made me prick up my ears. They had got wind of the fact that Livia was serving in the Army unit which was doing garrison duty in Avignon. Don't ask me how. But someone was trying to make contact. London said that it was 'someone close to her'. I did not at first think that it might be her brother, for he had disappeared so definitively from the scene that I wasn't prepared for his reappearance as a commando who might be dropped from the air in the LaSalle region, in order to organise Resistance groups which might later make an allied landing from the air a feasibility. As for me, only my hate for him surged up when I found that it was indeed he. Hate! Pure hate!

"It is not the most desirable or elegant of sentiments. I was surprised myself at its force, for I operated in a sort of blind dream-like automatism which seemed to absolve me of any direct moral responsibility. None of what actually came about was circumstantially planned in detail – or at least not by me. Circumstances fell out as they did, as if willed by destiny or fate or whatever. For example, even after I knew that it was Hilary and that he was going to be dropped in the hope of contacting his sister I did not say anything to Liv, though it would have been wise to see what her reaction might be. Would she, for example, have been capable of refusing these overtures on behalf of her brother – indeed, her lover? And then, what did Hilary really hope to gain in making contact? It was hard to see what London was really expecting of the operation. But for my part I was quite filled with exultation to think that I might lay my hands so easily upon the author of all my misfortunes, and that it was in my power to have him done away with the utmost ease, simply by betraying him to the Milice or having the Army arrest him and sentence him. But first we must secure his person. I selected a landing ground with the greatest care, high up in the forests of the Cévennes, and again there was something dreamlike about the ease with which the whole operation took place. He himself was not suspecting anything untoward, and he had received a message through me that his sister would make herself available for a talk. Of course we did not recognise each other after such a long lapse of time – indeed, there really was no reason why we should. We had perhaps seen each other once or twice but we had never actually met in the conventional sense. Indeed I would not now have been quite certain of his identity had I not known from London who it was. It was pitifully simple, his capture and transfer to a jeep to take him to Avignon, and of course by now he knew that he was a prisoner of war, that the plot had failed. I had involved both the Army and the French Milice in the operation so that in a sense he was everybody's prisoner, and this was the start of my troubles because I progressively lost control over him myself – he was locked up for interrogation in the fortress of Avignon where a number of agencies started to interest themselves in his identity and his fate. The fact that he had lived in Provence before the war and knew the place and the language was intriguing for the Milice and they started claiming him as a common-law prisoner – he had not been in uniform when captured. Of course either way it could spell death – both agencies could invoke a firing squad once they had finished their interrogation . . . which was all I really cared about. Unhappily with this turn of events Liv came into view.

"Of course you know that there had always been something equivocal about Livia's life and the way she chose to live it, and there were people who found everything about her somewhat suspect, including her political and philosophic views. In time of war, too, it is the fashion of intelligence agencies to suspect everyone of possible treachery. So that not everyone was friendly to Liv. And the more people knew about her past, and about the family relationship with pre-war Provence, the more intriguing they found her. And now her brother had flown in direct from England with the professed intention of locating her. Well, all these brainless but suspicious creatures who collect around intelligence agencies like a sort of intestinal flora – they began to ask questions, and so indeed did I. The trouble of course was that whatever they found incriminated Livia, a development for which I had not really been prepared. When I told her about the arrival and capture of her brother she went as white as a sheet and sat down, almost fell down, into a chair, possessed by a total amazement. And then of course came the realisation that a sentence of death would be practically a certainty for him. Can we do nothing to save him, she asked me ironically enough, and I did not know what to say in reply, for it was far from my intention to save him. But her emotion was so intense that I hesitated, while she now said that she must see him, she must have an interview with him. He had already been tortured by the unimaginative Milice interrogator and plied with a great number of routine questions worthy of a fifth-rate medieval inquisitor, to none of which did he give anything but evasive answers. It was not a very rich dossier as intelligence went. But I now persuaded them that there might be richer material to be found if one organised an interview between brother and sister of which a recording could be made if we placed microphones in the place of rendezvous. They found this reasonable enough, and as a matter of fact the spot I chose for the encounter was right here in this pew, where we are sitting! Yes, I know, it is rather queer to choose the same place again, but I somehow felt it appropriate to our story – or at least to mine, for I often come here and sit here alone in order to think about her. I regret so much – and yet our misfortunes do not seem to be the outcome of our acts but just due to fate, to destiny! The meetings duly came about, right here where we are sitting, and the whole thing was duly recorded by a powerful microphone which I had installed carefully to transcribe it all on to wax rolls, to which you may listen if you are so minded. There is hardly anything about espionage on them – it is all about their extraordinary, unholy love. It makes my blood curdle as well, for it explained why our own love miscarried . . .”

He had by now turned quite pale and strained and his recital had a tendency to flag as his story neared its crisis. He came and slumped down beside her in the pew and let his head fall into his hands. He closed his eyes and went on in a lower key. "Of course you may not want to hear it, it may seem too painful. But I was hoping to win your sympathy and confidence by offering the text to you; and, by the way, there is one passage which refers to you in it. It is where Livia says to him: 'You only settled for me because Constance was not available – she was in love with Aubrey: but it was she you really loved, really wanted!' Inextricable the strands of motive which make up the repertoire of a single human heart." (This was Constance's thought, and also: one can become morally responsible for things, situations, desires, of which one is ignorant.)

"Go on," she said in her dry tone of utter amazement, for the whole of this recital had shaken her to the depths. If asked to invent an answer to her questionings she would not have been able to devise anything as baroque as the truth. Hilary and Livia! And then, to cap it, the image of herself as figuring in this history, as accumulating Dharmic guilt for situations she was not even aware of . . . He had started talking again in his halting fashion: "Do you want to hear more, then? It is not a very happy story. Hilary had now become the prisoner not of the Gestapo but of the French Milice whose newly appointed head was a fervently anti-British expoliceman, avid for advancement. For him even a death sentence hardly satisfied his bloodthirstiness. It hardly satisfied his hate which was nourished on sentiments of secret shame and cowardliness. People who are cowardly enough to cut off women's hair are toneless souls and would cut off anything. That is why we Germans loathed the French so. This bleak and dreadful little man proposed to use the brand-new guillotine which Vichy had sent him to make an example of

Hilary! I wanted this, of course, but I had not worked out in detail just how I would like it; nor had I taken Livia into consideration! I tried to delay the judgement but there was a limit to what I could do, and besides I had lost control of my prisoner now – the French tried and condemned him to death. Meanwhile Livia herself had been picked up and imprisoned for further questioning. The French had been quite intrigued by parts of the interview which seemed to them to promise useful information – rubbish, of course! But meanwhile Livia found herself in the fortress in the next cell to her brother. From the priest who was sent to console them she now learned that Hilary was due to be guillotined on the morning of the next day but one. There was no hope for him as he had been judged by secret tribunal – at that time the police was a law unto itself, and many a private grudge was paid off in this way. There was worse to follow, for in order to punish her also for her resentful and non-cooperative attitude under questioning, it was decreed that she should be forced to witness Hilary's execution in the prison yard where this dreadful toy had been set up at last. The other day I found the day-book of the Milice with the most detailed instructions about the uses of the instrument. Vichy's special tribunals of 14 August 1941 had a military figure as a president and special laws – death sentences for all proven Communists and Anarchists. The first to die was the town tart, a gipsy called Guitte. I remember a few laconic phrases from this record: *M. Défaut, l'exécuteur des hautes oeuvres, a commencé son travail à l'aube, à echancrer la chemise autour du cou, entraver les pieds avec une ficelle et d'attacher les mains derrière le dos* . . . all in great detail. Hilary is there listed simply as *espion anglais*. The guillotine is referred to as *les bois de justice*, or as stags' antlers. Beside it were placed *deux grands corbeilles en osier* by the executioner whose assistant pinioned Livia's arms and dragged her to the site. He was called Voreppe and later he committed suicide because, his wife said, he could not stand the *bruit sourd* of the falling blade which he always seemed to hear in his memory. Hilary struggled and choked, and so did she; there was quite a fight before they managed to force his head into the half moon of steel and release the heavy blade. It was now that she inflicted the wound which cost her her sight, plucking a dirk from the belt of one of the guards. She intended to do away with herself but was forcibly prevented and carried back to the garrison infirmary where she was drugged and put back to bed. It was over!"

He gave a gross sob and fell silent; and so was Constance now, silent for what seemed an eternity during which in her imagination she relived this awful scene, ran it through repeatedly like a cinema film until she felt sick and apprehensive for her reason almost . . . But what could she say? It was she who had sought for answers to certain questions – and here they were, totally unexpected answers! Moreover answers which apparently cost him great pain to formulate and express. She looked at him with curiosity, wondering what the motivation might be of such a performance. Then she said, "What are you expecting of me? I am curious to know."

He sighed profoundly and for a moment seemed at a loss for words. They stared at each other – there were still tears in his eyes as well as hers. "I want," he said, "to meet Lord Galen if possible. I have something important to say to him – something which may make me useful, nay indispensable to him. I know that you know him and that he is somewhere in the region at this moment. Isn't that so?" She watched him with some curiosity as he wound and unwound his fingers, for his pallor was quitting him and this new departure brought a flush to his cheek. "Yes, but why exactly?" she said out of pure perverseness. "I feel you must tell me a good deal more before I trouble old Galen on your behalf!" He made an impatient gesture with his head and said, "Very well, then

I see I shall have to tell you the whole story. I was afraid of
boring you, for it does not concern you in any way. But it
could concern him, and I might secure his good offices in the
question of my trial for enemy activities – it is coming up in
Avignon in some months, and I need sponsors of his calibre.
It would not be at all compromising for him to intervene and
help me because after all I have quite a solid case in my own
favour. After all, I *did* work for the British as they will certainly
testify. But just to make the whole thing 100 per cent secure
I would like to offer Lord Galen something unique, something
that he has been looking for for years – the Templar treasure!
To go back a little way in history, one of the most helpful
collaborators was Dr Jourdain – it's from him that I know all
that I do about you all. And at some period in the war he had
to hospitalise and sedate a young French clerk called Quatre-
frages who had been working for the Galen consortium on the
whole Templar problem. It was from him – often it was from
his ravings because sometimes he wasn't all there – that I
found out how much work and thought had already gone
into the project upon which he hoped to found a whole
fortune – I suppose a second or third! Of course this interested
me very much. When Quatrefages was discharged I kept in
touch with him, and by mildly threatening him with the displeasure of the Gestapo I obtained all the historical and topo-
graphical material he had accumulated on behalf of Lord
Galen and the Egyptian prince who shares this interest. In the
meantime a new and different line of inquiry developed from
the discovery that the Roman workings of the abandoned
mines near the Pont du Gard could be transformed into
ammunition caches for all the stuff which was pouring down
upon us in the Rhône valley and which we must stack up in
some safe place against the day when the big battles for the
south of France became a reality, as the German Command
thought – and with good reason! But the sappers in charge

of the operation were Austrians with a bad record for mutinies and desertions and they went about their work with sabotage in mind. So it was that as fast as they cleaned out the corridors and stacked the incoming ammunition they mined the whole place very thoroughly and in such a way that from a relatively small central explosion they could cause a chain of secondary ones which might blow everything into the air – even the Pont du Gard itself! They wired the whole place up so scrupulously that the five master-keys or detonators could be set in place in a matter of minutes. It was at this time that they stumbled upon the door in the rock which opened into a hollowed-out group of five contiguous caves with cemented walls and stone masonry of high finish. From here they started coming out with precious stones which of course were difficult to sell except to the gipsies, and that is how I got wind of the find, from a gipsy who was 'helping' me with my inquiries into other matters. That is how I got into touch with the sapper Schultz, the drunken sergeant of the troop who together with one other-rank claimed to have made the find and who had locked up the cave, intending to keep this booty for himself. But meanwhile the general situation had deteriorated greatly and we were preparing for a wholesale evacuation. At this point the story of the ammunition train took over. As a parting act of revengeful vindictiveness the General commanding the retreat decided to inflict a mortal blow upon the city. He planted a train full of munitions on the railway bridge and commanded the unit of sappers to boobytrap it as thoroughly as possible so that when the troops had reached a fair distance from the town a skeleton rearguard could set alight to it and cause an explosion of unpredictable violence. Yes, there is no doubt, Avignon would have become a hole in the ground! And at this point the drunkard Schultz who had never performed a coherent act of magnanimity in his whole life, ordered his men to mutiny and refuse! They started to try and barricade themselves into the tunnels but the garrison was ordered out and with a couple of tanks they dislodged them and took the whole lot prisoner. The outcome was not far to seek. They were lined up against the wall in the public cemetery and executed for treachery. Later the townsfolk covered their mass grave with roses to show their gratitude. But while people were found to dig the grave the bodies lay along the wall for nearly a week and I gave myself the disagreeable task of picking them over at night with the aid of lanterns, in search of a map which I knew must exist, a map of the caves with all their secreted ammunition. Otherwise how dare to enter them and search for the treasure? Schultz was the last to die – he was forced to watch all the other executions. The map was on him!

"It took me a little while to work out the code he employed – parts of the glossary are in a kind of electrical shorthand. But I finished by comprehending it, and also the elaborate system of lighting which enables one to light up the whole place; also the grotto which houses the entry and exit system and the keys. There were some obscurities but thanks to what I had learned from my long dialogue with Quatrefages I knew a few things about the quincunx shape of the caves. In architecture the quincunxial shape was considered a sort of housing for the divine power – a battery, if you like, which gathered into itself the divinity as it tried to pour earthward, to earth itself – just like an electrical current does. This magical current was supposed to create an electrical 'field' around the treasure and protect it from being discovered until its emanations were fully mastered and could be used in the alchemical sense to nourish a sort of world bank which might enable man to come to terms with matter – his earthly inheritance, so to speak. It sounds utter rubbish, I know, and I am not personally very much concerned with that aspect of the business. I share Lord Galen's simpler and more practical view of things. I think that riches offer the only tangible safety for a man who has clearly seen how dangerous and horrible his fellow man is. There is no other way of protecting oneself against him except by amassing money and creating a protective power-field of money – that is my view. Well, I wish to try to interest the consortium he represents in my scheme. I am the only living person who can offer safe access to the treasure which otherwise would be out of reach of everyone because of the sheer hazards of the boobytrapping. There is no means at present of evaluating how much is at stake, but the sum must clearly be tremendous, and of course we must keep the secret if we can. I have even gone so far as to secure an official licence to reactivate this abandoned Roman mine with all its workings (fortunately the whole area still belongs to a single family which is delighted to accept a handsome sum for the licence) so that we could place the whole sector out of bounds to the general public while we went to work on the quincunx of little cells . . . You see why I must meet Lord Galen and put this whole matter to him? Of course I shall want equal membership in the consortium, an equal share of the spoils. Goodness me, can't you see the possibilities of such a thing?"

They stared at each other in silence for an eternity. "Yes, I see," she said at last. "I will tell him."

He burst out laughing with delight. So they fell to discussing the details.

FIVE

The Falling Leaves, Inklings

THE GIPSIES KNEW OF THE TEMPLAR TREASURE, EVEN to its location! The knowledge came from Egypt – landscapes of cork oaks ravaged by yellow ants. Honeysuckle grown clear into trees as if it had had a mad desire to perfume the sky. Desert cobras conferring king-hood, smiles like a breath over embers. Tawny dunes, rock doves, hoopoes. The Bedouin shared their love of gold ornaments, the spoil of rifled tombs, sold to the Templars! Lapis lazuli, amethyst, alabaster, tiger's eye, turquoise from the workings in Sinai, mummia!

Notes scattered to the winds of old Provence. Reality is what is completely contemporaneous to itself: we are not completely in it while we still breathe but we yearn to be – hence poetry!

Sutcliffe *loquitur*. A little tipsy? Yes.

Good writing should pullulate with ambiguities.

Whose dead body buzzing with flies?
The dimensions are four but the aggregates five;
Open-ended reality coming alive!

Questions concerning the individual's rights in the matter of buried treasure occupied the waking thoughts of Lord Galen for many weeks, months, now! He found the ideal man to cope with this ticklish matter – a dark, hook-nosed man – nostrils flared: a lawyer who smells the perfume of litigation. He was a Jew from tragic Avignon who had somehow escaped the searches. A Jew is only a Brahmin with a foreskin. Snip. Snip. Snip.

> In age of clones and quarks
> Bless our radioactive larks
> Quinx in her religious quest
> Will one day tower up o'er the rest
> A star-y-pointed pyramid
> To point to where the Grail lies hid
> Within the poet's begging bowl
> Last metaphor for the human soul!

Once poems were nuggets of inner time but we have become experts in not listening – experts in not growing up.

Sitting on his balcony in the Camargue Blanford thought: "The past has just finished becoming the present and here I am. I am still here un-dead. But the desert has covered the breathing and the night has covered the best. Everything (look around you) is as natural as it can be. All nature consents to the code of five. (Five wives of Gampopa, five ascetics in the Deer Park, five skandas.)"

Proust, so attentive to history as Time, as chronology, as reminiscence, never seems to ask at what point the limpid noise of the water-clock or the gravity of the sun-dial's long nose was replaced by clock-time marked by a machine; surely this must have registered the birth of a new type of consciousness? His immortal tick has become our tock.

Blanford sealed up in a poem like a virgin's womb.
"Subsiding from zenith like an old sand-castle,
The sea-lick washing me away balcony by balcony,
By keep and drawbridge, tower, bastion, ravelin and ramp,

By mote and sannery, and so back to dune soon
And then forever dune prime, and then sand, sand, sand,
The endless and uncountable sand."

"Eh, Sutcliffe?
"Can't you understand?

"I am blind sometimes, like old Tiresias,
My eyes are housed in my breasts
This interloping insight is all I have, outwardly
But inwardly whole new kingdoms are there,
Whole new kings and queens unborn,
But alas my eyeballs were scorched out by sea and sand.
Salt-burned, turned inwards upon the Shades,
While someone I may not name or love
Leads me about like a dog."

Her heart and mine have begun a whole dialogue of
sensation; is it possible after such a long time she is going to
acquiesce and love me? Our hearts are like kites with entangled
strings. (Blanford on Constance.)

Miss Bliss who taught him the piano long ago had a very
classy Kensington accent which when she had a head cold
transformed things – singing "The Berry Berry Bonth of
Bay", for example, or reading from *The Furry Tails of Grimm*
or *The Arabian Nates*. The Prince revered her memory. He
often thought of her and smiled puckishly. Lord Galen told
him about one of his business partners. "Someone told him
he looked Jewish when he was asleep, so with great astuteness
he stayed awake all through the occupation!"

Capstone of the sky, blue Vega the darkness
Like an unharnessed cat – blue star,
The vane and lode of sailors once was fixed,

Who now aim at Polaris, their masts
Vast in erection, riding the simple sea.

"Aubrey, you will soon be beginning your novel. At last! And I shall be leaving you after all this time together, body and soul plus soul and body. It's been great knowing you, and I hope the book works as a metaphor for the human condition, though that sounds pretentious. Only remember that those two seducers the striking metaphor and the apt adjective can turn out to be the poet's worst enemies if they are not held in check."

Tiresias, the old man wearing tits for eyes,
Deep in his vegetative slumber lies.

Her voice lives on in memory
A bruised gong spoke for Livia
Lessivé par son sperme was she.

In the Hotel Roncery the slip hatch
Into Grévin with its wax models
Showing more pure discernment than intelligence.

Sutcliffe took the Prince on a binge or
Spree – a pig in clover he rolled about in
A garden of untrussed trulls.

A sex in her sex like an alabaster dumpling!
Her knickers smelt of gun-cotton, a
Moth-bag of a woman shedding rice-paper,
Powder, cigarette ash and paper handkerchiefs
Which she had twitched once about her lips.
A characteristic groan as he paid in coin.

You'd have been surprised by the tone
He took, the young Catullus with Julius Caesar;
A Tory untrussing a parvenu, dressing down
A political bounder, a tyke. Then later,
A heart shedding its petals, Latin verse.

Sutcliffe's poetry hardly varies ever:

"Come pretty firework untruss
And let me grope thy overplus,
Between the horns of either-or
Be my dilemma, purple whore,
If spring be through, the season's pulse,
Let's teach each other to emulse."

The ego (Affad used to say) is only a sort of negative
for the superlative esoteric state – tiny glimpses of wholeness;
as if light passed through them, printing out a different reality.
He also said: "Love won't live on charity, its demands are
absolute. If she won't love you then your ship is down by the
hull. Aubrey overheard asking S: "What can I do to make you
seem more real?"

Birds do it like young Lesbians do
As lip to lip they tup their tails
In an adhesive swift caress,
The oviposter's carnal hue,
A member short I must confess
They cause each other sweet distress.
But arms thrust to the elbow up
Is how the modern hardies tup!

Mud . . . Merde . . . Mutt . . . love-bewitched in old
Bombay – my think is spunk when thunk . . . chunks of

thought thunk spill spunk. Blanford to Sutcliffe: "Reading your verse is like dragging a pond without ever finding the body."

Tomboy with a clitoris like an ice-skate seeks rational employ. Sutcliffe: "To oblige her I had to bark like her Pekinese long-dead, run over, buried at the bottom of the garden. Until I was hoarse, my dear fellow! Gustav was the name of the Peke."

Paraplegic frolics, geriatric revels! Once upon a time Truth Absolute dwelt with the Sublime and poets knew where they were or thought they did. Now?! And if you can't get your breath because of your asthma how will you cool your nymph's porridge? Man is so weak that he needs the protection of a woman's desire.

> I married a fair maid
> And she was compos mantis,
> We bought a third return
> On a voyage to Atlantis.
>
> "Happy New Year!" the roysters cried
> While clowning clones their cuddles plied.
> Gaunt Lesbians like undusted harps
> Hung up their woofs and coiled their warps.
> Woof to warp and warp to whoof
> They like their whisky over proof.
>
> And so one day we
> Reached Atlantis,
> Outside all peacock
> But inside mantis
> Ecco puella corybantis
> Primavera in split panties!

The new day is dawning – women have become sex

service stations: no more attachments, just distributors of friendly faceless lust. Modern girls whose body-image is smashed by neglect. Neither caressed enough nor suckled without disgust nor respected and treated with the awe they deserve. Pious loveless lives . . . Anorexia nervosa the name of tomorrow's nun – spite long ripened in a sense of inadequacy. Insolent lurching looks when flushed and a bit drunk. Man is noble, man is marvellous: he can be monogamous for whole moments at a time!

Poor Blanford with his eternal note-making and note-taking. "Proust, the last great art metaphor in European history, is relative and contingent in its view of life; ego, sensation, history . . . The sign manual is memory, the central notion is that being is advanced through memory – through what is kept artificially alive. History! But history is simply gossip from an eastern point of view – the five senses, the five arts, are its plumage. For after relativity and the field-theory bleakness sets in and the universe becomes cosmically pointless. Relativity does not bring relatedness! *Monsieur est ravagé par le bonheur!* As Flaubert remarks somewhere: "*Moi, je m'emmerde dans la perfection!*""

The fool waits for perfect weather but the wise man grabs at every scrap of wind, every lull. When he was young he headed for Paris, capital of synthetic loves. Tall beauties like well-trained rocking-horses. Love was a jubilant relation, placental in rhythm; we danced the foetal swirl, the omni-amni blues. A thirst for goodness becomes unhealthy. Let yourself embark on the music's great white pinions into Time!

The worldly life is the enemy of the poetic science! Alchemy will out! But holy structures when they go mad plunge into infamy!

QUINX

The vatic mule, our German Poet, where was he when the killing was rife? The language is so glutinous that it is like investigating the nervous system of a globe artichoke.

The post-war world has started to form itself in Provence. In the village, Tubain, they have started drinking *pastis* with the old tumefied air, and playing at *boules*. It is reassuring. Even the human type has come back – the true Mediterranean loafer – sleep eats into him like an antacid into a dissenting Anabaptist! A purse under each eye and one under his waistcoat which stirs when he breathes as if a mole were trying to surface. A huge brown nose like Cromwell, full of snot. A Protestant mind packed tight as Luther's big intestine with golden turds – alchemical fruit. The minority dream is to make the parochial universal – the whole universe a suburb with an *accent faubourgienne*! Whiffs of red wine and underclothes – the love calls of a mouthful of dripping crumpet. An analysis of figments! Here, honey, chew on this crust, death!

Problem of woman – lightning never strikes twice in the same place. That heavenly gloating walk, as sultry as Achilles upon a bed of glowing embers!

Today Sutcliffe was washing his hair and singing tunelessly – his theme was "What shall we do with a drunken sailor?" to which he had harnessed words of his own devising, namely, "What shall we do with our alter ego?" I suppose when the time comes you will force me to commit *suttee* – climb on to a pyre and disappear in a swirl of smoke and a delicious odour of frying bacon. My apotheosis will have begun – myself transformed into the Swami Utter Conundrum with his three free-wheeling geishas, preaching the way to Inner Umptiousness. Swami so full of inner magnetism that he sparks as he describes the new reality: "If you can leave it

1306

alone sufficiently you will discover that reality is bliss – nothing less! When the mathematical and the poetical co-exist as they were always meant to; a collision of worlds takes place and you write a hymn to Process. It's love that beckons, that huge axiomatic doll that we kiss to three places of decimals. In her arms you realise that happiness is just despair turned inside out like a sleeve. You ask yourself, "What am I as an artist but a whimsical poacher of stallion's eggs?"

To investigate what went wrong with the intellect of a civilisation one has to start with human perception ... i.e. sex, the original form of knowing which preceded language ... i.e. telling, formulating, realising!

> sweet thumbs up
> dark thumbs down
> life's for living
> says the clown
> nothing adventured
> nothing said
> slip off to join
> the laughing dead!

Smirgel took every kind of precaution against declaring where he was living or how, and for a while all trace of him was lost – so much so that the Prince began to wonder whether the whole rigmarole of his story was not invented, perhaps for obscure motives. Then the air cleared and he telephoned to Constance and offered them a rendezvous at the little bistro on the road to Vers which had recently changed hands and reopened. Sunlight greeted them under the olives. He was already there when they arrived in the Prince's great Daimler which had once belonged to Queen Mary! In the sparkling shadow and light of the glade with its green tables Smirgel looked what perhaps he really was at heart, a wandering German professor of history on holiday. But he rose to greet them and his ankles sketched the faintest shadow of a Prussian heel-click – out of respect for the two dignitaries who came forward to meet him full of a delicious sense of legitimate cupidity – the folklore of riches! The Prince's natural affability was very fetching, he exuded warmth. They all sat down and eyed each other for a long moment of silence, until a waiter came out of the bar and procured them drinks of their choice. Smirgel was nervous and ordered water.

After a silence during which the Prince politely toasted his guests in rather indifferent champagne Smirgel said, "Lord Galen, I feel we can afford to be frank now. I trust my reasons for wanting to meet you have become clear to you. I explained everything about the treasure to Constance and asked her to retail it to you in the hope of gaining your attention because I know that you and your consortium of interested backers are Geneva-based and serious – *des gens sérieux, quoi*! I am quite confident that what I have to offer them is of interest even though for the moment I cannot evaluate how much is actually at stake. The point is that nobody alive has access to it because of the pure danger inherent in the situation – the explosives and the mining! But what I can offer them is a detailed map of the boobytrapping with which one can gain safe access in order to visit and assess it. I have seen some of the precious stones and have spoken to the man who discovered it, so I know that it is not a fantasy but a fact. In exchange I would naturally wish to be represented among the other speculators, and entitled to my legitimate share of the booty."

"I must admit that the thought of an immense fortune makes me sentimental," said Lord Galen dreamily, but the Prince sounded a trifle reproachful when he said, "Yes, but think of the pure historical beauty of the thing – to rediscover this long-lost and far-famed treasure! We mustn't lose sight of the cultural aspect, for many of the articles must be things of great beauty and we must keep a careful record for the future of our find." The German sat quietly smoking and watching them with attention. The Prince's mind roved far and wide among the legends and folktales of his own land, Egypt where secret treasures buried in caves and guarded by malefic djinns were a commonplace. "It would be amusing," he said, "if the treasure had been filched away and had been replaced with feathers or sand!" He chuckled, but neither Galen nor the German found this line of thought funny. "How soon can we be sure?"

The German smiled and replied, "Just as soon as I am prepared to release to you the map of the workings. Then we can just walk into the caves and locate the door and force it. Presto! But this I will not do until the articles of association are signed and I am happy in my mind about my part."

"A limited company, based on Geneva, called Treasure Trove Incorporated," said Galen dreamily. "But how shall we describe the site? I have all the means to create the document."

The German pulled forth from under him – he had been seated on it – a battered briefcase which contained two documents of importance: a cadastral map of the workings with scales and numbers and the names of the owners.

The German continued his exposition in a leisurely style and in the tone of a lecturing professor, but the matter was impeccably organised and the English choice. "I have discovered that practically the whole section which concerns us is in the possession of one single family, and I have already made contact with them. They are peasants and pretty hard up so that they have been delighted to rent the whole section to me on a hundred-year lease; on my side I have been into the legal side of things and have obtained a government lease

QUINX

and a permit to work the land and exploit the resources. French law is coming back into force and civil considerations are coming to the fore. I hinted that what I had in mind was to reactivate the Roman quarry as there were many unexploited seams still bearing, and this would of course provide employment in the area which would be welcomed. Indeed this will have to be our cover-story, so to speak, as we would not wish to excite the French government with tales of buried treasure upon which they might have a tax claim. However, in the present state of things I see no major reason why we should not extract the treasure, bit by bit if necessary, and maintain a cover-front of quarrymen to work the seams in good faith. Do you see anything against it?"

Lord Galen saw nothing against it. "But the famous map of the quarry – where is that?"

"It is in my possession, in a safe place, and at your disposition when certain conditions have been fulfilled. Chief among them is of course my acquittal by the war crimes tribunal which have put me mistakenly on their black list. In two months' time my case comes before them, by which time I hope that Lord Galen will have acted for the defence and pulled the scales down in my favour. This whole business is due to the vanity and jealousy of the Milice. They would like to get me branded or beheaded or imprisoned because of all I know about their behaviour during the bad years. They have much to hide, as you may well suppose. But I think it will be possible to get a fair verdict in my favour especially because of the British members of the ruling committee. I am sure Lord Galen knows them all and can put in a word for me. I have their names on this piece of paper." He passed over the documents in question and Lord Galen saw with horror that there were several friends on the list, while the president of the tribunal was one of his shareholders! He swallowed and blinked. "As soon as I am acquitted you will have the map.

But in the meantime let us work out the articles of association and get everything ready for action."

He conducted them across the quarry to where the entrance was, picked out by the tall entrances to the caves, some quite profound. "We are concerned", he said, "with the sequence of caves which begins here, on the left-hand side. I have managed to get the family which owns the land to close off the entrance as far as is possible in order to avoid trespassers of any sort. I have had several scares concerning the place. On one occasion a shepherd used them to shelter his flock during a thunderstorm: drove a hundred sheep into the entrance. My blood ran cold – I happened to be across the way, sheltering myself in a cave-entrance. It was too late to stop the shepherd, for he had followed his sheep into the first corridor. When I told him the danger he faced he went as white as a sheet and started to whistle up his dogs to retrieve the sheep, which by this time had scattered into the various corridors. Psychologically we both kept our fingers in our ears and hardly dared to breathe for what seemed eternity, until the last sheep had been retrieved and chased back into no man's land. What an escape! One sheep could easily have fouled a trip wire and set off the whole place by a mass explosion. But of course once we start work seriously we must enforce strict security measures until we have cleared the place – or as much of it as is necessary for the work we have in mind."

(Blanford had noted in his Ulysses archive: when the Cyclops cries, "Who goes there?" and Ulysses nervously replies "Nobody", it constitutes the first Zen statement in the European literary canon!)

Walking back across the olive-glades they reached a working agreement as to the procedure to be invoked in order to harness all their interests together. Smirgel gave them a phone number where they might contact him if need be and then took his leave astride an ancient push-bike, melting slowly into the landscape with slow strokes of the pedals. "Well I never," said the Prince, summoning another drink in order to talk over the whole matter with his partner. "If this comes off it will be something quite unique, no?"

"Indeed!" said Galen with a sort of uncertain rapture. The Prince added, "Are you going to use your pull and try to get him off?" Lord Galen nodded vehemently. "He won't be any use to us if he's sent up for life and won't tell where the map is, will he? He must be kept cooperative, don't you think? The whole thing is far from settled, I think. But it's promising, I agree, dashed promising, and we must pursue it single-mindedly." He put on his single-minded look and gazed round him like a blind buzzard. He had borrowed the look from a bust of Napoleon on St Helena which stood on his desk at home.

SIX

The Return

WHEN SHE SAW HIM STANDING THERE IN THE HALL of Tu Duc beside his luggage, leaning on a stick and clad in his old much-darned Scotch plaid, she could not resist a wave of tenderness, so much did his presence evoke of their common youth – a whole summer passed here in these enchanted glades and meadows in that limbo before The Flood! He too was overtaken by an involuntary shyness and hesitation. "Are you sure you want me here, fouling up your life with my heavy sighs?" But they embraced tenderly enough and she put on her briskest medical tone in order to hide her emotion. "I really wanted you under my eye, in my hands, because I noticed that you are slacking off on the yoga and simply not getting the massage you need for your back. At least that I can guarantee myself, while of course here you can swim in the mill-stream every day which is a radical part of the treatment. I propose to take you in hand."

He could not imagine anything more delightful to contemplate and he settled into Livia's room with its old Freudian couch without very much ado; his few clothes and books and his clutch of notebooks found niches easily enough, and once his possessions were in order he descended with his queer swaying walk to the kitchen where he proposed to help her cook the lunch – she was expecting the Prince and Lord Galen after their interview with Smirgel. They were both good cooks by now, and this was a further bond which was ripening between them. Somehow a profound reserve reigned in a strange sort of way, for there were a hundred questions he was dying to put to her though the time and place had not yet somehow come into focus – it was not yet appropriate to do so. And of course when their guests arrived the redoubled activity absorbed them and provided a neutral background against which all conversation became not personal but general. The Prince for example had been highly exhilarated by his encounter with the German but was as yet not fully convinced of his *bona fides*. He plied Constance with questions about him. Galen on the other hand had swallowed the whole proposition wholesale. "What other thing could he have been thinking?" he asked plaintively, and, "One has to learn to trust *someone* or one never gets results. I think the story is true, and if we play our cards right we will win out!"

On this genial note the lunch party embarked on the dishes that Constance had prepared. "I shall see to it that your name is on the list of shareholders," the Prince told her, "if only because of the excellence of this *boeuf gardien*."

The Prince had spent the previous afternoon visiting the half-yearly fair of the city, some aspects of which had filled him with misgivings, such as the bold red inscriptions on the walls of the churchyard talking of alien matters. The first American tourists had arrived in Avignon!

> Skinheads Rule!
> Yes! Yes!
> Madness Reigns!
> Yes!
> Kill everyone!
> Yes! Yes!

It was the new world they had hatched beginning to stake out its claims on the future. The Prince permitted himself a premonitory shudder or two and allowed a chill to trickle down his spinal column as he visualised this hallowed countryside being invaded by representatives of the American industrial ethos. Nearer home, too, and hardly less disturbing was a British representative of Tyneside who at least had some redeeming touches of Golgotha humour to salt his act. This was a young man, Suckathumbo Smith by name, who sat in front of a curtain on which was depicted a scene from circus life – a dentist in frock coat extracting a tooth against the will of a young woman in a crinoline. Smith was a chunky young man and his eyes had been completely circled in mascara like the spectacles on the hood of a cobra. He looked tear-stained, as if he had cried all night, and when not using his voice kept himself corked up so to speak, thumb in mouth. He would suddenly remove the thumb and let forth a shriek of song, and then as suddenly plunge his thumb back into the aperture, sinking as he did so into a posture of despair and gloom. Blanford delighted in him as a curiosity, and would not leave his booth until the whole performance was at an end. The last act was a spirited rendering of the old Cockney classic:

> Uncle Fred and Auntie Mabel
> Fainted at the breakfast table
> They forgot the gipsy's warning
> Not to do it in the morning!

This at least had the hallmarks of true music hall on it and was as true to its tradition as Shakespeare would have been. But such manifestations made uncomfortable bedfellows for the folklore subsidised by tourist organisations in the hope of making foreign visitors feel at home. And indeed the first foreign visitors had hardly begun to show their faces as yet. The post-war city was a sort of limbo for the moment, quite uncertain of its possibilities, urged on only by the prestige of its past.

But spring was at hand, the sunny days not too far off, and this gave them the opportunity to transfer their morning therapies of massage and yoga to a more suitable spot, namely the flat rocks around the weir with its grave menhirs and abandoned threshing floor. Here the river swept by in a sudden convulsion of pleasure among the water lilies. Here one could lie and drowse or read, lulled by the water-music of the Roman weir. Constance was very businesslike about the work and Blanford grumbled but obeyed her, allowing the doctor full rights over her patient, though the feel of her capable brown hands settling on his back and beginning to manipulate the muscle schemes thrilled him sexually until he felt shy to feel the incipient half-erection which the therapy caused him, and wondered if she was aware of the fact. She was, and the thought gave her a twinge of irritated self-reproach. But it would pass – so she opined – familiarity would breed contempt! She need only persevere. And talk about other things. "I must say, Aubrey, they have done you a superb job of renovation." He grunted his assent and added: "All done up like an expensive tennis racquet with the best gut and steel wires. I am unbelievably lucky. And now to continue the massage with you . . ." Part of it, too, was the swimming. They took off side by side and paddled slowly up river among the lilies, talking, or else in a companionable silence betimes. A new kind of intimacy was hatching itself between them which, for the moment, they could not identify or classify. She spoke to him now quite wordlessly, while she was working on his back. "How strange that you should be my first love, my worst love," she told him. "The only one with whom I could make no progress whatsoever. And of course I yours – I would have been an idiot not to recognise the fact. What went wrong? I found you frigid, autistic and quite self-obsessed – but now, looking back on it, I wonder whether it wasn't simply timidity? Those English schools drive one back into oneself and remove all spirit of enterprise where girls are concerned." Blanford had fallen asleep like a cat under the effect of the massage. She frowned, for it was obvious that his psyche was reacting to the massage as if to caresses – and this was not what the doctor in her approved or had in mind.

"Aubrey! Wake up!" she said, "And let's go for a swim up to the point. The sun is westering." He grumbled but complied. "I dreamed we made love," he said grimly, "and that at last it worked between us. You were after all my first love." She frowned and acquiesced reluctantly. "And I yours?" After a pause, "Yes. Very much so!"

There was a long silence.

Then he said, "Christ! What on earth went wrong, do you think? And is it redeemable?" She laughed and spread out her arms in a rueful gesture. "Of course not!" she said, but gaily, "look at us both, so battered from the wars and the whole blessed attrition of time passing . . . We've overshot the mark!" It was depressing, nay, intolerable to believe that she might be right. It made him suddenly realise how permanent the image of her had been – even when she herself was not present, even when he had not been conscious of the fact, she had been overwhelmingly present in his mind, his heart. "You have always been so very much part of the décor; I don't think I have made any decisions or thought any thoughts without mentally referring to you – I mean, even when you were with Affad you were still a sort of lodestar to me! It's queer! In anyone else it would be accounted for by the word 'love'. But I don't dare! I am afraid you would protest!

"I can't flirt any more. But I can still dare, so in a sort of way I am still open to adventure. But so much has changed in my outlook. After he died I realised, but quite slowly, that I could not love again in the old way, in the literary way, as if from a dialectical frenzy. Yet paradoxically the new freedom which came to me from his death freed me to love more truly, more correctly, while at the same time remaining my own master. It was deeper and chaster despite its freedom. Yes, I could not any more enter into the great engagement and surrender myself wholly. I'm on the threshold of middle age, I suppose that is it."

He listened to her with the silence of misgivings, for what is more hopeless than for a woman to try and analyse the nature of love and its thousand forms and dispositions? He said, "I have been watching his wonderful little son to whom you have managed to bring so much that you have really succeeded in being a mother to him. In him I get a wonderful feeling of self-sufficiency, of estrangement from all formal joy. I feel sure he is going to be an artist. He looks about him with the disabused eye of one – the feeling of being able to see through things, to discern their coarse primal roots, their quiddity, and hence their boredom with God! It's only a manner of speaking, but how to convey his marvellous detachment? I was like he is, an autist, a complete virgin, which unluckily you could not possess – to my eternal loss. Had you managed to wake me from my death-sleep I would have blessed you for the rest of my life! But no, it was not to be, I had to sleep my way forward by years in order to catch up with you here, on this rock, after a long and miserable war. How strangely life arranges things!"

Another comic paradox of fate was the drift of Blanford's notes which he had so carefully emptied to the four winds; a large section had blown about the city until the curious gipsy children had started to amass them and show them to their parents. From there to the consultation of a bookseller was but a step, and it was not long before Toby was offered a bundle of scraps for sale, which he had at once recognised from the handwriting as belonging to Blanford who expressed himself prepared to buy them back, presuming that the mere fact that they had escaped destruction was a portent concerning their value for his forthcoming book whose presence had begun to loom up strangely over his future life. Now that he was more or less physically restored to daily life the question of an occupation had begun to nag at him. He was glad that his tiny income did not prevent him from addressing himself

to literature as a possible means of making money. It would
have been bad for him, he thought, if private means had freed
him from the onus of thinking coldly and professionally of
the novel as a wage-earner. And then there was another thing
– for how long could he support a brother-to-sister relationship with Constance? Their relationship could not forever
stay like this, in solution so to speak, without any sort of
physical development: or could it? His breasts ached when he
thought about her! How stupid people were! He lay softly
breathing under the determined thoughtful fingers which
prowled his back and shoulders while he riffled the latest
bundle of scraps to have emerged from the hands of the
gipsies. A novelist forced to buy back his own notes – what
a farce!

Is meditation an art or a science? Discuss.
Strawberries are neither classical nor romantic. Discuss!
By simple oxygen and silence slip
Into the Higher Harmlessness!

To this Sutcliffe had added a rider, which went: "But
the Hindu is as high-minded as he is long-winded. Heaven
preserve us from such a cataplasm, however much he may be
right theologically."

He added: "What a curse self-importance is! If we would
only shut up and give nature a chance to talk we would
certainly learn that Happiness, nay, *Bliss* is innate!"

But circumstances do not always show themselves as
cooperative to human designs and they were soon thrown
together without equivocation by a simple incident which
grew out of their habit of night-swimming. Despite the
relative earliness of the season they had enjoyed almost a
fortnight of hot weather, real summer weather, and this had
pushed them to revert once more to the once popular habit of
swimming at night off the stone, using as light the one hissing

gas-light of which the house boasted. This they propped on the rock. Its rather ghostly yellow light which flapped and flared outlined a small central circle of water among the lilies sufficient to constitute virtually a round shining pool of water. They tried to keep within its limits in the interests of good order and indeed safety, but it was not always possible, so strong was the tug of the water round the rock. Nevertheless that was the scheme, and they were sufficiently practised and confident, both of them, to embark for a swim even if alone. This is what had happened on the night in question – Constance had gone on ahead; crossing the dark garden with his slow swaying walk he could see the flap and flare of the light standing on the stone plinth above the water. He heard the sound of her plunge and then the noise of paddling and treading water – all perfectly in order. It would be difficult to say just what it was that alerted him to the fact that all was *not* in order; perhaps he overheard her gasp of dismay as she turned on her back – dismay to feel a sudden rogue cramp attack her thighs and legs, a reaction from the cold of the water. But with a current so formidable there was little time to be lost if the situation was to be redressed – and there was no shore to speak of, for the lilies were anchored in three metres of silt. "Are you all right?" he called anxiously, for he had sensed that something had gone wrong. "Yes! No!" she cried in her disarray. It was a double deception, for Aubrey in his present situation was not at the peak of his powers as a swimmer, and it would be unfair to call him into the water . . . Nevertheless her distress conveyed itself to him rapidly enough and he saw that the only thing to do was to throw himself in after her and try to help her master the tugging current which was trying to pull her downstream. In still water there would have been no problem – she could have floated for ever; but the current created a possible hazard. She heard him plunge after her and her heart misgave her – they might both be in trouble because of this rashness. But he was stronger than he himself had quite supposed and seizing her under the arms he turned doggedly back up-current, determined to put them both within finger-reach of the stone plinth, their point of entry into the water. At first, and for a long moment, the issue hung in the balance even though he put forth his utmost endeavour, stroke on slow stroke. Then with infinite slowness he began to gain against the water. It was a matter of a mere two or three metres but the issue was a critical one, for the water was trying its best to sweep them down river to where the Roman ford created a sort of small but vertiginous waterfall. Here the current might be strong enough to create an accident of sorts – a knock on the head, a broken wrist, something of that order. But his slow and concentrated stroke was sufficiently masterful to begin to gain on the current, and at last he had a satisfaction and relief of pushing his fellow swimmer to a point where her fingers could grasp the serrated edges of rock and haul herself clear of the current, but at the same time holding fast to his hand with the other arm. Thus with infinite slowness and infinite labour they at last managed to clear the water and crawl ashore to the safety of the rock – there to tumble in an exhausted heap. "I have never had a cramp before," she said, among her apologies for having dragged him after her, "I had no idea one could just freeze up, like that." And of course concern for his back now seized her – he might have sprained or dragged a muscle by his efforts, and nothing would satisfy her but to see for herself. But here something radical had changed – the whole cloud of inhibitions which had paralysed him in his dealings with her suddenly seemed to have lifted. Was it perhaps the fleeting terror of losing her for ever to the river that had purged him? A classical boldness now beset him, he took her in his arms unerringly, as if he were completely sure of her response. They stood like that, enlaced and

in silence for what seemed an eternity. Outside in the tall trees
the owls screeched and hunted; the lamp which usually stood
beside them on the kitchen table gave forth its buzzing commentary – like the noise at the centre of the chambered
nautilus. "How marvellous," he whispered, "not to be afraid
any longer of making a mess of you! You gave me such a
fright with your cramp that it shocked me back into sense.
Fear of losing you for ever! I realise everything now. You
have learned the most important thing a woman can learn
from a man – not from me but from Affad: the art of surrender
which assures everything. How grateful I am to him as well!"
Nor was this mere verbiage for it translated itself into caresses
later that night which were as generous as they were famished.
He could still make love then, still generate the power and the
glory of the complete sexual encounter. Where the devil had
it all come from? He was at a loss to tell.

And like lovers at any time and everywhere they
suddenly found the need for privacy overwhelming; so much
so that for several weeks after this critical re-evaluation of
their loving they almost went out of circulation as far as their
friends were concerned – preferring to dine early and lock
up at an early bedtime rather than dawdling over dinner, even
by moonlight, which was the time-honoured way of treating
the slow Provençal nightfall. He found himself jealous not of
her person but of her company. Nor was this change lost upon
the Prince whose intuition was Egyptian in its sharpness of
focus. "It's happened at last," he said with a chuckle in his
most pleased and shocked tone of voice. "I shall be writing
to the Princess, and I shall tell her that her worst fears have
been confirmed! The spectre of love has begun to hang over
this pious old bachelor's head. Eh, Constance?" But she was
sunk so deeply into the luxury of this marvellous pristine
attachment that she was not put out of countenance by his
banter. "She will be delighted," she said, "the Princess has

always had a soft corner for Aubrey and rather pitied his isolation." Indeed the Prince was highly delighted and was already writing his letter in his head. As for Lord Galen, he had not noticed anything and he became plaintive when the Prince pointed out the obvious to him. "No one ever tells me anything," he said with a sigh, "but I suppose it is a Good Thing, if you say so."

"I most certainly do," said His Highness with his characteristic tone, trenchant and cocksure. But it was less pleasant when the lovers disappeared from circulation for a few weeks, and rumour had it that they were somewhere secret in Italy. They were much missed by the Prince who was hopelessly gregarious and could not live without a staple diet of courtly gossip. Then, as if to complete the catalogue of unexpected happenings, Constance began to believe that she was pregnant and this provoked a further revision of options, a further period of reflection upon the future. It was marvellous to think about, and all the more so because neither had really foreseen such an eventuality, though at no time had any precautions been taken to obviate the fact. Blanford was highly delighted in a tremulous sort of way; he had begun to worry about being inadequate as a father and family man. "Does the man having nothing to do spend his time yawning and riffling a dictionary of Christian names? Surely you can set me to work doing something useful?" But for the moment she took her pleasure in encouraging his shiftlessness and the incoherence of his passion. She realised somewhere deep down that this sort of crisis would either make him or lose him!

To wake and find her arms round him – it surprised him to realise his former loneliness: how had he not been more conscious of the felicity of loving, the thrilling beauty of sharing? It was unnerving to find himself surprised like an adolescent at these departures into fine feeling, tenderness, passion. And then to find himself still thirsty and heartwhole after her love had passed over him, so to speak, parched anew like a landscape after rain. Sutcliffe wore a slightly reproachful air these days, but it was probably a case of sour grapes though he had never claimed to be in love with Constance himself, which would have provided an explanation of the fact. Fragments of rejected notebook material kept turning up, too, to add colour to the growing mountain of *obiter dicta* which one day would be polished and sited in the projected novel. He claimed to have invented the "extra-marital biscuit" as well as crumbless bread, not to mention the dildo called Recompense; it had wings and a snout which developed uterine suction by a system of spontaneous nibble. It was full of camshaft glory. Listen to the music of the spheres – the clash of Hercules' testicles. "Enough!" cried Blanford. "In God's name, enough!"

With the first days of summer weather the newly constituted tribunals set up to judge war crimes began to sit in the city, and the question of Smirgel's guilt or innocence would soon come under debate. The whole subject was still confused and riddled with suppositions and false testimony. A typical search for heroes as well as scapegoats was going forward. Two members of the Judge Advocate's staff were plied with attestations highly favourable to Smirgel, while the Prince found them places on the board of the treasure company and a promise of a share in the spoils. You would have thought from the way he went on that the German had been put up for a British DSO as well as the French Military Cross. It was hardly surprising that the case against him was quashed "for lack of conclusive evidence". Meanwhile the courts had the good grace to publish the figures concerning the missing, which showed very clearly that Provence had taken a terrible beating from the Nazis. Of the 600,000 forced labourers sent into Germany 60,000 did not return, 15,000 were shot or beheaded, while 60,000 contracted tuberculosis . . . But the tribunal's judgement on Smirgel was highly delightful, indeed was music to the ears of Lord Galen, for now nothing could stand in the way of their treasure-hunting. The company too had been set up to exploit their gains when the time came.

But here again unexpected factors came into play, among them the fact that rumours of their find had somehow leaked out – perhaps Smirgel had committed a calculated indiscretion? At any rate the city fathers and the authorities in Avignon made it known that they would expect to be kept informed and that any treasure trove which accrued from their activities should be brought to the notice of the museum authorities and the civic authorities. "Bang goes any hope of keeping it secret, but perhaps we can limit the affair to a couple of bribed officials?" said the Prince, swallowing his disappointment as best he could. "Anyway, let's not get worked up in case there is no treasure, or so little as not to be of interest." Lord Galen put on his wistful-alarmed look. At any rate Smirgel had now only to wait for the official judgement which would restore him to the world as innocent, and he was free to produce his map and lead the expedition into the caves. "I don't think we should be dog-in-the-mangerish about letting the officials come in at least for the initial discovery. It is of course a fact of great historic importance and under French law they might even consider impounding the whole thing in the name of the Louvre. Still, for the moment they have not gone as far as that and I think with a few judicious bribes we can get them to shrug their shoulders and declare the find of little interest – something like that."

The era of enlightened self-interest had dawned, it was obvious, and everyone was going to become a millionaire overnight! Yet there were pockets of misgiving here and there. "Are you really confident in the *bona fides* of your map? I wanted to ask you that before," said Lord Galen, and Smirgel cleared his throat and nodded vigorously. "After all, it is only logic for Schultz to keep a copy which would enable him to come back in peacetime and retrieve the treasure; can you see anything wrong with the reasoning? I can't. He would hardly have held on to a dud map, would he?"

No, it stood to reason the map he had hidden about his person was a valid one. It could not be otherwise! On this optimistic note they separated for a day or so to allow all the papers to be sifted into some sort of provisional order. Details for the treasure hunt would be dealt with very shortly. One of the strokes of luck had been the discovery of Quatrefages – his opinion on the affair would be, everyone felt, invaluable. The doctor had kept in touch with him, and he was proposing to come back and work for the Prince once again; but he had become very old-looking, and his hair was quite white. But he had retrieved a good part of his documentation concerning the Templars and hoped to round off his studies with a long essay about them.

Once or twice, in order one supposes to whet their appetites, Smirgel led them as far as the entrance to the main grotto which had been barred to the public with wooden palisades bearing the word "*Danger*" and the phrase "*Défense d'entrer*". They hung about in a desultory sort of way here, discussing ways and means and rather hoping that the German would decide to unburden himself of the famous map, but he was dogged and obstinate, and waited upon the document of the war crimes tribunal. Meanwhile there was another small flutter of excitement, for Quatrefages had unearthed a gipsy in Avignon who claimed to have wandered into the caves by accident and to have actually seen the treasure. According to him the door which Smirgel had firmly closed had opened again and one could enter the caves – or at any rate he had done so and had seen the massive oak trunks with their heaps of precious stones and various sorts of ornament. From these he had extracted a single ruby which he had had fixed in a nostril. Later on when he had learned of the danger he had run he had been horrified – but like everyone else he could not push the affair any further for lack of a guide or a map with the necessary instructions. Now, of course . . . But while his testimony sounded valid enough there was something about the man which did not inspire confidence – a suggestion of feverish hysteria which made one wonder whether he had not been fabulating in order to find out something to his profit.

A still further complication was the arrival on the scene of the new Préfet of the country who at once asked if he might address them all on a topic which concerned him as it affected law and order in the province. It was not possible to refuse, and the courteous elderly gentleman duly presented himself before the board which was holding its first executive meeting at the Pont du Gard in order to discuss dates and means for the final act. The Prince, Lord Galen, Smirgel and Quatrefages were the most important executives, while vaguer associates like, for example, the doctor Jourdain, played backgammon with Blanford and Sutcliffe in the garden. The Préfet who, like all Frenchmen, had a strong sense of occasion, ordered champagne all round, before rising to his feet to toast the Prince and open the ball with a polished little speech. "I expect you will wonder why I intruded upon your deliberations. Gentlemen, it is to ask you to have some charitable thoughts about my own problems. Avignon is a thorny place, and among other thorns I have always to keep our gipsies in mind. It is a quite large colony and they provide us with a number of headaches – worse really than Marseilles. But it would be ill-advised for a governor not to humour them because they are not only troublesome but also extremely useful to him. Practically all police intelligence of any depth and cogency has been sifted and evaluated by the gipsies before it reaches us at the executive level. Naturally one of my first tasks has been to make their acquaintance and find out if there is any way in which I can show myself as prepared to be an obliging and friendly patron to the tribe of Saint Sara – such a little gesture goes down very well as you can imagine! And in the course of these manoeuvres I happened upon a remarkable English woman turned gipsy – a daughter of a certain Lord Banquo who may be familiar to you. She has proved a mine of useful information and penetrating judgements, and it was largely on her advice that I hit upon the notion of visiting your organisation.

"It was from her that I learned that long before the Austrian sappers started their ammunition stockpiling in these caves the gipsies kept a grotto here as a chapel sacred to Saint Sara where baptisms and initiations took place at certain times of the year. Yes, the 'tenebrous one' was a flourishing cult figure – sometimes she even encouraged prophecy and the gift of tongues. Naturally the Germans threw out the gipsies when they started stocking the caves. I have been asked to keep these facts in mind if ever there should be a question of spring-cleaning the place and defusing the ammunition contained in the caves. Obviously your own preoccupations centre upon the same matters though for a different set of reasons. I am hereby asking for the sympathy and the good offices of your board when such matters are undertaken in the near future. You will understand that in my present position I can hardly refuse to return the grottoes to Saint Sara whose old mud statue and icons must still be knocking about inside. So far I have only made one approach – I have sounded out Herr Smirgel, and he is perfectly agreeable to a gipsy representation on the first exploration, who will follow him into the caves just as soon as he gets his clearance from the war crimes tribunals. Ouf!"

He paused, somewhat out of breath after so long a disquisition, and gazed from face to face with a self-confident diffidence – for when had his charm failed to convince? But the Prince betrayed a certain disconsolate dismay. There would be far too many people in the know, he opined, and most specially semi-official agencies like the Beaux Arts with largely undemarcated areas of responsibility. Suppose the treasure proved to be not only tangible but immense . . . The whole thing was becoming too swollen for his liking, it was sliding out of control, for now they were even talking of making a photographic record of the findings – to film each item as it was disinterred!

"O dear!" said Lord Galen who had been listening with an expression of ruefulness, for he had begun to enumerate in his mind the number of things which could or might go wrong and qualify their own hold upon the treasure. (And yet suppose there is no bloody treasure, he kept thinking!)

As for Smirgel, he had chosen his day after due and weighty consultations with Quatrefages, aware that it would have to satisfy certain mystical provisions. It must, for example, be a Friday Thirteen in order to echo not only the Name Day of Sara in her prophetic form but also to echo the fatal day when the Order of Templars was abolished. Why does one instinctively seek a continuity in things as if synchronicity satisfied some deep cosmic need? (The question was posed by Blanford to himself and answered with: "Because you fool the world of consciousness is a world of historic echoes which cry out to be satisfied. One grabs at every connection. For example the Templars were abolished in that dismal town Vienne where I once spent ten days in winter haunted by a simple historic fact which I had picked up somewhere – namely, that Pontius Pilate when he retired from the civil service chose Vienne as his town of residence because he found Rome too noisy and too sophisticated and too expensive for a poor pensioner of the state." The result of that visit was a little monograph purporting to be his memoirs written here. It was called "The Memoirs of PP" and it received a condescending but friendly review by Pursewarden.)

"For months afterwards," added Sutcliffe, "I dreamed all night of washing my hands in a silver ewer to the baying of a scruffy crowd of subhumans!"

At teatime the old Daimler of the Prince hove in sight with Cade at the wheel; he had come from the Tubain post office with a cargo of mail from the central sorting agency in Avignon which had only half-resumed its civil functions. With these heterogenous letters there was one familiar buff envelope superscribed OHMS and addressed to Smirgel. He had not given the Judge Advocate General his true address but that of Lord Galen since they were friends. It was the magical certificate for which he had been so anxiously waiting. It attested to his innocence of any war crime. He gave a sob as he unfolded the document. Then he tenderly embraced Cade, kissing him on both cheeks. Then he held up the paper and cried, "Look, everybody, this is the certificate of clearance – I am declared innocent, and can resume civil life again as an ordinary citizen of the world! Ah! you can't know what it means! But as for the treasure we can go ahead now and plan the event in all seriousness." To their surprise he fell on his knees and said a prayer.

SEVEN

Whether or Not

B LAN: "ADMIT YOU WERE JEALOUS: YOU DID NOT LIKE
to see me slipping out of your grasp, did you?"
SUT: "I admit it. I felt insulted that you would not tell
me the truth. I knew full well that you were not in Siena or
Venice or Athens . . ."

BLAN: "No. We were hidden in the Camargue in a little
cottage lent to us by Sabine. After this strange episode, the
kisses and the awakening I suddenly knew that this long-
heralded book had nearly formed itself. I would soon be
brought to term. Constance would insist. We did as all lovers
do, we hid. I did not want you looking over my shoulder.
Hence I sent out an inaccurate account of our whereabouts.
The silence and the heat were a wonderful backcloth to our
loving, while in the evening the gipsies came, or Sabine alone.
They brought us a flock of white-manes, the chargers of
heaven, with all the runaway tilt of Schubert impromptus,
immaculate as our kisses. On horseback we set out across the
network of dykes and canals and lakes; into a mauve desert
sunset, with a silent Sabine in between us who had much to
tell those who asked the right questions. (Man is the earth
quantity and woman the sky: man mind, woman intuition.)
Several times now I recognised that I nearly died of love in
the night for my heart stopped for appreciable lapses of time
and I felt myself entering the penumbra of the continuum, to
hover for a long while in an unemphatic state of mystical
contingency! Genius is silence, everybody knows that. But
who can attain it? With every orgasm you drown a little in
the future, taste a little immortality despite yourself. And here
I was hoping not only to tell the truth but also to free the

1331

novel a bit from the shackles of causality with a narrative apparently dislocated and disjointed yet informed by mutually contradictory insights – love at first insight, so to speak, between Constance and myself. An impossible task you always tell me, but the higher the risk the greater the promise! That is the heart of the human paradox. I did not want to fuck her at first, I did not *dare* to want to because there was so much as yet unrehearsed and unrealised between us. And it might never have been brought to book, so to speak, had it not been for touch – for her probing massage of my wounded back, for while her hands were modelling the repair of the flesh we often spoke of the past, and one day she confessed that she had always been in love with me! 'From the first look we exchanged on the slip at Lyons as we set off down the Rhône. But alas!' Alas indeed, for I was completely unfledged, completely cowardly, if only because I realised the importance of that look but could not believe that it meant anything to her. But my adoration must have sunk into her, for all our subsequent lives, the long detour we made, was informed by the force of that single look! Old Shakes was right – or rather Chris Marlowe. Whoever loved that loved not at first sight? And I was glad retrospectively that I had waited on the event in full cowardice and inexperience rather than risk spoiling it by a *gaffe*, for she too had been physically inexperienced, though of course psychically fully mature and aware of the dilemma. What a calamity ignorance is. And with the war and its separations hovering over us. You have no hold over destiny when you are young. How much better to wait. An enigma is more than a mere puzzle – and a premature marriage can become just intellectual baby-sitting."

From Sutcliffe's notebook

Femme à déguster	CAUCHEMAR
Mais pas à boire	COUCHEMAR
Homme à délester	CACHEMERE

Mais pas à croire   COCHEMUR

BLAN: "Here on these quiet lagoons or trotting the dusk mauve sands of the Saintes Maries I learned the truth about the significance of love and its making. 'Because fashions have changed, and the woman's freedom is confirmed. She has slipped the hook.' So Sabine says riding coolly and thoughtfully between us by the rustling sea, 'And now the new lovers will become at last philosophers. They will realise themselves in mating and sharing the orgasm. Nobody will notice that they are dying of loneliness.'"

SUT: "Don Juan, eh? No, Bon Juan the new hero. You will walk about in a muse, looking as if you had had your prostate massaged by leprechauns. And when you die you will go straight to the Poets' Corner of the Abbey. They will write on your plaque: 'Aubrey was not always his own best friend and sometimes got into intellectual positions his enemies could not have wished for more. Finally, exhausted with so much realising, he farted his way to Paradise.'"

As for the book it was a hopeless task, for what is to be done with characters who are all the time trying to exchange selves, turn into each other? And then, ascribing a meaning to point-events? There is no meaning and we falsify the truth about reality in adding one. *The universe is playing, the universe is only improvising!*

Sutcliffe says, "Who knows all this? You should say, in the interests of clarity."

"I leave you to guess."

"Sabine?"

"Yes, walking by the lagoon or in the hot crypt where the bitumen-black waxen figure of Saint Sara stands sending out waves of divination across the fumes of the hot candles. See? There are no sutras, no prayers, no literature to split hairs over. It's just wish to wish, need to need, like spittle falling

on a red-hot iron. You ignite the black doll and she answers
any question that does not concern the past or the future! As
for me, I am a bit of a fraud and an interloper. Why? Because
I joined them out of curiosity – and you can't really. You have
to be born one. So I remained outside, a vehement observer.
History rolls on but the gipsy folk follow an unconscious star
rhythm, they don't take part, they invigilate, so to speak. They
have refused to codify impulse like the Jews, to profiteer.
Now, with the slow breakdown of deterministic Christianity,
one wonders if Nietzsche was not right when he said that the
Jewish role historically was to unlock the gate from the inside
– the ancient intellectual fifth column of radicalism forever at
work with its messianic fanaticism gnawing at the roof-tree
of tradition and stability. Thus they did for the Goths and now
they have done for us. Divide and rue! There is no hint of
illiberality or partiality in these notions which are purely
philosophic. For us gipsies both Hitler and Stalin were children
of the Old Testament executing a blood programme inspired
by Moloch. There is nothing to be done to hasten its inevitable
disappearance and its transformation into something new,
thank goodness! People fall into these thought moulds from
copying each other. But we can with justice accuse Christianity of masterminding our intellectual disarray. As for the
gipsies, they have made no effort to capitalise on the tragedy
of their extermination in the camps as the Jews have done. A
total silence is all that has emerged – not a poem, not a song,
not a scrap of protest folklore! It's uncanny. But the old
aptitudes hold – basketwork, thieving, prophecy and the
telling of fortunes still hold out. The game of destiny."

   "Ah! That's what I want to discuss!" said Constance,
"because it all seems a pack of lies. The last time we came
down here we each had different fortunes, each by a different
soothsayer. Surely there must be some constant in the whole
business, Sabine?"

The swarthy woman shook her head and smiled.

"We each have as many destinies stacked up inside us as a melon has seeds. They live on *in potentia* so to speak. One does not know which will mature. But after the event one pretends that it was obvious all along. And sometimes the soothsayer is right, chooses right, skries the destiny which manifests itself! You have many discernible destinies – in one you are to die in childbirth; Aubrey divined this though he is no soothsayer, and it figures in the first draft of his novel. In another you will die together – this our tribal Mother saw. It is part of a great accident, something like an earthquake. All of you, all of us, have as many destinies as the sands of the seashore.

"But as for you, Aubrey, I saw something else of more immediate experience. Suddenly she has discovered in you the love she feared would never exist, since there seemed no hope of you ever snapping out of your coma. Suddenly she realised that if she staked her claim and risked everything you might get reborn, re-created. It was up to her to divine the meaning of the orgasm with complete female ruthlessness, to divine your metaphysical anguish, and then to respond to it – to yield and to conceive, that is what she is trying to do. You have both realised love as a future-manufacturing yoga with a child at stake in it, the consciousness of a child, which will be read in its regard! You know the old Provençal saying that a child anyone can make, but one must *round off or perfect its regard (faut parfaire le regard)*. This hints at the inner vision which will give the child a pithy heart and mind on condition that the dual orgasm is experienced simultaneously. She is going to rescue you!"

It certainly felt like that, though poor Constance, responding to the analyst in her, explained it all quite differently, indeed somewhat apologetically. "I am at the moment taking the male part, overwhelming you, almost I am castrating you, but the intention is finally to cause you to respond fully to me. You see you are still traumatised by the shock of the explosion and your image of your body is making you mentally cringe, as if you had pain to fear; whereas I know now that the wound is healed and while there are some muscular movements you can't make there is no more pain or stress. You can go the whole hog and act without thinking or hesitating. Last night I felt you for the first time in control. Sabine is right, we are moving into a fine dual control of the act." Yet he knew they had Affad to thank for much of this love-lore.

SAB: "Yes, there are precautions to be taken just as in the making of bread! By progressively conquering the loving amnesia of the orgasm and expanding its area of consciousness – adding more and more meaning to the eyes of the child-future. By this voluntary extension of consciousness you refine your death progressively, the death he will inherit from you. Once you start this process and realise fully what you are doing all stress vanishes, and all unbelief also. You become all of a sudden who you are, thanks to her, and she who she is thanks to you! But you must not make it sound too like a *constatation de gendarme* or Sutcliffe will be forced to redress the balance in his notebooks which presumably will be one day inherited by Trash. All these pitiful slogans of desire! (After intercourse show him amazement – advice to young brides.)"

But how to overpraise the gold body of Constance, dusted now by the dust-thunder of the bullrings and splashed with freckles of gold?

> Sweet as a rock-panther one day old
> Just come on heat and mateless
> Melts like a cat in rut unsated
> In vast desires unsublimated
> Freckles of coy gold . . .

BLAN: "Why should death have the monopoly, eh? *Il faut paufiner la réalité, faut bricoler dans l'immédiat!* Why remain a victim of uncouth wishes? As for love among the martial arts you must read my new study of Cleopatra, to learn the secrets of love from her. She buttered her breasts before intercourse while Antony honeyed his valves! Soft probe of human tongue – hysteria is a distress which does not come from blameless kisses exchanged between male and female adversaries. The new lovers have become philosophers and equal to the loneliness they inspire. The tremendous sadness becomes rich though the love seems profitless. *Something quite new is happening!*"

These philosophic considerations sound highly sententious, and one suspects that too many of them could easily spoil your loving to the tune of this lazy night and this quite momentous sleek jazz pouring up among the lamplit trees. Can't you be content with the soft goads of the simple flesh? Of that wonderful girl Blanford invented he wrote in his book: "Her husbands had tried to ring her like a wild swan but she was subject only to the gravitational tides of the seasons, flying north or south where the blood called, eluding settled ways and settled men. In lonely places I always found her, tide-borne, solitary, perfect, my lover and my deep friend. At night we dined by the light of a single candle, with olives and iced wine."

BLAN: "When Sutcliffe was born it was a time of grave portents. The doctor said, 'It is clear he will die young for he has no sense of humour.' But his French nurse (muse?) leaned over his cot and whispered, 'They have all brought gifts as spurs to the crib, Zeus a garlic-squeezer, Venus a foreskin-clip of purest gold portending loves without drawback. And now think: the white breast of chicken musky with dusky truffles, stippled like a trout's belly: a pot of black aromatic olives dense in the sweet introspection of their own dark oil, *pâté de foie gras.* Admit it, my dear, you are getting an erection!' The *démon du Midi* has him by the hair of a Sunday.

> Aborted Christians drinking blood
> A thirst which dates before the Flood.
> I'm sick of the thirst for becoming,
> The heaving and retching and humming,
> I will turn to a thirst to exist
> And catch up on all that I've missed!"

The private mind is never at rest, and always on the magic frequency of love.

SUT: "The formula seems to be *petit talent et gros cul.* Fond as a stableful of horses' bums polished up to mirror grooms' grins. They burn. They burn. But nowadays you must bring your own whip. But this is how the gentry do it. With us and our little white palaeolithic chargers it is quite different, for they behave like pets and live loose on the range when they are unsaddled, prodigal of their smiles and head-long tossing of white manes, as if they had leaped out of context and no longer respected the serial order expounded by nature. Think: old men's sperm makes not old men but infants-in-arms who will grow to form church fathers simmering in the raging paranoia of a punitive God. A thirst for magic rules. The schizoid states are uncrystallised mysticism. The kundalini of the unconscious accidentally touched off and set in motion, like an engine's pre-ignition; it comes from incautious thinking, incautious wishing."

BLAN: "Art for the Prince is the representation of a reality upon a plane surface – an artefact without volume or depth. It will not stand up to interrogation. You risk by poking at it with your questions to go right through the canvas into nothing: or else everything! There are limits even to everything. *Bien sûr que non,* as you can say in French, using the cryptic Buddhic double negative. As for the woman, she is a psychic scout and pathfinder through the flesh, a lieutenant, the ship's first mate who divides responsibility with the captain."

When the Prince overheard Constance say, "We have started getting a poor quality of human being for whom wisdom has become mere information!" he was entranced and begged her to teach him ethnology. Together they frequented international gatherings and wistfully compared cultures in search of a thread of historic significance. Certain symbols stood out and seemed to hint. The suffering Prometheus, for example, stood with its face to the rock while the vultures fluttered and pecked; while the suffering Christian stood with its back to the cross, arms spread like a radio aerial, with a crown of wild acacia on his head ... Two different approaches to human suffering! A professor had said, "The will to self-destruction seems more advanced in the more gifted nations or peoples." The Prince gave an exclamation of impatience, for he had begun to feel that they would never find what they were looking for in this way. Also the fortune-tellers had predicted the death of the Princess, and he had begun to dream of the funeral cortège – the long procession of Rolls-Royces, nose to stern, stretching some eighteen kilometres along the blazing desert road between Cairo and Alexandria. The screeching water wheels of Egypt are the country's cicadas. He would soon have to return to her, the one being without whom he did not think he could continue to live. "C'est une affaire de tangences," somebody had remarked to him in the midst of a cocktail party on the Lake Mareotis. And now that the thought of her dying had become an echo in his mind how boring all other women seemed, how shabby his sprees! They were tergiversatile and showed him their lily-white panjandrums, that was all! (The value of the hypotenuse of the Pythagorean triangle is valued at five!) Yet he must not be unfair. With some he had learned things which profited his love for his own wife, and in one – why, she had opened her legs and revealed the whole secret of the pyramids and, yes, that of entropy also. But there is also a principle of repair which contests the irreversibility of process for a short spell – the omnifact of omnideath, the ubique of human obsolescence. "I want you to go ahead and try out the child, one of your own, it's a great challenge," he said to Constance, who replied in somewhat oracular fashion, "Even though you know full well that lovers are selfish as arrows?"

"Even though! Even though!"

Blanford took her in his arms, which was still an unfamiliar purchase for the two unfledged hearts, unquiet presences. He said ironically, "With this future I thee wed." But they knew that the trick had long since been done and it only remained to live it out, to act it out. Reality is desperate for someone to believe in it; hence manifestation which is History's party frock!

> Dull carnivorous males in love
> A-playing the game of hand-in-glove;
> Projections of our self-esteem
> Reflected into love's young dream.
> Gonads rehearse the Primal Scream
> Man, sublime mud of all he thinks
> Sleepwalks in darkness with his jinx,
> Gaunt fellatrix with urban curves,
> Each gets the partner he deserves.

SUT: "Passing down the village street they were reflected in the shop windows, the three mounted figures; the gold leaf of her sunburn glowed against the blonde head like a declaration of intent. Living without awe is living without a full consciousness of reality – of its value. Men without awe will never be wise. Ah! for men who realise that reality consistently outstrips intellectual formulations. Sometimes we could not help seeing the world as a sort of farmyard – with humanity quacking or honking rather than talking. Ontology – the study of being! Ours is perhaps the first civilisation which cannot decide if the answers lie in art or in science. They appear to flow from different centres in the same animal, man. And a man now must realise himself through a sort of religious experience yet stay a man. But if a woman has a religious experience she is obliged to forsake her womanhood and become a nun. Can you have the grin without the cat? I am not sure. A suicide wrote recently, 'In leaving you I am inheriting the whole world!' For dinner he had eaten lobsters tender as Christian children and an overloaded conscience is as bad as an overloaded bowel – something has to give! Then bang!"

They had started to make love as if their embraces were extensions of their thoughts, and he realised the full extent of her power over him; it was a little frightening because he realised that later he would be called upon to take over this power, this domination – it belonged to the male demesne. She was only trying to waken him to his responsibilities. They hardly talked now. The long silent rides were wonderfully tonic beside bulky seas. And their little tavern was as abominable as ever, serving slices of ancient donkey badly cooked and served tepid, covered in rancid oil. The tavern should have been called the Bloodstained Toothpick instead of the Mistral. The proprietor had the specially dead look you see in the eyes of a fly. One knew it was no use arguing because he did not understand. Yet the wine was marvellous. It came from St Saturnin. Suddenly one had thoughts of pith. "*Oui, en toi j'ai bien vendangé ma mère!*" he told her. It was a declaration of love of the most absolute kind and she recognised it as such, good Freudian that she was, or seemed!

So they rode in sweet symbiosis, while the ravenous blue sea lopped at the land, honed down their horizons of sand, extended its bony contours cradled by the heartfelt blue meniscus which was sky. She had finally convinced him of the existence of lovers as philosophers, and of the need for a joint approach to time through the atom of their love. And this sometimes made them both a bit of a bore. "For me the *Aetiologie of Hysteria* is the great document of the twentieth century, the great Sutra, so to speak, and the Freudian denial of its truth is quite inexplicable; it is as momentous as the other great philosophic denial ('Thou shalt deny me thrice!') which ended with the crucifixion scene." What she meant was that the child would be clear-eyed and vigorous and unshocked in its beginnings – she knew it must be so. On the other hand . . . "I had this *dream* which suggested that it was going to be the ending of the whole book. You went back to Tu Duc to tidy up and I to England in order most appropriately to begin my opus. And there the telephone rang with news of your . . . I have never accepted the unique word." "Say it!" "No! It must be lived to be swallowed!"

Death!

BLAN: "Your consciousness bears witness to the historic *now* which you are living while your memory recalls other nows, fading slowly into indistinctness as they move into the prehistory you call the *past*. This temporal series, indistinct and overlapping, you attach to one individual whom you call 'I'. But . . . in the course of a few years, about seven I think, every cell in the body of this 'I', this individual, has been modified and even replaced. His thoughts, judgements, emotions, desires have all undergone a similar metamorphosis! What then is the permanence which you designate as an 'I'? Surely not simply a name which marks his ('its'?) difference from his ('its?') fellow men . . . A discrete sequence of rather disjointed recollections which begin some time in infancy and terminate with a jolt *now*, in the *present* – such is time as a datum of consciousness! (Despite this stone wall, I love you more than myself!) When all this raw material has undergone the strange refining process which we know as physical intuition it is transformed into something close to a meditative state – a version of 'calm abiding' as the Tibetans would say, and it becomes an ark or house for the love-child to inhabit, afloat upon the waters of the eternal darkness, backcloth of everything we do or every kiss we exchange. When if ever one has the luck to arrive at an inferential consciousness the steps of the reasoning process that preceded it are no longer necessary; one can let them go! Kick away the ladder, so to speak."

> Sutcliffe will write us epitaphs
> In poems acerb and wise
> In rhythms the pendulums adore
> And human metronomes despise.

Constance turned her smiling head and sighed: "You have not seen as much of death as I have in my work. Finally, I have got on to good terms with the ugly fellow! Somewhere in the middle of the whole thing there comes a sudden luxurious feeling of surrender to inevitability in the dying themselves. It belongs, this mood of gradually deepening amnesia, to the rhythms of plant life. It makes one realise that all love passes into obsolescence in the very act – it illustrates the nothingness we have decorated with our trashy narcissism. A soft withering surrender to a death without throes. Lying alone by oneself there guided by the merciful paralysis of fading thoughts which cradle one and lead on and on and on . . . until snap! Kiss me. Hold me. And then for some time the echo of an emptiness will follow you about the house, invisible as gravity but as omnipresent, the emphasis on a vanished presence."

Yes, Rob's poems will come all tension-charged with the original perfect illness to undo our knots and make us thrive on images of unimpeded loves . . . He knows that the flesh cools also like a pot of clay in freshly ovened silence, set out in gardens like women beautiful and purposeless as fruit but just as suave in their archaic silence as the grave.

> Faustus who held all nature in contempt
> Was punished, could not die,
> Instead he went
> Into the limbo of the death-exempt,
> Becoming everything he might have dreamt.

To him was granted the famous penis with three heads – the Noble Toy of the alchemists. From now on they made love, creaking like old tennis racquets, and he was able to note in his diary that "*le temps du monde fini a commencé*".

I have made a discovery but I can't tell you what it is because the language in which to express it has not been invented. I know a place but there is no road to it – you must swim or fly – thus the mage Faustus. What's to be done? Why, we must push on with reality, living in the margins of hope.

> the puckering of a thousand vaginas
> the groans and squeaks of minors
> the booming of ocean liners
> the sighs of aircraft designers
> the concentrations of water diviners
> well blow me down with mortal slyness!
> tickle my arse and call me Chomsky!

The adjective which is the prop of good prose is the perverter of poetry – except in the limerick which is its proper show-window. Ideally one could write a whole book in this concise and convenient form to sidestep memory's slow ooze, though perhaps the too rigorous beat of the metronome might lead to monotony. In slower prose one can let packets of silence drift about like mist. Truth is not only stranger but older than . . . The whole of reality dreamed up by a shaggy little god muttering in his sleep. *Eppur si muove!* He talks as if he needed hot rivets to clench up his prose – yes, aphorisms like rivets!

> Let him who writes with velvet nib
> Reserve a sigh for Women's Lib
> Confusions Imp, the God of Love
> Must ask them what they are dreaming of.

SUT: "Darling, soon they will abolish the male and you will have to consider joining the Sperm Bank, the most select form of civil servant, with a certain guaranteed sperm-count, and a uniform like a treasury official. They wear their gold chain of office proudly, simply. And the girls sigh after them – those who have only known the ministrations of the homely plastic syringe torn from a steel dispenser, the dose kept at blood heat, but often not quite fresh or even out of date. Oh for a real man, a small beef extract of a man to enliven the Effluent Society presided over by Madame Ovary. The taming of the screw.

"God's brush!" he cried, "with every lady kissed
The future is encouraged to exist!"

"Constance, you overpersuade me – perhaps we are the last specimens of an obsolete cult. (Cuddle the embers of memory and she'll be thine – so I tell myself.) All is not lost. I sit on the nursery floor of literature surrounded by the dismembered fragments of my juggernaut of a book, wondering how best to assemble this smashed telamon. The débris itself gives off light despite its incoherence. Some wise and disciplined girl like you with those inevitable eyes in shadow, disgusted by the petty transactions of time, suddenly finds plain love and its choice delights; so crowding on all sail she heads for the dark fronts where the great attachments hide. In the heart of the licensed confusion a sense of meaning. All beak and virgin's claws in girls of renown. Or in old men whose basic valves have shut; despairing silence holds them yet, though all but their earthly sun is set . . . And love's umbilicus is cut. Neurosis is the norm for an egopetal culture – Freud exposed the roots as a dentist's drill exposes the pulp chamber of a tooth – the aching root is guilt over uncommitted sins! Civilisation is a placebo with side-effects."

They made love again, secure in this despairing knowledge of a truth their embraces exemplified!

EIGHT

Minisatyrikon

"IT WAS PURE ROMAN SWANK, IF YOU ASK ME," SAID LORD Galen comfortably. "When you think that the whole of this huge edifice was brought into being just to convey a current of fresh water twenty-five kilometres away to a waterless Nîmes where the eleventh legion had been sent in as settlers . . . pure swank, that's what it was." They were taking a turn upon the bridge in the fading light, waiting for the festivities to begin, for at long last the great day had arrived for the unveiling of the Templar treasure in the caves. "Perhaps," said Felix Chatto who had joined the strollers in the dusk, "perhaps," as he gazed upwards into the evening sky where the felicitous honey-golden arches rose in an unpretentious explicitness, "it didn't represent very much for their architects – a mere hydraulic work, inescapably functional. Not even a Roman virgin bricked up alive in it as a sacrifice to the goddess of water!" The Prince nodded and added, "As far as we know! But could it not have been to create employment and prevent social discontent, and thus to ingratiate the Roman settlers with their hosts? Surely it was not just showing off, eh? It's exasperating that one doesn't know. Nor do we know at what point a purely functional object, a fort, a railway, a dam, becomes suddenly (as if by a change of key) aesthetically precious." It was not perhaps the place and the time for such aesthetic promptings, for since the prefectorial announcement of a festival and *vin d'honneur* in honour of the reconstituted niche of Saint Sara the gipsies had taken the hint and started to invade the valley with its tall cliffs and dense forest land which cradled the green river and its fast variable currents lapping at the stone-shingle beaches.

"We'll never discover," said Felix with a sigh. "Many
years ago we discovered a Greek monastery with a juke box
in it and were carried away by the charm of the unusual in
such a remote place. One of the monks had visited America
and brought back this cultural object as an *ex voto*. It was
delightful and quite incongruous. Several years later we
returned to discover that every monastery on the peninsula
had one if not more juke boxes which played canned music
all day long at full volume. The singular and charming had
become the horrible. How was it? Is the good, the desirable,
the admirable, dependent on its rareness and vitiated by
quantity? I have often wondered." Lord Galen felt unhappy,
out of his depth. He knew he had little talent for Aristotelean
casuistries. "Surely," he ventured, "more is better than less,
as with money?"

Felix shook his head.

"Or bacteria?"

"Oh dear!" said Lord Galen, "I hate this line of reasoning
because it never seems to lead anywhere. Would you feel it
was a bad thing if Greek monasteries invested more in sanitary
equipment? Myself, I should feel it admirable."

But while this pious wrangling went on in good-natured
fashion Sutcliffe was noting in his commonplace-book the
salient facts about the place and time – this might serve
Aubrey if for some reason he did not turn up or was late, or
whatever. The basic thing was that all the visitants, of whatever persuasion, were expecting something different from the
adventure. For the Prince and his associates material gain, for
the Beaux Arts aesthetic, for the gipsies a prophesying oracle,
and so on. Even the little doctor and the egregious Quatrefages with his strange epileptoid air and cadaverous physique
were expecting something in the nature of a revelation about
the Templar *mystique*, the Templar secret. All these matters
would come to a head – with any luck – after midnight when

the revellers would be led away from the scene of the festivities towards the dark quarries with their labyrinth of grottoes. As for the gipsies, they knew how to do things with subtlety, to penetrate by infiltration, cart by cart, tribe by tribe. The magic word had been uttered and passed along the bloodstream of the race so that tribes from as far away as the northern Balkans, from Yugoslavia, from Italy and Algeria, had found that there was just sufficient time in hand to send a few representatives to this important event which in the gipsy tongue was known as "an awakening" – that is to say, the inauguration of a tribal saint, a soothsayer and initiator. It was natural that the tribes in and around the city should be pre-eminent as being numerically the most important, and most closely in touch with the authorities. They smoothed out difficulties with the police and the various other departments concerned with public events. So far all the organisational side had been worked out with precision and aimiability, though as for the Préfet himself he had passed a sleepless night, for in the middle of it he had awoken from his sleep with a start and a chilly shudder of fright – for he had suddenly realised the fearful fire hazard which the surrounding forest created at the Pont du Gard. And here he had even authorised a brief display of *fireworks* to salute the risen Saint Sara! His blood ran cold as he realised all that might go wrong . . . a single imprudence by a smoker, an overturned lamp . . . With a vague if scared sense of propitiation he rose early that morning and went to mass, but throughout was preoccupied with visions of a Pont du Gard in flames. It was too late to change anything but he called for the fire brigade to send out a strategic work force just in case . . .

But nevertheless the whole event had been regarded as a municipal operation of some importance to the town of Avignon (to flatter gipsy pride) and it was envisaged that the whole hamlet and ravine would be occupied by sightseers and participants during the fête. The town *pompiers* had taken the matter in hand with despatch, beginning with the problem of lighting. Wires had been slung across the gulf with ribbons of coloured bulbs suspended from them, worked off a portable generator in a lorry, so for the first time the whole edifice was lit up against the night sky. This was in addition to its own lighting system which it was able to use on national days and events of a tourist sort. This whole area of swinging illumination created a sort of mesmeric village of light scooped out of the theatrical blue darkness of the night sky. On either side the cliffs mounted with their dense scrub and forests of holm oak, and here the gipsy bands had already taken root. (The blood chilled, for one could not prevent them from lighting small fires on the embers of which they grilled their evening meal!) They had brought all their own equipment with them, trade by trade, tongue by tongue; they travelled in ancient lorries or in slower carts with their verminous armfuls of keen-eyed children. They had even brought their own fleas with them, if one was to believe the municipal police on the subject! And then there was their music which, once the occupation of the site got under way, began to proliferate in a variety of styles and modes with different groups of instruments and differently cadenced songs and airs – whining mandolins purring like cats, quailing ailing violins, trombones like village idiots reciting their themes. And then to follow came the dances of the children. And as this invasion advanced the place was steadily filling up with little stalls where one could buy pasties or roasted meat dishes or fruit or scones, or even trinkets and baskets – fruit of the day-labour of the gipsies, for they neglected no chance to foster their wares. And here, manning other stalls, were farriers who could shoe you a horse or key-cutters who could cut you a set of skeleton keys to open an office safe or knifegrinders who could sharpen your kitchen knives in a flash. And sellers of scarves and lace and brilliant coloured napkins from Turkey or Yugoslavia. And lastly the army of fortune tellers, brilliant as parrots and all professing palmistry . . .

Meanwhile a central marquee had been run up, extensive as to size, for it was to house most of the notables and provide a centre inside which the Préfet could made his speech in honour of Saint Sara. He never missed the chance of speechifying in public. It was his job as well as his art.

The nexus of the gipsy organisation was centred in half a dozen old fashioned carts with small windows decorated by brilliant curtains and flashily painted sideboards. They were grouped about the loftiest and most gaudy which was the home of the tribal "Mother". The smell of joss and whisky hung about in it, to tantalise the noses of those clients who came to consult the old lady about their fortunes. All this smoke from fires and tobacco and cooking and Indian joss-sticks ebbed and flowed with the evening river-winds as they poured softly over the stony sills of the ravines and so down-stream.

"I'm on the look-out for that Sabine lady," said Lord Galen, "to try to get a really detailed and authoritative reading out of her. She was rather unsatisfactory last time when we went to the Saintes Maries; and yet there was sufficient truth in what she said to be very striking, and give me the hunger to know more if possible."

"Did she tell you if you would get the treasure?" asked the Prince curiously. "No! I thought not. Nor me exactly! But she defended her limitations very ably, I thought, by saying that she could only see what lay within her personal competence, just as a human eye can only see a certain distance. Yet I was like you impressed by what she had to say."

Felix Chatto who had decided to resign everything to fate and had a poor opinion of fortune telling was nevertheless just as anxious to see Sabine whom he admired deeply and thoroughly appreciated as a conversationalist. He had himself grown up so much and in so many unexpected ways that he felt the need to test out his new maturity upon someone whose sensibility seemed to be the equal of his own, whose notions echoed his. And he could see that the woman was hungry for good conversation in her own tongue which offered her the comforting support of humour and lightness of touch. But where was she? She did not reach the great viaduct until nightfall, owing to some minor trouble with the transport. She had lost a very great deal of weight within the last year or two – indeed, she already knew that she was starting a cancer; but for the moment she had gained much in simple beauty which she could offset with the dramatic apparel of the gipsy tribe in all its brilliant grossness; and her body answered the change, reverting to the old swinging walk of the past, her head slanted to one side, as if she were listening to her own beauty from some inward point of vantage. They heard her hoarse voice in the crowd and exclaimed (or Galen did): "There she is! Let's waylay her before she gets carried away by the French Préfet!"

Meet they did, but it seemed that Sabine had been on the lookout for Felix, for she advanced upon them with impulsive speed and took his hands, ignoring the arms of Galen, keen to share a handshake with her. "I must talk to you alone for a moment," she said breathlessly, "if your friends will permit me. I have something to tell you." And so saying she drew him aside into the forest and sat him down on a fallen block of golden stone, an ingot broken off the bridge. "When we spoke of Sylvie I did not tell you the whole of what I saw because I realised that there was something capital which you did not yet understand, and that was the provisional nature of prophesy. The fact that I see something does not automatically mean that it will come about, for sometimes it does not; yet statistically it falls out as I see it about seven times out of ten. You questioned me about her illness and her possible death by suicide and I turned the question aside at the time. I wanted time to consult my Mother as to what I had a right to reveal and what not – for I saw quite far into your future, or my version of it. In that version she does not die that way, but she is buried alive in a mountainous snowdrift somewhere north of Zagreb some years off, some years from now. In between you will experience absolute bliss with her, for you have, by recognising the nature of her so-called illness, given her the courage to reassume her reason. As a young Ambassador I see health and riches and professional success. But this catastrophe comes quite unexpectedly. They are there silent; the uniformed chauffeur is dozing. They are waiting for help to come in order to dig them out. She is playing chess with a pocket chess set. I hear Smoke, the cat, purring contentedly and also the soft tick of the dashboard clock of the great limousine. Help will come, but too late; the rescue team have laboriously dug a tunnel down to the bottom of the drift to remove the bodies but the car is jammed in rocks and incapable of being moved. It will have to stay all winter and wait for the spring thaw. By then of course the moisture will have blurred the contents of her last two note-books – a great loss to literature, they seem to believe." All this while holding his wrist and staring down at his palm with a trance-like expression. Then she sighed. "That is all. And now you must please excuse me for a few moments because I think the French have arrived."

Indeed the French had arrived; that is to say that representatives of the Press with their cameras had already started to put in an appearance, reassured by the promise offered by the more than adequate buffet which was still only halfway mounted. This creation had been confided to the great chef of Nîmes, Tortoni, who amidst a multiplicity of highly comestible cakes and pâtés had prepared the pedestal for the most important of his creations, a recumbent woman fashioned in butter with trimmings uttered in caviar of several different provenances and helpings of *saumon fumé* and an archipelago of iced potato salad to round out the offering. Venus rising from a Récamier of Baltic caviar with the smile of a redeemer on her lovely face, just to remind everyone that Tortoni had attended Les Arts before turning aside into a career as a gastronomic chef which had brought him fame and fortune. But all this superlative invention had to be kept chilled and here again great ingenuity came into play, for the whole creation was offered in a disguised thermal showcase upheld by captious looking Cupids with sweet erections and honeyed grins. "I must say," said Galen proudly, "you really do have good ideas sometimes." For it was the Prince who had thought up this little gastronomic frolic, as the Préfet's budget for such a feast was somewhat cheese-paring. "I only hope it wasn't too expensive," he added, for the Prince in his lordly way had sent the bill to the company. He shook his head reproachfully and said, "Ah! you and your money! I dreamed last night that you died and were incinerated and that your ashes were scattered over your bank in Geneva by helicopter." Galen laughed heartily: "And that you built a funerary memorial in the crypt of the bank itself!"

But Galen's mirth was superseded by a thoughtful look, as if in afterthought the idea didn't sound too unreasonable! The Prince continued on his mischievous teasing way: "I remembered Voltaire's advice to people visiting Geneva and wondered if you knew it." Galen did not, so the Prince obligingly repeated it: "Voltaire said, 'When you visit Geneva, if you see a banker jump out of a third-storey window jump after him. There will be three per cent in it!'" This put Galen in a thoroughly good humour. "Old Banquo used to say that if you put your ear to a Geneva bank you could hear it purring just like a Persian cat. The noise was the discreet noise of the interest on capital accruing!" Felix clicked his tongue reprovingly at so much flippancy, but he was only pretending to disapprove. The Prince said, "Admit it, Felix. It's a Mouton-Rothschild world with far too little merriment in it. As for me I'm dying to plunge my spoon into the buttery buttocks of the Tortoni Venus; but I think we will have to wait for the Préfet, no?"

Obviously they would have to, in the interests of correct protocol as well as a sense of occasion; but of course it was obvious that the gipsies themselves could only be allowed a limited share in this upper-class celebration. Though it was in their honour they seemed to accept the fact with equanimity. The Préfet's congratulatory speech had been copied and its distribution to the Press Corps achieved; its actual construction had proved something of a puzzle for he saw that it would have to be written in a manner which suggested that the statue had been in fact found – yet delivered before the fact, so to speak! It contented itself with expressing itself on a warm note of benevolence and goodwill – turns of phrase habitual enough in speeches of an official kind. But the actual gipsy participation was of a limited kind inside the official marquee, though in fact they completely dominated the musical fête which had grown up around the events: already the smoke from the flares and the lights and plangence of the music provided a wild note of romantic colour, a felicity and unbridled expansiveness to the proceedings which was reminiscent of other more important gipsy rejoicings – such as the one in honour of the original Saint Sara at the Saintes Maries de la Mer at the end of May every year. So much colour to delight the eye that Sutcliffe was drunk prematurely, without the ever-present aid of wine. He had asked Sabine if she would consider sleeping with him, and she had looked at him for a long time in a very strange manner. "But I don't know which one of you is more real – for Aubrey has already asked me that." To which Rob testily replied, "Is one not permitted a practising *alter ego* in the modern world? I am the ape-carrier of tradition, for in great houses the Fool customarily carried his Lord's ape! Why all the mystery? When you are writing from the hither side of a deeply privileged experience a certain hilarity is quite in order if only to express your elation. That is why I love you, for you have realised that as far as individual identity is concerned we only give an illusion of coherence. Your I, me, mine, has about as much consistency as a vapour. Sabine, I am turning into a rainbow! I can feel it. Slowly but gracefully. I am full of love and mis-giving for I have learned how to write poems. There comes a struggle, a feeling of suffocation, an agon, a convulsion – before you can take that vital step forward into the unknown! I want to escape from time through the perfect amnesia of the orgasm. Time! Have you not noticed how much one second resembles another? All time is but a uniform flow of process. It is *we* who age and disappear!"

"Come to my caravan," she said. It was an order.

But though they had not advanced upon the food they had started to broach the champagne, and were beginning to enjoy the twinges of elation it brought. Flash bulbs began to pop off and everyone began to feel that he was about to be immortalised. And the music soared together with the general conversation which had reached the pitch of coherence common to cocktail parties – as if a whole collective un-conscious had like a wine-bowl been overturned. Galen was saying: "You scared me so much with your talk of serpents and buried treasure – the Egyptian folk stories, remember? – that I bought myself a stout stick with a steel spike atop, and I shall take it with me just in case." The Prince chuckled: "How typical!" he said, "when the real danger is of stepping on a mine!" New arrivals began to put in an appearance, like the doctor Jourdain and the saturnine Quatrefages and even (surprisingly) Max, looking even more like God-the-Father than ever: it was as if the very spirit of old age had come to nest, to find its apotheosis in his white-haired gravity and beauty. Galen had paid for him to be present, since he also had been created a sleeping partner in the company. "What has happened to Constance?" he wanted to know, and was delighted when Felix replied: "The best and the worst! She has fallen in love with Aubrey and disappeared. But they promised to appear tonight for the ceremony so perhaps we shall see them here before long." The old man bowed his head. He was thinking to himself, "Love not disembodied must end in despair and forgiveness. One will ask oneself if that is all that life has to offer. But life has its own imperatives and everything must take its turn. So she was perfectly right to behave as she must. The only art to be learned was how to cooperate with reality and the inevitable!" And then immediately he reproached himself for this rather specious formulation, but at the same time he recognised that it came out of his yoga practice – the fidelity to insight and to oxygen! Nevertheless he was dying to see Constance again and hoped that he would be able to stay awake to talk to her; recently (and regretfully) he had fallen into the habit of dropping off to sleep in a quite involuntary manner after dinner, an annoying symptom of old age against which he was quite powerless!

The Préfet according to his rank was entitled to three kettle-drums for public appearances of importance, but out of modesty he only convoked two for this cultural manifestation. It was almost the only way of subduing a rowdy Mediterranean crowd, of announcing your presence, or making it clear that what you were about to say was supremely important, because official. Kettle-drums create the required hush before a public speech!

Tonight, however, he was possessed by a pleasant

fancy – of descending from his official car and effecting the
last few hundred yards to the bridge on foot, preceded by his
drummers. And this he succeeded in doing, walking at a calm
unhurried pace, clad in his frock-coat with decorations
proudly mounted. The drummers walked before him,
uttering their deep rallentando to mark the step; and as he
advanced the gipsies espied him and made way for his advent,
orienting their music in a manner of speaking towards a
welcoming demeanour. Meanwhile the experienced eye of the
official ran over the scene taking everything in – above all to
see if the leaders of the gipsy tribe were seated correctly in
consonance with that invisible and inscrutable element,
protocol. He was reassured to see that the old lady, the
"Mother" of the tribe, who looked rather the worse for wear
already, had been planted firmly at a side table which adjoined
the main one, with her implacable bottle of gin before her, and
some lighted joss to keep things savoury. Her husband and a
whole tribe of sons kept her company, though they were a
tiny bit ill at ease because of the light and the signs of
"officialdom": yet manifestly flattered also. The Préfet made
a slow official circuit now to shake the hands of the invitees,
noting with interest that some of them came from other time-
fields or other contingent realities – like Toby and Drexel,
who was there with his two charming and juvenile *ogres* who
seemed rather like impersonations of Piers and Sylvie of the
past. In fact there was hardly anyone missing except for the
two lovers who were still acting out the long detour of their
age – the biography of that first look exchanged on the river
bank at Lyons so many years ago!

The official presence now authorised the official arc-
lamps of the shrine, and suddenly it was possible to admire
the magnificent presence of the whole monument pressed up
against the sky and coloured by the white arcs in all its
perfectly proportioned grace. No, it was not possible to dis-

miss it as an adequate piece of Roman plumbing, thought Felix as he gazed at it with newly kindled emotions. It raised once again the old tormenting problem. (Beautiful is valuable against Beautiful is precious – which?) It was a question of market value against aesthetic or spiritual value. Max at his elbow spoke as if he had read his thoughts for he said, "No. It's full of spirituality; you could do a very good yoga here and it would be appropriate enough!"

The wine had done its work, the music exercised its charm, the leafy shadow and white light had expressed all the ample beauty of a late spring; and then to crown it all they stood to gain fortunes tonight and to revive the memorable saint who for years now had been forgotten. The roving and curious eye of the Préfet quested about for a moment, he was on the lookout for someone. Presently she came into view and threaded her way through the crowd to his side; it was Sabine, and he was obviously waiting for her. In her deep voice she said, "Monsieur le Préfet, I have made the inquiries you asked of me and the girl is available, and can come to your residence whenever you wish. Her husband has assured me that she is not ill – I appreciate your concern as so many of these folk have venereal troubles. The only trouble is that he wishes something from you *en contrepartie*, and you may not feel like giving him what he asks for . . ." "Anything, within reason," said the Préfet, who was blushing with pleasure, as the girl in question was a magnificent young bird of paradise – or perhaps more appropriately a golden pheasant. Sabine went on: "He wants the centre stall for the Avignon fairs, the stall which is to the left under the old bastion – stall G." The Préfet groaned: "But everyone wants that stall, it is strategically the best in the town. Very well. I shall speak to the *placier* in that sense and he can take possession of it as from tomorrow. And I hope tomorrow evening the girl will make herself available at about eight o'clock. I can't tell you how grateful I am for your personal intervention on my behalf. Sometimes these things are so hard to arrange when one is an official. Thank you a thousand times." Sabine smiled. One is always in a strong position when one is in need of nothing. But she knew that if ever she needed official help with any scheme she could count on her *piston* with the Préfet, and that was important.

But as yet neither had spoken of what was uppermost in their minds – the question of Julio's embalmed legs. It invested their silence with a kind of pregnant significance for on neither side was the conversation broken off, it simply tapered off into silence, into a pause. She left the official with the onus of referring to the subject. "Of course," he said at last, "I am fully aware of the political significance to the tribe of finding the shrine untouched and in working order. In a sense I am as much concerned as you must be – for my job is to see that nothing troubles good civic order."

"Indeed," she said, looking down at her hands as if the answer to the secret might be hidden in them. "Indeed!"

The official drew a deep breath and plunged. "Have you thought any more about my suggestion concerning the legs?"

"Of course I have."

"I am having repeated offers from the Musée de l'Homme; as you know they want to add the originals to their collection. It seems to be a matter of vital interest to them and I am sure the matter could be arranged without anyone knowing. After all with a pair of plastic copies who would be any the wiser?"

"That is not the question. I quoted them a price for the whole transaction. Will they meet it or not? If they will then I agree from my side. If not, not!" The Préfet coughed behind his hand. "They have agreed to your price," he said and his face broke into a smile. But not hers, there was no corresponding smile on her face. So *this* was the discreditable act she must perform according to the cards – for of course plastic copies could not, would not, conduct the lightning flashes of healing to suppliants! She took the proffered cheque and stared at it with puzzled amaze, dazed by her own behaviour. It was a ritual sacrifice of something, though she did not know of what. And it would lead, as the cards had warned her, to her murder by the tribe – ritual murder by stoning. She shook herself like a sheepdog with sheer disbelief. "What rubbish it all is!" she exclaimed. "Rubbish?" said the Préfet. "It seems a fair price to me for such a thing. It's all superstition anyway, so what are the odds?"

He moved slowly on and left her standing there in amazement wondering if she should tear up the cheque but knowing she would not.

Everything was unrolling in the most satisfactory fashion; an unruffled optimism reigned. It was time now to broach the food, and the official approached the gallant spread with all the ardour and enthusiasm of a true Frenchman who is confronted with something good to eat. It is practically a religious duty to do justice to the fare. And by now everyone had caught the mood, and started to follow suit. Fragments of thoughts and snatches of conversation floated about in the breezy darkness of the Roman treasure. Old relationships between acquaintances who had not met for years renewed themselves. Glasses were raised to Saint Sara, and "*trinc*" became once more the password!

"As for Saint Sara, I don't suppose we shall ever know for certain who she was: the repudiated wife of Pilate, the servant of the Virgin, or some forgotten queen of Egypt, reincarnation of Isis, who once ruled over the Camargue. Perhaps it does not matter except to these swarthy children who so reverently kiss her belly button during the fête." Thus the Prince who was enchanted by the excellence of the food and drink and the manner in which things were shaping.

Twinkling with love-bites Cleopatra came,
Saint Sara had resolved her of all shame,
The belly-button of a virgin's kiss
Transformed her very breathing into bliss.

In the unwinking gold of the candlelight all the brass-work in the little caravan twinkled and flashed. Sabine gazed at the two palms of Rob Sutcliffe, allowing her concentration to sink into them, to founder in them until they seemed to her as transparent as glass. "We will be saved if at all by the Jews coming into a new heritage; the persecuted make mistakes and they once made a false identification of interest on capital with safety; this translated into blood as a kind of alchemical investment plus material usury. There will be other ways of stabilising the finances of state and they will show us a new road." Sutcliffe was clad only in his shirt. In his notebook he had written: "The untouchable dreams of licit caresses." He had asked her to marry him, as he had asked so many people to do, and like so many people she had refused. (Can you (ex)change lives? Can you (ex)change deaths?)

Lord Galen was discoursing upon dreams. "Sometimes," he said, "I want prophetic dreams, lucrative dreams which come without warning. Last year, for example, I woke with a cry of astonishment to hear a voice say: 'The obvious thing at the end of a war as wasteful as this last one is a contract for scrap metal.' It was a revelation – the obvious always is! Within ten days I was negotiating with ten governments to take over their deserted battlefields!"

"Yes, I also used to be scared of snakes," Max was saying, "until I went to India to study. In the *ashram* there was a king cobra with a mate and they were quite tame; they came out at dusk and drank milk from a saucer with little flickering tongues. You could describe them as good-humoured when not alarmed and quite unaggressive. But in another part of India they killed snakes and there I noticed how faithful the female was and how deadly. She always returns to avenge her mate, and for days after a male has been killed the whole place is in a state of acute anxiety waiting for her certain reappearance. Usually she comes three or four days after the killing of her mate. They say that this is the better to plan her ambush because she is careful to execute her retaliation according to a set plan. She lies in wait in some place where people are bound to pass – on a thoroughfare or pathway, in a kitchen or at a shrine. If any unwary person approaches she strikes with all her might. But I was very impressed by the anxiety with which the whole household awaited her coming. My teachers used this as a metaphor. The state of watchfulness as if for this second coming!"

The noise of the music rolled over his words and he felt snatches of sleep invading his whole consciousness in little paroxysms of pleasure. The collision of different languages superposed and mingled gave a wonderful barbaric note to the fair. One could imagine whole conversations when one did not understand what was being said.

Who is your friend over there? The cannibal one?

Death!

He looks rather nice.

He improves on acquaintance. The man with a pocketful of deaths.

I thought he looked familiar.

The Prince's car was full of small gipsies – they had asked for a ride and were being driven over the bridge and around the leafy roads with their dapples of frenzied light. The great engine purred, soft as elephant fur, emissary from the world of Pelf and Vox Pop and processed citizen. "Everyone is here save the lovers and Smirgel," said the Préfet on a note of deep anxiety, as he wished to begin his alembicated discourse well before the advance into the caves.

"They will come," said Felix soothingly. And truth to tell they were not far off. As for the lovers, they had elected to ride up from the sea and with the falling of darkness had reached Remoulins when the meandering roads led them steadily towards the bridge; from time to time through the forest they caught glimpses of insinuating light against the distant sky. Soon the distant clamour of mandolins would greet them. They advanced like riders in a dream, his arm through hers. They had decided to separate for a while, perhaps for several months, in order to give themselves the possibility of concentrating all their forces upon the book which he had decided to begin at long last. But this could not be done without a finalising meeting with Sutcliffe for whom now the enormous sense of utter despondency had once more gained the forefront of his mind – the despair over the inaccessibility of Sabine. As they wound slowly through the dark glades he told her his plan and asked for her permission to execute it.

She was vehemently in favour of it; she felt, in fact, that the whole *oeuvre* for which he was going to try was as much her work, her responsibility, as his – which was indeed the case. To celebrate the mystical marriage of four dimensions with five skandas so to speak. To exemplify in the flesh the royal cobra couple, the king and queen of the affect, of the spiritual world. "My spinal I with her final she." Some of this they tried to express to Sutcliffe who remained somewhat unconvinced. "Very well," he said at last, "on condition that you don't write like a hundred garbage cans. But first we should clap eyes on the treasure, no? To console ourselves against the cold and damp of our native island – that barbaric place with its two tribes." The Prince explained the allusion. "At first you have difficulty liking the inhabitants. Then you realise that they come in two sorts, the British and the English. The first are descendants of Calvin, the second descendants of Rupert Brooke! Poets and Idealists against Protestant shop-keepers. Hence the divided voice which so often fills us with dismay. After all, in this hideous war we have just passed through never forget that Halifax would have treated with Hitler: it took Churchill to refuse. England over Britain!" It was one of his favourite themes, and one very congenial to a typically Egyptian temperament. As who should know!

The remaining two persons – Smirgel and Quatrefages – arrived in an old fashioned gig with a somewhat super-annuated horse drawing them. They looked somehow dazed in a vaguely triumphant way, and the German, true to his promise, had brought the Austrian sapper's map of the workings without which all access to the treasure would have proved impossible. But first the warnings, and here the Préfet could afford to wax somewhat rhetorical as he pleaded for care and circumspection and civic respect for the saint – if they managed to locate her. His voice was from time to time drowned by the moan of mandolins. But at long last the great moment announced itself; Cade manifested in a puff of smoke and a flash – an optical illusion which the light created as it flashed among the leaves. He had with him a whole bundle of lottery tickets which he wore over his shoulder like a bandolier. This had been Smirgel's idea. "It would be wise to keep a check on those who go in. The gipsies are such a rabble I am scared to let them in. But if you give them a ticket each we can do a count later on if something goes wrong." There were also torches to be distributed and fairy-lights . . . All these elements had to be coaxed into some sort of order. Slowly the mellifluous periods of the official French wound to a halt.

"And so, my children," – for he could not resist the avuncular note – "let us go in all humility in search of our Saint who alone will secure the well-being of all who live here. Viva Sara!" The cry went off like a pistol shot and for a long moment the music swept upwards towards the sky in a glorious arpeggio while individual voices barked the savage message to the shade of the Saint. "Viva Sara! Viva Sara!" And now the fireworks ranged upon the aqueduct started to splutter and whizz – crowns and globes of spinning light in a deep blue sky. The volume of the music turned itself down and a single plangent woman's voice started to sing a love-song, an Andalusian folk-tune with its curious peristaltic rhythm and alternative breaths suggestive of the human orgasm. Sutcliffe said grimly, "Sex – the human animal's larder." And his double said, "Yes. Or the fatal power-house. We could do so much with it if we learned the code!" But the Prince who had learned of the mortal illness of the Princess and was planning to leave for Cairo at dawn, was thinking of other things – of mortal sin, parodied by illnesses of the physical envelope! He could see so clearly into the future of her death, clearer than any gipsy. On the anniversary of it the telephone smothered in tea-roses – white roses and red. In this way to conspire against console, and hope in their love. Aubrey said, "When we separate shall we correspond, do you think?" Sutcliffe said, "Of course. We mustn't neglect to think of the collected correspondence – an exchange of hiero-glyphs between two cuneiform personages, what? A corres-pondence in Mandarin?"

The procession was forming; at its head would ride the Prince and the Préfet in the royal Daimler; then the official limousine; then the other cars and the ribbon of caravans. At the head of the procession walked the magnificent singing woman-gipsy in all her finery while the cars followed, slowed down to her pace. In this way they covered the quarter of a mile to the cave entry with its ominous hoardings with the inscription DANGER everywhere written large. Here Cade had taken up his position in order to give everyone a ticket before letting them through the barrier. The first cave was vast, like a cathedral, and was rapidly filled. Now it was time to advance down the inner corridors guided by Smirgel and Quatrefages. The lovers gave a shiver of premonition and Blanford thought that if ever he wrote the scene he would say: "It was at this precise moment that reality prime rushed to the aid of fiction and the totally unpredictable began to take place!"